Islandia

from maps in John Lang's notebook

The Co

Isla

ISLANDIA

THE
KARAIN
CONTINENT

Scale : 1 inch = 45 miles

N

Ardan

Niv

Beal

Deen

Miltain

Bre

Carran

Sobo Pass

Mobono

SOB

S

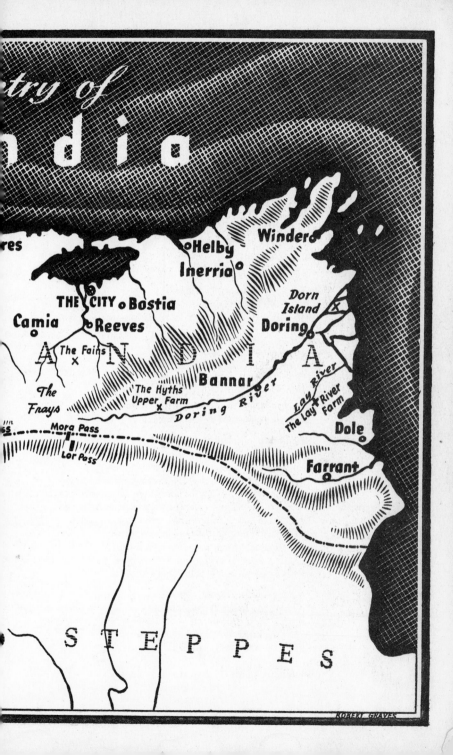

This edition first published in the United States in 2001 by
The Overlook Press, Peter Mayer Publishers, Inc.
Woodstock & New York

WOODSTOCK:
One Overlook Drive
Woodstock, NY 12498
www.overlookpress.com
[for individual orders, bulk and special sales, contact our Woodstock office]

NEW YORK:
141 Wooster Street
New York, NY 10012

Library of Congress Cataloging-in-Publication Data

Wright, Austin Tappan, 1883-1931
Islandia / Austin Tappan Wright.
    p. cm.
    1. Consuls—Fiction I. Title
PS3545.R155 I85 2001   813'.52—dc21   2001021934

Manufactured in the United States of America
1 3 5 7 9 8 6 4 2
ISBN 1-58567-148-7

Introduction

IN THE ATLAS OF IMAGINARY COUNTRIES Islandia stands apart. Austin Tappan Wright's creation is altogether more grounded in seeming reality than its fellows, and that sense of solidity and place has made it a destination quite as familiar to the many readers who have visited Islandia in the sixty years since it was first published as many more prosaic spots on the globe.

The years of Islandia's fictional birth must have roughly coincided with the years of John Lang's voyage to, and residency in that far away country. Perched at the tip of the Karain semi-continent, facing the unexplored wastes of Antarctica in the Southern Hemisphere, Islandia's story begins in the year 1906 when Austin Wright embarked on the course of Law at Harvard University. Nearly one hundred years ago the world was a larger place and the 'discovery' of a little known nation at the bottom of the world, one with few ties to the West, and embargoed from daily contact by distance and the will of its people was perhaps not so implausible as it is now. The race to the South Pole was breathlessly in the news, and the competing attempts to reach and explore the Pole, including Scott's Antarctic (Discovery) expedition of 1901–04, Shackleton's British Antarctic Expeditions of 1907–09 and 1914–16, and ultimately Amundsen's successful Norwegian Antarctic Expedition of 1910–12, brought the first tidings of an unfamiliar part of the world into many homes. Wright's Islandia, unfolding slowly in his thoughts and on thousands of pages of manuscript during this period, could not have seemed too farfetched. After the novel's publication in 1942 (eleven years after Wright's death in New Mexico in an automobile accident) the essayist and bookman Lawrence Clark Powell concluded that Islandia "attained a reality of absolute conviction."

The conviction was supported by the intricate care with which

Wright framed his world building—the construction of a fully real-ized culture and country, with a carefully established history (including the fully written, but still unpublished, *Islandia: History and Description* of M. Jean Perier), language, geography, and culture. Even the cartography was professional, supplied by the author's brother, Dr. John K. Wright, former head of the American Geo-graphical Society. Born of the daydreams and musings of a bookish child grown to be a meticulous and thoughtful man, Islandia owes its credibility to something more than the typical scene-setting of the novelist. C.S. Lewis, another great maker of worlds, also occu-pied his youth constructing the imaginary land of 'Boxen,' a precur-sor to Narnia. Both men must have sought to fulfill an inner need to fully realize an ideal place. One gets the sense that the writing of novels was almost incidental.

When Wright set down to describe his imaginary country he chose as his hero the somewhat unsteady and self-doubting young American, John Lang. Introduced to a country where foreign resi-dency was restricted by the Hundred Law, limiting access to Islandia to a bare one hundred visitors at any one time, Lang is the perfect foil for depicting the differences between Islandian and Western civ-ilizations. Hesitant and unsure in any case, Lang is confounded by what he encounters touring this unfamiliar land. In the process Wright delights in making Islandia real in its smallest particulars, and some of the novel's best moments are in the details. Lang spends much of the novel touring the countryside and making visits to the grand (and not so grand) homes of the Islandian nobility, joining a series of house parties, excursions, picnics, parliamentary debates and entertainments that might have stepped out of the pages of the novels of those two 'social' Anthony's: Trollope and Powell. His per-spective is an ideal one to reveal the broad sweep of Wright's imag-ined society, but Islandia also has Lang literally digging ditches while visiting Lord Some and learning, as gardening readers will ruefully agree, that double-digging muck, a spade-full at a time, is back-breaking labor but the only proper way to lay a new garden.

The subject of gardening, in fact, crops up frequently and teach-es about Islandian society and its cares and responsibilities. Not only does Lang learn with some dismay that it is perfectly proper to set visiting house guests, even American consuls, to manual labor on the family farm in this agrarian culture, but the work itself is regarded as a privilege. Indeed, when Lang is set to digging ditches he is also given the harder task of breaking ground first, since his host thinks it will give Lang pleasure to discover bulbs and roots lying hidden beneath the soil. In this culture farmers "look upon their whole farm as a great living canvas," and "consider how a field will look when [plants] first come up through the earth, and when they are full grown—and when they are dead and when they are stubble."

Sailing, architecture, music, even snowshoes bear a characteristic Islandian stamp and are described and explored in detail. Lang is given opportunity to compare and contrast the Islandian world and the familiar West in a profusion of small ways: in the shape of a reed basket or the way an Islandian yacht cuts the waves (Wright was a strong and enthusiastic sailor, and boats of all sorts figure large in the novel), but the most important differences are in the character of the Islandian people and in the society they evolved. Nowhere is this made clearer than in Lang's struggles to comprehend the Islandian language, and specifically to learn the language of love. *Apia, Alia* and *Ania* (corresponding roughly to Eros, love of place, and the mature love that comprises the closest marriage) define the three kinds of love that gradually overcome Lang's foreignness and draw him into the emotional life of Wright's imaginary land. In the course of the novel, Lang loves three very different women and is sorely tested by the experiences, although ultimately he finds contentment and a kind of acceptance from each.

One of the marvelous things about the novel is watching Lang's turn of the century Harvard reserve melt away as he grows closer to the Islandian culture. This is most clearly felt when Wright deals with sexual appetite, a subject examined in unblinking detail with respect to Lang and each of the women to whom he is drawn—and a different lesson is drawn from each relationship. Unrequited love begins the novel and exacts a melancholy that persists through all of Lang's conquests, but passion is also here in plenty, so much so that the novel has at times taken on the reputation of being a kind of early 'free love' manifesto, anticipating the 60's by a double generation but carrying the full weight of the protest movement, doubting the establishment on subjects as varied as sex, big business, big government, and the franchise. Still, Wright's message is not so simple as Sex is good and Big is bad. When Lang does commence an affair giving full vent to lust (*Apia*) his direct and unashamed mistress cries,

"My dear, my own Johnlang, my beloved one, it is perfect to have you want me and take me, as perfect as anything I will ever know.
I kissed her mouth, but it twisted away, saying:
But why, why am I not contented?"

Early in the novel, Lang occupies his time reading George Meredith's The Travels of Harry Richmond, but it is not so much that novel as that writer's very clear-eyed view of sex and feminism in his 'Modern Love' poem cycle that seems to be echoed here:

If I the death of Love had deeply plann'd,
I never could have made it half so sure,
As by the unblessed kisses which upbraid
The full-waked sense; or, failing that, degrade!
'Tis morning: but no morning can restore
What we have forfeited. I see no sin...

Islandia is in every way a bookish novel, and that probably lends to its cult appeal. There is a rather large bibliography imputed to the country and referred to throughout; titles such as Carstairs' *Against the Demiji With the Islandians*, Bodwin's *The Life of Queen Alwina*, and, of course, John Lang's *History of the United States*—but actual titles and authors also figure as touchstones in the novel: Mark Twain, Emerson, Plato's *Republic*, and a host of Victoriana that arrives ashore in Lang's fiancé's trousseau. Never mentioned but impossible not to be reminded of is Anthony Trollope whose Barsetshire and Parliamentary novel sequences seem likely models for Islandia. Wright, like Trollope, was the son of a successful novelist mother*, and also like Trollope pursued his craft from the sensible confines of an established professional career—in Wright's case the law, in Trollope's the British postal system. In fact, Wright's Islandia, despite its frankness about sex, bears many of the hallmarks of nineteenth century literature, concerned with testing the boundaries and niceties of human behavior against the responsibilities and inequities of society at large. John Lang's naive and groping public course as Consul to Islandia mirrors Phineas Finn's eponymous journey in Trollope's classic (and Finn, too, ends his days as an expatriate convert to a foreign system), while Lang's mistress, Nattana, seems to exude the same unswerving rectitude as Trollope's Lily Dale in *The Small House at Allingham*, even if Nattana's efforts are concerned with making it clear that sex for its own sake should not be confused with love, while Lily's position seems to be that love, once given, should not be confused with anything else at all.

Although conceived nearly one hundred years ago, and nurtured during the period between the wars that seems to have marked a long transition from the nineteenth century way of life into the tumult of the present, Islandia remains fresh and vital. The reasons are simple enough: Wright's invention is a stirringly *real* locale, not some utopian confection. Late in the novel, Lang's brother Philip, a sensible lawyer who surely must represent at least this one aspect of the author, argues with him, saying, "You have a prejudice in favor of the simple life—the Brook Farm, the Charles Wagner, the Rousseau fallacies!" He goes on to say "Islandia is an emotional Utopia evidently!" Lang counters that he shouldn't be accused of mixing up theory with reality—Islandia, for Lang, and for its many readers, is a form of reality. What Islandia represents is a reality familiar in some haunting way to all of us, but sadly lacking in most of our lives. It celebrates a life rooted in fixed things such as home and family, but argues that those concepts have meaning only if they extend beyond the nuclear family so often written about by late twentieth century sociologists and experts, and apply to a full understanding of the generations that go before us and stretch into the future. Wright's grandson, Austin Tappan King, tells a story certainly familiar to Wright about the rooftrees of Oxford University, his home for one year. When the provost of one of the colleges there makes his annual tour of inspection, traipsing from cellars to leads (as the rooftops are called) he discovers to his dismay that the vast timbers framing the Great Hall have weakened over the centuries since it was built and need to be replaced. Despairing that no such massive timbers are likely to be found at the local lumberyard he is directed by an old graybeard retainer of the college to speak with the woodsman in charge of a farm owned by the College. When he arrives there, on the outskirts of Oxford, he is led into a copse of tremendous oaks. When he exclaims that they are the solution to his problem the woodsman replies, "Yes, I know. We were expecting you about now." This sense of past, present, and future, sensibly commingled and informing every aspect of daily life lies at the heart of Islandia's attraction. Even in 1931, the year of Wright's death in an automobile accident, it was clearly too late to set back the clock to a simpler world, but what Islandia offers us is a chance to step into such a world for a short time, and contemplate how our lives could be changed by inculcating some of its basic truths. That is not a trivial legacy for this one book and author to leave behind, and not a trivial matter for twenty-first century readers to consider.

JOHN SILBERSACK

Contents

PA**I**RT

Appointed Consul to Islandia

IN THE YEAR 1901, it was the custom at Harvard for seniors to entertain the incoming freshmen at "beer nights," where crackers and cheese and beer, to those who drank, and ginger ale, to those who did not drink, were served. To one of these I was invited with a random selection of my new classmates. However much alike we would have seemed to older persons, we believed in our own heterogeneity and, having all of us social ambitions, feared meeting or being seen with the wrong man; but we also accepted the tradition that one of the greatest things in life was college and class spirit, and that knowing a great many men fostered it. We were therefore in conflict within ourselves, but did not know it, nor were our hosts aware of it either. Having no knowledge of anything naturally in common we were all ill at ease.

A spectacled youthful boy talked with me in eager friendliness, but he revealed the fact that he was a graduate of a local high school. I made my escape and realized that it was far worse to seem to know no one than to be seen with the wrong one. I wished I had never come.

There was, however, another man in like plight. He was tall, over six feet, and heavily built. His face was too square, too ruddy, and too rugged for good looks, but it was strong and noticeable, with magnificently arched eyebrows; he had thick brown hair, that was black at night, parted in the middle, brown eyes with very clear whites, a strong chin slightly cleft, and a mature mouth. Because he looked like an athlete and therefore not socially compromising, and because his clothes were well cut, I dared and spoke to him.

His voice was deep and strong and, though anglicized, was peculiar in that every vowel and consonant was roundly articulated. I was embarrassed by its unusualness.

3

"How do you do?" I said. "Are you a freshman too?"

"Dorn," he answered. "My name is Dorn. Yes, I am a freshman."

"My name is Lang."

"Lang," he repeated and smiled, showing even white teeth. "That is like one of our names. Many of your names are hard for me to learn."

"Aren't you an American?" I asked, and hoping to please him, added, "You look like one."

"No, I am from Islandia."

His voice without being loud filled the room. There was a hush and many faces turned in our direction. None of us had ever seen one of his nation before. We knew that it lay, facing the Antarctic, on the edge of the Karain semicontinent in the Southern Hemisphere, that it was inhabited by an obscure Caucasian race with perhaps some dark intermixture, that it was pagan and hostile to foreigners, that the Islandians had rooted out the missionaries who had settled there in the forties, and that our school geographies gave it only a few lines because it was ruled by a peasant oligarchy, was agricultural and primitive, and had no trade.

With so many watching us I could not resume a personal conversation. I stood gaping. The aura of the remote and different was upon Dorn. Our sudden silence did not trouble him as it did me. He was serene, smiling a little, quite at ease.

A senior attracted by his voice looked him over and came up to us. Our class was in disgrace because so few of us had announced candidacy for the freshman football team. This man, an athlete, was searching for "new material." He asked Dorn, without any preliminaries, if he had gone out for football. Dorn's statement that he knew nothing of the game was met by the reply that he could soon learn, and that a man of his physique owed it to his class and college to try to make the team.

"I do not wish to play football this year," said Dorn.

"That is no reason," answered the senior. "If you have got any other reason let me hear it."

"I have no other reason," Dorn began in his clear, strong voice. The senior had his audience and made the most of it. He lectured us at length upon our duties to class and college and did it rather well. While he was speaking, Dorn went to the senior in whose room we were meeting, said good night, and departed apparently unconcerned.

While not for a moment disagreeing with anything the senior said, I felt that he was a little hasty with a man who was after all a foreigner; and whenever I saw Dorn I made a point of bowing to him in the smileless fashion of Harvard lower classmen in those days, but did not speak to him.

After Christmas, however, when football was a thing of the past, I did an unheard of and exciting thing for me: I went to walk alone; and met him, also by himself, circling Fresh Pond with long strides.

He smiled; I hesitated; he was a classmate, he had not been fairly treated, and he was another human being. We walked back to college together and thus began acquaintanceship.

We talked a little of the courses we had taken and then of the occasion when we had met, and I told him suddenly that I was very sorry that the senior had spoken in the way he had. He was so quiet that I wondered if I had not either offended him or touched upon a matter of deep concern with him.

"But did I not violate your customs?" he said.

In answer I attempted to justify the senior, whose attitude was that of most men, but I added, though what he said was all right, still I did think that a man had a right to do as he wished about athletics.

"Then you do not think I have done what is contrary to your American customs?" he asked again.

The question was a curious one.

"You haven't done anything wrong," I said.

"No, of course not!" he answered almost angrily.

"I wish you had been·given a chance to tell your reasons," I said. "Then no one would blame you at all. But all you said was that you did not wish to play football."

"Wasn't that enough to indicate that I had reasons?"

"Hardly," I said.

"My reasons . . . ? I'll give them to you."

He explained then how difficult he found the work that he was doing and how little spare time he had, that he had come to America to learn its civilization and customs and that he believed the best way to learn was by study. I answered that work alone was narrowing.

Our acquaintance became friendship. We did not understand each other always, but we soon discovered that by talking long enough we eventually reached what was next best: a sense of mutual relaxation and good will.

In the summer he went to England to join a remote cousin who was at Oxford. In the fall we met again, and he told me that he would take my advice and not confine himself to study alone, but go in for athletics. As a football player he was fast on his feet, with perfect muscular co-ordination, immensely strong, and very intelligent. He played his first game late in October. The *Harvard Crimson* commented upon his play as "crude but powerful." The coaches, however, rejoiced. He was never hurt and never taken from a game for injuries. He played at tackle for three years and was the strongest man in our line. Our opponents regarded him as a savage and were always surprised because he played a clean game. He took football lightly and did not make other athletes his only friends; there was still time for walks and talks with me, who was most unathletic. Little by little he began to talk about Islandia, but most of our conversation was about America and her problems. History and economics were his subjects, language and literature mine, but he was so ignorant of fundamental things that I was useful to him in his own fields of study.

Junior year found us rooming together with two others, all good friends. This was a happy year for me, with some literary success, many social engagements, and not too much work.

In the early spring Dorn showed signs of homesickness. He would fill his lungs with air as though to burst their walls and pound upon his expanded chest with a sound like a drum, all the time smiling. I felt much the same way. I called it spring fever, a phrase that pleased him, but he declared that it was country fever. Were there no farms in the United States, he asked, where we city dwellers could go? I thought of the little farm of one of my aunts near Adams on the edge of the Berkshires. She had asked me to visit her, and there we went for a long week end.

Aunt Mary was tart and downright, but her opinions were sharper than her practices. Her manner puzzled Dorn continually. Almost as soon as we arrived he offered to work for her. She took it as a joke coming from a "college boy," and to test his sincerity, gave him a heavy task splitting wood. He finished it quickly and came back for something else to do. She understood then that he really wanted to work. Soon she was telling him all her farming problems and he was advising her. He departed calmly and quietly happy, much surprised when Aunt Mary kissed him and said that he had probably ruined her farm, if she took his advice. This worried him, until I explained to him the nature of a New Englander's sense of humor.

Summer came and he went on a round of visits, for he was now one of the great men of the class. I was unsettled about my future, having finished my college work in three years; and I was wondering whether to take another year in literature and become a teacher or to go to the Law School. Neither prospect allured me.

In August we met in Portland and set out on a cruise down the Maine coast in a hired sloop. For six weeks we sailed from place to place, Dorn quite at home in a down-East boat. There were calms and fog and strong smoky winds. We were baked brown by hot suns and drenched by spray, mist, and rain. We went ashore only for supplies and to stretch our legs, content with the variety of the sea. With it all came a mood that was strange to me—of living with something vast and of being at the same time too happily sleepy quite to understand what was occurring. When there was noise enough of wind and wave and creaking spars to give resistance to my voice, I would sing loudly tag ends of tunes, and Dorn would lie on his back between the windward coaming and the rail and hum his own odd melodies in an undertone of roar like the sea. I had unexpected shivers of exaltation. Now and then the sea dropped its summer mask and showed a face of hardness. I did not care. My life seemed very little. I was content, but I was also always on the edge of frantic restlessness.

Sometimes hours passed in silence; but often we talked with all our hearts in it, and thoughts pressed so fast as to outstrip utterance. At first I was the egoist baring my inmost self as I never had before to anyone, and finding in him a warm sympathy and a cool judgment. Eventually I revolted myself for so cleaning house in his presence. I became silent and it was his turn, but while I was personal he was impersonal, and his need was not to speak of himself, but of his country.

It appeared that his cousin, young Mora, now at Oxford, was son of the political leader of Islandia, also named Mora. The father, Mora XXV, the premier, was strong in power and influence. His theories, like those of his ancestors, were opposed to the theories of the Dorns, and there had been historic clashes between the two houses down the centuries. Without my companion saying so, I gathered

7

that he was in a state of anxiety lest another such clash be imminent.

As far back as Islandian history went, the nation had been menaced and occasionally overrun by the peoples of the north. These consist of a vast population of Negroes, primitive and savage, and of a coastal fringe of men of higher civilization—"the Karain"—formed out of the intermixture between the Negroes and Arabic settlers, who came after the Hegira. Until recently the Karain were most to be feared, but within the last fifty years they had come under English, French, and German influence, which drove their more turbulent men into the interior, there to organize the blacks and make trouble. Islandia's policy had been one of defensive self-protection. At times her borders had been extended beyond the natural lines, but afterwards she had always withdrawn behind her rampart of mountains. That she should remain there was Dorn's view. Lately, however, Mora had undertaken against the blacks and their Karain leaders, a great campaign, which was now in its second year and steadily advancing to success. This warfare was always in Dorn's mind, partly because of his many friends engaged in perilous duties, still more because of his wonder at the political consequences that it might bring. This was complicated by the fact that the country through which Mora's army was advancing was watched with covetous eyes by the Germans. It was hard for me to understand exactly what troubled him.

"Political contacts are for us unfortunate," he said.

"What are you afraid of?" I asked. "No strong European power is likely to invade Islandia."

"I am not afraid of war," he answered, "but I am afraid that Mora and his followers will change us from what we now are, and that we cannot help it because of all the political contacts."

A vague remark like this seemed to me expressive of the most unreasonable fears, for were not all countries changing, was not change inevitable, and was not change the true sign of progress?

"You are a hopeless conservative," I said.

He thought for several moments.

"Of course," he answered, with some surprise in his voice, and then he smiled and stretched himself out full length and added the bass of his humming to the roar of the sea.

Often Dorn seemed to feel the need of speaking his own language, and he would say aloud to me unrhymed verses of marked rhythm, or tell me fables, translating as he went along. Thus was I introduced to Bodwin, who wrote in the fourteenth century. College had made my literary consciousness acute. I liked all that was new and different, and longed to read Bodwin in the original. Knowledge of him, not shared by my compeers, would be a feather in my cap. This led me to wonder if I could learn Islandian.

As we sailed through the reaches and thoroughfares of the coast of Maine, skirting her islands that were like wooded shields on the surface of dark waters, Dorn began to teach me his native tongue. It was without declensions, conjugations, moods or tenses, or genders, except where sex required them. Before the cruise ended I had made appreciable progress. I puzzled out a little Bodwin for myself, and found an interest more valid than merely to exult over literary students. His fables were unlike anything I had ever read, humorous, wise, old in date, and yet thoroughly modern and sophisticated in their undogmatic morality. During all the next year, possessed of Dorn's dozen Islandian volumes and armed with dictionary and grammar, I spent more time than I should working my way through Bodwin's works and acquiring by myself a fair reading knowledge of Islandian.

Our cruise came to an end after a week of heavy, treacherous northwest winds that gave us our fill of excitement and peril. At the last moment I decided to enter the Law School, while Dorn began his senior year with the burden of football upon him.

Three days before the game with Yale, he told me that he had received a letter from his great-uncle asking him to return to Islandia at once, and that he was going to start on his way on the night of the game itself. I was almost dazed. I saw him to the train at New Haven and we said good-bye to each other there.

An important part of my life seemed to be leaving me. I could not quite believe that I should never see him again, though reason said as much, for he was quite certain that he would never return to America, and it seemed most improbable that I should ever be able to seek him. Our actual parting was brief and silent and I for one was tongue-tied. I went away with tears in my eyes and wondered if I were a fool and a hero-worshiper. He seemed aloof and remote just then. Politics undoubtedly called him home. He, aristocrat, moved in places out of reach of me, still immature, regarded as a boy, and given no power by circumstances.

His departure left me with a sense of emptiness which was not relieved by my attitude toward my work. Conscious that I had drifted to the Law School like many others, and that I had no inclination toward any one profession or business but a shifting interest in many, I felt myself to be a rather worthless young man. I was horrified at the dismal picture of myself enslaved by the law, and such eagerness as I had would turn to ashes at that vision, closing the many other alluring avenues I wished to follow. It was a most unhappy year, and at the end I was more subtly miserable than at the beginning. All efforts to force my interest into a single channel had failed.

To complete the disarray of my half-adolescent manhood, I fell in love. It was calf love, and I had a vague sense of guilt as though I were prematurely indulging in an emotion only proper for more confident and ripened men. I became feverishly absorbed in a younger, but much more mature girl, Mary Jefferson, and the compulsion toward her was so strong that I thought the "real thing" had come at last. So much time and energy was spent in thinking about her and in pursuing her that the spring examinations nearly floored me. It was almost a relief to be rather abruptly dismissed by her before I had half expressed myself, much as an importunate child would be.

After these experiences I felt myself painfully callow, envious of mature men. My Uncle Joseph upset me further with an attack upon my "chosen profession," in which he highly praised the businessmen of modern America. They, he said, were doing things; opportunity stared these men in the face; the day when the best brains went into the ministry or the law was over; and so on. He swept me off my none too steady feet, but I hesitated before entering his employment. My pride rebelled against any trade where the chiefs reserved the right to treat one like a child, merely because they knew more about one narrow phase of life. But my eloquent and vital uncle presented a picture of commerce, of the development of trade with strange exotic lands, that stimulated my imagination more than any single occupation had yet done. He played on my patriotism, latent ambition, and egotism, and I saw myself sailing my ships, laden with superlatively cheap commodities of my own American manufacture, upon the seven seas of the globe. Then—a master of trade and finance —I would help the charming young lady, who had thrown me over, out of the mire of poverty that was her lot for refusing in advance the proposal I had not really intended to make.

During the summer Uncle Joseph made use of me as a sort of

secretary. One day he remarked casually that there was a job that I might qualify for; didn't I know Islandian?

I said I knew a little.

"You are one of the few men in America who do," said he. "If you were well recommended, you might get the new consulship there. That might be a fine opening."

I was surprised indeed, for I well knew from Dorn that Islandia neither received nor sent consuls or diplomatic representatives. My uncle, after a few critical words upon my ignorance, explained to me that in the previous October, nearly a year ago, Mora, the premier, had concluded a treaty with the Germans somewhat similar to that of Perry and the Japanese. My attention leaped to Dorn, who had left college just a month later. The treaty must have been the reason. Mora had pledged his country to receive diplomatic or consular officers from England, Germany, Austria, Italy, Russia, France, and the United States, and to permit a certain number of commercial prospectors for a period of two years and nine months, that is until June, 1908, with the promise that at the end of that time, if not before, the government would pass upon the question of entering into full commercial treaties with the countries named. Until then, however, the old laws forbidding trade and limiting the number of foreigners permitted to visit Islandia were to stand.

"Our businessmen," said Uncle Joseph, "are as little awake to what this means as you were. There is a wonderful market there. Their agricultural methods are primitive, and the ground-down farmers will now have their chance to get modern machinery. Sewing machines! Automobiles! There isn't one now in the country. They are rich with gold and can afford to pay high prices. Besides, they have ore and lumber in unlimited quantities for export. It is a chance, my boy. Even if we have to wait a few years, we shall stand better than someone else if we know what is going on. Of course, you would not want to be a consul all your life. With your knowledge of the country, when the commercial treaties go through, I'm sure someone might jump to get you on their payroll as agent. I would think it over myself." This was Uncle Joseph's way . . . "As consul, you could spend nearly all your time looking over the field and sounding men out. That would make your reports to the government really worth while. You would lay the foundations! There are a number of us interested. They have their backs up in Washington to a certain extent

11

and aren't inclined to send anyone who doesn't know the language and can't pass an examination. That, John, is where you come in!"

I was diffident, somewhat against my will, and annoyed my uncle by disclaiming sufficient knowledge or ability. He replied briskly that it was politics or nothing that would get the appointment for me in the end, and, of course, it was all up in the air.

Here was something to think over. The prospect had an effect like that of strong liquor quickly swallowed, but there was something sinister in Uncle Joseph's manner—the suggestion that I must remember to whom I would owe my appointment, and that I must, but not too coarsely, show that I would recognize my obligations before he would move actively. I was on trial and would have to prove, so to speak, a willingness and ability to serve two masters. Later, on second thought, I explained this as the cause of my instinctive reluctance.

In the months that followed I remained with Uncle Joseph, abandoning the law as a career. As a clerk or secretary, I was fairly efficient, but with regard to the consulship I was indifferent and inconsistent. The exhilaration never left me, but no one would ever have inferred as much from what I said or did.

Uncle Joseph worked for me behind my back, however, and in June sent me off to Washington to take the examinations for which I was not unprepared. In July I learned that we all had passed, a surprise because I knew that few of the others had any knowledge of Islandian. Uncle Joseph explained to me that no one ever failed and that if I expected to obtain the appointment by merit I was mistaken.

A long time had passed since the plan was first mentioned and I was so discouraged that it became unreal, but there was no other hope to receive its lost glow. My uncle's office was a bore.

In the middle of October I was notified by the Department of State of my appointment to the consulship, and that I should begin my duties on the first of the coming year (1907). The journey before me would take nearly six weeks, leaving me but a month for preparations. A new president would not be elected for more than two years, and I would therefore spend a minimum of eighteen months in a remote corner of the world. It seemed a very long time. I resigned from Uncle Joseph's and spent my month in studying timetables, shopping, and making somewhat sentimental farewell visits. All this proved to me that I had no real sorrow in parting from any particular person, not even my family. On the other hand, I discovered a regret at the probability of seeing no young American girl of my own age for two years and more. As I bade each of my several present flames good-bye I was depressed as at an opportunity missed by my own act. Love, or rather the possibility of love, seemed at these moments the only true pleasure.

There was one girl, very young, not yet "out"—so young, in fact, that she seemed to have been recently made of the freshest of materials. Gladys Hunter was still very much a child with a mind that seemed almost naked in its simplicity and honesty. She had no airs, but she was both impersonal and enthusiastic. I found pleasure in seeing her long slim figure, still clad in rather short dresses, her slender youthful hands, her honest long legs, her candid, large brown eyes and crisp fresh features, and in trying to match her simple sincerity with one equally fine and clear. I had only just met her and I did not like to lose her so soon. At the end of two years she would be "out" and grown up. Perhaps I was flattered by her eager acquisitive interest in my journey and in Islandia—particularly by her frank taste for and insight into timetables of steamers, so fascinating to me. When the time came to say good-bye to her I lost my head a little.

"Would you mind if I wrote to you occasionally?" I asked. Her eyes grew still upon mine, in a surprise that I knew with instant relief was not personal or sophisticated.

"Why no," she said, and then added, "if mother doesn't mind, and I don't think she will."

Uncle Joseph summoned me with the rigorous courtesy of royalty, not to be disobeyed, but he treated me as an equal. He gave an elaborate lunch with important men to meet me. He captured my emotions as he had never done before, although I was always under his spell. The swinging wide of doors to the most vital of American things was hinted. He and his friends were near the beating heart of it all. The way was clear to me, still quite a young man, to open vast new fields for the glory and good of my countrymen and of world commerce, and to reap my reward in power and consciousness of pioneer work ably done in the face of able rivals—England, declining, but still the strongest; Germany, the growing giant.

My uncle may not have realized his hopes of having the Consul of the United States at Islandia devoted to his business for in one way or another, by no great merit of my own, I had escaped pledging myself to any particular interest; but if he had known my state of mind on the eve of my departure, he would have been delighted. I felt my nationality as I had never done before, I was resolved to serve my country, and I believed that the finest way to serve her was by extending her foreign trade.

These convictions brought a severe pang. Dorn had roused my interest in Islandia and to him I owed the knowledge of Islandian which certainly helped me to win the consulship. I was not merely going to his country as the exemplar of a policy opposed to all that he believed for her best interests; there was almost a betrayal of him in my grim resolve to further in every way what his opponents wished. I did not write him that I was coming, for I did not like to mention the consulship while it was uncertain and perhaps have to explain why I did not get it. Now that I had it, I put off writing, because I could not decide exactly what to say. Soon it became too late. I dreaded seeing again the best friend of my college days, and this was a cloud on my pleasure. Yet the thought of seeing him was also one of the components of my happiness, and he most of all drew me to Islandia.

2

New York—St. Anthony—The City

THE ENGLISH ROUTE to Islandia permitted a visit to the crown colony
of St. Anthony. I took my passage by a Cunarder to Liverpool and
continued by rail to London where I spent six days, busy, carefree,
and amused, presenting letters from my uncle and catching a glimpse
of a more ancient and professionally commercial world. On December 7th, 1906, I was whisked by the express boat train to Southampton. There, on board the Orient Steam Packet Co. steamer to St.
Anthony, I was at last alone—dependent solely on myself for a long
time to come and face to face with a future for which past experience
furnished me no guide.

I was much alone during the long leisurely voyage, but I enjoyed
the nineteen days at sea. As we worked south, all the seasons of the
year swept over us. We passed from the dim brief days, long nights,
and the harsh chill of winter to the full glare of a high sun and the
heat of the tropics. Dressed in flannels and white, we sailed over blue,
bright seas and saw the sun's course grow oblique in the north. At
moments I felt the year whirl around me and only by a mental effort
could recall that the calendar read December still.

It was a lethargic life, and I did not resent it. The idleness was
pleasant to every muscle and bone. My mind, inactive, did not desire
even a book. For hours I sat in my chair watching the line of the
horizon climb laboriously to that of the ship's rail and reluctantly
sink away.

But St. Anthony drew nearer inexorably. As we moved along the
coast of the Karain continent, I felt its presence over the sea's horizon, with all its demands upon me.

I heard much of this coast from those on board. St. Anthony had
been seized by the English to prevent another European power taking

it first to use as a base. Then English rule was extended steadily south, until in the last great step of establishing a protectorate over Mobono, English influence was brought squarely against the mountain frontiers of Islandia. To the north was the Caldo Bay, of deadly calms, across the mouth of which we were sailing, bordered by lands arid, sterile, and all but empty. Recently, however, attention had been turned upon this unexplored region; the Germans were nibbling, and there was said to be great mineral wealth.

This was immensely interesting to me. I was at the edge of empire, and I was learning the reality of problems that had been cold and dull in history books.

Christmas was a day of muggy heat and seas that heaved without a ripple. Always in my past that day had come with winter weather and had been spent indoors. Here we all lay in our deck chairs, spent and indolent, shading ourselves from the white glare of the sky and the dazzle of the sea. To celebrate the day there was an elaborate Christmas dinner and a concert. The heavy food, the wines, the rather wailing music, and the menacing needs of the morrow sent me to bed in an emotional state. I felt lost and far away, my own powers none too strong to grapple with the problems before me. Cold reason told me that there were no real difficulties in my way, but I could not convince my inner timidity.

In the morning, however, I woke, knowing we were near the land, with great eagerness to see its newness and strangeness; and after breakfast I beheld—beheld for the first time—the Karain continent, some thirty miles away. Through the white mist there loomed what looked like an immense field, pale brown, yellow, and green, tilted up to steel-gray misty mountains.

In this coastal plateau are two valleys, which narrow into steep-sided gorges, turning sharply towards each other as they approach the sea, from which they are concealed. In the northernmost St. Anthony lies, an elusive hidden city.

When we approached the shore, all the passengers gathered to watch, for there was fascination in the view before us. The sun, filtering through the white haze, made the air warm and damp. The cliffs glimmered, banded with hot, light colors. Near the top was a vertical strip of hard, buff-tinted limestone; below, rustier bands of softer rock, with a precipitous talus slope down to the edge of the pale-blue water.

A tug drew alongside and I saw my first "Lamb of God"—for so the St. Anthonians call themselves. The deck hands and stewards were pale mulattoes with large seal-brown eyes, soft features, and gentle smileless faces. They are of an immemorially ancient race—a mixture of a white people, perhaps the same as that which peopled Islandia, and the black Negroes of the far interior. History had it that white and black were separate when the Christians came, but that both races, taking literally the precept that men were brothers, intermarried as the only course of virtue, until in a few generations there were few whose blood was still pure.

Everyone trooped down the gangway into the tug. After landing on the quay and going through the brief and perfunctory customs examination, we straggled into a diminutive train of open cars, which set out with a high toot and violent jerk. At once we began to climb. There was a glimpse back upon the roofs of the warehouses on the quay, and then we were in a gorge with a brawling stream below us on our right. For a few moments it was impossible not to feel that one was in the heart of desolate mountains. High above, shutting out the sun, rose the rusty talus slopes of the cliffs; the air was cool; the train swayed and creaked and screamed on sharp curves; and there was not a sign of a human being except ourselves.

Presently the gorge narrowed and became wild and almost sinister. Then abruptly on either side the cliffs, like a portal, fell back, and we were in a valley shaped like a broad-bottomed U. Its slowly rising sides were everywhere terraced, with trees, grass, gardens, dark soil, sharply-climbing earthy roads, and here and there low, brown stone houses. Once more the sun was hot, and the valley air was close and muggy. A few moments later the train slid abruptly to a stop at a little station between the river and a low block of shops. The street was crowded with St. Anthonians, the men dressed in baggy, dark-blue trousers and loose, coarse jackets, and the women in somber browns. I smelled the famous smell of the place—humanity and half-rotten vegetables. Into the idle crowd, passive and quiet, but curious, I pushed with my porters; then I found a victoria and was driven up through steep streets to the hotel, a low building with wide verandas, a garden, and an air of age, dignity, and style.

It was a relief to be served efficiently, to be shown to a room, and to be able to settle my moist and enervated body into a deep chair.

After lunch on the hotel terrace all by myself I returned to my

17

room, still tired. The visit to the Islandian representative was an ordeal that I wanted to put off, preferring an afternoon of utter laziness on my back. There was no reason why I should go today rather than tomorrow, for this was Thursday and I had until Sunday to wait, but go today I somehow must. With a rather dizzy head I rose from my bed, freshened myself, and put my papers in my pocket.

I had expected to be directed down into the town to some office, but was instead dispatched in a victoria. In the glare of the sun we crawled up the limestone cliffs, on a road that looped back and forth upon itself. Halfway up the cliffs at the end of one of the western loops we stopped by a gate in a solid stone wall, beyond and above which rose tall trees. Here on a little shelf not fifty feet wide was the dwelling place of the Islandian representative, who was responsible for his country's few relations with England and for supervising the entrance of foreigners into Islandia. A board was nailed to the gate with directions, in English, Islandian, and the language of St. Anthony, to ring. I pulled a projecting pin and far off a deep bell clanged once solemnly.

The gate opened suddenly, and I was face to face with an Islandian—and so different from Dorn, my friend! He was a slight man wearing loose, rough-spun knickerbockers and a belted coat over a shirt with an open, broad collar. His head, covered with dark, curling hair, and his face had an almost perfect symmetry. His thin, straight nose, the simple lines of his cheek and jaw, his small mustache, and well-made mouth looked soft and mild, until I was aware of fine arching eyebrows and of clear, direct gray eyes upon me.

With an effort I spoke to him in his own language, stating my name and my errand, watching his expression lest he should not understand. But he nodded and smiled cordially, and at his invitation I followed him through the gate. On the left were the trees and directly behind them the cliffs; on the right was a low stone wall edging a sheer drop of two hundred feet with the valley below; ahead, along the gravel path edged with flowers, was a small stone house.

As we proceeded he told me his name, Cadred, and speaking in his own tongue, suggested that we arrange at once about my passport. I had to concentrate all my attention to understand, but a burden rolled away when I realized that I could do so. He guided me into a simple room furnished only with a bright-colored rug, a few stools, and a table on which was a pile of immense books bound in stiff, black, angular covers, with gold and red inlay. He offered me a stool and sat himself behind the table, leaning upon it with his slim refined hands clasped before him, and looked me squarely in the eye. He was very still. Heat and the novelty gave me a sense of dreaming, and he seemed a carved figure, vivid but unreal.

After a few moments he questioned me without a movement of his body, his voice leisurely and kindly, pausing to give me a chance to understand. It appeared that, as Consul of the United States, the exclusion laws did not apply to me, and that I would receive a passport as a matter of course, except for one thing: he had no power to suspend the requirement of a physical examination. I wondered to myself if it were not my duty as a representative of my country to resent such an ordeal; and I asked if this were required of all foreign representatives. He told me with a faint smile that he could dispense with it in the case of ministers, but not of consuls. Then quite abruptly I made up my mind. My real duty was to get to Islandia and not to bristle at imagined insults to our flag. I told him I would be willing, but that I only consented because he had orders to make the examination.

"Today?" he asked, and I nodded. "The doctor will be here this afternoon, and it will, if you wish, take place then."

Then he examined my papers, made entries in his books, and prepared and gave me a paper, stiff as old parchment, permitting me to enter his country subject to physical examination. After that he questioned me as to my age, my education, and my marital condition, all very courteously; but it was rather annoying, and I did not wonder at the hostility of the many who had come to Islandia and had undergone these examinations.

Our business was ended. For a few moments he sat motionless as before with hands clasped and eyes on mine. The room was utterly still, and I felt a little as though hypnotized. At last I was aware that he had risen, and I rose too, and followed him out to the veranda where we sat down near the stone wall edging the cliff.

After some minutes the gate opened, we heard a man's and a woman's voice, and two Islandians came along the path. The first was a young, pretty woman of about twenty-five, bareheaded and wearing a plain brown skirt and belted jacket with a blouse of the finest linen, orange-colored and striking, with broad collar. The second was a man, tall, slender, ruddy-cheeked, with black hair.

Cadred stated our names. The woman was Islata Soma, his wife; the man, Mannar, the doctor.

I knew that the Islandians had but one name and there were no honorifics, such as Mister, but my home custom made his introduction sound a little uncomfortably informal. The term "Islata"—of nobility—redeemed his wife's name of that embarrassment, and I looked at her curiously a moment. She, then, was an aristocrat—and in appearance she seemed a lady, simple and at ease.

The physical examination was mentioned by my host to Mannar. I said I was ready, and we two went through another door into the doctor's laboratory or office. The examination was extremely thorough and yet far less offensive to my modesty than I feared it would be. I winced at some of the intimate questions he put to me, but I also admired him for his tact and—against my will—for the way he dominated me. His methods were not quite those of our American doctors. He did things that were strange, and asked questions that were very personal; but I did not feel, as have some foreigners visiting Islandia, that he was guilty of the unscientific tricks of an ignorant and prurient medicine man. When, after about three quarters of an hour, we returned to the veranda, he knew more about my inner life than anyone else in the world; but I also had his certificate of fitness to enter Islandia, and I was sure I deserved it!

Islata Soma and Cadred were awaiting us at a table, unpainted and carved, upon which were a bottle of wine and a plate of cakes. This was my introduction to Islandian food. The wine, heavy and ruddy in color, was slightly sweet with a strange, resinous tang that left a pleasant taste, so that the mouth felt cooled and freshened. The cakes were short and a little nutty.

For a few minutes no one spoke. It was very quiet. In the valley beneath us long shadows were gathering and the greenery became darker and blue. The others moved little and their faces were grave. Presently the silence began to weigh upon me and I spoke to Islata Soma, telling her of my friendship with Dorn. She described to me the part of Islandia where he lived, saying that the home of her cousin, Some XII, the Lord of Loria, was on the road thither, and that her own home was about fifteen miles away in remote, hilly forests.

"But," she added, "we live almost as much at my cousin's house and he at ours. It is newer and has only been in the family one hundred and sixty years. Ours goes back nearly four hundred. You will go to visit your friend Dorn, and on your way you must stay at my cousin's house. If you are not hurrying you might go to my home in the hills. I will give you a letter. You will be welcome at either place."

I thanked her, sincerely pleased.

"It is nothing," she said.

A moment later her eyes kindled and she clasped her hands tightly and, speaking so rapidly I could scarcely follow, she described the ancient house.

"It was very small when we came to it. We were poor then. We had been driven out of Camia, where we had lived for hundreds of years. Little by little we cleared the land and added to the house. Ours is one of the few farms in the forest. We were very happy there as children, and whenever we wished to see more people we had only to ride to my uncle's on the highway."

For a moment I was puzzled, and then I realized that the "we" to whom she referred must be her ancestors for four hundred years. My mind turned inwards at this living evidence of Islandian permanency of family and tradition, and I saw in sharp contrast to it our own modern development, and in a new light the problem of Islandia's opening herself to trade. I thought again of Dorn and the policy for which his family stood, and of my position as consul—one whose very existence supposed a condition contrary to all that in which he believed. For a few seconds I hung balanced between reticence that seemed wise and conventional and a desire to state my trouble—and I stated it, and when it was out it was not half so bad as it seemed.

Islata Soma smiled at me.

"Do you fear that he will wish not to see you?"

"Not that—but am I not acting unfairly to my friend?"

"You could not be unfair," she said, "believing as you do. Go to see him soon."

A few moments later the bell clanged suddenly, and Cadred went to the gate, returning with a tall young man of small head and light, curling hair—obviously English. This was Philip Wills, brother of Gordon Wills, British consul, and just graduated from Cambridge. He was on his way to Islandia to visit his brother. He had evidently come to fetch his passport. He was introduced to me, and our conversations thenceforth were in English, a language in which

21

the Islandians were proficient. Islata Soma, with a little quick smile of humor, went to get tea for him.

Half an hour later we left together, and I had with me my passport and health certificate and a note from Islata Soma to her relatives.

That evening it was hot at the hotel, and after a day that seemed long and quite reasonably profitable I felt myself at liberty to do nothing. I was lonely, then, as I had not been before—lonely for young people of my own sort. I thought of the girls with whom I had arranged to correspond, and I wrote to Natalie Weston and Clara Bryant, constantly tempted to be sentimental; for in the night and heat and silence—the town below my window black—they lived before me, more and more vivid and provocative. Love was to me still a mystery. I did not really wish to end the mystery by marriage with anyone, but I wanted them, and the longing was hard to bear.

It was a relief to me when Sunday night came. At half-past nine I took the special boat train, which ran clattering and clanking down the gorge and around the bend in the cliffs to the station on the shore.

On the quay I saw Wills, my only acquaintance, tall and graceful, immaculate in his evening clothes, talking to a young girl so much shorter than himself that she had to hold her chin high. She showed against a light an aura of soft, fair hair and a profile cut with the sharpness of a cameo. She was eighteen or nineteen and very pretty. Accompanied by a middle-aged Englishman they boarded the S.S. *St. Anthony* together, while I watched them from a distance.

Early in the morning the cessation of vibration woke me. It was utterly still. The steamer was not moving and I remembered that there was a stop scheduled for a place called Coäpa, settled by the English. Sleepiness struggled with curiosity and finally the latter conquered, and I rose and looked out.

The little window opened upon a narrow deck. The stanchions were black against a background hushed and bluish, with that pervading, faint, translucent light that comes from nowhere shortly before dawn. The shore was visible and close at hand. There were high cliffs faintly touched with color, cleft by a valley that vanished into shadows. On the water's edge was foliage and a few yellow lamps already losing significance as the light of day increased. A group of these was moving, and I was aware by its dots of red and green that it was a launch coming off to us.

Footsteps sounded along the deck, and I drew back a little, not to be seen. The round of the porthole made a frame, and in that frame was the upright of a stanchion, which in the gathering dawn had become a rosy white. Against it leaned a head—a profile, softly lighted.

It was the English girl. I saw her from a distance of about ten or twelve feet, but the early glow was confusing, and her features eluded me. I could not see her eyes except as little pools with clear-cut lazy eyelids. My heart beat.

It was a matter of a few seconds. I saw come upon her features what might have been a smile, sleepy, amused, and indulgently annoyed at being got up so early. A man's voice said clearly and paternally:

"Well, Mary?"

There was the sweet, soft, sleepy answer of a young girl's voice. Her head vanished.

A few minutes later I saw the launch heading shoreward, and looking back over the stern was her face, receding in the distance round and minute.

I went back to bed, deeply moved, and slept soundly several hours more. I woke quite contented, for my memory was so bright that it gave color to the steamer that had otherwise become drab and cheerless.

All day we were in sight of land to starboard, arid cliffs and foreshores of pale ochres, lavenders, and pinks, faintly visible through the hazy air. Toward evening the heights receded and we coasted a desolate plain, rimmed by a faint line of mountains. Here the Karain lived, the enemies of Islandia, who organized the blacks of the interior and once in almost every lifetime set out to conquer, pillage, and enslave.

The next day we continued along the coast and Wednesday, January 2nd, found us approaching Mobono, the largest city of the continent and newly under an English protectorate.

On deck I found Philip Wills with M. Perier, the French consul in Islandia, a small man with a narrow beard and thick, curling hair of a dusty brown, and with limpid, intelligent eyes. He had traveled about the Karain continent and told Wills and me something about

23

Mobono, an ancient and sinister city, crowded and poverty-stricken, formerly the seat of the Karain emperors.

In the early afternoon the city emerged from the haze quite near at hand, lying upon a low shore. A stone quay lined the water's edge and, beyond, the town lay level and confused except for an immense palace, towering above all in rectangular steps of battlemented masonry.

It was the Palace of the Emperors, M. Perier said, and he suggested that we go ashore together to visit it. He engaged a boat with a crew of two Negroes, their sweating faces jet black in contrast to their white turbans and jackets and loose trousers.

Arrived at the city we were driven in an ancient victoria through narrow twisting streets, crowded from wall to wall. Life teems in Mobono as in Naples, and the smell is the same.

M. Perier told me that until recently no European had been safe there without a guard. I looked over the side of the victoria into insolent black and mulatto faces. Occasionally a Karain passed us walking disdainfully, his robes held tightly about him, and I felt hostility and danger surrounding me.

When we reached the palace, we climbed to a terrace in the sunlight, which was crowded with beggars and loafers. Leaning over the balustrade we looked down on broad, firm stone walls that surrounded the building. Beyond lay the tossing huddle of the city. Its borders and the harbor were hidden in the haze and it seemed immense.

"In the fourteenth century," said M. Perier quietly, "the Islandians captured this castle by storm. It was one of the great deeds of their history. The queen herself, yet a young woman, led them. After the capture, she remained here more than two years and at her court the great period of Islandian letters began. Here Bodwin, the fabulist, lived for many years. It is the 'high tower in an evil city' of which he writes. If it were clear weather we would see to the south the snow peaks of Islandia. They are a very great people."

"They seem opposed to modern ideas," I remarked.

"It is a question of taste," said M. Perier shortly.

Later, after we had made our way to a café on the water front, I thought again of that answer and wondered what his ideas were on the opening up of Islandia.

"Do you think the Islandians will vote for foreign trade in the next few years, M. Perier?"

He shrugged.

"If they vote against it," I said, "I suppose our careers as consuls would be over."

"Perhaps not. Some nation might find a grievance and force trade upon Islandia."

"I don't believe the United States would."

"Nor France."

"England?" I asked.

Again he shrugged.

"Germany?"

Then he looked me full in the eyes.

"Islandia possesses precious metals—metals the Germans need. And Germany wishes markets and a field for settlers and for investment. Africa and Asia are almost closed to them, but here . . . The west coast will some day be more German than Potsdam. There is much vacant land in Islandia. Very soon a German railway will be built from here to M'paba on the west coast. Iron will come to M'paba over this railway. Coal is needed and Islandia is rich in coal —and oil. Why not another railroad from the coal mines of Islandia to M'paba, which is only thirty miles from the boundary. Then German steamers to Ferrin, Islandia's island, with gold, silver, iron, platinum—platinum!—all coming to M'paba with a temperate climate, and only forty miles away fertile valleys with much room—in Islandia."

Mines, oil wells, and railroad concessions were evidently the big stakes. Before leaving New York I had been told of prospectors, who were thinking of Islandia and who would come during my consulship.

"If money is to be made, then, it will be by the concessionaire rather than by the merchant," I suggested, in order to have my conclusion confirmed.

"Yes . . . the concessionaire," Perier muttered in a brief, irritated tone.

We returned on board just in time for dinner, and our meal was accompanied by the clattering sound of the winches, the rattling of tackles, and the shrill signal whistles of the winchmen.

I went to bed when the sea was black around us, my mind crowded with thoughts and new impressions. Tired, I slept soon, seeing in my dreams the streets of Mobono, pursuing wearily a fugitive thing, both very sweet and unknown, and not finding it.

The sound of a long-drawn whistle waked me. It was repeated, and I knew we must be in fog. My watch read midnight and therefore we were certainly off the Islandian coast. An indefinable homelike feeling came pleasantly upon my drowsing consciousness. The air was distinctly cool and for the first time I drew up my blankets. In perfect comfort, treasuring the thought of another long, lazy night at sea, I slept, hearing intermittently the whistle, and woke with surprise to find that it was full daylight, and that the steamer was rolling as she had not rolled before.

Rising from my bunk in the expectation of sunlight, so bright was it, I looked out into a white, translucent fog. Overhead the sky was glowing and the rushing, windy water was unexpectedly blue.

On the deck, after breakfast, we did not as usual sink into our deck chairs. It was bracing without being cold, and the wind from off the land though dampened by the fog had now and then some of that peculiar land quality of warmth, dryness, and earthiness.

There was no sign of land, however, for though the sky was often blue overhead and though the fog opened to show wide vistas of sea and not infrequently the eastern horizon, it never thinned enough to disclose the land to the west.

I spent the afternoon in the smoking room with a group of Germans. Three of them, who looked like commercial travelers, had come from St. Anthony and had been joined by three others who had come overland on horseback from the German colonies on the west coast. One of the travelers, Hoeffler, was a magnificent man, over six feet, massive, burned to the color of brick, with a heavy jolly voice and gray, bloodshot, but friendly eyes, far apart under heavy lids. He was telling of his journey and I heard for the first time the words "Sobo Steppes," describing a dry, grassy region which lies north of and under the great range of snow mountains that form Islandia's northern boundary.

I listened, picking up enough to be interested in the accounts of the small walled towns dotted here and there in the steppes, inhabited by mixed races of blacks and Karain. Remembering the remarks of M. Perier on German plans, I sought, in what I heard, for confirmation. The route of the projected railroad from M'paba was mentioned once or twice, but there was nothing to rouse suspicion.

At four o'clock that afternoon we were off the east coast of Storn, the southeastern province of Islandia, which occupies a blunt peninsula with the sea on three sides, and nothing between it and Antarctica but an ocean, wilder and more stormy with every mile. The wind had almost dropped, for we were near the fog-bound, high-lying shore.

Suddenly blue sky opened above, and to the northwest sunlight struck down to the sea, brightening the wave crests and darkening their blue. Abeam, a billow of fog wavered, split, and rose. The sun vanished behind it and the water darkened, but there appeared, two or three miles away, a red cliff with its rugged base in white foam. The curtain of gray lifted higher. Disclosed for a moment were miles and miles of spacious moors, a deep rich green, except where the sun fell upon them in patches of emerald.

A great shoulder of fog hid it again.

Islandia! I had seen the naked rock of her shores, and her rolling moors.

Not long after a violent gust of wind swept over the deck, lifting our rugs and howling about the stanchions; the sky darkened, heavy lines of rain slanted obliquely from the southwest, drumming on the boat deck over our heads and splashing in the scuppers; and the steamer pitched heavily. The fog closed in around us in a rushing stream, making the dark sulphurous in color.

It was late when I finally went to bed, and later still when I slept. We were corkscrewing through heavy seas from the southwest, but I was wakeful as a result of an emotional excitement that had been growing all day. Tomorrow, Friday, January 4th, 1907, my long journey would end.

My only possible trouble in this new country would be loneliness, but the land I was approaching was Dorn's. He was there over the water. I saw him vividly with his strong, kind face, his steady sympathy, his power, and his mystery.

3

First Weeks in Islandia

WHEN I CAME on deck I faced a cloudless, lovely morning, brilliantly clear. We were headed almost due north and entering a broad, landlocked bay between jutting promontories of brownish rock. Over the bow, hanging low in the sky, was an immense white dome. Its lower slopes showed white fingers upon a background that was the color of the sky, so that the dome seemed to float ethereally. To the right and left, an equal distance away and seeming to face it like guardians, were snowy giants of sharper outline. Over one hundred miles away, so great was their bulk and height, they were tremendous, and the sea apparently reached their mist-hidden, colossal foundations. I did not need to be told that the dome was Mount Islandia.

Breakfast was not a meal to linger over. There was too much to be seen, and in two hours the anchor would be dropped. Because I needed advice and also liked and trusted him, when M. Perier appeared on deck, I confided my feelings about Dorn to him; and he, like Islata Soma, advised me to write at once and not to worry about our different views. There was something very friendly in his manner, and my cup of gratitude was full when he offered to take me in hand when we went ashore, suggesting that I present my credentials in his company that afternoon and then come home with him for dinner.

Soon the land to which we were bound became visible, a dark-green band on the horizon, marked directly where the bow was pointing by a pale dot—our destination. For over an hour, absorbed, I watched it grow. At first it was but a tiny dash of white upon which slowly mounted a dome that was pink; then to the left a lesser hill lifted a sunlit head, and the whole widened, and there appeared upon it faint rectangles in different tones of pale, bright colors. At last it was a city indeed, zoned and encircled on the water's edge by low brown walls, behind which a network of double masts like wishbones were visible; and rising above these were the square, simple façades of buildings of stone, ochre, gray, or rose, crowding to the summits of three hills.

But I had to leave it all, to collect my things and to tip the stewards, and while I was thus engaged I felt the surcease of vibration and a few moments later the rumble of the anchor chains.

When I returned to the deck a heavy barge, low and wide, was coming toward us from across the harbor. It was decked forward, and four rowers stood there facing us, keeping time with rapid, short, whiplike strokes. It came rapidly, pitching a little and casting out white foam on either side of its broad flat bow; but with a sudden backing of water on one side and with hard rowing on the other, it swung about and came up broadside to our gangway in as deft a "landing" as a sailor could wish.

A moment later two slender young men, bareheaded and in Islandian costume, were on our decks, going through our papers with courtesy and great expedition. Perier, Wills, and I were passed at once, thanks to our examinations at St. Anthony, and were sent down the gangway into the barge. Our baggage was portered down to us, and at a signal from the deck the barge was off with a rush. The four oarsmen and the steersman were dressed in close-fitting, dark jerseys, homespun brown knickerbockers, with bare legs and sandals. They were all slender and muscular, with fine small heads and sunburned faces, and the heavy craft was a plaything to them.

Ancientness, permanency, quiet—these were the first quick impressions; and then, activity. Here and there a barge was moving, rowed as swiftly as we were rowed. From a dock to the east slid a bluff-bowed, solid boat, with two wishbone masts; two huge spars rose to the crotch of the wishbones, great brown sails dropped and caught the wind; white water showed in a rushing line along her leeward side; she heeled a little, gathering speed, heading for the harbor mouth. On the docks and quay were tiny figures, varicolored, in quiet motion. It was almost unearthly still. We heard the dip and splash of oars, but from the docks and quay came no cries, no rumble of machinery, no rattling of tackles, nothing.

We came to a stop at a stone quay where fifteen or twenty persons were waiting—four or five Islandian officials, Gordon Wills come

29

to meet his brother, Madame Perier and her two daughters, and several other Europeans. I found myself in the midst of the group, being introduced to these people and to a sturdy, heavy German, Graf von Bibberbach, the German minister. Then my baggage, with that of Perier, was piled in a handcart, and we started towards The City on foot, followed by our goods, I with Madame Perier, and he ahead with a daughter on each side.

We crossed a causeway and looked down on our right into a narrow dock, crowded with two-masted boats of heavy build and of dark, varnished wood, from which open boxes of large, ruddy oranges were being unloaded. Their strong perfume filled the air. A moment later, came another odor, both resinous and sweet, from a large rectangular basin beyond. Mme. Perier, in her slow French, explained that each province had its own docks, piers, and warehouses, that on this island were those of Carran, whence came the oranges, and of Winder, the mountainous province in the southeast corner of Islandia; and that the sweet pungent odor was from the sugar gum brought from Winder. A moment after there came from the open door of a warehouse the smell of chocolate.

M. Perier insisted on coming with me to the hotel and I was glad of his company, for by this time the unaccustomed steadiness of the land, the sunlight, the novelty of everything, and most of all the strange stillness, had dazed me a little. Through his help arrangements were made for a room on the western side, at a price by no means small. There he left me, promising to call at half-past two.

My room was large, with walls of masonry over which were hung great, flat curtains of a brown, soft wool. On the varnished floor was a large, brown woolen rug. The furniture, all of wood, consisted of a low bedstead with a rather hard mattress, linen sheets, and very soft blankets of brown wool; three or four stools, a plain table, a huge, square wardrobe, a sofa with rush bottom, and a washstand with immense bowl and huge pitcher of brown earthenware. There was no ornamentation—all was square, massive, and well-made, and no color except the deep, ruddy, shining brown of the wood, and the soft, clear brown of woolen cloth, and two great trusses of scarlet blooms four feet high in dark-blue glazed vases on either side of the window.

My baggage was brought in by an Islandian, in the usual working costume of blue jersey, brown knickerbockers, stockings, and sandals, well-bred in appearance, strong, and quiet. He asked if I would bathe, and when I assented, brought in a large earthenware tub on wheels, a great pitcher of hot water, and an armful of soft, white woolen towels. He then asked when I would lunch. I suggested one o'clock at random. He smiled and looked puzzled, and I remembered that in Islandia there are no watches, only water clocks; but that everyone in consequence has a peculiarly accurate time sense, and that day and night are divided into twelve hours from sunrise to sunset or vice versa. I said six, which I guessed would correspond to noon. That he accepted as natural.

After bathing, and because I was to make formal calls in the afternoon, I dressed in morning coat, worsted trousers, and patent leather boots, and laid out top hat, gray gloves, and cane. By the time this was done, the servant arrived with my lunch on a tray, set the table near the window, wheeled out the tub, and left me.

There was a broiled fish steak like halibut and a small tender beefsteak, green peas, and a vegetable like carrots but with a chestnutty flavor. There was a large basket of fruit, oranges, peaches, and huge objects that looked like plums, a small cup of chocolate, and a pyramidal china bottle of wine, with a silver goblet.

Only the chocolate and wine had peculiar flavors, the former rather bitter, and the latter faintly resinous and very sweet.

I was feeling hungry and I never tasted anything better than the plumlike object—the famous Islandian *sarka*, with its melting, reddish yellow, juicy pulp faintly flavored with attar of roses. As to the wine, I was a little doubtful of the headiness of its rosy, pleasing volatility.

Lunch over, I stood long at the window in a dream. There was such quiet and peace! It was hard to believe that I was in an actual city, for in the sunlight and stillness what I saw was like a painted model. Below me was a block of closely built houses. Some had flat roofs, others pitched steeply with red tiles and skylights. Beyond, lay a stream with wooden drawbridge, and on the other side were docks, piers, and warehouses; then blocks of houses, the city walls, a glimpse of river, and further still miles and miles of green pastures, woods, and farms, with here and there a white, red-roofed house. To the left lay the blue waters of the bay. There was movement here and there—small figures on the quay or on the bridges or piers, barges coming down the stream with their four rhythmic oarsmen, a boat with two masts for which the draw was raised—but such sounds as came were faint and distant; far louder was the shrill twittering of some finchlike bird in the roof gardens below.

This bright, minute, and quiet land was that of my friend Dorn. It was hard to realize that to him it was home and natural. He too seemed alien. But I saw him, big, ruddy, kindly, and I heard his deep voice singing fluttering tunes against the hiss and rush of the sea and the creaking of spars. I knew in my heart that he would greet me gladly. I must write him at once.

M. Perier gave me countenance by appearing dressed as I was, but although our costume was unlike that of anyone else abroad on the streets, no one stared at us. Men and women passed us with only now and then a glance. All were bareheaded, walking with leisurely directness and silently in their sandals, which often had fiber soles. Their costumes were unusual, and it was I who was tempted to stare. The men wore trousers ending above their bare knees, shirts without neckties open at the throat, and, over these, jackets, more loosely cut and often without the lapels of our sack coats. The women wore short plain skirts that fell only a little below their knees, and jackets similar to those of the men, of a fine, rather loosely spun wool. The colors of the garments were striking—creamy white, gray, tan, green, light- or dark-blue, or sometimes red, or heather. Sometimes they wore wide lapels or cuffs of a different color, and of a different texture like broadcloth. The legs of about half of those I saw were bare, women's as well as men's.

There were two extreme types—men or women like Dorn, big, with massive heads, black hair, black eyebrows, dark eyes, and ruddy skins, and those more like Cadred with oval faces and heads and delicate firm features, hair of light-brown, often curling, and eyes of light-brown, blue, or hazel. Few were fat, and few of the men full-bearded.

M. Perier and I climbed to the summit of The City's central hill and emerged in a level square, paved with terra-cotta sandstone. A cylindrical tower, perhaps fifty feet high and slaty blue in color rose in the center. Five ancient two-story buildings with curving façades and steep roofs stood around the plaza. The governmental center of Islandia, it is startling in its plainness and austerity. Except for an incongruous victoria with two horses and coachmen in European livery standing before the low door of one of the buildings, the square was deserted. My own costume seemed quite as ridiculous in the presence of these ancient buildings with their flaking walls and blind windows with small, leaded panes, and I followed M. Perier, feeling as though I dreamed.

With clicking heels we climbed a flight of stone stairs with stone walls on either side and presently found ourselves in a dark anteroom with sofas on all sides. Half a dozen persons were seated there, among them two Europeans, and an immense black-bearded man, with brick-red face, his huge muscular hands clasping his knees like those of a peasant, but his thick hair parted sleekly in the middle with the care of a dandy.

After a few minutes of waiting a young Islandian came and spoke a word to this man, and I felt his eyes upon me, small and scarcely visible under his thick brows but hot as flames. He made some answer, and then the young man turned to us. M. Perier rose. We passed through the door.

The room was bright, its hangings were of buff upon which the sun streamed through its two wide-open windows. I saw a yellow table, a vase of great red roses, and behind it a man rising to greet us.

Lord Mora! Of course, I knew I was going to meet him, but I had not realized how instantly he would seem one of the great men of the world. He was more than handsome—a tall, rather spare man of fifty-five, active and graceful. His iron-gray hair was closely cut, showing the structure of a most beautiful head, proud, intelligent, and gallant. From beneath a serene forehead and fine, arched brows, his bright, steady blue eyes saw everything, but were too kindly and too confident to be piercing. The complex symmetry of his strong sunburned face fascinated me, and it seemed a great privilege to be shaking his hand, which was slim, small, sinewy, and warm.

It seemed but a single moment, and M. Perier and I were once more upon the plaza, full of sunlight now.

"Lord Mora is a magnetic man," said he with a laugh, and I laughed too, remembering bit by bit what had happened. I had been introduced and had shown my papers. The question of a place to live had been discussed. An aide was coming to assist me tomorrow morning. In addition he had made me welcome officially and personally. He had asked me to dine with him. He had made me happy

33

and at home. It subtracted nothing that our interview lasted only ten minutes.

The next events were official calls and M. Perier led me where I should go. We left our cards on Graf von Bibberbach and Count de Craillizi, the German and Austrian ministers and then climbed the west hill of The City by a long, narrow flight of steps upon which opened the doors of houses at various levels. The steps ended in a wooden door set in a garden wall. As at Cadred's house, there was a bell rope, and M. Perier's pull was answered by a sonorous clang far off. We waited, standing before the gate; and M. Perier broke the remote and perfect silence by describing the man upon whom we had come to leave our cards.

"Isla Farrant is Lord of the Province of Farrant in the West. He is of a very old and much ennobled family. He is nearly eighty and has held his present office for over forty years. I venture to call him my friend and the friend of France. In the forties we nearly came to blows with Islandia over the sheep trade with Biacra. It was illegal but very important to us. The trade was put down, but the Islandians made large gifts of sheep to us out of pure kindness. The Farrants were largely responsible. Since then, the present lord has helped us in various ways. He is probably not at home, now, but in his province."

The gate was opened at last disclosing a charming terraced garden, above which rose the Palace of the Lords of the Province of Farrant. As my escort surmised, the Isla was not in The City. We were, however, permitted to ascend through the garden and were let out by another gate upon the plaza on the summit of the hill. We descended by a flight of steps and emerged in an alley, which led us to the Russian Legation, where we left cards upon Count Wittersee. From there we continued to the British Consulate, in an Islandian house with a little walled garden on two sides.

We had planned to leave cards, but Philip Wills saw us and asked us in, leading us out to the garden where tea was being served. There I saw again Gordon Wills, the consul, in appearance like his brother, but older and stronger. I also met his sister who kept house for him, and a Mrs. Gilmour, a woman of about forty dressed in Islandian costume, but English in speech, manner, and appearance.

These people and my escort knew each other well and talked without explanation of things and persons unknown to me. Nevertheless I gathered that Mrs. Gilmour's husband was an English-born, naturalized Islandian, and a teacher at the University, who had prepared Dorn for Harvard. Her father, Sir Colin Miller-Stuart, was a famous engineer, who had planned and built the industrial town of Suburra, which lay east of The City. Here were the only factories in Islandia, which made ammunition and the materials of war as well as plowshares and other farm implements. For his services to the country he had been granted citizenship and had been given a farm. I looked at Mrs. Gilmour with interest.

"We saw Don today in Lord Mora's anteroom," M. Perier was saying, and I supposed that Don was the first name of some other Englishman.

"Don!" exclaimed Miss Wills with great interest. "What was he doing there?"

M. Perier shrugged and Gordon Wills looked noncommittal.

"He stopped with Colin two months ago," said Mrs. Gilmour. "He had climbed Bronder alone."

"As he did Mount Islandia," said Miss Wills. "Gordon thinks he is a fool."

"Sir Martin Conway says he is the best mountaineer he ever met —certainly the strongest."

"And the most intelligent," added Miss Wills. "These *tanar* are really gentlemen."

"Don is, if a rough one."

"He parts his hair!"

"Sir Martin says not one lock was out of place after that terrible night, and Don was bareheaded."

"A cock and a hen, two larks and a wren . . ." remarked Gordon Wills.

The ladies laughed, and recognizing the quotation I pictured Don as a man with a beard—and parted hair. He must be the immense man with the red face, great hands, and diamond eyes, who waited in Lord Mora's anteroom.

"Who is Don?" I asked. They all looked at me, hastening to explain, and I learned that Don was a famous mountaineer as well as an athlete and weight thrower; that four years ago he had attempted to climb Mount Islandia alone and had nearly lost his life, being overcome by blindness and exhaustion when he reached a very high peak, which might have been the top and might not, and had only escaped by a series of desperate glissades which by luck carried him to safety and not to death.

At the Willses' gateway M. Perier and I separated after he had pointed out to me his house, which lay across the river and higher up, and I started toward the hotel with two hours of free time and much to think about.

Once more in the hotel room I took out pen and paper to write to Dorn. Something was suddenly wrong, but what was it—homesickness, or nervous fatigue, or coming sickness? I tried to think what I should say to my friend. The will and the material of thought were there, but I could not at once loosen the latter into fluent words.

By the time I was finished it was time to dress and go to the Periers'.

M. Perier's secretary, François Bart, a man of about forty with dry and shriveled skin, was the only other guest. To us both Mme. Perier was friendly if somewhat absent-minded; Marie and Jeanne were attentive if guarded in manner as proper jeunes filles should be; but M. Perier himself was kindly and sympathetic. We dined in a sheltered corner of the garden on French fare that took a long time in the serving. Most of the conversation was carried on by the girls and me. They were bright, but their troubles with English and mine with French thwarted our efforts to shine. Good will made up these lacks. They were impersonal, but their rather beady, dark eyes glowed with intelligence, and their thin, nervous hands made quick eloquent gestures. It was good indeed to find potential friends of my own age, and it was no matter that they were girls who were not pretty—at least to me.

Sound, dreamless sleep is a wonderful thing. I woke cheerful, glad to be alive, and quite equal to the task of house-hunting.

Lord Mora's aide, Earne, was a young man of my own age, with a sense of humor, and we went about our task in high spirits and not too seriously. He had decided what I needed—six rooms and a kitchen, a cook, and a manservant, and his duty was to provide place and persons both. Armed with his list of rentable houses we visited them all, walking several miles of hard paved streets.

Three of them were in a part of The City as yet unvisited, and having a character all its own. Centuries before there had been a great siege and in order to quicken the movement of defenders and to avoid congestion in the narrow streets, bridges had been built from roof to roof. Now many of these remained and roof gardens had been built, connected by these overhead paths and bridges, which were independent of the streets below, and as confusing as a labyrinth.

As we searched for the houses on our list, we passed under several bridges—graceful stone arches two and three stories overhead, with flower boxes on their balustrades. The places we looked at were more or less satisfactory, but it was disappointing to find that they were not connected with the "overhead."

The next house eluded us. For some reason all his own, Earne seemed much amused and when at last we found it, we had threaded a narrow alley scarcely five feet wide for some distance. We visited the house, however, and found it charming. It had seven rooms and a pretty roof garden.

When we were once more in a sunny street, Earne explained himself, using unfamiliar words. It was some time before I understood that the region was for very obvious reasons not suitable for the consulate of a moral nation like the United States. We set out for the next house.

Neither as place for a consulate nor as a place for convenient housekeeping was it what it should be, but it did fascinate me. It was one of a row of houses, built against the city wall, and using the wall, pierced with windows, as its own. There were two tiers of houses, superimposed on each other. The house to which Earne led me was in the upper tier opening on a passageway, from which a bridge with steps sprang upward across the lane, a part of the system of aerial paths.

Earne rang the bell and we waited, leaning on the low ramp of the passageway. After a long time a woman came slowly up the steps. She was about sixty with white hair and a quiet, gentle face. She was Lona, and lived in the house immediately below, owned both, and let that above. We explained our mission, and she let us in. On the lower story were four rooms, including a kitchen on the west, fairly well lighted. Those on the east, however, faced the city wall, at least ten feet thick, so that the windows were at the bottoms of deep bays. Earne shook his head. In the upper story there was one immense room running the full length of the house, with windows to east and west. One corner was walled off to make a small bed-

37

room. From the larger room a flight of stairs ran to the roof. Here we emerged into quiet sunlight and a garden.

Toward the east one looked down the sheer face of the city walls to the river far below. On its further side was a towpath, and then came miles of flat farm land, reaching to a low line of blue hills ten or more miles away. To the west one looked down upon the flat roofs of innumerable houses—upon green, bright gardens, stone walls, twisting paths, little bridges, all seeming flat like the ground until one saw the rectangular clefts of the streets opening here and there.

"It is too small," said Earne. "Rooms for two servants and your office would fill the lower floor. You could dine and live in the large room upstairs and sleep in the small room. But where would you put a guest?"

"The lower rooms in the wall are dark," I added.

"Too dark," said he.

"It is a difficult place for a stranger to find and a consul should be near to the water front or to the places where business is done."

"That is true. It won't suffice."

"No," I added.

We agreed entirely.

"If I weren't a consul, it would be a delightful place to live," I said.

We were silent.

"I like it, though," I said.

"So do I!" he answered, brightening.

My mind clicked. I rented the house. There were excuses. Lona would cook for me, thus freeing one room; and she would accommodate my manservant.

"When will you come?" she asked.

"This afternoon!" But I was not any too happy. A feeling of tension was coming again and I wanted something to keep me busy.

With the aid of the efficient Earne, by six o'clock I was established in my own house. My belongings had been trundled across The City in a handcart, a manservant was to call upon me next evening, and I had been introduced at that Islandian institution, which in English may be called "The Agency," where my money was exchanged, all my purchases would be made, and where I arranged about delivery of mail.

It was seven o'clock. I was sitting in my living room at the western window. Downstairs Lona was getting my supper. It had been a busy day, with much leg exercise. The sun shone in and a pleasant summery air came with it. The City was profoundly still. Some fifteen feet below me lay the gardens, with their flowering shrubs, box borders, and gravel paths, and their density made it hard to believe that there were dwellings beneath them. From the vine-covered chimneys at a level with my eyes, wood smoke streamed thinly and lazily; at intervals its odor came in on the breeze, now spicy, now resinous, now faintly acrid, and a veil would be drawn across the distance.

It grew darker, and there settled upon the plain of gardens a shadowy blue haze. It was as though all this region had once been a lake, in which square and rectangular islands had been built close together. The water had been withdrawn between them leaving vacant hollows, now very dark, but the domain of gardens, of trees, flowers, and shrubbery, of graveled paths and high walls, bridges, and causeways, was at the true level of the lake's lost waters.

Overhead now was my own garden. The tang of wood smoke was like the country. I was hungry . . . I wondered why the Islandians were not fat.

Like a living presence I felt Uncle Joseph at my side, and I heard his voice, so real as to be uncanny.

"John, this is no place for a consulate. I had a fine time getting here! What were you thinking of? How can you expect to keep up your office properly here! The government pays you to. . . ."

I ran up to the roof, to my roof, and my garden. It was airy and cool in the low sunlight—the perfume of roses in bloom mingled with wood smoke. I strolled along the beds that lined the walls, filled with climbing roses, and roses on standards, dwarf larkspur with thick stalks and heavy sprays of dark metallic blue, and nameless evergreen shrubs. The gravel scrunched under my feet. I almost walked on tiptoe, all was so still. Was it a dream?

Lona's voice called me from the stairs.

"Lang!"—no more.

It was not good to play too long with that feeling of dreaming, for it could not be put away after a while . . . My supper was over. The living room seemed enormous. It was very dark, and the tiny flame of a little candle above the massive fireplace was very bright.

Dusk gathered, and The City became unreal in the shadows. In the gardens here and there were yellow points, and dim glows came up from the streets, but the roofs were dark and black. The air that blew in now smelled no longer of wood smoke, but of night and damp, illusively perfumed with flowers.

It was like a dream, but a dream that gripped like a vise and terrified. I lit my five big candles, and dropped the thick, opaque curtains over the windows.

My bell clanged. Taking a candle I descended into the black lower story and unlatched the door. The man standing in the night spoke.

"Lang?"

"Yes," I said.

"Letters."

Four letters! They were of that real world that slipped away from me so easily. Setting the candle on the table I looked at them one by one.

The first letter, from Mrs. Gilmour, suggested that Reeves was worth a visit, that it would give her and her husband pleasure to have me come and stay with them there, and said that her husband was very fond of my friend, Dorn.

The next was from R. C. Gastein whom I knew of from Uncle Joseph as head of one of the most powerful copper interests in the world. He spoke of having heard of me from my uncle and of being sorry he had not met me before I set sail. Would I be able to help his engineer, Henry G. Müller, who was arriving in February, to investigate conditions in Islandia? He (the great R. C.) would appreciate it personally. He wished me a happy and successful future.

Uncle Joseph wrote me a brief business letter asking for commercial information. Already I was being put to the test. He mentioned R. C. Gastein, who, he said, was a very powerful man. A word to the wise!

The last letter remained, the address was feminine, careful, and unformed. Which of the girls with whom I had arranged to "correspond" had been thoughtful enough of my loneliness to arrange that her letter should catch the same boat that I did and not leave me letterless for months? She began in the middle of things, telling of wintry weather in New York, of the play she had been to, of going to school, and of her journey abroad in the coming summer.

"I got mother to get me out of the library a book about Islandia," she concluded. "It is called *Travels in a Modern Utopia*, by John Carter Carstairs. You have probably read it. It is flowery, I think, but I like it a great deal. I study and study his quaint maps and pretend I am there. If you do any traveling about, I should like so much to have you tell me where you have been. I shall look it up on the maps and read what he says about it. Mother has promised to buy it for me, which is a lot better than a book one has to return in two weeks!

"I hope things are just what you want them to be there. It is very far away and it would be horrid to have things unhappy so far from home.

"Sincerely yours,
"GLADYS HUNTER."

I reread her letter. The writer was the same as the seventeen-year-old girl. She could not have evoked her image more vividly. There she was across the table from me, with timetables between us —long and young, fresh beyond belief, childish but dignified, and simple. . . .

On my third day in Islandia, Sunday, after dining with the Willses and calling on the Periers and being kept to supper, I started home across The City alone. The streets I followed were dimly lit with an occasional candle protected by yellow waxed paper on the corner houses. The last few blocks were full of narrow and misleading streets. Overhead the stars were brilliant in a summer sky almost warm in tone. I turned here and I turned there and thought I had gone wrong, but I suddenly emerged opposite my house.

With eyes unused to the light I climbed to my living room, and found one candle burning and a man sitting there. He rose slowly, and I saw the bulky silhouette of a bearded man, and thought of that immense, legendary creature, Don.

"Geroge," he said, for an Islandian, meeting a stranger will name himself and never ask the other's name. Geroge was his name, not our Anglo-Saxon "George," but an ancient name in his nation, meaning wheatfield. "George," however, will I write it.

This was our first meeting. He was the so-called "manservant" Earne had promised to send me, but after a few moments of con-

41

versation it was evident that I could not hire him as a servant. I found myself in an embarrassing social position. George was a gentleman. Earne had not warned me, nor had he explained to George—not because Earne was inept, but because being an Islandian he was quite confident that in such a situation one would instantly understand what had occurred. Luckily I did understand, but I came very near not doing so.

George was a man of about fifty-five and unmarried, and had served for thirty years in the Islandian army. His older brother was a landowner, in the Province of Hern, where he was known to the Earnes, and Earne thought that as a companion or dragoman George would be more useful to me than a servant would have been. Having served his time in the army, it was open to George to return to his brother's farm, but he did not wish to go back to a rural life so suddenly. He was, of course, pensioned and could live in idleness, but this was not in his nature.

Our negotiations were dignified but friendly. We found a great deal to laugh about. I engaged him, and he departed to get his belongings.

Needless to say, there was little for him to do in the first weeks. He amused himself in learning English, very slowly, in tending the garden on the roof, and in investigating various commercial problems that I set. I had foreseen a real manservant, but the more I saw of George the more I liked him. If he was not very bright, he was perfectly bred and full of knowledge of all sorts useful to me. If he treated employment with me as rather amusing, he also could be used as an adviser on matters out of a servant's ken. He had a naïve bonhommie. His big beard was thick and grizzled, but he was rather like a boy.

To the excessive quiet of The City I had become used, but there were far more subtle things that, as time went on, stole upon me with their queerness. I would observe and comment to myself, surprised, interested, or amused, quite sane and objective. Then, imperceptibly, a sensation of uncanniness would shiver through me. What was it that so affected me? Never one thing. Single phenomena could be isolated and explained, but in all things, everywhere—in streets, in houses, in the faces of the people, in the still roof gardens and the flat diversified country visible from my windows, in the sea itself, and in the motionless remote mountains—there was a difference in quality, slight here, greater there, but always present, and in the sum worse than merely puzzling.

I did not know what was the matter, but I know that something very real troubled my mind and reacted upon my body. Buds of pleasure would start beautifully, and then be blighted and shriveled. My attention suffered. I woke as from a daze to realize someone had spoken. The sky was clear, the wind summery, the air delicious, but I was encased in bronze, with a bronzy taste in my mouth.

Two Americans who had been traveling in the east dropped in upon me. One was tall and lanky, crude in dress, face, and manner, but with a veneer of culture. His companion was a rotund, dapper little man, having nose and cheeks with red veins. They were world-roamers and commercial travelers—not gentlemen, but on the edge of that class.

They entered my room precipitately and wrung my hand. They sat down and lit cigars. Conversation dragged. All at once they looked at each other. Recognition flickered between them and made them shamefaced.

"Is there any way of getting out of here before the middle of next month?" said the short one.

"Charley and I think this is one hell of a country," burst out the other.

I understood perfectly. The odor of tobacco smoke had its own peculiar stab, and brought with it poignant memories of Harvard-Yale football games, smoking cars, and of roaring, rapid, colorful life, dear and familiar.

"It is a queer country," I answered.

"You bet it is! We've nothing to complain of. Everyone has treated us white, but—" said the tall man.

"We wondered if there wasn't some tramp steamer—" Charley added with feeling.

"None—there is no trade, you know."

"And I don't care if there never is!"

"If we were highbrows," added Charley. "But we aren't. We are plain Americans."

"What are we going to do next, that's what I want to know."

"Well, I won't stay here."

"Keep a-going, I suppose."

I advised from my limited knowledge, and let them go. It would have been kindness to invite them to dine with me, but I shrank from them, in spite of the tie that bound me to them in an unexpected common emotion.

Like them I did not wish to keep still, for when I was motionless the silence closed tightly around me, and I had a waking nightmare—of nothingness, of smoothness, of eternity. The wind might flutter something or sigh, the water in the river splash a little, or some voice speak quietly, but there was nothing else, nothing—no sound of grinding tram wheels or clanking radiators, no whistles, never the romantic wail of a train, no cheerfully clattering footsteps except my own, none of the happy creakings of a wooden house, but only cold hard stone.

Nothing was real except the fact that I was feeling, and I was feeling nothing that I had ever felt before. I set my teeth and I suffered intensely, longing for my friend Dorn.

In him, however, I was disappointed. There was one really bad day—that on which I might expect a letter from the West. The day before young Calwin had asked me to come to his country home with him, dine, spend the night, and return on the morrow.

Calwin, to whom I had been introduced by M. Perier, was the son of the Lord of The City and his father's right hand man. They spent most of their time in their official residence in The City; but their real home was in the country, ten miles away.

Four of us made up the party and we set out from The City at four o'clock after young Calwin's work was done. Besides our host and me, there were Philip Wills, and young Mora, eldest son of the premier and a former student at Oxford, England. He and Wills, of course, had much in common, being contemporaries at college. He and young Calwin were furthermore first cousins, for the aunt of each had been the other's mother. The three, therefore, had connections with each other to which I was a stranger.

They were courteous to me, but that courtesy seemed scrupulous rather than warm-hearted. I did not "belong," not for political reasons alone but because I was too uneasy and too unnatural to comply wholly with their standards. Calwin's politeness was a little hard and overperfect—the others understood, but to me he must explain in ABC language. Wills was a chameleon and enjoyed being one with the right people. Mora was like his father, but less definite, less finished, and less magnetic. He had a charming smile and gave me full measure of it; but I wondered if he were not too confident and whether inside his able, handsome head he was not quite indifferent to the John Lang sort of person, but too polite and too proud to be critical.

We rode out of the northernmost of the eastern gates, across the bridge, and into the flat farm lands of the delta, where we were soon involved in all their intricacies of high stone walls, hedges, and patches of wood. The sun shone hot and the air was full of the warm fragrance of earth and of vegetation. It was a fertile region. Leaves of vegetables and grass in the meadows were lush and green; sprouting maize and grains held up strong stalks and full heads; and flowers in gardens glowed as though just watered. Even the road itself was invaded and sometimes our horses' hoofs thudded in the grass.

We rode along the river, following its gentle windings. Willows edged its banks and iridescent tiny swallows in hundreds skimmed its placid waters. Now and then a bulky boat lay on its smooth bosom, its dusky sails hardly swollen, and its crew taking life easily.

Shadows lengthened, and the loping horses quickened. The road wound away from the river, and ahead to the left, over the tops of a dense wood of enormous beeches, was the head of a cliff, brightly lit in the sun. We wheeled sharply into a gate between high stone walls. The woods were damp and dark. A moment later we emerged into bright sunlight with level fields before us. To one side lay a cluster of red-roofed buildings. This was the Calwin's true home, their farm, theirs for two hundred years.

In a clear bell-like voice, our host shouted our names: "Mora! Wills! Lang! Calwin!" and the last vibrated with pride and power.

Two men appeared, one to take our horses and another our bags. A white-haired old lady greeted us softly with her name, which I did not hear. I was shown to a quiet room on the ground floor, but only to remain a moment to unpack my things and slip my evening clothes back again into the saddlebag that George had bought for me.

The four of us set out to the river, stripped in a small stone boat-house on the water's edge, and then plunged off the end of its pier one after the other. Through the hard shell of unreality this natural event—swimming on a warm summer afternoon—broke its way. Mora, Calwin, and Wills were only young, human men like myself. If their bodies had slender beauty and mine was only a body, if the Islandians swam better than I, yet I swam far better than Wills, and I swam in cool water under an immense blue heaven, while swallows dipped wings in the water around me. And a good dinner waited.

But what a comparison between myself and the others when we dressed! While I, damp and warm, was struggling with nearly a score of garments and articles constituting formal evening costume, the others had to handle eight, including even Wills, who was experimenting with Islandian costume. Besides, my shirt and collar were badly starched—for starching was unknown in Islandia—and were like iron. The others had only to slip on their light linen under-garments, their stockings, their sandals, a shirt open at the throat, their short trousers like a boy's leaving the knee bare, and their jackets. They looked like aristocratic youths, cool and immaculate in shorts, while I felt like a waiter. They made a striking picture. Their shirts were of the whitest and softest linen, with broad soft collars; trousers and coats cut loosely, but fitting well, were a navy blue, matched by stockings and sandals. Wills's costume was without color except a red band in the turnover of stockings and about his cuffs; but Mora had red lapels and broad red bands on either side of a narrow white one in his cuffs and stockings, and Calwin scarlet lapels and scarlet and black bands arranged in the same way.

By the time we reached the house I was hot and moist, and my collar made my neck raw.

The table was spread in the veranda and dinner was served to us four. It soon darkened outside and a lamp with a waxed paper shade, burning clear white with a faint sweet aromatic fragrance, was set before us. It was a simple, elaborate meal and was eaten with the critical solemnity of hungry young epicures. The conversation was political and it was soon apparent that the Moras and Calwins saw eye to eye in the matter of foreign trade and removal of the exclusion laws. Over the question of whether the country would voluntarily make the necessary changes in its laws, they lightly passed, and agreed that if this were not so, the change would be forced upon them. Their interest seemed to be what would happen when the change came. A world over the head of me, the American consul, was revealed: the railroad that English capitalists had more than considered, from The City to Suburra, the industrial town, and thence to the great town of Miltain; the rival lines of the German promoters; steamers; exports; imports; banking; exchange. I watched Wills quite naturally play the role of the suave and admirable advocate of his country against the others, particularly Germany, and the two Islandians like diplomats committing themselves to no choice. They were far from nobodies, these young men, and in the confidence of their fathers, who were powerful men and united. Lord Mora controlled the East, and Lord Calwin had from his vantage point in The City strong influence in the center of the country. In the West was Dorn and his great-uncle. Judging by the former they seemed a little cruder and much less astute than my finished host, his cousin of the intelligent eyes, and their worldly, definite, and purposeful fathers.

Soon I felt the finger of Mora furtively probing me. A few questions to which I answered mechanically of his cousin Dorn, of Harvard, and of our friendship. Had I seen him yet? No, but I had written. They were good friends despite long standing political differences, he said cordially. Consuls meant trade. . . .

I became aware that he was suggesting that Dorn might refuse to answer my letter.

"Consuls do not mean trade unless your country votes for it," I said after a pause.

"Perry and Japan," remarked Mora.

"I should hate to see my country at odds with you," I answered, glancing at Mora and Calwin in turn.

Thereupon the former laughed honestly and delightfully and the tension was eased.

"I am only a consul," I said, "and I don't know what is going on in the minds of men at home."

Like a true diplomat I warmed to the safety of ignorance.

"Perhaps I shall learn, but, you know, the United States often forgets all about its consuls."

"What do you think is best for Islandia?" he asked.

"That is too big a question for me."

"At present we are outcasts because of our habits," he laughed.

"You have very good friends," I answered, smiling at Wills, who nodded solemnly.

"The only reason I was chosen consul," I continued, "was because I had some knowledge of your language. There were a number of applicants and I went in with the rest. My classmate Dorn's account of Islandia interested me. So here I am. And I am surprised to find myself here, for I am quite without diplomatic experience. I suppose the government wanted to have someone on the spot, but it can't have cared or expected very much, for it never would have appointed me if it had. You see other countries take the situation much more seriously. They send men like Gordon Wills, and Perier, and Graf von Bibberbach, men of experience and distinction."

"I have no doubt the United States is very well represented," said Mora with a slight bow.

After that, memory is of the white lamp, the black night outside, the chirrup of a cricket, and my tongue wagging, while at every moment all became more unreal. From the table we adjourned to the library. There we were served with a white liqueur, as smooth and sweet as a drop of pure honey. Candles lit the backs of hundreds of ancient books in mahogany Islandian bindings. There was talk, talk, talk, till a late hour.

It was a relief to go to my room with its window opening on motionless trees against a starry summer sky. The yellow candle flame rose up straight, and the hangings were dark and somber. The only ornament was a delicate, flat relief carved on the lintel of the door. It showed a man in proud posture speaking to three others, one of whom was listening doubtfully, the next turning away as if moved to action, and the third picking up a pitch fork. The event it portrayed I did not know, but the speaker, carved with minute care, was a Calwin, for his nose was hooked like that of my host. On either side of the group were trees and at the extreme edges behind a trunk lurked an evil Negroid figure on the watch.

When I slept I dreamed of that scene come to life and of terrible danger threatening and of Sisyphean efforts to avoid it. . . .

In the morning, after an early breakfast on the veranda, we all returned to The City. Today was the first on which I might expect an answer from Dorn. I steeled myself against the strong chance of disappointment.

At nine o'clock I parted with my host and the rest on the steps of the passageway that served my house and its neighbors.

George, studying English and mouthing the words in his great beard, looked up with quiet eyes and friendly smile.

I asked if there were any letter.

"It is too early," he said. "The carrier from the West will not reach The City until midday, and the letter will not be delivered until evening." Then he looked at me kindly. "But I will go for it myself at midday."

At noon we went together to the office of the carriers from the West near the Agency Building. We waited standing on a bridge over the harbor and looking down upon a complicated arrangement of protruding piers and sheltered docks. These served the Western provinces and George told me this little end of The City was very Western in character. Nearby, he said, was the official city residence of the Lord of the Province of Lower Doring, that is, of Lord Dorn, looking out upon the bay, with its own boat landing sheltered by moles.

George rambled on about the West, where he had often been as a soldier.

"The Westerners are not the same as the rest," he said. "They are always the furthest away from the center of things, not so much in distance as because of the mountains. You can't get more than thirty miles away from them anywhere, and usually they seem at your door . . . Then there are the marshes, stretching far, with here and there an island rising a little higher. You stand in a place as flat as can be, and you see mountains off against the sky, and a gale blows tears into your eyes. Put a Doring man on a bit of land there, and gunpowder and earthquakes and lightning and storm floods won't move him. There you will find him afterwards, he and his family whole and happy, tilling the soil and getting along very well, thank you. He fights till all that is left of him is the fist that holds the sword—and look out for that! When the other man has you down, it is the Doring man who turns up to save your life. Isla Dorn, your friend's great-uncle, is one of them—every hair and bit of flesh and bone, he is a Doring man. He is getting old, but age only toughens those fellows. They say he hasn't the brains of his father, but time will tell—There is the carrier now."

Along the distant quay near the hotel came trotting a little cavalcade of two pack horses and one man riding another in the rear. The leading horse knew his way well and swung around the curve from the quay to the bridge, cantered up to the office door, and whinnied.

The others followed nose to tail, the man on the last riding nonchalantly sidesaddle on a pile of leather bags.

We crossed over to him, and George stated our errand.

"Is there a letter from grandnephew Dorn to Lang?"

The man shook his head.

"One from Faina to Lang," he said, and with great courtesy he slid from his seat and searched through a bag till he found it. The name "Faina" stirred memories without releasing them. No one would write me from the West unless related to my friend. Had anything happened to him? I recalled the terrible tragedy, of which he once had told me, when his father and mother and his father's first cousin were drowned.

The stiff, cleverly folded sheet was sealed with blue and white wafers where the flaps met. Crossing to the other side of the bridge I tore it open.

> Lang, my grandson's friend:
>
> Three days before his friend's letter came my grandson went on a journey to the north, not to return until the end of Septen (about March 15th). His friend's letter must wait his return, for we do not know where to address it to find him. We have, however, sent word to those places where we think he is likely to be, telling him of his friend's presence in Islandia. It is most uncertain whether our messages will find him. Therefore his friend will not construe my grandson's silence as neglect, for if he knew that Lang were present in his land he would at once go to the place where he was.
>
> We, too, venture to say that we know Lang, though never having seen him. We heard of his coming as Consul of the United States the day after grandnephew Dorn left us and we sent a message to overtake our relative but without success. We know that he has for Lang *linamia* (a word I did not know).
>
> We do not know what Lang's duties are, but our house is his.
>
> FAINA

Below was written in English with a small but sharply etched handwriting in the blackest of black ink:

> John Lang's room is prepared for him.
>
> DORN XXVI

Disappointment went through me like acid, but almost immediately afterwards came unexpected relief. They knew I was consul and it never occurred to them that this fact could make any difference to their relative or to them. But the letter raised several questions. There was but one man who understood enough Islandian to explain, and that was M. Perier. I bade good-bye to George and set out to find him.

He was in his office, smoking a briar pipe cocked up at a high angle, correcting proofs. His limpid, intelligent, light-brown eyes looked into mine curiously and kindly.

"Has one of your countrymen committed murder?" he asked, noticing my red face, and recalling the fact that he had promised to guide me when consular questions were troublesome.

"Read this, please, and tell me the nuances," I asked. He complied with deliberation.

"You are a greatly honored man," he remarked, nodding at me and handing back the letter. "Have you ever heard of *tan-ry-doon?*"

Literally the words meant soil-place-custom, but their combined meaning I did not know.

"I know the words, but not the phrase," I answered.

"And you say you have read Bodwin! But no matter. What does *elainry* mean?"

"City, of course."

"Literally?"

" 'Place of many people.' "

"Did you ever know another language where the word for city is so expressive of the countryman's conception?"

I shook my head.

"Did you know that even the Islandian city man does not feel that the city is his home?"

"In a way. I knew from Bodwin that city men usually had some relative in the country at whose place they were welcome."

"More than that," he said. *"Every* city man has such a place. It is the same place for his grandfather that it is for his grandson; not only is he welcome but he has a right—a legal right—to go there and stay as long as he likes, though if he stays over a month he is expected to do some work. He may go and take all his children. Good taste controls the actual working out."

Perier was silent for a moment.

"When you marry," he continued, "a month or so before your

child is to be born you will put yourself and your wife on a boat bound for Doring, and you two will go to the house of Lord Dorn, and there you will find them expecting you and glad to see you. There your wife will stay until the child is weaned, and longer maybe, and you as long as and whenever you can. If the child later becomes sickly or bored in The City here, back you will all go to Lord Dorn's. That, and a great deal more, is *tanrydoon*.

"Madame Faina is cautious and besides the house is not hers. She says that 'our house is the house of my grandson's friend.' She invites you there as a guest—not as a transient guest, however, or as one at a specified time. That would have involved another formula: 'If you travel through our province our house is yours,' or 'our house is yours May 1st.'

"I suppose that having written her letter she showed it to Lord Dorn. He is her brother-in-law and head of the house, of course. He writes that your room has been prepared for you. He means it literally. Some room has been swept and washed clean. New hangings have been hung, and a bed, a chair, a stool, a table, and a washstand installed. Probably the lintel of the door or some stone over the fireplace has been extracted and even now Faina may be carving there some scene familiar to you—perhaps Washington crossing the Delaware, if she knows none of your own family history. You have your *tanry*—soil-place, now, my friend. None of the rest of us foreigners here can claim as much. I think Lord Dorn did it to please his grandnephew."

"What does *linamia* mean?" I asked.

"You should know that. What is *amia?*"

"Affection, liking, love—anything like that not sexual."

"And *lin?*"

"Strong."

"The compound *linamia* means those strong friendships, which are limited to one or two in a man's life. You are a lucky man! The honor done you is the greater because you may be sure it was done in spite of the fact that you were consul and not because of it. And you share *tanrydoon* at the house of Lord Dorn with only two other families and those great ones. May I give you some advice?"

I nodded.

"I think you did wrong to show me this letter, but it was natural and excusable. The Islandians have all sorts of understandings and courtesies as clear as crystal to them and quite incomprehensible to us. One has to learn them slowly. There is a famous story of a man who knew some fact about his friend that if known to the opposite party would mean his ruin. One of this party was obviously most anxious to learn that fact. The man knew this. In the course of a conversation it became perfectly natural for the man to mention the fact in another connection. To mention it seemed disloyal, but not to mention it was worse, for it showed distrust of the man of the opposite party. So he mentioned it, and the other did not take advantage of it. Now it strikes me as peculiar that young Dorn has gone where his family cannot find him for several months. He is not unknown nor is Islandia very large. It is a fact that may be extremely important, and I should not be surprised if Lord Dorn's opponents would be very glad to know it. They mention it to you, because it is the only way they can explain why young Dorn has not come to you. Being Islandian, it probably did not occur to Faina that you would tell anyone else. I think Lord Dorn must have seen the risk, but he is enough of an Islandian to prefer to run it rather than the worse risk of insulting his grandnephew's friend. So, as far as I am concerned, you never came to see me and I never saw that letter. Best keep the fact that you have *tanrydoon* to yourself, also."

I blushed. To my surprise, M. Perier was also red.

"Honor is not always a matter of pure instinct. The Islandian definition of a gentleman is one to whom it is such. Never mind. We are both embarrassed. Have I not broken the Islandian code by presuming to doubt that you knew what you were doing?"

He laughed.

"One more word of advice. When you go home, take one of your rooms, sweep it and wash it, and put in new hangings. When you answer Madame Faina's letter, say that you have *linamia* for her grandson—I know it is so. Say that you have prepared a room for young Dorn. I don't believe that Lord Dorn expects it for himself. But say your house is his and hers. *Tanrydoon* is reciprocal, you know. You can't accept it unless you are willing to keep the countryman when he comes to The City."

The Periers invited me to lunch, and later Marie and I took a walk. She at her father's suggestion, but without being given a reason, had undertaken to carve for me a bas-relief showing an event in the history of the house of Dorn. Now we wandered about through alleys

53

and streets studying the carvings on the houses, her hobby. Some were so ancient as to be almost worn away, others were new and unfinished. They were not the work of hired artists, but of some past or present member of a household who chose a scene from family history or a significant event and carved it in relief on a lintel or the sideposts of the doors or windows. Marie showed me her favorites: a hunting scene, suffering faces in a group of refugees flying from a burning house, and, covering nearly the whole façade of one building, a savage battle with men of Negroid faces. The skill of the sculptors varied from the crudest to the best, but sometimes the vigorous imagination of a crude piece gave it an attraction denied to one better done but overelaborated.

Later Jeanne joined us and we climbed by a winding street to the summit of East Hill to look at the statues and carvings of the cathedral. That done, they insisted on going up to the roof, from which we had a view of the mountains in the north, lifting their naked white shoulders through the late afternoon haze.

Immediately below us was the slate roof of the King's Palace, a plain three-story building. There was a hot argument that led to the subject of the king, and the girls told me about him, interrupting each other.

"He is young—"

"King for only two years—"

"Not much real power—"

"Father says he could have more if he chose to exercise it, but it hasn't been the fashion in his family for—"

"A hundred years—"

"But he can appoint people and he presides at the council meetings—"

"He has a vote!"

We all laughed.

"Have you seen him?" I said.

"He came to the house—"

"Not since he was king, Jeanne."

"You weren't there."

They quarreled for some time and then said in one voice:

"Anyway he used to come."

"What is the king like?"

They shrugged.

"Tall and round like a candle—"

"Very strong, they say."

"He has yellow curling hair and blue eyes."

"His nose—"

"Proud, ah!"

"Greek, with a forehead like that!" Marie swept down her hand in a straight line.

"Dangerous—"

"All the girls. . . ."

They looked at each other with understanding, giggled, turned to me grave faces, and proceeded solemnly.

"He is never at home. Nobody knows where he goes—"

"He is mysterious—"

"And very fascinating."

"But his sister usually lives down there."

"She will receive you in March when the council sits."

"I wish there were a Rumpelmayer's here," cried Jeanne, jumping up.

"Let's go home to tea!"

Perhaps the events of this day were a turning point. Certainly my sense of nervous brittleness lessened a little. The flattery in the conduct to me of Lord Dorn and the relief of knowing definitely that my official position meant no estrangement, removed one of the causes of my trouble—worry and doubt. But there remained other causes far more subtle. Maybe I missed the life that was mine at home, but that seemed hardly probable for I had a far more diversified life in Islandia. If there were no theaters or concerts, no baseball or football games, no tennis, no clubs, no shop fronts or bright-hued advertisements, no sense of swift journeys possible, no large dances, no restaurants, no young ladies of my own race holding out possibilities of flirtation according to rules familiar to us both, yet there was in Islandia a social life among the diplomatic colony more finished and worldly than I had ever known at home, where I had never been even on the fringe of the life of power, politics, and intrigue. Here I was a part of it but with no heavy stake of my own, and I found it interesting and dramatic, with a climax steadily approaching when the day for the acceptance or rejection of the Mora treaty finally came.

It was not boredom. It was something deeper and more sinister,

corroding the moment if not wholly tarnishing the memory. Egotism
—an inturned mind—the pangs of adjusting a too solidified personality to strange surroundings—lack of confidence—a mental kink
—nervous prostration—sexual need—laziness—weltschmerz—now
one or another generality seemed to explain my case for a moment,
but failed in the end. I did suffer, and I cannot even describe it. Tension—a sense of my whole being drawn tight to the breaking point—
and an inability to feel reality, to shake off a sense of dreaming a
dream always on the edge of nightmare, moving smoothly to some
hideous end, and happy moments blighted in the bud over and over
again by a harsh breath of brass and acid.

The end of January came, and the southwest wind was a daily
visitor, bringing now rain squalls, now long, mellow, sunny hours. It
was the height of summer.

Steamers were due in the middle of February and early in March.
The diplomatic colony showed a tendency to take a month's vacation.
In June (early winter) would come the most important meeting of the
National Council and the greatest social season. The March meeting
of the council would bring a number of lords to town, but it was less
important. To me, March was a month to long for, because it meant
the return of my friend. Meanwhile I marked time, working on my
hardware report, and collecting material for others, calling on the
Periers and the other diplomats, dining out occasionally, and every
day taking a walk alone or with the Mlles. Perier, George, or Earne.

Steamer time was approaching. My report and letters to relatives,
friends, and on business began to fill my time, and in occupying my
mind insulated me for many pleasant hours against nostalgia. The
sifting processes of narration and description were clarifying to my
ideas and, realizing the limits and limitations of my knowledge, I
planned a course of reading. M. Perier's good library was at my disposal, and I borrowed from him the great work of Carstairs, a little
ashamed that Gladys Hunter should have read it before I did. Of quite
as much interest and perhaps more value was M. Perier's own history
of Islandia, which he was kind enough to let me read in proof. After
a sympathetic account of the history of the country, he surveys her
institutions, social life, arts, and natural features, making use only
of the opinions of foreign observers. Adopting the classification of an
Islandian author, he ranged the latter into two classes, Utopians and

Alterators, showing how they were united by a common characteristic, the itch to change something somewhere. The Utopians were extravagant in their praise of Islandia, wishing to change their own nations to be like her. The Alterators wished to change Islandia to be like themselves. I was really an Alterator, for I felt that no country could stand apart from the rest of the world as Islandia did. Accepting alteration as an inevitable evolutionary process, I wished it to come to pass in a form that would do good to Islandia, to the United States, and to the rest of the world.

On February 15th steamer day came. It was my old friend the *St. Anthony,* and as was the custom for consuls, attachés, and the lesser ones in the diplomatic colony, I went out to the landing place late in the afternoon, with my pouch of mail. We were all supposed to keep track of our nationals in this way.

Henry G. Müller and his assistant, Roy Davis, were unmistakable, their Americanism clear-cut as a cameo. The former, dressed in blue serge with a derby hat, was a middle-aged man. His hair, nearly white, was close-cropped, and his features were sharp and determined. Behind steel-rimmed spectacles were a pair of confident, interrogative blue eyes. Men like him had passed through Uncle Joseph's office. Their intelligence was great; they were efficient in business; in religion good Methodists (but that was not obtruded); and men like myself were constantly being convicted of not having grounds to corroborate what we said, of saying it indefinitely, and of being generally out of the running.

"Are you Mr. Lang, the consul?" he asked, gripping my hand in a purposeful grip.

I admitted my name.

"Meet my assistant, Mr. Davis!" said Müller. "I understand there is a hotel here."

I pointed to it, rising over the Winder docks, and told him that I had arranged for a room.

"Thank you," he said briefly, "is there a cab?"

He seemed surprised to find there was none, but accepted it in good part, and we set out, followed by his luggage in a handcart. On the way his eyes saw everything, I am sure, for they roamed about while he talked without waste of time. He wished to leave Islandia early in March, and had only three weeks. Therefore, he must get to

57

Winder (the copper region) as soon as possible. He counted on my assistance.

"It will be a pleasure," I said, and I told him what I could do. Thirty-six hours later, with an interpreter, a guide, a cook, and two horsemen, and a letter of introduction from Lord Mora, he departed, apparently satisfied with what I had done for him, but taking it as a matter of course.

"I am sure that Mr. Gastein will be grateful to you," he said, as he rode away, khaki-clad, efficient, and spruce.

Three days after the arrival of Müller, the German steamer *Sulliaba* arrived from the east coast and at eight in the morning I was on the dock to meet her American arrivals, and get my first mail from home. I served my countrymen by escorting them to the hotel.

That first batch of letters! I retired to the garden under my awning. Only one was at all unpleasant, a blast from an angry man who was denied a bill of health by Cadred, on account of disease. He made these points: (1) he was cured of the disease; (2) he was a white man; (3) the disease was not regarded as cause for exclusion by any civilized nation, so what right had a heathen people? (4) he was a good Baptist; (5) the examination was insulting rubbish; and (6) it was my duty to act quickly. Under the circumstances I felt no sympathy for him at all.

Other letters promised me much work, for they contained commercial inquiries of all sorts. Among them was one from Uncle Joseph, who never failed to put me a task, and I felt that some of the others were due to him, coming as they did from men I knew to be his cronies.

There were also long, full letters from home, and letters from all my girls in answer to those written in London—among them another from Gladys Hunter.

Three days before his steamer sailed Müller came into my office with hustle in his whole manner.

"I have left Davis in Winder," he said. "He will remain until the middle of March. We need your help. All in strictest confidence! . . . We are anxious to get options on some properties we have seen. They seem to me valuable—worth the chance. My proposal is this: We will place a sum of money or a note in escrow to be paid over to the owner the moment that the Islandian government agrees to the open door.

If these options must be paid for in cash, cash it will have to be, and a shipment of money will have to be made. I hope, however, that notes will suffice. I have a power of attorney from Mr. Gastein which you may see. But I believe that notes are an unknown form of security to the mine owners. I think a certificate from you of some sort would do much to convince them that it is better than cash."

"What sort of certificate?" I said, puzzled.

"As to the effect of the note, the solvency of Gastein—"

"But isn't this violating the treaty?" I interrupted.

"I know, I know," Müller said shortly. "You mean that at present no foreigner has a right to hold an option. I have thought of that. The man to whom these options shall run may have to be an Islandian. There would be no objection to that—"

"But he would hold in trust for Gastein, and that would—"

"Suppose he does?" he asked me so sharply that I found my heart beating.

"I will give you the name of a lawyer," I said, "who will say if it is proper."

"Very well," Müller said. "Now you are consul here, Lang, and your questioning attitude is quite proper. Nevertheless, I don't see that the fact that options on certain mines are taken in the name of some local man need upset you. Where you come in is just here. Money can only come into this country on a traveler's person, or else through a minister or consul. If certain sums of money are to be paid at intervals to someone or deposited somewhere, neither Davis nor I can afford the time to bring it in. But you can receive it and pay it. That is just what you are here for. It is a service that would be appreciated very much by Mr. Gastein."

I said nothing.

"We Americans ought to stand together," continued Müller. "There is a race for these things, you know. I am quite sure there would be no trouble. You can carry scruples too far, Lang. Your part can be a perfectly proper one."

Something was wrong. I did not know quite what.

There was silence. Müller was boring me through and through with his eyes.

"Gastein remembers services done him," he said. "He knows about you from your uncle. He may make a big thing of the mines here."

There was a long pause.

"Well?" shot Müller.

"Did you ask me a question?" I asked, really confused.

"Good Heavens!" he cried. The scorn in his voice was stimulating.

"I am not sure whether I can receive money that way," I said. "If it were in exchange for goods I was sending out for someone, I couldn't—"

"You *can* receive it!" blazed Müller.

"Oh yes, I *can,* but ought I to?" I answered.

"How can I make you see that you ought to?" he said in a fatherly voice.

"You can't," I said innocently. "It is a purely legal question. I shall consult a lawyer before I agree to it."

"No need!" cried Müller. "This is business, not law. If you won't say now that I can count on your aid, we will let the matter drop."

"Do you know," I said, "it looks shady to me. I don't believe you see it."

"Not as you do . . . Do all you can for Davis, if he gets into trouble!" he laughed. "You and I don't see eye to eye, Mr. Lang, and it is no use my troubling you further."

He held out his hand. I shook it warmly.

He departed, and I thought it all over slowly, much disturbed, and bit by bit I saw the light. He abandoned the suggestion of the note, because certainly a promise by a foreigner to an Islandian was a "foreign relation" not yet sanctioned, and because he thought I saw that the option could not run to the maker of the note. Then pursuing the idea of money deposits, and finding me doubtful, he hinted at favors to come. Intuition, not sense, had carried me through—and in future I would get legal advice and be extremely careful.

March had now come. Something seemed imminent, but what I did not know. Islandia was beautiful and oppressive; life amusing yet terrifying; I had learned much of interest and done nothing worth while. Time was heavy on my hands until the middle of the month. Then the council would meet and then also my friend would return to his home in Doring, and there would be news of him. This event was a mountain peak. Would it bring me sight of level lands beyond? Or was I doomed still to climb up and down, getting nowhere and seeing nothing but other peaks ahead?

4

From The City to the Fains'

LINES OF heavy rain from the southwest were beating obliquely on
the windows of my office, and water, dotted with leaping rings, lay
in pools on the flagstones of the passageway outside. The shrubbery
crowning the wall of the roof garden opposite tossed in the gusty
wind, a dark wet green against a gray sodden sky. Twilight just beginning was almost sulphurous in color.

Dorn came in.

A dark-blue cape, glistening with water, covered him from head
to foot. He had thrown back the hood, and his face was thinner than
I remembered, its ruddiness sunburned to orange-brown. Drawn
slowly to my feet, I saw him as bright and as detailed as though seen
through an enlarging glass, standing against the vague tones of a
world suddenly grown dim.

His deep voice spoke with resonance.

"John!"

We gripped each other's arms above the elbow. We laughed and
we looked at each other. Then I was aware that George was also
present. I gave the name of each, and in Islandian fashion identified
them to each other by reference to their relationship to the heads of
their families.

"Brother—George of Hern; grandnephew—Dorn of Lower
Doring."

Dorn flung off his cape, and stood before us in all his muscular
bigness, but sparer than I had known him.

"Your room is prepared," I said in Islandian.

He laughed, answering in English:

"My uncle knew what would please me. He wrote me of your
reply."

61

"I am very grateful to him and to you."

"I first learned that you had come nine days ago; and I started at once for The City."

We were silent. He had not told me where he was when he received this news, but since it had taken so long for him to reach me, he must have been in a far corner of his land.

"I left undone one or two things I have to do," he said. "I hoped I could take you home with me and on the way I will do them. But it means much traveling, two weeks instead of five days."

"That is nothing," I said.

"When they are done, I shall be free for a time," he continued. "Can you come with me—two weeks of traveling and then to my home —and stay with us a long time?"

My duties as consul, my social obligations, my plans for studying the council in action vanished like ghosts in the sunlight.

"Yes!" I cried.

"If we go together, I can only stay with you here for two days. It will mean your missing the meeting of the council. If you prefer to remain for that, you could come to my home afterwards . . ."

"No! If I could come with you . . . But I don't want to be in your way!"

He looked at me smiling, and I was reassured.

"I would like to change my clothes," he said. "I have been riding all day in the rain."

"Are your horses cared for?" asked George.

Dorn nodded, and turning to me:

"I picked up one for you," he said diffidently, "one I used to ride myself."

His bag was in the hall, and carrying it I led him to his room, thankful that it had been prepared. I stayed with him while he changed and bathed, telling him of my life in New York and of how I came to be consul. He listened attentively without comment, until I had concluded.

"I think you will be happy here," was all he said.

Lona did well by us for dinner. Halfway through he began to tell of our proposed journey. The usual route to his home was to travel west crossing the mountains at the Doan Pass, taking five days in all; our route would lead us due north, through Reeves, to a high mountain pass, known as the Mora, opening into the head of the valley of the Doring River, down which we would ride to his home.

"We shall have to travel fast during the first few days," he said, "for I have an engagement I must keep. I am sorry, for I would like to show you Reeves, the Frays, and stop at my great-uncle's, Isla Fain's. But after that, we can take our time."

Once committed to making a journey away from The City it was a disappointment for me to miss anything. Perhaps George read me.

"How are your horses?" he asked.

"In good condition. A few days' rest would do them no harm."

"If I were to rest the horses I would prefer to leave them in some good green paddock, and not in a stable at The City," said George.

"Would you care to start sooner?" asked Dorn abruptly.

"Yes, very much."

"Tomorrow?"

It would mean a busy evening.

"What do you want to do?" I said.

"I would rather go tomorrow than stay," Dorn answered after a moment's thought. "Can you be ready?"

"Yes," I said instantly.

"So be it," he replied smiling. "I am ready."

"What shall I take?" I asked. "I have a saddlebag and a heavy raincoat."

Dorn considered a moment.

"Would you mind wearing our costume?"

"No indeed!"

"We'll fit you out at Reeves," said Dorn, "and can therefore start early tomorrow. Bring toilet articles, some money, and a few books; wear riding clothes and bring your raincoat. That is all you will need tomorrow."

Matters were thereby much simplified. Soon after, Dorn left us to settle the affairs of the consulate together.

I was in need of advice, and asked George if I were doing right in not letting my friend and his horses rest a few days.

"Dorn said he would rather go than stay," was the answer.

"But he might say that for my sake!"

George looked puzzled.

"But you asked him?"

"Yes, I know. . . ."

We did not understand each other, and I was face to face with another racial difference. Only after some time did it come to me that having asked my friend what he wanted to do, I could not question his answer with propriety. When I accepted this, George brightened and was willing to speculate on Dorn's attitude.

"He wants to go tomorrow, not alone to please you," he said. "You will be with him whether you go or stay. I think he has definite reasons for not wanting to be seen here. That is not our concern."

There was a hint of mystery in it all, but I was growing to be enough of an Islandian to accept a man's word without trying to solve his problems in my own head.

George and I worked several hours arranging affairs for a month's absence, with him in charge, and then I went to bed.

When I woke it was still quite dark and the rain was pattering gently at my window. My watch read a quarter to six; the coming events were like cold sharp wine.

Sounds outside told me that others were about, and when I emerged from my room I found breakfast ready. Dorn had already gone to fetch the horses to the door. Smoked bluefish, bread crisp like a cracker, chocolate, and fruit; the rain dripping outside; my leather saddlebag all packed with toilet articles, pyjamas, three books, and paper and ink; my raincoat lying at hand, and myself dressed to travel —it was all good!

At seven Dorn and I put on our coats and took up our bags and went out. How simple it was! No tickets had to be bought, no struggling for porters or long waiting at stations. We started, that was all.

The rain was steadily falling but the air was warm. Clouds gray and white came swelling and rolling up from behind the greenery edging the housetops. In the street below under the arch of the bridge three horses stood quiet and huddled. They were creamy white with rusty spots, and they all had thick bristling manes. The rain dripped upon the stone flagging of the street. A stray drop or two slid coldly down my neck, and I envied Dorn his cloak and hood, though in the back he looked like a huge little girl. In a few moments he had strapped his and my saddlebags to the back of the pack horse, and knotted a long halter-rein to the pommel.

Taking one horse by the rein close to its mouth, he turned its intelligent head to me.

"John," he said, "this is Fak. You won't win any races upon him, but he is as steady as a river. He is mountain-born and bred, and I don't know a better horse in bad footing. He is yours, if after you have tried him you want to keep him."

By some trick he made the horse whinny.

"If you don't mind," he said, "I'll ride ahead of you."

He called out a few guttural words that later I learned to use myself. While Fak pawed the ringing pavement with ears cocked forward, the pack horse, Hail, started off by himself at a brisk walk, Dorn followed close, and then Fak of his own accord set out with his nose a few inches from his fellow's tail. Thus we proceeded through rain-swept, empty streets, across The City, out the Reeves Gate, and across the west branch of the Islandia River, by a long curving bridge. Then we went north by a straight road between farms, full of glistening pools and a little muddy, but well built and firm under our horses' feet.

The sky, full of bellying gray and white rain clouds, was an immense dome over my head. The only sounds were the clopping and thudding splashes of the feet of the three horses, the creak of my saddle, the swish of the rain among the trees, and the occasional faint whistle of the wind around the corner of my hat. We passed fields and woods, and gardens of maize or grain, which were wet and green. Through the trees were glimpses of buildings; house, stable, and outhouses, the center of each farm, lying in the midst of pastures, meadows, orchards, woods, and market gardens, constantly repeated in varying arrangements. Dorn was a huge huddled figure, so large for his horse as to be slightly funny. My left cheek, where the rain beat upon it, was cool and damp, while the other side of my face was very warm with the exercise of riding. Fak's white coat was pitted and streaked and pointed by the wet. I liked to watch his velvety ears, alert, curious, questioning, while the rest of him walked steadily and mechanically.

Thus an hour passed, wordless and calm, and the world was an immense, spacious, rainy place in the very center of which our train of three horses and two men moved small and alone.

There was a faint bass hum; Dorn was singing to himself as he used to do. . . .

Now the air was warmer, and the sky whiter between the wet, darkening gusts of rain. Pools in the hollows of the road glistened, and the foliage of trees here and there overhanging the road were a vivider green. On and on we rode—two hours now—and I had passed into a dreamy state where thoughts were unsubstantial.

Blue sky showed in patches to the west and north. Dorn took off his cloak and rolling it up strapped it to the cantle of his saddle; I followed his example, but found difficulty in manipulating the straps behind me with the horse never still in his tireless, hurried walk. It was a strange gait, rather monotonous and not wholly easy, for the impression one had was of constant accelerations of speed about to break into a canter that never resulted.

At intervals we passed other travelers, for the most part single horsemen, but not infrequently pedestrians and caravans like our own. At every such encounter the first rider of the group held up his hand, and smiled and nodded as he passed.

We rode for another hour under a warm sun, now bright, now pale, and through pleasant, fertile, freshly wet country. The constant repetition of wood lots, fallow land, meadows, gardens, and well-built stone walls was a little monotonous. Then unexpectedly the road passed a heavy round tower on the right and came to the abrupt edge of a highland.

Below us lay the river, glistening in the sunlight, meandering in broad serene bands and reaches. About ten miles away, at the end of the valley, was a white broken line upon the summit of golden brown cliffs, and rising above it, over a background of blue haze was the white snowy dome of Mount Islandia.

"Reeves," said Dorn.

My sense of distance had gone awry. It was full morning now, between ten and eleven, and we had come eighteen miles. By train that was nothing—a pipe or two, a short story—but the eighteen miles we had just come was long, for every house, every tree, was exposed to a vision that could study and remember it as we wheeled slowly but steadily past.

We gave our horses a few moments' rest. The tower, Dorn said, was very old, built when the Islandians were winning their country from the Blacks, and was placed upon a promontory of the highlands to watch the river valley. It lay in the property of the Danning family.

"They are expert farmers," he said, "and their two houses are beautiful. I wish we could visit them. There are many people I'd like to have you meet. The Dannings are related to your friend Islata Soma, Cadred's wife." He laughed. "The Somes support us! Of course the Fains, also. You have fallen among the conservatives, John."

"You may convert me, but if you did I would have to leave the country."

"Would you? Well, so far as we are concerned, your views are nothing. You perhaps remember Carstairs could never get over the fact that his dearest friend, Lord Fain, was a heathen. That is more of a difference than politics."

It was the first time he had spoken of this matter.

"Consuls really have no politics," I said, "and this particular consul is committed to nothing."

We rode on. The road turned sharply to the left and made its way inland again among the farms. Another hour passed like magic, and then another. The sun had reached the meridian and passed it. I was tired, hungry, and sleepy, but content.

Just as unexpected as our emergence on the promontory that commanded the Islandia River was our arrival on the edge of the gorge of the Tamplin River, which flows in from the northwest to join the Islandia River at the foot of the cliffs on which Reeves stands.

The road to the water below seemed all but perpendicular, and was cut out of rock. Opposite the cliffs, touched by the sun, were a tawny yellow and the walls that edged them were of the same color, and behind them were roofs of red tiles or gray slate.

We paused only a moment and then went down into the gorge. It was filled with sunlight and wind. We crossed a stone bridge under which the water washed audibly, and rode up between two stone towers into a town very much like The City, with narrow irregular streets paved with flagstones and closely built houses decorated with carving. Few people were about and the streets were quiet under the high midday summer sun.

We crossed the town without stopping and passed through a narrow gate between two heavy towers in massive landward walls. Just outside the gate the ground fell away a little and then rose again in a gentle grassy slope to a hill crowned with walls, behind which was a confusion of stone towers, battlements, and façades, ancient, gray, and simple. This was the University.

Immediately within its low, plain entrance were stables, and beyond was an open grassy court, surrounded by shaded cloisters, and emerald green in the sunlight. An attendant took our horses. We waited until they were unsaddled, fed, and watered, and then followed him through confusing arches, along cloistered arcades and across little sunny courts, to a low building at the further side of the college and into a simple room with an open window. A warm wind blew in over a yellow hayfield, which came up to the foot of the wall, utterly empty under the blue sky. It was so still that the ears sang.

"We are too late for the regular lunch in the great hall," said Dorn, "but they will bring us something here. Isn't it a pleasant place to go to college?"

On the way to the tailor's we crossed the University enclosure again and Dorn told me something of our environment. Reeves was founded in 815 A.D. and was the first permanent, substantial Islandian town. Not till its strategic site was won did the leader of the Islandians, the first Alwin, call himself king and take a crown. The college was founded in 1035 A.D. by Alwin the Great, who himself drove the plow that marked the limits of its enclosure—some thirty acres in extent.

The students, from two to four hundred in number, are nearly all relatives of nobles, although the college is open to anyone with the necessary educational qualification. The course is two or three years, begun at nineteen or twenty, but those who go into medicine, law, army, or navy take longer; for the college at Islandia is not only Harvard and Yale, but Johns Hopkins Medical School, West Point, and Annapolis. It was termtime, but so large and complex was the place that the students were lost among the long arcades, which were as still as a dream, with geometrical designs of sunlight cast through the arches on their shadowy floors.

At the tailor's shop Dorn took entire charge, selecting materials and determining the cut; and at the end of an hour he had ordered for me a navy-blue broadcloth for dress wear, and a heather-colored "tweed" for ordinary use, each of which comprised jacket and knickerbockers. Then, too, there were a pair of riding breeches and leather coat; a waterproof cape like his own; a number of shirts; woolen stockings; a pair of sandals; and a pair of waterproof boots. It was a large order and the tailor was somewhat dismayed. It was arranged that my outfit should be shipped after me to Isla Fain's where we were to spend the next day but one.

When we returned to the University the sun was dropping, and there was an extraordinary sense of personality in the place, serene, still, lovely, and as definite as that of a human being.

A little later, washed and clean, Dorn and I left our room to visit the Gilmours. Their house seemed very English with its oriental rugs, large familiar photographs of the Forum, cathedrals, and Oxford colleges, and English furniture. So used had I become to Islandian houses that the Gilmours' seemed at first cluttered and overcrowded; but after a time it touched subconscious memories of similar houses at home. Though Gilmour was a naturalized Islandian, he was still an Englishman, wearing a dinner jacket, and smoking a pipe.

Our host, his wife, their daughter, a girl of about seventeen, their son, a year or so younger, and a student at the college, named Hyth, made up the party. The doors of the dining room, thrown wide open, brought in upon us the breezes of the little garden outside, planted with English flowers that glowed even after the soft summer darkness came. The Gilmour boy wore Islandian clothes, and though in appearance English was less so in manner than his parents. The girl, however, was a typical English miss in an English frock, serious and very much on her guard. My place was at her side and her near, fresh presence, young, wind-burned, and living, was warm against my senses.

Hyth was a boy of about eighteen, sandy-haired, with yellow eyebrows, freckles, a great deal of dignity, and a trace of uncertain humor when he ventured to speak. His aunt, now dead, had been the wife of Dorn's great-uncle, and there was evidently a close bond between the two families. He was familiar with our plans and told me that when I stopped at his uncle's house—which I did not know I was to do—I must not let his brothers and sisters run over me. "There will be seven of them," he said, "all wanting their own way."

After dinner, with my first cigar for several weeks—tobacco not being smoked by Islandians—we went upstairs to a spacious open room over the arcades and directly above the pond. Here in the dusk sat the older Gilmours, Hyth, Dorn, and I, talking in friendly desultory fashion of the differences between nations, of geography, and of other things. Through the round windows the night air floated in upon us, and the fatigue of the day and the wine of the dinner made me sleepier and sleepier, so that I was glad at last to go back through the dimly lit cloisters to our room.

Next morning Dorn woke me, and slipping on a few garments, we made our way down to the river, along a narrow path through the wooded grounds of the college. Fifty or more students were swimming there, naked, and many of these Dorn knew and named to me and me to them. At eight we sat down with the whole student body in the great hall of the college, vast, ancient, and hazy, with high-pointed timber roof and dark walls, and lit by round windows near the top, through which sunlight came in slanting lines of interweaving motes. There was a cheerful clatter of crockery and knives and forks and a smell of bacon and hot bread. Before nine, we were on horseback once more in the courtyard near the Reeves Gate.

"Do you mind if we change our order today?" asked Dorn. "It is more convenient for me to go first and you last with the pack horse between, but yesterday I did you an honor, though you may not have known it. You had no duty at all, you see." He laughed, and we started as he suggested. Later I learned that the honor was a real one.

We trotted through the gate and headed north, leaving town and college behind us, our faces towards the mountains.

We covered forty-five miles that day. The sun beat down on us and the glare reduced my eyes to slits. The country was more rolling, more sun-baked and rural. A haze lay over everything and there was no view, either of the mountains to the north or of Reeves to the south.

We lunched in the bottom of a broad valley through which ran a swampy stream, and for the first time I ate typical travelers' fare, the Islandian meat roll—a piece of beef, hermetically sealed in a close-grained casing of hard bread. Before being eaten this is softened by soaking in water, and it is then satisfactory to the hungry. Besides, a roll will keep from eight to ten days in hot weather and a month or so in cold. In addition we had *sarka* and hard bitter chocolate.

During the afternoon conditions changed. The land became more rolling and the monotony of the checkerboards of the farms was broken by patches of silent, deserted pine woods with sandy loam underfoot. The shadows became long and blue, the air damp and cool. We were among the foothills of the mountains at last. I drew deep breaths, happy though tired, yet not too weary to respond to the everlasting wonder of land steadily rising, and lifting one up to the high places of the world.

At last we reached a narrow north-and-south valley and suddenly at its end I saw the snowy dome of Mount Islandia—pink in the light of a low sun that was hidden below the hills. Dorn turned his horse off the highroad, between two stone posts into a damp, needle-strewn lane. As he did so he smiled and nodded a warning. I sat up stiffly just in time, for our horses broke into a canter. The darkening air rushed cool against my face. Great pines flitted by. Five hundred feet perhaps, and then there was an opening in the trees and a low stone house of two stories, ancient and gray. A door opened under the shadow of a vine-covered porch, and a yellow gleam came through. It was dark in the valley, though light still lay on the high slopes of the hills.

"*Kana!*" came a voice gentle and old, and two figures came toward us.

"Dorn and Lang!" cried my friend.

All became vague to me, and it was not till I had drunk a bowl of bitter spicy chocolate that I trusted myself to speak. It was the first time that this drink was really right.

A hot bath and a change of clothes lent me by Dorn, and of course too large, were restorative, but the good dinner that followed brought sleepiness. Our hosts were gracious. Lord Fain, whose gentle voice had called a greeting to us, was over eighty, frail and slim but with a straight carriage and alert step. His head was striking. Under bushy white brows were coal-black burning eyes. His nose was a haughty curving hook, and his skin, crossed by a network of fine wrinkles, was so dark that his thick, close-cut white hair was like a snowy cap. It was a savage face except for the mouth, which was smiling and sympathetic. He was Dorn's great-uncle, brother of the Faina who had written to me so graciously.

With him lived his brother, a man of the same general type, but gentler and less vivid, more humorous and less sympathetic. His wife, Mara, somewhat younger, was a clear-eyed, wise old lady.

After dinner we all sat about a wood fire. Besides the red flames there was only a dim yellow lamp. Outside the air was cold and the night black. Our elevation was quite two thousand feet, and north of us were empty rugged mountains. The firelight glistened on a hearth smoothed with ages of brushing.

Lord Fain was the son of one of Islandia's great generals, he who crushed the Demiji seventy-three years before, and who figured in Carstairs' first book, *Against the Demiji with the Islandians*. His father, too, was the man whom Carstairs visited and loved well. For my sake our host told of his own recollections of him.

As I lay in soft blankets I remembered all at once Gladys Hunter and her interest in Carstairs. What a letter I could write to her!

My sleep was deep and I woke to sunlight, utter stillness, and a view of trees—great pines with long needles in bushy, steel-gray bunches—ranked on a hill slope one above the other and motionless in the early air.

A cool bright morning followed. Lord Fain and Dorn, the latter on a borrowed horse, while ours rested, departed on some errand apparently planned the night before. The brother shouldered a hoe and went off on foot. Mara gave me a cake of chocolate, said there was a pleasant path and a view in a certain direction, and then she, too, abandoned me. Remembering Gladys Hunter, I took writing materials and set out in the direction indicated.

Beyond a gate in a stone wall an easy trail led up through cool pines, and I followed it slowly, realizing how leaden two days of riding had made my legs. After about half an hour's climb the trail led to the summit of an east-and-west ridge. Sitting down on a log I looked at the view.

Southward the winding course of the Frays River was visible as far as Tindal Valley, and beyond I could see its gleaming reaches winding through flat bottom lands. To the north the Mount Islandia massif, its summit perhaps twenty-five miles away, covered an immense extent of skyline, the gentle lofty dome a pure unbroken white.

Time slipped past. The sun grew warmer. Clouds gathered on the snow mountains. In the valley whence I had come the roof of the Fains' farm nestled among trees. Lying face down on a bed of pine needles, with a gentle hill wind sighing about my ears and warm sun on my back, I wrote to Gladys Hunter and became utterly absorbed in making precise the color and feeling of the place and of the Fains. . . .

Long afterwards I looked up, aware that inspiration was flagging, but the letter was nearly done. Emotions and desires, indefinite and nameless, were adrift. Horses' feet sounded; perhaps for some time I had been hearing them. The faces of Lord Fain and Dorn, as they came riding down the path from the higher ground, were for a moment those of moving puppets on a painted ground.

The afternoon dreamed itself away like the morning, but there was more activity. Lord Fain's brother, Dorn, and I went over their farm, the first two conferring as experts.

The farm lay along the west side of the river and was occupied by three families beside the Fains, who held the status of *denerir* to the Fains, the *tanar*. "Dependents" and "proprietors" is the nearest translation.

Our tour was leisurely, now through lush water meadows, now between rows of ripening maize, and through orchards of green fruit. The senses were filled with the sound of wind in the grass, green things growing, wooded hills, and the distant mountain; there was the smell of earth and of leaves and of vegetables. With feet caked with wet dirt we plodded back home toward suppertime along the road, the road that led down to the plain and up mysteriously into the mountains.

The carriers arrived that evening with the Islandian garments made by the tailor at Reeves. They were tried on and fitted well enough. My discarded American clothes were packed up for them to take back to Reeves on their way to George and The City. My letter, consigned to him for mailing, was also in their hands to start its journey when they left early next morning.

It was as though the cords that held me to my old life were definitely cut.

I was undressing for bed when Dorn came in and sat down for a talk.

"You will pass for one of us tomorrow," he said. "Even your name has an Islandian ring. If it were Higginson or Saltonstall or O'Brien! But Lang! There are Langs in Dole . . . I hope you don't mind."

"Of course not! I'm glad to do it. It will be interesting to wear your clothes."

"I suppose it was not essential, but it will help. I owe you an apology, for I have put you to expense. I am on a mission, as you know."

"If I am in the way. . . ."

"You won't be. If anything comes up that would embarrass you or—frankly—that I do not want you to know, you will be left out for a while. It will raise less question if you appear as an Islandian. One thing, John—you won't have to pretend that you are one. If anyone talks to you, don't feel you must play a part. Be yourself—

73

and if in addition you care to be guileless and innocent all the better. I mean . . ." he blushed, "forgive me, John, I can't ask any promise of secrecy."

"I won't give it," I said, suddenly understanding him. "I see a great many things and many of them, the look of places, the way people live, things like that. . . ."

I stopped and he nodded. There was silence a moment.

"Are you ready to go on tomorrow?" he said.

"Yes, are you?"

"Quite! We will go, then, and spend our next night out of doors."

"It will take some of the newness out of my new clothes."

At this we both laughed, quite contented with ourselves.

5

Incident at the Lor Pass

WE STARTED at eight next morning and all the Fains saw us off. It was good to be once more on the highroad, stretching in a straight line along the valley to its end where the pine-forested slopes met and where the river brawled and splashed down its boulder-strewn bed.

The back of Dorn, almost too large for his horse; the alert head, bulky burden, and white rump and tail of the pack horse; the surface of the road flowing under me; the trees wheeling past to join the ranks of those who stand at ease after inspection; the sky overhead growing bluer and warmer and bringing out the odor of resin in the trees; the sun looking slantwise upon us and keeping us company by rolling along the tops of the hills, or by rising above them and soaring through the sky—this is my memory of that morning and of many others that followed. It was perfect; if I wanted to look, there was much to see and plenty of time to see it in. I could sing if I wished, and if I wanted conversation I could call to Dorn who would ride sitting sideways if the spirit moved him. The horses seemed humorists in their tails and ears. If excitement were needed there was always the next thing around the next bend.

We emerged from the woods, and great, rolling, parallel hogbacks of grassland lay before us, sloping down to a blue-green plain to the southeast. Rail fences lined the road and scattered herds of cattle dotted the grassy slopes. For an hour we followed the road over the rolling hills and then plunged into another forest, with gnarled, mossy tree trunks, dense thickets of twisted branches, and damp hollows with ferns and mushrooms. When we had gone half a mile perhaps, I felt rather than saw an immense loom to our left—the cliffs of the mountain several miles away. Their height overawed and dominated the forest, with sheer faces of gray and yellow stone rising three thousand

75

feet. About two-thirds of the way up there was a step in the cliffs, where patches of green were dotted horizontally at intervals.

Noon found us still in the forest. We dismounted on the slope of a knoll, and climbing to its summit ate our lunches and then stretched out on our backs. The checkered sun fell upon us, a few small birds twittered, and an occasional insect hummed.

The Frays, Dorn said, were that greater shelf upon the cliffs opposite and we would be upon them by midafternoon.

I asked why the forest around us had not been cleared.

"Sentiment, perhaps," he answered with a shrug. "These woods were the first ground conquered after the descent. They were a sort of national park."

"Could we camp here?"

"Oh yes. There will be parties camping on the Frays."

"Life is rather pleasant here, isn't it?"

"I think so, John. Would it be pleasanter if we had come by train from The City? It is only ninety miles or so—say three hours. A railroad route has been surveyed, you know, and the line would come looping up the grazing land. The City, Reeves, and Mora Pass Railroad, scenery unsurpassed!"

"It would save time."

"Yes, in one sense. I like to travel at a horse's gait."

"If you were used to another?"

"I'm not. Why should I change?"

"Progress!" I said.

"Speed, is that progress? Anyway, why progress? Why not enjoy what one has? Men have never exhausted present pleasures." His voice had a bantering tone.

"With us, progress means giving pleasures to those who haven't got them."

"But doesn't progress create the very situation it seeks to cure—always changing the social adjustment so that someone is squeezed out. Decide on an indispensable minimum. See that everyone gets that, and until everyone has it, don't let anyone have any more. Don't let anyone ever have any more until they have cultivated fully what they have."

"Dorn, you sound like a socialist."

"Oh no," he said, and laughed, "not with us. We grew that way, because we enjoyed so much what we had that we never really wanted more. It is individualism—that is, the individual enjoys so much what he has that he does not crave other things from the community. And then comes Mora—and says, 'See how everyone else does. Let's copy them; they must be right. If not, they may hurt us.' " He laughed again. "Socialism is just another silly sort of progress and quite as footless. You will have to change the nature of your mankind before you will all be happy."

"To be unhappy is a sign we aren't stagnating."

"Nor are we. 'Happy' wasn't the right word. We are quite as unhappy as you are. Things are too beautiful; those we love die; it hurts to grow old or be sick. Progress won't change any of those things, except that medicine will mitigate the last. We cultivate medicine, and we are quite as far along as you are there. Railroads and all that merely stir up a puddle, putting nothing new in and taking nothing out."

"Dorn, you almost persuade me—" I said to tease him.

"No, I don't, John. There are hundreds of flaws in what I've said."

"There are!"

"I know it; yet I don't want my country changed."

"Are there no poor people, whose lot on the material side needs bettering?"

"Wait and see. There are no outstanding rich men. Technically 5 or 6 per cent of the people own 90 per cent of the wealth, but in practice and law they have such duties to the rest that they can't deprive them of a comfortable living and something over. Take the *denerir*. They are secure in their tenures."

"If they want to be proprietors—?"

"Nothing to prevent, if they set their minds to it for a generation or two; but they have then more to worry about. They marry us and we marry them. They are happy. But that is something to decide for yourself."

I don't know why, but this conversation made me wish for one of my own kind. I was glad when it ended, for the world around me seemed alien.

An hour later, arrived at the talus-strewn bases of the cliffs, we dismounted and began to climb on foot. Soon the rounded muscular bodies of the horses shone with sweat. Dorn was cool, but I was red and hot with aches in my calves.

After another hour we emerged from the trees on a rocky knob

77

projecting from the hillside. Here the road forked, one branch con-tinuing on, the other turning off sharply to the left. Eastward, at a distance of thirty miles or so, was the whole of an immense peak from its sloping foothills, up through its broad girdle of dark forest to its talus slopes, its glaciers, and its ragged rocky summit and white snow. We turned onto the road to the left, bringing the cliffs back again on our right hand, and came after several miles to a precipitous rocky slide, strewn with huge boulders up which our road zigzagged its way.

Soon heart and lungs were tried and every step up was a lift. The air seemed thin. Things became a little vague. We passed through a broken gateway in a crumbling white wall, and I caught my breath in surprise.

A meadow, flat and level, lay before us, perhaps half a mile long. On the left the green grass crowded upon the edge of a sheer dizzying drop of more than a thousand feet; on the right it ran to the base of cliffs that soared up as high again, sheer and straight. A trail mean-dered across the meadow to its farther end. We mounted our horses and rode on. The air was taking on the softer, richer coloring of late afternoon. The grass under our feet was vivid and dark; and the cliffs were a glowing amber-yellow. Here and there were ruins of buildings. One house was complete and whole, with a high-pitched roof and narrow windows opening into blackness. About it the ground was beaten hard as though many had stopped to look at it, but inside this ring was an encircling band of high untrodden grass. Within the un-passed barrier that imposed no physical restraint, it lay, ancient, solid, and intact.

At the end of the meadow we came to a series of irregular terraces, lying on the steep pitch of a rocky slide. Beyond them the path turned and ran along a ledge on the outer face of the cliff. We could see it all the way to the point where it turned into another meadow, and beyond, another and another extended for miles, until hidden by a curve of the cliffs in the haze of a great distance.

The eye recoiled from the drop on the left and skipped along these shelves, seeking a spot wide enough to rest on without fear of the sudden uprush of the forest carpet below—so detailed as to seem soft —treacherous because the eye could guess that a tiny feather of greenery down below was a huge tree, a pin point of white a boulder as large as a house.

Dorn went around the right-angled turn unhesitatingly, Hail followed, and then Fak after him with a nervous flick of his body. I did not let my eyes drop, but thought of other things. . . .

Unexpectedly, around a turn, the inner wall concaved. A semicircle of green grass, dotted with tall beeches, lay before us. A stream came down the cliffs in cascades, gathered its mists and drops into a deep pool under their shadow; and thence meandered through the trees to the outer edge, over which it swept in a smooth, green, glass-like fall without a sound. Here we dismounted. The horses were unsaddled and left to wander, and Dorn and I gathered broken branches and made ourselves a camp fire.

Our pillows were our saddlebags, our bedding their outer coverings and our great cloaks. The hot leaping flames warmed us. In the cool black night the cliff edge was terrifying and yet comfortably far away. Little owls began to hoot.

We ate our suppers in our beds. A night wind made the treetops hiss, and we talked with long silences.

The Frays, Dorn said, was the region from which the Islandians descended in 800 A.D., to found their nation.

"Before that, very little is known. We think that the Islandians were scattered very thinly over the whole continent, for they were not a gregarious race and the presence of fellows was an incentive to go elsewhere. Then the Negroes came, the *Bantir,* and drove them back into these mountains. In this place they made a stand and learned to live together. Gradually they became too numerous for the resources of the Frays, and they went down and drove out the *Bantir* and finally conquered the whole nation. But we don't know much about it, for when they descended they destroyed their houses lest they be tempted to give up their new adventure and return."

I recalled reading something of this in M. Perier's history.

"Wasn't there anything left?" I asked.

"Only the house of Alwin, which we saw on the way. He left it with the door unbarred, but declared it inviolate. We like to observe his command; it coincides with our own ideas as to the importance of respecting a man's privacy. You remember, perhaps, that his wife was buried there."

"Wasn't her name Dorna?"

"Probably she was the sister of some ancestor of mine. The Bants had somehow got a foothold on the Frays. The story is that they came up by one of the slides. She was outraged and killed herself, and this terrible event stirred us to action."

"What is in the king's house? Does anyone know?"

"Probably nothing. I don't know, and I know of no one who does unless it is some of your countrymen. Cornell University sent an expedition to study Islandia, and they spent some time on the Frays. Though our feeling was explained to them, I am told they thought they had a higher duty in the interests of archaeology. They certainly never entered the place openly, for there were many campers here."

Dorn made me feel small, and I recalled Mark Twain's story of the American who blew out the lamp that had burned a thousand years.

The fire died down and was replenished several times. The little owls came down close to us and then all departed. Occasionally the thud of our horses' feet sounded now near, now far. Frogs with a metallic bass croaked in the pool, and were silent. At last we too were still, and went casually to sleep.

For me there were many wakings, but not to discomfort—rather to a sense of strangeness and of peace.

The whinny of a horse woke me, and there were many layers of subconsciousness to be passed through before my eyes were open and I knew where I was.

It was a clear morning. I could see the hill that I had climbed at the Fains' and the broad expanses of grazing farms lying westward among the folds of the hills. Farther south the warped surface of the central part of the Province of Islandia was like a delicately tinted relief map, and The City itself was visible, a whitish shadow on the edge of something hazily and faintly blue.

We bathed in the cold clear water of the pool, ate a breakfast like the supper of the night before, saddled our horses, and went back the way we had come. When we reached the terraces we turned our horses up their slopes, and mounted by narrow trails until we were near the top. Here, surrounded by gnarled and twisted trees and surmounting them like a watch tower, was the king's lodge, the only habitation of the Frays, built of roughly hewn brown stone.

I asked if the king were there, as we rode by.

"I don't know," said Dorn. "He has customs all his own. He thinks it enough if he is present when the council meets. The rest of the time no one knows where he is or what he is doing. There is a great deal of criticism. He is young, only our age, and many people feel that he isn't performing his duty. But when he does appear he does his official and social work so well that his shortcomings are forgotten."

"Do you know him?"

"Oh yes. Our house is one of the places he visits two or three times a year, usually with his friend Stellin. He is attractive, very, but peculiar. You are sure to meet him some time."

A king!

About the middle of the morning we reached once more the tower, where, on the day before, we had turned aside from the main route on our way to the Frays. The great mountain to the east—Matclorn—had gathered a fleet of white clouds under its western shoulder. In the few moments that we watched they rose visibly, and I wondered if we were to be caught in mist and rain.

We set out, and presently the fog billowed up from below, and the sun turned pale and vanished. Sounds were muffled and dead, and ahead and behind the road faded into nothingness. It was cold, but there was excitement in our isolation.

An hour passed. The trees dwindled away leaving only gnarled gray remnants. I felt a freer wind and the rocks shone white through the fog. Abruptly the sun appeared as a pale round ball, then patches of blue sky behind bright white edges of twisting mist; the wind grew to a sudden gale, and wide expanses of rocky slopes appeared to the left. Southeastward, and a few hundred feet below us, Matclorn rose out of the clouds like a cape. Due south of it rose another mountain, from which a sharp ridge sloped down to the west to a snow pass. Still further west the ridge rose again and became a lofty, snowy arête, culminating in a sharp, rocky peak with snow fields and glaciers. Beyond it through a rounded saddle was a glimpse of ragged snow mountains fifteen or twenty miles away. On the farther side of the saddle was a gradual slope that grew steeper, became smooth and white, and rose in a serene sweep to a vast, smooth, snowy dome—Mount Islandia itself.

We rode on a little way, with the glare of these snowy giants cutting the sky full upon us, and stopped in a rocky shelter for lunch.

The smooth saddle to the southwest was the Mora Pass, through which we were going. It opened into the head of the Doring Valley, which stretched between two great mountain ranges all the way to the sea. Beyond the head of the valley were the Sobo Steppes, now under German protection, and inhabited by the bloodiest of the Mountain Negroes.

We rode on through a desolate region of barren ridges with the scantiest of vegetation, and arrived late in the afternoon at the Inn, lying in a little circular amphitheater below the Mora Pass.

Fuel was so scarce here that the usual custom of serving meals separately was not observed. There was a large hall with a huge fireplace, where six or eight people were already assembled. We joined them and everyone talked informally of roads and mountains, of weather, and of where they lived, of mutual friends, and of what they raised on their farms.

It grew dark quite early and the wind began to blow. A servant piled wood on the fire. A faint odor of broiled meat came from the dining room. I conversed with a man from Dole and his wife. They were evidently *denerir,* and yet in dress and manner no different from the proprietors of farms that I had met. They were a young couple not long married, and the wife had a slightly distraught air, for she had her baby in a nearby room and was listening for it instinctively all the time. They were bound for Brome, they told me, to stay with a friend.

It was nearly supper time, and I was telling my new acquaintances something of my own country, when I saw across the hall, in the doorway, three men in the European costume of mountaineers with the full paraphernalia of hobnail boots, goggles, and ice axes. The room was rather dimly lighted and hazy, but as they came forward I recognized Gordon and Philip Wills, and young Calwin.

"What are you doing here?" asked Philip Wills.

I smiled, for no answer was ready to my lips, and then I said:

"What are you doing?"

"We have just climbed the Moraclorn."

Wondering if they knew Dorn, I turned to where the latter had been sitting to make the introduction, but the place was vacant. My friend had vanished. With a feeling of emptiness, I wished for quicker wits and resolved if it were possible not to tell who my companion was. Quickly I questioned the Willses as to their climb.

Philip sketched their effort. Apparently the summit had eluded them, and not being prepared for a desperate effort they had given up perhaps five hundred feet below it. Soon afterwards they left to change their clothes. As soon as they were out of sight, I went to the room that Dorn and I shared. He was packing his saddlebag, and looked up with an amused smile, but questioning eyes.

"Forgive me for running."

"I didn't have to give away that you were with me," I said.

"Good! I would prefer not to have Calwin know my presence hereabout." His eyes were relieved. As he spoke he put on his raincoat. "I am going to leave," he added.

"I'll come too." I half stated, half suggested, anxious not to be left alone.

"No—if you don't mind. If Calwin has any suspicions and if you disappeared, they would be confirmed. You can join me tomorrow morning."

"Where will you sleep?"

He shrugged.

"I'll find a place in the open. I'm used to it. . . . John, I'm sorry to put you to some trouble."

"It's nothing!" I cried.

"Spend the night. Talk with them, if it is natural. If they ask you who you are with, say you are with a friend. Calwin will be too polite to ask more. Tomorrow morning leave early. I shall arrange to have the horses taken over the pass and down into the valley. You can go with them if you like, and wait for me down below; but if you prefer you can join me. I am going to spend a day on foot in the mountains."

I studied him, doubtful. I knew he had a mission of some sort and wondered if I would not be in the way.

"I think I'll go down with the horses," I said at last.

There was silence a moment.

"Will you let me decide?" he asked gently. I hesitated.

"Will you promise not to let me embarrass you?"

"I promise."

"Then you may decide."

"Join me tomorrow morning, that is, if you feel good for a day of walking. You may see some unexplained things, nothing dangerous—there is small chance of danger. I want your company. If it turns out embarrassing to you, to me, or to anyone else, you can go on alone. The way is easy to find."

"All right," I cried.

"You can leave with the horses, early, and go up over the pass.

About two hundred yards below the summit there is a trail off to the right—the northeast—leading to the Lor Pass—the pass over into Karain country from the Doring Valley—about twelve miles away. I'll be waiting for you three or four miles further on. Bring lunch from the Inn. I'll arrange to have it put up for you."

"What shall I wear?" I asked.

He told me to travel light, and as a last word, said:

"You may be put in such a position that you will have to say you are traveling with me. Use your judgment. If you are pinned down and a denial, or too much reticence, would rouse suspicion, be frank as the wind, only don't say that you are going over to the Lor Pass. I have friends hereabouts and my not stopping here wouldn't seem strange to Calwin. This Inn is peculiar and historic and all that, and such things interest you, don't they, John?"

"Very much," I laughed, "and I much prefer to be comfortable."

"Yes—but be careful. Good-bye. I shall envy you your bed."

He opened the door cautiously, looked about, and with a feline quickness and quiet unfamiliar to me he disappeared.

Dinner was being served at two long tables. The Willses and Calwin were not yet there and I took the opportunity to slip into a vacant single place, feeling deserted and alone. Across the board, however, were my *denerir* acquaintances from Dole. With these I talked and was so engaged when the Willses in evening dress and Calwin came in and took places far from me.

In bed before nine o'clock, I was satisfied. For over an hour I had chatted with these three lazily before the fire. True, I had had to say that I was traveling with a friend, and for one awful second I had been faced with Philip Wills's point-blank question as to whether the friend were anyone he knew. Calwin had saved me, changing the subject rather sharply. To him, as Dorn suggested, an answer such as mine closed all inquiry; and when his friends pressed me further he felt himself partly responsible for their behavior and interfered. Luckily, Philip Wills was not sufficiently interested to cross-examine me further, and I pumped him on his climbs in the neighborhood, a safe topic. I suggested also that certain Americans were interested in trade routes in Islandia and complained a little of my duty to make investigations of such matters. Perhaps this satisfied their curiosity.

I was waked just at daylight. Breakfast was brought to my room, and I left the Inn, finding all arrangements made. It was cold, damp, and misty under the pass, and I was far from warm as I rode the zig-zags slowly up to the top with the servant from the hotel on Dorn's horse ahead and the pack animal between. Fifteen or twenty minutes brought us to the summit, a green saddle. High on the ridge on either hand were towers, and a wall connected them. We passed through a gate and the Doring Valley lay beneath, with naked ridges of rock and green alps sloping down to the valley floor. I looked at once to the opposite side, where I knew the Lor Pass must be, but the passage through was not visible. North was a lofty spur of Moraclorn crowned with snow fields; northwest a long high mountain lifted a pinnacled crest with blue glaciers and white névé. Between these two was a wall of complex cliffs and ledges with no sign of a break. Somewhere, a way through existed. Later that day I would find it, and the thought was like wine.

A few moments later we came to the mouth of a chimney down which the main road zigzagged out of sight. On the right branched a trail, which the guide pointed out to me. I dismounted. He started on at once, waving a friendly hand, and I watched the horses turning and descending before I, too, went on.

Free and light, with nothing on my back or in my hands, but with my lunch in my coat pocket, I set out along the trail. In a few moments it had wound around a shoulder and I was alone in an immense amphitheater. The valley below was empty and still, and the shadows of the mountains upon it were vast. Nothing was to be heard, except my feet and the rubbing of my leather trousers; and there was no sign of man anywhere, except the trail, like a thin thread, looping around the slopes.

Dorn had gone one way, and the horses with all our goods another. The mountains were motionless and immense, their high snow fields were faintly rosy. The air was thin and cold.

My friend was really alien. There were great differences between us, and the warmth of our feelings for each other were always somewhat unexpected and surprising. He was working for a cause that was not mine and that seemed to me hopeless and misguided. He had said I was to see some "unexplained" things—a fact mysterious and a little frightening.

I quickened my pace; my inclination was to walk too fast, with a long day on foot before me.

After a time thought ceased to be a thing of words. Ideas and images shifted across the mind like the shadows of clouds over mountain and valley, as intangible and evanescent. The intelligence that kept me plodding along the path was an instinct half animal, divorced from memory and introspection.

Dorn said he would meet me three or four miles out—an hour's walk or so. An hour when one is alone, in unfamiliar mountains, seems very long.

My watch said that an hour and a half had passed.

The trail turned east into a deeply cut sloping valley filled with a glacier with a rippling broken surface, and ice-blue caverns. From the glacier's dirty foot a stream ran steeply down the valley to the greater, grassy valley below. I crossed the rushing pale water by a suspension bridge of heavy boards, which swayed and sprang.

Wondering with growing dismay where Dorn was, I went on out of the deep-cut valley. A half hour passed. Dorn had said three or four miles; and I had been walking two hours now and must have covered six, coming to a region of desolation. The trail wound between erratic boulders and shattered rocks of all sizes which lay singly and in heaps over the steep mountainside.

My hair stood on end. I listened. I had seemed to hear my name far off.

"John!"

It came again, much nearer. I looked up a defile between huge gray-brown boulders, hot in the sun, and saw Dorn sitting on a rock perhaps a hundred feet up the slopes, beckoning to me. Out of breath I arrived at the base of the rock where he was, four or five feet over my head. He reached down his hand. I took it and was drawn up to his level.

The rock where we stood was the lip of a slight depression in the bottom of which was a man with heavy high shoulders, leaning over a fire. He was bareheaded, but his thick black hair was perfectly smooth. Conspicuous was the straight, white parting exactly in the center. His head lifted, and I saw again the round, brick-red face half-hidden by a wide, bushy black beard, and the two hot flamelike eyes under heavy eyebrows of the man in Lord Mora's anteroom.

"Don, this is Lang," said Dorn.

The man rose and smiled. His eyes were faceted diamonds in narrow slits, and he showed large, even, pure white teeth. The "unexplained things" had begun to happen.

Don leaned over his fire again.

"Sit down," said Dorn. "We are just having breakfast. I would have met you sooner, but it turned out to be impossible."

Abruptly Don rose and with two springs climbed a high rock, looked about nonchalantly, and returned to his pot.

"In sight," he said, carelessly (of course in Islandian), and with a most unexpected voice, a high tenor.

"How soon will they pass?"

"Five minutes."

Dorn turned to me.

"Did you walk fast, John?" he asked.

Don most disconcertingly looked up and grinned.

"Yes," I said.

"I'm glad you did," said Dorn with amusement, and Don chuckled.

"Luck," he muttered in his beard.

I sat perfectly still, wondering if I enjoyed adventures.

Moments ticked by.

The pot over the fire bubbled cheerfully.

Don rose.

"Would you mind staying here and watching the pot? It may tip over," said Dorn, also standing. "We'll be back in a moment," he continued, and they disappeared.

I went to the fire and watched the pot. There was perfect stillness. The rocks hemmed me around and there was nothing to see but them and dark-blue sky overhead. Dorn's cloak lay on the ground nearby as though he had slept in it. Next to it lay another which must be Don's and a heavy pack, unopened.

Six or seven minutes passed. I watched the pot. Several times I thrust sticks under it from a pile at one side.

They appeared so quietly that my heart came into my throat.

"They have passed," said Dorn. "Now let's have breakfast."

Don brought from his pack three bronze bowls and spoons, and poured out the contents of the pot. It was a sort of stew, very hot both with pepper and fire, containing meat and carrots and peas, all in a thick liquor.

Don ate his portion quickly and then fetched water and sand from a spring and scoured pot and bowls and spoons.

While he was so engaged Dorn asked me if I objected to going to the Lor Pass by another route, a little harder but shorter.

A few moments later the two others were ready, their cloaks strapped on their backs. Don grinned once more and beckoned. Dorn nodded to me to go next, and we set out, he following.

They were trained mountaineers, and I feared I would prove a handicap. Don maintained a slow but steady pace. Our way led up the mountainside and westward in and out among the rocks.

After a while my legs lost their spring and I could not seem to draw into my lungs enough air. I suffered enough to feel dazed and a little faint and to lose all track of time, but I managed to keep up and always found a reserve of strength.

Relief came. We ceased to climb and struck off westward under high cliffs topped with overhanging snow. The Doring Valley, far below, was hazy seen through the veil of fatigue. We began climbing again, but I endured and struggled. It was a slope of gravel, its upper part cutting the sky. I stumbled, and Dorn took my arm.

"Are you all right?" he asked. "It is only about three hundred feet more."

"Up—or lengthwise?"

"Up," he said. "Let us give you our arms."

Each took an elbow.

"I see why you lasted a football game so well," I panted.

"Wouldn't he make a fullback?" he answered, nodding at Don.

We left the gravel slope for snow and came to a ledge under sheer rocks at the mouth of a forty-foot chimney.

"Rest!" said Don.

I stretched out at full length. Across the Doring Valley we looked down on the Mora Pass, six miles or so away. Don sat down and clasped his knees gazing across the gulf, cool and immaculate, every hair in place.

I don't know how long we stayed there, but it seemed none too long.

Don took from his pack a thin rope and knotted it about my waist. Then, taking the end in his hand, he started up the chimney. Dorn followed close behind me. I knew nothing of rock-climbing, but did as I was told. Up we went bit by bit with finger holds and toe holds to emerge breathless on a bold promontory, from which we looked obliquely down a thousand feet to a smooth, grassy col or saddle. Over and beyond it, the eye sank to light-brown foothills that gradually dropped into infinitely remote pale distance, where they were indistinguishable from the haze.

This was the Karain country, now German. The saddle was the Lor Pass. I forgot my fatigue.

Don, without a word, continued on perhaps a hundred yards. Dorn turned to go down to the col. It was not easy. Here and there were steep gravel slopes when every step meant five or six feet of descent; but more often there were ledges, a little too steep for comfort, with deceitful little cliffs at their foot.

Dorn stopped me. Don, to our right, was also motionless. Far down the mountainside a minute cavalcade of some dozen horses was slowly climbing up. A moment later all three of us were hastening to our left, and when the group below was out of sight we resumed our descent to the col. I had no idea what it was all about. In a surprisingly short time we had reached a point perhaps a hundred yards from the point where the grass began. Don had joined us, and here we stopped, concealing ourselves behind the rocks.

Moments passed. Gradually I regained my breath, but the throb of excitement remained in my heart.

A man was approaching from the left. He was tall and supple with bare head and yellow hair. At first he was but one with cliffs and sky and cloud, and then, sharply, my mind acted. Touching Dorn's shoulder, I pointed.

He started violently, and so did Don. They looked, and the latter half rose, and ran stooping to meet the newcomer. Then they approached us talking. As they drew near they also stooped, ran, and dropped at our sides behind the rocks.

Dorn and the young man nodded and my friend spoke my name. I bowed and looked for a moment into clear gray eyes. The brownish yellow hair curled like a girl's, the skin was an even rosy-orange, and the features the most beautiful I have ever seen, very like those of the Hermes at Olympia. It was a strange and fascinating face, strong and yet effeminate, and suggested a plane of existence utterly unlike my own. He stretched out his long, round, muscular body like the rest of us and seemed to be slightly amused.

We waited, the four of us in a row, Don, the stranger, Dorn, and I. The tingle of excitement in my heart was sometimes a desire to laugh.

Three men were near the col, coming along the valley from the Islandian side. They were dressed in European clothes, but at their present distance their faces were indistinguishable. They proceeded on a little way beyond the edge, looked over, and then sat down to wait. We watched them, utterly still.

Five minutes later there came in sight from below the head of a horse and of a man, and then another. The two groups joined, the riders all dismounting. Three or four of those who ascended from below wore white flowing robes and turbans and had dark faces; the rest were in European clothes and were white men.

There seemed to be much to say. The arrangement of figures shifted and changed continually. Wide gestures were made as though to call attention to topography. Finally, after a long time, activities became more specialized. One man, assisted by two others, set up what looked like a plane table. A group of four, after shaking hands with the others, mounted their horses and set out southwest along the valley. One of these was turbaned.

My companions all moved slightly.

To the south the valley sloped downward. The col was the height of land and the boundary must pass along it. A trespass into Islandia of a few hundred feet was permissible, but the four riders seemed to have taken permanent leave of the others. Was this an evasion of the exclusion laws or was it worse? And why, on a pass so easy, were there no soldiers, no guards?

The young man was on his feet, his face hot and red. Dorn and Don both seemed startled and dismayed.

He spoke quickly and in anger:

"This must be stopped!"

The others started to reply, but he was gone, and Don rose and followed. Dorn rose, but glanced at me in doubt.

"I must stay by him," Dorn said, "but you . . ."

"I'm coming too," I said cheerfully, but I was frightened.

We pursued and caught the others, and walked rapidly toward the col, the young man in the lead. The pace was too fast for me, and I fell into a trot to keep up.

It was some seconds before the eight or ten men left at the col saw us, and then the whole group became agitated and faced us. One man shouted loudly. The group of horsemen, now several hundred yards away, came to a halt.

We approached, nearer and nearer. The men at the col all turned toward us, were motionless, and their faces were white disks steadily growing larger and more distinct. Several wore military uniform and were armed. A shiver ran down my back, but I ran on after my tall long-legged companions, not unamused. The young man had taken charge, and Dorn and Don were overridden. I wondered who he was.

Among the group below was one who seemed more significant, a soldier in uniform, an officer, with a familiar face, a German face. They were Germans, I was sure, except the dark ones.

Our leader went straight up to him, Dorn and Don on either side, and I close to Dorn's. The clear cool eye of the officer rested upon me and I remembered his name.

"What are you doing here?" said our young leader in German, and then not waiting for an answer he continued, "Recall those men. They cannot enter Islandia by this route."

The officer thought a moment.

"Who are you?" he asked.

The young man seemed nonplused.

"That is of no consequence," he said at length. "I am an Islandian citizen. You do not need an official to tell you that this route into Islandia is closed, and that your country has agreed to keep it so."

"If we break the law it is no concern of yours," replied the officer. "As a matter of fact we do not break it."

"Have you a passport?"

"I decline to answer, since you are not an official."

He looked at me again. We were getting the worst of it. The officer smiled.

"It is not the intention of any of us to enter Islandia. We shall camp here for a day or two and then return to our base."

Our leader pointed to the horsemen far down the trail.

"Do you include those men also?"

"They will have to speak for themselves. They are not under my orders."

"Come!" cried the young man to us.

He led the way down the trail, and I was again forced to run and was humiliated by doing so with the eyes of those on the col watching me.

It would have been easy for the horsemen to have ridden away before we were near enough to recognize them, but they did not do so. In fact, one dismounted. The turbaned figure, only, moved on, and not far.

When we came near I saw two familiar faces, and knew that I was recognized in turn. It was evident from the heavy equipment on the horses that these men were prepared to camp and to stay.

The young man went up to them.

"You cannot enter Islandia by this route," he said.

"Have we trespassed?" answered the one I knew best, with unexpected acquiescence.

"The boundary line is the pass."

"It did not seem to us that a few kilometers in this valley was a serious breach of our treaty with your country. If it displeases you we will return."

There was a stir of dissent in the others, but they said nothing.

Our leader bowed politely. The German smiled and saluted and gave a word to the others, and they all turned about and cantered away, their spokesman nodding to me cordially as they went.

Dorn and the young man exchanged glances and laughed, but Don was solemn.

"We have no proof now," he said, "and nothing to complain of."

"The riders intended to stay," cried the young man, nettled by the covert accusation, "and we kept them out."

"It is a great deal that you believe so," Don replied with a bow.

"I believe so. You were right. I am glad I came and saw with my own eyes."

I felt that they would speak more freely, if I were not with them. I debated a moment whether to tell them that I knew some of the Germans, but an instinct bade me be silent. I strolled down the trail, leaving the others earnestly talking. The excitement was over, but I was still shaken by it. I sat down on a rock. I was tired and faint and very hungry.

Shortly afterward the others joined me, and I discovered that it was afternoon. At the side of the trail Don made his fire and filled his pot. I turned in the lunch that I had brought from the Inn. There was just enough for all. We were a silent group.

It seemed to have been settled that we were to separate, and when the meal was over Don morosely bade us good-bye, shouldered his load, and started up the mountainside. The young man who had been in a brown study roused himself suddenly.

"I am very sorry," he said to Dorn.

"We are glad you understand."

"I can do little. I have much to think of. I am going to my camp now. In a month or so I shall come to see you."

Dorn bowed.

"Good-bye, Lang," he said with a smile. "We shall meet again."

He held out his hand and I shook it. He, too, went his way down the valley.

Dorn turned to me and spoke in English.

"I'm sorry! I did not mean to get you into anything like this."

"I have had a very interesting walk," I said. "I have seen the Lor Pass. I have done some real climbing. That is all I remember."

"Someday you will know a great deal more!" he said with relief. "You are a true friend. Let us go on to the Shelter House. A load is off my mind, even though . . ." Dorn paused and shrugged.

"He is too impulsive," he added, nodding at the yellow-haired young man, now a diminished figure in the valley bottom. He said no more and we set out at a leisurely gait along the trail.

"I thought the pass was fortified," I said.

"There is a fort," he answered, after a moment's hesitation, "but it is concealed."

We walked on in silence.

"It isn't occupied now," cried Dorn, with such sudden bitterness that I was silent.

Presently he continued.

"Until Lord Mora became premier there was always a strong garrison at the Lor Pass, but he withdrew the garrison when he made his treaty. Germany agreed to police the Sobo Steppes, and Lord Mora wanted to show he believed in their good faith and efficiency. There have been no raids by the Mountain Negroes, but that has not been wholly due to German police. I think there will be some interesting disclosures at the meeting of the council in June."

I was interested, but I asked no questions.

He grasped my arm.

"As soon as we get out of this region there will be no more things that I cannot tell you! I wish you were an Islandian and of my party. How mysterious we must all seem to you."

"You do, but I am enjoying myself," I said.

It was midafternoon when we arrived at the Shelter House, but I regarded the day as over, tired out. After changing my clothes I slipped into one of the many bunks that lined the wall of the main room. I took a book with me, Meredith's *Harry Richmond,* and found myself in a mood to be absorbed; but behind the interest of the printed page was consciousness of mountains and remoteness, of weary muscles, and of an inner clutch of excitement straining my heart.

We supped early, and immediately afterward I turned in for good and slept a broken sleep in which I relived in troubled, distorted form all that I had done during the day.

6

The Hyths

WE BOTH ROSE LATE, and it was ten o'clock before we were ready to
leave the Shelter House. Dorn was like one who had finished a piece
of work. He was franker about his plans. That day we would travel
down to Doring Lake, twenty-two or -three miles away and sleep
at the upper farm of the Hyths.

Then would follow two days of traveling, bringing us to the
lower or home farm of the Hyths, where we would stay several days.
"It is spacious," he said, "and very beautiful. They are all good
friends of mine. You will like the Hyths."

For two or three hours we rode in checkered light and shadow
through the dense forests of a wide valley. Between the pines, bluish
dark vistas opened and closed, shot with parallel lines of hazy sunlight. Doring Lake gleamed like silver through the tree trunks before we reached it. Coming out of the forest on its southern shore
we looked down on the water, blue and cool and sparkling in a fresh
west wind.

On the opposite shore was a low white house around which a few
trees huddled, lying on a low bluff above the sparkling water. A path
led down to a boathouse on the western edge and beyond, downstream, ample rolling fields stretched for miles. Except for the
snow-capped Doringclorn behind, it was very like New England.

Dorn stopped his horse.

"That is the Hyths'," he said. "I don't think any of the family are
there. I can tell by the look of the place."

We were, however, welcomed by the dependent in charge. I wondered why Dorn wished to stop there when the family were all away.
It seemed strange to be eating meals in the house of an absent host, to
use his hay and oats for our horses, and to borrow his boat for a sail

on the lake. Late in the afternoon Dorn borrowed a horse and set off alone. Perhaps he had some duty to perform.

Next day we followed the river around the base of Doringclorn and descended a gradually widening valley between high snow peaks. Toward night we left the road and turned off into the forest where we camped on the edge of a brook. We had brought meat from the Hyths' and this we broiled over an open fire. It was a still and wonderful night.

The following day was hot and windless. A yellowish haze gathered, hiding the mountain tops. The road and the fields were dry and flocks of Islandian sheep passed, surrounded by dust clouds.

Dorn pressed the horses and we did not stop for lunch.

At two o'clock we came to Hyth, a solidly built village in the center of the sheep and cattle country. We went around it without stopping and turned off the main road onto another leading south over the mountains to the Tamplin Pass. As we rose out of the river valley we were met by a hot gusty wind and a cloud of dust enveloped us. The west was yellow-gray and there was a rumble of thunder.

At a canter we crossed a flat plain with dry grass beyond the wooden fences. We began to climb and after a while a stone gate loomed out of the haze; through this we turned, riding hard.

All at once, low buildings of pinkish stone emerged from the haze, and ahead of us another building of two stories unnaturally large in the murk.

Dorn called our names.

A flood of people were already leaving the house, a boy, a middle-aged woman, and four girls in their twenties.

Short greetings were given, and quick glances at me, a stranger.

The eldest girl cried out something about the cattle and panic, and that they had been sent for by Father and the men.

"John," Dorn cried to me. "We can be of help here."

I waved my hand.

A tall girl with a round striking face ran toward Dorn, spoke to him, and started toward a low building on the left. Another girl came up to me and smiled, and, taking my answering look for assent, stepped on my foot in the stirrup, plucked her skirt above her bare knees, clutched my arm, and all in one motion drew herself up behind me.

"Follow Dorn!" she said in a strong clear voice. "I'm Nattana."

Fak did so without being directed. The dismayed face of the mother, the laughing ones of the others, vanished in the haze.

The girl's strong, small hands gripped my arms. We followed Dorn around the corner of the low building.

"Stop, please," she said, "and wait a moment."

She dropped from the horse before he stopped. Dorn was also waiting, smiling broadly, a light in his eyes.

"Go with Nattana," he said. "She knows what's wanted. I don't."

The tall girl soon appeared with her horse, and they disappeared together. Then the one who had climbed behind me appeared on hers and ranged along side.

"Please follow me if you don't mind," she said.

We set out in a different direction, she in the lead, and galloped over the dry hard ground while the sky grew darker and more sinister. Thunder grumbled louder and nearer.

Unexpectedly she drew up her horse and Fak, imitating, threw me forward on his neck. Ahead was a pounding roar not of thunder. She swung her horse to the right and shouted to me and I followed. A drove of cattle passed close, running and tossing their heads. A young man on horseback followed them and she and he shouted to each other. She called to me and we moved on again at a canter.

Suddenly I was aware of nervous pawing cattle around us. She had stopped her horse. She called to me several times, but it was by doing what she did that I guessed our task—to round up and drive home the cows and bulls left out of the half-stampeding herd that had passed us. Glad of the height of Fak's back, I yelled and shouted and slapped the sides of the huge, heavy excited animals, watching her, encouraged by smiles and wavings of her hand. Little by little the cattle gathered. She shouted and they lumbered off, and we followed.

Then the rain came in sheets and driving lines, drenching us in a few seconds, but at the same time the dust was driven down and the air cleared. We were in the midst of an immense sloping field. In the lower corner, dim through the rain and small in the distance, were the houses we had left, a compact cluster. From various directions other herds of cattle with attendant horsemen were proceeding thither.

The cattle moved more quietly and the girl came up to my side, her bare tanned legs showed the grooving of smooth muscles as they pressed the sides of her horse. Her hair, which had been bright and rippled, was dark and stringy, flattened upon her round head. Her clothes were plastered to her body showing the shape of her thighs and breasts.

"I am Hytha Nattana," she said quietly.

"I am John Lang."

"Can you understand me or should I speak more slowly?"

"I understand."

"Dorn said that you would . . . It was very kind of you to come with me and to help us."

She looked at me with momentary careful scrutiny of her green eyes.

"You are the first foreigner I have ever spoken to," she said. . . .

We drove the cattle into a large corral behind the house, where a *deneri* took charge of them, and then rode to the stable. There we stalled the horses, rubbing them dry with enormous towels of coarse unbleached linen, dripping water as we moved about.

"We are very wet," she said, when we finished. "We had better go to the house."

I picked up my saddlebag and we went through several rooms with grain in bins and harnesses, and came out upon an arcade. On the right the courtyard into which Dorn and I had ridden was now a sea of muddy pools in which large raindrops fell from a leaden sky.

The girl gave me a charming smile as we entered the house.

"Thank you for all your help," she said.

The older woman, Airda, was in the hall before an open fire with cups and a pitcher of hot chocolate. She was a sister of Lord Dorn's dead wife, and the second wife of Lord Hyth.

She suggested that I change and I went to my room. There I stripped before another open fire, wrung out my wet clothes, and spread them out to dry. After changing into clean dry clothes, I went downstairs again.

The cattle drivers had been arriving one by one. Dorn and the tall girl were the last to come. She was Nekka, twenty-six, next to oldest of the four sisters. She entered with her flushed face glistening with rain. She named herself and smiled at me over her cup of chocolate. I stared at her, not so much because she was pretty as because she had been with Dorn, and had an original face.

I went to speak to her, and, at Dorn's suggestion perhaps, she held out her hand, long, slim, still wet, and unexpectedly strong.

"Lang, Dorn's friend, I am glad you have come," she said in a voice clear and resonant, but somewhat mannered.

At supper I met the rest of the family: Lord Hyth, with red hair, mustache, and pointed beard, and freckled face, who talked politics and farming with Dorn, who showed an informed interest in the United States, and whose reddish eyes roved over the table preoccupied with other thoughts than those he discussed; Hyth Ek, his oldest son, Nattana's older brother, a quiet man of thirty-three, small, self-contained, and tired, with green eyes and reddish hair; Hyth Atta, taller, looser, darker, who asked many difficult questions and looked at me with eyes friendly and inquisitive; Ettera, the eldest of the four sisters, with the same reddish hair and the most muscular figure, twenty-eight, unappealing as a woman, with eyes that stared one down and flashed as with suppressed anger, but with a suave, pleasant, and intelligent voice; Nettera, the youngest of the four, so slender as to seem unsubstantial, with large eyes of a robin's-egg blue, beneath which were shadows like those of dissipation—certainly the prettiest of them all. They were all Lord Hyth's children by his first wife, Stellina; Airda being the mother of Hyth Pek, whom I had met at Reeves, and another son, Hyth Patta, a boy of fifteen.

The names of the Hyth children were not first names in the American or European sense, but were numbers which indicate their order in the family with a feminine ending added in the case of a girl. Thus Hyth Ek meant Hyth-first-child, a boy; Ettera, third child, a girl, and so on.

After supper we went into the living room. Lord Hyth soon led Dorn away into his study, Nekka dozed in a corner of a bench, but Hyth Atta continued his questions seconded by Ettera; while Nattana and Nettera watched from their jade-green eyes, saying little, their arms around each other. In answer to Atta's questions I told what I knew about the raising and marketing of cattle at home, of the Chicago stockyards, and how dead meat was transported everywhere; and all the time I was conscious of the two younger sisters who seemed to listen but made no comments, now and then whispering together.

Ettera wished to know how in an existence so complicated one knew when to do what. I answered that there were more timepieces. In Islandia the people relied on a native time sense. We had clocks and watches. I brought out mine to show them, saying that I did not know whether it was right or not, having nothing to set it by.

"How can it be wrong?" asked Ettera to whom I handed it.

"The hour it indicates may not be the hour it really is."

"It is pretty," she said, "but what is the use of it?"

I tried to explain.

"Old people need to be told the time when they begin to forget," she said drily.

"And musicians," said Atta, glancing at Nettera who promptly looked down. Nekka had waked up and was watching with sleepy curiosity, Nattana had leaned forward, her elbow on her knee, her chin in her palm, but Nettera remained withdrawn. The watch was passed about from one white hand to another. They were a little like children. One by one they held it to their ears to listen to its ticking, all but Nettera who was passed by. Because she had been left out, I rose and went to show her the watch when it came to me again. She leaned back on the bench putting her hands behind her.

"Would you like to see it?" I asked.

Her eyes lifted to mine, showing the white beneath the clear blue-green with an expression I did not understand.

"I don't want to touch it!" she said.

Thinking she was afraid she might break it I held it toward her. She shrank away but stared at it as though fascinated.

"I can hear it," she said in a thin voice.

Believing her interested I put it toward her ear. She sprang to her feet.

"Don't touch me!" she cried. "You are a foreigner!"

There was a silence—and then the voices of the others broke out all at once.

"You don't know what you're saying," cried Nekka. "Dorn brought him."

"Don't misjudge her, Lang. She often doesn't understand." Nattana's voice trembled.

"She is unpardonable," Ettera declared angrily. "Nettera, you ought to be whipped!"

"You had better go before you do anything worse," came Atta's calm masculine tones.

"All right, I'll go!" Nettera cried. "Lang, I am sorry . . . If you think. . . ."

She choked. Her eyes filled. She fled from the room, her rapid bare legs thin like a child's.

"Don't mind!" I called to her.

They all began speaking to me. Atta explained her conduct.

"Foreigners have been the cause of women's diseases here," he said. "Of course, we all know that this applies only to a few, but Nettera often does not think reasonably. Stories about foreigners were in her mind."

"She is a fool!" Ettera said.

"No, she isn't!" Nattana cried hotly. "But it is true she doesn't always think."

"I don't blame her," I said. "I know the stories also. You have a right to fear us."

"But we don't fear you, of course!" Ettera said.

"That's not necessary to say," cried Nattana. "Don't you see he knows it!"

I nodded to her my thanks. I was rather shaken.

They continued their explanations and apologies for some moments longer, and it was a relief when Nekka said:

"Let's not talk about it any more. Everyone knew what everyone else thought long ago."

"I am going to speak to Nettera," the oldest sister cried, rising and starting away. "Good night, Lang."

"Good night," I answered, "but tell her not to care. . . ."

"That can't be helped," Nattana was saying. "We all care, perhaps more than you do. Forgive us! . . . But I have got to go, too, or else Ettera. . . ."

Her eyes flashed at me and she ran after her oldest sister, calling to her. Only Nekka was left, and she looked at me with her droll smile. Then we both laughed.

"What will you think of us?" she said.

"You go too fast for me. I am sorry for Nettera."

"She is the one to pity, not you . . . She repents so hard. She was probably a hundred miles away when you spoke to her. Tomorrow she will understand . . . I think I had better go also, in case Ettera and Nattana quarrel. Good night."

I went to bed. Dorn was still closeted with Lord Hyth, discussing the important matters of which we had agreed that I was to remain ignorant. Try my best, I could not rid myself of hurt feelings and a sense of shock, wondering if all the sisters did not feel as Nettera did, but were too polite and self-controlled to show it.

101

Next morning clouds with sagging gray folds hung low, misty showers blotted out the distant view, and all was dark and wet.

During the afternoon we rode in the rain down to the town of Hyth, returning home for supper or dinner—too hearty a meal for the former word, too simple for the latter.

Just before supper Nattana drew me aside to tell me that Nettera was very sorry for the events of the evening before.

"She quite understands now," said Nattana, "that you are just like one of us."

I had not seen Nettera all day, but when we met at supper she smiled at me a faint and charming smile, and I answered it, knowing that the unpleasant incident was ended.

At this meal everyone wore the colors to which he or she was entitled. The only ones not thus privileged were Dorn and I, for he was only great-grandson and great-nephew of those who had been ennobled, and I was an American. We therefore dressed in plain and somber blue. Hyth wore a suit of brighter blue than ours, but the broad lapels of his coat and his cuffs were white with a broad, dark-blue band in the cuffs. His sons were similarly dressed except that the bands were narrower. The girls wore skirts and loose jackets of the finest white wool, white sandals, and fine white stockings that did not cover their knees. Their cuffs bore the same narrow blue band as their brothers; but there was further color in their shirts, which were of white linen open at the throat with soft collars and pencil lines of blue. Their braided hair had been brushed till it shone and their faces glowed with cleanness, their complexions bright in the candlelight.

The table was of brown oak without a cloth, the dishes plain in shape but ornamented with geometrical patterns in terra-cotta red and blue and green on a white ground. Candles gave the only light and the walls of the room were of a pinkish white stone.

When dinner was over we assembled in the living room where a low fire burned. Rain drummed on the windows, but no one doubted a fine tomorrow. It would be our last day at the Hyths' and a picnic in the mountains was planned.

From a cabinet against the wall Nettera brought forth an instrument of black wood and metal stops with a high clear tone like a clarinet. She began to play, her mouth solemn, her eyes absorbed but alertly watching.

The notes came in a rapid flood. The melody was difficult to follow. I guessed that it was one well known to her family and that she elaborated and played tricks with it impromptu. The rhythm, though marked, shifted from two-time to three-time in a disconcerting manner.

Everyone stood and paired in couples. Airda suggested that I watch and join later. Two groups formed and Nettera, never ceasing to play and never seeming to draw breath, took her place with the rest.

At some turn in the music they all laughed. The tempo quickened and they began a dance that resembled a rapid and more fluent lancers, but no person touched another until the end when they all clasped hands in the course of a ladies' chain that mingled both sets.

The yellowish tone of the candlelight brought out vividly the golden threads in all the red heads of hair, and the greens and browns of eyes. The girls' faces had an expression of smiling dreaminess. Dorn looked happy. From here and there in the room came the music, itself a part of the dance.

It ended on a low note as deep as that of a bassoon, followed by a humorous run like a squeal. Everyone laughed again. Nettera's face, which had become flushed, at once began to grow pale again, but she did not seem out of breath.

The dance was repeated and then I was asked to join. With the assistance of Ettera, my partner, I somehow got through. On the third performance I began to move freely, but Isla Hyth and Airda had had enough and without them this dance was no longer possible.

Nettera, however, continued her playing. The five girls took off their jackets and danced what might be called a breakdown, their skirts flaring out and folding down like the long fins of a Japanese goldfish. They were as unconcerned about their bare legs as American girls were about their ankles. I wondered what people at home would think.

Then the three older girls with Ek, Atta, and Dorn danced a more sedate square dance with intricate figures, while Nettera played slow and lovely music with eyes half-closed, absorbed in it, not watching them.

From these I was left out and all the while the rhythm of the dances, Nettera's perfect sense of time, and a throbbing quality in her music, stirred in me a wish to dance that I found hard to endure in quiet; and when she ceased playing and I found myself among the dancers, warm, flushed, with bright eyes that indicated a mood like my own, I asked if they ever did anything like our waltzes and polka. I undertook to show them a waltz, humming the "Blue Danube." Nettera caught the rhythm and time and improvised or built up from melodies she knew a waltz of her own. The other girls imitated me. In fact, waltz steps appeared in their own dances. Soon several of us were circling about the floor practicing singly.

I asked if one of them would try it with me. Dorn and Nekka had gone to a bench and did not seem interested, but Ettera and Nattana stood ready. The first, after some hesitation, volunteered, and I took with her the position properly learned at dancing school. At first she was very stiff, but she was naturally too good a dancer not to learn to move in time with me. Nevertheless it was not a success. Nattana was the one I wished to dance with, but when Ettera said she had had enough it was Nettera who stood waiting. She had handed her instrument to Airda who, after a little trying, produced a fair waltz. I was touched by Nettera's offer, believing it to be an effort to make amends, and I put my arm around her so lightly that it scarcely touched her and held her hand gently. She seemed the nothingness of a feather and moved with me perfectly for half-a-dozen steps.

"I can't do it!" she said in a breathless voice and slipped out of my arms. "Try it with Nattana. I'll play." This was what I waited for. I went to Nattana. She hesitated, her head lowered a little, her eyes shining green in her flushed face.

"Will you try it with me?" I said. Nettera was playing a waltz that was strangely stirring.

Without a smile Nattana nodded. Like Ettera she was for a moment wooden, but I was determined to have my dance and to make it a good one. I took her firmly and beat time, told her with which foot to begin. Suddenly she yielded. For a few steps we were awkward, our knees bumping, and then we really waltzed and I was happy, beside myself, wholly absorbed.

It seemed a matter of time lost in space. . . .

"Please, please, I must stop!" she said in my ear and reluctantly I let her go. Nettera continued to play. I was in the mood to dance all night. Someone had opened a window, admitting drafts of fresh damp air. Colors everywhere were brightened, the green in the girls' eyes, the blue in their dresses, the fire in their hair.

Airda took the instrument from Nettera who looked up with wide eyes. She suggested that since we were going on a picnic next day and preparations were still to be made. . . .

The girls all at once looked meek and sleepy like children at bedtime. They said good night and left.

Later, in my room, I was in no mood to sleep and was glad of a visit from Dorn.

We talked about the picnic next day, our future travels, and then he asked me if I were having a good time at the Hyths'.

"So far it has been perfect!"

"In spite of Nettera?"

"That is forgotten. Nattana apologized for her."

"Do you like Nattana?"

"Yes, I do."

"I don't know her very well," he said, and there was a note of warning in his voice.

"She seems like girls at home."

"You can be proud of yourself," he said, laughing.

"What for?"

"Persuading them to dance with you."

"Why is that?"

"Don't be bothered, because it is all right. They quite understood. But they aren't used to the sort of embracing that goes with waltzes."

I felt slightly faint.

"To them it is—embracing," he continued. "Of course, they are human and women. They probably liked it in a way. I think they realize that to you it is not."

"Have I made a break?" I asked, uncomfortably hot.

"When you get away with a thing like that it is not a break. It is quite all right."

Are you dropping me a hint?"

"Yes, in a way I am. I believe our sensual emotions are a little keener than those of Americans and Europeans in general. We are perhaps simpler animals. We take more care not to do halfway things."

What he said gave me much to think about. It increased my satisfaction in having danced with Nattana, it roused vague amorous speculations, but it also filled me with acute embarrassment.

The Hyths were weatherwise. My eyes opened to a gleam of sunlight. The break of the evening before was a thing to laugh at in the morning.

From my window that faced west down the valley, the wide expanse of sky was full of great clouds in fleets with white tops and dark flat bases, and beneath them were miles of grazing land, browns and greens, mottled with bright patches of sunlight.

Near at hand was a vegetable garden freshened by the rain with pools between the furrows. The air that blew in was warm, smelling of earth and rain. From the room below, perhaps the kitchen, came the sound of a gentle clatter and young feminine voices.

I leaned out and looked down the rough wall of the house.

A voice said, "Someone ought to wake Lang."

Another answered, "Let him sleep."

There was laughter.

Later, when there came a knock at my door, I was already dressed.

It was nearly ten when we gathered. Seven horses were hitched to the bar before the front door. The girls were packing the saddlebags behind the cantles. They were all bareheaded, their hair done up on their heads and held in place with green or black ribbons.

The four older ones, Hyth Patta, Dorn, and I were the party. Our route lay over the half mile or more of pasture land to the stone gate, where we turned to the right upon the road that led over the Tamplin Pass, into the central provinces, a day's ride away. In the valley the town of Hyth, in shadow, resembled a medieval fortress in miniature. Everywhere else were immense pastures with only here and there a cluster of trees and houses dwarfed by the distance.

After a time we turned to the left from the road and followed a trail that wound upward through the pastures. It was too narrow to ride abreast and we strung out in line. A little later, however, the trail became wider and Nattana dropped back to my side. We were high above the valley and leftwards she was outlined against the sky of white clouds and blue.

"We are last," she said. "We shall have to put up the bars."

After that there were several dismountings. She let me make the first one and led my horse through the gate, but at the second she was too quick for me. It was evidently the custom to take turns.

There were three gates. At each we dropped still farther behind.

When it was my turn again it was lovely to look up at her vivid color against trees and a wet green slope of coarse grass.

The woods became dense, and we rode through stands of iron pines. Raindrops upon them flashed back the sunlight as we passed.

"When the Demiji raiders came over the mountains a hundred years ago," said Nattana, "the women and children took flight in woods like these. At the warning they dropped everything and ran and hid for days. Grandfather remembered one such flight when he was very little. The cavalry came just as they were about to fire the house. The Demiji were buried in a corner of the vegetable garden. Sometimes we still dig up a bone."

"Is there any longer any fear of them?"

"Not of them since Lord Fain beat them."

"You are safe now with the Germans in charge across the mountains."

"I know," she said. "The Mountain Negroes still live there, and though they aren't as daring as the Demiji they are worse in some ways. Only five years ago a band got over. We were all ready to run, when we heard that they had been captured up the valley. Once when I was little I actually saw a chase of five raiders by cavalry . . . I think I did. Ettera says they never came so near then."

"The Germans do things thoroughly," I said. "They make good police."

"I don't know anything about them."

"They are civilized, Nattana."

"What does that mean? They are soldiers. They are there. I am not a man . . . They are just another group of men across the mountains, and every group that has been there has wanted to get over into Islandia. From the beginning we have fought off people from the north."

The withdrawal of troops from the Lor Pass had a new significance. It was a personal not a political matter to the people in this region.

Quite suddenly we came upon a spur, thrust out into the Doring Valley, two thousand feet below. High snow peaks, from which the clouds had lifted, were visible to the north. These were the mountains across which the raiders had come.

The others had already dismounted. It was the end of our ride.

The horses were led to a natural grassy meadow and left there tethered, and we went on carrying the saddlebags.

Nekka now walked with me. Taller than I and rather long-limbed she moved with an ease almost pantherine.

The path we followed was but vaguely marked, leading steeply upward through shady damp woods and over sunny open ledges. There was much to see, the flash of birds' wings, insects on a stem, flowers and seed pods, glistens of mica in the rocks. Walking with Nekka was effortless and there was a sense of rhythm in our progress as in a dance—I part the bushes, she passes through; I follow and she steps aside; I offer her my hand, she glides up a step in the rock; I follow again—all in tune.

In the stillness and bright fresh air I found myself moving upon another plane. The world was beautiful and she adorned it. There was nothing to say and no need for words. The sun beat down upon us and we were warm with exercise. I felt pleasant sweat and mild fatigue in my legs, but my strength bore me on and up . . . The meadow where we had left the horses seemed far below, and time was a memory of changing woods, ledges, sunlight, and brush.

"Climbing makes me feel that I am dreaming," I said.

"Isn't it rather that you find a different self in yourself?" she answered quickly. "There is not one 'you' who is awake and others who dream."

"That is what I meant."

"There are many 'me-s,' " she said softly.

I would have liked to say that the present one was lovely to look at, but lacked courage.

We came to a ravine into which the others were already descending down root-laced mossy ledges with twisted trees overhanging. At the bottom was a grassy circle and a brook full of water running over brown stones and sandy pools. Above towered stately pines so high as to make the sky seem far away. The sun struck down through blue shadows in luminous pale-white lines.

Sitting on the grass we ate a brief lunch. We were all together again, a silent group. Eyes wandered upward toward the sheer rocky cliffs to the southeast, bright in the sun.

"Who would like to walk?" Ettera asked, turning to me first.

"I would," I said, but she and I were the only ones so choosing.

We moved without haste, but without rests. Our direction was up the ravine of the brook that bisected the cliffs. It was very steep but so full of great boulders and roots that a way could always be found even though often hand over hand. After an hour or so we emerged somewhat breathless on the top of the cliffs, five or six hundred feet above the circle of grass, a dark-green patch in a hollow among treetops.

The return was more rapid, though the inward look of climbing had not revealed the steepness as did the outward look of descending. We came to a deep pool and Ettera announced that she was going to bathe. I went on to a lower one and was naked and warm amidst the confusion of great boulders, then icy cold in the clear water, then glowing and relaxed. But I did not dare to bask long in the sun lest Ettera so find me.

The sense of peace and contentment became fixed and continued after we had reached the grassy spot. Leaning back against a tree I watched the gently moving treetops, the far blue sky now bare of clouds, and the cliffs, seeing them with eyes that translated no impressions into words. A little distance away, Ettera, indefatigable, aided by Nekka and Patta, was getting supper ready. They had declined my offer of help. Dorn had gone downstream. Nattana and Nettera had climbed the side of the ravine opposite to that by which we had descended, and though not to be seen, their voices now and then came down to us and finally the sounds of a woodwind instrument, floating in the air like the song of a bird, cascades of high shrill notes, abruptly beginning and ending.

This, I thought, is like the Golden Age. Picnics at home had so often meant a circle turned inward, away from the lovely spot chosen as its scene, with much talk and laughter and "jollying" and some disputes. . . .

The fifelike bird on the hillside was human. It could not be amiss to join the two sisters. As I climbed the song stopped abruptly and when I came near they were both looking at me in silence. They were sitting side by side on a fallen log, like two birds on a branch, with a low green bough arching over their red heads. They made room for me between them, but as I sat down Nettera rose.

"Perhaps I am needed," she said, and went down the hill.

Nattana giggled, and when I glanced at her, her eyes were instantly elusive.

Because I had stopped Nettera's music I was tongue-tied. Nattana's hands were clasped between her knees and I saw only her profile, glowing as from an inner alabastrine light, against the shadowy blue woods.

From below her sister's fife burst out again and she stirred and uttered an exclamation like a groan.

"Nettera, don't!" she called, and the music abruptly ceased.

"Did you have a good walk?" she asked in a dry voice.

"Oh, yes, and a swim on the way down, which I enjoyed."

"Did Ettera swim?"

"At an upper pool."

"I thought of going."

"I wish you had."

"So do I, now . . ." She laughed a little. "I ought to have gone."

"Why, Nattana?"

She seemed to shudder.

"Oh!" she said through her teeth. "Walking is good exercise!"

There was silence for some moments.

Her eyes were upon me. The air seemed to quiver, and I felt myself on the edge of something either very painful or very sweet, and I wished I had words by which to protect myself.

"Day before yesterday," she said, "two days seemed quite long. How quickly they have gone!"

"Yes, that is true."

"You know us a little better and we you."

"I am glad of that. It has made me feel more at home in Islandia than anything else."

"What has?"

"Meeting all of you."

"We seem like those you knew at home?"

"Oh, yes, Nattana. The differences are very slight."

"Perhaps you will find deeper ones as you know Islandians better."

"Do I seem different from the men you know?"

"You do," she answered, in a low thrilling voice.

"In what way?"

"You really want me to tell you?"

"Yes—you make me afraid it is something unpleasant."

"Oh, no!" she said.

"Won't you tell me?"

"It is only that your feelings about things seem to be pink rather than red."

I drew back amazed, and her eyes widened in alarm.

"It is not just you," she said hastily. "I think it must be true of all foreigners. Their lives. . . ."

"What makes you think so?" I asked.

"It is a guess."

"You have something in mind. You ought to tell me."

"Lang, I am sorry! I have hurt you."

"Not at all! But you have given me something to think about."

From below Nettera's fife blew a call.

"They are ready," Nattana said, rising.

"Tell me one reason before you go," I cried. I reached for her hand to detain her, but restrained my impulse.

She turned and faced me.

"I *have* hurt you," she declared.

"If you would only tell me one reason?"

"Last night—your waltzing. Our men would feel very differently from the way you seemed to feel."

She turned.

"But, Nattana," I cried, "it has been usual with us so long. I know now that it is not customary here. Dorn told me. . . ."

Her face flushed.

"I am very sorry now that I made you dance with me," I continued.

"I was glad," she said. "But I think it a strange custom that makes a man and woman embrace without feeling anything!"

She ran down the hill and I followed.

Under the towering trees we ate supper in a circle on the grass. The lines of sunbeams were more horizontal and the air cooler and more rich in color. A fire sent up a thin, waving stream of smoke and gave off a sweet resinous odor.

There was a salad of lettuce, vegetables, and chicken or turkey, thin toasted bread of a slightly nutty flavor, meat rolls, a clear, light, red wine, brown cookies with raisins, grapes, and early apples.

It was more like the Golden Age than ever, but Nattana's re-

111

mark had put me outside the picture. And as though guessing this Ettera spoke with regret of our departure.

"It is always the way," she said. "Just as we find we know Lang he goes."

"I hope he will come again," said Nekka.

"So do I!" cried Nettera, and Patta looked at me with a friendly smile. But Nattana said nothing.

"I should like to come again if I may," I said.

"Why, of course you may!" Ettera declared.

"You are likely to pass this way again," Dorn suggested.

"We hope you will make a special trip," Nekka said warmly, "and not wait till you pass."

"Do!" said Nettera, looking at me with her head sideways, "and stay longer."

I was happier, but not sure that I would return.

The meal was eaten slowly. Conversation lapsed and was resumed. There was a little talk of politics which I did not follow, wondering why my emotions were pink, not red . . . Was it true?

When supper was over no one moved or spoke, and there was a long charmed silence.

Nattana rose and came to where I was sitting.

"Would you like to take a walk?" she asked, a little past my face.

"Remember," said Ettera, "that we have to start down before dark."

We walked away down the ravine in the enchanted light among the tall trees. From behind us came the sound of Nettera's fife, playing softly like a flute, and Nattana uttered a low gasp.

I could think of nothing to say. It was more and more beautiful as evening took the place of afternoon. The shadows under the trees deepened in tone and in the brown pools of the brook the water was so transparent as to be visible only as a thought of clear freshness. We crossed the stream on flattened stones and started up the hillside.

Nattana leaned over a flower blue like a gentian and put her white hand under it.

"Isn't it pretty?" she said, looking up. She was so beautiful as to be unreal, doll-like.

"It is beautiful," I answered, wishing I dared to be personal and tell her that it was she who was so.

We moved on.

"Our house is yours," she said in a low voice. "Do you understand?"

"Yes, Nattana. I shall come again."

"I wanted to tell you by myself, not with the others all around us."

"Thank you, Nattana."

We climbed slowly among the tall trees.

"I am taking you to a place all my own," she said. "No one else knows it."

"I shall be glad to see it."

"I am sorry you go tomorrow."

"I don't want to go."

"What shall I call you? Dorn calls you 'John,' not Lang."

"I would like you to call me 'John.' "

"It is not a special name, is it?"

"It is my real name, my first name."

"You have two real names?" she asked in surprise.

"Yes, Nattana. Your family call you by your first name and people who know you well. Others use your last name."

"In your country would I call you just 'John'?"

"I think we know each other well enough."

Already we were above the ravine's cool and darkening bottom, paralleling its downward course, but also climbing slowly. She led the way. The grass was tall and I felt the damp through my shoes.

"You will wet your feet," I said.

"Of course I shall, in this grass," she answered. "But they always dry."

As she walked she stepped high, graceful in the upward thrust of her knees beneath her skirt, her shoulders square. She looked over her shoulder and smiled, and in the amber light her face glowed.

I followed. At the lower end of the meadow we came to a rocky ledge leading down into the trees. She descended, was sunlit, and passed into shadow, and seemed herself to be the light.

We came abreast of a steep rock wall, above which, ten feet from the ground, was a step. A dead tree lay tilted across the step, its broken branches protruding.

At once she began to climb upward along the tree, sometimes on all fours. I followed her agile fluttering skirt, and soon we arrived upon the ledge. The shelf where we were was only five feet wide and ten feet long. A sturdy pine grew upon its edge buttressed with heavy roots, one of which lay half-buried in soft grass. There she sat and leaned back.

"There is room for two," she said.

I took my place at her side.

The tree shaded us and one branch hung so low that the peaks of the northern mountains lay behind it.

"Lean back," she said; "watch the branch sway."

I obeyed. The feathery pine needles and twigs moved slowly up and down, tracing in the air a dark design through which the white and flushed snow fields of the mountains seemed to rise and fall. The branch was near; there was height and great distance.

We did not speak. Time passed. Soon I must thank her for this lovely thing she had brought me to see. The pine needles waved, were still, waved again as with new life. A gentle breeze touched my cheek. It was so still that I could hear her breathing and wondered if it were always so quick.

"I hope you won't be sorry that you came to the Hyths'."

Her voice was low and by its sound I knew that her head, but a foot or so from mine, was turned toward me.

"I have been very happy," I said.

"I have been happy too. But I am sorry all the same."

"About what, Nattana?"

"About what I said as to your feelings for one thing."

"Don't bother about that."

"It was unkind."

"Don't say so, Nattana. You may be right."

"I don't want to be unkind to you." Her voice was low and vibrating. I sat up and turned to her. She was facing upwards, her hands clasped behind her head pushing her hair forward on her cheeks.

Our eyes met and hers let mine go deep.

"There is another thing I am sorry for," she said, "the way Nettera treated you."

"She tried to make amends. It is nothing."

Her eyes widened with a look of pain.

"She did a cruel thing. It ought to be made up to you."

Her eyes softened. Her bosom stirred. Her face seemed to lift.

"There are some who don't mind what she objected to."

I did not know what she meant, but my heart knew and was hammering.

"I am not like Nettera," she was saying, "not to you."

Her eyelids covered her eyes. I saw her closed soft lips and burning cheeks nearer and nearer. . . .

Something seemed to have broken. . . .

"Hytha Nattana," I was answering. "It was all made up to me. Really it was!"

Her eyes opened wide.

"I am glad you think so, Johnlang. I am glad you have forgiven us."

She sat up abruptly.

"You? It was only Nettera, not you."

"We have pride. Mine is as great as yours." She smoothed back her hair. Her eyes, which I tried to see, avoided mine. "It is time we went back," she added.

We returned in a silence that was for me misery, but just before we reached the others she spoke quickly:

"You will come again, won't you? I would like you to be my friend."

"Oh, yes, Nattana, I will surely come. Will you be my friend too?"

"If you wish."

"I do. I have been lonely here . . . And just now, there on the ledge, Nattana, I. . . ."

"Please!" she cried. "Please!"

She went on quickly.

7

Dorn Island

THE DAWN NEXT MORNING was cold and dark, for clouds lay heavy in the valley to the east. And in a cold dream I rose when my friend called me, and with cold fingers and slow mind dressed myself.

In the somber dining room Dorn and I breakfasted. Only Nekka was about and she waited upon us. She was as silent as we, and her face was round and smooth with recent sleep.

The sun was whitening the tops of the piled-up clouds in the east, but the valley was breathlessly dark with shadow, and the courtyard was a still place. Our familiar rusty white horses, small and friendly compared to the greater ones of the Hyths', waited for us, rested after two days' idleness.

We set off down the valley.

At noon we rode down to the river and took a swim before having lunch. We dried ourselves in the sunlight and in a world of water, reeds, dipping swallows, and wading cattle, we ate our meal and then went on.

All afternoon the valley descended and widened until the mountains were pale masses on the horizon, and the river, whose course we followed, became broader and deeper, and navigable for larger boats. At twilight we trotted into Manson, a shady town, built without walls. At its quiet, vine-grown Inn we stopped and ate our dinner in the garden. The twilight flashed an amber glow over everything and then it grew dark.

"May I say something?" said Dorn, out of the darkness. "The Hyths seemed to like you. I wondered if they would find you too foreign, but evidently they didn't . . ." He paused as though to choose his words. "Other women may feel the same way . . . Well,

I am sorry. Don't let yourself care for an Islandian woman. Don't let her care for you."

A startled answer was on my lips, but he had not finished.

"One very good reason is that no Islandian woman would be happy in the United States, however much she loved you. You may not be able to stay here."

He was silent.

"How did you like Nekka?" he said abruptly, as though to change the subject, but he continued before I answered. "I have known her a long time. Before I went to America I wanted to marry her. But while I was there my parents and my great-uncle, Lord Dorn's son were drowned. My father had expected to succeed my great-uncle as provincial lord and to inherit our land, and I had expected to succeed him; but now in order to maintain our succession the title should pass to Lord Dorn's grandson, my cousin. If this happens, I should transfer my rights to the land to him and retain only residential rights. Nekka knows that my prospects have changed. I have talked to her. . . .

"Matters aren't wholly clear," he said with a slow smile. "It is not her fault. I don't blame her. She has several admirers. The king has come to see her more than once. He is a very handsome man. The Hyths are ambitious. Nekka—" He broke off suddenly. "He is a dangerous man—not one a woman can play with. After he has come or when he is coming she is not the same. She has never been the same since my father died. I wished to marry her when I was eighteen. No other woman has taken the place she had then. Since I came back from America—there was so much to do, and with my future so different . . . I don't blame her for anything! There is nothing she has done."

This conversation gave me much to think about. An Islandian woman, he had said, would not be happy in the United States. Love by itself seemed not to be enough and I wondered if Nekka's possible hardness was typical.

Next morning, instead of continuing on toward Bannar, the capital of Upper Doring, we crossed the river and set out for the mountains; for the Dorns owned a grazing farm on the slopes of the main range, and my friend wished to visit it on the way home, to see how it was progressing.

During the morning we traveled through the foothills and at about three o'clock we reached the Hail River and turned south onto a road that led through a high pass over the mountains into the central provinces.

All afternoon we rode beside the river, through a forest of oak trees on up into the mountains. It was not until night had fallen that we approached the grazing farm. A quarter moon hung in the sky and the Hail River gleamed in its rushing rocky course. As we came nearer the farm, our horses began to run. Dorn shouted something which I could not hear. I held in Fak, who seemed excited, hastening toward his remembered home, for he was mountain-bred. It was a canter, a gallop, downhill in a dark forest! All three horses whinnied at intervals. Moonlight bathed us and the mountains towered black under the stars. Then level fields, warm and smelling of grass, stretched their pale expanses before us, and on a knoll to the right was the dark rectangle of a house. Another with a yellow light was ahead.

"Dorn! Lang!"

The cry rang out.

"Hold him! Don't let him make for the stable."

I pulled hard and mastered Fak.

Soon after, dazzled from the recent night, we were sitting before a bright fire in the house of Donal, the head *deneri* of the two who with their families managed the farm.

Early next day we set out again, riding through the meadows, past barns and orchards, back to the road. It was a serene bright morning.

I thought of Dorn's warning and his remark that perhaps I could not stay in Islandia, and the farm and the hills that lay around it seemed to turn cold eyes upon the alien.

What would my life be when the consulship was over? I saw the wide suburbs of an American city, of Boston, in the muggy heat and lifeless air of overinhabited places in summer; men watering lawns in their shirt sleeves; the shriek, clang, and grind of electric cars; Sunday newspapers scattered about . . . In a dream of home, I saw Dorn himself as the alien, now jogging along ahead of me, broad and red-necked on his sturdy small horse with its switching tail. . . .

Midmorning brought us down to a branching of the road where we turned to the left, and were once more upon the road of the day before, which continued on to Doring Town, skirting the foothills of the mountains. Toward four o'clock we turned into the hills and rode for nearly an hour towards the farm of the Notters, friends of the Dorns.

The evening was calm and clear, the farm very quiet. This was our last day on the road, and our traveling into new places was nearly over, for next day we would reach the Dorns' island home and settle down.

We left early and rode down again to the Doring Road. Soon we had our first view to the west. Beyond a dark plain of variegated green, near the misty horizon, threads and patches of white water lay intermingled with the land. Dorn pointed out a tiny dark hillock, rising out of a patch of water, which he said was Doring Town. His farm lay in the network of land and stream fifteen miles further away.

We descended into the plain and rode through mile after mile of flat country, covered with farms, passing stone walls and gardens, orchards in fruit, hayfields and wood lots, surrounding the farmhouses. Soon after midday we crossed the Doan River and lunched on its further side; then we passed into a forest of ancient beeches and oaks, quite six miles long, from which we emerged into the pale sunlight on the banks of the Doring River. A mile away, rising out of the green windy water, was Doring Town.

Everyone had said that this place was unique. The dramatic suddenness of the vision may have had something to do with its surprise.

The town lay on the water like a ship, her bow pointing upstream, her length half a mile. The islet farthest upstream is the highest, rising steeply from the water a hundred feet. A steep cliff was the ship's cutwater. Above this was a pink granite wall and higher still were irregular concentric tiers of substantial separate houses deep in trees. Highest of all was a square, solid, gray structure, with high-pitched roof of blue slate, and a central tower. A cove was let into the side of this islet, and at its base was a steep-terraced garden, above which was a great gray palace.

Downstream ran a river wall with battlements and square towers, behind which the same arrangement of irregularly concentric rings of houses, gardens, and trees, was visible. The whole made a compact group in the pale sunlight, and was so colorful as to be gay. The water, darkened by catspaws, was a foreground of dark-green, above which the walls of the houses had every tone from pale-pink to orange, from light-gray to blue; the roofs were red or blue, tiles or slate; and about and over and under was the foliage of trees of every shade of green, from pale-emerald to a dark, wet seaweed color.

We paused only long enough for Dorn to ascertain that his great-uncle was still at his farm, and set out again for the town of Earne, in the same direction that we had come, crossing the National Highway that came down to the ferry from the Doan Pass to the southeast.

We pressed our horses, soon leaving the woods. On the left were farms; on the right sometimes the stream itself was only a few feet away, ruffled by the wind, and sometimes there was a strip of salt marsh, either low and reedy or higher and covered with salt grass or cut hay. From this side blew a strong west wind, fresh and damp and smelling of salt and marsh grass. The marshland stretched indefinitely to the horizon. Many waterways broke the opposite shore and disappeared, curving, into the flatness. It was a wind-swept and salty land—a watery land at this season with the sea water of the winding channels and the rain water from the skies.

Trot and canter for mile after mile, until I was spattered all over with mud. Our horses were sturdy and consented to be urged, giving us an honest, unwearied, if not breathless gait. It was the end of the journey for them.

Earne Town crouched in the flat corner between the bordering stream that we had been following and a substantial river of the same name that came down from the mountains. It was a low, walled, wind-bitten town—the place of supply for the most thickly settled parts of the marshland. We made our way at once to the quays along the river, which were crowded with sailboats, of which a few were adapted both for river and sea; but most were smaller—broad-beamed and shallow, decked from end to end, with hatches forward and aft of the single mast.

Dorn was well known here, and everywhere we were met by smiles. In a short time our horses were led away, our saddlebags were placed aboard one of the smaller boats, and we were thrust out into the stream by strong arms.

The rigging of this boat was wholly strange, but I did the right thing with the tiller, while Dorn raised our single lateen sail. A keen wind blew into the harbor. The sail filled with a snap, the cordage strained, we heeled, and the water began to foam under our counter. Dorn took the helm, and excitement and responsibility were over.

Memory vibrated but without recalling any definite event. The wind whistled, the water slapped against the bow, and the air smelled salty. The absence of the straight sky-pointing pole of a yellow-varnished mast was strange. The singular wishbone that sprang from the two sides where the shrouds should have been and arched together could not take its place. The curving, steeply sloped spar, suspended from the apex of the wishbone seemed a Damoclean thing. The brown sail was softer than the familiar duck, and the unpainted broad deck, with coamings a foot high, had proportions to which I was not used. But the rope was the same sort of rope, there was a familiar faint odor of tar, there were blocks and cleats like those of home, and the boat heeled and responded to the gusty wind with the same lift and sweep.

Without tacking we slid out of the Earne River into the broader waters of the delta river. Dorn loosened the after sheet, and we headed more off the wind. At home we would have reefed. The water was a dark-green crested with whitecaps, and spray began to come aboard in fine showers.

Westward, in the eye of the wind, about a quarter of a mile away, were the low, floorlike lands of the marsh, stretching mysteriously to limits hidden by a white, thickening mist. Somewhere over there lay the Dorns' farm.

We followed the delta river north for about a mile. Quite suddenly a channel, running somewhat south of northwest, opened a wide reach of wind-swept water, straight for at least a mile. The great sail cracked like a pistol as we headed into the wind to haul close the "main sheet," a tripled rope that led from the leech of the sail to blocks and cleat at the stern. The port tack was a long one and the starboard a short run across and somewhat back. The sail lay arched and our speed was not great, but we went closer to the wind

121

and made less leeway than I would have expected from so wide and shallow a craft.

Dorn steered standing, with his feet braced on cleats set for the purpose, while I sat on the deck to windward. We talked about the boat, comparing her with those of the United States. In hull design and rigging, Dorn said, she was the common type on the marsh; one man could handle her, and she could carry drily a considerable cargo.

A long leg and a short leg, a freshening wind, choppy sea and head tide—how familiar and how strange. Behind us the mist had reached long enfolding arms, blotting out the mainland with its farms. We sailed in the center of a great circle, perhaps a mile across, and moving with us. Pale sky, pale mist, the dark blue-green of the marsh, the green and white of the sea, the mud beneath the edge of the grass—all else was eliminated. At intervals I heard again, when the wind lulled, the bass drone of Dorn, humming to himself. My face was wet with spray.

Twilight came and the mist drew closer, decreasing the circumference of the circle. The wind lessened minute by minute, and spray no longer came aboard. There were pauses in the slapping of water against our counter, and we glided rather than swept. But we were near home, he said.

Many channels had opened into the marsh, but now there appeared to port one of a different kind—straight not curving, obviously cut by men. At its entrance was a triangular beacon painted white, and here we turned on the starboard tack, as close-hauled as possible. Ahead the mist hid the land, but to the right over the marsh were dense firs and the beginning of a low knoll.

"The Ronans' farm, our nearest neighbors. Ours is there!" Dorn waved his hand toward the bow.

There appeared a low belt of marsh across the end of our channel, and then out of the mist loomed an embankment, and behind it a windmill like the Dutch, and a row of pollarded willows. This was Dorn's home, the place that I had so long been approaching and was reaching at last.

Channels opened diagonally to left and right, and out of the latter wind blew freshly again. We sailed to the low spit which lay in the apex between, so near that I could touch the muddy bank, and then tacked to starboard into the right channel, which curved away into the mist. It was only a little over a hundred yards wide and tack followed tack as we zigzagged our way into the wind, now closing Ronan's shore and seeing his low evergreen forest, and now going back again to the marsh of the Dorns and the embankment.

The windmill was left behind, and a line of willows made an angle almost to the water's edge. At last slightly higher ground appeared, edged by a gray stone wall perhaps six feet high with round towers a few feet higher every little while. More and more of the wall appeared, approaching nearer and nearer the water, and suddenly turning out into it upon a stone pier, which narrowed the channel to half its width.

The quickening of excitement that always comes with a landing at a new place! A short tack took us to the quay on Ronan's side; we came about smartly, payed off, gathered way, and then, with sail flapping, shot around the ends of the pier into a little rectangular harbor. Gently we edged up to the quay wall at the bottom of the harbor between two boats. I scrambled up the three feet of wall that topped us, felt solid ground of broken clamshells under my feet, and made fast to a mooring post. Not a soul was in sight. From the stern, Dorn flung me another line and we were moored.

I returned on board and we furled the sail. The process was familiar, but not the feeling of the soft, almost woolly cloth. Dorn went below for the saddlebags, and a moment later we had scrambled to the quay wall again.

No one saw us come or helped us. A warehouse loomed over us with closed doors, and the wind sung around the edges of the building. The low sun had made the mist whitely luminous, banishing all shadow. This was the home of the most ancient of all the nobles in Islandia. We shouldered our own luggage and set out on foot toward his house.

For over a quarter of a mile we followed a white road, until it turned suddenly at right angles, and I looked along a beech-lined avenue, straight as an arrow. Mist and darkness at the further end did not wholly hide the façade of a stone house.

Wind made the leaves rustle and the branches sway over our heads. The sun was falling below the level of the tops of the mist belt and it darkened quickly now. By the time we had reached the end of the alley of beech trees the mansion had become obscure and shadowy.

123

It was low and irregular. Directly ahead was a plain two-storied part with steep-pitched slate roof; to the left and in front was a similar structure, but lower, with smaller windows and much more weathered ashlar. In the corner at this side projected a three-storied pepperbox tower. On the right a series of low buildings in echelon ran back from the road.

We entered a dim, empty hall, paneled and ceiled with dark wood. Opposite the door was a smoldering open fire. Not a soul was visible and not a sound was heard. Two candles burned above the fire.

"Wait just a moment," Dorn said, and disappeared upstairs. The house itself was so still as to be ghostly, and the gray squares of the low windows added no light to the interior. I went to the fireplace and watched a red eye of flame in a log. The dark stone mantel was richly carved.

Again that note of deathly quiet, all about me like an intangible prison! I felt the flat reaches of the marsh, wet and windy and dark, on every side and I was aware of the stirring of sea, faintly salty, damp, and cool.

There were rapid footsteps on the stairs and out of the darkness into the candlelight came a woman's face, the gray, bright eyes intent on mine, a stern but kindly face, spare and strong. My friend was just behind.

"I am Dorna," she said. "John Lang's room is prepared for him."

After a moment she held out her hand and I took it.

"Thank you," I answered—all I could think to say.

She smiled a very little.

"Would you not like to change?" she asked. "Let us show you your room."

I followed her and Dorn up the stairs, and then on through corridors lighted by an occasional candle set in the wall, bare of all furniture and hangings with only rugs to relieve the coldness of the stone. At last we came to a door set deep in the wall. Dorna, taking a candle from a nearby bracket, stood to one side. The room was large and low with a ceiling of dark, polished beams; two small gray-blue windows, deep-set in thick walls, were opposite. The hangings were a dark crimson. On the right-hand wall was a fire-place, with mantel of carved stone, and on the left a bed with blue woolen spread. A table was set between the windows, a high wardrobe in one corner, and a few chairs, all of dark, varnished wood. Next the fireplace was a door, a little ajar. Dorn, bringing my bag, laughed.

"Harvard crimson, John," he said.

"Thank you for all you have done," I said, facing them.

"We will all be waiting to meet you," Dorna told me. "We are glad you have come."

She left us.

"I am next door," Dorn said. "I'll fetch my things. We'll light a fire and dress. I am glad you are come at last. It had been a dream of mine to have you here."

He left me for a moment and I began to unpack. The fire he had lighted blazed up, and the room, warm and livable in its dancing flames, began to reveal itself. The lack of ornament and pictures made it seem bare, but bit by bit surprising things came to light. It was the wardrobe where I went to hang my clothes that first showed how truly this was my room. A great cloak hung there, and in one corner was a pair of wading boots, a shotgun, and a rifle, each marked with my name. There were sandals of felt and a dressing gown. The door ajar led to a dressing room, and here was all in the way of toilet articles that one could wish: razors, brushes, towels, and soap —all Islandian in style, different but usable. In the table drawer was writing paper, pen and ink, chocolate, a bottle of wine and glasses, and a book of Bodwin's, *The Life of Queen Alwina*, and *The Discovery of Ferrin*, by Dorn XVI. Gratitude, loneliness—or was it Islandia herself?—played tricks upon my self-control. . . .

Stairs nearby led us to a dim corridor on the ground floor, at the farther end of which was a lighted open door. My eyes were a little dazzled by the blaze of an open fire, brighter than the candle flames on the heavy mantel above. The farther corners were filled with jumping shadows. It was a plain and large room but not forbidding —the meeting place of the family of Dorn. On either side of the fireplace were two immense, rough oak benches with high backs, and in the corner of each sat a woman.

I was named to Faina, my friend's grandmother, sister of Lord Fain, and like him—small, white-haired, gentle, with bright, black eyes. Dorna, his cousin, was the other. Faina motioned me to one side and Dorn to the other. She had a frail, precise voice and great kindliness.

Marta, Lord Dorn's daughter-in-law, came in and took her place next to Dorna opposite to us. She was a rosy-cheeked, healthy young woman of about thirty, pleasant and rather commonplace.

A few moments passed in which we told them briefly of our meeting and journey, and I, rather moved, of my happiness in receiving Islata Faina's letter and in being among them. Then my friend suggested that I meet his great-uncle, and led me through a door behind one of the benches.

A wood fire of large radiating logs burned ruddily on an elevated platform. For the moment I saw only that and the four squat, heavy pillars that enclosed it, supporting pointed arches and a huge, columnar chimney. It seemed to furnish the only light. In the background, some distance away, a shadowy wall encircled this central hearth, and the beamed ceiling was high in the darkness.

Trying to see into the shadows, I followed my friend to the farther side of the fire. My feet clicked noisily on the stone floor and then nearly stumbled on a deep, soft rug. A young woman was sitting cross-legged on the floor in front of the fire, and behind her a frail but broad-shouldered man sat on a bench. These two, aloof from the rest and apparently in silence, seemed to be the vital heart of the Dorn family.

My name was spoken. The girl rose, rather awkwardly, her long dark braid swinging over her shoulder and for a moment lying against a cheek warmed by the firelight.

I had not pictured Lord Dorn thus—a thin face, parchment brown, with strongly marked cheekbones; iron-gray, wiry, slightly curling, close-cut hair on a beautifully round head; a drooping mustache; a forward-thrust square chin; highly arched bushy eyebrows; and clear light-brown eyes, with a strange sparkle from the fire.

"Dorn," he said, in an unexpected deep voice. "Welcome, John Lang."

He did not offer me his hand, but he bowed a little and smiled in a way that made his face flash.

"We have made your room ready."

I turned to the girl, my friend's sister, who said her name—Dorna—in a maturer voice than her appearance indicated. Her serene, clear brown eyes studied mine, dancing a little in the fire-light.

Lord Dorn laid his hand gently on my shoulder.

"I am glad you are here, Johnlang," he said, in a voice that seemed a little amused.

"Johnlang isn't his name," she said. "My brother says we should call him 'John,' as he does, now that he has come and is one of us."

Her voice was unexpected in its clearness and power. Her smile became friendly and then it changed; her lids narrowed and her chin was thrust forward; her face became that of another sort of creature, an elf trapped, with a look of wildness and some inner ravenous feeling.

It passed in a second, but it was a shock to see. Her face was human again, and she was lovely. Every feature was strong and fine and delicately modeled. Her eyebrows—the Dorn eyebrows—were two proud dark arches, and it was her skin that made her seem less than twenty-three.

Lord Dorn asked me to be seated, and I took my place at his side. My friend found another beyond him, and Dorna dropped to the rug again, her face toward the fire and away from us, her hands in her lap, utterly still.

"Tell us when my nephew met you and how you came, John," said Lord Dorn; and I told them of our meeting and journey. He interrupted for questions and comments on things on the way.

When we had got as far as the Mora Pass, I hesitated, and glanced at Dorn, who caught up the thread and with a brief word said that we visited the Lor Pass. His uncle nodded gravely.

"Tell me what you and John saw," he said, and I was as excited as I had been then, forgetting the more recent emotions that had overlaid that sharp experience.

At once Dorn took up the narrative in detail. The name of the stranger was not mentioned nor was it asked. "A fourth man joined us," was all that was said.

At the description of his behavior, however, Dorna moved for the first time and looked suddenly at her brother with surprised eyes. With something that might have been a shiver she turned back to the fire.

When he reached the point where Don and the stranger went their several ways, his uncle interrupted.

"You haven't told John who this fourth man was?" he asked.

"No," said my friend.

"The fourth man did not name himself?"

"No. That is the reason."

"You will learn some day," said Lord Dorn to me. "You must forgive us for making a mystery of it."

"I am curious," I said, "but I am quite content to be ignorant."

"You do not have to answer if you do not wish. Think before you do," said Lord Dorn. "Did you know any of the Germans?"

I went through a process that may be described as thinking, but finding no ready reason for concealment I nodded my head and was about to name them.

"Don't tell us who they are," continued Lord Dorn. "I would rather you did not." Then he sat back and looked into the fire. I held my tongue. After a moment he asked me to continue.

While talking I glanced over the room. It was evidently the lower story of the pepperbox tower at the northeast corner of the building. Its walls were quite five feet thick and the windows were lancets at the bottom of tapering depressions three feet above the floor. Close to one wall was an immense table, semicircular in form, with curving benches all around it. Besides this, the bench on which we sat, and half a dozen stools, there was no furniture; but the walls between the windows to a height of ten or fifteen feet were lined with cases full of books in dark leather bindings.

While we were talking a *deneri* appeared at the doorway, and we went to supper, back through the room where Faina, Marta, and the older Dorna were, picking them up there, and on through the corridor down which I had come to a room beyond.

The family had much to say to each other, for Lord Dorn had arrived only the day before from The City and the meeting of the council. He told of his journeys, of the weather, and of the houses at which he had stopped, and there were inquiries as to how innumerable people were, their families, and friends, all strangers to me.

Dorn's sister never said a word and did not look at me, nor at anyone else. She had thoughts of her own and her profile slumbered. Her beauty grew upon me, though her face was a bare one. Her dark-brown hair was smooth as silk, but the arrangement was of the plainest, the hair brushed back to the braid all over her head. The forehead was almost too high and smooth, but the dark wonderful eyebrows redeemed it. Her spirited nose with an aquiline break at the bridge would have been manlike were it not so finely made. The mouth was firm and the chin strong, yet the curves of these and, above all, her wonderful skin—a creamy rose overlaid with a delicate orange-brown—were a girl's and only a girl's. Her hands were slim, shapely, and strong, and her figure seemed a little heavy. I would have liked to watch her face, and did hold it in the corner of my eye when turned to listen to Lord Dorn; but this gave me no chance to study its changes, significant, but unfathomable. Something was always going on in that head, so plainly dressed, so glowingly clean, though what it was lay beyond my power to guess.

When supper was over Lord Dorn and his great-nephew went to the circular room. Marta took me in charge and asked me to sit by her in the anteroom. Faina with a smile, and then the elder Dorna, left us, and I was left alone with Marta and with Dorna the younger, sitting as before on the floor facing the fire.

Marta had little to say, but her round, red-cheeked face beamed with good will. There was a question, an answer, silence, the dropping of an ember, another word, silence again, and then a roar in the chimney as the wind blew overhead brightening into white the red sparks.

There was much to think about.

In the next room with its extraordinary fire open on all sides, was my friend, Dorn, Harvard '05, at home at last. This was as familiar to him as the frame house, miles away, with its incongruous furniture of all periods, was to me. A draft in a corridor, an odor, a nick in a step, were all home to him.

That girl on the floor was his sister, better known to him than I was. In the next room was one of the greatest present-day Islandians, former premier, second only to Mora now. Perhaps his task was too large for him, and he had not the force, ability, and intelligence of his great father, who in the forties had beaten the proponents of foreign trade and re-established isolationist policies. Lord Dorn had not affected me as Mora had. He was frail, already in his late sixties, different from other men, it is true, with much force in reserve, but after all only a man, quite my equal, my friend's equal.

Marta was now telling me about her son, who, she said, bore little resemblance to any of her own relatives except for the redness of his cheeks. For conversation I asked her where they lived and she made a vague gesture to westward where lay the marsh and the sea.

"We are one of them," she said.

It was the first time I heard the idiom, used by the dwellers in the marsh among themselves to describe themselves.

Dorna raised her head for the first time and looked at me squarely in the eye, her head tilted, and glowing and lovely in the firelight; but she said nothing, and after a moment looked shyly away. Curious as to what had moved her I wished to speak to her, but could think of nothing to say.

Marta excused herself, for she wished to cover up her boy as it was foggy. Alone with my friend's sister I felt my heart quicken. There was no reason, except her unusualness. Resuming my seat I resolved with a certain amusement that she must speak first—at an advantage, for I could watch her from above and she could not see me.

The silence was so deep that I found myself listening, as I had listened so desperately during the first weeks of my stay in Islandia. For a moment came back that mood of brittle nerves and tension that had caused so much intangible but acid suffering. I shuddered, and Dorna was an unreal being, eternal and calm like a Buddha.

The wind roared in the chimney and the embers glowed whitely.

A girl becomes uncanny if stared at too intently. The attraction withers. It withers, but it returns subtly. It is not there, and then it is there.

Ten minutes must have passed. The vaguest of impressions and images floated through my mind, as changing and unsubstantial as clouds above a quiet lake. The mystery of love among these, abashed by her presence yet permitted by her stillness, but not love for her . . . The mystery and shame of love gave place to other things: visions of the day, the sail through the marsh, the narrowing circle of fog, our landing in the shadowy white light on the deserted pier, and the unexpected broken clamshells, waking old memories. I listened, and I felt the flat watery plains foggy and damp, extending into endless distances about us; I listened, listened, but my nerves were not brittle and I was quite content.

Her soft, deep voice came from a distance, precise and clear.

"Let us like each other," she said. "Let us like each other always and very much, John."

"That is my wish, Dorna," I said.

She rose and so did I.

"Good night," she remarked. "I am going to bed. Tomorrow I shall be up early and away."

"Good night," I answered. She smiled lightly, held up her chin, and gravely departed.

It must have been this that I wanted. I wished no more and I was happy, sitting in the corner of the bench, and thinking with impatience of tomorrow, and daylight and a view over the marsh.

After a long night of sleep there was the presence of Dorn sitting by my bed, and the sight of a patch of sunlight on the wall. I went to the window. The view was eastward. The air was fresh and bright, unstaled by too long sunlight. Below was a rich green paddock, hoary and glittering with innumerable drops left by the fog, at the farther end of which was a row of dense trees, perhaps beeches, in autumn colors. Farther yet, perhaps a quarter mile away and also to the right, at a lower level, was a row of ancient pollarded willows enclosing a hayfield or pasture; and beyond that lay the marsh, flat and even, stretching on and on with bright arms of creeks to a low band of pink thick fog crouching against the land. Overhead the sky was blue; on one of the creeks was a small white sail; and far away above the fog, sprang the dark, high, serrate line of mountains, out of which towered one giant with rosy-white, pure snow fields.

While I shaved and dressed Dorn talked to me. Two days from now Lord Dorn was going to Doring Town for a month and my friend must go with him, for they both had to attend the provincial assembly over which Lord Dorn presided. After a day in Doring, Dorn was going north for a week or so. I inferred at once, of course, that he could not have me on his journey.

We discussed our plans. It was now March 26th. To reach The City in time for the steamer arriving there on April 15th, I must leave not later than the 10th. From March 28th to April 6th, Dorn would be away, thus giving us together only the next two days and three in April. He suggested that I come to Doring with his uncle and himself; after that I could return to the Island; or else I might ride three days north and visit Lord Farrant, from whom I had an invitation and to whom M. Perier had given me a letter, returning about when Dorn did. This suggestion meant that I must travel alone, but it would bring two new provinces under my observations.

By the time it was settled that I should go to Farrant, I was dressed and ready; but my friend hesitated, embarrassed, and suddenly blurted out what was on his mind.

"My uncle," he said, "doesn't think I treated you quite fairly that day at the Lor Pass. He thinks I was rather heedless of your interest when I exposed you to the attention of those Germans in my company and Don's. The situation is this. Lord Mora has withdrawn the guard at the Lor Pass, to show the German government his good will, and that he really recognizes their protectorate over the Sobo Steppes. He is thinking, perhaps, of the unguarded frontier between the United States and Canada. We think he is wrong, because we do not believe that the Germans can police the Sobo Steppes so as to make us safe. Everybody in the valley is apprehensive. . . ."

Nattana's remarks came back with new understanding.

"Besides, we don't believe in taking the Germans, or anyone, on faith of mere promises. You know that Lord Mora's Treaty has not wholly abrogated our old laws that the number of foreigners in the country shall be limited, and that no one can enter without a medical examination. We are afraid that the opening of the Lor Pass will mean the letting in of unauthorized and unexamined Germans and also marauders. That is what Don and I went to find out, though he—the fourth one—rather spoiled things."

I had surmised all this.

"The Germans," continued Dorn, "must have guessed our purpose. How will it affect you, asks my uncle, if you are seen apparently hand in glove with us? Some of the Germans know you. Everyone in the diplomatic colony, everyone in the government, will know it. My uncle asks what can be done to explain your presence . . . Mora is working hard to abrogate the exclusion laws altogether. If we had only caught those men red-handed in Islandia as Don and I planned! The fourth man spoiled that—they had a chance to lie. Our case is weakened. If we could show the council what effect Mora's policy was having—how Germans were sneaking in—that would have helped us in our fight."

He was forgetting me. Dimly I had realized the embarrassment that might come of being found in Dorn's company at such a place, but there was too much happening to John Lang, the individual, for John Lang, the consul, to give it much thought. Now, I saw clearly, and though I was amused, I was also alarmed, for I might be recalled as one who mixed in politics.

"We talked about you a long time last night," Dorn continued. "I did do wrong by you—"

"Don't!" I cried suddenly.

"I was excited! You see, if Don and I had worked things out our own way, you would never have figured at all. We would have trailed those Germans until there was no doubt; then you could have gone on to the Shelter House and we would have arrested them—"

"Don't worry about me—"

"I do. My uncle does. We decided to do this—to write Mora and tell him the whole story and how you came to be with us. We can trust him to do the right thing, but he will probably have his laugh at us. The letter has already gone."

A perambulation of the farm is an established custom. I had already made the circuit of the Fains'. On this clear windy March day, corresponding in season to the latter part of September at home, Dorn, Dorna, his cousin, and I made the round on horseback.

The island was roughly about a mile and a third east and west and a mile north and south. We rode first to the north through the avenue of trees under which Dorn and I had come the night before, and then turned east into a great meadow, bordered at its lower edge by an embankment on which grew pollarded willows. These I had seen yesterday looming out of the mist. East of this we rode into another large meadow filled with Islandian cattle and emerged on a creek from which opened a little harbor called the "Fisherman's," with a stone pier and dock and the house and boathouse of a *deneri*. A sloop lay in the dock and there was a faint smell of fish and clams.

From this little settlement, a firm clamshell road ran west through a wood of low pines and firs perhaps a quarter of a mile to a branching. We took the road to the south, between a pasture for horses and a hayfield, past the house of the dependent in charge of the horses, then west through woods, a wide circuit of a mile or more, to another creek and pier and dependent's house. A wooded island lay opposite, and a flat scow was moored below. The way back led us for another mile to the piers and harbor where we had landed the day before.

Having ridden around the borders of the island farm, we returned through its heart—paddocks, grain fields, hayfields, and orchards, separated by low stone walls, brought bit by bit from the mainland, or by rows of beeches or willows—past the great hay barn, past the vegetable garden and the rather straggling vineyard on the hill slopes, back to the rambling main house.

We had traveled slowly with many stops and conversations. Though I had known there were some fifty people on Dorn Island, and even more when ships were in, I had not expected quite so large an estate or one with so many functions and interests. These included the occupations of fisherman, sailor, forester, herder, agriculturalist, horse breeder, stock raiser, and house servant. M. Perier's book had not led me to expect an estate in Islandia so feudal, and I asked Dorn and Dorna about it. They told me that there were other places like theirs in the marshes, some even larger, and a few in the rest of the country; but these were exceptional and had each its peculiar reason and history. Their own estate had come to be as it was because, in the early days of raiding Karain pirates, Dorn Island had been a strong point and place of refuge. Farm owners had come there, abandoning their own places. These men had not all become dependents as dependents were elsewhere, for the contract between them and the Dorns gave them a more secure tenure and greater privileges. Only two of the families ranked as *denerir*. The rest ranked as proprietors by a custom hundreds of years old.

"We all get along perfectly well," said my friend, "because we have been adjusting our conflicting claims for hundreds of years and have reached a settlement that is satisfactory to nearly everyone. We are in many ways a large partnership as you understand that word."

Lunch came soon after our return. My friend's sister had not yet come back from her unexplained errand, but all the rest were present, including Lord Dorn's grandson, the boy of seven who was to carry on the "succession." He already possessed the strong fine eyebrows of his family, but otherwise he was an ordinary enough child in my eye.

No place could have been more quiet than my room that afternoon. The windows faced east, and though a fair west breeze was blowing no eddy of it disturbed the trees near the wall. At a distance beeches and willows tossed their branches, already partly stripped of leaves, while those that remained were golden or ruddy. The still air was distinctly autumnal. Beyond the pastures and about a mile away was a winding creek and beyond that a strip of flat, dark-green marsh, and then another creek.

I did not want my stay to be so short as seemed likely.

I had the sensation of having traveled far, more than the actual three or four hundred miles warranted. Doring and the West seemed true country—remote from The City. There was a sense of vacation and of autumn in the dropping leaves and smoky air. Echoes of past emotions came back with delicate melancholy, and I thought of Nattana and then of Dorn's warning not to care too deeply for Islandian girls or let them care for me; and again it brought the feeling of a door slammed in my face.

A group of horses and men were coming over the farther, wider expanse of marsh, so minute as to seem like toys. White sails glinted in the sunlight near the town of Earne, and a smaller one was making its way through a broader creek to the northwest.

After all, America was my country and its people my own. I turned my back on the view and began to write a letter home.

There was a brisk footfall outside my door, which was instantly flung open. It was Dorn.

"I hoped I would be free for a walk or a sail," he said, "but my uncle needs me. If you care to, why don't you go to meet my sister? She will reach the Fisherman's Harbor soon—I can see her boat—and I think she would like it."

From the window he pointed out to the north a small white sail, close-hauled, moving south along the creek beyond the pastures. There was no time to lose, and as soon as he had guided me to the south end of the ell in which was my room, and pointed out the path I was to follow, I set out. The air was briskly cool and fresh.

My way led me along a trail through a dense wood of beeches. Dead leaves hissed overhead and around my ankles.

Rustling leaves under foot and their dry smell, combined with that of salt air and damp earth, set vibrating memories beautiful and vague. Could I ever hope to have my own New England acres of beech and pine and maple, and to walk there in the slow-gathering darkness of fall afternoons, smelling newly plowed earth?

The path turned left, out of the woods and through an arched gate. I saw a vista of broad pasture, infinite miles of level marsh, and level plain, and far haze, and snow mountains. This was not New

England, for it was too spacious, too immense, too aloof, empty, and indifferent; and when I set out across the grass, I became a mere dot upon it moving slowly—minute and lonely.

The white sail of Dorna's boat was gliding along the creek nearly a half mile to my left. I quickened my steps, and in the cool, clear sea air my blood tingled.

The sail did not move as fast as I did, for the wind was light. As the sun went lower the white linen sail became dusky pink. I wondered if she saw me, for I could not see her—the banks of the creek were too low. She was some two hundred yards away when I emerged from the pasture and came to the stone pier with its crackling clam-shells.

Here a cove opened from the creek with an entrance perhaps two hundred feet wide. Directly opposite the entrance was the harbor, cut into the shore and lined on three sides and a part of the outer one by a stone wall. The stone pier to which I went projected from the northern side about halfway across the entrance.

The sail was still outside the cove, moving very slowly in the failing wind, and there being nothing better to do I sat down on the outer face of the pier, dangling my legs over, and waited.

The tide was low and in the northern and southern ends of the cove flats of a dark-gray mud were exposed. Here and there upon them were mounds of earth where clams had been dug, and I could see a line of footprints. The water was perhaps ten feet below me, oily, opaque, and smooth, but making a faint wash-splash and gurgle against the massive stones.

I cursed the fate that had so shortened my stay, and filled my lungs with the salty fresh air in which was mingled the odor of spruce woods, of clams, of marsh, of mud flat, and of grass. As the craft slowly tacked and entered the cove the dark-brown hull became visible, and standing in the stern was a still figure with round head.

The wind "headed" the boat, and she bore off toward the mud flats to the north, moving perceptibly but very slowly. Wondering whether to row out and tow her in, I rose. It was a signal for Dorna, now about a hundred feet away, to wave her hand in a fashion familiar and friendly. I called to her, asking if she needed help. She shook her head.

When she was near the flats I saw her lean against the tiller, and, considering the lack of wind, the boat came about smartly; but she did not make the harbor on this tack either. When abreast of me she smiled and waved again and then gave herself sedately to her duties, sailing past me to the mud flats at the south end of the cove. The third tack, however, pointed the bow at the end of my pier, and I watched her come toward me, more slowly than ever, for she was close under the lee of the land.

It was a little provoking, as though she were consciously eluding me, and I went to the end of the pier to be ready to do what she wished; for it seemed likely that she could not enter the harbor with the wind but could only just reach it. She had her own methods, however, and when off the entrance she let the sail fill and the boat gently gather way, and then with a vigorous swing shot it into the eye of the wind.

Again she passed me, the sail flapping idly not twenty feet away, and there was nothing to do but run around the inner wall toward which she was heading.

When I reached it, somewhat out of breath, her boat was motionless in the center of the harbor, which was quite glassy, with melting rings of blue and pink and a reflection of the boat inverted beneath, shattering and re-forming.

This time I would ask no questions. I descended by a ladder to a skiff waiting below, and sculled out to her. Meanwhile she had dropped the yard of the single lateen sail and was furling it when I came alongside. She looked up with a smile.

"Thank you for coming to meet me," she said in a voice always unexpectedly low.

She gave me a rope and with some difficulty I towed her alongside the wall and at her command made fast bow and stern lines. When this was done she came nimbly up the ladder and was near me. Her dress was stained and damp and on her temples salt was crusted. She looked weather-beaten and a little disheveled.

Giving herself a little shake, as though she were stiff, she looked up at me.

"I am glad you came, 'Zhohn,' " she said. "Would you like to take a walk?"

"Why, yes. But aren't you tired? You have been gone a long time."

"I'm not tired." Her lips closed almost primly, but she smiled a vague smile. We set out at once, and Dorna moved at my side with easy, swinging steps, more free than I expected from one who had seemed so restrained.

There was strangeness in finding her at my side, keeping abreast of me. Why was there flattery in so ordinary a thing as that? She awed me a little and was very beautiful. The low sun made her face luminous so that the warm, rose-golden tones in her skin glowed. Sedate, serene, friendly, and happy—so she seemed; but her lips were shut firmly as though she had decided not to speak, and wanted me to know it.

The white road flowed under us and we were soon in the shadow of the trees. The clear light was translucent like amber and the needles of the pine trees were a vivid brilliant green. Some minutes passed.

Abruptly she left the road and we were soon in a bewildering and shadowy maze of criss-cross branches, with brown, dark needles under our feet, and feathery dark-green ones against a blue sky over our heads. She led and I followed. She was taking me to some definite place—I guessed the tower on the hill—but why did she not speak to me?

The woods gathered densely around us. She seemed capable of some mischief. And yet her plain dark-blue skirt, fluttering ahead of me unerringly, was ordinary enough, stained with the white residue of salty spray.

There was a dark loom ahead, and we came upon a gray, moss-grown stone wall, about eight feet high, and directly in our path. Abruptly Dorna stopped at a flight of steps, steep and high, with narrow treads leading up to an open gate near the top of the wall, through which was a glimpse of trees and sky.

She pointed without a word, and I assumed that she wished me to go first, perhaps to help her. I climbed through and turning reached down my hand.

"I don't need help," she said, and her voice coming after the long silence startled me. I looked down into her upturned face which was puzzled and intent. Then she held out her hand. I took it. She came up without any aid of mine and did not draw her hand away, but left it where it was. I could not let it go, of course, and we went on hand in hand.

My heart beat and my head was dizzy and confused. The trees were more open, grass lay on the ground between them, and a few hundred feet away was the tower, lifting a round cylinder of gray stone about twenty feet high with narrow windows and a battlemented top.

After so plainly saying that she did not need help, would she, I wondered, have given me her hand and have let it remain in mine unless she wished me to hold it? Was this some dumb way of hers to show the liking that we had pledged to each other the night before? Were the Dorns, greater people, simpler than the Hyths with whom, as at home, this would be flirtation?

My head whirled, my heart throbbed, her hand was a thing of soft fire, and all colors sharpened with brilliance.

Thus linked, we walked to the foot of the tower, neither speaking nor looking at each other. We stopped before the low, closed wooden door. I looked up and saw the sharp upper edge of the tower against the sky. Dorna's head was lifted also.

"Shall we go up the tower?" she said in a clear precise voice.

"Yes, Dorna." I answered shakily.

"You will have to let go my hand. It takes two hands to open the door." Was there mockery in her voice, or merely an effort at steady articulation?

Released, she stepped forward and pressed on a loose board with one hand, raising the latch with the other. The door opened with a creak, showing a dark interior and the beginning of a narrow, steep, winding stair. She stood aside for me to go first, but just as I was about to enter, she said:

"Do you want to take my hand again?"

Of course I offered mine, my heart leaping, and we went up, awkwardly, sidling along in the darkness. She was somewhat below me, and when we reached the top, I was out of breath and I was dusty where my back had brushed the walls.

The island, the whole marsh, the barrier beach of sand hills, ten miles or more to the west, the dark-blue sea beyond, toward which the golden dazzling ball of the sun was dropping, the border of farming land east and southeast, and Doring Town a glittering spot of bright colors riding like a ship in the river—all were spread before us.

My hand held hers and hers mine with light but firm tenseness, and we walked slowly around the tower, and then there was a movement in my heart and a blur came before my eyes. The beauty of wide waters and land was remote. It was too much, and suddenly I placed the hand I held upon the parapet and left it there.

Promptly she clasped it with the other. Down the wooded slopes of the hill the great main house lay like a model, sharply clear in the amber-rosy brilliance of the twilight.

I was not to care too deeply for Islandian girls, but when they gave me their hands to hold, what was I to do? A moment would have been nothing, but this had lasted too long. They were all cruel and unkind, and I was unhappy and angry; not at her, but at the situation that made me alien and unacceptable—angry at this beautiful, spacious, and self-sufficient land.

"Dorna," I said, "your brother told me that I must not care too deeply for any Islandian woman or let one care too deeply for me. It is dangerous for me to hold your hand."

"Didn't you want to hold it? If you wanted to hold it what was I to do? I do not know your customs, John. I was trying to do what you wished." Her voice was very quiet.

"I offered you my hand to help you up the steps through the wall. That is customary in my country."

"That was the only reason?"

"The only reason then."

"Oh," she moaned with half a laugh, "I thought you wanted to hold it. That made me wonder, but, still, I thought it was probably your custom."

"I wondered also," I said.

I looked at her, but her face against the low sun was so scarlet that I felt like an intruder. I turned my head away to the cold east, where the great mountains lay dark and high against the sky.

"That is what comes from trying to act according to other people's customs which one doesn't know, instead of sticking to one's own," I said.

"Yes," she answered, "but that isn't all, for if your customs are like ours, to you—perhaps me—a thing like that . . ." Her voice dwindled away.

"We know it was a misunderstanding—"

"Yes, our minds know—and there is no blame." She was dumb again.

"Don't ever be concerned about me," I cried.

"Perhaps tomorrow we shall laugh about it. I cannot laugh now," she said.

"Nor I."

"Let us keep it to ourselves."

"Dorna, I'm sorry!"

"Why be sorry—now?"

Side by side but looking in different directions we fell silent. The fire in my heart cast a golden glory on the wide view. I saw with new eyes a new world imagined dimly in dreams and become a burning reality: marsh, sea, and sand—scattered white island dwellings—the minute distant barque of Doring Town riding buoyantly on the pale river—infinite miles of mainland farms dappled in greens and lavenders and yellows—and far high lines of dark mountains.

"It is very beautiful," I said.

"Yes—yes," she whispered earnestly.

Smoke was rising from the chimneys in the ell of the main house, and from the farmhouses in the valley. The odor came to us of wood smoke faintly acrid and sweet.

"I come here for hours," she said. "I must come here, for here I feel our farm as a whole. Do you understand?"

"I'm not sure," I answered.

"An Islandian might," she said half to herself. "I wonder how different and how alike you are. I have known very few foreigners, Perier's daughters the best."

No "monsieur," I noticed.

"I don't think anyone could understand who has not lived on a place for hundreds of years as we have. I feel our farm as a whole, as it is, as it was, as it will be—ours—our land; and I feel ourselves and its past and future as one thing—not me, not us, but one thing by itself. . . .

"Let us go home," she added suddenly. "I'm hungry. I have been sailing all day."

Homeward we went, scarcely speaking, down the tower and through the woods to a wooden gate that opened into the upper end of the garden. As we descended the sun set and the shadows became blue. The tang of wood smoke was heavier and the air was chilly, and I thought of open fires and dinner. Dorna became luminous in the shadow, her face golden with a light of its own. She was so beautiful I could hardly bear to look at her.

She stopped at a flower border as yet unplanted, newly dug with dark, damp, rich earth.

"I shall plant bulbs here soon," she said. "If you were going to be with us longer you could help me and tell me about the flowers in your country. There must be some that would grow here."

"Perhaps I could get you some seeds and bulbs."

She pondered.

"They would come too late to plant outdoors. . . . But will you tell me about them someday?"

When I reached my room to change my clothes, I found myself trembling.

Later that evening we made plans for next day, my last at Dorn Island—a sail to the great barrier beach and the western sea, which drew me like a magnet.

8

Dorna

A FRESH WIND was bending the beech trees away from my window, dislodging their leaves in flocks and sailing them eastward over the pasture. The wind was west, therefore, and the sail was on! The air that came in was warmer and damper than that of yesterday. Did it mean fog? Eastward the air was clear. The town of Earne was sharp and minute, and the farm lands behind it rolled on and up, free from haze and without loss of detail, into the glare of the sun. Had that dreaming freshness of sensation, mine as a child, come back?

I breakfasted with the elder Dorna and Faina, for the rest were already up some time. Lord Dorn had gone out, and my friend was at the harbor. His sister was in the kitchen, getting our lunch together. She came in before I had finished, and when I spoke of fog she shrugged.

"Oh, very likely we shall be caught."

Soon afterward we left the house together and walked down the alley of trees, their branches tossing and their leaves hissing. She looked up and I wondered if she thought the wind were too strong. Did she really wish to go on this picnic? Most young women would have had something to say, but scarcely a word and not a smile had I had yet. But the material substance of her was with me, vivid against the trees, marsh, and green grass, colorful upon the white shell road.

Our boat was ready—not the one in which we had come two days before, but one a little smaller, more yachtlike, and more comfortable. She had the same flush deck and low coaming, but her woodwork was dark and polished, her sides white and fresh, and the big sail already raised and flapping clean and unstained. She could carry cargo, but now she was fitted for passengers on deck and also below, in the roomy

143

cabin furnished with bunks, lockers, curtained ports, and a mirrored table.

We pushed off and the sail filled, the *Antara* heeled over and water seethed along the side, with all the wind we could wish for. A moment later, however, the sail was flapping again. We were close to the stone wharf on Ronan's side of the channel and a young man was standing there hailing us. We edged in. He asked where we were going, Dorn invited him to come, and at once he accepted. He was a slender man, dark-skinned with clear light-brown eyes, shy and reserved, and in his early twenties. He named himself: Ronan, and was in fact the Dorns' neighbor's second son.

I sat on the deck, leaning against the windward coaming, with Dorna at my side, it is true, but with Ronan beyond her, and all three of us wordless, neither looking nor speaking to each other.

Dorn, standing erect, steered the *Antara,* eastward to the artificial channel and thence north through that. The wind, therefore, was at first astern and then abeam. The water was a heavy opaque green, wrinkled by innumerable catspaws, and breaking here and there even in these narrow marshland creeks. It would be almost a two-reef breeze at home, but our boat was made to endure such winds with full sail. Close-hauled, our weather coamings under water, heavy waves hammering under the bow, we headed westward along the main channel that ran out into the marsh from near the town of Earne.

Back and forth we three inactive persons shifted on each tack, soon quite wet, for though the *Antara* did not ship broken water, she threw high clouds of fine spray. We were chilly, too, and our sitting position with water flowing under us was not particularly comfortable. We did not complain; at each shift Dorna smiled at some inner amusement of her own, the quickest and deftest of us three to change her position. We said nothing to each other and only when we changed across did we look at her—she never looking at us. Standing erect, her brother was aloof and rather magnificent. I began to be amused. Were not Ronan and I like two shy jealous boys, rivals with regard to one girl, perhaps as shy?

We were now well out into uninhabited marsh. Dorn and Ronan Islands were several miles astern. North and south were flat marshlands.

Here were wind, and dark-green sea channels, wet salt water, and a sturdy boat beating her way to the open ocean—and what was a little jealousy in so vast a scheme? Soon Dorna and I were talking, and Ronan, just beyond, listened with his dark handsome face not uninterested.

After an hour and a half, perhaps, the channel we were following widened into a lake of green windy water dotted with whitecaps. The channel left this area at the northwest corner, through narrows only a hundred yards wide. The tide was with us and we foamed through against the wind, the water swirling around us. Beyond the narrows the channel turned and widened again, and with sheets eased we sailed northwest.

The constant pressure of the wind, the creaking of spars, the clop-clop of waves under the counters, and the bright glare of the sky and water, slipped me into a trancelike mood. Dorna at my side became sharply detailed and colorful but unreal. We had to tack now, and I was lazy, disinclined to move. Half of me fell asleep.

Not long after, the channel became rough and choppy. The wind increased and we lay far over, all the cordage tightening till it sang. Spray in clouds swept over us, our faces ran wet, and the taste of salt was on our lips. With a sensation of being overborne by this tumultuous weather I clung to the thought of the adequacy of Dorn. Dorna, holding fast to the upper coaming, was gasping, with bright eyes. She was not wholly a superwoman.

At last I saw, between two headlands of sand, the straight dark line of the horizon of the open western sea—a line broken here and there with the great waves heaving up on a distant bar.

We came about sharply, wallowed heavily, and shipped water, the sail filling with a loud twang. My heart came into my throat. We headed directly for the northern headland; the white teeth of the breakers were there. But the force of these was broken by a sand spit, behind which an inlet led into the marsh behind the dunes. We were soon under the lee of the dunes in smooth blue water and glided alongside a wooden wharf on the westward or dune side. Ronan went nimbly ashore with a rope. The *Antara* was made fast and her sail lowered. Dorna beckoned me below.

She gave me a basket, and it, like all Islandian things, was different, long and deep and closely woven. That was all, and we returned to the deck and went ashore. There was no house within miles. Ahead, a hundred yards or more away, rose the rolling smooth lines of the dunes. Between us and them was a level of dry light sand with tufts of pale-green grass here and there. Ronan took the other basket. Dorn plodded ahead. Dorna came to my side and made harder the carrying of mine by irregularly helping me. It was as it might have been at home on a picnic. The walking was tedious, for at every step we sank deep and slipped back. Under the dunes it was almost windless, but overhead streamers of sand blew off in level lines from the summit. Most unexpectedly we came to a marshy spot, in the center of which was a shallow stone-rimmed well; a pole and dipper lay on the sand. A skin was produced from one of the baskets and filled, and we climbed into the dunes, leaving a trail of soft gigantic footsteps in the sand behind us.

We went on, with good firm footing in the hollows and loose soft sand on the slopes, which we ascended painfully but descended in great strides. The basket was heavy. Dorn with the skin of water seemed tireless, but Ronan and Dorna as well as I were a little out of breath and heavy-footed.

At last, through an opening as smooth as a saddle, the beach appeared, a crescent three or four miles long, steeply shelving, with vast high breakers thundering against it. Of one accord we retreated from the wind into the dunes again and in a sheltered spot, lay on the sand, while Dorna opened the baskets.

Picnics! So often the spot though carefully selected means nothing. As quickly as possible, everyone chatters, summoning back the world that was deserted. But here the place where we were was dominant. We said little, we were happy and hungry, and our eyes were filled with the vastness of the great dunes, and our ears with the bass rumble of the surf behind us and the soft whistle of the wind through the grass just above our heads.

After lunch, Dorn, Ronan and I went again to the beach. The sea and shore were empty. The wind was blowing so hard that when our lips parted it pressed into our mouths. Close to the water the sand was firm, but the beach was so steep that the curl of the breakers was as high as our heads, and the spray from their tops was leveled off and blown upon our faces in fine mist. Dodging the wash of these waves we walked north for perhaps a mile. Looking back we saw Dorna coming and waited for her—a minute figure, between beach and water, gradually enlarging. Ronan spoke a word to her that I did not hear, and then she and he turned away into the dunes, and I found myself hurt.

The beach curved westward and became less steep, and finally Dorn and I rounded a great blunt point. The surf on its outward edge was colossal, its roar deafening. Around this headland I saw what he had brought me to see. Before us was another beach, seventeen miles long, a vast crescent with a broad flat strand—surely one of the great beaches of the world, pure, flawless, and utterly empty, except for a lighthouse at its far tip.

We returned as we had come, and due to the others' desertion it was necessary for us to carry both baskets and the waterskin back to the *Antara*. Shadows had begun to lengthen and the wind to drop. Dorna and Ronan had not yet arrived. At last they came, Dorna bright-eyed, and Ronan, to a suspicious eye, self-consciously calm. We set out, and the wind grew less and less as the sun sloped down. Pale-pink clouds were in the sky. The light-brown sail became orange when the sun fell upon it and purple in the shadow. The air was fresh and cool, and I felt happily sunburned and tired.

In the narrows was scarcely a breath of air, but the tide carried us through and a sunset breeze bore us the rest of the way, on into the channel between Dorn and Ronan Islands. It was a satisfaction to drop Ronan at his wharf, and to have no competitors as we drifted across to our moorings. Dorna and I walked up to the house under an opalescent sky with a wheeling afterglow behind us, a moon gathering light in the east, and, now that the wind was gone, the air summery again.

After supper, before the open fire in the living room, it seemed that autumn chill had come again. The warmth was welcome. Dorn and his uncle were in the tower room; Dorna sat tailor-fashion on the floor, staring into the fire, saying nothing, with her hands limp in her lap. Faina and I carried on a slow conversation.

Then Dorna looked up and asked me to go for a walk with her. I agreed gladly, but turned to Faina for her assent, because it was night. After a moment she smiled.

We went as we were and at once. Outdoors it was unexpectedly warm and still. A faint mist rising from the marsh diffused the moon-light and softened the shadows, but the moon itself was high and silver-bright.

"Let's not talk for a while," said Dorna, "unless you really want to."

"I don't, unless you do."

147

She made no answer.

We walked down the long alley of beeches. Darkness hung under their branches in black folds. At my side Dorna moved smoothly and silently with her supple long steps that swung her hips a little. When we came abreast of the gate leading through the wall into the pasture she turned without a word. Under the open sky it was brighter, and the mist, not dense enough to conceal anything, was faintly saffron. Dorna moved soundlessly over the soft grass of the pasture. Her head was to the front, her chin was lifted, her eyes were a little narrowed, and her face seemed to be receiving with rapture the mild night air.

Dorna, moonlight, an unfamiliar place, and most of all, Islandia, vast about me, were suddenly unreal. I must remember that I was of the United States and would return there, and that all this lonely strangeness was but an episode in my life. When the season was like this at home, football would be beginning. I visualized the somberly colorful thousands at a Harvard-Yale game; smelled tobacco smoke again; saw rushing trains trail clouds of white steam back from the engine over the roofs of the parlor cars; thought how it felt to buy a new hat at Collins and Fairbanks; of turkey and Thanksgiving dinner; of dances, friendly faces, familiar waltzes. . . .

Dorna's feet made no sound. She herself had become a wraith. And it was not fall at home; it was spring. The year was all awry. We came suddenly upon shadowy cattle. A cow's head moved. . . .

Against the sky ahead rose an odd structure—the windmill with its long vanes motionless and its squat tower very dark. The water of a ditch gleamed ahead, and our feet sounded on a narrow bridge of planks. I followed Dorna up the slope of the dyke.

I watched her open the door, but she did not enter. Instead she sat down on its low threshold, her back against the jamb, and pointed to the opposite side. Obediently I took my seat and looked into her moonlit face; but she gazed past me eastward, saying nothing, while I searched my mind for the safety of small talk and found it empty.

Her face, warm in color in spite of the paleness of the white moonlight, was beautiful in its simplicity. It was relaxed now. Her head was resting on the jamb of the door and her throat was softened. I stared at her face, and my heart beat because she was so lovely and so unreal. I could not make her seem friendly nor feel any consciousness of a familiar and usual contact. One hand lay in her lap, palm upward, the fingers curved over it. I wanted to take it, for I had held it yesterday, and to recapture her, but I did not dare. Though her head did not move her eyes glittered and came slowly upon mine and held them. She stared at me. There was no flicker in her eyelids. She examined me. No girl at home would have done what she was doing. Her eyes, into which the moon shone, held mine powerless, and she saw all of me that there was to see; and I saw nothing but eyes, Dorna's eyes, and felt the very substance of my being drawn out of me painfully, leaving me weak and shaken.

Then, as though satisfied, she looked away over the pasture. Her eyes narrowed, and mine, released, wavered over her face. She smiled, looking away from me, that odd unhuman elfish smile that had no warmth and no friendliness to me.

"John," she stated to herself, with a little buzzing Z in the J, almost a lisp. "John Lang. Lang."

"Yes," I answered, "that is my name. . . . Yours is Dorna."

"Dorna to everyone," she said in a low voice. "But you are only John to a few—Lang to everyone else."

"John to my friends and family. You said we were to be friends."

"Oh, yes, but it is strange to call you John. Is it really your custom that I should call you John? I am only the sister of your friend."

"It is really our custom."

"It doesn't seem that way to me. And I am afraid of trying to follow your customs which I don't know—after yesterday."

"This is one you can follow . . . I wish you would. Ask your brother. Dorna, I wish you would."

She shrugged a little.

"Don't wish to marry me," she cried suddenly, her eyes full upon mine again, and realizing what she had said I could scarcely breathe.

"I might," I said, "but I—don't be afraid!"

I wanted to reassure her, but I was hurt with a pain by now familiar, yet deeper than it had been before.

Her eyes looked down.

"You may not wish to marry me," she said. "Oh, I know what I am like!— But you may and that thought fills me with fear! And if it had to be said, it is best to say it at the beginning."

Why did it fill her with fear?

"You have warned me," I said slowly, "and it was not easy to do. You have not given me any reasons. But I am grateful to you, Dorna. Your brother said much the same thing. I can't expect to live here always, and an Islandian girl would not be happy in the United States."

"Oh," she cried, "it goes deeper than that." And again I wondered wherein I was defective.

"As to me, I mean," she added, and I looked at her averted eyes, a little comforted.

"Whatever I do, you never need worry, Dorna," I said.

"John! If that were my fear, do you think I would ever have spoken?"

It was painfully confusing.

"I don't know what to think," I cried. "I *am* grateful, but—"

"I had you in mind."

"Dorna," I said. "Am I unfit to love an Islandian girl?"

"I don't know!" she answered hastily.

"I think that *is* your reason!"

"I have not told you my reason, and I will not. Oh trust me, John!"

"Dorna," I said. "You are very different from other girls I have known. I don't understand you as I seem to understand some of them. I think perhaps you are thinking of me. I am grateful, but what you have said is not a pleasant thing to have to think about."

It seemed a proper and flattering speech as I made it, and it gave her the freedom, which I knew she wished, to say no more; but I craved her reasons and waited in hope that she would be kind and give them.

"I am sorry," she said, and there was some comfort in the warmth of her voice. But she was silent. The moonlight streamed on her impassive, lovely young face. And I knew that I was not to know what was wrong with me in her eyes—at least not now, if ever. Nor could I tease her to tell me as I had teased Nattana.

After an interval she spoke again, asking me if I liked the windmill, and I roused myself to answer. It seemed very old, I said, a place one would like to come to and be alone in. It was old, she told me, four hundred and twenty-seven years, built at a time when the Dorn family was in eclipse. It was now exactly as it was then but probably included none of the original woodwork, for every year some wearing part was replaced, and much of the stone, owing to collapse of the foundations. "Was it the same windmill?" she asked with a smile, and something prompted me not to view this materially—the old jackknife problem of schoolboys.

It was the same, I said, for the important thing was not the substance of which it was made, but the service it rendered and how it seemed to those who knew it. It was in use continuously, she answered, pumping the water that seeped through the dyke or accumulated behind it from the drainage of the pastures, over into the marsh creek—at work year in and year out, winter and summer, in all sorts of winds and weathers, rarely still.

And it was a place she came to as a child—and still did—being so isolate and quiet, and yet a vantage point to watch the vessels coming to the Island or passing along the Earne River. She had long kept a box inside full of her belongings, lying in a corner out of the way of the spare parts and machinery of the mill.

As she spoke quietly in the voice in which a child explains things, a light gust of wind made the great spokes move, imperceptibly at first and then gathering speed. There was not a sound for a few moments and then we heard the rhythmic pulsing hiss and splash of water. Dorna's eyes closed, and her face in the glare of the moonlight became simple, bare, and blind. Something stirred deep within me.

The moments slipped away. The noise of the water rocked me into a trance. Her eyes did not open. Her head was pillowed on the lintel of the door, and she sat utterly relaxed, both hands loose and open in her lap. I began to wonder. What was wrong? Why was I wrong? Why did these people so carefully warn me? And then I wondered if Dorna like Nattana was a flirt, unconscious of it, or only half unconscious. I felt near to anger at this girl, who closed her eyes and dropped her guard so flagrantly and ostentatiously before me.

In pique, largely, I rose and went around behind the mill. The water was flowing down a narrow stone sluiceway in waves that dropped into the dark arm of the creek below. I sat down. It was good to be alone. At a sharp angle I could see the dark woods at the eastern end of Ronan's Island, which lay in the moonlight like a black quiet monster. Ahead the beacon showed a white triangle. I leaned back against the stone wall of the windmill and closed my eyes, and resolved that it would be Dorna who must come and find me.

I don't know how long it was, but it was long, before I heard

"John" called softly, and I knew it had been called before and I had not grasped that it was my name. I rose instantly and returned around the tower. Dorna rose as I came.

"It is damp," she said, "let us go home."

I smiled at her, and she looked intently into my face.

"I cannot take back what I said," she stated gravely, "but I am sorry, John."

Her eyes made me unsteady.

"It is nothing," I answered. "You are probably quite right."

"I want you to be happy in Islandia."

"I shall be happy," I said lightly.

"I shouldn't want you not to suffer," she added, "but I don't want you to suffer too much. I want to be a true friend. Remember that, John."

"That means a great deal to me," I answered. "And I wish you would believe that I am your friend, too."

"I think I shall," she said after a moment. "Come, let's go. I'm cold and stiff."

We returned across the pasture. And watching her silently moving at my side I asked myself if I could or would love her, finding no crisp answer in my blood or heart; for she was to me strangely simple and bare and a little hard, and beautiful as nothing else had ever seemed to be.

We came to the house door and paused a moment in the darkness.

"It was very good of you to ask me to walk," I said.

"It was an act of love (*amia*). I feel so much when I am at the windmill, I don't ask many people to go with me there." She drew herself up, and moved through the door into the light.

"I'm coming back a little later," she continued. "I think my uncle and brother would like to talk things over with you."

She smiled vaguely and went up the stairs, while I turned leftward and sought the great round hall.

There, when I came into the center of the room, three men, instead of the two I expected, emerged in the firelight. The third was a slim tall man of about fifty-five, with a long oval face, a wide mouth, overhung by a thick brush of a mustache over a rather loose chin. His eyes, the color of Lord Dorn's, a light brown, lay under heavy eyebrows. It was a face almost grotesque, caricaturing that of my host by overaccentuation of the noticeable features, but nevertheless it was kindly, intelligent, keen, and consciously humorous.

"Dorn, of Grase Bay," said its owner, smiling in a way that won me and yet made it hard not to laugh. In return I named myself and took my place before the fire.

Once he had named himself I knew this man to be a collateral of my hosts, a noble himself also, being a judge, and third of the family. He had been on his way to Doring Town to hold court, having come from Winder, the fiord province south of us, and had stopped for the night.

Next day we four were to sail to Doring Town, and I would not return again until April 6th. It was arranged that Dorna should meet me at Doring on my return and sail me back to the Island in her boat; and I looked forward to this as the climax of the days of traveling ahead of me.

After some chat Dorna entered, a paper in her hand. This she showed to her great-uncle, and after he had gone over it she brought it to me. The paper was heavy like parchment, and drawn upon it in the blackest of ink was a sketch map of my route to Lord Farrant's with all the intricate places indicated and the places where I was to stop marked. Her comments were colloquial and amusing. It was beautifully done and I thanked her as best I could, while she regarded me with pleased and teasing eyes. Then she abruptly left us.

9

The Marsh Duck

NEXT MORNING we left for Doring Town and after spending the night there I set out alone for Farrant. My trip was uneventful and I accomplished what the Dorns and I had planned.

The climax of my trip—my visit to Lord Farrant in his ancient castle above the ocean—left me somewhat subdued. He was old and very feeble, with bright, dark eyes, and for a man on the eve of death he was contented. He had listened with grave courtesy—although he himself supported the Dorns—to my ideas on politics; that a country so civilized as Islandia in a world growing so small could not avoid commercial contacts; and he had told me of the history of his family who had lived for nine hundred years in the same spot, of their *tanrydoon* with the Dorns. These were bare facts, but behind them was something so ancient and so powerful that I was dazed. Lord Farrant had, in some subtle way, made me feel the reality of a great inheritance, an inheritance I did not completely understand.

During the two weeks on the road I was in a fever of impatience to have the trip over, and the last days of travel seemed weary and long.

It was dark when I came to the ferry at Doring Town. Over the water the yellow lights of Doring glowed in design like the aftersparks of fireworks. I had to wait. Fak hung his head. I was tired out.

An hour later, giving Fak to the stableman, I shouldered my saddlebag and climbed up the steep way to the Lord's House, the Dorns' official residence in Doring. I went to my room unobserved, changed and bathed, and went out to seek my hosts. My heart came into my throat. I entered the living room and saw Dorna, and she seemed at once very plain with her skinned-back hair, and exactly what I hoped to see.

Dorn was absent; the judge had gone to Upper Doring; and besides Dorna only Lord Dorn remained. They were sitting before an open fire, doing nothing. He greeted me kindly and sent her off to see about my supper, and as she passed she looked me in the eyes without a change of expression.

After supper, which I had alone, I rejoined them, sitting together as quietly as before. There was a mystery or secret which they shared, for it was some moments before they could bring me into their ken, and they were almost awkward in doing so. The great dark room was uncannily still to tired nerves. I felt obscure forces working around me, exerting a pressure upon me in some nameless direction; and I heard my own voice as a stranger's. I told them in detail about all my experiences.

On first seeing Lord Dorn, I had doubted his greatness and ability, contrasting him to Lord Mora. Now some new element figured, something not ordinarily estimated in making such comparisons, a quality, a power, pressing for admission into my brain.

Dorna departed in her usual abrupt fashion. Speaking for her, her great-uncle said that it was planned that she and I leave after breakfast, so that there was no need of a hasty rising.

I went to bed and lay trying to bring into the focus of reason the shifting emotions I had experienced. They existed, that was all I knew, and affected by them was my feeling toward Dorna, different from any other feeling I had ever had. It, also, existed, beautiful yet also bare and plain, without mystery, not happy nor unhappy, yet full of tension. And as I sank into sleep it lay in my mind tangible and hard, and I felt it all night, a presence in me.

I woke to a bright room, not because the sun was high but because the sky was filled with light thin clouds that held and diffused a white glow. The warm air that drifted into my window smelled fresh. The distant water of the river was pale and shining. I washed and dressed to look my best, for the day I had looked forward to had come. The wind was light, and I was glad, for we would not reach the Island quickly.

The others had already breakfasted. The servant said that Lord Dorn would like to say good-bye to me before I started, and that Dorna was at the gate in her boat ready to start whenever I was. Therefore I ate in haste and immediately afterward sought my host in his office in the southwest wing. He was in conference with half a dozen men, but seeing me through the open door came out to me. I told him I was going and expressed my thanks for his hospitality and kindness.

He smiled quietly.

"We all love (*amia*) you, John," he said. "We are glad you are one of us. Remember that you are always free to come and stay and go whenever and as long as you please. Don't wait until we invite you. Think as the Islandians do, who have *tanrydoon*." He paused. "I am quite sure Lord Mora will prevent any false understanding as to your being seen in the Lor Pass with my nephew and the others. I advise you to visit Lord Mora as soon as you can. See the other side of the country."

Awkwardly I stumbled over my good-bye and went outdoors into the diffused white glare.

At last!

My saddlebags had already been carried to the boat. I ran down through the gardens, thrilled by their beauty, my heart beating. The gate was open and beyond was the harbor, almost glassy. I passed through and saw to one side Dorna's boat, its sail already up. She herself was sitting on the deck, utterly relaxed, patiently waiting; but when I approached she looked up and saw me, and slowly rose.

"Come on board," she said sleepily. I obeyed. We cast off the moorings, and at her bidding I shoved off at the bow. "I don't know where we are going," she added. "There isn't any wind and there won't be. Do you mind? I don't."

"I don't either," I answered.

"I'd rather not drift around Doring Town all day," she continued, "but perhaps the tide will carry us past. After that . . ." She went to the tiller and gave it a shove, and the boat slowly turned. "I like the marsh. Maybe you will."

We sat down side by side. Dorna leaned back against the coaming, her finger tips on the ball at the end of the tiller. Inch by inch we moved away from the wharf, the sail hanging loose, but an occasional gurgle sounding under the bow.

The day had begun.

Dorna's boat was perhaps twenty-one feet long on the water and about twenty-seven over all. The hull was a dark brown, highly varnished. She was decked all over, but the deck was neither painted nor varnished. The rail of the coaming, about a foot high, was painted white and so were the two curving spars, rising from the sides a little forward of amidships, which made the wishbone mast. The great spar that hung from their apex was, however, highly varnished and the big sail was a buff-yellow, very fine and soft, not made of canvas but of linen and wool. It was too rich a piece of cloth, as all Islandian sails seemed to me. Amidships was a hatch, from which a ladder led below. Just forward and aft of this were low skylights. Except for these, the rigging, an anchor forward, a grapnel, and coils of rope, the deck was without furniture. The freeboard was at least two feet amidship but she had some sheer fore and aft. Her name, translated into English, was "marsh duck"; and because Dorna herself liked the foreign sound of these words and so spoke of the boat herself, I think of her as the *Marsh Duck*.

Dorna was hatless, her hair brushed back so tightly that I wondered it did not draw her eyes into slits. She wore a linen blouse of light orange open at the throat with a wide collar and her skirt was the color of the sail, of the same material but a little finer. It flared rather widely but was quite short. She had a long, loose, sleeveless jacket of white linen. Her feet were shod with brown leather sandals, but she wore no stockings. Because we sat on the deck, with our legs straight before us, her ankles were prominent, neatly crossed, bare, smooth, each with its little round anklebones. They were tanned a delicate brown, with the veins towards the toes showing in faintly blue lines near the surface.

The confused sky was bright. The intermingled clouds and patches of blue were never the same, and the whole cast a glare, reflected back by the pale smooth water, which made us both sit with squinting eyes. A breath—it was no more—blowing from the Island carried us slowly out of the little harbor, but died at its mouth. We hung motionless. Behind us the terraced heights of Doring Island were mirrored, each hot wall, house, bank of flowers, and tree, having its cool inverted counterpart. We did not even drift. Slow silent moments passed, and then gradually we swung around in a complete circle, the current or tide caught us, and we moved, now stern now bow first down the river, so slowly that we seemed to lie for long minutes without movement before each bit of shore.

"The *Marsh Duck*," said Dorna, "has sweeps which I ought to have brought, but I am always falling over them. I hope the tide does not turn while we are here." Then she had a spasm of energy and churned the water with the rudder.

The ferry passed us, rowed by two vigorous men. We rocked gently in her wake. We looked under the two beautiful arches that join Doring Island to the rest of Doring Town and then little by little we passed and were abreast of the sea wall.

"I wish we would drift alongside," she said. "Then you could tow the *Marsh Duck.*" She smiled at the name, and her eyes quickened, and she went below returning with a piece of board about three feet long and six inches wide, slightly curved—a loose piece of the cabin flooring, which could be taken up and the bottom reached. She began to paddle with it, but work of this sort was my job and she let me take it from her.

A moment later she came and leaned over me, so close that I felt her breath, and gently removed the board from my hands. We were both kneeling on the deck opposite each other. Without a word she rove a bit of twine through the hole in the board.

"Your wrist," she said.

I held out my hand wondering. She tied the twine to my wrist. Her hands were beautiful. Then her eyes, wide open, looked into mine.

"If you dropped it," she said gravely, "we might never get it."

I could breathe again when she moved away.

I worked hard and sweat gathered, but at last the *Marsh Duck* crept toward the wall, steered by Dorna. When we came alongside she had a rope ready. I climbed on the coaming and when I had pulled myself up the mast a little way, and stepped through an opening between the battlements, she threw the rope.

The openings between the battlements were not wide and could be jumped. I managed to progress, drawing the boat after me, while Dorna remained on board to steer. Whenever I looked back, she smiled. She was amused, and so was I—and also very hot.

The only real difficulty came at the four towers which we passed. When I reached these she hauled in the rope and coiled it; I ran around the tower; and she flung the rope back to me—throwing it as a girl throws but with dexterity and skill.

Fishermen sitting on the wall and loiterers watched us, taking it all in, but they did not even smile at us. Perhaps others had done as we were doing, or perhaps they were naturally polite. Some of them Dorna knew and greeted by their names and they answered her as "Dorna."

Soon after we had passed the last tower the rope slackened and she called. The *Marsh Duck* was moving by herself. When she came alongside the wall I jumped aboard, hot but well content. Here at the lower end of the tower near open water, a faint breath of east wind and a strengthening of the tide sent us onward with a soft gurgle under the bow.

While thus slowly passing the lower or southeast end of Doring Town, Dorna asked what we should do. If we followed the Inner Arm of the Doring River, the usual route to Dorn Island, we had no strong tide to contend with and only twenty-three miles to go—but we probably would find no wind to propel us; if we followed the South Arm directly out into the marsh, we would find whatever wind there was—but we would meet the full strength of the flood tide soon to turn and have nearly thirty miles to cover.

"You decide," she said. But how could I?

"I don't know these waters."

"What would you like to do?"

"What would you like, Dorna?"

She watched me for a moment.

"We will follow the South Arm. You haven't seen it."

She ported the tiller and our bow swung to the west instead of the south.

A point of the marshes comes to within three-quarters of a mile of the town and is the nearest land. We passed slowly through this opening into a spacious expanse of open water, several miles wide and long. Its northern shore was forested, but westward the forest line receded inland from another projecting marshy point.

"It is good sailing," she said. "There is usually plenty of wind and the water is smooth, but the tide!"

A steamer lay anchored, so natural to me that I thought nothing of it. She was a vessel of perhaps two thousand tons, rather weather-beaten, not heavily laden, yet not empty. She was a tramp perhaps . . . But what right had a commercial steamer here?

I asked what she was.

"She is German," Dorna answered, "and put in here in distress. My great-uncle thought her distress unreal, but she had permission from Lord Mora to come up the river and to stay here until some new parts for her engines arrive. She has been here a month already. Her crew spend much time fishing in their launch. That is all I know . . . I am sure there is more to it than that, but my uncle won't tell me!'' Her eyes flashed.

We sailed within a hundred feet. A man leaning over the rail in a white uniform waved to us and called something in bad Islandian.

"Did you understand?" I asked.

"He wants us to come aboard," she said, and raising her voice she cried, "Not today!"

"Come some other time," he shouted back. "Don't forget."

"I won't!" she answered.

He walked along the deck shouting what sounded like pleasantries.

"I should like to find out what they are up to," she said, when we were out of hearing.

Her calling to a man who obviously wanted to pick her up was not what an American girl would have done. Islandian girls were strange. . . .

The sun was warm and the light airs, off the farm lands to the east, carried land odors and heat, flowering the water here and there with sparkling ripples, while in other places the surface was as smooth as glass. The sheet was slack but the sail remained quietly distended, and we moved steadily though slowly. Dorna steered with her finger tips, her eyes half-closed.

I began a calculation. We had covered two or three miles of our journey of thirty and were moving at the rate of three an hour. It was half-past ten . . . Nine hours more . . . Dorn Island by half-past seven . . . But soon the tide would turn, and Dorna had said there would be no wind. It would probably be later than that.

The sun and glare were subduing, but my eyes, though not very wide awake and carrying little to the mind, were full of the bright picture before me—of Dorna with her bare, sandaled feet crossed at the ankles, her translucent slender fingers on the tiller, her figure outlined against a background of pale-blue shining water and dark-green marsh, her face looking forward or averted, and her skin with its inner orange glow showing no flaws even in the day's intense brightness. Her arched eyebrows were a dark, rich brown, her hair was so smoothly done that its darker brown bore but one glinting golden highlight, and her eyelashes were black against the even tone of her skin.

The naked simplicity and plainness of the way she did her hair, drawn tightly back from her forehead, was her only defect, but after a while it did not matter. She became too beautiful, and I shifted my position and looked elsewhere.

The river arm had narrowed and marshland was close to us on our right. The wind had increased; we were really sailing. We might not be out late after all.

But after a while I looked at the shore again and we had not moved.

"The tide has turned," she said. Her voice came out of an utter stillness.

Time passed.

There was always the impression of pleasant motion when I watched the water, and of standing still when I watched the land. Nevertheless we inched along, at last rounding a point with a wall on the further side, the only visible sign of man in many miles. The channel had narrowed to a quarter of a mile. We hugged the shore. Further out the water raced, and when the river widened again we moved a little faster.

Two or three miles beyond, the wind died out abruptly, the great spar creaked and slowly swung inboard, and our bow turned shoreward and then upstream.

Dorna rose and ran forward, there was a splash at the bow, and the anchor.had been cast before I was aware what was happening.

She watched the shore for a moment, paying out the line, nor would she let me help her.

Unless wind came again we were likely to remain here for four hours. When would we reach the Island? Could the marsh channels be navigated at night?

"Let's have lunch," she said, and with the movements of one accustomed she descended the ladder and twisted and ducked out of sight. I followed her.

Cabins opened forward and aft of the well beneath the hatch, and she called me into the latter. It was perhaps seven or eight feet square and five feet high with a bunk on either side, narrowing the floor space to less than three feet. Further aft was a cupboard and beneath the bunks were lockers. Ports on either side and a skylight above lit the interior. Reflections from the sun on the water played liquidly on the low roof overhead.

Dorna, kneeling before the cupboard on one bunk, produced three large bottles of wine, a dozen meat rolls (two making a meal), two large, lidded bowls of salad, a basket of fruit, a loaf of bread, and a box of small cakes. With all this before her, she sat back upon her heels.

"I wonder if there is enough," she said.

"Isn't there more than enough?"

"For three meals perhaps, but how about dinner tomorrow?"

There was a subtle jar in my heart.

She apportioned the provisions for our lunch and put the rest back, produced plates, cutlery, and glasses, and served me. We began to eat, sitting upon the bunks opposite to each other.

"When do you think we will reach the Island?" I asked as casually as possible.

"Tomorrow afternoon perhaps—not before."

There was silence.

"You look frightened," she cried. "Do you mind?"

"Oh no! I am glad, but I did not know. I was taken by surprise."

Her eyes were watching, but mine lacked daring.

"Have I done wrong by you again?" she said in a voice that seemed to harbor a little annoyance.

"Of course not, Dorna."

"Maybe I've been selfish. Do tell me if I have done wrong. Sometimes we don't seem to understand each other at all! But I knew my brother would not reach home until tomorrow night. Of course we could have ridden to Earne and have been ferried over, but I had brought my boat specially to take you and I wanted to go back in her."

"So did I! Dorna, I wouldn't have wanted to ride."

"Are you sure?"

"Absolutely sure."

"But you did not think it would take so long?"

"No."

"Well, I did. Would you have come if you had known?"

"Of course I would, Dorna."

"Is anything wrong?"

"Of course not!"

She sighed a little.

"I don't think my uncle really objects," she said slowly. "He did ask me if I did not think it better to ride. I said 'no,' because he did not tell me what he meant by 'better.' If he had asked me whether I thought we would reach the Island today, I would have had to tell him the truth; but he did not ask that question and later he said to be sure to have enough to eat and drink on board."

She uttered a nervous little laugh.

"I wonder what he would have said if I had made it perfectly clear that we could not reach the Island today."

"I am glad you didn't," I dared and said.

"Really?" she cried, leaning forward.

"Of course!"

"I thought you might like it."

"Oh, I do."

It seemed better not to tell her that this would have been an unconventional if not an improper thing at home. Were Islandian standards different? . . . But perhaps we would spend the night at some marsh farm on the way. I could not trust myself to discuss what we were to do nor its propriety.

Here was a new Dorna and a disturbing one. She had been guilty of a subterfuge practiced upon her great-uncle. Perhaps he also had been guilty, but was accustomed to let her do as she pleased, spoiling her. His failure to object suggested that in Islandia the unconventionality was not so great. . . .

The *Marsh Duck* bobbed now and then in tide rips and at intervals the lapping of water sounded along her sides. All afternoon we sat in the cabin, each in a bunk with pillows behind our backs and our feet extended before us.

We talked about her brother's college days, and I told her what she had not known, his difficulties in his first year and his great popularity later. She in turn described what he had done when he came back to Islandia immediately after the defeat of his great-uncle on the matter of the Mora Treaty, and how these two were working as their ancestor, Dorn XXV, had worked in the 'forties. Then with momentary but strong feeling she cried that she wanted to help them and was only half-accepted and often repulsed. It was flattering to be told so much. I asked her to tell of earlier days. She described and made vivid the happiness of life at Dorn Island when her parents still lived, and then told how the drowning of them and of Lord Dorn's son altered and blackened the lives of everyone. Dorn had never spoken as freely as she was doing.

She asked me to tell about my coming to Islandia, and settled herself to listen, crossing her ankles and leaning her head back. Seeing more throat and chin than face, I began at the beginning and told her how I had come to learn Islandian, and then of life in Uncle Joseph's office. She asked many questions and I was glad to satisfy her curiosity as to details of life in New York. But when I came to the subject of the consular examinations and of the way in which I was appointed, I became confused, for the part I had played seemed worse than vacillation, and a betrayal of her brother as well.

She sat up and watched me; and I told her of these feelings. Leaning back again she said that when it was known that an American minister or consul might come, her brother had expressed a wish that I be the man, although not thinking that there was much chance of it.

"I don't see anything that need trouble you at all," she added. "You surely don't think that he believes that you should not have come."

"No," I answered. "He has reassured me."

"Then what is there to worry about?"

"Do you think I did right to come?"

"I?" she exclaimed, and her cheeks became pink. "You yourself know, don't you?"

"I am not at all sure."

"You ought to be!"

It was like a rebuke, and my face was as red as hers. She bit her lip.

"We don't understand each other," she said, and dropped back on her pillow. A moment later, however, she cured it all by a smile.

"Tell me what changes foreign trade would bring," she said.

"A good many," I answered. "It is rather hard to tell it all."

"Tell me part."

"Foreign vessels would come with goods to sell," I suggested.

"What sort of goods?"

I mentioned agricultural implements, knowing something about these things, their functions, and their costs, from work at Uncle

Joseph's, and I stressed their adaptability for communal use and the time they saved the farmer.

"They increase the output of his farm," I said.

"Why should his output be increased?" she answered.

"He can make more money."

"But what is the use of that?"

"There would be greater power to enjoy life."

"Do you think so? There is no lack in that power now, Johnlang. But I don't want to seem prejudiced. You said these machines would save time. That's worth while. If ever your countrymen try to sell us agricultural implements let them sell those that save time. They will be listened to!"

"I'll remember that," I said, thinking of the suggestion of Uncle Joseph that I might be an agent in Islandia for American firms.

"No," she said, "don't remember it!"

For a while longer we discussed this subject, and then she asked me what I thought about those who wanted concessions to develop natural resources, and how the concessions would be worked out.

"Suppose that a concession were granted to work a copper mine," I said, thinking of Henry G. Müller. "The mines would produce raw copper."

"Where would it go?"

"Abroad mostly."

"Good-bye to our copper."

"It would be paid for, Dorna. And if the mine was owned by the proprietors of a province, the money could be used to develop the province. There would be better roads, schools, libraries, finer public buildings, electric lighting and power, railroads, lots of things. . . ."

She asked me to describe these things, and I was as glowing as I could be.

"But no one may want any of these things," she said. "Of course it is simpler to just press a button to make a light, but all the complications of wires stretched everywhere . . ." She sighed.

"There are two sides to it," I said. "You would get used to wires."

"Never!" she cried with a laugh. "Threads going everywhere tying everyone to someone else!"

"It isn't so bad in practice, Dorna."

"It's not our way," she answered. "And I don't see the gain. We work some of the time to make candles. Someone else would have to work to make wires and burning things and mills. There would be just as much work."

"But each person could spend more time on one thing."

She shuddered.

"Why should he?"

"You can accomplish more doing one thing. You become more skillful."

"But you touch life in fewer ways."

"You have more leisure to touch life in ways that aren't work."

"We have all of that we need," she said.

What was the answer? She gave me no time to think it out.

"Do you think it good for one man here and there to get rich, the man who happens to own land where there is a mine?"

"Of course there is a bad side to that," I conceded, "but remember that greater wealth in a few men means greater wealth in all. The money received would be invested—"

"What would it be invested in?" she asked.

"Mills, mines, electric light plants, railroads."

"Foreign railroads?"

"And Islandian ones in time."

"These men would get richer and richer."

"They might, but they might lose money. Some enterprises would be failures."

"Why have enterprises that are failures?"

"It can't be helped, Dorna."

"We don't have failures unless there is a landslide or a great storm or a very bad year for crops. We don't have failures as a result of starting out to do things people don't want and aren't ready for."

"Most enterprises would not be failures. These men as a class would steadily become richer. At any rate they would be causing new enterprises in Islandia and everywhere . . . But there is another side. There is a need for change in other countries, Dorna. There is great poverty. The value of this mine going there will help to cure that."

"But when the mine is exhausted?"

"Other things will have been started."

"Until the whole world is used up! And won't there be hundreds more people than there ought to be, all living by exhausting what the world has, and all doomed to die when the world goes barren?"

"No," I said. "Science will keep ahead, finding new sources of supply."

"That seems to me a very long gambling chance," she answered. "But you have said one true thing. We here must take into account what the world outside wants. If it wants us to play its gambling game we may have to do so, or else have everything taken from us. But I don't see how foreigners can play such a game. They cannot care for their families as we care for them. With us it is not just our parents and grandparents and children and grandchildren, but all that are back of us and all that are to come, little Dorns and Dornas and Langs and Langas hundreds and hundreds of years from now. Foreigners don't think of working to make a place for them that will be at least as happy as the place they live in. They are quite willing to start some new, terrible, changeful thing, not caring about them at all or else trusting blindly to luck. That is the difference between them and us—some of us. If we go on here as we have been, and are let alone, life hundreds of years from now will be as it is now; and life now, with growing things all about us and changing weather and lovely places kept beautiful and new people growing up, is too rich for us already, too rich to endure sometimes. We haven't half exhausted it, and we cannot—we cannot so long as young people are born and grow up and learn new things and have new ideas. All that is to us the vital thing, John, and the changes foreigners propose—railroads to carry us about, new machines to till the soil, electric lights, and all that—are just superficial things, and not worth the price we have to pay for them in changing our whole way of living, in threatening our children with the chance of ruin!"

She was out of breath, laughing a little but also very serious. I wondered if her words were not a speech learned by heart. It was exciting to see her excited and glowing.

"You assume that Islandia will be happier unchanged," I said. "But is that proved?"

"To us it is perfectly clear, but it isn't clear to the Moras. But it will be proved someday! I know it will. But if you want to beat us, Johnlang, talk about saving time and not about making money."

Her confidence in the ultimate victory of her side was more than dismaying. The possibility of exclusion from Islandia made me slightly sick.

"What do you think is going to happen?" I asked.

"I know what we are trying to make happen," she answered, and she must have read my thoughts.

"It is odd," she said, "that we are fighting for something that will mean your banishment. We have thought of that often. Do you see now why my brother and I don't want you to love Islandia too much, nor an Islandian woman, which is the same thing."

"Is it the same thing?" I asked.

It seemed much darker than it had been.

"It is the same thing—if she is a real Islandian."

There was pain in this.

"Suppose I am banished," I said, "maybe you and your brother would come to the United States."

"It is very improbable. Even you do not make me want to go there, but you do make me think of it. But you could visit us again. The Hundred Law allows you one year in ten. We don't want to repeal that law. You would never lose your right in our house, even if it were illegal for you to stay in Islandia more than that."

"I understand much better," I said. "You and your brother are quite right; and I hope I shall never be so anxious to stay that I shall let it affect my judgment as to what ought to be."

"That is surely impossible!" she cried, as though surprised, and in her surprise was a rebuke, and I knew that I had been a little bitter.

"You perform your duty as consul," she added. "We don't mind that. We understand of course . . . Would you mind seeing how the wind is?"

The western sun was entangled in soft masses of gray-white clouds. The darkness that I had felt in the cabin was real. The marsh on all sides was empty. The nearest object breaking its flatness was a low line of trees, southeast, four or five miles away. Another settlement was visible at a longer distance, southwest, but to the north nothing could be seen except the eternal dark plain, bluish green, extending under the cloudy vault of the sky.

I searched for wind as directed. The channel was without a ripple, but air stirred somewhere for I felt it elusively on my cheek. I went forward and tried the anchor rope and found it slack. Evidently the tide was about to turn. Indeed, Dorna had timed it within a few minutes, for as I stood there the *Marsh Duck* began to swing, and with this change came another. Northeastward in the narrows two miles away a boat was approaching with distended sails, slowly but perceptibly moving, and beyond her the water seemed darker.

I waited a little longer and then went to the hatchway and called the news to Dorna.

She came on deck. I raised the anchor, and we moved off down the channel to the southwest. It was nearly five o'clock and the sun was due to set before six. In its battle, however, with the clouds, it was winning, and long bright beams radiated from rents in the gray masses; some fell in a long slant on the marsh making the grass there a vivid dark-green, and lightening air and water. The wind came up to us and sent us along faster than we had yet gone, perhaps three miles an hour. This, with the current adding another two, made me afraid that after all we might reach Dorn Island that same night.

I remarked that we were going well.

"The wind will drop at sunset," she said and her eyes flashed. My heart became uneasy.

"If this were the United States, Dorna, if your country adopted foreign inventions, they would send out a motorboat from the Island to tow us in."

"I am glad it is Islandia," she answered.

"Don't you like the idea of a motorboat?"

She laughed and said nothing.

We slipped along steadily, outdistancing the heavier boat behind us. When the sun shone it was warm, but the moment it vanished the air grew damp and chilly. Dorna gave me the tiller and went below. I could hear now and then the sound of her moving about but only faintly, and I felt alone—alone under a vast dome of sky amidst an utterly flat world. And it began to grow darker almost in jerks, like the coming of night upon the stage. The wind freshened and the sheet tightened. For a few moments it was exciting, for I had the boat to handle by myself, and the wind being behind, the great sail was in danger of a jibe.

Dorna's head appeared suddenly.

"John," she said, "it's going to be quite damp tonight. There won't be any open fire. Wouldn't you rather stop at a settlement? We pass the Amans' quite soon."

"Would you?"

"I asked you."

"No," I said.

"We won't then."

The head vanished.

A little later the sun won the fight and emerged below the sail, a red round ball on the level of the marsh. The light it cast had an orange tinge, and the sail with this glow behind it became luminous. The water caught the light on every ripple, so that the whole marsh was shot with long arrows of color and shadow. Steering Dorna's boat I watched the glow soften and the sail slowly turn a dark-blue when the last flaming edge of the sun disappeared.

As she predicted, the wind grew less, the ripples died down, the gurgles lost their rapidity, and we moved with the tide past two shadowy settlements back in the marsh a mile or so from the channel. Darkness came steadily; the shore was indistinct, and the windings deceitful; but the water retained a luminous glisten and I steered as near to the center as possible. A strange yellow glow was dancing along at our side, and this after a moment's wonder I knew to be light coming from the cabin through the porthole. It became damp indeed.

At last Dorna appeared, scarcely distinguishable, and studied the shore; then she came and took the helm from me, and at her bidding I drew in the sheet. We headed shoreward and a faint channel opened, into which we moved slowly, anchored, dropped and loosely furled the sail—two shadows moving in the darkness.

And while we were at work tying the stops, my fingers quite cold, touched hers, warm and living. I worked on and so did she. And I felt that if our fingers touched again, I would take her hand.

When all was snug, she ducked below, calling me to come. In the cabin the four lanterned candles were dazzling. The bunk on my side was soft with blankets. Dorna was closing the door as I looked up at her, her hair loose and soft about her face. Her eyes met mine a moment and dropped, and her face reddened. She was utterly beautiful.

We ate supper almost in silence. The cabin was warm; within there was candlelight; outside there was dark sky, marsh, and water for limitless distances. Water now and then slapped the sides of the boat, but otherwise there was no sound but that of our own movements. Dorna was sedate and lovely in the candlelight, her face dreamy with inturned look, her bright, dark eyes with their black lashes strongly marked against the even color of her skin. Her stillness and that of the cabin and of the night enforced silence upon me also, and I scarcely dared to speak; each motion had to be considered and made slowly lest it be noisy.

There was great peacefulness, and yet every once in a while consciousness of our situation intruded and, like a rock in a smooth swift stream, broke the even flow of my contentment. The unconventionality of our presence together all night in this little boat might be less in Islandia than at home, but Dorna had been confused when telling of her conversation with her uncle. And the blankets were spread in the two bunks as though she intended that I sleep in one and she in the other! Oughtn't I to assert myself and sleep outside or in the other cabin, on the hard floor if need be? Didn't I owe it to her? Should I let her do this? At home it would all be very clear. . . .

There came a moment's dizziness and a baffling ignorance of where I was. Dorna, making no sounds and with inturned eyes, was like a painted doll. This was not home, not the United States, but another land. A dark, flat marsh was all around me. . . .

I spoke.

"Dorna, do you know—"

"Know what?" her voice was low.

Conversation was launched, and must be continued.

"I have been thinking. You seem quite sure that your side will win."

Her eyes came upon me, and the inturned look lessened. She nodded her head.

"How about the majority that Lord Mora has had in the council?"

She seemed to wake up. She smiled and showed her even white teeth.

"I'll tell you all about that!" she said; but first she must clear away the remains of our supper, bidding me stay where I was. She moved about with an expression of inner amusement, bright color in her cheeks. I waited in suspense, unnerved by what I had been thinking.

"Let's be comfortable if we are going to talk," she said when she had finished, and made herself so, her feet crossed and a pillow behind her back.

The first vote, when Lord Mora was authorized to conclude the treaty with the Germans, was not much of a surprise to her great-uncle. The war had been successful; Lord Mora was considered by many as the proper man to conclude it and to make peace terms. Her great-uncle, Dorn XXVI of Lower Doring, Marriner XV of Winder, Farrant XII of Farrant (whom I had visited), Some XI of Loria, and Fain II of Islandia Province (these being stalwart supporters of Dorn policies), together with Hyth IV of Upper Doring, Dasel III of Vantry, and Drelin IV of Deen, nine in all, had voted not to entrust the making of the peace terms to Lord Mora. On his side were himself, Mora XXV of Miltain, Calwin VI of The City, Robban II of Alban, Baile XI of Inerria, Borderney V of Brome, his most consistent followers, together with Benn of Carran, Tole of Niven, Farnt of Hern, Dax of Dole, and—a disappointment to her great-uncle—Stellin V of Camia, and Bodwin VI of Bostia, only two more than Lord Dorn had had. So among the Lords of Provinces Lord Mora had as small a majority as was possible. But, of course, these eleven were increased by the votes of most of the military lords: Dasel II, the Marshal, Bodwin VI, a general, Earne II, a general, Branly, a general; and of most of the judicial lords, Belton XVII, Chief Judge, Granery V, a judge, Tory V, a judge, and Chessing, a judge. This made Lord Mora's vote nineteen, and at his suggestion the then King Tor XVII also voted, making twenty in all.

Of these, Dorna said, only Earne II was an irrevocable follower of Lord Mora. On the other hand, her great-uncle's nine were increased to fourteen by the votes of all the naval lords, Farrant XIII, the Admiral, Dorn IV, commodore, and Marriner II, commodore, and of one judge, Dorn III, and one general, Some, all of whom were committed to exclusion policies except possibly Dorn the Judge.

Between this vote and that in which the treaty with its provisions for admitting foreign representatives to Islandia was ratified, Dasel II died, Bodwin VI became marshal, and Mora, a brother of the premier, was appointed general to succeed Dasel II; Some XI died, and his nephew Some XII was elected to his place. This added one irrevocable Mora man to their ranks, but otherwise caused no change in the parties.

Three men who had supported Lord Dorn shifted to the Mora side at the time of the latter vote, but this was not because they believed that the treaty was right but because they felt that, Lord Mora having made it, it should be confirmed and his proposals given a trial. These were Dorn III, the Judge, Drelin IV, and Dasel III.

Since then the Dorn party had suffered further losses. Some, the general, retired and Brome XIII, probably a Mora follower, took his place.

She became animated. It looked very black, didn't it, she asked, but wait! Drelin, Dasel III, Dorn the Judge, Stellin, and Bodwin of Bostia were probably all against foreign trade. That alone would mean eighteen Mora votes and fifteen Dorn votes. But wait a little longer! There was doubt as to Bodwin the general, Granery, and Belton. A shift to the Dorn side of two of these would mean a victory. If only one shifted, then the king could make it a tie, and a majority was necessary to put into effect Lord Mora's plans for foreign trade!

"It isn't black at all," she said, but I wondered. Suppose some Dorn follower did the shifting? Suppose the king voted with Lord Mora?

"How does your king stand?" I asked.

She looked at me quickly and laughed.

"I don't know, but he won't do as his father did and vote merely as Lord Mora tells him. Not he!"

The king ceased suddenly to be a political figure and no more. Dorna's manner brought back all that the Mlles. Perier and Dorn had said about him. There was brightness in her eyes and she was watching me.

"Your brother told me that he was handsome and dangerous," I said.

She clasped her hands.

"He is! He is!" she cried. "There is no other man like him. Oh, we all of us have *apiata* for Tor."

Apia means sexual desire. So I thought. It was true that she had used a diminutive. My face was hot.

"He for us, too," she added quickly as though to get it said, and she went on rapidly and I wished I were surer of the exact significance of Islandian words. "But he has such an opportunity! His father really was stupid, but his mother wasn't. The Banwins are often very intelligent if a little unstable. He is intelligent. What will he do with it? At present he is always on the go with his friend Stellin. He does only what business he has to do. No one knows if he is really interested in anything—except us. He does seem to like us . . . Oh, he likes high mountains and the outer islands. He likes danger. He appears at Dorn Island unexpectedly on his way to Ferrin, or Kernia, or Carnia, or the mountains, or anywhere."

So the king came to Dorn Island and liked girls, and they felt *apiata* toward him.

"The Hyths said he came to see them with Stellin, who is their cousin." Perhaps Dorna also was a cousin.

"He does not go there as a friend of Stellin," she said, sharply.

"I think he comes to see Nekka," I began, and stopped, wondering if it were any business of mine.

"Very likely," she said, and quickly changed the subject. "Didn't you like the Hyths?"

"Very much."

She watched me for some moments, and then said, "Tor comes to Dorn Island three or four times a year. It is to see me mainly, I suppose. There is a fact for you, Johnlang. But don't think I want to marry him."

I laughed hesitatingly, not knowing how to take this frank statement, but her last words were a great relief.

"Nor anyone," she added, "not yet."

There was a pause.

"How about you, Johnlang? Do you want to marry anyone?"

Before the inner eye ran the figures of my American girl friends, of Nattana, and then Dorna. What was the truth?

"No," I answered, "not really, but there are several girls who, I think, would make me happy."

"For life?" she asked, sitting up suddenly, surprise in her voice.

"Why, yes."

We looked into each other's eyes. Hers dimmed those of all other women, and I tried to make mine say that she was the only one.

She smiled a little and looked away, leaning back again. . . .

What exactly did *apiata* mean, used by this girl with whom I was to spend the night and who confessed to having felt it? Did the diminutive *"ta"* added to *apia* change its significance? . . . There was tremulous suspense and in me a wish to go on as we were going.

"Well," she said, her eyes bright upon mine for a moment, "I'll admit several men have made my heart beat, but there certainly are not that many who could make me happy for life! . . . We have a good deal to learn about each other, you and I."

"Yes," I answered, "there are differences." She nodded her head. "It is partly language, Dorna. I miss the meaning of some words." But when it came to asking the meaning of *apiata* the word stuck in my throat . . . Several men had made her heart beat. . . .

"You understand and speak very well," she said, as though bored. "What differences are there?"

"Hytha Nattana thinks foreigners have pale-pink emotions! She believes we differ from Islandians in that respect. What do you think, Dorna?"

She seemed to be pondering her answer. She smiled, looked at me, was about to speak, dropped her eyes, and said nothing. Her expression changed and became amused, then mocking and elfish. As before when she appeared in this way it was a shock to see her, but now it also stirred me, teased me. Then abruptly her features softened. She turned her head toward me and was relaxed, all but her hands which began to twist and play together in her lap.

"Do you think your emotions are pale and pink?" she asked. "I wouldn't have said that, John."

"Why, of course not!" I cried. "But it made me wonder. What do you think about foreigners, Dorna?"

Her eyes were upon mine, intent and still, dark and very deep, but her face was all gentle submissiveness. Her eyes were tender, denying me nothing, and she stared until I was dizzy and hot, blood throbbing in my temples. Her nervous hands invited mine to quiet them. Her lips were parted.

"Dorna!" I whispered, leaning forward.

Her eyes widened a little but without hostility or surprise. . . .

Then I was sitting back in my bunk, with heart racing as the screw of a vessel races in the air, powerless to drive her forward, racking her structure. I could not touch Dorna, and the desire to do so died in the shattering of nerves and strength.

She had turned sideways, with knees drawn up and heels bent back, and her face looked up at the ceiling. She was overpowering in the vigor of her beauty.

"I don't know whether Nattana is right or wrong," she said coolly, as though unaware of what had happened. "You are almost the only foreigner I have known—young man, I mean. Maybe the

175

life you lead in the United States makes emotions more scattered and thin than does the life we lead here."

"Why, Dorna?"

"Oh, I haven't worked it out. I am guessing. You yourself said there were differences. That must be because the life is different . . ." Her voice was uninterested. There was a long silence and then she said suddenly, "What will it do to you to live here?"

"I don't know."

"If I were you I would stay American."

"You have said that before."

"I am sorry! I didn't want to hurt you again."

Water lapped against the sides of the boat. One of the candles had guttered out and the outer damp was penetrating the cabin . . . The impulse to move to Dorna had been unexpected, coming like a summer storm sudden and violent. Now there was quiet again. . . .

Dorna's face was turned away, and all I saw of it was the bright curve of her smooth cheek, warm and sweet. To be drawn to her as I had been was an odd experience. After all, the rules imposed by convention had some reason—we ought not to be here together. . . .

"Shall we step ashore for a while before we go to bed?" Her voice was sleepy, but startling. On deck a damp mist muffling the boat added blindness to darkness. She went forward and I followed, feeling along the rail with my foot.

What was she doing? She was invisible but there were faint sounds and a gentle splashing. I stared at where I thought she was.

"Can I help you, Dorna?"

"No, thank you, John."

Her voice was all there was of her. It came from a level with my waist.

"I wish we had the sweeps," she said, "but we will probably drift against one shore or the other."

"What are you doing, Dorna?"

"Paying out the anchor line."

"It ought to be my job."

"Why?"

"I am a man."

"Does that make a difference?"

"There are things men ought to do."

"This doesn't require a man's strength."

"But it is a man's kind of job."

There was a pause. The *Marsh Duck* was moving but almost imperceptibly.

"Are there men's jobs and women's jobs in your country?"

"The men feel that they ought to do the physical work on trips like this."

"But—" I could feel that her head was turned toward me. "How funny that is!" she said. "Is it the clothes your women wear?"

"Partly, perhaps."

"Of course men are often stronger," she pondered. "But I wonder if you are stronger than I am."

"I ought to be. I'm taller and a little bigger."

"You are slimmer for a man." After a moment she sighed. "Probably you could beat me in the end. You would wear me out. But I would give you a good fight. I am rather strong, Johnlang."

It was not a boast. I seemed to feel her strength in my senses.

There was a soft jar and a checking. Dorna brushed by me in the blackness, so that I felt her breath, her solidity. Her feet sounded on the deck, and a light laugh.

"I am ashore," came her voice from near the stern.

Feeling along the rail again, I went toward her.

"You can step ashore," she said farther off. "I've moored the boat with the grapnel."

The glow from the cabin lights made a faint yellow circle on a shelving bank of black earth and coarse blades of grass close to the side of the boat. I stepped from the rail upon the marsh and went onward. The blackness pressed upon my eyeballs. Dorna had already drifted away.

Silence was absolute. Flatness was ahead of me and on both sides. The *Marsh Duck* was my refuge. It was not well to go far. The chilly damp penetrated my clothes. . . .

Then, after a little while, the ground beneath my feet quivered in a rapid rhythm and there was a hollow sound. My heart leaped and raced and cold shudders went up into my hair. Footsteps, and then Dorna's voice:

"Where are you?"

"Here. What is that sound?"

"The marsh is hollow. Some are like that . . . Oh, did it frighten you?" She had come near, but was invisible.

"It startled me."

"I was running. I didn't think."

She moved toward the boat. A glow from the skylight made the mist immediately above it luminous. Against this paleness came her shadow, and then her feet sounded on the deck.

"Shall I cast off?" I called to her.

"Just as you like. No one will come aboard."

She was descending the hatchway.

Somehow it seemed more proper to remain attached to the shore.

Should I go down into the cabin? When once more on the deck of the *Marsh Duck,* I hesitated.

Moments slipped past. It was worse than awkward and embarrassing; there was tense distress. . . .

"Johnlang, aren't you coming to bed?"

Her voice sounded from the hatchway.

"I am coming, Dorna."

But I waited a little longer before descending and entering. I did not mean to look at her, but my eyes went instantly to her side of the cabin. She lay under the soft gray blankets, her head turned away. A bare arm was outside the covers.

Taking a candle and my saddlebags into the other cabin I undressed there. When I returned, Dorna looked up at me and smiled, her face already that of one half-asleep. Her arms lifted to the only candle that remained lighted. Hastily I climbed into my bunk, and nestled down in the soft blankets shivering from the chill that had come from damp air on my hot skin.

Darkness . . . I turned my face to the wall. On my eyeballs was imprinted the image of Dorna's lazy bare arm reaching up to the candle.

Her bunk rustled and there was a thump as she too turned over and nestled down.

"Good night, John," came her voice, innocent, sleepy, serene.

"Good night, Dorna," I answered, and my voice shook.

I thought that I heard a faint laugh or a sigh but I was not sure.

10

Return to Dorn Island

SLEEP WOULD NOT COME. Dorna on her side of the cabin did not stir again and made no sound, perhaps already asleep. On the planks close to my head water chuckled and lapped; died away; ceased; resumed again. Otherwise there was utter stillness—blind, deep darkness. The *Marsh Duck* was a frail but perfect shelter, shutting out the immense empty night. Though the bunk was hard, the blankets were soft as fleece and warm.

Dorna was sleeping in the same room with me! Of adventures like this I had dreamed. This was the reality, unbelievable, and therefore unreal again and like a dream. In the dreams all was perfect tunefulness; I was usually, as I was now, playing the part of a gentleman. To sleep in the same room with a girl was in itself enough. The girl was sweet—at my mercy, but safe and trusting. Dorna was safe, but her safety was in her own keeping as well as in mine. Other men, perhaps. . . .

At last, sleep began to weight my eyes and to muddle my thoughts. There was truth in the warning not to love an Islandian woman. In all that made them lovable they were my own sort, but they brought wonderment, confusion, pain, and glimpses of unfathomable deeps . . . I was sleeping in the same room with one of them . . . But why, oh why—if she wished me to follow the warnings that she had given me—had she taken me with her for so long, to eat with her, travel with her, and sleep in the same room with her?

She was too lovely, too dear already; she made my eyes burn and sting by her beauty. And yet . . . She was so dear, so enchanting, so kind to me . . . Sleep deepened. The blankets were soft and warm. I lay relaxed. . . .

179

My eyes opened with my face close to the planks. I was wide awake, conscious that day had come, bright day, filling the cabin with light. On the deck overhead was the brisk rapid tapping of footsteps . . . Dorna! She must be out already, I thought, and I sat up, in haste to dress; but deep in the pillow of her bunk lay a head the roundness of which was blurred by disheveled brown hair with bright gleams; and the blankets softly outlined Dorna's body, motionless, apparently asleep, so unprotected and abandoned as to hurt. As quietly as I could lest I waken her, I went to the cabin where I had left my clothes and quickly dressed.

Cool freshness! Overhead the mist was so thin that the blue of the sky was visible. Around the boat the pale damp air was suffused with white glowing light, beneath which fifty or sixty yards of marsh were to be seen, a dark, rich green. A big dog, his tail between his legs, was loping off into the denser air. I had mistaken his pattering feet for Dorna's. I would tell her so! It was a thing to laugh at.

The marsh called to me. The air was salty, fresh, and quickening. Already the mists were thinning and the sun shone as a white ball through the pale shifting vapors.

The heated puzzles of the night no longer mattered. As I walked over the flat damp grass I moved in a wide circle enclosed by white mist. The *Marsh Duck* was soon lost to sight. Dorna might wake and wonder where I was. At least she would have a chance to wash undisturbed. Would she get up, set the cabin in order, and prepare breakfast? This was what it was like to live with a woman; hours together, and a going apart that was not separation . . . But the night was over and there might never be another. It had gone. It had been pure happiness but it left pain. Her beauty, unseen, gathered force and became a magnet that drew me back.

Dorna was waiting on deck and breakfast was also waiting below. The cabin had been cleared and ports and skylight were wide open, but a little fragrance of Dorna lingered in the air. Her hair was loose, gathered with a bit of twine at her nape. It was dark and a little ropy and wet. She had had a swim, she said. The water was very cold. Her skin glowed and sleep had softened her face and made it smooth and childlike.

While we ate, it lightened steadily but with occasional lapses into darkness like the winking of a great eye.

My mistake about the dog's footsteps made us laugh. The will to laugh took the place of wit. We were not as we had been, for many hours together lay behind us and a night and sleep, each with the other as a companion. We were used to each other. We ate and smiled at each other, laughed at nothing, and were silent.

We did not hasten. There was no sense of pressure from time. The wind was not blowing; the tide was wrong. We sat in the cabin long after we had finished the meal, and then went on deck for no reason at all.

The mist was rolling away in streamers, some still flat on the marsh and others uptilted, rosy with sunlight, pale-blue in shadow. The marsh was checkered in dark greens and yellows and had become wide and spacious again. Eastward, less than a mile away, was a settlement, and its fenced marsh pastures came to within less than two hundred yards.

"That's the Amans'," said Dorna. "It must have been their dog."

We laughed again.

Their house would have been easy to reach.

The sun was warm and it was well on into the morning. Dorna seemed restless and so was I, and although there was only a light air stirring, we decided to start. She was willing to let me be American and to do the physical "work" necessary, standing watching me, a little impatient. This was also something at which to laugh. I unhooked the grapnel and drew the boat up to her anchor. The line brought on board a soft gray mud. I raised the sail—really a man's job—and thought she must be strong to be able to do it herself. When I raised the anchor, she also had to do something and she fetched a bucket to wash the mud from the deck, taking off her sandals and having bare feet as well as legs. And it required her skill and knowledge to set the sail to the faint breeze.

We moved with occasionally a ripple at the bow. The channel was narrow and winding and deep, the tide was running out against us, and at times the shore did not move. Such wind as there was came in light puffs from the south, sometimes heading us, but more often over the starboard side.

The morning stole away. The sky was a changing patchwork of soft white clouds and firm dark-blue. We sailed and drifted in sunlight and darkness and on the marsh surface great shadows moved.

Our eyes were full of light and color. Southwest three or four miles away was a settlement low in the middle of the flatness, its trees and mound little more than a vivid rough edge on the horizon. Dorna told me of these places. This one was accessible only by a branch of the channel we were using. Northeastward was a lake, she said, five or six miles away with an island farm in its center, just visible. Thousands of duck gathered there. It was fed by springs, and dams had been built to keep it as fresh as possible.

"Are they marsh ducks?" I asked.

"Yes," she answered, "most of them, but there are other kinds. They are the neatest of little birds, well dressed with bright blue wings and brown and white bodies and a black head."

"Are they good to eat?"

"Now and then."

"Do you hunt them?"

"If we need food."

"Not for pleasure?"

"What is the pleasure?"

It had to be explained. It was no pleasure to kill them, she said, except when one was hungry and saw in them a satisfaction of appetite; but they were very interesting to watch. They were fascinating! She described their habits, their businesslike and unexpected ways.

Hunting only for pleasure seemed to be outside her comprehension.

Noon came and a high sun. Four or five miles away Ronan and Dorn Islands broke the even horizon below the intermingled blue and white, but we had twice that distance yet to go. The wind dropped and to avoid drifting backward the anchor was cast to wait the turn of the tide in the early afternoon.

The end of our time together was coming nearer, and it was hard to face, but though sailing brought it nearer still, I was restless and wished to be moving.

Dorna, however, seemed at peace, sitting on the deck with her ankles crossed. Her feet were still bare. How rarely had I seen a girl's bare feet! They did not seem natural. These pink-soled things with toes were not the proper way for a girl to end off. Nor was I used to the shortened look of the legs of Islandian women, who wore no heels or very low ones. And it was hard to believe that Dorna's bare feet were not flaunted at me—that she was unconscious of them. Yet I knew that she was quite ignorant of the feelings of an American, glad that she did not know the pricking disturbances she caused.

She sat with her elbows on the rail and did not look really comfortable and yet she was quite contented. What did she think during her long moments of idleness and silence, or did she think at all? Rather she appeared to be absorbing the air and sunlight. Sometimes she lifted her head and looked up, and her hair, still loose, fell back from her serene forehead and hung in a soft loop behind. Her face, turned to the sky, seemed to be waiting.

Staring at her did not diminish her beauty. Her bare feet became a natural part of her. She was complete and perfect, and her beauty increased in power until it was bewildering and stunning. It was not good to gaze too long upon her.

Our journey—our glimpse of life together—could not end with a casual good-bye. The wonder of it demanded its climax. I must tell her something. I would have liked to kneel to her, and to kiss her foot . . . But what could I say? How tell her that she was beautiful? Would it interest her to hear this from me? And anyway such words were a form of flirtation—and was not flirtation a disloyalty, an unfair advantage taken of the adventure into which she had brought me? And yet, at the other extreme, was the possibility that she expected more of me. But she had warned me against loving. Could she be so cruel as to expect me to make love?

The only path to follow was that of my own conscience, which told me not to flirt with her, not to tell her that she was too beautiful and very dear. She wanted to be a friend—she had said so. A friend I would be, impersonal, and loyal to my friend, her brother, and to her great-uncle who trusted her with me.

Dorna slowly turned and looked at me. Her eyes seemed to wake and became intent as though she had seen something unexpected in my face. After a moment she rose and without a word went below. She had left me. I leaned back and half closed my eyes. The sun beat down, warm and subduing. The tide lisped along the boat's sides. Was I not in love with her—in love in spite of the warnings? It was pain and it was beauty—a prism giving a sharp edge of color to all things.

After a long time she called. In the cabin she had spread out the last of our food. Had she guessed my thoughts? In her manner was a quiet restraint that signified the loss of something precious we had had.

Her impersonal manner I matched with one as impersonal. My plans were discussed. Should I stay one or two more days at Dorn Island? If two, there would be no time to visit both households of the Somes. She advised me not to stay.

"There will be many chances to visit Dorn Island and to stay a long time, but it is worth your while to meet the Somes soon . . . I would rather have you stay," she added lightly.

"I want to stay, Dorna."

"I hope you will come here in the spring." But it was now only the fall.

"My visits must be timed to the steamers. I have six weeks in May, July, and September."

"Be sure to come in September. In July it is very cold and raw."

"It is a long way off, Dorna."

"Oh, come other times, too, Johnlang."

"Will you be here in September?"

"Probably. In that month my garden begins to bloom. I make my visits in the fall and winter. Spring and summer are the loveliest times to be at home."

"Do you make many visits, Dorna? Are you likely to come to The City?"

"Not to The City, but I may come to the Council Meeting in June. I make a good many visits. . . ."

Regularly each year she went for a week or more to her cousins at Thane Island and Grase Bay, to the Farrants, the Somes, and the Marriners of Winder. She also often visited the Stellins in Camia and the Beltons of Carran, the Drelins of Deen, and the Airds of Storn, every other year or so. There were families all over the marsh upon whom she frequently descended for a few days, particularly the Marts, the relatives of Lord Dorn's widowed daughter-in-law. And every spring, she said with a quick glance, she spent a few days with the Ronans—ever since she was a baby. Besides this she went to The City once or twice a year for a Council Meeting and often to Doring Town to keep her great-uncle company.

I loved to hear the tones of her voice with its shifting of pitch and individualities of accent and to watch the changing curves of her mouth. She was willing to talk, this silent one. Lack of words was not her trouble.

She had been everywhere at one time or another. There were occasional visits besides the regular ones—a memorable one to the Moras when she was fourteen. They had ridden to the northern end of Carran and she had set foot outside of Islandian soil—for a few yards! At seventeen she had gone for two years to the girls' school at Thale, Camia.

Her face lighted with her memories. The pleasure of traveling in a country so beautiful, various, and homogeneous became vivid and real. I was grateful to the Dorns for putting me in the way of traveling as they did.

"Who visits you at the Island, Dorna?"

She mentioned her cousin, Dorna of Thane Island, Drelina, the recent bride of young Dorn of Grase Bay, the two Beltonas, daughters of the Chief Judge, Soma, until she married and went to St. Anthony, and Stellina, daughter of the Lord of Camia. All of these except the first were girls of her own age. Were there no young men except Tor?

I asked if they ever had houseparties. These were rare except with the Moras; guests came singly, and infrequently were more than two present; and the only gatherings of groups of friends came in The City when many attended the meetings of the council.

"When do you meet men of your age, Dorna?"

"At other people's houses and at The City—and some come to see me."

I wished that she would name them, but did not like to ask. Then, as though guessing my wish, she continued:

"Young Stellin comes once or twice a year. Some, the brother of Soma at St. Anthony, rides over unexpectedly at least as often. There is Granery, a brother of the judge. There are men in the marsh who drop down on us for a few days. Of course there is Ronan. Sometimes a man will come to us, and I know it is to see me, but he won't come again. There was young Mora!" She laughed and watched me as though to say: are you satisfied? But she had not mentioned the young king. These men had the same sort of wishes that I had and a much greater power to attain them, for they were native and I was a foreigner who had to be warned. There was dismay and bitterness

185

at the thought of them. But it was kind of her to be so frank about them.

"Stellin is the one with whom I have most in common," she continued. "He is perhaps the handsomest. His sister is certainly the loveliest of all my friends. I hope you will meet her soon. Maybe she will be here sometime when you come."

"Is she dangerous, Dorna?"

"No more dangerous than you choose to find her, Johnlang— no more than we all are!"

Her words stung for some reason.

"Perhaps you are thinking of what I said about not wanting to marry an Islandian woman, and are wondering why I want you to meet one who is so beautiful. Is that why you asked if she were dangerous?"

My remark had not had so much conscious thought behind it.

"I don't know, Dorna."

She waited several long moments.

"I still think that you will be happier if you don't ever want to marry one of us," she said.

"Do you mean that it would be hopeless?"

"Oh, no!"

"Then why is it any different from wanting to marry a girl at home?"

"It is, Johnlang!" she clasped her hands tightly; and I knew that what we were saying troubled her.

"You say that I'll be happier if I remain heart-free in Islandia. I wonder if I want to be merely happy!"

"It is the best way to be."

"What is happiness, Dorna?"

"It is to be so much in tune with your life as a whole that every moment that comes is untroubled and full of interest. It is what I want—to be serene, to enjoy wind and sea and earth and sky without any worries forcing themselves upon me."

Her wish sounded empty and was disheartening.

"It is a lonely wish, Dorna."

"Oh, no," she answered with honest quickness. "I want my friends, men and women both."

"Just friends?"

She looked at me.

"Someday I shall probably want a great deal more, and that may be good-bye to happiness. I have had heartbeats over men, Johnlang, and they have been pleasant and they have hurt. But I don't want to marry before I'm ready, and I'm not ready yet to be a wife and to bear children."

The earnestness of her voice raised a dreadful suspicion.

"You don't have to be anybody's wife until you are ready, Dorna!" I said. Her head dropped a little. After a moment she raised her eyes.

"I don't know."

"Aren't you free to marry when and whom you please?"

"Do you think I am?" she asked, as though wanting reassurance.

"Dorna, you are one of a great family. I see that. You may be under obligations that do not apply to ordinary people."

"It is not exactly my family," she said slowly. "There is nothing definite, but I am afraid something may be demanded of me—not by any person, but by circumstances and by myself."

My throat choked with love and pity intermingled, and waiting until sure of my voice I said:

"I understand why you want to be happy—and to be serene, Dorna."

Her eyes grew wide, and her lips parted to speak, but she checked herself abruptly and looked down again. Then after a moment she said calmly:

"Thank you, Johnlang. It is a problem that some time I may have to face, but don't think that it confronts me now. I am quite free. But until I know whether that problem is going to have to be decided, and until it is decided, I want to remain free and to be happy."

"There is something definite, Dorna?"

"As definite as I have said, something that I may have to face, but something that will be settled one way or the other."

Was this her way of telling me that she was engaged to be married—of warning me off again? I had no rights, but it was cruel. She must be told something of this pain in my heart. An abyss opened before my feet, and I wanted to plunge dizzily, to say I loved her and to ask her to marry me. But could I say it on such sudden impulse, and was it fair, after what she had just told me?

When I spoke it was near to but not quite what I wanted to utter.

"You said I must not wish to marry you. Is that the reason, Dorna?"

"It is a reason, isn't it?" she said gravely, and I knew by her voice that it was not the only reason. There was still this heart-breaking, sickening, impalpable other fact that Nattana and Dorn himself and she had emphasized and never explained.

"It is not the sort of reason to deter a man, Dorna. You say you are free."

She sat with bent head, her hands palm upward in her lap, with curved fingers that worked and spread.

"Perhaps you are right," she said, "but it is in your power to make my problem harder. Yet the real reason why I told you not to let such a wish come to you, concerned you, and not me."

"Because it would be hopeless if I did, Dorna?"

"Johnlang!" Her voice shook a little. "Do you think I would say that it would be hopeless unless I were absolutely sure? I would like to say so, but I am not going to tell you an untruth. You are a man like other men, but there are reasons—reasons—"

"Can't you see how hard this is on me, Dorna? There is something wrong with me in your eyes—and you don't tell me what it is."

"Nothing is wrong with you!" she cried and her eyes blazed. "But there is something that stands between you and us. Don't make me tell you what it is. I am not sure that I know. I would only talk and you and I would argue and we would each be hurt and get nowhere. But it is real, Johnlang. It may not always exist. I don't know."

She sprang to her feet and went toward the door, but on the threshold she turned back and faced me.

"I understand some of your troubles. Believe me, I do. I am your friend now and you are mine. But I don't wish to marry you and I don't think I ever will, and I don't believe you really wish to marry me, or know what you do wish. I want you to be happy in my country, and I see dangers before you so clearly. Oh my friend, don't let yourself wish to marry one of us, and don't try to make one of us want to marry you if you value her happiness."

"You have this feeling, Dorna—"

"Yes, it is a feeling—"

"And you can't tell me?"

"Does that make a difference, because I can't put it into words? It is just as real!"

"It can't be, Dorna, if you can't explain it."

She looked at me for some moments, studying my face, puzzled, concerned.

"I don't understand," she said. "If I have a feeling and it seems true, do you mean because I can't express it in words—You can't mean that! The ability to say things isn't what makes things true."

"The feeling exists?"

"Oh yes." She turned her head away, and her eyelids lifted in pain. What was there to say? The flow of all emotions was to set her at ease again.

"Never mind, Dorna."

She turned upon me suddenly.

"Why should we harass ourselves in this way, Johnlang? I have told you as clearly as I can what I feel about you. We don't know each other very well. There is lack of knowledge as well as difference of country. You don't want to marry me, either, I know. But do think of me as your friend."

There was a long pause. The wish to tell her that she was wrong was violent in my heart, but it could not be uttered—not when she felt as she did, not now. The moment passed. I had hesitated. It was too late. The delay would ruin whatever I said.

"Let's go on deck. The tide turned long ago," she said quickly and went out.

I followed her, passed her, and began to pull in the anchor line.

Time had moved as silently and as swiftly as the sweeping of cloud shadows across the flat marsh.

There was a light breeze from the north and it carried us along steadily if slowly. The shelving banks on either side of the creek slid rearward and the level green surfaces wheeled as we passed. The sky darkened, for today it was the clouds' turn to win over the sun.

Dorna steered standing, her bare feet planted a little apart on the deck. The sail was to starboard and I sat on the starboard rail, but the *Marsh Duck* was so broad that my weight heeled her over only a very little. My task was trimming the sheet.

Overhead were patches of blue sky, but around the horizon the

189

clouds were heavy and dark with rain. Distant settlements that had
broken the clear edge of marsh and sky with their lifted roughness
of trees and low mounds were blotted out in grayness, but Dorn and
Ronan Islands were still clearly visible. They were not far away now,
and our two days together were ending.

Did it matter very much? An ending was inevitable and was it
not due? Yet I was in the mood for a cruise and wanted days of just
this—of boat and sky and water channels, of the even green surfaces of the marsh, with occasional scattered settlements—and to
visit the fresh-water lake of the wild ducks, to sail seaward to the
dunes, and to be serene and happy as Dorna had said.

"I am never tired of sailing, nor of all this," she said, suddenly,
waving her hand across the horizon, and she smiled a little shyly. "I
would like to go on and on. There are too many things to do!"

She held the tiller under her arm and steered by swaying her
body, lifting now one heel and now the other, showing her pink
soles, a little wrinkled. Hers was a pretty foot, in proportion with
the rest of her.

"I have been thinking the same thing," I answered. "I would
like to cruise all over the marsh."

My thoughts had been of cruising without respect to the companion and so had hers, surely, yet the image of cruising together
and the possibility that her wish included me intruded upon serenity
and troubled speech.

There was silence for a long time.

"It is going to rain tomorrow," she said, "and it may sprinkle
before we reach home."

"Your brother told me that you were a sure weather prophet,
Dorna."

"I have studied the weather. I love it. I've always thought I knew
what was going to happen for a day or two ahead."

"Have you ever cruised in the marsh, Dorna—long cruises, for
several days?"

"Oh yes. I have lived on the *Marsh Duck* for weeks!" she cried.
"But not so often these last few years. When I was eighteen and
nineteen!"

"Were you alone, Dorna?"

"Sometimes—and sometimes a friend came, and my brother before he went away to your country, or Dorna, my cousin, or Dorna

of Thane Island, or one of the girls on our Island. I have been with young Ronan, too, and once Stellin and I sailed into Great Marsh."

My heart beat uneasily. She was suddenly silent.

After some time she said:

"I don't believe in being with a man for more than a night or two. *Apiata* is almost inevitable. Some people don't believe in it at all, but it seems to me unfortunate that a man and woman can't be together in that way!"

"It does to me, too," I answered.

"I wondered . . . What do people think in your country?"

Honesty was hard.

"They don't approve," I said at last, not looking at her.

"I almost turned back." Her voice came over my head. "You seemed so upset. But it was too late. We would have had a hard time reaching Doring Town again. And I did not want to! . . . I make *such* mistakes with you! This time it was through following our customs. Before that it was trying to conform to yours."

"Do you think it has been a mistake, Dorna? I don't."

"Not for me, Johnlang!"

"Nor for me, Dorna."

"I hope not," she said in a low voice.

"I have been very happy."

"Oh—So have I!"

She laughed, but not quite naturally.

"Let's not bother now," she added. "We will only harass ourselves again . . . When two people are together like this for so long, one ought to be to the other just a pleasing part of the background for a great part of the time. I am getting bored with ourselves. Aren't you?"

"With myself, not with you."

She sighed a little.

"It doesn't matter," she said.

She wanted to be mere background to me and me to be in the background for her. I said no more. . . .

Twilight came early while we were still in the channel; and when we passed into the broader waters of the Earne River it was beginning to be dark.

The wind was freshening and the *Marsh Duck* heeled. Dorna

191

was above me, a dark figure against a dark sky; but she seemed to give forth a subdued light; the yellow of her blouse and her skirt was vivid, the duskier color of her cheeks was warm, and a highlight played along the calf of her legs as she swayed upon the tiller. The air was growing colder, and yet she, hatless, coatless, with bare feet, did not seem conscious of it.

Her eyes flashed, intent on what was ahead.

"Ready, Johnlang! We are going to jibe."

She glanced behind her quickly. The water was dark astern with white gleams rushing toward us on the wave tops. She swayed away from me and I could see the line of her back and hip and leg, strong and lovely. The *Marsh Duck* turned with a swirl of foam and the great sail came inboard and swung across, but I had been warned and was ready. I let the sheet fly, spilling the wind, and then hauled it in quickly.

The *Marsh Duck* foamed into the creek. Over the bow I saw the familiar outlines of Dorn Island, and Dorna's windmill revolving its great arms against a dark-gray sky.

Dorna was laughing. Her voice was high.

"We are going to jibe again, Johnlang! Ready! It's blowing!"

Yet she held on until the shore was almost under our bow. Around we came, and again I let the sheet go and hauled in again.

"Good! Oh, good for you!" she cried. "Oh, isn't it fine that we have some wind at last!"

There was only just light enough to see when we jibed for the last time and slid into the harbor, where the wind, broken by Ronan's Island, was much less strong. She was captain, I was crew, but I knew fairly well what to do and she gave but few orders, in a voice that sounded more like requests and suggestions. And I remembered how others gave commands on their boats.

We made a perfect landing and she was pleased, laughing and saying:

"Oh, we are good, Johnlang. We make a good crew!"

A harbor furl was the next thing, and every rope must be neatly coiled. The *Marsh Duck* was stationary at her mooring and it was over, all but a few moments more. Dorna seemed very happy.

I brought the saddlebags on deck, hers and mine, while she

quickly put the cabin in order. When she came on deck she reached for her own.

"Let me be American and carry both," I said.

"Let me be Islandian and carry mine."

"No—not this time."

She laughed and gave way.

"It is kind of you, Johnlang. I can walk more freely and I am a little stiff."

We stepped ashore and the shells crackled under my feet.

"Have you got your sandals on, Dorna?"

"Yes, I have." Her voice was almost humble.

Soft raindrops began to fall. She walked, swinging her hips in her way. Good sailor, good walker—I would like to see Dorna on a horse.

The great beeches over our heads made a black tracery against a sky only a little less dark. At the end of the arched alley was the lanterned door of the Dorns' house.

At my side she was a shadowy figure. The wind was tossing the branches of the trees, and it was difficult to hear, but I think she was humming to herself.

Her voice came out of the darkness and was a little hesitant.

"I have been very happy with you, Johnlang."

"And I've been happy with you, Dorna . . . I have never been so happy in my life!"

"Wasn't it beautiful? And I am so glad that the squall came and you saw how my boat can sail!"

We walked on. The door came nearer. We had been the only persons in the world for two days. Others were behind those walls, and with them we must share our lives.

"I wish it wasn't ending," I said.

"It had to end."

She was silent for a moment.

"Let me tell the family how we came to take two days," she said. "There are some who may not approve."

"All right, Dorna."

We came to the door. It closed behind us and the night and marsh and all good things of open air and boats were shut out. The hall was empty and dimly lighted.

We climbed the stairs and walked along the corridors. At my door she stopped.

"My bag," she said. "Thank you for carrying it."

"Can't I take it to your room?"

"It is my turn to have my way."

I gave her the bag.

Suddenly she touched the back of my hand with her finger tips. With a quick turn that swung out her skirts and showed the backs of her knees, she walked down the corridor toward her room.

Dorn was sitting in my room and his presence was a shock, for I had expected to be alone with time to prepare myself to face others. He raised his head and though his face was in shadow, I felt the hot glow of his eyes. I smiled and said "Hello," yet I felt naked and guilty. Turning away I set down my saddlebag. Perhaps when Dorna said that some would disapprove, she had him in mind; but he began telling me that he had come in only a few hours before, and then he asked about my journey to the northwest. I recounted my experiences while I changed and washed. My skin was hot and sunburned. The two days just over seemed exhausting rather than restful, and my wandering mind wished to cling to Dorna—What was she doing and thinking? Was she washing as I was? Was she tired and sunburned too?

We went down to supper. Faina, Marta, and the elder Dorna were waiting for us. After we had sat down, my own Dorna came in wearing a green dress, with cheeks that looked scrubbed and that were flushed, and with her hair done tightly again and in a single braid.

Our eyes met for a moment. I tried not to look and feel guilty again, and had a feeling of happy excitement mixed with apprehension. She and I were for the moment united against the others— against those who did not approve.

Questions were asked about my journey to the Farrants'. Dorna put many of them, perhaps hoping to keep me going until the meal was over. There seemed to be reserve in the attitude of the other two younger women. They did not encourage me very much. Dorn had already heard my story. It was impossible to string out my adventures to the end of supper, and before I knew it I had got myself back to Doring.

"Was that last night?" asked Dorna the elder.

"No, night before last."

"When did you leave?"

"Yesterday morning," I said, trying not to blush.

"There wasn't any wind," interrupted my Dorna. "It took us two days."

There was sudden silence.

"Wasn't that a little hard on Lang?" said Faina gently.

"I didn't mind," I said, but was this safe?

"You did a little, John," Dorna interrupted again. "You didn't expect so long a trip."

"No, but I did not mind."

Dorna laughed with what seemed assumed amusement.

"Wind is very uncertain at this season. It was calm when we started, but we went well for a while, and then it died out completely."

"You usually know what the wind is likely to do," said her cousin.

"Sometimes I make a mistake. Your father knows the wind as well as I do. He sent us off."

"He is more of a landsman than you are. I suppose you stopped somewhere. Did you go to the Amans'?"

"No," said my Dorna. "We did not get near enough until it was foggy and dark. I saw no reason why we should flounder around in the marsh at night."

"Nor I," said Faina unexpectedly. "I hope that you were prepared and that Lang was comfortable."

"I am always prepared on the *Marsh Duck* . . . Were you comfortable, John?"

"Oh, very!" I said.

"How did you like the boat?" asked Dorn. "How does she compare with the one you and I had in Maine?"

But Dorna the elder was silent while we discussed this question. Clearly she was one of those who disapproved. Faina did not seem to be of their number. Who was or were the other one or ones— Marta and my friend? . . . But the latter had now drawn the conversation into other channels, and I felt that I had been through an ordeal and was not very comfortable. His disapproval mattered a great deal.

After supper, however, when he and Dorna and I discussed our plans in the anteroom, he said nothing about the sail across the marsh. Instead the question was when I should leave, on the next day but one or the day after.

"I advised John to leave day after tomorrow," Dorna said to her brother, "so that he can visit both of the Somes' places."

When Dorn agreed and it was settled I half regretted and half was glad. Reason advised me against too much Dorna; my feelings dreaded her a little; but it was also hard to lose a minute of her.

"Will it rain tomorrow?" he asked his sister.

"Until late afternoon, and it will be a heavy rain."

"Are you sure?"

"Oh yes—quite sure."

"As sure as you were about the wind yesterday?"

"Yes, just as sure!"

She met his eyes squarely, but her cheeks burned. He watched her with a look that withheld I know not what. Her expression became at once angry and humble.

Her next remark was that she was sleepy and was going to bed. I rose, but Dorn did not.

"John and I had a very happy time," she said, and she went without a glance at either of us.

There was silence, and then Dorn suggested that I come into the library. I followed with the sense of guilt strong again, but his only apparent purpose was to show me maps and to discuss stopping places on my journey, to arrange for the stabling and care of Fak at The City, and to discuss the complicated situation arising from my being seen at the Lor Pass in his company.

A fire burned upon the central hearth. The logs were long and laid so as to radiate; when the blaze slackened they were thrust inward. Now and then the embers hissed as rain came down the chimney. Sitting on a bench beside me, Dorn read me Lord Mora's answer to his great-uncle's letter, containing a cordial assurance that my presence at the pass was understood and would be explained. The significance of my seeming share in the plot of Dorn, Don, and the other man was clear but I was cold to it, and at the moment I did not care.

"I made a blunder," he said.

"Oh no," I answered.

"I have kept many things secret from you for that reason. I haven't told you what I am doing. You will be able to say that you learned nothing about our plans and our policies."

I nodded, seeing the point.

"I shall talk of places that I visited and of views and of how kind everyone was."

He paused for a moment.

"I am glad it seems so . . . If you weren't a consul we would hide nothing, and I would try to make you see things as I see them."

"I have a much better understanding of your point of view than I had, by being with all of you."

He looked at me sharply and then seemed to muse.

"Don't let any of us influence you too much," he said. "We are prejudiced. And anyway I don't believe anyone can really understand us who is not one of us."

"Why not, if a foreigner is honest and fairly intelligent? What is so difficult about your point of view?"

"It goes deeper than honesty and intelligence. There must be an emotional knowledge."

He was rather annoying. Why did they deny me an ability to understand them?

"Are you so very different?"

"I suppose we are all human beings, but our sense of values is not the same as yours."

"Suppose a man remained in your country a long time and lived exactly the sort of life you live?"

"That would be only a beginning. He would have to do more. Of course, he must be quite contented without many things he had at home. He must enjoy our way of life for its own sake and not merely as a subject of study. And he would have to be stirred to the depths of his nature by something that was Islandian through and through."

"You don't believe that a person can understand a thing by studying it?"

"Not a way of living. He must feel it as well as know about it."

"What sort of a feeling must he have?"

"As part of him . . . I can't describe it."

"You are like Dorna. You believe in mere feelings. They are untrustworthy things when they can't be expressed."

"What difference does that make?"

"How can you know what they are?"

"You have them!"

I laughed, half at him, half because it was hopeless.

"Dorna and I are alike in some ways but not in others," he said shortly. "It works both ways. I had a very hard time trying to understand—I mean to feel—how you in America thought and why you behaved as you did, and I never succeeded. That taught me a lesson. I think it almost impossible for a foreigner really to understand us."

"I'm glad you don't say 'quite impossible.' Have we some lack of sensibility?"

"I don't think that exactly."

"Dorn, I should hate to think that I never could understand you. You are discouraging. When I came I did have the strangest puzzled feelings almost like terror, but lately I've seemed to be less puzzled."

"Dorna thinks you might understand our way of life in time."

"She does!"

His remark quickened my heart.

"So she said. She and my great-uncle were discussing the ability of foreigners to understand us the night before you came back from the Farrants'. He would not express himself and I was very doubtful, but she thought a few might, and she mentioned you as one."

"I wonder if she still does."

He was silent for a moment.

"Did you seem to understand each other?" he asked.

"Now and then we didn't, but we talked a great deal about the effects of foreign trade and about politics and we seemed to understand perfectly then. We differed of course. She can be quite eloquent. But are you really doubtful?"

He rose from his seat unexpectedly and turned to face me, his back to the fire.

"Why do you want to be like us?"

"Maybe I don't—but I want to understand you anyway."

"It is the same thing! What is it you want to understand?"

All I could think of were moments of confusion with Dorna, nor could I remember the details of any of these except that there was something that disqualified me in her eyes.

"I don't like to feel myself an alien, I suppose."

He did not tell me that I was not one.

"Why do you mind?" he said at last. "Why don't you think of us as the aliens?"

"Because you don't seem alien to me, and I do seem alien to you."

"I should think we would seem very strange to you."

"Strange sometimes, yes, but not alien!"

"It is because you are here, and you have to live as we do, and you see only us."

"No, because you did not seem alien to me in the United States."

"We have a simpler and a more self-confident civilization," he said slowly.

What was there to say to that?

"The Greeks and the Barbarians," I remarked.

"The Greeks and the Romans, perhaps—but we aren't Greek. Look at Plato's *Republic*. They believed in rules and in a strong state guiding the lives of everyone. But there is one thing that is not affected, and that is your and my friendship."

"It seems the only solid thing."

"It is solid."

There was no answer to make, but I felt the reality of it strong between us. There was a long silence. . . .

"I have been wondering what you thought about Dorna's bringing you here in her boat when she knew it would take two days," he said. "Is that one of the things that seems strange? We weren't any of us deceived at supper. She knew she couldn't make it in a day when she started."

I flushed to the roots of my hair, but he was pushing the logs toward the center of the fire with his foot.

"Yes, she knew it," I answered, "and she told me soon after we started."

"Not until you were well on your way, I'm sure."

"At lunchtime, but the tide was favorable for going back."

"But it was a dead calm."

"The *Marsh Duck* goes with very little wind."

"I'm not blaming her. You don't have to defend her."

"I am as much to blame as she is. I did not want to turn back. She gave me the chance." She had not spoken of returning, and this was half a lie.

"I'm not blaming you either. I only asked if you thought it strange. And you don't need to answer."

"I had conflicting thoughts. At home it would be regarded as extraordinary, but this place is not the United States."

"I know how it would be thought of in the United States," he said.

"Dorna told me that here some approved and some did not."

"When did she tell you?"

"Today."

"There is no rule," he said. "Some approve of one pair going off like that but not of another pair. I suppose you thought you were doing something quite usual in Islandia because Dorna would not have got you in for such a trip unless it were usual."

He glanced at me as though wishing me to confirm this analysis, but I could not.

"I did not think anything so definite. I accepted the situation."

"You couldn't very well have suggested that you turn back without seeming to accuse Dorna of doing what she should not have done."

"I don't believe I even thought of that."

He busied himself with the logs.

"I wish she hadn't done it," he said, giving one of them a vicious kick, "but it makes no difference now what I wish."

The fire in my face became hot again. Questions rushed to my lips, for clarity seemed vital. But he stopped them all.

"John, I care a great deal more for you than anyone else here. Let's not talk about this any more. Don't blame yourself and don't you blame Dorna."

"I won't blame her."

"Nor yourself."

"I have nothing to blame myself for."

He uttered a short laugh, but his face was dark.

What he had said was both a great happiness and a pain.

PART II

11

The Somes and The City

ON DORN'S ADVICE I had planned to visit the Somes in the province of Loria on my journey back to The City. It was late on the third day of travel that I arrived and the sun was descending when I came to the "stone gate on the left carved with two wolves' heads" which Dorn had described. The evening was cool, the air autumnal, and everywhere weaving threads and spirals of smoke rose from dead leaves burning.

Fak quickened as we went through the gate. The smooth, well-kept road plunged at once into dense young spruces, through which the road wound this way and that.

Out of these woods a little ahead of me, so suddenly as to make Fak shy, emerged a man and woman. The sun was nearly down now, and the light was ruddy. Against the dark green of the spruces they stood, so vivid as to be unreal, the man bareheaded with black hair, and a young smooth face, his buff shirt open at the throat, and his heather-colored jacket unfastened; the woman young as he, her brown hair braided down her back, flecked with golden light, and both with faces flushed and glowing.

I named myself, drawing up my horse. For a moment they did not reply, but stared at me. Then, suddenly, he came forward and spoke: "Some!" and she said quickly, "Broma."

"We expected to see you today or tomorrow," he added. "Dorn-nephew told us of your coming. Our house is yours."

I knew enough now to understand these last words, and I thanked him. He laughed. "You startled us. Those little horses which the Dorns breed walk as lightly as cats. We were running through the woods."

So I laughed too, and Broma who had come up smiled showing

white even teeth; and she was young, younger than I, not more than twenty-two or three, and his wife.

"You would like to go to your room, wouldn't you, Lang?" he said. "You have been on the road three days, have you not? The house is some distance yet. You need not walk with us. They are ready for you, I know. You will find my father and mother there. We are coming as fast as we can."

The road wound out of the trees into arable land, and the house came into sight, set on a knoll in wide lawns shaded by great trees. The road led me around to the back where a man, hearing my explanation, left my saddlebag on the doorstep and took Fak's halter, but did not lead him away. I guessed he expected me to come with them to the stable, and I did so, and saw my faithful horse made comfortable.

Then I returned to the house. My bag had disappeared from the doorstep. I was embarrassed, for no one was in sight to greet me and ask me in, nor was there any knocker or bell to ring. But guessing again what an Islandian would do, I entered and found myself in a low-ceiled, flagged hallway with closed doors and a flight of stairs. Several moments passed and then I heard footsteps above. Soon a man of middle age appeared on the stairs. I named myself again. He was Some, he said, and a room was ready for me. Would I come?

The room was in the front of the house, above the veranda, looking over the lawns to the cultivated ground, and beyond that to the grove of spruces into which the road disappeared. My bag was on the table ready to open, and a great copper tub was set in the corner.

The man said that water was coming for my bath if I wished it, and that his wife would bring us a glass of *sarka*. He was the father of the Some I had met on the road, a rather stocky, dark-haired, blue-eyed man, weather-beaten and quiet.

We talked of my journey, and of the health of the Dorns, and then his wife, whom he named as Danninga, appeared with a tray and three glasses and little shortcakes. The liquor was like a dry peach brandy. It was certainly strong and I felt it warm and comfortable in the center of me. We chatted a little of my visit to Lord Farrant, and then a man appeared with two enormous copper ewers of hot and cold water, and a light. They then left me telling me I had all the time I wished.

Baths are never so pleasant as after a long journey on horseback.

I lay and basked, warm within from the liquor, utterly relaxed. Man and nothing else I lay, scarcely thinking, rather sleepy, certainly tired, conscious of my naked, interesting self.

Comfort! That is the way to describe many of my Islandian visits. I was often road-weary. My hosts were unexacting. The meals they served did not overtax a travel-tired appetite, conversation was easy and without too great demands, and I was free to go to bed when I pleased.

In the house was Lord Some, the young man I had met on the road, his wife, and his mother and father. He resembled Soma, wife of Cadred, whose first cousin he was. He had been married only a few months, and was elected provincial lord only the year before, succeeding his uncle, who was Soma's father. He seemed to me younger than he really was (twenty-seven) and almost as it were in tutelage. He was jolly, carefree, and showed no signs of taking his duties seriously. Broma, his young wife, was twenty-one, still in many ways a young girl, looking like the unwedded girls I knew. She was fresh, rather than pretty, with her rather broad face, thick brown hair, and clear blue eyes. I wondered to myself why this young man was elected provincial lord, rather than his father, or his uncle whom later I met, and who was a retired general. These men were older, more stable, and their election would not have broken the succession. Young Lord Some seemed to have no special qualifications nor was he trained to the office. Lord Some's father was perhaps too negative and was certainly engrossed in the farm. The young spruces, he told me, he had planted himself fifteen years before.

It seemed to me that the people of Loria were supine. Obviously young Lord Some was the family's candidate, but surely there must be in that large province many others better suited to hold office than he was. I was all the more surprised when I learned that his election was practically unanimous. Perhaps it was merely a case of boss-rule.

Next morning, as the Somes had planned for me, I was sent off with one of their dependents, Cerson, a boy of fourteen, as guide. I was mounted on one of their horses, and Fak, unburdened, with a leading rein, ran behind. The way I never could have found alone. The Somes' wood farm was perhaps fifteen miles away and a public provincial road led there eventually, but it would have been hard to follow. Cerson and I left it and rejoined it, cutting through farms by farm roads, and though I did not lose my sense of direction altogether, I could never have retraced my steps through the intricate, distorted, irregular checkerboard of groves, pastures, hayfields, and gardens, walls and gates, that we crossed during the first part of the way. But finally this pleasant, complicated, gently rolling farming land ended and we abruptly reached Loria Wood, a forest of all but untouched trees, in the heart of Loria Province, perhaps fifteen miles long by seven or eight wide.

Dorna and Soma and Dorn had all told me of this forest. It occupies a vestigial plateau of less fertile soil than the greater part of Loria around it. In places there are fine cliffs, tree-topped above the farm lands. We entered the forest after a gradual ascent through pastures. The prevailing tree was the beech, at this season half-bare, but on the rockier hills were pines, and here and there oaks.

In clearings in the forest there are three or four farms, surrounded by dense woods, and widely separated from each other. The Somes' is one of these.

I did not regret seeing this forest in autumn instead of in full leaf as Carstairs had seen it and well described it. A strong wind was blowing, white clouds sailed in the sky, the air was chillier than below, and the woods were singularly full of light. The narrow road was rutted in places and with grassy patches, not in regular ridges as at home where wheeled traffic is so much more common, but in patches here and there, soft under the horses' feet. And quite unexpectedly we came upon three of the Islandian gray deer, with their short antlers and round bodies and long coltlike legs. Cerson said that a few bear were in the forest and that two years before a large wolf had been seen.

For four or five miles we followed this track and then came suddenly upon the clearing of the Somes' farm. There were open pastures bright in that cold sunlight sloping down to a little stream and rising again on the farther side. Here it was that the house stood, and along the banks of the stream, which descended quite perceptibly to the southwest, were the orchards and cultivated ground fenced in with heavy wooden fences.

Within its forest cincture the farm had a character of newness, different from the other farms I had seen, perhaps because of the wooden fences and the look of America outside the stone-wall region. We rode up to the house through apple orchards of trees with bare twisted twigs. It was but one story high though long and rambling,

—standing out almost nudely with its white coarse stone, except for one wing which stood in a dense grove. As we came near, however, it took character and became dignified. Lintels of doors and windows were of a darker stone richly carved, and green grass came up to the wall itself. In the center was a veranda of stone, with stone seats on either side of the door.

Cerson called my name and his in a loud, ringing, boyish voice, and scarcely had we reached the porch when the door opened, and Some, a young man of twenty-two or -three, greeted me. He was almost the twin of Soma, Cadred's wife, with a smile so charming and an acceptance of me so instantaneous and friendly that for a time I quite forgot his sister's letter of introduction. He introduced me to his mother, Hytha, who was great-aunt to Nekka, Nattana, and the rest.

It was lunchtime soon after that and we three were the only persons present. Some, the retired general, the young man's uncle, his wife, Marrinera, and their children had by chance gone to visit Lord Some that very day. Had it not been that my guide Cerson had a fondness for short cuts that were longer than the usual way but more interestingly intricate, we would have met them on the road.

Hytha had a little of the robust, jolly quality of her nephew, Lord Hyth, but also less of his quality of facile bonhommie that had made him seem like an American politician. She was quick to talk of her great-nieces, when I mentioned my visit to them. She told of various escapades of theirs and refreshed and enriched my memory of them.

We also talked of the farm, which belied its look of newness. The family, young Some said, had come there nearly four hundred years ago, exiles from Camia, because, as he remarked with a smile, they had tried to obtain election to the provincial lordship by methods that were unpopular. They had no right to settle in Loria Wood, he said, but settle they did, living largely by hunting and eventually legalizing their claim. They were very poor then, and because of the harshness of the winter and poverty of the soil they never had been able to live with much margin. Only one hundred and fifty years ago had the other farm been acquired, and they were only now bringing it up to the condition they wished. That was thanks to "Some second son" (the father of Lord Some) and his wife. He had given himself to the land, setting aside other ambitions, often traveling back here to wrestle with the age-old problem of wringing enough from the forest farm. When I heard this I knew I had the reason why his son rather than he had become provincial lord.

Young Some that afternoon had work to do, and I volunteered to go with him and help him. I felt I was truly Islandian. I was a guest, but as such it was more natural but not any more obligatory than at home for me to turn to and aid, if aid were wished, even though that aid was manual. But for all that I had an uncomfortable feeling of awkwardness. He took my offer as a matter of course, and after fitting me out in an old pair of leather breeches and waterproof boots, he set out with me following.

On the way down the stream he told me that they had had bad luck. On the farm was one family of *denerir* now in the fifth generation. Old Park—the English sounding name was natural, then odd, then natural again—had had three sons. Since only two were needed one had gone into the army, and then of the two remaining one died, and the other was crippled by a falling tree. Old Park himself, over eighty, worked a little, and the cripple could do some tasks about the barns; but he, Some, and his uncle, the general, were the only able-bodied men on the place. It was a great relief when his other uncle came up to help. "There is less leisure here than on some other farms, Lang, but it won't last very many years. Park third (the cripple) has two sons. We are content."

He had not told me yet what he had to do. Perhaps it takes a farmer really to learn Islandian, for its vocabulary as to all matters of husbandry is rich and various with several words where we make one do. My farming experience was of the briefest and most casual. Aunt Mary, who had only a garden, had taught me all I knew. When two Islandians were talking farming matters I was hopelessly lost. Also, Some was one of those grave-faced persons whom we do not credit with a sense of humor until acquaintance deepens and we become familiar with his personal oddity of expression and own particular savor—the sort of person who with convincing feeling calls the mysterious task he has to do a "bore," the task turning out to be digging a hole.

After following the stream for some distance below the house we came to a level considerably lower. Above us the little stream had deeply trenched a steeper slope, below which it had evidently spread out over a small plain of perhaps half an acre in extent following a varying channel, and thereby making the plain useless.

The soil was red, almost purple in color, in some places thick and gluey, in others coarse and sandy. Some surveyed the plain and I waited. The stream looked quite innocent, and I noticed that it had been confined between low dykes and that the plain at a little distance was gashed with a trench. It was soon evident what our work was to be, to deepen and prolong that trench—in other words, a job of heavy digging. He talked in his solemn quizzical way and I pieced out this much. In six weeks or two months the heavy southeast storms of winter would begin, and before then, before the ground froze, the trench must be dug and lined and the stream turned into it or the work done would go for naught. He loved digging, he said, and therefore he did exactly so much every day. If he missed one day's work he had to make it up. He was up to schedule. If I saved him the amount he had prescribed for himself for tomorrow, he would forgive me with difficulty. Therefore I must not work too hard.

Heavy spades stood upright in the trench. He "hefted" several of them and then handed me one. I watched him carefully and gripped it as I saw him grip his. Ahead of me for perhaps thirty feet the trench was about a foot deep. My task was to deepen it. We dug upgrade, so to speak. The undersoil of the little plain was by no means dry; for behind me the lower parts, already completed and lined with flat stones, contained pools of water. In these he took his place, but where I stood it was only damp.

I began to dig. I heard him sloshing in the water behind me, and the squelches of the wet spadefuls that he flung out upon either side. My own spade cut out large and satisfactory chunks of the damp earth. It was rather fun at first, but quite soon my unaccustomed muscles rebelled. I went slowly, therefore, wishing that he were not behind me but in front of me—yet more anxious to keep on digging as long as he did than to move much earth. I wanted to explain myself, yet did not know how to do so without seeming unsporting. To tell the truth, I was a little indignant at being put to such a task as this, for I could not really convince myself that it was natural for an Islandian to make use of a guest in this way; or rather for a guest without a subtle social coercion to do this sort of heavy manual work for a host he had never seen before. But I dug on, putting my whole mind on the task of doing a reasonable amount of work in a way that would not wear me out too soon and compel me to quit.

As I swung out the spadefuls, I thought of Lord Mora and of

young Calwin, and wondered what they would think if they knew the United States Consul was thus trapped on a backwoods farm. They, I was sure, would never put me to such a task. There was too much "farm" to Islandia. This was a job for a steam shovel. I thought of Uncle Joseph and ideas of labor-saving machinery, of its importance, and arguments for its introduction stirred in my head. I thought of him as scornful of me for letting myself be inveigled into this, and I felt also a sudden anger at Dorn for getting me into trouble in connection with the Germans at the Lor Pass. My friends were a group dangerous to my future if I became too familiar with them.

The spade was heavy. My back ached and my palms stung, but still I went on digging. Nor would I rest or stop until Some did!

Behind me he began to talk. At first I resented it for it distracted my brain, which I was trying to use. He told me of the little plain, and how once the stream had behaved itself; and because the place was sunny (though now with the sky gray and overcast it seemed a chilly place) and the subsoil damp yet with good drainage, they had grown here certain flowering plants, bulbs, and vegetables which require a dry soil but thrive if their deeper roots are wet; how three years before the stream after heavy rain abandoned its bed and ruined the plain; and that it was the only place on the whole farm where conditions were favorable to these growing things. This stirred my sympathy, but suppose there was a traveling steam shovel in Loria, hauled by a tractor? All such jobs as this would be done in a few days. Why not do some advertising for my country's products and be a true consul? I told him of steam shovels. They would scoop out this ditch in short order. It was his turn to listen, and to ask questions. He seemed impressed. I became eloquent and broadened my sales talk, and as a result was perhaps a little less earnest and careful in my digging.

He said he would like to see a steam shovel or at least a picture of one.

I remembered Dorna's remark that Islandians would be interested in devices that saved time. Here was a man really interested in the things we had to offer. It seemed that as one went East one found more progressive people. The conservatism of the West had overcome me for a time. I was too loyal to the Dorns and to their friends not to be impressed while in their country, but I had not really changed my point of view.

Then I became aware from Some's questions that he was not thinking of a steam shovel as suitable and useful for the sort of task we were doing. We had been misunderstanding each other. He had been assuming that I had his sense of humor and that my suggestion of a steam shovel which moved large quantities of earth wholesale for this job was a joke.

"I don't see at all," I said, "why this isn't exactly the job for a steam shovel."

He paused as though fearing to insult me, and then he spoke rapidly. It was a little too intricate for me, but it came down to this: in slowly digging by hand a trench through the little plain one would gain a knowledge of the soil and of all its capabilities that could not be gained if a shovel were used; a shovel would arrange the different sorts of earth in a wrong way for the best results; the weight of the shovel would pack the earth too hard where it had been; oil and coal droppings from the shovel might do other harms.

It seemed to me that he was spinning things a little too fine, but he was a farmer and I was not.

Then he added in an unexpectedly shy voice that here at any rate there were bulbs and perhaps even some herbaceous plants that would be turned under too deep or destroyed if a shovel were used. Intuition served me and I knew why he was shy. My digging was not such as would preserve bulbs or roots. I stopped short and decided to be honest again.

"I had not thought of that. I may have lost you several things already."

"No," he said after a moment. "I have been watching. Nor would there be much in the soil you are digging."

I feared that this was politeness on his part, and that he had suffered behind me.

"Islata Some," I cried, "tell me! Have you not been apprehensive watching me at work?"

"Yes," he answered, "a little. You thrust in the spade so hard. You would cut any root or bulb that was in the way. You would not feel them before your spade."

"Would you?" I asked.

"Why, of course," he answered.

"I could not possibly feel them," I cried.

"Wouldn't you know the soil and everything in it by the feeling in the handle of the spade?"

"No," I answered.

We looked at each other and we both laughed. Then I told him of the extent of my experience in digging.

"I am not the man for this job," I ended. "Are there any bulbs or roots where you are?"

"No."

"Let me try it there?"

"It is heavier and wetter work, and much less interesting."

"Let me try it for a while."

He hesitated.

"I gave you what you are doing, because I thought it would give you pleasure to find bulbs and roots that have survived the floods."

"It would have, but I haven't your touch to find them, and it would be a real pain to me to ruin anything." I told him of the bulbs I had sliced in two while digging for Aunt Mary, and he perceptibly winced. It was like casually talking vivisection to a member of the S.P.C.A.

But he let me come down into the trench. We understood each other now. He ventured to make suggestions as to my handling of the spade—suggestions anatomically helpful. I set to work with zeal.

I suppose I was tired. I ached in a good many places and my hands burned and were a little blistered, but I felt an unexpected power. There was a strong smell of earth. I was absorbed and content. Dimly I looked forward to the stopping time, to a bath, and to supper, with an almost passionate but not impatient pleasure. From the trench where I dug, with my feet in the water, I saw the earthen bank in which the stream had cleft its V-shaped gorge and through that opening the wonderful, rich, deep-green of a field. On either side the forest was close. Behind me the valley of the stream sloped down, the view outward blocked by the dark ridge of the woods.

I felt, rather than knew, with a sudden keen taste and appetite, what it was to be a farmer in Islandia. I sensed the absorbing interest of the immediate task that also is integrated with all other tasks of one's life into a rounded whole, because one's land and one's farm is larger than oneself, reaching from a past long before one began into a future long after one is dead—but all of it one's own.

A quiet voice spoke to me from the edge of the trench above my head.

"Islata Some of Loria Wood. Is this Lang, Dorn grandnephew's friend?"

I looked up into the face of Some, the general, uncle of Cadred's wife, and of the young man with whom I was working.

He was not tall. His dark hair was grizzled and was cut short. His head had the same beauty and nobility as that of Lord Mora, and it also had a gallant quality all its own. His face was handsome, regular, and strong, but his eyes were extraordinary. There was something in them at once savage, passionate, and deeply hurt.

He smiled charmingly, yet his eyes did not lose their gleam of ruthlessness. After a moment I acknowledged his greeting.

While he was welcoming me, young Some, his nephew, uttered a sudden cry.

We both turned to him.

"You remember that *darso* that came up about here in the spring?" he was saying. "I think I've found it!"

His spade was half buried. He slid his hand along the blade into the earth. We both watched him. Much later I saw the *darso* in bloom. Then I was wondering where I had heard of it before, but the excitement of the others I felt myself.

Young Some drew from the ground a large bulb nearly round, and brushed the earth from it. He and his uncle bent over it, examining it. I could not quite follow them. I merely knew that it was rare if not unique.

"We must send it to Dorna grandniece," said the uncle.

"Yes," answered his nephew with feeling.

"There must be bulblets."

The younger man began feeling in the earth again.

I leaned against the wall of the trench, exhausted yet happy, and at the same time vibrating with longing.

That evening after I had gone to my room, the memory that had stirred at the mention of the *darso* became suddenly clear. In one of Bodwin's natural history fables there is an account of finding this plant in the neighborhood of an army bivouac. The idea of the fable is the suggestion of the continuance of strong rural interests and feelings in spite of the excitement and upsetting dangers and hardship of

213

war; and the description of the flower with its dazzling white perianth and crimson, open trumpet was so vivid that it glowed as the flower itself must have glowed to Bodwin's eyes.

As it would also glow in Dorna's garden, I had no doubt! The thrill and ache came again as it had come that afternoon, but I could not sharply visualize her any more, across the mountains, not seen now for four days and nights. It was like a sudden blindness. I strained for a vision of her, but her face would not come. My idea of her was the purest, rarest thing I had ever had, but the life I had to live away from her changed me subtly and veiled her image. The East to which I was returning was sordid, but it had its temptations. I would be more at home there. I was not equal to Dorna, nor to the West which was her home, but I knew that I loved her.

Next morning I left the Somes. Day after tomorrow I would be back in The City again. It would seem like home.

Young Some himself took me out of the wood and left me at the edge of the forest with directions as to how to find the National Highway a few miles southwest of Loria Town. I made a valiant attempt to be truly Islandian and to remember his instructions; nor was I badly lost, nor did I stop to ask my way more than twice.

It was a relief to leave the Somes behind, and to turn my back on all the conservative Westerners—the Fains, the Hyths, the Dorns, the Farrants, the Somes—all of them opposed to the Mora Treaty, exclusionists, barring Islandia to me and my sort of life. Judging by them one would believe that their country would refuse free intercourse with foreigners, deny them settlement, deny them the right to trade, and admit only a few for limited stops as visitors. However, I told myself, as I rode through the flatly rolling, heavily farmed country of eastern Loria under a rather pale but glaring sky, there was another side to this problem and I was not its sole exponent. There was Lord Mora, young Earne, young Calwin, young Mora, and there were the inhabitants of their provinces. I rode all that day, prey to reaction, planning how to do my part in the struggle to come.

The only dark cloud that hung over my homecoming was the effect on my position of my presence at the Lor Pass. Lord Mora had written that the reason was known, but I wanted to see him personally and make certain how I stood with him, and above all with the Germans. The premier's letter had been reassuring but I felt ill at ease.

On the evening of the next day, I arrived at The City and went straight to the stable on Mony Square where Fak was to live and saw to his care. I was more than fond of him and more than grateful. Then shouldering my saddlebag, like one at home, I climbed to the aerial pathway over the roofs and among the roof gardens. I reached my door, above which flew my own flag, and walked in; and George was there to greet me, after an absence of over a month and that a long one. I had left March 10th and it was now April 14th.

I dropped my saddlebag and slumped into a chair. It was good to be at ease again! And to have a bath in my own tub and to dine at my own table—and to drink a little too much of my own wine was better still.

George did not pin me down to business that evening. He let me do the talking as to my journey and I told him all that was tellable, including the whole Lor Pass matter. At that he produced my mail. There was none from abroad, of course, because there had been no steamer, but there were several local letters, one from Lord Mora himself. It was the only one I looked at, for I was aching for bed.

The great man himself was not to be in The City on my return, but he suggested that at my convenience I call upon his son. He said that so far as he and the government were concerned my presence at the Lor Pass was regarded as of no significance at all; that he had taken pains to tell Count von Bibberbach how I came to be there and was quite sure that the count understood the situation; and that he had asked his son and the count to explain the matter to any persons who seemed to misunderstand. He hoped that I had enjoyed myself on my travels, trusted that I had not let his very good friends the Dorns convince me of their point of view on certain political questions, reminded me that I was to come to visit him, said that he would be at home in Miltain until May 20th, and hoped that I would come and stay with him for a week or more before then. The letter had a quality of impersonal and kindly good will. I was of course relieved by it, but I was also a little disappointed. There was a suggestion that certain persons might misunderstand persistently.

Well, then, I would call on young Mora.

I went to bed and for a little while lay awake. Somehow Lord Mora's humorous suggestion that I should not let the Dorns convince me threw me back to the feelings I had had when in their part of Islandia. They came fresh and sharp, and brought with them the image of Dorna. What business had I to say that their life should be changed? Was I not an interloper? If the Western part of Islandia wished to remain exclusive, why should it not, whatever else the rest of the country thought? . . . And Dorna? For a fraction of a moment I wanted Islandia to change its character in order to punish her for the things she had said to me, the warnings, the criticisms. In a changed Islandia, a defeated Dorna might turn gratefully to a powerful Lang.

Wine is a loosener of restraints. I dared think of what I wanted to win: her eternal company, of course, satisfied with me; her lips, the first woman's lips I had ever kissed, and all the rest of her, too, to be loved as my wife. She became real, and because she was real she was as overwhelming as her actual self. I was treated by her image as the living Diana treated Actaeon. In a way incomprehensible to me, I felt as though strong irresistible hands had shaken me violently and flung me down. It was the same feeling that I had had in the cabin of the *Marsh Duck,* when she seemed so yielding and was in fact so safe.

She had a power over me that seemed more than natural for a mere human woman. I could not even rebel against it. I comforted myself with the thought that one has curious thoughts when one is drunk—or rather, curious feelings.

One of the great advantages of drinking a good deal lies in its power to end an old mood and to start one anew. When I woke the next day, all was subtly changed. I had slept well. I had traveled far, learned much, and seen more. I felt eagerness and vitality for my various affairs.

It was steamer day, and at the landing place there was Count von Bibberbach whom I dreaded, although he "understood." He stood in a group of his countrymen, all talking with animation and loud joviality. The minister was always dressed in style. There was nothing to do but to walk up nonchalantly, my hands in my pockets, prepared to greet him, but with a heart that beat uneasily.

The count spied me, said a word to his companions that caused them all to stop and look at me, and himself hurried forward, a broad, slightly mocking grin on his florid face, and his hand out.

"Hello!" he cried in English, and he grasped my hand and gave me a heavy slap on the back. "I am glad you are here again, and not on the frontier." He laughed. "Isn't it your country's policy to avoid foreign entanglements? But they were not officials, your friends on the frontier." He squeezed my hand. "My dear Lang, I quite understand. You must have had some uncomfortable minutes with your headstrong friends, but no wrong was intended by any one, and no harm has been done with us. We all know that young Dorn was your old college chum."

"I had no idea what it was all about," I said. "He wanted to show me the pass, and when we fell in with the other two of our party I began to be surprised, and when I was a witness of what happened at the pass, my breath was quite taken away."

As I said it, I had my doubts.

The count still held my hand. He looked at me narrowly.

"By what?" he said, just a little angry.

"It seemed such a remote place. To find so many people gathering there."

"Your companions believed a wrongful entry of their country was intended."

"Was that it?" I said, trying to look half imbecile. "They told me nothing. It all seemed rather strange to me. You know how secretive Islandians can be."

He had me tightly. He was stronger than I. He was staring at me. I wondered if my flushing cheeks betrayed me.

"No wrongful entry was intended."

"Of course not."

"The boundary line in those parts has not been settled yet."

This was a new idea to me. It had been quite obvious that the saddle which the German riders crossed was the highest point in the pass. From there it was downhill on both sides. The saddle was the boundary line and it could be nowhere else. This was mere pretense on Count von Bibberbach's part.

"Lord Mora admits our right to make surveys."

"I wondered if it weren't a surveying party," I said innocently.

There was a pause.

"I have not been there," said the count. "I understand it is an interesting region. I envy you your youth and your agility. I would like you to meet my friends."

Among the men whom he courteously presented to me were two men whom I recognized as of the three persons who had been on foot on that exciting day—Herr Meyer and Herr von Stoppel. They looked at me closely but were cordial. Every one of us was making reservations and thinking his own thoughts.

I was among these men when the four-oared boat came alongside. The passengers were few, none Americans, but among them was the splendid, broad-shouldered, jolly Hoeffler, whom I had met on the *St. Anthony,* and who also was a leader of the party of riders whom we had pursued in the Lor Pass. The others shouted to him effusively and with much laughter, but he saw me very quickly, and before he stepped on shore he smiled a smile maliciously amused and full of good humor.

"May I land, Herr Lang?" he shouted to me.

The whole party looked at me, I think a little dubiously. Here, I told myself, I shall be a true diplomat; so I ran forward and shook his hand before anyone else.

His laughter was loud above my head.

"I must see you again," he said. "The others of your party misjudged me. What else could I do? I was only seeking the height of land. But they were right. We had crossed it."

He turned from me.

Then and there I resolved to do some detective work. Hoeffler arrived in January with me. He did not leave on any steamer. Yet somehow he must have left Islandia for he rode up from the Karain side. It seemed to me unlikely that he would leave by any other pass than the Lor. If it were the Lor Pass, he knew the height of land at an earlier time than the day when I saw him. One did not need surveying instruments to find out. I surmised that he had slipped out of Islandia and hoped to slip in again unnoticed, but being noticed decided to enter again properly by the front door.

I went home with a good deal to think over, for I had really had a glimpse of my German friends behind the scenes.

Among the local letters that I had put by last night was one that was a complete surprise. Hytha Nattana, for reasons of her own, chose to write me, not just a note, but a real letter, and without any request on my part that we "correspond" with each other.

Her letter ran like this:

Friend of mine,

In John Lang's country do young women write letters to young men without being asked? In Islandia they sometimes do. And though John Lang will be very busy on his return from Dorn Island and will be full of thoughts of what happened there, I, his friend, Nattana, am sure enough of his friendship (*amia*) to know that he won't mind listening to me for a little while, and that perhaps he will answer my letter. I feel that I ought to say a good many things to him in explanation, but I don't know how to say what I am not at all certain of. Maybe I merely want to talk to him and to be reassured. It was this not knowing what to say that kept me in bed when John Lang rode away early in the morning, probably for a long time. He will go all over Islandia before he begins to repeat his visits, I am sure, and it won't be my turn to travel for some time. I stayed in bed when he rode away and of course I was sorry as soon as it was too late, and I was not a bold enough girl to throw on my clothes and ride after a man as though I could not bear not to see him once more. I wish I had not stayed in bed now, for I am sure that without saying these things I would have been reassured. Please will John Lang not judge other Islandian girls by me, but judge me as I am? He has said he likes me (*amia* was the word I had used to her). Will it be too much for him to prove that by writing to me, who was so unkind to him?

A few days after he went away Stellin our cousin came with three horses, and next day, as we suspected, his friend, our greatest and most handsome young man, the king, young Tor, with one horse, only one, and no companions. Nekka knows all the whys and wherefores, but none of the rest of us do. He stayed with us four days and he worried my father, because he ought to have been in The City at the meeting of the council on March 15th and for a week later, and evidently he had "cut it." (The phrase she used was the equivalent in Islandian of breaking an obligatory social engagement, but softened by the convenient diminutive, *ta*.) But father himself had also "cut it." He spent hours with Nekka and was away with her once all day, and Nettera played her flute all the time, playing tunes which we all know and which she ought not to have played—which however, he would not know, but which made Nekka very angry, so that she wanted Nettera punished; but Ettera and I voted against it, and Nekka would

219

not take it up with father, of course, for it would have meant his knowing the meaning of her tunes.

When our gloriously handsome young king left us, Nettera went out on the stable roof and played her tune of triumphant joy, and I danced to it, and Nekka hearing us took her horse and rode up into the hills.

There is no other news for John. No one else has come to see us. No one has come over the unguarded passes. We may be foolish, but we do not ride often on the other side of the river, and we are all training ourselves to examine the hills across the valley whenever we go outdoors—as our ancestors did. Perhaps it is needless.

I say there is no news, but perhaps there are things that might interest John Lang. If he will tell me, I will write them. There is much he can tell me, but I am not hinting that he write me much or often. Is there no history of his country in Islandian? I would like to read it.

But if he does feel that he is still my friend, will he not write me at least a line to say so, to reassure me and to forgive his true friend

HYTHA NATTANA SOLVADIA

I read and reread this letter, and gave up my attempts to elicit from it the exact nature of Nattana's feeling for me. It was no use, but one thing at least was sure. What she asked for I could sincerely give her, assurance of friendship and of the kindest feelings.

It was to me a fascinating letter. My translation cannot give the peculiar tang of her account of the king's visit, but there was something underneath the words that spoke directly to my feelings. Evidently Nattana was troubled and puzzled. So was Nettera also, in her own way. My heart was sorry for Dorn, my friend, as somehow I knew the hearts of these two girls, his friends, also bled. I felt strongly again the flavor of that household, and I seemed to hear Nettera's fife-flute-clarinet; and I wondered what the significance was of the tunes she had played on the hillside above the place where we picnicked—and exactly what those she played during the king's visit signified, since they made Nekka so angry that she wanted her younger sister punished. And though somehow angry at Nekka, I also sympathized with her, wondering if her feeling for him might not go deep, worrying lest she be his plaything.

There were other things to wonder over in this letter, and above all the significance of the last word Nattana had written. It was a built up word. *Sol-* was an intensive prefix; *di* or *dee* was green; the final *a* was feminine; but the *va* puzzled me until I had a happy thought. *Va-* or *van* was the word for eye; a far-seen thing was *vant-;* *Vantry* was the place seen far away. In this word, *Solvadia,* that Nattana had perhaps made for herself, or someone else for her, the idea conveyed to me, more and more able to think in their language, was that of the girl with the very green-green eyes—and as such it was most apt. I remembered also that many Islandians had a secret name of their own used only by those closest to them, though sometimes becoming common. I wished I knew the exact significance of Nattana's revelation of this nickname. Perhaps she had a more secret one still, and Solvadia was the name she flirted with, or gave to her friends. I had heard Dorn call his sister *Aspara* or sea gull—the lovely swift-flying, long-winged sea gull of the Doring Marshes, agile as a swallow, with vivid scarlet beak, and brown-backed, the rest dazzling white . . . But unless I learned from someone what privileges this mention of the pet name of Nattana gave me, I resolved to do no more than recognize it indirectly—to mention a green which I had seen matching her eyes, the dark-green of shallow water over sand in a strong sea wind under a bright sky.

And I felt in my heart that, flirt or not, Nattana was my friend and I hers, and I was happy in that knowledge.

That same morning, with no eagerness, I went to see young Mora as his father directed. He was at the Home Building on City Hill, keeping office hours and holding down the government in this quiet period. I walked in nonchalantly, I hoped, and greeted him as an equal.

I told him of my travels first of all, where I had been and whom I had visited. That was, of course, only a preliminary. I suggested very briefly my efforts to talk up foreign trade and indicated the reactions of those I had talked with. He answered exactly as his father would have done. I must hear the other side, see other parts of the country, and spend at least a week with them while his father was there. I would come in May, I said, after the 5th (steamer day), if that were convenient to his father. It was, he said. I could write a few days before I arrived. He smiled. There were no telephones nor telegraphs as yet.

He supposed that I was no doubt thinking of means to interest my countrymen in Islandia. Anything he could do . . . I nodded, and told him I was making reports which anyone could look at. But, I said, Islandian products would seem very costly to my countrymen, because gold was comparatively cheaper in his country. He came back at me with a list of what might be called quality goods, which it seemed to him Americans (rapidly becoming so rich) would like— wool products particularly, Islandian textiles, some food products; and then he suggested that at first Islandia would import more than she exported and this would increase the value of gold in Islandia. That must happen slowly, of course, he said, or it would too greatly upset local prices established for years. I asked him if Islandians would want to buy foreign goods. Some would not, but there were many . . . and gradually the rest, he answered. Of course a credit system was a necessity, but they had the skeleton of that ready to hand, and Lord Calwin was concerning himself particularly with that problem.

These were only the preliminaries. I remembered what M. Perier had said to me before I reached Islandia. The buying of foreign products by Islandian farmers and the selling to foreigners of what they produced was only a minor matter. I was quite sure that young Mora knew this to be so. I began to be annoyed at his stressing with me this minor matter as though it were the big thing.

I decided to have it out.

"It seems to me," I said, "that such foreign trade as would grow up would not effect great changes here. Your people have nearly all that they want and need. What I should fear, if I were in your place, would be exploitation of Islandian natural resources in timber and minerals by foreigners whose only interest was in getting out and taking away what was in Islandia, making as little return as possible. I should think the investment of large amounts of foreign money in Islandian resources and enterprises—without at least an equal if not a greater investment of Islandian gold, dollar for dollar, in each concession granted—would not be something you would care to have happen."

I watched him. He looked troubled.

"Yes," he said. "We must, of course, take care of a great many such problems." Then he shrugged. "We are neither a very rich nor powerful people," he added, and abruptly he changed the subject.

He told me that Lord Dorn had given his father a full account of my participation in the Lor Pass matter. He wanted me to know that an investigation had been made and that his father was convinced that the party which we had seen come to the pass from the Karain side intended no more than to make a survey to find the height of land that is the true boundary.

I knew what I was expected to believe, and that perhaps I ought to believe it and say no more, but I answered according to my feelings:

"The height of land is obvious. That pass seems to me one place where no survey is needed."

"So we think," he said sharply, "but our generous friends, who are charged with the duty of policing that region wanted to see for themselves. They do things thoroughly, you know, and will not let themselves be misled by appearances."

"Not even the appearance of water running downhill?"

"No. Such water may later disappear under ground."

He eyed me with a shrewd smile.

"Your companion acted too quickly," he said significantly. "The only result was an unpleasant situation for a number of people including yourself. You may be sure that your part in it as a surprised spectator rambling in the mountains with a very old friend is understood by everyone. And my father has charged us younger men with the duty of telling how innocent and surprised you were, and that you merely followed behind—"

"—rather out of breath!"

"Yes—and said nothing at all!"

Young Mora laughed.

"Someday I should like to hear more about what happened, but not now, for I know all I care to know."

Our eyes met. He had won me. He asked me to lunch with him, but I wanted to lunch with the Periers.

They welcomed me, all four of them, and asked me to lunch with such promptness that I was saved the embarrassment of asking myself. I told them all about my travels, including of course more personal details, and needless to say I mentioned meeting the Hyth girls and Dorna. Afterwards, over a cigar, I had a long talk with M. Perier concerning the Lor Pass matter. I told him exactly what happened, because I wanted to arm him against any suspicions about me and I trusted him implicitly. Then I hunted up Jeanne and Marie, and asked them if it were proper for a young man and a young woman in Islandia to "correspond."

"How should I know?" cried Jeanne.

"Why not?" cried Marie.

The truth was that they knew their own etiquette but not the Islandian. They were very little help. I tried to make them use their knowledge and feminine intuitions. Jeanne thereupon hypnotized herself into being an Islandian girl. To be in the proper mood she dressed herself in Islandian costume. Her name was Jeanna, and she was the daughter of Jean, a proprietor. When she declared herself at last feeling thoroughly Islandian, I went out and came back, sat down by her, and after a little conversation in the Islandian mode I asked her if she would let me write to her and would write to me; but instead of answering she fainted. It was all very silly. Marie revived her with difficulty, and when she came to herself she pressed her hand to her heart, and cried in a deep passionate voice that she would write to me until death, one hundred pages a week and that I must do the same or she would *kill* me. I shivered, she was so dramatic. After that declaration she closed her eyes and when she opened them she was French again, declaring that she had really been Islandian for a while and that everything she did and felt was exactly true. She argued from this that you could not safely make such a request of an innocent Islandian girl. Marie argued the opposite, but that you must not expect her to write too much. Thus they teased each other and me, but when I tore myself away Marie advised me to try it and Jeanne not to.

On my way home, I hunted up the only other American in The City at that time. His name was Robert S. Jennings and I had met him at Uncle Joseph's in New York and liked him. I also wanted to obtain his help with a plan I had for introducing American products to the Islandians.

He was the type of man seeing whom you know exactly what he looked like as a boy—a rounded boy filling his clothes tightly with a fresh chubby look long after the time when he would, if self-conscious, wish to look more sophisticated; with round face, round head, round cheeks, bright coloring, and clear rather impertinent eyes, physically harder than he looked, mentally more precocious—a boy other boys respected, with a knowledge and a vocabulary which his parents would not approve of. And as a man Jennings was still rounded, fresh, and knowing.

There are many men like him in the United States, young men of about thirty, who have made their own way from their teens, who love money and are very intelligent in acquiring it, who also love adventure and do not hesitate to cut loose from an assured position and promising prospects to embark on some enterprise more colorful and interesting, confident they will come out on top somehow; men who, avoiding college, and never seeming to have had much opportunity, are yet perfectly capable of being presentable in any circle, full of what might be called native wit, self-contained, lusty, with many indecent stories, with a low opinion of women, and not much better of men, yet true to the promises they rarely give.

Jennings had set out as a sort of free-lance commercial agent, and had moved along the west and east coasts of the Karain continent a little more than making his way, looking for a place to make a killing of some sort. Then, on impulse, I gathered, he had left his samples in bond at Mobono, and about the middle of February had come to Islandia to look things over. He had given me no trouble, being quite able to fend for himself, and in the last two months he had been traveling about visiting the provinces of Bostia, Loria, Camia, Brome, Miltain, Carran, and Deen.

That evening over cigars (his) and wine (mine) we talked and talked on the Mora Treaty and commerce. We saw pretty much eye to eye, except in one particular. He believed that the Islandians were human and susceptible to good advertising. I was not so sure, but we both agreed that the foreign trade "game" was less of a "game" than that of the concessionaries. The best pickings were theirs. Jennings no doubt had ambitions to get in on some concession, but he frankly admitted that it was probably too big game for him. The other game, that of a trader, appealed to him also, even though less profitable. After all, W. R. Grace & Co. in South America, he said . . . He wanted to find out from me how much advertising he could do and how he could go about it.

His coming was a happy coincidence, for a man like Jennings was needed to help carry out my plan.

I told him of it that evening, making it seem a development of his ideas on Islandian susceptibility to advertising. I told him of my talks with various people. His round, clear, dark-blue eyes watched me intelligently. The idea was this: to charter a boat large enough to take the sea, small enough to ascend the rivers, to load it with samples or diagrams and literature of every sort of thing that America had to offer the Islandian, and to send this exhibition ship on a tour; taking no orders, of course, but showing the people at various places what foreign trade would enable them to get and what it would do for them; and so far as permissible indicating to whom they could address themselves to obtain these things, if and when Islandia became open to trade. We got out a map and I showed Jennings where the boat could go, stopping at at least two ports in every province, including even the wholly inland ones of Islandia and Bromé. The enterprise ought to be in charge of one not in the official position I was in, but my share in it would necessarily be a large one: on me would rest the task of obtaining the necessary permissions from the government, the preparation of the "literature" in Islandian, instructions in that language to the men on the boat, the chartering of the boat, and other similar things. And, I said, I would endeavor to accompany or to join her in certain places.

I told Jennings that he was just the man needed for the job, and I pointed out that those who participated in it were likely to become agents in Islandia for American firms.

While Jennings was making up his mind on this plan of mine I was busier than I had ever been before. In the two days that intervened before the *Sulliaba* came in from the East bringing, I hoped, a large mail (and also dreaded official communications and inquiries from Uncle Joseph and his friends), I completed my reports on costs and answered all inquiries made of me up to date. I wanted a clean slate so as to be free to work on plans for the Exhibition Ship, and Nattana's brief history of the United States in Islandian.

I was somewhat tired by April 18th when the steamer was due. Early that morning Jennings appeared and invigorated me anew. He had made up his mind to undertake the exhibition if we could obtain the necessary governmental permission. He had satisfied himself since I had last seen him that Islandia was an interesting enough place in which to remain for the necessary time, and he had a sheaf of letters sounding various persons whom he knew in New York. Promptly, therefore, I wrote to Washington to obtain the sanction of the Department of State for my part in the proposed enterprise, and he and I rushed off just in time to meet the steamer and send our letters.

Among mine was one to my brother, Philip, asking him to obtain for me various seeds and bulbs. These were for Dorna, whom I had scarcely a moment to think of for several days, who seemed utterly remote and lost, left further and further behind as I rushed on planning in every way possible to bring about the state of affairs that she was fighting.

Jennings and I waited on the pier, with Gordon Wills and Miss Wills who were apparently expecting a number of their countrymen.

Over the water came the four-oared boat with its usual dash and boatmanship, and as always I felt a thrill as this craft, our only connection in a land without commerce, cables, telegraph, or proper mails, swept in between the castles from the steamer lying outside. It was perpetually interesting to see what it would bring—to know that soon I was going to read what friends thinking of me had chosen to say to me.

As the boat came nearer, I saw Philip Wills's fair uncovered head. Evidently he had gone out to the steamer. He was talking to a young woman, a girl.

Others were between me and her for a little while, but as the boat swung in to the landing place I saw her profile looking up to the debonair Philip Wills, for she was short. My memory was of early morning and of silence following a steamer's stopped engines. The cameo features, the perfect profile, and my disappointment when I saw she was leaving the steamer—all this I remembered vividly. She was Mary Varney, whose father had an estate at Coäpa.

The *Sulliaba* brought me much mail and for the first time answers to letters I had written. It was a good mail. The State Department's cablegram was unexacting, and there were no annoying reactions to my business and official letters. There were several inquiries, but no difficult ones. The best part of this mail to me, in spite of Dorna, was that it brought an answer to my letters, mailed in St. Anthony, from Clara Bryant, Natalie Weston (the last letters I received from them), and from Gladys Hunter.

Gladys Hunter wrote two pages of answer to my account of my voyage (I liked that); four pages on Carstairs with real interest and several questions; and two more, very schoolgirlish, about her experiences at school. I told myself with satisfaction that two letters on my visit to the Fains and my visit to the Farrants were on their way to her, for in her questions she had touched some of the very matters I had written about in those letters. That coincidence stimulated me happily. Her letters always elicited answers and made writing to her pleasurable.

That evening when Jennings had gone I made it my duty to write to Nattana.

I told her that in my country young women did write to young men, and that I had just received letters from some of my country-women. Usually they talked it over together, and I hoped she would write me again as I surely would write her. I thanked her warmly for doing so.

I then said I really knew nothing about which she needed to be reassured although, of course, I was disappointed that she did not come down to say good-bye. I hoped to come to the Hyths' again. I told her that her account of the king's visit was very vivid, and that the description of herself and her sisters made me miss them. I sympathized with her over her feeling as to the unguarded passes, but she must not tell anyone I did, because consuls were not supposed to have any such feelings. I then said that her inquiry as to a history of the United States had stimulated me to write one—very brief of course. If I had time I would begin it soon.

I concluded by a brief account of my doings since seeing her last, mentioning the green of the windy sea matching her eyes, and I signed myself "John Lang" with a space between the two words.

Before I could go to sleep I must begin that history in my head, planning what to say, realizing that our own extermination of the Indian bore a resemblance to Islandia's expulsion and destruction of the Bants, and thinking on and on. . . .

Next day was the last of the Islandian *Sorn* or summer, four months long, and next day began the two months' season of "Leaves" or fall. It was a warm day, clear and beautiful, and I went up into my roof garden; and finding a place in the shade I mapped out the work I had to do, and later began my brief history with a description of North America. In my mind constantly were reminiscences of the fables and essays of Bodwin and these as far as possible I allowed to influence my style.

Thus occupied I was peaceful yet impatient, happy yet restless. The City lay westward, the moat and flat farms to the east. It was clear and almost windless, characteristic weather of the season. A delicate north wind just fluttered now and then the leaves of my shrubs. Much of the garden was bare, the flowers nearly over. Lona, my landlady, was too busy to give it much time. Another year I would try my hand. There was, however, a vivid red flower of the Compositae in full bloom.

To know that one is doing the job for which one is hired brings serenity. When that job leaves one a certain latitude and, within the limits allowed, one does something new and original, one is entitled to be happy. So my plan for the Exhibition Ship seemed to me then. My peaceful happiness was consular and American, though there were so many things to do that I felt under pressure. The impatience and restlessness were, therefore, not connected with my job. They were the personal feelings of the American dot of life, John Lang, sensitively quivering in a land no longer strange and alien, but queer, very queer.

If Dorna with distance had become vaguer, if I could no longer visualize her or hear her or remember details of her and her dress with microscopic accuracy, nevertheless in her remote and isolated West she became a goddess condescending to me. She made me feel too much. I dreaded her as too strong for my sensitivity. And yet nine-tenths of her always, and all of her when she wished, was comprehensible to me and within the ambit of my manhood. Dorna's bare, crossed ankles on the deck, with the rounded anklebone, and penciled light-blue veins on the instep . . . The vision of that small aspect of her danced before my eyes that morning, and of the glassy river and hot sun overhead. But she was too much for me. Some of my serene happiness came from not being exposed to her any longer, though my restlessness lay partly in not having her.

Marrying her would turn my life into a golden age, but I must be as heroic as I was in dreams and knew I was not in fact. The mere idea of eternal companionship with Dorna, we two, a unit against the world, me become her major interest, as she would, of course, be mine, dizzied and frightened me. It was what I ought to want rather than what I wanted.

When Jennings had come to see me after my return from the West, at the end of our long conversation and after a silence of some minutes he had said with a smile and a trace of shyness, "Lang, do you know where I can pick up a woman?" I did not know and I said so. It did not seem to be one of my duties as consul. Jennings told me that I was no good, and then I suddenly remembered my experience when house hunting with young Earne and why the fifth house we looked at was unsuitable. I thereupon told Jennings where the house was.

Several days later he came in to see me and after having become a little mellowed with *sarka* described his experiences in that locality. I had not thought he would go there on so vague a description, but I did not then know his adventuresome nature nor, perhaps, did I realize his need. He told me that except for the back-street character of the region and the narrowness of the alley it did not look like a red-light district. He wandered about for some time, explored other alleys, went away, and came back. But it was a red-light district all right, he said. A door opened and a middle-aged woman came out, and talked with him. He gathered that she wanted to know if he was a stranger and what he wanted. He said he was an "American," and what he wanted was a girl. That was all he said. That was enough, for she smiled and invited him in by signs. It was a nice-looking house. He sat down and she talked a great deal, and finally he began to understand. She wanted to know if he had ever had any sicknesses. She was apologetic and quite embarrassed.

He said, no—which was the truth. Nevertheless, he gathered, she wanted to examine him. He let her do it, and "would you believe it, Lang," he said, "she took a drop of my blood and went out with it?" He waited and waited. It must have been over an hour before she came back smiling. Evidently everything was all right. The trouble and delay seemed to be because he was a foreigner. She invited him into another room where there were two girls. She served him a sort of meal with a little wine. He made up to one of the girls and spent the night with her.

He and the girl had somehow managed to converse. He learned

a great deal from her as to how it was done in Islandia. Apparently there were some fifteen or twenty men, single men for the most part, many in the army or navy or at sea, of all ages, who when in The City came to see her. That was a new idea to him. A man had a regular girl. It was customary when he wanted a girl to come to her only. "Your Islandians," he said, "are not a promiscuous lot. They stick to one woman until she gets tired of the life, and then if they come back the old lady finds them another." His friend, he told me, was frank about herself. Her father "worked on a farm"—a *deneri* evidently—and there were too many at home. She liked men and saw no chance of marrying. Besides she did not want to marry and never would. She had a good time as she was with very little work to do. She did not like work. But she was getting tired of it. They all did sooner or later. Someday she would tell the old lady that she could not stand it any more, and they would let her go home, and if she behaved herself—as she would—she would not have to come back here to earn her living.

Jennings told me more of his experiences, and mingled with a sensation of ugliness and disgust was much curiosity and some envy for a man who obtained so easily what I had never had. Yet I knew it was impossible for me, made as I was, ever to get it in such a way. But I knew in my heart that in my restlessness and impatience this desire lurked, and I had a feeling of degradation. Jennings's easy acquisition of a girl in stirring my envy made me ashamed and in my shame I could scarcely let myself realize the existence of Dorna or of Nattana, and then only with an unpleasant shrinking or sensation of physical unworthiness.

One evening, when I was sitting alone by my fire working on my history, my bell rang. I went to the door myself, and saw with some surprise the Mlles. Perier accompanied by M. Bart. They told me that Ansel was to play that evening. Father, they said, had at the last minute been unable to go and had suggested me. Would I come? There was very little time. Of course I said I would and prevailed upon them to come in. In a few moments I had dressed and we set out.

The City has a theater, Alwina's Theater, built by the great queen nearly six hundred years before. I had passed it and looked in, for it always stands open. Its seats are like those of the Greek theater, of stone set in a steep semicircle, with a rather shallow stage, but over all is an amazingly light and airy half-dome that makes the stage very high. The theater, however, is not used as theaters are, for Islandia has no drama. M. Perier told me that it went against the grain to mimic another person, even an imaginary one. And Dorna said that it was belittling to pretend you were someone else. But if anyone has anything to say or show to a large public, he uses the theater when it cannot be done out of doors, and in addition the theater was used for concerts. Annually in June there was a sort of music festival, but at other times there were solo concerts as well. To such a one we were going.

I never was much of a concertgoer. I always felt that if listening were not so acute and strainful a performance I would love music, and I always planned to go more than I did. But I never missed music at all and knew very little about it. I knew of concerts in The City, but I had never bothered to investigate until the Mlles. Perier took me in hand.

Ansel was a fife-flute-clarinetist like Nettera. His instrument, however, had a greater range than hers, which was more fife-flute, his being more flute-clarinet-bassoon. The theater was perhaps half-full. The performance was free. Ansel was not a professional, but anyone who wanted to pay something could do so, and what was paid went for the benefit of professional music. Ansel was brother of a *tana* of old family and residence in the province of Brome. The family was so placed that Ansel's services on the farm could be dispensed with. Had it been otherwise he would have been a professional. His talent would have necessitated his being a musician, and his earnings as such would have gone to provide for a substitute for his hands at home.

There was no visible program. He played without notes. I constantly thought of Debussy. There were strongly marked rhythms, and there was melody elusive to my diatonic ears. When the concert began Ansel rose nonchalantly from a group of friends in the front rows, walked on the stage, faced us and began to play. Evidently he became tired, for later on, without stopping he brought a chair from the back of the stage and sat down. It was most informal. He played for perhaps an hour with no pause for more than a few moments. It seemed all one piece, for there was one theme that constantly recurred. I listened at first with curiosity. During one of the pauses someone spoke from the audience, but I could not catch what he said. Ansel laughed, and played a few bars that seemed to me a repetition and there was a faint rustle of recognition and applause. In another intermission he said, "This may puzzle you for a moment." In another he said, "Upper Doring." I was reminded by what followed of Smetana's "Moldavia."

According to Jeanne, who was intensely excited, there was no virtuoso like Ansel. She seemed a little annoyed at me, as true music lovers are, for not realizing that this was an extraordinary occasion. I dared ask no questions, and, debarred from learning through my brain what it was all about, I had to listen with my ears alone.

Perhaps it was association of ideas rather than true musical appreciation. The passage like Smetana's piece continued for a long time, and suddenly my hair stood on end and I felt cold tingles down my back, and for a long while I was carried away, deeply moved, and wholly absorbed. The music touched the obscure roots of my emotions and I thrilled with a feeling akin to agony. One is supposed to enjoy that scraping upon the sensitive core of one's being. At least those who have had it, seek to have it again. I wanted more of this unbearableness, I know—that is, I wanted it then. It was as though I were being painfully readjusted deep within. But when it was well over I dreaded exposing myself to Ansel again.

On the way home Jeanne was very silent, her dark, dark eyes bright, her cheeks flushed, almost pretty. When Marie said he had worked up an effective climax, she snubbed her with rude sharpness which Marie took in good part with a glance at me, and when M. Bart showed an inclination to tease Jeanne, Marie in turn snubbed him.

I accompanied the Mlles. Perier to their door. I was very tired, and deeply shaken. Until then I had been getting along very nicely for a man in love with a demigoddess, impatient rather than unhappy; but Ansel had stirred in me suppressed forces. I suffered a crisis of longing. I felt that I could not live without sight and sound of Dorna again, and yet I dreaded seeing one who would so overstrain my emotions.

Next day common sense set me to work on my reports, which were good discipline for my lacerated soul. I had to go on living until June, when I would see Dorna again. In the meantime I must have something to bite on.

On the third the *Sulliaba* came from the German colonies and

on the fifth the *St. Anthony* from that town. I met them both. They
brought some mail but not much, and that was easily cared for next
day. But the *Sulliaba* brought two Americans—Andrews, a businessman, and Professor George W. Body, a geologist. They came to see
me, and I dispatched them on their way, of not much use to them.
Body had been in Islandia before and professed to know his way
about. They were the first sign, beyond Henry G. Müller, of the
prospector and concession hunter. It annoyed me that they did not
take me more into their confidence.

12

At the Moras'

ON MAY 7TH, at an early hour, I left for Miltain, wearing Islandian
costume for the journey, but with all my American best clothes with
me to wear at the Moras', for I wanted to be thoroughly American.
Because I planned to travel fast and did not want to overburden my
horse with all my baggage, I traveled well, with an extra horse of
Fak's breed which the stable man had found for me. I brought with
me my diary, my history of the United States, and an edition of
Bodwin's *Fables* to brush up my style. And I set out in good spirits.

Lord Mora inspired me with awe. The Dorns in the West were a
slightly older family, but they seemed of the same sort as other
Doring and Western men. The Moras on the other hand stood out
from other Islandians in wealth, in family customs, and in the way
they lived. They entertained ducally and treated their guests more
as a European nobleman would, and their house was usually full.

Even before I started I had a foretaste of their way of doing
things. The distance I had to go was at least two hundred miles. My
stopping places were all arranged for me. The first stage of fifty miles
would take me to Camia Town where I was to be Lord Mora's guest
at the Inn. The second stage of sixty would bring me to Brome Town
on the Matwin River, where a certain *tana*, an agent, Panwin, would
receive me. The next stage was to one of the eight establishments
of Lord Mora, again sixty miles away, their so-called Brome farm.
The last stage of all would bring me to Miltain. All but this last were
long days for Fak, and were more suited to the horses of the Center
and the East. He had endurance enough but he was slow.

There was little that was new in my four days' journey. Camia and
Bostia are as like as two peas, with endless farms and nothing else.
It was warm and Fak had to be urged a little. For the most part he

walked, but every little while I made him trot. Riding was already
instinctive. I could think as I rode and my history filled my head and
I composed long paragraphs. In the evening or during the long rest
periods I wrote what I could. It was never as good as what I had said
to myself. But such intense preoccupation gave to this journey a
dreamy, half-remembered quality.

Late in the morning on the fourth day of travel I came to a rise
in the road and saw about a mile away over flat meadows the gray
walls of Miltain, with here and there red roofs rising above them.
To the right the blue waters of the broad Haly River edged the walls,
and far across the city was a round battlemented tower, and in the
center a cathedral façade, with two square western towers, crenellated
with low pyramidal spires.

Like Doring Town, Miltain Town is unique. Both are riverine
settlements, but Doring is set on hills in the river and Miltain stands
in flat meadowland at the junction of the Haly and Miltain Rivers.
It is the most Europeanized of Islandian places, the most liberal,
where the foreigner feels most at home.

I rode through the meadow under a full dome of sky and then
across a drawbridge over the Miltain River through an arched gate
into the city. The houses, built directly on the street and nearly all
of white limestone with pointed, red-tiled roofs, were uniform in
height, and the streets were wide for Islandian towns. A curved street
led to the center of the town, where I passed the ruddy brown mass
of the cathedral, built by Christians in the eleventh or twelfth century, pre-Gothic, a basilica, heavy, imposing, massive rather than
beautiful. Here I turned into a straight street leading to the Mora
Park, which stood at the southeast corner of the town, jutting out
into the Haly River. It contained the Old Capitol of the province,
the great tower which I had seen rising above the city, and the Mora
Palace, my destination.

Shortly before I arrived at the palace I caught sight of a carriage,
and I stopped at the door just as Miss Varney and Mrs. Gilmour
stepped out of the carriage.

We separated to our rooms, to change our clothes and prepare for
lunch; yet it was not here that we were really to make our visits,
which were informal ones, but at the Moras' principal country seat
—their great farm—six miles down the river. Nevertheless we
were first received at the palace in Miltain as a sort of formal honor.

My room contained some European furniture and I changed into my American clothes seated on a Chippendale chair. I heard afterwards that when the missionaries were expelled, in the 'forties, the Lord Mora of that time, to minimize their losses, bought many of their goods at high figures.

There were no more perfect hosts than Lord Mora and his wife, Calwina, though her consideration was just a little mechanical. He was a great man. He had everything, a fascinating face, magnetism, charm, a sympathetic kindliness, and a personal simple manner. He made me feel that I was welcome.

He and his wife and younger daughter had come up from their farm for the purpose of meeting us. He had other guests, but he did not at once mingle us with them, himself giving us this special attention first.

After lunch in the sumptuous dining hall, under Lord Mora's guidance we visited the Old Capitol and we climbed to the top of the Mora Tower, which ought to have two stars in any Baedeker. It was built with the idea of being the last refuge of the Moras and their followers in the days when Miltain was a frontier strong point in the East. The tower antedated the Old Capitol building and rose above it; and from its top one looked to the south down onto the town and for miles over the flat meadows that surrounded it and the farms beyond, and to the east directly down the broad channel of the Haly River, with its sand bars and long arms of blue ruffled water.

As we all stood there, caught by the view, Lord Mora told us briefly some of the scenes witnessed from there. The siege of Miltain in 1066 (strangely reminiscent date!) shortly after the town was built, when the founder of his family and builder of the tower saw the Saracens sweep over the country and the fire rise from all points of the horizon; and the several great sieges in the reign of Alwina, when, from this tower, a Mora had seen the oared galleys of Kilikash, the Karain emperor, ascend the river to invest the town by water for the first time, and had later seen the relieving squadrons of Islandian vessels come up to the town by kedges and under sail. Since then Miltain had seen no enemies except as prisoners.

To me the account—very simply made, and always with an ancestor of the man who spoke figuring in it, as real to him at least as the grandparents of most people, but grandparents in his case contemporary with the Battle of Hastings—touched something deeply responsive. Here with the Moras as with the Dorns and others in the West was the same feeling of family solidarity, so strong that the Islandian language reflects it, having two pronouns to represent the first person plural; one for use when the aggregate involves the speaker and those not of his blood, and another when the "we" or "us" refers to members of the speaker's family—a different "we" to the Islandians. It surprised me a little to find the Moras in this respect as native as the Dorns and the Somes, and I felt suddenly that for all their great political differences they were closer together than any of the foreigners could ever be to the Moras, who at times seemed so like ourselves. And because Lord Mora was an understanding man and drew from one the utterance of unformulated thoughts, I told him how this feeling of family had struck me, and how I had encountered it with the Dorns and Somes. He was somewhat enigmatic, yet went straight to the core of my feelings. He spoke in his own tongue.

"We (the family pronoun) consider ourselves as Islandian as they are. The difference between us is not of end, but of means." Then lest I seem to take too much of his attention, and yet still with what I had said in mind and for my special sake, he pointed out the cathedral to us, and spoke of Christianity in Islandia; and told how the founder of his family was brought up by a priest, and, if never quite a professing Christian, came near to being one. He had made Miltain, the province he conquered from the blacks, a refuge for priests. "Our split with the Dorns began then," he said with a smile. "Later Moras were sympathetic with Christians, and Mora V was a little more. He was baptized. The priests, he said, introduced into Islandia the alphabet, the written word. They were foreigners. There was much to be learned from foreigners. Even the present Lord Dorn's father thought so, though apparently all he was willing to borrow from them was means to keep them out."

We were to travel by water to Lord Mora's farm and we left soon after. The boat had two masts and was yachtlike. Its sails were snowy and carried on immense yards, and its lines were finer than those of the sturdy boats of the Doring River Marshes. The wind was light and the journey took two hours. We all sat in a well or cockpit lower than and before the tiller. I enjoyed that ride immensely.

We made a pretty landing at a stone pier in a cove at the foot of a green lawn. The house was masked in trees, and we were met by most of the others at the Moras'. The season corresponded to mid-October at home, and the weather to Indian summer. If the lawn was green, the magnificent lofty beeches and other trees beyond it were bright in their autumn foliage, reds and yellows, with the scarlet twigs and white stems of birches already bare of leaves. Two small houses of buff stone with red tile roofs stood near the shore end of the dock, with gardens behind, where flamed some of the red Compositae. On the dock itself those who waited for us added their color, among them a girl all in white except for red cuffs and lapels with a white band.

It was like landing at a summer place that takes pride in concealing its luxury and comfort behind an exterior of simplicity—like Mount Desert without the mountains.

We landed and introductions were made. I saw again young Earne who had helped me in house hunting, and met his mother, who turned out to be Soma, somewhat to my surprise, for the Somes were Dorn stalwarts and the Earnes Mora followers. She was the aunt of young Some with whom I had worked in Loria wood. Apparently political differences did not prevent intermarriage. There was also young Earne's sister, a girl of twenty-one, and Lord Robban of Alban, a man of forty-six or -seven, and his wife, Delan and his wife Enninga, a couple of perhaps fifty; Morana, the girl in white, elder daughter of Lord Mora, Morana Ettera or "third" and her sister, Morana Nekka; Mora Atta, Lord Mora's second son; and last, but not least, two of my German friends, Herr von Stoppel and Herr Meyer, the walkers on foot at the Lor Pass. Later, at the house, still more persons appeared: Lord Mora's uncle, a man of eighty-six, Morana, his sister, and Bordernia, wife of Lord Mora's brother, a general, and in addition a number of children.

To find oneself one of so large a house party of strangers, all friendly, and to keep them straight, was a strain.

"It is as bad as in England at a house party," said Miss Varney, "only there some of them are related to you."

However, by the time I went to bed I had them all straight.

Of the daughters of Lord Mora, the eldest was a beauty. Their resemblance to their father was striking. They were tall and well made with his aristocratic symmetry of figure, with finely featured faces, spirited, proud and full of fire, with rich pure brown hair and blue eyes, all except the elder Morana whose eyes were dark-brown like her mother's. There was something about this girl that said to me all the time, "I am a prize, I am rare and lovely. I am well bred and fine, and it is my lot to have to marry greatly." She reminded me of some New England girls, but was without their self-righteous stiffness, nor was her conscience so obviously at work. She was a Great Lady in the making.

European as Lord Mora's sympathies might be, in his treatment of his guests he was as much Islandian as European; that is, he attended to his normal concerns, including his guests when he could, and leaving them to their own devices after first indicating what there was for their amusement. There were no plans for our amusement made in advance. Yet he or his wife, his son or his daughters, took good care of us all with a certain unobtrusive tactfulness and I never felt neglected.

Across the river in the Province of Deen, about fifteen miles away, were the Yovel Hills, a tract of rugged forested country. A picnic there was decided upon. We were to be ferried across the river, to ride to the hills and climb among them on horseback, and to lunch there.

At dinner the evening before when the picnic was under discussion Morana Ettera, who sat two places down the table from me, suggested to me that I ride Fak. I might start a little earlier than the others and get back a little later, but in the hills, she said, Fak would feel at home. My pack horse was of the same breed, wasn't he? He could be ridden? I said that he could and dared to ask if she would ride to the hills with me. She accepted at once.

We started nearly an hour before the others. The horses had all been taken over the night before. I rowed Morana over in a skiff, or rather we both rowed.

The river, almost half a mile wide, with a narrow sand-bar island to be avoided, was ruffled blue with a light, cool wind. There was autumn in the air. Last night there had been a light frost, Morana said. We landed in a little cove, tied the skiff to a tree, and walked by a narrow path to the farmhouse where our horses were. Morana wore a soft longish coat, and also knickerbockers, and wore these last so naturally that I, unused to girls in such costumes, was not too conscious of them; she was so slender and graceful that such a costume became the long simplicity of her figure.

We had a little dispute as to which should ride Fak, obviously the better horse, and finally agreed to take turns, she professing with a smile to prefer the pack horse to make up to him for our thinking him inferior. We drew lots. I remember vividly her pretty, slim, brown hand, two blades of grass protruding from the crotch of her thumb. She drew the pack horse.

She led the way, and I followed. The chill passed out of the air and it became warm with a bright sun. There was a long pleasant silence while we followed grassy farm roads between stone walls, or edged pastures, taking turns opening and closing gates as she insisted, telling me gently that on a trip like this an Islandian girl was much happier if she did her share, but that it was nice of me to want to open all the gates. After some time we came to a public road that followed the Yovel River, which was really a brook but a vigorous and busy one, often rapid but sometimes in pools and shallows—the sort of stream that delights the eye of the trout fisherman.

So we went on, duly changing horses when she said, in good but silent companionship, I no longer worried because there was little between us to talk about. Indeed she, like some other Islandian women, sealed my lips. I must do them the honor of talking only when I had something worth while to say.

But when we crossed the National Highway that runs south through Deen and Hern to distant Ardan in Storn, and the road began to rise a little, the brook to brawl more on our left, and the woods, mostly birches, to become denser, she dropped back to my side and began to talk to me; and we had one of those time-winging conversations that establish a sort of relation ever afterwards between two persons—something that cannot necessarily be named friendship, for it may occur between those who remain strangers, but that gives to each a knowledge of the other's key, so to speak, and a memory of having sounded in unison. Yet we talked of no very deep things. She drew me out, and I said more than she did, speaking with an absorbing painful precision, avoiding insincerity, the assumption of knowledge, and all posing, speaking almost with bareness. I was flattered by her interest. I told her of my coming to Islandia, of

241

Harvard days with Dorn, and of my visit to the West; and as though to match these and reveal the same side of herself that I revealed, she told me that she had never been outside Islandia like her father, older brother, and younger sister; that her father and mother had very much wanted her to go to England, but that she had resisted being sent (she did not say why). And then speaking of my friends, the Dorns, she said that she had visited them once and they at the Mora farm once.

The sun dappled the road we were following. The Yovel River brawled and bickered; and suddenly the image of Dorna burned in me, a dweller in some deeper part of my being, where she was hidden but always there.

The road became steeper and ridges appeared, and around a turn we came to an opening and saw ahead and above us limestone cliffs hot against a pale sky; and the green that crowned their flat tops and dotted their slopes was dark and made them glare.

Fak quickened his pace and the pack horse responded.

"I doubt if they overtake us now," said Morana with seeming pleasure.

We came to the last farm and the road became a trail winding up into the hills. It was her turn to ride Fak, and she was reluctant to change.

We began to have views back and down. We climbed with what seemed to me extraordinary rapidity. Morana was leading, for we had found that with Fak ahead the pack horse was put on his mettle.

The trail wound out along the cliffs. The drop was a little breathtaking, but not dangerous or disturbing to one who had traveled in the Frays.

The plain of Deen, the gleam of the Haly River, and Miltain lay flat beneath us, misty, in pastel shades. It was true Indian summer, and the sun beating on the white cliffs made them glare whitely.

I saw Morana wind around what seemed to be a turn into space. She swung about in the saddle and waved her hand, and I turned my eyes where she had indicated. Down the steep slope I looked a little dizzily and saw below me, minute and foreshortened, the rest of our party emerging from the woods in single file; first came a man (young Earne) and then a dot of bright white a little softer than a man would be, probably Miss Varney; then the unmistakable bulk of von Stoppel; two women; a boy; a couple; and then pack animals and lastly two men. They wound out of the woods to their right and on one by one, the bottle shape of the horses seen from above giving them the appearance of having their bellies to the ground; and then we saw the infinitely tiny pin points of faces turned our way, and a faint shout floated up to us. I chuckled to the pack horse to catch up with Morana, riding serenely ahead on jaunty-footed Fak.

It was nearing late morning and the sun was high and hot. I was drowsy. Finally another turn far above the last one brought another view of the road below and looking steeply down we saw the others, every one on foot, toiling along in front of their horses. And yet our two were not overtired, hot as it was.

Morana dropped back to me. We both, I think, were a little dismayed, and we discussed the others. She wondered if they had not ridden too hard in the heat to catch us and had brought their horses, spent, to the climb. It was young Earne who led. He was a little inclined to compete, she said.

Of one accord we asked each other if we ought to wait for them. They would be rather tired, she said. She did not want to wait, I knew, for she also enjoyed competition, and so did I, proud of my horses, whose day and whose country this was.

If we waited, we decided, we would wait in the shade, and so we rode ahead, tied our horses to a shrub, and sat down in a little edge of dense shade. Then for the first time I realized how very hot we were. The air was utterly still and I burned moistly, feeling the blood in my temples and hot clammy places under my clothes.

Morana leaned back, folding her hands behind her head, smiled a faint little smile, and said nothing, her eyes remote and serene.

We waited and waited. A soft wind touched us now and then with a breath always about to be but never cooling. Morana sat with amazing stillness. I don't think she stirred anything but her eyelids for a full half hour. She never looked at me. Her bosom rose and fell softly. She half reclined, half sat, perfectly relaxed, so inert that she seemed almost intentionally flaunting her feminine receptiveness. Vague thoughts, vague feelings . . . If one were alone with any reasonably good-looking woman long enough, could one help but feel slow warming of the masculine in one, though another be the right one and not she?

Her stillness was hypnotic. It seemed to me that I was in a trance not really awake from sleep—not able to wake—when I saw young

243

Earne come into sight, smiling but his face flushed and wet, leading his horse, and then Miss Varney, her face very red indeed, and after her von Stoppel, Morana Nekka, Earna, young Delan, Robban, and Calwina, and after these and the three pack horses, to my great surprise, the German Meyer and Lord Mora himself.

Miss Varney was attractive, the femininity of her figure flagrant in her rather close whipcord riding breeches, long oiled riding boots, her soft white silk shirt, and her white low helmet. The masculine cut of her clothes was belied by her stocky body within, her small hands and feet delicate in spite of shoes and gauntlets, the soft wings of her hair, and her hot, angry, little face. And as I came nearer she exhaled a definite and not unpleasant odor of perspiration.

I was too hot also, and long sitting in absolute stillness had left me dazed. There was nevertheless a curious sensation of ease and co-operation. Morana, her father, and I—I don't know which of us suggested it, but it was soon all arranged. Miss Varney was mounted on Fak, and Calwina on my pack horse, and we all went on, all on foot except these two, Herr Meyer and young Earne, whose horse even to my untrained eye was superb and equal to his weight uphill for a long time more. Those of the others were obviously tired, sweating heavily.

With curt thanks to me, Miss Varney rode off on Fak following Earne, and I led her horse rather unexpectedly finding myself at the head of the procession.

Fak's rear view with Miss Varney astride him, his sure little feet, and the muscles of his buttocks and flanks rippling with energy and wiry power, obviously determined not to be left behind by the tall, strong, black horse ahead, filled me with pride.

I led, but the way was easy enough. I did not look back, for if I had I might have got in the way of my horse. Earne and Miss Varney soon disappeared. We reached the foot of a cliff and the trail became stiff and exciting, a wall on one side, a drop on the other, but no great danger. The plain far below was almost invisible, drowned in a pale shimmering. But view or no, hot or cold, I was in good condition, and I was glad of the exercise of walking for a change, glad to be very, very warm and to feel my muscles.

I don't know how long we walked. We ascended the cliff face, the trail taking advantage of ledges and curving back and forth several times.

Looking up I saw a sharp edge of cliff against the sky and moving upon it three small figures, one in white. They waved to us as we climbed upward leading our horses. I assumed that Earne and Miss Varney had met someone. Still leading, I looked back on the train following me, down and over them. I noticed without much thinking that Calwina was leading a horse as well as riding my little pack animal. At the end of the procession, Herr Meyer with a felt hat over his eyes was talking to Lord Mora who was walking by his horse, with the easy swing of the athlete. It thrilled me to see him— pleased me to go on this rough picnic with him and to be so intimately a part of his group of acquaintances and friends that he could think with me as to lending my horse, and could trust me to lead.

When I looked ahead again, I saw to my astonishment that the third person in the group waiting for us was Morana. Von Stoppel boomed his surprise behind Morana Nekka, who said nothing until asked directly by the German how her sister had got ahead of us. She answered noncommittally.

"There are short cuts for those who haven't horses. Isla Calwina led my sister's."

Soon we were all on the top and for a few moments were busy tying the horses in the shade. Lord Mora himself, Lord Robban, Earne, and I cared for them, while the women spread our lunch, and von Stoppel and Herr Meyer looked at the view.

After lunch Lord Mora told us how, when Miltain was captured in 1305, "we" escaped to these hills and hid for a short time in some of the limestone caverns.

"Morana," he said, smiling at her, "passed them on her short cut, I think."

She nodded.

"For some reason she does not want anyone to know where they are," he added.

Von Stoppel looked up at her. He was reclining on his side.

"Are you afraid that they may be useful again, Islata Morana?" he said in his Germanic Islandian.

There was a slight flash in her dark eyes.

"I am not at all afraid," she said, "but I like to keep them secret."

She twisted his words. He had not asked her if she were afraid, but if she feared a particular occurrence.

I was reminded of Nattana and her fears, and was pondering over Morana's feelings when I heard von Stoppel say to Lord Mora:

"I would like to find an authenticated instance of an inherited fear six hundred years old. You must have told your daughter stories when she was young." He was slightly ironical. I think it piqued him that Morana did not offer to tell him where her caves were.

As the sun sloped westward a breeze sprang up. It seemed to blow in from open spaces to the north, and under our eyes a miracle happened. The haze that made the plains of Miltain and Deen look submerged in cloudy water, vanished. The city of Miltain, its meadows, the gleaming reaches of the Haly River, were a bright cluster and a line of silver threads in this dark-green and yellow carpet. The whole was dotted with farmhouses, tiny spots of white; and unexpected, breath-taking, finest of all, on the horizon to the northwest hung the pink-white snow fields of the Great Range. Von Stoppel voiced his delight loudly.

But it was time to go.

That evening Lord Mora and I had what might be called a political conversation. I asked him if I might talk to him and he was cordial, leading me to his library full of books in all languages. There was a fire, and tired from my day of heat and chill I was glad of the warmth.

I told Lord Mora of Jennings's and my plan for the Exhibition Ship. It meant, of course, bringing into Islandia foreign goods, but not to remain there nor to be sold. I made a full statement and a careful argument, concluding with the remark that in the event that Islandia was not opened for foreign trade it would all go for nothing, hoping thereby to draw from him a prophecy. But he gave me none, at once asking me many questions that occurred to him. We talked a long time. The idea pleased him, he said, but it was not a matter he could rule upon offhand. He realized that it was not a matter that we would want to have generally known lest other countries imitate us and perhaps precede us. He promised me an answer by the middle of June, and told me that he thought it would be favorable, saying that, although the present laws forbade exports or imports of any kind, he thought an exception could be made in the case of the samples needed for the Exhibition Ship.

"But does the present law prevent the making of a gift?" I asked, suddenly remembering the bulbs for Dorna. "I should like to send my aunt a packet of the seeds of some Islandian garden flowers. Can't I do so? Can't I import into Islandia seeds and bulbs?"

"No," he said, "the law forbids importation or exportation of any sort, except books and the like. Gifts are not excluded. But as to the seeds, send them to your aunt and say no more about it. And if you are expecting seeds and bulbs of your own native plants, don't destroy them, but don't plant them without sending them to the University for examination for pests. We will forgive you that much."

I blushed hotly. He had read me. His clairvoyance with regard to the seeds and bulbs I had sent for touched an inner sensitive fiber, and I wanted to stay with him and tell him all my personal troubles . . . His peculiar magnetism transcended our difference in age and position and nationality. I felt it physically. But I did not say a word about myself to him. Instead I told him how much I was enjoying my visit and how kind they all were, but I said that I thought I ought to go after two more days. He pressed me, not too insistently, to stay longer, making me feel a little more than a mere guest.

After a slight pause he asked me if I were going directly back to The City, and I said that was my plan, mentioning the various irons I had in the fire. The mention of my monograph in Islandian upon the history of the United States quickened him. He was tactful in his questions. He offered to help me. How far had I progressed? I found myself offering to show him what I had written and he seemed really pleased.

I fetched my manuscript and notes to him, and left him reading them and went to bed.

Soon after breakfast Lord Mora asked me if he might show my manuscript to his elder daughter, to try it upon her who had never been to Europe and thus to ascertain whether it had in it the sort of thing she, a typical Islandian, would want to know about a foreign country. I was pleased to think of her reading it. He made me a pretty compliment on my facility in Islandian, and asked me if I would object if he and his daughter made a few notes and suggestions.

In the afternoon it rained, a gentle but persistent wet rain. There was my diary, letters to write. I went to my room and shut myself up. At about half-past four, there was a knock and I found Morana. When I opened to her I did not know whether it was proper to ask her in or not, and she settled that problem of etiquette for me by asking me if she might come in.

She sat down, crossed one limber knee over the other and clasped her hands upon it, strong pretty hands. The swelling at the base of her thumb was somehow fascinating, and the open-air texture of her fine skin. Morana was twenty-two and yet she seemed to me older than myself.

She informed me with a smile that it was raining, but since I was going so soon, and there would probably be some trip tomorrow, there was not much opportunity for a talk with me; that she wanted quite a long talk, and would I care to go for a walk, for the house was stuffy and she was tired of being indoors and perhaps I was also.

We set out in the semidarkness of the low, gray, rain clouds, and our faces were soon cool with the chilly wet rain. I wore my Islandian cloak and boots, and an American felt hat—an incongruous combination—but she encouraged me to please myself. I told her how Americans whose position compels them to wear uniforms, like postmen and railroad conductors and brakemen, as soon as they are off duty put on some article of civilian wear, usually a hat, to remove the stigma of the uniform. That amused her, walking straight into the rain.

But she had taken me out to talk about my history. Slender, tall, graceful Morana, the drapery of her cloak in gusts of wind and rain, now against her body, now billowing: her profile that seemed to lean a little forward, fresh, wet, and young as a child's, serene, friendly, and royal; the background of trees, meadow, gray ruffling river, under low skies—these things brought a sensation of time floating on wings. The expression of one country to another—personal because each cited each or the other as an example—became absorbing. We walked along the edge of the river for perhaps two miles, on the right its waters ringed with raindrops, on the left meadows and then low banks; country, river, rain, open air—and over all that peculiar sensation of isolation and distance that comes from walking along an uninhabited strand with the shoreward view masked by dunes or bluffs. Gulls wheeled over the water. A boat passed foaming upstream with all sails set. I did not know where we were going, but we had a definite objective—a little one-room cabin on the cliff edge, about twenty feet above the river, with a grove of beech trees close behind it.

Morana went straight to it and pushed open the swollen door with her knee. Within was a fireplace, two comfortable chairs, a couch or bed, a table, and a little wardrobe. She flung off her coat gracefully, and at a smile from her I took off mine. We hung them on hooks. Then she knelt to make a fire and would not let me help her. As soon as it was blazing she produced rather stale nutty cookies from the wardrobe and a light thin wine, and from the folds of her coat my manuscript; and we sat down on the two chairs, and went over it page by page and note by note, and also over the finely written suggestions of her father and herself.

Behind us the door was open upon a blue-dark world of rain, cloud, river shore, windy waters, and trees. Our fire was to dry us and the room rather than for warmth.

If Dorna had her windmill for retreat, so had Morana this cabin, a place to be alone, yet sheltered and comfortable. I had not been inside Dorna's windmill, but I had no doubt it had two chairs and a couch, where she could lie and think with her hands clasped behind her round head. She would hear the windmill's rhythmic clank and clatter, smell the salty air of the marsh, and closing her eyes feel timeless age and become one with her ancestors for a thousand years.

Morana was kind, but she was thorough. I received more suggestions and criticism than praise, but all were illuminating; and she never criticized anything that it was in my own power to better.

And as we talked and argued a little, I felt more and more strongly her native quality; so that she, though daughter of a modernist and traveled man and herself experienced with foreigners, became to me in one part of my perception one with and the same as Dorna, and I had a sudden surge of love for her—of unexacting love which when its crisis passes becomes the cement of deep, permanent affection. If I had met her first, would she not have been my Islandian beloved, and Dorna the friend, because I was fated to love someone in that beautiful, elusive country? And I wondered if this love was really love, the love I would feel for girls at home. Perhaps it was beauty that ached, so that I thought it love and mistook my need.

Finally all was said and she handed me my manuscript with her notes and her father's; and she did what I had pictured Dorna doing —she clasped her hands behind her head, revealing its sleek symmetrical roundness, and she smiled at me a friendly, unforgettable, charming smile.

Her eyes drifted away and there came a long charmed silence, broken only once when she poked the fire with her foot. It grew darker and rain drummed on the roof above us. I shifted my chair a little to avoid the constraint of so directly facing her, saying nothing —moving as quietly as I could not to disturb her. From my new position I could look through the open door.

Her voice broke a long silence, clear, cool, and gentle.

"You are like one of us in your willingness for moments of no conversation."

I was grateful to her for pointing out a likeness instead of a dissimilarity, but I could not utter it, thinking of what Dorna and Nattana had said. I only nodded and there was silence again. Yet I knew I was not Islandian, for in these silences I was more often waiting to talk again than contented in speechlessness. . . .

"We had better start home," said Morana.

The rain and wind were behind us as we walked along the shore. Morana leaned back in her cloak, which billowed ahead of her like wings. She held it out and said it was her sail. Thinking of other things I was not giving her her due, unable any longer to realize her except as a charming image floating at my side.

Yet at the end she won her victory over me. I had to thank her for what she had done for me, and in doing so I was carried away, telling her what I thought her to be. I said that we in America were brought up on fairy tales of rare and noble princesses, so that a princess to us meant the kindest, most courteous, and most charming of all women, and that I felt that in her I had at last really met such a princess.

"I know some of your fairy stories," she answered, "and you say to me more than I deserve. Yet it will give me great pleasure to remember, Lang. I will tell you what I really am. I am my father's bad girl, who would not go away to school, who always wanted to hide when foreigners came, who knowing he is right in his ideas and policies has always been afraid of them, and who is almost a failure to him."

She repeated her offer to help me with my history, and we arranged that I should send it to her. She suggested that her father was interested in it and was too busy to help me all he wished himself and had asked her to do it for him.

That gave me my chance fairly to catch her, and I cried:

"If he is so interested in it, would he have asked that of you, if he thought you a failure?"

She laughed her honest laugh. It was some time before she said that he was always giving her one more chance to redeem herself, being a forgiving father.

So we parted good friends with the prospect of continuing our friendship in a common task.

13

June, 1907

THERE WAS MUCH to be done on my return to The City. I had not been present at the meeting of the council in March, and although I had not missed much of political importance (for the greater meetings were those of June and September), I had accumulated a great many social obligations, which it was customary to return at such times. George had already begun to plan lists of guests for dinner parties I should give when the council met in June. There was work to be done on my history, which must be published soon to have any effect as propaganda, for in a year the council would vote on the Mora Treaty. And there was Jennings to see and plans to be made for the Exhibition Ship.

On the afternoon of June 11th, when I was impatient over the Council Meeting that evening, over the three dinner parties I was giving, over my clothes, over the possibility of having to look at Dorna, and over the job of finishing a first draft of half my manuscript, the bell rang. I had no thought of Dorn at all. Then he stood before me. Of course I had known that he was likely to attend the Council Meeting, but I expected that I should have to look him up, not that he would find me. But there he was—big, broad, ruddy, with bright steady eyes.

Dorn made himself at home in his room. He was going to stay there one night now and perhaps visit me again later. He had reached The City with his great-uncle only shortly before, coming directly to me, the latter going to the Dorn Palace on the outer wall. He mentioned no one else as being of their party. I asked no questions, assuming that Dorna was not with them.

We dined together and dressed for the King's Reception that preceded the Council Meeting. I wore full evening dress, which was beginning to seem more and more ridiculous and out of place in this country. His clothes in cut did not differ from those of every day, but there was something "full dress" about them all the same. He was very striking in his dark-blue knickerbockers, coat, and magnificent cape, all of a material like the very finest of light-weight serge, his linen as white as white paper, and his stockings also of white. The cape had a white lining and when we set out he flung it back over his shoulder. His head was bare, mine was surmounted by a tall hat. I wore gloves. His hands had none. We laughed at the contrast between us. I told him that his costume was the more sensible.

"Yours would be the regular thing if foreigners overran us," he answered.

It was a windy, dark, overcast, but rainless night. The air was damp yet bracing. At the street corners, the flames of the candles in the lanterns were twisting and struggling as if to escape their wicks. The occasion and the season were festive. The fall and early winter always seem the time for parties! Open-air days are still fresh in the memory. Walled places are not yet tedious prisons, but welcome shelters from stormy, exhilarating weather. My spirits rose. My feet were light. The wine at dinner warmed me.

And Dorn also was excited. He walked with long strides, his head thrown back. We talked of those who were to be there and those who were not, but his sister was not mentioned. Of the Hyths there would be Lord Hyth, Airda, the eldest son, and Nekka. He had not seen her since March, he said, and it was a confidence. I would also see the famous Stellin and his sister, Morana, Lord Fain, the Somes, and others. We also talked of my dinner parties, to the second of which—for contemporaries—he promised to come. I could not know about many of my Islandian guests until tonight or next day, but I had all the foreigners "booked" already. I felt not unimportant, being sole representative of my country at the reception.

Street lights were dim, but other figures, men and women, black splotches, were moving toward the shadowy palace, which was seemingly unlighted except for a blaze in the doorway. As we walked toward it, dark figures came into that white glare and their costumes showed as a brilliant scarlet.

"The Calwins!" Dorn said instantly; and I realized with some-

253

thing like a thrill that they would be all together, East and West, Dorns and Moras, exclusionists and foreign traders, all Islandians.

Once within the door the light was dazzling. I found myself among foreigners and acquaintances, the Periers and M. Bart, and the little Italian consul, S. Poloni and his wife. A certain area of the reception hall was reserved for us, and thither we went, Dorn deserting me as he had warned me he must.

We entered the great room by a different door from the Islandians. It was very large with a high, dark-timbered roof. The walls halfway up were of a stone of a warm buff color and the stones of the floor were covered with rugs of the same warm tone. The room was lighted by rows and rows of candles set so high that one was not blinded by them. The walls and the rugs took light from them and diffused it through the room, so that the effect was of a rich golden glow in the air.

And the color of the King's Reception was enough to take one's breath away. Every Islandian present wore the colors of his or her province or position. Each province, the army, the navy, and the judges have two colors, the major one worn solid in the cape, with the minor one making a band along the hem, broad in the case of the Islas and their wives, narrow in the case of the Islata, omitted entirely in the case of those with no rank at all, like my friend. The minor color, or else some tone of white or any other color harmonious with that of the major color and with the wearer's own color, showed in the lining, often displayed, for one half of the cape is frequently turned back. The coat or jacket, the knickerbockers or skirts beneath the cape, were also of the major color, with bands of the minor color at the wrists in case of those of rank, such as I had seen at the Calwins', the Hyths', and elsewhere. Shirts, blouses, and stockings were of white or of other colors to suit the wearer's taste, chosen always with a view to correct disharmonies between his or her complexion and the colors which custom compels him or her to wear. The extraordinary thing is the way many women or men by some daring note in lining, collar of shirt, or blouse, or stockings, will enhance their looks, good or bad, rising triumphantly above what would seem a most unbecoming color combination.

Along the two sides of the hall were stations or boxes, eighteen on each side. Of these thirty-six boxes, each province, and each military, naval, and judicial officer had one, their position being determined by the date when a province became part of the nation, or the date when a professional rank was first created. Therefore the old provinces of the Center were at one end of the room, those of the West next, and those of the East last, set on alternate sides; and below these the boxes of Chief Justice, Marshal, and Admiral, and then those of judges, generals, and commodores. These boxes were separated from each other by braided ropes of dark-green held up by standards of dark wood. They were open behind and faced into the center of the room. At its lower end were similar boxes newly established for the diplomatic colony and set in a single tier at right angles to those of the Islandian nobility. At the upper end there was nothing but a closed door.

The nobles were gathering in their boxes, facing more or less into the center of the room. Similarly we foreigners gathered in ours. For some time I was alone in mine, with vacant boxes for the Germans, Austrians, and Russians, separating me from those of the Periers and Polonis. I waited for George's company to give me countenance. My box was eight feet square and there was nothing on which to sit down. But I soon forgot these minor worries in the pageant of color filling out before me. I discerned faces I knew, faces sharply vivid upon that rich palette of contrasting colors, lighted by the warm diffused golden light—faces distinct and detailed like those of miniatures, faces heretofore seen against backgrounds of fields and woods or simple interiors, unexpected faces, changed but familiar, faces that seemed those of friends.

To my right I saw the familiar odd countenance of Lord Dorn III, the Judge, in buff with white bands, saving his face from too dark a contrast with his cape by a dark-blue shirt. Beyond him the boxes were filling fast. Face after face I did not know; yellow, terra-cotta red, pink, scarlet, capes with the harmonizing contrasts or conductive colors of shirts and blouses; and then I saw the cameo, Roman profile of the Calwins, and just beyond them Lord Fain, in the end box, the box of greatest honor, in scarlet with gray bands, his frail, high-bred, tired face that of an unexpected friend.

The other side, I thought, must contain the boxes of those I knew best, the Dorns, Hyths, and Moras. I was about to turn my head that way when Gordon Wills's box, next to me, filled. He and his sister entered, and there was Mary Varney in a low-necked dress of muslin sprigged with flowers, a frock from London or Paris, fitting her like a sheath, and rather frilly across her bosom. Her arms and neck seemed flagrantly bare in contrast to all those other figures in capes and coats. At the same moment George appeared, rather red-faced and flustered, but with beard and hair well brushed. He had worried over what to wear and finally came in cape and suit of splendid material but a plain dark-blue. He could not wear the colors of his province in my box, and he saw no way to sport my colors, red, white, and blue. I introduced him to the Willses and Miss Varney, but he was a little distraught and preferred to see what was to be seen; for this was the first time he had attended such a reception, as it was my first time also.

All the diplomatic boxes were now filled and I glanced along them over her head. The uniforms of the Germans, Austrians, and Russians were brilliant and sparkling, and the dresses of the women anywhere else would have been striking and to be admired. They had done their best. Their jewels gleamed in facets of light. But in contrast to the Islandians we were a tawdry lot, our blacks a dusty brown, our whites like skimmed milk, our blues dead, and all the bright gold lace and jewels and decorations seemed like mere bits of faded color and bad glass. The rioting colors of the Islandians would have reduced the most brilliant assemblage elsewhere to nothingness.

Wondering if Dorn had come in I raised my eyes and looked along the other row of boxes. On that side were many more faces that I knew, and though farther away and more minute than those on my right hand they were vivid and recognizable. Near at hand, standing a little behind another couple in the army gray and brown, were Lord Some, the retired general, in the same colors, and Marrinera, his wife, in dark-blue and green. Farther on was young Earne's friendly, youthful face, with Soma his mother, and a man who must be his father, Earne II, a general. But beyond was a striking-looking man, Farrant XIII, the Admiral, son of Farrant XII, whom I had visited, in the navy gray and blue.

My eyes leaped along searching for Lord Dorn and my friend, and suddenly I saw the Moras, in red with white bands, Lord Mora's high, handsome, spirited face standing out from all others, and with him his wife, Calwina, and young Mora who was to follow him and Morana, my princess, tall and lovely with eyes looking off and a smile, like my memory of her and yet exceeding it.

But it was the Dorns for whom I was looking.

Beyond the Moras' box were two of persons I did not know and then an empty one, and farther still toward the other end of the room were the Hyths in white with dark-blue bands, Lord Hyth himself with hair very red, and Airda, and his eldest son by his first wife, his replica, and Nekka—Nekka looking exactly like herself with her quizzical smile, and her tall, half-self-conscious, half-graceful figure turned toward the still closed door at the end of the room.

And then, and then. . . .

In the next box stood my friend and his great-uncle, in dark blue and white, much frailer and quieter than Lord Mora, and just beyond them Dorna. I had not expected to see her. I had dreaded seeing her. I had not dared to think I would. Like her brother she was in dark-blue without white bands. She looked as though she had just come in from the windy marsh and stormy bright waters of Dorn Island. She was so simple! She stood very still, her eyes on the door. Her hair was brushed smooth. Though almost a hundred feet from her I seemed to see every detail of her face. My memory was plowed deep with it. She seemed changed, unhappy. Her small face even at that distance lost none of its color, as bright as enamel against homespun. I said to myself with a sudden feeling that it was rather funny after all. "This is the end. She has got me."

Everyone was looking at the door at the end of the room. My eyes turned that way also. With Dorna in the room I could gladly look where she did.

The great moment had arrived.

The door swung open and a tall couple stood outlined within the rectangle of its sills and lintels. They came forward into the light, both young, both dressed in green, the only solid green in the room. Their two heads were a glistening gold. His skin was as pink and fresh as a child's, but there was nothing of the child in his splendid confident body nor his haughty poised head. His sister, Tora, the Royal Isla, was as haughty as he, as true a princess as Morana.

I had seen him before, for he was the fourth man at the Lor Pass.

Tor, the King, went straight forward to a position between the boxes. He waited some moments, as royalty should, and then he spoke.

His words were an ancient formula of greeting from the king to the council. He did not speak of the members as his, but of himself as theirs. He declared the council to be assembled, and then called the names of all those entitled to attend it, and each one in turn stepped forward and bowed to him and he to them. He did it all with dignity, but with a certain lightness of touch.

"Tora!" he first called, turning to his sister with a smile, and she with a smile almost flirtatious bowed to him and he returned her bow very solemnly.

"Dorn!" I watched that greeting and saw, not her great-uncle, but Dorna standing with bent head.

"Mora!" Lord Mora stepped forward. The two most striking and most majestic men in Islandia bowed to each other. But Dorna was not watching.

"Belton! Marriner! Brome!" Thus he called them in the order to which their rank entitled them, the succession of the Dorns going back to 1003, of the Moras to 1008, and of Beltons to 1472.

Then he called the name of Farrant, and Andara's husband stepped forward and bowed.

"Farrant!" he called a second time, and there was silence, and the young king bowed to the empty box, and I thought of Lord Farrant in his castle with the great windows facing the sea. . . .

Dorna did not seem to be interested. But I half forgot her, busy fixing faces to names—forgot her because she was present and so easy to recall and to see.

When the roll call was over, the last name being Tole, Lord of Niven, Tor, the King, came toward us with his sister at his side, and addressed us briefly in French.

We were here. We were the guests of Islandia. As guests we were always welcome . . . That was the gist of his remarks. They seemed to me simple, cordial, and sufficient. Then he paused a moment and continued. Would we remain in our stations so that the others could meet us? As doyen, Count von Bibberbach bowed and replied formally to the king.

I had not looked forward to what followed, nor had anyone else of our colony; but it soon became apparent that all the Islandians were going to march past us in a procession headed by Tor and Tora, and then by the occupants of the boxes, not in the order in which their names were called, but in the order of the seniority of the office which they held. Thus Lord Fain, eighty-two years, accompanied by his sister-in-law, Mara, followed immediately behind the king, as Lord of Islandia Province, the oldest.

The procession proceeded from left to right across the front of our boxes. As a result, S. Poloni, a mere consul, was the first to be. greeted by the king, while Count von Bibberbach, a minister, had to wait. I wondered about it at the time, myself last to be greeted, very much interested in the colorful line gradually taking form in the center of the room, losing and finding Dorna several times, and catching a gay happy nod from Nekka, whose eyes searched for me as she stepped from her box.

The German minister was keeping the royal party for some time, perhaps to make up for the slight of not being greeted first. Dorna was somewhere in that long brightly colored line. I was going to see her face to face. . . .

Close behind the royal party, after Lord Fain and Mara, and behind a handsome couple with intelligent faces in pale grass-green with buff bands, was a young man and a young woman, obviously his sister, who caught my eye, less because of their resemblance to their parents, as because they reminded me of more familiar faces, but whose I could not tell. The young man was slender and tall with perfectly balanced features though with rather a wide face. He had an air of intelligence and of gentleness, but with a reserve of power held back. His sister was lovely. She was tall also, her head was rather small, and her face oval. Her pretty, youthful lips seemed a little compressed with a suppressed smile. Her skin was of a texture so delicate that one wondered how it could endure exposure even to ordinary weather—in tone a pale, faint, buff-rose, a little warmer in the cheeks. Her eyes were a wide blue, almost violet, so bright and so clear as to flash like water in sunlight.

The line had moved. Count de Craillizi, the Austrian minister, did not hold the king so long. He came abreast of the Willses' box.

Behind him, Lord Fain smiled to me, and that was good.

The king's coming seemed very amusing. After all we had met before.

At last he moved away from the Willses and stopped and looked at me. Closely seen, his face had a certain effeminacy, beautiful as it was—a look edging upon the dissipated—but his eyes were a clear, intelligent gray. He said nothing for a moment, and then smiled a smile that exactly answered my own feeling.

"No," he said. "No, Lang, I was not there."

I bowed.

"Sir," I said, "you were not there at all."

His sister was looking over his shoulder. Her eyes smiled a little and her face was pleasant.

"Some day we may be in the same place," said Tor.

"I hope so," I said.

"So do I," he answered, and with a smile turned away.

Lord Fain and Mara, next behind in line, were friends, asking me with cordiality to come to see them whenever I could, both looking warmly into my eyes.

They moved away, saying they would attend my first dinner party. I was greeted next by the man and woman in pale-green and buff and by their son and daughter. He named himself: Stellin and his wife Danninga.

They smiled a greeting and withdrew for their children. These then were Dorna's friends. We were for a moment a little constrained. I had the feeling of knowing them without having met them.

"We feel that we know you, Lang," Stellina said at last in a voice that had a warm, matter-of-fact quality.

I could think of no answer at all, and then suddenly it came to me.

"Would you come to dinner at my house on the sixteenth?" I asked. "There will be others you know, I think."

They considered it, they thought they could. They would let me know. I wondered if I had been precipitate. If all I asked came, George would have a difficult time seating and accommodating them. I wondered if Dorna would come. I had asked her, of course, not sure that she would be in The City.

I wanted to see Dorna and the procession dragged.

There were the Calwins in their scarlet; and Some and Broma, in gray and pink, the pair whom I surprised upon their driveway, and who asked me to come again; and then Robban and Calwina, of Alban, in white and green, whom I had met at the Moras'.

It took a long time. Count von Bibberbach, loquacious and flushed, detained everyone. There were pauses when I talked to George impatiently.

And then I saw the familiar face of Lord Dorn before the count's box, with Dorn and Dorna standing at his shoulders, the latter looking bored.

A man appeared before me, by himself, in gray with pink bands. "Baile of Inerria," he said gruffly.

I answered in Islandian, and he stopped as though grudgingly. I told him that I had crossed his province and that it had seemed like the more arid midwestern part of the United States. I wondered why I held him. He seemed noncommunicative and irritable, but he stayed, he listened, he asked questions.

In the corner of my eye I was aware of Dorna at the Willses' box. I heard a word in her unexpected, low, mature voice. With all concentration possible I finished what I was saying to Isla Baile.

But suddenly he broke it off, looking over his shoulder, and saying with real warmth:

"Here is Lord Dorn—and Dorna! They are more worth your while, Lang . . . My house is yours. You understand that?"

I thanked him, pleased, and at last I was free, really free, to turn, to turn to Dorna.

There she was. Could anything have been simpler or better?

It lasted but a moment, yet it was all I wanted. These were my nearest, dearest friends. My room was ready in their house—mine to live in. Under it all, the foundation was young Dorn, my friend . . . He said nothing. His great-uncle asked me to dine with him on the seventeenth, but declined my invitation for the fourteenth. Dorna said she was coming on the sixteenth, and then, as they turned away, she looked back.

"Can you find time to call on me? I am only here for five days."

I suggested various hours. We held up the line trying to find one in which we were both free. It was a delight to talk with her, whatever the result, for she was apparently as anxious as I was to arrange for our meeting. I was incapable of working it out, and so was she. Then Dorn came to the rescue.

"Day after tomorrow following the Council Meeting neither of you have anything to do," he said as to children. "Come to our house then, John."

Dorna looked up at him, a flash almost angry in her eyes, and then turned to me.

"Yes, come then. I'll be there."

They moved away. The back of Dorna's head was sleek and

round, her braids within her cape. She looked a little like a French schoolgirl in a school uniform. She was as plainly dressed as the plainest there, she seemed all but out of place. Her face was changed. Her expression was perhaps an unhappy one. . . .

Having greeted two men and a woman without even noticing their names, I found the Hyths before me, friendly and smiling. Nekka was radiant and excited. When was I coming again? How had I liked the East?

I could not see that tall girl's odd elusive face without seeing a little through Dorn's eyes. I wondered, as we talked, what he was thinking, and realized the unusual and extraordinary good looks of his rival, the king, and I knew that she was perhaps as unfathomable to Dorn as she was to me. Over her shoulder as she moved away she gave me a troubling glance, but the quizzical smile followed it almost immediately. She leaned back toward me.

"Nattana told me to tell you that she liked your letter," she said.

"I liked hers," I called.

Nekka made a little face and was gone.

Others followed the Hyths, more and more of them, some already known to me, almost as many as the strangers. In the center of the hall the Islandians were talking in groups. There was a faint sound of their voices rising and falling, but none of the noisy babble of a tea party at home. I wished the reception were over, and that I were alone in order to take a look at the astonishing place to which I had come. I was a suitor for Dorna.

Nevertheless it was a great pleasure to see Lord Mora and my princess, who came past after an interminable detention by Count von Bibberbach. I had just time to tell level-eyed Morana that I had a sheaf of manuscript for her, and I found myself invited to call on her with it after the council adjourned. But she could not come to my dinner party the next day. Lord Mora, however, accepted for the fourteenth.

When the last man had gone by, the reception was technically over. The members of the council met privately. Their wives, sons, and daughters went home empty, but a spread was served to us. However, I decided to go home, to wait for Dorn, to dream and to hug to myself my new intention.

I strode lightly unaware of my feet. Oh, the wild joy of knowing where I was and what I wanted! The wind whooped. The dancing candle flames in the lanterns on street corners fought to remain upon their wicks. Overhead were black night and vast skies. My heart was in tune with the universe.

Dorn came in some time after I did. He was flushed and his eyes smoldered. We sat down together, each with much on our minds. He was the first obstacle that presented itself in my path. I knew that after all he had said to me the news of my feelings and my intentions toward Dorna would trouble him; but I also felt quite sure that he would tell me to go ahead. We looked at each other, he and I, and I knew that he had similar matters on his mind. But we said nothing to each other. We felt warmly toward each other and held each other in reserve, so to speak.

That night in bed I felt somewhat sobered. I was doing exactly what I had been told not to do, in spite of the warnings and criticisms. Nattana had told me that I was in effect a creature of pale-pink emotions; Dorn, my friend, had said that an attempt deeply to understand Islandian life would make me suffer, that I had better not try to do so, and that it would be a misfortune if I were to fall in love; and above all, Dorna herself had warned me to the same effect and that I was not to wish to marry her nor to make an Islandian girl love me. Now I was in love with an Islandian girl and I wanted to make her love me, a thing that I had been told would cause her certain unhappiness. For this I could see no reason, as I lay wide awake in the darkness, nor any reason why I should not myself love and seek to win. The objections became shadowy. I almost forgot them, being very happy.

Next morning at ten o'clock, dressed in cutaway and with my tall hat—for today I was a diplomat—I took that half of me which was a consul (the other half being Dorna's suitor) to the Home Building, there to attend the first business or open meeting of the National Council.

The meeting took place in a large whitely lighted room, with timber roof, and stone walls carved from ceiling to floor with flat reliefs. Along each side were two rows of dark benches. At one end was a raised platform with a heavy chair, but this was not taken. On the two sides were large open fireplaces with brightly burning logs, and at the other end were benches for diplomats and spectators in several rows, each raised above the one in front. I was early and found a place in a corner. I had my notebook ready, for Washington would want a report. Nothing much of international interest was expected, but no one was sure. Lord Dorn was an unexpected campaigner.

One by one the members of the council gathered, some with their sons or other assistants, they sitting in the front row, and the latter just behind them, all in the same order in which their boxes had been arranged at the reception.

In groups also the diplomats gathered. The Islandians were without their capes, but most of them still wore their colors. The picture they made was bright and pleasing, with the brilliant and somewhat hard effect of a Turkish rug, in which the ivory is strong, newly come home from the cleaners.

At last, Tor, the young king, entered with his sister, and a number of other men with books and pens. These last sat at a table in front of the throne. She, the only woman on the council—pretty, a little bored, and haughty—sat at the end of the front bench on the right, next to Lord Fain. Tor had a chair set for him before the table facing into the center of the room. All rose when he entered, but once the proceedings started, he stood as often as he sat, and no one felt bound to stand when he did.

His duty was that of presiding officer or speaker. Lord Mora though premier had no special place, and he and Lord Dorn, his political opponent, sat on the same side.

Tor took his seat and Lord Mora at once rose. He began in a low voice, but I had no trouble in hearing him. As time passed his voice became louder and more vibrant. Its timbre was so musical and clear that one could listen to him with pleasure even though not understanding. His speech began as a report, at first about matters of routine concerning international relations, the number of foreigners in the country under the Hundred Law and holding diplomatic passes as business prospectors, and the number of diplomats and their families. There followed an account of the results of medical examinations. Five or six persons had been excluded, but only two had complained. Here my ears began to grow red. One, a citizen of the United States, had objected very strongly. He had addressed himself to Lang, the consul, but Lang had—quite properly it seemed to the speaker— refused to intervene. It was understood from Cadred at St. Anthony that this man had taken the matter up directly with Washington (unpleasant news to me), and it was possible that Lang would receive a communication from his government very shortly.

I saw eyes steal in my direction, and a smile on the lips of Lord Dorn. I felt important but troubled.

From these matters Lord Mora went on. No ships in distress, he said, had entered Islandian ports since the last meeting of the council, and but one foreign ship was in Islandian waters, the German steamer *Altgelt,* moored off Doring, about which the council knew. (I thought of my sail with Dorna. . . .)

He then took up the activities of the foreigners in Islandia and mentioned those who were sightseers and pleasure travelers, perhaps thirty in all, and those who were there pursuant to the permission given in the treaty, eighty-five persons. He stated the figure precisely and paused a moment and then described the activities of these men.

His next remarks were on the subject of various foreign communications, largely concerning the administration of the laws relating to the coming in of persons on diplomatic passes. Requests had been made either that the medical examinations be dispensed with or else that an examination by a doctor of the national in question be allowed. This was a matter which would be presented to the council for action.

From this Lord Mora went on to a matter which he considered of great importance. It concerned the arrangement with H.I.M. representative Count von Bibberbach regarding the frontier. There was a general quickening of attention. As the council knew, said Lord Mora, in the interest of friendly relations and as a result of strong representations by the count acting on instructions from Berlin, garrisons had been withdrawn. Of course this left the frontier unguarded so far as Islandians were concerned, but he was sure that it was in fact safer than it had ever been; for the Germans in the Sobo Steppes were removing by destroying them the menaces that previously had existed more or less undisturbed and that had merely been prevented from entering Islandia by defensive measures. For many years the frontier had been wherever the Islandians had chosen to put it. Now, of course, with a civilized power across the mountains the line must be drawn exactly. The Germans were engaged in making surveys. They would soon present their proposals, he was informed. It seemed to him that the decision whether the line should be here or there was not one whose every detail should come before the council. He was going to ask them to give him permission to settle these matters himself, of course with the advice of the Marshal (Bodwin, I remembered, who had followed Lord Mora but was not one of his stalwarts—Dorna in the cabin of the boat had told me this).

One of the fears expressed, when the garrisons were withdrawn, was that unscrupulous persons would enter Islandia in violation of the Hundred Law and the law regarding diplomatic passes. There was no evidence whatever of any violation! Lord Mora spoke emphatically.

All faces were turned upon Tor, the King. To my surprise and perhaps to that of others, he was smiling with the delight of a naughty boy, but Lord Mora fixed him with his eye. He blushed slightly and at once made a somewhat mocking bow of agreement. There was a little rustle all over the room.

An ill-advised attempt had been made, said Lord Mora, to discover whether or not such violations had taken place. Of course, it was the right of every Islandian to enforce these laws. That right would not be surrendered, though suggestions had been made that it should be withdrawn from civilians and limited to the military—suggestions on which he wished the council to act later. But granting the right it was far better for obvious reasons that civilians should not become aggressive in the matter, but should defer to the military except in flagrant cases. A party of Germans, said Lord Mora, had ascended the Lor Pass for the purpose of making a survey. They had met by pre-arrangement another party of Germans rightly in the country. While these Germans were at least in disputed territory, perhaps in German territory—(I looked quickly at Tor and saw him apparently bored)—a party of Islandians three in number had rushed upon them apparently to arrest them; but saner counsels prevailed, and since the non-violation of law was quite obvious these Islandians withdrew. Their behavior, said Lord Mora, is much regretted.

As he spoke he looked at the young king smiling, but, I think, a little angry.

"It was most ill-advised," he added significantly, a hit, I knew, at the Dorns. Tor flushed hotly and then smiled and interrupted, his voice easy and amused.

"Ill-handled," he said pleasantly. "Ill-handled!"

There was a little angry buzz among the Germans.

"Ill-advised *and* ill-handled," said Lord Mora sharply and in a way that deprived Tor's remark—half an apology to the Dorns and half a sarcastic contradiction of Lord Mora—of much of its sting.

It was an exciting moment. I was sure that Dorna would enjoy it. But Dorna and the king? He would score in her eyes.

For me it became even more exciting, for Lord Mora in the handsomest possible way and not without humor exonerated me from my participation in that affair. There was some laughter in which I tried to join naturally, feeling, however, very much a silly child.

It was a great relief when Lord Mora began to make a most eloquent address on the problem of foreign intercourse. In a year only the council would have before it the most important question perhaps in all its history. He pleaded for deep consideration of all that was involved, suggesting rather than saying that the choice before the nation was not so much a choice as making the best of it. Then in very general terms he pointed out some of the advantages of foreign trade, the enrichment that inevitably followed intercourse with foreign nations—not only material but spiritual, not merely commercial but conducive to the good of a troubled world as a whole and to each part of it.

There was a rustle among the diplomats.

The rest of Lord Mora's address concerned national affairs without international implications. They took the rest of the morning and the early part of the afternoon. When the morning session ended, I went to Count Wittersee's for lunch—the first of my many engagements. On my way I was stopped by Andrews and Body, my compatriots. They wanted my aid in obtaining permission to export ore samples and wanted it quick! They wanted these to go on the fifteenth. When, they demanded, could I see them? I suggested that they come late that afternoon; but that would not do for them, nor would early next morning. They seized upon the afternoon, the very time of my call upon Dorna. I said I had an engagement. They answered that the day after was too late. I insisted again upon tomorrow morning. Ten o'clock? they answered. No, I replied, I must attend the Council Meeting. Didn't I keep any regular hours? No, not while the council was in session. Well, said they, tomorrow afternoon.

"No, I have an engagement."

"I'll bet it's with a girl," said Andrews, really angry. I was myself too angry to speak, the more so because I blushed hotly. I walked away, thought better of it, and came back.

"I can see you tomorrow morning between eight and half-past nine, or the day after," I said. "I have got to go now because I have an engagement."

When I had met them on their arrival in May I had liked them, and had I known they were to be in The City I would have asked them to one of my dinners, but that thought vanished out of my mind.

The afternoon was soon over. Lord Mora ended his speech and next morning he would subject himself to questions. Lord Dorn seemed tired, uninterested, lacking in the force so strong in Lord Mora, who seemed full of power in reserve, and had certainly been pleasant and charming and clear-headed all day.

Tea at the Periers' and then a grand dinner at the Calwins' given to all the diplomats and to some Islandians swept me on with scarcely a moment to think of myself. Slightly dizzy with my host's wine, the busy day whirling in my head, I went to bed as soon as I came home and slept long; waking late I had to keep Andrews and Body waiting while I dressed, and to talk over their affairs with them while I ate my breakfast. I also had to disappoint them in part for it was obvious to me that some of the samples they wished to export were more than samples. They wanted me to frank things through, they said, but the law was too clear, and I refused to countenance breaking it.

At the Council Meeting that morning Lord Dorn as leader of the opposition began his questions. Back in the 'forties, when the question of foreign trade was fought over and the party of Lord Dorn's father won a victory over that of Lord Mora's grandfather, the then Lord Dorn had made his own investigation into all the facts upon which the then Lord Mora, the premier, had reported. It was soon evident this had also been done at the present time. When Lord Dorn began to ask for information, it was apparent that he had many facts of his own in reserve. He turned often to my friend close behind him and to Lord Fain who had moved over and sat next to him. It was interesting to me to see Lord Dorn in action. His voice had a carrying quality which I did not expect of it. His questions were very clear. He knew exactly what he wished to elicit from Lord Mora. His manner was courteous, but also obstinate. He suggested latent power in an unforeseen degree. I was pleased to find him so strong, but at the same time I had a wish that Lord Mora would win the day that was to come next year, for his victory would largely clear the way for me.

With mixed feelings, therefore, I heard Lord Dorn bring out the fact that, excluding members of the diplomatic colony, there were probably in Islandia nearer one hundred and thirty persons than one hundred and fifteen, with the implication that either Lord Mora had made a mistake or that persons were entering in violation of law. Lord Mora promised to check the figures.

"You ought to be so sure of them that a check would not be necessary," said Lord Dorn. "The Hundred Law is still in force and diplomatic passes are still required by your own treaty."

This seemed to me unnecessarily curt and rude, but I later learned that Lord Dorn in the council, if nowhere else, often made such remarks. This one, to me, was quite telling. Nor did Lord Mora seem comfortable.

The next fact brought out was that the Islandian doctors were of the opinion that medical examinations by foreign doctors were often a mere form, that certificates were issued without examination, and if there were to be any examination at all it ought to be a real one. So it went all morning.

There was an informality in the way the council carried on its business, and a closer relation of that business to actualities than seemed to be the case when our own Congress debated matters. I listened closely. Time went fast.

After lunch with Earne at his father's palace, I hurried back to the meeting. The matter being argued was whether Lord Mora's suggestion that the fixing of the boundary be left to him, should be adopted. Lord Dorn made use of the fact that the alleged German surveying party had passed beyond the obvious height of land. There were some rather acrimonious disputes as to topography. Lord Dorn seemed to be floundering a little. Lord Mora suggested that it be put to vote, and Lord Dorn most disappointingly backed down. He said it was not time for a vote; for if the proposed line was in the main reasonable, details could be left to the premier with advice from the army.

Lord Calwin spoke for the first time, suggesting in a voice not wholly pleasant that perhaps Lord Dorn would like to have the navy also advise. I remembered Dorna's voice telling me that the admiral and the two commodores were her great-uncle's supporters. The innuendo was clear.

Lord Dorn answered pleasantly that he would like nothing better. Lord Mora asked him if he would consent to a vote now if the commission to decide included a representative of the navy, but Lord Dorn merely laughed.

So it went on during the afternoon, and as the time for my call on Dorna came nearer and nearer I began to feel more and more impatient.

No action was taken on this matter, nor on any other. At the moment the council adjourned I left. It was long past four o'clock and I ought to be back at my office by half-past six to dress for the dinner at Count von Bibberbach's.

The southeast wind blew in my face, strong, chilly with occasional sleet, as I ran down the street that led to the quay. The water in the harbor was an angry gray-green, and the boats at the docks seemed huddled there. There was sure to be an open fire, and Dorna was expecting me!

Past the Agency Building and up over the bridge across the Suburra Canal, where the wind almost checked me and the sleet made a cold wet surface on my hot face, past the office of the Doring carriers where I had waited with George and had received Faina's letter months ago, and then down upon the mole and along the gray wall of Doring Palace. At last I reached the gate and swung open its heavy panels. Across the half-frozen garden, every tree stripped bare, was the long low façade of the palace itself. I crossed to the door and rang the bell. In a few moments, Dorna—Dorna herself for all the rest of this darkening wintry afternoon!

A dependent let me in. My face was stiff and my ears began to tingle. My coat and hat were taken. She would have to endure me in my cutaway coat. I hoped my shirt would not creak as I breathed. . . .

I was directed up the stone stairs and to the left. My feet clicked on the stones of a long corridor, at the end of which was an open door.

I found myself in a large bare room, but at the farther end was a blazing fire, and before the fire a bench; and rising from the bench was Dorna, not in plain dark-blue this time, but in a tan dress that brought out all the flush in her ivory skin, and with hair done softly. I went toward her quickly. It seemed a long way. I heard her voice greeting me, and I found myself seated by her on the bench, and the call had begun; and to make the fire warmer and our intimacy greater, the southeast wind from off the sea blew angry sleet against the windows.

Dorna, so silent the first time I met her, three long months before, began to talk to me at once this time, just as a girl at home, well trained in entertaining men, would do. She wanted me to tell her all that had happened since she saw me last. I told her of my visit to the Somes' households, of how much I enjoyed working in the trench, and of the bulbs, and that I had written for seeds and bulbs for her. She listened quietly, and I continued my story, coming finally to my trip to the Moras'.

I knew that this was what she wanted to hear most about, for when I began she looked away from the fire to me, sitting with legs crossed, her elbow on her knee, her chin in her palm—seeming folded a little in this position, her figure balanced and enchanting. And her clear eyes watched me and speculated, showing the activity but not revealing the nature of her thoughts.

For a moment my concentration faltered.

"Didn't you like Morana?" she asked. So a girl at home might ask a leading question . . . I told her what I thought of Morana, and of what I had said to her, of my history, of her help with it.

"I would have helped you," she said.

My impulse was to desert Morana for her.

"You are of the wrong party," I answered, and continued my narrative.

When I had finished I asked what she had done. Her reply was brief.

"Nothing much," she said. "I have been at home where I was busy. I help my uncle, you know. Stellina came to visit me two weeks ago. I didn't think I would come here, but I changed my mind after my uncle and brother left. We came on alone, she and I. We made it in four days, though there was a good deal of snow in the pass. We may have trouble getting home . . . I am very glad you have asked the Stellins to your dinner. Who else is coming?"

I told her, reassured as to my invitations. Our conversation shifted to the reception two days before.

"What did you think of Tor's speech?" she asked, and I told her that it seemed brief but sufficient. She looked me in the eyes, as though there were a significance I had missed. The king's words ran through my head.

"He spoke of the diplomats as 'guests,' " I said. "He did not tell them that Islandia was theirs."

Dorna's eyes contracted in the corners with that elfish, mischievous look of hers. She nodded her head.

"It is as though he said to them that they were only temporarily here and would not necessarily be asked to come again. They may not have understood but we all did." Her face broke into a smile. "I am surprised that you did not see, John."

Her eyes were intent on mine, and then she looked down. So happy had I been that I had not really searched her face at all, for she was here, and it was enough. Last night I had thought her changed and unhappy. There seemed to be a shadow under her eyes. I wanted to know why.

But Dorna had her own ideas as to how our conversation should go. What did I think of the Council Meeting yesterday? I told her my ideas and again it was the young king's behavior that she had in mind.

"It was scarcely diplomatic," I suggested.

"Of course it wasn't, but it was just like him. Lord Mora had coached him, of course, and he agreed to it all, but he could not help rebelling and showing how he felt. It was not mere mischief. He was sure that the Germans were going farther than a surveying party ought to."

She seemed to know Tor's mind.

"Is he of your party?" I asked.

Her whole face lighted with amusement.

"I don't know," she said, "but he won't let Lord Mora make up his mind for him. He will be a real king, not a figurehead like his father."

"Would you feel as glad if he showed leanings the other way?" I asked.

She was sobered, and her eyes dropped.

"I think so," she answered slowly.

Then she was amused again and we talked of Count von Bibberbach's behavior and of his obvious effort to assume leadership of the diplomats.

"There is a threat in that, you know," Dorna said. I made her be more precise, and she admitted that sometimes she thought the Germans wanted to establish a protectorate over Islandia, and that their occupation of the Sobo Steppes territory was a move in that direction. "I must not tell you too much," she added quickly. "I forget that you are my enemy."

"Never!" I cried.

"Yes, you are, so long as you are a conscientious consul. I would not want you to be otherwise . . . And if you resigned as consul, you would have to go away sooner or later. The Hundred Law only allows you one year in ten."

I felt we were nearing the painful subject of my fitness to understand Islandia, to love an Islandian girl, and to make her love me.

The reception, I said, was very colorful, and I told her how the beauty of that brilliant gathering had impressed me, how quiet Islandian voices were in contrast with those of a similar group at home, and how dowdy their costumes made ours look. Unwittingly I touched upon a sore point with her.

"My brother and I were the plainest people there. We have to wear the plain dark-blue. It is so hopeless that I don't even bother what else I wear."

A new Dorna and worried about clothes! I looked her over. It seemed proper to tell her that I thought her present dress exceedingly becoming.

She smiled.

"*I* think it is," she said, and seemed pleased. "It is hard for me to find colors that suit me." We discussed what would become her. It gave me a chance to stare at her. I loved her more and more.

"Do you think green would look well?" she asked me. I was not sure about green.

She insisted again that she dreaded a reception when she had to wear that plain costume. She had not even done her hair for it!

"You looked," I cried, "just as you ought to look. You seemed yourself, as though you had just come from Dorn Island. You brought it and the marsh, and the sea and fresh air with you. Other people looked like faces set on top of clothes! You were perfectly lovely, Dorna!"

She laughed.

"I am glad if you thought I looked as though I had just come from 'there.' I felt that way, John. Dorna of Dorn Island and of nowhere else."

This was her cue. Dorna of Dorn Island, of the West, of the conservative party . . . We were talking politics again. She had her ideas on all the subjects before the council. She spoke with precision and force, not unlike her great-uncle. I was delighted again, happy to find her so definite, so clear-headed, and so strong.

I told her of various conversations I had had, including that with young Mora. She fell at once upon his suggestion that an excess of imports over exports would mean a flow of gold out of the country, and, making it scarcer, would decrease prices in Islandia. She spoke with scorn. That was only a minor result of foreign trade in their eyes! Everything would work out all right in the end, of course! How exactly like the Moras! After a moment she became serene again, and she pointed out very clearly the disruptive effect in the country, so long stable, of a change in prices.

"Of course," she concluded, "if the question were solely one of making the best of a change that we can't prevent, we would have more sympathy with them."

She stared into the fire and said slowly:

"I despise the Moras for obscuring that issue by their arguments that foreign trade would be good for us. Dear John, if the change must come, some of us might be happier fighting to inevitable death for the ideal of being ourselves in our own land. Some of us can breathe free only in our own air."

She used the words of her ancestors. The problem as she made me feel it was greater than the trivial chess game of politics, too great for me to speak upon it.

"Dear Dorna," I said, "I hope that never happens!"

There was silence, and then abruptly she spoke in a different voice.

"How do you enjoy the busy life that we all live at this season?" she asked. "What are you doing?"

I told her of my many engagements, and of the dinners I was giving. She approved of the guests invited and said she wished she could attend all of them.

"So do I," I answered, thinking of her as opposite me.

"But there is one thing left out," she said. "There is no music. And this is your only chance in the year to hear one sort of Islandian music."

She told me of her engagements. There were many meetings when girls of her own age came together, renewed friendships, and planned visits. There were several dinners of young people like the one I was giving. One of these by the Calwins I had had to decline, because it conflicted with my first party. She was attending it and that was a regret. "But soon I shall be riding home again," she said, her eyes lightening. "I shall be out on the road and not in stuffy houses all day long. It will be bad weather probably. My fingers will be cold. There will be open fires at stopping places. . . ."

"I envy you, Dorna," I said. "I shall be here—indoors—and I shall work."

"You must come to Dorn Island in the spring," she said with real feeling.

I told her earnestly that I would come.

"You don't know us in the spring," she continued. "I am a different person."

"What are you like?"

She merely laughed.

"But you must hear some music, John. I should like to take you to a concert. There is one every night."

We both had engagements for every evening during her stay, but Dorna on this occasion found a way. The concerts took place late in the evening. Guests at the shorter, less formal, Islandian dinners were quite free to leave early. She selected an evening when both of our evening engagements were Islandian and not foreign—the fifteenth.

It was getting late. Several times I had thought it time to go. This seemed to be the only occasion when I would see her alone. I wanted to take advantage of my opportunity, but with no clear idea of what to do with it. But we would walk through The City at night on the fifteenth.

"I ought to have gone long ago," I said as I stood up. Dorna's alacrity in also rising was disconcerting, but she also had an engagement that evening. I had forgotten it.

Wishing it were the Islandian custom to shake hands, I said good-bye and departed. The strong wind pressed my back and whistled past my ears as I ran home. The need of hurrying and the realization that I might be late to Count von Bibberbach's very grand party were sobering. I had spent golden unforgettable hours, but the dismal warnings clanged in my head.

Later that evening, at the German legation, when the dinner was ending, and my waistcoat was tight and my head a little dizzy, when wine and food were still coming, voices sounding a little far off in my ears, and colors very bright, I had a definite sensation of myself as rather a pig and of everyone present as rather like pigs also. The dinner was so obviously the thing to most of us—even to Lord Mora, even to Isla Calwina, quite obviously so to young Tor who was bright-eyed and flushed, mischief on his face.

For the hundredth time I thought of Dorna. Suppose she had come, would she seem a little piggish too?

Not she! Dorna, slightly intoxicated, would be a maenad in the open air, not a sedentary woman at a table. Oh, Dorna, Dorna, I thought, you are not for me! And I felt blue, for someone had told me once that drink accentuates one's true feelings. If drink makes the seemingly unhappy laugh, it is because they are really at bottom happy; if drink makes one in an ecstasy of happiness feel hopeless, then hopelessness is indeed his true mood.

So I ended in melancholy as happy a day as I had ever had.

The next day, the fourteenth, was a busy one. Lord Mora withdrew the matter of medical examinations and postponed action for six months, agreeing that perhaps the time was not ripe without a fuller consideration of the opinions of Islandian doctors. This seemed a triumph for the Dorns. The matter as to the commission to fix the boundary was not mentioned again. The council proceeded to matters of national rather than international concern. An air of greater accord instantly settled upon the meeting, and the diplomat watchers began to slip away one by one.

I myself left early, my dinner on my mind. And that night, almost frantic, I saw seat themselves at my table all the ministers and consuls and their wives, Lord Mora and Isla Calwina, Lord Calwin and Isla Morana, Lord Some and Isla Broma, and Lord Fain and Mara. Conversation instantly sprang up, the food and wine appeared when it should, and I gradually ceased to worry. Nevertheless there was an amateurish quality about my dinner that embarrassed me, but seemed to do no harm. At the close of the evening Count von Bibberbach, a little flushed and unsteady, put his arm around me, and called me the baby of the diplomatic colony, but the best host, the best host!

The fifteenth of June . . . What a day it was!

It was steamer day, and I cut the Council Meeting to meet the *St. Anthony* coming in from the West. The weather was fair but cold at eight o'clock on the customhouse quay. No one of interest came or went, but she brought me a most unsatisfactory mail.

The government communications I read first. There was cabled assent to all I proposed with regard to the Exhibition Ship, but the rest was utterly disconcerting. The man excluded on account of disease had taken up the matter "with Washington" and I was directed to do all I could to bring about a reconsideration with a suggestion, by no means veiled, that I had not done all I should. I was also informed that I should do all I could to assist Americans in making reasonable arrangements with Islandians in anticipation of the adoption of the Mora Treaty. The implication was that I had not done so, and I knew that Henry G. Müller had also taken things up with Washington . . . I was frightened, and I felt a little sick. A rush of angry explanations ran through my mind.

Uncle Joseph's letter was in a similar vein. It was dictated, but the typewritten words read as though he were speaking to me. "See here," he began, "you are getting in wrong." He told me I must not pussyfoot, referring to the diseased man who, he said, was a person for whom, after all, it was wise in this not wholly ideal world to do all I could. He also told me that irrespective of the rights or wrongs of the matter it was at least good policy to keep my temper with the representative of a man like Gastein. After all, in this not wholly ideal world (he repeated the phrase), there were times when wise, foreseeing persons took a look ahead and without stretching a point too far made a point of doing more than they ordinarily would. I was very young, he said, my future was at stake, I had no one to advise me but himself, who got me the job, a few plain words were not amiss, and I ought to understand that I could not have everything as my fine New England conscience wanted it. Above all, I must stick to my job, I must make a point of pleasing people; big issues were at stake, and now was the time for me to make or mar myself and my future. I must not forget that I was an American, nor neglect other Americans for my Islandian friends—and so on, and on. Then came the usual annoying requests—to keep me busy, I knew.

No sooner had I received these letters than I sat down to answer them. The letter which I sent off on the eighteenth was much more restrained than the first draft, written in a "go-to-hell" spirit.

After lunch I looked in at the council still engaged in noninternational matters. Seeing me Dorn came over and advised me to attend next morning. It was good to have a word with him. He stayed only a moment but when he went he squeezed my arm, and my feeling of angry worry lessened.

Somewhat tired I dressed for dinner and walked to the far north end of The City to the house of the Earnes. Young Earne seemed fast becoming a real friend, and he and his family were more than cordial without that suspicion of political reasons that I had with the Calwins and young Mora.

It was a small dinner, but a pleasant one. The guests were chosen with no political motive, but rather, I think, to give young Earne a chance to entertain those whom he liked, and his parents to see some friends not often seen. We were both young and old.

My impatience to see Dorna was a distracting, almost unbearable thing. Our two hours together would pass quickly, and there would be none like them, with Dorna all to myself, until spring, months away.

On edge, afraid that I was late, I left the Earnes' rather abruptly, for I had a long way to go to the Camia Palace on City Hill where Dorna was dining with the Stellins. It was hard to put the warmth I really felt into my thanks to young Earne and his parents. And then, I was out in the damp chilly night air, running down the steps that led to their palace. They were forgotten. Dorna only existed, separated from me by a tangle of dark twisting streets.

I loved her and I also loved the darkness, the wintry air with a sharp dampness foretelling snow; I loved The City, I loved Islandia.

I had ample time, and I walked slowly up City Hill, deliberately holding myself back. The square on the summit was bleak and empty. The Council Building, by day the scene of so much activity, seemed to be alive although no light showed in any window. A gust of wind almost stopped me, and my face was cold with rain or snow. When I passed a street lamp at the corner of Norm Street, which would lead me to the Camia Palace, flakes were sweeping across the pane and were already clinging to its windward side.

I would have Dorna with me in the privacy of a snowstorm.

My heart beat as I came to the door and rang the bell, and my voice shook when I told the dependent who opened to me that "Lang" had come for "great-niece Dorna." He departed and I stood waiting in a small square hall from which a dimly lighted corridor seemed to extend indefinitely.

She came running toward me, already in her cape. Her feet clicked on the stone floor of the corridor.

She rushed up to me. My impulse was to shake her hand. I thought I had learned to restrain it, but I had not.

"Dorna, am I late?"

"No, John. You are on time. Why?"

"You hurried so."

"I hate to keep a person waiting. I know how it feels. Is it snowing yet?"

"Yes, Dorna."

She drew her hood over her head and we went out. She was like a monk, or like Red Riding Hood in dark-blue. The street light over the door shone down upon her. The flying snowflakes ruled white lines against her and against the darkness. Cold white, dark-blue, black night—and a glimpse of Dorna's face, vivid, flushed, and warm within her hood . . . I had her again at last, and the two hours of this meeting were still ahead of me!

We walked down the hill. The ground was becoming soft underfoot. By my side moved a dark cape, usually faceless. But what did it matter? I should see her at the concert hall, Alwina's Theater, and she was with me now and wholly mine.

The distance was short, the way sheltered, except when we crossed the park where the river arm used to be. There the wind blew her almost backwards, and she struggled against it with bent head. When we were in the lee of walls again she came close to me.

"Suppose it is like this on the way home?"

"I hope it isn't," I answered, and that was all we said.

We came to the theater and entered. As at home tickets were taken up, but at home she would have handed them to me to present to the collector, even when I was her guest; but here the slight shame a woman feels at being a man's host, or perhaps thinks he feels as a mere guest, did not exist. We went in, Dorna ahead. She flung off her cape as we moved through the quiet, slowly gathering Islandians, and her skirt and jacket were of a dark burnt orange, her blouse of orange bordering on yellow, and in her braid which was wider and flatter than usual was a ribbon of the same color. Her skin looked browner, darker, and more flushed. She was vivid and brilliant—a contrast to the Dorna of the reception.

She went straight to the seats she had in mind, and we were side by side. We had come together, and she was mine and I hers for over an hour . . . Dorna glanced once briefly around the room, and then turned to me and gave me a lecture on what I was to hear.

Only in The City and only in June are there orchestral concerts. Islandian talent does not run to compositions for large choirs, but rather for solo instruments or for ensembles of two or three. She told me not to try to find any meaning in the music, but to empty my mind of all feelings, and to listen. It was a little irritating because it implied that I did not know how to hear music.

"Very well," I answered, "I will make my mind a blank."

"Do, please!"

I told her about Ansel's concert, and how he had labeled a certain piece "Upper Doring."

"He is very different," she answered, with a trace of contempt which I resented, for Ansel had stirred me deeply. "He plays his own things and he is always thinking of some definite place or feeling describable in words, or visible to the eye, or knowable with other senses."

"His music is very moving."

"Did it make you want to cry?"

"Yes," I admitted.

She laughed shortly.

"What was so sad?" she asked.

"I really don't know."

"Were you thinking of someone?"

"I don't know . . . One of the pieces was 'Upper Doring.' "

"You pictured Upper Doring and it was all very much more beautiful than you remembered it?"

"I am not sure that was it."

"But you had a lot of thoughts?"

"I don't think so—just feelings."

"Sad, sad ones, John?"

"Yes," I said with almost a groan.

"That is what Ansel wanted you to feel," she answered, again with a touch of scorn, "lovely, beautiful, sad feelings . . . This will be different."

I tried to do as she said, to listen in a blank mental state, merely as a pair of ears with receptiveness within, and for a while I succeeded. The music had a crystalline simplicity, weaving pattern after pattern of sound. But Dorna stirred. I glanced at her brooding profile, her dark eyelashes. I loved her too much, or else it was not in my power to listen properly. The music became a mere accompaniment to thoughts intensified by it to an almost unbearable poignancy—immense love, immense will to achieve happiness in spite of obstacles, complete realization of the tremendous barriers between us, despairing grief, then love and happiness again.

My eyes roamed over the hall once or twice. I saw, looking like any ordinary couple, young Stellin and Tora, the Princess. She was leaning a little back, aloof, but his long, refined, intelligent face was concentrated on what he was hearing. I also saw Jeanne and Marie Perier with M. Bart. Marie's eyes stole in my direction, and it pleased a perhaps not wholly worthy pride in me to be seen by her with Dorna . . . My heart became softer. They also were dear to me, these French girls. We were all an intimate group together, and I wanted to be part of it beyond possibility of separation. Loving Dorna, I adopted Islandia as my home. I loved Islandia. I could never leave it. I was one with it. Love had changed me. Immense love—Dorna!—power to surmount any obstacles, obstacles unsurmountable, grief, real grief, the first I had ever known. . . .

The music ended somewhat to my surprise. There was no applause—a rustle of pleasure and relief.

Dorna did not move. She leaned forward, one elbow on her crossed knee, her chin on her palm, her other arm across her lap.

I wondered if Marie were watching us, and were seeing us two wholly dumb together. Stellin and Tora seemed to be talking. There were passionate things I wanted to say to Dorna, but what they were I did not know. Somehow in some way, but without saying too much, I wanted her to know what I felt. Yet it was not quite that, but rather to make sure that matters were as they were at Dorn Island—that the problem she might some time have to face but which had not come to her then, was still in the distance. I heard her voice, "I am quite free. Until it is settled one way or another, I want to stay free." I understood better now. It was a hint to me to leave her alone emotionally. I would do so! I would say nothing. I loved her, and her freedom was precious to me. So, passionately, I resolved.

The concert went on. I listened to the other pieces in the same mood. Dorna was quite wordless; she might pretend not to be thinking, but I was sure that she was. I would have given anything to know of what it was. Maybe it was of this problem of hers.

The concert ended and I had only a little while longer with Dorna. The perfect two hours had all but vanished.

I held her cape for her, and she drew the hood over her head. The ground was covered with an inch or so of soft snow. The air was white, and softly stinging flakes clung to my eyelashes and half blinded my eyes. The snow diffused the light of the street lamps so that we could see our way, but the footing was slippery. I stumbled, then Dorna did. I reached out my hand to steady her, and quite unexpectedly she slipped her arm through mine. I wanted to take her hand which I knew was bare. I could feel it on my forearm through my sleeve. Once I had held it, and the vivid memory of that fact broke down barriers that otherwise would have existed. But I did not, intent to keep my resolution not to be emotional.

It was only a quarter of a mile from the theater to the Doring Palace. It seemed but a moment and we were passing the Agency Building on the canal. Here with the snow-hidden harbor to the right and the sea so near, the wind was stronger and the flakes cutting and blinding. We had to fight our way against it up the steep slippery bridge, closer together, helping each other, our bodies sometimes touching—united by the isolating, salt-smelling privacy of the snow-storm.

On the other side of the bridge, where the road began to descend to the mole, it was suddenly quiet, but the snow had drifted deep. On the right, below us, in a blue haze of snowflakes against a blacker distance, was the gleam of a ship's light on a varnished mast, and the dim outlines of the docks. Dorna drew upon my arm to save me from a wrong turning. I felt her steady strength. I loved her for it, her follower.

It was very near, now. The wall that enclosed the palace grounds was a blackness on our left. Only a few moments more, and we came to the gate beneath the feeble lamp. There was a hissing in the snow-flakes along the top of the wall; Dorna was passing through the gate and I was following over the frozen garden now dumb with soft white snow; and then we were before the palace door itself.

"Good night, Dorna," I said, passionately, hoping that after all she would ask me in. I moved to open the door, but her arm, still through mine, checked me.

"I want to tell you something," she said in a low hurried voice. "Nothing has happened since I saw you at Dorn Island to make anything different from what it was then."

My heart leaped. She had answered my unspoken question.

"Still free?" I asked in a shaking voice.

"Still free, with the same problem but no nearer."

"Thank you, Dorna."

She withdrew her hand quickly, and opened the door herself, and stood in the yellow square of light facing me, a step above me.

"Good night," she said in a voice that trembled. Though her still-hooded face was against the light and invisible, I could feel the outline of her features, burning and lovely.

"Good night," I cried.

She stepped back and the door softly closed.

I turned away in exaltation. Of her own accord, she had told me she was free, told me the one thing which I most wanted to know. Homeward I surged, with no consciousness of the storm except its privacy and silence.

But when I was once more before my own fire, I realized that among the things which were no different was her warning to me not to love her, nor any Islandian girl, nor to let any one of them love me —that I was still unfit. I made great resolutions that evening as to how I should handle my life, and more in particular what I should do in the next few months.

There were letters still unread, from relatives, and one from Gladys Hunter. It was the only one which I was in the mood to read, for she did not remind me too much of the unpleasant ties that, binding me to home, held me away from Dorna. She was a child, and a charming one, entitled to have her letter read promptly and not put aside. I was glad that neither Natalie nor Clara had written me.

They were busy days, for I had to placate Washington, but I vented my suppressed rage more or less on Uncle Joseph, telling him how utterly impossible it had been for me to do anything differently without being a dishonest man. There was also Jennings to see before his departure on the eighteenth for the United States to arrange about exhibits for our ship. He went with reluctance and seemed less of his spruce confident self, but he did not tell me of his personal affairs.

On the sixteenth, following Dorn's advice, I attended the Coun-

283

cil Meeting and had an interesting but disturbing morning. Lord
Dorn made his answer to Lord Mora. His position was perfectly clear.
He proposed no action but merely presented facts, content for the
present, he said, with laws as they stood. But Lord Dorn had a report
to present, a report that made Count von Bibberbach extremely red.
There was strong evidence that since the Germans had established a
protectorate over the tribes of the Sobo Steppes the natives there were
much better armed than ever before, that the German police-soldiery
were few and widely separated, and that there was considerable unrest
among the natives. As yet, however, none had crossed the boundary.
But, Lord Dorn said, as the natives woke up to the fact that the
Islandian garrisons were really gone and were not merely hiding, it
was likely that the Upper Doring Valley would again witness scenes
which had for some years seemed impossible. No doubt the Germans
would do their best at the task of policing the steppes, but in spite of
their promise, they would not have the same motives for keeping
Islandia safe that they had for keeping the steppes safe. The Mountain Bants would behave properly on one side and not on the other.
Unless the German police crossed the boundary, Islandia in such cases
was helpless. And as for him and many others of like mind he would
be almost as sorry to see German soldiers following Mountain Bants
into Islandia for the purpose of arresting and restraining them, as he
would be to see either coming alone.

It seemed to me that there was a most unwise display of hostility
in his speech, and that he almost went out of his way to insult the
Germans; but he certainly made it evident that the frontier situation
was one of great danger and that that danger very possibly went
deeper than the peril of native raids.

Count von Bibberbach wrote a reply in the form of a letter to
Lord Mora, which was read two days later. It was full of facts, German honor, and anger, but it was not one that entirely did away with
the feeling of menace in both of these different dangers. To me the
thought of Nattana and Nekka in peril was one that constantly recurred. Lord Dorn had impressed me, who had friends in the Doring
Valley, very much indeed.

Following the reading of this letter, Lord Mora ably explained
that the situation which Lord Dorn had so graphically described was
one that could not occur. The sources of Lord Dorn's information
were unofficial. They were certainly not at all in accordance with what

official investigators had discovered. The German promises were being more than merely kept. The frontier in his opinion was never safer.

As I listened I felt myself more and more reassured. I no longer saw pictures of black men on horseback pursuing Nattana and Nekka on foot. Yet neither Lord Mora nor Lord Dorn had stated the facts on which they based their conclusions. The discussion ended with a duel between the two leaders.

"Granting for the sake of argument that a band of Mountain Bants crossed the frontier, who would stop them?" asked Lord Dorn.

"It only wastes our time here to argue questions that have no reality," replied Lord Mora. "I will tell you privately if you want to know."

"The council has all the time in the world. I am willing to go to a vote upon the question whether it wants my inquiry and some others I should like to make, answered or not."

"It is no secret that there are about one hundred cavalry soldiers in garrison at Tindal, one hundred at Hyth, and two hundred at Bannar."

"These, then, are the only men who would stop and destroy any Bants who came over the frontier?"

"Your question was 'stop.' Destroy is another matter."

"Do you mean that their extermination like vermin could not take place?"

"They would more properly be turned over to the German government for punishment."

"Is that provided for in your treaty?"

"Not *my* treaty, but in the laws of our country, Dorn—not expressly but as interpreted by us and Count von Bibberbach."

"Mora, you are going very far with Count von Bibberbach in breaking down ancient safeguards."

"We have never before had a civilized power across the mountains."

"In the past the more civilized our enemies the worse the danger we have been in."

"Lord Dorn, I beg you not thus publicly to refer to Count von Bibberbach's people as enemies. You threaten the good will that we have built up with the Germans."

"I know that in other countries the foreign office has curbed the tongues of those who would speak honestly what they think. That has never before been true here. It is one of the consequences of the treaty you presented to us, Lord Mora. The passage of the law ratifying that treaty contained no clause requiring me to curb my tongue. To me and to those who follow me, all who wish us to do and to be what the German and other foreign governments who have accepted the treaty wish us to do and be are enemies. Let them come here as our guests and we will welcome them, if not too numerous and not making demands improper for guests to make. To me they are guests still and no more."

Lord Mora listened quietly to this harangue.

"They are not enemies," he said. "They merely wish a state of affairs that you disbelieve in. So do I. Am I your enemy?"

"No, not mine, but your country's enemy, Mora."

The two men looked at each other speechless. The council was very still.

"Forgive me for my question," said Lord Mora, "for I knew the answer. To me you seem, not your country's enemy, but her fatally blundering friend."

They smiled at each other with real affection. Finally Lord Dorn spoke:

"I have one more question. Do you concede to the Germans the right to cross the frontier in hot pursuit of Bant marauders?"

"We do."

"A violation of the Hundred Law, Lord Mora."

"Not that—but a necessary consequence of the provisions of the treaty as to the policing of the steppes by the Germans. They undertake to protect us. They must be allowed all proper means to do so."

"I am glad that the council knows this fact and this interpretation," said Lord Dorn. "Let none of you forget it. German soldiers have, according to Lord Mora, a right to enter Islandia, provided only that some black men are running away before them."

My two remaining dinner parties were successes. That on the eighteenth was given primarily for the Islandians who had been kind to me in one way or another. All those at whose houses I had stayed were asked and many came—both the Somes and their wives, and among others and best of all Lord Fain and Mara, his sister-in-law. On the sixteenth came the young people's dinner.

On my right was Morana, my princess, and on my left Dorna. To give the dinner the atmosphere of foreigners for Islandians I placed Marie Perier at the opposite end as my hostess, a position that seemed to embarrass her a little but gave no concern to anyone else. On her right around the corner was Jennings, sprucely dressed but with dissipated eyes, and at her left at the end my friend Dorn. Along the left side from Dorna were Calwin, Stellina, Mora, and Miss Varney; along the right side, next to Morana, Stellin, Jeanne Perier, young Earne, and Nekka next to Dorn.

I had seated them thus after much thought. I gave Dorn, a busy man, a chance to talk with Nekka; put Miss Varney and Jennings, two foreigners, together; counteracted myself for Morana's sake by Stellin, and handed to Jeanne the attractive and spontaneous Earne; and separated successfully all whom I knew to be intimate friends, except Dorn and Nekka. This last was my only mistake. They seemed to have nothing to say to each other. Earne engaged Jeanne, and Dorn Marie. Nekka was often left out to sit beaming absently and thus to worry me.

Across me talked Dorna, whom I loved, and Morana, for whom I had every warm feeling but love. They seemed to draw each other out and with them young Stellin. As host, I had nothing to do but enjoy myself. A new Dorna manifested herself. Once I had thought her shy. She was the most intelligent and brightest person there, not excepting young Mora himself. Little by little the conversation became more general, Dorna leading it. Only Miss Varney and Jennings stayed outside because of their imperfect knowledge of Islandian. The subject that held us all was the difference between foreigners and Islandians, one of unfailing interest. Everyone had ideas, of course, and Dorna's willingness not to conceal her own made others equally frank. No one was too serious, but the conversation did not degenerate into teasing. The point that Dorna made, and made in innumerable ways, was that we were "unplaced," we wandered about alone in the world as homeless as fish in the sea; whereas the Islandians really had a place from which they came and where they were buried at death.

The evening ended too early. Some left for the concert, the Stellins, the Moras, and the Periers with young Earne, caught by Jeanne. The others left together. It was my good-bye to Dorna until spring three months and more away. I could only treat her as a guest, and yet she gave me a little bit of her personal self most sweet to go upon.

"I have meant to write you a note, but I have been very busy. My brother will give it to you," she said. "Good-bye, John."

She smiled over her shoulder the brightest of smiles. Her eyes were dark fires and her cheeks were flushed. She looked pleased with herself, not unaware of the success she had made.

The council adjourned on the twentieth, and that night Dorn spent with me as he had spent the first. He came in late, a tired man, with many worries on his mind. One was his great-uncle, whose fatigue and feebleness disturbed him. I let him talk and fed him and wined him, and tried to make him comfortable.

There was not a word about Nekka, though I knew that she was much on his mind, but he said things that enlightened me as to the political situation.

The idea that the Germans were tricking Lord Mora into opening the frontier, so that in case of war an excuse could be found, was not one to laugh at, he said. Did I think his great-uncle went too far? It was not, of course, diplomatic (he used the English word).

"It is more a victory for us than for them, however," he said. "It always is when the government hesitates and refuses to put a matter to a vote for fear of a defeat. Lord Mora would have carried every measure he presented, I think. There are all those old fellows who from a sense of honor and a sense of fair trial believe in backing him up. What they will do next June I wish I knew, but meanwhile they think that Mora ought to have what he wants. But he was afraid. My uncle bluffed him out of all his proposals."

If he did not talk of Nekka, neither did I talk of his sister, nor did I mention my troubles with Washington. I persuaded him to go to bed, because he was to be early on the road next day. I should miss him deeply. There was no certainty of my seeing him again until spring.

He was gone. Dorna was gone without having had time to write the letter she promised. Jennings, congenial in a way, had left on the eighteenth. The Hyths, of whom I would have liked to see more, the Stellins whom I wanted to know better, the Somes, Lord Fain, and Mora, and everyone else particularly interesting, except the

Periers and my princess, had departed. The last named, on whom I was to call soc u with my history, was a comforting anticlimax.

To the history I turned. I set my teeth and refreshed my resolution to win Dorna. Hard work!

But she kept her promise after all. Her letter written at the Somes' came on the day her brother left.

John:

I broke my promise, but if John had known all that I had to do and to think about, even at the concert, he would forgive me at once. I know that he will. What I want to say to him is this: When I told him that nothing had changed since he was at Dorn Island, I wanted him to understand first of all that the very cruel things I said to him then still were true. He seemed so very happy that I became afraid. I don't want him to suffer, and I know he will if he does not steadfastly remain an American, and if, when he wishes to marry, he does not choose an American, or French, or English woman. He must not let himself wish to marry any of us, and he must excuse me for saying it again.

There is much more that I would like to say, but I have ridden hard for two days on frozen roads and I am too tired.

Of course what I said about being free is also true. He may be glad to know that the problem which I feared so much at that time does not confront me any more closely now than it did then. He still wishes, I am sure, placid enjoyment, which will come at Dorn Island to

His very dear friend
DORNA

14

Winter: The Stellins

THE COUNCIL HAD RISEN, The City was all but empty of close friends, no steamer was due for a long time, and the consulate demanded little attention, for an hour or so a day irregularly given sufficed. It was full winter with lovely clear cold days alternating with those of snow, sleet, and strong southeast winds. I had a coal fire burning nearly all the time. I took a few walks and made a few calls. I exercised Fak less often than I ought, usually riding along the tow path outside the walls and thence among the farms in the flat delta. But far the greater part of my time was spent upon my history of the United States, and my life was sedentary and indoors.

So at home in winter it had often been, and the strangeness of Islandia was burned away by the reality of love for Dorna. Long hours passed when I was conscious of that country only as one is conscious of home, all things familiar, in the background, freeing the mind and heart.

With that love, it seemed, I had at last grown up. I could feel it tangibly within me, and I had known nothing like it before. It integrated me with all mankind. Life was all at once simplified. I had discovered a purpose for myself and an end for which to work.

Into my history I tried to put some of the greater sensitiveness to all stirring and beautiful things that Dorna had brought me. I thrilled as I had not thrilled before over various events of our American history—the doggedness of Washington, the westward surge of the pioneers. And I labored long to make the form of the telling in itself fluent, vivid, and graceful. I worried greatly over details of style.

My problems I took to Morana once or twice a week during June and July. No one could have been kinder to me than she was, and I was welcome at her house whenever I chose to come. The cordiality of her welcome made me fear to abuse it. I would go to the great towered Miltain Palace with my manuscript, and, having asked for her, would rarely find that she was out. I would go to her own reception room. Sometimes she was there already, with others, such as her cousins, young Calwin, or young Earne, or their sisters. Once there was Stellina, whom we admitted to help us with the history for two happy hours—a lovely girl, but not so acute nor so constructive a critic as Morana. Before a pleasant open fire we would talk, nine-tenths of the time on the history. She never hesitated to say what she thought, sometimes a little bit to my discomfort; for she had an unerring eye for a sort of emotional extravagance and overemphasis of which I was frequently guilty. I wrote in a high pitch of excitement at times, deeply conscious of my love for Dorna, as a pressure on my brain. It was not wholly pleasant to have pointed out to me overwritten passages.

We had only one difference of opinion. Rather suddenly it occurred to her that she might be doing more than merely helping me in making my history readable to Islandians; and that instead she was giving it a character that would be partly hers, not wholly mine. The truth was that she had done just this. She found great difficulty in expressing her fear, and her cheeks became quite red. I not only had to protest that the history was turning out to be exactly what I wanted it to be, but to thank her without thanking her so much that I seemed to confirm her fear. For a dreadful moment I thought she was going to withdraw her aid entirely, but eventually we settled everything satisfactorily.

If Morana said she missed my calls, I certainly missed her when she returned to Miltain. I sent her sheaves of manuscript twice and had them back promptly with notes and suggestions; but I did not have the Miltain Palace to go to, nor her calm welcoming face and voice to see and hear.

Was I soft about her, I asked myself several times, I who was in love with Dorna? It was troublesome to find that love for Dorna did not wholly immunize me against the seductiveness of other women nor against adolescent temptations not yet wholly outgrown.

Sometimes in those dark wintry, indoor days I doubted whether I loved her sufficiently, or rather I saw with a sort of horror that the fibers responsive to that love did not always vibrate within me. My history absorbed me entirely. I often felt a happiness not traceable at all to any feeling about Dorna. Was I, therefore, a leaky vessel out of which love drained leaving me empty and ordinary?

Much alone and advancing little on the road to winning Dorna, I also found being in love an interesting phenomenon; and because this was so, I had an additional reason for doubting its intensity. For some reason it did not seem quite what it ought to be.

But at first there were few such lapses and no such doubts, and never was there a period of more than a day or two at most when I was not acutely conscious that I loved Dorna—happily, unhappily, pleasantly, painfully, but certainly with a burning intensity. There were moods of wild exhilarated responsiveness to all things emotional or beautiful; and moods of a teeth-on-edge sensitiveness to the sensual implications of being in love, when, knowing that I desired her because in love with her, I shrank from all sensual suggestions in books, in my own body, or in my thoughts, loathing myself for the lack of self-control that made it impossible for me not to associate one idea with another.

But there were often moods which I deliberately indulged, dreaming for hours of all the innocent things pleasant to do with Dorna—of travel, of showing her my own country, or having her show me Islandia, of home occupations, of endless conversations—in all of which, of course, she was mine, loving me wholly.

These were the pleasant phases. There were others disheartening and troublesome, when emotion stimulated my mind to worry itself into a condition of semisickness over the obstacles in my path, which at times seemed so irresistible that I despaired and wept.

I was not penniless, but I was too poor to be a match for Dorna. My capital at home was perhaps fifty thousand dollars. Even if I a foreigner as Dorna's husband were permitted to become naturalized, I had scarcely enough money to buy an Islandian farm. These were only rarely for sale and then only when a family died out. True, very gradually, new farms were being created and I might conceivably have enough money to finance one of these, but this was no life for Dorna, nor for me with no farming experience at all.

As to taking Dorna to the United States, I shrank from the idea. I did not see Dorna comfortable and happy among my relatives and friends. They would not understand her any better than they had understood her brother. I hated to think of Dorna as the wife of a young man in business, a clerk, to whom Uncle Joseph would speak as he had spoken to me.

There was but one way in which I could attain a position which would be sufficient according to my personal wishes for Dorna. If the Mora Treaty were ratified, I, as agent in Islandia for American exporting houses, might really be somebody. I often dreamed of that consummation, but always with an aftermath of discomfort; for I could not forget that she had indicated that she might prefer to die rather than to see anyone established in her country in such a way.

There was also another cause for worry—Dorna's problem. There was someone, someone definite, who was not a present problem but who might become such. There were many possible factual explanations of this tormenting mysterious generality. Of these the one that seemed to me most probable was the existence of some man who had "spoken" to Dorna, who certainly loved her, and in whom she was at least "interested"; but who could not at present marry her because of some condition that might disappear.

A sword of Damocles hung over my head. At any moment that condition might cease to exist. Indeed, perhaps at the very moment when I sat before my fire writing my history and thinking about it, the man might be on his way to Dorn Island to tell Dorna that he now was free to ask her to marry him!

In addition to other obstacles were those—so damaging to my pride—that were implicit in the warnings I had received; not those as to my own suffering if I loved an Islandian girl (it was too late now), but those as to her suffering if she were to love me. Something was wrong with me in Dorna's eyes—some defect in me personally. What? Was it some racial trait that made me physically repulsive?— I could not believe it that. Was it some mental characteristic? What was wrong with my mind, my character? Did Dorna feel herself a superior being? And why had she not told me?

At times I worked myself into a state of real anger at her. It was cruel of her to warn without giving any reason. It is better to know the worst and have done with it than to be left to imagine causes worse still. No woman had a right to be mysterious to a man in matters of this sort!

"Oh, Dorna," I would cry out to myself, "if you realized what you have done to me, you would never have done it!" And I thought of writing to her and asking her to explain.

I kept silence, however, writing her in all that long time between early winter and spring but one brief note thanking her for hers to me, telling her that I had understood perfectly at the time (a lie!), and wishing her a happy winter with no worries to trouble her; and only giving way to the passion in me by adding at the end that I looked forward to seeing her in the spring more than I thought she knew. I had no word from her and no news of her from June 21st until late in September. It was indeed a long, long winter.

It is a strange situation to be in love, and to be cut off, and to have that silence self-imposed. I could have written her without ill grace. I could have made a flying trip to Dorn Island, but she imposed silence upon me in her request to be left undisturbed and in her emphasis that I come in spring, that is, not sooner.

Three months—three months during part of which, at least, I might have been seeing Dorna now and then without troubling her at all. I longed for her, for the look of her, for her voice, for her smile. I felt that merely that much would be quite enough. Explanations, protestations, certainty, and all the rest that I, at times, so passionately craved, would dwindle into insignificance if only—if only. . . .

I became a recluse during that long, dragging winter. Every day I heard the sound of my own voice talking to George, but only for a few minutes.

There was an influx of Americans on the July steamers, but they let me alone to an unexpected degree, using me merely as a sort of Cook's agent to procure means of travel for them. Prospectors for concessions were becoming more numerous and more active, but I was out of it. I did not really care, though I felt that I ought to care more. Uncle Joseph would have approved of my having dogged these men, whether Americans or not. "Pick up all you can, John. Don't be too fastidious. Take advantage of your opportunities. You may learn something to your advantage and make some valuable friends." I could write his letters of advice for him and save him the trouble! And yet . . . and yet . . . I knew that by letting these opportunities go, I also let go a chance to better myself in the one way that would make me materially able to support Dorna. Why not invite them to meals, hang around the hotel, give them drinks, get up a party for them, show them the way to the district Jennings visited?

Why not do so in no mercenary spirit at all, but as one robust American to another who did not know the ropes, and who was in a country without any theaters or dance halls or other pleasure places?

I ungrudgingly told them all I could think of, to help them to move about and concerning conditions in Islandia. I did my duty, as I saw it, to my country and to the expansion of my country's trade. But when the question was squarely presented to me, I made up my mind that I would not seek for myself a position wherein I would be one of those against whom Dorna might feel like fighting to the death, even though I lost, perhaps, the only way possible to me of winning and supporting her.

There came a dark period early in August. To long for a person is in itself a normal condition, but worry combined with longing is hard to bear. My various worries seemed to dwarf all the pleasant things in loving Dorna. They gave me no peace and wore out my concentration. The history began to fail me.

George, who must have guessed my depression, persuaded me to go away. His methods were slow. He never presumed to advise me, but he wondered, he said, if I wouldn't enjoy going into the country more often, for he felt much better for his vacation. "After all, Lang, though you are city-bred apparently, we are all alike in this world. I don't believe there is a man who isn't better for a change from city to country or *of* country now and then."

He argued it with me purely on theoretical grounds. The habit of being a recluse was hard to break. It took some fighting against a sluggish will to rouse myself enough to go to the Stellins', though their farm in Camia was only eighteen miles away. But I went and furthermore I did not ask them if I might come or even warn them in advance that I was coming. I simply went one day—on an impulse, partly prompted by the fact that Stellina was Dorna's friend. They had told me that their house was mine, and I knew what that meant to an Islandian. I packed my saddlebags for a week, mounted Fak, and rode away in a snowstorm. As soon as I was outside the gate, I felt happier; delightful it was to feel snowflakes on my face, hot with riding, and to feel them tangling in my eyelashes.

I had heard of the Stellins from various persons and had been led to believe that they had in high degree some quality which Islandians especially esteemed. George had spoken of them almost with reverence in his voice. They were the oldest of old families, living on their present farm for a thousand years.

I rode out to visit them with some curiosity, with some warmth because of Dorna's friendship for and high opinion of Stellina, and also with a little of the hostility of one who wants to be shown.

The storm was over by noon and the sky cleared. I took my time, not wishing to arrive just as a meal was being prepared, and not sure whom I would find at home. Young Stellin was likely to be with Tor, the King, who was said to be in the East. Stellina·might well be making visits. It did not greatly matter, however, who was there, but if there were only older people I would stay not more than a day or two.

Fak was rather fat and the snow had a tendency to ball under his feet. We went slowly and I often walked and found myself also heavy and sluggish and disinclined to exert myself. A man in love likes to think of himself as fit and at his best. I did not want Dorna to see me plodding along the road, panting, stumbling, and perspiring. And yet I had a hope, which I knew to be unreasonable, that she would be visiting the Stellins.

Fak and I! I had neglected him and had not exercised him enough. What would I do if I had to go away from Islandia and leave him behind? Or, if I could take him with me, where would I keep him, myself a clerk in Uncle Joseph's office? "These, John Lang," I told myself, "are the golden days of your life whether you lose Dorna or not. The first task for you is to get yourself into proper physical condition again. The spring is coming." So I arrived at last, tired, but in a chastened and serener mood.

A stone wall capped with snow bounded the road on the left. Beyond was a field untrodden and gleaming white, bordered on one side by a wood of tall, bare beech trees, which swept away in a great double curve that returned upon itself in the distance. The field sloped gently upward from the road and from this grove, and on the highest part, stood the simplest of houses. It was of gray stone, two stories high. The roof was white with snow, and the snowy field seemed to reach its walls. There was something lovely in its proportions and in its relation to the slopes of the field and to the curves of the beech wood.

At the door which was in the rear of the house Lord Stellin himself came to greet me, after I had conquered my shyness and called my name; for to shout in that snowy stillness seemed an intrusion. I wondered if he remembered me, but even if he did not he showed no signs of it. He made me welcome and in a few moments I was before an open fire talking to Stellina herself, Dorna's friend, and to her brother. They both knew me without question. Nor was it much longer before all sense of strangeness left me and I was being floated along most happily in the stream of their life—with Dorna strangely remote, and the pain of worrying like the memory of a toothache.

There I remained for seven days, too sure of my welcome to ask myself whether it was too long. Life was of the simplest. There was no music as at the Hyths', no books nor talk of books, no carvings as at the Dorns', nor any sign of graphic art. Nor was there much conversation. Why did I have so happy a time? I spent some hours on my history, I took several walks and rides with the younger ones, separate and together. I was alone a great deal. Nothing exciting happened.

Perhaps it was the beauty of the place, a suave serene beauty in the massing of simple elements, a grove, a house, a field. Nowhere in the whole farm was there a place without charm or even a certain fascination that drew one there again. Beneath the simplicity was something very rich, for I knew that with the changes of season there this loveliness would change but remain. Changes of seasons and of light in an infinite variety of combinations!

The morning following my arrival, I made the perambulation of the farm on horseback with Lord Stellin. The day was bitterly cold and I was glad to get back to the fire. Stellina was making a dress, the cloth over her crossed knee, her slender back in a pretty curve, and her small graceful head looking up as she spoke and then down. Young Stellin was simply loafing and watching his sister. They asked where I had been, and when I told them as well as I could they both suggested other places to which I must be taken.

"But we crossed that field," I said.

"Yes, on the west side, but you ought to go to the other side and look back," Stellina answered. . . . What was so special about this field, I wondered.

"We ought to cut down those birches," young Stellin remarked.

"Not at all!" said Stellina with a curious eagerness.

They argued a little, and I found that what interested them was the effect upon a certain view, rather than the value of the wood. They

297

were in exact agreement as to the end to be obtained, though differing as to the means, and that end was the intrusion upon a spacious composition of a complex tangle in the foreground. It came to me quite suddenly that they looked upon their whole farm as a great living canvas, whose picture changed from moment to moment and hour to hour, and to which they as artists made only little changes from time to time; for the larger picture was painted mostly by nature and by generations of Stellins before them.

It was strange that I had to be in Islandia eight months before I learned that no farmer merely farms but is an artist in landscape architecture as well, of course with greatly varying skill. That morning and all during lunch I questioned my hosts, and I learned.

"At home," I said, "a farmer plants things where he thinks they will grow best."

"So do we."

"But you also consider how the field will look when they first come up through the earth, and when they are full grown—"

"And when they are dead and when they are stubble."

"Which consideration is the most important?" I asked. But they could not tell me.

I told them how men at home ruined lovely views by unsightly structures. It never occurred to anyone that an ordinary view was worth saving when put into competition with a commercial interest. The only views considered were unique ones and those concerned with their preservation were few.

They smiled.

It appeared that one hated to destroy or even to change an aspect of things found pleasing, and never did so without trying to create another in its place.

"But there must often be men who do not feel that way and change a farm greatly."

"Not the old ones. The great changes become fewer and fewer as the farm grows older; and after a time one can give attention to details."

I asked about farmers with a perverted artistic sense.

"They do harm, of course, but upon an established farm as most are no one man's errors are going to spoil it except here and there. No man will do much, you know."

I suggested that therefore those with artistic talent were frustrated by the insufficiency of their opportunities.

"Oh, what one can do is infinite!" they said. To my questions one was as likely to answer as another, and the one speaking was never interrupted, nor his or her views qualified or amplified. Nor, often, could I remember which had said a given thing.

That afternoon young Stellin took me for a hard walk. We returned tired, both of us. He was the most worldly of all of them and seemed the best to understand my ignorance. He told me so much about the principles upon which crops were planted, fields changed from pasture to meadow, and wood cut, that I felt as though I had been to school. The art in which I was instructed was neither agriculture not architecture but a combination of both; and the Islandian word connotes both aspects of a farmer's effort, just as the word agriculture does if one stresses a certain meaning in the last two syllables.

I tried to set down what he told me, and was so interested in this new phase of Islandian life that I wrote a long letter all about it to my remaining girl correspondent at home, who was the only one to show real interest in the place where I was.

Because Stellina had seemed pleased when drawn into my conferences with Morana over my history, I offered to read parts of it. They all seemed delighted and set aside the next evening. No author ever had in advance a more cordial audience. The author in question, John Lang, hoped, however, for something more than a chance to show off. I was coming to believe that Dorna, Nattana, George, and the others were true in their judgment of the Stellins as their best. The best should be the best critics.

I invited criticism, but I got none. They were as responsive as they were cordial; and stimulated to talk more than usual, they furnished me with several new ideas as to Islandian similarities or contrasts to our conditions. But not a word did they say as to any faults in expression, proportion, or emphasis. Nor could I force persons who gave me such a charming hearing to pick flaws. Yet my head was not turned, nor did I feel flattered. They went straight to the subject of the United States and discussed it rather than my history of it. Nevertheless I was encouraged to read to them on several other evenings.

Stellina and I took one long walk. She was dressed in high gaiters, without visible buttons, which fitted closely her slender legs, loose knickerbockers like a skirt, and a long coat, all of the same material, a wool, and in color, a dovelike gray with a faint flush in it—an extraordinary and fascinating color against white snow and dark winter evergreens and leafless hard woods. On the back of her coat was a hood of linen, edged with the material of her coat, of a slightly lighter color, and the shirt that showed over her collar was white. Sometimes she drew the hood over her head and was rather quaint, but more often the hood lay back on her shoulders like a handkerchief.

The day was a dull one, eliminating contrasts, and Stellina was the vividest thing I saw, but of a subdued vividness, blending into her backgrounds, setting them off as they in turn did her. Her large, lucid, violet eyes were the center of every picture, and they bothered me all the time. I would not say that they had no depth and no particular expression, but they certainly had none of that responsiveness that is exciting and often dangerous. They were always ready to be looked into, and it was I that did the withdrawing and dodging.

Stellina was fragile and slim. Sometimes we walked through deep drifts. I worried over her strength a little, but in the end it was she who was fresh and I tired, mentally as well as physically.

She was impossible to talk to in commonplaces. Constantly I lost her attention. She was always stopping, turning away, listening, or looking. I found myself doing just as she did. Her remarks were brief. She would point out a tree with a graceful wave of her ungloved hand, and smile. She would look up and draw a quick breath and smile. Her eyes would flash into mine an unexpected cold flash. Her lips were sweet, the only part of her seductive.

On the snow was a dead bird, a disheveled bunch of white and slaty blue feathers with darker markings.

"Look at it!" she cried, in a tone that was either ecstasy or acute distress. "Look at it, Lang, and my dress." . . . Dress and bird made the other glow. "Is it entitled to burial? The ground is frozen."

"We could put it under the snow."

She shook her head and stood staring at the bird.

"It hasn't thought enough of life to wish that its body be buried when it dies. Let's leave it. It does not care whether or not its body goes on being useful." There was a long pause, and then she added in the same tone: "My sister died, of course. Most of us do. So we did what she wanted. There was a shady place on the Inly farm in Niven. Her husband was young Inly. There were all sorts of flowers, wild ones, growing there. Father took charge himself and young Inly helped him. They were very careful and they took out the sods whole, and scarcely disturbed the roots at all. It was hard to do, for the ground was frozen. But she will be there in the spring when the things start. She would have liked that idea. And I do, too. Of course, I would like to think of her here not there, but it was her *alia*. She wanted to be buried there. I will show you the place I have chosen, if I don't marry. You would understand better if it were midsummer and the trees were in bloom." She named the name of a certain tree. "Do you know it, Lang? It has large red flowers."

"No, I do not, Stellina," I answered, most unexpectedly shaken.

"I like to think of some of me part of these flowers."

The sudden thought of Stellina dead, above all of Dorna dead, of myself, too, was for a moment unbearable.

"When did your sister die?" I asked.

"Oh, ten days ago," she answered lightly. Then as though guessing my curiosity, "She was thirty. She had been married ten years and had had three children. She was killed by a fall—Oh, Lang, look!"

And I looked where her hand indicated and saw a soft gray blur slide between two trees and vanish.

"What was it?"

"A little wolf," she said. "He was so pretty."

We went on.

"What do you do with dead people in your country?" she asked. I told her in an unsteady voice.

"Don't you think it better to be unmarked, Lang?"

I argued that relatives and friends liked to know where their dead were. She nodded her head.

"I had forgotten," she answered, "that you are not buried on your own places. If all people are buried in one place—" She broke off. "Whose place is it?"

I gave her a truthful answer. It usually belonged to some company. Stellina shuddered, and her eyes grew wide.

"Lang, I'm sorry! You can't like it that way."

"Some do. Your way is rarely possible. And there must always be a stone."

"Here those who care, remember," she said. "And everyone knows you are there. Why does the spot matter? And after ten years, if things change, why not change with them? That tree of mine will only live about one hundred years more. When it comes down the field will be plowed and I shall be shifted, but I will always be here—unless I marry, and then I'll be on my husband's place somewhere."

"I should think that bones would often be plowed up."

"If they are, they are broken up and put back in the soil . . . Oh, you must be so different from us, Lang! Probably you have many reasons which I don't understand."

I longed for a change of subject . . . Dorna dead . . . The idea of death! Yet something in me fluttered in an effort to rise to Stellina's serenity. Or was it merely her callousness?

I could not tell. Continually she turned to something she knew, or found some new thing to look at. It seemed to me almost a pose. If you can conceive of monosyllabic gush, that was what I thought of Stellina's raptures some of the time.

That evening a neighbor brought the news of Lord Farrant's death. Besides Lord Stellin, Danninga, and their two children, several others were present. It was the Stellins' "day" when those who wished to call upon them came with a greater freedom and with the expectation of finding others. Conversation was desultory and of local affairs. I sat near the fire, listening but not taking part, tired and rather subdued.

The neighbor did not state his news at once, and when at last he spoke it was in a casual manner; but there was an instant hush, which continued for at least a minute, and then Lord Stellin spoke easily:

"It means the loss of one of Lord Dorn's surest of followers."

Though the minute had seemed long, this remark, made without any transitional tribute to Lord Farrant's character, surprised me. Of course he lived far off and was not perhaps well known to the people of Camia; but it seemed to me that he was entitled to more homage than to be classed merely as a follower of Lord Dorn. But none was paid him. Conversation was continued, now along political lines. There was interest in Lord Farrant's successor, and in his probable affiliation. One man seemed to think it likely that if there were two candidates for the vacant office, one favoring Lord Mora and one Lord Dorn, the vote would be strongly for the latter. With this another man took issue. Though the West was conservative, he said, nevertheless Lord Mora's views were gaining adherents all over the country.

Lord Stellin listened for some time as these two men amicably wrangled, smiling at each other in friendly apology whenever one thought he had scored on the other. Then he asked a question that interested me greatly. Did any of those present regard it as a problem which the people should settle rather than the National Council? I thought of the arguments at home over the referendum as opposed to the pure time-honored principle of representative government guaranteed by the Constitution; and I heard back and forth the same arguments—that the people are directly concerned and therefore should vote directly; that the people are not well enough informed to vote intelligently on complicated questions; that this question was, that it was not, complicated.

The discussion was a long one and I felt myself becoming tired and sleepy. Interested as I was, vital as the whole problem seemed, because connected with the Dorns, my best friends, and with Dorna, whom I loved—though tonight in person she seemed painfully remote and unreal—I felt those present with their constant differing voices slip into the distance. Perhaps I dozed, but if I did it was into a consciousness deeper than words, of what Stellina had said of death and of burial, and I shuddered. This feeling clung to me.

It was nearing the end of the week which I had allowed myself. My house in The City seemed a forlorn and dull place to which to return.

In the afternoon Stellin was going out to cut the birches about which he and his sister had talked, and I went also, provided with a dangerously razor-edged ax. It was a day of damp chilly haze, the temperature being only a little above freezing.

He chopped with a lazy effortless deftness. I trimmed the trunks, afraid of the efficiency of my ax. He asked me my opinion upon the subjects discussed the night before; and in the course of our conversation he told me casually that he expected to leave in a few days to join Tor, and that they were likely to travel into the West and to find out the temper of the people there for themselves.

Would they go to Dorn Island? I dared not ask, but it was likely. Dorna and the king! That image was enough to kindle my emotions again. Through a twinge of jealousy I recaptured again all my intense longings, and I was glad to feel suffering and love once more.

We became warm and stopped to rest. Stellin looked about him, sitting on a pile of brush. The haze thickened, and the snow became gray in the distance; but near at hand the red twigs of the birches were vivid against its fleecy whiteness. I also sat down, stiff in the back, but comfortably aware of being in far better condition than when I arrived five days before.

Then Stellina appeared.

She came out of the haze and over the trodden snow, light, slim, with a jauntiness that seemed almost self-conscious. She was dressed in a white that was almost buff-colored in contrast to the snow. Her head was bare, but about her neck was a bright scarlet handkerchief, loosely tied. Her eyes were unexpectedly blue—the only blue things to be seen anywhere. She brought us a flask of chocolate, welcome with its hot, strong, bitter sweetness.

While we drank she busied herself gathering up the scattered twigs, graceful and limber. Her brother and I watched her with the same feelings—a quiet pleasure in the color of her and in the rhythm of her movements. But to me, acutely aware of Dorna again, she was not the right one, and her loveliness only seemed to make that fact more painful. The damp chill began to penetrate in spite of the chocolate. I shivered. It was nearing dusk. I was invited by her to come to the other end of the field to see how it looked with the birches down. This was also the way home.

We tramped through the snow to the place she had chosen and when we turned, Stellin at a lower level was almost lost to sight in the haze. We could see his dim figure moving, and then a yellower haze rising, and finally the ruddy wavering flames from the lighted brush, all against a shadowy background of distant trees.

Stellina at my side drew a sharp breath. I caught her eyes, and she smiled suddenly as though hurt.

"We can't tell how it will usually look," she said, "because it is so dim . . . Shall we go on?"

We walked in silence, Stellina seeming to float at my side, half a ghost and half a treacherously close friend. I wanted to tell her all my troubles.

Her mind, however, was running on burials. She asked me what our cemeteries looked like. I told her rather cynically that they were a series of disorderly little arrangements of turf, gravestone, shrub, or vine, no one in any way related to another.

"Aren't there trees?" she asked.

"Yes—sometimes quite beautiful ones."

"Some of the plots must be quite lovely," she said hesitatingly.

I admitted it, adding, however, that there was always present the fact of death and of hopeless loss.

"I wasn't thinking of that," she said, "but of how one could really make a little square plot of grass with shrubs and trees and a carved stone a pleasure to look at."

I remembered her incomprehension of a few days back. Evidently she had been turning over in her mind the fact of cemeteries, thinking of them less as places in which to dispose of the dead than as places on which to exercise one's artistic talents; and it seemed to me that she evaded the grim side of life in her constant concentration on its visual beauty.

I looked at her wonderingly and also critically, and found her eyes waiting and questioning.

"What have I done?" she asked suddenly, her voice cool but with concern.

"To us," I said, "a cemetery where dead are buried is not a place in which merely to create a lovely thing. It is a place full of grief for us, and we try to make it peaceful and restful."

"Of course, you try to make it lovely too!" she cried.

"Some people do. Others merely try to put up something that will tell all about the dead person, symbolically or in words, and preserve his memory as long as possible."

"No one could hold a memory of him rightly except those who knew him," she answered. "But I am sorry! It is hard for me to understand, Lang."

She won me.

"You would understand perfectly," I answered, "if you saw a cemetery."

We went on in silence. My thoughts rushed back to Dorna.

"Death," said Stellina at last, "seems to be more painful to you than to us."

"Perhaps you merely feel it in a different way."

She pondered a long time.

"What do you do in America when someone dear to you dies or is lost to you, Lang?"

It seemed to me an astonishing question.

"We try to bear it," I said.

"Yes, but what do you do?"

"Why, we go on with what duties we have to perform in the world."

"I understand that," she said slowly.

There was another long silence.

"Is it very beautiful in America?" she asked. "Tell me about places there that aren't like places here."

I talked with Stellina until suppertime—on the way home and then before a blazing fire. She listened with apparent interest while I described the prairies of the farther Middle West, the sage brush regions of the great basin, the Grand Canyon, Niagara Falls, the Great Lakes, and the desert west of Salt Lake. I knew no counterpart of these places in Islandia, and though my personal knowledge of them was slight I had read and seen pictures of them.

"It seems to me, Lang," she said, when supper was so near that I had to go and change and wash, "that even if cemeteries and the places where you live aren't all you would wish them to be, there are wonderful things to be seen in your country."

"Yes," I cried, "but when you have suffered a loss, they only make it worse!"

Her eyes became very wide.

On the day that I left, Stellina and her brother came to the gate with me. Fak followed us and being a well-bred horse he did not overrun us. It was cold, but not so cold as to chill us after the first few moments of walking. The sky was a cloudless deep blue. In the night more snow had fallen, and all things on earth were freshly white, with pale-rose and pale-lavender lights and blue shadows. Only here and there was anything uncovered—tree trunks, almost red in the glowing, pale, clear air, the façade of the house beneath its white roof with its gray stone ruddy, and the dark tufted leaves of the evergreens.

Bareheaded and in dark clothes against the snowy fields, glittering in the sunlight, the two Stellins were more fragile and more slim than ever, but they strode along freely. Limber and light yet strong, they could both outwalk me, but it would be the last thing they would ever do. They were almost like twins, their smiles the same, their eyes having the same expression.

Stellina's small lovely head turned here and there. She looked off over the fields and up among the trees and back to the house, or else watched the sun-bright spray of powdery snow made by her moving feet; and I knew that there was nothing beautiful that her eyes missed, and that beauty flowed through her like a clear stream sweeping her clean and empty of all but the loveliness of itself. And meanwhile her brother, not so perceptive, and I, less perceptive still, looked to her to make us see and feel it also, finding reflections of it in her face, or following the direction of her eyes to behold what she saw. Aware that we were staring at her, she smiled at both of us in the same way, giving us each the pure clarity of her eyes. Her head dropped and she swung along, the smile fixed on her lips, her knees gallantly throwing her dress forward, her long figure like a child's, and the white snow-spray rising about her feet.

And her brother and I, after thus watching her, glanced at each other and smiled with sudden complete comprehension.

We reached the gate, Fak came up to us, and her brother went to his head on one side. Stellina on the other turned and watched us. I mounted and settled myself. She came forward, her eyes on mine —wide-open, simple violet eyes as clear as bright water. She had some thought in her head, I knew, wondering what it was, hoping that she, who seemed to know so many fresh beautiful things, would this time be able to express them so that I could understand. Still looking at me she stroked Fak's gray nose, and he nodded his head. And then she smiled and her face seemed to suffer a little. She turned to her brother as if for his consent.

"I think I shall kiss Lang," she said, and she came forward like a child. I leaned down. Fak did not move. I knew enough to be kissed and not to kiss, just touching her shoulder with my fingers. For an infinitesimal fraction of a second I felt her small soft lips on my cheek, but she really kissed me, and then stepped back, smiling, not flushed, quite serene.

I could not speak, but I looked at them both and nodded, and Fak walked away with me.

According to the Islandian calendar, *Windorn* or winter, beginning on the shortest day in the year, lasts four months. *Grane* or spring, which follows, is but two months long; *Sorn* or summer, another four, and "Leaves" or fall, two more. *Windorn* began on June 20th corresponding to December 21st in the Northern Hemisphere, and it was not *Grane* until October 20th, the same as April 20th at home. During these four months the southeast winds blew and blew sometimes for several days, often with sleet or snow, sometimes with overcast skies. When the wind ceased it was clear and cold. The water in the river arm below my window skimmed over, and Mount Islandia was visible on the horizon. When the wind resumed, it became warmer. It was the first winter of my life when I did not have a bad cold.

Soon after my return from the Stellins', though the winds still blew as strongly as ever, they brought more sleet and rain than snow. The farms across the river showed pools that reflected the sky when it cleared. I went out more and slopped about either on foot or with Fak, in mud and water. It took some effort to go, but I was improving my own condition and getting my horse ready for the long journey to the West.

On September 2nd and 4th, steamers were due; and then there would follow six weeks without any. I made plans to leave on September 10th and to spend nearly a month at Dorn Island, to be there when spring really came.

It was hard to wait and wait for the day when I was to see the girl I loved. I was nervous and impatient, perhaps the more so because my love for Dorna had lapses. Perhaps by dreaming ahead too intensely of my meeting with her I wore out a little the sensitive fibers of my emotion. And I also worried because early in August, having heard from Nattana and having received an invitation to visit the Hyths in the spring, I had foolishly accepted, the time at my disposal seeming at that long distance endless, but now all too short.

All the same I worked hard to finish my history, and had a completed manuscript on the day that the steamer arrived. All it waited for was Morana's final approval. I sent it to her.

Then came a bitter disappointment. The particular gentleman in the Department of State who wrote me as to how I should behave directed me to attend the Council Meeting on September 13th, which concerned itself solely with local matters. Washington many thousand miles away knew better than I who was on the spot! I must be there and report. Furthermore I was informed that it was undesirable that I should be away from The City and my office for more than a few days at a time. Someone had filled the ears of this gentleman with tales about me. I wondered who it was. There were several persons who might have been annoyed at me: Müller, or Andrews and Body, or the diseased man.

To make matters more unpleasant but no worse, Uncle Joseph wrote me in his usual vein. He was evidently aware of the letter from the Department of State. He had happened to be down in Washington, he said, and had dropped in at the State Department. The time had come to speak frankly. They weren't wholly pleased with the way I was handling the consulate. My reports were all right, but not of much practical use. Yet there was no complaint on that score. He was sure I did not need to have him tell me what was wrong. "You had better buck up," he wrote. No doubt I was having a good time, making long visits, but was I sure I was getting in with the right crowd? Of course, no one grudged me my friendship with the Dorns for the sake of old college days, but had I gone to Islandia for a reunion with a classmate? He was sure that I knew as well as anyone that Dorn was of the wrong party. Had I been wholly careful? Was I doing all I could for so-and-so and so-and-so? Uncle Joseph knew nearly everyone who had come to Islandia . . . Then he said over again in almost the same phrases what he had written me three months before.

If I literally obeyed the instructions from Washington, I could not go to Dorn Island at all; and yet there was nothing to keep me in The City. Two groups of Americans had arrived, it is true, on the September steamers. One was interested in the possibilities of oil, and was easily satisfied by my usual provisions for their traveling. The other group was interested in oranges. All it wanted was to examine and study methods in Carran. It also was no trouble. By September 8th they both were on their way, to be gone five weeks; and yet I must stay at The City until the twentieth to attend and report upon the meeting of the council, which would concern itself solely with questions of roads and local land laws.

My rebelliousness did not carry me so far as to make me disobey the injunction to attend the Council Meeting. On the other hand as soon as the council adjourned I was going to leave for Dorn Island and I was not going to be back at The City before October 16th. I wrote the Dorns on the sixth to say that I was coming, and had an answer from Faina on the eighteenth that they would all be there. I would have two weeks with them if I broke my engagement with the Hyths—one if I did not.

Having thus made up my mind to disregard my orders I was, however, far from comfortable. The very act of going to see Dorna might mean my dismissal from the consulate and thereby lose me further opportunities to see her. I fretted for hours in speculations upon the influences at work in Washington. At times I was inclined to think that it was only Uncle Joseph's way of compelling me to follow the lines he wished me to follow; but at others I felt the ground caving in under my feet and I was really badly frightened.

The council duly met and I attended every meeting. An attaché from the German legation was equally faithful, and at moments as rebellious, but there was no other foreigner. Only about two thirds of the provincial lords were present. Young Tor was there the first day and no other. His sister did not come at all. Yet in spite of my rebelliousness I had an interesting time. Business was conducted in a most informal way, and everyone was in great good humor. I never heard one Islandian really chaff another, yet they teased each other a little like the good friends they were. Lord Dorn was present for three days only and invited me to dine with him. I told him briefly of my instructions from Washington. He made the remark that Dorna would be disappointed because of my shortened visit, and for a moment my heart expanded, and then collapsed—for was this more than a polite remark? Lord Fain, seeing my loneliness upon the benches reserved for spectators, asked me to sit behind him on the bench reserved for his secretary who had not come. I felt almost a member of the council, and when the meeting at last adjourned on the twentieth I really knew all those who had attended, and had gained knowledge of Islandia's internal affairs.

There was another advantage in my staying. My history was returned by Morana with a charming note of praise and congratulation. She wrote that she had enjoyed every minute she had spent in connection with it. Before I left I had placed it in the hands of The City's one printer, and its publication was assured.

On September 21st when I set out for Dorn Island I could not help feeling that it was rather creditable to have become an author in a strange language within a year. The history was short, it is true, but printed it made a book of one hundred and fifty pages of the usual octavo size. I was, I say, proud, though I knew that it was not what I intended it to be when I began it. It was to have been a work of propaganda aimed to convince Islandians that the citizens of the

United States were not so very different from themselves, that these citizens were pleasant to know and to deal with, and that they had (for sale) many things of the greatest possible use and benefit for Islandia. As I wrote it, however, the propaganda became more subtle lest it defeat itself by being too obvious, and finally disappeared. The book became a brief history and explanation of the United States. In some matters I described in some detail our methods, such as in agriculture, in transportation, and in the use of electricity, oil, coal, and gas. But there was so much that had to be explained to those who had no vehicles moved by mechanical means (except the ships of the navy), no telephones, no telegraphs, practically no shops, no advertisements, no credit system and therefore no banks, that very little space was left me to argue the desirability of all these things. Morana said several times that the best thing I could do was to present as clear a picture as I could of life in the United States, and to leave it to my readers to judge whether or not they wished to emulate us. And I agreed with her. Certainly it was more to my taste to write the sort of book I did write, but I hesitated before deciding to tell Uncle Joseph about it. It would not be advertisement enough to suit him. On the other hand I could send Dorna a presentation copy of it without any shame. Gladys Hunter had sent me her usual letter by the September steamer, and I decided to send her a copy, even though she could not read it.

15

Spring: Visit to Dorn Island

SPRING HAD BEGUN when Fak and I started our journey to Dorn Island. The day was clear and warm and the grass, wet, lush and growing, was a new and lighter green than at other seasons. The orchards were either in a mist of blossom or else had twigs edged by vivid little leaves. The air was full of the smell of warm earth, and the road glistened with pools from recent rain.

Our first night was spent at the ancient farm of Bodwin, the new marshal, where Bodwin "the younger" had lived and written in the early thirteen hundreds. The second night was spent at the Somes', the third in the Inn at Inerria Town, and by evening of the fourth day, I had reached the Inn at the Doan Pass.

Descending the pass next morning we went back to a different spring. There was less water in the Earne River than there had been in the Cannan, less mist in the air and cloud in the sky. All was stiller and quieter, and plant life seemed in suspense.

From the mountains could be seen the marshes of the Doring River delta, flat and dark-blue against the high horizon; and that sight, with nothing between my eyes and Dorna, except miles of air, told me that this was the West again, the home of friends and beloved.

The ride to the town of Earne through the flat farms was tedious. Perhaps Dorna would be at the ferry!

Hope and worry and all else became trivial as the long afternoon wore itself away. I was going to see Dorna and hear her voice. For two weeks I would be near her and see her daily. When the first shock of seeing her was over, there would be nothing but beauty and peace. I would hold my tongue, for she did not want to be bothered, but I would be as delightful a friend and companion as I could be.

My heart was beating when we rode through the gate of Earne, out of the green world of countryside into streets of close stone houses. It seemed only a moment before the road curved out upon the quay. I smelled the fresh salty air of the marsh. Boats with double masts lay moored alongside the stone wall.

Tired and stiff, I slipped heavily down from the familiar saddle and went to the water's edge to look for the boat that was to come—really, however, searching for Dorna.

A slim dark man in blue jersey and short knickerbockers approached me and stated his name. He was the fisherman at the little harbor on the southeast side of the Island where I had gone to meet Dorna.

He had been asked to come for me, he said. There was not wind enough for sailing, but he would take me across the river and ride with me to operate the intermediate ferries.

There were three ferries in all, and the third brought us to Dorn Island itself just beyond the little harbor where Dorna had landed.

The three months of waiting were over.

Mounting Fak again, I set out. There awaited me a room which was my own. To arrive like a member of the family seemed best. I rode to the stables and unsaddled Fak and gave him a vacant stall before entering the house, but my eyes looked everywhere for Dorna and my heart beat. This was her place, her home, and every stone in the façade of the house, every breath of air, every aspect of tree and field was full of her.

The corridors were quiet and deserted. I went to my room without seeing anyone. "Your room has been made ready for you"—so they had said six months before. Ready it was, literally, on this strange spring day. I was expected, and that was a great relief to me as I stood in the utter quiet, my ears singing from silence and fatigue. It was near suppertime. When ready I gathered myself together and went downstairs to the little room where I had been welcomed by Faina on the day that I first came to Dorn Island.

The door was a little open and a fire was burning. Faina, herself, was the only person there. She greeted me as though I had never been away. But she was a dream-person to me. Where was Dorna? Where was my friend?

Marta came in, and then Dorna, the elder. They were friendly. Little by little they gave me news. Lord Dorn was at Doring. My friend was expected back from Hoe Bay in Winder tonight or tomorrow. . . .

Dorna was visiting the Ronans. . . .

I asked a question or two quite naturally, but my heart hurt. She spent a week with them, it appeared, every year. She had not been able to fit it in before, because of visitors and visits. She had gone two days earlier. (After my letter came!) She was, however, coming home to supper tonight, and had suggested that if I arrived in time I might like to go over to the Ronans' to fetch her. It was probably too late now, but I might try.

I went out. The Ronans lived near. It was not as though she had gone wholly away, but it was cruel. Dusk was gathering. I walked along the white shell road under the arching beeches, with their small new leaves fluttering in the wind. The smell of salt marsh and sea was elusive—rather the smell was of earth and grass. Dorn Island seemed very much the farm which it really was.

I walked quickly with a heart that beat faster and faster. The moment for which I had waited so long had come, and it was half-spoiled. Had not Lord Dorn himself said that Dorna would be disappointed because my visit was to be short? But annoyance soon dissolved in dread lest she was deliberately avoiding me.

Just before I came to the deserted warehouses of the little harbor, Dorna, dressed in dark-blue, emerged from between the squared walls, walking in that easy, limber, casual way of hers.

She gave me the quick smile of one who had seen me shortly before. She said nothing and I fell in at her side.

She was just exactly what I expected her to be—perfect because utterly herself, herself and no one else. All worry, anger, and dread drained away. Nothing mattered.

It was Dorna who spoke first, not lifting her head, her voice deliberate.

"I wanted to welcome you, John."

"Thank you, Dorna," I answered.

"Oh, don't thank me! You have a right to blame me a little. I am partly responsible for your being here at this time," she continued, "and I don't like having to be away."

I held back the words I wished to utter, waiting to hear her go on.

"But, John," she said earnestly, "I promised them this visit, and I don't see any other time when I can fit it in. And it is not as though

I had gone from the neighborhood. I have told them that you were coming, and that, if you want me, I shall give you some of my time."

Her little speech was ended.

"I have wanted to see you very much," I said.

There was a pause.

"Well, I have wanted to see you," she answered. Her face was turned towards me in a question, but I did not look at her.

"You can take me back this evening," she added after a moment.

I was the only man at table. Faina was opposite, Marta and the elder Dorna on my right, Dorna on my left. *Tanrydoon* gave me place at the head of the table when the men of the household were away. It was as though I were a member of the family. Dorna seemed flushed, vividly bright and young. Hope kindled to an extent which was unreasonable and dangerous. I made a resolution to say nothing, and doubted my ability to keep it. She valued the placid enjoyment of her life at home—it must not be broken. Though not presuming to be able to trouble her peace of mind, I must love her peace of mind more than my own.

Half of me, however, talked easily of The City and my life there, and (for Dorna's ears) of my history and its impending publication. I felt grave eyes upon me. Was she curious and surprised? I waited to hear her speak, but she said nothing. It was the three older women who kept the conversation going.

After supper it was the same.

We sat before the fire in the little room, Faina and I on one settle, the elder Dorna and Marta on the other. My Dorna sat on a stool, her elbows on her knees, her face between her hands, looking into the fire and seeming to pay no heed.

I talked on and on, but whenever I looked at her I lost the thread of what I was saying. I waited impatiently for the time when I would escort her to the Ronans'. Marta yawned, then rose and went to her boy and to bed, I suppose. Faina, too, seemed to wander. Only Dorna, the elder, wanted to talk, and I suspected her of mere politeness.

There came a pause in the conversation. Was it my duty to whip it alive again? Silence fell upon us all.

Faina after several long minutes said good night and left us. I thought that the elder Dorna started to rise, but that her cousin motioned to her to remain.

But it was Dorna who broke the silence. She asked what the council had done at its meeting, and I told her all about it in great detail, having it in my memory because I had had to write a report for Washington.

She listened without turning her head, yet I felt that I had her attention. So suddenly that she startled both her cousin and me, Dorna pushed her stool back from the fire.

"It is so hot!" she cried, and I wondered if she had been listening as intently as I thought she had. She rose to her feet. "The Ronans go to bed early," she continued, "I ought to be going back."

Looking up at her in surprise I forgot my American politeness and did not rise also. Her face dazzled, younger than I remembered it, and with a vivid burning freshness—fire in her cheeks and a hot light in her brilliant eyes.

She was at the door before I realized that perhaps she might be intending to return without me. I ran after her and followed her along the corridor.

"You need not come," she said shortly. "There is really no need of it at all."

"I am coming if you don't mind," I answered, too disturbed to think of a politer way to put it. She made no answer, and I went with her.

We moved out into the night. The dark sky was powdered so thickly with stars that it seemed unfamiliar—the sky of the Southern Hemisphere. We passed into shadow under the beech trees. The sky was blotted, but the white road had a glimmer of its own.

My tongue was tied. I had her to myself, but did not know what it was I wanted to say.

At my side her face was only a vague whiteness, that yet was warm, living, and desirable. I heard what I thought was a laugh, and then she spoke.

"When I first learned about that book of yours," she said, "I wished that I could have helped you with it."

"I wanted your help," I answered, really pleased.

"Morana could make it more what you would want it than I could."

"I don't think so, Dorna," I replied sincerely.

"I wanted to help you because I wanted the book to contain things I wanted to have said. You chose the right person, Johnlang."

Her voice made me uncomfortable. I knew of no way in which to tell her that I really would have liked to write the book with her, without seeming in turn disloyal to Morana.

We emerged from the alley of beeches and the stars were over our heads again. Dorna took on form and solidity. The starlight made her face white, and yet I could feel it glowing, and the wish to speak became a choking thing in my throat. But all I could do was to ask her a question.

"When shall I see you again, Dorna?"

She made no answer for a long time.

"My brother will be here tomorrow," she said at last. For a moment it sounded like a rebuke, but there was a low note in her voice of explanation and almost of regret. "I work with my hands at the Ronans'," she continued. "I become one of the family. I wash dishes and I cook. They have only one family of dependents. And I work in their flower garden . . . Let's meet again day after tomorrow."

I winced, but there was nothing to be said.

"All right, Dorna."

"Come over after breakfast." She spoke as though she too were sorry, and her name leaped to my lips, but I did not utter it. She wanted to be let alone. She did not want to be bothered with my emotions. Perhaps her warnings were for her sake as well as for mine. In her manner was something that had never been there before—a gentleness. . . .

I looked up at the powdery clouds of stars. I was at Dorn Island with Dorna again. If I had come to love her in the winter, I loved her more now; time and absence had merely deepened it. I was miserable with an excess of happiness.

We came to the harbor. At the foot of a narrow flight of stone steps were moored several rowboats.

"Wait a moment," she said. "I'll go down first. They have drifted out from the step."

It was properly a man's task to bring in the boat.

"Can't I do it?" I asked, stepping forward.

"You might fall in. The steps are slippery."

"So might you."

"I know them better. Let me, John."

We both were at the top of the flight, blocking each other's way down. Our voices were low. Something seemed about to happen.

"Please, John!" she cried in a sharp voice.

I stood aside with throbbing heart. A moment later she called to me.

"You can come now. Be careful! Can you see?"

The rowboat was dimly visible. She was in the stern, holding to the steps.

"Will you row?" she said.

I took my place at the oars. It was strange to handle them at this season with winter so recent. A glassy cold came from the invisible, black water. I pushed off with the oar blade and we drifted out into space.

"I'll guide you," she said. "I will steer by the trees against the sky. We will have to allow for the tide."

So I pulled, following her directions. On my left loomed a black wall and a tower, and then the tide seemed to sweep it from us sideways.

"It is only the neap," she said. "Sometimes in spring tides and a wind it is hard to get across."

Her voice was enchanting. Coming from her face, which was almost featureless in the starlight, it was a warm intimate thing that united us. My own in answer sank to its tone.

"Pull on your right hand, John."

I obeyed.

"You row well," she said after a moment, and I was happy, because it was not only Dorna who said it, but Dorna who knew boats from childhood.

"Oh!" she cried suddenly. "What a night! What a night, John!"

My heart quickened. Why need we land? Could we not row into the Earne River and have darkness, space, and water all around us?

"Can't we go out to the river, Dorna? It isn't late."

"The poor Ronans," she said softly. "They are probably sitting up to hear all about you." There was silence. "I think it better not," she added suddenly.

We came to the Ronans' stone wharf. The house was not visible, for on this part of their island was a dense grove of low-growing pines. They made a dark mass on the land.

"You need not come ashore," she said. "I can find my way. Allow for the tide on the way back, and be careful on those steps . . . Day after tomorrow be sure to come."

Her voice made me quiver. I knew I must speak—at least say something. She was changed indeed. I was not afraid now.

"I will take you to the door if you will let me," I said.

"Why yes," she answered as though surprised.

We climbed ashore. It was utterly dark except for a star path, where the trees were open, above the road. The smell of the pines was fresh in the night air. Dorna, not even a blur at my side, was manifest only by her faint breathing and faint footfalls.

My voice sounded strained and unnatural.

"Dorna, in the letter you wrote me last June you said that the problem, which you feared, did not confront you any more closely than it did last summer. Are things the same still?"

There was a long silence, and her voice out of the darkness seemed deeply moved.

"Yes. Things are quite the same."

Was her emotion for me? I could not believe it. But she was again speaking and in a firmer lower voice.

"The rest of my letter is also still true."

Thus she repeated her cruel warnings. And yet . . . she might merely refer to the last lines. I spoke to a living invisibility moving at my side.

"You said at the end of your letter that you were sure that I still wished you placid enjoyment. . . ."

"Do you?" came her soft deep voice.

"Of course!" I cried, and my own words nearly choked me. "It is the one thing I wish you most of all. But . . ." I stopped, for it was difficult to say.

"But what?" she asked, and there seemed to be a strange amusement in her tone.

"I wondered if you really wanted me to come," I burst out. "Dorna, I hesitated about coming."

The silence was almost unbearable.

"You have as much right to be at Dorn Island as I have," she said at last, slowly. "If wonderings like that should keep you away I should be very sorry."

"I know"—for some reason her words hurt—"but I did not want to come if it interfered with your serenity, Dorna."

"Why should it?" she asked.

The blackness ahead suddenly opened, and on the right a little

319

way off was the low bulk of the Ronans' house, with one ruddy yellow window.

"Does it, Dorna?" I cried.

"Oh, John!" she said in a voice of pain. "What are you trying to make me say?"

"I only want to be sure that you want me here!"

She uttered a strange cruel laugh.

"Didn't I ask you to come at this season?"

"Yes, but perhaps only because it is so lovely here then. You said so. It is . . . !"

"Isn't that enough? I wanted to please you."

"You have, Dorna. You do, but. . . ."

We had stopped near the door, facing each other, and I could now dimly see her face and the dark brilliant gleam of her eyes.

"What do you want me to say?" she asked in a voice, half-gentle, half-annoyed.

"That you yourself would rather have me come than not," I answered, trying to laugh a little.

"Why of course I would! What did you think?"

She turned to the door and opened it quickly.

"I didn't know," I said.

"Good night, John. It is too late to ask you in."

"Good night, Dorna," I called to her. The door closed upon me, shutting her within the cottage of the Ronans, where young Ronan himself was probably sitting up to talk to her. I went plunging down the black road following the star path.

I rowed back to Dorn Island, finding my way somehow, and almost running into a two-masted boat anchored in the middle of the harbor. I rowed around her and made for the steps, where I found my friend sitting in a rowboat waiting for me.

I came alongside before I was aware that he was there. He spoke quietly, but I was wholly unprepared, thinking of other things. He seemed enormous in the darkness and very much a stranger. His voice spoke to me from another world, and like one under hypnotism I answered him and walked back to the house with him in a dream, feeling rather like someone who is nearly caught red-handed while secretly acting against his conscience.

It was a relief to have him talk. He told me of his journey, and I listened enough to remember it for future use. He had gone and come by boat, having fine weather. He did not tell me the reason for his visit. He had been up in the mountains of that long peninsula that is the spine of the Province of Winder. He said that that region never failed to impress him and that I must see it some day.

He came up to my room and made himself comfortable. We talked till late. Bit by bit I recovered my poise, forgot my sense of guilt, and was able to feel him as something real. All the time I regretted overlaying my memories of Dorna with new impressions, and longed to be alone and to recapture her again. Yet I was glad to have someone to talk to who was a friend, and who, though Islandian, nevertheless understood all I could say. I told him about everything, my troubles with Washington included, my history, the Stellins—everything but my feeling for his sister. As I talked I could feel readjustment taking place within me. I emerged from that conversation with certain definite ideas—I would keep to my resolution to be impersonal with Dorna. I had learned what I most wanted to know; the part of our conversation to remember was that "things were quite the same."

Dorna was mentioned but once.

"When did she go to the Ronans'?" he asked.

"Two days ago."

"How long is she to be there?"

"She says a week."

He was about to make some remark, but he checked himself.

"I'll take a few days for myself, John," he said instead. "We will do something together."

He yawned and departed soon after. I wondered if I had not talked too much. But after all he was my nearest and dearest friend. I wondered about Nekka as I undressed, and wished that I did not, for some reason, feel uncomfortable about Dorna. I was sure that I loved her, and yet talking with Dorn had changed things. If he had made the world seem workaday and colorless, after all it was the real world, my world.

Exhausted, almost as soon as I was in bed I fell asleep.

The room was full of warm light. Awake only enough to know that I was at home, or rather at Dorn Island, and that in the east the sun had risen just above the mountains and was sending his level rays through my window, I chased an elusive dream without success— wondering whether it was a dream, and not merely consciousness of

321

enrichment and fresh beauty. Had I dreamed? Beauty flooded my heart, too painful to bear. It was early morning. This was a day without Dorna. But what was it that in sleep had seemed so much happier a thing than merely loving her—as though there had come to me something new?

I remembered that on the night before I had talked long with Dorn, and that I had made resolutions then. The sensation of gladness receded. I reaffirmed my resolutions. But all day long I wondered how *she* was amusing *herself* at Ronan's Island. She was in my thoughts and before my eyes—hidden and enringed with pine trees, busy and domestic, perhaps washing dishes, or working in the garden. Was young Ronan hovering about her? Was Dorna looking up and smiling at him?

Nevertheless, I gave myself with pleasure to my friend. Taking our lunches, he and I rowed across the Earne River and walked over the inner marsh to the South Arm of the Doring River. It was a lovely bright spring day, with cool air and warm sun. Overhead the sky was blue with little white clouds, and on our human level the dark marsh was flat and empty.

We did not talk a great deal. On our return Dorn had some business with the farmers through whose settlement we passed. I sat in the sun and daydreamed, playing with a young dog that was large and wire-haired, with a big melancholy black muzzle that belied his playfulness.

My impatience next morning gave me no time to chase elusive dreams. I woke with knowledge of what I was to have, full of nerves and eagerness. When breakfast was over I waited fifteen minutes lest I arrive too soon, and then told Dorn in as casual a voice as I could that I thought I would be going.

"Don't feel that you have to come back to lunch," he said. "You had better take the rowboat with the sail."

The colors of all things that morning were like those of yesterday, but very different! The same sky of intermingled white and blue was overhead; the same beeches swayed against it in a capricious wind; the same blue water gleamed in the creek, and the same pines were motionless on Ronan's Island; but today all things were sharp-edged and brilliant.

Ronan, the father, a man with a gray and brown beard, was outside the house caulking a rowboat, inverted on two logs. He looked more like the hard-worked farmer at home than did others I had seen in Islandia. We greeted each other and talked of the weather. At this season, he said, there was not rain enough. They fared better across the mountains and up the valley. It put everything back. There was no use planting now, though some did so. Perhaps he ought to be planting, and not getting this boat ready. Still . . . He smiled a quiet smile. I listened politely, but I was impatient, for Dorna was in the house that was so near to us.

"Still," said Ronan, "Dorna says that this boat rows more easily than any they have." His voice changed. "She is expecting you," he added.

I left him at once and went to the door. The house was low and small, and its surroundings seemed unkempt and forlorn.

"Go right in!" called Ronan, and I heard his caulking hammer sound again its metallic note on the pawl. I entered what was evidently the living room. It was paved with worn red tiles, most barely furnished, and had an unswept hearth and a stale odor of breakfast. No one was there, but a door stood half-open and I heard movements beyond.

I said my name aloud.

I heard two feminine voices speak and then Dorna's rose gaily. "We are out here!"

So I went into the kitchen. There she was again, washing dishes as I had surmised, while young Ronan dried them, and Parna, his mother, cleared up the kitchen, and Ronana, his sister, a girl of about twelve, read a book at a table.

Dorna was a little disheveled. Her sleeves were rolled up above the elbow, and her wet arms caught the light.

I greeted Parna and young Ronan. His eyes and mine met and lingered a moment, but, I think, we warmed to each other rather than otherwise, as men do who are in the same plight. Neither of us would have been surprised to learn of the other's feelings.

Dorna was obviously the center of their life whenever she was present, and I am sure that she knew it. She smiled; she was very busy; and I suspected that she posed at the Ronans', and that she overdid a little the role of entering into their life.

They gave me a chair at the table. Ronana raised her eyes once from her book, smiled in friendly fashion, and buried herself in it again.

Parna and Dorna and young Ronan began to discuss something that was to happen that day, but I realized that Dorna was, so to speak, clearing her morning, saying that though she could return before lunch, the afternoon was better . . . I thanked her in my heart.

At last the dishes were done and she turned to me, rolling down her sleeves. My eyes watched the covering of her firm smooth arms. "Would you like to see the place where Dorn XV hid?" she asked. I said that I would, trying to remember why he had done so. "We will take Ronana across first. She goes to my cousin to school."

Soon afterwards we three set out. The girl had been studying her lesson. She and a number of other children went daily to Dorna, the elder, and we landed her at the steps.

There was a light breeze from the east that ruffled the water now and then. I put the mast in place and shook out the sail. Then with Dorna at the steering oar, now drifting, now really moving, we departed, but for where or for how long I did not know nor did she explain.

We slipped out of the harbor and into the creek, and thence westward with the wind behind us. Slowly I relaxed. She was the same and yet new, very much a close friend, and yet she was compulsive in her attractiveness. She led our conversation and drew me out without my knowing anything except that I was telling her all my problems with Washington.

Dorna asking me searching questions was another new experience. What reason had the Department of State for calling me to account? I told her about Gastein, Andrews and Body, and the man refused admission because of the medical examination. She seemed puzzled. I told her that my proper behavior was nevertheless insufficient to those at home.

She looked at me a long time, with concern, but also something judicial and questioning in her eyes.

"I am sorry," she said. "What makes you so out of tune with them, John?"

She put me in a dilemma. I could explain myself better by adversely criticizing the attitude of my countrymen toward all laws that were of no apparent direct benefit to them, foreign laws particularly; but I did not like to do so. Her intelligence was dangerous, for she had jumped from explainable specific instances to the basic emotional fact that I was out of tune.

"I think they dislike what I have done, because I have not made much of an effort to entertain and make friends with those who have come here."

"They expect that of you?"

"Yes, they do." I told her then about Uncle Joseph, and that he and his group of businessmen were the persons who were principally interested in my consulship; that these men had commercial ambitions, and had probably procured my appointment; and that my uncle was personally anxious to have me advance my business acquaintance, not only for my own sake, but perhaps as a future employee of his own, who would be more effective the greater his friendships.

"His hope, of course, is that some day I may become a commercial agent for him and for others here in Islandia. He regards the consulship merely as a steppingstone."

As I spoke, I remembered all I had thought in this connection, and particularly her words to me at the Doring Palace. She had said that there were some who might prefer to fight to the death. I watched her expecting to see her stiffen, and to hear, perhaps, another such quiet outburst of strong feeling.

But Dorna's eyes continued to study me coolly.

"So you aren't here just as consul, John?" she asked. "You say that your uncle has acted partly for your sake?"

"Yes, Dorna. But I am here merely as consul. That is how I see it."

"Has your uncle any children?" she asked.

"A son who is a lawyer, and a married daughter."

"Perhaps he wishes you to succeed to his 'agency.'" There was no Islandian word for "business."

"I don't think so, but I don't know," I answered. "But I know that he is disappointed because I haven't been more friendly with American prospectors, and because I haven't tried to stretch the law for their benefit; and it may be that he has had something to do with the attitude of the Department of State. He wrote me a very similar letter to theirs."

"Why don't you feel that you are here as more than a consul, John? Why haven't you done as he and they have expected you to do?"

"Dorna," I cried, "I think I shall tell you! I made my uncle no promises before I came here. Of course I knew the consulship might be used as a steppingstone, but I am under no obligation to anyone to be more than a consul. Dorna, there are strong reasons why I want

325

to be!"—I had to pause to breathe, for I felt the reasons strongly then —"But when I learned how you felt about commercial agents, Dorna, I couldn't—I can't—do anything that would tend to make me one."

Her eyelids dropped abruptly over her eyes.

"So it is for my sake?" she asked in a low voice.

"Yes, Dorna."

"Not for my uncle's or my brother's?"

"I'll be honest!" I cried in shame. "It is for your sake, Dorna."

"I am sorry," she began. I watched her. Her mouth became pinched. Lines, hard and almost old, deepened around her chin which lifted a little. My heart throbbed, and I felt that I had done wrong. If I could only say that I loved her!

But I found that I was thinking in English. Could I say in Islandian that I felt *ania*? That would indicate that I wished to marry her, I who had nothing to offer. Nor could I say that I felt *apia,* which would indicate only that I desired her, though this was true. . . .

But Dorna had looked up, her face calm. Her eyes were upon me, and she smiled an elusive, sweet smile.

"I am also very glad, John," she said, and instantly she added, "We are hardly moving. Don't you want to row?"

So I got out the oars and pulled hard. It was a relief. I could scarcely have told her more plainly that I loved her. The look on her face showed that she understood, and now she was gentle with sympathetic eyes, as she sat in the stern, steering with an oar, smiling when our eyes met.

We were among the narrow creeks to the west of Dorn Island. The great half sphere above our heads was nearly all blue now.

I looked at her. How easy to say, "Dorna, I love you!"—the setting of marsh, blue water, and sky called for the utterance.

She sat with her side toward me, watching the wake behind us, her strong browned hands firm upon the oar, her profile against the blue water. Her bare head was round with smoothly done hair, the braid within her coat.

After some time Dorna steered the boat to land, and we disembarked upon the marsh, mooring it to an oar thrust into the fibrous soil. Before us was a low hill densely covered with pines. We were upon a wooded island lying to the southwest, separated from Dorn Island by a creek.

We crossed a belt of marsh. Dorna moved in her free, limber way, almost too revealing of her body. My love had taken to itself a new quality, and the desires that I had had in The City seemed figments of my mind, futile and nervous, compared to this dark compulsion in my blood itself.

With a smile she went ahead into the pines along a narrow path like a deer run. The trees were soon dense about us, shutting out the marsh and reducing the sky to a tent above our heads. They stood as stalwart pyramids, with close-knit twigs and branches, and short, hard, dark needles in tight bunches. Then we emerged into a small clearing, where grew a coarse grass, brown and winter-killed but with the new green starting.

Dorna stopped and lifted her head. Her eyes half closed, but she gave me a polite, absent smile. I stood still also, watching her; and she was glowing with the inner light of one's beloved, unlike any other, which makes of her a burning, brilliant thing, and sharpens all other colors. The dark pines were her background.

"I think this is where they hid," she said. "Of course, there were other trees, but this clearing must have been here then. There are places where the pine won't grow, that remain sterile for hundreds of years. This is just the place."

The clearing sloped upward and she climbed to its higher end, turned, and beckoned to me. I came to her and looked in the direction that her hand indicated.

"They could watch the farm," she said. "It was more open then."

What I saw was a wide pine wood a little below us, but beyond it were the hills of the farm—above them the hill with the tower.

"They could watch it burning," she added in a low voice. "And if the Karain, who searched everywhere for them, came too close they could crawl among the trees and hold their hands over the baby's mouth. But they say he slept most of the time."

The story came back to me in part. There was a Dorn, Lord of Lower Doring, who during a raid escaped with wife and seven-months' child and two servants.

Dorna sat down on the grass and then without a word stretched out at full length, her arms behind her head. I could not remain standing and seated myself at her side.

"This is one of the places I come to," she said vaguely. "My uncle says I am too sure that this is the exact spot."

I watched her upturned face, her throat relaxed. Innocence had gone from me . . . So easy to lean over her and to slip my arms beneath her unguarded body.

"Do you know their story?" she began.

I told her what I knew.

"He was a bad sort," she said. "Perhaps he was the worst one of us since the Descent. He let everything else go and tried to save his own farm at the expense of everyone else's—and he lost that, too." Her voice became deep and vibrant. Suddenly she sat up. "But he saved the last Dorn, John, the last one of us! That was what was strongest in him. He kept us going. They call him selfish, and later he was disgraced. But he could have saved himself alone so easily! What is a seven-months' baby? He had a wife. He could have begot another child. But he would not take that chance. The baby was a good Dorn. It was the one he wanted to have go on. It wasn't just risking his life, but the way he planned it all, and stuck to it. He was so clever! He put the baby in his hood and tied him there behind his head with straps around his forehead and another in his mouth. He crawled at night down to the water and swam across the creek. He saw farms burning to the westward, and he turned north. He swam the Earne River. There was a big wind blowing and waves went over his head. The baby was very still when he landed. He could only feel the weight of it. He was exhausted and he lay on the ground. He felt it with his hands and it did not stir. He cried out to it, 'Kick if you are alive!' And the baby kicked its two legs. He felt it move that way and he rose and went on. He saw farms burning to the north. He turned east. There were farms burning there also, but the mainland was his only hope. He walked and he swam and he spent the daylight standing in water up to his shoulders, for the Karain were moving all over the marsh. The baby was hungry and he had nothing for it. When night came again, he went on as fast as he could, because he did not know how long a baby could go without food. About midnight he came to a burnt farm, but there was an old woman there, and a cow recently killed. They took milk from it and cared for the baby. Next day he went on beyond the reach of the Karain.

"All the Dorns were in that baby! Of course I know there might have been another one, but that was the precious one. It was a good baby and he knew it. I was in that baby, John, and my great grandfather, who drove out the settlers, and the Dorn who wasn't afraid of firearms although he had never seen them before—and my great-uncle, and my brother. I don't care if he was a selfish man. He saved us all for hundreds of years. The thing he wanted went on in the world!"

She sprang to her feet.

"Let us go from here!" she cried.

We went back to the boat, and this time Dorna took the oars. Her feet apart, and braced on the ribs on either side, she rowed with a firm catch and a snap as the oars left the water. Her face was grim but with a smile not far away.

She told me to steer, and when I asked her where, she answered "anywhere except ashore!" We went on southward into the marsh, and I could never have pulled so hard nor rowed so long.

We came into a region where the banks were high and the creeks narrow, a region where I was lost, too busy steering to keep track of the turns we had made. All my attention was needed, because Dorna pulled harder now on one side and now on the other, and I would not have let the boat strike the banks for anything!

Finally, however, I steered into a cul-de-sac. I saw the banks close ahead of us, and cried out to her.

She let the boat run, and laughed, drawing long breaths. . . .

"Did you bring anything to eat?" she asked.

"No! Should I have done so?"

"It is a good plan, but I didn't expect it. I have some chocolate."

This was our lunch.

We turned homewards. She admitted that she was tired and sat relaxed in the stern while I rowed, tired also—not merely with exercise. Of her own accord she said that next day but one she was coming home to lunch, and unless Dorn planned something better, would I hold the afternoon free to plant the seeds which had been sent me?

At the Ronans' wharf, I bade her good-bye. It was almost relief to have her go, but relief that vanished the moment that I saw her disappear into the pines—walking lightly and fast, her fatigue apparently forgotten. It was only midafternoon and I had nearly two whole days to get through.

Time passes, however, even time of waiting. There was much to do, and I felt, and was made to feel, completely at home. Attaching myself to my friend next day I went about with him all over the

Island. An accumulation of small matters needed his attention—repairs to a certain dyke, growth of weeds in a pasture, and details of the farm, the budding of fruit trees, the coming-up of planted things. He made it a point to utter many of his thoughts, and I listened and learned and counted the hours.

That night the clouds gathered and it rained—a warm, busy shower, long enough to make me afraid the seed planting would be postponed. Next day, however, was perfect. The sun rose in a clear sky, and I waked early, very happy.

Dorna, the elder, had asked if I would not talk to her school-children about the United States, or about anything else I wanted. They met in a big room at the southeast corner of the house, overlooking, on one side, Dorna's garden, wet and glistening with last night's rain, and on the other, a pasture, with the mainland bright under the sun a long distance away. A great table stood in the middle of the room, old and heavy, polished with the rubbings of restless arms for many years. There were no desks, and no apparent formality as to where the children sat; but there were many books—in the Islandian bindings that look as though an amateur had done them to last—a map of Islandia on the wall, and a number of comfortable chairs near the windows. But it was like a school for all that, perhaps because the children, in age from seven or eight to fifteen, were—children, about a dozen of them.

I had expected to talk for half an hour or so, but found that no time was set to end. Sitting at one end of the table I began my lecture and was listened to with attention that seemed the result of good manners. After a time some of the little ones were bored and retired to the chairs by the window. Dorna went to them there. The older ones began to ask questions. I forgot that it was a school with other duties to be done. When we had recess, two boys and one girl wanted to be told about American games, and seemed interested in track meets. Back in the schoolroom once more, somewhat out of breath from running with them, I had more questions to answer.

At last it was lunchtime. When I apologized to my hostess for interrupting her program so completely—as any American would have done—she seemed a little puzzled, and I discovered that she had practically no program to be disrupted. Apparently anything interesting that came along was seized upon.

I ran upstairs to my room to wash. At last the time had come round again, and I was a-quiver with happy impatience.

Dorna was late, slipping into her place at table after the rest of us had begun. Dorna, the elder, proved herself a different person after a morning of teaching, flushed and more alive. She had much to say, and the rest of us listened to her. Methods of teaching, the characters of particular children, problems, amusing things—she talked about them all.

After lunch Dorna, the younger, suggested that we wear heavy boots, and ran off like a girl to change her clothes. When we went out into the garden, she was dressed like a man. Her boots, of fine soft waterproof leather, came above her knees, so that she could kneel in the wet soil. Her knickerbockers, which falling naturally would have had something of the looseness of a skirt, were tucked into them. Her coat reached halfway down her thighs, but because it was warm she soon took it off. She coiled her braid upon the top of her head and pinned it there with a splinter, which she whittled from a twig. Then she was ready for work.

She was an amusing, brilliant, and disturbing object. I was not used to her so two-legged—a little ungainly and heavy—nor in a garment that fitted her so closely about the hips, nor in a blouse without a jacket. I was not sure I liked her this way. The end of her braid, loose upon her head, dangled about like a scalplock, making complete seriousness impossible. Perhaps I wanted to be serious, but she did not—she wanted laughter.

"It is a perfect day for it!" she said, as we walked around the garden, considering planting places. Now and then she knelt and turned over the damp earth and leaned down and breathed in its smell.

Foolish things! What did we laugh at? Within, I laughed so much that it became like a spasm—at Dorna saying English words, not with conscious mockery of them nor of my pronunciation, but in a way that savored them and made them amusing to her and me: "Alys*sum*, Sweet Weel*yum*!"—No Islandian words end in *um*— "Armeria, Arabis!" She gave to every vowel and consonant a tuneful precision. Kneeling at last to prepare the soil she said:

"Weelyum—a man's name! Do you know any more names?" I tried various ones upon her to hear her utter them. "*A*rthür! Reech*ard*! Deeck! Jos*e*ph! (Not Josiph)," and then my name in various ways,

"Zhahn! Djahn!" She never got it quite as others did, but she seemed to like to try.

"Let us plant the Alys*sum*—here!" she said, pausing on the *um*, and I wanted to kiss her closed lips.

She rose. I had in my hand the packet with its brightly colored picture of ideal flowers and directions in fine print beneath. She came close to my side. The warm sun beat down upon us, and there was an odor of earth and a little of Dorna herself. Her knees and her hands were earthy. In one was a muddy fork. She asked me to read the directions in English, looking over my shoulder. If either of us had moved we would have touched. I drew a breath and began solemnly as though it were poetry. She leaned forward to follow and I felt the firm but light pressure of her arm—and her breath on my hands.

"What does it mean?" she asked in a low voice.

I translated.

She looked up into my eyes with an expression intent and concentrated. On the words? On what?

"May I have it?" she half whispered. I gave it to her. We were awkward, our fingers blundering with it and touching.

She glanced at the house, drew herself up, and walked away, and upon her knees again planted the seeds. I looked down at her ridiculous topknot, dangling over one bare ear.

"My *darso* ought to be out in four or five days," she said.

"Did the Somes send you one from Loria Wood?"

She pointed with the fork to a vigorous sheaf of bladelike leaves, above which were tall stems with long buds at right angles.

"Will you see it?" she asked. We had not yet discussed the length of my visit. "How long can you stay with us?"

"I must be back in The City by October 16th."

"Then you will surely see my *darso*. They are lovely!" She seemed pleased, and I was very happy. I watched her hand, finer-grained and more glowing because of the dirt upon it, deftly and quickly smoothing the soil and sprinkling the seeds.

Why did I ever mention Nattana's invitation? At that moment I had no intention of going to the Hyths'. I told her of the date when the invitation had come, and how I had accepted, thinking that I would have more time, not really working out my plans.

"They expect you then?" she said, in the voice of a friend about to give advice.

"I haven't told her that I was not coming."

"Did she ask you herself?"

"She said that they all wanted me. We have written to each other several times since I was there." I did not say, as I was tempted to do, that Nattana began it.

"Do you think it was her invitation sanctioned by them or their invitation through her?"

I hesitated to say which I thought lest I seem to commit Nattana, but Dorna gave no time to answer.

"Of course, they told you that their house was yours last March?" she added.

"They did."

"I don't want you to go," she said in a low voice, and my heart beat again as it had the day before. Again came the sharp impulse to speak and to have it said.

But I heard Dorna singing to herself, as she edged along upon her knees to smooth new earth with her hand.

"—if that helps you to make up your mind," she added cheerfully.

"It does!" It was settled. I would not go to the Hyths'.

Dorna unexpectedly laughed.

We worked together at the planting, now near each other, now apart, while the sun gradually sloped westward. Her singing became louder—spontaneous and unpremeditated like a bird's. Her singing voice was deeper than her speaking one, and reminded me of her brother's when we cruised along the coast of Maine.

Dorna rose suddenly. I looked up to see her pulling at the splinter hairpin in her hair, watching me as she did so.

"I almost forgot!" she said. "I promised Parna to come back and help her. It is the Ronans' day. All the Parns and Cornings will be there. Do you want to come? They would be glad, but they will talk about last night's rain for hours!"

"Shall I come?" I asked. Thus I put it upon her.

"Yes," she answered briefly. "Come at suppertime. I'll tell them."

She could not disengage the splinter, and asked me to help her. Her eyes watched as I approached. With arms raised, she left herself unguarded, and I wanted to clasp her round on a level with her breasts. She leaned her head down obediently. It was easy to remove the splinter—but some hairs clung to it.

As she straightened her eyes looked into mine and instantly dropped away.

She thanked me, and I said:

"I'll stay here to finish, if you trust me alone?"

"Of course. Today's the day. You will be at the Ronans', won't you, at suppertime?"

I said that I would, and she turned to go.

"You have left some hairs behind, on this hairpin of yours!" I cried after her.

"I know it. Keep them!"

"I'll plant them too."

We both laughed, but I was trembling.

Dinner and the evening at the Ronans' were long. They were glad to see me, but the conversation, as Dorna said, dwelt for hours upon the rain and could only leave it for a little while. The whole marsh would now quicken into life . . . It was soon apparent that I was to have nothing of Dorna, who constituted herself assistant hostess. She was talkative and easy and familiar and too much at home.

It came time for me to go—one of those bitter moments when a man wonders if social confusions will not prevent the saying to a particular person of the word he needs. I lingered until the Parns, who were also leaving, should be well down the road; and then I said good-bye and my thanks to the Ronans and to Parna. I turned to thank Dorna also, but she came forward instead of listening and out into the night with me.

"You were very good to come," she said, stopping on the doorstep and closing the door.

"I wanted to come."

"And I wanted you here."

Our voices were low.

"When can I see you again, Dorna?"

"Give tomorrow to my brother, and give me the day after."

"All of it!" I cried.

"We will walk or ride or sail, according to the weather. I'll come over to the harbor after breakfast. You had better bring the lunches."

I did not know what to say . . . After a moment she said good night softly and went in, and I ran down the path in great happiness.

As directed, I gave the next day to Dorn, and we spent the morning in a trip to Earne and back, for mail and supplies, sailing and drifting in a wind that blew between fresh and none at all, and from all quarters; preoccupation with Dorna spoiled me as a companion for someone else. I might have driven her from my mind, but it was too pleasant to hold her there.

In the afternoon Dorn and I exercised horses over the farm. Becoming hot, we rode westward into the pine wood to a place where there was the semblance of a beach, took off our clothes, and had a brief icy swim. The ride back restored enough warmth to leave me, at any rate, just warm enough, tired, but refreshed.

It was between four and five o'clock, but like my hosts, I had become used to a clockless existence, rarely bothering to wind my watch or to try to set it by the big waterworks affair in the Tower room (which always required a long calculation), but relying upon a developing time sense. Unless something unusual happened I could, or thought I could, guess meal hours within twenty minutes, which was near enough.

I went up to my room and found Dorna there.

"I thought you might like to go to walk," she began. "I came over here because—" She stopped short, and after waiting a moment I asked her if she wouldn't sit down. Promptly she did so, and from my chair I watched her, waiting until she could finish.

She laughed.

"The Ronans are good friends," she began, "but I'm not one of them! I try to pretend that I am when I visit them, because I know it pleases them—and yet I don't want to please them too much that way." Again she stopped and flushed a little. "If I do, old Ronan and Parna begin saying how nice it would be if they had a grown-up daughter. So I ran away this afternoon."

I smiled.

"You have noticed it," she asserted.

"Yes—it seemed hard for you to be natural there." Her eyes widened and then dropped.

"It is worst when some 'of them' come in." I remembered that the idiom, "of them," meant men of the Doring Marshes.

Thus she explained her coming and came back to her first suggestion. But if I were tired from riding?

I told her that the swim quite refreshed me.

"I wish I had been there!" she said. "I haven't been in swimming since last autumn. Let's go to the Tower. The marsh will be worth seeing."

We departed, through the garden where the newly planted places were still smooth and brown, and then on into the pines. . . .

We looked out from the Tower. The sunlight came at a slant, and the marsh was a flat and spacious plain of pale glowing green, of darker emerald, and of purple shadows of clouds. Dorna turned away and leaned her elbows upon the parapet. When last we were here, she had voiced her intense love for Dorn Island. So she must be feeling now. I held back from her, for though through her I could respond to the beauty and feel a little as she did, the marsh was hers not mine. I was an alien. But our presence on the Tower also brought back what I had never forgotten. Dorna's strong smooth hands, a translucent brown, were firmly clasped on the top of the parapet. I looked at them and at her, relaxed and absent, one foot behind her on tiptoe, not graceful then, but most dear and too desirable.

"I never want to leave this place!" she cried in a voice deeply moved. "I never loved it more."

"I understand, Dorna."

"Do you really think you understand? Do you love it, John?"

"Oh, Dorna, I love it with all my heart—and not just because of you."

Then came a long breathless silence. She laughed with a catch in her throat. Her hands unclasped.

"Do you remember what happened when we came here last?" she said in a sudden shaking voice.

My heart beat slowly—then faster, harder. Her hand which lay open on the parapet moved towards me.

"Yes," I whispered, trying to make a joke of it. "This happened."

I took her hand. It came loosely and without reluctance, and then knit firmly into mine. All colors brightened with fire, all the doors that shut me in were flung open. Now I could speak if I could find the words —if it mattered. I had her hand.

I had her hand, warm, tremulous, holding nothing back. I saw the curve of her flushed cheek, averted, sharp to my senses like a sword edge. I felt, through her arm, her deep breathing. . . .

"Dorna!" I began, but where was I to find the right word in her tongue. I hesitated. . . .

"Please!" she moaned, and her hand struggled and sharply drew away. She turned from me, and I found that we were descending the winding stairs, she ahead, and I pursuing.

"Dorna!"

We were out in the open, and her shoulder seemed to interpose itself as I tried to look into her face.

"Dorna, listen to me."

"No! No!" she cried. "No!" She choked. She laughed! "No, John! No—no—no!"

The pines were around us, and then the beeches. I could have held her and made her hear me, but this was not what my will would allow my hands and voice to do with Dorna. I let her go.

Dropping back I merely followed and her pace at once slackened. We passed through the gate as though nothing had happened, politely holding it for each other, but Dorna's garden beyond was swimming and vague.

"I am going back to the Ronans'," she cried in a high hard voice. "Don't come with me any farther! I should never have let it happen!"

"Dorna, tomorrow—"

"Oh, no! We can't! I can't now! Let me go, John!"

"Good-bye," I said, to tell her she could go.

"Oh, not good-bye yet! I'll see you again, I'll explain, but I want to go now."

She moved away. I turned not to see the agony of her disappearance . . . After a time I tried to see whether the *darso* buds were any nearer opening. She was walking down the alley of beeches by this time. My mind's eye saw her with burning vividness, moved, troubled, hastening away. . . .

It is hard to throw oneself into the stream of ordinary activities after such a shock, after seeing all the doors opening to find them closed; but I had to do it, and did it well, proud of my power to be natural. I talked as though nothing had happened. No one guessed anything, but when Marta made the casual remark that Dorna had come over from the Ronans', apparently hoping someone would ask why, I was dizzy.

And all that night my mind wandered miserably in torturing mazes that yet could not dim her beauty or the beauty of what had been mine.

Morning came, and when I went downstairs, too early for breakfast, the house dependent met me with a message. Dorna wanted to see me after breakfast at the harbor. Perhaps we would have our day together after all. . . .

There was a touch of iron chill in the air. Open fires had been made again, and outside a surly breeze blew from the west bending the branches of new leaves on beech trees and willows into fleeting patterns.

Dorna was sitting on a stone bollard, facing the harbor, when I came from between the warehouses. I hoped to see her with cloak and basket prepared to go with me for the day, but of course she was not.

Never before had I seen Dorna with a line on her forehead between her brows, nor with eyes so deeply shadowed.

She rose and faced me.

"John," she said almost at once, "we must go back to where we were before you came."

My heart leaped because it was an admission that we had moved, she as well as I.

"Not just for your sake but for mine too!" she added. "I can't tell you why, except what I have said before—there is my problem."

"Will it ever be settled, Dorna?"

She turned half away from me.

"Yes, by the time the council meets this summer—one way or the other—by then or a few weeks after."

Her words meant that I must wait three months, with no greater hope to sustain me than before.

Dorna's hands were raised and clasped before her breast. She was looking at her knuckles.

"I have been unfair," she said.

"Don't feel that way!" I cried.

"It is true. I have been guilty of showing *apiata*. I'm sorry."

She looked unexpectedly into my eyes.

"Sorrier than I can tell you!" she said. Her face was drawn and humbled, and I could not bear to see it so.

"Don't be sorry, Dorna!"

"John, don't be so kind to me!"

We spoke as though we were angry, and her eyes seemed to be praying for some right word or deed, while my whole heart craved of her an easier sentence. She had doomed me to three months of misery worse than that passed through, with desire sharpened because of what she had given and taken away.

"You must not worry about it, Dorna."

"Oh, John!" Her eyes blazed, and she turned her back upon me, and spoke over her shoulder. "There is nothing that I can do for you—nothing, nothing now. I wish there were. It is so unfair! All that is left is for you to do something for me—something you ought to do. But it is not because you ought that I'm going to ask you. It is for my sake! Will you go to the Hyths'?"

For a moment I did not realize that she was sending me away.

"I will go if you want me to go," I said.

"Want you to go? John!" She paused, and spoke in a controlled voice. "I want you to stay here, but for my sake please go—and perhaps it will be better for yours also."

Why did she rob my renunciation of its purity? What was for my sake did not matter.

"I'll go tomorrow," I answered, "since you ask it."

"Is it because I ask you?" she cried in a choking voice.

"Of course, Dorna!"

There was a deathly silence, for this was the end. I knew how long three months were going to be. At last she spoke.

"I must go back to the Ronans'. You will probably leave early. I'll come over and say good-bye to you."

"If it is too early—"

"John, I want to come!"

She moved away to the steps where was moored the boat which old Ronan had been painting.

It was my pride to betray nothing to the others. I rehearsed the announcement of my departure and uttered it coolly to Dorn and Faina.

In the afternoon Dorn took me sailing. The wind was at last strong enough for him, blowing in flaws fresh from west and northwest. Out in the Earne River we gradually overtook a smaller boat, heeled far over, nosing into the streaked waves and casting up such clouds of spray that more than half its sail was drenched. We passed close to leeward. Dorna was sitting on the windward rail, steering. She waved her hand to us before the sail hid her. She was very wet, her hair in strings, her bare legs in water that washed about in the bottom, her dress clinging to her body. Young Ronan was with her, and he was bailing.

She could spend my day with him but not with me.

Not until the last moment did the hope vanish that something would arise to cancel my departure—that Dorna who wanted me to stay would ask me to do so. The morning was cool and cloudy, and I was up and ready to go by half-past six. Dorn was coming with me as far as Doring Town. Just as breakfast ended Dorna came in, bright-cheeked, fresh, her face as though smoothed out.

There occurred a half-quarrel between her and her brother.

"Did your boat fill up?" he asked her, and his voice was not exactly pleasant.

"No," she answered shortly, "but we nearly capsized."

"It was no weather for that little shell. You ran a risk."

"Of what?"

"Of ending up in the water."

"It wouldn't have mattered," she said, and seemed really angry.

"You might have drowned. The water is still very cold."

"There was more danger of losing the boat. We expected we might have to swim." Her voice was controlled again. She turned to me, and her eyes gave me a steady look, saying I know not what, but grave though not reproachful, perhaps a little ashamed, and then becoming gentle, exposed, and sweet.

We had no moment when we were really alone. I did not know how to manage it, and she made no move.

We said our good-byes after I had mounted and while Dorn was still adjusting his saddlebags.

"Good-bye, Dorna."

"Good-bye, John."

Her eyes without expression slid from mine, and when we started, she was already halfway down the alley of beeches, walking fast, a jaunty figure, and yet pitiful.

16

The Hyths and The City

NEVER BEFORE had there seemed to be degrees of intensity in the reality of what I was experiencing. The present was always real, today no more and no less than yesterday, and surely tomorrow would be the same. But while I was at the Hyths', the atmosphere of a phantom existence persisted. The place had lost the stark vividness that it had had during my first visit, and all the many Hyths, even Nattana, seemed but painted dolls unexpectedly moving before me.

At first it was disturbing, like a condition induced by an illness; but I became used to it, and in the plane of my existence apart from Dorna, lived not unpleasantly.

Nattana, after all, was a friend. She was a friend, or rather she was like a sister whose company is soothing when one is deeply pre-occupied with something else—a sister who has an always perceptible charm.

The first day, however, was almost a failure. I could not put my mind upon Nattana. She took me for a walk, began by being talkative and friendly, and ended as dumb as I was. If she were displeased she did not show it. She did suggest that I seemed tired after my jour-ney and had better go to bed early.

Next morning was lovely and springlike, and Nattana—and I too—felt drawn away from the house. The whole valley was spar-kling, the spacious simple slopes of the pastures all a fresh green, and on its further side, above the forests, the peak of Hythclorn was a dazzling pure white against a dark-blue sky. Nattana's enthusiasm roused at least restlessness in me, and taking lunches we mounted two of the Hyths' horses and set out for the slopes of the mountain—down into the valley floor, down into the trench of the river, across the bridge over its foaming, swollen, turgid waters, up again to the great levels of the valley, around the town of Hyth, with its brown walls rising directly from the plain—civilization set in emptiness—and on toward the foothills.

In her first letter, she had said that they did not often ride upon the other side of the river—which was what we were doing now. When I reminded her of it, she laughed.

"We might have brought a gun," she said. "I don't think there is any real danger. I meant that we don't often ride this way unless there are several of us, and never girls alone."

"Do you and I make 'several'?" I asked.

"No, hardly."

There was no thought of turning back, but I had a feeling that was quite new to me—of empty-handedness and of unprotection, of real desire for a weapon, and of a sudden cherishing of this woman who was with me. I did not want her out of my sight.

Nattana, I think, liked to play a little with the image of danger.

On the other side of Hythclorn—not thirty miles from the farm—was the settlement of Sho, inhabited by several hundred of the Mountain Bants. Although there were no snowless passes within a good many miles, and the Mountain Bants avoided snow, they seemed to people the mountain and to hang over us. I imagined them lurking in the forests up to which we were climbing.

We were following a rough road. Leftward, still below tree line, was a cluster of houses and sheds. The trees were now not far above us. I remarked that the people who lived there might feel timid.

"They have gone away," said Nattana. "They have relatives across the valley who have taken them in. They will come back if the garrisons are re-established." After a moment she added, "You know that the mountain tribes desire Islandian girls."

Alarmed inner watchfulness sharply increased.

By a narrow trail we wound upward to the point at which we were to leave the horses. For an hour or more we climbed on foot still higher. The air became thin and cold, and the trees smaller and more stunted. We came at last to our destination, a slope of scree above tree line with a hollow in it down which came a brook of milky water. The snow was near, its cold breath apparent, but the sun shone hard and bright upon the rocks. In hollows between them little alpine flowers of blue and white were blooming above their close bunches of blue-green leaves.

Nattana found herself a spot in the sun, sheltered from the wind, lay back and closed her eyes, but I turned to look at the view.

Far below us the town of Hyth was like a rusty finger ring, with white and red sugar in its circle, set upon a green cloth. Opposite us, at a higher level, thirty miles away, was the Great Range in all its beauty.

I shivered with a sudden premonition and turned around sharply. Nattana lay limp with closed eyes, not pretty exactly, but precious and much to be protected. My eyes swept the slope that cut the hard blue sky above us.

But, of course, no evil head appeared there.

Nevertheless, while we ate our lunch, I sat facing up the slope.

Nattana had told me that some months before she had decided that she had been idle too long, that it was not good for her, and that she was going to have from then on a regular occupation. She was going to make the most of her talent for cloth weaving, and during my visit she must work half the time.

Next day brought showers and for Nattana it was a day of work. Not to go to her shop and talk to her seemed impolite, but to go and sit all day doing nothing but talk would be a strain. I left Nattana alone, writing letters home, trying vainly to think up something to say to Dorna that was at once sufficiently personal and impersonal, wandering about the house, and trying to read.

Nattana came to lunch with absent-minded eyes, hair a little disheveled, and a look of having been absorbed. She was also very hungry. After the meal, I went back with her to her workshop, with a firm resolve to be less unsatisfactory.

It was on the second floor of the wing which ended in the stables, and was entered by steep stairs from a storeroom below. Nattana had a loom with a treadle before which she sat on a high stool, like an organist. There was a workbench, a carder, spinning wheel, bales of wool and vats. Windows opened in both directions, and today they were open. The room smelled a little of carded wool, of dyes, of spice, and of warm earth and rain. She motioned me to a bench with a high back and went on with her work. I made myself comfortable and watched her.

She sat straight, poised rather than seated upon her stool. Her movements were deliberate, but rhythmical, in a series of threes: her right hand tossed the thread across, her left moved the lever that pushed it evenly down, and her outthrust foot pressed the treadle— clickety-clack; her left hand tossed the thread, her right moved the lever, her foot pressed—clickety-clack, and back again.

The fabric was an ivory white, and Nattana was dressed in tan and green. Her head moved as her hands did, ever so little, like a nod of recognition to the loom, and the high-lights changed upon her hair.

Between the clickety-clacks was an interval for speech. Soon we caught the rhythm, stopping as her foot moved, and resuming again.

"I have finished the his—" clickety-clack! "—tory of the United States, Nattana. It is going to be pub—" clickety-clack! "—lished."

The room was peaceful. Rain now and then drummed overhead, and on the edges of the red tiles of the roof, visible through the windows, water gathered and lengthened suddenly into long gleams and dropped.

The great eye of daylight half closed and it was shadowy and dark. I forgot Nattana. For a moment hope was so strong that I envisaged the reality of Dorna in love with me, looking into my eyes, mine—and I, John Lang, permitted to learn with her the mystery of completed love. I perceived a dim burning miracle as possibly mine to experience—something very different from and infinitely more beautiful than the unions, always guilty, that once I had thought I wanted with other women.

Perhaps it was a vague feeling of shame, perhaps it was reason telling me that, whatever she felt, my own alienage and poverty stood as a hopeless barrier between us—but the fire died suddenly, and I found myself miserable. . . .

"I can hardly see."

Nattana's voice did not sound in my mind until several moments after she had spoken. There was an echo of other words not heard at all.

I came back with an effort to the dim world where I really was. Nattana was a dark silhouette against the gray window, her feet halfway up the stool with heels on a round.

"What was it you said, Nattana?"

"Oh—nothing much. It is too dark to work. Father is worried about the bridge across the river, but he always is."

"The river seemed high yesterday," I suggested after a pause.

"Father fears the melting snow. It is so warm today."

We remained sitting silent for some time.

"John?" She spoke doubtfully.

"Yes, Nattana."

"There is something on your mind, my friend."

My heart throbbed, and I stood half-revealed. I had had no thought of speaking to her or to anyone about Dorna.

"Yes," I said in a low voice.

Her head was turned toward the window.

"You need not tell me if you don't want to, John." Her voice sounded indifferent.

"Nattana?"

"Yes, John."

"I think I'll tell you. I have not told anyone."

"You need not!" she said quickly, "but if you do wish to tell me. . . ."

"I think I do."

"I would be glad. Maybe I . . ."

She seemed embarrassed. I chose my words carefully, avoiding Islandian terms for love, and I said:

"I want to marry Dorna."

"Have you told her, John?" Her voice was even and cool.

"She would not let me," I said, and then I groaned.

"Not let you?" she asked softly.

"No—I think she guessed what I was going to say."

"Is she—?" Nattana began, but stopped.

"She is not engaged to someone else," I said guessing at her unfinished question, "but she—" I also checked myself.

"Is it *ania*?" she asked with sudden pain in her voice, but she added with feeling, swinging around to face me, "Oh John, forgive me. Of course it is!"

What was there to forgive?

"Yes, Nattana," I answered, and felt hot blood rush to my face.

"And she would not let you tell her?"

"No!" It was confessing this that hurt.

In the silence I could hear the raindrops falling. I could not see her face, for her head was a dark round against the shadowy light, with a soft glowing rim of fine hair about it.

"It was good of you to come here, John." I saw her shoulders rise and fall. "I don't know what I can do," she added.

"You have done a great deal, Nattana."

I felt her smile, rather than saw it.

"No," she answered. "I have done nothing—I wish I could." She paused. "Shall I say what I think, John?" she added.

"Yes." I waited in fear, for her voice warned me. She spoke with hesitation.

"I don't know Dorna very well, but I don't think you will win her."

I knew it, but her opinion was crushing.

"I think she likes me," I began, using *amia*, the word for friendship.

"Of course she likes you!" cried Nattana, so positively that hope quickened.

"What makes you think so?"

"Oh—she would!"

Hope died again.

"Don't take too seriously what I said about your not winning her," she continued gravely. "I really don't know. But she is the only Dorn girl—even if she isn't close to the succession. . . . Oh, I oughtn't to say anything. I don't know enough. . . . I hope you do win her. You really may. I don't see why you shouldn't."

"There are several reasons," I cried, and I unburdened myself bitterly, telling Nattana of Dorna's manifestations of feeling against foreigners, of my lack of prospects and of my poverty, of the trouble with Washington—of everything. She listened, speaking now and then in a kindly voice, and all the time her face was dark, but I felt its warm friendly pain and concern.

After it was all said, Nattana cried out that she could work no longer. We would go to walk. She herself would get my cloak and boots and her own.

"Your eyes would give you away, if anyone saw you," she said.

There was a gusty wind from the west which whipped our cloaks about us, but the rain was not heavy. We walked directly into it with bent heads. The air was warm and the ground soggy, so that our progress was something of a struggle. I felt exhausted and exposed, but in the hands of a true friend; and Nattana, though rather quiet, seemed as it were to be staying by me, her sympathy and her *amia* apparent in her voice and manner.

We went as far as the ravine of the Hyth River, which descended from the Tamplin Pass, but we did not go down. The river below was a yellow flood that sent up a persistent brawling roar.

Having solemnly looked at it in silence, we turned around and came back to the farm. It was not yet suppertime, and I went up to my room.

Why had I told Nattana about Dorna? There were several moments of regret, and of a vague feeling of having cheapened my love; and yet I was glad Nattana knew, for in some way my relationship with her, our friendship, seemed now based on firmer foundations. She knew my secret. No one else did. She would keep it. She had said so, and I trusted her; and I knew that, as the only person who knew, she would help me if she could.

On October 12th I started upon my journey back to The City, back to steamers and mail and criticism from Washington, back to being a consul and to being alone. It was going to be as it had been for three months waiting for spring to come and to see Dorna, and it was also going to be harder to bear. I had loved her then, but it seemed a child's love in comparison.

The day was clear again. Nattana rode with me. We were to lunch together at noon wherever we were, and then she was to return. We started early when the sun had only just risen in the haze at the eastern end of the valley. The snow mountains on the other side were still pink against a dark, robin's-egg-blue sky. The wide valley itself was full of a rosy hushed light. Nattana's face, smoothed and simplified by recent sleep, with her green eyes bright and dewy and still a little heavy-lidded, was really lovely; and when the sun struck upon her in golden shafts of light through the iron pines, her hair glistened like shining copper.

It seemed to me, city-bred, a wonderful thing to live all one's life in a place as open, as unmarked by man, and as beautiful as this.

A morning passed in which there was no pain in my heart and no confusion in my head because I loved Dorna. She seemed remote and I let her stay so, knowing that the strength of my feeling was merely dormant for a time. It was more courteous to Nattana to seize my present mood and not to be preoccupied.

It was still early when we emerged above tree line into that hard bright realm of thin air, deceptive distance, and sharp heavy shadows, of rocks with alpine plants among them and snow tongues on the slopes, and of lofty white summits nearer, but still remote.

The road looped its way up a steep but widely open ravine. The Hyth River was now a swollen brook of milky water.

There was little chance to talk to Nattana. Her horse, of the larger type, was at this kind of work slower than Fak, who bent his head a little and walked fast. I had to hold him in, for on looking around several times I saw my companion dropping behind. When behind me she was below me also, and I saw her vivid face and hair against the far green background of the valley floor.

We reached the highest point of the pass, overhanging the Doring Valley, in less than three hours. It was midmorning, and the sun was well up.

We dismounted for a few moments. A mountain summit is something satisfactory accomplished, but once one is there nothing remains but to come down; whereas a high pass is not only an achievement, but it has another side and is a stage in a progress. Passes therefore are much more interesting.

This vague generalization I tried to express to Nattana.

"Not for me," she said, "I am going back."

"I wish you were coming farther with me."

"So do I! I thought of coming as far as the Andals'—"

"Why didn't you?"

She uttered a little laugh.

"No," she answered, "I couldn't. But I agree with you about passes—usually."

"It is kind of you to come with me," I said, suddenly aware of the honor I was receiving. She was giving up her whole day in order to ride half of it with me.

She gave me a clear questioning look.

"You don't have to thank me quite yet. I am going on with you until lunchtime . . . You don't have to thank me at all," she added, as she mounted her horse.

We rode down from the col into the shallow valley beneath,

deep enough to shut out the view of everything but rocky slopes. A brook, which gradually grew larger, was at the bottom.

I called to Nattana that a valley where the stream was not at the bottom would be really interesting, and that made her laugh as I hoped it would.

Stunted, willowlike shrubs, not yet green, appeared in the hollows, and then others began to show upon the lower slopes. The cold brisk air of the col became milder. An hour or two passed, we reached trees, and it was lunchtime.

The Hyths had so often come this way that they had a halting-place used by them for many years, and preferable to all others near. A flat ledge of rock, a little way from the road, sloped from a group of dwarfed old pines to the stream. The roots of the trees made seats with a back. The sun shone warmly on the ledge, and behind among the pines was a place out of the wind for the horses.

We made ourselves comfortable and opened the lunch that she had brought. There was enough, there was variety, and there was not too much. We were both hungry. There were meat rolls, a nutty bread, plain hard bread, cheese, preserved fruit, and a flask of red wine, rather stronger than usual. I was a little chilly and its warmth was welcome.

It seemed ungracious not to tell Nattana that she had been more than kind in the way she had treated me during my visit, and particularly in coming with me on this day. She leaned back, listened, and eyed me now and then while I said all this. When I had finished, she smiled.

"I will do what you taught us all when you were here in March." She raised her cup. "What do you say? Here is to your success."

So I drank to hers.

"You had better take the rest of the wine with you," she said. "I have also brought you a book to read. It is in my saddlebag. Don't let me forget it." She laughed for no reason at all.

We had risen early and had ridden long without much breakfast. Mountain air and climbing, even on horseback, was subduing. I was sleepy, and said so. Nattana admitted that she felt the same way.

"But there is no time for us to sleep," she said. "You have a long distance to go, and you ought to be on your way soon."

She yawned behind her hand.

"You ought to be going," she said indifferently, and her eyes, a little teary from the yawn, smiled.

We went to the horses. She packed the rest of the lunch including the wine flask in my saddlebag. I did not want to say good-bye to Nattana.

I told her so suddenly.

"I have been a help, have I?" she asked.

"Yes, indeed!"

She considered a moment.

"Well, if you should not get what you want, don't forget the Hyths."

"I shouldn't anyway," I said.

Nattana laughed.

"I was forgetting the book," she added. She was vivid in the cool, sun-flecked shadow of the trees, standing by her roan horse, with her green collar and rusty glistening hair. Finding the little volume she thrust it into my saddlebag.

"Thank you, Nattana." I went to her horse.

When she was seated, she said, "If you don't want to bother to write me now, don't."

"I do!" I answered quickly.

"Now and then would make me happy," she said, and swung her horse around. "Good-bye, John."

"Good-bye, Nattana."

I watched her as I mounted Fak. She and her horse moved along a rocky slope. She had a long way to go. She was dear to me, a friend indeed, and I had not thought of the right thing to say.

That evening, at the Andals' near Tamplin, when I was unpacking my saddlebags, Nattana's book fell out, face down. I picked it up, but a scrap of paper was left on the floor. Whether it was to mark a certain passage and whether or not put there by her, I could not tell.

It was a book of fables by Godding, who lived in the early eighteenth century. Opened at random it showed this: "There was a *tana* named Alan, who thought he would die if he did not have a certain woman. . . ." In no mood for that sort of thing, I closed Godding's book quickly. Nattana had shown lack of tact, but it did not matter. My mind was full of Dorna, and I was anxious to end this solitary traveling and to be at my own house again. I was going to leave no stone unturned to advance myself now! It was my only hope. As consul I was not rich enough, and the tenure was precarious. Whatever Dorna's attitude was toward foreigners as a class, I was nowhere unless a fairly prosperous one. She had been sorry because I had let my opportunities slip. It was this or nothing if I wanted to be in a position to support her.

The next morning I continued my lonely journey, filled with a new happiness at the thought of Dorna and of the resolution I had just made. Fak required little pressing, and when, after a night at Reeves, we set out on the last stretch of our journey, I was as glad as he to be returning home where I could begin to work for Dorna.

According to George, nothing had happened during this absence of three weeks that required my presence at the consulate. Disobedience to the instructions of the Department of State had harmed no one, nor, furthermore, was it likely to be known, for rightly or wrongly I was going to say nothing about it. Nor did the steamers, which arrived on the sixteenth and eighteenth, bring any unpleasant letters of criticism and of instruction from Washington. I was merely informed that a party of men were expected to arrive at The City in the latter part of the month upon the yacht of Mr. Roderick Latham, and I was asked to arrange that all possible privileges be extended to them. There came a long letter from Jennings about the exhibits for the Exhibition Ship. He wrote amusingly and was keen to be back, he said. The steamer also brought two of my countrymen as commercial prospectors, and a party of four sight-seers. It was well that I returned at this time. Busy days were ahead, bringing with them an opportunity to put into effect the decision made at the Andals'.

The American, John Lang, therefore entertained every American that he could find, seven in all. He went to see them at the hotel and pressed them with offers of assistance. The head of the party of sight-seers was a man of wealth from Chicago, bringing with him a daughter, a companion for her, and a secretary. All that could be done for wealth was done, including the usual work of a Cook's Agency. The two prospectors were given even better treatment. They were interested in automobiles, and were anxious to see what sort of roads Islandia had.

All this took time. Though Jennings was not due for two months, the prudent thing was to make as early as possible all arrangements for chartering the Exhibition Ship, for manning and equipping her, for her itinerary, and for such advertisement as was possible—taking still more time. So also did my efforts to smooth the way for Roderick Latham's party. The medical examination which would have to take place was the principal thing to worry about. I tried to arrange to have the doctors who examined the Latham party headed by a certain man who had great dignity and humor as well.

These occupations took me out of the consulate and involved hours at the Agency Building. Broadening my acquaintance there would certainly be useful if ever the day came when I was an agent myself. Besides, there was Fak to be thought of, necessitating a certain amount of exercise. The mistake made in the winter must not be repeated. Neither he nor I should become fat and sluggish again.

The days passed, not quickly, but with a certain inevitableness that was comforting, bringing slowly nearer the long-distant day that I dreaded. Within a week of my return I had written to Dorna. It was hard not to spill over, not to say indirectly if not directly that I loved her. Passages in which there was a compromise between saying it and not saying it seemed false on rereading, and were torn up. In the end the letter was much cooler in tone than I had meant it to be. It seemed a pallid thing of mere words when at last it had been sent. It contained an account of the journey to the Hyths', and of my doings there, and of my hours with Nattana. Of these Dorna must know in detail, but she was not informed that the other had been a confidante. I wrote also of the beauty of Dorn Island, trying thereby to show her how deeply I felt with her in her love for her place. Lastly I told her of my resolution to advance myself in every way possible. Here only was the letter personal: "Whether you can ever forgive me for doing this, I do not know, but there is nothing else for me to do which will put me in the position where I must be in order to be able to have the thing in life that I want more than anything else. You said you were sorry that I had let my opportunities •slip. That has encouraged me to do as I am doing. I mean by this only that I don't think I shall have your disapproval. Even though you also said you were glad, I do dare to think that you will understand that I am not taking this course in any way intended to make you unhappy. I wish there were some other way, but I don't know of any."

The letter was sent. The fact that it was finished after such effort was like another good-bye, for while I wrote we talked; but the fact that it was on its way to her, to be read and later answered, made her much nearer than she had been in the winter.

Of course, a letter was also due to Nattana, easier to write and easier to be satisfied with. It told of my journey, of my present life, and it thanked her again.

The *Daphne,* Roderick Latham's yacht, arrived at the end of October. We were ready to do all that could be done. Word was brought to me as soon as she cast anchor, and I went out to her in the boat that took the doctors to examine her passengers and crew. My purpose, of course, was to stand as a buffer between the Americans and the Islandian inspectors, easing the shock upon the former as well as I could.

It was not a pleasant morning. All my efforts to facilitate the examination of his party and their entry into the country stood for nothing in the face of my admission that I had made no effort to have the medical examination entirely dispensed with. It was no use protesting that such an effort would have been unavailing. Because I had not tried, how could I know? You never can tell until you try!

It would have been useless to try, but it would not have been improper to do so. In spite of myself, I felt guilty in not having made the vain attempt.

The examination proceeded. The humiliation of my countrymen required a compensation, and this they found in blaming and complaining to me. Nor did I find much solace in the fact that when it was all over I was Latham's guest at lunch, and that he magnanimously said, when the examination was over, that after all no harm had been done.

The next week was spent largely in the service of the Latham party. It was not a satisfactory task, for I had a subtle feeling that I was prejudged before they arrived, and that I had begun upon this course of conduct too late.

For some weeks the yacht lay anchored within the sea walls, a conspicuous object, and about November twentieth departed for Ferrin.

My half-failure made work less of a release than it had been. The arrival of steamers on November 2nd and 4th, with mail from Washington, brought increased depression, for all my sins as consul were raked over at length, and it was borne in upon me again and again that I had begun too late to make an ingratiating businessman of myself.

The turning of spring into the summer, the first that I had witnessed in Islandia, mocked me with a beauty which I could not feel. Almost daily I rode into the flat delta lands. The waters of the bay sparkled more and more blue and summery. There was a charming road along the shore westward about ten miles to a pretty recessed bay, enclosed by a barren headland. There was always the ride north in the direction of the Calwins' farm, becoming daily more and more weighted with the verdant richness of summer. All these rides I took, but I saw them with the eyes of a condemned person. Washington was displeased beyond cure. Oh, the ghastly irony it would be, if, when Dorna's period of probation were over, she turned to me who had in the meantime forfeited all right to remain in her country!

Two weeks after my letter went to her, her answer came. It was all I could desire. She was glad, she said, that I had decided to advance myself as consul, and to make as good friends as possible with all the visiting traders. There was no question of forgiveness. She did not disapprove, nor did it make her unhappy to know that I was trying to establish a position for myself in Islandia, in case the Mora Treaty were ratified. Much as she would hate to see that happen, she would dislike still more the thought that she had prevented me from being true to my American destiny. Then, having disposed of this matter, she wrote with unexpected ease and length of her garden, of the seeds we had planted, and of summer weather coming over the Marsh, making Dorn Island achingly clear to me.

Almost at once I wrote her again and tried to be as amusing as possible about the Latham party, and to reproduce for her some of the beauty that had eluded me on my rides into the country.

On December 9th, the council met, and, as I have explained before, this meeting like that of June is of more importance, there being a greater attendance and international matters being discussed. The season was now late spring.

My first year in Islandia had nearly finished its round. The flowers that had been in bloom on my arrival were now in bud. My garden was just ready to let itself go, and those into which I had glimpses from my west parapet showed dots and banks of yellows and blues and some few reds.

Without announcement, on the evening of the eighth, Dorn appeared. I had felt quite sure that he would be present, but I was not prepared for the message he brought me. He delivered it almost at once. When one expects either a pardon or a warrant for execution, and receives instead a reprieve, one suffers simultaneously relief and disappointment.

I had made him at home in his room, and he talked as he washed for supper. His great-uncle was already in The City. He had himself come with Lord Hyth over the Tamplin Pass, with Airda, Hyth Ek, and Ettera. They had met Lord Fain at Reeves. Nattana had sent me her love (*amia*), so had Nekka, and Nettera. His voice grew a little grave.

"My sister wants you to come to Dorn Island when the council rises," he said.

"She is not coming to The City?"

"No, not at this time. She is very busy with her garden, she says. She told me to be sure to bring you back with me."

My mind was a blank. What did she mean? It might be that her decision had been favorable to me and that Dorn Island seemed to her the place to tell me so. But the council would sit for ten days at least, and steamers which I must not miss were due on January 2nd and 4th. I could not leave The City until the latter date, nearly four weeks away.

"Did she send any other message?" I asked.

"No," he said shortly.

"Is she well?"

"Oh, yes. She is well and she seems happy. She is anxious to see you, I am sure of that. If you can come back with me, I can give you some of my time. I shall have a week or so free, I think, but I shall not be there after the first."

I told him about the steamers. He laughed a little.

"She said that anyway you are to come as soon as you can," he answered.

It was more a relief than a disappointment. Dorna's invitation to come to the Island presaged something hopeful. I could hardly believe that she would have asked me to make that long journey merely to be told that her problem had been decided against me. Sustained by this reasoning, and free of an immediate grief, I was better able to give myself to the weeks of activity that followed.

In themselves, they were full of excitement and interest. The reception at the palace next evening was as brilliant as that of six months before. The young king did his part with that slightly nerve-wracking air of mischief that I was coming to expect. But there was no Dorna on this occasion with whom to talk it over. There were, however, other friends in plenty, and as the Islandians moved past our boxes it was delightful to see again Lord Fain and to be pressed to come and spend a long time with him; to see all the Stellins; to realize with an uneasy treacherous heart that this slim, clear-eyed young woman had kissed me; to see Lord Baile, who scolded me for making him no visit; to see the familiar faces of the Hyths; to see Lord Dorn, the Somes; to see Lord Mora and his wife, and my princess, and all the many others I knew.

The day after the council opened my book was published. It was a small, thin, amateurish-looking volume, and almost at once its white pages showed a few staring blunders; but it was my own child and I was proud of it, proud of the twenty presentation copies that were delivered at my door, and I spent a happy evening dispatching these to the proper persons with messages from "the Author." Four went to America—one to the Harvard Library, one to the family, one to Uncle Joseph, and one to Gladys Hunter. The rest went to Islandian friends.

On the seventeenth the council suspended its session so that we could attend the athletic meet at The City's Fair Grounds.

It was the first time that I had seen a large Islandian crowd. The oval, which lies in the northern part of The City not far from the Miltain Palace, has no grandstand, except on one side. The spectators were seated here or else stood around the track or in the windows or roof gardens of the surrounding houses. They were silent except for a low hum of conversation between events and applause, wholly vocal, at their conclusion. No one cheered until the last runner had crossed the line. Then the sound made was friendly, bass and pleased, rather than vociferous and shrill and excited. The spectators included quite as many women as men. The athletes who competed were the winners of events at provincial fairs, and therefore were the best in the country. On previous days there had been short dashes, hurdle races, runs of medium distance, broad jump, and fencing matches. We witnessed a long run of about five miles and the hurling of the great shots. No women competed but I was told of a remarkable girl runner who had done well in, though not winning, the short dash. The running race which we saw included about forty competitors from all over Islandia. They wore sandals and shorts in the colors of their province, but were without shirts. Their bodies were browned and lean, and the race was close among all of them. I could not judge of the pace, but one of my companions declared that it must be very fast.

The hurling of the weight took place in the center of the oval. The athletes wore the same shorts, but were barefoot. They were magnificent. The shots weighed about twenty-five pounds. Two of slightly less than half that weight were connected by an iron rod, and were thrown, not "put" as in America and Europe.

Watching them I saw a familiar figure, with a black beard and smooth black hair parted in the middle—Don of Upper Doring, whom I had met at the Lor Pass. Others were heavier and bigger and seemed stronger, though he was a man of more than the ordinary size. But his perfectly proportioned body, so beautifully made as to seem small, had that extra quality of skill and co-ordination that made him the winner for the seventh consecutive year. I was glad to think that I knew so splendid a champion.

On December sixteenth, S.S. *St. Anthony* arrived from Biacra, bringing Jennings and two barge loads of objects for the Exhibition Ship, which was lying at the Winder Docks, waiting to receive them, fully equipped with provisions, master, and crew.

Jennings himself was full of eagerness, more spruce in appearance than when he left six months before. He brought with him an assistant, Harry Downs, and they could scarcely wait before inspecting the Exhibition Ship, the *Ace*. In fact, no sooner had the necessary customs arrangements been made than they were at work upon her, and I could leave them to climb the hill to the Council Meeting.

That evening had been reserved for them. They both came to dinner, but no conversation was possible with Jennings. Everything was ready, everything was perfect, he said, his round cherubic, sophisticated face beaming. "John, you are a wonder. So are we. So is everybody!"

Immediately after the meal he departed, leaving Downs with me to discuss details. He smiled, he winked, and did not conceal at all the fact that he was going to see his girl.

"I have been waiting six months for this," he said, "and nothing is going to stop me. Harry and you can settle everything. She's reserving tonight for me."

357

Off he went with a frankness in his impatience that was disturbing to a man in love.

Downs made it plain that he had no interest in that sort of thing.

Our most serious problem was to make our exhibits understandable to Islandians. I could not be with the ship often, Jennings knew a little Islandian, Downs none at all. I spent hours writing descriptions of agricultural machinery, of cream separators, and of similar things in Islandian and English in parallel columns. Downs undertook the arrangement of the exhibits on the ship. We put aboard a large number of copies of my *History*. We planned in detail our sales talks. Betweenwhiles I attended meetings of the council and dined and entertained. These were the busiest days yet spent in Islandia, nor were they unhappy ones, but the pressure of work was too great for serenity. I resented activity that seemed to erect barriers between Dorna and me.

After ten days, on December 26th, we opened the ship to visitors. There was first a private view for agents and members of the council and of the diplomatic colony. Of the Isla there were few, because the meeting ended on the twenty-third; but every consulate and legation was well represented, and the agents came in force. I made myself showman on that occasion. Downs was of little use, and Jennings disappointed me. The fact that he was to leave The City with the ship preyed on his mind.

After five days the ship set off up the river to Reeves. I did not go with her. Certainly, so far, the enterprise might be called a success. Visitors were numerous and seemed really interested. When Jennings gave his mind to it he could hold his audience in spite of his imperfect knowledge of Islandian.

For the first time I found myself something of a figure in local life. Nearly everyone foreign or Islandian had heard of my book. Unexpected persons spoke of reading it, such as a farmer from Deen at The City for a holiday. The *Ace* also brought me many congratulations and, I think, just a little envy from some of my fellow diplomats, for they praised us for our ability in concealing it until too late for imitation.

With the departure of the *Ace* came a few days of comparative quiet, and then a blow fell. Just a year after my arrival in Islandia, the *St. Anthony* brought a letter from Washington that nearly ended all my hopes; and this came just the day before that on which I planned to start on my journey to the West.

The gentleman who ruled over my destiny at the State Department reviewed my whole career as consul in a series of numbered paragraphs, which read like the clauses of an indictment. I could not complain of not being informed as to the particulars wherein I had failed. In ways the cleverness of which I admired, my failure to protect the diseased man who was denied admission, my failure to render all assistance that I could to representatives of various American business houses (not mentioned by name, but clearly Müller, Andrews and Body were intended), my identification to an improper extent with persons and a political party hostile to American interests, and my frequent absences from The City, were all brought up against me again. It was no comfort that my own conscience was clear as to each of these charges, and that the same facts would have justified a very different story if someone else had written it. There were influences hostile to me in Washington, and no defense or explanation of mine could alter their point of view. The last part of the letter pointed out that, in view of the important political developments now taking place in Islandia, the presence of a man there of greater diplomatic experience was regarded as desirable. It was clearly intimated that my resignation as consul would be accepted. In the meantime, of course, I would continue in my present position. Nor was there any suggestion that I do otherwise than remain upon the job.

For a moment I almost wished that I would lose Dorna, for then this defeat at home would have less sting. The sting of it, indeed, hurt me not at all except in connection with her. As a consul who failed and had been displaced I saw little chance of becoming an agent for American goods in Islandia. There was no letter from Uncle Joseph to explain or to ease the blow. In a twinkling of an eye the fabric of hope which I had been laboriously constructing in the last few months fell to pieces. I had begun too late. My whole career as consul was one of futility and vacillation.

But I was going to see Dorna as planned. Nothing would prevent me!

17

Summer: Dorna

SOLITARY JOURNEYS of several days' duration were familiar now. It was the easiest thing to pack my saddlebag and to leave The City, January 5th, 1908, on Fak's back, bound once more for the West upon a road already thrice traveled, a road never followed without Dorna very much in my consciousness and full of reminders of her.

Summer had truly begun, and the weight of its sunny leafage and growth and of its long warm days was heavy upon the rolling farm lands of Bostia and Loria. The unhappiness of my position depressed me, and the shock that I had received renewed itself every little while. Fak's feet, plodding in the dusty road and sending up a light, yellowish cloud behind me, rhythmically beat the news: I had failed, I must resign, I had lost my job, Islandia was not for me.

After the first interminable day The City with its practical and logical realities had sunk behind the horizon. The road brought back the world of love, freshening the heart and all the senses.

On the fourth day as Fak and I walked up the defile of the Cannan River, which roared and boomed, making the hillsides echo, there came a sense of freedom so new and so complete that it was as though I had moved into a new plane of existence. Soon I would no longer have to play a part.

On the ninth we crossed the Doan Pass and as we faced the descent we met the southwest wind, a vast powerful breath that seemed to lift and to lighten the hills and to deepen the tones of all colors.

Impatience to see Dorna came as a great hand smoothing out and blurring all other thoughts and worries excepting only the one fact that I was on my way to her.

Late in the afternoon I rode once more across the flat farmlands and saw the low gray walls of the town of Earne; and as before, I longed to have Dorna meet me, and yet discounted so much this hope that when I came upon the quay and saw her boat, the *Marsh Duck,* lying moored to the wall I could not believe it.

Yet there she was sitting on the deck, leaning back against the bulwark, her arms straight out on either side of her, a relaxed and brooding figure, waiting—waiting for me.

The blue waters of the little harbor sparkled in waves that slapped against the quay wall. Beyond, the river was streaked with whitecaps, and farther still the opposite shore of the marsh was low and a dark green.

I saw Dorna before she saw me, looking down upon her from the quay. Her head was bent and she was thinking some elusive Dorna-thought, I knew, the stillest of still figures. I called to her:

"Dorna, here is John Lang!"

She looked up and smiled sleepily and rose like one reluctantly waked to some duty, and came to the wall. It reached above her waist, but before I could bend to help her she had placed her hands upon it and had sprung high enough to swing up her knee. Then she scrambled to her feet awkwardly, but unconsciously.

The world went slowly round and round. Three months of absence from her had falsified her image a little. If she were not so ideally lovely as I had remembered her, in her reality, solid, and occupying space, she struck upon my heart and my senses with the violence of the perfect and of the wholly natural.

"Did you see my brother?" she asked—and oh, her voice, Dorna's voice, vibrant, young, unlike any other sound!

It appeared that Dorn was riding from Doring Town, coming to spend next day with me. She was to sail us both back to the Island. Fak would be brought over next day by one of the men.

Having stabled him we sat down on the deck of the *Marsh Duck* to wait for her brother. I had come—to learn from Dorna the solution of her problem; but I had no wish to ask it now, nor, apparently, had she any wish to tell me. She resumed her seat on the deck, leaning back once more upon the bulwark, her arms straight out along the rail.

Without preliminary she asked me to tell her my impressions of the meeting of the council. Her uncle and brother had been too busy to give her a full account. I wondered if these two did not leave her out in a way she rightly resented. I was on her side now. It did not take all my mind to discuss the council and I could watch Dorna.

She seemed younger, more a girl, and in some dim underconsciousness a little more my own. Her eyes seemed to look at me with openness. Her bare legs—the skin was of the finest smooth texture, tanned a little—were not flawless, and I was glad. Across her uppermost shin ran the line of a scratch, evidently recent, for along its edge was a row of little beads of clotted blood. There were several bruises and a spot of dirt on one ankle.

I laughed, forgetting what I was saying. This was the real Dorna, the woman I loved, made of flesh, blood, and bone, as ordinary and as real as my own.

The moments passed as they always did with her. Time moved at a different rate of speed. With Dorna, smoothly flowing peace lay under all other feelings.

Her brother appeared at last and we three set sail. His coming made her abruptly silent. He and I talked now, and though the boat was hers she gave the management of it over to him, she and I crew, he skipper. We had to row the *Marsh Duck* out from the wall to get under way, for the wind was directly on shore; but soon we were foaming along into the river, the great sail full, and the short little waves dashing violently upon the bow and coming over upon us in a fine soft spray like a drizzle.

It was too lovely and I was drowned too deep in happiness to intrude upon it my own troubles and to bother about hers. Seeing Dorna again, I had refound my love, far deeper and far richer than I had known it to be.

That evening, toward bedtime, I had one word alone with Dorna. "You and I must have a talk, John," she said, "but let us wait until after my brother goes."

Apprehension quickened in me.

The next day I gave to him and did not grudge it, for there were other days to come with Dorna.

It was warmer, with less wind, but still clear. He and I went on the water soon after breakfast and did not return until midafternoon, and only then because the wind died out. In fact, we came drifting back into the harbor upon its last breath. I told him all my troubles with Washington, revealing to him the fact that I had been asked to resign and planned to do so. It would, of course, be some months before my successor arrived and even then I would have to stay some time to familiarize him with conditions. Dorn blamed himself in part and I tried to describe to him my feelings of release and freedom. It was hard to convince him that these were not inspired by a wish to minimize the harm which he believed that he had done me; but I at least had no doubt in my own mind that a burden had fallen from my shoulders, now that duty was no longer going to compel me to adopt a particular point of view toward the opening of Islandia to foreign trade. Naturally we also discussed my next step. Even when my official position no longer existed, I could, he said, continue in Islandia as a visitor under the Hundred Law, which would allow me a year's additional residence. We agreed that it would be a pity if I left before the Mora Treaty came up for rejection or acceptance. For that at least I would stay. He pressed me to write an account of my experiences in Islandia and to describe dispassionately whatever happened in connection with that treaty, offering me Dorn Island as a place for retreat and work. And he added sagely that when my salary was cut off, I could live for practically nothing at all if I spent my time on visits. There were the Hyths and the Fains. At either place I could stay indefinitely if I were willing to turn to and work a little. At Dorn Island, of course, this was not necessary.

We returned in the middle of the afternoon. The talk with Dorn had somehow strengthened me. With him I had been at grips with the facts of actual living, and in him I had found reaffirmed the strong support of our friendship. I felt solemn, but only a little less happy.

There was still half the afternoon to be got through.

We found Dorna also at loose ends. She had worked all morning and half the afternoon in the hot sun in her garden. She was in the big circular room, the coolest place in the house, flat on the floor on a rug, her arms straight out, and her face red and flushed. She sat up slowly as we came in.

We all sat in the dim silence of that big room with its shadowy ceiling, wondering what to do, talking in desultory fashion of my history, which both Dorn and Dorna had been reading. I had said little about the United States that he did not know, but there were a number of facts new to her. He spoke a kind word as to my style, and she said that my country was a much more comprehensible place than it had been before.

"Is it hot like this?" she asked.

"Hotter," I said. "This isn't bad."

It was Dorn who suggested to me that we go swimming. The delta waters would still be cold, he added, but it would be a relief.

"May I come too?" asked Dorna. He hesitated just a moment before saying yes. She sprang to her feet and was gone.

"I will fetch towels," he said, "and we will meet outside."

The usual swimming pool was on a creek opposite the island of Dorn XV, at which place there was a sandy beach instead of the usual steep bank where marshland ended above the water.

Dorna appeared with a towel folded over her shoulders like a shawl. Her braid was wound in a bun upon the top of her head. I saw no sign of any bathing suit. Neither had Dorn nor I any, and I assumed that we would bathe separately.

We passed through the heart of the farm, cut across a field in the full heat of the sun, and then took the road that led westward, first through pastures and then through the pine wood.

"It is just the day for a swim," she said, in a voice eager and contented. The heat was not too oppressive and humid, but acted directly upon the skin in that tingling drying way which makes it crave the soothing contact of cool water. And the walk on the dusty road in the hot sun was a sort of purgatorial preparation for grace to come.

Little was said. Dorn hummed. Dorna strode along in her free easy way, smiling a little. She wore a linen suit of pale-blue, and a blouse of white. I noticed the dust gathering upon her smooth white calves.

The sun had not yet sloped low enough to lengthen shadows, and the little tight-leaved pine trees, quiet always, were very still in the windless air, sharp-edged and vibrating with dark colors. Something in Dorna and in my love for her gave natural things seen in her presence a quality which they had at no other time, so that I seemed to see the essential quality of them doubly vivid and as it really was.

We came out of the pines upon the creek quite suddenly. There was a low wharf where a small boat could lie. Opposite was the low hill of Dorn XV Island, where I had landed with Dorna and heard of his escape with his child. Leftwards from us the beach curved for about one hundred yards, rather steep, of a coarse yellow sand.

She moved a little away from us, her towel about her neck. Dorn began taking off his clothes. I hesitated and saw Dorna unwind her towel and drop it on the sand. The water in front of her reflected the pale, hot, blue sky.

Dorn's coat and shorts were already removed. I held my breath, and looking away from Dorna, began to undress myself, the blood pounding in my temples.

To them evidently this was natural, or they never would have done it, and they assumed that I was enough one of them to find it natural also.

Quickly I undressed. I had never seen a naked woman nor to my knowledge had I been seen by one. The thought of a woman without clothes was associated with thoughts of desire. To them this surely was not so. Could I put myself upon their level?

Dorna was mine to see, but I could not turn to her, yet it was as indecent deliberately to avert my eyes all the time as it would be to stare.

Dorn walked past me toward the water. I knew his body, long, muscular, brownish in color, and covered with dark hair. His foot touched the water. Then Dorna called.

"It is cold!" she cried. To keep my head turned away made painful and embarrassing what otherwise might be the simplest, easiest thing. She was standing with her feet in the water facing us, unconscious and at her ease. Without clothes she was more slender. Her skin glowed like a clear, brilliant flame against the background of pale-blue water, orange beach, light-green marsh grass, and darkgreen pines. There was nothing of her that I did not see, nothing of her simple nakedness.

She walked into the water with long steps and much splashing, lifting her feet high like a child. The white foam rose up around her. She sank quickly, leaned forward, and struck out, at first toward the Island and then toward her brother, her arms splashing. I rose, knowing that she saw me. It no longer mattered.

Soon we were all three swimming. That occupation gave me countenance, and I could look into her eyes and smile and see the wet gleam of her bare shoulders and for a moment her breasts, frank, honest, and full.

The water was cold. We did not stay in long. We swam across to the island, but did not land. Then we swam back again, and Dorna

365

went ashore in front of us, walked out upon the beach with me behind her, and then moved in the sunlight, wet, gleaming, to the place where she had left her clothes.

Dorn and I landed, and a weight as of paralysis rested upon my muscles, and it was only with an effort that I rubbed myself dry and dressed again. To Islandians this might be a natural easy thing, but the force of my traditions and of my training was too strong. Dorna's beauty was greater than I had dreamed possible. She was one of those women whom clothes make heavy. Naked, her body was revealed in its natural lightness, balance, and grace. I tried my best to take it all naturally, but I was deeply shaken.

As soon as we were all clad again, we three lay in the sand. My eyes were very shy of her, and I was tired and subdued. There was cruelty in what she had done to me, an American. She had made herself too dear. So Dorn, also, had gone deeper in my heart. I was with these two persons whom I loved more than all others.

We talked a little. The island opposite lay like a low dark shield upon the water. When the sun had sloped much lower, we walked back, slowly lest we lose the cooling effect of our swim.

Early next morning, just as my room was growing gray, Dorn came in to say good-bye. Though the night had seemed long I had really slept and slept well.

He repeated to me that the busiest of days were before him for the next six months.

"I tell you this," he said, "though you know it, because, while you do understand, I want you to hear the words said once more. I wish with all my heart that I could spend a great deal of time with you in the way we used to live before all this political trouble came upon us. I have many dreams of what I want to do. One is to live the life of a farmer somewhere for a long enough period really to know it. You would like it, John, at least as we live it here. And I want to travel with you . . . Let's not give up hope."

He paused, something more on his mind.

"If you need me," he said suddenly, "promise to send for me. I can always make time to see you. I mean that. Do you understand?"

He leaned over me.

"Yes," I said.

Then he laughed.

"Don't be too much a conscientious New Englander in deciding whether you need me or not," he added. "It may not be any material thing, John. Don't think it has to be! Have you taken that in?"

I said that I had. He departed, telling me that the caretaker at the Doring Palace in The City would always know the quickest way in which he could be reached.

For a little while I remembered what he had said, very much moved, and then the whole focus of my being turned upon Dorna. Today I was sure that she would tell me that for which I had so long waited. My heart felt like a wind-tossed balloon, so dizzily lifting within me that I was half-sick.

The day was overcast and yet not cold. An uneasy damp wind, smelling of salt, blew in from the sea, and the clouds, which passed like shutters across the sun, trailed light rains over the farm and the marsh.

Dorna was late to breakfast, coming in when the rest of us had nearly finished. In an odd way her clothes did not seem so essentially part of herself as they used to. I noticed them as separate things—her buff-colored skirt and jacket and pale-green blouse with loose collar, which made the skin of her face and neck, her arms and hands and legs, a brown, slightly dusky, but full of warmth and color. Her face was simplified and smoothed of all expression.

She yawned and tears came into her eyes. She said that she had not slept very well. That also was a surprise, for her face seemed most serene. I wondered why—wondered if she would tell me. The balloon of my heart tossed again, and I could eat no more.

"What shall we do?" she asked calmly. "I thought we might go for a sail, but I am lazy today. And it would not be much fun. The wind is too uncertain. I don't feel like drifting about."

This hurt. Once she had been content to drift with me for two days.

"Haven't you things you want to do? Letters to write?" she asked. "I have several. There's plenty of time. Let's go for a walk in the middle of the morning."

So it was settled, and I spent two interminable hours of waiting.

About eleven we met again. Dorna was dressed as before, but with a great loose cloak of light blue in addition. It was raining gently, but patches of white glowing cloud here and there seemed to promise clearing skies. We walked slowly because it was warm, and the errant wind made her cloak unruly.

"I would not mind getting wet," she said, "if this dress did not spot so easily . . . How are things with you, John?"

Her voice was friendly, but personal. I would tell her now all the things that she ought to know. It seemed only proper to acquaint her with the attitude of Washington toward me. I began to explain.

She walked at my side, grave-faced, listening, but not looking at me. I told her the whole story at length and from the beginning. Some was repetition, but I wanted her to be aware of all the facts. She let me speak in my own way. She only raised her voice once. It was when we came to the gate in the old fortification wall north of the house.

"Let's go to the windmill, John," she said. "We can't walk and talk very well in this wind. There is much to be said."

We passed through the gate. Level and flat for a full quarter of a mile the pasture extended before us. Low on its further edge was the dyke with its row of willows, above which rose the windmill revolving its four great sails, now fast now slow, against a white sky, which at any moment seemed about to break and show the blue.

"I think I'll go barefoot," said Dorna. "Why don't you? The grass is very wet. Why do you always wear stockings, John?"

She put out her arm and I held it, supple and strong yet slender, just below the elbow. Her pose was graceful as she stood on one leg, the other crossing over the knee like the figure 4, and removed her sandals, first one, then the other. Because she bade me, I drew off my own sandals and my stockings. We walked on over the wet lush grass. With our shoes in the pockets of our cloaks, I had a vague feeling of going to dancing school with pumps ready to put on upon arrival; but I was not barefooted then, nor were the little girls I walked with. It was several moments before I could resume my explanation, for my heart was not in it. Her bare feet were pink against the dark grass. She stepped firmly, not half so squeamish and tickled upon the soles as I was. I noticed that each toe was straight and flat, and that they spread a little, fanwise, before her foot lifted. My own feet were distorted by years of narrow boots.

Her young perfection was a painful thing. I felt myself maimed and incomplete. The explanations I was making seemed beyond my power. It was as though a great hand had swept over the world, dimming my mind, darkening the sky—and Dorna, the center of all things, became unreal. It had stopped raining, and she had swept off her cloak as she walked and was carrying it on her arm. Her supple, slender young chest did not seem large enough to hold me, and yet the only comforting place that life had for me was there; and I remembered her breasts as I had seen them, so unexpectedly full and round, unfamiliar things to my eyes, and yet part of her, the very substance of Dorna, creature of another sex. It hurt me then to know her so completely, nothing hidden—the hair, golden-brown, upon her groin, everything.

She was speaking.

"So it really has brought you a sense of freedom, John, to know that you will no longer have to work against us?" she said. "Is that really true in the bottom of your heart?"

"It is absolutely true!" I cried. "It came over me suddenly as I was riding along the Cannan River three days ago."

"It isn't because you want us to feel more happy?"

"Oh, no, Dorna! I wasn't thinking of that when I realized it. It isn't for your sake at all!" I tried to laugh.

"Is it because you have come to agree with us?"

"I don't know," I said, trying hard to be absolutely honest. "I don't know what I think yet. I mean, taking everything into consideration, I don't yet know what I want for Islandia. There is a great deal to the Mora side."

I could hear my bare feet and Dorna's swishing through the wet grass. To our right gleamed the water in the straight cleft of a drainage ditch, reflecting the white sky like mother-of-pearl.

"Of course," I said, "I realize that I have lost a chance I very much wanted, as I explained in my first letter to you. It has gone glimmering. I don't believe anyone will want to employ as an agent here one who has made the sort of failure I have. I have given up all hope of being able to support you in that way, Dorna, but it doesn't make me any less glad to be free."

I did not realize what I had said until I had spoken. I found myself drawing slow deep breaths, strangely weak, and yet released. I had proposed to her without knowing it. She was very quiet. There was no need to look at her. She was there at my side, moving quietly with me.

The air darkened. Westward over Ronan's Island all was opaque

369

with gray mist. Dorna, with a single sweeping movement, wrapped herself again in her cloak. The rain came in slanting, silvery lines, cool and wet on my cheek. The windmill, perched on the dyke, loomed over us, its great sails spinning around and rattling, against the dark-gray mist. Dorna went ahead across the plank bridge over the ditch upon the inner side of the dyke.

"Let's go inside," she said, as I came up.

We entered the windmill. Two small windows on the sides lighted the hexagonal interior. In the center a straight rod of metal was revolving, and close to the floor was a complexity of heavy cogwheels. Two other rods alternately rose with a sort of shuddering reluctance and sank again with a rhythmical rattle and clank. There was the sluicing rush and splash of water beneath us. Spare sails and parts of machinery leaned against the wall, and opposite the door was a copper stove with a pile of wood billets beside it. For furniture there was a sofa, a chair, and a low square chest.

The light was dim and dusty. High above us, in the center of the room was a little hole, revealing the sky, through which passed the metal rod to the vanes of the windmill. Dorna's place of retirement did not have the quiet and peace of Morana's; she must always hear the squeak and whirr of wings, the sighing clatter of wheels and rods, and the swishing of water.

Taking off her cloak she emerged from it, glowing like ivory in the shadowy light, and sat upon the sofa, curling her bare legs around sideways beneath her. There was room for me, but some vague scruple made me select the chair. The rain drummed upon the roof. I could feel her eyes upon me, but I did not look at her. The moment of my ordeal had come, and I waited, dreading it.

It became lighter again, and I knew that if I raised my eyes I could see her in her buff dress distinctly; but I did not want to look at her face. My eyes lifted and stopped at her shins. The scratch upon one was like a close-lipped mouth about which the skin was drawn tight. She hurt me—she would always hurt me. I held myself still and my rigidity became fixed as in a dream. Words were useless, for in words might be my doom. And yet I drove myself to speak.

"Dorna, I have nothing to offer you now—no place."

It was a meaningless cry.

"Don't say it! Don't say it, John!"

Her answer meant nothing. The Islandian way of uttering what was in my heart was like a tight knot at which my mind plucked with vain fingers. There was nothing left but English.

"Dorna, I love you. I love you. I want you to marry me."

I was standing over her, and she seemed to be cowering, her legs folded more closely beneath her. Her eyes were wide and bright, but I could not read them.

Would she mind if I sat next to her?

Her eyes did not waver from mine as I dropped to her side. I laughed a little.

"Dorna, I had to speak in English. In Islandian it means—"

She shrank from me. I saw her lips twitch and her brows knit. She seemed afraid. The world fell away and there was nothing but her eyes, dark, intent, incomprehensible. . . . Beneath the woolly fabric of her jacket her arms were smooth and round and firm. Her hands could not be grasped. They were supple and strong, twisting from my own, but if once I held them firm and still, I could speak. Was it I who was shaking? Her bosom rose and fell quickly, but her lips were closed. I could not gain her warm, quieting hands. She denied them to me.

"Give me your hands, Dorna!"

If once I had them this torment of wrestling would end.

Suddenly she slid away from me. Her fingers, half-held, slipped like snakes out of mine leaving fire where they had touched me.

"John, John, don't! don't! Let me tell you! Let me tell you!"

She dropped into the chair where I had been, swiftly, like one exhausted. My arms sank, empty of her. Her moving away made me impotent with an unnerving inner chagrin. . . .

Rain drummed on the roof.

"Don't be afraid of me," I said.

"Don't make me struggle with you again, John."

I waited. Nothing mattered.

"Don't be afraid, Dorna."

"I am not afraid," she said.

My hands burned where hers had touched them. Through the small dusty square of the window the sky showed gray and rainy. I knew what land I was in and what place. It was strange to have bare feet.

"I understood you," came her voice, cool, tired, kindly. "I know enough English."

Everything paused, even my heart. I knew before she spoke, but I did not want her to say it.

"I cannot marry you, John."

She could not have said it more gently. I loved her for the way she refused me. I loved her for her voice. She was sitting with bent head, not looking at me. I saw her clear and distinct, and then all edges became blurred and burning.

"I want to tell you why."

Something in me stirred. Dorna had some problem that she was waiting to have settled. I had forgotten it. To learn of its solution was the reason why I was here.

"Is it—your problem?"

"Yes."

There was utter silence, and then her voice began explaining.

"My problem is settled. It has been settled for a month now." Her voice rang out sharply. "I don't want to be married any more than I did last fall—not to you, not to anyone! I want to remain single, but I am going to be married, John, in May. I am going to marry young Tor, the King. He has asked me. I have said I would . . . It is a fact not known anywhere. We both wish it so. . . ."

What I heard was her outcry. It sounded through all else. "I don't want to be married!" She must not marry! The burning wickedness of her marriage was more vital than my own loss. Her youth, her dearness, and her beauty must not be given to a loveless thing.

"Dorna, don't marry then! Don't! You must not."

"I must," she cried. "I must! That is just it. I must!"

"No, no—I am not thinking of myself."

"I know you are not."

"I'm not thinking of myself," I repeated, "but you must not, Dorna!"

How could I say what I felt in Islandian? What did I want for her that could be expressed in that language? It was not *apia*, sexual desire, that she must feel, or was it? And *ania* seemed merely to connote the desire to have a proper married life with a particular person.

"Why must I not?" she demanded, and her voice seemed angry, like a child's.

"You will only be happy and complete," I cried, "if you marry with 'love,' Dorna—with *ania*, as you say."

Our eyes met. Hers were dark and bright.

"Of course, John! I have *ania* for him."

My head turned in torturing confusion. She had said that she did not want to marry anyone, that she wished to remain single.

"Do you want to marry him?"

Her eyes half closed, and her face twitched in pain.

"No!" she cried, "though I ought not to tell you. But I do feel *ania!*"

"For him?"

"Of course! For him only."

An indestructible hope raised by her denial of the wish to marry was trampled again . . . I could not understand her. She contradicted herself. I wished to ask her this question: "Will you be happy?" But the Islandian word was too light, not equivalent to "happiness" in English.

"Will you be contented, Dorna—in tune?"

She raised her head proudly.

"Yes," she said, "my will is strong."

"Will you have to use your will to be contented?"

"Of course, John. Everyone does."

"You break my heart," I cried. "Oh, not for my sake, Dorna!" I saw a dreadful life stretching before her. It was unbearable that contentment had to be fought for and would not flow over Dorna as naturally and as simply as the breathing of the wind.

Her hand reached out and drew back.

"Don't cry, John," she said in a sharp, hurt voice, "and don't break my heart also. Of course I must use my will. I must not pity myself nor think of myself. Nor must you pity me nor think of me as uncontented. My task will be not to think of 'here'—of 'us.' "

She looked about her with eyes suddenly grief-stricken. Her voice steadied.

"And I must not think of you, nor of the Tower, nor this windmill. I must not dream of having things which I shall not have. Nor must you! I must give myself wholly to my new life, John."

She clasped her hands tightly. I wanted her to break down and to weep.

"I can!" she cried. "I can give myself to the new life. I feel *ania.* Realize that, John. It is what I have been waiting to be sure of. There will be so much that I can do, and see, and let come to me. It will be a rich life, John! And if I yield myself, and don't worry about myself, or what I am or what is happening to me, if I just listen and look and utter what is in my heart, have my babies, and become part of my new life, and give myself wholly to all I shall have—"

She broke off. Clairvoyant, I saw her forcing herself to hug sterile satisfactions in order to save herself from despair. There was a wild bright light in her dark eyes.

"Dorna! That is not what you want. What do you really want? What do you really care for most of all?"

Her eyes fixed mine.

"I care most of all for 'ourselves,' " she said, and the word she used was the family pronoun.

It seemed to me a false word, and I clutched my head.

"What do you mean, Dorna—your brother, your uncle, your young cousin?"

"More than that! All the Dorns, and here—this place that is in us all. All the Dorns that were and that will be here in this place. It is all one thing. That is what is strongest in me!"

"I see why it is so hard for you to marry and to leave this place, even if you do feel *ania.*"

There was silence.

"I wonder if you do see," she said slowly. "My love (*alia*) for the Dorns and for this place demands that I, a woman, do what all Dorn women must do—take my love in my hands and yield it to someone somewhere else for whom I feel *ania,* and to carry into the life of those of whom he is one something Dorn. Women must do that here, John. Our love for home and for what home stands for is just as strong as a man's, but if we marry we must take it to a strange place. My love would not be what it should be unless I could do that gladly. And I can! Believe me, John, I can! It is what I must do—what I ought to do." She drew herself up stiffly. "You don't know me!" she cried. "You don't know me!"

"Do you know yourself, Dorna? Aren't you trying to persuade yourself that you can do something impossible?"

"No!" she said in a loud ringing voice. "I know myself. I know what I can do. Of course I'll look back and suffer—perhaps more than some other women. But there will be so much in the new life, John. I shall forget myself in them and in what I have. It will be hard at first—"

I winced to see her shudder.

"Dorna!"

She raised her hand.

"Listen to me," she cried. "Suddenly some day I shall wake up and find that for a long time I have forgotten all about myself. I shall learn how to yield and to be free in yielding. I shall wake up, I say, and find myself too deeply contented ever to want to change."

She laughed. Dorna laughed. Our eyes met, and hers burned wide and bright.

"There may be moments of regret," she said steadily.

We stared at each other. She had drawn her bare legs beneath her again, and she was sitting upright like a child. Her breasts were rising and falling. It was strange to see her legs, the calves pressed wide by her position, the scratch still upon her shin. In a whirl the words of explanation seemed nothing. All that mattered was the fact that she was doing a wrong, headstrong thing. The only reality was the suction of her beauty, drawing upon my flesh in a way that made her mine—mine to save from her folly. I swayed toward her, and she did not shrink.

"Dorna!" I cried. "You must not do this thing! Last spring you cared for me!"

Her face changed suddenly.

"No! No!" she cried. "John, don't touch me!" It seemed that she laughed. "I am right! I really am. I have thought about you and me, and we are not for each other. We would each make the other miserably discontented."

A moment passed, a moment of power. She was stronger, surer, than I. Force drained out of me, leaving only a desire, forever to be sterile . . . All grew white.

"John," she was saying softly, "have I done wrong to ask you to come here to tell you this? It seemed fairer to tell you rather than to write it—to give you a chance to ask me questions. But I have brought you on a long journey for nothing."

I wanted to laugh. She knew nothing of what I had felt.

"I would rather hear it from you," I said.

"I could not write it," she continued. "One reason is that no one knows—not even my brother and my uncle. Only young Tor and you and I."

It was clear what she wanted and I gave it to her.

"It is safe with me," I said. She drew a sharp breath.

"What a burden to put upon you!"

Her hand reached out to me. She knew how safe she was and her power over me. I did not want her hand as a sop.

"Thank you, Dorna," I said, and I clutched my head again lest I too impolitely refuse her hand. "Don't worry about me."

But suddenly she sobbed. The spasm of anger that I had felt vanished. I heard the padding sound of her bare feet and closed my eyes not to see them.

"I think I shall go back to The City at once, if you don't mind," I said. "I really ought to be there. I'm worried about the Exhibition Ship. Jennings is not so trustworthy as he seemed."

"Perhaps you had better go," came her voice from above me. I had not known she was so near. "And not see each other again," she added.

"Yes," I said.

"I'll go back to the house. I'll make it easy for you to go without seeing anyone. I'll arrange to have you taken over the ferries."

"Thank you, Dorna."

I heard the thud of her footfalls, and then there was utter silence, except for the pattering of the rain, the rattle-clank of the windmill, and the soft rhythmical swishing of the water under the floor.

It was as though I had never done anything else. Riding Fak and watching the road slide past at a walking pace was the only existence I had ever known or would know. I was an automaton guided by a little mechanical device, the size of a watch, ticking in my brain. It informed me that I was a consul bound toward the consulate to do my duty there. It was a minute functioning machine that was sanity.

The worst was not to be today, but tomorrow, and the day after, years and years—all my life—for a period perhaps three times as long as I had yet lived. Today was full of glory and fire and beauty. I had seen Dorna only a few hours before, and I could see and hear her still, vivid, edged with fire, her voice a music that coiled around my heart; but when all that faded, when memory dimmed, when she was no longer hot upon my senses, but merely a shrouded and elusive memory, for minutes, hours, days, years—I wondered how I would endure and go on.

Tears dropped upon Fak's mane. But the little guiding machine of sanity ticked on. It was comforting to be normally able to choose the right road, to stretch my face in a smile, and to hail cheerfully those who passed on the road.

It was a warm afternoon, more humid and more still the further I rode from the sea. The salty marsh fragrance began to die from the air.

I listened for Dorna's voice and could not hear it any longer. It was unique, but I could not hear it.

We spent the night at the Inn at the foot of the pass near where the road from Winly joins the National Highway from Doring Town. I dreaded sleep and the ending of this day on which I had seen Dorna, and I dreaded crossing the Doan Pass and putting the mountains between us. With waking would begin the morrows without her— days that were to last forever.

The first morrow came. I knew that it was upon me before I opened my eyes, and I wished I were dead.

All that should have been said had not been said. She did not yet know what I really felt about her. I began to say to her what I had been cut off from saying.

I rode, I walked. Fak plodded along methodically whether I was on his back or not. We wound slowly upward through the forests. We met many travelers. They were vague and unreal. Once I walked so slowly that Fak, close behind me, gave me a violent shove with his nose. For a moment I did not know where I was. A river was roaring far below me in a deep gorge, and to the right and left high forested slopes cut the sky. I was talking to Dorna, saying all the things left unuttered, planning them, arranging them.

There was also much that I wanted her to tell me. "Dorna," I said, "I do not really understand you. You say you want to remain single and do not wish to marry, and yet you also say that you feel this thing which you call *ania*. How can that be, Dorna? I wish you would explain to me. Is it that you dread sleeping with that man? If you do, Dorna, you must not marry him. You must not marry anyone until you want to sleep with that person and be loved by him. It is foolish to talk about *ania* when you can't bear the thought of that . . . Dorna, you have only one life to live! If you aren't afraid of sleeping with him, and merely want to remain single because your life at Dorn Island is so happy, I wish you would tell me. It would make a great difference to me, for I love you and want you to be happy."

The strange thing was that talking to Dorna after a time brought utter weariness. I would climb on Fak's back and ride in exhaustion with half-closed eyes. Yet I did not want to overfatigue my little horse, for I was going to press him hard and reach The City in four and one half days instead of the usual five. I wanted my own walls around me as soon as possible.

"Fak," I said, "it is good that this road is so easy to follow or I would be lost."

It seemed quite possible that my mind would give way. There was one thing that I must do—stop at the Inn in the pass and feed and rest Fak and obtain food for him for the evening and morning. I must not forget to stop at the Inn.

We came at last to the corridor through the mountains. Ahead of us was the col marking the height of the pass. Somehow we had reached it. Fak knew the Inn was near, and he cantered up the last loop of the road. I saw through a cleft in the mountains the far blue plains of Inerria.

"Good-bye, Dorna," I said.

It was folly to be sentimental. I doubled over upon Fak's back, shaking and weeping.

Nevertheless the little ticking machine of sanity guided me. Fak had his meal and his rest at the Inn. I found a quiet secluded place in a dark stable, ate a meat roll, and began to compose a letter to Dorna.

We rode on. Behind us the mountains lifted their barrier higher and higher, interposing their vast, insensate bulk between me and Dorna. She was gone. I had not really known it before, for my heart and my senses had been benumbed, and filled with the feeling and sight of her and with the sound of her voice. Now realms of consciousness that had refused to believe were irresistibly invaded and laid waste. Walls closed in upon me more and more tightly.

The long, deliberate approach of twilight was like death. Night was to be dreaded, for sleep would never come again. Yet all I planned I did, glad that I had a plan to go by, for I could not really think. Dusk came. We were in the gorge of the Cannan River and turned from the road to find a level spot close to the stream. It was later than I thought, and difficult to see. Fak was led to the water. He wanted to drink! But he did not want to drink, merely to nuzzle the water! I tried to draw up his head, but he resisted and nearly shouldered me into the stream. I waited. He had his own life, and his will was perverse, and there was no comfort in him.

Dark came quickly in the deep gorge. Against the sky high above me the treetops were hard and black. The opposite slope, heavy with shadows, was utterly insensible. Once a night out by myself would have been full of quick interest, but the loss of Dorna had made all things remote, unreal, and dead.

I rolled myself up in my cloak, made myself as comfortable as possible on the unyielding ground, and closed my eyes; but it was so dark that whether they were open or closed things seemed the same. Fak stirred now and then. There were sounds in the woods.

Time became a slow, deliberate, sliding thing—a horror. To feel time moving, flowing like a quiet, half-stagnant stream, was to realize what I was going to have to endure. An hour was forever, a night an eternity. There would be thousands and thousands and thousands of these . . . thousands of slowly ticking hours without Dorna.

Yet I slept for a little while, sinking slowly and deeply into quiet oblivion. When I woke all was gray, and for a long moment I lay in peace. The form of Fak, standing with head drooping at an unusual angle, asleep, seemed more motionless than any inanimate thing. For a moment I did not think, and love was fresh and sweet and good. It was only thinking that hurt. Love, when without thought, did not accept defeat.

Perhaps Dorna would find that she had made a mistake before it was too late. Perhaps all my misery would be for nothing. . . .

But in my heart I knew that she was of the unchanging ones. She had made up her mind and she would be inflexible. I writhed on the ground. If only she were doing something that would bring her happiness. . . .

We were on our way before the sun struck the slopes above the river. We moved in a gray mist. Fak was sluggish.

The night on the bank of the Cannan River was not the worst.

379

Misery has as many aspects as pleasure. The little machine of reason and sanity continued its quiet functioning.

The next night we spent at the Inn at Helby, then journeyed by way of Some Town and Botian, spending the fourth night in a field halfway between those places. Next day, January 15th, toward evening we reached The City.

PART III

18

The Exhibition Ship

THE JOURNEY from Dorn Island had been a flight. It was late afternoon when I came to my house, empty and utterly still. My ears rang with a fatigue that was only partly of the body, and partly of the wearying tension of endlessly thinking of one thing and of being aware of one pain. I had wanted to be within the quiet of my own walls, but on the road there had been enforced movement, and now there was nothing except soundless vacancy.

In the twilight a pile of letters on my table glowed with a peculiar whiteness. The busy life of sterile daily affairs called to me, sunk in brooding shadows. That other life had to go on. To live it I had come home.

There were invitations, and three letters from Americans in the country needing one thing or another. There was a letter from Nattana, which seemed an intrusion, and I put it aside, and felt that I was unfair to her.

Later I would answer, think, and decide.

The garden on the roof had been well cared for. The paths were raked and the earth in the beds was moist. As twilight deepened the glowing deep reds and yellows of the flowers remained, and deepened also, darkly, in pools of shadow. The loveliness of the garden, the plains of the river delta to the east dimming with the invasion of blue, still darkness, the rich tapestry of the roof gardens sinking also into shadow, and the hard, chiseled outlines of the buildings on City Hill motionless against a saffron sky—all struck me with beauty, but beauty brought Dorna; and she was lost, and beauty died.

Downstairs again, I lit candles and wrote letters. My brain would not fail me if I held my thoughts very still. I accepted the invitations that were not too late. There was no reason why life should not be lived as usual.

There came a sort of peace, or rather ease. I knew that it was because I would soon no longer have to live a life at cross-purposes with freedom to think and do as I wished. Though I had lost Dorna, I need no longer oppose her unless my own will bade me. I was saved from the shame of seeking to win her in ways that would thwart her wishes.

I drafted, then, my letter of resignation or rather request to be relieved, not attempting to justify myself at any length. I begged that my successor be sent as soon as possible. Though the letter would not reach Washington for quite two months, I drafted a cablegram stating the gist of it to be sent from Mobono, and this would be in the hands of my chiefs much earlier. Release might be hoped for in three months. In the meantime I would do my best as consul. Afterwards? It did not matter. There was nothing to work for, merely living to do.

Thus writing letters I looked outside myself a little, and found that I could read what Nattana had written me with the warmth of friendship due her. Her note was brief:

> I have been thinking so much of John's problems that I must write and tell him again that I wish him happiness in Islandia. I feel that we Islandians owe it to him. And I also want him to know that my sister, Hytha Nettera, has been married. Her husband, Bain, is a man of thirty-five. The Bains are dependents on the grazing farm of our neighbor Ensing, five miles west of ours. She has gone to live with the Bains. We are not very happy over her marriage. There is more which I could tell John, but will not write. He must not forget that he will always be welcome in this lonely place.

> HYTHA NATTANA

Of Bain I had never heard before. What underlay Nettera's marriage? So kind a note demanded a prompt answer even though the warmth that should be there would not come into my words. I said that I was sorry that Nattana's sister's marriage did not please them. I thanked Nattana for thinking about me, and said that I had just come from Dorn Island and had learned there that the happiness she wished me never could be mine. Having written that down and seen it in ink, I could write no more. But the news was her due, since she had heard my confidences and had been sympathetic.

I lived on as usual, saw the Americans, dined at the Periers', rode Fak on the towpath. If grief held my attention bound at times, so that, when George or others spoke to me, at first I did not answer, sooner or later I did answer. The little ticking watch of sanity functioned and a me not my real self was intelligent, saw jokes, made them, laughed, moved about, dressed and undressed, shaved, went to bed and slept. The weapons of suffering, now bruising, now hammering, now cutting with a sharp edge, never stopped the ticking of that watch, never became quite unbearable, but were always nearly so. My ability to go on, living a double life, seemed really remarkable.

On February 9th came a letter from Downs on the Exhibition Ship at Doring Town. Would I come at once if I did not want the ship to be a failure, a scandal and a disgrace to the American flag? He did not go into particulars.

Though steamers were due in the next two weeks, perhaps bringing countrymen and certainly mail, the Exhibition Ship was the first consideration. But to travel again through the Doan Pass at Fak's slow pace! It was hard enough to have to go into the West where Dorna was. I arranged to go by a different route and to ride hired horses furnished by the carriers. This was expensive and exhausting, but I wanted to move and to move fast.

There was, however, no way of escaping the familiar National Highway as far as Bostia. It was a hot, dusty, parching day, and my room in the Inn was close. I dreamed of the road, and waked, and dreamed again—of Dorna, distorted, unattractive, but still Dorna whom, of course, I loved—of this dream woman acquiescent and shameless—and I imagined savorless kisses, and her body mine—and then suddenly gone, too soon, too late.

That night, at Loran, in the upper part of Loria Province, where it was cooler, sleep was good and the dream was no longer a curse.

Late on the fourth day I rode through the woods and came to the Doring River. The town lay like a leviathan on pale glassy waters. Beyond its downstream end was the mysterious blue-green plain of the marsh. I delivered up my horse to the carriers and took the ferry.

In the blue haze that veiled the distance was Dorna. I kept my eyes from it, holding tightly to the fact of the Exhibition Ship.

The *Ace* was moored alongside a quay in Moor Town, the farthest downstream of the six islands which make up Doring Town. It was warm and windless and the boatman had to row all the way. We followed the open inner channel between the islands, resting on the glassy, oily blue water like elaborate embossed shields.

Steps had been lowered on the outer side of the *Ace* for those who came by water. Saying good-bye to the boatman, I climbed directly on board with my saddlebags, prepared for the worst, with head ringing and oppressed, and with no confidence in my ability to settle difficulties.

The low sunlight streamed upon the bare, hot deck. The reflection of a white warehouse on the shore was almost blinding. I thought no one was about until I saw a girl, rather slight, in a pale dress, walk along the deck and go down the afterhatchway with an assurance which no visitor would have had. Just before she disappeared she looked at me for a moment. Her face was pale and rather small, her hair a neutral yellow, but her eyes seemed large and strange.

I wondered who she was, and dropping my saddlebags I too went below. She had disappeared. The air in the aftercabin was close. No one was in sight.

The exhibits were placed around the walls; a reaper, a mowing machine, a sewing machine, meat slicers, coffee grinders, typewriters, and things of that nature. There were tables with books of photographs and piles of "literature," and explanations in Islandian which I had written were tacked on the walls. It looked like a fair at home —a commercial exhibit which was partly a selling and partly an advertising scheme, but on a small scale.

Voices came from one of the cabins, the door of which was ajar. I went in. The interior was messy, the air bad, with shirts and boots and papers on the floor. Jennings was lying on the bed, and he and Downs were in their shirt sleeves.

The latter showed no surprise at all, but Jennings jerked sharply.

"Hello, John!" he cried. "What are you doing here?" He lumbered to his feet and wrung my hand. He was unkempt, untidy, his face no longer had its cherubic freshness, and his eyes were watery. Nevertheless he had the easy manners of a host, and offered me a chair.

"On a little tour of inspection?" he said.

"I came to see how things were going," I answered.

Just then the door opened and the girl whom I had seen started to come in, but her eyes fell on me and she instantly withdrew. Jennings was up and off the bed in a moment.

"Mannera!" he called.

Behind his back Downs caught my eye with a look full of information.

At Jennings's call the girl came in reluctantly. I rose. She was slight, even frail, and though her skin was smooth it was so close upon the bones of her face that the veins showed blue. Beneath her large, pale, clear eyes were penciled shadows. Her mouth was small.

She was Islandian, I was sure, and so I named myself, and in a low voice she said, "Mannera," and her eyes dropped. She made a little movement and I knew she wanted to go. She was graceful, delicate, and pretty in a fragile way all her own.

"Well!" began Jennings in English. "So I don't have to introduce you. Mannera is here, John, to show the exhibits that interest women to our women visitors. We have needed a woman demonstrator all along. We men don't know what will interest the women. She does, being a woman, naturally. She's learning by herself to run a sewing machine. Aren't you, Mannera?"

She looked up at her name, but not above his chin. He told her in his now fairly fluent Islandian the gist of what he had said to me, and that I was John Lang, the American Consul, of whom she had heard him speak.

She looked at my chin with a little twist of a smile that wrinkled her cheek and made her look old. She stirred uneasily, and I knew that she wanted to get away from us. Her eyes lifted to Jennings's and begged permission. He stared into them, smiling intimately, and he swayed a little. He seemed about to kiss her, and her large, pale eyelids at once covered her eyes. There could be no doubt now who she was; but it was not pleasant to see her hide her eyes.

"It's all right, Mannera," he said, and with a darting awkwardness she was gone.

"Close the door!" Downs said sharply. "Let's have this out."

"I'm willing," Jennings answered. "Let's be seated, gentlemen, before we go into conference. It is damned hot."

His voice was not very assured.

Downs began at once.

"She oughtn't to be here," he said. "She lives on board, Mr. Lang. A sort of a cabin has been fixed up for her. She is the only woman on the boat. That in itself. . . . Personally I don't care—"

"Say it all," Jennings remarked from the bed. "Don't mind me." His voice was both jovial and bitter.

"You have guessed who she is?" Downs asked me.

"She's the girl I've been going to see in The City. You know about her, John. She is the same one."

He had tact in sparing me an answer to Downs's question.

"She is all right!" added Jennings coolly.

Downs was silent for some moments.

"I said I must speak out." He turned to Jennings.

"Go ahead, man!"

Downs began again.

"Mr. Lang, there will be a scandal. There already is one, I am sure. Our visitors have been dropping since she came. She has been here four days. Mr. Jennings must have arranged it while we passed through The City, but I did not know then. He went to meet her about ten days ago and came back with her. He was gone nearly a week. He oughtn't to be gone like that! He told me what he was going for. I'll say he has been frank enough. I did my best, but I couldn't stop him—he said he was boss here and that we needed a woman to explain the exhibits to the women. So I wrote to you. I can't make him see that he is wrecking the whole thing. It is beyond me. I'm not the boss."

"John, who is boss, you or I?"

It had never been discussed between us. The fatigue and heat of the room and the strain of my own preoccupation made my head impotent and confused. Jennings having put his question went on.

"All friend Harry says is quite correct. Poor old Harry. John, Mannera is really useful. She has caught on like a wonder. The one thing I bank on most to get these people is sewing machines. The Singer people put up a lot of money. I have got them on my conscience, because I certainly talked things up to them. I can't really sew on a sewing machine! Of course I can make it work, but she is a woman and she can *sew* with it. She does. You ought to see her! It's very different from having me explain it, to have her sitting there sewing away, making real things when women come aboard."

"It is all right to have a woman demonstrator," cried Downs, "but not a woman like her!"

"See here, Harry!" shouted Jennings, sitting up.

"Hold on!" I said in pure self-defense. "She is the girl you have been going to see in The City, isn't she?"

There was silence. Jennings lay back and laughed unexpectedly, but the laugh died away, and he turned his red face upon me.

"John," he said, "I'm sick of this. I'm sick of this job and of this country. It's one hell of a place!"

His voice, which began as though he were being humorous, was overmastered by a burst of angry feeling that changed everything. It rang in my mind and then touched and released a memory of the two Americans, who, in my early days as consul, had been so eager to get out of Islandia. I understood them then, and I half understood Jennings now, and thinking sharply of myself realized that I was miles away from them and him. The problem was deeper than one of scandal.

"Downs," I said, "let Jennings and me talk this over for a while."

He hesitated and then left us, closing the door significantly.

Jennings was lying motionless as though his outburst had exhausted him.

"I don't know which is boss—you or I," I said. "I am here because Downs sent for me to come—if I did not want this enterprise of ours to be a failure and a disgrace to the flag."

Softly and without any real feeling he cursed Downs, and in cursing him was thinking less of him than of his own situation.

"Are you bored?" I asked.

"Bored?" he cried. The word released him and he poured out his story. There wasn't much doing for him anywhere else and though he was out of the big things, still the Exhibition Ship seemed an opportunity to kill time anyway and perhaps get somewhere. But what had really tipped the scale was Mannera. Of course, he knew and I knew what she was, but it was different in Islandia—the life wasn't so hard and a girl could get out of it. She was, he said, more like a girl in the United States with several friends, who had not steadied down yet.

I reserved my judgment and waited, and at last he continued.

"When I got back to New York last July, I nearly let you down, John. I never was so glad to be anywhere in my life! God, man, I didn't realize how much this country had got on my nerves. I said to hell

with the Exhibition Ship and John Lang and his schemes, and Mannera and everything else, for New York is the only place for me. Well,
after enjoying myself for a while I decided to do as I had promised.
So I got down to work—and I did work! I passed by several good
offers. And back I came, and, damn it, the only good thing in this
country was Mannera."

Jennings raised himself on his elbow.

"I have sold goods to a lot of people in a lot of places, and I've
run up against some queer people with queer ideas, but I never ran
up against the sort of thing I've met here. There is no getting anywhere
with these Islandians. They come, they look, they smile, they seem to
listen. I'm talking about a mowing machine, let's say—how much hay
it can cut and all that. A man will speak up and say, 'No pair of horses
should pull a heavy thing like that with the pole and whiffletrees
where they are.' 'Well, they do,' I answer. 'Oh yes,' the man will
answer, 'but it is wrong. The drag comes in the wrong place.' And he
and his friends will stand around and eventually damn the whole
thing because it is not a comfortable arrangement for a horse or a
pair of horses to draw. They wouldn't condemn any horses of theirs
to that sort of a contraption, they will say. It is impossible to make
them stick to the point! That is the trouble. I was explaining how
simple it was to keep up. I showed how it was oiled. They all began
to smell the oil and look disgusted! And they are always asking about
the noise. And doesn't it break? And things like this: if the ground
is rough isn't some of the stubble left longer than the rest? They will
begin talking crops. It will get beyond me. The fact that you can't
cut a field mathematically even all over is the end of it. I argue and
argue—as you told me to—about saving time. They listen, they smile
—they are so polite! Then they smile and smile and slip away. They
won't even take any of our literature. I guess I could stand it," he
burst out, "if it wasn't that—"

He stopped abruptly.

"Wasn't what?" I asked after a moment.

He sank back on the bed.

"God knows," he said. "The damn quiet. So set in their ways. So
dead. I don't know. I don't know what it is. Stuck on themselves! I'm
sick of the place. I'm sick of it!"

Again I waited.

"Do you want to quit and go home?" I asked.

"I'm no quitter," he answered in a low voice. "I have undertaken this job."

"Suppose Mannera could not be here?" I suggested.

"Mannera?" Softly he swore, and it seemed to be at her, but he took up the thread again: "She makes life livable, or I thought she would. Since I got her here from The City she has changed. She has gone dead. She had a lot of go to her there, but here!—She hasn't laughed since she has been here. She doesn't care for anything but working that sewing machine. She doesn't give a damn for me. But she's all right. She's no quitter."

"What do you want?" I asked him, for Mannera, at first a shame and a shadow, was becoming very much part of the whole tangle.

"I've said I'm no quitter!" repeated Jennings. "I'll stick. But Harry Downs and his talk of a disgrace to the flag! I tell you I pin my hopes on sewing machines and getting the women interested. No one need know where Mannera came from. No one in this neck of the woods knows who she is. She says so herself. Whose business is it anyway what she . . ." he paused and then said, "was."

"So what you want is to have her here, and yourself to keep on with the *Ace?*"

"That is what I said I would do."

I tried to think and to decide, and could not. Therefore I made an excuse of my tension of fatigue.

"I am going to give Downs a chance to tell me his side of all this."

"For God's sake do," Jennings answered indifferently.

"I'm going on deck for air."

When I opened the door, I heard a purring sound. In a corner of the cabin was the figure of Mannera at a sewing machine. I watched her for a moment. Her back was toward me and her head was a little bent. Every motion she made was cautious and deliberate. Her feet moved slowly upon the treadles, and the purr of the machine had not the rapidity and assurance I had known at home. I could almost count the tick of each stitch.

As I went on deck I passed her and saw her profile, pale and ex-pressionless. Her eyes were wide and absorbed, but unintelligent. Her lips were set sedately. Fatigue—or something—made for a clairvoy-ant understanding of her. She had changed, Jennings had said, and laughed no more and cared for nothing but the sewing machine. She was one to whom reality was lost in crosscurrents of conflicting feelings. From her no help could be got. She, like Jennings, probably did not know what to do or what to strive for, or what she wanted.

Downs was pacing the deck. His attitude was easy to learn. Personally he did not care. He repeated it so often that I knew he was irked and offended; but either because he was a subordinate or wanted to appear a man of the world, he pretended to have a moral callousness which he did not feel. But the disgrace to the flag was a real shame to him. Pinned down as to the diminution in visitors because of Mannera's presence, he could not prove what he alleged. In truth, Downs knew so little Islandian and could communicate so unsatisfactorily with others that he was really in the dark as to what was happening, and as to how people felt. But of one thing he was sure, he said. One night he could not sleep with worry. It was late and he heard Jennings's door open. He felt it his duty to make sure, so he jumped out of bed and looked out of his cabin. He saw the girl coming from Jennings's room. She uttered a gasp and ran like a rabbit, he said. She had little on and the air reeked of the liquor they drank. Its name sounded like *sarka*.

There was one person who might help me—the Islandian captain. He had been my own choice. I told Downs that I was going to talk with him.

Banning was in the forward cabin of the ship, taking his ease in one of the sailors' bunks. He and the mate had cabins aft, but they spent most of their time with their compatriots in the forecastle as we would call it. This may be a shock to seagoing, non-Islandian traditions, but discipline did not seem to suffer in consequence. I asked him to come on deck with me, and he climbed out of the bunk with a smile. He was a tall man, over six feet, with a heavy beard, once black, and now grizzled. He wore blue shorts like a boy's knickerbockers, and jersey, and that was all. His bare legs were long and muscular.

He suggested that we sit down. The deck was hard, but its hardness was a relief.

The sheer of the boat—we were in the very bow—raised us so that we could see over the bulwarks, past the end of Moor Town and of the seawall, across the water to the marsh upon which the bluish haze of dusk was already gathering. Over in that direction was Dorn Island. I was on the edge of Dorna's domain, seeing the very marsh that she saw daily, near to her, so near that her presence seemed always about to manifest itself out of the shadows. And at the same time the problems of Jennings, Downs, and Mannera, and of this ship which was partly mine, went round and round like interweaving pin wheels in my head.

A little breeze floated in. Past that point of marsh over yonder, Dorna and I had half sailed, half drifted. . . . It was hard to have to come to the West again, for its glamour and familiarity penetrated every joint in my armor.

Banning saved me the trouble of wondering how to begin. He waved his hand toward the after part of the *Ace*.

"Troubles," he said.

"Yes," I answered, "troubles about the success of this ship and about the people there. What do the Islandian visitors think about our having Mannera on board?"

He pondered.

"They see a woman. It does not surprise them."

"An Islandian woman?"

"Have we not an Islandian crew? What is the difference? She works on that thing which sews."

"Do you know where she came from?"

"I know. The crew know. Those who visit us do not know and do not ask."

"If they knew, would they stay away or think ill of Americans?"

Banning was silent for a long time.

"Why should they think ill of you? They would say, 'Their ways are their own, ours are ours.' "

This was not wholly satisfactory.

"Would any of them stay away?"

He seemed loath to answer.

"Some women might," he said at last. "Not many."

"So we are acting in the Islandian way?"

"No—but what does it matter? You are Americans."

Was this merely politeness?

"We do not want to live in your country in a way opposed to your ways."

He brightened suddenly.

"I will tell you what I think. When those girls end the life they lead with many men, they usually go home, at least for a time. There they live like the unmarried who have nothing to do with men. Later they may marry. But there is always a time between—a time of peace. Because this is so, the crew wonder. They wonder if she is still as she was at The City. They will talk when they are ashore, and others will wonder. No one will really trouble her, I know. There is no great harm." He was silent. There was some objection in his mind, though by no means what Downs with his American prepossessions thought.

"What is wrong?" I asked.

"Nothing is wrong. Jenning"—he left off the final "s,"— "brought her here. He keeps her and she gives him what he wants. That is not wrong, since she has chosen that life." There was a doubt in his voice, not of the right or wrong of Mannera's conduct, but rather of something else. I could feel that all was clear to him, but that he was groping for the difficulty of that alien and incomprehensible American who was talking to him.

"Banning," I said, "I don't know your Islandian ways in matters of this sort. Ours are different. Do you think she ought not to be here?"

"No," he answered, "not that." He studied my face, wondering, I think, whether it might not be an insult to explain what was so obvious.

"Is his keeping her the trouble?" I asked.

"Yes!" he cried. "If a woman lives the life she has lived, she may live by it, leaving her family; but no man should keep a woman— support her in return for her body. We do not do that here."

The surprise in my face led him to utter what was so simple to him.

"When a woman marries she goes to the place of her husband's family, and becomes one of them, and is as secure as anyone there. Thus she is provided for as she should be. When a woman becomes a man's lover without marriage she still has her family. It may not be as some would like it, but he does not keep her. She is secure in her family and is provided for in that way. If a woman chooses to lead the life that Mannera chose, those who keep the house where she lives look out for her, even though she has cut loose from her family. But when a man does as Jenning has done and takes a woman from the place where she is provided for, it only leads to grief. Mannera has abandoned her family. She has no safety. She cannot be herself. She must act so as to please him, give her body whether or not she feels *ania* or *apia*, or else her bread is gone . . . She should go home," continued Banning. "If it is *ania,* let them marry later. If it is not, that is for them to settle at her home. If she wishes the old life, let her go back to The City."

He had told all that was necessary to know, but the problem was no nearer solution. Downs, however, was at least three-quarters wrong. The Exhibition Ship was in less danger than the individuals who went with it.

An odor of cooking came from the forward hatchway. It was desertion of the troubled three in the aftercabin to have supper on deck with Banning and the mate, but I could think of nothing to say to any of them. Mannera was the most to be pitied. Perhaps she had rebelled against her life in The City. Perhaps Jennings was to her something different and had opened her eyes to new worlds. But he had persuaded her to adopt a course of action that was contrary to the traditions of her country and her own instincts. No wonder she had gone dead. He was making her do what to an Islandian woman was wrong. For Downs also I was sorry. He was a puritan and a patriot at heart; he was really shocked and he saw his flag being smirched. As to Jennings, he had lost his grip and gone to pieces. He also was to be pitied.

After a while I went aft, wondering where I was to sleep. It was quite dark. In the direction of the marsh was a heavy opaque mist. The memory of the night on the *Marsh Duck* was all at once unreal.

In the cabin Mannera was at the machine, and it seemed as though she had never left it. The light was dim, and she sewed a little and then searched and peered at the machine like one half-blind.

Jennings's cabin was open. The light there was bright and he was lying in his bunk. Downs's door was closed, as though reprovingly.

It was right to speak to Mannera. I stood by her waiting for her to look up. Her feet slowly worked the treadles. I spoke her name, and her head moved a little, but she did not look at me.

She stirred unwished emotions. What a man could have of her for a little money could not be forgotten, and this realization made it hard to be at ease with her. There was an attractiveness, unpleasant and unexpected.

I spoke of her sewing. She indicated what she was doing.

"Do you enjoy sewing on this machine?"

She did not answer, and I knew not what to say.

"Do you want to stay on the *Ace* and live as you are living?" It seemed a strange question.

Her hands dropped. She was utterly still.

"What do *you* want?" I asked.

Her voice which I had not heard before except in a low spoken word was strangely hard and clear.

"What do I want?" She laughed. "To sit under a tree on a hillside in the sun and see no one, and to do nothing."

She was either joking or intensely honest.

"Do you want to go home?" I asked.

She was dumb.

"What you want, Mannera, is very important."

She bent her head.

"Can't you tell me? Don't you know?"

She lifted her hands to the machine and peered at the needle. After a moment she shook her head. Her feet moved on the treadles.

Banning's voice sounded at the companionway.

"Visitors!" he called.

Jennings swore in his cabin and called to me:

"John, you see them. I'm tight." He slammed his door.

I turned to the figures descending the hatchway. A man of about sixty, a woman of the same age, and a younger man—they seemed fresh and simple and clean. He was a farmer from near Tory. I took them about.

The sewing machine held them longest, perhaps because it was being worked. They asked Mannera questions, and I was afraid that she would not answer, the pause was so long; but eventually a reply would come as brief as possible and not illuminating. She did not really understand the sewing machine.

Finally the visitors moved to go. The older man thanked me courteously. The woman went to Mannera and thanked her. They departed.

I decided to talk to Jennings, drunk or not.

Mannera had risen and was standing looking at me. We were alone in the cabin. Her figure was slender and charming, and I knew in that unwished, unpleasant way what drew Jennings to her.

What was in her wide, strained eyes? Was it a question she wished to ask, or resentment, or shame? Or was I in the way in the cabin, and did she want to go to Jennings?

I smiled. There was nothing else to do. And her face twitched mechanically. She walked away, but looked back over her shoulder as though wondering what I was doing. Then she disappeared behind a curtain that I had not noticed before between two machines. Was that the "sort of cabin" they had fixed up for her?

Jennings was not really drunk. I told him the substance of what I had learned from Banning. And in the end I said that the scandal and disgrace which so disturbed Downs did not bother me half so much as the problem of Mannera herself; and I made it as clear as I could that it seemed to me wrong for him to bring her here.

"The reason she has gone dead, as you say, is probably because you have put her in a position which she feels is all wrong to her as an Islandian."

"The hell you say!" That was Jennings's answer. He sat up to make it, and then he lay down again.

"Let's talk it over tomorrow," he added later. "I'm drunk and you are tired, John. You look it, anyway. What does that damned captain know?"

The morning seemed a better time to go on.

"Where am I to sleep?" I asked.

"With Harry—the chaste Harry."

Downs was expecting me. There were two berths in his cabin, and he had made up the second one for me. I went to bed at once, but not to sleep, for he had to tell me his side again and then again. He added nothing new. He was a patriot and a puritan. After that he talked about himself until I was nearly asleep with the effort to keep awake. He unfolded his whole life, his struggles, his marriage, how fine his wife was, his poverty, his enemies . . . He was lonely and wanted someone to talk to. It was only kind to listen and to say a word now and then. But I could think of nothing but the miserable tangle Jennings was in, and the pitifulness of Mannera; and under it all was my own private misery, aching all the time with a grinding painfulness.

We had talked so late that we overslept. When we had dressed and were ready for breakfast, Jennings's door was still closed. Downs was unwilling to disturb him, saying that he often was late, sleeping off a "jag"; but Downs was surprised that Mannera had not appeared, for usually she was up early. He said he had breakfasted with her once or twice before Jennings was up. He was in a kindly mood on this morning and obviously wanted to say a good word for her, but could not, lest it compromise him in his own eyes or mine.

"She is the real problem," I said. "She is pathetic and likable."

"Let's call her," he suggested after some thought.

We called, and the curtains that hung before her shelter hung as silently as ever. We called again.

"Is she with Jennings?" he asked.

It seemed possible and that both were still asleep. We decided to leave them alone.

Later, however, we began to wonder about their silence, and I went to Mannera's shelter, called her several times, and, getting no answer, parted the curtains. Within the enclosure there was only room for a bunk and a chair. Jennings and Downs had given her miserable quarters in which to live. She was not there, the bunk was made, and all was neat . . . Too neat! There was no sign of any things that might be hers.

We knocked on Jennings's door, but no answer came. He too was gone. On his table, however, was a note addressed to me.

Dear John,

I am going to quit after all. Mannera and I have talked it over. We will be gone before you are up. There is a steamer on the 18th and we are going to make it. I am anyway. I have failed in this job. I am going home. Islandia is hell to me. You are sole boss now.

R.S.J.

They had been gone at least four or five hours. It was possible for them to have taken an early ferry, to have obtained horses, and now to be so far on the road that they could not be overtaken. The impulse was to pursue, not because Jennings had gone, but for Mannera's sake. Yet what could we do? There was a crying need for something, but what? To persuade Mannera not to go to the United States with Jennings? But it was not sure that she would go.

Downs and I talked and vacillated. He was dismayed by the responsibilities which Jennings's flight put upon him. He also needed my attention and time. We gave up the thought of pursuit and set ourselves to planning how best to continue the enterprise of the Exhibition Ship. Someone who spoke English and Islandian was needed to act as Downs's assistant. The demands of the consulate, with ships and mail arriving, as well as the task of finding such a person, made it desirable that I return to The City next day.

We had visitors in the morning and afternoon. Downs and I showed them about, and he made an effort to talk to them, aware that now, as chief upon the *Ace,* he must learn their language. I felt like a shopkeeper—curiosity as to who would next come in, tedium at saying the same thing over and over, and speculation afterwards upon the profit made. We talked a great deal as to whether our visitors had been interested or excited.

It was midafternoon and warm in the cabin. A group had just departed and we were trying to decide whether their polite manners veiled a real interest in what we had to show or the opposite. The task of being showman was tiring, and I wished the day were over.

There were footsteps on the deck above us—of a party. More visitors!

Sandaled feet appeared upon the topmost of the companionway steps—a girl's feet—and then bare ankles and strong bare legs; and in the way they stepped they were individual, familiar, insolent—and then a green skirt. Behind them came a slimmer pair of sandaled feet and longer, slighter legs, more white, less golden-brown, and a lavender skirt. After these were a man's shoes and a man's legs in gray stockings, in their way as individual. Before their heads appeared I knew them all.

Dorna, Stellina, and Lord Dorn descended into the cabin of the *Ace.* I went to meet them, my eyes upon his. Their faces lighted with friendly smiles. There were greetings and laughter—Dorna's voice. I thanked them for coming, pleased that they should visit this ship that was largely mine, when it was a symbol of what they were fighting. They expressed surprise at finding me aboard. My head was dizzy, my throat choking. They were unreal like painted dolls—very near, then far off—and their voices were loud, then sounding from a distance. I was faint and dizzy, dizzy. Dorna glowed like fire, but my eyes must not ignore her. They found hers and she smiled quickly. The smile said nothing, but her eyes were caught, and in a flash all I knew and all she knew went back and forth between us. Lord Dorn was speaking. Her eyes released mine. They were glad, he said, very glad that I was here. Would I not come back with them to the palace, dine with them, stay the night with them? Something in me was crying to me not to yield, not to go. . . .

Downs, standing near, was a way of escape. I had said my thanks, only that. My forehead was cold. I was naming him to them. I heard them naming themselves. Dorna's voice sounded again, saying "Dorna." I told them who he was, smiling, and explained to him who Lord Dorn was, and that Dorna was his niece, and Stellina, her friend, and daughter of Lord Stellin of Camia. These were facts he would like to know. He rose to the occasion. Stumblingly he said in Islandian, that Lord Calwin had visited the *Ace* at The City, and Lord Fain at Reeves. Dorna was a flame growing in the edges of my eyes, impossible to face again, if I were to carry on, for she stopped my heart and my breath. But Stellina—there were Stellina's eyes. They met mine. Her eyes were as clear as pure water, blue with an undertone of violet. She was real for a moment, not a doll, with her small delicate face and her small, sweet, firm lips. My head went round. Dorna's face, not looked at, was a golden-orange flame.

Did they wish me to show them our exhibits? The watch of sanity had gallantly ticked again and made me say the right thing. It was what they had come for. I moved and they followed. I explained, talking and talking, blood burning in my face, even being humorous, with a pulsing excitement that must be repressed. Dorna was near me. She was near. She was at my side. She was listening, moving, breathing. I saw corners of her as I explained it all—the flutter of her green skirt, her feet in her sandals, so open as to show the divisions between her toes, her dangling half-closed hand; and, when she looked at something and there was no danger of meeting her eyes, I caught the flushed smooth curve of her cheek, the slumbering warm beauty of her profile, her long dark lashes. Each aspect of her thus seen struck like a blow and sent over me a wave of pain and fire. She was a burning flame, and all our exhibits glowed in the light of her and became rich and interesting.

There was the sewing machine! I saw it suddenly and it was magical. I led them to it, wishing to say that it was a truly wonderful thing. Downs sat down to work it. He, too, was excited. We all watched him sew two pieces of cloth together, turning it over to make a proper seam. Dorna was close to me. He handed the cloth to her, and she examined the stitches. Her hands, holding it uplifted, were warm with an inner fire—hands once given to me, and once again twisting out of mine. I wanted her hands, I wanted everything, all of her.

Downs said she could keep the cloth.

Stellina must have her piece to carry away as an example of the work of an American machine. I spoke to Downs.

She smiled at me. Her clear eyes saw deep, and she was so simple and fearless within that her eyes let one see as deeply. Because she had kissed me there was a tie uniting us, and always would be, but one that exacted nothing. Her eyes seemed to ask a question, and a shadow passed.

Downs handed her the second piece of cloth and she gave to him her complete lovely smile and thanked him in shy English, perhaps the only words she knew.

Lord Dorn wished to have the mowing machine explained. This was a subject studied at Uncle Joseph's. There was much to say, but I could not plead for mowing machines nor argue, but only say what they accomplished in the United States; adding that the oil smelled, that they made a noise, that they did not cut as evenly or closely as a well-handled scythe, that the problem of repairs in Islandia presented difficulties, and the arrangement for its traction by horses had been criticized.

I was talking to hold Dorna on the *Ace*. Our exhibits were nearly exhausted. Why not return with them, dine with them? Then I would see her alone. Her hands were tormenting. She seemed to flaunt them. And of her strong, soft, full lips I had dreamed. I would say all that was unsaid, all I had thought of, and that I loved her.

It must never be said. I wanted her to go.

Lord Dorn was repeating his invitation, and must be faced. Dorna was hanging back, leaving it to me and giving me no help. I felt myself yielding, too weak to think of excuses. He asked to have Downs come also, and on this little thing I seized, and was talking, talking, explaining that there was another man who had this very day deserted us, that I was leaving early next day, and had much to arrange with Downs, and furthermore, if visitors came. . . .

Would I not come for dinner then, and return to the *Ace?* There seemed to be no answer. Then Stellina moved. It seemed . . . I do not know . . . Words of excuse came back again. He did not over-press his invitation. Suddenly my excuse was accepted and they moved to go, all three. My chance was gone, but I could accompany them to the gangplank as near to Dorna as might be. I moved with them, straining to lengthen seconds, to draw into myself her nearness. Across the cabin, up the companionway stairs, across the deck we went, and the seconds dwindled away. At the gangplank I stopped. Words were being said, but it was over. She moved from my side and it was a breaking.

Only she turned to look back. The others went on. Her dark eyes were in mine for a second. I thanked her in my heart for not smiling.

Downs was rubbing his chin. They had vanished behind the white warehouse.

"Now those are nice women," he said. "They are evidently friends of yours." He pondered for some time upon that fact, and then added, "Well, they stayed a long time, didn't they?"

It had passed in a breath. I held myself as rigid as iron.

In the hot sun, fields and groves and houses and walls and fields and groves and houses and walls slowly turned as I passed. These were the plains of Lower Doring on the road to the Doan Pass. Why avoid the shortest way to The City?

It was despicable to go to pieces as Jennings had done. He was false to himself, false to his job, unfair to Mannera. Islandia was too much for him. It must not be for me. Therefore to think about the consulate was the proper thing, and of the Exhibition Ship, and of finding the man who could talk English and Islandian. . . Grief walled the mind with glass which nothing even scratched. . . I could not think the proper thoughts now.

The Doan Pass. . . Forested slopes and diminished trees far up, cutting a blue sky. . . Beauty was there, but it was held away across an abyss. The Doan Pass was merely a way through mountains, and the Inn a place to change horses and go on.

At night the tired mind loses its hold and love is a torrent of bitter waters closing over the head of the lover. The wind sighed in the trees and said "never," and "never" was the only reality. . . The road was plain at night, the horse sure-footed, and a day was gained, and sleep did not have to be wooed in a bed into which one feared to go. The body was too tired for loving and could only hold to the thought of "never." "Never" was like the stars overhead, as infinite and as deep as the dark spaces between them.

There was no act in life however little and no act however great that was not related to Dorna. She blocked every road except the road to her, and that road she had closed also. No pleasure could steal upon me without being blighted, because she would not wish to share it. She put a clear vision in my eyes and then blinded them; she put desire in my body which she alone could satisfy and gave herself to another. And all this she did because she was herself and existed. Pallor stole down from the sky upon the slopes of the mountains. The angry roaring of the Cannan River still came up from darkness.

It would be despicable to break, despicable to break. The feet of my horse said it over and over.

Faint and pale were the plains of Inerria.

Light struck the upper mountain slopes with cold fire. The whole world grew warm and bright as the sun lifted.

A night without sleep for Dorna. . . .

19

The Visit of Dorn

A PAIR OF HANDS, my own, lay limp and inert upon the table. If I turned my head the delta lands would be visible through the window. In the sunlight flooding the out-of-doors world was an imminent change, perceptible even in the suffused daylight of my long room. This expectancy in the air placed me in time, and the aspect of the stone walls with their hangings, in space. A man named George had gone for the day; a woman named Lona would soon bring something called supper. A memory existed: for two days, under the stimulus of George, who assumed that work would go on as usual, a mechanical being had followed habitual paths and had done work with human intelligence.

On winter nights, when darkness is coming, the cold, moment by moment, increases, and the world steadily becomes more rigid and still. Despair was the same, growing imperceptibly. There would come a time when only the fact of existence existed.

There were steps on the stair. Ears heard them, but they were a sound from another world and were no concern of the frozen existence that was myself. But a man turns to face those who at unexpected moments are heard approaching from behind. Reason said that the tall figure with sunburned face and tired, but brilliant dark eyes, carrying a saddlebag and coming forward, was a friend—was Dorn. It also said that men do not usually sit at a desk doing nothing. Reason was aware that such idleness lays one open to curious questions and, to what is worse—sympathy.

My heart was beating, and therefore I knew that his sudden coming was a shock, and to feel so little of the old warmth and gladness—to feel nothing at all—brought a vague regret.

He spoke first. His eyes glanced quickly and inquiringly into mine, but he asked no questions and showed no surprise. After saying that I was glad to see him, I smiled and took him to his room.

"Lona saw me coming," he remarked, "and she knows I am staying to supper." It was always a relief not to have to speak to strangers—and Lona was become a stranger.

As soon as he had put down his things, without looking at me, he said in English: "Five days ago I came home to the Island. I had not seen my sister for over a month."

At the mention of Dorna my blood stopped and then ran swiftly. She was real again. A fire burned in the cold deadness and pain came once more. Dorn's voice was continuing from a greater distance: "She said to me that after I left the Island you told her that you loved her and asked her to marry you. She told me what her answer had been. I don't know whether you want me or need me, but I left next morning and came as quickly as I could."

What he had done was clear. I saw it as an act of friendship that somehow I must recognize. He stood, looking out of his window. Not to want and not to need him seemed unkind and treacherous.

"Don't force yourself," he said. "Don't pretend to be glad if you are not. But we in Islandia believe in a friend's making himself manifest, even though he says nothing. So friends have a way of suddenly appearing. I have appeared."

"I am glad you have come," I said, and quite coolly I decided to tell him my side of everything.

We went up to the garden. The mountains were not visible, for the plains of the delta melted into a pale-blue haze. That far flat view was again lovely to see, vibrating with a beauty given to it by Dorn, because of his kinship and nearness to Dorna; but the surge of feeling in my heart lifted me only for a moment and then flung me against the high stone walls that enclosed me.

"Let's sit down," I said, turning my face away. We sat on one of the benches, and at once I began my story.

"I shall tell you everything," I said.

"I should be glad to hear," he answered.

It was strange to be speaking, strange to find myself steadily shaping in words what I had felt. The form which it took was somehow new, and it became during the telling less unbearable. I gave Dorn the history of my love for Dorna from the beginning—how she had warned me at the very start not to love her; and how I had

gone away from Dorn Island at the end of my first visit and after
our two days' sail in the marsh in love with her and yet not really
aware of it; and how in June at the winter meeting of the council, I
saw her again and knew that I did love her. I told him how kind she
had always been, how fair, and how straight, and of her telling me
of the problem that left her free and yet barred me from her; of my
visit in the spring, and of my effort not to bother her with my love.
I said that I thought that she must have guessed it and that she seemed
to like me a good deal, but that, of course, she had shown no sign of
loving me. Then I described my coming in January, now six long
weeks ago, and said it was really a visit to find out how her problem
had been settled. Then her beauty became too vivid to permit any
more words.

"Will she be happy?" I cried. All sense of time and place had
ceased.

He answered me at once, slowly and carefully.

"I can only guess, knowing my sister quite well, but not so well
lately as I used to know her. In all this matter of her engagement
she has acted by herself, consulting no one. I think that she and Tor
understand each other very well, and that he and she will work har-
moniously together. My sister wants more of life than merely to be
the wife of a man she loves. Tor, as a man, is, I think, the only man
the mother of whose children she has ever had any wish to be. The
wish to have work to do and the wish—or willingness, perhaps—to
be the mother of his children are so strong that they are to her enough.
She will have and be what she wants to have and be most strongly.
Perhaps that is—'happiness.' "

He paused, and I saw that only an unusual combination of circumstances would ever have given to Dorna a complete fulfillment.

"Do you mind," he continued, "my telling you what I think
about you and my sister?"

"Oh, no!"

"Perhaps you could have given her something that he could not.
Of course, if she had loved you, I would have been glad in many
ways. She likes you very much and she always will—and not just
as a friend, I think. To women there is a special class of men who are
more than friends—men whom they have seen as possible lovers if
their feelings deepen a little more. They don't really love those men,
for their feelings have not in fact taken that necessary further step.

My sister, I know, dreaded you, and it may be that she feared that in spite of herself she would move nearer. But she knew, I think, that with you certain sides of her nature would never be satisfied. . . But I am only guessing. She has left me in the dark. I don't think she wanted to tell me what had happened, but did so for your sake."

Nothing that he said sounded strange or was really new. His doubting surmise as to his sister's feeling for me had for a moment the tang of bitter-sweet; but the walls that shut me from feeling and enjoyment and blocked all paths worth following encircled me again. A prison can be comfortable, but in mine there dwelt with me a torturer—Dorna's own unhappiness, which her brother had made me see as incurable.

"The fact that there are sides of her nature which you could not satisfy," he continued slowly, "is not much comfort to you now, but it means this, John: there is a certain rightness in her refusal of you."

It was as though he had cut me sharply like a surgeon.

"And that rightness is a reality that may help you to go on. It isn't as though two persons, each feeling perfectly matched to the other, were separated. There is some excuse for feeling that life is futile in that case."

This was beyond bearing. The very fact that I could not satisfy Dorna was futility itself.

"For her, yes!" I cried. "I can see that I am not the right man."

"Suppose she would have you, but you knew that she did not love you and that your ability to satisfy her was doubtful, would you take her? Oh, don't answer me! Put as a principle in words, there is only one answer and that is 'no'! But the reality is different. The hope that she will love you and that you may satisfy her is very strong. But it seems to me wrong for any man to take a woman not sure of her love. His desires give too much color to his hope for it to be reasonable and honest."

Was he telling me that I had done wrong to seek to marry his sister? He must have seen me wince.

"You did right," he said, "to tell her that you loved her and wanted to marry her. She needed that telling, perhaps, to know her own heart. It helps a woman to be told fully what a man feels. And it equally helps a man to know what she feels."

"She told me what she felt very clearly," I said.

"She would do her best." He paused a moment.

"You and I," he continued, "would both be happier if we knew that she was going ahead with complete assurance and without any reserves or doubts. We can't have that, however, but we do know that Dorna is brave and strong. That is something worth while."

I nodded.

"I'm trying to tell you what you still have, as I see it. There is rightness in the fact that you and she are not embarking together on a dangerous sea in a boat in which there are not enough provisions. You haven't forced her to take such a voyage. Does it matter that she saw it more clearly than you?"

"It hurts my pride that I am not fit!" I cried.

"I don't blame you. But don't you love her more for her clear-sightedness? Don't you love her for her adventurousness, for the attempt she is making to grow and to fulfill her nature? You have loved someone worth loving. That is a great thing! You have not cheapened yourself. It takes two who are in accord to make a union good. It is no fault of yours that she does not feel as you do. Your half is good in itself."

"What good is it?"

"What good is love unsatisfied? Don't you feel that the love is good? Oh, you do! What is painful is its frustration. The love is always good—and it is better still if the one you love is worth loving. . . Do you mind my talking to you in this way?"

"Of course I don't!"

"I was afraid this was coming, and I have thought about it a great deal. I can't make you think one thing or another, but my ideas brushing upon yours may quicken them into growth. That is all a friend can do."

He moved me deeply. What I thought dead was alive and painful again.

"Tell me all you are thinking," I said.

"You don't want to die, do you?"

"No—but sometimes I want to be dead and to escape."

"Isn't that because you are out of tune with the life you are compelled to lead?"

"Yes," I answered, "I know I am." But I had not previously thought of it in quite this way.

"There is a fable about a little gray wolf. He hunted by night and caught enough for his needs, and by day he hid himself and slept. He had a hunger that recurred and recurred, and he felt dimly that if once he could make a great killing and gorge himself he would be satisfied forever. Once in the daytime there was a forest fire, and it sent all the animals he fed upon flying through the woods. He woke and fled with them in the strange daylight. And then it occurred to him that now was his chance to make the great killing. . . The moral is not that in consequence the fire caught and killed him. That would be the moral if your European fabulists had written this one. But no European did write it. No, this wolf made his great killing and gorged himself and slept a happy sleep of repleteness and great satisfaction. When he woke he decided that he had made a great discovery. He would hereafter hunt by day! This he did. But he could not sleep at night. He lay wakeful, feeling strange familiar promptings. Thus he wore himself out and in the end a little antelope killed him in his weakness. He was a night hunter and a day sleeper by nature. He put himself out of tune with the life he was born to lead and that was the end of him!"

I listened as best I could. There was an elusive moral that the mind did not make precise. Instead it wandered. I pictured again the little gray wolf that I had seen with Stellina, and remembered the curious pain of that visit, and wished suddenly that I had walked in the snow with Dorna and had seen the wolf with her. Beauty leaped up complete and wonderful—and was shattered on the enclosing walls.

"Haven't you done a little as the wolf did?" he was saying. "We have been unkind to you. We have tempted you to hunt in a way that is not natural to you. It is no question of better or worse, but you aren't one of us. Yet you are very near to it. There are feelings that are common to all men, of course. There is friendship and there is love. You can be friends with us, and you can love and be loved by us. But when it comes to marriage you and we think differently, and thoughts—ideas—play a large part in marriage."

There was the old torture in this. Islandia again turned upon me its alien, stony face. In my heart I rebelled.

"I find you very strange beings," I answered. "I seem to understand you and to be one with you, and then suddenly I come upon something utterly unfamiliar which I can't understand. It is as though all at once you were another thing, another animal, not really human."

"We are all human," he said. "If we were simply animals we

none of us would feel any difference." He paused, considering what
he had said. "But perhaps habits of thought do differentiate humans
into species as markedly as panthers are differentiated from, say,
leopards."

"Or horses from donkeys!"

Then we both laughed, and laughter eased the tension. Those
bright playthings—words and ideas—had suddenly become amusing.

"I didn't tell you the fable to show you that horses don't belong
in the donkey's pasture," he said.

Each knew what the other was thinking—that asses beget mules
out of mares and that mules are sterile.

"I want to tell you Stanning's fable called 'The Perfect Life.' Do
you know it?"

"No."

"In a ravine there was a stagnant pool and a rock on which the
sun shone all day long. The pool bred many fat and sluggish flies.
The place was isolated and protected. Here dwelt lizards, safe from
their enemies, with all they wished of flies to eat. There were no
dangers and no pinch of hunger. They were fat and sleek. Most of
the time they slept a hot sound sleep in the brilliant sunlight. Now
and then a male stirred and a female became submissive. There were
always plenty of each for the other. They were all alike to each other,
all males the same, all females the same, and they had no yearnings
for differences. The males slept again or fed a little. The females as
sleepily laid their eggs which the sun hatched, and slept or fed a
little. All was a perfect tunefulness. Everyone had everything that
he or she wanted. They all died in their sleep, so death was unknown.
Stagnation, food in plenty, sex in plenty, and no fears—that was the
Perfect Life to the lizards. One day, however, the sun was perhaps
hotter than usual. Everything was exceptionally perfect, and a lizard
was hatched with a special desire for the exceptionally perfect—a
differentiating lizard, with the concomitant of special desires—ideas.
That was the end of the perfect lizard life. . . The fable ends at
this point."

Another elusive Islandian fable and moral! The little warmth
of amusement and pleasure was dying. Dorn's words touched something deep in me that was sensitive and full of dismay and pain.

"These lizards," said Dorn, "were wholly in tune with their environment, which included each other, of course. Men crave that very

tunefulness at times and at times some of them have it. We are animal enough to need it and to want it and to be better for knowing it and having it. But men are able to endure such a pause of tunefulness for only a short period. They are not really in tune with their environment, and so with themselves, unless they feel out of tune with it some of the time."

He laughed softly at his paradox. But, oh, how did all this concern me?

"It is a question of balance with me," he added. "Perhaps that is true of animals also, but they have minds less consciously striving. But with men it is as foolish to strive for continual animal tunefulness as it is to deny the excellence of it because one cannot have it all the time—and therefore to despair."

Thus subtly—and perhaps unawares—he struck me a vicious blow; but I knew, I knew in my heart, that my love for Dorna was not a desire for "animal tunefulness."

"Do you despair because you are out of tune?" he asked, startling me, but gave me no time to answer. "Despair as a phase in one's moods can't be helped, but if one really continually despairs the only logic is to die. When a person wants to live, it is absurd to nurse despair."

These were commonplaces, but they hurt. Was he thinking that I deliberately nursed my grief?

"We are put in a world of nature, of wind and sun, rain, clouds, growing trees and plants, of other animals and of other human beings. We are out of tune if we alter our natural environment too much. At least so we think here, though you foreigners often don't think that it matters or don't think at all. In this natural world we have natural desires—hunger, love, exertion of our powers in our minds and in our muscles. If the natural satisfaction of those desires is in any way checked we are out of tune. But we have simplified our problems greatly. We have a mode of life that gives us satisfaction of hunger and as full an opportunity as we wish to exert our minds and our muscles. You foreigners have built up for yourselves an environment that makes the satisfaction of these desires less easy, for its complexity makes the desires complex, and its diversity makes the desires of the mind confused and obscure. John, it is so hard for you—harder for you than for us. No Islandian young man is handicapped by 'having his way to make,' as you say, when he is in love

411

and wants to marry. He has his place where he can bring his wife, whether he be *tana* or *deneri*. For a woman, also, the choice is between men, not as it is so often with you a choice between two social and material offerings with which the men are clothed and altered, and which lessen their intrinsic importance as men. For you there is a confusion which it is hard for us to understand. But I think I know. I have lived in your country. I have seen men and women overweight scales fitted only to weigh love with all sorts of other weights and considerations. . . This is cold comfort, but give me a chance."

He paused. I felt his smile, but did not look at him. The evening air had moved and dark was beginning.

"Do I hurt you?" he asked gently.

"You couldn't hurt me."

"Yes, I could, but only by being untrue. . . Never mind that! The way that aids a person in an affair like this is hard to find. I want to help you to find it. We have our methods. Nature is nearer to us than it is to you foreigners because of our simpler environment. We have habituated ourselves from childhood to losing consciousness of ourselves and to sinking into the depths of natural things—air, sun, rain, our growing crops, our trees in the wind and rain, our friendships, our unelaborated arts, and each other as beings not apart from nature. We know what to do when we lose what is most dear to us. . . Oh, don't let me go on if it hurts you, but there may be something here and in our ways for you!"

Was there anything in a land the very air of which breathed of Dorna? Was there anything in my own country so empty of her? . . . I closed my eyes. To go home and to do and to be—what? It seemed then that I had drunk so deeply of the drug of Islandia that in it was the only cure or death. Under thoughts this feeling moved. Reason, however, spoke in my words.

"I may have to go home," I said. "Maybe a complete change is what I need most."

"I don't know," he mused. "I don't really know. . . There would be in the United States a greater battery of sensations and ideas upon you. You would be more likely to forget, but if you can't forget it is not the better place. Your grief will remain in your being a thing apart. You cannot put the force of it into the life you lead. It might work havoc with your life. . . I don't know if I am clear to you. But anyway, you don't have to go for a year at least. There are ways to be found to keep you here."

He was silent, and I thought suddenly of Jennings. He had caught the steamer which he had mentioned in his note to me. He had not taken Mannera with him. In a letter which I had found upon my return he said that at the last minute she decided not to come with him.

"I care more for her than I have ever cared for any woman," he wrote. "I am going to miss her like hell. I know I am a damn' quitter, but I am going home, and I will be all right there and get over my troubles."

Dorn was speaking again, more about the little gray wolf, and it was hard to hear and to follow him.

"In spite of Darwin," he was saying, "you Europeans haven't yet become accustomed to thinking of yourselves as animals, and your philosophy has not yet shown much consciousness of the fact that this is what we all are. But it has never occurred to us here that we are anything else. We are more like the little gray wolf—before the forest fire. If he had lost a pretty female gray wolf that he wanted, it did not become a disease in his brain, I am sure. He yearned and longed for her sleek gray sides. These were at the moment the perfection of tunefulness. Perhaps in his little brain for a long time there was a knot of agony at the loss of her, but he hunted *at night* moved by the old instincts, true to himself, and he found therein the familiar, good, comforting rewards. How much harder for him to adjust himself to his loss if he had turned to hunting by day and all was subtly false! It is quite possible that nothing ever again came to him equal to that lost perfection, but he continued to live the natural life of little gray wolves. An Islandian in your situation would go on with his life. He would not be uprooted as you are, for he would have a place of his own, an environment natural to him for genera-tions—his *alia*."

His voice deepened and it moved me.

"I want to give you the nearest thing to that which is possible for you," he said. But what was there at all comparable to an *alia*?

"I have no farm to go to," I said. How far away from Islandians and their ways of thought was I, an American! "And I think that if I had a home of my own it would be the last place to which I would want to go!"

"Isn't that because you can see it only as the place to which you

413

had planned to take the lost one? Forgive me! But think of what our farms are to us. They are not retreats from the world. They are the greater part of our world. Nor are they nests built specially for one person—one little unit of a man and woman and their children. They are the world of a family past, present, and to come, a growing place, many years old, the concern of all of us. No personal loss can spoil such a place for a man or for a woman."

"I have no such farm," I said. "But I see what you mean."

"You have a much harder problem in lessening the disharmony in your present life. You have no natural life to which you can turn. What are you going to do?"

It was a cruel question.

"I don't know!"

"You have a great, good longing that is unsatisfied. You don't want to die."

Very gently he touched my knee. I turned to him, torn two ways, despairing because of the relief which Islandians had but which I had not, deeply moved by his touch. I saw clear, steady, brown eyes, lighter than they really were because of his ruddy face—eyes with the whitest of whites looking into mine with a hot bright glare. They stared at me from another world, almost from another kind of creature. Then for a moment they had the look of Dorna's eyes—her look of independence and pride. There was no contact between us, and I looked away, longing for her eyes which his resembled and caricatured.

He spoke with sudden strong emotion, his hand tight upon my knee.

"I know what I am saying to you," he cried. "Let life come to you. Don't shrink from it however much it hurts. Don't withdraw. Don't be afraid of what reminds you of my sister."

Words! words! What was the use of them? I wanted peace and silence.

"I know what you mean," I said. "You are right, of course."

"Don't pity yourself. You are not to be pitied."

"I don't pity myself!"

"Be glad you feel so strongly. Don't be sorry!"

"I'm not sorry!" I cried, really angry.

"Don't feel any bitterness, for that is a form of self-pity."

"I feel no bitterness! Of course not. She never led me to expect anything."

But I was bitter for a moment, remembering what she had done, and that she had condemned herself as a flirt.

"Keep your love strong and good!" he said.

"It is!" I cried; but to keep it alive meant endless suffering.

"You can't ever really forget her. You don't wish to do so. Your love is no *apia*. The flames of one's *apias* die down and can be forgotten, but not the steady glow of one's *anias*. Hold to it, John!"

What he said was exalting, but the sudden increase in emotion merely accentuated the loss.

"I must not hold to it!"

"You can never lose it! Don't think that I am advising you to cherish vain hopes. You have seen in my sister the woman through whom the life that is in you can gladly go on in new lives that would be yours and hers combined."

My cheeks burned. I had had no such definite thought, and I was ashamed because I had not.

"Don't hope, but don't vainly try to forget. Don't check any emotion that rises from depths within you, like water rising in a spring."

He rose.

"Of course, it is foolish to tell you not to hope," he said. "Hope comes as naturally as the wind blows. It may die for a time as the wind dies, but like the wind it rises again."

It was growing dark. The trees and fields and isolated houses in the flat plain were enfolding themselves with shadows as with cloaks for the night, and all were sinking down together. There was the strange fact of sudden stars.

"I have definite things in mind for you," he said. . . .

Lona had come softly, her face a moon in the dusk, and she told us that supper was ready. We went down to the bright candles and sparkling china and white linen. We sat with darkness behind us. Dorn stood dimly for hope, a new hope, not that which would rise and die and rise again like the wind.

The definite things that Dorn had in mind were three—first, that having no farm of my own I should go to the farm of someone else and become a member of the household and live and work there indefinitely; second, that he and I should travel together when the

415

chance came; third, that when relieved of work at the consulate I should watch and report the political struggle, expressing my own views, and publish my writings in some newspaper or magazine in the United States. These suggestions were concrete, and if adopted would occupy body and mind. They seemed futile, but worth trying, because I was committed to staying alive. Therefore I put myself in his hands and agreed to do as he said, feeling toward him a little as one feels toward a doctor who is none too confident himself but who prescribes a course of treatment that may do good and can do no harm. My only doubt was in remaining in Islandia. When my successor arrived why not go home? The answer was a shudder. There was nothing there.

Dorn could stay with me overnight and no longer, but he was to return in two weeks; and then we would ride to the Fains' and I would make my home with them, with journeys to The City whenever affairs at the consulate or politics demanded my presence. There was no real need that I·be continuously there. The fact that I had been criticized for my absences and directed to remain made no difference. Having asked to be relieved, I would do my job according to my own standards as to what was sufficient.

With a goal to approach—the goal of going somewhere else—even though it were a futile one, my life was suddenly easier. The rails were laid down and upon them I mechanically moved. There was much to do in the two weeks of waiting. For Downs I found a retired soldier who knew some English and was intelligent enough to make up for his lacks. Consular business was put as nearly in perfect order as possible, and I did all I could in return for following my own standards and not those of Washington. George moved into the house on The City's wall. If he wanted me to return I could be with him again on the third day after his message started, which was a short time as business was transacted in Islandia.

Two weeks later, on the seventh, Dorn arrived, and next morning he and I set out for the Fains', the University at Reeves to be our night's stopping place. A journey in company is very different from a journey alone. A year ago he and I had followed the same road upon the same horses, but there was no memory of what had happened then—merely knowledge of the experiences of another man whose life was separated sharply from my own.

It was hot and we took our time, and arrived at our destination dusty with parched skins and a great thirst. During the journey it was evident that Dorn had something on his mind. I knew him well enough to know this much and not so well as to guess its nature. He was both cheerful and distraught. But what did it matter?

At the University we were assigned rooms in the graduate quarters on the farther side of the enclosure. We reached them through the same intricacy of open courts and roofed cloisters. There was the same stillness and the same submergence of the students in the place. From our windows was the same grainfield, yellow and ready for cutting. As before, there was nothing between the complex but quiet place of learning, thought, and architectural beauty and the open farm lands under the sky. Each element in Islandian civilization was strictly itself. There was no intermediate zone, just as there were no suburbs around The City or the towns. The City, the University, the towns on the one hand and the farms on the other, each held itself true to type. They were separate, but they adjoined.

Dorn asked me what I wanted to do in such a way as to indicate his own preferences clearly. This was just what I wanted. We would not dine in the great hall with the students and professors, nor would we drop down upon the Gilmours. We would take a swim and later dine in our own rooms at dusk. It was his mood, as it was mine, to keep apart from others.

We took off all but our underclothes, and with clean ones to put on after the swim and with towels set off for the bathing place. It was still a hot sunny summer day when we passed out of the River Gate and at once entered the woods that cover the slope down to the river. When we returned, however, after a lazy swim all by ourselves, twilight was beginning and a gentle breeze was blowing.

Our meal was begun in waning daylight. We were still a little too sunbaked and tired to be really hungry. The swim had almost quenched our thirst and we were just in the condition to respond to and to enjoy the light dry wine that Dorn had ordered.

There was something on his mind. Of this I had no doubt, watching his ruddy, open-air face as he lighted the candles in the middle of supper. The light by which we had previously seen suddenly became darkness, all but the square of the open window. His eyes were bright with sparkling points from the candles. He refilled my glass and then his own, which he raised.

"Why not change our moods?" Saying this he drank.

417

Why not indeed? My mood was a somber one, but might it not, instead, be intensified and hard to bear?

"Will it change my mood?" I asked.

"Try it and find out."

So I drank also.

"There was a man at Harvard," he continued. "He did not drink, and his reason was not the danger of becoming a drunkard, nor the fear of setting a bad example to the weak-minded, nor the fear of injuring his health, nor the fear of going too far and making a fool of himself. It was because he felt it wrong to do anything that would change his moods. He thought it wrong to do anything that would change what he naturally felt to something else."

"Don't you agree to that?" I asked, for some such reason had always weighed strongly with me.

"I think he was a fool," said Dorn. "We are always trying to change our moods one way or another. This is a good way, if it doesn't go too far."

"Doesn't it sometimes make a bad mood worse?"

"If you feel that happening, stop drinking and take a walk or do something else."

We filled our glasses again.

"I've a mood to change as well as you," he said. "Several in fact! I'll tell you later. . . It is all a question of balance." At this he looked at me quickly and laughed, showing his white teeth. "Why did that friend of ours ignore the real reasons why one should not drink too much—one's health, one's self-control? Moods must be changed sometimes. We would perish if certain ones continued indefinitely. Moods are just as unfortunate, if not more so, when one is sober, especially when one is out of tune with one's environment."

His eyes looked quickly into mine. He was reopening matters that we had discussed so painfully two weeks before, and I suspected him of a definite purpose. Very well then!

"You would recommend, then, that your little gray wolf take to drink if he had also taken to hunting by day.'.'

"A question of health," he said vaguely. "Otherwise what is the harm?"

"It doesn't make one forget."

"Who really wants to forget? That isn't the way! You forget or you don't forget depending on how deeply you feel. To resolve to forget—is nonsense!"

He looked at his glass.

"This wine," he said, "won't give us bad heads tomorrow. Come on, John Lang! I don't know where it will lead us. Who cares?"

"I'll come on," I answered. Ahead of me stretched a dismal and sterile vista—the drinker's dread of tomorrow which he hopes to forget in a bright false mood today.

"Puritan!" said Dorn.

"Why 'Puritan'?"

"You are one at heart."

"Perhaps," I answered, and I wondered.

"Don't be a Puritan in this country," he was saying, and he was a little far away at one moment and rather too near and too loud at the next. My ears sang not unpleasantly.

"What is the matter with the Puritans?"

"They hope to find salvation by the control of their feelings. That is what I learned about them at Harvard. The reason that that man objected to drink was a Puritan reason. Of course, much of Puritanism is derived from your Bible. 'Whosoever looketh on a woman to lust after her hath committed adultery with her already in his heart.'—That is Puritanism. It ignores the realities. . . John, we study a little speculative thinking here at the University, but not half so much as you do—or can do—at Harvard. This place always reminds me of that sort of thing. There is an Islandian philosophy of a kind—or perhaps it is only a formulated suggestion as to how to live most happily. Various Islandians have tried to reduce it to generalizations. I wrote an essay myself once, but I could not do it again—not tonight anyway. No foreigner ever wrote it up that I know of, but Borden Cartwright said that he had talked philosophy with an Islandian, and that as far as he could judge, this man declared that hedonism with a kind heart was the Islandian philosophy. The real Islandian philosophy waits to be expounded to the world by a trained philosopher."

He laughed and his face had the malice of Dorna's elfish smile. . . Drinking would merely intensify a mood already somber. There would not be the relief of a change. . . So I thought. . . Philosophy?

"Why don't you be the man?" said Dorn.

"I'm not trained."

"Take a year or two more at Harvard. Get a Ph.D. Forget it all, and come back here." His eyes became very bright. "Live like one of us. Read our fabulists, especially Bodwin, while doing so. Do that anyway! You'll find all his books at the Fains', and also those of others. I know the work that they will give you to do—mending fences. Take a book with you. There is no eight-hour day obligatory even upon your conscience. You will be much alone, and when you get tired of digging holes and planting posts in them and all that, find a sunny place and read as long as you like."

He could not know how deadly dull seemed all that he proposed!

"We don't believe at all in being critics of our feelings. The more there are the richer is a man's life—so we believe. We don't analyze our own too closely. . . Oh, we can generalize about them as I am doing now! We believe that the stimulus to more and richer feeling comes from external things—things outside ourselves, and not from playing with the feelings we have had and are having, weighing them, measuring them, and thinking how to describe them. When things go wrong with us we advise sufferers to seek external things—to seek them consciously. One can find those things on one's own farm by working there, and when that becomes too much the same sort of thing over and over one can travel. If one is creative, one can create new things out of one's external experiences, careful of course not to express merely one's personal grief. The consequences of conscious externality are self-forgetfulness and a sense of being in tune. Perhaps this is what Cartwright meant by hedonism. Other people are externalities, of course—the woman a man loves most of all, and certainly they are the loveliest ones—Oh, I'm sorry!"

"It is all right," I answered. Talk did not really matter, nor anything else. I was a little sleepy, and his voice was pleasantly remote, until he said he was sorry. Then it was like an explosion.

"There really is something in what I am saying," he remarked as though surprised. "It sounds like my essay. But of course one can carry externality too far."

"Then what happens?" I asked, surprised at my own voice.

"You become so impersonal and unselfish that you are merely a shell. Others want to treat you as an external object, and find very little there. I love the Stellins, but they are somewhat like that. They have carried it so far that they are rarely conscious of themselves at all, merely of you and of what you are feeling and wishing for. Externality carried too far eliminates self and its productive desires and forces too much."

I laughed, for he robbed Stellina's kiss of all flattery. His eyes were upon me, and he paused a moment.

"How is a person like that ever to have a real *ania?*" he said slowly. "They defeat themselves by their interest in others and their desire to please, and they defeat those who love them also. . . No, one can carry externality too far. It is like everything else, a question of balance.

"How's yours?" he added suddenly.

"All right, so far."

He filled our glasses, rose, and slowly walked around the table. I followed him with my eyes, a little dizzy.

"So is mine," he said, and drank. We were both a little drunk. Certainly his lips were loosened, and my head was not like its familiar self. I had suffered a great grief and loss, I knew, but even that seemed rather remote—now. But Dorn's eyes were perfectly sober. What was he thinking?

"I wish I had my essay," he said, "but I gave it away. But you don't need it and I don't need it. What you need is to be an Islandian and to have a farm. If the Moras beat us, why don't you settle here? We'll help you to find a farm."

My heart was warm toward him, but I was loyal.

"I hope they don't beat you. That is the only reason I would want them to."

"Would you like to settle here for good?"

Grief came back again.

"There is no other place."

"If that is really true," he began, but did not finish. He seemed much moved. Then in a more cheerful voice he added, "Even if we do beat them, perhaps we can find a way to keep you here for some time . . . though I can't think of any now. So don't hope too much, John."

"No, I won't."

"I think you would fit," he said. "I really do. And that is not because I am a little drunk and feel strongly about you. You have much to learn, but you are learning. You are learning much better and more easily than I learned the merits of your country. You aren't

421

as provincial as I am. But you are, if you will forgive me, a little soft yet."

"How am I soft?" I asked, but I was not annoyed.

"We have hurt you quite enough in the past! I have nothing definite in mind. Do some Islandian living and you won't be soft! It is your vile job, not you yourself. You, inside, are all you should be. You really are one of us!"

This was a warm, happy thing to hear, but I made reservations.

"I am not yet sure I want to be," I said.

"Well, don't until you are sure."

The sense eluded me a little. He laughed.

"I tell you that what you need is a farm, and I know what you really need but can't have. I don't know how clear-headed you are but I think I'll say it. You may be one kind of man. You may be another. Some men have needs that—"

"Don't say it!" I interrupted, for I had guessed that he was thinking of women—other women.

"Be sure of that also," he said slowly, "before you condemn yourself to sterility."

For a few moments we neither of us were at all drunk.

He filled our cups.

"It might be worse for you," he said.

"Yes," I cried. "She might be dead."

Haze came again, through which I watched him shaking his head for a long time.

"Her death would be like the sun going out," he began at last. "So would Nekka's death put out the sun for me and turn the world into an ash heap . . . But that isn't what I meant. It is Dorna's will that you lose her and that makes for a certain rightness. It is far worse to turn your back on the woman you love when she will have you. That is what I have done."

The air seemed to throb. The room turned around slowly. This was a desperate matter, and I was not sober enough really to understand.

"Why? What is the matter?" Then it came back—his confidences when we stopped at Manson. "I'm sorry!" I said, and I wanted to weep.

"I told you what I feared, last year. Don't ask me to go into it again. I cannot see Nekka as my wife at Dorn Island—my wife in the

life I must lead—doing and feeling and thinking as she has done . . .
I know she will have me. She has said so. I want her. But I am not
going to take her. There is rightness in that also, I suppose. But it is
worse, I tell you, to turn your back on a woman than to have her refuse
you."

I was very angry.

"Worse! You can always have her. You don't have to turn your
back. She is always there waiting for you. And I can't have Dorna!
She won't have me!"

"You have a purpose—"

"What purpose?"

"To live—to integrate the beauty that she has given you into your
life. You don't have to think that she is—waiting."

"I have no purpose. You have a purpose. I haven't! You have
your place to build up. You can't really mean you think it worse! She
is waiting for you. She is there, I tell you!"

"Yes, she is there, and that is what makes it worse."

"You have a reason—"

"So have you—Dorna's reason."

"I want my own reason. There is no reason in anything else."

"Are we going to be helped by deciding whose fate is the worst?"

The sense of what he said stole upon my anger like fog over a hot
sun, and the cold that came was horrible and unreal in a world that
was whirling.

"Let's agree that it is bad for each of us in different ways," he said.
He could have it so.

"All right. That is true."

"Today is a bad day for Nekka." His voice came from far off, and
after a long time meant something.

"Why, for Nekka?"

"Today the man she wanted to marry is marrying someone else."
There was breathlessness.

"What man?"

"Tor and my sister."

"Why aren't you there?" It seemed a wrong to Dorna for him, her
brother, not to be present at her wedding.

"Because I was to see you today. . . ."

On this very night Tor had Dorna's body, and I was drunk. The

423

room was going round faster and faster. I oughtn't to be drunk when Tor possessed Dorna.

I tried to rise.

"I'm steadier than you are," said Dorn's voice.

"I thought it wasn't to be until May."

"They changed their minds."

All things were turning around together so fast that they were a whirlpool sucking me down.

"Thank you for coming to see me," I said.

The whirl was going over my head.

20

Fall: The Fains and the Hyths

ANOR AND I SET out on the morning after my arrival at the Fains'. He was a stocky man of forty-five who walked with a roll, dark, and often unshaven. With his family he lived about a quarter of a mile from the Fains' farmhouse near the road to the Mora Pass, and also near the houses of the other two families of dependents, the Bodins and the Larnels. He was to show me where fences were and how to go about mending them. We departed immediately after breakfast on horseback with our lunches. Anor hoped that by the end of the day I would know all there was to know. He treated me a little as though I were a child. His explanations included the obvious and were very simple and slow. It seemed strange to him that any man should have to be instructed how to mend fences. Even if a man had never done it before, he ought to have done so many similar things that the art was second nature.

The hot weather had continued, but here among the mountains the air had a dry, clean freshness, and the odor of the pines was strong and bracing.

First, according to Anor, we must ride from end to end of the farm along the highway, from the point at the south end where the hills closed in upon the river and where the road led down to Tindal, to the point at the north end where they closed in again and where the road led up toward the Mora Pass. Nearly all the way, on both sides, were stone walls.

The road was dusty. It had not rained for some time, Anor said. We stopped at intervals.

"Look," said he. "Stone out. See? Stone needed. Stone of the right size. A little mortar on this wall. You know what mortar is?"

I said I did.

"I will show you how to mix it. Other walls don't need mortar. This one does. When stone falls out you hunt for it. If you find it you put it back. Sometimes stones fall out and vanish. Who knows where they go? When that happens you find another one. There are stone piles. I shall show you where they are, and there are also stones in the brooks. I shall show you the brooks. The stone walls are one job. In the flat land—stone walls. One job. On the hill slopes, post and rail fences. Very different job. I shall show you."

We rode on.

"Where do the lost stones that fall out go?" he asked. It was a puzzle.

When we came to the northern end of the farm we dismounted. The stone wall ended, but a fence came in at an angle ascending the steep wooded hillside. The horses made much of the climb up through the rough ground, and soon horse and man were hot and sweating.

"No place to bring horses," said Anor, stopping in the hot leafy shade. He pointed to the fence that ran through the dense woods seemingly without reason, and gave me a lecture upon it. There were posts and rails ready for use at the mill, which would have to be hauled to places where needed, but of these there were by no means enough. So trees must be cut down and taken to the mill for sawing and tarring. These latter arts I must learn. When working on fences I would take a horse with me, packed with the necessary material for some places, hauling a wagon loaded with it for others. To me the fence we inspected seemed sound and strong, but Anor found weak places and taught me how to find them. He gave me instructions how to repair them when discovered.

For a third of a mile we followed the fence which ran in a straight line descending or ascending a little above the valley; and as we went we probed posts and rails for rotting places. It was a pleasure to discover ones that Anor had overlooked. Perhaps after all fence mending would be within my powers. It might even be amusing.

"There are stones on the hillsides and wooden fences," said Anor. "There are no stones in the flat lands and there are stone walls. Why don't the stones grow where the stone walls have to be? The subsoil wetness rots the fence posts in the flat lands. Still, there are trees on the hillsides. There is balance in that."

He seemed pleased, and a little later I heard him singing to himself:

> *"For man there's the bird's song to hear;*
> *For the bird there's the tree branch to light in;*
> *For the tree there's the soil·of the earth;*
> *The earth is itself and needs nothing.*

> *"For the heart there is beauty to feed on;*
> *For beauty there's love which it springs from;*
> *For love Om gives us each other;*
> *And love is itself and needs nothing."*

He was utterly unconscious of me, poking with his knife at the head of a fence post.

"Sound," he said, and moved along the rails examining them with careful eyes.

In his song, for "love" he used the word *ania.* . . .

Next morning Anor and I went down to the mill and looked over the stock of prepared rails and posts, and he explained the working of the saw in case I wished to make new ones; and he told me that under the arrangement with the Catlins, who occupied the other side of the valley, it was proper for the Fains to use the water power.

I was one of "the Fains" now, and there was pleasure in so being.

After that we rode to the workhouses that lay on the highroad not far beyond the dwellings of himself and the other dependents. Here he explained how to mix mortar, and before his eyes I replaced a stone in a wall and cemented it there. Then armed with rails and nails, hammer and saw, I demonstrated my ability to mend a rotting rail.

"I am going," said Anor suddenly. "You are not as quick as some but you will make no bad mistakes. Come to us on our day, or whenever you like."

The season was like mid-September. The days were as warm as in summer, but in the air was a sense of summer passed, and the nights were cool. Others worked to harvest the fruits in the orchards which frost endangered. I went off to my fences every morning and returned at evening; walking to work, for Fak was burdened with rails, but usually riding back in the misty chill of twilight.

The fence at the northerly corner was the point of beginning, and I moved slowly south along it. The first three or four days were therefore spent in the woods. They were a pleasant peaceful place early in the morning with the sheen of low sunlight on the rustling leaves; but as day advanced and the sun became high and hot, the foliage, which was becoming yellow here and there, closed in tightly, and I wanted to move rapidly and to go away from spots that were soon too familiar. Dorn seemed cruel to have recommended that which made me so much alone, with nothing to see but motionless tree trunks, leaves fluttering aimlessly and aimlessly falling, ground moss-grown and littered with old and new dead leaves, and—all day long close to my eyes—the monotonous fence always repeating the same design, but demanding foot by foot attention and care. The noise of my hammer rang loud. I talked to myself, understanding how loneliness and the desperation of an irrevocable loss makes men queer and edges them toward the brink of the incomprehensible and insane.

Lord Fain had gone down to The City for the Council Meeting. His brother and Mara, the latter's wife, were quiet and old, courteous but distant. I told them what I had done and where I had been. They in return talked of the work proceeding elsewhere on the farm. It had been a good year, but a little too dry. No crops had failed but the yield was not great. They seemed neither delighted nor worried, pleased nor displeased.

One day Mara came out to see me at noontime, bringing her lunch with her. It was hot, and the distant cattle had sought the shade. The farm, as we looked along and down upon it, seemed vague and oppressed in the heat and the haze.

She suggested that some time before lunch I go down to the pond. The Larnels had a son and daughter about my age, and there were young people at the Catlins', and when days were hot some of them were sure to go in swimming. It was not good to be too much alone.

"We are all good friends here," she said, with a faint smile, and I wondered if she were thinking the thought of the old—that young people can cure their griefs by seeking out each other.

We ate our lunch in the shade of a great oak, and it was not only no effort to talk to her, but I talked and talked of the most insignificant of personal things and thoughts.

It was kind of her to come, for she was old and the day was extremely hot.

Lord Fain came back from the Council Meeting on March 23rd, after I had been at his farm for two weeks. The outer fence that ran from the northern corner of the farm was in good repair for nearly half a mile, and I had confidence that my work was good and would last for years. I was thin, sunburned, and hard, and also tired.

He told of the Council Meeting on the evening of his return; bringing into the household what it lacked—the vigor and style of his definite personality. Old as he was, he seemed decisive, powerful, and strong. His white hair was like a white cap above his dark face. His eyes gleamed on either side of the hook of his nose with wisdom and with interest. He quickened life in all of us.

He mentioned Dorna once:

"When Tor received us at the palace," he said, "his new queen was with him. She was very handsome. And she came to all the meetings of the council."

Having been a statesman Lord Fain as easily became a farmer. He gave us his news, and then his mind wheeled its attention upon this land of his where I was working. I made a report.

"You seem to have worked hard," he said.

"I have enjoyed it."

"What else have you done?"

There was nothing else, but a little conversation in the evening and sleep.

"No reading?" he asked. "No writing? Young Dorn said that you were thinking of telling about us in your country."

In his voice was a kindly and gentle rebuke, and deep understanding. I could think of no answer.

"Don't work too hard on our account," he continued. "What you are doing need not be finished for years. Take your time, John Lang. Carry books with you while the weather is still warm, and work when you wish and read or write when you wish. That is a good life."

That night sleep did not come at once. When Dorna appeared with Tor at the reception to the members of the council, she doubtless wore the royal green, a color that became her when not too dark. She had worn green when I last saw her—green of her own choosing as an independent young woman. Now she wore green in the right of her husband . . . I wished Dorna would wear her own colors, not Tor's royal green. All day I worked surrounded by green. It would be good when winter came and the grass turned brown, the trees were leafless, and snow came.

Next morning when I set out with Fak loaded with posts and rails to repair the fences south of a little brook called Singing Water, Lord Fain came with me. I showed him some jobs of mine and he examined the fence and shook it and smiled and nodded. The sun was hot over our heads, but coolness lingered in hollows. Fall had really begun. Behind the fence leaves came down in light showers when the wind blew. The trees swayed as though glad to be rid of them.

He was a small man and held himself straight. He went bare-headed, and his hair was as white as the whitest parts of the sailing clouds above us. His face became darker in the heat and was almost mahogany, and there was something proud and ruthless in it. When he shook the fence with his strong small hands, it was as though the fence were an enemy. There was power in him.

We worked together for an hour or more. At midmorning he suggested that we mount our horses and we rode up into the hills by a narrow trail that became steeper as we ascended. We came out upon Singing Water above a steep fall. The farms were far below us, and the view wide, reaching far over the opposite ridge to the snowy peaks of Matclorn.

We tied the horses and from his saddlebag he produced books and papers. He had letters to write. Before he went to work he leaned over the stream and drank deep. Then he moved away and leaning against a tree was soon absorbed. It was a little strange to see that dark face with its aspect of power and command placidly writing words. I picked up the book he had given me and made myself comfortable and tried to become as still and as mentally concentrated as he was; but it was hard to go from one thing to another.

It had only this for a name: *A Collection*. It included fables and verses and odd paragraphs, some by well-known authors, but others with no signature at all. These perhaps were by the unknown maker of the collection.

I did not read. Singing Water was a little brook at this height, but it had a capacious runway ready for seasons when there would be a greater flow. On this day it came trickling and dripping down from above, over and around moss-grown rocks, gathered in a pool, passed through a groove in a rock and without a sound vanished below.

Where I sat I could watch this ceaseless, soundless passing and disappearance of the water. Somewhere beneath us the water fell and gathered again and went on.

Later in the morning, when Isla Fain had finished his letters, we went for a walk higher up the stream. It made us warm, and I stripped and bathed in a pool that just covered me. He sat on a rock and watched me, saying nothing and thinking I know not what thoughts about the day, or Islandia, or his farm, or me, or my nakedness, or life.

We returned, lunched, and then rode down to the valley again. I stopped at my fences.

"Keep the book," he said. "Read it. Don't work all the time."

It took two persons to teach this lesson: first Mara by her visit, and then Isla Fain by his. Thereafter I did not always work all day, but idled when I felt like it or wrote.

The book was not one that could be read straight through. Evidently some man made this collection of various things that had met some need of his soul. He was evidently of a speculative turn of mind, troubled, and in need of comfort, yet I imagined him as a serene person.

Early in the collection was a poem called "Holding the Fort," of which this is a translation:

"While those they loved fell everywhere,
Although unhoping of relief,
They held the fort with steadfast care
And yielded neither to despair
Nor to the lassitude of grief."

Isla Fain's presence and less fatiguing days changed the character of my evenings. He had a large correspondence, which he encouraged, particularly at this time. He wrote to many of his constituents asking them their views on the Mora Treaty, and he had letters from as many more persons with opinions of their own or wishing to know his. These letters became so numerous that he let me help him with them, for at his farm he lacked the services of a secretary. Writing for someone else I was inspired to write for myself also. I began an article on the political situation for an American newspaper to be released as soon as my successor arrived and I was free to say what I thought.

431

A day in the open air, not all of work, to which I was now accustomed, and an evening of two or three hours as secretary or writing my own things until I was too sleepy to do any more—this was my life.

Hot days came again, but the heat had an autumnal tang. Near the apple orchards there was the smell of rotten windfalls and discarded fruit. The strong thick odor of the burnt straw in the blackened stubble fields hung above the ground. The smoke of burning leaves rose, and its pungent, nostalgic smell was always in the air.

On such a day as this it was hot work repairing the fences that bordered the *denerir's* fields just south of Singing Water. Not only was it hot, but it was dry also—dry to the skin and dusty. When the sun reached a height which I judged to mark noon, I mounted Fak and rode down to the Larnels'. The Larnel daughter, a young woman of twenty-six or -seven, solid, dark, and healthy, came to the door.

"Mara said that you and your brother went swimming on hot days," I explained. "She suggested that I join you some time. It is very hot today."

She laughed, eyed me, shrugged, and then answered:

"My brother has gone, but it is too cold for me. The water is like ice . . . We hoped you would come some time."

"Won't you come?"

She shook her head.

"Too cold," she said.

I rode away. Clouds of dust rose around Fak and me and settled down upon us. We turned off at the road to the mill. Left and right behind willows, already turning yellow, were flat green meadows. I placed Fak in the shade of the mill itself, trusting him to stay there. Beyond the mill the road curved and crossed the Frays River on a bridge below the dam, and from there I saw the swimmers, standing on the stone embankment just beyond the sluiceway of the dam. There was Larnel, a dark, heavily built young man; the two Catlin girls both in their early twenties; Catlin, their father, a man of forty-seven or so, with grizzled hair; and Tolly and his sister somewhat younger than he. They showed no surprise at my coming. No one as yet, Larnel said, had dared to enter the water.

I took off my clothes and joined them. At Catlin's suggestion we lined up on the shore and he declared that he would count six, when we all were to jump in.

"Ek—atta—"

The water beneath the wall looked black, deep, and cold. Dead leaves drifted on its surface. The blue haze of autumn lay over the meadows and the pond, and the air was strong with the smell of burning leaves. Hot as the day had seemed, there was a chill lurking under the dry heat. It was not like the full heavy warmth of summer when nakedness was less chilly.

"Etteri—nek—"

Catlin's voice was slower and more ominous. The slender but solid young bodies of his two daughters standing in profile beyond him were like ivory. Their heads were crowned with chestnut, their breasts were small and round, the nipples were carmine, and the tufts of hair in their groins were rust color. I met the dark bright eyes of one, and her smile was of amused dread and despair.

"Natta—netteri—Stell! (Jump!)"

I leaped out into space, the black water rushed up, and its breathtaking iciness went over my head. Down, down into darkness I sank until my feet touched soft cold mud. I sprang up, with lifted open eyes, and saw radiating green, light, and fine bubbles above me, and at last my head emerged into warm smoky air, while all the rest of me, every inch naked and free, felt the sustaining numbing touch of the water.

No one, losing courage, had remained on the wall, and with much splashing for warmth's sake all seven of us struck out for the opposite shore where just beyond the mill was a shelving place. It was scarcely wide enough for all, but the water was so icy that we came out together near enough to touch each other.

It was almost too much. There were too many bare pink bodies. While the others walked back to their clothes, I plunged in again. Larnel followed, either because he did not wish to be outdone or more probably because he did not like to leave me, a stranger, swimming alone.

Looking over our shoulders we saw the others, men and women, streaming across the bridge in single file against a background of yellowing willows with blue sky above.

Larnel lent me a towel, and in the sun just behind the wall we all dried and dressed ourselves, and the talk was rapid—of the cold water, of the weather, of my fence repairing, of Fak who had wan-

dered over the bridge to us, and who was known to Tolly and to
Catlin as of the Dorns' breed.

The black water nearby was still flecked with the brownish yellow
bubbles and foam of our splashing. The unbleached, coarse linen
towels flickered. Honest bare flesh was pink until the whites and
dark reds and blues of clothes began to cover it.

The care that we at home take to hide our bodies was forgotten,
and when remembered again for a moment it seemed needlessly false.

The Tollys and the Catlins went their way, naming their days
and asking me to come and see them, and Larnel went his.

After giving Fak his midday meal, I ate mine sitting on the wall
in the warmest, sunniest spot to be found. The swim was refreshing
and subduing, but the small of my back was cold and my fingers
numb. Only a return to work made me really warm again.

I labored on the fences in peaceful but heartbroken quiet. Dorna
was very remote.

During the afternoon great clouds rolled in from the south and
formed over the valley like a roof, hiding the tops of the hills, but it
did not rain until morning.

At the mill next day I sawed rails and fence posts, grateful to
the rain that assured to us in the valley water and water power. A mist
of sawdust was in the air, and the faintly spicy smell of sawn wood
mingled with smells of wet dust drifting in at the open door. Anor
had come to teach and to help, but he left at noon satisfied that, though
slow and a little wasteful of wood and power, I would do well enough.

The semi-twilight of the mill, the privacy of the gray-blue steady
rain outside, and its quiet pattering on the roof overhead made concentration possible. After lunch, I read.

Opening *A Collection* at random, I was caught by a title and read
this fable of Bodwin's:

THE YOUNG SEE IN PICTURES

"Pictures have only two dimensions. The art of the painter gives
an illusion of depth, but it is only an illusion. The young paint their
future in pictures, and the more vivid their imaginations the more
vivid the pictures. When a picture of the future is thus painted by an

imagination vigorous and hungry but brought up in ignorance, it is truly misleading.

"There is nothing unusual in the story of Amera, the young daughter of a *tana* in Miltain. The pictures of her future which she painted were bright and lovely and false. Her mother, somewhat bruised by life, encouraged her, recapturing in the glow of Amera's imagination a romance that she had hoped for and lost. She also wished her daughter to marry well, for the Amers' house was crowded.

"A suitor came, Danling, a *tana* of Brome, a widower, with a fine farm. As many maturing young women are, Amera had been disappointed by the inconsequence of young men, busy painting and repainting their own pictures. Danling was solid—in his wishes, established and content. She painted a new picture. Large upon it was his farm and life there; Danling figured also but only in two dimensions and rather small in size. She gazed upon this picture often, and, living away from her present life in a crowded house, lived in its spacious flatness as deeply as that flatness allowed, unaware that it was only a picture. Danling she saw as a companion, a guide, an older brother, sitting across the table at mealtimes, or away at work in the fields. She herself would make his farm, already lovely, more lovely still. There were marriage mysteries, but she had heard of no woman who suffered from them. Nor is a man of only two dimensions fearful, and during his courtship Danling so remained. It was all pictures and words. Childbirth was painful, but she was a woman and brave and this was her fate. The important thing to her was the picture that she painted, aided by Danling and her mother. She made it vivid and beautiful, cherished it in her heart, and, absorbed in contemplating it, married Danling.

"She was charming and young. He was kind in heart and wished for her happiness; but no amount of kindly feeling can make acts of love a kindness to those who do not want them. Danling, emerging from the flatness of the picture as a creature of three dimensions, tore it into shreds. To her senses he was like sharp salt on the tongue, which thirsts and wishes it not. She had a man, clean, honorable, and noted for his kindness. Those who think of the mating of human beings as they think of the mating of their animals, and who having two healthy specimens of opposite sex resent their not functioning as they are expected to with the resulting foals or calves, will blame Amera and will be annoyed by this fable. She should have accepted

435

gladly the fact that she, a woman, had a man and a good one. She should have lived according to nature's design. But how much better is the stallion or mare which can if so wishing decline the other, while the man or woman married and ruled by the will and convention and custom cannot! No doubt many women could have attuned their desires to the man whom life gave them, but Amera was not, and could not, become one of these. When Danling made love to her with his mature desires, it was impossible for her to retain any part of herself for herself, and not loving him she had no wish and no power to give him all that was herself. There was no giving. It was all taking. In her shame and grief she would have given anything else she could, even her life, but something of herself must remain as her own. He invaded her and left her nothing, not even empty, but his and filled with him. The dead have no consciousness; Amera was alive and conscious and not herself any longer. When painfully she found her soul again, Danling, casually and lovingly, professing kindness, destroyed what she had recreated. The child he gave her was too much his to be her own. So they lived.

"Oh, the misleading, lovely pictures of the young! He was not to blame, nor she; each true in what was felt to the nature within. Yet the falsity of their lives might have been prevented. Hide not from the young who are of the age to marry the reality of the life upon which they expect to enter! It is hard to teach those who believe in flat pictures that life as lived has other dimensions. We older ones spend many years in becoming aware of this mystery and never wholly grasp it. But let us do our best to give the young the ability to recognize many-dimensioned *ania.*"

Amera was Dorna. She had painted a picture and was misled by it. Wise in part she knew that she did not want to be married, to be a man's—not mine nor anyone's. But she was not wise enough. She said she had *ania,* but she was misled by the bright falsity of her picture, and did not know that what she felt could not be true, many-dimensioned *ania.* The fable made Amera's, and Dorna's, sufferings almost too vivid to endure.

The rain pattering on the roof was like the rain on the roof of the windmill at Dorn Island. Life at the Fains' had diminished grief in nothing. The pain was the same, increasing as time went on and knowledge deepened. The misery Dorna was doomed to suffer was no longer a future thing as it had been then, but a present, daily one. . . .

On April 13th, I mounted Fak, and rode down towards The City, taking a day and a half for the journey. On the fifteenth and eighteenth steamers arrived, bringing mail. The most important news was that my successor, Oswald Lambertson, would arrive with his wife and secretary by S.S. *Sulliaba* on May 3rd—about two weeks hence. His coming was tangible proof of my failure, and I felt one sharp twinge of regret and perhaps of shame. Nor at the moment was the thought of release welcome. The official position that had been mine gave me a right to be in Islandia. Thereafter I should be only a tourist subject to the exclusion laws and condemned to leave in a year from May 3rd, or whenever it was that my resignation took effect. There was, however, evidence of an effort on the part of Washington to save my face. My successor came with the rank of minister. If I were a good young man and pleased him, I might remain for a time at least as consul.

My first dispatch as a prospective correspondent was mailed on the eighteenth. It was sent to a friend, with directions to hold it until I cabled to him. In that case he was to offer it to a certain New York newspaper on my behalf. At least it would be in the United States available for use as soon after my release from an official position as I could send word.

The Lambertsons arrived, the man himself carefully dressed, and his secretary and his valet, his wife and her maid. I had arranged rooms in the hotel.

The first days were busy ones. I changed back into my unfamiliar American clothes in order to look more like one of his entourage. He made his official calls in my company, and I took him about with his wife and secretary leaving cards on all the other diplomats. I talked more than I had talked for months, telling him and Mrs. Lambertson everything I knew of Islandia and her customs and politics and leading men; but he knew more than I about the various syndicates and would-be concessionaires.

Daily intercourse with him was not very pleasant. His manners were perfect. He condescended at times to be familiar and even hearty. But he pumped me until I felt exhausted and sucked dry. There was not a crumb of information that bore in any way upon the Mora Treaty

437

which he did not draw out of me, and even when I was empty the suction continued. He also had to know all about the Lor Pass matter, including every trivial item in the behavior of the other diplomats afterwards, and I spent long periods vainly trying to think who smiled and who did not.

About a week after his coming he said suddenly that the acceptance of my resignation was neither necessary nor to be thought of, and he became all at once more affable and less cross-examining in tone. I lunched with him at the hotel and his manner was echoed in that of Mrs. Lambertson. Apparently I was useful and competent enough to be retained.

When lunch was over and we were alone for a moment, I said that I was willing to be of any assistance I could, to remain in The City, and to be at his call through June, but only in an unofficial way; and that I would be greatly obliged if he would use the special power that he had and would accept my resignation.

"To take effect when?" he asked.

"This afternoon."

We argued for several days and I might not have won if he had not had so many engagements.

Free! I was really free, but did not feel the full effect of release until May 15th, when once more bound for the Fains'. The City was no longer in any sense my home, for I had given up the lease of my house on the wall, and I had left it for good; with relief at never having to enter again a place of so much suffering and disappointment, but also with a sharp regret at losing its familiar quiet, and its romantic view over the roof gardens. My last acts there were to arrange for the sending of a cable to the friend who had my manuscript, stating that it could be published; and to write a letter to Uncle Joseph telling him of my new plans, and one to Gladys Hunter, my only correspondent left in the United States who was not a member of the family.

Free, I was a little too free. I had no house of my own any longer and was adrift. The Fains' farm was the nearest thing to home that I had, and it seemed a precarious one. But I was mounted on my own horse whom I loved, an Islandian with whom I had been for more hours than with any other. No one was my master. I had work to do and good friends. I loved with all my heart a woman who liked me though never to be mine. It was not so bad after all. . . .

It was colder at the farm. Few trees had any leaves left, but the ground was not frozen, and there were warm Indian summer days. Fence mending was an absorbing, pleasant occupation. It was good to be at work in the open air after softening hours indoors in American clothes at The City, and good to live a life where talking was of only secondary importance.

A day or two after my return came a letter from Nattana, with an invitation to visit her in which I thought I saw Dorn's hand.

"The weather is lovely here now," she wrote, "so lovely that I hate to be indoors even though I am working at something very interesting to me. I am weaving the cloth for new clothes for myself to wear at the Council Meeting, for I am going. What is going to happen then? We think and talk of nothing else. I shall be glad to be present, but I am often uneasy and afraid. Perhaps the old time is ending, and great changes are coming. I am not ready for them. I don't want to be snatched into a new life . . . Dorn has visited us. He and Nekka went off together for one day, but what that means no one knows. Nettera isn't unhappy. She is going to have a baby in June. She has said John Lang may be told . . . I am hoping that John Lang will come to visit us also, or if he is going to the Council Meeting, he could meet Father and me at Tamplin on the evening of June 8th, and ride the rest of the way in company instead of alone. But if he is going to be with the Dorns or the Fains, don't bother about us. Oh, what will happen? Will everything be different, even for us in the Doring Valley?"

HYTHA NATTANA

In three weeks hence the Islar of Islandia would meet to decide whether or not to adopt the Mora Treaty. Lord Fain told me in confidence that those persons on whom Lord Dorn counted were to meet several days before June 11th when the council met; and that therefore he was leaving on the first, only ten days away. He wanted me to understand that whatever action was taken his farm was mine, even in the event of a war in which my country was involved.

439

His voice was quiet. War sprang out of the category of things talked about but known only as ideas, and became an ominous reality; and I had a sharp sensation of paleness and shock.

"Is war likely?" I asked.

"Attempts at coercion are not unlikely," he answered, "if our party prevails."

The days slipped by, and I went on working, reading, and writing, becoming hard and fit again.

Islandia had had her full share of wars and yet hers was the least aggressive of peoples. I found a verse by Mora, the poet who lived in the sixteenth century, which expressed what was perhaps the country's attitude toward warring:

> *"The stunted pine that strove in gales*
> *Has done as much of growing*
> *As have tall trees whom naught assails*
> *But summer breezes' blowing.*
>
> *"Its seed will thrive in peaceful soil,*
> *Releasing strength it stores.—*
> *This is the guerdon of your toil,*
> *Man battered in the wars!"*

I sat on a rail, rather bored with mending fences. Coming events made us all restless. Sooner or later every conversation turned to the meeting of the council, to occur in less than two weeks. Isla Fain had already gone . . . I ought to send word very soon that I would meet Nattana and her father at Tamplin on June 8th.

It seemed that I suddenly found and knew myself. The urge to go on living was irresistible, a force that was good. Though I owed nothing to anyone and was as free as the air, I had no wish to die and be blind to the world shining about me. Grief was a wolf whose teeth often gripped, closed tight, and caused agony, but I was accustomed to his attacks and knew him well. Without Dorna I was only half myself, but there was beauty all around me, there were rich things to do and to see, and the world seemed full of good friends.

When I opened my eyes early June 4th, just a week before the council convened, I resolved to do something, to travel, to go. An hour later, Fak and I were on the way.

The sun had risen high enough to make the dome of Mount Islandia a glowing pale rose against a sky still dark-blue with stars. Was there any country lovelier than this one now that its aspect was becoming familiar and no longer seemed remote and alien? The flat land below lay at the bottom of a quiet lake of night shadow. Mara was still going about the house down there with a candle.

A little above me the forested heights began to glow. The shadow cut them with a hard line, all below still cool and quiet and sleeping. As we ascended this line slipped downward also, Fak and I rode up out of the darkness as from a pool into the bright early sunlight.

It was almost night and raining when on foot I came to the Hyths' stone gates, mounted Fak, and put him to the trot in order to arrive in style. The house loomed ahead dark and low with its wide wings. Yellow panes gleamed in the central part, and there was a single window faintly lighted to the left, which might be Nattana's workshop. She did not know I was coming, nor did anyone.

Under Fak's feet the ground squelched, and he spattered himself and me with mud and water.

When I shouted my name Hyth Atta appeared with a lantern. He showed no surprise, for which I was grateful, saying that he would take care of Fak and that I had better go in and change. Then he turned the lantern on the horse's body and observed the color of the mud.

"You came by the Tamplin Pass, didn't you? How is it up there?" he asked. I told him I had run into snow and he added, "Father is afraid he won't get over."

He laughed and went off with Fak.

Airda was waiting inside the door. She also showed no surprise and gave me little time to speak. I was wet, she said, and would want a bath; and not long after, in the same room that I had already twice occupied, I was sitting in a tub of hot water, at ease.

Downstairs Isla Hyth was waiting before the fire in the living room. He stood with legs apart, his hair and beard very red. His words of greeting were uttered with smooth and hearty cordiality, but something else was on his mind.

"How was the weather in the pass?" he asked.

I answered, wishing that I had been more observant of the snow and its depth, for he examined me at length.

Airda had come in.

441

"You are going to the Council Meeting, aren't you, Lang? You are planning to ride with me and my daughter Nattana?" he said.

"I hope to, if I may."

"I am glad to have you. But if it continues to rain tonight, there will be so much snow up there that it may be necessary to start tomorrow and go by the Doan Pass, if we are to be there on time. I don't know whether Nattana will be ready or not."

"She has been sewing all day," said Airda quickly.

"She knew we might start tomorrow," he answered turning to Airda. He seemed somewhat on edge. "If need be I'll have to travel without Nattana. If she does not go, do as you please, Lang. But I shall be glad to have you with me," he added over his shoulder, walking away.

Airda sighed faintly.

"Hyth is tó meet his eldest son, who has been at the Upper Farm, and my son, Hyth Pek, at Reeves four days from now. If he goes by the Doan Pass . . ." She did not finish, but began again. "Nattana is trying hard to be ready tomorrow. She is the only one of the older girls here. Nettera—you know. And Nekka and Ettera have gone up the valley . . ." She paused once more. "Nattana would like to know about the condition of the pass. Supper won't be ready for some time. She is in her workshop . . . I am very glad to see you here again, Lang. It has been a long time . . . These are troubling days. At least we find them so."

She gave me a chance; and I said that I thought I would go and tell Nattana that I was here and about the weather.

"Don't distract her from her sewing," said Airda, and I wondered how she thought I would.

In the storeroom beneath the workshop it was dark except for a faint glow at the head of the stairs. I felt with my feet for the bottom one, and ascended.

By three candles Nattana was sewing. She did not raise her head when I came up and in. The light was on the other side of her and her round head was outlined by a mist of fine, gleaming, coppery wires. Her back made a simple curve, and her braids were over her shoulders. She looked smaller than I remembered her to be. Her legs were crossed, and the lower part of the upper one did not hang down alongside its fellow but pointed out at an angle, looking a little as though it had kicked something. A dark-green fabric was on her knees, and her hands, rosy-white and translucent, were busy.

"John Lang," I said lightly, so as not to startle her.

Her head turned, but I could not really see her face.

"You came!" she said in an unexpected high voice.

"I wanted to come all the way rather than meet you at Tamplin."

Her head turned back to her sewing.

"I thought you were my brother to tell me Father wanted me. I'm glad you have come."

Her hands moved again.

"Can you find a place to sit?" she said.

On every chair and on the bench where I had sat months before were cloths and garments of different colors, mostly tans and greens. A new piece of furniture—a narrow cot or bed in one corner—was covered with them and with stockings, sandals, linen, a cloak, ribbons, comb and brush, two saddlebags, books—all of Nattana's belongings, it seemed.

I found a place on the arm of the bench.

"How are you, John Lang?" she asked.

"Very well indeed," I answered, and there seemed to be some inner significance in saying so. "How are you, Nattana?"

"I am very well—and very busy . . . I'm so glad that you have come."

"I ought to have written you."

"It is quite all right. You are here! Father thinks of starting tomorrow, and I am going to be ready, even if I have to sit up all night, whether we start then or not."

The candles made a straight line of light, soft and youthful, along Nattana's nose, and other highlights indicated the contours of her forehead and chin. As always she sat lightly as though about to move away at any moment.

"Do you mind if I go on sewing?" she said. "But I know you won't. I must be ready tomorrow even though we don't start then."

She offered no reason, but I surmised some difficulty between herself and her father and was uncomfortable at the possibility of intruding upon a quarrel.

"I don't mind, but I don't want to distract you. Airda told me not to."

She laughed and leaned over her work.

"Once we are on the road it will be different . . . You have seen Father. What are his plans now?"

I told of the conversation.

"It would be rather fun traveling six days instead of three." She waved her hand toward the south, and the needle caught the light. "But it won't be bad up there day after tomorrow. There may be snow, but it is too warm for the snow to be deep in the ravine on the other side . . . How's Fak?"

"He seems in excellent condition."

"Could he stand six days more?"

"I think so."

"Father might prefer to have you ride one of our horses. They are faster. You may have to leave Fak behind . . . Then you would come back for him; or maybe I could ride him to you. Do you expect to go back to the Fains'?"

"Yes, I do," I said, and told her briefly of the work I was doing; and from that beginning conversation moved to my resignation and to my plans of writing. Soon I had told her nearly all there was to tell about myself.

"You have got a year, haven't you?" she said.

"A year from Noven 22nd (May 12th)."

"It seems long now but it won't soon, I'm afraid."

"That is what I have been thinking."

The shadowy round of her face turned toward me for a moment, and then looked back at her work again. The highlights resumed their places on her profile.

"Well, anyway," she said, "you will have been with us in what may be the worst days of our history. It seems to me that each time we have enemies they are a little more powerful and a little more deadly. Will you some day tell me what you really think about it all, about us and the rest of the world and everything?"

"Yes, when I know, if I ever do. I'll be glad."

"Whom do you talk with at the Fains'?"

I told her of my life there, but in the middle she interrupted.

"It is suppertime," she said. "You had better go, or they will think I kept you."

"Aren't you coming?"

She waved her hand at all the things in the room and shook her head.

"Come back and see me for a little while if you get a chance," she said.

She had guessed to the moment. The rest of the family were about to go to the dining room. I explained that she was not coming, and Isla Hyth looked annoyed.

When supper was over he became momentarily the hearty, cordial man whom I had known during my first visit. He took me to his room and kept me for more than an hour. His conversation led to Lambertson, and what sort of man he was. What instructions had he and what attitude would the United States take? I ought to have known, but I did not. Lambertson had not taken me into his confidence, and I said so.

All at once I was wondering, almost with a shock, why Isla Hyth was not present at the meeting of those loyal to the Dorn policies to which Isla Fain had gone. Dorna had mentioned him as one of the stalwarts, I thought.

It took him some time to believe that I had nothing concrete to tell him, but once he was convinced, his interest in me ceased. He asked me quickly as to my plans, and then said that he was glad to have had this talk with me; and if we were willing to make something of an adventure of the journey to The City, we would not leave to-morrow, but would wait until June 7th.

I rose to go, but he detained me for a moment.

"When all this worrying business is over," he said, "I would like a talk with you on your country. I've read your *History,* and I've read other things about the United States. I've picked up a reading knowledge of English, and when I go to and from The City I make a point of spending a few days at Reeves and of reading there. We lack very much something that you have, not in a commercial but in a 'spiritual' sense."

The word "spiritual" was uttered in English, and sounded strangely amid the Islandian which had no such term.

"I'll be glad," I said, wondering. "May I tell Hytha Nattana that we don't leave till Decen 17th?"

"If you wish!" he answered shortly.

The light still shone in the window of her workshop. Rain had ceased and the damp air was very still. She was sitting exactly as I left her, and her hands were sewing.

445

I explained that her father had wanted to talk to me, and said that we were not to start our journey until the day after the next.

"There was no real need," she said. "And I'm glad, for now I can take you to see Nettera—if you would like to come."

"I would—if she will want to see me."

"She won't care."

Nattana's voice was tired.

"Have you had anything to eat, Nattana?"

"No."

"Nobody brought you anything?"

"No—when I skip meals I'm supposed to go hungry."

"I've got some things in my bag left from my lunch yesterday. Would you like them?"

"I would!"

I went to fetch what I had, a meat roll and some chocolate. When I returned and gave them to her she ate them while she sewed.

"Why don't you stop?" I said. "You have all day tomorrow."

"Father told me that I could not possibly be ready by tomorrow and that he would not take me unless I were, so I am going to be ready whether we go then or not."

"How long have you been at it?"

"All day."

"You are pathetic, Nattana."

"You are not to distract me, John Lang."

She did not seem far from tears.

"It oughtn't to make any difference, since we are not leaving then."

"If I'm not ready Father will have a grievance, whatever day we go. And things are such that it is just as well that he have none. Of course, he may be annoyed because I insisted on being ready although it was not necessary! I'm so glad you are going to be with us."

Her voice was a little unsteady, and suddenly she jerked and changed her position.

"I shall be glad to be with you. It is going to be fun."

"Tomorrow," she said, "I'll be so dead tired that I won't be any fun. But once we have started, I'll be a different person."

"You can be anything you like."

There was silence for a moment.

"Is there anything I can do to help you to get ready?"

"You can oil and polish my sandals if you don't mind that sort of work."

It was pleasant to be busy. There were two pairs, one brown, one green, and a pair of boots lined with fleece for the snow. It took some time for I wanted to make a good job of it. She could think of no more tasks—unless I would read aloud.

"What shall I read?"

"Your *History*—about the Revolution. It is there waiting to travel with me." She pointed to the cot.

She was the quietest of listeners. I finished the Revolution.

"It is so different, I find it hard to picture," she said. "You are the only American I've ever seen. It will be interesting to meet at The City another one, and to see an American woman. What will she wear?"

I described Mrs. Lambertson's clothes—the dress, close about the hips and flaring around the feet, that reached the ground, with fitted waist, high lace collar and lace cuffs; the big hat on the high pompadour; and the gloves.

"What is underneath all that?" Nattana asked, and I mentioned the undergarments of an American woman, making some guesses, puzzled for Islandian equivalents, amused and a little confused.

"That makes at least nine things besides the dress!" Nattana exclaimed. "We wear much less underneath. I'll show you."

She put down her work, rose, and without hesitation lifted her skirt and showed the linen bloomers she wore. Then she went to the cot and held up a band for the breasts and a light woolen garment for very cold weather.

"That is all except what you usually see," she said.

She then showed me the dresses that she had made and was making for the journey.

"If you weren't coming with us, I would try them on, but I would rather surprise you," she said.

Nattana did not come to breakfast. No one commented upon her absence. At nine, perhaps, I went to the workshop. It was in perfect order; two saddlebags packed and ready were upon the bench; and Nattana lay on the bed covered by a dark-green robe. Her scattered hair was a copper-bronze. She was asleep, her flushed face as still as wax.

447

I went to see Fak in the stable and sat there on a pile of blankets looking out through the door. Mists were everywhere rising from the wet ground and the sun was winking and trying to shine behind them. Trees on the hills above appeared and were hidden again.

Lest Nattana waken and fail to find me, I returned to the house. But we did not go to see Nettera until afternoon.

Isla Hyth was busy getting ready for the journey, but I had come prepared, and she was prepared already. This fact and the leisure that resulted seemed to please her. The sky had cleared except for light fluffs of mist. The higher slopes were powdered with snow. We rode the high, brown horses of the Hyths.

I was reluctant in going to see Nettera, whom I remembered vividly, light-footed, slender, absent-minded, playing her fife-flute with absorbed eyes.

The Ensings' ranch was six miles to the west and on the same side of the Doring River as the Hyths'. On the way we rode down into the ravine, crossed on a wooden bridge, and then climbed to the level of the pastureland again.

Nattana let her horse go and mine followed. The Doring Valley was a spacious place reducing men and their structures to minuteness. We rode a long time before there was any change in the relative positions of natural objects. It was too big and simple to seem wholly real.

There was a quiet charm in the low stone house of the Bains, with its dense pines as windbreaks and its garden, now bare of flowers. We dismounted and tied our horses to the white fence. Nattana went ahead and I followed.

Nettera rose from a chair in the small low-ceilinged living room, where a timid fire flickered on the hearth. Her face was thin, appealing, and lovable. The shadows under her eyes were darker than ever, but her eyes themselves were bright with a vague look of suffering, of absent thoughts, and yet of contentment. She looked taller and her slender figure was much misshapen. She smiled the smile of a child.

We all sat down, and then she on impulse rose quickly to fetch us wine and cakes. She moved as she always would have done, forgetting her pregnancy, and then was forced to remember it and became suddenly awkward.

Nattana and I sat silent and looking away until she returned.

After that we talked, but with many pauses. Nettera, serving us, made explanations. Motioning with her hand, she said that Bain uncle and "Bain" were "off there." Another Bain, his cousin, was fishing; and Barta his aunt by marriage had gone over to see one of the other *denerir*.

"Ought you to be alone?" asked Nattana.

"I'm all right," she answered. Beyond a few questions this was all she had to say. She sat as though dropped down, smiling a vague smile, listening to our talk with polite attention and far removed, yet seeming more one of us than one of those with whom she lived. Nattana chattered, rapidly telling her sister the news of the Hyths, and about her new clothes, and the impending journey, and her father's unreasonableness. Though the older, she seemed to have lost something to Nettera, and to be the inferior and aware of it. She switched the conversation to my resignation and my life at the Fains', while Nettera looked at me with a smile and a shine in eyes that might not have seen me at all. A woman pregnant and so near the time when her child was to be born was an unfamiliar being. She seemed out of men's reach in a world of her own and yet was attractive. I wanted to do something for her, something special, or else to have from her a smile that recognized me—a personal word.

Nattana abruptly declared that she did not want to stay away from home—and Father—too long. She objected to Nettera's coming to the gate with us, but the latter came notwithstanding and stood smiling and holding tightly to it with both her thin hands while we mounted. Things I would have liked to say occurred to me too late.

Behind us the settlement of the Ensings' dependents—of whom Nettera was now one—sank into a low green mound and the vast U-shaped valley became spacious again. A golden light had softened all its colors; and the mountains on the other side were light and unsubstantial and of soft tones above the upward sweep of the yellow pasturelands.

"It's upsetting to see Nettera," said Nattana. "I don't quite know why. What do you think, John Lang? Do you mind talking about it? You are a foreigner and different. Everyone here has ideas as to how it ought to be; and there is no one else but you."

How to formulate in words feelings that seemed to go beneath them and in which grief, attraction, interest, and pleasure were inextricably mingled?

"It is hard to say . . ." I began.

"Isn't it!" she cried.

We fell silent, and our horses walked.

"She seems to accept it," I said at last. "And I would not say that she looked unhappy."

"Nettera accepts too much," she said. "She never complains."

"Does she still play her fife-flute?"

"Oh, yes—and she always will. There is that!"

"What do *you* think, Nattana?"

"I am miserable."

"Is Nettera being criticized? Is she going to suffer for that reason?" I asked.

Nattana stirred uncomfortably.

"Father," she said.

"Why don't you tell me what is bothering you, Nattana?"

"Oh!" she cried. "You tempt me!"

"Why shouldn't you? You have said that I was outside, and that there was no one else.'"

"If you were an Islandian, what would you think about Nettera?"

It was only safe to be honest.

"If I did not know her . . . Well, I would wonder. But I do know her."

"What would you wonder?"

"I might think her—light, easy—not to be respected especially. But I know her, Nattana."

"How does that change what you think?"

"She is not like most women. I can't judge her."

"But you think she has done a thing a woman can be judged for?"

"Yes . . . hasn't she? Don't Islandians judge women who have done as she has?"

"Some, but not all. Don't you judge Bain, too?" she asked.

"Yes, I do! He hasn't been fair to her."

"So you judge them both, or would if Nettera were different and like a more ordinary woman. You would judge me, perhaps. I'm ordinary, am I not?"

"More so than she is."

"Would you judge me?"

"It wouldn't seem like you."

"No, it wouldn't . . . for I know enough not to have a baby!"

She spoke with strong feeling and with anger. "And I'd never do what she did, for there was nothing in her toward him at all! She liked some men, but not him specially. There would have to be that with me! What hurts me is that it is wrong that it should make such a difference in her life!

"Of course," she continued, "he has wanted her for a long time. It is real with him—real *ania*, I think. . . . It was his way of capturing her. But he was not kind enough to let her go, knowing how she felt about him. A love all one way isn't enough. Of course, it is a temptation when one person knows that he has all the love that can be—or thinks he has, for he can't have such a love when he lets it override the other person's lack of it. . . . You say she accepts what has happened. Oh, acceptance isn't enough!"

She spoke as though I were to blame.

"Of course, John Lang, she is different from many women. Maybe she never would have had a strong wish to be any man's wife and the wife of no other. She may be incapable of that sort of feeling. Some women are. We all used to think she ought to be married. How foolish we were! We got it from Father. She isn't the kind to marry and have babies, and live in a man's house as his wife, and be his when he wants her, and do housework. She ought to have been allowed to grow her own way and live in her music, and, oh, have her affairs if she wanted them. They would never be the main thing with her. And she might have had just that life if it wasn't for Father. It is his fault, really."

Nattana stopped.

"You see I am telling you everything," she said in a different voice, "and I don't see why I shouldn't."

"Nor do I."

She rode to my side.

"I might as well tell you about Father," she said. "I would do it sooner or later. He has many ideas, John Lang, which he picked up somewhere. I think it began when he went to the University. He did not expect to succeed my uncle, and he wanted to do so very much. He wanted to rule. I don't know whether he had a lot of children in order to have someone he could rule—but he certainly did rule us after he had us! One of his ideas was that husbands and wives should not take measures to prevent having children. He has preached that to us, but nearly everyone does in this country and has for hundreds of years. And if he felt that way he shouldn't have had two wives or he should not have gone to them so much. . . . But that was not Father! He must have everything just as he wished it." Her voice became high. "It is selfishness, John Lang. I think it is because he is weak, and could not bring himself to do one thing or the other. He won't suffer for it, but we do and we will! There are too many of us for the farm and it is very unfair to us."

"People at home think that children in a large family have a better time and are better fitted to meet the world," I said.

"That is not true here. We are a restless and unhappy family and not like others in this country. We have only two farms, and no money with which to take up new land. Soon the farms can no longer be owned as one—and they ought to be, and the cattle driven back and forth as the seasons change for change of pasture. Ek is planning to settle at the Upper Farm and Atta may go with him. They aren't rich farms and there are already enough to work them. And if we girls marry that is one thing, but if we don't . . . we will be very crowded. And Father was glad to see Nettera married although he knew she had no *ania*, because there would be one less of us to worry about! Of course he gave other reasons. But why couldn't she have had her baby without being married? I argued and argued. It was unfair to the baby, he said; unfair to Nettera, I answered. But she had no right to be considered, being to blame herself, he said—or meant. And do you know what I am afraid he is thinking, which is worse than all the rest? I am afraid he may go with the Moras in the hope that conditions will change and all of us will find opportunities in the new life that will come. Do you wonder that I'm unhappy? If I did not exist, if there were only three or four of us, he might never have these thoughts in his head. He is not now with Isla Dorn and the others. He would not go! He must be thinking of deserting them. He has not said, but. . . ."

She put her hands to her face.

"Oh, John Lang!" she groaned. "It may not be so at all. I oughtn't to have told you all this."

"Yes, you ought!" I cried in nervous distress. Islandia had never shown me this face before.

"No. . . . I'm not sure about him."

"You ought if it helps you."

"It makes me ashamed! I wish you would hit me and make me angry."

She leaned forward on her horse and put him on the run, leaving mine as though standing, but soon he started after her.

She looked back and laughed. She wanted to be pursued, and I did so, hoping that I would not be able to catch her. The hope was realized. She disappeared where a trail led down into the ravine of the Hyth River. Racing was no longer possible here. I thought she would wait for me, but when we reached the edge she was already crossing the bridge. I dared not ride a borrowed horse at such break-neck speed. When I reached the level ground on the other side she was streaking away across the pasture far ahead. She did not look back. It was rather annoying to be left in this way, and still more so not to find her in the stable when at last I arrived.

Next morning, however, when Nattana, her father and I set out for The City, she was serene and happy again, and our friendship seemed to have been cemented now that we both knew the other's troubles.

We took three days for the journey, arriving late in the after-noon of the third day. I parted from Nattana, promising to call on her at the Upper Doring Palace, and rode off to stay with the Fains, and knowing that Dorna would surely be in The City now, I looked for her on every corner.

21

June, 1908: Lord Mora Speaks

THE PALACE OF ISLANDIA PROVINCE, that of the Fains, faces upon City Square together with the four public buildings of the nation. My room was in the second story looking out upon the square itself, and I was truly in the thick of things, with every advantage that a newspaper correspondent, even a self-appointed one, could have.

The Fains had not yet come. My time was my own until evening. I planned my work. It must be ready to send by the eighteenth, when S.S. *Sulliaba* was due.

The thing to do was to keep on the move. Next morning I called on the Periers and was asked to their dinner on the fourteenth. M. Perier was nervous. He felt that the occasion was too serious for dinner parties, but everyone was entertaining almost as usual and he must do as the rest did. He shrugged his shoulders and made me tell of my affairs. At the end he said he envied me, but that it was necessary for him to live. When I inquired what he thought would happen, he asked to be spared. His colleagues, he said, were in no mood to have the Dorn Party prevail, and that was all.

At my room writing my narrative I achieved with effort a detached attitude, but when I talked with anyone it was impossible.

According to M. Perier, who knew everything, the adherents of Isla Dorn were arriving on this day, the tenth. Restlessness sent me to the Lower Doring Palace late in the afternoon to do no more perhaps than to pay my respects. A conference of some sort was just breaking up. I saw in the hall Marriner, the Lord of Winder, Some, and Fain. In addition to these was Farrant, the Admiral. He had not been among the Dorn stalwarts, and his presence was interesting news.

Isla Dorn spoke to me. There was a flush in his cheeks and his eyes were bright and tired. He was cordial, but absent-minded.

"There is room for you here with us, Lang," he said. "Come if you wish. And don't neglect us at the Island."

Dorn came out of an inner room. He seemed in the prime of condition, but with the same bright flush, and by contrast he made his uncle look frail.

We shook hands.

"I came to lay eyes on you and to see how you all were, and no more," I said.

"We are well!" he cried. "And you, you are well, too! And I have some time to spare!"

He was like a war horse.

We went into another room and he closed the door, and asked what I had been doing. Briefly I told him, ending with the ride back to The City.

"Hyth left us," he said. "He wrote us that he was not sure enough that we were taking the right path to be of any use to us. I don't doubt that it did not please Nattana."

"No," I answered, believing that she would not mind my saying so.

"Nor Nekka!" he added with a laugh. His eyes fixed mine. "Nor Nekka," he repeated, and his strong hands clasped and unclasped.

A confidence was imminent and I waited.

"She is one of us," he said, "or will be in fact when the country is quieter. Nekka is somewhat hurt, but all is as it should be."

There was a flash of pain in the eager happiness of his face.

"For a time," he continued, "I thought either I would be weak or she would come to see things my way, and both have happened."

What he said caused a shock of gladness and of relief in which a sensation of sudden isolation mingled.

"I am very glad!" I said.

"She will do you and me no harm," he answered unexpectedly. "I want her very much, and she wants me—enough. She will make my life whole for me, as it has not been. I shall be a freer man, and she will be more solidly based in her life. It is as it should be."

Was there not a doubt in this reiteration? I wondered and was hurt, begrudging him nothing, but he made sharp again my loneliness and thwarted longings. The curatives of farming, travel, and writing seemed dull, arid, and trivial.

"For me," he was saying, "it has been Nekka or no one. Another woman would have been—not really a complete woman, for she is all my *apia* and all my *ania*—everything. I've seen clearly what I wanted for a long time—life with Nekka as she can and promises to be. She fits into my heart and my senses and my house. No one else ever has. . . . I know that some other woman might perhaps become as dear nine or ten years from now. I never quite gave up, of course, though we have been so far apart that I had little hope of her. There have been no others. I'm not exceptional in that. I've had too clear and too real a picture of what life with her could be really to want second bests. If a man does not have so clear a picture, if he does not see as a whole the life he is to lead with a woman, if he merely wants to love her and have her, then when he cannot have her, other women may content him for a while, and he can turn to them more easily. But I could not, and sometimes I was sorry for myself."

He laughed and stretched his strong, long body.

"I am not sorry for myself now," he added.

"Nor am I sorry for you. I am glad."

"You are good to say so," he answered. "I know how you feel."

"I do feel great gladness!"

He drew a deep breath.

"It was a little hard to tell you. As soon as I have time enough for her I am going to her, and that depends upon what happens in the next few days. She is at the Hyths' Upper Farm."

He rose suddenly from his chair.

"What can I do for you?" he cried.

"Nothing now."

"Later we will have another journey. And the Island—you will come?"

"Of course!"

"Will you come to our dinner on the thirteenth? My sister will be there."

"Oh no, if you don't mind."

"No one will be hurt. All of us, Tor and Dorna, and also Mora and the diplomats, will be present. We have left out Hyth. The dinner is too frankly one of our party. Tell Nattana why her father isn't included if you have a chance. I'm not likely to have one."

Soon afterwards I left him. . . . Perhaps the thirteenth would be a suitable day in which to call upon Nattana. Dorn was now a little lost to me, or so it seemed, though I tried hard not to feel that he was.

It was bewildering to be full of eager interest in what was to happen and yet to have that interest made remote and theatrical by personal loneliness; and it was hard to sleep knowing that I was to see Dorna next day, wakened from nervous drowsing by the beating of my heart.

The eleventh of June, nineteen hundred and eight! It was not a day on which to be worried and to wonder, caught in the entangling web of one's own personal loss and unhappiness—not a day in which to feel that the great events that were to take place were things seen in a dream. Soon would occur the most important event in Islandia's history, also significant in that of the world: this test of a nation's right to be individualistic, to work out alone her own way of living, to refuse to yield to the new Western civilization, commercial and industrial, and to hold for herself material things, which other nations coveted, because the touch of the foreigner upon these things would endanger what she believed to be good. Yet all day writing I could not feel the real, which my mind knew to exist.

An invitation came from the Moras to their great dinner next day. I declined it, fearing that Dorna would be there—sorry almost immediately afterwards.

At last it was time to go to the Lambertsons'. The prelude to my narrative was written and the rest must be completed from day to day. We dined at the hotel, all in European dress, and went to the palace in carriages. The minister and his wife, his secretary, a woman who was a friend of Mrs. Lambertson, two Americans, and I made up the party, a more numerous group than George and myself a year ago.

We were only just in time. All the boxes except one or two among the Islar were filled. The colors of cloaks and costumes were for a moment those of the palette of a painter gone quite color-mad and squeezing out all his tubes. Individual faces were indistinguishable. Above it all the upper, empty parts of the room were quiet but with a breathless golden glow as exciting as the colors themselves. The faces of the rest of our party had a peculiar orange shine, and their eyes were very bright.

Lambertson placed me on his left with his wife on his right, and her friend beyond.

My heart beat like a hammer, and all the colors became remote and swayed. Faces were like tiny miniatures.

The door, the little door in the silent blank wall, opened. Tor stood within its portals, in green, his head held high. At his left side and a little behind him was a figure also in green, small and slight. They waited for a moment and then came forward in step, like a machine, like dolls—a high fair head of yellow curling hair, a brown head at a lower level, but held as proudly.

They stopped between the boxes. His eyes gleamed as they swept over us. The figure at his side, smaller than he, was half a step behind him. Her chin lifted. Her expression was cool, but a little amused. So was his—as though they had been laughing together before they entered and had not made their faces wholly solemn.

They stood there side by side for long, long seconds.

He spoke the ancient formula of greeting in a clear resonant voice: their leader welcomed them, representatives of the people of Islandia. . . .

He and she knew each other now as intimately as man and woman can. I forced my knees to uphold me.

"The council is assembled," he said in his easy voice, and stepping a little to one side he turned to the woman as the first on the roll of names to be called.

"Dorna!"

Her name re-echoed, full of love, it seemed, and yet playful. She bowed to him graciously and yet with a touch of mockery. Ice and fire . . . I felt them both.

"Tora!" He turned, unconscious of the magnificence of his supple tall figure, to his sister who was behind him.

He was the man who had loved and taken my Dorna.

The princess answered with a bow that was a little stiff.

"Dorn!"

"Mora!"

So the roll continued.

Mrs. Lambertson leaned to her husband, and whispered:

"The queen is a very pretty woman. . . ."

Dorna was pretty on this day. Her hair was very softly done. She stood with her hand on her hip, holding back her cape, showing its tan lining and revealing the long curve from her waist to her knee. She seemed slighter and more slender, softer, and younger. Even her expression was that of the pretty girl, a little spoiled.

She was herself and not herself. There she stood, Tor's girl, his wife, not a queen at all. I had seen her austere and cold; stunning and beautiful; as a companion in out-of-doors activities with bare feet and blue skirt stained with white salt; ridiculous with her braid turned back on top of her head; naked and unconscious against blue water and sky and orange sand; brooding speechless before an open fire; in many, many phases; but this was a new one—Dorna doll-like and pretty.

Tor at her side, calling the roll, had lost all his effeminacy and never before had looked so strong.

The last name of all was Shane, Lord of Farrant, successor to the old man whom I had visited more than a year before.

Tor's greeting to the diplomats was brief. He did not describe them as "guests," merely saying that the ministers and consuls of foreign nations were welcome. Lambertson asked me to translate and I did so in a whisper.

Tor finished, and I saw him coming toward us. Last year the parade had begun at the other end of the row of diplomatic boxes. There was no time to move myself.

He came straight to Lambertson. The others were falling in behind him. Dorna was half-hidden by his body. I heard his voice, then hers—remote, yet the one familiar thing in a world that had become a dream. She said no more to them than a greeting in French. Tor spoke for both.

He was speaking to me. I held my eyes upon him. A green blur with a vivid face watching mine was at his side. He had shaken hands with Lambertson and his wife, and now he took mine. He said in Islandian that he hoped I would remain as long as I could—no more —and moved on.

I looked at Dorna. She was what she always had been, and seemed no longer only half herself, but her face was subtly aged and changed. Like her husband, polite to the stranger, she gave her hand, and the hand that I had for a moment—warm, nervous, well known—was reality amid a whirl.

"How do you do, John?" She spoke in English, and her accent made her foreign.

"I am well," I answered. "How are you, Dorna?"

"I am happy." Her English was slow and careful.

I looked into her eyes. There was something that we had together. . . . Was her happiness true?

"The Island misses you," she said suddenly in her own language, and her hand tightened for a second, and then she also moved on.

A moment later I was introducing and interpreting. I had caught a glance from both the Lambertsons when Dorna called me "John." There was a mean triumph in my heart. . . .

Tora passed us and she gave me a quick smile almost shy. She was lovely and haughty, and I wondered if her brother's marriage was what she wished and how friendly she and Dorna were.

The Fains came. They, I explained, were the persons with whom I was staying. Then the Stellins were before us, and the friendliness of the faces of these four, cool, purified, was a solid thing again.

As last year, Count von Bibberbach held the royal party in conversation for a long time, and in the interruption the Calwins were equally long in front of us; but they knew some English.

Movement began again. The Bodwins, the Somes, the Robbans, and then Isla Baile by himself passed by.

"You have not come to see me," he said severely and went on.

Isla Dorn and my friend appeared, and I was "John Lang" to one and "John" to the other. Lambertson seemed to be making a special point of hearty cordiality.

Dax of Dole, his wife, and Tory, his predecessor, were next, and then quite suddenly the red heads of Isla Hyth, his son, his stepson, and of Nattana, more golden and bronze than theirs. Her face emerged substantial and familiar. I introduced and interpreted, holding her in the corner of my eyes.

They began to move, and I looked at her, and she remained. Dasel of Vantry and Banwina his wife were standing before the Lambertsons. I spoke their names quickly and turned to Nattana.

"Are you free in the evening day after tomorrow?"

She seemed ill at ease, her eyes continually jumping to Mrs. Lambertson.

"Aren't you going to the Dorns'?" she asked.

"No."

She uttered a laugh, half of surprise, half of understanding.

"I'll be at home all evening," she said.

Dasel and Banwina passed her; and her eyes widened in dismay and embarrassment.

"I've got to get back into line!" she cried.

"Your dress is perfect!" I answered to her back as she fled. She was awkward, shy—a country girl! She looked over her shoulder and smiled. She wore the dress she had made, blue with a white blouse whose collar was edged with buff and embroidered with green, and she had woven green threads into her braids. The bronze-gold of her hair upon her round head was brilliant above her green eyes and soft red lips. She was pretty—and a needed friend.

I turned to rescue the Lambertsons, stranded with Isla Shane of Farrant.

Several others filed past us, and at last came Lord Mora and Calwina, and both of their sons and daughters. With him the Lambertsons did not need me, and I could talk to Morana and the second son, and include Mrs. Lambertson's friend, because they all knew some English.

Morana spoke of my book. It was being read by many people in Miltain. I had half forgotten our friendship, and it was a pleasure to find it again.

"Do come and see us," she said as she left. "Not all our visitors are political and our house is yours, you know."

There came others with many invitations cordially given. Though I had lost Dorna, her country as a whole was most kind.

But I had lost her. With her husband she drove home in my heart like a nail a fact which my imagination had sought to escape.

That night, in the room overlooking the dim oval pavement of City Square, I wrote of the reception, trying to reproduce in words its brilliant colors.

All things in Islandia were turned toward tomorrow's meeting. I also turned, seeking not to be submerged in my own personality. My mind responded, but when at last I put out my candles and went to bed, I saw again vivid colors and faces as vivid, the glow of amber light, and a shifting and changing procession, with sudden flashes startling in their detailed reality. Dorna's was not among them. The

461

memory of her was of a pretty girl, a young thing, a man's enjoyment. It hurt to remember her so, and not to see her. But Nattana's round head came again, and Dorn's ruddy face, large, strong, contented. . . . He thought of Nekka to whom he was going soon. . . . There was Tora's unexpected personal smile, but perhaps the Tors had been told of my vain wooing—and the faces of the Stellins, clear, thoughtful, Emersonian. There was no longer any strangeness in Islandian countenances and expressions. Myself half one of them, I longed for that which would bring them greatest happiness; and yet, half an alien, I stood apart and lonely, but free of prejudices at last. Why should they swim with the world? But I, John Lang, a stranger, wanted passionately to go deeper into their beautiful, ample life, that was so free and still seemed so mysterious. . . . The great day had already come, for it was long past midnight.

The atmosphere of the whitely lighted Council Room, with its timber roof and carved stone walls, was electric. It was so crowded that there was not a vacant place, and behind the benches on which the members were seated some of their assistants had to stand. All wore their colors. In the second row of benches, just behind Isla Dorn, was my friend and two men whom I did not know, and two others were erect behind these. There was a similar group at Lord Mora's place.

Lambertson with whom I sat asked many questions.

At last Tor entered, with his sister and with Dorna. In a plain green dress and with hair done more severely she appeared no longer as a merely pretty girl, but as an intelligent woman under the handicap of too much youth and of a loveliness that distracted men's attention from her mind. She seemed to be playing a game! And for days I must sit in the same room with her, seeing her at a distance, and always longing for her beauty and to have her as mine, and always aching because of her palpable wifehood.

She and Tora went at once to the right-hand row of benches and sat together in a striking contrast to each other, next to the snow-white cap of Isla Fain's fine head.

Tor took his seat and Lord Mora rose. The crowded room was instantly hushed, its bright colors as still as flowers in a windless garden.

The usual report was briefly made. Then he stated that he had many communications from foreign governments, but that all of these related to the same thing: what action would the council take upon the treaty which he had concluded with the German government now nearly three years ago? The day for such action had at last come, and he and many others had no uncertainty in their minds at all.

He paused. This was only preliminary.

Lambertson buzzed questions in my ear, and I tried to translate significant parts, but I wanted to listen and to do nothing else, and not to be a mere interpreter.

Lord Mora's voice was warm and resonant. He spoke with deep feeling and perfect control.

"What is the natural unit of society? We have discovered that it is not the individual, nor the family, nor the tribe. The Descent from the Frays would have been impossible if single men, or families, or tribes, had acted separately. We lost our land because we lived selfishly as individuals, but, compressed into unity in the Frays, we acted as a nation, and we regained it.

"So it has been throughout our history. We have fought as a united people for the sake of all. We want freedom, which we know can never be absolute, but we are more free through subordination to a common purpose than through individualism.

"We are isolated, and we are very different from our near neighbors, and it is not strange that we have come to regard our nation and the people who live here as a natural and final unit of society. But is this so?

"We have met foreigners from overseas and we have found that we have much in common. We differ more from the foreigners across the mountains, Bants and Karain; but even they are changing, and the continent is absorbing the spirit of the overseas foreigners who sit on the diplomatic benches and are our friends."

Lord Mora then spoke for some time on the similarities between Islandians and Europeans. He described instances of brotherliness, derived from his own experiences, experiences which had a common moral—that all men are fundamentally alike.

"Why should we fear increased contact with foreigners? You may argue that so far our contacts have been social—contacts where we have met in the free realm of ideas and not as competitors; but

463

where is the strangeness, the difference in kind and species that some believe to exist? If we meet them with opposing interests, can we not resolve our difficulties as Islandians resolve theirs, and have resolved them in the past?"

The noon recess came, and I went to lunch with the Lambertsons and told him as much as I could of what he had missed. We agreed that we were hearing a great speech, and we found this to be the common opinion of the diplomats when we returned. Lord Mora was a broad-minded man.

In the afternoon he traced the history of Western civilization, speaking not of nationalism, but of the spread and development of the Western way of living as a whole. He pointed out its striking characteristics, common to Europe, the Americas, Australia, and large parts of Asia and Africa: industrialism, commerce, and ease of intercommunication. These things led to various results: increased dependence of a man upon the work of many others unknown to him; specialization in labor; standardization in manner of life and in ideas; and complexity in a man's contacts with his fellows. In many ways the life of the foreigner was richer than that of the Islandian, and was it not enrichment of life that made for vigor and freedom?

He then graphically described the infinity of things that the average man had and the Islandian did not: trains and automobiles which could take him hundreds of miles instead of tens in a day; foods from many climates preserved in numerous ways; literatures of different nations; a panorama of music and of painting; more various recreations; conveniences in his home; power to communicate within hours instead of days, or within minutes by telephone and telegraph; more to see, more to think about, more varied people to talk to, and sometimes in his work a wider scope for his activity and ambition; and as a young man a wide choice of paths to follow.

"This civilization is still growing and changing, and for those who accept it, life is vivid, active, and various. It is spreading through the world, peopling its waste places; primitive peoples are drawn within its culture, and other civilizations have felt its impact and adopted it. It is a great stream of irresistible power. Conscious of its strength, it knows no barriers to its extension, and, conscious of its rightness, it sees no other civilization but as its inferior. Shall Islandia stand alone against a force so strong and so full of promise for mankind? And if she wishes, can she do so? This is a civilization of many hungers and Islandia has great unused riches, needed by the rest of the world."

It was near the shortest day of the year and dark came early. Attendants went about lighting candles, and waked me from an attention that was as absorbing as sleep and that had made me forget Lambertson entirely. Looking around the gathering I saw everyone still and listening. Lord Dorn sat erect in his seat, his eyes never leaving Lord Mora, shadows in his cheeks. My friend had crossed his long legs and had made himself comfortable. Nattana, unnoticed, had come in and was sitting close behind her father, whose head was high and who looked inspired. On the other side of the hall, Dorna sat with bent head and flushed cheeks. Lord Fain's white head was also bent.

I seemed to feel myself moving and many moving with me. Lord Mora had made the march of progress a living thing. Islandia was an island in danger of being submerged. A spell was upon us all.

"These things—the reality of the outer world—must be clearly visualized by the members of the council. This is why I have dwelt so long on Western civilization. What it is, what it wishes, and its strength, must be well understood."

He then spoke upon its strength: the intensification of industry, the increase in wealth, and the increase in population; and the enormous power of modern armies and navies. Hundreds of millions of people, and Islandia had but three!

"And what does it wish?"

The time to adjourn for the day had come.

"At this rate," Gordon Wills said to Lambertson, "he will speak for a week; but he is magnificent. His idea of our civilization as a whole is worth hearing. It comes rather a surprise to find that to him we are all much the same."

Lambertson looked sleepy.

I went to my room at the Fains' and wrote all I could remember with a flying pen.

Lambertson came next morning for a few moments only, and I listened undisturbed to Lord Mora's account of what Western civilization wanted.

465

It wanted all the resources of land and water, of the air over them, and of what lay beneath. Its needs were enormous and its progress so great that there was no natural wealth which it could pass by and remain consistent with its ideal of growth.

The wealth of Islandia!

He made statements as to the known mineral riches of the Island of Ferrin and of Winder, and to the known coal wealth of Hern and Niven that astonished many of us. The unknown wealth was probably as great, notably the oil of Dole. And there was more unutilized valuable timber near navigable waters than anywhere else except in Northwestern America.

"Our agricultural possibilities are almost as great, and because we are a nation trained to subsist alone, we can buy what we want, and our gain can be turned to enduring things. We will enter the stream of progress not as a beggar, but as a nation of great wealth. Thus our position will always be strong, and our bargaining power as favorable as that of any other country.

"Western civilization—a unity, though represented by ministers and consuls from different nations—needs, wants, demands (in my opinion rightly demands), and eventually must and will have full use of Islandian resources. In the same way, it demands the opportunity to spend its surplus vitality in making these resources useful to the world. Foreign nations are crowded and their vigorous young men go elsewhere. It is this that has brought about the great development of the German Karain."

Lord Mora then described the colonies growing up to the northwest and enumerated their needs: coal, iron, timber, live stock, and foods.

It was well done. From the general he moved to the specific.

He spent the afternoon in describing the results to Islandia of ratification of his treaty. Islandia might buy and import whatever she wished and foreigners could sell whatever they could find a market for. Certain ports would be designated as ports of entry. Banks would be established to finance trade transactions. Foreigners must be allowed to come and go under the conditions the rest of the world found sufficient—substitution of the ship's bill of lading for the present medical examination and there must be no limitations on their time of residence.

He concluded by painting a picture of Islandia under these conditions, saying that no man would be hurried into a new way of living.

Returning in a hurry to the Fain Palace, I wrote rapidly and had supper by myself, for Lord Fain and his brother had both gone to the Dorns' dinner. One who declines too many cordially given invitations for personal reasons not inimical to his hosts feels lonely and a little bitter at no one in particular. In this mood, and also tired by two days of sitting and listening and several evenings of writing, I went to see Nattana.

The distance was short, but the night was dark with a penetrating damp cold wind. The Upper Doring Palace stood in a garden frozen in winter sleep. It was a large stone mansion nearly two hundred feet long, two stories high, and simple in outline. Most of its rows of windows were dark with only here and there a faint glow. The low door was lit by a lanterned candle; and its flame, flickering and twisting in the wind, seemed to be striving to cling to the wick, knowing that if once it lifted it would expire. I rang the bell and heard a distant clang within.

Markan let me in and showed me to a small room with dark hangings, an open fire, and a high-backed bench facing it. Two candles on each of two low tables at the sides gave a soft yellow light.

It was some time before she came, and being still cold I brought the fire to a bright blaze, even though I had not known her the seven years necessary to permit interference with another's hearth. There was no one in Islandia whom I had known so long, not even Dorn. Friendships were all new, but this life seemed a natural one though still only a beginning. Was it going to be merely an episode? So would it be if I returned; so would it be if I remained, but foreigners also came introducing their way of life.

Nattana entered, a little breathless. She wore a tan-colored skirt and a jacket of the same color, rather closely belted and having broad green lapels and cuffs, a blouse the color of cream, tan stockings rolled down below the knee, and green sandals. Her face had a clean-washed look, and her hair shone, sleek with brushing. She was stylish and the care she had taken of her appearance was flattering.

She at one corner of the bench with a leg beneath her and the other hanging, and I at the other, watched each other and talked weather. The fire was bright and warm. Her father and brothers were

467

busy elsewhere and we had an evening before us. Each had confided in the other. We had a past that gave color to our present.

Conversation was slow, a little difficult, and very pleasant. Soon we had asked each other what we thought of Lord Mora's speech. Neither of us had anything but generalities in mind, and our answers were of the vaguest.

"I don't know what I think," she said after a pause. "I don't believe that I am thinking at all."

Nor was I, and I admitted it. Yet the speech was the most critical and interesting event in years.

"What is the matter with us?" I asked.

"Is anything the matter?"

"We ought to have something more than this to say about so important a thing."

"Why ought we?"

"Maybe we are a little overwhelmed by it and can't wholly take it in."

Her green eyes dwelt on mine and she laughed, but soon she was grave again and her eyes dropped.

"There are reasons," she said. "One is that we have each been under a strain."

"Do you mean that we are a little dazed by the great decision that is going to be made?"

"I ought to be more excited by that."

"Aren't you, Nattana?"

"Are you?"

It was something else.

I suggested that we might be "fatalists," but knowing no equivalent term in Islandian, expressed the idea by saying that we might be those who, impotent to influence a result, reconcile themselves to an unfavorable happening in advance, and are calm in consequence.

"But I'm not calm," she cried. "Are you?—And I don't like your 'fatalism.' "

"No," I said, "I'm not calm."

"You must be suffering, Johnlang!"

"You mean . . . seeing Dorna?" I said.

She nodded.

"I'm not suffering so much that life is spoiled," I said.

"I'm glad," she answered with sudden feeling.

"Are you worried about your father, Nattana? Is that the strain you are under?"

"It is a strain . . . I don't want him to desert the Dorns. He is with Earne and Calwin and the two boys and Amel, the Upper Doring agent—that's why I am receiving you in this little room—and he has been seeing Mora people every day!"

"A person can honestly believe with Lord Mora."

"Oh yes, I know, and if he does he must vote as he believes; but I am so familiar with what he thinks that a vote for the Moras means that he has come to have beliefs that aren't going to make for his happiness or ours. He talks about more order and more rules so often, Johnlang! It is the sign of the growth in him of a mania for that sort of thing. Of course, it is his way of working out a solution for a bad situation, but it is so unfortunate a way!"

"You have reason to suffer," I said.

She frowned with what seemed annoyance. She smoothed the base of her palm along her leg. Her spread fingers were pretty, and her bare knee, upon which the hem of her skirt lay lightly, was pink in the firelight.

"Don't think I suffer," she said, "but I *am* under a strain. One doesn't suffer when life is almost too full to bear and one is not afraid."

"Aren't you afraid of change, Nattana?"

"No! I don't want it, but I'm not afraid."

"Does life seem very full?"

She shifted her position so suddenly that it was startling.

"Yes," she said. "Full of things I want to do, and to see, and to know, and to feel."

She sat now on the edge of the bench with both feet on the floor, her elbows on her knees, her face between her hands, looking into the fire, and sighed profoundly.

"Nattana . . ." I began, but what was there to say? "I think I understand . . ."

"It is nice of you to say so," she answered. "Nothing special is the matter—only youth and being a Hyth!"

In her voice was a hint of laughter, and for obscure reasons I envied her.

"I don't see how being a Hyth is a trouble, Nattana."

She uttered a sharp little cry.

"We have red hair."

"It is red and gold and bronze—several colors."

"Do you like my hair?"

"Yes, I do. It is always interesting. But what is the matter with red hair?"

" 'Red hair—a hot heart.' "

"Instead of 'pale-pink emotions,' Nattana?"

"Oh, don't please remind me of what I said so long ago!"

"Does it seem long ago?"

"Years! So much has happened."

"To you, Nattana, as well as to me?"

"Not quite the same," she said with a little laugh; yet there was a distressing suspicion in my heart; and a memory of what she had said after the visit to her sister sharpened it.

"Is 'red hair—a hot heart' an Islandian proverb?" I asked.

"It is a family saying."

"Because you are bad-tempered?"

"Johnlang, it is not merely that!"

"You have never shown bad temper to me. You warned me of your temper, you may remember."

"I would be ashamed of myself always if I ever did," she cried.

"Nattana, that is nice of you!"

"It is the way I feel about you. Did you ever show bad temper to anyone?"

"Of course."

"I don't believe you."

I wondered if sweet temper was not in her mind a concomitant of "pale-pink emotions."

"Try me," I said.

"Oh, don't tempt me, Johnlang. Don't lead me to make our friendship a common thing! It is too fine."

"It certainly is, Nattana."

For a while we sat looking into the fire. Her suggestions that she had a hot and troubled heart and that she had had experiences not dissimilar to mine, combining with recollections of her frankness and freedom, were disturbing and caused a pressing desire to know more about her. . . .

"You have perhaps only eleven months more of Islandia," she said.

The time seemed short—eleven months in a lifetime!

"I know it," I said.

"Your *History of the United States* made me realize how far away your country is and how long the journey is . . . It would be ten years before you could come back again."

"Would you like to visit the United States, Nattana?"

She lifted one shoulder and hesitated.

"I don't know . . . I don't think so!"

It hurt a little.

"I am sure you would be interested," I said.

"It is impossible for me ever to think of it! Coming only to The City is a great event!"

"We can write to each other." But it was a futile compensation.

"There are still eleven months, Johnlang—and you will be at the Fains' most of the time, won't you?"

"Yes," I answered, "and I will come and see you. Do you remember that you suggested that I make you a real visit and I said that I certainly would."

"That wasn't just politeness?"

"No!"

"I like to feel sure . . . A real visit—a month?"

"Yes, Nattana."

"There may be a few difficulties—but we won't bother with them now."

"What sort?"

"Father's ideas," she said shortly, and it made me uncomfortable. The room was very quiet, but there was a faint ringing in my ears and a feeling as of having moved swiftly in a dream and of waking up to find myself here, with Nattana. I had looked at her round head for a long time and I wanted to see her face again. Hers was a good strong back, but saved from heaviness by the suppleness of her waist.

After some time she said:

"You know, I have said things to Father—my bad temper!— which may make it hard, for him and me both, to live together if both of us are at the Lower Farm—that is, if he should vote with the Moras. I may move to the Upper Farm for a few years."

"Would you dislike that very much?"

"I would miss the openness and bigness of the lower valley. It is more shut up in there. One can't see so far or ride so far." She

471

paused. "But it might simplify your coming on a visit. You would not mind working a little, would you?"

"Oh no!"

"I would be working. I am going to weave and weave and make lovely things! Hyth Ek and Hyth Atta would not mind your coming. Atta likes you a great deal. And if you helped us all—oh, it would go so well!"

"I am coming," I said.

"Of course, the Mora Pass will probably be closed to horses within a few weeks. If you come this winter . . ." She paused. "You oughtn't to come alone," she continued. "There is no regular travel, you know. If you were caught in a storm . . . But Don has his own route and knows the snow and knows the mountains. He crosses over several times a winter. He could guide you. I know he would like to. Are you fairly strong, John?" She said "John," not "Johnlang."

"Stronger than I was," I answered.

"It would be wonderful to have you come that way during this winter and not to wait until spring. Days go by without anyone passing. Snow falls and the road, instead of being marked with tracks, is clean and smooth between the trees."

"I'll come, Solvadia," I said, and my heart beat with the sudden impulse and the daring to use this name. Nattana faintly sighed, and there was silence again.

She went to fetch the little nutty cakes and the wine that is served between meals. And, as if released, we talked of Islandian food and of American food, and compared diets and wines; and this led us to statements that Lord Mora had made. There was no longer any difficulty in "thinking" about his speech. She wanted to test these statements in the light of my knowledge. We did not decide anything or argue. It was the perfect conversation of two persons interested in one thing, with varying theories and degrees of knowledge, glad to exchange with each other all they thought and knew. Time was winged. It was late when I left Nattana, and the hint that made me go was the passing of footsteps in the corridor outside the door, which marked the breaking up of Lord Hyth's conference with Earne and Calwin and Amel.

Yet once more out in the darkness and penetrating damp, bound to the Fains' mansion on City Hill, I felt the ties that bound me to them to be the stronger; and I knew that through them, rather than through Nattana, Islandia was partly mine, for dear as she was the ties that held me to her were like those established in drunkenness, evanescent and on sober afterthought unreal. She was charming, and she was most kind to me and truly a friend; but when I was gone from her brightness and color the old grief came back again with grimmer hardness, and I was more alone than ever. It was dazing to realize freshly again with wonder and despair that I was not to have what I wished, that Dorna was not mine and never would be.

Soft large flakes of snow were falling outside the Council Chamber, and the light within was intensely white. Lambertson was in attendance again, because, as he said, he had been told that the premier was to speak on very important matters today. He had had a good time at the Moras' dinner and at the Dorns'; though one could see easily that the premier was a man of the world and a statesman and that his other host was provincial—but nevertheless a gentleman! . . . Had I heard any rumors as to how the council was likely to vote? There was a good deal of talk going around. At the Fains' and Hyths' little was to be learned. Nattana's prognostications were too vague and perhaps too feminine to be mentioned. Nor had I discussed this matter with other Islandian friends. I said that I had heard nothing and did not know.

"Monsieur Perier thinks the Dorn Party has a majority. Count von Bibberbach declares the opposite," said Lambertson. "As for me, it seems incredible that a country so primitive and yet so wealthy should pass by its opportunities. Look at Japan!"

"Their minds aren't primitive," I said.

Tor and his sister and Dorna entered to interrupt our conversation.

Not once had she looked toward the benches of the diplomats, and she had few smiles and glances for anyone except Lord Fain and, more rarely, her sister-in-law; but she had listened closely all the time. Day by day she seemed less pretty and soft and more firm and strong. She had lost nothing of her look of youth, and yet the shadows of thought were upon her eyes and in her cheeks.

I seemed to see her with new eyes. She was not merely a wife and a man's pretty enjoyment. She was an intelligent young woman with a will and a purpose. She was one of the council, her best given to its problems. I had loved her, greatly daring. I had wanted to marry her, but she was too much an Islandian and too vital and too strong for the only life I had to offer her. There was rightness in what she had done, and though its recognition had crossed all the currents of my heart, my mind fully realized it. I was not the man for her. It was unimportant whether my lacks were inherent in me or lay in my training as an American. It was hard to admit it. I had loved her deeply and had desired her with all the force of which my manhood was capable. Loss of her had made death welcome—and this I would never forget. It was hard to see her in her beauty and power and youth as a stranger, but a stranger she seemed, yet one who was still a little a friend. The rightness of the cleavage between us was a chilling thing. My heart ached, for I loved her still.

It seemed to me that Lord Mora was a little nervous. He began hesitatingly, and re-enumerated the advantages that would accrue to Islandia as a result of that trade and intercourse which was the very soul of Western civilization; but as he spoke his voice gained in power. He described the "primitiveness" of Islandian life (I translated this to Lambertson, who smiled with satisfaction). Horses or legs were the only means of land transportation; horses on towpaths, or wind or oars the only means of moving by water. The navy alone used steam. The machines to aid agricultural life were few. . . .

He was an artist. He described vividly the advantages to Islandians of time-saving and production-increasing devices upon their farms, and of steam vessels and of railroads. These latter he particularly stressed.

"So far," he continued, "I have confined myself to the effects of trade, and the abolition of the exclusion laws. There is another side, however, perhaps the greater one. As Western civilization has developed, enterprises have been conducted more and more by large groups rather than by individuals.

"Over the mountains, in the German colonies on the west coast, coal and iron are needed. But if we supply them, will they be content with the surplus of such goods that we do not use, and with our methods of transportation and handling which are sufficient for our own needs? They wish to operate the mines by their own methods, which are less slow and more productive. A group of Germans wish to construct mines in the Herntock Hills, to build a railroad from there to Shores, to build docks at Shores for their steamers. Another group wishes the concession of iron mines in Ferrin."

Rather hurriedly, he described other requests for concessions, a large number—the syndicates of varying and mixed nationality; and then went on to describe the elaborate machinery of banks and laws necessary to the functioning of these enterprises, operations of which Islandians knew nothing, and which would take years to set up in Islandia, if Islandia refused to use foreign means and capital.

"We can forbid such activity within our borders and limit ourselves to the buying and selling I spoke of yesterday. But if we do so, we will still be holding ourselves apart from the great stream of world progress. I have said that the true unit of society is no longer national, but international. The ideal of Western civilization is the interrelation and close cohesion of men all over the world. If we sell, we must sell in the ways to which foreigners are accustomed, and it is inevitable therefore that we grant them concessions.

"You will say that if we grant concessions our way of life and the face of our country will be altered. This is true. Some spots will lose their primitive beauty, some farms their privacy, because of the near presence of mills and mines and docks and because railroads will run through them. I deplore this result, but in this loss, we will give back to the whole community—to the world—a good that wholly outweighs the harm to a few. So, although some are killed, the fruits of a victorious battle are enjoyed by all; but we need not fear death, merely personal inconvenience to some who will be benefited in other ways."

At noon Lambertson wanted to know all that had been said.

"We have got to the real issue at last," he cried. "Of course, all that long preliminary was necessary in a country so backward. What Lord Mora says is absolutely true. Mr. Lang, the pressure being asserted by business is very great. This country is so rich—the Island of Ferrin alone contains billions. If Islandian enterprise were up to the mark—that is one thing; but as Lord Mora and we all know from past history, it never has been and is not likely to be. There is a wonderful opportunity here for the investment of foreign capital. Of course the distances to the great centers are long, but this is a part of the world that can grow to be another United States!"

We returned to hear Lord Mora describe the benefits that would accrue from the granting of concessions.

"I have mentioned," he said, "only the general benefit—that Islandia will not stand in the path of world progress. If this were the only one, I am not sure that it is not enough; but there are others, for every concession will give back more than it takes away.

"Lord Calwin and I have discussed the terms of the concessions with foreigners and have made our own suggestions. In every case where mineral wealth is taken a royalty will be paid; if land is used for mills, docks, or railroads, it will be paid for. This is to be expected. In particular cases there will be other direct benefits. If we grant an exclusive concession to the coal mines in Niven to the German syndicate, they will build for us a railroad from the coal fields to Suburra and The City, with the privilege of extending the line to a western port—Doring or Grase Bay. Eventually a continuous railroad will be built from Carran through Miltain, Brome, and Camia to The City, through Bostia, Loria, and Inerria, through the Doan Pass into the West to Sevin in Vantry; and our whole country will be linked together, and we shall be able to pass from one end to the other in twenty-four hours."

He described similar proposals by other groups. These direct benefits were not all, he said. They were only minor compared to the indirect benefits that would follow.

"The presence of foreigners among us and of their enterprises in active operation will give us a world consciousness we have always lacked—necessary in a world becoming more closely knit by cords of communication, a world from which an individual may try to retire, but a nation cannot."

He paused a moment.

"Every nation that has adopted Western civilization has developed as a result a more active, more powerful, and more centralized government, for without such a government it could not respond to the demands of that civilization. This will be true for Islandia.

"Problems arising from the granting of concessions require such a government for their solution. Islandian resources are owned in different ways: privately and by the one business group with which we are already familiar—the proprietors of a province. We cannot allow resources to be withheld from utilization because of the caprice of individuals or groups. We have recognized already the right of the government to take land for army and navy purposes and for roads; and we must concede its right to control natural resources for those broader purposes I have mentioned, making of course due compensation to those whose property is taken.

"There has been too much individualism—too little awareness of a larger world. With such a government, strong and centralized from the necessities of commerce, we can set up a system of national education to give Islandians the ideas and ideals they should have as citizens of the world.

"We cannot casually repudiate the necessity for a strong government, because it will curtail the freedom of our private lives. Under Western civilization the contacts of man with man are closer and become more complex, and to control these contacts the individual must subordinate himself to the state. And this centralization of control over human destiny is full of hope for the world, for it brings order to the lives of men—order necessary in this civilization."

Lord Mora was tired. His voice was a little husky and dark lines had appeared in his face. Lord Dorn's eyes never left him, with an expression that seemed to me both somber and malevolent. He at least was not agreeing, and never would. Dorn looked a little sleepy and bored. The faces of other members of the council betrayed nothing. They were quiet, all were listening, but there seemed to pervade the chamber a sense of uneasiness.

"You may disagree on the benefits of such a government, but you cannot deny that the other consequences of foreign trade are for the national good—if you wish to think in terms only of the nation and not of the hungry, striving world. We have so much to give that, giving, we can never be impoverished. What is good in us is too strong to be overwhelmed. If there must be sacrifices, let us all make them for the good of others within and without our borders."

Lord Mora was moved, and his speech lost a little in clarity, but gained in emotion. He had begun his conclusion.

"I have told you of Western civilization, of its vitality, its complexity, and its richness—of what it has to offer Islandia and what we can give in return. I have spoken of how this must be brought about, how it will affect our nation and our lives. In this flow of progress we have been a barrier, standing against the current. We have clung to the life of the past, believing it the only good life for us, because it is the only one we have had; and we have clung to the con-

477

cepts of the past, which give first place to the wants of the individual and the family and ignore those of the world, which has already moved past us to broader and more rewarding ideals. To bring us into harmony with the outside world, I ask that the council vote to ratify the treaty."

He ended suddenly. Candles had already been lit. He staggered a little as he went to his seat. Had all been said that could be said for his point of view? I wished that he had spoken longer and that I felt in my mind wholly convinced by his logic, not for any other reason but that for his sake I wanted him to have done all that was humanly possible.

After being seated for a moment, he rose again.

"I am, of course, open to any questions that may be asked," he said.

Lord Dorn slowly stood, and lifted his head.

"I do not speak for all," he began, "but I know that those who in the past have agreed with me have no questions to ask. Unless others have such questions, I am prepared to say what I have to say at once."

But Tor suggested that it was late and that the council adjourn.

That night I dined with the Periers, who were kind enough to include me, for the dinner was a large and formal one and their house small. The diplomatic colony was present in force, including the Lambertsons. Of Islandians there were only Lord Mora, Calwin, and Farrant the Admiral, and their wives. These latter left early, and as soon as they were gone Lord Mora's speech was the subject of conversation. All agreed that it was a great one, a very great one, a most interesting speech—not exactly what one would expect from a Bismarck, or a Roosevelt, or a Chamberlain, and yet no doubt perfectly adapted to the hearers. Mora was a farseeing man, a man of broad vision, certainly far ahead of most of his countrymen; and yet the trouble with men of that type sometimes was this: a lack of that practical knowledge, which the narrower man often has, of the right moment for showing the mailed fist. "Or the big stick," said Lambertson, whom Roosevelt had appointed. Roosevelt and the Panama Canal and the United States of Colombia . . . The Island of Ferrin was a world necessity like the canal. . . .

The air was blue with smoke from cigars which the smokers were too busy with talking to smoke. Maybe I was a little drunk, maybe a little tired, and certainly with a longing for something fresher and clearer.

The "mailed fist," the "big stick"; one man choosing a moment and then, although only a man like others, suddenly procuring the coalescence under his control of many forces and turning them all one way, and seeming a giant in strength; Roosevelt, Bismarck; cleverness, opportunism; a flash of understanding of mass feeling because of an acute sympathy with it—this was political genius. Mora, the diplomats felt but did not like to say, had failed them in some way. Was it because he had reasoned too much and threatened too little? Or had treated Islandia as too reasonable to be seduced by eloquence and too stubborn to be affected by coercive arguments? I cannot remember their words but I felt their feelings. He was too much a man among his peers, not enough a strong man, honored by the backing of those who sat around the table dictating their wishes to his inferiors. He could have said this; he could have said that. There was a spirit of uneasiness among us.

We all sat facing inward around a table. The ladies were in the drawing room. We could hear their occasional gusts of mild laughter. Ours was much louder. Our faces shone and we all drank and smoked. Outside our circle we saw nothing. Behind us were the vacant spaces of the room. Beyond the walls of the house was a city dumb with snow, and further still more than a hundred thousand farms with people living upon them, all wrapped in winter cold.

Our conversation was inconsecutive and confused in feeling, with interruptions for broad stories, but it had one trend and one centralizing interest. Something must happen. Islandia must change. We were present to produce a change. It was our mission and our duty. . . .

Monsieur Perier, with a voice that sometimes reeled on mechanically, spurred all to talk. There was no difficulty in his French, but it was a foreign language, and because it was foreign the effort to understand it seemed to squeeze out intimacy of meaning. German was no better. The English into which Gordon Wills and Lambertson occasionally lapsed was unexpectedly quite as foreign. To translate any of these languages into Islandian would have been most difficult. There were so many words of elusive meaning that the pause necessary to find the sense in which they were used, and to fit to it an

Islandian equivalent, meant losing the rest of the speaker's utter-
ances. Suppose I tried to describe to Nattana what had been said? . . .
For example, the word "good." In Islandian there was a word that
meant good for growing crops and plants and trees; another that
indicated good for the development of *alia;* another good in cases
of illness; another good for health, physical and mental; and many
more each with a specific effect inherent in the word itself. Lambertson said to Wills that the Islandians certainly ought by this time to
have learned that foreign trade would be "good" for the country. It
could not be translated. A broad story was told, the point of which
was an embarrassing situation to a "good" woman. But how put it
into Islandian? Did "good" mean that she was a good promise-keeper,
a good housekeeper, or good as a lover?

Conversation was like a breeze rising and falling.

Perier suggested that Mora might have expected to bring out in
the course of Dorn's questioning those various matters omitted from
his speech. Everyone had an answer to make. Lord Dorn's action was
looked upon as an adroit political trick. But could it have been a trick,
Gordon Wills asked, for there was nothing to prevent Lord Mora
continuing his speech when he found that no questions were to be
asked? Yet if not a trick it was at least a political move. Great issues
should not be decided by moves or tricks. The political trick of the
'forties, when the then Lord Dorn gave foreigners an opportunity to
present their views to the council with disastrous results, would not
be repeated. The Dorns were notoriously tricky as politicians.

The Moras had never resorted to such methods, they all agreed,
and had never adopted extraofficial means to influence the opinions of
the council. But Mora had not made of his case all that could be made.
It was a little disappointing. Not enough force. . . .

Monsieur Perier wondered if the speech of Lord Dorn would be
similarly ineffective.

"I sincerely hope so," said Count von Bibberbach, and Lambertson agreed.

We joined the ladies, and John Lang, ex-consul, was sleepy and
heavy-headed with burning eyes. Conversation was now like the sound
of remote waters. They, the ladies, were of course interested. . . .
The men explained what the opinions were. They nodded their heads.

At last it was time to go. In the lull of getting wraps my host had
a word with me.

"What do you think of all this, now that you are out of it?" he asked, and I tried to think and be awake and answer.

"I want Islandia unchanged," I said.

He seemed about to speak, and instead asked another question.

"What do any of us want? We represent others. . . ."

Marie Perier said that it was a pity that I was not hearing any music. "He has become too rustic," said Jeanne.

The night air was fresh and The City lay hushed under several inches of snow. I walked with the Lambertsons and because it was slippery she took my arm as well as his. She seemed large and good and soft and unsteady and she exhaled a sweet, strong perfume.

I left them at the hotel and climbed the hill. Darkness, the quiet of The City, the breath of fresh air, and the peace of my room, made writing possible.

22

June, 1908: Lord Dorn Speaks

NEXT DAY, June 15th, I came early to the Council Meeting, because I wanted a good seat and had inferred from the excitement at the Periers' that the diplomatic benches would be crowded; but few were present. Perhaps the diplomats expected as long a speech and thought that there would be time enough later to hear Lord Dorn; perhaps also they hoped to accomplish something by the tacit disapproval in their failure to come to hear him. Or perhaps they absented themselves on the grounds that it was steamer day. At any rate they did not come. On the other hand, the benches of the Islandians were packed, and some persons invaded the back rows of the seats reserved for foreigners.

Any member had the right to ask questions of Lord Mora, but no one rose to do so. There was a long, rather tense pause. Tor asked for questions a number of times, and silence followed. Everyone was either pro-Mora or pro-Dorn. . . .

Lord Dorn finally rose and was recognized, and he began in an easy and almost casual fashion.

"I am surprised," he said, "that no one asks any questions, though to me and to some others the omissions from Mora's speech are so obvious that there is little or nothing to ask.

"There is a possible exception. We are familiar with the proposals to internationalize the Island of Ferrin. These are not mere suggestions of metallurgists, but definite requests presented by foreign governments in concert with Mora's government. They ask that Islandia surrender all but nominal sovereignty and all actual control of Ferrin, in return for which we are given a fixed amount in gold and a small proportionate share of the ores mined. We are asked to give up a supply of minerals sufficient for our needs for almost limitless generations. We are expected to play the gambling game of the rest of the world, caring only for the near future and trusting to man's ingenuity to invent something new to replace what is exhausted."

Sharply I remembered similar observations made by Dorna on the *Marsh Duck,* when she was not a wife and a queen; and looking at her profile at the end of the long row of benches I saw her cheeks brighten with color, as though she recognized her own idea.

"Mora has mentioned many requests for concessions, but not this one, so I ask no questions, assuming that this is not an issue and that he has not made up his mind to assent to it. But I speak of it because it is the next step Islandia will be asked to take, perhaps will be asked to take in any event. The foreigners may believe that the tentative adoption of the Mora Treaty two years and nine months ago gives them a basis for such a request, and that if the treaty is not finally ratified now they will have lost some of their rights and should be compensated.

"Is there such a feeling among them? Mora has not confided in the council."

Lord Dorn paused and Lord Mora looked as though he were about to speak. He glanced at the diplomatic benches and remained silent.

"Once," said Lord Dorn, "a man applied for work to a certain *tana,* who gave him a trial. His work proved unsatisfactory and he was told that he must go. He refused, answering, 'You gave me a trial, and I've been thinking of nothing else but working with you for good. Therefore I have a right to stay with you.' The moral is: do not give a trial to that sort of man; and if you become involved with him, the blame is your own. History has made clear that the foreigner seeking fields for his businesses is that sort of man. And if we are in that situation the blame is with Lord Mora and with all those who have supported him."

I was suddenly sure that Lord Dorn was doing more than surmising, and that as a price for nonadoption of the Mora Treaty Islandia might be asked to internationalize Ferrin. He paused again; then with a sudden step forward he lifted his head and began to speak in a full, firm voice.

"No man here should make up his mind as a result of what he feels in this crowded place with its excited and emotional atmosphere.

To do so is treachery to himself, his family, his *alia*. The basis for each man's decision must be his state of mind in his daily life. The use of meetings like this is to learn new facts, not to stir emotions and force decisions under their stultifying influence. To win action by exciting the emotions of an audience is to achieve results by falsity and trickery.

"Generalizations as to world civilizations, world purposes, world needs, are particularly deceitful. The outside world is not the unity Lord Mora describes, but a complex of forces pulling in different directions. The force that pulls hardest and in the direction of Islandia is a group of businessmen. Foreign businessmen are clever in capturing other forces and directing them to their own ends. Among those captured is what is called the government in foreign countries, but this is very different from the Islandian government. Businessmen become so rich that by the indirect if not direct influence of their money they make the government their servant.

"It is not true that the world is interested in Islandia. A group of businessmen is interested, and their governments, who are behind them, send these foreign diplomats. Their demands are not the demands of the world upon Islandia. The voice of a foreign government is not the voice of its people, for the people are too diverse in their lives and aims to have a single voice. 'Government' abroad is merely a mask with a terrible face put on by different groups at different times.

"Shall we allow ourselves to be exploited and changed by a particular group of active foreigners? They do not ask us to enter a world stream, but to permit them to come upon our soil and satisfy their ambitions here. To them these ambitions are good and they have the faith in them that the Christians had in their religion and way of life. What opposes them is wrong and should be destroyed. They are not concerned with the inner life of Islandia; they will take, not receive. I see foreigners in the mass as no different from Islandia's former enemies—slayers, destroyers, ravagers, pests, describing their real purposes in the pleasanter words of their business religion.

"It may be unimportant to vote yes or no, because Islandia is too strong to be changed by this disease of commercialization and industrialism, and would destroy it as the germs of disease are destroyed in the blood of a healthy man; but consciously to submit to contamination is an unwise risk.

"If the majority wishes it perhaps we should submit, but whether a majority has a right to expose a minority to such a risk is a question that need not be decided now. I make this statement for the following reason:

"The majority of the people of Islandia wish the situation to be what it was before Lord Mora made his treaty."

Lord Dorn's voice rang out confidently and Lord Mora looked at him in surprise. Was this a rhetorical figure? It seemed to me with a sudden feeling of dizziness, that if Lord Dorn could prove what he had said he had won.

"If the council votes in favor of the Mora Treaty," he continued, "it will be the wickedest arrogation of power in Islandian history. In other countries, legislative assemblies decide such questions, but for the council to make a decision risking Islandia's way of life is wholly false to our tradition. The true source of power is the National Assembly where every Islandian can vote for himself.

"It is implicit in Mora's argument that the council is like the legislative assemblies of other countries and has a right to act in this way. He will tell you that it is a deliberative group of experts, representative of the people, and that here we learn facts and exchange ideas that the average man does not learn or properly consider. It is true that we need a governing body to save time for the average man. But we do not need an umpire to resolve the conflicting interests of a heterogeneous and complex civilization. And the question before us is simple and comprehensible as a whole to every man. We need no deliberation nor expert knowledge. We must decide: shall we continue the old way of life or adopt a new one full of risks, and if we wish to continue the old way, are we willing to fight to preserve it?

"If Islandia expels the foreigners, there is danger of coercive measures, perhaps war; and Mora believes that only the council can weigh and appreciate this danger. So they think abroad in such questions. Mora believes that at best the country will gain, at worst we must balance two risks; and for him the risk of harm from foreign intercourse outweighs the risk of foreign coercion. For him the council only is competent to consider these choices. But the individual will fight and die, and if he wants to risk his life to preserve what he believes is good, he should be allowed to do so.

"This is what the majority of Islandians want."

Had Lord Dorn, I wondered, some knowledge as to the attitude of the country which Lord Mora did not know or, knowing, concealed? Were not the diplomats foolish not to attend on this day which was surely the most dramatic one? The tension of excitement was tighter moment by moment.

"It will be a crime to adopt the treaty without consulting the National Assembly. It is a crime to make a treaty that leaves so vital a question to the council alone. . . ."

There was suddenly utter quiet.

Lord Mora was on his feet, but neither impetuously nor angrily.

"You accuse me," he said in his beautiful resonant voice, "of committing a crime, Lord Dorn."

"Yes, but with the purest heart!"

They faced each other, as they had faced each other a year before when they had similarly clashed. They looked at each other with no hostility in their eyes.

"Can one commit a crime with a pure heart?" asked Lord Mora.

"Not to another man, perhaps, but to the people of a nation, yes."

Slowly Lord Mora seated himself; and after a long moment Lord Dorn continued:

"If I am wrong in saying that no group of Islandians, but merely individuals here and there, favor the treaty, Mora can so prove when his turn for asking questions comes.

"Later I will present certain facts to the council, but before I do so I wish to state what must be apparent to all.

"Mora's position is such that half his arguments defeat the other half. How far does he believe that what he proposes is good in itself? How far is he influenced by a feeling that it is wise to bow to the inevitable? Can a man declare strongly that a thing is good when he feels that it does not matter if it is good or not, since in either case it is wise to accept? Why did he say so little of foreign coercion? Because it is not diplomatic to mention the unpleasant? Is it left to me to declare how real is the danger?

"But does it matter how great that danger? Not to me and not to some others here. Granting that we may have to fight, we would rather fight and die than expose ourselves to the risks of the foreigner's way of life. To us the extremity of the danger is therefore unimportant.

"Mora spoke of natural units of society. We will all agree that the individual and the family must give up some of their desires, but how much? The answer is: as little as possible. But Mora answers: all to the state! all to the world as a whole! In foreign countries they believe this, but in Islandia the state is a servant created by the family for its ends."

When the council adjourned for the midday recess, I went to Lambertson at the hotel, and found him with a heavy mail and several newcomers, a busy man. It was some time before he asked as to the happenings "on the hill." I reported what Lord Dorn had been saying, and he did not seem much interested.

For my own mail there came a brief interval after lunch. Most important was a cablegram from my friend in New York stating that the paper I had sent him had been accepted and that more was wanted. I was thus transformed from a would-be to an actual foreign correspondent, and the feeling was pleasant. There was also a letter from Gladys Hunter, who had followed mine and was aware of the important events now happening.

Back to the Council Chamber with renewed interest, I saw more faces on the diplomatic benches, but they were largely of strangers who had arrived that morning and had come to see a show. As Lord Dorn resumed his speech they whispered together, their escorts from the legations pointing out Tor, Dorna, Mora, and other important persons.

It was a gray chilly afternoon and the room was rather dim, colors glowing somberly; and as though influenced by this, Lord Dorn spoke more quietly and with less of what had seemed to be rancor, as though he had been angry at having to play the part he did.

"In Islandian life, the natural unit is the family and all else is subservient. This is not true in foreign countries. They often announce that the family is the foundation of the state: but by family they mean the small domestic group of husband, wife, and children, not the continuing of generations on the same land; and when they say that this group is the foundation of the state, they mean that if husbands and wives are faithful and have many children, the state will flourish. For them the family is good because it is a foundation for something more important."

He then spoke at length upon the effect of foreign intercourse on Islandian life. If trade alone were involved he believed that no great changes would come, because Islandians would not readily become buyers and sellers. "But," he cried, "the foreigners would live among us and would bring their diseases and pests to ourselves and all our growing things," and he then graphically described them and their effect. Advertising would be necessary, and he told of the changes it would bring to the face of the country. But it was not trade that was to be feared so much as concessions; and for the rest of the afternoon he worked out in detail exactly what would happen if concessions were granted: the gradual substitution of wealth in money for wealth in productive agencies like land and ships and flocks; the development of the indirect ownership of such wealth through ownership of securities; the introduction of banks and credit transactions; and as a consequence the gradual detachment of large classes of people from the soil and the destruction of the Islandian family and of *alia*. Then he described what would be the aspect of the land in places where concessions were in active operation, with railroads, factories, mills, and docks, and the noises and smells and invasions of privacy. And lastly he discussed the changes in government that would arise, the increase in rules and regulations, and in causes for contention and litigation, and in governmental interference with daily life.

The picture he painted of a changed Islandia was not one that complimented a foreigner's love of his own country.

At the Lambertsons' dinner, which was given in the hotel, and which consisted mostly of Islandian foods but served in many courses and therefore enormously filling, Lord Dorn's speech was not the subject of conversation as Lord Mora's had been at the Periers'; for Lord Mora himself was present. He seemed a tired and a worried man, and there was something choking to the throat in his courtesy and friendliness, not because it was an effort but because it came naturally from the man himself.

I came to the dinner as a polyglot and my duty was to jump into stumbling conversations between Islandians and foreigners, and to supply missing words, watching as a waiter watches for empty glasses. This made me feel an outsider with all the advantages of impersonality. Here were men who differed and did not understand, and yet in their hands were great forces. It seemed a casual way to decide questions that might vitally affect the future of millions.

Lord Mora had spoken for three days and Lord Dorn for one. Next morning he announced that he would conclude that day, and that although he had more to say, it was all on one subject.

"Sixty years ago Islandia was confronted with a similar situation. My grandfather, Dorn XXV, did not trust the facts stated by the government and he investigated the attitude of the people. In this case Mora has been opposed to calling a National Assembly, so it has been necessary to find out what the people feel in some other way. This has been done."

To me this was the most dramatic moment so far, but most on the diplomatic benches seemed uninterested. Among the Islandians, however, everyone stirred to listen.

"A poll has been taken," continued Lord Dorn, "on two questions, which were: (1) Do you favor the adoption of the Mora Treaty? (2) Assuming that rejection of the Mora Treaty involves Islandia in wars not likely to be successful, do you favor its adoption?"

In a tantalizing way he described the methods taken to secure the fairness and completeness of the results.

The long absences of Dorn were suddenly explained. He had been in charge of the vote-taking.

"The results can be summarized as follows," said Lord Dorn. "In the Western provinces 98 per cent voted 'no' on question one, and 90 per cent 'no' on question two; in the Centre 89 per cent voted 'no' on question one, and 75 per cent 'no' on question two; in the East 75 per cent voted 'no' on question one, and 60 per cent 'no' on question two.

"Even in Miltain, 65 per cent voted 'no' on our first question. Only in Miltain was there a majority against us on the second. Forty-eight per cent voted 'no' . . . Mora, you have affected your province with your fears. Calwin, in your province of The City, which includes the places most in danger and the men most likely to profit by concessions and foreign trade, the figures are 80 and 65 per cent."

Dorn went forward with a sheaf of papers and handed them to the clerk. They stated in detail the results that he and those assisting him had spent two years in obtaining. They had taken the votes of 145,000 persons. They had stated the problems in terms which never varied and which presented the views of both sides. They had refused to state their own, and the votes were cast in such a way that the voters were freed from fear that others would know how they voted.

Lord Dorn stated that he and his great-nephew would submit themselves to the fullest questioning desired. He ceased to speak, but remained standing. The room was quiet and all waited. Dorna with her elbow on her crossed knees and her chin in her palm watched him closely.

"I am nearly done," he said. "This afternoon I will be yours to question. There is little more that I can say. I repeat what our ancestors have declared: 'We Islandians can breathe free only in our own air.' At intervals in our history we have cleared away the dust storms that rolled in upon us from outside, choking our lives, and have breathed again. More than once these storms have been so dense that it seemed all but certain that those Islandians who survived would thereafter live in the murk, but we were always successful. Four hundred years ago it was said, 'Let us be ourselves in our own land.' From that principle some of us have never moved, and we proclaim it again. Our way of life is an ancient one; the way of life of the foreigner has changed completely in the last few hundred years, and changes daily at what seems an accelerating rate. Who dares tell us that a thing so new and so unfixed is good for us? With them the son and the father are of different civilizations and are strangers to each other. They move too fast to see more than the surface glitter of a life too swift to be real. They are assailed by too many new things ever to find the depths in the old before it has gone by. The rush of life past them they call progress, though it is too rapid for them to move with it. Man remains the same, baffled and astonished, with a heap of new things around him but gone before he knows them. Men may live many sorts of lives, and this they call 'opportunity,' and believe opportunity good without ever examining any one of these lives to know if it is good. We have fewer ways of life and most of us never know but one. It is a rich way, and its richness we have not yet exhausted.

"We are an ancient people and like all ancient peoples have an inner life of our own, incomprehensible to peoples whose ways are new and changing and still upon the surface.

"They cannot be blamed for seeing nothing good in us that will be destroyed by them. The good we have they do not understand, nor even see.

"We ask no more than what we had in the past. We seek nothing of them. We merely wish to be let alone. Our area is relatively small. Do we ask too much? Lord Mora thinks so. I do not. We are ready to have the council settle our difference of opinion now!"

Abruptly he seated himself. It seemed as though he had become suddenly wearied with words—for a moment almost as though he had failed.

In utter silence the council adjourned. Dorna went out with young Tor, her head bent. I had a sudden choking fear lest the forces that threatened Islandia were too great for Lord Dorn and those who followed him to meet and resist.

When I told Lambertson at lunch what had happened, he laughed.

"A straw vote! We all know what that means. And what difference does it make anyway?—When will the council vote? I want to be there."

There was cause for dismay. Something was in the air, ominous and strange. Men gathered together, but what were they, and what mattered their decisions? Forces that seemed outside their control moved according to a will inherent in these forces themselves. There had been no real clash between the arguments of Lord Mora and those of Lord Dorn—if arguments they were and not merely strong statements of opinion and feeling.

An afternoon of questions followed. The details of the vote taken by young Dorn were brought out more and more clearly, and its significance became from moment to moment greater. Suggestions that a man voted more lightly when not voting officially as a citizen, and that only those voted who agreed with the views of the men who conducted the voting, merely served to bring out facts that made the reality of the opinions expressed more solid. It seemed that the people had spoken with as great a clarity as they would have spoken if the means for obtaining their opinions had been one sanctioned by the government. The fact that it had been obtained by a group in opposition was a small ground of objection. To discount the vote because the government had not authorized it was to hide a truth behind a technicality.

Nor did Lord Mora seek to do so. He seemed sincerely anxious to bring out everything that would affect the significance of the vote

491

in any way. He was not a cross-examiner seeking to give his own color to the answers of witnesses, but was an honest man trying to increase knowledge. Differences of party and of opinion were forgotten. He, Lord Dorn, and my friend, who answered many of the questions, were three persons engaged in common pursuit of the knowable truth.

Lord Mora's sincerity and honesty shone like a strong light. More and more did it seem that whatever happened, and however great the difference between him and Lord Dorn, they were more like each other than he was to any foreigner. He was quick to admit what enhanced the significance of the vote; and Lord Dorn as ready to concede what diminished it.

It was dull to those who came expecting to watch a battle between two doughty fighters.

And yet Lord Mora gained rather than lost. His position was more and more clear. The council were guardians of the nation, to which the government was entrusted. The vote indicated a strong feeling and a fine courage, but it was a vote of the ignorant who were provincially conservative and unaware of the outer world and its great forces. The council must act as it thought wise. The desires of constituents were to be considered, but they were no mandate. It was the duty of a parent or guardian sometimes to cross the wishes of a child. Members of the council had thought of little else for several years; the people of Islandia immersed in the preoccupying currents of their busy daily lives at best uttered merely an offhand opinion; and whether the vote was official or not this would be true.

He made no formal reply. The session was one of informality, so great that the importance of what was to be decided seemed to be overlooked, at least to some of us, accustomed to the staged battles of our own legislating groups. At the end of the afternoon when the council adjourned to meet next day to hear any others who might wish to express themselves and to vote, the opposing-opinions of the Moras and Dorns seemed each as coherent as they could be; and yet because Lord Mora and Lord Dorn viewed the situation so differently and believed in such very different things, I for one, if I had been a member, would have wanted something more before I made my decision. This was not further information upon the likelihood of attempts to coerce Islandia, for dangers of war seemed irrelevant. If exclusion of foreigners was best for Islandia it was worth fighting for.

The more that I wanted was of a different nature. What really was the soul of Islandia? What was this inner life of which Lord Dorn spoke? Was it something that would be sacrificed by living as the rest of the world lived? Was it so good that it outweighed the losses due to national isolation—possible stagnation, and certain distrust and envy?

It was the sixteenth, and on the eighteenth a steamer sailed. An account of what had happened must be complete by then. Two nights of dinners had left me behind. In my room I wrote till late, and it was hard to condense and to generalize with a mind so full of questions and doubts and a heart so dismayed and so excited. Mora had stirred me deeply. He was the one man if any who could safely lead Islandia into new paths. He was of the world and he was great. But my friends, the other Islandians, whose life was happy and who wished to be let alone! I was no longer one of the foreigners convinced of the rightness of their demands and of the inevitableness of their way of life.

On the morning of the seventeenth the diplomatic benches were as crowded as those of the Islandians. The room held as many as it could hold. The Islandians wore the colors of their offices, and all of us who had them their uniforms. There was a buzz of excitement. Count von Bibberbach in the center was a busy man, coming early and holding brief conferences with all the rest of the diplomats. There were no exchanges between us and the Islandians; they were one unity, we another. Across a gulf I saw my friends, and it was hard to believe that I knew them so well and so intimately. My head was light with long hours of writing, and I was foreign and weak, a unit in a group that had a group force of its own. I was one of those who would be accepted or rejected, and who if rejected might make demands and use their force.

Lord Calwin rose and was recognized. He spoke briefly, informing the council that sixty years before when it was faced with a somewhat similar problem the bay was filled with warships and a bombardment of The City seemed imminent. No such immediate menace threatened now. He described the armaments that could have been used, the naval stations of the Germans and English to the northward, and the soldiers there. It was to the credit of foreign governments that they had been so careful to avoid all suggestion of coercion.

Several others spoke. They added nothing and increased the tension. The diplomats were restive. One could feel in the air the pressure of desire for decision and action instead of words. The faces of the Islandians gave little sign of what was in their hearts, but some were pale and among these Lord Hyth. Nattana standing against the wall had a drawn, tired face. Lord Mora sat motionless, watching the speakers. Lord Dorn had sunk down in his seat and with bent head seemed to be thinking of other things.

The time for the vote had come. The last speaker had sat down. The eyes of Tor were running along the benches to see if others wished to be recognized, but no one rose.

I looked for Dorna. How hard and tense must her excitement be if mine, a stranger's, stopped my breath! She was leaning far forward, her arms at her sides and her hands clutching the front edge of the bench. Her head was turned toward young Tor, intent upon him, and the curve of her cheek and throat was young and lovely. Her fingers were working with impatience.

His glance traveled along the benches at the end of which she sat. Lord Fain whispered to her and she quivered. Tor's eyes came upon her. With a bound she was erect.

His face did not change. He bowed to her, and she stepped forward with suppressed violence.

"Once you had a queen," she cried in a voice like a child's, "and against your wills you listened to her. For her sake listen for a few moments to me, your new queen."

Bright color came with a rush into her cheeks. There was a stirring like a sigh throughout the room and then perfect stillness. Her voice became lower and stronger.

"We have our life. Our families, for generations past and to come living on the places that are their own, are the centers of our life. We women who love one place and must transfer our love to another know this more deeply than most men can ever know it. For this reason, also, listen to me.

"Abroad there are no such centers, and there life is adrift. There, it is true, men have places and families. Sometimes a place and a family are united, but even then the place is but temporary and the family a thing of a generation.

"Our whole way of life is based upon these centers—upon family and place as one. The roots of our being grow in the soil of our *alia*. Family and place intermingled as one make that soil. These roots go deep. Firm in the soil, our lives are not cast loose by grief and disappointment as theirs are.

"I pity them!

"With them as with us the forces that draw a man and woman together are the greatest forces of all. No one has said so here, but let us not forget and decide for lesser reasons.

"Each foreign nation has a single word for these forces. The English call it 'love'; the French 'l'amour.' Our conception of these forces is different from theirs.

"We have our *apias*"—her voice rang out—"but we have *ania*, also—*ania*, the love which is so glad of its beloved that it would mix with her or him and create new life, his and hers together, and send it on in these centers of our being—place and family as one.

"*Ania* is never aimless; but to us their 'love,' their 'amour,' is vague and aimless.

"Man demands an aim for his life; without it he weakens and is out of tune with all about him or else he comes to envy the animals who are unconscious of their ends. It is the curse and glory of man to be conscious of a striving toward an end—to have an aim, or, if hopeless, to wish that he had one.

"They, the foreigners, also have their aims—many more than we have, ambitions and desires for service, for sacrifice, for renunciation, for wealth, for power, for conquest; but their aims are beyond the mark of human possibility . . . Oh, I pity them! Our aims are of the earth and of all growing things. They are of the earth earthy, as they say with contempt and we with gladness. They aim for other lives beyond life on this earth and they imagine heavens in the empty skies. They long for such heavens on earth. They always long for something else beyond their reach! But we sound the deeps—the deeps of our natures, of dreams, of what we feel, and of our growth, and of the growth of all that grows about us, men and women, animals, grass, and trees.

"Life is a mystery to us as it is to them; but the mystery that troubles them is only half of earth and of growing reality. The other half is the sterile, unreal mystery created by brains distorted with impossible aims. They are moved to explore their mysteries; they

495

doubt the reality of all since half is unreal. We have no such impulse; we can accept our mysteries and sink into them. But they—they build heavens and put gods into them, and unsatisfied with the gods change them. Or else they turn to another god with the godless name of 'science' and destroy these heavens of their own invention, and think that in this new god they have found the universal, which they call 'truth.' They rebel against the tangles that they spin in their own aimlessness and they crave the relief of the so-called absolute. Yet all the while they are suffering not from complexity but from unreality.

"Oh, they are to be pitied! They are forever seeking to find and to name an aim that will absorb and justify the promptings of the forces that stir within them. All their efforts are fruitless because they have no good soil for the roots of their being. The soil that we have is so natural and so deep that we, satisfied with our aim, are content to leave mystery mysterious.

"They are far from natural things—from wind, sun, and rain, from growing things, trees, plants, other animals, and from each other. When they seek to come nearer, their ways of life, their theories of society and of state and of the duties of man toward man and woman, and most of all their habits of thought and their desire for the comfort of universal rules and truths, forever defeat them. They cannot understand each other. Their lives are chaotic.

"The evil which they will do is this: if they come among us as freely as they wish to come, if they use our land and what is in it, erecting upon it their factories and mills and railroads, then the face of nature that we love so well will be marred and stained. If we deal with them, buying their toys and machines and selling them what they want, they will force upon us their way of life. For they will always live among us according to their way and not according to ours. Two ways of life cannot exist side by side in a nation as small as ours. Theirs will at least crowd upon and narrow our own. More, probably ours must conform to theirs: to live at peace with them we must adopt their manners and ways and think as they think, for they have no wish to learn and to adopt ours. Whatever happens we can no longer live completely the old life as we began it and now have it. We could be useful to them as an experiment in a way of living worthy of watching and perhaps of imitation; but this aspect of our lives does not interest them, for they wish us to make changes that will destroy that outward simplicity of ours which permits the inner life to be free and to go deep. If we do as they wish, place will tend to become only temporary and family a thing of a generation. With the loss of *alia*, *ania* and *apia* will become confused. The house of living may become more ornate, but its air will be impure and its foundations unstable. There is little hope for them. Unless they come seeking to follow our ways of life as well as to enforce their own, they come as enemies. We have always fought what struck at the roots of our being. It is better to die than to endanger what we know has made existence worth continuing."

Dorna ceased, hesitated a moment, and turned. Her eyes sought those of her husband as if for approval, and perhaps he gave her what she would most wish to have. His face was blank with surprise and he rose and bowed to her as though a little dazed. With sudden, quick shyness she found her seat again.

Lambertson was whispering in my ear.

"The queen was against the treaty, wasn't she?"

"Yes."

"Has she a right to speak?"

"She is a member of the council, but she does not vote."

"A clever trick of your friends, the Dorns, to have a queen and a pretty woman speak for them. It was really dramatic. What did she say? Anything new?"

"No," I answered. "Only the feminine touch!"

He laughed, and I had peace from him.

Long stillness followed. No Islandian moved or spoke. A low buzz began among the diplomats and became louder. Heads were together, no doubt discussing the unexpectedness of Dorna's speaking.

Tor remained standing looking along the lines of his countrymen. With a start he seemed to collect himself.

"Are you ready for the vote, Mora?" he said.

"Yes." The answer was almost inaudible. "Accept or reject."

"I shall call the roll," cried Tor.

To breathe seemed impossible.

He turned to Lord Fain and called the name of his province, the oldest.

"Islandia—Fain?" The white head rose.

"Reject." There was no hesitation.

497

"Camia—Stellin?"

"Reject." Previously, Lord Stellin had voted with the Mora party.

"The City—Calwin?"

"Accept."

"Bostia—Bodwin?"

"Reject." He also had been a Mora follower.

Each man stood as his name was spoken and their seats were so placed that they rose alternately on each side of the hall.

"Loria—Some?"

"Reject." This was expected.

"Alban—Robban?"

"Accept." He was a Mora stalwart.

"Inerria—Baile?"

"Reject." There was a movement among the Islandians, for Lord Baile had been staunchly with Lord Mora. The ranks of his stalwarts were broken.

"Lower Doring—Dorn?"

"Reject."

"Dole—Dax?"

"Accept." He was a Westerner, and yet a former follower of the Moras. His vote was no surprise, but it was a cause for dismay.

"Upper Doring—Hyth?"

"Accept." It was a sudden shock to hear, for he had once been one of Lord Dorn's closest allies. I saw Nattana's head drop.

Lambertson leaned to me and whispered, "How does it stand?" I had pencil and paper and was taking notes.

"Six to four against the treaty."

"Hm," he answered.

"Vantry—Dasel?"

"Accept." Dorna had counted on him to vote the other way.

"Farrant—Shane?"

"Reject." His opinion had been unknown. The gap in the Dorn ranks caused by the death of Lord Farrant was filled again.

"Niven—Tole?"

"Reject." Another Mora follower had turned to the other side. Was it because of Lord Mora's threat to expropriate the coal owned by the proprietors of Niven?

"Brome—Borderney?"

"Reject." He also had been a Mora man.

"Deen—Drelin?"

"Reject." Dorna was right as to him!

I whispered to Lambertson, "Ten to five against the treaty."

"Looks bad," he answered, but did not seem concerned.

"Hern—Farnt?"

"Reject." Another lord of a province rich in coal had changed sides.

"Carran—Benn?"

"Accept." He had voted this way before.

"Miltain—Mora?"

"Accept!"

"Storn—Aird?"

"Reject." So it was expected.

"Winder—Marriner?"

"Reject." Lord Marriner was certain to vote in this way.

All the provincial lords had voted—thirteen to seven against the treaty. Excluding the king but four more were needed to ensure its rejection, and the three naval officers were Dorn stalwarts. I began to tell Lambertson, but Tor was no longer calling the roll.

"For many years," he said, "your leader has only cast a vote in case of a tie, or else as a makeweight to a cause he thought good; but his right to vote as an ordinary member of this council has never been denied. Unless my vote is challenged, I shall vote now."

"What's he saying?" whispered Lambertson. I told him, and he uttered a short laugh, and answered, "It is not parliamentary."

"Reject!"

"That means 'no,' doesn't it?" Lambertson asked.

"It does, and the treaty is surely beaten."

"Are you sure?"

"Yes."

"Well, it is what we expected."

Was it what everyone had expected except John Lang, not taken into the confidence of the diplomats because no longer one of them, and not taken into that of the Islandians because a foreigner?

It was decided at any rate, and I was dazed.

"Marshal—Bodwin?"

"Reject."

"Chief Judge—Belton?"

"Reject."

"Admiral—Farrant?"

"Reject."

The majority against the treaty was established. A movement which was half a sigh stirred in the room, first among the Islandians and then along the diplomatic benches. The faces of my dearest friends were happy, Dorn and Dorna, and Lord Fain. Nattana's head was lifted again, but her father's was bent and he was very white.

The room was blurred to me by an exhausting relief, which was in itself another tension, but I set down the rest of the votes.

Twenty-three votes against the treaty, eleven for it.

One wakes and believes that the night is still deep and cannot sleep, but there is a quiver of light and day is dawning. So it was with me. I had not known that I cared so much or would or could be so glad.

Dorn was speaking to his great-uncle. They were quiet, but there was a gleam on their faces. The eyes of Nattana standing against the wall behind her father caught the light and glittered. They must be full of tears. Dorna looked tired, dark under the eyes, and suffering.

"The treaty was voted down, wasn't it?" whispered Lambertson.

"Yes, it was, by a two-thirds vote."

"What a fool thing to do! But I'm not surprised."

Tor was making a formal announcement of the result of the vote. His eyes were upon Count von Bibberbach whose face and head were crimson.

"More work for us," Lambertson was saying as though to himself, and then to me, "What was that about submitting it to the people?"

"There is no chance, and you would lose anyway."

"We would gain time."

"What do you need time for?"

He looked at me shrewdly and did not answer for a moment.

"I suppose your friends, the Dorns, are to be congratulated," he said. "They have been clever. How did they learn so much about conditions abroad?"

"Young Dorn was four years at Harvard."

His eyebrows lifted, and I understood his insinuation, but it mattered nothing. Even if I had told the Dorns all I knew and thought about life outside Islandia, whom had I betrayed? But Lambertson himself had become unpleasant to sit with.

"Mora, what do you wish?" Tor was saying.

Lord Mora rose.

"If it is the pleasure of the council—to be relieved of my office."

"Do you wish a vote?"

Lord Mora looked at his various followers.

"It does not seem necessary," he said.

"Will Dorn take the office?" Tor asked.

Dorn nodded without rising.

"Does anyone wish a vote?"

There was no answer.

"The government has fallen," I whispered to Lambertson. "Lord Dorn is now the premier."

"What, so quick! Lord Mora ought to stay on. We can't deal with your friend."

"Didn't you expect that also?"

"Yes, but, for a time at any rate. . . ."

"What are your wishes, Dorn?" Tor was saying.

Lord Dorn rose.

"The treaty," he said, "has been rejected. All the old laws are in force. Persons present in Islandia except those who have qualified under the Hundred Law have no longer any right to be here; for the treaty does not provide what they may do in case it is rejected. But they are here with our consent. The policy for which I stand is that the foreigner shall have nothing more than what he had before. Whatever he has hoped for, his hopes were only hopes and were not promises, and he can justly make no demands upon us. We will, however, give him time to settle his affairs and depart."

A look of unbearable pain crossed Lord Mora's face.

Lord Dorn continued and presented a resolution which legalized for three months the presence in Islandia of diplomatic officers and their families and of those holding passes, and accorded to the

501

former the privileges given them by international law. The resolution was passed without a roll call.

He then stated that Islandia was now in no treaty relation with any foreign power.

"We stand alone," he said.

The council then adjourned on his motion until next morning.

Immediately voices rose and the whole room was full of movement. Count von Bibberbach started forward to speak either to Lord Mora or else to Lord Dorn, and then thought better of it.

Lambertson was asking what the latter had said and I had to shout to make him hear me.

He uttered some remark about a slap in the face.

Count von Bibberbach was summoning his colleagues about him, and beckoned to Lambertson.

"Do you need me any more?" I asked.

"I don't think so."

"Then good-bye."

I shook his hand, not expecting to see him again, and he left me.

Lord Dorn, Lord Mora, and my friend were standing talking together. Tor and Dorna were moving away toward the door behind the throne by which they entered. Her face was lifted to his. Before she left the room she looked back, and standing on tiptoe I waved my hand to indicate to her my admiration and gladness, but I was not sure that she saw me in the milling crowd.

I must tell someone that I was glad, Isla Fain, or Dorn, or Nattana. Most of the Islandians were now standing in the open space between the rows of benches, talking with an excited animation that I had never before witnessed. Islar Stellin and Calwin were talking together, and Dorn and Chessing, the Judges. The groupings had no relation to the way they had voted. Would it be in any way wrong to go among them, to seek, and to speak to my friends and to tell them how glad I was? Dorn was busy with his great-uncle and Lord Mora, and I did not like to break in upon them. Lord Fain was not to be seen, for the groups changed and re-formed, but Nattana was standing against the wall and she was alone. I would go—let the foreigners think what they would if any of them noticed. The Islandians would not care.

The secretaries and wives and guests of the diplomats were crowding out of the door, and one or two spoke to me as I made my way among them behind the rows of benches from the domain of the foreigners into that of the Islandians. At last I came to Nattana. Her face was pale, the freckles more marked than usual. She raised her head and her wet eyelashes were gathered in points and her white skin seemed oversoft.

"I wanted to tell you—" I began, but suddenly remembered the apostasy of her father. He was not in sight. "Nattana!" I cried, but it was too late.

"Tell me, Johnlang."

"I wanted to tell someone how glad I am the way the vote went, but you . . . I forgot—"

"I am glad, too," she cried. "Why not tell me?"

"I wanted to tell you, Nattana. I have found out how glad I am!"

"No gladder than I! Look at them!"

She swept her hand toward the group of ministers and consuls around Count von Bibberbach.

"They look—surprised," I said. Our eyes met. We laughed. But a cold shiver ran up into my hair. These men were not to be despised . . . If there were war would the Islandians allow me to enlist in their army? Then, if I survived, might I not remain with them?

Looking into Nattana's face was not enough.

"Oh, I'm glad!" I said, and I seized and wrung her hand. But who might not see it? . . .

"Nattana, I forgot you don't shake hands." Hers had remained quite limp.

"We do sometimes." The hand tightened a little.

"I can't say how glad I am that your country has done this, Nattana!"

Her hand disengaged itself, but gently as though apologizing for doing so.

"What are you going to do now, Johnlang?"

"I must write all afternoon and finish my article for the mail. Tomorrow or next day I'm going back to the Fains'—unless something unexpected happens."

"I am going to the Upper Farm," she said, dropping her eyes. "I don't know for how long. Father said that I had better go."

"I'm sorry!"

"So am I. I don't like to be punished."

Her head lifted.

"I'm going day after tomorrow with Ek. It is the same road as yours."

Impulse was checked for only a moment.

"We could go together."

"Will you, Johnlang?"

"Oh gladly!"

"Send me word if anything happens. Otherwise we will come by for you shortly after sunrise. But now I want to go home."

Part of me was absorbed in what I was writing, but another part, seething with gladness and excitement and some fear, continually threatened to rise up in a wave and drown the first part. Elsewhere, foreigners and Islandians, both, were doubtlessly engrossed in their own affairs, the former planning how to circumvent their exclusion and to overcome the new government, and the latter building up their defenses. As a mere observer I was a stranger to both sides. City Square, white with snow across which there were many tracks, lay under pale winter sunlight. It was a temptation to watch the coming and going of people to the Home Building where Lord Dorn must be now. It was hard not to feel that the attitude even of my friends would be changed and that I was unwelcome. The aspect of The City was not the same but colder and more remote, going its own way with its own life which was not mine. But in my mind was serenity, my pen flew, and the afternoon moved past.

Downs came to say good-bye. Next day he was to sail and he was delighted to be going.

"I have made a fairly good thing out of this," he said, "though it probably won't lead to anything. Will you write me a to-whom-it-may-concern letter? It may come in handy."

I promised and in return he offered to act as courier for my article and to send a cablegram to my newspaper from Mobono, which might be the first news to the world.

"I'm leaving just in time," he continued. "You had better come, too, Mr. Lang. This is no place for us Americans now, and won't be for some time, I guess."

He went, and the Exhibition Ship and all that had been connected with it was a closed episode. What had it accomplished? It was my best effort to alter Islandia.

City Square had become dark. Such other Americans as there now were in Islandia had their common center in Lambertson to whom I hoped I had said a final good-bye . . . There was the journey with Nattana day after tomorrow and a sure welcome at the Fains', and eleven months more—of what? Fence mending? idling? writing? trips with Dorn when the intense first months of his marriage were over— that is, if he were not too busy with public affairs as seemed likely? a visit to Dorn Island? to the Moras perhaps? more certainly to the Hyths?

What would relatives and friends at home think of such an existence? But I was going to continue it all the same as long as I could.

Before I did so, had I not better make sure of my welcome and dispel all doubts? If the Dorns wanted me to go, would it not be best to go tomorrow with Downs or at least on the next steamer in early July? Thus realized, the prospect of leaving brought sudden sickness. I wanted a word from Dorn and wanted it at once. To remain at my room and to write was no longer possible.

At the Home Building I learned that he and his great-uncle had gone shortly before to the Dorn Palace. Surely our friendship was deep enough to justify a demand of a minute with him even at this time? Then I remembered my *tanrydoon,* and with lessened doubts I ran down High Street to the quays, past the Navy and Agency Buildings and over the bridge across the canal. It was dark but I knew my way. The harbor was black, but it was almost windless and quite clear and the lights of the boats made shimmering yellow spears in the water.

The garden of the palace was as it had been when I brought Dorna home after the concert. The air smelled of the sea.

The man at the door ushered me in as though I were expected. At least he saw no strangeness in the coming of this foreigner. Isla Dorn and "great-nephew" were in the reception room with others, he said. They were not having a conference, merely seeing friends. I went on, up the same flight of stone stairs and along the long corridor to the left and into the great room where I had called upon Dorna.

Many were present standing around the hearth. Most of them I knew, among them Islar Fain, Farrant, Marriner, Dorn the Commodore, Dorn the Judge, Isla Dorn himself, my friend, the wives of some of them; and in a green dress Dorna, but with her back toward me, talking with Andara, Farrant's wife, and young Stellin. They were all busy together, all Islandians, but I walked forward and Dorn, seeing me, came at once and took my arm to lead me into the group. The question I had come to ask seemed almost needless.

"I am glad you have won," I said. "I didn't really know before, but when it happened it was exactly what I wanted. But, Dorn, shall I stay here or not?"

He stopped short.

"Stay? Why, of course! Had you thought of going?"

"You don't want foreigners here."

"We want you, as long as you can be with us, for many reasons. You know what we don't want as well as I do."

"That settles it then," I answered with relief so great that it brought faintness. "I shall stay, as long as the law allows."

"We would like it to be longer—but making exceptions is the very thing for which we have criticized the Moras. Isn't it detestable to have to be consistent?"

Others were around me. I was sure Dorna was aware of my presence, though I had not yet had a chance to meet her eyes. Lord Dorn seemed changed, the lines deeper in his face, and his expression one of preoccupation and power. He awed me and his welcome was good to hear.

"I have told John to stay in this country as long as he can," said my friend.

The clear light-brown eyes looked into mine and he read my doubts.

"We are glad you are here, Johnlang. You are not what we wish to exclude."

Was Dorna listening?

My coming had caused silence in several groups. Now conversation resumed again. There were cakes and wine on a side table to which we went. Lord Fain appeared, and said that he thought that the council would only sit for a day or two more, and that on the fourth day he was going back to the farm.

"Shall we travel home together or are you going sooner, or later?"

The question was not asked for an answer but to inform me, not too obviously, that his home was still mine. I told him of my plan to ride there with Hyths Ek and Nattana next day but one.

"Tell them our house is theirs if they care to stop for more than overnight—one or both."

He left me. It was evident that some of those present had matters which they wished to discuss with others.

"Don't bother with me," I said to Dorn. "I have learned what I wanted."

"You never need have thought otherwise."

"I did not think . . . I merely wanted to be reassured."

He asked my plans and I told them, adding that I wanted to stay in The City if anything more of political importance were likely to happen. It was not easy to talk nor to listen with Dorna so near.

"There is no more important business scheduled to come before the council. I can now let you in to some of our secrets. We expect a renewal of the request to internationalize Ferrin, but the foreign representatives won't be likely to agree for several days. Therefore if we adjourn tomorrow their proposals can't be acted upon for another six months. We need time to undo some of the things Lord Mora has done and to prepare to defend ourselves."

"Are you going to be as busy as you were?"

"I'll know better in a few days, but at least I shall have time to go to Nekka." His eyes lighted. "Perhaps in a week I shall pass by the Fains', and I shall see you on the way. But even if I am free, we are going to have to curtail our expenses. The Dorns have paid a large part of the cost of the poll and at present we are rather poor. But you and I are going to see more of each other soon, I'm sure."

"You think I won't miss anything interesting to a correspondent if I go day after tomorrow?"

"No, but I'll send word tomorrow if anything arises. We can talk more freely now. I am glad of that . . . Would you like to speak to Dorna? She won't come unless you want her."

I had been waiting for her to make the move. Must I make it? Did I want to speak to her? My wound was half healed and the cutting weapon was close to it again.

I looked in his eyes, without will, afraid of what I would feel if I spoke to her, equally afraid of the misery following a lost opportunity. He watched me.

"You had better speak to her," he said. "That is my guess. Talk freely. She will give you a chance."

He called her name, and instantly she left the group of which she was one and came to us. She was standing by the table. Dorn had gone. I looked a little past her, afraid of her eyes, unprepared, confronted by her too suddenly.

"What you said this morning seemed just the right thing, Dorna."

"Was it? I don't know. It was what I felt, anyway . . ." There was no voice like hers, never to be quite remembered, but so perfectly true to memory that I wanted to laugh with pleasure.

"It must have taken courage."

"It did—all I had. And after Lord Mora and my great-uncle, too! But there were things he didn't say."

"That is what I was thinking."

"Did you understand?"

"Perhaps not quite as an Islandian would have done, Dorna."

There was silence, which was terrifying.

"I am not so sure," she said slowly. "I thought of you, too, and I faltered for a moment. It was hard on you."

"Oh, no!"

"Yes, it was, John." In her contradiction was something dangerously flattering, but I did not understand why.

"Dorna . . ." I began and lost the thread of what I was saying. To feel her waiting was torture.

"Did what I said sound true to you?" she asked.

"Quite true—and the right thing."

Again came silence, and my eyes and hers slipped at the same moment and became entangled. She was real as she had not been, penetrating all armor. Like her voice she was perfect, and there was nothing else perfect or desirable in the world.

She smiled a faint smile and her eyes slid away and came back again.

"We don't seem to be able to talk," she said.

"No . . . I can't talk."

"Nor I. I hate to feel this way with you."

"So do I, Dorna . . . But your speech—"

"My poor speech?"

"It wasn't poor! It was perfect!"

"I am glad you think so. My great-uncle and my brother were so afraid that I would spoil things that they haven't yet got over the shock!"

"Didn't others like it?"

"Oh yes," she answered and looked at me quickly, and was silent.

All had been said that could be said about the speech, and there was nothing else.

"Won't you have a cake or something, Dorna?"

"No . . . Yes, I will."

I offered her the plate.

"I am going to stay in Islandia eleven months more," I said.

"I hope you will be happy."

"I think I shall be. I hope you are happy, too," I said.

She laughed a little.

"I'm happy," she said lightly. "I miss my boat and the Marsh, but I shall have them again."

We could discuss only unimportant things, while all the important ones clamored in me for utterance.

"Well, good-bye, John."

"Good-bye."

Dorn stopped me as I was going out.

"Will you be at the meeting tomorrow?"

"I may come for a while."

"If you don't, I will see you at the Fains' in eight days."

He would be going to Nekka!

"I shall want to see you there," I answered, and doubted.

"So do I want to see you, but you don't need me." There had been a time when I did need him without knowing it, but that was four months ago.

"I don't need you this time." It was true, but the futile talk with Dorna was not to be thought about. Memory of it lay like razor blades in my hand, deeply cutting if I stirred my fingers.

There was little more to be done upon my article. A few corrections, and it was ready to go, but time was heavy on my hands. How could it be better employed than in repaying Gladys Hunter for her interest and faithful letters? It would please her, perhaps, to be told of events before they were generally known? I wrote her a long letter and shorter ones to the family and to Uncle Joseph stating the news and telling my plans.

Next day, after seeing Downs off and dispatching my mail I went for a few moments to the Council Chamber. The diplomatic benches were nearly empty. The arrangements for legalizing the foreigners' presence and providing for their departure were being discussed. Lord

Mora pointed out that in many respects his treaty still stood. All that the council had done was to end a period of probation and to terminate diplomatic representation of other countries in Islandia. The agreement made with Germany in 1905—whereby the integrity of Islandia was recognized and similarly German rights in lands across the Great Range, and whereby the Germans undertook to police the Sobo Steppes and to prevent raids—was still in force. To this Lord Dorn assented. The matter of Islandian garrisons at passes through the Great Range was not mentioned; but the need of some person through whom Germany and Islandia could communicate was much discussed. Lord Dorn saw the need of but one foreigner resident in Islandia as had been the case before 1905. M. Perier was still acceptable. But, insisted Lord Mora, the Germans would want a German.

There was no hostility between Lord Mora and Lord Dorn. The former accepted the defeat of his hopes without bitterness and without seeking to reopen the question. He spoke rather as an adviser than as one in opposition. It was evident that no action was to be taken.

I rose to go. Had I come hoping for a last look at Dorna? She was in her place—a quiet listening figure, unaware of those who came upon the benches of the foreigners at the other end of the room. A woman's absorbed interest in public matters was her rightful privilege, but I grudged Dorna hers, for she was so lovely and so young.

As I tiptoed out, Lord Mora's voice arrested me.

"Dorn," he said, "before we leave these matters, let me offer you my services. I will remain here in The City if you wish. I know these men who are leaving Islandia. I can perhaps make their departure easier for them and less troublesome to you. They are my friends."

23

Return to the Fains'

NATTANA HAD SAID that she and her brother would come shortly after sunrise, and the sun was already high enough to light the snow in City Square, but the dark-blue shadows of the buildings still reached all the way across. Fak was at a hitching rail outside the door, and by leaning forward at the window of my room I could see him. He would lift one hind leg and hold it up as though hesitating whether to stamp or not, shake and toss his head, and then put the leg down gently. He was stretching his muscles, impatient to leave city life where no one paid much attention to him.

The council had adjourned. Dorn had sent a message that nothing more of interest was likely to happen, and that he would give whatever news there was when he stopped at the Fains' seven days hence. The ground would be snow-covered there, preventing fence mending for long periods. I wanted some new outdoor job and some physical indoor job. Writing all the time with only walks or rides to break it would be a bore. Fain had promised. . . .

There they were, two red heads, on tall brown horses, with another carrying their saddlebags. They emerged from around a corner, and the sun fell brightly upon them.

It was good to be going away from The City! With a thrill in my heart, I ran downstairs not to keep them waiting.

Nattana was astride Fak, watching to see how I took it. Ek with a smile was holding her horse. I paid no attention at all, but promptly mounted him. Nothing was said. After all, it was easier for us to hold back for her than for her and her brother to do so for me, and she was lighter than I and Fak smaller than her horse.

The pack horse first, then Ek, then Nattana, and lastly John Lang —thus we rode down City Hill, out from the troughlike enclosures of stone streets and unbroken stone housefronts, out into the country again, fresh, windy, spacious, snow-covered, but with brown dry grass showing through the snow.

Twilight was deepening when we came to the Y-shaped gorges near the town of Reeves. On the opposite side sparse yellow lights were dotted along the cliff edge, and the steep slope below was a dark blue. Thick blue shadow filled the hollows; the bridge and towpaths were in a deeper blue, and the waters of the river were faintly silver. We descended the steep road, into this darker region, but Nattana's bright head continued to glow, only a little subdued.

Where were we to stop? We discussed the question. Ek was not a graduate of the college. The Gilmours would take me in, and perhaps two of us, but not three, Nattana said. There was the house where she had stopped eleven days before but it was too small for three, Ek thought. They both baulked at the Inn, perhaps because of the cost. The Calwins had a farm several miles on and had suggested that I stop there on my journeys, but this was when I was a consul. This suited the Hyths, but I betrayed a little reluctance. Nor did we want to separate. All agreed to that.

We stopped in the center of the town and though making light of our indecision we all felt a little forlorn. Then Ek, who was also perhaps annoyed, said that he would find a place and rode off.

Nattana sat limply on her horse. The town was dark around us. There were a few passers-by, dark shadows moving against the black walls and the white trodden snow.

"Tired, Nattana?"

"And sleepy."

We waited. It was quite cold.

"And hungry," she added. "Anyway, tomorrow night there will be a place where we can all go. I wish Ek hadn't ridden off so suddenly. It's cold and bad for the horses."

She drew her hood up over her head.

"I'm sorry I did not seem to want to go to the Calwins'," I said.

"Neither did I—really, though there is no reason; but he and Father. . . ."

"I am sorry about your father. Are you really going to have to live at the Upper Farm?"

"He said I must, unless I—"

She broke off, and I waited.

"Unless what, Nattana? Do you mind telling?"

"Oh, unless I made certain promises. I spoke my mind too much to suit him. But I told you all about it."

"I am sorry that you have to suffer this."

"So am I—more than you know. Partly for Ek's sake. And my loom and all my materials are at the Lower Farm."

"Can't you make the promises, Nattana?"

"I tie myself too much. I can't speak. I can't . . ." She stopped again.

"I hadn't thought of your workshop. That must be hard."

"Oh, don't let's talk of that! There is a little loom at the Upper Farm. Ek has promised to bring up some of my things—all he can. He is very kind about it. But the big loom! . . . Oh, it isn't wholly that! There will be enough to do, and when spring comes there will be the lake. Don will take me up into the mountains. There are compensations. What hurts me, Johnlang, isn't just because Father and I haven't got along, but because of the way he thinks of it. He believes in certain rules and because I don't and say so and haven't obeyed them, I am being punished."

"Have you differed about other things than— Nettera and his vote?"

"Oh, yes. That's only part of it, but it is typical. The main trouble is that he believes that he should be the ruler of the house and the maker of its laws, and whenever anyone disobeys them or questions his right to make them, that is a crime. I'll be better off at the Upper Farm. And yet I don't want to go there either."

Ek interrupted us by his arrival. He had been to the Provincial Palace, which was of course a residence of Lord Fain's. There was only a caretaker there and we would have to wait on ourselves and have a rather meager supper, but there would be all that we needed.

"And we won't have to leave 'Green Eyes,' " he added.

Next morning, we rode from the Provincial Palace without any bother over tickets or times of trains or bills to pay or money or tips. I told Nattana the many things one would have to do to make such a journey as this at home; but the methods of the United States had their revenge long before the day was over. A train would have taken us to Tindal in an hour without effort on our part, but we three had hard

513

work to make our way. The weather was overcast and gray. The temperature hovered around freezing and then rose. There were flurries of snow and then of rain. The roads were slippery, both frozen and muddy. We walked many miles. We became tired, muddy, wet, and bedraggled. Yet no one minded, even though there were moments when it seemed unlikely that we would reach our destination.

Nattana became silent with fatigue, but she did not complain and her face was always serene and her smile ready, though the slippery road, the slow pace, and the risk of falls were trying to patience and temper.

It was night when we reached Tindal, but though a man at the Inn, where we fed and watered the horses, said that the road was bad we decided to go on.

At the entrance of the ravine of the Reeves River we dismounted again to walk the long ten miles, spare the horses, and avoid the risk of dangerous falls for them and for us. Because it was moonless and overcast and therefore too dark to see where our feet fell, we knew that we were to suffer the wearing fatigue of walking blind on an irregular and treacherous surface. Ek took the lead with a lantern. The horses strung along nose to tail, trained to follow each other in this way. Fak was at the end of the procession, the faint whiteness of his sturdy rump a mark for Nattana and me to follow. Our task was to prevent the horses from becoming too widely separated. The departure from Reeves seemed to have occurred many more than twelve hours ago.

Ek's lantern moved in the blackness. The ascent began. Nattana had drawn her hood over her head hiding the last bit of whiteness that she had; and as we walked I could not tell where she was except by her somewhat panting breath, by the sound of her feet in mud or on stones, or when one or the other of us staggered on a slippery spot and we brushed against each other. I walked at her side and was so anxious to encourage and help her in some way that it was a continuous sweet pain. I began to tell of life at home and of the family. It was a desultory narrative that she could listen to or not as she pleased and that required no answering thought. I forgot my own weariness and leaden swinging legs. After some time I wondered what she was thinking.

"Does this interest you? Do you want me to go on?"

"Yes." Her voice came instantly from an unexpected place in the blackness. I continued, telling her of my childhood, contrasting it with hers, mentioning friction with parents, rules, and childish misunderstandings, describing glowing moments and black ones.

When the road turned rightwards we saw plainly the yellow glow of Ek's lantern some distance ahead, jogging along slowly but without a pause. When the road was straight, it was often only a faint radiance. When it turned to the left, the steep slopes of the hills sometimes came between, and the darkness was absolute. If the lantern seemed too far away, I interrupted my story to make that unwritable sound which is the Islandian equivalent of "get up." The horses usually responded by an unseen commotion and for a few moments Fak's white rump went faster. When there was no such answer, I left Nattana alone and moved up the line finding the gaps by hearing, feeling, and smell, and closing them by talking to and slapping the straggler. Then I would stop and let them pass me.

"Where are you, Nattana?"

"Here."

I would take my place at her side again. I lived a double life, all the senses alive to our progress, to the night, to Nattana, and to the horses, the mind so alight with memories that it did not seem dark. I became franker than I had ever been even to myself. My listener was unseen, and these things uttered aloud must be honestly said. I told of adolescent loves and of my ignorance and something of my troubles as a growing boy. I described the futile affair of Mary Jefferson.

She said hardly a word, but when she spoke it was a phrase or a brief question, which showed that she was following closely. I wondered often if later I would not regret such frankness, but there was something in the silent listening figure at my side that seemed to validate it.

So time passed. I was not finding the journey tedious, and without any idea of how long we had been walking or where we were, I came to the end and knew it was the end. All that had gone before were just passing things. With Dorna it was different. This I told her and here I left it and was silent.

Darkness seemed to close in more blackly, and I became more aware of the shrouded unseen land. The road was level. We must be passing through one of the areas of flat land below the Fains' farm, which was occupied and used in the same way that their land was. Leftward a little above us was a yellow spark that must be at some distance because we passed it so slowly. If I were truly Islandian I would know better where I was.

"Do you know whose that light is, Nattana?"

"No, I haven't been noticing where we were."

So even an Islandian lost sense of place.

"I've been too interested," she added. Her voice was husky and slow with fatigue.

She stumbled and bumped against me and as several times before I caught her arm and steadied her and let her go.

"I can't talk," she said.

"You don't have to. Why don't you ride here? It is level?"

"I couldn't walk again."

I hoped we were nearing the Fains', for what could I tell about now? Perhaps college life or our literature, translating poems I had learned by heart, or else. . . .

She was speaking.

"I want to say one thing. You have not possessed any woman. No man has possessed me, but I think I have gone a little further than you seem to have, Johnlang."

"I think," I said, "that at my age in my country it is a little exceptional in a man."

"That is not true here. Most men find it more natural to wait for *ania.*"

I remembered Dorn. . . .

"I can't talk any more," she said.

"You need not, Nattana."

The road began to ascend under our feet. Her breathing quickened and there was a sound like a sigh.

I plodded on. College life and our literature seemed irrelevant.

The glimmer of Fak's white body was not to be seen. I searched for and at last descried the glow of the lantern a long distance ahead. I had been keeping abreast of Nattana and we were going very slowly. I tried quickening my pace but hers did not respond.

"We ought to go a little faster," I said.

"I can't."

"I'll call to Ek to slow the pace. You ought to ride."

"No, don't!"

What should be done?

"I'll take your arm."

"Oh, will you?"

I found it in the darkness, and slid my bent forearm under hers. Our heights were such that they fitted, and I supported all the weight she chose to give me, and gently I quickened our steps. After a long time the pallor of Fak was all at once close at hand.

She leaned more heavily. . . .

"You could ride," I suggested.

"This is all I needed."

Her round, firmly soft arm was becoming familiar. . . .

"We can't be far," she said.

"I'll ask Ek," I said.

"No, don't."

My fingers slid without hesitation among hers, which gently responded. My heart seemed to lift with new strength that flowed between us.

We could hardly believe that we had arrived, although it was a long time afterwards. Ek was calling to us that the horses might make a break, and that we had better ride. Our hands unclasped. I gave Nattana a lift to mount Fak and then found the horse which I had been using. The smell of the pines was strong.

It was near midnight when we reached the house, which was dark. We left Nattana there in the hope of preventing Mara from disturbing herself too much, and Ek and I stabled the horses. Nevertheless when we returned Mara was up. She gave us warm milk. Nattana had already had hers and gone to bed. Ten minutes later I was in my own room again and not long after asleep.

Next day it was much warmer and everywhere mist was rising from the soaked ground and melting snow. This was a new aspect of Fains' farm, but all familiar things were there, and the place was merely an old friend in different clothes. I had breakfast with Mara and Ek. Nattana was staying in bed that morning and perhaps all day. She was tired, Mara said.

"She does her best," said Ek, "but her legs are too short."

He spoke of Nekka—a great walker—and said he would have liked to have Nettera with him. She became tired but did not know it. She would have played march tunes!

He was staying over a day to rest his horses. Nattana, I learned, would be present five days more, or until Dorn came, and maybe longer if there were heavy snow in the pass. Evidently she had received an invitation and Ek did not need her. I was delighted to have five more days of her company.

I spent a lazy morning, encouraged by Mara, but I thought of the fences and at least wanted to look them over. Though there was mud on the surface, the ground would be frozen beneath and it was not the season to set posts; but I could work on the stone walls and on the new tasks that Isla Fain would give me and that were mysterious and promising. Mara was eager to know all about the Council Meeting. She sewed by a window and I told her everything that I could remember. Outside, the air grew clearer and patches of blue appeared. It was like fall or spring rather than winter. Though I was leg-weary and somewhat inert, there was deep contentment in being at the Fains' again.

Lunchtime came. Nattana still remained in her room. She had books and Mara had brought her some sewing. She sent me a message that she was perfectly well, merely tired.

The day drifted on. The outdoors was too alluring to resist. Ek also was restless, and we walked along the highway examining the wall in a casual fashion. He made suggestions, which were precise and likely to be useful. Having become master of the Upper Farm, he was aware of his responsibility and thought of it constantly. Our talk shifted back and forth among three topics: his farm, the Fains' farm, and my future. Fences ceased to interest us but occasionally we reverted to them also, and he was watching the weather and the land all the time.

He faced serious problems at the Upper Farm. Though for the present it would still be used partly in connection with the lower one, it must cease to be a summer camp and must be a complete permanent residence, for the day was coming when the two farms could not be used together. A new line must be started at the Upper Farm with no dependence on any other place. He regarded himself, Atta, and Ettera as the founders, who would work together and build for the future. Nattana did not figure in the visions that he saw. He would marry, or Atta, and the line would go on.

He indicated their plans and the difficulties involved. Vegetables and grains and fruits must be grown for the family. These things could not be got in any other way, and the climate was rigorous. The Fains' granary, a reservoir against lean years at a place where seasons differed greatly in their yield, interested him a great deal. We visited it, and he examined its dim, cool, dry interior with a considering eye. The farmers who did not raise cattle had an easier time, he said. They had no worry about buying and selling and going to market—but it was a much duller life.

"We can't hope for much leisure for ourselves or the next generation, not for forty years," he said, but he smiled. "By that time there won't be any trouble. I would rather like to live to see it."

The situation which his father had caused became clearer to me. Had there been at the Lower Farm a family of normal size, life would have been a different thing, easier, broader, pleasanter—at least for those among the Hyths whom Fate had selected to be born.

Ek and I climbed up into the hillside pastures. Now and then he asked questions about my own life, directed to my future; how long I would remain in Islandia, what I would do upon leaving, and what sort of home I would have?

We leaned upon a fence. Often I had stood at this spot during fence-mending days of autumn, for from here the twin farms lay under the hills in a long panorama, and one saw all of both. When Ek meditated the lines of his face deepened.

"I saw your *History of the United States,*" he said, "but did not get a chance to read it. Nattana says you are writing in English, too; and you work on the farm here. That is a good life, isn't it?"

"I think so. . . ."

"Yes, if one has a mind that wants to busy itself in that way. I haven't that kind of a mind. Whatever thoughts I think that aren't part of the work I am doing I don't feel any need to express. Most of us are the same way, but Nettera has music, and my father, now. . . ."

He paused and thought about it.

"He has thoughts that he wants to express about how people ought to live. It is the same sort of thing, but he doesn't write . . . He ought to."

The lines in his cheek deepened in what might be a smile.

"If you express yourself in words or in paint, or in music or in stone, you aren't using materials that suffer; but if the material you work in is other persons' it isn't the same thing. Of course, ours was a confused household with special problems, and there is some excuse for him; but he is merely doing the same thing that others who have to express themselves do, only the material he works in is ourselves. I have come to see that, and so has Atta. I wish he would write a rule book instead of making rules and wanting us to obey them—and everyone else . . . On our place we are going to get back to the old ways. Atta and I aren't like him, though Ettera has some of his ideas. We feel that the old way is best; it is quite clear what is worth while doing in this life, and there are the old customs to serve as a guide when in doubt. Rules aren't needed."

He sighed slowly.

"I thought that you might like to know this when you come to see us. It won't be like visiting at the Lower Farm . . . Will you come and stay with us?" he continued. "It is always a lonely place, and more so in winter when there is no travel over the pass. It is all right for us older ones who are there for good, but Nattana is young and has not long been a grown woman. She has her way of express- ing herself—she is already a good weaver—but it is a way that re- quires other people to make it grow. I know she thinks the Lower Farm an isolated place, but it is very different from the Upper Farm; there are people passing all the year, more farms, and the town is close. There won't be the same interest in and requests for work to encourage her. She will need something else. And Atta and I would be glad to see you, too. We don't find you strange, Lang. He likes you. You will have what a man wants up there, for there is work to do there as well as here: we will be building a new stable, and when we can't work outdoors because of the cold or snow, there will be stones to be shaped and beams and boards to be cut indoors. Of course, as yet there won't be so many cattle and sheep to occupy us, but there will be enough work of some kind to keep us all happy . . . And you write, too . . . I was forgetting that."

He offered work as an inducement, and so it was—but at home would a host have used this method of persuasion? I told him I would surely come.

We walked home through the center of the farm past the or- chards, where the twigs and branches of the bare trees were black and sharp against the mist. We had done what had been done on all my first arrivals upon Islandian farms—we had surveyed the establishment. In the early days it seemed a ritual, and I was silent and a guest; now I was the host and could talk, and the walk was so natural that I had not realized that it was the same thing.

At last Nattana appeared. Faint shadows were under her eyes, which made her fleetingly resemble Nettera. She wore the dress in which she had received me when I called at the Upper Doring Palace. Ek had become a friend, but she had not ceased to be the one whom I knew longest and best. Nor had my own fatigue wholly gone; a feeling of indolence remained . . . What I would like was to spend this evening upon a bench before a fire, much at ease, and to talk to Nattana about anything that came into my head.

Instead, however, after supper, half of the inhabitants of the two farms arrived—Catlin, his wife and two daughters, Tolly and his sister, Bard and his wife, Keeping, and Anor and his wife, Bodin and all the Larnels. They came to hear about the Council Meeting and Ek, Nattana, and I were kept busy describing and answering questions.

The Larnel girl assumed the role of a rival. She also was a weaver, and Nattana made an engagement to visit her next morning, telling Mara that she would sew with her in the afternoon. I had assumed that all her time was mine; evidently she did not intend it to be.

Next morning large flakes of snow filled the air, falling slowly and rather sparsely, but the pines outside the window were burdened. Nevertheless, Ek had gone before anyone was up except Mara. The ground was white again, and it was not a day to mend stone walls. Instead I would work at the mill, for some physical work was necessary. Besides, Nattana had other engagements.

After breakfast we set out together, she for a morning with Larnella, I to the mill. Soon her cloak and hood were dotted with large melting snow crystals. When I asked her how she was, she said that she was tired still and would not be herself for several days, and that she would show me what a good walker she was at some other time . . . Her thoughts were full of her brother riding in a snowstorm to the Mora Pass.

"I don't know the weather here," she said, "nor what it will be like in the open spaces up there. We have no such region on our pass. I wish I knew he were safe."

The distance to the highroad was short and our paths then separated.

"Shall I see you at lunch?" I asked.

"The Larnels may ask me to stay. I told Mara I might. Shall I?"

"I have no objection."

She leaned back against the gate post.

"If you should object . . ." she said slowly, looking at me with her green eyes.

"Nattana, your time here is your own."

"If you want me to give you some of it, why don't you say so?"

"I do want some of it."

"You can have all you want of it."

"Today you have made engagements."

"Did you mind my making them?"

"I said I didn't!"

It came so suddenly—this half quarrel. . . .

"Is that true or not true, Johnlang? Think! Be honest!"

I paused.

"Nattana," I said, "you want to sew with Mara. You want to see another weaver. What I want is some of your time for my own."

"Are you asking me for some of it?"

"Of course I am! Tomorrow—"

"I shan't want to do anything very active."

"Give me the afternoon."

"Yes."

"I don't know what we shall do."

"We'll see what the weather is. What we do doesn't matter."
The quarrel was over.

"Wouldn't you like to look at the mill, Nattana?"

"I'll call on you on my way back."

"This morning?"

"No, this afternoon—after lunch."

"I'll be there."

She moved on her way. She was vividly colored, making all else somber.

"You are very pretty, Nattana," I called after her.

Her eyes flashed back at me.

"Sometimes," she said.

"Always!"

"Oh no!" She laughed, waved her hand, and went along the highway, hidden in her dark cloak, and her feet made neat footprints in the white sheet of the snow.

The mill pond was full almost to the top edge of the embankment from which the swimmers had leaped three months before. The snowflakes in the pale air and the white fields around the pond made the water blacker than ever by contrast. Over the dam just above the bridge the water curved in quiet green glassiness to break into spray and rise up in foam from below. The persistent roar of this waterfall would be an accompaniment to the morning's work in the mill.

I lingered on the bridge. There was water enough, and no need to be sparing in the use of its power. I planned my work, to cut and shape perhaps a dozen or more rails and posts, and to stand them up to weather; and later to tar those cut when I was here last, examining them first to make sure they had not rotted anywhere, for they had gone a little longer than they should.

The interior of the mill was damp but the air was not cold, and there was no need to light a fire of chips, bark, and shavings in the wide stone fireplace at one end of the long room.

Examining the saw, I found it a little rusty. Therefore my first task was to clean it. The spirit of work, learned from Anor, was one of deliberation and thoroughness usually resulting in absorbed attention. Time passed, and the room became lighter as the moist snow outside whitened the windows.

This mill was typical. The overshot wheel in its sluiceway turned an oaken axle from which power was carried into the mill by wooden cogwheels turning a shaft. Within was a flywheel with different radii. It revolved whenever the mill wheel did, and it could be connected by cowhide belts, fitted to its varying sizes, either to the machinery of the saw or to that of the millstones. The mill wheel itself was set in operation by depressing a great oak lever inside the mill, which raised a gate and released water upon the wheel. As an Islandian worked, so did his machinery, simple, long-thought-out, deliberate.

I brought in logs, studied and trimmed them, and then measured and marked them for cutting. It was heavy work. The morning was nearly over before I was ready for the sawing itself, and I decided that I had had enough and went home to chat with Mara for half an hour before lunch.

In the early afternoon, back once more at the mill, I fixed in place the belt that was used to connect the flywheel to an idler wheel which could be enmeshed with that operating the machinery of the saw. Then I sat on the great oak lever which lifted the gate and rode it to make it work. Slowly it sank and there was that thrilling and somewhat frightening roar of power let loose. Seconds passed and then deliberately the flywheel turned, as though it had first to consider the matter. Its revolution was slow but the belt ran fast and the idler wheel raced. The mill was filled with the clatter and jar of wooden machinery. This was an exciting moment. I swung the lever that meshed the idler, and after a moment the saw moved with just the motion that a man would make back and forth with a slightly circular thrust on the upstroke. One watched for the cut of this stroke upon the line along which one wished the saw to move. Stopping the saw, I adjusted with screws the first log in a slide that traveled in a groove along the saw. I swung the lever again. Then for some time I dared not turn my eyes, guiding the log with my hands, for there was no artificial feed. If the cut began to deviate from the line, it was necessary to stop the machinery and to readjust the log in the slide; but this would not happen if the log were properly placed and the cutting marks "trued up" with guide lines on the slide.

The first cut was the hardest, for after that there was a flat side to go by. It was pleasant work, and a deep satisfaction to produce from a round bark-covered tree a square-sided beam, with "shakes," smelling of bark and of the woods, for by-product. Yet no beam ever came out perfectly square. This was not in my power as yet.

Time lifted itself like a runner and moved swiftly. The saw never slid the whole length of a log or beam without the coming of a memory or an echo of a memory of Dorna; but I was so used to these now that they stirred no ruffle of pain and scarcely a thought.

As the saw cut it uttered a little shriek down and a little shriek up with sighs between. The air smelled of fresh sawdust and became hazy. On one side the pile of beams increased, and on the other that of slabs, like boards on one side, bark on the other. As background to the sound of the saw and to the clatter of machinery there was the distant, continuous, low thunder of the water going over the dam and the nearer swishing in the sluiceway under the mill.

I finished a cut and swung the lever, when a voice spoke from behind me.

"Nattana."

She stood just within the doorway outlined against a white swirling world of snow. As I went nearer I saw that she also was white, plastered with snow from her hood to the lower hem of her dark cloak. Snowflakes were melting upon her lashes, her cheeks, her eyebrows, and upon the red-gold lock of hair that hung looped upon her forehead. She threw back her hood and began flapping her cloak like wings. Her tan stockings were sheathed with snow below her bare knees. She looked wet, warm, happy.

"I met a man!" she cried. "I met him just beyond Anor's. He said it was much worse down here than up there. He had met Ek on the road and said he would have no trouble at all. . . . And then on the way here I fell flat. Look at me! . . . I came as soon as I could. They kept me and kept me . . . The snow is so sticky, and it is wet too! . . . Do you mind my being so late? But I couldn't help it."

She took off her cloak and looked about her.

"I have never been here before," she added.

To Nattana I had said that she was always pretty. It was not true, but she was pretty most of the time, and particularly so now with her face pink and warm, her eyes green and brilliant, and the waves and curls of her glowing hair flattened upon her round head by the damp and by the pressure of her hood.

"It is chilly in here," she said.

"I'll make you a fire."

"I won't interfere." She laughed. "I want to dry myself, too."

Soon there was a roaring blaze of slabs. She spread her cloak upon a sawhorse, and standing close to the fire she turned herself to dry different parts of her body and her dress, holding out her skirt, taking different positions—fascinating to watch.

"I'm glad about Ek," she said.

"So am I."

"He is kind."

"He seems so—very. He asked me to be sure and come and see you all at the Upper Farm."

She nodded, and after a moment said:

"You will come?"

"Oh yes."

"Next month?"

"Yes, but it depends on the pass—"

"And on Don."

She shuddered and sighed.

"I'll see him soon after I reach home. May I tell him that you would like to cross with him next month?"

"Yes, won't you please?"

"I wonder what is going to happen," she said after a moment.

"You mean—about the treaty?"

"Oh no, at the Upper Farm . . . You may find things different —and me changed."

"I'll take the risk."

She smiled and turned to me.

"There is such a noise," she said. I went to the lever and raised it. The flywheel stopped turning reluctantly, but the distant roar of the water over the dam increased.

"Did Ek say anything about—Father?" she asked.

I repeated his analysis of his father as nearly as it was remembered. "But," I concluded, "he said that at the Upper Farm they were going to return to the old way because he and Atta thought it the best one."

"He told you that?" she said, looking at the fire again.

"Yes, and he said that he thought I might like to know it."

She uttered a low wondering ejaculation half to herself.

"I didn't quite understand what he meant," I said.

She spread her fingers to the fire.

"Oh, I suppose he was thinking about all of Father's rules. Rules aren't the old way, you see."

"What does the 'old way' really mean?"

"Oh, there are customs—"

"He said there were customs which served as a guide."

"Yes, but not as rules."

"What is the difference, Nattana?"

"Oh, customs you follow yourself when it seems best for you to do so, which is usually the case, or when you are in doubt. They are only what most people believe to be the best course most of the time; and you don't have to follow them when you have a good reason. But you always have to abide by rules whether there is any reason for it or not. And those who believe in rules, as Father does, think you ought to be made to observe them. . . . I can't tell you any better."

It was rather vague.

"About what kind of thing are these customs, Nattana?"

"Oh, about the way one lives."

"I wonder why he told me what he did," I said. She made no answer for some time. Then she began in a different voice, "I promised to sew with Mara."

"Oh, don't go so soon!" I said.

"I can stay a little longer. It is a quiet pleasant place to work."

"Are you getting dry, Nattana?"

"I'm beginning to burn! My legs!" She looked at me with simulated pain and a smile, and stepped back. "Do you know, I haven't made a visit for years to an entirely new place long enough really to know it. Of course, I have stopped here overnight, but we came late and left early. It makes me so happy! And I suppose with the Upper Farm near, next spring, perhaps, I can come again."

"Do you like it here?"

"Not for too long. It is so shut in. But it is a peaceful, happy place, don't you think so? Wouldn't you like to have a farm like this and be a *tana?*" She turned to me.

"I have wondered if I would not, very much."

"It seems to me so strange that you have no farm! I find myself thinking that you have one and that I am wondering what it is like—as though you had it! I have even dreamed about it. In my dream it was this kind of a farm, and not a grazing farm like my home. There were thick woods all about it. I came to visit you there and we walked all over it. But the dream was odd in one way—I don't remember any house. Where did you sleep, Johnlang? . . . Perhaps the dream is one reason that I think you must have a place. It must be strange to have no *alia!*"

She turned her head away suddenly. I looked around her cheek and saw her chin working.

"What is the matter, Nattana?"

"It is not the dream. I thought of my home, and I want to cry. There isn't a crueler punishment than sending a person away! It is all right for the boys and Ettera to be at the Upper Farm, for they will remain and build their lives there, and their *alia* will be where they are; but mine will be down in the valley, where I can never go— for years perhaps! You have no place. You can't understand. . . ."

"Nattana, I do!"

"I don't see how you can!"

"I can be sorry, very sorry."

"I know you are, and it helps me."

With a sudden thudding in the heart I took her hand. It seemed about to resist and then yielded, and I slid my fingers among hers. There was sudden stillness, and all words and thoughts were washed out of me by a benumbing wave.

I heard her sigh.

"I didn't mean to make you do that."

"Do you object, Nattana?"

"Don't force me to think whether I do or not."

Before we left the mill we scattered the charred and still flaming slabs. The room became dark as the flames sank. Nattana buried the burning pieces in the ashes with the poker. One by one they went out, and she herself faded into darkness. The light in the door was now a pale, dying blue.

I held her cloak for her and she put it on quietly. Having wrapped myself in my own I took her arm.

"Let me guide you," I said. "There are all sorts of things scattered about and I know where they are better than you."

The round, softly firm arm which I held seemed yielding and a little mine.

The outside world still held a glimmer of diffused light. There were a few flakes in the air. She stood motionless and dark on the doorstep, while I swung shut the heavy door.

There was a faint sigh.

"Would you like to walk a little way?" I suggested.

"Yes," she answered in a thin voice.

We moved toward the bridge. The glassy edge where the water first curved over glittered quietly, but the fall itself was only movement in darkness and a heavy roaring that cast dampness on our cheeks.

She moved slowly, a dark blot against the white glimmer of snow, which was cold and soft over our ankles. We followed a road that wound through a black corridor of trees. Every little while there came the damp chilly touch of a snowflake on the face. The sky overhead was opaque, but visible against it now and then were drifting black specks. It was hushed and still, except for the distant purr of the waterfall. . . .

Somehow it was dreary also, and we returned to the house.

Isla Fain and his brother were at the house when Nattana and I came in from the damp snowy night. They had left The City early the day before and had traveled far beyond Reeves on the road to Tindal, and therefore, today, June 22nd, they reached the farm at the end of twilight.

That evening in the living room they told us of later political happenings. Nattana sat in her usual light way, a compact graceful figure, one knee over the other and her upper foot pointed out. She was sewing with a lamp set near her. Her head was a little bent, and the light on her hair made every red and golden thread glisten. She looked very young, a sturdy little girl, with her braids and bare knees above the tops of her stockings. It was a wonder that so many thoughts and so much knowledge and intelligence could be inside her head. Ek had said that she had not long been a grown woman. She was twenty-two and I would be twenty-eight in three more days. She seemed more valuable than she ever had before.

Isla Fain and his brother each sat at the corners of two high-backed settles set at a little more than right angles to the fire, with Mara next to her husband and I to Isla Fain. We had often grouped ourselves in this way. Nattana, a quietly glowing interest, was a little apart.

Isla Fain's face was always darker than I remembered it and the cap of his hair whiter and more dense. His brother was like a reflection of him in a mirror a little false.

On the day after we had left The City the council adjourned. The session, more important than any in sixty years, had been a short one. Isla Fain said that whenever important measures came before them he doubted the ability of any representative assembly to decide wisely. He deplored the existence in any small body of men of power to shape the futures of large masses. The function of the council should be as it had been in the past—to adjust irreconcilable differences between small groups and individuals. In an ideal world there would be no national questions at all.

But, said he, there was this to be realized on the other side, whether it was better or not: the council had not really decided the

529

matter in the present case. Individuals and families had become alive to its significance partly as a result of the referendum conducted by the Dorns. Members of the council consciously and unconsciously reflected what individuals felt. The feelings and wishes of single human beings had risen as water rises and had submerged the national point of view which Lord Mora strove to keep to the top. He was less right than the Dorns were. As to future consequences perhaps he was the wiser, but, declared Lord Fain, great and far-seeing man that Mora was, he was not in heart like the majority of his countrymen. The Mora family for generations had kept alive a different tradition. In other countries it was one usually in the ascendancy, but in Islandia it never had been for long. "What we really decided," he added, "was that we did not want to be a nation. A dread of being a mere part of a whole influenced many minds. We seem to differ from the rest of you. There is less of the gregarious instinct in our heredity, and more of the individual, as though we had descended from animals who lived alone rather than from those who lived in packs."

I had a passing wonder as to how the Islandians came to reason in the terms of the doctrine of evolution, propounded by Darwin not so very long ago. Had it filtered into this country or had they long ago themselves discovered it, their speculations not stopped by a brain full of inconsistent religious and other dogmas?

But Mora might be right, Isla Fain was saying. The menace to Islandia was a real one in his opinion. The most important thing that had happened aside from the vote on the Mora Treaty was an intimation presented by Count von Bibberbach that the re-establishment of garrisons along the border would probably be regarded by his government as an unfriendly act. This was perhaps the largest problem that the new Dorn government had to face. It was all the more unfortunate because the Germans had now less interest in doing their part—that is, in keeping raiders out of Islandia. Another problem, almost as difficult, would certainly arise, for proposals to internationalize Ferrin were almost sure to be presented whenever the diplomats could agree upon their terms.

Nattana spoke suddenly.

"Fain, do you think there is any greater danger of the Bants making a raid?"

He hesitated for a moment.

"It is all guessing, Hytha, but on the whole I think that the danger is greater than it was before we repudiated Lord Mora's policies."

"Is the Upper Farm less safe than the Lower Farm?"

"It is nearer the Lor Pass, Hytha."

She shuddered a little and bent over her sewing, and I shuddered also feeling her fears with new force.

Next morning Nattana sewed and I went to the mill to finish my sawing. As the morning advanced it became clearer and colder, the temperature dropped below the freezing point, and the air was dry again; but it was not yet so cold as to freeze the machinery of the mill, which I was told sometimes happened. It was good to be at work with an afternoon of Nattana to come. There was a little throb, partly of dread and partly of impatience, in my heart.

Toward noon Fain, the brother, came to see me and for a while we sawed together. Then we discussed work to be done. Fence mending would be at best a spasmodic occupation during the winter. Did I want to be a roofer and stonemason? he asked. The granary had not been repointed in his generation and there were places where the tile roof leaked. There was also similar work needed upon the workshop and upon the mill. These were both indoor and outdoor tasks and could be done whenever it was not so cold as to freeze the mortar. It was a relief to know that there was real work for me.

The afternoon came at last. No one at lunch asked about our plans, and it was not necessary to tell our hosts that we had an engagement and were going to be leisurely.

Nattana played somewhat the part that Dorna had played at the Ronans'—the young woman-visitor eager to help her older hostess in domestic ways. Bodina, aunt of Bodin, was the only regular house *deneri* and therefore Mara often cooked, waited on table so far as it was necessary, and washed dishes. Nattana thought she must do the same. I went to the living room to wait for her, and thought of Dorna at the Ronans'. The lost wonder was a fire unseen behind the curve of a dark hill. I was older, less romantic, less stirred in the heart. Life at the Fains' was an everyday sort of life, familiar and natural now.

At last Nattana entered, and went to one of the settles, sat down, and relaxed with her head resting on the high back, as though tired. Her profile was lovely, with its balance and sleekness; face to face

531

she was more commonplace. Her profile suggested the existence of a unique elusive spirit; her full view was that of any girl.

"What shall we do?" she said suddenly, as though irritated by the silence.

"We'll do something," I answered. "There is no hurry."

"None at all."

It was pleasant doing nothing.

"What would you do in your country if we were visiting at the same house?" she asked.

My imagination quickened. Here was something to talk about. The date was June 23rd, 1908. After some time I worked out that it was Tuesday, and therefore there would be no matinee to which to take her; but there was the Art Museum, perhaps a music recital, or else we could walk and go to tea somewhere. I assumed that we were in Boston, or if it were New York there might be some play even on Tuesday.

All these things I told her, thinking aloud.

The house at which we were staying was my brother Philip's on the south side of Beacon Street.

"What would I wear?" Nattana asked.

I dressed her: a long skirt—which would make her look smaller—a svelte waist, a gray fur coat because it was winter, and gloves, and I put on her head a little squirrel fur toque whether in the fashion or not. On her feet would be arctics, over a little pair of pumps, with high heels! It took time to make her clothes precise to her eyes. . . .

I saw her face against a background of Beacon Street houses as she and I set out for a walk and for tea at the Touraine. I would have bought her a corsage bouquet of violets. . . .

"You would say, Nattana, 'How noisy it is!' "

"Why would I say that?"

She laid herself along the length of the settle, her chin between her palms and stared at me. Her braids hung over her shoulders, and bright color had come into her cheeks.

In answering her question it was necessary to describe a city street at home. Almost yard by yard I led Nattana along, down Beacon Street to the Public Gardens and across them and the Common and eventually to the Touraine. As I spoke the quiet living room and the open fire became a dim and unreal background, and the snowy silent farm lands outside with their encircling forested hills were a dream;

I saw only Nattana's actual face and her two pretty hands spread along her flushed cheeks, her short little skirt lying flat upon her rounded body and occasionally a sandaled foot lifting in the air; and also—quite as vivid as she was—the scenes which I was imagining and the Americanized Nattana that I pictured as with me. . . .

"Does this bore you?" I asked.

"Oh no! Go on! What is your brother's house like?"

I described it in detail, the three floors, the arrangement and use of rooms, the lighting and heating, the furniture, the outlook, and its servants.

"What is your brother like?" she asked.

I described Philip and Mary, and their children.

"What does he do?"

I told her about his law practice and that he was successful, and how much time he spent at his office and how much at home and at leisure.

"When you go back to the United States, will you have a house like that?"

I said that I would not—not for years and then only if I were successful and married; and that if I did not go to New York I would probably live at home. This led to a description of our house in Medford, and of Father and Mother and Alice and of their occupations.

"Is there no country?" she asked. "Is all city?"

Our ways, I said, were cast in cities and suburbs, and I described the country and how city dwellers visited it on vacations and I mentioned something about rural life. She understood quickly, reminding me of my *History of the United States* in which these things were treated.

"I had forgotten," she said. "All you have been talking about is city life. Why wouldn't you rather be a farmer when you go back?"

The reasons I tried to make clear. I did not know enough and in New England there was little chance to make money. Our family tradition was one of professional and business interests.

She nodded her head.

"You would be an agent-kind-of-man, wouldn't you?"

"Yes, Nattana."

"Suppose you married and weren't successful like your brother, how would you live?" she asked.

I had as model his suburban house in Winchester, before he moved to Boston, and this I described to her and something of the worries that he and Mary had had, and of their pleasures. Then I told of his move.

"You all move so much!" she said. "I keep picturing your places and then I discover that you are somewhere else."

To make it complete, I said that if I went to work in New York I would probably board. Boarding had to be explained to her.

"Would you 'board' if you were married?" she asked, lifting her head when I had finished.

"Probably not."

"I was thinking of you as being married. How would you live then?"

"In a flat," I said, "or else I would 'commute.'" Then I told her that if I commuted it would be like the life I had already described but with longer distances to go. After that I embarked upon an account of life in an apartment in New York, making it as real and as accurate as I could.

Nattana's head dropped upon one of her arms. She asked questions but they became fewer.

"If I married," I said, "that would probably be what I should do." And I told her that Uncle Joseph's office seemed to be the place where I would end.

Her voice was a little muffled.

"You would be there all day doing one kind of a thing and she would be in the flat all day doing something entirely different?"

"Yes, that is the way it is. She keeps house. He makes the money. Of course, she wouldn't be in the house all the time. Housekeeping would not occupy her wholly."

"Where would she go?"

I indicated what her interests might be. Then I realized that my hypothetical wife might have children. They would take a great deal of her time.

"Where would they live at first?" she asked.

"In the flat."

"Not in the country?" she exclaimed in surprise.

"Only during vacations."

"No place in the country where she could go to have them away from the city and give them a start?" she asked, raising her round head.

"No."

"Never the country?"

"Only on vacations."

"If the children did not take all her time, could she do something herself—oh, carve, or weave?"

"She could, but most married women do not; and weaving is done in factories."

She dropped her head again and asked a few more questions, which I answered briefly. Then they ceased.

"You have made it all very clear," she said in an absent voice.

I explained a few more details that occurred to me. She was silent. . . I wondered suddenly what she was thinking. She lay limp as though dropped, asleep or brooding. I could not see her eyes—only a few inches of cheek and a round head of disheveled hair.

"What are you thinking, Nattana? Is there more I can tell you?"

"No more! I see it all," she said in a low voice.

Her mood was unexpected. She seemed to have become disturbed and melancholy. Abruptly she sat up. The cheek which had rested on her arm was much redder than the other one.

"What do I think about it—I, myself, who am not one of your women? I think it is dreadful, so confused, no place really to live in, only a few rooms belonging to someone else, no *alia!* I don't see how you can live that life or ask a woman to share it."

"There is no other way for many people, but it is not so bad. There is a great deal that is interesting. It can be a full life."

Her prejudice was dismaying and I resented it.

"And as to asking a woman to share that life," I continued, "if she loves you, she is willing. It is hers as much as yours."

"I don't see how she can be willing."

"You are Islandian."

"I don't see how *you* can, Johnlang!"

"I am not Islandian," I answered, but my feeling that I could live such a life was one of sudden pain.

She looked at me and her green eyes blazed with anger. We seemed on the edge of a quarrel, but her eyes changed. They softened and in their corners was a wet flash. She turned her head away.

Something had hurt her. I moved towards the settle to say what I could. I saw her hand. I would take it.

But as I came nearer, she rose and went to the fireplace. Sympathy for her unknown hurt was blurred in a hot wish for her hand. I caught it, hanging at her side; it stiffened, resisted, and twisted away, and she interposed her shoulder.

She edged away a little and turned to face me.

"I'm sorry!" she said in a clear strong voice, and her eyes met mine. "Johnlang! Oh, Johnlang! you are a heartbreaking person!" she cried. "Let's not talk of this any more!"

"Let's go outdoors."

"Oh yes!"

We separated to fetch our cloaks and waterproof boots. The pause gave us steadiness.

When she returned, her face looked as though she had washed it, and her eyes were bright.

"I've an idea!" she said. "The Fains are sure to have a sled or a toboggan. There must be a place where we could coast."

We found Mara, who told us that there was a toboggan at the granary, and she recommended a hillside.

"You are starting rather late," she said. "Why don't you take your supper with you? There will be chocolate warm for you when you come in."

The supper was quickly prepared and we set out in haste to get the toboggan and to find our coasting place before it was dark. The sun was already gone and the valley in shadow, but the upper parts of the hills above the Catlins' farm were still in sunlight. The air was clean and cold, the sky cloudless and blue. All things vibrated with dark, rich color.

"We should have gone out long ago!" said Nattana, turning to me as she strode through the crusted snow, which crumpled under her feet. It glistened, and beneath, the snow was fine and powdery.

The sharp fresh air was bracing and pure. The troubled feverishness of our long talk of home drained away, all but the wish for her hand.

We found the toboggan, which was really a sled with two broad flat runners like skis supporting on stanchions a rectangular framework crisscrossed with cowhide like a snowshoe. It was very light but long enough for both. We set out for the hill to which Mara had directed us, opened wide the gate in the rail fence that separated pasture from orchard, and climbed the flawless snowy surface, each drawing the toboggan by a cowhide thong. It skittered over the crust without sinking in. When we reached the top a descent was before us, extending down for two hundred yards to the orchards, where the distant trees stood above the snow like hearthbrushes of twigs with thin stems. The surface had no mark upon it.

We were both bareheaded and warm from our climb. We took off our cloaks. I turned the toboggan around.

"I shall steer," I said.

"Do you know how?"

"I have coasted before."

She sat astride the toboggan bending her feet to place them upon the runners. I kneeled behind her, trailing one leg.

We seemed a little top-heavy.

"Are you ready?"

"I am ready." Her voice was high and excited. I pushed off. . . .

The toboggan gathered speed. The air was swift and keen. The orchard which had been below us was rising up.

We slewed. The necessary little to straighten us escaped the giving. We tilted and I let go, my arms before my face—and came to rest with mouth and eyes full of soft fine snow.

I was on my feet. The toboggan was going on by itself. A little way off Nattana was rising. She was unhurt, laughing, white from head to foot, her eyebrows and hair like an old man's.

We recaptured the toboggan and climbed the hill again, agreeing that we had been top-heavy. I apologized, but it was not necessary. Her only hurt was snow down her back, and she writhed and laughed as she walked.

"Do you trust me to steer again?" I asked.

"Of course!" she answered. "I'm not afraid."

She laid herself upon the toboggan and was so long that there was no room for me except resting upon her legs. Once more I pushed, and the bow of the toboggan tilted down and moved and went faster. The air began to rush and then became breath-taking, but I was learning the technique of steering—a light pressure and shift of my foot. There was a moment of excitement when we came to the place where we had spilled; the toboggan tipped; but it straightened and went on. At the edge of the orchard the ground dropped from under us. We flew in air but landed erect with a springy jounce, sped among the trees, and came to rest.

We rose, a little breathless. Down the hill were two parallel tracks ruled in the snow, and we had come nearly to the road through the center of the farm. It at once became our objective to reach and cross it and to penetrate into the orchard on the other side.

The subject as to which she had said, "Let's not talk about it," came up again, and we began to argue.

Each time that we climbed the hill the darkness was a little greater and there were more stars in the sky. On the ascents we were in one world, our minds busy, looking beyond what we were doing to another life; on our descents, a brief rush in the dark, this world was forgotten, and we were in another, Nattana half embraced, my body against her firm and rounded hips and thighs, and for a few seconds, I knew her well; and then we were walking up hill again, and she would be saying, "I don't see how people can go into marriage when it is all so uncertain!" and I would be answering, "When people at home want to marry each other, Nattana, they are willing to let the future take care of itself."

"I don't see how anyone in your country can ever dare have children," she said, "since there is no sure future for them, and all is changing so rapidly—unless they can't prevent them!"

"People at home want them."

"Just to want them seems to me disgusting!" she cried. "To have them to satisfy yourself is worse! To have them blindly is so unfair! Have you ever really wanted a child, Johnlang?"

Instantly I thought of Dorna—and no more.

"I take that question back!" Nattana said sharply. "I have never wanted a child, though I have half wanted to want one at moments a long time apart!"

"I can't answer," I replied.

"I am sorry. . . I won't bother you any more. Your country may have many interesting things, but we shall never agree about it, you and I. It is no use trying."

"I shan't give up hope."

"Of what?" she demanded.

"That you will understand my point of view."

"I know it exists. It is natural to you, an American."

It was night, and there were so many stars that they lay in drifts like spangled clouds. The Milky Way in this hemisphere still seemed out of place, and the star arrangement so unfamiliar as to be artificial, but the same immensity yawned.

Nattana suggested supper. We agreed that it was warmer down in the orchard, where was also a pile of brush which we might persuade to burn. We wrapped ourselves in our cloaks and she put the lunch basket on the front of the toboggan, and we embarked; and for a few seconds we were a close-knit unity rushing down through darkness with the seething sound of the runners and the icy keen air upon our faces.

We found the pile of brush and shook the snow from it. Nattana, a dark heap seated on the toboggan, watched my efforts to light it without making suggestions. At last the flames caught and began to lick upwards and at the same moment the night became a black wall around us. I sat next to her and she explored the basket by the sense of touch. She put a meat roll into my hand, her cold fingers brushing and resting upon my own. The flames rose higher and lighted our faces and we felt a definite and palpable warmth. We were hungry, a little leg-weary and subdued.

We wondered if we should have burned this pile of brushwood. We realized that we were both guests at someone else's house.

"My home is not very far but I am an exile and yours is on the other side of the world," she said.

We ate our supper quickly. She wished there were something warm to drink. . . .

Our fire was dying down. Nattana held out her hands. Her profile was lovely in the ruddy-orange light, her hood only half upon her head.

Islandians so rarely wore any covering upon their hands. I asked if her hands would not suffer. She said that she had a lotion in which she would immerse them on her return. They became chapped sometimes, she admitted, but gloves. . . .

"Are they cold now?" I asked, my heart beating.

She looked at me, her face becoming dark, and nodded.

"Mine aren't," I said, and I took her hands. She gave them to me, turning a little towards me; and holding both in one of mine I drew my cloak over them, and then I made upon my knees a sandwich of the cold smooth things between my own.

There came a sense of quiet and peace.

"Was it necessary that they be cold?" she asked.

"I wanted them," I answered, "and I thought an excuse might help me to get them."

"I think you like my hands," she said.

"I like them a great deal, Nattana." Words stirred wishing to be uttered. Moments slipped by, and peacefulness deepened.

"Last night I dreamed again about your living here," she said. "Perhaps it was because we talked about it. . . You would like to be a *tana*, wouldn't you?"

I was thinking that I would not let Nattana leave three days hence without having kissed her.

"Oh, Nattana, it is so impossible that I have not let myself think deeply about it. I don't really know."

I explained the law and told her what Dorn had said about making exceptions to it. "Nor," I added, "am I sure that I want to abandon my own country."

"But what does that mean? If you could have a place of your own! You don't know how you seem to us, Johnlang—like a strange lost creature who has wandered in from another world!"

Her hands gripped mine.

"I want the best for you!" she cried. "The only best I can think of is what I am used to. You are just like one of us, Johnlang. . . I can't see your face, but I know what it is like. It is the kind of face we know. It is a good face. I like to look at you. Your eyes are so clear!"

Her hands relaxed, quivered, and then quickly withdrew.

"My hands are warm now!" she said and she rose. I started to my feet also. She was stooping in the darkness to pick up the thong of the toboggan.

"Nattana," I cried, "you are dear to say that to me!"

"It is true. . . Let's go up the hill again."

She went on, and I caught up the other thong lest she drag the toboggan alone.

We ascended the hill in silence. Her words were a delight in my heart. . . Down we came through the darkness, and the toboggan—as though with new life—went on into the further orchard.

Nattana snatched up the thong. "We'll go further next time," she cried, and then she laughed aloud.

It was colder, with a rising wind. We were glad of our cloaks. We walked with lifted faces and the stars above us were winking brilliantly.

Up the hill we toiled. The need for words had gone from us.

She took her place upon the toboggan, and I took mine. The toboggan shot forward on the harder snow. I embraced her, she could not but know it. She was quite still. The sharp air caught my breath away, but I held her, and there was far more pain and mystery in a woman's body than I had ever dreamed. The cold air blinded my eyes with tears, so that I was afraid that I could not see the gate and the trees. We had never gone so fast.

We raced through the higher orchard, jounced across the road, sped under the flying trees of the lower one, and on into the open stubble of the maize field. There in a shower of soft snow the toboggan came to a stop.

She rose quietly, and slowly leaning down lifted the thong.

"That was a record, Nattana!" I cried. What was she thinking, this dark shadow of a girl whom I had held so closely that I knew the very substance of her?

"We can't break it again," she said at last.

"We can try!"

"All right," she answered, "once more, but then let's put the toboggan away and go home."

It was a long way up the hill. She was right—it was time to leave, for we were tired and perhaps overwrought. She plodded along in silence at an irregular pace, quickening her steps and then dragging back.

We reached the high fence, and above us the woods beyond hung over us black and rustling with wind.

"I would like to feel my hair flying," she said.

She was a long time taking it down, and I was restless. When she went to the toboggan she seemed reluctant to place herself upon it, but she said nothing and with a surge in my throat I embraced her again.

Her hair whipped backward upon my face and it was hard to see, but the toboggan had made a furrow and steered itself. I closed my eyes, not caring what came, laid my head upon her and held her tightly. We traveled through the night as through the air. But we did not reach the stubble field again.

What was there to say? On the plod to the dark granary silence hung heavy upon us, and we were tired, tired. . . She was right, we had not broken the record. We walked back to the farmhouse, and on the way she slipped her hand into mine. On the doorstep we hesitated, our hands still together. Within were the Fains.

"We will sleep well tonight, won't we, Johnlang?" she said.

"Are you sleepy, Nattana?"

"Almost asleep now. . . ."

Nattana opened the door, disengaging her hand.

Mara brought us warm chocolate diluted with milk. Nattana drank hers with hair loose about her head and face. Her eyes were heavy with sleep and they looked at no one. She set down her cup, said a brief good night, and immediately drifted away to bed.

24

Early Winter at the Fains'

THE WIND BLEW HARD all night and the air became much colder. Next morning the windows in the downstairs rooms were white with frost. Breakfast was over and Nattana had not yet appeared. I dreaded her a little and left without seeing her. Hunting up Anor, the expert in repair jobs, I went about with him inspecting granary, workshop, and mill, finally going to his house for lunch. The morning in the bitter windy cold had seemed long. At first it had been almost a relief to avoid Nattana, but now I wanted to see her again. Tomorrow Dorn would arrive and next day she would depart with him. Less than forty-eight hours remained. I left the Anors' early to make up for lost time, and returned to the Fains'. The tracks of our toboggan were still ruled upon the empty snow.

Breathless with cold, a little numb, and eager for Nattana, I entered the house expecting to find her. But she was not in the living room nor in the empty kitchen nor at the stable. I knocked at her door but there was no answer.

Angry with disappointment, blaming her for no reason at all, I went to my own room, made up the fire, and lying on the bed opened the little book of Godding's *Fables* which she had given me. Its sense, however, did not bite into my intelligence. Twenty-eight tomorrow and once so much in love, now I was behaving like a youth, preoccupied with holding a girl's hands and hoping to get a kiss. I must not make a fool of myself with Nattana.

There was a knock at my door and she entered. I scrambled to my feet and asked her to sit down. Her cheeks were glowing, her hair was neatly done, and while I poked up the fire she told me where she had been.

She had sewed all morning, she said. The Catlin girls had come to see her and she had gone home to lunch with them. She liked them. They were pretty. Did I see much of them? Very little, I answered. On the way back, she had thought I might be at the granary or at the workshop or the mill, and she had visited all these places. Not finding me she came home. In return I told her what I had done and of my search for her.

"Let's not go out," said Nattana. "Let's read and talk."

The little dark-green volume of Godding's *Fables* lay upon the brown blanket of the bed. Her eyes fell upon it and she began to laugh.

"At last?" she said. "What did you read?"

My mind was a blank.

"I had not started when you came in."

"Let's read from that. I'll get some sewing," she said, springing up. I heard her calling in the hall to Mara that Johnlang was going to read aloud, and had Mara any sewing to be done? Her voice seemed a little excited.

She returned quickly.

"You would rather have the chair, wouldn't you?" she said, and she made herself comfortable on the bed, sitting with a pillow behind her back, her ankles crossed, the sewing in her lap, and her face expectant.

"What shall I read?"

"Oh, open the book at random."

I read a fable about a woman who refused a man in marriage but always retained a deep affection for him. She married another and had all the children they wanted. Then, some years later, pitying the first man who still longed for her, she gave herself to him. It was a failure to both. Her pity could not take the place of what was needed to make their union successful. She was a giver of the wrong gift; he was a thirsty man who receives bread.

"That is clear enough," said Nattana, who seemed less embarrassed by the frankness of the fable than I was; but I was thinking that a man might want a woman so much that her motive in yielding would make no difference at all.

"As to her, yes—but suppose he merely wanted her?" I asked.

"What do you mean by 'her'? Her body only? He wanted more than that!"

"What he had was better than nothing."

"No, it was poisoned. Pity always poisons that sort of thing to anyone who feels deeply—pity or kindness, or doing it for the other person's sake!"

"If you don't feel so deeply—" I began.

"If you can be sure that neither of you do! But the trouble is that two human beings can rarely both be—oh, purely pleasure-seeking."

I wondered where she picked up all these ideas—as confident and as sure as those based upon morality.

"How do you know, Nattana?" I demanded.

"It is part of my education to know," she said primly.

"You mean," I continued, "that usually one of two people will have *ania*—"

"No, I didn't mean that at all. I was thinking of any two people who have any kind of feeling for each other. Whether it is *apia* or not, both aren't likely to be mere pleasure-seekers."

"Isn't *apia* mere pleasure-seeking?"

"No—it may be more."

I was puzzled. *Apia* and *ania* did not fit the categories of love that I knew—the purely physical on the one side and the spiritual justifying the physical on the other.

"*Apia* may be merely that," she was saying, "but *apia* may also be a desire that lacks only a wish that you two go on in the world. . . It is really very simple."

"To you it may be," I said.

"The idea is simple, but not the thing itself," she said. "Read me another fable, if you would like to."

I took the hint and turned the pages. The next fable was about a woman who loved a man with a past of experiences with other women. She was cursed with curiosity as to these but respected his reticence. Becoming aware of her trouble he showed willingness to tell her anything she wished to know. Her curiosity ceased abruptly. It was enough for her that she could know if she wished.

"I always liked that one," said Nattana.

I admitted that I also liked it, and yet it seemed to me that a greater love would not even have been curious.

"You wonder about me, don't you?" she said.

"I do, but less than I did."

"I knew you did from the way you told me all about yourself when we walked from Tindal."

"Did you wonder about me, Nattana?"

"Very much until then, but I was not surprised . . . Would you like to know more about me?"

"Are you willing to tell me?"

"Yes, I am," she answered slowly.

I waited.

"You don't seem ever to have—oh—kissed anyone."

"I haven't, except very long ago. I have held your hand, Nattana, more than that of any other woman." The embrace was not to be mentioned.

"I have been kissed," she said, "several times. Only once did it seem important. That was two years ago. I felt suddenly grown-up and I wanted that man to have me. But he did not want to marry me, nor I him, I think. He taught me what it was to want to give myself. There weren't only kisses, Johnlang. We talked about my giving myself, and thought we would not. We decided it together, and it did not leave much hurt. I am fond of him still, but he is all over me. And I am all over him that way."

"It did leave a hurt, Nattana?"

"It made me grown-up. Perhaps that is a hurt. It was unfair in him to teach me to want something I was not to have. That is the only harm done. I have forgiven him that. . . We could make a fable, couldn't we? The point is that you oughtn't to do halfway things."

There came to me a sudden sense of shame. Was she indirectly rebuking me for what I had done? or was she perhaps suggesting that we go on?

"Nattana," I said, "are you also thinking of us?"

"I don't know," she cried sharply. "I was thinking of us a little. . . You were planning to come to see me at the Upper Farm, unless you have changed your mind. We go further and further. . . At least, so it seems to me." She stopped.

"To me, too, Nattana," I said quickly.

"And it is not as it is with others where the way is clear to work it out and there is a choice of marrying or not marrying. Oh, we are far from that, I know, but can't we face it in advance?"

"Yes, we can, Nattana, and we will," I answered, but the thought of marrying her made me feel faint and I felt as though I were trapped.

"I will tell you what I think about that if you will tell me. I couldn't go to your country and live there, Johnlang. I could not want to marry you enough! Unless I changed completely—and I don't see how I could—that can never be!"

Suddenly I felt no longer pursued and trapped, but eluded and denied, and I was angry.

"Suppose the impossible happened and I stayed here?" I cried.

"Then we would be like everyone else!"

We watched each other with fiery, loving hostility.

"Shall we face it?" she demanded.

"Face what?"

"What we feel now."

"Yes, Nattana."

"What do you feel, Johnlang?" She made a gesture with her hands that clearly said, "You like these." And my heart quickened and I looked at her soft lips. But how could I say it in Islandian where there were so few muffling words?

"I feel at least *apiata*," I said. Blood flamed in my face, and it suddenly seemed that I had uttered a brutal, indecent thing. Color mounted in her face also.

"So do I!" she declared, as though gallantly resisting me. There was silence, and then we both smiled weakly. "There!" she continued. "That is said! And *apiata* either dies or becomes something else, Johnlang."

Her eyes suddenly slid away from mine, and she straightened with a deep breath as though weary, and resumed her sewing.

"Read me another fable, won't you please?" she said. I opened the book, waiting till sure of my voice.

It was about a man who wished to marry a woman, but she caring for someone else would not have him. To another woman, a friend, he told all his troubles and she was sympathetic. She also made clearer to him the feeling that the one he had lost had toward him. She disclosed to him matters concerning herself to illustrate the nature of the problem from a woman's point of view. Becoming wiser, he found that his loss was less unbearable. . . .

Reading on, careful of my voice and pronunciation, I wondered about the visit that I was to make to the Upper Farm next month and remembered that she spoke as though I might wish to change my mind. Did she mean that if my feeling increased I ought to want to do so? It was hard to hold to the sense of the fable.

Thus, continued Godding, this woman rendered the man a great service of which he was fully appreciative. He often told her of his gratitude. "You are," he said, "of great value to me. I hope I may be of value to you." She answered that she enjoyed seeing him. . . So he came often and told her about himself and about his love, which he wished to see clearly. He frequently described the beauty of the lost one most poetically.

"Sometimes," read the fable, "we see upon the road a figure of another. Our thoughts are elsewhere and that figure is unfamiliar to us. We approach and suddenly find that one whom we assumed to be a stranger is one who is close and dear. It is like the emerging of a bright light where one thought only to find darkness."

I turned over the page, but there was no more. Where was the point? I raised my eyes to Nattana to ask her.

She was watching me, very still, her hands in her lap. Her face was scarlet and her eyes a hot green, and her expression was one of guilt and apprehension. I stared at her in amazement wondering what had happened.

Her eyes wavered and dropped, and then looked at me again; and my heart began a slow painful throbbing. Yet though absorbed by her emotion, I mechanically asked the question:

"What is the point of that fable, Nattana?"

Sudden relief came into her eyes, which shifted away.

"It is rather vague, isn't it?" she said.

"Do you see any point?"

"He found a friend, I suppose."

"Did he find more, I wonder?"

A sudden surmise leaped in my mind. At the Andals' months ago I had dropped this book and a piece of paper that might have marked a place fell out. Shortly before this, I had told Nattana about Dorna. . . But could she have done such a thing as designate this fable for me to read? Did I seem to her like the man who confided in the second woman?

Nattana must never know what I had guessed.

"I don't see any point in it," I said.

"Nor do I!" she cried.

"Shall I read you another?"

"Oh, do, please!"

I read on and she sewed. We did not analyze any more fables, merely stating whether or not we liked them. It grew dark and I lighted candles, two for her and two for me.

She was on her feet.

"I have just time to wash and change my dress," she added, "and thank you very much for reading to me."

She was gone before I realized that our afternoon together was ended. Until I read that miserable fable about the man who confided, all had moved smoothly. Then came her telltale blushes. . . But why did she run away? We had drifted, happily, upon a swift stream and then the water became broken and all the distance we had advanced seemed to be lost.

It was the Tollys' "day," and at supper Mara suggested that some of us might like to visit them in the evening. Her husband volunteered, and so did Nattana, looking across the table at me for a moment but not waiting for me to speak. I did not want to spend the evening in a crowded room talking to many people and answered that I thought I would stay at home—and regretted it when Nattana departed gaily with her ancient escort.

If an obscure and perverse impulse prompted me to punish her, I punished myself even more, and spent an impatient, absent-minded evening with Mara, waiting for Nattana's return. She came in late with bright eyes and pink cheeks. Both she and Fain trailed a faint odor of sweet wine. She seemed most unpunished as she stood before the fire warming herself, a little rakish in attitude. She had had a good time, she declared. She did like the Catlin girls and Larnella, whom she had promised to see again. She had had a long talk with young Larnel. She liked him, too!

She gave me scarcely a glance.

"I think I shall go to bed," she said. "The cold air after the warm house and the wine—I'm very sleepy. . . Mara, I'll sew for you tomorrow!"

She passed me on my end of the settle, and as she went by her skirt brushed my knees and her fingers just touched them. It might be intentional or it might be unsteadiness.

"Hytha," Mara was drily saying. "You have sewed for me all that I am going to let you."

Nattana's face did not seem pleased as she passed through the door. . . . Could it be that she was a little drunk?

It was June 25th, my birthday, and I was twenty-eight. The wind had dropped and the air seemed warmer, but the sky was still cloudless. Nattana had not come down when I began my breakfast nor had she arrived when I finished. Should I go out and begin work as I ordinarily would, or should I hang about until it was her pleasure to appear? It was her last day.

While I was making up my mind I heard her voice calling from upstairs.

"Johnlang! Johnlang!"

I went to the hall and looked up the stone staircase.

"Don't go out before you have seen me!" Her voice had a trace of reproach in it.

"I won't, Nattana!" I cried, and I waited in the hall. She was slow in coming, but at last she was running down the stairs, vivid and alive, and—as always—a stronger, dearer person when actually present than when only in my thoughts.

She had no braids, and her hair was done up on her head in a way that I had never seen and that made her look older. Her eyes caught and held mine. She smiled at me.

She came down the stairs—this lovely new Nattana who revealed for the first time how pretty was the pillar of her neck and how gracefully her head was balanced upon it. And I knew suddenly that unless I moved aside she must either stop or else come straight to me and be kissed, for I barred her path. She came steadily toward me and showed no intention of stopping. My heart was in my throat. She knew what was coming for she lifted her face.

Mara's voice sounded from the dining room calling Nattana. I stepped aside instinctively, hot and then cold. Nattana ran past me, her cheek warm with color and a gleam in her eye that might mean, "Oh, what bad luck!" I drew a deep breath and followed her.

She was fluently disputing with Mara about being waited on when she was late. Apparently the fact that within a few seconds she had almost been kissed had not disturbed her at all—but, I remembered, kisses were no new thing to her as they were to me. Nor, very likely, did she care as much as I did. I sat down limply, while she, overcoming Mara's wish to wait upon her, went to fetch her own breakfast from the kitchen. . . Perhaps, also, she was unconcerned because not aware that I was going to kiss her. But I was going to kiss her, or to try, before she went away! So I determined, and felt better, having a purpose.

She returned.

"May I sit with you while you have breakfast?" I asked.

"I hoped you would."

I was looking at her head, not yet accustomed to her round white neck, nor to the unexpectedness of her ears.

"Are you wondering why my hair is done this way, Johnlang?"

"Yes, I am."

"Do you like it?"

"Yes, but I shall have to get used to it."

"I thought I would take my horse out and it is more comfortable not to have braids flopping."

But she had ridden from her home to The City and back to the Fains' with braids.

"You ought to take Fak out also," she said.

"Shall we go together?"

"Would you like that? I would."

"Very much, Nattana. . . When are you going to see Larnella?"

"Oh, sometime."

Soon afterwards our horses were saddled. The light upon the snow was rose and lavender, the sky a hard wintry blue. The horses blew clouds of vapor from their nostrils. Bracing ourselves to the sharp cold of the air we drank it like wine and made our way through the pines towards the trail that climbed the hills southwest of the house; and then, passing through the gate, we rode up a white-floored aisle of dark trees in fresh cold sun, the farm lands dropping behind us and the hills marching down to meet us. Under the horses' feet the sparkling crust crunched and broke, but the snow beneath was soft and powdery and there was no treacherous ice on the ground.

How different had this trail been less than a month ago when I set out on impulse to meet Nattana! How different was everything! I told her that I had ridden this very path to join her.

"Would you like to be making that journey again?"

"Alone?" I asked, "or with you?"

"Suppose we were starting out now?"

"I wish we were!"

"Very likely the Tamplin Pass is blocked with snow."

"That would mean eight or ten days more!"

"We might be making that journey if I had not quarreled with Father."

"Together?"

"Why not?"

"What would he think?"

"Oh he!" She shrugged.

"How about other fathers? Would it be customary?"

"They might or might not object, depending on what they thought of you . . . or me. There is no custom about it. But there's a custom against such a journey being too long."

"Our custom would not permit any journey over night," I said.

"I don't understand it!" she said and laughed. "But it is too lovely a day to let our minds become tangled again."

"I agree, Nattana!"

The air was crystalline and it was good to ride again. We had in effect declared a truce.

To declare a truce was one way to be happy together—for a time at least and as long as there was so much to be seen. We did not ride far, because Nattana's horse faced two days of hard traveling, and only climbed until we could look into the north, whither her route lay. The great dome of Mount Islandia was magnificent, but we were not interested in its beauty alone. Its lower slopes were not whitened with snow. The heavy fall had evidently been confined to the valleys.

We discussed Nattana's journey, which seemed very near. There had come no rumors that the Mora Pass was dangerous, and our view in that direction confirmed what had been heard from passing travelers.

Turning around, we rode down the trail. The question of Nattana's visit to Larnella arose again.

"I wish I had not said that I would go, but last night, well . . ." She laughed a little.

"You promised?"

"Yes, I promised."

"I suppose you will have to go."

"She will want me to stay to lunch," Nattana suggested.

"Stay, and I will come and get you afterwards."

"All right!"

"It *is* all right, Nattana."

"If you think so, it is."

We agreed to ride to the Larnels', and that I should take back both horses, and return on foot for her soon after lunch. Thus tacitly it was understood that we would spend the afternoon together. At the Larnels' door she swung down from her horse and we said good-bye.

On the way to the Larnels' in the early afternoon I turned aside to make sure of firewood at the mill. The air was dry, cold, and motionless. The dark gleam of the pond drew my steps. It was frozen smooth with scarcely a bubble, hard black ice, unscratched from shore to shore, and perfect for skating. I could manufacture skates at the workshop and introduce the art into Islandia, where for all I knew it was unknown.

My heart was beating hard when I reached the Larnels'. Larnella opened the door. Her cheeks were flushed and she was smiling.

"Why didn't you come to lunch too!" she said as she ushered me in. "We have had a happy time with Hytha."

"Hytha" herself was seated on a settle before the fire with young Larnel. Her cheeks were pink, and also those ears of hers to which I was not yet accustomed. Raising her head a moment she looked at me with an absent "oh-here-you-are" smile, and Larnel abruptly stopped talking when he saw me. Nor could I be sure that he had not been close to Nattana and had not leaned away quickly upon hearing me come in. I was suddenly struck with unreasonable suspicion and jealousy.

I was asked to sit down and reluctantly did so, afraid it would mean delay. Larnella offered me a glass of wine, but Larnel was saying something to Nattana, and it was some seconds before I realized her question. I declined and thanked her. She seemed to want to talk, and I made an effort and answered. Larnel was earnestly speaking to Nattana who was looking at her hands in her lap with a little smile. Interminable minutes passed. . . .

At last she rose. I could not have given the signal, trapped by

Larnella, but was on my feet in the middle of a sentence. Larnel fetched Nattana's cloak and held it for her, saying something that made her laugh—and at last, at last, we were in the open air and outside the house.

Nattana was at my side but I was speechless. I wished to be at ease, and could not; I wanted to be reasonable, and could not free myself from an angry misery.

"Wasn't it clever?" she said with a laugh.

"I don't know."

Her laughing stopped and there was silence, as we walked out into the highway.

"What's the matter?" she asked in a cool voice as to a child.

I tried to say that I was jealous but would get over it—and there was no word for jealousy in Islandian.

"I have no right—" I began.

"No right to what, Johnlang?" she asked.

"—to object, but I do for some reason. What is the matter with me, Nattana? I mind coming in like that and seeing you. . . I don't know why."

"There is nothing for you to mind about," she said. "And if you do mind, you do. Why do you think you have to have some right?"

"But I have no right—"

"Why, of course not! But you ought to have some knowledge of me!"

This was a rebuke.

"What you want is to know about me and Larnel—whom I have seen just three times!" she continued.

"I want to know what you thought so clever."

"Why, his sister, of course. She wanted to give him a chance to talk to me; so she sat down by you and kept you occupied. It was obvious!"

Relief began to come.

"Nattana," I said. "You need not trouble to say anything more."

"It is no trouble. And I don't blame you. . . I'll tell you about Larnel. If he saw more of me, I think he would really want me. It has been very quick, and it has gone to my head! I don't see many men, Johnlang, remember that, and when one goes so fast. . . But I'll tell you how I feel about Larnel. Last night he asked me to put my hair up. And I did and I wish I hadn't. And at lunch I began to be bored and I longed to have you come and take me away—and when you came I saw escape at last; and so I was willing to stay a little longer and let him finish what he wanted to say."

I wished to know what Larnel did say, but checked myself.

"I did not tell him that our house was his," she added, "because I did not want to."

"Don't bother to tell me what he said."

She laughed.

"Well, I would rather not give him away."

"Don't," I said.

"Now I shall say something to you! Some men and some women may have *anias* or *apias* or *apiatas* for two different persons at the same time, but I don't think I can! I think very likely you can, but I don't know. And it doesn't matter now. If it ever does, oh, you will tell me, won't you?"

Was she thinking of Dorna?

"I will tell you," I answered. . . .

But she had put her hair up on Larnel's request, and had in the morning lied as to her reasons. Her lie was a shock, and I was angry for a moment, but it did not really matter. She was no less attractive.

"Where are we going?" she asked. "We are walking as though bound somewhere."

"We are going to the mill. We will make a fire and talk."

"Dorn will be here this afternoon," she stated. "You and I know him! He will plan his journey so that he won't have to come up from Tindal in the dark."

"He will also be here this evening, and we shall want to talk to him."

"And he to you. . . All right, let us go to the mill."

We understood each other, and there was delight in finding the wish to avoid Dorn a mutual one.

"And tomorrow morning early," she continued, "you will say good-bye to Hytha Nattana."

Pain was in her voice and answering pain in my heart.

"I don't want you to go!" I said.

"I don't know whether I want to go or not. . . But I am going. Let's not bother over what we feel about it."

"Let's walk on to the pond and see if the ice will bear us, Nattana."

"If you want me to go sliding, I can't. My shoes have rope soles."

"I wasn't thinking of sliding. We can walk on it."

"If it is safe."

We passed the waterfall where hung a white and brown beard of ice over which the water flowed. At the embankment I descended on the smooth black surface, tried it with my heel, and found it firm. She stood on the embankment watching me.

"Be sure it will hold us, Johnlang!"

"It is quite safe. Come on. I'm heavier than you."

"I feel very heavy now!"

She stepped down carefully, walking as though on eggs. I laughed at her.

"I am not used to ice," she exclaimed.

"This is solid enough."

Taking her round arm above the elbow I walked her boldly towards the middle of the pond. The glassy black flatness became extensive around us and we were in a more open world. She went on steadily but I could feel timidity in her arm.

"Do you ever put sharp edge runners on your feet and go on the ice, Nattana? We call it skating."

"No, but we have 'shoe sleds.' The edges are round."

"How do you make yourselves go?"

"Someone pushes us and we slide; or else we have poles with sharp points. But I don't know much about it. There are no ponds or quiet water near the Lower Farm."

The lake at the Upper Farm would be ideal for skating. Perhaps I would make skates and take them with me and teach her to use them.

We came to a point where all the shores seemed equally far away, their whiteness making the surface very dark, but it had shining reflections.

"Nattana, don't you like to be in the middle of an absolute flatness?"

Releasing her I stepped back so that by herself she could really know the feeling.

She stood as though unable to stir.

"I am afraid that my feet will go through!" she cried. "I want to raise them."

She acted upon her words lifting first one foot and then the other, but she lost her balance, the rope soles slipped, and she fell. Before I could help her, she was sitting up.

"I am always falling!" she said angrily. "Johnlang, I don't like ice."

Catching her hands, I steadied her. One cold hand I kept.

"We will go back to the mill. Are you hurt?"

"I am not hurt—of course!"

"I knew what you meant," she continued, as she walked carefully at my side. "I love the feeling of flatness you spoke of. I have found it in the valley." Her fingertips, which extended beyond my hand like little faces above a high collar, fluttered and pressed.

But when we came toward the embankment they twisted free, and she ran ahead and climbed up to safety.

"At last!" she cried.

"It was quite safe."

"Oh yes, wise Johnlang, but I can't help what I feel!"

"Not angry at me, Nattana?"

"Why should I be? I needn't have gone."

She moved along the road with a shrug and a laugh, going towards the mill.

Within was a cold odor of sawdust and freshly cut wood. Everything was as it had been three days before. The fence rails lay in a high pile, more neatly squared than I remembered having made them.

"It is damp," she said with a shiver, and she huddled her cloak around her.

"It won't be so for long, Nattana."

Carrying wood to the fireplace, I crouched before it, laid shavings upon the soft cold ashes, and piled slabs upon them.

A spark snapped from the flint upon the oily wicking of my lighter, and a yellow flame leaped there out of nothingness. I held it under the fibers of a shaving.

"I am not used to thinking of Nekka as marrying and going away," she said behind me.

"Will you miss her, Nattana?"

"Oh, I shall feel her absence very much. Only Ettera and I will be left. Nekka is older and has always kept her thoughts to herself, so that we haven't been very close, but I shall miss her."

Little flames began to run among the shavings.

"Does Nekka really want to marry Dorn, Nattana?"

She did not answer at once.

"It is going to burn," I said. The progress of the flames was hypnotic and held my eyes.

Coming nearer and standing above me, she answered:

"Nekka is ready to be married. She wants that life. She knows it. . . Women do, Johnlang. . . And she knows that as a companion with whom to live there is no one finer than Dorn, your friend. But that is not enough."

An edge of flame stole along one of the slabs.

"What is a woman like Nekka to do?" she asked. "She knows that married life is the best one for her—to be used and to have children. There comes a man who wants her very much. Should she say 'no' to him because she is bruised?"

"I didn't know that she was hurt," I said.

"She wanted something else very much, Johnlang—Tor and to be queen. And she broods often and thinks that if she had done this or hadn't done that everything might be different."

"But she does want to marry Dorn, doesn't she?"

"Of course, but her wishes are all so crisscrossed that she can't follow one without going contrary to another."

"Do you think she is being unfair to him?"

"He knows it all. She is not deceiving him."

The flames were widening over the slabs; dark-brown smoke was rising from the bark; and there was a sweet, pungent, oily smell of burning tar and resin.

Still kneeling before the fire I looked up at Nattana. She had thrown back her hood and opened her cloak, her hands on her hips. Her eyes dwelt on mine for a moment, and her lips smiled, moved by other thoughts than those relating to Dorn and Nekka—friendly, shy, more personal.

The fire had become too hot to endure. I rose and stepped back and watched the broad sheet of forked red flames. . . .

"When will they marry?" I asked.

"She will be ready when he wants her, I think. Dorn and I

should reach the Upper Farm day after tomorrow. They will probably say what they intend that evening and sleep together and go down the valley next morning."

"Who will marry them?" I asked.

"Who? They marry each other. . . I don't understand."

"In my country, two persons who want to marry go before some third person who is given power by the law to declare them married. Unless they do that, they aren't really married."

"But what has the law to do with it?"

"Unless there is something like that," I answered, "a marriage seems to me very casual. And unless the state takes an interest, how can a person prove that he or she is married?"

"They usually say what they intend before other people. Dorn and Nekka will. In fact, one wants others to know. Then she would enter his life as one who adopted his *alia* and that would prove it."

"Suppose a man brought home a second woman?"

"After he had married one already? He would be married to the first one."

She sighed deeply.

"You put such strange cases! I try to remember how things are with you. You haven't any real homes; so I suppose a man could take one woman one place and another another place. But don't you see that it would not happen here? A woman knows who is at a man's house. If another woman were already there, she would know she could not marry him. Everything is so confused in your country." She pressed her face with her hands. "And there are such differences—oh, such differences."

Her distress brought sudden tension.

"Between you and me, or merely between your country and mine?"

"Both. . . You call our marriages casual. Your marriages seem to me much worse. You have nothing to found them on, and therefore you have laws and all sorts of things to make them what they can't be.

"You foreigners are like my father who has got the idea that confining yourself to one person is the one vital thing in a marriage. You may need some such idea to give your marriages value, because there is so little else there to keep them good when they have started. But there are other people here besides Father, people who know they are not always sufficient and who understand the needs of those they marry, and they don't begrudge the others whatever will not destroy the *alia* they have together."

"Our marriages aren't loose ties—"

"Nor are ours!" she cried. "We have something on which a man and a woman can work together. With you they work separately—or he does. Our marriages give us a full satisfying life. It is the best life there is, and the most complete and interesting. Everybody knows that from childhood. We see it all the time. Our marriages aren't casual. They aren't *apias* propped up to look like *anias* by rules and laws! Our marriages give the two strongest feelings there are, *ania* and *alia,* a full opportunity to work together."

She rose suddenly and went to the fire and stood turned away from me. I watched her, a little dazed by her passionate speech, admiring her for her eloquence and intelligence.

"As usual," she said, "I have talked you into dumbness. Do you agree with me or don't you?"

"You are rather hard on my country. But you have also worked things out very well for yourselves."

"I am only hard on your way of life, Johnlang."

"I can't tell you all at once what I think."

She put her arm against the stonework over the fireplace and leaned her head upon it. Her hair, drawn up, gave the back of her head the appearance of a girl too young to have her hair done up; but there was nothing childish about the supple fullness of the rest of her figure.

I rose slowly, and felt steal over me that sense of placelessness and timelessness that comes from intoxication.

"There is suddenly a wide stormy sea of difference between us when we talk about your country. I don't hate your country, but I hate that sea. I couldn't hate the country you came from. But I sound as though I did."

"Go ahead and hate it," I answered, not really aware what I was saying, for this white-necked girl still bore the appearance which she had assumed at the request of another man.

"I don't want to hate it. . . ."

"Nattana," I said, "I want you to do your hair in braids again."

"Don't you like it this way?"

Slowly she turned.

"Yes, but I want it in braids."

Her eyes gave me a quick, half-doubtful, questioning look, and then at once her hands went to her head. I watched her, but her gaze was sideways, her face sedate and composed. Her hair fell in heavy masses of red and gold, against which her hands were white, pretty, slim.

She went to the bench and placed the pins there. Her prompt obedience increased my drunkenness, and I was both faint and warm.

"I can't very well part it up the back without a comb."

"Do your best."

"I will, Giver of Orders. . . And I haven't anything to tie the ends."

She glanced at me, shaking loose the flowing mane of her hair with her hands.

"Your hair is a beautiful thing," I said.

She laughed and began dividing her hair with her hands, thrusting out her head, and slowly turning until her back was towards me.

"Is the parting straight?"

There were strands that went crosswise.

"Not quite, Nattana."

"Will you. . . ."

She came nearer, and I straightened the locks that were out of place, feeling on my fingers the fine soft wire of her hair and the firm roundness of her head. . . .

She braided her hair, first one side, then the other, tossing back the ropes when they were completed, facing me, watching me.

"There!" she said, standing straight and putting her hands behind her. "How do you like me?"

"I like you," I said. I moved towards her, and she swayed back but not far. Her face became grave and dropped a little but her eyes never left mine. I took her arms just above the elbows, and held her firm.

"I must kiss you, Nattana." Her expression did not change.

There was a swift rushing in my blood, and she became more and more burningly bright. I saw her two flushed cheeks and then her lips and only them, wickedly offered to me. I kissed her mouth, not knowing that her eyes, close to mine, would be so brilliant and so drowning, that I would feel her warm sweet breath, that her lips would be so crisply soft, and that for a moment I would possess the strong dizzy-

561

ing reality of Nattana. I had kissed her, but her mouth suddenly pressed mine in her own kiss, more clever and more intimate than the one I had given her, and it left a little of herself on my own lips.

We looked at each other, and her lids dropped and then lifted again for a moment. Her eyes were wide, hurt, and they seemed reproachful. They looked down again, and her lips, which I had kissed, slowly parted. An expression of pain crossed her face. She trembled, and turned. I let her go. She went quickly to the bench, and sitting down bent her head, both hands limp in her lap.

Seeing her hurt I forgot the wonder that I had had. I went to her and sat by her and she was quivering. I took her inert hand, which was very warm, between both of mine.

"I did not know you would mind," I said in a voice not familiar. "I took you by surprise. I did not mean to make you suffer."

"Oh, Johnlang!"

She bit her lip and turned her head away.

The familiar aspect of the mill suddenly struck upon my consciousness, the pile of rails, the white windows opening upon a snowy world.

"Nattana, I didn't know . . ." I began. But what was it? I tried to think.

"Nor did I!" she said, and I felt her hand tremble.

English words were the only ones by which I could express myself, and she would not know their meaning.

"I can't say anything, Nattana."

"Let's not try!"

I wished that she would look at me again. She left her hand in mine. I closed my eyes and held her hand tightly. No idea completed itself.

"Nattana, you are so dear. That is all I can think in your language."

"It is enough," came her voice.

I opened my eyes and looked at the smooth bright curve of her averted cheek. Her hand was not still. Though limp, every little while it quivered.

"It is strange," I said.

Her face turned to me.

"Does it hurt you too?" she said.

I had not thought of it as a hurt, but so it was.

"Yes, Nattana."

"Poor Johnlang!" She laid her other hand on mine. All four were together.

"Poor Nattana just as much."

"Why are we hurt?"

There came a feeling of tension and dread.

"Let me kiss you, Nattana."

She held up her lips, and this time I put my arm around her and did not let her go so soon. I learned that I did not know how to kiss and that she did. It was sweet to have her show me, but bitter that she should have had another teacher.

"John, dear John!"

Her face was only a little way from mine and our knees were touching.

"Why are we hurt?"

"It isn't all a hurt. . . ."

"Is it because you are not one of us?"

This was too much. Tears ran out of my eyes before I could stop them. Her chin lifted, and her mouth became ugly, and then her eyes were brimming. Her ugly weeping face broke my heart and I kissed her, and tasted the salty wetness on her cheeks.

Her hurt, greater than mine, was a menacing thing that might make me lose her at any moment. I held her close and kissed her many times.

"Isn't all a hurt, Nattana . . . It really isn't!"

"We must think," she said.

"Yes, but I can't."

"But we must."

"Oh, we will."

"It is no use thinking what we feel, but what we are going to do."

Again came desperate fear, and I kissed her and held her tightly.

There came a certain exhaustion. . . .

"Nattana, did you know it is quite dark?"

"I saw the windows becoming a strange blue."

"It is queer to be here, Nattana."

"In the mill?"

"In Islandia . . . I don't know where I am."

"Oh my John!"

She held me.

"Nattana, dear Nattana, our fire? There are only red sparks."

"We can make it burn again."

I rose before I thought. The world seemed to spin and come to rest. I found myself John Lang again with a mind in which problems sprang alive.

Feeling for shavings and slabs I carefully placed them on the embers. She was almost invisible on the bench. There had been more than kisses. I realized it now. We were closer than those who merely kiss. Without thought of its intimacy my hands had been upon her thighs, and my fingers though not seeking them knew that her breasts were full and round.

I blew on the embers. . . . A shaving caught fire.

"How near is supper, Nattana?"

"I am trying to think."

I laughed and so did she.

"I trust to your time sense, Nattana."

"It's not destroyed, John. We need not go yet."

"I wonder if Dorn has come."

"He must be at the house."

The reality of Dorn leaped before my eyes. He was so near that he could almost call us.

The flames were spreading.

I rose and looked at Nattana. The firelight flickered on her face, and though I saw her eyes I could not see her expression. She was all at once very strange and then as instantly so desirable that I wanted to seize her and hold her and find her flesh. Yet out of nothing had grown a barrier between us.

"You are going away tomorrow, Nattana?"

"Yes." Her head dropped.

"Oh, my dear!"

I sat down beside her and put my arm around her and kissed her. Because I had desired her so much, I was gentle, and she, though unresisting, did not give me her lips and I had to find them.

"We ought to go," she said suddenly. "We oughtn't to come in just before supper."

Our afternoon together was over and there was heavy sorrow and deadness. We scattered the burning wood in the fireplace and the mill became dark and cold. For a moment we lingered. I ran my arms around her and held her and kissed her. It was sweet to feel her body along mine and to know her in a new way. Then we put on our cloaks and went out into the night.

The road was a pale track in the darkness. As we moved the ice in the pond cracked with a hollow ringing boom. . . . She seemed a little reluctant to give me her hand, but I possessed myself of it.

We were among the pines near the house, a soft wind was blowing in their invisible branches, and there were no stars in the sky.

She drew her hand away and stopped.

"It feels like snow," she said.

"I don't want you to go tomorrow," I cried, but she was silent. . . . She did not say that she was sorry also.

"My cheeks are burning." She spoke in an absent voice. "They will give us away."

"What are you doing?"

The dark blur that was Nattana had seemed to shrink. Her answer came from a lower level.

"I'm kneeling and cooling my face with snow. You kissed me so much!" There was hurt reproach in her voice. I leaned down to her and found her arms and then her hands, but they twisted away, and she rose by herself with a hard little laugh.

I followed her rapid figure.

"Nattana, before we go in—"

"What is it you want?"

"Let me kiss you!"

"Oh no—please!"

The perfect understanding and the unison of the afternoon no longer existed. They had seemed eternal, and they were gone in a breath.

Nattana called to those in the living room that she was going to change her clothes, and ran up the stairs, escaping unseen with her telltale cheeks. I entered, and Dorn stood before me large and vivid, but it was hard to change the current of my emotions and to make him real. All the Fains were present.

We shook hands according to our custom. He seemed thin but happy.

"How was your journey?" I asked.

He told me of it. Nattana and I had correctly guessed how he had planned it, and he had arrived just at dark. . . . Was he wondering why I was not there to meet him?

There came a lull when the Fains were speaking together, and he said quickly:

"Dorna sent you a message. She wants to have a long talk with you some time."

But I did not want it. I feared her still, and knew that I had not ceased to love her.

At supper Nattana wore her best dress—that of the king's reception. I wondered if she appeared to the others as she appeared to me. She seemed marked by my kisses, and I felt marked in the same way. It was hard to believe that our loving, so warm in my senses, was not apparent to others' eyes, and yet in spite of this feeling of exposure and in spite of the cleavage between us, there was a deep proud contentment.

Dorn's wise gaze was upon Nattana often, and she returned it with only now and then a glance at me too quick to be caught. He and she were to be together two days. They were both so attractive! I resented his telling her that she looked pretty and that he thought her visit had done her good.

"I have been very happy," she said. My heart leaped—but I realized that she might be speaking only for the benefit of her hosts.

We sat in the living room after supper. I wanted to be alone with Nattana and waited and schemed for an opportunity, but she herself defeated my hopes. Quite early she went off to bed saying that she wanted a full night's sleep before her journey.

It was Dorn with whom I was left alone. He was my best and dearest friend and in two days he was to be married. It was painful not to be able to avoid preoccupation with Nattana and to give him my full interest.

He told me his plans. Nekka and he would ride down the valley to Dorn Island, taking five days to the journey. There was much to be done at the farm there and he hoped to remain for at least a month, but if his great-uncle needed him he would go to The City. Whenever I wished to visit him I must be sure to come. In the spring he and I, and Nekka perhaps, would travel together. Nothing must be allowed to interfere with this plan which he and I had already made. All he said seemed remote and colorless.

He asked about my plans, and I told him that I planned to stay with the Fains until I had to leave Islandia, working for them and writing, with occasional visits to various places—to Dorn Island again, of course, and maybe to the Hyths'.

His eyes were upon me and I did not want to meet them. Yet if only I had his mind, impersonal and part of myself, to advise me what to do about Nattana . . . But in all likelihood all was over even now. Perhaps in an unguarded moment she had let me come too close and repented of it.

We did not mention her, and we were both silent. Then he said:

"Several times I have thought of asking you to come with me and to be present when Nekka and I declare ourselves to each other. That is what would happen in your country. You would be my 'best man.' And I would like to have it so, but I don't think she would, and I am not going to take the chance. Do you understand?"

"Oh, perfectly!"

We were silent again, and then I told him that I was very glad of his marriage.

"So am I," he said, "and not worried." He looked at me for a moment and although what he was thinking was withheld, it was not concealed from me as though he wished me to be ignorant. "I have in my hands the life I wish," he added slowly.

Our friendship existed as strong as ever, and when we called upon it we would find it again.

My room was cold, and I could see my breath. I laid a fire for the morning and quickly undressed, but the blankets soon made me warm.

There was a dream that continued endlessly, of dark places, of endless talk and of questions, of half-wakings, to find it night, of problems always on the point of solution and never solved, of Nattana weaving in and out, now a dark shadowed figure, now a vivid one, burning, painful, and too sweet, and of a knocking, and of a long night and day not yet come . . . of a knocking . . . of a square of blackness only a little less black than night itself, of a square that

567

was my window in my room at the Fains', seen in reality and not in a dream. . . .

The knocking was a memory that became a present fact requiring action and decision. I struggled to cast off sleep, and pushed myself upright. The window was so dark that it must still be the dead of night.

"Who is there?" I asked, and my eyes remembered direction and found where my door would be.

A dazzling point of yellow light moved and was reflected along the edge of the opening door. A face appeared above the light, black shadows cast upward upon it.

"Nattana!" I said in a low whisper.

"Yes, it is Nattana," she answered quite calmly. She came forward, and her hand guarding the candle was of rosy fire. The light touched her here and there; she was fully dressed. It must be nearly morning and time to rise.

"Mara is up and Dorn is getting up. I've been dressed a long time. I said to her that I would wake you . . . Shall I light your fire? It is a cold morning."

Her voice was sweet and remote. I tried to brush away the sensation of dreaming.

"If you would," I answered.

The candle flame floated to the table. Red and gold sparkled in her hair.

"The flint is on the mantel," I said, and leaning on my elbow I watched her dim figure stooping before the fireplace.

"You are kind to light my fire for me, Nattana," I said.

"Anyone would," she answered.

"But you are kind all the same."

"I thought you might stay up late with Dorn and oversleep."

"Is it very early?"

"There is time to dress and have breakfast, and for us to leave at the first daylight."

"Shall I get up?"

"No, stay there till the room is warm. There is time enough."

Flames began to rise and her figure took form, becoming less cold and vague. The firelight was on her face, and her profile seemed contented and half slumbering.

"What waked you, Nattana?"

Her lips moved, and she held her hands to the blaze.

"I have been awake a long time." Waiting, I wondered. Had she come to tell me some bad news about my visit?

"It is snowing," she said.

"Will you go?" I cried in sudden fear.

"Dorn says so. He is not afraid—and I'm not afraid with him. I am to ride his horse. He will ride mine."

On impulse sudden and sure, I said:

"Your horses aren't so good in snow, are they?"

"Not quite."

"Would you like to take Fak?"

She was silent for several long moments.

"I could not. You would not have him all winter. This may be the snow that closes the pass."

"But you would have him, Nattana. He would be useful to you at the Upper Farm. I could come and get him when the weather was right again."

"I wish it wasn't snowing," she said. "I will tell you: Dorn did say that he wished we both had mountain horses, but we weren't going to speak of it. Now you have spoken. What would you do without Fak?"

"You could leave me your horse. I won't have much use for one this winter." I drew a deep breath. "When I come to see you next month it won't be on horseback."

"I have been thinking about your visit."

"It has nothing to do with your taking Fak," I said.

She rose and stood before the fire.

"I have been thinking and thinking," she said.

"I am coming, Nattana," I answered with sudden desperate willing.

"If yesterday when we came from the mill and in the evening, I seemed . . ." She spoke with effort and her voice ceased as though stopped in her throat.

"Nattana," I cried, "I am coming."

She was silent. The firelight shone upon her sturdy graceful figure. She already wore the snow boots halfway to her knees. Her calves, in woolen stockings, were round and strong.

"You must remember to tell Don," I said.

There was no answer. The candlelight gleamed on the back of her head.

"Promise me that you will speak to him, Nattana!"

"The snow is early," she said. "It may be a long time before he would be willing to come."

"Is it safe for you to go today, Nattana?"

"Dorn thinks so. It will take several days of snowing to block the pass. And we could turn back, of course. But that is not the point. . . ."

"You will take Fak, won't you?"

She uttered a gasp.

"If you would let me have him—Oh, no, Johnlang!"

"Wouldn't you feel safer? I should. Take him so that I shall feel safer, Nattana."

"Do you want me to take him?"

"I do! It is the one thing I want."

"I can't say 'no.' I ought to. . . ."

"You are not going to say 'no.' You are going to take Fak."

"I'll take very good care of him," she said. "I'll send him back in the spring, because, Johnlang—"

"Nattana, I am coming to see you."

Her body quivered, and I watched her. She put her hands to her face and suddenly dropped them.

"I've several things to do," she said, "and you ought to get up . . . I am going. I will light your candles."

She thrust the points of my two candles into the flame of her own, and in the upward light her chin and throat were lovely.

She started toward the door.

"Thank you, Nattana," I said.

She stopped in the doorway.

"It is a hard journey over the mountains. You ought to practice climbing on snowshoes and skis."

She was quickly gone, closing my door softly behind her.

Dorn was in a hurry to be on the road. Breakfast was a confused meal, no one remaining at table for more than a few moments but running off to do some last thing. The weather was discussed; the journey of Dorn and Nattana would be a race against the snow. I worried lest she be a victim of his haste to reach her sister, fearing for her and loving her well; but I was also happy, for I was to cross the mountains with Don. She and I were going on with our adventure together.

The Fains and Mara and I assembled outside the door to see them off. Outside it was quiet and not yet full daylight. The air was gray-blue with snowflakes falling softly. They seemed few but they made the distance dark. I was afraid for my two dearest of friends departing in that long shadow upon a dangerous journey.

Mara and the two brothers remained in the shelter of the veranda, but I went to Fak and said good-bye to him, and held his head while Dorn fastened Nattana's saddlebag to the cantle.

"With these two horses," he said, "I know that we are safe. We are sure to get through now. Your lending of Fak is a service to Nekka and me as well as to Nattana."

She herself appeared, in snow boots and cloak, her hood over her head. She said good-bye to her hosts and then came to me.

"Mara has given me mittens," she laughed. "You need not worry about my hands."

We looked at each other for a moment, a little pain and the hint of things unsaid in her eyes.

"Thank you for Fak!" She turned and stroked his nose.

"I am very happy that you have him."

"I love him," she remarked, and he nodded his head and blew vapor through his nostrils. She sighed, and straightened as though weary, and looked at me.

"Shall we?" she asked. "Why not?"

Dorn and the Fains saw us, I am sure, but they paid no attention. I kissed her crisp soft lips. They and her breath were warm but her cheeks were cold. She kissed me, she was mine for a second, and then instantly she turned and went to Fak's side, glancing at the Fains and Mara and laughing as she mounted him. She settled herself in the saddle, called her final thanks to them, and gave me a last quick smile.

Dorn was already mounted.

The two gray-brown horses with the dark figures upon them moved into the blue haze of snow and became dim. Her hooded head was turned towards his.

PART IV

25

The Upper Farm

THE ISLANDIAN SNOWSHOE is lighter and more fragile than the Indian shoe, and is made like an elongated tit-tat-to mark, the foot resting in the central square which is solid and the other open spaces being woven across with a fine, waterproofed rattan. The Islandian ski has also features of its own. It is shorter and wider, and in front of and behind the foot are cut rectangular slots, in each of which loosely fits a block of wood about eight inches long and an inch square, sharpened to a beveled edge at the rear. These can be pegged at both ends so as to fit evenly in the slot and to make the bottom edge of the ski smooth; or the rearmost peg can be removed, in which case the block slides upward into the slot on a forward movement of the ski, and drives backward and downward into the snow if the ski tends to slip backward and prevents or at least decreases such motion. It is therefore possible to climb with Islandian skis in a way impossible with those of the rest of the world. The disadvantage which I found was that in certain conditions of snow the block became stuck in one position or another.

When I mentioned snowshoes and skis at lunch on the day of Nattana's departure, information was forthcoming. Everyone knew about them and had them and sometimes used them. Tolly at the Catlins' farm was the local expert and would fit me out and teach me as far as was necessary. A few days later my own pairs were ready and thereafter I snowshoed or skied wherever I went.

The lending of Fak to Nattana was justified on the day after she left. Late in the evening two men from Dole arrived at the house somewhat exhausted. They were welcomed for the night and then reported the news: they had seen Dorn and Nattana at the Inn in good spirits and condition after a hard day; on the other side of the col, however, the descent was dangerous, almost impassable except for mountain horses. While we talked to them Dorn's marriage might be taking place. Three days later another party stopped to tell us that it was a fact. These were the last to come down from the pass. On July 1st it was closed.

This particular winter, a closed one, was of a sort that occurred every six or seven years. When the early snow did not melt away but remained, the road to Tindal as well as that to the Mora Pass could not be traveled. If human beings wished to get away or to come, they must go on foot, or better still upon snowshoes or skis, up over the hills and down again.

I worked in good measure. Fence mending in the open became impossible, but rails and posts for the spring began to fill the mill. Whenever there was thaw enough for water to run, I sawed wood. At other times I worked in a pleasant antiseptic odor of tar, preparing what I had sawed to resist rot, or else did mason's jobs on the walls of the granary, workshop, and mill. I tried to work manually at least four hours a day, which was no less than those of many others on the two farms, never long enough to be bored nor short enough to feel myself unduly a sponge on my hosts. This with an average of two or three hours a day of writing upon magazine articles describing experiences in Islandian life completed the steady work which I did. There were other spasmodic labors, a pleasure to do, such as secretarial work for Isla Fain, domestic tasks for Mara, helping Anor at the forge in the workshop, lecturing at the school on history for Tollia, helping her brother make skis, and many others. In addition, I was often called upon as a sort of entertainer. At our evening gatherings it seemed to please those present to hear descriptions of the United States and such tales as I could remember, borrowed for example from Aesop, Uncle Remus, and mythology. Whenever I went to anyone's house where several were likely to be present I prepared myself with a few such stories in advance.

This way of life required as a counterweight a daily hour or two of outdoor activity that could be called recreation and not work. The need and the good sense of keeping hard and fit and an expert on skis and snowshoes coincided. I must be no drag upon Don in crossing the mountains, and I must not become sluggish with indoor life as I had a year ago. Companions were easy to find; I was too restless to wish to be alone. Sooner or later all the young people singly or in groups joined me in the afternoon's ski-running up into the hills and down again. As we climbed the brakes in the slots of the skis made a peculiar click that soon became associated with the game itself. The weather was often lovely, with glorious views of Mount Islandia, a snow-covered dome uplifted in the sky, its pedestal as white as the flawless summit. Such trips of an hour or two before dark or else by moonlight became almost a valley custom. It was a pleasant way to see friends, and often afterward we went to supper at someone's house.

Larnel always wanted to come, and as a result I saw more of him than of anyone else; for he appeared at the skiing hour whenever his work permitted and sometimes, I think, when his work did not. We had a common interest, Nattana. I soon decided how much to tell him, forced to such a decision by his curiosity. Therefore he was informed how often I had seen her, and all I could remember of the outward features of the environment in which she had lived; but I told him no more, and he never pressed me for personal matters or feelings. He was particularly interested in Nettera's marriage to Bain, an example of the daughter of a provincial lord, an Islata, marrying the son of a dependent, and to him, perhaps, an indication that among the Hyths such marriages were not unusual. His thoughts were easy to read—he might have the same good fortune.

My reticence did not match with an equal one. Talking to me, who knew Nattana quite well, was apparently the next best thing to talking to her herself. He had seen her four times to speak to, but that was enough for this isolated young man. It was evident that he thought about her constantly and wanted her very much. Her flirtatious act in doing up her hair at his request was a cruelty because he built hopes upon it. He was not aware how obvious he made his desire. The fact that it existed so strongly in this good-looking vigorous man, nearer Nattana's age than I was, stirred my own.

Dorna for long periods was merely a color in the sky, a pang of beauty in the light upon the snow, not wholly realized as herself, not actively in my thoughts. Desire for her was frozen. Our thoughts could not touch, and together we were dumb, on different planes; but her absolute rightness was imperishable.

Yet I was happy, restlessness the only flaw! Life was like a satisfactory machine which every day produced as it should a large number of good hours and moments to be enjoyed like new books and toys. There was a troubled feeling that I was wasting time; but northwest across the mountains, on the further side of the high white dome of Mount Islandia, only thirty-five miles away as the crow flies, there was the bright fire of Nattana.

Days became weeks and weeks a month, but I lost no faith in Don's coming. He would want a week of settled weather when it was not too warm nor too cold. Such weeks were more likely to come in August than in July. Meanwhile life was full of good things where I was.

Work was one of these, writing another, and social life, not overemphasized and not complicated, was perhaps best of all. I was usually too restless to sit down in the evening at the Fains' fireside. There were eight families in the valley each with one "day" a month, and I never missed anyone's "day." If it were not a "day" I made a call trying not to be too attentive to any one family or person and not really preferring one to another. I dropped in and talked with whoever was there—sport with young Bard who had been something of a runner and still competed, politics with Catlin, poetry with Tolly, mechanics with Anor, education with Tollia, Nattana with young Larnel, and art with Catlina Attana.

Besides calls there were moonlight skiing parties in July and early August, and twice there was dancing at the Catlins', where we did square dances like those at the Hyths'—but I did not attempt to teach anyone the boston. Then on two occasions parties of us attended the "days" of neighbors, setting out in midafternoon and returning late at night by moonlight, once up the valley to Grayling's farm, the last one of its kind on the road to the Mora Pass. There were nine of us: Catlin and his three older children, young Larnel, Tolly, the younger young Bard, Anora his wife, and I. Catlin and his family were proprietors or *tanar*, the others dependents or *denerir*, and myself, unclassed; but these distinctions had no significance. Isla Fain did seem of a different class still, but that was because of himself and of the authority and wisdom that his political position, traditional in his family, had given him.

Oh, the black and white night when we returned to our valley below this higher world! I walked with Catlina Attana, my favorite, who was only twenty, who talked on equal terms with me, an older man, as though it were an accomplishment recently acquired and still new to her, and with whom there was always enough to say.

She was enthusiastic about carving, a young sculptress. I had seen her work and liked it. It was childish, pure, intense—flat reliefs of leaves, of a dog, of a kneeling naked boy, a portrait of her sister suggesting all her charm, and one of her father, a caricature very like him. The best of these would be built into the walls of her home. People, she hoped, would want her to make things for them. She wanted more to do! She would like to put up my face somewhere, she said; there were many carvings of much more trivial things than my visit to the valley. A small square bas-relief of me for the mill, where I had sawed so much wood. . . . Would I let her try? She was charming, shuffling along on her snowshoes, eager with her thoughts, unself-conscious but with self-consciousness never far off, familiar and like the nice girls at home but full of latent strangeness because Islandian—shy, impersonal, but willing to bathe before men naked, innocent, enchanting.

Our talk went on, but I was thinking about Nattana. Six weeks had passed since her departure. She had said "next month," and next month was July, already over.

Another week passed. The moon became full and began to wane. I induced Anor to help me make skates. In the end, he, not I, made them—two pairs.

On August 13th, a cold clear day, toward five o'clock and not long after sunset, Larnel, his sister, and I, were on our way home from skiing, and had come to and climbed over the fence west of the granary.

"Look!" he said in a voice that swung her and me around.

A man with a heavy pack on his back came swiftly down out of the woods behind and above us, seemed about to crash into the fence, but stopped short in a cloud of snow. In an instant his skis were off, dropped on our side, and he had vaulted over and was upon the skis and coming toward us. He was bareheaded and his raven black hair was parted exactly in the middle.

"Why, that is Don," said Larnella. "What is he coming here for?"

Don was seated at the Fains' dining table and seemed to fill the whole side of it. He had come for me. Day before yesterday he had left his farm and had climbed to his Doring Valley hut; next day he had crossed the Mount Islandia Pass west of that great mountain and had reached the grazing farm of one Tanar; today he had come to the Fains'. The weather was good. Would I leave the next day?

He was an extraordinary person, reducing all others to insignificance. He was huge and ugly. He was also strikingly handsome, and almost beautiful. His forehead though rather low had serene nobility, and his hair grew out of it like two strong black wings. His black eyebrows were bushy, irregular, and overhanging. His upper eyelids drooped at their outer edges, and his eyes were small and rather far apart. They themselves were pale green but had the glint of faceted yellow diamonds. His nose was short with wide nostrils, but well cut. All the rest of his face was hidden in a black beard.

One felt the menace of his strength as one feels that of a gorilla. His hands were huge but with tapering fingers beautifully kept. His speaking voice was a quiet high tenor that did not seem to belong to him. He looked a gentleman and almost a dandy, but he also resembled pictures of massive cavemen. He smiled beautifully, his whole face abandoned to it, but in repose that same face was like an angry storm about to break.

He said what he had to say in few words, yet he never put one at a distance. One could ask him questions and receive prompt and willing, if brief, answers. One got along with him perfectly but he was impossible to know.

His coming was expected, yet I was not ready for it, nor ready to visit Nattana; but the fact that I was to climb a high pass in the dead of winter made it impossible to think too much about her. There was the unknown and the dangerous to be faced first.

"The first day will be an easy one," Don said, and it was almost the only remark that he made. But there could not have been a better guide. When I was going well he let me alone. When help was needed he gave it quickly and did exactly what was required.

I said good-bye to no one except the Fains and Mara. I took only one change of clothes, toilet articles, the skates, and writing paper. When I would come back I could not say, perhaps in two weeks, maybe much longer. I felt that I was embarking on the wildest adventure in my life. Nothing about it was ordinary. It constantly hovered on the edge of a dreamlike unreality.

We set out at an easy pace on skis, our snowshoes strapped to our packs. I was in good condition, but the climb to the level of the grazing farms took a good deal more out of me than I cared to think, with days that were not "easy" yet to come. But we went only eighteen miles and climbed only one thousand feet in all; most of the time it was not at all exhausting and I arrived at the Tanars' fresher than when I started, and that night I slept.

The name "Tanar" is the commonest in Islandia, there being twenty-five families bearing it. The only dwellers at the house where we stopped were a woman of a little over thirty, daughter of Tanar, a judge, but now dead, and her husband, Orlan, somewhat older. Of these two I have only the haziest recollections, for the next two days were so exciting as to send them quickly into the past.

We left at dawn with only ten miles to go in a straight line and four thousand feet to climb; and at first it seemed "easy" again. Our route lay up through woods west of the Frays, and eventually reaching a point well above timber line at seven thousand feet where Don had built himself his "south side" hut. There we would spend the night and cross the pass next day, descending to the Doring Valley hut or all the way to the Hyths' if we had time.

There was a trail to follow for only a short distance, and then climbing ceased to be easy. The trees were often dense and the snow deep and full of soft places. How Don knew where he was going I cannot say. All I knew was that the way was up. There were no blazes on the trees, no visible landmarks, and the line of the Reeves River was soon crossed and abandoned. Nor did we follow the way by which he had come, because he chose "one sort of route for ascending and another sort for descending always." Progress was in large part climbing out of a snow hole into which I had fallen, disentangling my skis that hung on my back, or extricating my snowshoes that were sometimes on my feet. We advanced steadily however, at an average rate of a mile an hour. I am sure that alone he could have gone much faster. Nevertheless he left me to myself most of the time and therefore I knew that I was going well. And it was wonderful to be with him, for he was wholly absorbed in the forest and in the snow, in what he was seeing and hearing, in signs of animals and of birds. In a few words or by a smile and a gesture or a lift of his eyebrows he made me see and hear also, so that we did something more than merely climb.

At one o'clock we reached timber line after seven hours of progress and one of resting, and we had our first real view. Eastward was Little Mount Islandia, seen endwise, a high rounded peak, gashed with ledges and covered with snow. Mount Islandia, however, was not visible, but the plains of Islandia were at our feet; below the belt of woods down which we looked were the descending white slopes of the grazing farms; and beyond these were the plains themselves less white and more blue as the distance increased, with a far dark horizon like the sea.

Above us were icy ledges and snow fields cutting at a high level a deep-blue sky, but we still kept our snowshoes on our feet, Don fitting them with the metal points of "creepers," and we roped ourselves together. The way he chose was a winding one but it was unerring. There were few places where we could not walk freely and only two where the snowshoes had to come off. By midafternoon we reached his hut.

It stood in an utter waste half buried in the snow, sheltered to east and west by shoulders of the hill, facing south into the air. It was about eight feet square and built of heavy stones. Every inch of the space within was utilized, and there was but one small window facing up the mountain. There was no place to sit except the bunks on either side. It was better still to lie out flat. Don made a fire in a little fireplace. I was tired but not too tired. When this wearing, exciting, and wonderful journey was over it would be delightful indeed to see Nattana again.

I fell asleep.

Such cold as we had that night I never dreamed possible. The mountain cracked with it. Outside our hut it was like a black monster waiting for us in utter stillness. Don slept placidly. I wondered if he were warm, for I was not. It took all the courage I had to get up and make the fire again. My toes and fingers ached so that I thought I had frozen them and my eyes wept from pure cold, not from pain. . . . Then perfect bliss when I was warm, and I thought of Nattana again, as I could not do when I was frozen.

"We climb today," said he at dawn, and when we had finished a breakfast of his thick meat soup that welcomely scorched my insides, he strapped both pairs of skis and snowshoes to his own back. Before we set out he insisted that we warm the insides of our clothes.

Outside, the still shadowy air was like a knife in the lungs, and all the time that ache continued.

Three times I doubted my ability to go on. Don did not know it by being told, but on several occasions he said that I was not used to this, and that he was.

"I know the limits of your strength," he remarked. "They are a long way off yet."

He made me want to laugh, but I had not breath enough. Nor was it worth while telling him that it was the damned cold! "Oh, Nattana," I thought, "you have let me in for a pretty bad sort of hell! You will have to make up for it."

There was worse to come. . . .

"It is colder than I thought it would be," said a voice, and I realized that I had been walking asleep. What a ghastly place to wake and find myself in! There were nothing but rocks and slopes of ice and snow, a hard blue sky, and a rope dragging me on.

Yet when I reached the col and realized where I was, I was as proud as though I had done it myself.

The Mount Islandia Pass is a little short of eleven thousand feet. No trail crosses it. Some use it in summer as a short-cut from the Province of Islandia into Upper Doring, but no horse can go over. Only Don made use of it in winter, preferring it to other routes. It had one great advantage to him who knew it so well. There was no rock-climbing necessary; the wind usually blew so hard as to prevent the freezing of snow and the formation of treacherous ice; and the ground was so broken into small fragments that though the climbing was steep a way could always be found by one who knew it. To him, I think, it was like a rather long flight of steps; he was aware of the lesser capabilities of others, but in an impersonal way like a doctor. No one received any sympathy from him but he gave aid, and he knew how others felt.

He knew that with the strain of climbing removed and with my lungs no longer obliged to breathe deeply of thin, icy air, I would be headlong on the descent. It was at first hard to understand why we went so slowly, for we were looking down into the Doring Valley, its floor only five thousand feet beneath us and a few miles through the air. The white expanse of the lake within its nearly complete ring of dark woods seemed only an hour's walk away. The buildings of the

Upper Farm were plainly visible, and Nattana was there. I had no doubt that I would see her at the end of this very day. To be with Nattana, to rest, and to be warm again would be perfect happiness. . . .

We came suddenly to Don's Doring Valley hut, which like the one on the other side of the pass was built above timber line. The two were twins except that this one faced north.

"We stop," he said.

"But it is morning," I answered, surprised that my tongue could speak.

He waved his hand to the west. The sun was descending into the flat sea of the valley!

Disappointment at the postponing of my arrival at the Upper Farm was unnerving. Temptation to act like a child was a sign that Don was right and that I was exhausted.

To my body, aching in every inch, a bunk, warmth, and relaxation were delightful. Had we not crossed the pass and were we not now on the other side? Fatigue was only temporary. We would reach the valley floor by noon next day, Don said. And then, Nattana!

There was a sensation of pleasant leisure and of accomplishment on this last night of traveling with Don. Lying in our bunks we talked, and he spoke more than I had ever heard him. He put me a number of curious questions about the United States. Do not trains and swift boats and automobiles change one's feeling as to the size of the country? Do they not alter one's interest in natural things? . . . He would listen to my answer, consider it, and ask another question as though drawing a slip with the question upon it from some cabinet in his brain, where he had filed them until such an opportunity as this.

He also of his own accord told me that physically I was strong enough for such mountaineering, quite a different man from the one whom he had guided to the Lor Pass. All I needed was more experience. Then like a teacher handing back an essay, he commented step by step upon my methods of climbing and made suggestions.

Our conversation was broken by long silences. Just as I was dropping asleep, he spoke again.

"You have no family," he said.

I answered that I had a father and mother, a brother and a sister. "I mean no home."

"Not yet," I replied, wondering if I were going to have to go through a discussion of *alia* with him.

"Do you know German?" he asked.

I told him that I could understand and make myself understood in ordinary conversation.

"Would a German mistake you for a German?"

"Oh no!"

He pondered upon this a long time.

"Do you like adventure in a good cause?" he asked.

"I have had very little in my life."

"Have you ever been near death?"

"Never."

Again there was silence.

"Do you think you would like adventure in a good cause?"

"With a chance of death?"

"Yes."

"I have thought several times that if this country is attacked by other nations than my own I would like to fight for her."

"You may hear from me," he said.

What did it mean? Something dangerous in which a knowledge of German played a part? It might well be some sort of spying over the mountains to the north of us.

They hung high in the sky across the valley. The Hyths' Upper Farm was coterminous with the foothills of the giant Doringclorn. On the other side were the towns of the Mountain Bants. It was winter now and they avoided snow, but in the spring? There were no garrisons and the Germans cared less to keep them in order.

Don's hints had somewhat the feeling of a waiting trap. Perhaps at heart I was not naturally adventurous, but there was also a strange and terrifying response. To adventure and to die was a good way of ending a life with a happy present but no future. And Don was a man whom one could follow with the great happiness of an adoring loyalty.

This brief conversation lay under and colored my thoughts that night and next morning. A call might be made upon me and I might have to heed it, unworthy if I did not. Were all prospective adventurers frightened as I was? Fear could so easily destroy the pleasure of the adventure. But to be considered by Don as one with whom to work filled me with pride—and intense surprise.

We breakfasted on hot soup again, but in an unhurried way. I could not let slip matters which he had left so vague, and yet he was a hard man to whom to speak.

"Last night," I began, "you said that I might hear from you. I don't know what it is all about, but I have my guesses as to the cause you had in mind. I hope that if you need me I will hear from you."

Thus half to commit myself was terrifying and a wild excitement.

"You will," he answered. "Guess, but don't think that you know. Before you leave the Hyths' come to my house anyway. It is yours."

I bowed. I would be as brief and reticent as he.

How casual it seemed! How important it might be! Anyway I was going to see Nattana. How strange it was that this should happen on the very day when I was to see her!

The distance down to the forests was longer than seemed reasonable, and the mountain stretched as we descended, the valley coming no nearer. Nevertheless after long hours of steep and fatiguing walking and climbing, when the rope and ice ax were often useful, we came at last to a great snow field. There we put on our skis and in a few moments of swift breathlessness left its high, white purity cutting the sky behind us. Not long afterward we were among the iron pines that grow so well above Doring Valley. Progress was steep and a little treacherous but fast. The snow was less deep than it had been on the other side.

From these woods at about noon we suddenly emerged only a few hundred yards above Don's farmhouse. The floor of the valley was within easy reach, the Hyths' Upper Farm not two miles away. Once again the Doring Valley was a vast and spacious corridor, U-shaped in cross section.

There was no need of Don's coming any farther. How could I thank him? He had given me a week of his time and I was much in his debt. Pay was unthinkable and words were inadequate.

"The trip was of use to me," he said. "I saw to my huts."

"We used up your firewood and your supplies."

"I gained knowledge of Lang."

He smiled, and parried all suggestions of indebtedness.

With my pack and snowshoes on my back and my pole in hand, I tilted my skis off Don's veranda. It was hard to believe in the mind that I was here at last and that the meeting with Nattana was a matter of minutes; but the fact of my surroundings was stronger than thought itself. The Fains' was far away; I was cut off from all my past life in Islandia and elsewhere. Don had changed me to an adventurer; Nattana also was an adventure.

In a few seconds the hill slope on which Don's house stood was left behind, and I was on the floor of the valley. It was a relief to shuffle along at the side of a road which was level, and to have miles and miles of flatness to the west. It was good to be on the ground again.

The Upper Farm, hidden from Don's house by a spur of the hills, came in sight less than a mile away and at my own level.

I came to the gate and went through quickly not wanting to spoil the rhythm of my skis. I was tired and wanted sleep and rest, for the nights at the huts had been cold and broken ones; but the muscles of my legs moved easily, and I could go on for miles.

Horses' feet marked the snow of the highway. I had come back again to a world where men could move freely from place to place, though eastward beyond the lake the road was surely blocked by snow. The lake itself was a snow field and probably useless for skating.

The road dipped down into the trench of the Doring River. Water was still running but the rocks scattered along its bed were capped with ice. The sides of the trench were a dazzling white in the sunlight. Tracks of skis and snowshoes were imprinted on the thin layer of snow that covered the bridge.

The road ascended to the floor of the valley again. It turned to the left and went on for hundreds of miles, to the towns of Hyth, Manson, Doring Town, and the Marsh. This was the West and it seemed like home.

The main house of the Upper Farm was a long, low building of two stories. Its situation, near a bluff over the lake, was isolated and windswept, with only a few tall pines at the farther end for companions. The stables, the barns, and the houses of the Ekklys lay in a cluster some distance away against a grove of evergreens and at the foot of slopes steeply ascending into the mass of Doringclorn.

I passed through the gate. At the gabled end was a window where

Nattana might be watching. A pure white field extended from the gate to the house. Along ski tracks already upon it I shuffled.

To dash up to the front door of a house on horseback shouting your name was a gallant way of arriving, but I had no horse, nor had I breath enough, and my heart beat too heavily. Instead I kicked off my skis on the paved veranda and knocked.

Ettera opened the door, so like her sister become plain that it was as though I saw Nattana changed in a dream.

"Lang!" she exclaimed, and then quickly added, as though the surprise in her voice was a dishonesty requiring correction, "We have been expecting you."

Her eyes regarded me shrewdly, but not unkindly. I remembered that she was the one, who, according to Nattana, had ideas similar to those of her father.

"Would you like to go to your room at once?" she asked. "You have had a hard journey, I know."

Across the square hall was a narrow flight of stairs leading up to a landing, from which two other short flights branched, one to the left and the other around a corner to the right. This last, which we followed, led to a square hall only large enough for two doors. The one of these opposite was ajar, and from within came the familiar rhythmical click and jar of a loom.

"Nattana," said Ettera in a loud voice, "Lang has come."

"Oh! . . . In just a minute!" Through the noise of the loom sounded the well-known, clear, young voice—expressive of an expectation realized if of nothing else.

Ettera had opened the second door to the left, and it led into the room which was to be mine.

"We have no house dependent," she was saying, "and we do everything ourselves. It won't be so comfortable as at the Lower Farm."

"I shan't mind—and while I am here you must let me help in every way I can."

"Oh, we will let you help," she said with a laugh slightly acid. "I'm sorry this room is so small, but it is the only spare one we have. Nattana's presence here means giving up the other one because of her weaving . . . You will want a bath, won't you? If you need hot water, would you mind bringing it yourself?"

"Of course not, Ettera."

There was only space enough in the room for a bed, a wardrobe, a table with a woodbox under it, a washstand with copper utensils, and one chair. Nothing could be moved without making something else inaccessible. But the single window, which faced northwest, commanded a wide view to the westward down the valley for thirty miles to the snowy peak of Bronder; and to the northward to the stables and barns a hundred yards away, backed by dark greenery and lying beneath the steep white slopes of the foothills. Just in view to the right were the tall pines that acted as sentinels around the northeast end of the house.

I freed my shoulders of my heavy pack and set it on the floor. There remained only room for Ettera and me to stand.

"I'll go and fill a jug for you," she said. "If you turn to the left at the foot of the stairs you'll find the kitchen—and usually me."

Casually Nattana appeared in the doorway, smoothing back scattered locks of red-gold hair from her forehead. She looked domestic, at home, and absent-minded with recent work. Ettera, leaving, passed her and she came in and stopped, looked at me and smiled.

"Here you are!" she said, and I was drawn toward her, without any thought at all, by her great dearness, but she shrank back with a quick movement too slight to be an affront but definite enough to check my impulse.

"Here I am, Nattana." We watched each other. . . .

"Wasn't it very cold last night and the night before? I wondered about you in Don's little huts. You didn't freeze anything, did you?"

"Nothing at all."

"Are you quite all right?"

"Yes—a little tired."

"You can rest here. Life is rather slow! Well, I am very glad that you are safe."

"Aren't you glad I am here?" I asked half as a joke.

"Oh, that's another matter!" she answered with a laugh, instantly adding: "Of course, I am. And I do hope you will be comfortable. You won't starve and you won't freeze, but we are very poor. If you want something more elaborate you will have to go to the Ekklys'. They are much better off than we are. The boys made the decision to run the farm independently too recently to lay in a stock of food. There'll be enough, but it will be very simple."

"I don't mind," I said.

"I did not think you would, but I wanted to warn you."

Her eyes had looked at me only for the briefest of impersonal glances.

"You will want a bath, won't you, Johnlang?" she said. "I'll get you hot water."

"I'll get it. Ettera told me where to go."

"Well, I'll find you a tub anyway."

She turned on her heel.

The tub was in my room when I returned from the kitchen, and Nattana's loom was jarring with a click of satisfaction at the end of each rhythmical shift.

Wearing the only other clothes that I had, I went to the door of her workshop. Hearing me she called cheerfully to come in, and gave me a nod and went on with her work. The room was only a little larger than my own on the other side of the house. Her loom was much smaller than that at the Lower Farm and was set sideways to a window with a view southeast over the snowy surface of the lake to dark forests on the other side; and above these were foothills over which the white dome of Mount Islandia, narrowed at this angle, was lifted like a white bubble.

If Nattana wished to turn her eyes from her work, she had a view as gorgeous as that of the Yosemite with this marvelous white bubble in addition; for farther to the north she could look between the great portals of vertical cliff through which the Doring River broke in its descent from the alpine highlands at the foot of the Lor and Mora Passes.

I watched her. Her eyes were intent on the dark-brown fabric before her, her pretty hands moved with mechanical regularity, her foot pushed the treadle and a groove appeared through her stocking on the side of her calf. As always, she sat poised lightly on her stool. She was like a machine in her movements, but every little while she became a girl at work and pushed a lock of hair back from her smooth forehead, not taking the trouble to make it stay.

"I want to finish this," she said between clicks; and therefore I found a seat on a low bench against the opposite wall. The room was as crowded as my own with her loom, her spinning wheel, her carder, a small dyeing kettle, a rack, piles of cloth, hanks of wool, a designing table, and all of Nattana's tools. A second door, a little ajar, opened into a room beyond, and I could see a chair with a dress upon it.

She wore a dark-green frock, new to me. Only her face and hair were disordered and domestic. She herself was neatly dressed and trim.

The loom shuddered to a stop, and she swung round on her stool.

"I had to finish what I was doing," she said.

"That deep brown is a beautiful color, Nattana."

"Oh, do you like it?" Her voice was high with pleasure.

"I like the color of your dress, too. It goes with your hair."

"I tried a long time before I got this green."

"Did you weave and dye it here?"

"Oh, yes! But this is not like my other shop. I have no space to turn around in. And I want to work, Johnlang!"

She laughed, but her eyes shifted away.

"You have a fine view, Nattana."

She glanced through the window, and again I was captured by the symmetry and distinction of her profile.

"I know I have, but I wish the Lor Pass were not so near."

Reminded of the Mountain Bants, I wondered whether or not to tell her now of Don's offer.

"There is no danger in winter," I said.

"It won't be winter always. This would be the first house they came to . . . But let's not talk of it."

"Very well . . . Nattana, you are prettier than I thought you could be."

Her eyes met mine for a moment with a green questioning flash. She laughed.

"Let's not talk of that either. How was your journey? How are the Fains—and Larnel? And how are you, Johnlang?"

"How is Fak, and Ek, and Atta? How is Nattana?"

The one I did not speak of she mentioned.

"Nettera had her baby not long after I left the Fains'—a girl."

"How is she?"

"She had little trouble. She was well ten days ago. News does not come often. I wish I were with her . . . Tell me about your journey."

I had scarcely begun, when she rose and said that she must set the table for lunch.

From my room came the sound of Nattana emptying the tub which I had left standing. I had meant to ask her.

Lunch was a simple meal as she had predicted: a stew of meat and dried peas, bread, apples for dessert, and chocolate, which was specially in honor of my arrival and not usual, Ettera said. Ek and Atta were not present, for they were working at the new stable and had taken their lunch with them.

"They usually do," said Ettera. "It saves trouble."

"And food," added Nattana, "but don't worry. There are enough peas to feed an army, and we had a fine harvest of apples."

Having lunched with my hostesses I went out to greet my hosts. What Nattana meant when she called the Upper Farm shut in became apparent. The masses of Mount Islandia, Bronder, and Doringclorn, in all their greatness from valley to summit, were hard and sharply bright against an intense blue sky and in the thin air hung near. The valley corridor was closed at both ends, and there was no view to a horizon.

The barn was a spacious building, but the dusty haylofts were half-empty and there were rows of empty stalls. At one end were the horses of the Hyths and a few cattle. Fak was there, blanketed and well cared for. Part of the long cowshed had been partitioned off as a workshop. Ek and his brother wore garments of heavy linen over their ordinary clothes, and these were white with stonedust. Outside the windows the new stables were visible at right angles to the barn and as yet little more than a ground plan. Today it was too cold to labor outdoors, and therefore the brothers were at work squaring stones, a great pile of which, carted down from a quarry nearby in the foothills, lay outside the door.

They provided me with a suit of their "overalls" and I went to work with them. Our mallets and cold chisels clinked, now together, now separately, making a rhythmic pattern for periods of time. At intervals we stopped for a few words. Ek and Atta seemed happier and freer than they had been at the Lower Farm, full of plans, and contented with their lot. I felt at home; and this was a good place to be.

A little after dark, having seen to the horses and cattle, we walked back to the house in the hard, still, cold twilight air, entering through a woodshed and by the kitchen. Ettera, a little red-faced and grim, was getting supper, moving rapidly about the room. Nattana walked in and out in a more leisurely way, setting the table in the amateurish offhand manner of a lady of the house when the maids are gone out. I stopped in the dining room to tell her how I had spent the afternoon.

"Don't feel that you must enter into our life more than is natural to you," she replied as she moved about the table. "I have been afraid that I have talked too much about our being poor. We want you to be happy with us."

"I shall be happiest if I may enter into your life, Nattana."

"You may, of course," she said absently. "We will be ready soon," she added, and I took the hint and departed.

The evening was a short one. All of us were sleepy. We sat in the living room when the dishes were washed and put away, no one saying much, even Atta, the questioner, silent. He and Ek and the two women began to seem remote.

They did not waken me, and when my eyes opened the bright light in the room was that of a day already aging. I felt rather than heard the jar of the loom, and knew that breakfast must be over and Nattana already at work. By the washstand was a tall copper vessel of hot water swathed in a towel to keep the heat. Someone, Ettera or Nattana, must have brought it in so quietly as not to waken me . . . Care must be taken lest I be a trouble to these two. On other mornings I would be up and about with the rest.

There was utter stillness except for the faint regular reverberation of the loom. Passionate friendly love for Nattana flooded my heart.

Shaved and dressed I went into the hall. The door to the workshop was closed.

I rapped on the door, and her voice called and I entered. She was sitting before the heavy wooden frame and the vertical threads of her loom like a musician before a harp. Her eyes lifted, and she smiled. Twice more the shuttle ran across, the bars clicked and jarred, and her arms made their regular graceful gestures. Then the machinery stopped, and she turned on her stool.

"Don't bother to knock when I am here," she said. "Come in!"

Her clasped hands were between her knees, and she was looking up.

"How did you sleep in a new house, Johnlang?"

"Wonderfully, Nattana."

I went forward, and her eyes followed me, but she did not move. Greetings of mere words were incomplete.

"How did you sleep?" I asked.

"Oh, very well. I always do."

I was close to her, but she had not stirred. I looked into her eyes; words and theories and ideas were merely veils that had been snatched away; and we both stared again at the same thing, our confused problem.

I bent over her, my hands on her shoulders. Her head turned a little and she gave me her cheek, hot and soft, but it pressed definitely against my lips . . . She stirred, and her movement and her manner declared that she wished this to be all.

"You haven't had your breakfast," she said. "Ettera has gone to the Ekklys'. I'll get it for you."

She rose, and my heart came into my throat, for her hands were clenched, and she had bitten her lip, pain in her eyes.

"Nattana!"

"No—please!" she said quickly, and she eluded my hands and started for the door. I followed her rapid steps down the stairs, seeing suddenly the whole thing in a new light: my presence hurt Nattana; I thought only of my own pleasure; I should not have come if I valued her peace of mind.

But in the kitchen she turned to me a face so serene and so easily smiling that I wondered if I really had hurt her.

"I'm sorry to give you all this trouble," I said.

"You need not be. I'm glad to take it."

She set before me warmed milk, bread, honey, and an apple.

"This afternoon," she said, "we will go out and see the place, if you would like that, or do something together."

I told her that it would be a pleasure, and that I thought I should join Ek and Atta. With a glance back, she went off to her weaving.

It was a busy household, in which I must do my part. Therefore, before going out, I washed my own dishes.

Returning upstairs to fetch my cloak I found my bed already made.

The loom was making its busy racket. I looked in on Nattana to say good-bye, and she smiled and nodded without stopping her work.

Long mare's-tails streamed across the valley from the direction of Mount Islandia, and the sun behind their high white feathers gave out a pale wintry light.

Ek and Atta had returned for lunch; they were riding down the valley to the farm of Samer, who had a forge, and asked Nattana and me to join them, for she had announced that we were going somewhere. Ettera had her suggestion: that we return a kettle which she had borrowed of Elwina, Don's wife, and that if the cloth which Nattana was making for Elwina was ready—as it ought to be—we take that over also. To each suggestion Nattana was noncommittal: we might do it. I had no ideas of my own, except to be with her, preferably alone. I mentioned skiing, riding, walking, and skating, watching for some response in her. When we rose from the table many things had been talked about and nothing decided.

The two men left for the barn, and Ettera went into the kitchen. Nattana began to clear the table.

"If we want to go with them, Nattana," I said, "we ought to tell them."

"Would you like it?" she answered, going into the kitchen with plates. When she came back I made my reply.

"I would like to go with them if you would."

"And I would if you would."

She departed with more plates.

"I want to do what you want," I said when she reappeared.

"So do I . . . ."

"I would love to go with them if you would, Nattana." What more could I say? Time was going fast.

"It will soon be too late if you don't tell me, Nattana."

"I've told you: if you want to go we'll go."

"But do you really want to?"

She was carrying out the last of the plates.

"If you and Ettera would like me to help you, I'll be glad," I said.

"Oh no! not this time," she answered from the doorway. Our impasse had the horrid feeling of a quarrel. There was nothing to do here, and I went into the living room where a fire was smoldering.

Through the window I saw Ek and Atta riding away.

After a long time Nattana came in.

"I wondered if you had gone," she said. It seemed almost insulting. I had risen when she came in. She went past without glancing at me, poked a log with her foot, and stood looking into the fire.

"They have gone," I said.

"Have they?"

"We could go down to the lake," I suggested. "There may be hard ice under the snow and we could try the skates. Perhaps you would like that, Nattana."

"If it is what you wish."

"It is, if you like the idea."

"Do you?"

"If you do, Nattana, of course I do."

She was silent.

I suggested that we go skiing and then that we ride, each time with the same result: she would not say what she wanted, only that she would do it, if it were what I wished.

It seemed likely that we would do nothing, and I felt a hot flicker of anger. Nor had she looked at me since she came in.

"You haven't said that you wanted to do anything," she said. "Tell me what you want, and I'll do it."

"It must be something you will want also."

"It will be, if it is what you want."

"But I would like it to be something you wanted also, not just to please me."

"Tell me what you really want," she said, and her voice was high and dangerous.

There was one thing that I desired. Anger made no difference in that longing. There were other ways of settling difficulties than talking. I sat down by her and put an arm around her and caught her hand.

"You want to know what I really want . . . I want this."

"I don't!" she cried and twisted away from me, and went to the fireplace, where she faced me and stood like one at bay, drawing long breaths, her hands behind her.

"I had better go back to my workshop," she said, a deep frown on her forehead, "and finish that brown cloth I'm making."

"I am sorry!" I cried, angry and astonished at the sharp repulse.

"What are you sorry for?"

"I am sorry I did the wrong thing just now."

"Oh—you don't understand!"

She turned away suddenly, and was a forlorn figure with her head bent, her round head, and two braids.

"I am sorry," I repeated in a gentler voice.

"If you apologize for that, I don't know what I'll do!" she said furiously.

"Then I won't apologize—but I *am* sorry that it was the wrong thing."

She turned sharply, her face angry.

"What do you want of me, Johnlang? I don't know. You never say."

"I don't want to hurt you," I said.

Her eyes grew wide, and then softened, but her voice was still angry.

"Just now—you wanted to kiss me, didn't you?"

"Yes, Nattana."

"Like the afternoon in the mill at the Fains'?"

"Nattana, I was happy."

"I was too! But—oh, Johnlang! And—I am not speaking of just now—you wanted to do what I wanted, to go with Ek and Atta, or over to Don's, or down to the lake, but only if it were what I wanted —to please me!"

"Yes, I did."

"And I wanted to do any one of those things if it pleased you. Ours were Unmeeting Wishes. And you seemed to get angrier and angrier. I could hear it in your voice. It made me angry, too."

"What do you mean by 'Unmeeting Wishes'?"

She looked surprised.

"Why, when I want to do a thing if you want to do it, and you want to do that same thing if I want to do it, and neither of us has any other reason for doing it than to please the other, our wishes don't meet. When we find that this is our state of mind, we certainly do not do that thing! You did not say you wanted to do anything for its own sake."

"Neither did you."

"Yet I think we were agreed on one thing. I was—until I got angry."

"I wanted to go somewhere with you, Nattana—I did not care what it was."

"So did I! I suppose I could have decided what we should do, and

597

perhaps that is what I ought to have done, for you are my guest . . . But, oh, Johnlang, you don't know half the things that have been going on in my head!"

"What things, Nattana?" I said, rising toward her.

"Oh, the same old things."

She drew back from me, crying:

"If you kiss me, I think I shall scream—but it is not that I don't want it, Johnlang."

I thought of the first thing that came into my mind as a way to help her.

"Let's do something. I want to go to the lake and try the skates. Will you come?"

"I'll come gladly."

"But some time I will kiss you, Nattana."

She shrank back against the stonework of the fireplace as though I were about to strike her.

"What do you want of me?" she cried. "Tell me what you want! Oh, I won't say it . . . You wished to come here; you insisted—I know that much. And you want to kiss me sometimes. Is that what you really want?"

"I want that . . ." I began.

"Let's have it out. Some day we must. Is that all you want?"

It was a deadly thing to utter. The room went white.

"I have wanted you."

Her face winced and she put her knuckles to her teeth.

"And I have wanted you," she said.

The snow outside was cold and hard under the white sun.

"What are we going to do, Johnlang? Do you see why you must not kiss me? I could not stand it. With me, that is everything or nothing. But if it is to be nothing I think I can still be your friend. But how is it with you? Would you be happy with my kisses sometimes, going no further?"

Was my passion milder than hers?

"I want your kisses if I cannot have more, Nattana."

She started to speak, became white and checked herself. After a moment she turned to one side and went toward the door.

"Where are you going, Nattana?"

"We are going to the lake."

We seemed to be in calm waters after a storm that left us subdued and dazed and yet not unhappy. The mare's-tails in the sky had become more dense and the sunlight was chill and pale. Nattana thought that it would snow and grow warmer. She wore leggings and breeches and a heavy coat like a lumberman's jacket, but with a hood, half the time off her head. They made a better costume than mine for outdoors in winter.

It was only a few steps to the edge of the bluff above the lake, the pure white surface of which extended eastward for five miles toward the portals that marked the beginning of the habitable parts of the Doring Valley. These were always in the view, black, unchanging, their simple immensity apparent even ten miles away.

We walked down to the boathouse and out upon the lake. To the south, the east, and the north, were dense and splendid forests.

I remembered the lake in summer and my sail upon it, and thought as I had thought then that this region had all that a summer resort needed; but I knew better than to speak aloud such ideas as these lest they remind Nattana of my country. Yet there was one solution of all our troubles—troubles half the pain of which was now gone because we shared them, both wanting the same thing—and that solution lay in changing Nattana's attitude toward the United States: in Nattana as my wife. But I would not speak of that now, for we were getting along together too well. We were each in love with the other.

The surface of the lake was heavily crusted snow through which we sank a few inches to the ice beneath, but the surface there, even with the snow removed, would be impossible for skating. She suggested, however, that sometimes the lake melted and froze again along the edges of its warmer southern shore, while the rest remained snow-covered ice all winter. For this shore, two miles away, we set out. Under our feet the crust crunched, but with a certain springiness that made walking easy. The flatness was so perfect all around us that it was like a voyage on a sea.

Nattana's face became serene again, and though her cheeks and nose were a little red, I loved her no less. It was true love, for in her plainer aspects I was drawn to her most.

The walk was a long one but she was a gallant walker; and when at last we came under the overhanging forested slopes we found what we wanted. Either for the reason she gave or because strong winds from the east had moved the ice sheet from the shore, along a cliff was a dark strip free of snow, strong enough to bear us, and smooth enough for skating.

I put on my skates while she watched me, sitting tailor-fashion on the snow. Their balance was not quite what it should be; but after sprawling about for a little while I became accustomed, heard again the familiar click and grind, felt the bite of the edges, the rhythm, the speed, and made for Nattana in as good form as possible a figure eight, a grapevine, an anvil, and a spread eagle—which caused her to laugh. Then I went to her, took her ankles in my hand, and shod her with skates.

Nattana, usually so deft with her feet and hands, was awkward, unsteady, with ankles that wobbled . . . I pushed her along, told her how to strike out. She fell many times and pulled me down with her.

However, she learned quickly, and no one could have been more delightful to teach . . . She was persistent, and did not mind being hurt, she was good-natured, and eager. And I had always loved skating.

The shadows grew longer and the white surface that edged our strip of good ice became blue, but before it was time to go Nattana could skate forward with both feet and was trying the edges, her ambition a good figure eight; and when skating together with crossed hands she moved of herself with some rhythm.

The time sense in her brain did not fail her. At a certain moment she said it was time to go. I unshod her.

She said that "feet" were a relief after skates and that she was rather bruised, but she added:

"I shall love skating, and I shall thank you all my life."

We started homeward. The far shore of the farm was gathering darkness rapidly but the snow field of the lake made a pale glare. A spark of light appeared above the bluffs.

"Ettera has probably put a lamp in a window to guide us," Nattana said.

"Are you tired?"

"A little."

I took her hand and slipped it through my arm, where she let it remain, light but definite . . . We walked in silence. I was strangely happy. The pain of our difficulties was outweighed by the happiness of knowing what she felt.

There came a faint drumming and we both stopped, and my heart quickened. Her hand gripped my arm. The sound died away and then became louder.

"It sounds like horses," I said.

"Yes, but what horses?"

"Somebody riding on the lake. . . ."

"I see them!" Her voice was almost a shriek, and she turned and clung to me with both hands. Dark figures emerged from the shadows of the shore and were moving towards us.

There was a throbbing in my throat.

"No one could cross the high passes on horseback at this season," I said.

"They may have taken our horses."

I put my arm around her and held her, and she came close against me.

"I know it is probably Ek and Atta coming to meet us, John," she said, "but I am afraid."

"They probably see us." I was realizing that it was impossible to escape these riders if escape were necessary, that I had no weapon, that I did not care what happened if Nattana were safe, and that all these fears were most likely quite foolish and needless.

We stood quietly waiting for several long seconds. . . .

"Let's walk," she said. "If it is Ek and Atta, they will wonder at seeing us holding each other."

We went towards the approaching figures, now obviously men on horseback . . . It took courage on her part.

"I see Fak," she cried sharply. "He's a different color. He is being led."

She laughed with sudden shrillness.

"How foolish of us, Johnlang!"

But I was thinking of Don's proposal and of the need of serving under him, and that I would tell Nattana of it in time. Her fear gave Don's cause a new reason.

The two riders were Ek and Atta. Ettera had seen Nattana and me departing over the lake. Afraid that her sister might be hurt skating, she suggested to her brothers on their return from Samer's that they take spare horses and come for us.

Certainty made them welcome, yet for a few moments they were

601

as strange in their normalness as an enemy would have been. Nattana was glad to ride.

We all four rode to the stables and returned to the house through the kitchen, on the way Nattana telling Ek that skating was quite wonderful.

Ettera met us.

"Are you all right, Nattana?" she asked.

"Oh, perfectly—a little bruised by falling down."

Ettera made in her throat a sound in which sisterly animosity, disapproval, and pleasure in the thought that Nattana was hurt and ought to be were all expressed.

26

The Vaba Pass

Nattana and I were friends; and being friends consisted in being very careful with each other in all we said and did and in seeing much less of each other than we wished.

Days slipped by. Life at the Upper Farm was different from that at the Fains'. There all was well-established, leisurely, and comfortable. The intelligence and energy of many men and women for long years had been directed toward the development of a way of living in which all had work to do but were never under pressure and all had leisure. The extent of spring planting, the amount of wood to be cut, the hours of labor needed on each thing, had all been worked out. There were no changing markets in the outer world continually destroying the adjustments evolved at the farm. Set free by a stable life in which no effort prescribed by circumstances was ever wasted, each individual worked out his own happiness. So far as concerned that part of living which relates to shelter and food all were untroubled. Yearnings to create, to love, to see the world, were free of the handicap of too complicated living. They found that newness, which their souls like those of all men craved, in the study of natural life around them, in their friendships and loves, in perpetuating their families as institutions, and in making all work they did sound and beautiful, whether it was mending a fence or carving a bas-relief.

Life at the Hyths' was different, but had the same end in view. Ek and Atta worked to achieve, if not for themselves then for the next generation, what the Fains already had and what they would have had if the pressure within their family had not compelled them to go elsewhere. They were pioneers, and yet unlike many pioneers in that they knew so clearly what they wanted to build that they were without restlessness. They worked without that frustrating waste of

603

energy that is expended in rebellion—itself often the result of an aimless urge to be active. Ettera worked with them but not so contentedly, for the work she did had less tangible results. Ek and Atta could look at a new tier of stones lifting the wing of the barn a little higher, she only at another meal consumed. But Ettera, if given the choice of working in this way or at home or not working at all, would have chosen what she was doing. She also was deep in her *alia*. These three were the nucleus of a new Islandian unity.

Nattana stood apart, a little of an exotic. She was a weaver of cloth, a designer and maker of clothes, and demanded a scope for her activities larger than that of a single farm. There were many like her in Islandia, who filled the needs of those in the neighborhood. Nattana would make clothes only for members of her family, but she would be consulted for ideas by others, and would manufacture cloth on order for still more, for which she would be paid. The money she would receive would be her own, but there were few ways to spend it on herself; and she would contribute it to her family as a matter of course, and it would go to pay for those things that had to be bought. Her interest in her *alia* was therefore actual but less direct than that of others who worked for the farm alone.

All this would have been true if Nattana had remained at the Lower Farm. The local weaver was old and retiring, and there was a need for someone in her place. Nattana had at least talent and aptitude, and perhaps more. Those who lived in the neighborhood knew what she could do and were numerous enough to keep her as busy as she wanted to be. At the Upper Farm, however, there already was a weaver ten miles down the valley, and upon him Nattana did not like to trespass. Furthermore if she were long absent from the Lower Farm, someone else would take her place; and if she returned she would not like to intrude on that person's business and goodwill. She did not earn money to contribute to the Upper Farm household, nor did she work for it as Ettera did, nor could she have the same satisfaction in labors because her stay was only temporary. Nevertheless she set the table and helped wash the dishes, and in addition to caring for Ettera's room and her own rooms, took charge of mine. But she was a weaver, and if she gave up this work which satisfied her creative eye, brain, and hand, she would be most unhappy. So Nattana went on with it, and avoided the waste of producing too much by consuming time in making what she did unusual and perfect in every way.

The custom seemed to be that every other day was a half holiday. Sometimes the holiday portion of the second day was spent only in a different sort of work. This was the case with Ek, but Atta mounted a horse and rode off for at least part of the afternoon. Ettera went for a walk by herself, always returning in a good humor. Nattana and I spent ours together, skating; and when we set out from the house, life changed its character. I was absorbed in her, who became daily more desirable. Sometimes desire was too strong for happiness and sometimes happiness too great for desire to matter. But we scrupulously pretended to be friends, often understanding each other so well that without any words about it we laughed at our pretense.

After a little over a week, a portent of mare's-tails streaming from the direction of Mount Islandia was followed by a storm. Wind and snow forced themselves over the barrier of the mountains. In the morning we rose to the tune of a raging gale from the east roaring and singing around the house, to drafts of cold through the rooms, and to air outside so dense with snow that nothing was visible except a driving white curtain. I spent a busy morning bringing wood and tending fires, with trips to the barn when the wind blew me from my path and the snow seethed around and burned my face.

It was Nattana's and my half holiday. Skating was, of course, impossible and to go out dangerous. At lunch Nattana said that when she called me I was to come to her workshop, for she had something to give me and to do.

Waiting in the living room, trying to read, wondering what she had planned, I heard the sound of the loom; but after it had ceased there was a long silence before her voice called.

I ran up the stairs. She was waiting at the door, her eyes bright but doubtful.

"It has seemed a long wait, Nattana."

"I wanted to finish undistracted . . . I don't know whether you will like or not what I have done."

She had gone to her worktable; and the loom was empty, the fire burning warmly. She held up the cloth that she had been weaving, draping it over her arms and shoulders like a tailor, and all of her dress was covered except her open green collar. She turned this way and that and the light shifted and ran on the soft folds of warm brown. The snow was driving upon the window panes, and against its white background her round and red-gold head was outlined.

"When you said you liked this cloth, I was so pleased! I was making it for you and I had been doubtful, for I had not talked to you about the color. I knew what I thought was right but you might have your own ideas. Yet you wore nothing but dark-blue as though you had not bothered to work out your own best colors. If it is wrong or doesn't suit you, you don't have to take it."

"Nattana, it is just what I want and exactly what I need!"

"Yes, you do need new clothes . . . May I, Johnlang?"

She came nearer and wrapped the cloth around my shoulders; then stood back and surveyed the effect.

"I wish you could see yourself," she said. "I like you too much already . . ." She paused. "Will you let me go on with it?"

"Of course—what do you mean, Nattana?"

"Will you let me make for you what you need?"

"Nattana," I cried, "you are so good! I can't begin to tell you what a kind thing it is for you to do . . ." I caught at her hand, and gratitude and love intermingled. "You are so dear to do this! It is just like you. You are wonderful. . . ."

Color rushed over her face, and she stood like one being scolded, drawing back a little, her hand tense and her lips set, but her eyes were extraordinarily bright.

"Let's begin!" she said, and her hand pulled and I released it.

There was enough cloth to make knickerbockers, shorts, jacket, ulster, and cloak, the last two with hoods. She took no measurement but used a suit of mine for a pattern. She knew exactly what to do, and in a short time the cloth was laid on the table and she was cutting it with unhesitating, rapid shears.

My part of the job was to sit on the bench and talk to her. She was so absorbed that she was absent-minded. She moved quickly, but no motion was wasted. She was enchanting to watch, leaning over the table, measuring the path of the shears with intent eyes, her whole body busy, the hem of her skirt quivering with the eager movement of her arms.

The art of making clothes, however, was one about which she could talk while exemplifying it.

She explained that the brown cloth was made of a special thread of wool of long staple and of linen for strength. She had begun working on it as soon as she arrived from the Fains'. She had had a hard time dyeing the yarn to suit her, handicapped by lack of materials until Atta made a special trip in a cart to the Lower Farm.

Nattana had given nearly all her time for six weeks to this and to nothing else. I was dazed as the extent of her interest and her labor unfolded.

I began to thank her all over again. I told her that she was a friend in need, and she interrupted me saying that the need was real; I told her that I deserved no such kindness, and she said that it was time someone paid attention to my wardrobe. She parried my thanks and yet seemed pleased by them, saying several times, "I am glad to do this! I have been happy working . . . Because you are pleased, I am happier still."

I watched her at work, thinking that what she had done for me and her spirit in doing it was a sure indication that she and I could be happy together, if I could match the strength of her interest and devotion with strength as great. It seemed more and more that I could. Interwoven with these thoughts was desire to love Nattana, to have her, and to have her now; and it became clear that I was where she had been a whole week before: it must be everything or nothing—kisses were a futile halfway house.

Conversation slackened. I made myself useful by keeping up the fire and by now and then holding the cloth for her to cut. The pile of pieces to be sewed grew higher, and the floor became covered with snips.

She said she was hungry, and when I went to fetch her a glass of milk in the kitchen I surprised Ettera sitting at a table doing nothing, her face in her hands. She started violently when I entered. To carry us through the shock of my catching her off her guard, I told her what I had come for and what Nattana and I were doing.

She rose to get the milk. When she returned she looked me in the eyes.

"Lang, I have thought I would not speak—but I worry about you and Nattana. I want you to promise . . ."

Blood rushed to my face, and my instinct was to reassure her, to deny all intention of doing, to promise that of course I would not do—anything guilty.

"What do you want me to promise?" I asked.

"You know, Lang!"

I felt insulted, misunderstood.

"Ettera . . ." I began, and thought of Nattana. I would entangle myself in promises and obligations to no one except her.

"Ettera, have you asked Nattana to promise?"

"I have spoken to her." Her eyes dropped. Nattana had refused to bind herself. I would spare making Ettera admit it.

"I don't want to displease you," I said. "At present Nattana and I are friends. We have agreed to work out together whatever we are to be to each other. I cannot make promises to you and still keep my promise to her."

She turned aside, her teeth on her lip.

"No," she answered, unexpectedly. "I see that you can't. But oh, Lang, you and Nattana, do be careful of each other! You have other years ahead of you."

"I want her to marry me," I said.

"I am sorry for you both," she answered.

I returned to Nattana. To Ettera I had said more than to her. She must know what I wanted soon.

She took the milk. Our fingers touched. I trembled, but she seemed untroubled, relaxed—her hair a little over her forehead, her eyes absent and absorbed. She drank the milk slowly, but the moment that it was done she spun around to her task again.

I sat down on the bench.

Nattana was threading a needle. She drew out her stool, perched herself upon it, crossed her knees, and began to make a seam.

"The tedious part of this work," she said, "is the sewing. Nevertheless, I rather like it."

She looked up for a quick smile. She was so innocent of what I was thinking that I was checked. It was an advantage to have a job to do.

"You ought to have a sewing machine."

"What is that?"

I explained, adding, "If you had gone to see my Exhibition Ship you would have known."

"Father went when she was at Bannar, but he would not take any of us younger ones—only Airda . . . Tell me about making clothes in your country."

In her voice was a gentleness that offered an apology for past anger when we had discussed such matters. I told her everything that would present a clear picture of how clothes were bought and made, stressing what was obvious to us but not to her, such as the differences between cheap and expensive, "made to order" and "ready to wear," "stylish" and "unstylish."

When the picture was painted, she said:

"I have one question. You have seen my work and have an idea of what I can do. With what I know and what I can do where would I be in your country?"

"If you were married, Nattana?"

"Either—if I worked."

I thought some time before answering.

"Weaving is what interests you most. As a weaver I see no place for you with our manufacturers of cloth, unless after some time and a good deal of luck you were employed under others as a designer for the sake of your ideas; but you would not weave yourself. As a maker of clothes, Nattana, you could always find employment, for you are a good needlewoman. I can tell by the sureness and quickness with which your hands move. But you would lead a confined city life —a poor one if you were only a seamstress. There would be no half-holidays every other day, no continuous fresh air, no countryside, no horse, no freedom to do your work in your own way. The thought of you, Nattana, in a small room with only walls visible outside your windows, harassed by continuous noise of which you have no idea, and doing all your work subject to others' orders and decisions and whims, wrings my heart!"

She listened without a word, while I told these hated truths.

"But Nattana," I continued, "if you married it might be quite different. You could make cloth for your family—and clothes, too. You would study fashions and make them more reasonable. It might be fun for you. You could be a reformer."

"And of course," she said, "I would have the man I had wanted to marry, and that would make up for a great deal. I could give up the weaving, perhaps . . ."

My heart leaped violently in agony and happiness.

"Nattana, listen to me—"

But she held up her hand and continued:

"I love you for your truthfulness, Johnlang . . . But if I gave up my work there would have to be something else. I have thought and thought about it. It is not just work I would need."

She ceased abruptly, in doubt. Her hands lay on the brown cloth across her knees and were tremulous. The room was very quiet for the wind had ceased.

"If you had the man you wanted, Nattana, wouldn't it be possible?"

"Do you mean: suppose I were married to someone like you?"

"Yes, Nattana, someone you wanted."

"Suppose it were you! You make me doubt myself. You make me weak . . . Oh, don't touch my hands, please, Johnlang. I need all my head!"

I stood before her, not knowing I was there. Her eyes looked up into mine and her face was quivering.

"Not yet!" she said. "You must listen to me. I have thought about it so much—of you and me married and in your country. If I married you and we lived in your country, all would be well with you, I know, for you would find nothing strange in the life we would be leading. Can't you see how tempted I am! But our life would depend on me being something I am not. It is a greater burden than I could bear! Your life would change my values, and I would have no chance to be myself. I may be a coward, but I would fail you and our marriage, Johnlang. I would be so unhappy without this. . . ."

Her hands flung outward, came back to her knees and clasped tightly.

"I am not afraid, Nattana. I want you. I want to marry you. If you want me, how can you doubt our happiness?"

She drew back.

"Johnlang, answer me this: do you want a child by me?"

For a long moment I was silent.

"Yes, Nattana!"

She wrung her hands.

"It was not your instant thought. I'm no better."

"Oh, I wish I were an Islandian!"

"Would it make a difference? It might have once, but it doesn't now."

"Then there is something wrong with me!"

She sprang to her feet and put her hands on my shoulders and shook me.

"Don't say that!" she cried. "Don't you dare!"

She was weeping and I held her unresisting, closer and closer to me.

"Yes!" she said, "there is something wrong with you and wrong with me, and it is not our fault. We are both perfectly true people but we haven't got *ania*. Somehow we can't have it with all our differences!"

Her head dropped forward, her forehead on my shoulder. Her hair was against my cheek; her hands moved over my arms, and I held her to me with all my force, crushed but resilient.

"You are the strangest being that ever was," she said in a muffled voice.

A voice had been calling my name from somewhere far off, "Lang! Oh, Lang!" breaking the wings of our dream.

Nattana raised her head.

"Ettera is calling you," she said in a dazed voice.

The sound came from the landing.

"Lang, are you there? Don has come. Don wants to see you."

We had let each other go. Now she seized my arms with small strong hands.

"What does he want of you?" she cried.

"I don't know definitely," I said.

"But you won't go away, or anything like that?"

"No, Nattana."

"Go to him," she said suddenly, pushing me away. "Talk to him; but don't commit yourself to anything without good thought. Promise me!"

"No, Nattana."

"He has no right—but go to him. He is waiting."

She was standing in the center of the room watching me with wide eyes. The cloth on which she had been sewing was a brown heap upon the floor.

Don's coming was a cold wind. He was waiting in the living room with two other men, and though they were large he was taller and wider, and yet seemed spare in his close-fitting ulster.

They named themselves: "brother" Gronan, Samer "nephew."

He explained the reason for his coming. The storm had ceased; the new snow made skiing possible in places formerly bare; there would be a few days of fine weather. Would I come with him to a pass and down the other side a little way?

"Can you tell me what you need me for?" I asked. "Before I go with you I want to know."

His answer was brief. Ever since the garrisons were withdrawn he and others had patrolled the passes to the north. He needed more men, for it was not unlikely that German vigilance would be relaxed and that when spring came there would be raids by the Mountain Bants. There were signs of preparation among them. For his band he selected men with as few ties as possible, whose work was least needed at home. At present there was little danger, but later the danger might be great. This expedition was to accustom Gronan, Samer, and Lang, if he would come, to mountain-climbing, and to familiarize them with the lay of the land. We would leave as soon as I was ready and climb for a few hours to a hut in order to make an early start next morning. We would be gone three nights and days.

"Will you come?" asked Don. "Will you try three days with us?"

"I will come," I answered.

"We will go as soon as you are ready."

Ettera entered with candles, for it was becoming dark.

"Lang goes with us," said Don in his high voice, and her face winced.

I ran up the stairs again to dress, to pack my knapsack, and to say good-bye to Nattana.

She had lit candles and the brown cloth was in her lap again. At the moment I entered her hands moved suddenly with the needle as though she did not want to be caught in idleness.

"What did he want?" she asked without looking up. I repeated what Don had said, and her hands were busy as though it were ordinary news.

"What did you say to him?"

"I said I would go."

"Had you thought about it before?"

"Yes, Nattana."

"And my not marrying you?"

"It makes no difference. I love your country . . . And there is another reason. It is you yourself. I have never forgotten what you told me about raids when I visited you at the Lower Farm and we rode across the valley . . . Don is inspiring, Nattana. I want to follow him . . . And of what use am I here or at home? As an American I am no one. I am not an Islandian. This is a chance. . . ."

She thrust her needle into her sewing with a deliberate purposefulness that silenced me, and laid the cloth on the table. Then she rose and stood before me, her hands behind her.

Her eyes were fixed on mine and her breast was rising and falling.

"Don't say such things!" she cried in a high strange voice. "Don't say you are no use! Don't! Don't!"

I caught her, thrusting my arms under her own and around her. She hung back inertly and her eyes were wide and astonished. I drew her against me, and she yielded so simply and came so close that it was as though she gave herself and were mine.

"We must not keep Don waiting. Can't I help you in getting ready to go?"

"You can help me . . ." but I still held her.

"You are wonderful, Nattana."

"And you are dear to me, Johnlang."

I kissed her and her lips met mine, and there was rushing fire and peace.

"You make me happy, Nattana."

"I am happy too. I don't know why. But you must go."

"My Nattana . . ."

"I love your lips and your clear eyes."

"I love your hair."

"You must go," she said, and she pressed against me and clung to me. "You must go."

She strained away and I released her. Instantly she became practical, hurrying to my room, neatly packing my bag, while I changed to the heavier clothes that I had worn crossing the Mount Islandia Pass.

"While you are gone," she said, as she moved about the little room, "I shall work hard on your things. You will need them more than ever. Some will be ready for you to try when you come back."

"In only three days, Nattana. It won't be long."

"Not very—and I shan't worry about you."

She helped me on with my knapsack, and then we faced each other.

"Good-bye, Nattana. You were always lovely and kind. Now you are more." I took her hand, strong, firm, yet trembling.

613

Our two hands drew us together and we kissed each other. From the landing I looked back at Nattana, who was standing at the head of the stairs.

"You said you would not marry me, but it does not matter, for you seem to be mine."

She leaned toward me with an outward gesture of her hands, of giving, of withdrawal.

"I am," she answered, ". . . oh, I think I am."

With Don in the lead, Gronan, Samer, and I, Lang, shuffled our skis in the darkness through powdery, new-fallen snow. The wind had lulled, and it was not cold. Our direction, Samer told me, was to the north toward the broken peaks that lay east of Doringclorn in the direction of the Lor Pass. We ascended through pastures with here and there a slight change to left or right, meaningless in the dark. We came suddenly upon fences and found gates. Overhead, stars appeared but were quickly lost in a scudding mist. There was no moon.

Time passed in leaps rather than as a flowing stream. Nattana's kisses on my lips and her body against mine remained like an armor to make me strong. At the farm supper was probably over and she was washing dishes in the kitchen with her sister. What were they saying? What was she thinking, my new-found one, who gave me such happiness?

We came to dark forests and followed a trail so narrow that the branches brushed against us. I walked easily as one walks in a dream. Two or three hours had gone by and it was between eight and nine as time is reckoned at home. Don now and then uttered his name, lest we lose each other in the darkness. Our names passed down the line like a roll call at school, no two voices alike: "Don! Gronan! Samer! Lang!"

My legs ached with the strain of sliding my skis uphill, checking their backward slip before the pegs caught. I was tired and not myself, transported too suddenly into an existence where for the first time I faced the unknown, an actual enemy lurking in wait, hatred in his heart.

In another hour we reached a hut in the forest, one of many scattered among the mountains. Of these some were very old, built from time to time by soldiers who guarded the passes. Since the withdrawal of the garrisons they were maintained and supplied by private persons, among them Don and his patrols.

It was large enough for eight men. Three bunks were placed in tiers on each side; these, a fireplace, a woodpile, a chest of supplies, and an armory were its only furnishings. A warm fire was soon blazing, and all of us except Don retired to the bunks to be out of his and each other's way. He who was our leader was also by his own choice the cook. His hot meat soup and melted snow with red wine were our supper.

Silence fell upon us. No one of these men were truly friends, but our common cause united us with bonds as close. Emotions of interest and mutual loyalty stirred in the tones of their voices and in the impulses of my heart.

Gronan, who was tired, fell asleep. Samer hummed a little while and then was still. Don sat before the fire. I was alone to think of Nattana again, and longing for her I, too, fell asleep. . . .

Much later I woke. Don was still sitting on the floor, his large black head bent forward between his knees; but he was not asleep. A long-fingered, strong hand went out to a log and tossed it deftly into the fireplace. There was a shower of sparks. Then he resumed his brooding. . . .

He may not have slept at all. Next morning before daylight he awakened us.

Stars powdered the sky over us when we left the hut but light was beginning in the east. Following the course of a frozen stream we ascended to the upper edge of timber, and by this time the snow was pink and the sun just rising.

Then began timeless hours of climbing steep snow slopes with axes and ropes from the armory in the hut, of rocky ledges, of a great snow field several miles across and almost level, and of a scramble upward through boulders and treacherous ice. There was no time to think of anything except what we were doing, no wish but to learn the ways of mountaineering and to remember the structure and contours of a region where later some of us would always be.

All morning Doringclorn hung over us to the west, a complex mass rather than a peak, with high black ledges and white snow fields sharp against a deep-blue sky. Northeast of Doringclorn and still to the west of us was a lower sharper peak and between the two was the gleam of a vast white field seemingly level, hanging over the Doring Valley and feeding a glacier. East of this second peak was the hidden Vaba Pass toward which we were going.

Facing inward as we climbed we saw the view to the south only in glimpses. We were high above the valley, the lake a small round pond. On the further side was Mount Islandia from base to summit; and peak stood behind peak in diminishing perspective to east and southwest.

At the head of a talus slope of icy boulders we came to cliffs that seemed vertical and that were overhung with snow, but there was a way by ledges and chimneys with artificial aids here and there. To an expert it was an easy ascent; to all of us but Don it stirred that dizzy fearfulness that dares not think; but sooner or later we all had to learn to make it alone. Up we went, Don watching every movement, quick to direct us and to steady us with the rope. The final twenty feet almost stole the last of my courage, and then when least expected, we hauled ourselves upon a snow field that sloped downward into a ravine running to the north. We had reached the highest point of the Vaba Pass. If the boundary line followed the height of land, as the Germans said it did, we were in German or Karain territory, and the ravine before us led directly to the region of our enemies.

We made a short run on skis, which would ordinarily have been the easiest, but now, to us with knees weak from fatigue and nervous strain, was painful and seemed dangerous.

At the entrance to the ravine, on a shelf above the snow field, which here merged into a small glacier, was a hut so blended with the rocks and whiteness that I had not seen it.

"No more today," said Don. We, the newcomers to this region, were glad to rest, to eat a little, and to sleep, while he built and tended the fire.

"This wood," he had remarked, pointing to the north with a smile, "comes from down there."

In spite of his statement that the day's climbing was over, late in the afternoon we went on skis down the glacier, which was deep in snow and fairly safe and wound along the ravine like a river. At the end of two miles it overhung a steep descent, and we left it for the rocks on the right-hand side.

The Sobo Steppes were at our feet, free of snow, a shimmering pale-yellow plain, far, far below us, but extending to a horizon that was uplifted. Immediately beneath us but higher than the plain which they seemed to overhang were dark forests; and upon their outer edge, just visible beyond the bastion of the mountain to the west, were white dots. This was the Mountain Bant town of Fisiji ten miles away. Our enemies were there and supposedly our friends, a few German police, to keep them in order.

Don described the duties of the patrol when spring came. There was a station a little higher up than where we were from which the ascent to the pass could be watched. From sunrise well on into the day a lookout must be on duty watching Fisiji. The Bants would not climb at night, but at dawn they would start. At the first sign of their coming the lookout must give the alarm. With all the speed he could make he must return to the edge of the cliff which we had ascended and light the signal fire visible in the valley at the Dasens' and the Hyths'. Eyes there were trained to watch for it. Then he and his companion—for there would always be two of us at the hut—would act according to the size of the Bant party. If small we were to wait in chosen places that he would show us later and fire upon them. If large we would light two fires and descend to an appointed rendezvous near the hut in the forest. Four men would be assigned to the Vaba Pass, and as soon as the snows began to melt in five or six weeks our duties would begin. Each man would spend six days at the pass and then would have six of relief. Every third day the guards would be changed. The fourth man of our patrol was one of the Ekklys at the Hyths'. Of our six days at the hut three would be spent as lookout and three as caretaker, cook, and forager. The man who came as relief would bring new supplies of food, but fuel we must get for ourselves. The nearest place was the forests at our feet, and this was the most dangerous duty of all.

We returned to the hut. We were on the other side and had seen our enemies' town. Nothing was between us and them except winter. That night I dreamed uneasy dreams when all was threatened and insecure, and I climbed impossible places always pursued and in danger of ambush; but their character changed, a sense of fearlessness and mastery and of confidence in Don took their place; and then this, too, changed to an incredible, tangible, lovely thing not out of my reach, and I woke from a happy dream of Nattana in which I heard her

617

voice and saw her vividly. It was no longer day after tomorrow that I would see her again but tomorrow.

Don was a good leader with whom there was always a sense of accomplishment. By nightfall we knew the pass as well as we could know it under snow, having visited the places of the signal fires, the lookout station, and various points of vantage on the slopes above the glacier where we could lie in wait for the Mountain Bants, sheltered, but with a way of retreat open to us higher up into the mountains. And for me there had been a real adventure.

In the middle of the afternoon, when our exploration was over, he said that wood was needed and looked at all of us.

"Lang is the quickest," he said. "Lang and I will go."

I learned the ways of fear, at first stultifying to heart and strength and then becoming a tension hard to endure, but absorbing and quickening every sense. How great the danger was he did not say. Part may have been imagination, but some was real, evident in his watchfulness and the care with which he moved. On skis we descended from the pass and from the glacier toward the northeast, pausing every little while to look around us. It seemed far and long, for our retreat to safety was upward. Finally we came to a shallow ravine which we descended to the edge of timber at seven thousand feet, acres of trees half-dead and dying, gnarled old conifers of a variety not growing on the Islandian side. With a hatchet and straps Don made two piles of faggots, setting me to watch the broken but quite open slopes below us. There were many places where it would be easy to imagine a dark head.

On the long tiresome climb back again with shoulders galled by the weight of logs I was carrying, it seemed that I had perhaps made more ado about nothing than it deserved. He was still watchful but less so than formerly. While the Bants, he said, delighted in taking a shot at an Islandian trespassing on their side, they would never do so when there was danger of detection; furthermore, none lived in these woods and except when on raiding parties none would spend the night in them; at this hour, when dark was coming quickly the few that were hunters, armed, and to be feared, were already far away in the forest bound homeward to their town.

That evening, the third spent together in the mountains, united by our common task, we were closer friends than we had been—Don, Samer, Gronan, Lang—and there was much to plan and to talk about.

My enlistment with the others was no longer tentative. I included myself and was included as one of the watchers of the Vaba Pass. As a consequence I needed a permanent dwelling place. The Upper Farm would become more truly my home than even the Fains'. Until I left Islandia I might have to remain on duty, all projects for travel put aside, six days in the mountains and six at the farm working with Ek and Atta. It was a great and unexpected change.

We lay in our bunks. The night was cold. In six weeks our vigils would begin. The wood that I had helped to gather lay piled on the hearth, and I took pride in seeing it there and was ready to repeat the risk of going down into Karain territory to fetch more. Fear, like a fickle love, came and went. Men not afraid of snow could easily reach us from the enemy side. The descent to the Doring Valley also had its perils. Would I ever climb with as little nervousness as Don had . . . ? But that night fear did not trouble me. Nattana would approve of my joining Don's forces, though the fact that I had done so had a definite bearing on our future which she could not fail to see, for it established me for a long time in the house where she was. I could no longer cut the Gordian knot of our problems by going away.

There could be no more drifting and trying to be friends. Two paths lay open. One was of words, argument, and persuasion to induce her to marry me—likely to be vain and resulting in an intolerable situation between us if she persisted in refusing. The other was the path of daring and action—to take her if she would have me and to seek to win her permanently once we were lovers. She might not have me—but I could try again. She might refuse to be won. It would be a deathly defeat . . . But I would have had Nattana.

Don was in no mood to let us go any sooner than he had promised. There followed a long, impatient, trying day. He gave us instruction in the route to the top of the pass from the Doring Valley side. We spent hours upon the rocky slopes under his watchful eye, becoming familiar with every ledge and hand- and foothold. And when at noon it seemed that we were homeward bound, we stopped at the hut where we had spent the first night and replenished the woodpile and put in order the equipment that we had used. Only then, and having agreed to be on call and given our addresses (Lang at the Hyths' Upper Farm), were we free.

He left us, our pace being too slow, and we followed, again delayed, for Gronan was a tired man and held us back. It was suppertime when, weary myself, I said good-bye to the other two and shuffled on skis up to the stone-flagged porch of the farmhouse—a dark shell enclosing the dreaded and painful, yet peace-giving loveliness and fire of Nattana.

I entered. The dining room was lighted with candles and the table half-set, but she was not there. I took a light and went quietly up to my room to leave my things. It seemed a most ordinary homecoming, and I was tempted to let decisions slide and to drift again.

Then I heard her voice calling:

"Johnlang, have you come back?"

I answered and her footsteps sounded, running up the stairs.

"Are you all right?" she cried. "You aren't hurt, are you?" And she burst into the room without knocking, out of breath, and stood just inside the door.

"I am well, Nattana—not hurt at all."

Seeing her again, strong and proud, I knew that she was not one who could ever be taken solely as the result of any man's will; rather must she give herself because she wished it. I loved her because she was herself, so glad to see her that it hurt my eyes.

"I came from the kitchen to finish setting the table. I saw snow on the hall floor. I knew it was you . . . Are you sure you are all right?"

"Quite sure."

"I am glad you have come back."

"Nattana!"

I went to her, but she flattened herself on the door as though to escape me.

"You said you would not marry me, Nattana. Take it back."

Her eyes did not flinch, but her face became obstinate and sullen. She shook her head.

"You must take it back."

"No! Never!"

I laughed, and her eyes widened. Then she also smiled. I put my arms upon her shoulders and kissed her, and realized only then how starved I had been and how much I desired and needed her.

"You are mine, Nattana."

"Let me go," she answered. "I don't want Ettera worried."

"You are mine!"

"Must I say it?"

"No—not now, but later you must."

I stepped back so that she could go.

"If you are quick," she said, "you will have time to get ready for supper."

They gave me time enough to shave and bathe, and I was freshened, strengthened, and relaxed. At supper I told of our experiences including the trip with Don to fetch wood. The others asked many questions, but Nattana merely watched and listened. The ordinary household work continued. After supper she went with her sister to wash the dishes, and Ek and Atta and I made up the fire in the living room.

The older brother said the necessary word.

"You will be at the pass off and on until next winter's snow. That will keep you at our house, I am glad to say."

"So am I," Atta added.

Ek looked into the fire.

"You will also help us to make Nattana contented," he said after a pause.

How much of our relationship had he guessed? He was my real host, and his wishes had great importance.

"I have asked her to marry me and she will not," I said.

"That is your affair and hers," he remarked in his slow way. "Maybe she will change her mind. If she does, you will take her to your country, I suppose?"

"I should have to take her with me, for I can't live in Islandia."

"You will have to work it all out together, you and she. We won't interfere."

"No," said Atta, "but look out for Ettera."

The two brothers gazed into the fire.

"Don't make each other suffer if you can help it," Ek said at last, "but I shan't advise you about anything."

There was no more to say. He had left me troubled but free.

"When I am not on duty at the pass," I said, "I will do all I can here."

He seemed embarrassed.

"Oh, of course," he muttered, "but that writing of yours—don't let that go by."

Atta asked how we had arranged the watches at the pass. He

criticized the schedule that Don had proposed, not approving of the combination of Samer as lookout and Gronan as cook and forager. Both were too slow. . . .

Ettera and Nattana entered and sat down near the fire. It was nearing bedtime. When could I speak to Nattana?

Ettera had questions to ask, and then conversation lagged.

"Lang is tired out," she said suddenly. "We must not keep him up."

Nattana's eyes were upon me and they seemed to reproach me, shifting away the moment that mine met them.

"I *am* tired," I said rising, and I went to each one and said good night, Nattana last, waiting until she looked up. Her eyes expressed nothing, the whites showing under the green irises.

I went up to her workshop, closed the door, and opened a little way the one leading into her bedroom. Then placing my candle on the table, I sat down to wait. I must see Nattana alone and tell her what was in my heart. The sickening unpleasantness of having to scheme was merely a surface matter. Desire was a deep river, which I could no longer resist even had I wished to do so. The river must carry her away, also.

I was afraid that I must wait a long time enduring the suffocation in my heart, but soon voices sounded from the stairs and then died away; Nattana as usual was going to her own room through that of Ettera. A moment later there came through the door which I had left ajar the sound of the farther door opening, then of her voice cheerfully saying good night to her sister, and at last, to my infinite relief, of that door closing. She was in her bedroom alone. Soon she would discover me. I watched her door.

She was humming, but there was a sudden silence. Then her footsteps came nearer. Her head appeared in the doorway and instantly withdrew. The door, held on the other side, seemed about to close, then opened wide, and she came quickly and quietly into the workshop, shutting it softly behind her before she faced me, her hand at her throat.

"Johnlang, what do you want?"

"I want to talk to you, Nattana. Come over here."

She hesitated and then moved toward me. I made room for her on the bench. Still reluctant, she sat down.

"What is it?" she said.

"I ask you again to marry me."

"No," she answered curtly. "And it is for your sake as well as mine."

"I shan't stop asking you, Nattana. Remember that!"

I sat down at her side, and took her hand.

"Poor Johnlang!"

I waited, gathering strength; and she also was waiting for me to speak. The candle on the table burned with a motionless flame. It was quiet, and yet the deep river carried us both upon it.

The words that I must say would be irrevocable, changing all things, but if I did not utter them my life would be sterile with cowardice forever.

"You are mine, Nattana, even though you say you won't marry me."

After a second's pause she answered in a low voice.

"Yes . . . I seem to be."

Strength came slowly and then like a great wave. Turning to her, I embraced her.

"I don't care whether it is *ania* or *apia*. I want you. You are mine —for always. I will make you marry me."

"You want me?" she said, and she was trembling. "I want you."

I kissed her in breathless torture. Our teeth clicked together and we were clinging to each other.

"Be mine, Nattana." The words were said.

She drew back her head.

"You can have me," she answered.

It was too simple to believe.

"We must have each other, Nattana. This can't go on."

"No, not with you here—and you can't leave now."

"I didn't have this in mind when I agreed to join Don."

"I did. I saw it all."

To quiet her trembling I held her more and more closely, but it was hard to say the definite thing.

"I was so afraid you would not come back, Johnlang. I knew I would have to give myself to you, if you did . . . and if you asked me."

I held her with all my strength.

"But it won't make me marry you," she said suddenly. "Don't think it will! I value you too much!"

623

"I shall not give up hope."

"Oh, you must, Johnlang."

"Never! You are mine!" But she was only half mine and it was hard to bear . . . "I want all of you, Nattana."

"You can try to persuade me," she said softly. "But don't hope."

"I shall always hope."

We seemed separate again. I was tempted to let her go, but my arms held her in spite of myself . . . Was this desire?

"We are afraid, aren't we?" she said in a low voice.

"It is not merely fear, Nattana."

"Nothing will happen. We won't have a child. We don't want one. I know what to do."

"It is more than that, Nattana. . . ."

She quivered and her voice was sharp and high.

"Johnlang, don't make what we are doing wrong!"

Only one thing could be said.

"I want you. Come with me, Nattana."

She hesitated, putting her hands to her face.

"If you think it wrong . . ." she cried.

"Come with me!"

She strained away, trying to look in my eyes.

"I will come," she said, "but you must go first and let me join you."

I released her, and thus took an irrevocable step.

The door of my room opened without a sound. She came with her candle, barefooted, wrapped in her cloak. Without a word or any hesitation she closed the door and placed the candle on the table. Swiftly she unfolded herself. Her bare arm went out to the candle and the light gleamed upon her body.

We lay in the darkness, warm under the blankets, with kisses, which we knew, to comfort us, but only slowly daring each to come closer to the strangeness of the other. She was slender and little and simple. We clung to each other and she wept and did not know the reason. We found that we were happy and that it was natural to be together.

Desire, forgotten in the new wonder that we had discovered, came like an intruder. We faced it together and she trembled and wept, but was steadier than I. For her honest shamelessness and her pluck I adored her.

What we did was suddenly simple. A mystery that had long harassed our imaginations ceased to be. In its place came another one, utterly deep, never to be solved. We were one, united in unbelievable natural intimacy, and we were still separate, loving each other with a love that held within itself all the happiness and longings we had ever known. We descended into soundless depths never to be forgotten but never to be remembered with the mind. There we blended together in pain.

We came slowly to the surface again, but to a new life, a new world. We lay dazed and wondering.

There was nothing that could be said, but she was mine forever after such a giving and taking. I held her close, willing that she know this truth.

She spoke first. She must leave before Ettera was up. Sooner or later Ettera would guess . . . but not yet . . . It was early still. We had long hours, we could sleep; but we must wake in time. We must!

The weariness of days in the snowy mountains weighed upon me like lead. There were decisions to make, problems, troubles, but they were in the distance, for now at last she was truly mine. She could not escape me. I told her so, and went to sleep holding her.

Coming out of depths of sleep, soundless, dark, and empty of dreams, thinking myself alone, I found her still with me, more familiar now and better known, but more burningly sweet when thus discovered again with no thoughts in my mind at all. She had been awake a little while, she said, her voice confused and drowsy. She clung to me, whispering that she wanted me. Her desire matched mine, and the fact that her need and her response equaled my own was a new but natural miracle. . . .

She lay as though I had slain her.

"You will marry me now, Nattana."

She did not deny it. She could not answer me. I slept again, sure that I would never lose her.

There was a pale light in the room. Her stirring had waked me. She was sitting up brushing her disheveled ruddy hair from her eyes.

"I must go," she said in a startled voice.

It was agony to be without her. I embraced her and held her, my head against her soft, full breasts.

"We are married, Nattana. We must tell them."

She looked down into my eyes, her face softened, full of love, not pretty, but utterly dear.

"No, Johnlang," she said gently, and tears ran down her cheeks.

"Yes, Nattana! It must be."

"No—but we can be happy together now."

Would we be happy? There came a sudden doubt. She saw it in my eyes, and her face winced and grew old.

"I am not good enough for you—or else I am too wise! Let me go, Johnlang."

Slowly I released her, but could not take my eyes from her face. She slid from the bed and in the pallor of early morning her body was white and less slender. She had her cloak around her before I was aware that I was losing her.

"Nattana, we must live together always."

"Don't make me feel wicked, Johnlang! Oh, I am yours as long as you are here. You know that, don't you?"

"I shan't give up hope," I said, but hopelessness had begun. It was unbearable, until I realized that I would be with her for many long months.

"You had better give up hope soon," she said. "We will be happier."

Hope unreasonably returned.

"We are happy, Nattana."

"Oh Johnlang!"

She came to the bed and I held her and kissed her.

27

Hytha Nattana

WINTER BROKE EARLY. On September 7th, eight days after the return from the Vaba Pass, Don stopped at the house to tell us that it might be necessary to establish the watch within two or three weeks. In season the day corresponded to March 10th at home. Everywhere the snow was melting and diminishing. The portals of the Doring River often lifted their sheer rocky walls above a soft white mist. There had been but one crisp, cold, winter day when Nattana and I, on our half holiday, could skate under the cliffs on the southern shores of the lake—skate and daringly be lovers.

Work continued serenely. Nothing had happened to Ek, Atta, and Ettera and they were just the same; and though Nattana and I had changed the nature of our lives, we also lived as we had lived before, she weaving in her workshop and I acting as handy man or else laboring with the two brothers upon the new stable. Sometimes when I thought of the step that this woman and I had taken, it seemed unbelievable—as significant and incomprehensible an event as birth or death itself—and that whatever plans we made as to our future we were truly united and married; but at other times—and more and more so as the days passed and our relationship became less of a shock and more familiar—it seemed an ordinary and natural fact that I, a man, should have found a woman whom I could love and have; that mine was merely the experience of nearly all men, and that my life and my nature were really not changed at all. Nor did the new relationship prevent us from having the same blind misunderstandings. Close as we came, we could be just as far apart. In my heart I had expected that we would never be troubled and puzzled by each other again.

On the day after Don's visit I took my lunch to the barn with Ek and Atta to work with them all day at building the walls of the stables. In the task of laying the stones three pairs of hands were useful—one to spread the mortar, one to place the stone, and one to work the little derrick that they used. And I wanted to be away from the house all day and not see Nattana, and to accustom myself to the amazing facts that she and I, who had often misunderstood each other but never angrily, had almost quarreled and had certainly lost our tempers, and that last night, for a trivial reason, she had not come to me.

It was a misty thawing day, the air full of chilly damp. Brown, bare ground already appeared in the fields west of the barn, and in the roads mud was mingled with the snow. This spot was likely to become better known to me than any other in Islandia . . . I wished that I were free to travel again, taking Nattana with me to a place where we need not be secret in our love. But it would be eight months before I could leave and then I would have to go without her, unless, as seemed unlikely now, she found that she could not live without me.

She had told me that she thought Ettera was suspicious.

"She came to my room after I had gone to you last night," she had said. "She asked me this morning where I was. I said I had gone down to the kitchen. Luckily she did not hunt for me. I don't know whether she believes me or not. We have got to be careful."

I answered what she had asked me not to say any more.

"If we were married, Nattana, we would not have to be furtive."

"If you are ashamed, Johnlang, I'm not!"

"I am not ashamed, but it is all wrong."

She resented angrily my last words, which I intended to apply not to our relationship but to the deceit we practiced.

"If you think it wrong, I don't have to come."

I tried to explain.

"You do think it wrong," she had said. "You are ashamed—of me and of yourself. I am only trying to make things easier for Ettera as long as possible. It will hurt her. She is like you!"

She would not listen.

"Well," she had said in the end, "tonight I am not coming to your room!"

It seemed useless to tell her that I wanted her. Dimly I was glad that I was to be alone, but I hated to have her assert a right not to come to me.

Atta was in charge of the mortar, which he spread deftly. He had become a humorist with a tendency to be ribald. Ek superintended the placing of the squared blocks of stone, a task requiring skill, in which he was wholly absorbed. My job was to stand by the derrick and to hoist, to hold, or to lower away as signaled. I wore no coat for my work was vigorous enough to keep me warm, and though there were waits they were brief ones. Nattana's lover was a laborer, and a laborer I felt myself to be most of the time. My hands were coarsened by handling ropes and stone. The John Lang who had written so fluently was another man, for my mind also seemed dimmed and less perceptive.

The day passed like other days, and yet it was not like them. The happiness and the miracle still existed to astonish and gladden me, but they no longer filled me to the exclusion of other thoughts. Before this day the only pain was impatience—quickly cured. She loved me so much that fear that I would lose her was no great worry. But now there had come a sense of grief. Why did we quarrel? Why did my thoughts wander beyond Nattana and leave her behind . . . ?

The three laborers returned to the farmhouse.

Unless the quarrel still rankled in Nattana's heart and she wished to punish me further, I knew how she would greet me: with a nod and flick of her eyes. When we were together in the presence of others, she was so perfectly the mistress of herself and so much at home that it was hard to believe that she was willing to give herself to me and that she had been mine; but in ways deeper than those of the mind I knew it was true.

The laborers were tired and hungry and their feet were heavy on the kitchen floor. Ettera, whom I dreaded because I was doing what she regarded as wrong, was busy at the fire and did not turn. The brothers went to their room. I entered the dining room on the way to mine. Nattana was setting the table and at the sight of her my breath stopped. I loved her.

She ran to me and caught my hand.

"I have been thinking of you all day," she said.

"And I of you."

Our voices broke. She raised my hand to her lips, but the honor was too great and I caught her arms.

"Ettera may come!" she said in a quick low voice. My hands dropped . . . It was no longer hard to say, but my heart beat in my throat.

"Come tonight, Nattana!"

"Of course! But you must hurry now, for we are nearly ready with supper."

Happiness had returned and with it impatience.

Nattana was slow in coming, but at last she stepped noiselessly through the door.

She slipped off her cloak and cried my name, but in tones of nervousness and excitement and not of love, standing before me unconscious of her nakedness. I knew her body well, all of it. It had no mystery now and was the more desirable.

"Ettera would not speak at lunch," she said. "I have been alone all day, thinking. I could not work! I was tempted to come out to the barn to talk to you, to say I was sorry."

"I'm sorry too."

"We both are! If Ettera doesn't definitely know, at least she suspects. I know what you are thinking, but, oh, don't say it again."

"I won't say it. Come!"

She obeyed and slipped into bed. I kissed her and held her close, but she was restive, and she said:

"I know you are thinking that we quarreled because we are hiding from the others what we are and that it is a strain upon us—"

"It is, Nattana! I wish we could go away from them."

"So do I, but we can't, and if we could, where would we go?"

"Nattana, let me say it. It is the solution."

"Why can't you be contented with what you have, Johnlang?"

"Are you, Nattana?"

She was silent for a moment, thinking, and I hoped she would give me peace from words, but suddenly her voice was answering.

"No, I am not contented, Johnlang, though I ought to be. But to pledge myself to you for always would only make it worse."

"Be contented," I said. "Why do you bother?"

I tried with caresses to make her lose herself, but she lay inert.

"Oh, I had doubts, Johnlang, and I was afraid it would not be perfect, but all the time I was sure inside that it would be."

"And it is not perfect, Nattana?"

She was in my arms, and the burning flame of present desire darkened all other light.

"No, it is not perfect for me," she said, heedless of my wish and of my need, and I half hated her. "But it is not your fault that it is not perfect, dear Johnlang. You have done all you can to make it so."

"It is perfect," I said. "This is perfect." And I kissed her. Desire could not be resisted.

"You want me?" she said in a changed, surprised voice, and she gave herself.

Perfection was in my grasp, but just when I held it, it eluded me. I possessed her and it was a pleasure and a relief, and that was all.

But it overcame her and captured her, and she clung to me weeping and seemed broken.

The grief which I thought lost returned. Love was merely a drunkenness in which all values were blurred. For a little while it drowned grief in sensation. I held her warmly lest, clinging to me and weeping, she would think I did not love her.

Then came Nattana's low, broken voice.

"My dear, my own Johnlang, my beloved one, it is perfect to have you want me and take me, as perfect as anything I will ever know."

I kissed her mouth, but it twisted away, saying:

"But why, why am I not contented?"

At her suggestion we remained apart for several days. Work went on and was dully absorbing. Nattana and I met in the evenings and spent one afternoon in her workshop saying all the intimate things about ourselves that only a man and a woman who have been lovers can say to each other and we both learned much. We found in each other a new and tender understanding based upon pity as well as love, and we were careful not to bring up again the matters that had troubled us. It was easier because we were letting each other alone and because her condition was unfamiliar.

The thaw continued. Above the mists from melting snow the high mountains sometimes showed themselves and were still pure and white, though there were places that were snowy one day and black the next. Sometimes we saw the slipping of avalanches and heard their distant roar. In the valley the ground was a patchwork of brown earth and decaying snow. The roads were deep and soft with mud. Nevertheless the carrier came through, mainly to examine the condition of the Mora Pass, but also to bring letters. The Fains had evidently assumed that my visit at the Hyths' was to be a long one and had forwarded my mail with greetings of their own.

There were letters from home and from Uncle Joseph, reluctantly acquiescing in my resignation of the consulship, deploring that it had to be, hinting that more information would be acceptable, and asking what I was going to do now. They blew upon embers that were to me long since dead, but they made real again the life that later I must lead. A day would come when Islandia would be but an episode. I must cling to it the more intensely now that it was still mine, lest it dissolve in this breath from the outer world that threatened it; for while reading these letters I momentarily saw with Nattana's eyes. Philip and Mother, Uncle Joseph, Father, and Alice were all consciously or unconsciously trying to entangle me in the life that I had abandoned; and if I brought home with me a little of Islandia in the person of Nattana, they would seek to catch her in the net of their ways. Though I still wanted to marry her and not to lose her and her country, I found myself suddenly half on her side in refusing me.

The John Lang who had lived until a few weeks ago was vague and romantic, hoping for impossible perfections. I was he no longer. Life was more bitterly flavored and more commonplace than he had ever dreamed. The having of a woman for my own had merely solved a physical mystery and made desire a familiar fact; the task of daily living was no less complicated and no more happy.

But there was another letter, from another woman, a much younger one. It was from Gladys Hunter and written in haste, for her mother was ill and needed much care and they were not going abroad as planned; but in spite of the hurried handwriting the letter was satisfactory, for she kept the ball of our correspondence traveling back and forth, interested in and responsive to what I wrote her and adding of her own what I was glad to know and wished to answer. Nor was it the letter of a child as her first ones seemed. I read it with a little shrinking, for would her letters continue if she were aware of what I had done . . . ? Though not knowing her well at all, I guessed that, though she would wonder, she would accept me simply for what I manifested myself to her, and having promised would write to me as before.

Next day after breakfast, when Nattana and Ettera were washing dishes in the kitchen and the two brothers and I were about to go to work at the barn, I found Nattana's eyes dwelling upon me with a persistence that made it impossible to leave her without a word. Therefore, saying that I had forgotten something and looking at her meaningly, I started back for my room. I went slowly and she overtook me in the hall.

"Have you forgotten something too, Nattana?"

"No," she answered. "Have you?"

I shook my head. Our eyes met and we understood each other. She trembled as I held her and she kissed me violently. After a little time she said:

"Do you want me again?"

With a twinge of hesitation, I answered:

"Oh yes, Nattana."

"I will come to your room tonight, for I need you, Johnlang."

All reluctance was blurred in an impatient happiness, and the blue of the sky was deepened as though I had drunk wine.

We intended to work all day, but in the afternoon Ettera called us and we returned. In the living room was Amring, one of the dependents at the Lower Farm, spattered with mud and telling the two sisters of his journey.

He had come on business connected with the transfer of cattle later in the spring and would confer with Ek and Atta at length. Therefore the day's work was over.

Just as the rest of us were about to withdraw he produced a packet of letters. Ettera divided them. There were several for her and her two brothers from their relatives, and one for me in Dorn's handwriting, sent to the Lower Farm on the chance that I was there.

Nattana stood expectant until the last one was delivered.

"None for you, Nattana," said Ettera with cruel cheerfulness. Her sister's shoulders twitched, and without looking at anyone she returned to her workshop.

I sat down to read Dorn's letter.

It began with political news. The diplomatic colony was breaking up without having come to any accord or having presented any proposals with regard to the internationalization of Ferrin. Count von Bibberbach, however, was to remain for a few months longer. Negotiations were continuing with regard to disputed matters. Lord Dorn was seriously considering the re-establishment of garrisons on the frontier whether he could agree with the count or not.

Here was news that affected me deeply. If soldiers took over the duty of watching the passes, it was the end of Don's patrols and I would be free. I felt an electrical sensation of gladness, not because the news promised relief from something I feared—for I still hoped and wished to render the service and to undergo the danger—but because I might no longer have to live indefinitely at the Upper Farm.

Nattana, upstairs in her workshop, must be told this news.

I read on: Nekka had taken over the housekeeping from Faina. She was one of them now. He had been very happy. . . .

At the first word of the next paragraph my heart quickened:

> Dorna has been staying at the Western Palace and I have seen her several times and she has visited the Island. She is very well and I believe that she holds her life firmly in her own hands. She is going to have a child in March and wishes you to be told. . . .

Her marriage had a sudden, wicked significance and I realized its completeness. All that Nattana had experienced with me, she had experienced with young Tor, but Dorna was also to have a child.

I read on.

> Soon after the roads can be easily traveled and the Mora Pass is open, she is going to the Frays where she will remain until her child is born. In this she is imitating Queen Alwina. She will go by the Hyths' Upper Farm and may spend a night. If you are still there she will be glad to see you.

The life I had been leading received a subtle jar changing a little, but definitely, all its values. And tonight Nattana was coming to me again. I wished that this letter had arrived a day later. But it contained news that should not be withheld from her.

Going up to the workshop I gave her the letter. She was sitting near the window sewing on the clothes that she was making for me, her knees crossed and her foot pointed out.

"Shall I read it?"

"Of course."

I sat down and watched her. She read slowly and in silence, her pretty profile against the light. It seemed older, stronger, a little set, but it was truly lovely. One hand went up to her throat and idly dropped again.

Her head turned and she looked at me intently but with no expression on her face. I knew that she had come to the statement that the garrisons might be re-established. I waited, but she said nothing and resumed reading again . . . Her expression seemed to have changed. Her profile was remote, and it was her own—independent, strong, enchanting.

She folded the letter, her lips placid, and held it out to me.

"Thank you," she said.

I rose and took it, answering:

"I thought you might be interested."

Her eyes lifted suddenly.

"Didn't you think more than that, Johnlang?"

How could I tell her what had been in my mind? I could not lie, but the truth was not clear enough to utter. The simplest, truest thing was present love, and this she must know.

"Doesn't it change things?" she persisted. "What Lord Dorn seriously considers he does."

"Whether things are changed or not is for you and me to decide. I know that you never seemed to me dearer or more desirable."

She winced as though hurt, and her bosom rose and fell.

I leaned down and kissed her, and because she was sitting I dropped to my knees and embraced her.

"You still want me?" she said. "I seem to want you more and more." Her hands slid over my face and she trembled . . . "Johnlang, if the soldiers come back to the passes, there will be no work for you. Will you go away?"

"I don't know," I answered, telling the truth, and adding, "but if I do you must come with me."

"Oh no, my dear Johnlang. It is clearer than ever that I cannot marry and go to your country with you."

She took my face between her hands and her expression was angry and loving and strong.

"Don't you think so too?" she demanded.

"Nattana," I answered. "I have had letters from my family disapproving of my resigning the consulship and wanting to know what I plan to do. They have reminded me very clearly of what life at home will be for me and would be for you. We don't wholly disagree, my Nattana! I can't see you as happy there, but even so you want to marry me a little."

Her lips became a thin line and her face hardened with pain.

"I knew this would come," she cried, "and now I wish it had not!"

I held her with all my strength, and after a few moments she relaxed and held me with her close, strong arms. . . .

"We still want each other, Nattana!"

"I will go with you now if you ask me."

Rising I caught her hands, but she hesitated and resisted, half laughing, half crying, until I was mad with desire for her, and picked her up.

Dusk was beginning. Our clothes lay scattered about my room. We were violent and shameless lovers.

The light was mournful and somber. She lay quiet in my arms and we had together for a little while a heavy peace, all desire drained from us. . . .

"It isn't the same, is it?" she whispered.

"It is for me," I said, but her words showed that she did not believe me.

"We were happy and untroubled at first, and now I want to be possessed more than I did but I am always sorry."

In her honesty she described what I felt also.

"Do all lovers feel this way?" she said vaguely.

"Perhaps it is merely the sadness of the evening, Nattana."

"I have loved being yours," she whispered.

Looking up at the ceiling I resolved to try once more to make her marry me. It would be the last attempt, but a hard one for her to resist. . . .

"Well," she said, "the day isn't over and I suppose we have got to get up and finish it."

The room was not large enough for us both to dress at once. She should be first. As always she was quite unconscious of her body. I watched her and knew it well and it did not seem either beautiful or attractive.

My feeling for her, once a unity, was split in two. One part, desire, waxed and waned and now was troubled and sick; the other part, stronger than friendship, a deep heartbreaking affection, grew from day to day and was never so great as now, but desire for her did not color it. It would continue though I wanted another.

When later I went downstairs Amring, Ek, and Atta were still talking in the living room. Nattana who was setting the table called.

"Ettera wants to speak to you," she said, making a wry face.

In the kitchen Ettera faced me with averted eyes and I was afraid of her.

"Don was here to see you," she said sharply, and her mouth twisted painfully and grew hard and she continued with contempt. "But I would not disturb you and Nattana for anything on earth. So I lied and said you had gone for a walk. He has been over on the other side close to their town—in great danger. He thinks they are preparing an expedition. The watches are going to begin tomorrow and he wants you to be ready early. I said that you would be. Was I right?"

"Of course you were."

"I thought you might be unwilling to leave here."

"Thank you, Ettera."

We looked at each other both angry, but with affection not wholly lacking.

After supper I went with the brothers and Amring into the living room, but heard nothing that they said. A little later, with violently beating heart, I returned to the dining room. It was a long time before Nattana came in, bringing a pile of washed plates. Her smile was gentle and gave me courage. When her hands were free I went to her and took one of them.

"Come!" I said, but was unable to go on. She resisted.

"Come where? What is it?"

"We will be married your way. We will go in and tell them."

Her hand became limp, and I thought I had won her, but suddenly she snatched it away.

"To take me by surprise like that! Oh, Johnlang!" Her fists were clenched and her face was like that of a small child about to cry. Then her eyes filled with tears. . . .

"I beg your pardon," I said.

She turned and went from me and I heard her feet running up the stairs and the banging of a door.

There was no place to go but the living room. Returning I smiled and took a seat in a corner near the fire, praying that no one would speak to me. . . . I had tried to make Nattana marry me and I had failed. I would not try again. Nor would I be a coward. I would face her refusal and accept it as a fact in my life. Another might have her. That fact also must I accept.

Amring wanted to know of pass-watching. I told him all about it, and it was a comfort to go over the situation, realizing that others were with me and in the same danger, and that Don was our leader.

An hour passed. The way that Ek and Atta and later Ettera, who had come in, spoke of Don's patrol and of its members, not praising but valuing us, was enheartening.

"Nattana is calling you," said the older brother, who seemed then my dearest friend. I had not heard her voice.

She met me at the top of the stairs, outlined against the light, young, graceful—my darling.

"I have been crying," she said, "and could not go downstairs with red eyes. . . . It can't be like this between us."

"No, Nattana, we care for each other much too much."

We went into the workshop closing the door and sat down together on the bench.

"I was trying to sew," she said, pointing to a pile of cloth on the chair and table. "I will have everything finished for you when you come back."

We were silent, and I held her hand. It seemed enough.

"Shall we talk it all over?" she asked gently. "Or would you rather wait till you come back?"

"We will talk," I answered, "but first I want you to know that I am very happy with you now."

"So am I."

"I am not going to ask you to marry me again, Nattana."

Her hand tightened.

"I don't expect it of you," she said with a sigh.

We were silent again and then I kissed her. The air seemed clearer, but the fact that she and I would eventually separate was like a wound that is quiet for a time and then hurts savagely.

"What do you expect of me now?" she asked, putting her other hand on mine. "Tell me what you want."

I squeezed her hand.

"Don't be afraid to tell me," she said. "Why should we be ashamed of our *apias?*"

"You are very desirable to me, Nattana. And I want to know you are my friend always and to be with you often holding your hand, or not holding your hand—just with you—talking to you, telling you things. . . ."

"You can have all that," she answered. "It is what I want, I think. . . . But only while you are living at this house, Johnlang."

"Why 'only while I am living at this house,' Nattana? Why not while I am in Islandia?"

She was silent.

"I don't really know. I think it is better. Everything is not clear yet."

"Nattana, when I go away what will you do?"

"Live here."

"You may marry."

It was better to clutch the sharp iron than let it cut me of itself.

"I may, but probably not."

"Why, Nattana?"

"Because an *apia,* and a strong one like ours that goes all the way, burns out a woman's ability to have a stronger, better feeling. She gives herself too completely. She can't again."

"Nattana, what have I done to you?"

"You have made a woman of me. You have proved that many things that were only theories to me are true. . . . I don't think I can ever feel for another man as I have for you, and I shan't marry unless I am quite sure."

"You say it has only been *apia.* It need never have been only that. It did not begin as *apia,* not with me."

"It is *apia* all the same—with both of us."

"Not with me, Nattana. . . ." Yet as I spoke *apia* became real as an emotion that men felt.

"You never once said 'Nattana, give me a child,' and if you had I would have been frightened to death. To you, I was all of 'me' there was. You didn't see anything beyond—just me, and somehow you and me managing to live. That was enough for you, because—because you are American! Forgive me! But you would grow tired of just Nattana's body and her friendship. And I would become tired of just Johnlang. You are dearer to me than anything else has ever been. Don't forget that! But I am an Islandian and if I am to marry I must have my *alia*, too."

"You are the dearest one I have ever known," I cried.

"That is not true," she said gently.

She was right.

"But I won't make you admit it," she added. "Just tell me I am dear now. That is enough."

I told her she was dear and I kissed her.

We were silent and when we talked again it was of the pass, and of my duties, and of the extent of the danger. She gave me assurance, showing concern but not alarm.

I could not bear to be separated from her for a moment, and she said she would sleep with me, and I was strengthened by having her. Waking in the night I put out my hands and found her and was at peace again.

Early in the morning I rose and dressed. Nattana was with me to the last minute, and when I departed in the damp mist, her kisses were on my lips.

We carried heavy packs of provisions, Don, Samer, and I, who would be gone for a week. The valley was hushed and full of shadow; the sun low and behind gray clouds. Under our feet the ground was rutted and frozen, but with a surface skim of mud. We followed the road that led along the lake past the house of the Dasens' and then turned upward into the mountains.

We plodded in silence, soon warm, for the air was not cold. At times every enterprise, even the most important ones, seems footless. This was like being dragged out of bed by some dominant, hopeful person to go on a tedious picnic to which one had foolishly committed oneself, and for which the weather was utterly unfavorable. There was, of course, danger. It lay like a cold little stone in a corner of my heart, but I was still wrapped in memories of Nattana. Men all the world over went forth to duty or work or upon dangerous enterprises from the arms of their beloved ones. Hers were heavy upon my senses. Our passionless but intimate night of sleep together had been sweet beyond believing. . . .

Rifts came in the dark vapors above the valley, but as yet there was no blue sky—only the bright sunlit whiteness of other clouds beyond.

The night had been a little wearisome, a little cloying . . . There was a need of freshness. The mountains, and days spent there, would give it, but I would always be grateful to Nattana. It would be hard to let her go, but I could. . . .

Later, when all the ice was out of the ground, the way to the pass would not be so toilsome, for the road from the lake had been built by soldiers and was basically good. Then when I went on duty I would leave the Upper Farm on horseback late in the afternoon and would reach the hut in the evening. As soon as it was light next morning I would climb the pass. The man I relieved would descend and ride my horse down into the valley reaching his home in midmorning. We would soon fall into a regular routine. But today, when there was not enough snow for skiing in the foothills and the roads were bad and the higher slopes were still icy, it was nearly noon before we reached the lower hut and evening before we were settled at the upper one above the glacier. Here it was still winter.

Don remained with us to inaugurate the watch next day, and his presence seemed to make us safe.

At sunrise the first lookout was posted. It was September 17th. Don and Samer left in the darkness with a lantern. The air was still and bitterly cold. I remained behind. They had taken guns and one was left in the hut where I could reach it quickly. The cold stone of fear was larger in my heart.

But the man whose duty it was to take care of the hut, to cook, and to forage for wood had the busier if less responsible task. He must inspect the material for the signal fires at least twice a day, and more often when it was stormy; he must make certain that it would catch fire surely and quickly; prepare breakfast and dinner; keep the hut fire going with wood split and ready; look after the hut; watch at intervals for signal fires in the valley indicating the recall of the watch or else warning us of danger; carry lunch to the lookout; and, most dangerous duty of all, descend on the Karain Valley in the late afternoon to the place where I had gone and return with wood. There was enough to keep me busy in the morning and it was better not to sit and brood, for the trip which I must later make, this time alone, was haunting.

In the middle of the morning Don returned. He was on his way to organize a similar watch at the Lor Pass thirty miles to the eastward.

Already I had spoken to him of Dorna's journey and he had said that he would arrange to have her movements known and followed, and that on the day when she passed the watches would be doubled. Now, before he left the hut, he repeated what he had said, adding:

"They at Fisiji may not know that she is to pass so near to them, and yet they may. There is no telling how they find out such things. It might come to them through the Germans, who would learn it from one of us. Some fool might send word to the German police to watch the mountain men."

His sharp bright eyes fixed mine.

"They gain merit with their gods," he said, "when they capture one of us, especially when the captured one is a woman. They would be sure of a happy afterlife if they captured our queen. Would you give up your days of leave when Dorna goes by?"

The answer was instant and inevitable. I might miss seeing her but it was unimportant.

"I am going now," he said, rising. "It is unlikely that they will come yet a while, and not unlikely that they won't come at all, but do everything as though you expected them at any moment. Be watchful when you go for wood and leave as few traces as you can. If you see one of them without a German with him, shoot quick unless he runs from you. I have warned them. I left a letter on the door of their temple ten days ago. They know me. *Kana.*"

His farewell word was 'Peace.' Was it meant as a grim joke? He stirred us all, and his presence remained palpable behind him, although his going took safety from us.

It was a relief to know that Samer was still near but hard to wait to go to him with his lunch.

At last I went down the canyon with food for us both in my knapsack, with hatchet, straps for the faggots, gun, rope, and ice ax. Don had marked with piles of stones a trail that lay now on and now along the snow fields and glacier . . . I wanted to run.

Samer was as glad to see me as I him, and neither of us concealed our feelings. Without Don we were frightened. The responsibility was too great, and the fact that it was not *likely* that the Bants would come made the burden no less.

On the Karain side, below the heights of the mountains, the snow had wholly gone. We looked down upon another season and climate. It was high spring upon the far plain of the Sobo Steppes, a deep emerald carpet beginning at a dizzy depth beneath and extending and lifting to the horizon; and the forest, on the edge of which stood the white dots of Fisiji Town, was no longer a wintry blue-gray but was here and there fresh with new light-green.

The important hours had passed and it was more than improbable that there would be any raid today, but we still watched the approaches to the pass, talking of our duties, of Don . . . And Samer told of Don's raids on Fisiji and Fupù to the east. Once or twice a year he went into these towns and left a message. It was not done out of bravado, but because such daring acts inspired the Bants with fear, and their success made him seem supernatural to them. It was said, though Samer did not vouch for the truth, that once a Bant hunter had shot at Don. The man was never seen again, but his gun broken and twisted was found nailed to the temple wall covered with blood.

Samer told me other stories as gruesome.

At last time came for me to go down for wood.

"I will keep my eyes open and shoot if I see anything," said he, but added, "I don't envy you."

"It will be your turn tomorrow," I answered.

"Good luck," he called after me.

I had come back; I was safe. Samer was refuge and security. I was breathless with fear and fatigue, and thanked God that I would not have to go through it all again for forty-eight hours. The loneliness, the upper silence, the hostility of every stone and tree had been a horrible nightmare. . . .

The danger was supposed to be over for the day. We returned to the hut, but the darkness gathered behind us and we wanted to run from it, for there was no physical barrier between us and them, only frail human reasoning.

Next morning, while it was still night, I set out for the lookout station. Samer had prepared hot food; it was his day at the hut. The light of the lantern jumped ahead, picking out the little heaps of stones one by one. The cold made me numb. But it was easier to walk toward danger in the dark than to have it at one's back. And daylight was beginning when I mounted to the station, carefully extinguishing the lantern at the last turn. The dark abyss of the Karain country lay at my feet. It was too black to see anything, too cold to stand still.

I walked and swung my arms . . . But there was freshness in the pure cold air, and magnificence in the coming of the sun. The snow peaks, a hard white against a dark-blue sky of stars, became tinted with rose. I thought of Dorna. It was she whom I really eternally loved. . . .

Streaks of yellow light stole upon the plain between long, cool, dark shadows. The rocks near at hand emerged from the night. I began the watch.

Sunlight came upon my back and was warm. My eyes saw well. No one, coming to the pass, but would be seen a long way off. The task of being lookout was not footless after all. Every moment that I was there I rendered a service to all those who were behind me. No stillness had ever been so great, no view as spacious. Danger merely added to its fascinating wonder. Oh, the glories mine to see! I thanked Don again and again for trusting me and for putting me to use.

But it seemed a whole lifetime from youth to age before Samer came—a sign that the morning was over and the dangerous hours past.

We were becoming friendly and were on the brink of the personal with regard to other matters than our immediate present and its reactions upon us. Here at the pass there were many opportunities to talk. In the valley below he was not a man whom I would have chosen for intimacy. A little older than I, he had a hard confidence and conceit in himself. His words slowly edged around to women. He told stories, not quite those of smoking cars at home but inspired by the same feeling—futile attempts at vicarious satisfaction of promiscuous desires . . . Why did I have to endure this sort of thing? It almost seemed that the step I had taken was subconsciously known to this man—the same had been true of Atta—and they treated me as one with them. And I was a different man, for the stories had an insidious meaning that I had not known before.

Perhaps he was merely diverting his mind from dread of his journey for wood. I knew his fear. I also knew the vague teasing need that inspired the stories of men and girls; but I wanted peace in which to watch and to see and to feel freshness free of taint.

That night, by telling myself that if I were to be murdered I would be murdered whether we kept a lookout at the hut or not, and that I had twice made the trip for wood and Samer once and Don many times without any harm, I slept as soundly as at home except for dreams in which I endlessly searched empty rocky slopes.

Samer had gone to the station. Inspection was made and chores done, and I had an hour to myself. Having brought a few sheets of paper with me I began a letter to Gladys Hunter, expressing regrets over her mother's illness, thanking her for the satisfactoriness of all she had written me, and telling her of my present occupation. As I wrote she became real and her image more attractive—Nattana had changed a little my feelings for all women . . . There was a great deal to say to Gladys, so much that I could do no more than state mere facts, leaving her to guess their color. How different were our lives at this moment! And yet through our letters the two streams of living, hers and mine, were unbroken in our absence. I thanked her for keeping hers continuous in my sight, and felt it a duty and privilege to show her mine; and to be honest with her I described Hytha Nattana and said that we were good friends and that I was very fond of her.

It was the fourth day and I was on watch again. Samer had cooked the breakfast. He would be relieved that morning by Gronan who would bring me my lunch.

It was misty and bitterly cold. We were to use our judgment as to weather; if it were so bad that we could not safely remain at the station or else such as to make it highly improbable that anyone could gain the pass, we were at liberty to leave the post until conditions changed. I used mine and stuck to my post and suffered acutely from cold, and was dull and numb when Gronan, looking old and wan, finally came. He was the senior of all of us, even Don, and was less able to stand the hardships than we were. I had liked him from the beginning.

It was obvious that the trip for fuel would try him greatly, nor had he ever made the journey before and the way was obscured. I went for him—and warmed myself by doing so—and fear was much less troublesome in the mist.

We also became friends though reticent ones, and that evening I continued my letter while he rested in his bunk.

"To a girl in the United States," I explained.

"Are they as fine as ours?" he said.

"This one is, I think, but she is little more than a child."

A day at the hut followed and then another on watch. Life at the pass had become familiar and had endured so long that it seemed almost natural; but the cold stone of fear never left my heart, weighing upon all my thoughts, palpable in all my dreams.

Returning with Gronan after the watch was over I knew that my term of duty was over. Early next morning young Ekkly would arrive to take my place, and I would go back to Nattana. Impatience made the night's sleep broken.

Not long after sunrise Ekkly came with a load on his back, ready to take my place. He was about twenty-five, slender but strong, familiar with the mountains, and our second in command. He had fine brown eyes rather far apart, was outwardly simple and friendly, but also reserved. He had come on horseback, he said, the horse was at the lower hut, and I could ride him down again.

For the first time I descended the steep ledges below the pass without a rope and alone. Familiarity made it easier than expected, but my mountain technique was improving also. Once I would have been terrified, but now I was cheerful, and the thought of Nattana helped me down.

In the week during which I had been away, spring had begun in the valley. The trail and road down to the lake, though muddy and slippery, were passable for Ekkly's horse. As we descended the snow under the trees changed from a sheet to patches, steadily becoming smaller and less frequent. There was a mist of green buds in the forest depths and the air was from moment to moment warmer. The lake was still frozen but the ice was pitted and covered with pools. I saw birds flying and on a sunny bank green weeds newly growing and flowers like harebells.

To make it almost too much to bear Nattana rode out to meet me. The road was edged on both sides with bushes, the buds of which were swelling sheaths of green. Leftward lay the lake, and expanses of water upon the ice bore mother-of-pearl reflections of clouds and blue sky. And Nattana was riding toward me upon Fak, whose sturdy legs splashed in the mud. She was lovely, she was mine, her bright hair red and gold, bareheaded, her dress white and green.

She waved her hand, laughing.

"Hello, soldier!" she cried.

I must wait before I could kiss and hold her—a new and sharp impatience.

We rode together toward the farm.

"Oh, I am glad to see you!" I said, watching her and nothing else. Every part of her burned with teasing fire, her mouth, her white hands, her bare knees. "You look like spring itself, Nattana. You are too lovely."

"It is spring," she cried. "The days are longer than the nights. I am glad I am lovely."

"I have been away a long time."

"And you are all right? You weren't shot at? You did not freeze anything?"

"I am very much all right."

"I knew you would be. I had no worries. Nothing has happened here . . . except . . . I told them all about us."

It was a shock. They would now be hard to face.

"And Ettera said that she knew it all along, and that she would have felt very differently if we had not tried to hide it."

"And Ek?" I asked.

"He seemed surprised, and he told me to be sure of myself before I married you. I told him that you had wanted marriage, but there was no question of it . . . And Atta—he made a joke!" Her voice was angry, but suddenly she laughed.

We rode toward the stables, the house on our left. The brown of the fields was free of snow and already showed hints of green. The two brothers, without their coats, were working on the new wing, the walls of which were perceptibly higher. They waved their hands, shouted, and turned back to their labor.

"They miss your hands," said Nattana. "You have helped us so much."

We dismounted and I moved to her.

"Wait till we have stabled the horses," she said. She was demure, and seemed needlessly deliberate, showing no sign of emotion, and all the while I trembled.

"I will care for you," she said to Fak, "even if he doesn't want to," and she patted Rolan, young Ekkly's horse.

I caught her arm and drew her away, and embraced her, kissing

647

her mouth and cheeks and eyes, and my hands moved over her. The wonder of her was all new, and her desirableness was agony.

"Come, soldier," she said. "We will go to the house."

She retained my hand as we crossed the open space between it and the barn.

"Ettera is probably watching us," she remarked lightly, "but it does not matter now . . ." But it did matter. . . .

"Why do you call me 'soldier'?" I asked. She laughed.

"You seem like one. You are one, aren't you?"

There was more behind it . . . Another thought intruded.

"If they know, the news will spread," I said.

"Not far."

"Your father will learn of it."

"Oh, yes, *he* will. Ettera will tell him—and I shan't have to do so myself."

"Is that why you told her?"

"The main reason was that later it will be easier to live without a secret, but Father was another reason . . . It simplifies things. Where do you want to go now?"

I led her upstairs to my room and closed the door.

"I want you," I said.

"I thought you did."

"You are mine!"

"You can have me," she answered, with no apparent feeling.

In no way did she resist me, but she checked my great impatience with common sense too cool. At last I held her and possessed her, but she was merely submissive, too inert to be really mine. Her body was given, no more.

It was over and I was a different being, but what had I had? A sensation and relief from an obsessing desire and, as a result, a heavy physical peace that darkened my mind but could not wholly blur a feeling of misery and self-betrayal. Some might call such a thing an act of love, but I could not. Was it even *apia?*

And she who had been so sure of herself became aware of what had happened and spoke as though in explanation.

"I am glad to give this to you," she said. "You seemed to need me. It makes me quite happy."

"But you? You?" I cried.

"I . . . ? What about me?"

"It was nothing to you."

"It was what you wanted. Isn't that enough? I can't help what I feel."

Anger flickered in her voice.

"It is enough." I lied to end words, for a quarrel now would be shame unbearable. She drew a deep breath and stirred and I gladly gave her body its freedom, but she did not go from me and we lay side by side.

"I could desire," she said after a long time, patiently and regretfully, "and desire just as much as I have, but it does not seem to be naturally 'me' any more . . . Oh, Johnlang, I do still wish to give myself when you want me."

"Thank you, Nattana."

She moaned sharply.

"You aren't satisfied!" she cried.

Unmeeting Wishes in this most intimate moment of all! I wanted the unison of love and not a mere act of sexual sensation and relief solely my own. Her heart must take part even though her body could not. I, a man, must betray passion if I possessed her, but she a woman could be cold and withhold hers.

"You aren't satisfied," she said passionately, "even though you have done *this* to me!"

"I am satisfied, Nattana."

We lay silent for some time, quiet, and far apart, and then suddenly she said that it was lunchtime and she must go.

Ek, Atta, and Ettera were full of interest in my experiences at the pass. Nattana was very quiet, dodging my eyes, looking as though I had wronged her.

I offered to help the two brothers, but they were taking a half holiday. There was, however, always wood to be chopped. I would work until my feelings were cool and then I would go to Nattana. I knew that the initiative in settling this trouble must be mine. As I worked steadily becoming more and more serene, Ettera appeared and stood in the door. I waited for her to speak.

"Spring really seems to have come," she said. "I would like to get away for a few days."

"Can't you go?"

"Who would cook?"

"Nattana or one of the Ekklys."

"Where would I go?"

"To the Lower Farm."

She looked at me shrewdly.

"These are exciting days," she said, "with the young men going to the pass and rumors of raids—and Dorna coming."

"Is there any later news in the last seven days?"

"Oh, no," she said with a sigh, and after a moment she remarked, "You would get along better, Lang, if you used the other hatchet . . ." Then she withdrew.

She had come to tell me that we were still friends . . . It was not such a bad world, but the hurt existing between Nattana and me must be cured.

The door to the workshop was closed, but in the hall was a smell, slightly acrid but not unpleasant, a little like that of quince-jelly-making at home. Hot from work, I took a bath, made myself as neat and presentable as possible, and knocked on the door.

"Come in!" she called in a high voice. I entered, and she said cheerfully, "Oh, it is you!"

Half the battle was over.

The room was in disorder. The dye kettle was bubbling on the fire, sending forth a thin steam. The smell was much stronger, but was still vegetable and not unpleasant. Nattana's hair was disheveled, her great apron much stained, her fingers brown as with iodine, and there was a smear on her cheek.

"It is a critical moment," she said. "If you don't mind I'll go on." She waved her brown fingers toward the bench where there were a few inches of space in which to sit, and went to the kettle and leaned over it. I watched her with a catch in my heart.

"I am afraid it is too dark!" she said impatiently, "and it can't be made lighter. You will have to remain the nice color you now are, Johnlang, and not get pale again as you were when you lived at The City."

"What are you doing, Nattana?"

"This is for your shirts."

"Are you going to make me shirts, too?"

"Yes, and stockings and everything except shoes."

"Nattana, you mustn't give me so much of your work and time."

"It is the greatest pleasure I have. Let me fit you out, Johnlang!

. . . I have been afraid to tell you I was going on with shirts and things."

"You are too kind! You give me too much. There is nothing I give you."

"Think, Johnlang . . . But does it matter? It makes me happy fitting you out with clothes."

"Nattana," I said, "it is really too much, but I am not going to stop you. I need everything you are making."

"You do."

"But I will give you something some day."

"You are doing so . . . There will be brown shirts and green ones and I have a lovely buff dye . . . But please don't talk to me for a while . . ."

She was busy over the kettle testing the color on strips of cloth. After a little while she was satisfied with the mixture.

"You can help me," she said. And for some time we were quietly busy. One by one I handed her hanks of thread which she dipped. Her face was relaxed and yet absorbed, and she seemed unconscious of me except as an assistant. Yet the work she was doing was for me . . . And I wondered whether a man was not always conscious of the sex and attractiveness of a woman he cared for, while she, though caring no less, became unaware of his for long periods of time when something else was on her mind. . . .

The hanks were all dipped and were drying upon a rack. Nattana poured off the remainder of the dye and began to scour her kettle, talking her thoughts aloud as she did so: the color seemed too light now instead of too dark . . . it was always that way . . . one never knew . . . except once in a while. . . .

At last she sighed and straightened and took off her apron, and began to put the room in order.

"There! That's done," she cried with relief.

It seemed unfair and unkind to trouble her, but unless I did so falsity would occur again.

"Nattana," I said, "you did not really want me this morning."

She stopped abruptly and faced me.

"I was glad to have you possess me," she answered.

"Aren't we in danger of Unmeeting Wishes again, Nattana?"

Her face was scarlet and my heart beat faster.

"But you did want to possess me, Johnlang!" she cried angrily.

"Yes, but is that enough?"

Nattana turned suddenly and went to the window. She seemed to be trembling, but her voice was calm.

"I know it is not enough, not with you. It might be with some men . . . But you want more of me than I want to give."

This was an announcement of a death and the pain of loss was sharp and deep.

"Why don't you want to give your whole self any more, Nattana?"

"It doesn't seem to be me."

"What do you mean? You must tell me."

"*Apia* is not me. Is it you? I don't think it is, Johnlang. We have had to learn it. You have been away, and I have been thinking all the time. I have been thinking of other men, of what you and I have done, of what it would be like with them—of Larnel, if you must know." She stopped, confused, and I felt a stab of jealousy and rose to my feet. She backed away.

"And you!" she continued. "You had that letter from Dorn about Dorna. I watched your face. You wondered how it would have been with her. Forgive me for saying this . . . We must be honest!"

I remembered Gladys and the talks with Samer.

"I thought of someone else, too," I said.

Her eyes flashed.

"Now I am angry! Isn't it funny? It is as though I pulled a string and you jumped and you pulled one and I jumped—like toys. That is what *apia* does to one, Johnlang. And I have more reason to be—oh—doubtful than you have, for you felt more strongly for Dorna than I ever did for anyone. I knew that a disappointed *ania* breeds an *apia*. That was my chance!"

She was telling me unexpected things.

"I have been curious about you from the beginning," she continued. "You did not kiss me, you know, and I knew it was not because you disliked me. Most men here, even though they had all kinds of scruples, would at least have kissed me, oh playfully perhaps, so that I would not have been ashamed of myself—as I was. I asked myself what kind of a man is this who is so scrupulous that he is not even polite?"

"Nattana, what are we going to do now?"

"I know what I am going to do, and this last week has taught me. I have been afraid for myself—thinking of other men like that. And it must be the same with you, for you are like me. We have learned exactly what it means to our senses to do what we have done. You will want just women, John, and I just men. That is an evil path to follow and I won't follow it. So I worked hard and did not think about that thing at all with you or with anyone. And when you came back, something in the way you looked at me, the way your hands touched me, then I knew you had gone through what I had and like a soldier wanted just a woman—any pretty woman, not especially me . . . Isn't that true?"

"I only thought of you."

"I knew you would be thinking of me . . . Only, I was not going to respond to you just because you were a man and I had been wanting a man. Yet all the time you were dearer to me than you ever had been. I knew how hard a time you were having up at the pass, and why you went there. I wanted to give myself. I have met you halfway, Johnlang! . . . This morning I did want to give myself. Oh, do you understand?"

"I understand. I care for you more than I ever did, but something is dead in you, Nattana."

"Did it ever really live?"

I bit my lip.

"Something is dead in me, too," I said.

She uttered a cry, and then a hard, short laugh.

"I was right, wasn't I?"

"About what?"

"It has been only *apia.*"

"Something still lives," I cried. "It has lived in me and still is the same, and it is *love.*" I used the English word.

"*Love,*" she said in a strange, gentle accent. "All right—it was and still is *love.*"

After a while she said in a different voice, "Now that spring has come you and I must take some long walks. We will find happiness." She paused. "It is all perfectly clear to me now: you and I are not persons who really wish to be sensual without *ania.*"

There was silence.

"Are you miserable, Johnlang? I'm not. I think I like you better."

"I am not miserable, but I wonder how it is going to seem never to have you again, Nattana."

"Let's not make any stupid rules about that, my dear. If while you are here you ever want me so much that you think it better for yourself to have me than to refrain, ask me to come to you and I will come gladly."

"Will you do the same if you think it better for yourself, Nattana?"

"Yes, we will make it mutual . . . And I may come, but I don't promise."

"I will understand."

"Of course, you will. We always do." She lifted her face. "Kiss me," she said.

She was right and she was wise. Instead of being constantly aware of an imposed restraint, I was free to find out what sort of man I was and what I really wanted in this life, immediately or later.

Days slipped by. Work continued on the new building, and Ek and Atta were just the same, the former absorbed and thoughtful, the latter jocular. They made no secret of the knowledge they had but they offered no advice, accepting it as a fact; and only mentioning it indirectly as when Ek suggested that as soon as the weather became warmer Nattana and I might like to move out of our little rooms and sleep in the boathouse.

It came near the twenty-eighth, when I would return to duty again. On the day before, Nattana and I took a half holiday and walked in the mud along the road south of the lake and leading eventually to the Mora Pass. We talked of our futures in different countries, agreeing that we would always be friends and would write to each other now and then. Under a flaming sunset we walked home in a spirit of exaltation and utter misery; and I gave her to another man for whom she would have *ania,* and she expressed the hope that I would find a woman in my own country whom I would wish to marry and really love and who would marry me. The walk had all the feeling of an eternal parting.

But that night when I was almost asleep she entered my room.

"I wanted you," she said, "and I have come."

I saw her white body again and I took her in my arms.

"We must not think about anything," she whispered. "Ask me no questions and I won't ask you any. And let's not talk."

Our passion seemed greater than ever and was equal. We were wiser in the ways of love and less restrained. The old hopes and longings revived. It seemed I could not live without her, but I said nothing. I possessed her—and it seemed so no longer, but we said nothing.

Suddenly she kissed me and slipped away, and I wondered whether after all she had come because she thought it better for herself or because she thought I wanted her . . . It did not matter. Wounds might be reopened, but next day I would return to the pass. In any case, she had done a simple, lovely thing.

28

Don

FROM WEATHER like April in its bright, showery freshness, I rode
Fak up to the edge of winter again and spent a cold night alone at the
lower hut, where the steep ledges that must be ascended to the pass
hung above my head ominous and dangerous. Six days in the valley
had blunted mountain keenness, and next morning it was a hard
ordeal to climb alone and overbalanced by a heavy pack up these
ledges with only narrow footholds and sheer drops at my feet. At
last, however, I looked up the horizontal V of the last chimney to
the hard blue sky, and soon after stood on the rim of the little snowy
cirque.

Ekkly was waiting, seated on a flat rock that overlooked the valley.

There was no news, he said; Samer was on watch, waiting for me.

He departed promptly and seemed to drop out of sight on his
way down the ledges to relief, rest, and home.

Once at the hut I soon fell into the routine again. In the valley,
life at the pass had seemed but an episode and life at the farm the
real one; but there, within an hour, the Hyths' farm was merely the
place where I spent brief vacations and I was back at the permanent
task of living. Though there was nothing to see but rocks, snow, and
sky, and though the hut was a confining place and cleanliness hard
to maintain, it was nevertheless familiar and not without comfort.
There was the pleasant sensation of something good accomplished,
the tasks were accustomed ones, the view from the station would be
beautiful, and habit would carry me through the dreaded descent for
wood. Only six days, and then relief and vacation and freedom from
danger would come round again.

When I took Samer his lunch he greeted me eagerly and began
complaining of Ekkly's dourness. The latter did his work well, Samer

said; he admired Ekkly and had a high opinion of his abilities and felt safe with him on watch, but you could not get a word out of him about anything but the business on hand.

Samer wanted to talk.

How was everyone at the Hyths'? How was the new wing progressing? What had I done during my absence? And what had ever brought me an American to the Upper Doring Valley? Where had I met the Hyths?

I felt the probe of a personal interest, and knowing his thoughts I dreaded his coming to the subject of women, of Nattana, perhaps.

Men who work together in changing pairs soon develop a strong preference for one companion and a distaste for another. I wished to exchange Samer for Gronan as he wished to exchange Ekkly for me.

Nor that afternoon did it seem that he was particularly watchful as it was his duty to be. It was I who scrutinized the quiet, empty approaches to the pass and the sinister carpet of forest spread beneath, greener than when I had seen it last, a place where anything might lie concealed.

Distaste for Samer's company was so great that it was almost a relief to go down for wood.

The nights were so still, the cold air so clean and fresh! Who would not sleep? It was an escape from Samer also.

The three days with him were long ones, my own morning on watch the quickest moving period of all. I was used to the thrill of fear, and danger seemed unreal. I saw the sun rise and the mists lift, and I wondered at the life of the mountain people whose town lay below to the west—and never one of them I saw! It was hard to feel hostile. . . .

But on the third day when he went to the station I was nervous and fearful, sure that he was careless, and when I took him his lunch, I was tempted to tell him so and only with an effort held my tongue. He was an endless talker; and he drew words out of me in spite of myself, for I could not be deliberately rude and dour like Ekkly. Life would be too unpleasant with this man whom I was doomed to have as companion.

At first his questions and conversations seemed the purposeless ones of a man interested in personalities, but it slowly became apparent that they had a recurring tendency and a progress . . . When was I going back to my country? Had I a girl there, or here, perhaps?

It would be a very different place, wouldn't it? The same sort of women there? Would an Islandian woman like it there? Was it going to be hard to leave Islandia and my friends? I must have made many, and close ones—very close ones maybe, girl friends?

He was clever and for a time merely caused discomfort, but at last I guessed his purpose and was angry and alarmed, and I began to lie. He wanted to find out about my relations with Nattana, and what sort of woman she was, thinking of the days when I would be gone.

Had rumors come to him, or was it my mere presence in the house? If *apia* bred other *apias*, as Nattana said, it was equally true that women who had *apias* were of interest to men like Samer—to all men, perhaps. He made all things cheap, myself, Nattana.

I thanked God when, on the fourth day before sunrise, I said good-bye to him and left for the lookout post and knew that at noon Gronan would join me for lunch.

Time passed. Samer was gone, Gronan even now at the hut. The forest was so far beneath that a gust of wind, changing a little the tone of the green as it bent the tree tops, crawled very slowly. . . .

Why bother about Samer? Why consider him detestable? There was a desire in him and he wanted to know if it could be satisfied in a certain way. The desire was natural and not wrong. And I had had the same feelings and differed from him only in the way I proceeded, quite as ill self-understood.

Gronan's slow and heavy figure came toiling up the rocky path which our feet had already worn. It was good to see him and there was much to tell. We ate our lunches together, and in turn he gave the news from the valley. He had passed by the Hyths' and in ten days or so they would be putting on the roof beams of the new wing. I was tempted to discuss my meditations. Some time perhaps I might.

Next day he was on watch and in the afternoon it was my turn to fetch wood. This would be the eighth time I had made such a journey, and when I set out I realized that I had not been anticipating it with fear.

A haze was spread over the steppes, and their dark color was dim. The forest lay under a slanting sun that roughened its texture. The day had been warm, almost hot. I descended quickly, running past places, now well known, where because only near objects could be seen it was a waste of time to stop and listen and be on guard; but there were other spots, equally familiar, where I always paused, stood still, and looked carefully in definite directions.

I had never seen anything yet.

At last I was near the end, running along the bed of a brook that followed for a hundred yards a shallow ravine. Reason told me to have no fear, because from the height above, a few moments before, all its approaches were visible. It was the return up this ravine that was most disturbing.

There was a shot . . . one . . . and then stillness.

It meant nothing, a mere sound, far off, but I could not move. The sky was as empty and as blue, the rocks the same.

A shot from a gun, but not near.

I had a gun on my back. Carefully I swung it around and cocked it with a loud click.

The ravine was a place of walls and retreat would take me into open places. I went on. I had come for wood.

A single shot, only one, and no sound of a bullet. If I were the mark, there would have been a second shot . . . Had Gronan fired? He was too far above to have been heard so clearly. Was the shot at him? He was out of sight from all this region.

Therefore the shot had been fired by a hunter. The ravine was an echoing place. He might be far away. He had shot but once, perhaps finding his mark—a deer. If so he would be preoccupied with his quarry and with getting home, for it was near twilight.

This was only a guess, but I went on. My suffering journey must not be a vain one.

The ravine ended upon a slope open in every direction. I stopped again and could not move . . . But the paralysis of indecision was more to be feared than danger itself.

A hundred feet below were the skeletons of dead trees, whose shapes and forms I knew well, and beyond began the darkness of the forest. An aisle opened among the trees, but no one was there—nor anywhere. I looked long, and then ran down the slope on tiptoe. As quickly as possible I gathered faggots, not wasting time to stop and stare and become more frightened.

Cold sweat was a queer feeling. The blows of the hatchet were so loud in the stillness that they seemed to hammer upon my brain. I wanted to fire my gun.

I was probably a fool to run such a risk, but perhaps the hunter was as afraid of me as I of him. The hatchet was dull. I swore. . . .

I had reached Gronan again, climbing with such haste that I reached that point of breathlessness where the breath catches and the lungs cannot be relieved; but the load of faggots was no smaller than usual. I lay at full length, recovering as I knew I would in time.

Gronan's face was white.

"One can't be reasonable," he was saying. "My first thought was that the shot was quite far to the west. The air is still and sound carries uphill. But I got to thinking they had shot you. Well, I wanted to leave the post and go down there, but knew that it was not orders. So I stayed here. I thought, 'They have killed our young American.' It was not reasonable, but I wanted to go down and kill someone."

I had never heard him say so much before.

We waited till dark before returning, and it was long before we reached the hut, talking then and during the evening of nothing but the shot. There was no certain explanation; but probably it was some hunter who if aware of us paid no attention. This at least was reasonable.

Gronan cooked the supper, saying:

"You had the worst of it, Lang, and you climbed hard. And you got wood for me one day, so stay in your bunk and leave this to me. . . ."

Later after we had eaten and the light was finally out, the fire smoldering ruddily, Gronan's voice came from his bunk:

"Why did you climb so fast, Lang?"

"I don't know," I answered.

"If you don't mind my saying so, that was not reasonable."

"No, it was not. It was panic!"

"Down in the valley it is natural to be reasonable, but not up here. That is why this sort of thing ought never to be in the world."

There was a long silence.

"Well, good night, Lang."

"Good night, Gronan."

"It is reasonable to sleep, but whether I do is another matter."

But I heard his heavy regular breathing not long afterwards.

As Ekkly had waited for me, so now I waited for him, for my six days were over, and in a few hours I would be riding along the shores of the lake toward the farm. Oh, the pleasure it would be to find it spring and green again, and to smell earth and grass and the water of the lake, and to see what new leaves were out and how far the buildings of the stables had advanced! And hot water and clean clothes, and a lunch at a table seated on a chair!

The lake at the bottom of the valley was like a little pool from this height. The water seemed alive and the ice must be gone. Perhaps Nattana would go upon it with me, and if the boats were not ready for launching we would put them in order and paint them together. . . .

Ekkly's brown head appeared and then another head, glossy black, with a straight white parting. Don had come, and his appearance was ominous of the unforeseen. Both brought heavy packs. He strode up to me.

"Lang," he said, "will you remain?"

There was no question, but I was sick with disappointment.

"A fool thought it wise to ask the Germans to double their care because the queen was going by. Therefore we will double the watches, for they may attempt to steal over by ones and twos. I have seen them."

We watched toward the hut.

"When does she pass?" I asked.

"In five or six days. Will you remain for eight? Then she will be safely over the mountains."

"As long as you wish."

"Gronan will be relieved as usual," he said. "Ekkly and you are the men I want up here. I shall come and go. Ekkly will be leader when I am not here, then you."

I was content with the part I played.

Don remained only a few hours and then left to inspect his post at the Lor Pass; but before he had gone we all knew that he had scouted in the neighborhood of Fisiji again, that the Mountain Bants were certainly preparing for something, and that he had seen a party of them in the snow on the northwest slopes of Doringclorn. The alarming nature of this news I did not at first understand; but that evening Ekkly made it clear: heretofore one could safely assume that the Bants would keep away from ice and snow.

The character of life at the pass changed under his leadership and the new conditions. There had been a certain ease which we now knew no longer; the danger that we sometimes forgot was always with us; instead of the watch arriving at the station just before sunrise it was posted night and day at irregular hours, because the moon was nearing the full, and it usually consisted of two men instead of one; the wood gatherer always went with a guard holding a ready gun; and Ekkly spoke his mind when anything did not suit him. We were, of course, volunteers but he created a real discipline. One hated to be found remiss, and yet because of the impersonal simplicity of his fault-finding bore him no grudge.

Gronan and I for three days, and then Samer and I, alternated as lookout and as houseman. Ekkly spent his mornings on watch, acted as guard for the wood gatherer, and on one day when there was a heavy storm from the north made a daring descent to the lower hut and returned with provisions. He was active and untiring, intent on what he was doing—which was never anything else but watching the Vaba Pass—unruffled by any occurrence, and unsmiling. It was clear why Samer disliked him, but it was not a feeling that I shared, though something in me reserved a right to rebel at any time not prejudicial to our cause. Privates in the army spend hours dreaming of telling the sergeant what they really think of him. Ekkly inspired a little of that same feeling, and I wanted to tell him that he took himself too seriously, but knew quite well that it was the only way to take anything at this time. And he was intelligent, "taking seriously" not our danger so much as our task of being effective watchmen, and keeping our purpose steadily before us.

The days were hard and long. The watch left and returned at all hours. The other man's work was doubled; he was subject to sudden calls to prepare or to carry a meal. The trail from hut to station became one that I could walk in my sleep. Of sleep there was not enough and it was constantly interrupted, and during the day there was no chance to think or to sit down.

Nevertheless twice, when it was my duty to inspect the ready-laid signal fires, I stole a moment and looked down into the Doring Valley. It was the road that we were guarding, leading like a great corridor to the West, its lower reaches barred by the bastion of Doringclorn. Dorna in my mind's eye was a tiny figure, already moving and slowly approaching—a living presence at the bottom of the deep gulf though still several days' journeys away.

She was no less there when the valley was cleanly filled with white mist above which the mountains rose unclouded.

On the second time that I deserted my duties, however, the air was clear and I saw the contracted circle of the lake and looked down upon the minute white dots of the buildings at the Upper Farm. Nattana was perhaps working at her loom—but my present life had dislocated time; what was recent and what long past were confused. Sometimes it seemed that I had come to the pass directly from home and that Islandia was a dream. My mind was blurred by strain and fatigue.

I turned from my idle gazing in haste and did not go again, not wanting Ekkly, whose comings and goings were unexpected, to catch me looking at a view and thinking of a girl.

Fear was like an ache, so long continued that if for a moment it ceased to hurt, the nerves nevertheless felt it still aching. Sometimes I thought that nothing mattered and that I was desperately bored, only to discover in myself a tension increasing almost to panic, urging me to slip over the rim of the cirque hemming me in and to escape.

If Ekkly would only make a joke or at least smile! Once, when Samer told a story, I saw the point of it and would have laughed but for Ekkly's unheeding face . . . Samer was the more human . . . I wanted to talk to him, even of the things which once seemed unmentionable, but there was no opportunity.

To the six days before Don's coming, eight more at least were to be added. Two weeks seems short, but not when time ticks by with every second acutely felt. Nothing would make it move more quickly. Even the beauty of the outlook from the station over the forest and the steppes brought no relief; watching was disciplined and methodical; one walked back and forth, for sitting might bring sleep; and one surveyed certain places before turning in a sort of rhythm, fear always present as companion.

But I followed a train of thought that released me sometimes from tension, fatigue, and fear: in my mind I followed Dorna's journey step by step. She would surely travel by easy stages, for she was with child—the one mystery besides death still unsolved in a stale world . . . For a few minutes before going to sleep and for a second or two now and then during the day I would work out her present where-abouts. On October 5th, the day when Don came, I pictured her as at Bannar; on the sixth, at Manson; on the seventh, somewhere between that town and the town of Hyth; on the eighth, at the Lower Farm, talking with Airda and the younger children. As she came nearer she grew larger. By day I thought of her as on the road. Her cavalcade crawled, for time moved so slowly that I visualized each step of her horse, and sometimes counted them . . . But on the ninth, to follow Dorna became a new burden, for she was now abreast of one of the passes. The valley had narrowed; Doringclorn was northwest, Bronder south. Even now . . . now . . . now the Bants might be surrounding her.

I could not sleep. October 10th was harder yet, for she was drawing near the pass which we were watching. My heart would not leave my throat while I was on lookout duty, staring down at the Karain country—a poor watchman. Had it been my luck to be at the hut, I could have seen—not her for she was too far—but the spot where she might be, and know her safe. . . .

Ekkly, coming up behind me silently, asked in a low voice if I saw anything. I had not known he was near. I believed that in this most critical moment there was at last something to see, but he only spoke to test my alertness. He saw nothing, nor did I, but it was a long time before my nerves were quiet again.

After sunset, when it was quite dark, he said that I should leave the post, but that he was going to stay on watch all night, for it was very clear and the moon, only two days past the full, would soon rise. And would I send Samer to him with something to eat?

Returning up the canyon I thought I saw shadows moving—just as I had thought so many times before.

Don was at the hut with my friend Samer, having arrived at dark and eaten his first meal since the day before.

"I borrowed your horse Fak," he said. "He is a good climber and I was in a hurry to get here. He is at the lower hut."

I was pleased that he felt free to use my property, and was so relieved by his presence that I relaxed, became aware of my exhaustion, and trembled—and almost forgot Ekkly's message.

On hearing it Don told Samer to go, to inform Ekkly that he had come and that he would appear at the station later. Samer took his gun and departed.

Don lay down in a bunk and stretched his long body.

"I was at the Doring Pass last night," he said in a voice already growing vague. "I want to sleep for an hour. Please wake me."

With Don asleep the sense of security vanished. It would be I who guarded him.

He spoke again:

"Lang, I was forgetting. Dorna and her party are safe at the Upper Farm. I joined them on the road. She sent you this." He fumbled in his cloak and handed me a twisted note. Almost before I had taken it his eyes were closed. . . .

Suddenly he said, "The moon!"—but he was asleep.

By the light of the hut candle I read Dorna's message. It seemed it was her voice speaking:

John, my friend:

I thought that I should surely see John at the Upper Farm and I am deeply disappointed. What he is doing frightens me a little, but of course it makes me glad also. I cannot now tell him why. I very much wish to see him soon for my own sake.

DORNA

By Don

During these last days we kept watch at the hut. I went outside with my gun. The moon was just rising over the rocky slopes to the east, and all was black and white, cold, and hard. . . .

As often before, Dorna said a little and suggested much, and I who had been at peace till she spoke was hurt with wondering. There was something she wanted of me. . . .

Time had moved again. Beneath the moon the opposite edge of the cirque, in shadow, was black and hard as iron, but the light on the white snow was bright and soft. Rising I walked away from the hut. The Vaba Pass would never be forgotten, for its beauty lay underneath all else that had been experienced there. To the right the snow field sloped up to a white rim like a sword blade drawn against the sky. Over that edge and down long rocky cliffs, past forests, and a farm, not many miles away, Dorna and Nattana, both, lay safe and asleep. It was near ten or eleven and time to waken Don. I turned to go back.

Beyond the white rim and higher on the mountainside, where there were ledges and rocks, the moon shone brightly. Up there were the signal fires ready to be lit. . . .

A black rock moved and then another. From down the canyon came the distant sound of three rapid shots and then a fourth.

"Don! Don!"

I raised my gun and aimed where the rocks had stirred. At the spot where the signal fires were laid a yellow flash winked. There was a report and then the loud explosion of my own gun.

It was a dream with the reality of death.

Don was at my side. I was aiming again, when another flash winked, and there was a report, and the air above our heads whistled.

I fired and so did Don.

We could not see them, but were ourselves etched upon the snow.

"We must go down!" he said. "We cannot reach the fires."

He ran and I followed. He stopped and knelt and shot at the hillside, leaped to his feet and ran again, and I imitated him. The yellow flashes were nothing, but when the air whistled my head reeled.

It was all quite clear. There was a way of escape that called to me —behind the hut, and up the mountainside, out of range of the flashes, to one of the refuges Don had showed us; but both of us must attempt to make the descent to the valley, one covering the other, for while there was little chance of both of us escaping, there was none for one. We must attempt to escape that way and give warning.

The snow had a springy crust. We ran upward seeking to gain the chimney by which we climbed up and down from the pass.

I knelt and fired. There were flashes on the hillside. Don was running, bending over, lower and lower, and was almost on all fours. He was coughing. I saw him fall.

I ran past the spot where his black head lay in the snow. I thought of nothing except to gain the rim and to go down, for I was the only one.

There were flashes. . . .

I was among the ledges and above me were the narrowing walls of the chimney. There had been a shock and my side was burning.

I could not remember, but a memory that was only half-conscious guided my feet when the shadows were too black to see.

And now it was utterly still again, and I must not spoil my escape and the safety of those in the valley by a fall from too rapid a descent. I must move with steady caution as Don had taught me, and not think of him, for that way lay panic.

They would try to follow me, but I knew the path and they did not. There was a space where looking down from the rim they would see me; it was short. . . .

I was in the open again with room to run in zigzags. Reports sounded high in the air, but there was only a faint whistling.

Now I must run, yet though they were behind me it must not be so fast that I would exhaust my strength, which must be just enough to gain the hut, to saddle my horse Fak, and to ride.

I must fight the panic that urged me to run till I fell.

I had seen death . . . I had shot to kill . . . but I must think nothing, not even of what I was trying to do. My intelligence was a precious thing and its loss was the greatest danger. . . .

What had happened? How long had it been?

The forest closed around me, dark and secret and safe, and the white moon, sailing high, showed the way.

Unless I walked I would faint, and yet my stopped breath was a condition, not a pain; but how strange it was to be walking as though all were well and I had been relieved from duty and were on my way to rest—to walk, to breathe deep, with death behind me.

The hut was a quiet place and dark. In the stable at the side, Fak's body was warm through the blankets that covered him. He moved over in his stall to let me reach his head. I felt it nod, and my knees sagged and I clung to his firm neck.

The stirring of his life made me aware of my own. To lift the saddle was almost beyond my strength, but he was very quiet. . . .

I was in the saddle and could rest.

"Fak, you must go! It is your turn now."

He would find the way; my task was to remain upon his back.

The moon flickered along behind the trees. His pace was steady, faithful.

A man I loved was dead . . . But when it was known, there would be no hesitation any longer and the garrisons would be re-established. It was what he would have wished . . . My eyes became blind. . . .

"Fak, we must go faster, faster than a man can follow us!"

He quickened into a trot, but would not go at a speed to endanger his footing. I felt them drawing nearer moment by moment. It was a race with the opponents whose whereabouts were unknown. The goal was the road which led down to the lake. There Fak must run, if I had to beat him.

The trail became the road, like a wood road at home but built by soldiers and firm.

It was safety and escape! Fak responded to my panic and doubled under me. The moon raced among the trees and the air, grown warm, rushed past my head. It seemed now that it was the act of a fool to have deliberately held back the pace, to have let them draw near. The round ring of a pointed rifle seemed close at my back, but I was not quite lost, and did not try to make my little horse outrun his surefootedness.

Safety lay in speed which seemed to be the greater because it was night . . . A time came when I felt that if they had been once close, they were far behind me now. I was content to let Fak slacken, but it was his turn to be unwilling, and I had to draw the rein. . . .

Time was like a stretching band that suddenly broke. The flashing yellow fires at the pass, the black figure prone on the snow, the flight on foot, and breathlessness, were no longer a part of the life of me who lived and rode. Time had begun anew. I was free—and I was riding my horse down into the valley to give a warning, leaving Don in death or dying, but as he would have wished. Ahead there was more to do. The Dasens must be roused and not forgotten. Ek or Atta should carry the alarm so that armed men could gather as they had in the past and hunt down the raiders. All others must leave everything and mount and ride down the valley. The danger was not over. The mountain men controlled the pass and were perhaps even now running along this same road, pressing the pace because I had escaped.

Fak had rested. I made him run again.

Oh, my wise, dear horse! His gallop was steady but without strain. He had never been ridden so hard and therefore knew the danger, but he also knew that he must keep going for a long way and not break his heart too soon. I wished I could share a burden that was all his.

From a forest utterly peaceful and still in the moonlight we emerged upon the shores of the lake, and we were down, down upon the floor of the valley. He hesitated and then slowed to a fast walk, for the road was muddy underfoot. The road turned from the water to cross a little headland. The ground was dryer and without urging but with a quiver he galloped again. We ascended and descended. The lake opened wide again, lighter than its further shore which was the Hyths' farm, a little over a mile away. I drew Fak from the road where I had met Nattana, in another life, eighteen days before. He fought the turn for a moment but yielded, and breasting the rise to the Dasens' quickened to a gallop. The house was dark for it was long past midnight.

I dismounted. Fak dropped his head and stood trembling.

I banged on the door, in terror lest I be delayed too long. A window opened above and I heard old Dasen calling.

"Lang," I shouted, and it was not my voice that spoke and the head in the window was unreal. "The Bants have captured the pass. They are coming."

"When?" he cried.

"Now! I must warn the Hyths!"

I ran to Fak, and as I mounted looked back over the fields, but they were peaceful and empty in the high moonlight.

Turning my head toward the Dasens' afraid I had not said enough I saw lights move in the windows.

Fak galloped again but heavily, yet he must break his heart now. There were many at the Hyths', and they might be slow to move. If they escaped, it would be he who saved them. I could not have out-run the mountain men, but I wished I were suffering with my horse. It was unfair, for he had given me back my strength, nearly gone at the hut. I had now only that side-ache which hard running leaves.

Fak toiled over the road through the fields. The half-built wall of the new stable was white with the moonlight upon it; but the farmhouse was dark.

I climbed from Fak's back and left him standing with feet apart, and ran, not daring to look back and to see him sink.

I shouted my name, in panic lest the black, still house would not rouse and show lights.

"Lang! Lang! I am Lang! They are coming!"

I flung open the back door. The woodshed smelled as it always did—of wood rotten and dry. I entered the kitchen and it also smelled the same. It was black, but feet were on the stairs from the brothers' quarters.

Ek's candle was dazzling, his face uncanny, like a mask. "The mountain men!" I said. "You must all go."

He asked no questions but shouted to Atta, who answered from above. . . .

"How much time is there?" Ek demanded.

"I don't know. They were at the pass when I came down. I ran and rode as fast as I could. They are on foot, but they may be close behind."

Atta came running down the stairs.

"The Bants?" he asked calmly.

"They have got over. There is nothing to stop them," I cried. "There is no time to talk. Go waken everybody."

I turned to Ek, but he spoke first.

"We will go saddle the horses," he said.

As we ran to the stables, I looked back to the east, but no running figures were visible on the quiet fields . . . no yellow flashes.

"Are you all right?" he asked.

"Quite—a side-ache."

"The others up there—Don?"

"Shot. I don't know about Ekkly and Samer."

Fak stood with bent head at the door of the barn waiting to be let in, and I shook violently . . . For a moment all else seemed unimportant but the relief of his life and naturalness.

There were many unknown horses in the barn.

"Someone ought to tell the Ekklys," I said.

Ek dropped a saddle and ran out.

Among these new horses was Dorna's. I saddled Nattana's horse; others must find the appropriate harness for these of Dorna's party.

Two men came in, one I did not know, but the other was young Stellin. They set to work on the horses at once.

Ek returned, and a moment later old Ekkly entered half-dressed. Lanterns moved about. My head began to swim.

There was something that ought to be done. . . .

I saw Ek cinching a horse; he was the steadier one.

"Atta ought to start at once down the valley to warn others."

"Yes, of course."

Questions were shouted to me: how near were they? where was Don? were we taken by surprise? I made half answers. Later I might really remember and tell.

The horses were restive, hard to quiet and handle.

I saw Ek speaking to Atta, and Atta leading a horse toward the door.

My mind was on Fak who had entered with us and gone to his stall. He could not be ridden as the other horses could be, but I would not leave him to be killed or misused by the mountain men. We might find the nearest woods and hide. . . .

The horses were already being led out by Stellin and Ek. The barn was full of stamping and of high whinnies.

I took the bridles of Nattana's horse and of my own, and went out into the moonlight again. The fresh air was reviving.

On the porch of the house were lights and many persons were gathered there, moving about. Eastward there was still nothing. . . .

I could not see faces. All was confusion. I heard Ettera's voice:

"Has everyone their most precious things?"

There was another voice speaking to someone else, familiar, clear, unlike any other:

"Where is Lang? Where is Lang?"

"Here I am, Dorna!"

She was in a crowd and I could not see her, nor could I go to her, because Nattana's horse was nervous and unruly. Her voice called again, cool and fresh.

"Are you all right?"

"Quite! Safe and unhurt!"

Another voice spoke:

"Can I help you, Dorna?"

It was serene and well known, and after a moment I knew it to be Stellina's.

There was a figure at my side, quite close.

"I am only half-awake," said Nattana, "but are you really all right? Oh my dear!"

I felt the touch of her hand on my arm.

"I've a side-ache from running," I said to show how well I was.

"You have got my horse!" she cried.

"Can't you mount him?" I said. "He is giving me trouble."

"Can you hold this?"

She thrust a heavy bundle under my arm, and was quickly on her horse and above me. Her legs were bare.

"Give me my parcel!" she cried. "How is Fak?"

"I don't know," I said, but her horse had danced off sideways with her. I turned to Fak. Others were already mounted.

Stellin rode up to me.

"What had we best do?" he said. The answer was obvious.

"Ride down the valley as fast as you can."

"That, rather than hide in the woods?"

"Yes. I don't know how many they are, and you are a large party. And go quickly!"

"Will you come with us?"

"I'll follow you—but I have another task."

He rode away to a group already mounted.

I spoke to Fak, wishing he could tell me how he was.

There was but one figure on the porch, and I led Fak nearer.

Ek came up with four horses, three saddled.

"Come on, Ettera!" he shouted.

"If they burn this place," she cried, "I'll fight."

"Fak must be ridden out," he said to me. "You mount one of these."

"I will lead Fak. I shan't leave him."

"Oh, the cattle!" he cried in despair.

"Never mind, my dear," said his sister.

The porch was empty. We were all on horseback.

Voices shouted in the distance:

"Dasen! Dasen! Dasen!" and a group of riders rode up from the fields to the east.

One of them cried, "We were shot at. There is no time!"

"Ek! Ek!" I called. "You and I last!" There seemed no one else to start the flight, and I gave the word:

"Ride, all of you, and ride hard!"

There was movement. A compact group set off at a canter. Others followed. With an effort I held in my horse and saw Ek doing the same.

Nattana rode up.

"Go with them!" cried her brother.

"No! I am going with you."

"You go, Nattana!"

"I won't!"

"Oh, Nattana," I said, "go with them!"

"You make me!" she answered. "I could hate you!" Her voice was breaking, but she obeyed.

We gave them a lead of a hundred yards.

"Shall we follow?" said Ek quietly, and we did so, holding in our horses and looking back. And Fak came after us.

I was torn two ways, for I had committed myself to being rearguard, and if Fak could not go at our pace he must be shot and left behind. The others were outdistancing us, but so far this was as it should be. They were already on the highroad, a long cavalcade, six in Dorna's party, Ettera and Nattana, six from the Ekklys', fourteen from the Dasens' including their dependents, and a dozen or so led horses in addition.

Ek spoke. He doubted that the Bants would come far beyond the Upper Farm, even if they were in large numbers. "But they will undo much of our work," he added calmly. "Still I am glad that most of our cattle are still to come."

I told him a little of what had happened, but it was hard to speak. The thought of Don reminded me of his wife, and my heart stopped still. She lived across the river, off the main road. How would she be warned? It was too late now, for we were already a long mile to the west.

"I thought of her and the Gronans and the others on that side," said Ek. "Atta sent Ekkly's second son that way."

We looked back often. The road that unrolled behind us remained the serene empty road of a peaceful moonlight night. Fak, my chief concern, often dropped away from us, but when I called he came up to us again. He was unburdened and he was strong, and we did not ride hard. The others were often out of sight.

"I think we are all safe now," said Ek. "There are no horses left for them to ride, and they have come a good many miles. . . You must be tired yourself."

"Only a side-ache."

"Maybe you strained something."

But with the relief of escape had come a dreamy fatigue in which I heard shots and saw yellow flashes and ran past Don again. . . .

We went by other farms, all empty, for Atta had preceded us. There must have been many on the road before us, all riding west.

The sky became paler and the moon less bright . . . But before it was dawn we came to Renner's Agency at the side of the road about ten miles from the Upper Farm, and the rendezvous of the men of the valley when raids came from the east. Fifty or sixty men were gathered, including the Dasens and the Ekklys. Dorna's party and the women had, however, ridden on. Ek and I, the last of the fugitives, reported that we had seen and heard nothing.

A *tana* named Gorth, a large, vigorous, gray-haired man, was recognized as leader.

Ek spoke to me.

"You ride on," he said. "You have done enough. But I am going to join these men."

"I will go with them also," I answered.

We offered our services.

"The more the better," said Gorth.

I was pointed out to him as the man who gave the alarm. A few questions were asked. I told of Don's death—if death it were—and many deep breaths were drawn.

But we were numerous enough to advance and there was no time to be wasted.

I saw Fak stabled at the agency—the only one within miles, and went with the main body. An advance guard had already started.

In the east, below the sunrise, was a red glow, which might be the buildings of the Upper Farm burning.

Ek rode at my side.

"You are hurt!" he said suddenly.

"I did not know it."

"Your whole side is covered with blood!"

I put my hand there and found my clothes stiff and the side-ache at a definite spot. I became faint, but it was foolish to be upset by mere knowledge of what I had long unconsciously endured.

Ek, however, insisted on stopping to examine the wound. My side was grazed, no more, and it had almost stopped bleeding. A man who seemed to have surgical knowledge was called and he applied a burning antiseptic and bound it up. The pain was worse than if I had been let alone, but worst of all was the fact that this man rode with me and held back my horse so that the others outdistanced us.

I was no use, and would have done as well if I had gone on to join the women! It was a bitter disappointment thus to be left out.

The man and I wrangled, and finally I had my way and we rode hard and caught up.

"You will open it up again," he said.

I answered that I had ridden with it for hours. . . .

We reached the Upper Farm at last. The mountain men had come and gone. The roof of the barn was burned away, the hay lost, and the cattle there killed. Attempts had been made to fire the farmhouse, but these had failed. Within, however, all was wreckage and confusion.

The surgeon was right. The wound had opened again, and I was too faint to go on with those who were advancing toward the pass.

I was helped upstairs. Everything in Nattana's workshop was smashed. I was not myself and wept with pity and rage. In my own room all was upside down, and the clothes she had made for me were gone, but nothing else was taken. One leg of the bed was broken, but the man who had been left to take care of me propped it up on a log of wood.

I lay down and sank into white, cold oblivion. Sleep was a long nightmare of shots and horrors and impatience to be doing something which must be done.

It was a relief to be waked in the late afternoon with word that young Ekkly wanted to see me.

He was pale and deathly tired. He had come back with Gorth's men after the latter had ridden as far as the pass. A strong guard had been left there and others were still scouring the woods, but he believed that the Bants had all returned to their town.

We exchanged our stories.

He was on watch, waiting for Samer. By chance he looked up toward the slopes across the glacier, and not down as usual, and he saw moving figures in that direction. In his opinion the Bants had not climbed the slopes where we watched for them, but had ascended to the snow field to the west and had come from there. Don—Ekkly's voice winced—had told him that the Germans had been training a native police, in the course of which they had probably familiarized the Bants with the ice and snow which they previously feared and avoided. In short, the Germans with the best of intentions had made it possible for the Bants to surprise the pass.

Ekkly had been fired at by the moving figures and had had a duel with them. He heard Don and me shooting. He knew that the Bants were in force, and climbed upward in the hope of making his way to the south and down into the valley. He eluded the Bants but became caught in too dangerous places to proceed at night. When the sun rose he cautiously went on, stopping at a spot where he could look down into the cirque on the edge of which the upper hut was placed. A few Bants were there on guard. He climbed a height and saw the barns of the Hyths and Dasens burning.

He thought only of himself, he confessed, and knowing that sooner or later the Bants would return he remained where he was.

In the middle of the morning they began to appear in the pass going north. There were no women among them, and for the first time he hoped that the warning had been given, though from where he was he could see that the signal fires had not been lighted.

He had some shells left for his gun and was quite sure that they could not see or find him. The range was about two hundred yards.

His eyes flashed.

He had made them run, he said, and he had got two of them and was glad of it for a special reason.

When he was quite sure that there were no more of them he made a rather difficult climb down into the cirque. He found Don's body. Don was dead. But they had not touched it. . . With Samer's body it was different. Samer had evidently seen Ekkly's shooting and had returned to the hut to fall into the hands of the Bants already there. He was stabbed to death. . . . .

But, he continued, he had examined the body of one of the men he had shot.

Ekkly looked me in the eyes.

"That man wore a uniform and in his pocket was this. Can you read it?"

He handed me a stiff folded card. The words upon it were in German. It was a certificate that "Todo-es-fisijin," having taken an oath of allegiance to the kaiser, etc., and having served his training, had been appointed an officer in H.I.M.'s constabulary stationed at Fisiji in charge of protecting the frontier and had power to make arrests; and it was signed with the name of a German officer, on special duty as commander of the police forces in the protectorate of the Sobo Steppes.

"It is what I thought," said Ekkly, "and it means that their own police are the raiders, and that means that the garrisons will be re-established. I am going to Lord Dorn at The City at once. Will you come with me?"

I said that I would, eager to go. Between us we could give a complete history of the watch at the Vaba Pass, for one or the other of us was there from the beginning. We could testify that no one had been molested by us, and that when the surprise came in each case the Bants fired the first shot. He would give his account of the men he had shot; and I mine of the shooting of Don.

We planned to leave next day.

When he had gone, I found myself exhausted. I tried to get up but could not.

Ek and Atta were my next visitors. They were already putting the house to rights. They were not dismayed. The loss of cattle was not so great, they said, because some were already in pasture and had not been found. Neighbors had promised to skin those that were killed and thus save the hides. "We will supply everyone with meat for a time," said Ek, "and they will make it up to us in some way."

Nor was a great amount of hay lost.

The roof of the barn was the principal thing, but spring had come, and they had received offers of labor from all sides.

"The rest help those who suffer on a raid," he said. "The Dasens are worse off than we are. Nattana is the chief sufferer. I hate to look into her workshop. There is nothing that can be repaired."

"What shall we do about her?" asked Atta.

Ek sighed.

"She would be better at the Lower Farm. Father's heart is not so hard. When he learns her loss he will want her back. It takes things like this to jolt him. What do you say, Lang?"

"Tomorrow I am going to The City," I said, and I told of Ekkly's and my plan. "He is certain that the garrisons will be re-established."

"We all are."

"In that case I shan't be needed at the pass, and I should not live with you unless you needed my services."

"We will have labor enough, but of course we want you."

"I am not so sure," I answered, "not while Nattana is here— because you are afraid that she and I will marry."

"It is for you and her to decide."

"If you had the decision what would you say?"

"Do I have to tell you? It is not my affair."

"You need not—but I think you want us separated."

"I do," he said, his face red. "She will be upset by all this."

He did not continue. It was all becoming tangled.

"You mean that she will be more likely to marry me than she was because of losing her workshop?"

"You saved her from the mountain men."

I held my head. It was true, and it seemed to give me a claim, but it was no reason for changing the decision we had both made. The fact that I violently wanted her in this room with me now must be partly because I was not myself. . . Yet I was tempted to ask her to marry me again.

"There is another thing," Ek was saying. "This is a chance for her to return home. If she does not marry you, she will be happier there."

"Unless your father makes life a misery to her because of me."

"I'll see to that," said Ek. "I know how to appeal to him."

It was hard to think clearly.

"It seems that she had better go back to the Lower Farm," I said.

"I think so, too. But if you and she want to remain here until you return to your own country, I want you here. You have no other place to be, you and Nattana. . . ."

"No!" I answered. "Give her the chance to go home."

"All right! I shall see that she gets it. Meanwhile she shall be here temporarily. In ten or fifteen days I am going for cattle and I'll see Father—if she so decides."

They left me.

While Ek was talking, Atta had straightened the room, and it was home again.

With an effort I sat up, and all grew white and slowly spun, and came to rest. Through the open window I looked into the sunset down the valley and saw the same road upon which we had fled by moonlight. Sleep had intervened between. I ought to feel normal again, but did not. Shots still sounded in my head, too heavy to hold up, too light to think with. I had been lonely in Islandia before, but never so lonely as now.

My present task was to gain in twelve hours strength enough for four days of riding. The man who had dressed my scratch said that I had lost some blood. Food was the means to replace it. I was hungry.

The brothers managed to cook a meal, my share of which Atta brought upstairs. With great care I sat up, and when the room ceased to revolve I forced myself to eat. It was galling to be a trouble to them at this time.

Atta was searching the room, and I asked him why.

"Dorna and all her people left many of their belongings behind. I am gathering them together. Dorna had this room."

From under the bed he drew a worn brown sandal, but could find nothing else.

"If this is all, she did well," he said. "Stellina left half her belongings. . . Trust Ettera to take the right things, but Nattana did not take anything but the dress she wore and a pair of shoes."

"She had a large bundle," I said.

"It probably belonged to someone else."

"How about you and Ek—what did you save?"

"We—oh, we left everything."

He went out, taking Dorna's sandal, which I wished he had left for company. . . .

Next morning I felt much stronger. Ek made a tight, strong bandage and he and Atta saddled a horse and saved me from all exertion.

The time came to go.

I hated to leave them with so much to do; but Ettera and Nattana would soon return, they said, and the neighbors would come.

"You must visit us again before you go back to your country. . . Where will you be after you have gone from The City?"

I did not know, and said that I would write to them—and to Nattana also.

There was so much to be said that we were dumb. I thanked them and they me; and then I rode away from the Upper Farm.

Ekkly as companion on the road was very different from Ekkly in command at the pass, but just as intent upon the business in hand, discussing continually what we would say to Lord Dorn.

We rode slowly for the sake of my wound, which would surely be better healed in a day or two, our objective for that night the Inn at the Mora Pass.

Behind a man's intelligence and concentration there was in my companion something boyish and simple. Friendship grew between us, and all at once I wondered if he were not the man for Nattana. . . I worried about her future. She had said troubling things.

The sun rose higher and the air became warm. The strength that had seemed sufficient in the early morning ebbed quickly, and long before it was noon I was so tired that I was tremulous and the splendid mountain scenery was pale and remote; but the worst of such fatigue was that it made memories more vivid than the reality, and particularly those of Don. . . .

We rode by places which I knew from having seen them more than a year and a half before—the magnificent gorge through which the Doring River passed in its change from a mountain to a valley stream, and much later the shelter hut where Dorn and I had spent the night, but I saw it dimly like something in a mist. I gave up speaking because my lips trembled. On the other hand, the stiff ache in my side had ceased entirely.

"Ekkly," I said, "I think I may faint. . . ."

I came to myself, cold water on my face. The wound had opened again and had been bleeding some time. Luckily the Inn at the Mora Pass was not far, but there was no possibility of my going on for several days.

That night, after a dead, white sleep, I could think again, and he and I talked things over. We decided that he should proceed without me, carrying a statement if I had strength enough to make one. Meanwhile the Inn would take care of me. When there was no doubt of the healing of the wound I would go on, though exactly where seemed unimportant unless Lord Dorn wanted to see me or the watches were to be continued.

Fortified with *sarka* and other stimulants I dictated my narrative to my new friend. He read it over to me and I signed it. All was in form.

He had made arrangements for attendance, and asked what else he could do for me. I was afraid that if Nattana heard that I was ill at the Inn she would come, and although I longed for her company I dreaded what we might say to each other. Therefore I asked him to see to it that my presence at the Inn remain unknown. This was not difficult, for meals could be served in my room where I was in the mood to stay, doing nothing peacefully, for days.

It was then very late. He planned to leave at sunrise and would not see me again.

We also had so much to say that we were dumb.

"There is nothing more?" he asked. "I wish you were one of us. It is hard to think of Lang as a foreigner going away."

"I have been one of you."

"Don liked you."

"Did he ever speak of me?"

"He said that he had seen you in an unpleasant situation and that you behaved well, and that he had liked you ever since."

This must have been at the Lor Pass.

"It is hard to think of him as—"

"Let's not!" said Ekkly. "He is too vivid in my mind."

He rose to go.

"Is there nothing more?"

"Yes," I answered. "Will you leave word to have Dorna told that I am here if she should stop at the Inn?"

We said good-bye.

I closed my eyes and saw Don, not disgraced by death and prone upon the snow, but as I had seen him striding erect during our trip together from the Fains' to the Hyths'. Every memory of him was more sharply bright than the reality of other men, and had become intensely precious. It was as though I had been privileged to live on friendly terms with a legendary figure, with Thor, or Sigurd, or Hercules.

The room at the Inn was small with a single window facing the mountainside. It was warmed by an open fire, and the nights were cold. On the day after Ekkly left I lay in bed unwilling to move even my hands and dreading exertion. It was extraordinary to realize that once I had been able to run! Late in the evening a real doctor appeared, arranged for by Ekkly. He rebandaged the bullet wound

and said that nothing was the matter but loss of blood. He prescribed a diet and departed, saying that he would charge me nothing
because of the way in which I had been hurt.

After a long night's sleep strength began to come back, but I
spent another day as I was, for if I lifted my head the room went
round dizzily. Thoughts, fragmentary except by an effort yesterday,
became consecutive and quickened. . . Unless the watch were re-
established at the pass—which was improbable—I had come to the
end of something, and must make for myself a new way of life.
Nattana had ceased to be my mistress. It was somehow satisfactory
that there had been no good-bye. I remembered her vividly—young,
bright, charming, with a jaunty manner all her own. We had separated, but we were still something special each to the other, and in
the parting of our ways there was grief, which however was painless.

What would the future be? Should I remain in Islandia the seven
months more which the law allowed? Or should I visit all my friends,
live with them for a while, and then say good-bye and go home? What
would home be like? Time would show and I would have to live
there anyway.

There was but one thorn in my side, one uncured pain—Dorna.
Her note delivered to me at the pass puzzled and teased my thoughts
and would not let me alone. She said that she was deeply disappointed
not to see me at the Upper Farm. She wanted to see me very much
for her own sake. . . Every word was significant and every word
started endless conjectures.

If she really wanted to see me, I had given her the chance. . . . .

Next day in the forenoon there was a knock at my door. When
I answered she entered unattended. I had dressed but was lying on
the bed, because I still felt faint when I stood. She entered shyly, but
seeing me came swiftly, told me not to move, and sat down on the
bed—and I was looking in Dorna's eyes again.

She asked at once how I was, and I told her. . . .

She seemed to have grown in height. Her eyes were larger and
very bright, her lips firmer and less young. Her face was stronger,
more mature, more noble, and she was prettier than ever, her skin
as lovely, a bright color in her cheeks.

She sat for a moment, smiling, looking at me, saying nothing, and I remembered her silences in the past and how they had worried me, but now I wanted to laugh. And she laughed too, and then threw out her hands and cried:

"What can I say?"

"What is there to say?"

"I want to say something. I know quite well what I owe to you."

"What do you owe to me?"

"I would be dead by now," she answered.

What I had done became clear, and it was wonderful to know that her beauty, her serenity, and all her living existence hereafter had been safeguarded by me.

"We have talked of nothing else," she said, "Stellina, Donara, Nattana, Ettera, and I. We did not fully understand in the haste of leaving the Hyths' farm, but we know now. We realize what they would have done to us. We would not have had a chance! They would have been in the house without anyone being aware. . . And I had your room near the head of the stairs."

She spoke calmly, but suddenly her eyes dilated in a look of dazed fear and she turned away.

"It is not good to think of, Dorna."

"No, it isn't, John!" she cried. "We think of it too much. I know I do. Stellina is more calm. Nattana was almost hysterical."

"Is Nattana with you?"

"Oh, no," said Dorna, relief in her voice. "She came with us only as far as the farm. . . They all thought you had gone to The City. Why didn't you send back word? She would have wanted to come here and take care of you."

"I wanted to get my strength back by myself."

Dorna looked at me gravely and then down.

"Let's be clear with each other," she said. "I happen to know what you and Hytha Nattana have been to each other."

I felt a sudden violent shock, and then quite abruptly it ceased to matter whether Dorna knew or not. I opened my eyes again, and she was still there, farther off, but real.

"Ettera told me," she was saying. "It was when Nattana was hysterical. We were all together for two days at a farm down the valley. Nattana was the one who really made clear the part you had played, and she was much upset about you. She did not expect you to ride back with Gorth's men. When she learned you had been hurt, she lost control of herself. Ettera took her away, and in explanation said to me later that Nattana and you had been living together. She need not have said it, but she was disturbed also. . . Why didn't you want her to come here?"

"Because it is over, Dorna."

"With her, too?"

"Unless she has changed."

Dorna looked at me again, her eyes shy.

"What was it?"

"I wanted to marry her," I said.

"And she would not?"

"No."

"*Apia?*"

"I would not have thought so at first, but I think she did all along."

Dorna sighed.

"I have no right to resent it," she said. I bit my lip not to ask her if she did. She answered the unasked question.

"But I do resent it somewhat. If you had known it was *apia* from the start—but never mind that! I am not here to talk about Hytha Nattana, and I can't stay long. . . And I am really glad that you and Hytha Nattana have had each other. I know it must have been good."

"How is she?" I asked quickly.

"She is quite herself. She is busy again. Her workshop is ruined, but she says she has plenty of sewing to do until she goes back to their other farm. She wonders where you are because she has a bundle of clothes belonging to you which she saved and she doesn't know where to send them."

Dorna was forgotten. . . .

"I must go!" she said suddenly, and she rose. "They are all waiting for me. We are trying to reach the Frays tonight. I came to ask you to visit me there for a few days as soon as you are well enough to leave here and before you do anything else. Will you come, please?"

Her voice was humble and yet oppressed.

"I will come, Dorna."

"We shall have much to say to each other."

What was there to say?

She was at the door before I realized.

"Don't let word reach Nattana that I have been here," I called to her.

"Oh! Trust me! That is obvious."

She was gone.

29

The Reckoning

TWO DAYS LATER I felt so strong that I left the Inn, on my way to see Dorna, at the Lodge upon the Frays.

The horse of the Hyths was not Fak and had ideas of pace that were unfamiliar and bothersome. After two hours I was all at once very tired. I wished the journey were ended and that my hostess would not want to talk at once of the much we had to say to each other.

Patches of snow lay on the alpine grass, already bright green. There were little flowers of white and blue, which were lovely, but the mountains were too magnificent and bright not to be oppressive.

My wound was stiff and to ease it I rode stiffly and ached all over. . . .

There were gnarled dead trees all around me, but I refused to look at them for they brought back a memory of fear and then of a place—a single shot. . . .

At last, however, came the real forest, which was like a homecoming after the five days of illness spent above timber line with only a bare rocky slope outside the window.

I reached the promontory with the tower, and the journey was more than half over. I risked dismounting, because it was lunchtime, though not sure I could climb to the saddle again. I tried to eat and could not, but I drank some wine, which gave me strength.

After what seemed the customary time of rest I rose to go on. By good fortune some travelers came by. I hailed them and a strong man lifted me upon the horse. I explained that I had been hurt and ill.

"Are you Lang?" he asked.

When I assented to my name they gathered around me. They

seemed to know all about the raid and of the death of Don, and of the escape of one of the watchers, who gave warning just in time.

"You saved our finest," said one man.

"The soldiers at Tindal march tomorrow for the passes," said the strong man.

My head reeled with sudden gladness. Ekkly had done well—and Lord Dorn had acted promptly! The men crowding around the horse seemed to become far off and then to shout very loudly, but the faintness passed soon.

One man offered to accompany me, but it did not seem necessary. I rode away by myself, realizing suddenly that now, no longer needed at the pass, I was truly without an occupation in Islandia. . . .

My horse stopped. When previously we had come to the rocky slide by which one ascended to the Frays I had dismounted and walked, but today the horse must take me up. I urged him on and he began to climb with reluctance.

The world opened and the forest beneath became a dark-green floor. The steepness and height of the Frays was greater than memory believed possible. I rode through the gate by the Tower and emerged upon the first meadow, which swayed like a green carpet with the wind beneath it.

It was not far now, and it was time that I arrived, for my strength was ebbing. It seemed a long time before we crossed the meadow and followed the winding trail in and out among the boulders of the slide. At last, however, we came to the terraces—irregular, covered with trees, and with trails up and down.

A man appeared on foot and hearing my name had turned back with me. I was glad of his company for I was very faint.

The brown stone of the Lodge with its high peaked roof and verandaed upper story was suddenly before my eyes. I slipped down from the horse and caught the man's arm.

"I have been hurt," I said.

Trees were rocking overhead in a gusty wind.

We entered the low door into a long, dark, low-ceilinged hall. At the end an open fire was blazing.

"John! Johnlang!"

She was so kind! She did not insist like a nurse that I go to bed and rest, but placed a long chair with rugs and cushions near the fire and yet facing toward a window; and when I was at ease she asked no questions but sat nearby, serene and lovely, and spoke only of simple things—of my journey and of hers, of the raid, of the Frays, and of Queen Alwina's living here. . . My eyes gradually closed; the last thing I saw was Dorna's darkened head against a window with small panes opening upon the waving branches of a pine tree and blue sky beyond.

The return to consciousness was devious. It was dusk. My position and the rugs were strange and the room unknown, but her head against the window turned, black now and perfect in its youthfulness and grace.

"Dorna!"

"Yes, John?"

"How long is it?"

"I don't know at all. . . You slept very quietly."

"It was not very courteous—"

"Let's not! There are other things. . . Are you all awake now? Don't you want to sleep again?"

"Oh no, Dorna."

"Are you ready to listen to an explanation? Or would you rather wait? We have all the time we need."

"What needs explaining?"

"Why I asked you here. . . You were so kind to come!"

"Why did you ask me, Dorna?"

"Because we separated hurt. Why should we go on through our lives with that hurt still in us? I thought that if we took our time and were patient we could really understand each other, and we would not dread seeing each other any more, and the hurt would be cured. Once you were nothing but a sore spot to me, Johnlang, and I would have done anything to avoid you, but all that feeling is gone. . . I don't claim all the credit. It is partly Stellina. You owe something to her and so do I. I had told her about you; and after that day on the Exhibition Ship at Doring, she spoke to me, saying I ought to tell my brother of what you felt about me—that he was your one close friend. And he went to you as soon as I told him. . ." She stopped suddenly, and then said, "What is it? You look so pale."

"Go on, Dorna. I am quite well."

"About Stellina? She is kind and wise—too wise sometimes! She said that every man and woman who have cared but who do not have each other for any reason at all owe each other a full reckoning in which nothing is left mysterious. She also said that no woman but a cruel one will be obscure to any man who wanted to marry or desired her. That applied to me! And the first to us both! Let's have our Reckoning, John. I am not sure where we will come out, but don't you think it worth trying?"

Beneath an instantaneous dread of the result of talking too freely stirred all the old pain and wonderings; I saw only her dark head, but I felt her bright burning eyes, deeply concerned.

"I do think it worth trying," I answered.

"We must be honest and frank. We must hide nothing. We must not be silent in order not to hurt each other's feelings." She seemed to droop and then flung out her hands and straightened. "I will tell you anything and everything!" she said. "It was for this I asked you to come."

"Was it what you meant in the note which I received at the pass?"

"Yes. Did my note trouble you, John?"

"It made me afraid, Dorna."

"Of what?"

"That I would care too deeply again."

"Maybe I do want to get you back a little but not too much, John-lang. Maybe I knew my note would trouble you and make you wonder. Perhaps I did not mind being unkind to that extent. I thought I could cure it all later."

"Dorna, you must tell me exactly what you mean when you say you want me back a little but not too much."

"I don't quite understand, myself. There is a feeling in me that I can't get rid of. I try not to act under its influence. You are my Johnlang, and I want my Johnlang to desire and to wish to marry me only. I resent his sleeping with any other woman. I don't want him in that way myself, but I reserve the right to change my mind. Yet there is another feeling just as strong: I do want him to be happy and glad of life. If another woman really good enough for him can give him happiness I cannot begrudge it."

Did she wish to learn more of Nattana? There was nothing in my heart to tell her. Whether or not Nattana and I had found happiness was our affair. . . .

Yet her frankness was as it should be. I felt deeply her strong effort to be honest, and it was this that mattered more than what she said. In return, if she wished, I would tell her what I felt—when I knew.

There was a long, long silence. The sky outside was steel blue and the window frame, the pine, and Dorna's head merged in one blackness. . . .

"What more do you want me to tell you?" she said.

"Nothing now, Dorna. You have been thinking of this before-hand, but I am still dazed."

"Very well. You can sleep on it tonight. . . Would you like to go to your room and not have dinner with the rest of us?"

"I will dine with you."

"Only with Tor and Donara and me. He is here for a few days. He was at The City and when he heard of the raid he came at once and reached here last night. He knows that you and I are going to have long and intimate conversations. He has mixed feelings about it, but the stronger one is the wish that we have them. He will be glad to see you because you have saved what seem to be his two greatest happinesses." She laughed lightly. "You know I am going to have a child?"

"Dorn wrote me."

"I am another *myself,* a very real one, but not one I know very well. . . Are you glad I am to have a child?"

"Yes, because I don't want you to perish in the world."

"I won't perish—because of you. John! I am glad as I have never been glad of anything before."

She rose, a dark shadow, and moved to the fire. There was a ruddy glow on her face and her profile bore a look of contentment and a brooding smile.

"I wonder if we can talk so well by daylight. . . We do under-stand each other!" she said happily.

The room to which I was shown was at the southwest corner of the Lodge on the second story. South upon the veranda was a door and two windows, and west was another one. It was too dark to see anything outside but the black masses of pines and a starry sky. The room had a faint ancient odor of cedarwood with a trace of some-thing fresh like violets.

Before dinner Donara, a young woman of about thirty-five and Dorna's companion or lady in waiting, tried to say her thanks, a hard task because of the nature of the peril from which she had been saved. It was a relief to have it over.

More handsome persons than Tor and Dorna surely never married. His beauty was greater than hers, with the perfect symmetry of his head and figure, the nobility of his face, the gleam of intelligence in his clear eyes, and the look of strength and of gentleness in his expressions. It was hard not to stare at him and to study the perfect modeling of his features—surprising to have Dorna outshone. When I turned to her after looking at him she smiled as though pleased. Seeing these two together I felt, as not before, the excluding nature of the bond between them. Tor was her choice and they now were three.

He spoke of the raid, and again I told the whole story, seeing it more clearly after nearly a week had passed. He asked many questions as to how the watch was conducted and as to such details as trips for wood. I described the episode of the single shot and how we dreaded that journey.

"I knew Don well," he said. "It seems a needless risk, but he may have believed it good for the watchers who would wait long and see and hear nothing. Danger had a different meaning to him from what it has to most men. He liked it as some men like a game, because it quickened his senses and demanded the exercise of skill and thought."

Finally my narrative reached the night of the raid itself. I told of Don's arrival and of the unusual fact of his fatigue. Dorna interrupted saying that he had spent the previous night awake and on watch at the Doring Pass, had left at midmorning and descended into the valley, overtaking her party on the way to the Hyths', had traveled with them as far as the Upper Farm, stopping only for a few moments, and then had gone at once to the Vaba Pass.

Continuing I told how he went to sleep and that I had gone out into the moonlight, that I had seen a figure move and heard almost instantly a shot. Tor asked where I was.

"Near the hut."

"Why didn't you run for shelter?"

"I didn't think of it. My first thought was to rouse Don."

"Then what?"

"To return the shot. Don came at once."

"Could you have found shelter?"

"Yes. The hut was a few yards away. But what good would it have done? There were no windows on the side the shots were coming from."

"Would you have been penned in and easily surrounded?"

"Yes, if I had gone into the hut. It never occurred to me. Then Don gave the word to make for the rim of the valley at the place by which we descended."

"Was there no other choice but to be penned in at the hut or to run across the open?"

"We could have gone around to the other side of the hut and climbed the hill there, or else run down the valley, but that did not occur to me."

"If you had run down the valley the men who killed Samer would have got you?"

"They might."

"Suppose you had climbed the hill?"

"We would have got away from them, I am sure. There was a steep shoulder that would have protected us from them. But what use would it have been? We could only have reached the lower valley by a most roundabout route too late to give warning."

"Was the way to the rim of the little valley where you were quite open?" Dorna asked.

"Yes, it was."

"It seems to me," Tor said, "that you and Don had a very good chance of safety and chose a great risk in order to give warning."

"He may have thought it all out but I didn't. It seemed quite clear what we ought to try to do. He gave the word and I followed."

"It was a splendid deed," said Tor.

"We were there for a purpose. They prevented our signaling. We had to do the next best thing."

Of the actual death of Don they asked no questions. They wanted to know of my flight and I told them, and also of Fak's stamina and intelligence.

Conversation turned quickly to the action that Lord Dorn had taken. He had gone at once with Ekkly first to the palace and then to Count von Bibberbach's although it was late.

"We all three went," said Tor. "The count asked for delay and an investigation. He was quite nonplused when Ekkly showed him the card found on the dead mountain man. Lord Dorn replied that longer delay was impossible, that the queen was in danger as well as the whole valley. . . Dorna's peril deeply impressed the count and made it difficult for him to reply. We said the guards would be posted within a few days. He answered that he did not know what the consequences would be. He could only report to his government. Efforts would of course be made to punish the guilty persons, though loss of life seemed to be equal on both sides, and so far only one side had been told. The armed guard at the pass was doubtless a provocation, and an insult to the sufficiency of the German police. If there had been no one there, the story might have been a different one. Nor was the guard at the pass military. . . He did his best to make a case for himself. Whether there will be any trouble or not, I don't know." Tor looked at Dorna again. "But I am not going to stay here more than a day or two. I am going back to The City. . . Lang and I might go together. Lord Dorn wants to see him."

Dorna stirred uneasily.

We left the dining room, and went to a long low hall. The walls were lined with books, some of them ancient. There was a large fireplace and one very old and dark long-chair.

Dorna reclined in the long-chair and clasped her hands behind her head, and relaxed. Her pregnancy had as yet changed her figure but little. Her beauty was no longer outshone by his. Her hands pushed her softened hair forward on her cheeks and temples. Black lashes lay on her cheeks. Her expression was one of pause, ease, and contentment. Her lips were placid and lightly closed. They seemed riper, expectant of kisses, familiar with them and yet innocent.

Tor came and stood over her, smiling.

"Alwina's chair," he stated with a touch of teasing.

After a moment she answered his unexpressed thought.

"I want my baby in my own way," she said. "He is mine now. He will be yours later. I like to think of Alwina and to do as she did. She is the only really great woman we have ever had."

"Greater than any king," he said gently.

"Not all. . . But, Tor, I am here to stay."

Because they had forgotten me I effaced myself further and went to the far corner of the room and pulled out a book, but I heard their voices. They were having some mild dispute, continued from the past. It seemed that he wished her to be with him for some months longer, particularly because he must be at The City for political reasons. . . .

I tried to read the book.

Their voices were lower. . . .

Curiosity turned my eyes. She had risen and they were standing before the fire. His hand, on her shoulder, slipped down to her hip. She looked up quickly and leaned to him a little.

I wore good armor. Most sword thrusts did not even dent it, but now and then one found a chink and the sharp point went deep.

In my room with its faint sweet odor of cedarwood and violets and its utter quiet, sleep was long and deep. I woke from a dim dream of Nattana—and it was as though she, dwelling in unconscious memory, asserted herself though my thoughts were preoccupied by another one. The morning air was fresh and cool on the veranda, which extended the length of the house, but was partitioned off in bays with doors in them.

Dorna sent word not to expect her before midmorning. Tor had gone hunting and Donara and I breakfasted together. She was not "one of them"—that is, a marsh dweller—but she was closely related to several families who lived near Dorn Island. She was a widow, her one child was dead, and she had left her husband's farm where there were others, finding a new interest in life with Dorna, whom she had known as a baby.

A walk was so tiring that I returned soon, but with an idea of the surroundings of the Royal Lodge. Behind it and separated from it by a dense grove of pines was a bay in the steep slopes, covering five acres or so, and containing a farm in miniature. At the inner end were cliffs beneath which was a little pond, fed by a series of cascades coming down a ravine cut in the cliffs.

On my return I chose the long low room in which to wait for Dorna's pleasure, but I avoided the chair that was Alwina's and hers.

At last she appeared and came down the room walking as she always did, easily and a little pantherine, and her face was bright with the loveliness that was new and yet no different from that which I had known and loved.

"It is too beautiful to stay indoors," she said. "Let's go out. We can wrap ourselves in rugs and find a sunny spot."

The place she had in mind was at the east end of the veranda.

The sun came over the tops of dense pines. The air was cleansed by breaths of their sharp odor. We made ourselves comfortable in two long chairs as though on a steamer. The light was bright and warm. When we wished we could look to the straight horizon.

"Here we are," she said, "like two invalids recovering. Shall we talk or shall we be silent?"

"We shall talk," I answered. "But does it really matter?"

"Not to me now, but if we don't we shall regret it later, I suppose. It is our chance. We have long lives before us. We shall both of us be happier if we really know each other. . . Don't you think so?"

"There is one thing I would like to know, Dorna. Why did you and your brother, and even Nattana, all warn me against loving an Islandian woman or making her love me? In your eyes what was the matter with me?"

"I wondered if you would ask me that!—I can't speak for them. I hardly know myself. . ." She pressed her hands to her face. "How much will this hurt you, I wonder?"

"I don't think I can be hurt now by what you thought of me."

"Will you let me go back to the beginning?" she asked. "And please forgive me. . . When my brother came back to Islandia he talked often of you. He was not very definite but I made a picture of you. . ." She paused.

"And I wasn't like it, Dorna?"

"You were and you weren't. . . I already saw my marriage as a problem. I had a hope, I suppose, that you might be an escape. . . At times I looked everywhere for a way out."

"When I came I did not appear as an escape, did I? You were disappointed!"

"Yes, I was, but it was not your fault—yet I was drawn to you. Really! When you held my hand on the Tower you thrilled me—and I was much moved and wanted you to know my deepest feelings, my *alia* for Dorn Island—everything."

"I was moved, too."

"Oh, I know it! If you had not been . . . but never mind." Again she was silent.

She pressed her hands to her face, crying, "How can I do this? I owe you my life! How can I be so cruel? And you have been ill!"

"Was I a dreadful disappointment, Dorna? Answer my question. You won't hurt me. . . ."

"You were such a purposeless person, quivering with feelings. I could not see you as strong enough to make a woman happy, and I could only see unhappiness for you. I was afraid you would want one of us to desire you, and that no one would.—There, I've said it."

I laughed, and thought of Nattana and a little of Dorna herself.

"Why purposeless? Because I had no *alia* as you understand it?"

"Yes, just that. Before you came it did not occur to me that you would not have any. I thought *alia* natural to everyone. . . But that isn't all! My uncle and brother were finer than I. It really made no difference to them that you were working against them, but it did to me! I saw a horde of unplaced persons with no aims but with merely a desire to agitate about changing things, all swarming over my country—and so attractive, too, in a way. I saw you spoiling everything. . . I half hated you, John, and I felt vengeful and angry inside much of the time—"

"You never showed it, Dorna."

"Thank you for saying that. It went far at moments. . . I wanted to hurt you and to change you, and, if I could not, at least to spoil one enemy. . . But don't think that I was not attracted by you, too, John," she added.

The wound of lost opportunities ached again.

"Why didn't I know it, Dorna?"

"Ask yourself, Johnlang. I felt I showed it too much."

"When, Dorna?"

"That whole trip of ours in the *Marsh Duck!*"

"We were happy, weren't we?"

"It was like a bright dream. It was all good!"

"There was only one moment when I thought you might . . ." I could not finish.

"Why didn't you kiss me?" she demanded. "You could have done it. . . I had made myself as pretty as I could be."

Lost opportunity, eternal frustration—doubly hard to bear because she blamed me!

"Too much 'quivering with feelings,' Dorna."

"That wasn't all.—You did not think it right!"

"I did not—that is true."

She uttered a bitter, short laugh.

"You could have kissed me. You could have gone further and put your hands on me, very likely. I was fascinated by your hands.

So many of our men have large hands, hardened and broadened with work. Yours are fine and small and yet strong. Oh, John! . . . But it wasn't merely attraction to you. I was miserable! I could see that I was leading you to do the very thing that I had warned you not to do, and I blamed myself. Yet all the time I was driven on to make you want me, to get you in my power, and to spoil you as an enemy."

"Dorna, it all seemed so happy, so natural—"

"But I wanted to make up to you, too. I thought if I let you kiss me, touch me, I might do so. . . I said I was a little fascinated by you. It is true; I was. But I was innocent, Johnlang."

"We both were, Dorna."

"I was grateful to you for not kissing me and for not making a scene. You were right and I was wrong. We would not have gained anything by thrilling our senses—and stopping. We would have stopped, you know."

"You would have stopped me, you mean."

"You would have stopped yourself, Johnlang, my dear."

I would have liked to think I would have gone on to the end, yet it was not true.

"Other men had kissed me, Johnlang, and held my hand also, as you did, so why shouldn't you kiss me? Sometimes kisses are a drug. Even when you don't feel deeply, they change all your values. . . But to you they would have been more significant than to me. I knew that. And you were wise—"

"Not wise—weak!"

"Wise in the end. You did not suffer after you went away from the Island, did you?"

"No, Dorna."

"You might have, if we had kissed and held each other, and played that little game—and stopped!"

"It would have been a very happy thing, Dorna."

"In itself, yes. It always is, but it is the involving of one's emotions afterward and the creation of wishes that can't be fulfilled that makes it unwise. You went away with your emotions uninvolved in that way."

"And yours also!" I said.

"Oh, yes, mine too, of course. But you did get over wanting me, didn't you?"

"Partly. . . Remember that you had warned me. I did not think of you as one I could marry—not then, Dorna. . . You practically asked me to let you alone."

"Not really. . . ."

"Oh, how can a man tell!" I cried.

"By not taking a woman's statement as to what she wishes too seriously if he really wants her. You don't win us by deferring to our wishes too long, Johnlang. That sort of attention soon palls on us."

"Dorna, how easy it is to make mistakes! A man must know when to defer to wishes that may be vital ones to a woman, and when to overrule wishes that she wants to have overruled. And she states both sorts of wishes in exactly the same way."

"We want you to have more than human intelligence, John, and resent it when you don't; but we suffer just as much by misstating or not stating our wishes as you do by failing to guess the ones unstated or the ones to override."

"How wise we are after the fact!"

"There was one thing you did . . ." she began in a hesitating voice, "that I never could quite understand. You wanted to marry me, I know. That was your purpose, wasn't it?"

"Oh yes, Dorna."

"You knew I had a hatred of the idea of Islandia becoming foreignized. That was a wish of mine you deferred to, but you did it at the cost of your own chance to win a place for me. You sacrificed your *alia* for me. When you told me that you were making no effort to build a place for yourself, to build up an *alia* to bring me to, I could not understand. You cut out from your *ania* the one thing it needed. I still try to understand. I suppose it is hard for me because here all *alias* are the same, all good, and all fundamental, whereas with you what takes the place of them aren't all good and are often changing. But think what it means to an Islandian woman to have a man seeming to want to marry her and at the same time disqualifying himself . . . !"

"But you hated this *alia* which I could have worked for."

"Of course I did, but it was better than none. It would have upheld my *ania*, but without it there was nothing. Johnlang, I remember when you told me. We were rowing. . . Afterwards, I wept. And I triumphed, too, for I had disarmed at least one enemy. I was touched to the heart. . . And don't you see, when I most wanted everything clear and simple, came this dreadful confusing act of yours!—I understand better now. Your way of life and mine were at hopeless cross-purposes. But your mistake was in trying to please me rather than in working to win a place for me to go to. If I had wanted to marry you, which would I have rather had, do you think?—There is no doubt at all!"

"Dorna, you are an enchanting person. You seem to me right as you go along, but I make reservations. When I come to express them, however, I can't remember what they are."

"Each of us tries to see the other's way, but our own native way is bred in each too deeply for us to understand the other's way long."

She looked at me as though wishing approval, her head tilted a little, and I nodded. She smiled and then her expression changed and she leaned over the arm of her chair, the back of one hand in the palm of the other. Her hands were not like Nattana's, which were smaller, more sensitive, and knew me too well. I turned my eyes from Dorna's too lovable hands.

"May I scold you?" she asked, shaking her head.

"Of course!"

"Oh, John, let me tell you this, please. When you came in the spring a year ago I was all upset. I had thought about you a great deal. I'll confess now: I went to the Ronans' to get away from you because I knew I might easily care for you too much for my peace of mind.—Oh, my peace of mind! My serenity! I begged you to protect it, and you did, but I half offered it to you to destroy! You longed for me, but it is not interesting just to be longed for even when it is beautifully expressed. You were careful of me, and oh, so tender. It is boresome to have a person always so tactful!

"Do you remember that night when you took me back to the Ronans'? I tried to leave the farm without you, but you asserted yourself and came. That thrilled me. It was what I wanted and did not want. Then on the steps in the dark finding the boat—I will use your word—I nearly 'loved' you. I did love you! That was our night, our moment. We thought of rowing out into the river. I said, 'The poor Ronans!'—Why didn't you row away with me anyway? Didn't you see that every time you did assert yourself I was meek and let you have your way? Do you remember I did not want you to come ashore? I was afraid I would do something wild! Yet when you came, I did not object. Then what did you say?—That the one thing you wished for me was placid enjoyment. You did not wish that! I can't believe you really did. If a man wants a woman he wants her to want him, whether it makes her serene or not! You asked if your coming interfered with my serenity. You hoped it did. If I had said yes, you would have been thrilled! And it did, Johnlang, and I wanted to say so. Of course, I tried to put you off. But you were put off so easily. Why didn't you pin me down? I gave you the chance—twice! I asked you what you wanted me to say—twice. You did not insist on knowing, but I would have said what you wanted. But you were being tender and tactful. You asked if I wished you to be at Dorn Island. Think of that question! You were trying to please me, not really trying to win me. I don't think you could have known what you really wanted, or you would not have been so afraid of hurting me."

"I wanted to marry you," I cried. "I wanted to tell you so, but I did not want to hurt you, too. I knew you were in trouble. I did not want to add to it. You had asked me—warned me."

She leaned forward again.

"What do you mean when you say you wanted to marry me? Don't be afraid to tell me. You won't shock me."

I was silent.

"Did you want my body?" she asked.

"Yes, Dorna."

"What else did you want?"

"To live with you always."

She clasped her hands tightly.

"Did you want children and me to be their mother?"

"Yes, Dorna," I said instantly.

"Did you think of it then?"

"No!" I cried, and the question made me angry. "I loved you. I wanted you. I would have loved our children if I had thought of them, but why should I think of them? It was all so beautiful, so new, so complete!—That seems to be the test question you Islandians put to each other. With us 'love' makes us accept children gladly. As 'love' goes on it grows, and gladness in being parents of the same child comes with that growth. We don't think of them in advance!"

"No," she said, "you don't, but we do. The idea is in our minds, you see, and there is nothing more wonderful than to see a person and to know all through your being that 'this person, so different from me, is the one with whom I wish to share my powers to make new life.' "

I felt dimly the reality of such a feeling and would not defend "love" against *ania*.

"Don't think that your 'love' is not something very beautiful, John. It is delightful not to think in advance, to know your moment good and to seize it, to be so confident of your happiness that you know that whatever happens it will continue. But we also can give all to the moment. We lose nothing by feeling deep in our hearts that the normal consequences are what we also desire."

"Oh, I understand—only partly perhaps, not being one of you—but I can't help resenting anyone thinking that they have anything greater than 'love' as we know it."

"Greater?" she said. "Did I say *ania* was greater? It is our way. Yours is yours. Maybe yours is the greater because it is simpler and more like animals and less thought out. . . I don't know, and I don't much care. Both are beautiful. Your love for me was a wonderful thing for you to give me. There have been men. . . They saw me as the mother of their children, I know, but their *ania* did not seem beautiful or interesting—and what you felt did. I knew it was not a mere *apia*."

A few moments before this all the old misery and ache of frustration had come back again, but it had passed like a flash of hot wind in summer. I was merely tired, thinking how good it was to sit on a veranda in the sun with Dorna, having nothing more active to do than to talk.

"You are so kind!" I said. "I somehow knew in my soul all along that you could be perfect in spite of misunderstandings and differences."

"Am I perfect?" she asked gently.

"Absolutely, Dorna. . . ."

I closed my eyes. . . I heard her voice from far away.

"I have dragged you through enough, dear Johnlang," she said. "I'll tell you about myself after we have had lunch. I'll go to see about it now."

We did not really talk again until lunch was over, when we had gone our separate ways for an hour or so, and I like a real invalid had taken a nap. We met again in the long low room of the books, because a chilly mist had swept in.

"Do you want me to tell you about myself, Johnlang?" she asked when we were comfortable before the fire, she in Alwina's chair.

"Yes, I do, Dorna."

"First," she said, "I want to scold you for one more thing."

"Go ahead, Dorna."

"It is about your *History.*"

"What did I do?"

"Weren't you satisfied with the help Morana gave you?"

"Of course I was."

"Yet you wanted me to think you would rather have had me."

"I would have loved having you help me."

"Why?"

"Dorna—to work with you!"

"Didn't you want the *History* to be a certain kind of thing?"

"Yes, of course."

"Would I have helped you to make it that thing?—I am of a different party. You were fighting me."

"You would have played fair."

"Would I? I wouldn't have helped you, anyway.—Why did you let your resolution \to make the *History* a fighting document go slack?"

"You mean it was not strong as an argument for trade relations with us?"

"It was weak! I am sure Morana never intended it to be anything except what you originally meant it to be—a fighting document— but she was too little interested in your propaganda and too much of an artist to hide what she felt. And so were you. Here and there in the *History* were indications of your original plan, but they were like little islands left by a rising flood. All the rest was just an account of the United States without any argument at all. I looked for a strong plea for foreign trade."

"Did it interest you, Dorna?"

"Oh, it was clear, simple, well told—but it was not one thing and it wasn't another. I was disappointed."

"I am sorry. . . ."

There was no escaping her criticism.

"Try again another time, without any bias, Johnlang."

I wanted to say I was done with all such things.

"I did not like Morana helping you, if you must know it. . . I could not help feeling that if you had met her before you met me, you would have 'loved' her, and she would have treated you much better than I did. . . ."

"You have been fair."

"She mightn't have—cared for you as I did."

My heart stopped. We were careful not to look at each other.

"I knew you cared for me, but never knew how much, Dorna."

"I don't want to revive any hopes . . ." she began after a moment.

"There are none to revive."

"Don't be too sure," she said sharply. "I have a little the same problem, too."

I bowed to her and made no answer.

She had bent her head and sat quiet, seeming to stare at her hands, but her eyes had looked beyond.

Color came warmly into her cheeks. Then suddenly she raised her head, her eyes very bright.

"When you came in the spring I knew you 'loved' me—at least I thought you did. I knew it wasn't *apia*, but I wasn't in the mood for anything deeper. I pitied you. I felt treacherous as I have told you. But there was more than pity. It was not *ania* for you. It never has been. . ." She suddenly clasped her hands and the knuckles went white. . . "Oh, the truth is I wanted you to make me feel *ania!* And you fascinated me. I wanted to touch you. I loved your balanced clean face, your clear, honest, puzzled eyes! I liked all there was about you. I was not afraid at all—of you, I mean—but I was afraid of myself.

"Do you remember when we went up the Tower? That day I felt that I could never leave Dorn Island. I wanted you and the Island both. You offered a way by which I could keep the Island. Your reserve, your sweetness, your willingness to go on with me whatever kind of person I was, made me weak—and led me to do what I did.

"I was thinking how beautiful the Island was and wondering—not for the first time—if you might not become one of our agents, living at the Island. The nearest one is at Earne, a long journey for those to the west of us in the Marsh; and we had often thought of having an agent making his residence with us. . . And you were standing by my side so quietly, wanting me, seeming to understand.

"I gave you my hand. I thought, 'This is what I shall do. I won't marry Tor. . .' Then it all became so clear. You had faith, but you did not know me. I lacked faith. I would make you unhappy. I would not be happy myself, for I would always remember my lost chances. I would have married you because I loved my home most. I would put you in an inferior position as a sort of pensioner of the Dorns. You were too dear, too innocent, to be taken that way. But I wanted you, John—I wanted you then to be my man—oh, to have me, I suppose, for always.

"I said to myself, 'If I were an American woman, this would be enough to settle it. . .' I took my hand away and I ran from you. I had to get free from you quickly, for fear I would break and not see clearly any longer. You were like a kind of sleep. . . If you had not let me go, I don't know what would have happened. I might have broken and been yours. . . .

"I thought it all over and decided to go on, and to tell you a lie. . . Do you remember? I apologized for flirting with you. It hurt you, but me more. It hurts to belittle what your heart has felt!—But I had made up my mind not to be beaten by the foreigner, not to be made an American woman. . . .

"And all the time I was on the thinnest of thin ice, hoping it would break with me, hoping you would take charge of yourself and me . . . !

"But you did not. I could only half spoil your chance. You yourself spoiled the rest of it . . . ! And though I half hated you I admired you, too, for you were true to yourself, true to the nature of your 'love.' It was an unselfish 'love,' and thereby it defeated itself. And it was not your fault. Your love would have been cruel if it had been selfish. I can only put it my way: You were Islandian. You knew in your heart that you had no certain *alia* upon which my *ania* could live, even if yours were satisfied. You had your chance. I think you half knew it, and let it go for my sake. That was an act for my sake!

"But, oh, poor John—and poor Dorna, too—isn't it miserable that we did not have a clear way open to us, at least to see if we wanted to follow it, and that instead of that simple problem we had to consider all sorts of other things?"

Knowledge that I could have won her made memory of the loss of her seem like a present breaking with one who had been mine.

"I did not know I came so near, Dorna!—It is a hard fact to learn now."

"Do you blame me?"

"Not you—myself!"

"But you were true to yourself."

"I wanted you. I've lost you."

"That isn't the important thing. . . ."

"Oh, Dorna! I could have had you and I never shall! It makes me want to die!—I wanted you. I wanted to have you. It is like a knife in me."

"Please, please, my dear, don't be angry! Don't be hurt! You don't want me that way now!"

I had been seeing her as she was, on the *Marsh Duck,* with bare arms at the Ronans', swimming naked. . . .

"I don't know. . . ."

Her voice was speaking through a haze.

"We are close to each other, Johnlang, and we always will be, but to us desire is only a rage that interrupts our friendship. Be honest! You did want my body. You don't want it now. There is something else you want of me—"

"Why don't I want you now, Dorna? Is it because I am half-ill and you with child?"

"You will have to answer for yourself. . . But have you been wanting me these last few months—at the Fains' before you came over the mountains? Ask yourself that. Didn't a change begin when my brother went to see you? Be honest!"

"Life became livable again."

"Don't forget Nattana."

"Oh Dorna!"

"I know it doesn't mean you ceased to want me. I can't hold you to that high standard of singleness. I don't blame you. I understand!— I even understand your wanting to marry her, made as you are, loving only as you can with no real *alia* and your traditions—even if what you felt for me were true *ania.*"

"It was, Dorna, as nearly as I can ever know it. But it was good having Nattana . . . Am I all wrong?"

"I don't think so."

"*Ania* should never die!"

"It never does—wholly. It remains beautiful always, a picture fixed in your life."

"What makes it become only a picture?"

"A state of mind, Johnlang—any strong intervention or change in your life. Not necessarily another woman."

"What change or intervention have I had?"

"Haven't you changed a great deal? Several things have happened. You have an aim now—you never had one before."

"I have no aim, Dorna."

"Are you sure?—You have lived as though you had."

"What aim can lie behind what I have done?"

"The aim to live in a certain way—not to quiver with feelings. Aims come before you are conscious of them. They are not wholly thoughts originating in your mind."

"I don't see yet any purpose in my life."

"More important still, my Johnlang: your love was unselfish and therefore eager to make a gift. You have been close to death in giving my child and me our lives."

"I don't understand."

"Wait, my dear . . . And you and I are now having what most men and women do not give each other—a complete understanding."

"How can these things make me 'love' you less?"

"Not less—only not to acquire and have me . . . I don't know either—and perhaps you cannot know until you have met and wanted someone else."

"*Ania* twice in a lifetime, Dorna?"

"Yes, when some strong new thing has intervened. These things that have happened may be enough to free you. You want to be free, don't you?—And don't mind admitting it to me!"

"If I am never to have you."

"You will never have me."

"Cruel Dorna!"

"Don't shrink, Johnlang. Don't let me thwart your new aim."

"An aim which I don't know!"

"Wait! Oh please wait!"

"Wait till when?"

"Until you are sure. You are not sure now."

She was silent.

"I will wait," I said. "There is nothing else to do."

"Don't keep an old love alive when it is natural for it to die."

"You mean: let these interventions you talk about kill it."

"Let them have a chance to kill it, so that you can live unhandi-capped by me.—I don't want to say this to you, but it is the only truth I can tell you."

"How can I know that it is natural for my love for you to die?"

"I can only say: wait!"

"Wait for what, Dorna?"

"For what life brings to you. It may bring you something good. And I may be able to help."

"How can you help me? You will never be mine."

"Perhaps I can give you something better than a woman whom you would not make happy and who would defeat your own happi-ness."

She rose.

"Let's not talk any more now," she said, tension in her voice, and she went away quickly without looking back.

After waiting to be sure that I would not cross the path of her flight, I went outdoors into the mist that veiled the Frays, and which from below would be clouds in the sky. One hears music and is deeply moved, but afterward there sometimes comes a more blessed serenity than was known before. Dorna now was like music, exalting, heart-breaking, but heard from a distance. Yet despair has a sister, Indif-ference, and when Despair drives one too hard she comes and the relief she gives has a deceitful resemblance to happiness. How pleas-ant it is to have her and to be goaded no longer!

Dorna said, "Wait!" I had answered, "There is nothing else to do."—It had not seemed funny then, but it did now. Yet a life spent in waiting for something to come eventually decays . . . I wanted to do something! . . . Perhaps this was what she meant by having an aim without knowing what it was.

I did not see her again that day, and saw Tor, on his return from hunting, for only a glimpse; but she sent me a note with these words: "Tomorrow I have two things to tell John." She thus stirred a curi-osity, which was pleasant because at the same time she promised to satisfy it.

That evening Donara and I dined together, and she talked of

Dorna as a child, a rather unruly, difficult one, headstrong, bad-tempered sometimes and sometimes sullen, but always lovable and beloved. It was good to have this knowledge and thus to make more definite the details of the picture of the woman I had loved, which I would always carry with me.

The clouds had risen higher and a hard rain was falling next morning. The brook that passed near the Lodge was full of roaring muddy water.

It was tedious waiting to see Dorna again, but evidently she, once an early riser, lived like a queen. It was midmorning again before she came into the long room.

She approached me and I rose. She came a little nearer than I expected. We looked in each other's eyes a moment. Neither planned it in advance, but in a sudden wordless flash both understood. I kissed her—a straight kiss on her lips—and she kissed me honestly. In that moment I wholly knew and possessed the strong sweet violence of Dorna's desirableness.

Her eyes questioned for a second, shy, pleased, and then she turned to Alwina's chair.

"You have two things to tell me," I said.

"Oh yes! And one is something really good!—And the second . . ."

She paused and looked at the fire, laying one hand on the other.

"What is the second, Dorna?"

"My marriage. I wondered what and how much to tell you, and what he would think. Last night I said to him that I wanted to be free to tell you anything, even about him and me, even things he did not know. He asked me why. I could only answer with what I have said to you: that I have made you very unhappy, that you wanted me and had lost me, that you were now finding yourself again, that the mystery of half-known things prolongs grief, and that you would go on more peacefully knowing just how happy or unhappy I was. I told Tor that I could not control what you would feel if I gave you reality, but at least you would no longer be suffering over imagined possibilities for which there was no reason.

"Well, he agreed. He said it really did not matter to him what you knew or did not know. And then I told him how happy I was with him and did all I could to make it seem true."

"Dorna—" I began.

She held up her hand.

"Don't stop me. Don't say I need not tell you. I want to tell you. It is really very simple. He began coming to see me three years ago—that is, to see me first of all. It was through his friend Stellin. Once, when I was quite young, I thought I could be happy with Stellin. We decided to wait and—oh, it was a little as with you. You were ineffective . . . You won't mind my saying so now, for you won't be later. . . ."

"This aim which I don't know, Dorna?"

"Yes, exactly. Don't scorn it . . . He was ineffective in a different way. He was too impersonal, too little ambitious, too wise—too perfect a flower! I wanted something more assertive and strong and vigorous, I suppose. So we parted—and are friends. He got over it quickly. He would. He knew just what to do in such cases. You could not disturb him for long!

"But I did not intend to tell about him, yet it may explain things a little. Tor began coming to see me. He is very handsome. Like others, I was affected by that and despised myself a little for it. One day we had a scene. He is simple, rather like an animal. There is no wickedness nor deceit in him. When he wants a thing he goes for it perfectly straight. If the thing objects he has no scruples against coercing it against its will—not like you and Stellin. But I am not so weak, either. What he wanted I did not . . . ! I thought that scene had ended everything and I did not greatly care. Yet I thought about him often, not in that way, but because of the strength in him. He is different from most of us, I know. That was partly the reason. I told you I was different. I liked him for being a true Tor, not a weak one. I liked his type, his intensity when he has some purpose. I liked the power that is latent in him. I felt that he matched me!

"He asked me to marry him, before you came. And, oh, I saw a vision! I saw myself helping him to use his powers. We understood each other, though we differed often. We recognized a likeness. I saw us founding a new line of Leaders, whom the Moras could not dominate."

She looked at me quickly and then away.

"Somehow he was the man I wanted to live and work with, the only man who could ever satisfy one side of me. He seemed to give me scope to be myself. Stellin did not. You did not. Only Tor!—I know what you are thinking—that he was Leader and had the most to offer of you all—a position possibly of great power; that Dorna was ambitious for power, political power. I am not going to pretend! Those things did enter in, but they were not all of it by any means. . . .

"Why was there a doubt in my mind?—Can you understand a woman's wanting to marry a man because of his qualities and the life he offers her, and yet not wanting to be his wife? *Ania,* Johnlang, but no real desire, only a sort of dread . . . ? Can't you forgive me for being a little unkind to you with this problem in my mind all the time? Then you became dear. . . .

"I decided to go on with it! I have. There is not much more to tell. It was *ania.* I am glad I am to have his child. That justifies it all to me. If I weren't glad of his child in me—and mine too—I would know it to be a mistake and a failure. But the desire has not come, and I am afraid it never will. I save myself for myself. I want to give; I cannot. Oh, sometimes . . . but it would be so with anyone.

"That is the unhappiness. But I can make up for it in other ways. He and I work together, agree, live together better than I thought possible. It is going to be enough . . . That is all there is to tell."

It seemed that she had told me nothing I did not know. My own loss of her was very little. There was a perfection, a naturalness, which she had missed—and which Nattana and I had missed also.

"*Ania* is not enough," I said.

"That is what I wonder."

"Maybe you mistook something else for *ania,* Dorna."

"Don't say that, Johnlang, don't! I have faith in my *ania* for him!"

I held my peace, but at that moment knew what *ania* was better than she, caught in the toils of a self-deceit—Dorna, who seemed so wise and was so sure, herself false to the theories she taught me!

"Let's not talk of this any longer," she said. "There is no more to tell! But I want you to know one thing: I haven't lost faith in *ania* that is perfect, even if I have missed it."

"If I had married you?"

"If I had married you!" She looked in my eyes, and shook her head. "It might have been," she said, "but our marriage would have been false for other reasons. What we are thinking of is not the only perfection. *Ania* must be rounded and complete in all ways."

We disagreed only about the meaning of a word and were one as to the fact.

"I am not a true Islandian," she continued. "I am only Dorna.—
You be a true one!"

She held out her hand. I took it, retained it for a while, and then
gave it back to her. All that we did not utter was understood and lay
within us for the future.

Dorna fled for a second time, but she said, "This afternoon I have
something more to tell you." But there was nothing more that I wanted
to know.

With the new knowledge which she had given me, I sat alone for
a long time. She and I had once had quite enough for a marriage at
home; and but for something hard in her, not wholly typical of her
country, she would very likely have yielded that little more which I
needed in order to be emboldened to win her. I would always treasure
the fact that we had come so close; many old hurts were cleanly
healed; but it was bitter to have lost her by so narrow a margin, and
what she had said raised for the future unforeseen and troubling
hopes. At present she was deep in her marriage and her will was intent upon making it complete and successful, and I must not now
render difficult the path she had chosen; but might there not come
a time when she would no longer wish me to let her alone?

In my room I heard the rain and enjoyed the darkness of the low-
hanging clouds; but the rain ceased and the grayness gave place to
a bright sunlight shining brilliantly on wet grass and leaves. Rain was
better, more quieting.

We sat upon the veranda in the sun, and she had been thinking
the same thoughts and was troubled in the same way.

"I believed it right to tell you everything," she began. "But I
wonder if I have not said too much, starting something new rather
than ending the pain of something old." She looked me in the eyes.
"I am Tor's now, bearing his children. There may be three or four
of them in the next eight or ten years."

It was almost as though she said, "For the present I shall be
faithful, but when the childbearing period is over. . . ."

Ten years did not seem long, and at the end of that period of time
I could return to Islandia.

"After that," she went on, "the relation of a man and woman is
really a different one. They have completed one phase of their lives.

Their house is built. Thereafter they maintain it. But their comings-together are of a different nature. I don't know how I shall feel then, but I know what is best for you and me."

She looked down at her hands, bending back her fingers, and waiting for me to ask her what it was.

"I have been wondering also, Dorna. Tell me what you think."

"What I know!—You must not live for any hope ten years away —nor must I. Such a hope must be no active factor in your life nor in mine. It is not worth it, Johnlang. It destroys too much and gains too little—for we can never start a new life together. We would be at most—oh!" She shrugged her shoulders as though in disgust. "If my nature demands that sort of thing," she said, "I would do better to have it with someone else!"

"I shall have no hopes nor expectations," I said. "Nor is it probable that I shall ever return to this country."

"Don't say that!" she cried. "Don't commit yourself to such a thought on account of me . . . I said a cruel thing, I know, because it isn't only the married who prize fidelity—but what I said is true. You and I must break clean, dear Johnlang, with no ties at all, because all is before you. You are young; you are unmarried; you have lost me; interventions have occurred; you must be wholly free to find the best life for yourself."

"How about you?"

"I have chosen my path. You play no part in it."

"And yet you said. . . ."

"I know what I said. It makes no difference!"

Her eyes blazed. I did not disagree with her at all: I wanted to be free of her; but she was too recently mine to be given up so easily.

"Suppose I come back in ten years, Dorna, and suppose we love each other?"

" 'Love' each other how?"

"*Ania.*"

"It would not be that with me—only desire."

"Have it that way! Suppose it is *ania* with me still and just desire with you?"

"I would leave you alone," she cried, "if I had any really kindly feeling for you at all! I would be cruel if I let you have me. It would only sharpen your suffering. Nor would I delude myself into thinking, as some do, that my *desire* might change into *ania;* nor would you be wise or kind to try to persuade me, saying, 'It is only *apia* now, I know, but it may *grow* into *ania*.' Such a growth isn't likely, Johnlang. Just as lovelessness doesn't turn into love merely because a person has you. You agree to that, don't you?"

"I do," I answered, "but there are some who don't. Those who love are always trying to persuade those who do not that love will come."

"It never comes in that way to the sensitive and strong . . . But you won't have *ania* for me ten years from now, Johnlang!"

"I may. Anyway, even suppose I don't—suppose it is *apia* only—"

"Both of us?"

"Yes, Dorna."

"Oh, if you were free and it would not hurt Tor, I am not one to say an absolute 'no' to us. Men and women always gain something enriching from each other when they are sincere; but often they lose more and are started on false trails. And wouldn't it be for us a dreadful descent, for we have both felt a stronger thing than that, Johnlang?"

"You may feel *ania*, too, Dorna."

"I won't!"

"Suppose you do? You may!"

"All right. Suppose we both feel *ania* . . . Then, I tell you, I pity both of us. What is there for us to do if I can't break with Tor and you aren't free either? It might be better for us if we once came together, and really knew each other, settled all doubts, solved all mysteries; but if we came together at intervals always aware of the complete life we did not have, we would suffer more than we gained. Our position would be a hopeless one. The best we could do for each other would be to be very careful friends, ready to help each other with a word if needed. But that won't be our case, not mine, not yours!"

"How can you be so sure?"

"Your age, mine, time, the need to live a full life that is in both of us so strong. I am hard, Johnlang. So are you going to be—hard and strong and one of us."

I laughed at her, and then she laughed. Our eyes met, and we both flushed a little. It was, after all, mere supposing, playing with an idea.

"You know what I want you to do, don't you?" she asked.

"Yes, Dorna—to be free.—I am free."

She watched my eyes for a moment and then smiled as if with great pleasure, but each knew that the other had made a reservation, and each felt it wise to say no more.

In spite of the rain Tor had gone hunting and had again given Dorna and me an opportunity to be together uninterrupted. His avoidance of us was a marked kindness and I was conscious of him and in consequence of the reality of his and her relationship.

Instead of remaining indoors that fine afternoon of clearing after rain, we walked away from the Lodge to a grove of pines eastward from the house about one-fourth of a mile. On the edge of a steep, boulder-strewn descent to the terrace next below we sat down together with pine boughs and blue sky overhead, and the wide lands of the Central Provinces far below at our feet and rising to the clear straight horizon of the sea. For a while we pointed out places we recognized. There was Reeves and there the Islandia River in its trench; farther on was The City and to the west was Bostia, a faint white patch in the blue plain.

"It is not like the Island," she said. "Yet it is a wider, finer view and more like this country."

"The Marsh is just as spacious, Dorna."

She agreed without saying anything.

"I love the sky to be a complete dome over my head—and the smell of marsh and salt sea and strong winds from the ocean. . . ."

The pines recently wet with heavy rain gave off a strong damp pungent odor in the high hot sun. The one with whom I sat was transplanted from the place where she was native and natural.

"Do you like it here, Dorna?"

"Yes," she answered. "I think I like it. It grows on me, but I loved the Island without thinking and as I breathed, an easy natural love. A conscious love is never quite the same . . . But you—do you like it?"

"The Frays, Dorna?"

"More than that—Islandia?"

"With all my heart."

She and her country seemed one.

"Do you wish it to be yours?" she asked.

"Islandia? I shall never forget it."

"Don't you want more than a memory? Wouldn't you like to have it really yours?"

"To live here, Dorna?"

"Yes, Johnlang!"

Her voice trembled and there were tears in her eyes, but I did not know why she was so greatly moved. Trying to imagine Islandia as mine, as my home—the United States permanently abandoned—I felt a deep pain, something lost, something immensely rich acquired.

"I have never thought of it as possible, Dorna, and I don't know." The pain sharpened. "I don't want to think of it as mine," I added.

"Why not?"

She held out her hand as though imploring.

"I might want to live here too much. I am going away fairly soon, you see, and it may be very difficult."

"You need not go!" she cried. "Oh, why is it so hard to tell you that you can stay?" She pressed her hands to her face for a moment and then flung them away and faced me. "Stay here," she said, "and be one of us! If you wish it Tor and I can make it possible. If he and I ask the council when it next meets to give you leave to become one of us, I know it will be so. Please wish to live among us, Johnlang. You do love Islandia, don't you? Doesn't it sometimes seem your own? You are naturally one of us. Tor and I want you here, and there are others. Let us give you Islandia. I want to give it to you."

"You make me love you, Dorna."

"Love my country," she said.

"What have I done to have it offered to me? Why should the rule be overridden in my case?"

"What matters is what you have given me, Johnlang. The warning you brought from the pass is only part of it, but it is a very lucky part for it gives the council a reason for treating you as an exception. Believe me, I do not belittle that gift, but I wanted you to have Islandia long before then."

"It is you who have been the giver, Dorna, and now you add this!"

"I believe I have given you something, and it makes me very happy. But let's not balance our mutual gifts. Let me complete mine!"

"I would love to take your gift, Dorna, but I don't know what to say. So far all my plans—and the purpose which you say I have—have been connected only with home—"

715

"Because you did not know what you could have. Isn't this really your home?"

"An adopted home, Dorna."

"Your real home discovered at last, Johnlang, my dear."

"What could I do? What use would I be? Where could I live?"

"I have thought of all that. The gift would not be complete if we did not offer you an *alia* also. Oh, I have had in my mind many things. Remember I have thought of you as an agent at the Island, but probably that would be unhappy for you now and for me to think of. But the best life here is as a proprietor of a farm, as a *tana*. You could buy or establish a farm, Johnlang. We could help you find a farm,—one already in running order with dependents capable of working it until you have learned enough and until the next generation of Langs has grown up to carry it on, knowing it from childhood."

"Where could I find a farm?"

She hesitated and spoke in a low voice, her face no longer turned toward me.

"The Dorns have three," she said, "one too many. They could sell you one, not the Island, but the Mountain Farm or the farm on the Lay River which you have never seen. I spoke of this with my brother and Nekka not long ago."

She clenched her hands tightly and spoke as with relief.

"If not that, we will find a farm that you could buy—Tor and I. You told me once what money you had and its equivalent in our own."

It was clear what would have to be done if I bought a farm: I must turn my investments into gold and import the specie into Islandia— and the idea was a little repellent.

"I could begin as a dependent," I said.

"I have thought of that also," she answered. "The main thing is for you to be here as one of us—as *tana* or *deneri* does not make a great difference."

The life of a dependent would mean such work as I had done at the Fains' or at the Upper Farm and such a house as the Anors, the Ekklys, or Nettera herself lived in. There I would be alone, the sole member of my family; but as such, whether a dependent or a proprietor, I would as a normal Islandian eventually marry, for otherwise my family and with it my *alia* would end with my death. For me the full life could not be lived without children. If I remained I would wish to carry on my line. One of the ingredients of *ania* was present, but with whom should I live? There came an instant thought of Nattana and a repulsion . . . I loved Nattana, but she was not the one. She must be someone with whom I had in common that peaceful and continuing perfection which I never had had with her, but might have had with Dorna were she less hard and ambitious, someone new and of my own kind, who would adventure with me, a stranger in a life I only half understood. . . .

"Do please stay!" Dorna said.

She began to cry, silently, with shoulders shaking, hiding her face and turning from me.

Again surprised by the strength of her emotions, I wondered whether or not to attempt to comfort her in some way, and in a detached spirit refrained, watching the strange spectacle of Dorna weeping.

Looking off at the distant plains I told myself with amazement that this land was through Dorna potentially mine. But her offer also marked the ending of my visit; the time to leave the Frays had come.

I turned my eyes to Dorna again. She was quiet now, but her face was averted. It was not for me to search it out until she was ready. So I leaned back and tried to make real the fact that I could be an Islandian, and found that to something in me it was quite natural but that the rest was dumbfounded.

The odor of the pines was strong and hot, the glare of the sun stupefying.

Dorna was mine. The gift of her country had removed the last barrier. Of what importance was the fact that the privileges in her body and the fruits of her childbearing were given to another? Every man and woman, interested and for the moment absorbed in each other, become one another's when together, however strong the social ties that have united them in the past and will unite them in the future to different persons. She was mine and I was hers, not only in this way but much more deeply.

Reaching out my hand, unknown to her I took between my thumb and first two fingers a fold of her skirt. With this contact established I was at peace, and would have been content in a little while to return to the Lodge, pack my bag, take my horse and ride down to the Fains' if there had been time before night fell, for I needed nothing more.

She sighed and I knew that she also had relaxed. We both were ready for what came next in our lives but it did not concern us now. We had said all the important things. We had had our flashes of perfect understanding so brilliant and so all-illuminating that the inevitable obscurities which remained were untroubling. Now was our time to be silent together, taking the place of being lovers, and for us as good.

She leaned back also, her arms behind her head, and we lay side by side, looking up into the detailed tracery of a dark swaying pine bough against the blue sky. All along my body was the sustaining contact of sun-hot earth, pine needles, gravel, with here and there a root or larger stone to tell me that this resting place, though natural, was not a soft, man-made bed.

After a long time of silence Tor, returning from hunting, passed near, saw, and joined us. He brought the reality of a world that required active thoughts and decisions to be lived in. Dorna had been content when sure that I knew she wanted me to remain in Islandia and I was content knowing that I could; but after she, sitting up again, had told him of her offer, he asked what I was going to do.

"Lang has only just heard that he can become one of us," she said. "He has had no chance to make up his mind."

But the decision was already clear.

"I love Islandia," I answered. "It may be the place where I shall wish to spend my life, but I would be sorry if I did not give my own home a trial first—for a year perhaps. Then I should really know."

"You need not decide at once," said Tor. "Let us through the council invite you to settle in Islandia if you wish to do so. I think you are wise to delay your decision."

What would Dorna say?

"If you go home, what will you do?" There was no disappointment nor surprise in her voice.

"Go to work as though I intended to remain. My uncle might give me a job. If he did I would take it."

"You might never come back," she said gently.

"That is true, Dorna, but if so, it would be because I knew where I wanted to live."

"Lang is right," said Tor. He paused a moment and then continued, "Dorna claims that the idea of the invitation is her idea and I claim that it is mine."

She flushed a little.

"You will receive it in any case," he went on, "and we both will wait anxiously and hope for your return."

His words must be taken literally.

"If I return," I said, "I hope I shall be worthy of Islandia and of you and Dorna."

"There is no doubt," he answered quickly, but her reply was a different one.

"That is unimportant. Islandia is nothing real, Johnlang. It is merely a place. Live true to your *alia* and to such *ania* as may come to you."

Tor laughed.

"We mean the same thing—all three of us."

I nodded, but Dorna was silent.

After several moments he spoke again. Next morning he would leave for The City and hoped to make the journey in two days. As soon as possible he would see Lord Dorn and would arrange for presentation to the council when it met on December 9th the matter of an invitation to Lang to remain in Islandia. He had no doubt of the outcome, he said, and his eyes grew bright; there would be no opposition! Nevertheless action by the council was a necessary formality.

He gently touched Dorna's hand.

"We shall be glad when it is definitely settled, won't we?" he stated.

"Yes," she answered with lips a little compressed. . . .

Whether the idea of the invitation originated with Tor or with her, he would be the one who put it through.

"You will be with us until after the council meets, won't you," he said, "at least that long?"

An important decision predisposes one to making lesser ones.

"I think I shall leave in the middle of December," I answered and felt Dorna's eyes upon me. "May I ride with you tomorrow?"

He did not answer at once, his clear gray gaze steady upon my face.

"And not stay with Dorna a little longer?"

Both waited for the reply. I did not seek any sign in Dorna's face and she proffered no audible help, but I knew that it was time to go.

"I wish to see the Fains soon," I said. "Their farm seems like home to me. It is less than two months before I sail. I also want to visit Dorn and Nekka, and there are others."

Looking in his face I said as plainly as I could that I wanted to leave with him. His eyes shifted to Dorna, but his expression did not change, and I knew that he also found there no help.

"Come with me then," he answered. Thus we settled it between us.

Dorna remained silent and after a little time we all returned to the Lodge.

All that could be uttered had been said and yet there was hunger for something and the feeling of a sudden rift between Dorna and me.

At supper that evening she was very quiet, but at the same time the decisions that I had made became firmer and more right-seeming. Tor led the conversation and spoke mostly of my plans and future. What Dorna had said as to the acquisition of a farm he repeated, and he also wished to know more definitely what I expected to do in the fifty-five days that remained before I left Islandia and after I reached the United States again.

He helped me greatly, and as we talked my own mind became clearer as to details and as to the fundamentals of my decision. I would go home and work hard and give to the American life all I had in me to give without reservation. If it proved the best, I would choose it. Meanwhile I would visit the Fains for a week or two until my full strength returned and then ride to The City and see Lord Dorn, who wished at some time a personal account of the experiences at the Vaba Pass.

After supper we went to the long room. Dorna sat in Alwina's chair, saying little, relaxed, brooding, thinking her own thoughts. The ache for something more increased, but at the same time the conversation of Tor and me deepened and broadened. Eagerly we discussed the differences between Islandia and the United States, both making sweeping generalizations, both interested and absorbed, saying nothing new but reclassifying and making more readily available for future use what ideas and knowledge we had. We half forgot Dorna. Sitting silent she heard two men playing with such a subject in a man's way, not greatly affected by her presence; and yet all the time I was aware of my debt to her and of how much through her I had learned, sure that she also was aware of it; and I wondered whether she saw with amusement what she had taught me thus reappearing and whether she noticed that some of the things I thought and felt came not from her but from others, among them Nattana. But all evening long her expression never changed and for some of the time she was surely in a world of her own where husband and lost lover played only a small part.

She left us for bed in the sudden simple way that she had shown at the Island, and when she was gone I knew how much I had hoped to see her alone again, nor could I talk easily to Tor any longer.

Not long after I went up to my room. Two candles were burning on the table; the fire had been lighted, for the nights were chilly on the Frays; and Dorna, sitting before it, was leaning forward adding a fresh log, when I entered. Her hair, in which gleams of light were enmeshed, was loosely done; her eyes were shadowy, very bright, and a little sleepy; her skin was warm with the glow of the afternoon in the sun; and she wore, not the buff and tan dress of supper, but a soft robe of bright new green.

"You are going tomorrow," she said as if in explanation.

"I am glad you are here," I answered, "for I was afraid I would not see you again."

She made no answer. I drew up the other chair.

"You have made a friend in Tor," she said slowly, watching the flames. "I was afraid that his interest in having you settle here would be only for my sake. But he likes you, Johnlang, and himself wants you here. I am glad it has happened that way."

"So am I, Dorna."

"I am only going to stay a moment," she said, and was silent.

The log that she had added to the fire was wet and hissed. Its flame waned and her eyes became darker. She pushed it with her foot, the flames increased again, and her face was illuminated, her eyes brilliant and glittering.

"There doesn't seem to be much to say, Dorna."

There was another silence.

"Do take to heart what I said about being free, Johnlang."

"Yes, Dorna, and you—"

"What advice have you for me?"

"Be a real queen, Dorna, all the time and as strongly as you can. That will make you happiest."

She bent her head in assent.

"Shall I see you again before you sail in December?"

"I think not, Dorna."

"I understand, of course," she said.

"I think my visit has been a success, Dorna."

"So do I—and we won't spoil it."

"We both like Tor."

"And my marriage is all in the making . . . And as to you, if I have ruined for you the way of life to which you were born, you still have Islandia."

"It will be what you have given me going on, Dorna."

"But only because you are what you are, Johnlang."

Then came the longest silence of all, and I drank deeply of her presence, and the draught was beauty, strength, and freshness. . . .

Her voice broke it suddenly.

"I am going, Johnlang. Do you want me to get up and see you off tomorrow?"

"Shall we, Dorna? Wouldn't it be—"

"Rather forlorn!—No! Begin your new life now, Johnlang."

"I will, Dorna."

She rose and faced me.

"How can I help you?" she asked.

"I am strong in myself, Dorna. How can I help you?"

"We will be friends in reserve always," she answered, "and that will be good to think of and treasure."

We watched each other and the moments flowed by, leaving us powerless to move.

"May I give you an idea to think about?" she asked. "A man's affection for a woman is in his head and in his flesh, and though the two affect each other they are also separate; but a woman's affection for a man, Johnlang, is a force in the middle of her, and what happens in her mind and what she feels in her flesh are often of less importance to her than to a man. He has more control over what he feels than she has."

"Is that a request, Dorna?"

"Yes, a little—if you come back."

"I will think about your idea, Dorna."

"That is all I ask."

"Let's kiss each other, Dorna, and say good night."

She drew a quick breath. Then I held her and kissed her mouth. For a second she was loose and yielded in my arms, but I released her lest I learn too much of what I had lost.

She moved toward the door slowly and I went to open it for her. As she turned to go out, she looked at me and smiled.

"That will have to satisfy us, won't it, Johnlang?"

"Yes, Dorna."

A flicker of amusement lighted her face. I held the door wide and she passed through, wrapping her long green robe about her.

30

Leave-Takings

THE LODGE at the Frays had been a quiet place, but my room at the Fains', where I rested after a hard ride with Tor and his attendants, was utterly silent. There had been the noise of words and the excitement of Dorna and of knowledge acquired; here, my hosts were old and said little, no wind stirred, it was midafternoon and sound and emotion were only a clamor remembered in the distance.

On my table lay an opened bundle but its contents had not been taken from the wrapping. It was the heavy parcel that Nattana had rescued from the Upper Farm, taking nothing of her own and only half dressing herself, so intent was she in saving what she had made for me. She had sent it to the Fains' by a carrier, charges prepaid, with no letter or word of explanation. It had been the work of months and contained thousands of threads all dyed and woven by her hands and thousands of stitches made by her needle. Nor would any of the clothes she made me be suitable at all in the United States except at a fancy-dress party or on a vacation in the woods or in a museum of textiles.

They would wear forever! They were so beautifully, so carefully, and so cleverly made!

What acknowledgment could I make and how repay her? She would protest, dear believer in equality, but the debt seemed all one, not for this alone but for all that she had given me. I must acknowledge the receipt of the parcel, thank her, and tell her my plans.

As I lay resting that afternoon I composed the letter in my head. There were also other letters to be written, announcing my homecoming. Steamers sailed early in November. It was now October 21st, and these they must catch or they would reach home no sooner than I did.

During the rest of my stay in Islandia I would wear the clothes that Nattana had made.

Ten days at the Fains' would be long enough to restore strength and health and also to recapture the life lived there which had been so good.

Everyone knew of my approaching departure and possible return, and many had plans in the last event, general and specific. The happy thing was that I could easily find some sort of niche, or *alia*. Kindest of all was the suggestion of Lord Fain that he would build a house for me if I cared to be one of his dependents; but it was an offer not to be accepted because his farm already had three families which were quite enough. Larnel was full of ideas, some impractical: he wanted to keep me in the valley and shyly suggested that he would probably never marry, and that there were only him and his sister at home, and that she was really a very nice girl . . . Larnella as a wife! Tolly took the trouble to make inquiries and to inform me of several farms on the foothills where a new dependent family would be welcome.

Life with them would not be incomplete: the Fains gave aristocracy, calm, and wisdom; Catlin was a man of information; Anor had knowledge of earth, folklore, and local life; Larnel was eager for activity; Tolly was a man of my own age, speculative, well read, poetic; the Catlin girls brought youth and loveliness. There were temptations to spin binding threads with man or woman that would be hard to break. . . .

Tolly was potentially an intimate friend. With him I talked late one night upon this region as a place to live. He denied that he found it dull and spread before me his philosophy. He would not admit that his *alia* was a millstone around his neck as I suggested. We both became rather heated, and I went home with these words ringing in my ears:

"You won't know anything about our way of life until you have lived it as we do, having what we have, and with no thought of moving somewhere else all the time!"

For Catlina Attana I sat for my portrait in flat relief to be set up in the mill commemorating my visits to the valley. It represented a. man leaning over and measuring a fence rail, the face in profile. To me it was not I, but Anor whose criticism she valued was pleased; no Islandian, he said, would look that way or work that way, and it was Lang all over.

Inspired by success she undertook a large relief of the Vaba Pass episode to be set up in my house if good enough and if I returned. For this she made many sketches, commanding my time. She wove a thread uniting me to her country. My house would have one ancestral carving if . . . This was the most ambitious work she had yet undertaken and would include many figures and require a year.

Two days before my departure came Nattana's answer to my letter:

Lang, my dear:

I am glad Lang is well again, but may I say he makes me laugh, because he treats the saving of his clothes so seriously and thanks me so profusely? That night of the raid I was waked suddenly. Hearing he was safe I was very happy. What difference did it make to me what I lost? I could not take my loom on a horse. Of course I thought of his things first of all. I worked on them so long.

I shan't try to thank him for what he did for me and the rest of us that night. It is beyond words.

So he returns home, not sure whether he will come back to Islandia or not. I don't know what to say about that, either. There is nothing to say, really.

Lang is under no obligation to see me before he goes. Of course I would be happy if he came here.

I shall be at the Upper Farm for a month longer. We are all hard at work becoming settled again. I am needed for a time. When the need is over I am going home (which means the Lower Farm).

How is Larnel?

Write me if I don't see Lang again, telling me how Lang is. I have worried a little, but shall no longer.

Think of all the things not said in this letter!

N. THE WEAVER

With the letter came three shirts, and to one was pinned a note saying, "More later."

On November 1st, I left the Fains' for The City, planning to return for one day to make final good-byes. Strength had fully returned, and the bullet wound was now only a catch in my side when I drew deep breaths.

Travel had most of its old charm, but perhaps never again would the moment-to-moment change of road and landscape be wholly absorbing. A purpose, even an unknown one, made one too impatient for progress, for the next thing on beyond.

While riding from Reeves to The City, I decided to tell no one at home that I might return to Islandia. The trial of the American way would be much simpler if relatives and friends supposed that I had no choice; for if Islandia came under discussion they would regard it objectively and utter fairer opinions.

I lodged at the Doring Palace which was open because of the presence of Lord Dorn at The City. On the evening of my arrival I told him in detail of all my experiences at the Vaba Pass. He in turn referred to Tor's visit and said that he was sure that the council would act favorably upon the king's request.

"Your wish to return home before deciding will not prejudice you in anyone's opinion," he said. "As to finding you a place to live, we will leave that to my nephew. Both Tor and I have written to him."

All the diplomats had departed except Count von Bibberbach, M. Perier, who as before represented in a semiofficial way all nations except Germany and England, and also Gordon Wills, who would remain, Lord Dorn thought, as long as the count did, to watch the Germans.

I inquired about the proposals to internationalize Ferrin. They were being considered at a conference in London, he said, which young Mora was attending on behalf of Islandia.

The choice was a little surprising, but Lord Dorn said drily that young Mora was not likely to give anything away.

Then with a change in manner he asked me more of my hopes and plans, and without advising me one way or the other made it quite clear that he would be glad to see me return, and thought that I could live a full life in his country.

"You are young," he said, "and are still pliable. You are not yet so bent by American ideas and ideals that you could not adapt yourself to our ways. You have made no definite American ambitions part of yourself and therefore essential to you."

"At home," I answered, "lack of ambition is deplored."

"That is natural, for the feeling that you have less than you want and must work to acquire more is in the air itself."

"Ambitions are sometimes concerned with the good of other people," I suggested.

His eyes were shrewd.

"An ambition to eliminate the need of such ambitions is the worthiest one," he said. "Concern over the lives and behaviors of others is not the best life. A reformer at the beginning is far more of a realist than one who has continued at it for some time."

His doctrines seemed to me scarcely Christian. Perhaps he was aware of a silent criticism, for he said:

"Spontaneous acts of kindness based on an actual need stand very differently. It is the generalized impulse to help and change that is to be suspected."

There was another matter which I had upon my mind, a surprise gift for Nattana, who sewed so often; and with much diffidence I suggested it to Lord Dorn, and obtained his leave to make one importation into Islandia. I told him the story of her saving my clothes, saying:

"It would be a spontaneous act of kindness, Lord Dorn—instead of an application of your rule against importations which is a generalization for the good of all."

"You are entitled to a few favors," he answered. "Of course we are inconsistent, but it is the foreigner who makes us so."

Two days were spent in arranging for my departure, now only six weeks distant, and in seeing friends, the Willses, Tor, the Periers, the Calwins, the Moras.

On the third day, still using the Hyths' horse, I rode eastward through Suburra and on into Camia. On the other occasion when I had visited the Stellins the ground was white with snow; now all was of a fresh, early May green. The discussions of brother and sister as to trees and shrubs had new significance. The Stellins' farm was as natural as Nature herself but also with that intelligent and satisfying touch which only a real artist can give. They were fortunate people thus able to combine so successfully two great beauties.

Tor had said that his sister would be at the Stellins'. He said no more, but something in his manner caused surmises. Perhaps Dorna's entry upon an active marriage had released Stellin, not from actual bondage to her for he had been dismissed some time before, but, as it were, from the habit of singleness. I also was released by her marriage and by our two days together.

What I surmised was true. Stellin and Tora were recently engaged.

Lord Stellin, Danninga, Tora, Stellin, and Stellina knew all about the Vaba Pass matter, and they also knew of the invitation to be extended to me.

At supper and afterwards in the living room, the raid, my escape, and the warning were discussed again and again, the conversation being kept alive by Danninga, Tora, and particularly Isla Stellin, who seemed to wish to eliminate chance as a factor in his daughter's safety.

She and her brother became silent, and after some time of answering questions I looked at her, and her eyes which always heretofore were open gates, met mine squarely only for a moment; she became suddenly no longer Stellina, but a woman who had escaped a terrible experience; and her eyes hid themselves. The fate from which I had saved her gave her to me too much to be talked about by either of us.

Lord Stellin began to utter thanks.

"Chance played a large part," I said, "chance and Don's foresight and training of the watchers. For us who have lived through it, it was too unusual to understand what happened. It wasn't as though a swimmer had saved the life of someone who was drowning. Then thanks would be natural; but what happened in the Upper Doring Valley was very different. I think Stellina will agree. Thanks are not due me for the part I played. I was there and I know."

"You ought to be thanked all the same," said Tora, "and I would thank you."

"Would you, after what Lang has said?" Stellin asked instantly.

"He would have made it a little difficult," she answered.

"He has had and will have the equivalent of thanks in other ways," said Stellin. "Everyone knows what everyone else has in mind. Thanks are only disturbing to all concerned."

Welcome silence followed. If Stellin understood me, his sister, so like him, would also.

Next morning, when Stellina and I met, the whole subject of the Vaba Pass was settled and done with and there was no need to mention it. We could talk and we did, drifting over the farm seeing again in the spring places previously seen under winter snow. It pleased her to remember how they had looked then and to contrast the two aspects. She asked my plans, listened while I told them, but made no comment. What we talked about was mostly the look of natural things. Her eyes lost their shyness. Her slender figure moved again with its supple ease.

Clear water hides nothing and seems the simplest thing and yet is a mystery, present to one sense and not to another, its invisibility cool and flowing. It cannot be grasped, but it quenches thirst, and all that its limpidness covers or touches is washed clean and changed and heightened in color. . . .

Evening came. There was chill in the air and we sat in the living room and at long intervals someone rose to the surface out of brooding thoughts and made a remark. Yet they all seemed content with dullness—and for me the beauty of the two young women and of the other young man was enough. Stellin and Tora had walked far, and his finely drawn face was the more handsome because a little fatigued; and she, for all her haughty, spoiled-child loveliness and her look of disdain for the status of visiting fiancée, had flushed cheeks and sleepy eyes and an air of willingness to be kissed.

The moon was one day past the full and when it rose its white light was perceptible in the uncurtained room, making the yellow candle flames and ruddy fire artificial. Stellin spoke of the moon, asked Tora to go out with him, and then looked at his sister and me. The two women fetched wraps at once and we four went outdoors.

The moon itself was a bright, sharp-edged disk of molten silver, but there was haze on the fields and among the trees, nothing on earth was hard, and all was flooded with soft white light.

Stellin and Tora drifted away arm in arm, and their departure made us a pair. We wandered out into the field where in the winter the birch trees had been cut down. She took the arm that I offered and her fingers felt like the touch of a fallen leaf, and she moved so easily at my side that she seemed to float without solidity.

"The moon!" she said, and walked with her face lighted by it, pale, rapt, every feature sharply clear, delicate, and balanced.

"Stellina, may I say what I feel?"

Her voice was cool.

"Why not?" she said, and her tone indicated that for men to utter what they felt was nothing new.

"You are lovely. You have done much for me."

"What have I done?"

She was not discouraging. I could go on.

"Today, this morning, you did not talk about the pros and cons of my returning to Islandia, but you made your country's beauty live again. I had lost it a little. That is your gift."

"I am glad you think so."

"Oh, you know it yourself, Stellina. You are a key to the loveliness in natural things."

"Am I?"

"Yes, of course you are!"

She did not laugh.

"You are something special, Stellina. You are not a sister. I haven't had any *ania* or *apia* about you but—"

"I'm content to be something special."

"If I come back . . ." I began.

We moved on. The beech trees rose up before us, dark and opaque like hills, almost as high as the moon. Her lightness made my own feet effortless . . . But she did not ask what would happen if I came back.

"If I come back . . ." I said again.

"You will find me here—a friend."

Her fingers gently guided our direction over the undulations of the meadow, lying smooth and rounded in the moonlight.

"I never thought I should be talking with you this way. You add to Islandia something it lacked."

"You will add something to our life also, when you return."

We moved into the shadows of the beeches, and gently her fingers turned me round.

"Look back at the house," she said.

It lay upon its knoll, blurred a little and its form simplified by the mist, the stonework opalescent in the moonlight, and behind it a high dark mass of trees. . . .

"You have done it again, Stellina!"

"What have I done?"

"Given me beauty—a beauty that starts a thousand hopes and wishes."

We moved along the high, clifflike darkness of the trees.

"You want something else," she said. "I wish I knew what it was and could give it to you."

My heart beat suddenly.

"What do I want, Stellina?"

"I don't think that kisses—and the rest—would do you any permanent good, not from me, nor could I give them to you, nor to any man unless I were quite sure for him and for myself . . . Perhaps you are curious—"

"No, Stellina."

"I have never wanted anyone really and no one has had me."

We drifted on and the house sank behind a rise of ground.

"Thank you, Stellina."

"You want a full complete life," she said. "Consider well where you will best find it."

Her hand trembled a little, and she spoke as though it were hard to express herself.

"If you come back, it will be for you an adventure . . . Let me also say what I feel . . . If you make it with another person, undertake it with a woman to whom it will be as great and as new an adventure as with you."

"You mean if I marry I should marry an American?" There again were the old bitter warnings.

"Wouldn't it be much more fun?"

"Stellina!"

"One of us," she continued, "would be too much at home, too much your teacher."

"Oh my friend!" I took her thin hand and held it tightly.

"What have I done?" she said.

"You have taken the pain from something that always hurt me."

"Have others told you the same thing?"

"In a different spirit."

"Do come back," she said softly.

Her hand fluttered and I let it go. We turned toward the house. After a few moments her hand came back again upon my arm.

"I would like to help you," she said. "If you do bring here an American woman let me come and see you soon."

We mounted a slope of meadow and the moonlight glistened on the moisture left by the mist. The ground was cold under our feet. Stellin and Tora, two slender figures arm in arm, were ahead of us, perhaps unaware that we followed them.

Near the door of the house they stopped without apparent pre·

meditation and for a moment were face to face and close together. The door made a square of yellow light through which they passed quietly, man and woman, black silhouettes.

We came to where they had been and went on and ourselves entered the house, content with what we had.

Next day I returned to The City. A letter from Dorn was waiting, containing a pressing invitation to come to the Island as soon as possible. Fak was three days' journey away at the Upper Farm, and I wanted him on the rest of my travels. While exchanging him for the Hyths' horse I would also see and say good-bye to Nattana.

Next morning I was once more on the now familiar road to Reeves and on the second night at the Fains'. There I spent a whole day and said farewells to all in the valley.

On the following morning I set out for the Mora Pass, and thought often of how easy it would be to turn aside and spend a day or two with Dorna. If the horse pointed his feet in the direction of the Frays, would I not lack the power to guide him back upon the main road? And yet in my heart I knew that it was all finished and over, and my reluctant temptation was not so much to continue an old affair as to begin a new one.

In early afternoon we reached the tower and platform where the road branched. The horse showed no intention to turn aside, and I knew that I also had none; but it was a relief to feel the path that led to her dropping behind me with every step forward.

"I am out of your power, Dorna," I said, "and it is to your credit that, not wholly wishing to lose me, you yet chose the best way to set me free. You stripped yourself of mystery, and revealing yourself as not wholly true proved that the human Dorna was more noble than my imagination, idealizing you, believed you to be. . . . But, oh, how I could have loved you!"

To her I owed the opportunity to claim her land as mine, but there were others to whom I owed as much or more. I thought of those who had helped me most—Nattana, Dorn, the Fains, Stellina, Hyth Ek, George, Morana, Tor. All of these would still be friends if I returned, and each with a particular value of his or her own. The only one with whom my relationship was still unsettled and doubtful was Nattana. I had been out of her power but the gift of Islandia had put me within it again. . . .

Once more at the Mora Pass Inn, I had great pleasure in walking about fully possessed of strength and vigor, no longer a bloodless invalid. It was also gratifying to be somebody in this part of the world, where men knew me as one of Don's watchers at the Vaba Pass and as the man who gave warning, not as an oddity and a foreigner. Best of all, however, was the sight of soldiers at the Inn, where they came on leave from the nearby passes.

Next morning early when I left the Inn a light hoar-frost whitened the ground. It was cold riding up to the summit of the pass, from which the Doring Valley lying at my feet appeared murky and dim, not yet reached and brightened by the rising sun. In haze its length seemed greater, and I pictured all the changes in its hundreds of miles from the mountains to the marsh and the sea. The West was perhaps the Islandia within Islandia most naturally my home. Suddenly and strongly I desired a place of my own within this inner Islandia.

The brown haze in the air presaged windlessness and heat. Though it was only November 13th, the seasonal equivalent of May 16th at home, the valley was under the spell of premature summer weather. As soon as I had passed through the great vertical portals that marked the end of the alpine region and was in the forest east of Doring Lake, it was hot, the pines breathed strong of resin, a clear blue sky was overhead and a dusty road underfoot.

Fifteen long miles were yet to be traveled before the road came to the lake itself. I rode, half dreaming and content, half troubled and restless, and at last reached the water, a pale ruffled blue under a warm, dry, up-valley wind. In the far hazy distance the knoll of the Upper Farm and the white dot of the house were just visible. Memories of life there flooded me, all set against a background of winter, the daylight short, the fields white with snow, rooms cold at night, blankets welcome in bed, and open fires to warm chapped hands; memories of the cold stable with powdery stone dust in the air, on my clothes, and on the faces of myself, Ek, and Atta; of Ettera in the kitchen, of the smell of sawn wood in the woodshed, of the workshop and the click of Nattana's loom, of everyone tired including myself, of sleepy domestic conversations with all of us one family; of Nattana in bed with me, each keeping the other warm, of her kisses, and of the feeling of her hair on my face.

I was riding to her with no clear purpose as to what I would say or ask. The Islandian Johnlang was Nattana's again as the one who had perforce maintained his Americanism was not. Though our wills and intellects had repudiated a permanent union and our separate nationalities had seemed a gulf between us, all the time our bodies knew otherwise.

But I must not forget that she had her own ideas, and that desire creates false semblances to delude a mind that opposes it so that the whole man may move its way. Whatever I said or asked or did, I must be truthful and frank.

The road followed the shores of the lake for several miles, now close to the water, now dipping back into the pine woods, with glimpses over the pale water to the farms of the Dasens and Hyths under the faint high mountains and gradually becoming larger, more detailed, more green and less blue as we drew near.

The horse's feet beat his home ground, familiar also to me in form and outline but changed in color now that spring was merging into summer.

No one knew I was coming.

My heart was in my throat and I was hot and parched, with dust thick on my skin and on the brown clothes Nattana had made.

How would she take my coming? She had been hysterical when she heard that I was hurt. Might not my arrival be a shock?

New beams showed on the roof of the stables. Men were working there, but I rode to the front door of the house which faced toward the lake and called my name.

No one answered.

I tied my horse, who was eager to break for the stable, and entered. Order had been restored. There was little trace of the damage done by the raiders. All was just as it had been, and memory was like a ball rolling into a hole which it exactly fitted. No one was in living room, dining room, and kitchen. I peered into the woodshed and it was empty. I went upstairs and looked into my room and saw there signs of recent occupation. In the workshop the loom had not been rebuilt, but there were two mattresses on the floor, and saddlebags. Knocking on Nattana's door and hearing no answer, I entered; it also contained mattresses and bags. The house was evidently crowded with guests.

Through an open window came the sounds of hammering and of voices from the direction of the barn. Thither I rode the Hyths' horse.

The new roof was a skeleton at one end, but at the other slates were being laid. Up in the air was a hive of workers. One of them saw me and called my name to others. The horse carried me into the barn on the run. Overhead was open sky, crossed by beams, and the sound of hammering and of voices, but Ek caught the horse's head and I dismounted. Others were approaching.

"Welcome, Lang," he said. "We hoped you would come our way again. All the neighborhood has gathered to help us put a new roof on the barn, as you see. We hear that you are going away. Stay with us a while."

"Your house is crowded—"

"That makes no difference. There's room for you."

What seemed a red-haired boy, barelegged, bare-armed, in shorts, shirt, and sandals, approached, but he spoke in Nattana's voice and was Nattana—her face streaked with sweat.

"Hello, Lang," she said. "We are glad you have come."

There was no sign of hysteria or shock. Having spoken she stepped aside to let others have their say: Atta, Ettera, young Ekkly, Gronan came up and men of the posse that had gathered under Gorth at Renner's Agency, and all seemed glad to see me.

I offered Ek my services.

"The more the better," he said, "but you are leaving Islandia soon."

"I can stay several days if I can be of use."

"No doubt of that. Stay!"

There was a lull. Some of those who had spoken went back to their work. I heard Nattana's voice at my side.

"Fak is well, but needs exercise. How are you?"

"Quite recovered, Nattana. And you?"

"I am a carpenter's assistant. Look at my hands!"

She held them out and they were covered with scratches. My eyes went beyond them to her face and her figure.

But Ettera was speaking.

"I know where I will put you," she said. "Come to the house with me. You can help me with supper if you aren't too tired. . . . There are so many of them."

"I must go to work—passing things," Nattana said, and went away without looking back.

Ettera gave me a bedding in a corner of Ek's room, now occupied by him and Atta. She and Nattana had the latter's quarters. The other bedrooms and the workshop were tenanted by the neighbors who had come to work on the barn, nine in all, and there were six more at the Ekklys'. They came and went giving what time they could. This condition had lasted two weeks and might continue several weeks longer. No one drew pay and some contributed food, but most were fed by Ettera and she was the cook for all, assisted by chance helpers. She was a busy woman. Soon I was as busy as she was and there was no time for thinking.

Time passed, shadows lengthened, and the air became cool. The workers returned and bothered Ettera by tramping through the kitchen and drawing water from her supply. She worked in the midst of confusion, and though her patience was a little grim it was to her credit that she was so restrained. Nattana came in, a jaunty boy, talking with a large, genial, bearded man; she also drew water, went upstairs, and after a little while came down again, a girl in a skirt, with braids.

Supper was late and candles had to be lighted. Eleven sat down to table, all men. Ettera and Nattana waited on us. Their faces were tired but both seemed happy, sustained by a good-humored excitement. Ek and Atta were soon finished and their sisters took their places and were waited on by them.

Across the table I caught Nattana's eyes and had a friendly look and a smile so quickly withdrawn as to hurt a little. Men leaned forward to talk to her, and she answered all of them, at ease, laughing, flirting a little perhaps.

After the meal was over there were more volunteers to wash dishes than were needed. My offer was a tardy one and was declined by Ettera, the general, who said that I had done enough; but those who were allowed to help seemed the favored ones.

On the porch the rest of us sat in the darkness, and, as the most recent comer from The City, I told them what I knew of political matters. Yellow light streamed through the open kitchen window and from within came voices and laughter, among which was Nattana's.

There were a few questions. All seemed to know that I was potentially an Islandian. Nothing at the Upper Farm was as I expected it to be, but there was gain in the consciousness that I felt, and was accepted as, one of these people.

Soon they began to drift away for bed. I returned to the house

but was too late. Ettera was still at work, but Nattana, she said, was
tired and had already gone upstairs. I also was tired, and it did not
greatly matter. She let me help her with the last of her many chores.
She was familiar again and like my older sister. I told her why I was
going home, and that I could not be sure whether I would return or
not, and it was a comfort to talk.

We were the last to go upstairs. She opened her door and holding
up her candle pointed. Nattana lay asleep, her hand under her cheek
and her hair over her face like a child's.

"She is so tired," said Ettera.

We said good night, and I sought my corner. Ek and Atta, my
roommates, were already asleep.

The house stirred. The valley was fresh and still in the early
morning light. Breakfast was eaten rather silently; no one was fully
awake.

The opportunity to speak to Nattana had not yet come. With the
men I went to the barn, and acted as assistant to the two who were
laying the slates on that part of the roof where beams and boards
were already in place. Each slab was almost as large as a tombstone.
Some of them had previously covered the roof, but most of the old
ones had cracked with the heat or had broken when the roof burned.
The rest had been brought from a quarry down the valley, and all
lay stacked in piles on the ground and were hoisted up by a derrick.

As a place to work, the roof was high in the air with a wide view
up and down the valley over the farmhouses and on the level with
the tops of trees. The green earth seemed far below, and the figures
there were foreshortened, so that when they walked their legs went
forward and trailed behind from a dwarflike roundness on which their
upturned faces were disks. The sun was bright and hot, the dry air
from the west still blowing. The two Hyths were not the only ones
dressed in shorts and shirts and sandals.

We, the roofers, were on the outside and for much of the time
looked down upon the carpenters engaged in setting up the beams.
After a time Nattana appeared among them. As "carpenter's assistant"
her job appeared to be to hand tools to the genial, bearded man, to
talk to him, and to keep him amused. He laughed, showing white
teeth. Apparently they were good friends. Once she sawed a board
for him, and he stood over her. When she kneeled and leaned over,

her shorts became tight. As half mine I wished that she wore something else, but was she mine at all?

No one hurried. The work was deliberate and solid, the new roof being built to last. The raising of a beam or the laying of a new slab was an important matter. Nevertheless as the morning passed the advance was perceptible. There was a feeling of light-heartedness, yet no one loafed.

At noon everyone ceased work and made for the lake. Others, mostly women, with some children and men, wives and relatives of the Hyths' guests, had come on horseback, bringing food.

Clothes came off everywhere, but the advance into the water was timid for it was cold. I plunged forward rather than wade in the iciness and swam to where Nattana was standing up to her knees trying to gain courage to immerse herself. Rising, I saw the whole of her again.

"I want a chance to talk to you," I said. "When can I have it?"

She looked at me with considering eyes.

"How long do you want?"

"An afternoon."

She studied me, and it was impossible to tell whether her look was hostile or tender.

Suddenly she became conscious and ducked under the water up to her neck scattering cold drops all over me. I looked down on her round head and white neck. Her body was froglike in the green water.

"How long will you be here?" she asked.

"Three more days."

"An afternoon is a long time when there is so much to do."

"It is not too long, Nattana. Give me an afternoon."

"I'll do this," she said. "Soon we are going to have to drive to the quarry for more roofing stone. You and I will take one wagon. There will be others but we will have a chance to talk, and it will take an afternoon."

We could talk no doubt, but we would be under observation all the time. But was more worth the battle?

"When will that be, Nattana?"

"Day after tomorrow or the next day."

"Thank you," I said.

She uttered a short laugh.

"I'm cold," she said, and rose and turned toward the shore, her body pink and wet. She glanced at me over her shoulder and her eyes were reproachful. I wanted to follow her and tell her that she was mine and must give herself again. . . .

Lunch was eaten on the boathouse wharf. A bonfire had been built, and was welcome after the coldness of the lake. I put myself under restraint and resolved not to pursue Nattana.

We all trooped back to work. The strangeness of the tasks had passed. Some day I might have a farm and the roof of its barn would be a personal concern; there was much to learn. Nattana could flirt with the carpenter whose assistant she was. For a long time I forgot about her, absorbed in the nice placing of heavy gray-blue slabs of stone.

It was a new experience to see Islandians adapting themselves naturally to a communal enterprise. The raid had been an extraordinary disaster falling heavily on a few households. All were concerned in restoring a normal condition. Once equality existed again, the individualistic life would be renewed.

Gronan and others and I talked of these matters in the twilight after supper, sitting on the porch, while Nattana, Ettera, and Branda, whose husband was one of the volunteers, worked in the kitchen with those men whom they had chosen to help them, including the big, bearded carpenter, Dorth.

He was an artisan like Nason, one of the two whom I assisted, and he lived at the town of Hyth. On such enterprises as this, men like him were really working foremen. They were paid for their services, for by such work they lived. As a citizen of Hyth he must have been known to Nattana from her childhood, but I did not like the fact that he was a widower. She and I had declared that the bond which once united us was broken, but we had swung an ax against a tough root.

Nevertheless on this day and the next two for no very good reason we played the game of Mutual Avoidance. Its unadmitted purpose is to lure the other on. Each hopes to be accused of avoiding the other and has excuses, an air of surprised innocence, and countercharges ready. It is equally part of the game to pretend that everything is perfectly normal. Each, however, lives in the hope that the other will weaken. The winner is the one who weakens last.

When there was a vacant seat at meals next to Nattana or to me, the other would refrain from taking it and would go somewhere else and talk to the person there as though having something important to say; but all the rules of politeness were carefully observed: we were scrupulous in saying good morning and good night; we even smiled now and then but never waiting to see if the other returned it. Sometimes each caught the other secretly staring and scored a point. . . .

It is a miserable game in which both players suffer as long as they play it, and both always lose.

On the third day, however, the pile of slabs was so far depleted that roofing must cease unless the supply were soon renewed. A consultation between Ek and Nason took place on the roof in my hearing. I heard that five wagons were to make the journey to the quarry, four belonging to neighbors and one to the Hyths. Next morning, which I had planned as my last at the Upper Farm, the wagons assembled, but not till lunchtime did Ek tell me that Nattana had suggested that she and I drive their wagon.

The game was played to the end. During the meal she did not look at me, and when at last it was over and the time had come to start she did not speak until I went to her.

"Well," she said shortly, "shall we go?"

She did not smile, and it was as though she felt that she had done her full share already.

I had seldom ridden in a wheeled vehicle in Islandia. It was odd to be rolling along a road, even though in a jolting springless fashion, instead of being on foot or on a horse.

Three wagons were ahead and one behind, but spaced at wide intervals to avoid the dust that drifted up from the wheels and from the horses' feet.

She held the reins and presented an impassive profile. I weakened and looked at her every little while and marveled that we who had been so close, our bodies enlaced and our tongues free to say anything, could be so far apart. It was as though our very closeness created in reaction a repulsion.

"Nattana?"

"Yes?" she said shortly.

"Look at me and smile, and say something."

She turned her head slowly before giving me her eyes, fighting against a smile, but her eyes at last met mine and dwelt there, and we recognized each other for the first time.

"Is there really anything to say?" she asked.

"I have something to say, Nattana."

She looked away and drew herself up wearily as though I put a burden upon her, and her smile was gone.

"You wrote me a very nice letter of thanks for saving your clothes, and I have been thinking how well you look in them."

"It isn't that, Nattana."

She sighed.

"Has it to do with the fact that you may return here?"

"Yes." My heart throbbed heavily.

"I hope you are not going to ask me again to marry you."

"Yes, Nattana. The hopelessness of my ever being Islandian was what kept us apart."

"No," she answered quickly, as though already prepared. "Nothing has changed. If I say I will marry you you will feel that you must come back here to live, and you don't want to have to do that. You told Ettera on the day that you came all about how you hoped to go to the United States, and when there to make up your mind whether you ever wanted to be Islandian or not."

"If you marry me, Nattana, we will go to my home and we will decide that question there together. Knowing we could return, you would look at my country with different eyes. You might even like it there—but if you did not, I would return here gladly. Having you would be the main thing; then the place would not matter at all. It would be our choice. That was not true before."

She gave me a swift look.

"Oh!" she cried. "Oh, Johnlang! I did not think you would put it that way. All I saw was what I said: you wanted freedom to make a choice between two homes, and if I married you I would force your hand."

I thought I had won her and was stunned with a deep dismay. She continued:

"But when you say *we* would decide, *we* would choose, you and I, *we! we!*—oh, Johnlang! your *we* melts me so!"

All the love for Nattana that had been, that had united us, and that was still in me, rallied.

"I want you, Nattana!"

She looked at me. Tears were in her eyes. She uttered an odd little laugh. She clucked to the horse.

"You are so dear!" she said. "You did it so beautifully! I thought you might—oh, hand me the opportunity to marry you like the honorable person you are, but I did not think you would make it so convincing. Thank you, Johnlang! There will never be another like you. But I am not going to marry you, and we both know it in our hearts."

"Nattana, I really want you!"

"I believe you; but we must not make the mistake of marrying."

"Why, Nattana?"

"It isn't the difference between your country and mine. That was not the main thing. If it were—oh, I would have married you long ago. Other reasons are stronger."

I felt relief and fought against it, and at the same time was deeply disappointed.

"Won't you marry me, Nattana? All these objections of yours aren't real. . . . . Here we are! We like each other! We get along so well—when we know where we stand with each other."

"Please!" she said. "It is settled. You have asked Hytha Nattana to marry you and for reasons of her own she has answered 'no.' "

I measured her with my eyes, wondering as to her resistance.

"How obstinate are you?" I demanded.

"You know. You won my body against my better judgment, but you haven't yet conquered my intelligence!"

"You are mine, Nattana. You have seemed mine all these days."

"Oh, I know what you mean—but, my dear, you have done the honorable thing. Don't go on with it! It is no use. Believe me, please. Let's not argue it."

"Marry me, Nattana!"

"I won't, won't, won't marry you!"

She began to laugh.

"You must!"

"You can't make me. I won't! And kissing me and holding me won't help you in the least. That has failed before."

She pushed away my arms, but the shaking wagon made a proper embrace impossible. She laughed and seemed happy. She made me furious and then in spite of myself I laughed also, and was furious again and did not want to give up.

"When I come back—" I began.

"No! No! You are free if I am. . . . ."

Within myself I had surrendered, but I talked on.

"Are you free, Nattana? I thought I was free until I learned that I could come back. The possibility removed a barrier."

"I am absolutely free, so free that if I want to marry someone—or give myself—I shall. You don't stand in the way, just as I don't stand in your way."

"Are you thinking of it, Nattana?"

"Are you?"

"No!" I shouted. "I have proposed marriage to *you*."

"I'll tell you only if you will promise to give up all hope of marrying me."

"How can I? If I come back here, and find you single—"

"And are single yourself, and if you want to marry me then and I want to marry you!—That is true of any man and woman! Is that all you hope?"

"Yes, Nattana, but it isn't so little as you think, because you and I were lovers."

Color spread over her face. She shrugged and uttered a short laugh.

"Is there someone else, Nattana?"

She jerked suddenly.

"Why do you need to know? What good will it do you? I have no *apia*-after-curiosity about you. We are free, and being free means freedom to do as we please. If your question were only a friendly one—"

"It is!"

"I hate to tell you."

"Tell me! Is there someone else?"

"No!" she cried in fury. "There is no one else, and there is not likely to be, for I know myself better. I am not what I thought I was; and I don't want men to come too close. I want other things—to be at home, to work. Through you I have had my glimpse at marriage and *ania*. I am going home to make everything up with my father—and to live single hereafter."

"Have I ruined marriage for you, Nattana? If so—"

"Ruined it? Of course not! But my eyes have opened. I like the thought of being single and restrained—and of working hard. What you have done for me is to make me want to work!"

"You have some of your father in you, Nattana."

"Yes—some of the same ideas but for different reasons. I want no second-best things with men."

"Was what we had second best?"

"Of course it was, or we would be married now."

"Don't say that, Nattana!"

"Our liking for each other is not second best. Don't confuse the two things, Johnlang!"

"I hate to think of anything we had as false."

"So do I!" she cried. "Therefore let's not! Let us think of what we now have and of what comes next, and of what you are going to be and of what I am going to do."

The wagon jolted on, loose boards rumbling. The dry warm air was full of dust and of the strong odor of the horses' sweat. The high snowy peaks were sharp and white and cold against the sky. Ahead of us down the road was a drifting yellow haze left by the foremost wagons, themselves out of sight around a bend.

The strong power of the sun was mingled with desire for the woman at my side, but at the same time my being was falling away from hers, the ties between us breaking.

Nattana and I rode for a long time in silence, sunbaked and dusty. The five wagons made no haste, for they were heavy even when empty and would be heavier still returning. Halfway to the quarry all of us stopped together at a brook, watered the horses, ourselves drank, and exchanged a few words. For a little while we seven men and one woman were comrades, conscious of the pleasure of working as a unit in a common enterprise; but, starting again, we were in our thoughts and interests and conversations separate wayfarers once more.

The work that Nattana had done in the barn had made her brown. In the hot sun that poured down upon us as we rode, her face was flushed and her bare legs and arms were pink beneath the tan. I loved the honest human quality of her revealed skin, and strove to hold her in my thoughts as a friend like any other lovable woman with whom I was thrown for an afternoon. I talked of home-going and of what I would do there, but because of the ending of the intimate personal relationship we had had, our conversation seemed impoverished. She in turn told her plans: she also was going home. Her father already knew of her affair with me, and yet had sent word that she might return.

"You stand clear in his eyes," she said. "He knows that you wanted to marry me and that I refused you. He regards me as the wicked one. I don't know how he is going to take me, but I think he will realize his impotence when he learns that we have settled and ended it ourselves."

Then with a gleam of quickened interest in her eye, she told of the weaving that she was going to do. . . .

We turned from the highway into a cart road leading toward the hills, climbed a little, and came to the quarry. The slabs had been already shaped by Nason and others before roofing work began. Two men could just lift one. Loading the wagons was heavy work and we were soon wet with perspiration and very thirsty.

Nattana went to a pool and returned with water. She was lovely with her body flexible and arched to resist the weight of the pail, a bare arm extended, her flushed face smiling, and her teeth white, with the blue-gray walls of the quarry behind her red head and high above her, the sharp blue sky. She brewed us a drink with a slightly acid wine, and we all drank deeply.

The wagon train started home in the same order as before, but she gave me the reins telling me that I ought to learn how to drive Islandian fashion in case I returned and had a farm of my own. We talked of this imaginary farm, and it was a pleasure to make known to her the fact that such a farm was a possible reality. I told what Dorna had said of the two other Dorn farms.

"You saw Dorna lately?" she asked, her voice guarded.

"I spent several days with her and Tor."

"At the Frays?"

"Yes, Nattana."

She was silent for some moments, and then said:

"I was always second, wasn't I?"

What answer could I make?

"Don't mind admitting it, Johnlang. It won't hurt me now. I knew it very well."

"Each of you was something that the other could never be," I answered.

"But you have given me what she never had. Isn't that still true?"

"Yes, Nattana—and in a deeper way than the fact that I was yours."

She pondered.

"I would like to think," she said, "that I understood you better."

"You never left me in the dark, Nattana."

"It was easier for me—I cared only for you. Still, I think I was more suited to the sort of man you are. Do you think I understood you better?"

"Yes, Nattana."

"Really, Johnlang?"

She was hard to convince, even at the end, saying, "You wanted her more than me."

"Not any longer."

"Is your *ania* all over, Johnlang?"

"I am out of her power."

"Are you sure? I knew too much ever to hope that *apia* for me would end it, for to one who has *ania* for another, *apia* is only a drug, a temporary anodyne. . . . It made it hard for me sometimes."

"But for Dorna would you have married me?"

"Not unless we had felt differently—as we might have. But thank you for asking me to marry you after your seeing her!"

"I want to ask you again—now that you know it is all over with her."

She laughed shortly, surprised.

"That changes nothing. I won't marry you."

The wagon, loaded with heavy slabs, moved no faster than a walk. The sun was sloping lower behind us, but the windless air was hotter and drier. I was parched and tired. Thoughts wandered away from Nattana. I was ready for the next thing, for Dorn, the cool sea, the Island, and a talk with him about the future.

After a long time I looked at her again. She sat relaxed, her hands in her lap, joggled by the wagon. She did not seem very pretty, but I knew her from head to foot, and she was dear, complete, desirable.

"I can't shake myself free from the feeling that you are mine, Nattana."

"It is a feeling, isn't it?" she answered. "Will we ever really get over it?"

"We aren't going to see each other for a long time."

"Marriage—or work—or both," she said vaguely, "and separation."

"But there is always this longing for something more!"

"It hurts to know that a good thing is good no longer, but we mustn't forget that we are quite happy apart!"

"That hurts too!"

"It has left a wound in each of us, which the presence of the other excites."

"What can we do, Nattana?"

"Haven't we had and don't we still have a lovely, valuable thing? We neither of us really know the other—no man and no woman ever does—but we have had many flashes of understanding. The understanding of men and women is like lightning in the black night—for a brief second the world is bright in every detail. All is much more brilliant than at any other time, much more so than when man and man or woman and woman become friends and learn about each other. Theirs is a steadier but dimmer light. I don't know what you think, but to me it seems we have had more than our share of perfect understanding—and that, I believe, will always be ours."

"When we meet—if we meet."

"I am not afraid to face the truth. We may never have it again, but we have had it, Johnlang!"

"And we have it now—this afternoon."

"I think we do," she answered.

When the five wagons one by one passed through the gate at the Upper Farm twilight softened the glare, the sun had already set, and the west behind us was flaming. The workers had returned from the barn to the house and were waiting for supper. There were yellow candles in the kitchen. But the wagons were still to be unloaded and the horses to be stabled and fed. Nattana remained, doing her share, and it seemed a great kindness to have her with us.

When we had finished the heavy tasks and had left the slabs of stone piled ready alongside the barn, the sky was thickly powdered with stars.

She and I drifted together and followed the others toward the house. Though cool evening had come the weight of the hot day and of the hard work we had done was still heavy upon us. From the dining room came the sound of voices.

"Tired, Nattana?"

"Very—and you must be tired too."

"Yes. We are both tired."

"I don't want any supper," she said, "nor to go in with all those people."

"Nor do I. Let's stay together."

"I will steal something from the kitchen in case we are hungry later."

I waited in the darkness outside, and the stillness of the night was so deep that the voices did not destroy it. When she returned I took her hot hand and we wandered out into the open, under the stars, and then our feet led us toward the lake.

In the pallor of the starlight we found a rowboat at the wharf and paddled out upon the liquid glassy water, so dark and so smooth that it was another starry sky inverted beneath us.

After a while we came to the point where we had skated, and landed on a narrow steeply shelving beach beneath a cliff crowned with dark pines.

We sat on the shore and I took her in my arms and we kissed each other. There was desire which was not desire and which wanted no union, but I wished to be near her and to hold her in some way and she to be held.

We lay down, our faces to the infinite deeps of the stars, and the touching of feet and shoulders and the clasp of hands was enough.

"Nattana," I said, "this is good."

But there was no answer.

I spoke her name, listened, and heard again her even breathing.

My own eyes closed. Sleep came quickly and I still held her limp, unconscious hand. . . .

Long afterwards, like persons drugged, we rowed back to the house, Nattana in the stern of the boat as still as a sleeping bird.

Everyone had gone to bed and only a single light burned in the kitchen.

The return was but a dreaming interlude between two heavy sleeps, and in sleep we found a peaceful ending.

It was night when I awoke again, but whether near dawn or not, I was going. Atta slept on, but Ek opened his eyes in the candlelight while I was packing my saddlebag. To him only were good-byes said. No one else stirred.

When the dark house was behind and the road, a pale yellow glimmer, was slipping past under Fak's feet, I knew that now the danger of farewells and explanations was truly over. Nattana would understand, nothing else mattered, and I was free.

My existence hereafter would be empty of her face, her voice, and of all that made her dear. She left a hollow void, but the nature of our love and our parting was such that life would fill it again without pain. She would be remembered with happiness.

31

Departure

On November 23rd, after six days of traveling, Fak and I came to Earne in midafternoon. Only light airs were blowing, the water was a summer blue, and the marsh was bright, dappled with the shadows of white floating clouds and stretching smooth as a floor for limitless miles. It seemed like a home-coming.

Fak and I were taken over to the marsh in a boat, and then we made our way towards Dorn Island, crossing and operating the other ferries ourselves.

This was Dorna's abandoned *alia*—which would never have been abandoned and which would have been mine also had she loved it or me a little more. Perhaps, if I returned to Islandia, it might still be mine, for her departure did not lessen the need of an agent at the Island. I played with the idea of this place as a permanent home, and in the glowing lovely light of late afternoon the Island became heart-breaking in its beauty.

From the Fisherman's Harbor I rode around the hill of the Tower and through the rural heart of the Island, a light smell of the sea in the air. Leaving Fak at the stables I carried my saddlebag to the house, entered unseen and went to my room, which was ready for me.

Whatever happened this corner of Islandia was always mine. I did not feel myself a mere guest. The custom that gave me the privilege of the Dorns' house as long and whenever I chose had at last become so real that I felt it. . . . Perhaps this, rather than Dorna, was the reason why the West seemed home.

This, and Dorn!

He entered, tall, ruddy, and brown, the whites of his eyes very clear. He had heard me singing, he said.

751

"What was I singing?"

"One of our tunes."

"I did not know it."

He sat down while I finished dressing.

"We expected you three or four days ago," he said.

"I stayed at the Upper Farm longer than I planned, helping put a new roof on the barn."

"What else have you done since the raid?"

The narratives of my wanderings emphasized the fact that they were in the greater part a series of visits to girls—to Dorna, to Stellina, and to Nattana. For a moment it was embarrassing and then we both laughed, and laughed again.

"How is it with all of them?" he asked.

"Perfectly satisfactory," I answered.

"Are you more or less likely to return to Islandia?"

"More—but not for the sake of any of them."

"I hope you come back. I have been anxious to see you, and I hope we can help you to a decision. Nekka wants to see you also," he said, and he went out to fetch her without waiting for my answer.

I was glad that I had saved my last visit for him. He was continuously satisfactory; with the others it had been a matter of much talk and painful adjustments to make them seem so. They each gave something that he did not, but his gift was as good as theirs and was always in my possession. . . .

At supper the many-times-told story of the raid had to be told again. The telling was easy because of practice and because Dorn was a listener. My narrative was for him. Faina, Marta, Dorna the elder, and Nekka were figures in the background.

Afterward we went into the circular room and left the four women.

"You are very fortunate," he said, "to have Dorna, Stellina, and Nattana your debtors."

And again, for some reason definite in the feelings but hard to explain, we both laughed.

"Nekka looks well," I said.

"Doesn't she!"

We smiled at each other.

"Since I saw you last—" I began.

His eyes questioned me.

"Both of us?" he asked.

"She would not marry me. I asked her.—She was right, I think."

"They are sisters," he said, as though the fact had deep significance, and we both smiled. A unity of masculine understanding existed between us from which all others were excluded. . . .

"I owe much to your sister," I said. "She was very kind. I spent several days at the Frays and we talked about everything."

"She has paid her debt," he said, "but if you come back I would be careful with her."

"We discussed that," I answered, and realized that she and I also had a unity of understanding from which all the world was excluded. . . . So also he and Nekka, no doubt.

The world was a shining, happy place. . . .

"Why are you going home?" he asked.

"To learn if I really want Islandia. I am an American still, you know."

"And one of us also."

"The warnings you all gave me when I first came were true and untrue."

"Remember that Dorna had faith in your being able to adjust yourself to our ways before the rest of us did."

"She is a queer girl," I said.

"They all are."

"I am suspicious of Dorna."

"So is she—of herself, and she is tragic for that reason."

"She is very lovable."

"Too much so . . . Ronan is worse off than you ever were."

"Stellina is an enchanting and wise woman."

"But can you imagine . . . ?"

"No," I answered. "I should have to be more rarefied than I am."

"That is the trouble with her. But what went wrong with Nattana?"

"Nothing. She believed it was only *apia*."

"I wonder about that. She may have thought separation best for you. She is capable of such a renunciation."

"I think she would be incapable of giving a false reason."

753

"She might deceive herself."

"It is hopeless if that is so," I said.

"They are all hopeless," he answered.

"I've no doubt we are as unsatisfactory to them."

"Of course! Nevertheless," he continued, "if you make your wants perfectly clear to them, much of the hopelessness disappears. They like to be shown a straight line, to follow or not as they please. Remember that."

"I have learned that lesson," I answered. He was a little saddening, for he seemed to have no faith in what I still believed possible— a relationship in which each did an equal amount of proposing, and in which no difference based on sex existed with regard to the choice of courses to be followed. . . .

"It is a relief not to have to choose for someone else," I said.

"They like to think you choose, but you merely propose and they choose."

"Do they never propose . . . ?"

"They may learn that it ought to be equal," he said, "—in time."

"Then—" I cried.

"Yes!" he answered.

"I have hopes!"

He flushed suddenly, and said:

"I have more than hopes!"

But I did not envy him because he was married and had faith in the success of his relationship with Nekka. It was good to be free at present.

"Now," he said, "tell me your plans, for I have been thinking of you long and often."

I talked and talked, trying out in my mind the things I intended to do, and in the middle of the long and ill-arranged statement Nekka came in and sat down next to Dorn. She was changed—slimmer, more quiet, less self-conscious. To me her odd face and her expression had always been a mask; so it still was, but a simpler one. I was drawn to her, partly because she was of Nattana's flesh and blood, her sister, and, through Nattana's relationship to me, familiar to me, like a relative; and even more because she, for all her elusiveness, was clear to Dorn and had chosen to follow the straight lines that he laid down for her. As his, she had a new quality that endeared her to me.

For the present Dorn was no longer in politics; he was manager of Dorn Island, which meant farmer, ship operator, and horse and cattle breeder. This he told me next morning as we rode about. The Dorns were poor, he said, reminding me that they had used their personal resources in connection with the vote they had undertaken, and much careful planning was necessary. All this he explained in the manner of a president making a report to an important stockholder in a corporation. The report, furthermore, was detailed and when it was finished I had a clear knowledge of his financial condition and of the fact that within a year or two the Dorns would be in need of money.

He then informed me that Nekka had been perfectly splendid, and he apologized for the judgments he had passed upon her eighteen months before. Once she had decided to marry him she accepted him and his ideals wholly. If he were not to have the political position that once seemed likely to fall to him, it apparently made no difference to her. She was even reconciled to the transfer of legal title to the Island from himself to Lord Dorn's line. He would retain the Mountain Farm or the Lay River Farm, he said, and would ultimately retire to one of those two places, unless—as was quite possible—he had to remain as manager of the Island as well until Marta's child grew up. He might even run for office himself, if Lord Dorn died before the boy was old enough to succeed him.

"You see what my life is likely to be," he said. "It is going to be a busy one—and Nekka is proving an ideal person to live it with."

There was a long silence.

"You have seen the Mountain Farm," he said to me at last. "I would like to show you the one on the Lay River. We have too many farms, and if you settle in Islandia you might like to buy one of them. . . . It was Dorna's idea first, but I am sure it would have occurred to me."

This was a great moment.

"There are other possibilities," he said rapidly. "There are other farms that you could buy, I am sure, here or elsewhere. If you return to Islandia many people will be interested in finding you a place. You could also establish a new farm—be a pioneer—but I doubt if you have the experience to do so without some capable man to help you. I have also thought that you might become an agent with your offices at the Island. One is needed there. Your previous training might fit you best for such a position."

"Did Dorna suggest it?" I asked.

"No," he said. "She mentioned many possibilities, but this was not among them."

I was grateful to her for not doing so. The idea with which I had played while riding to the Island on the day before now appeared in its true light.

"Let us rule it out," I said. "It is what I might have been, if your sister had married me. It was what she thought of for us when she was still in doubt. She wanted to keep the Island. I had better have an *alia* all my own, not one which I might have had with her."

"I suppose so," he answered, "but I think if it became your *alia*, it would be so strong in itself that memories of what might have been would not hamper its growth."

"Americans," I said, "are more sentimental than Islandians."

"I was forgetting . . . But we will rule it out, of course. At a farm, even one of ours, there would be no question, would there? You can't avoid all reminders of Dorna."

"I don't want to," I said.

He laughed in my face.

"We will visit the Lay River Farm," he continued, and he began to describe it with a flow of the technical terms that once had been incomprehensible.

We left for the Lay River next day but one and were gone nearly a week.

To give the trip an air of vacation and holiday, we went in his boat similar to but larger than the *Marsh Duck*. Winds were fickle, ranging from calms to heavy blows. We were held up and advanced by the tide. We had long hours in which to talk, and the fact that we were bound upon what might be called a business trip did not concern us greatly.

At noon of the second day we reached the house of Lord Dorn, the Commodore, and stopped for lunch. In the afternoon we sailed past Thane and into the Lay River. The character of the banks changed from that of the familiar flat, treeless, salt marsh to that of an inland river with meadows, overhanging trees, and continuous farms. Just before dark we moored the boat to a tree at the head of navigation. The air was no longer that of the sea, yet a boat could be kept here, Dorn said, and the whole marsh would be open for sailing. The farm was only eight miles away.

Early next morning we set out on foot by paths, following the river which was placid but with occasional gentle rapids. The farms, along the edges of which we passed, were fertile and quiet with rich meadows and fine trees along the water. The form of the land was masked by the vegetation, but was evidently of a mild relief though not flat like that of the valley of the Doring River. In a little over two hours we passed through a gate in a fence and had reached the Dorns' farm, no different from all the rest.

The main house, of ten rooms, none large, stood upon a low knoll about one hundred yards from the river, which was here a broad quiet brook overhung by magnificent willows. From the upper windows there was a pleasing but not extensive view to the south, with high stands of trees on other farms as the most striking features—a land-scape all green, except for glimpses of low blue hills.

We remained at the farm for two days and walked over it from end to end. It was not unique like the Mountain Farm or the Island, nor had it a single unusual feature, but was like a thousand others. Yet it had much variety and was everywhere pleasing. Away from the river toward the hills was a ridge crowned with pines giving a finer, wider view than at the house. The dwellings of the two families of dependents, the Stanes and the Ansels, occupied a little valley of their own a quarter of a mile from that of the Dorns. There were several springs and a little brook, dammed to make a small pond. West of the house was a fine grove of tall beeches. Orchards, truck and flower gardens, pastures, and meadows made the farm complete.

With eyes a little more professional than they once had been I observed all these things. Dorn and I talked "farm" from morning to night, not merely of its capabilities for raising crops nor of its suita-bility as a dwelling place, but of its charm and quiet beauty. He pointed out a lovely aspect or the places where wild flowers grew quite as often as a fine stand of timber, a rich pasture, or a fertile growing-place.

We walked back to the boat on the evening of the second day by a moon at the first quarter, and not until we were aboard again and lying in our bunks by candlelight did we, so to speak, get down to business.

"You would be like everyone else," he said, "if you lived here. It is a typical farm. It lies off the main road as most farms do. Thane is eighteen miles away. If you want to sink deep into our life this is the place for you. The Mountain Farm is often visited because it is unlike any other. It is also near a road through a pass much traveled in summer. You would be likely to see Dorna now and then when she and Tor went from the Western Palace to The City—if that is an advantage or disadvantage. People bound from the Central Provinces to lower Upper Doring, Dole, Farrant, and Vantry usually go that way. You have been brought up to see striking and varied regions. For that reason you might prefer the Mountain Farm."

"Which would you rather sell?"

"I cannot tell you. It is an even thing. You could, however, run this farm any way you liked. If you took the Mountain Farm I should hope that you would continue to breed horses."

"What would the price be?"

It was an important question.

He told me instantly. The prices of the two farms were about the same, both exceeding by several thousand dollars the present value of my investments. I answered as much.

"It doesn't matter," he said. "You could send us from here part of your produce or from the Mountain Farm some of the horses and cattle you bred until the difference was paid. . . . There is no need for a decision now. If you decide to return to us, consider which farm, if either, you prefer and let us know. We won't sell to anyone else for a long time yet."

On the way back to Dorn Island, the Lay River Farm dwelt vivid, rich, and tangible in my memory, impressed there by the fact that the eyes that had seen it visualized it as a possible *alia* and observed each thing like an owner . . . Dorna had given me Islandia, but Dorn made the gift solid and real—as she knew he would.

We spent two quiet days at the Island. December had come and in two weeks more I sailed, and the steady approach of the day of departure filled me with a happy, passionate regret. I did not want to leave. True summer was close and the Island touched innumerable quivering strings of beauty. But neither did I wish to accept Islandia without a surer knowledge of what I wished my life to be. . . .

On December 3rd I set out for The City, my last Islandian journey and my last ride upon Fak. The shortest road to follow was the familiar one by the National Highway through the Doan Pass, a place of deeper misery than any other ever known. But if I returned to Islandia and lived in the West I would ordinarily go there many times. Because Dorn and Nekka rode with me as far as the Inn, dread was less; and the splendor of the ride from the plain to the pass was not corroded by memories.

Many were on the road, going to The City for the meeting of the council, the first important one since Lord Dorn had become head of the government again.

The Inn was too large to be crowded; it was, however, full but we obtained two adjoining rooms, and there we had supper with a flask of special wine that Dorn had brought with him.

Nekka, sitting with us, hearing what we said, seemed one of us and not a hostile influence. Old matters were discussed again but her presence gave them new color. We were all happy, full of words, facing the future eagerly.

Bedtime came. Nothing much had been said, but there was nothing important left to say. The significant thing now was the proof that she would and could be a partner in the benefits of Dorn's and my friendship. Neither she nor I would hereafter regret his relationship to the other one.

After they had gone he nevertheless returned to my room. We agreed that we had no final speeches to exchange. Yet he remained, tall, thoughtful, strong in himself—splendid as an animal, a man, and a husband to the woman in the next room; quite as splendid and valuable as a friend to me.

He sat on the bed where I lay, already sleepy, contented with the present and its possessions, and quite as much with the future and its possibilities.

After some minutes of silence he belied what we had agreed.

"In your country," he said, "the ties between person and person are so strong that the tie between a person and place—*alia,* or whatever is necessary to make him his real self—are often too much obscured. You half-Islandian, John Lang, you run a real danger. If you need this country—that is, if you are really Islandian—that need will be the most powerful force to make or spoil your life; and if you cannot satisfy it you may pass into a sort of lethargic living death. Don't let any personal tie lead you to sacrifice a need for Islandia."

"Are you thinking that I may love some American woman who will not come here?"

"That is the most likely way that you will be tempted to sacrifice."

"Love," I said, "is enough."

"Yes, if each of you loves the other for what you are and what she is; but if she did not want to come with you and you were truly Islandian, and you tried to make of yourself an American, you would ruin yourself and thereby make yourself useless for her."

"I could be an Islandian in America!"

"Only a shadow of one, John Lang!"

"Suppose she were as purely American as I was Islandian?"

"Toss up a coin," he said, "and live where it decides, if you aren't content with a passing love affair—as I think you both would be."

Was he thinking of Nattana?

"The danger is," he continued, "that some woman of strong will and ideas will love you as material that she can mold into the image of what she believes in and adores. Don't marry a molding woman, John! They are what some men want, but not a man like you any longer. There are many such women in your country who the moment they become interested seek to compel you to be a certain thing and to live a certain way. They hold up to you the picture of you they have painted and reproach you if you do not resemble it."

"Dorn," I answered, "when I first came here you warned me against your women and now you are warning me against my own. Must I remain single?"

"No—seriously! If you return here you must have a complete life . . . I am groping to express an idea."

"Perhaps what you mean is that one should find one's truest self in oneself, and let others love you or hate you for it, however much it hurts, without trying to change yourself to please them?"

"That sounds more selfish than I like," he answered, "but it comes near to what I mean; and after all, one is only selfish in what one does, not in what one is."

He said good night; and a little later, lying in the dark, I heard for some time the sound of voices from the next room, the words indistinguishable, but Nekka's clear, simple, and childish and his a low buzz, and hers the more continuous. Was Nekka a molding woman? Dorna was surely one, and so might Nattana have been. Were not all women a little of that nature, and for that reason no less to be loved? Their character was as significant in the world's progress, and men hated to crack their precious molds. But it was very good not to be in the process of being fitted to any mold at the present time.

Next morning when we separated to ride our different ways Nekka also had her last speech to make.

"Do come back," she said. "It would make Dorn very happy—and me too, of course."

I rode down the steep ravine of the Cannan River, eyes to the front, glad that it was summer not winter. I spent the night in the Inn at Inerria, and the next two at both households of the Somes, the fifth at the Bodwins' near Bostia, and on November 8th reached The City and went to the Doring Palace in time to attend the King's Reception as Lord Dorn's guest.

The council met next day but I did not attend lest my presence affect the freedom of debate. That evening, however, Lord Dorn said that there was none. Tor had stated what had happened at the Vaba Pass and had presented his request in the name of himself and Dorna; and the council had at once voted to invite Lang, American, to reside permanently in Islandia. Lord Dorn himself had then told the council that Lang wished leave to make one importation, a certain machine, which he believed would neither be in itself harmful nor an entering wedge for foreign trade. Again the council voted favorably.

"I suggested but did not say," Lord Dorn said, "that it was a gift to someone."

PART V

32

The United States: Spring

THE CITY, dropping astern into a pearl-gray haze, contracted in jerks whenever I looked back. Dirty brown smoke trailed off to the left from the *St. Anthony's* funnel and hovered over the blue water which it shadowed. The rail on which I leaned vibrated and ceased and vibrated again in rhythmic bursts. A vessel with her lug sails wing and wing, proceeding in leisurely fashion toward The City, was passed so close that our smoke swept across her decks and almost hid her; but after a moment she emerged, her sails a clean bright orange above the blue water. She was Islandian and Islandia was being left behind. I was on the edge of passionate regretful hunger for what I was abandoning, but in fact everything was as it should be and my only worry was as to clothes. I could make myself presentable for a formal dinner or a wedding, but ordinary suits had long since been discarded as shoddy and worn out. I had nothing but the clothes that Nattana had made to wear by day and I must buy a new outfit and a hat at St. Anthony.

The steamer was a floating piece, all complete, of that occidental civilization which extends from eastern Europe west to San Francisco, with islands elsewhere all over the world. A machine moved us, not wind or animals or ourselves, and made a racketing, trembling, continuous clamor in doing so. I listened for silence all the time expecting the noise to cease, trying to select sounds that were natural, such as the hiss of the sea washing against and curling back along the steamer's side. On board were men, commercial or military or political, with tight white collars around their necks and hats on their heads; the three women on board wore long close dresses that swathed and made mysteries of legs, guarded from sight with all the intensity of purpose of a boy hiding a precious marble which he fears some larger boy may covet.

It was all rather queer and somewhat of a strain. Forgotten memories awoke for a moment and made everything natural; but I had been so long accustomed to people differently dressed and to less noisy and artificial surroundings, that the *St. Anthony* seemed like an interesting but nervously troublesome dream. Nightfall, soon coming, brought distress. Sleep in a creaking, unfamiliar, swaying stateroom was a sleep of dreams in which I was still ashore and in which gladness and regret alternated. Morning was a welcome relief with the will alive again, dominating the conflicting feelings in different layers of subconsciousness. We were skirting the shores of Storn and I saw again blue sea, a white line of foam, red cliffs, and rolling dark-green moors, with sunlit clouds floating low over them. This, my first sight of Islandia, was also my last. I said good-bye to her as to a friend, and she did not answer "I am not for you." In my trunk was the formal expression of the permission to reside, graciously worded, written in the blackest ink on stiff white paper, and signed by Tor as King. The red cliffs and moors diminished to a line on the horizon and disappeared behind its hard blue edge. Islandia, now, unseen, was a dot hard to find in a wide world, existing only in the mind. My senses began to lose consciousness of her as a continuous reality. For a while I was neither there nor here. But I knew that it was best to leave her at least for a time. To remain, feeling as I did, would have been to drift unsatisfied. All was well, the world a shining, fascinating place.

I hunted up someone to talk to.

The men in the smoking room gave Islandia an hour of attention, because I had come from there. The discovery that I was American in spite of my dress loosed their tongues. I was the only person who joined the ship at The City and no one had left her. The repudiation of the Mora Treaty deterred even those travelers who had no mission except their own pleasure. It was rumored that the steamship companies planned to abandon The City as a port of call, the suggestion being that this was a deserved rebuke to Islandian pretensions. A commercial traveler gave the Dorn Party five years of power, by which time the country would have learned its lesson. Another doubted this last statement, but thought the Powers would intervene. As to Ferrin, one of them declared that Islandia was a dog in the manger. They referred to the fact that relations between her and Germany were a little strained; there had been some sort of a clash on the frontier in which a body of Islandians who had crossed the boundary line were attacked by a number of Mountain Negroes and several of the former were killed. The talkers then passed to other subjects: the new railroad from M'paba across the Sobo Steppes to Mobono, the rapid growth of the German colonies, a scheme to establish German settlers in the steppes, an idea for a German Simla near Mount Omoa, the personalities of various governors and native leaders, and then trade, commercial rivalries, and markets for goods. I listened like one who has half forgotten a once well-known tune and gradually picks it up again.

On the *St. Anthony;* at the city of that name where I waited five days, most of which were spent with Cadred and Soma; on the *Doverton* which carried me from there toward Southampton, cosmopolitan and also very English; and at her varied ports of call, life had a pageant-aspect not only in things seen but in the characters and words of men; yet it was a pageant too swiftly moving for any one complex, colorful scene to be really beheld and known. So long as we talkers at dinner tables, in deck chairs, or in smoking rooms stated facts known to us, described experiences, or told stories, all was harmonious; but as soon as any of us ventured opinions or mentioned beliefs there were differences and wranglings. Each of us held within himself a set of convictions, not very well formulated, which were sore to a contradicting touch and which we therefore carefully guarded. Silence was often the better part. I had to learn again what I could not say and to hold within myself many thoughts which in Islandia I could have freely uttered. The heterogeneity of men compelled one to look out for innumerable "no trespass" signs. One could not tell a commercial man, who was so instinctively and naturally a creature of faith that his beliefs in the life he led were dogmatic and religious in nature, that the repudiation of the Mora Treaty was not a sign of backwardness, that backwardness or forwardness had nothing to do with it, and that it was merely a question of living one life rather than another. To him trade and intercourse were the inevitable, the normal, and the right. . . .

On a half-empty steamer from Southampton to New York, I was among my own countrymen again, and they were suddenly as recognizable and as well known as pictures in a room where one has spent many years but which one has not seen for some time. The discovery of their familiarness was like new experiences, and I loved to sit with them, to hear their voices, and to talk as they talked. There was a buyer for a Boston dry goods store who lived at Malden and had heard of Father. . . .

The tall buildings of lower Manhattan, pearl-gray against a brownish haze, lifted their hunched-together squares and rectangles directly from the busy, windswept water. There was the flat arch of Brooklyn Bridge seen as a whole for all its size.

A group of us stood together on the deck. Except for the water, which was not very clean, man had succeeded in covering nearly everything with his erections. The slopes of hills where they appeared looked strange, unkempt—as out of place as a patch of nakedness through a rent in a garment.

There was a prophet among us. The day of Europe was ending, he said. Soon the New York that we saw before us rising out of the water would take the place of London as the center of the world.

We began to warp into the dock, and I saw with a sudden shock the home reality of Father and Alice standing together in the crowd on the wharf, searching to see me. Their dearness brought tears to my eyes. They were familiar like nothing else.

At last we found each other. I waved; they answered; after a while they waved and I answered. There was the usual pause of anticlimax, but finally we met and I found their faces paler than those to which I was accustomed.

Mother had a cold and could not come, they said. There was an epidemic of colds going round.

"You look well," they both said, "but thin. . . ."

They stood near while I brought my few belongings through the customs. The huge wooden shed seemed flimsily built for all its great beams and had a musty smell of a thousand commodities.

There was not much to carry and therefore to save cab fare we went by the elevated and a trolley car. The noise was terrific: a big dray with rails moving over cobblestones, the rattle of the elevated and the shriek of wheels rounding curves, riveters at work on a new building, and a continuous roaring noise of seething people. Having stood it before I could stand it again, but for the present it beat so violently upon my nerves that I was desperate for quiet.

Alice took my hand and squeezed it and leaned close. The velvet brim of her large and extraordinary picture hat brushed against mine. Her skin looked too soft, too white.

"You are quite brown," she said.

"I have been in the open air a good deal."

"On the voyage?"

"All the time."

"What have you been doing?"

"I wrote you all."

"You told where you were but—" She broke off as her voice became critical and instead spoke pleasantly, "You do look well, but your clothes! That funny high waistcoat! And haven't you an overcoat?"

"I'll have to get one."

"It's winter. You must be tough!" She shivered. "The Braytons are giving a tea tomorrow for Marjorie who is coming out. I want you to take me. Will you? Have you proper clothes?"

The train, running on the same schedule from New York to Boston, full of people of a Bostonian cast of countenance, with a tendency to stare as though it were important to them to decide whether they had seen me before and what my place was in the scheme of things, was like home itself, touching unexpected depths.

Father had little to say. He looked tired, old. But Alice's eyes dwelt upon me and she was eager to talk but did not seem to know what to say. The parlor car was very hot and close with an acrid smell of oily smoke. The flickering scenery from the window jerked upon my eyeballs. There were innumerable frame houses set close together, sordid and temporary, wheeling views of large factories, back yards, fields, scrubby woods, houses again, and everywhere letters and words telling something to passing eyes without any consideration of whether they wished to read or not. . . .

"What are you thinking?" asked Alice.

Should I tell her or not? She was my sister and this was her country.

"I am not yet used to the noise," I answered.

"You look fidgety. You seem changed."

"I'll get used to things, but remember that except for two days in Southampton I haven't been in the middle of such noise and I haven't seen public advertisements for over two years, nor have I traveled on a train like this."

"You will have to get used to it."

It was true, and after a time I would cease to be so sensitively and nervously aware of my clamorous and blatant surroundings. Consciousness of strain would cease, but would not the wear and tear continue notwithstanding, dulling perceptiveness? There came a sudden dread.

"We will take walks in the Fells," she said. "Islandia is all country, isn't it?"

"Alice," I answered, "you are a darling."

She had taken off her coat and hat. She wore a brown dress somewhat Empire in style but with a princesse waist. The long sleeves were tight. Crossed folds of silk upon the breasts made the front of her seem oversoft. The folds of the skirt, which reached to the ankles, were so heavy, so voluminous, that Alice herself emerged as little more than a head and bust. Yet her costume was graceful.

We looked in each other's faces. Her eyes and forehead had a curvature and familiarity that meant "sister" ever since I could remember. She was not much my junior. We had spent hours together in play, in study, in expeditions. We had been both frank and reticent about our affairs. We had been close and remote. We had exasperated each other deliberately. We had quarreled and had hit each other. We had each found refuge in the other. Once she had confessed to a fault that I had committed to save me from being kept from a trip which she knew I ardently wanted to make; but she had so mishandled it that, not only did I lose the trip, but we both were spanked soundly by our puzzled parents for being liars. Once I had saved her from persecution by small boys but in the struggle had hurt her more than they would have done. During both these occurrences we were passionately attached to each other and very happy, immune to the pain we suffered. At other times we had called each other as stinging names as we could think of. What she declared was my "superiority" was always a sore point with her; and with me it was her "wishing to know everything."

But now she had traveled to New York to meet me and had come more than halfway in welcoming me home. The same mixed feelings were rekindled; I feared the probe of her critical curiosity and was also sorry that during my absence I had scarcely thought of her at all. She was twenty-seven with no suitors that I knew of. She was not particularly attractive or pretty, just a sister but a nice one. I thought of how Ek and Ettera had joined forces. If I returned to Islandia I might take Alice with me. The invitation permitted me to bring my "family." Then it would be my turn to tell her that her clothes were not suitable. How much healthier she would be! But what would she do, she who was so busy with social service? What would she think of Dorn and Nattana, Tor and Dorna? Of the Doan Pass and the Frays?

The train pulled into the South Station at Boston, and we took the elevated to Sullivan Square and thence by trolley to Medford.

The sight of Alice and Father on the pier had brought tears to my eyes. Mother was just as I remembered her, just as dear, with a lovely familiar look and charm like nothing else in the world. She wept and hugged me, crying out:

"I am so glad you have come home at last!" But I did not weep, tired in a way not experienced for a long time that confused my head and falsified what I felt. I could only think how hot the house was.

She sat on the sofa and held my hand.

"Back again," she cried, "my boy! My dear boy! My John! You don't look as though it had hurt you. I've been so afraid. It is so far —from your letters so unlike any reasonable place. Oh John!"

She made a gesture of relief and misery.

"I was happy there," I said, "and the people seemed to me quite reasonable."

"How lonely you must have been!"

"Only at first."

"You liked it?"

Her voice wanted me to say "no."

"I had a good time, Mother."

"And now you are back—oh, my boy, back again for good!"

She hugged me again and wept again.

"Back again for good!" she repeated.

There was a question in her voice, but it was not the time to mention the document in my trunk.

Supper was served. Father said grace. The maid entered, and I found myself thinking of her as a *deneria*, not as a mere servant. It was hard to realize where I was with the eyes of the family watching me from faces so white.

We sat in the living room, and again Mother held my hand. They seemed expectant of something and I told them bits about the journey and about things in Islandia, trying to ascertain what they wanted. My major experiences there were my love and loss of Dorna, my affair with Nattana (about neither of which had I written), the resignation from the consulate, and the experiences at the Vaba Pass, which I had not neglected to describe and of which I was willing to tell more if they wished; but they asked no questions as though I ought to know the right thing to say. I talked on and on, about Dorn, work at the Upper Farm, life at the Fains', the visit to the Moras, and they listened and waited. There came a pause and Mother said:

"You look older, John, my poor boy."

"Why poor?"

She hugged me. Had she in some way heard about Dorna? But that was impossible.

They decided that I was tired and I went off to bed with relief. My room, my own, was unchanged, filled with familiar dog-eared books, trophies, bric-a-brac, and photographs, all with memories of college and school and earlier days. Many had once been living possessions, but now the recollections they evoked, though whole and intact, were mummified and uninteresting. The air in the room was hot and drying to the skin from the steam heat.

Something was wrong; something was expected of me that I had not done. I wished that I were anywhere but at home. Taking off my clothes and putting on pyjamas I felt better. The trouble after all might be nothing but fatigues due to the assault upon my nerves of new sensations and impressions.

Alice at least would be frank. I went to her room and knocked on the door.

"Who is it?" she asked as though startled.

"John."

"Oh—wait a minute."

I waited several minutes. At last she let me in. She looked simpler and shorter in her nightgown and wrapper, with her hair smoothed back from her forehead.

"Come in," she said, looking me over. "But you ought to have a dressing gown on."

"The house is so hot, and I haven't any."

"Well, all right. But you ought to have something on your feet."

"I'm not cold."

"But your feet on the floors!"

I remembered that at home one wore slippers for cleanliness because of coal dust and not for warmth, and I went to my room for a pair.

"Alice," I said, "what is the matter with them? Why am I a poor boy?"

"Don't you know?"

"What have I done wrong?"

"Oh nothing—but of course you know."

"I don't know, Alice."

"You do know. You are in disgrace. They are really hurt."

"About what?"

"Oh John!" she exclaimed impatiently. "About being forced to resign as consul, of course."

"Oh that!" I cried, and I laughed.

She looked surprised.

"Aren't you—sorry?" she asked.

"Not a bit."

"Why?"

"Why should I be, Alice?"

"But you weren't a success."

"No, I was not."

"You are hard to understand. You are so . . ."

" 'Superior'?"

"Yes . . . Anyway they expected you to be unhappy and discouraged. Evidently you are not. Of course, most people suppose that when that treaty matter came up a man of greater diplomatic experience was needed and you resigned because a consul was not necessary, there being no trade. That's what Mother and Father are telling people. She had been proudly telling them you were in the diplomatic service . . . You really have hurt Mother and Father, John. Uncle Joseph told them the truth—that you did not make a go of it and were asked to resign for that reason."

"I was glad to resign."

"I don't see why. Then why didn't you come home last June? What were you doing there? You never really explained. You only said you were going to make visits and write articles and work on a farm. . . ."

"I did all those things."

"And only about a month ago a letter came that scared Mother to death. You had been camping in the mountains with a lot of men, and seemed to be a member of a band of guerrillas and there was evidently some kind of a fight and you just got away. That wasn't making visits or writing articles or working on a farm. Why did you mix yourself up in that sort of thing, John? Had you no respect for the way Mother or Father would feel? What kind of people were you with?"

I saw Don coming over the snow, a shine of light on his sleek, parted hair.

"The finest," I said.

"Well," she replied, "if you think that way! But it was—so unlike us!—like some adventurer."

"Do they feel as though I were the prodigal son returning?"

"A little—only they did not expect you to take the fact that you were asked to resign so lightly. After all. . . ."

"Alice, give me a tip how to behave."

"After all they are your father and mother. They are getting old and—you have disappointed them. Why didn't you come home? Apparently you did nothing for six months, and before that didn't do much. Uncle Joseph said that one trouble was your frequent absence from the consulate. What were you doing?"

"I wrote you. . . ."

"Oh your letters, just facts, so impersonal, so little about what you really felt, a list of outlandish names, suddenly someone appearing for the first time whom you apparently knew well! We have had many talks about you."

"After I resigned I wrote several articles."

"I've read them."

"What is the matter with them?"

"John—well, I'm no critic—but you seemed to be saying all the time 'You don't know about this, I do'—they sounded so . . . ."

" 'Superior,' Alice?"

"Well, rather. Uncle Joseph said you missed the point of the whole matter in your article about the treaty."

"What was the point I missed?"

"Ask him. All I know is that he has been quite angry at you. He can't understand why you stayed on in Islandia after there was no reason. Why did you?"

Should I tell her?

"He will forgive you though," she added significantly.

"What has he got to forgive me for?"

"Oh, John!" she cried. "You are so ungrateful!"

"Alice," I answered, "here I am back again in the United States. Do please tell me what Mother and Father want me to do."

"They don't want you to *do* anything, but at least they expect you to feel . . ." She paused. "Think of them," she continued, "not of yourself. You are nearly thirty. Apparently you have wasted two years. You aren't anywhere, John. You have made a failure of the diplomatic service. Yet you come home quite jaunty and self-satisfied, apparently. You were cold to Mother. You did not say there was no one in the world like her and no place like home and that you had missed her terribly. You just talked about what a nice time you had had. Naturally Mother—"

"Naturally Mother did what, Alice?"

"Wonders. She has wondered all along."

"About what?"

"Your lack of purpose for one thing, your lack of ambition, and what made you like that country so."

"I made good friends."

"Is that all?"

"I learned a great deal."

"What?"

"A way of happiness and contentment."

"Oh John!" Her voice was full of rebuke.

"Alice," I said, "don't be contemptuous of what I learned until you know more about it."

"I am only trying to tell you how you strike Mother and Father."

"How do I strike you?"

"You seem a brother I never knew before. Something has happened to you. I don't believe it's just the resignation. You look thinner, stronger, better looking, as though—"

"As though what?"

"Something did happen, didn't it, John?"

"A great deal happened."

"Tell me."

"I may sometime, but it is late now."

Alice had given me the needed cue. I had a "talk" with Father and Mother and told them that I was sorry to have been asked to resign the consulate and that I had come home to go to work. The air instantly cleared. They then told me that Uncle Joseph wanted to see me as soon as I returned, and perhaps . . . I answered that I would stay a week or two with them and then go to New York.

Having made up my mind to give America a fair trial I could only do so by going to work and by being ambitious to make a success. In my trunk was the yet unmentioned anchor to windward in case I failed or in case success proved to be not worth while.

Meanwhile at home I was a prodigal son turned earnest and anxious to please those who killed the fatted calf of their disapproval. The fact that I was going to work was apparently all that Mother and Father demanded. They regarded my Islandian experience as time wasted for a young man of my age and were not particularly interested in what I told them about it. A pained, patient look came upon their faces whenever I talked with pleasure of some beautiful or happy thing remembered, as though I were indulging a side of my nature that ought to have been abandoned. Alice, however, was curious and several times hinted that she would like to know what I meant when I said "a great deal happened."

Home neither was Islandia offering a path to follow nor was it work. I was impatient to put into effect the decision made more than three months before, knowing that only by living in the fullest American way could I learn what I wanted my life to be. There was not much to do at home. Such friendships as I had with people in the neighborhood were quite satisfied by brief meetings which reaffirmed them without making them closer. Except such seeing of friends there was little else to do for one who did not go to business every day. Therefore while having the time I undertook a task pleasant and interesting because associated with Islandia and with one whose personality and charm were still vivid. Needing help I asked Alice to give it. She was a good sister and was entitled to have some of her curiosity fed.

Persuading her with difficulty to take a few hours off from one of her missions I invited her to lunch at the Parker House. She met me, neatly dressed, but weighted with the flowing robes of the present fashion, bearing up under them gallantly. She was unselfish, diligent, and well-meaning. Seated opposite to her and seeing her face pale, tired, but determined I thought again of Ek and Ettera and my heart grew warm.

She wanted, she said, only a salad and some coffee, but when they were ordered she ate as well sweetbreads and mushrooms, puree of spinach, and potatoes Julienne, with an ice afterwards, though complaining of the expense.

"This is an occasion, Alice," I said. "You are a good sister and I haven't seen you for a long time."

She looked at me and her eyes said that she might think me a good brother, but was not going to say so—at least, not now.

"What is it all about?" she asked.

"I want to make a present to a friend in Islandia and I want you to help me to buy it, for you will know more about it than I will. She is a maker of cloth and also of clothes. She is a seamstress—"

"A seamstress!" The tone of her voice gave the word a connotation of class which had not been in my mind.

"She is the daughter of a Lord of a Province, Alice."

"Does she sew for a living?"

"She is principally a weaver, but she also makes clothes."

"What is her name?"

"Hytha; Hytha is her last name, but people call her Nattana."

"Do you?"

"Yes."

"Nattana," said Alice, and the word on her American lips sounded strange and I felt as though I had given away something I wanted to keep.

"How old is she?" Alice asked.

"Twenty-three."

"How well do you know her?"

"Quite well. She was a good friend."

Alice looked at me steadily, suspiciously, and her pale face became a little pink.

"Was she the reason?" she asked.

"For what?"

"You know!—for staying on in Islandia when there was no reason, after you resigned."

"Oh, no! I had decided to remain until next May before we became good friends."

"John, tell me, how good friends?"

I did not know what to answer.

"John!" she cried. "You are blushing!"

"Alice, what is on your mind? She was a friend."

"We have all been wondering so—"

"About what?"

"Well about whether you didn't get into trouble there. It seemed unlike you—unlike us. But your absences from the consulate and your staying on so long with no reason except perhaps somebody . . . We were afraid you had got mixed up with some native woman, as men do."

"I am not mixed up with anyone there."

"*Were* you? We have heard they weren't specially virtuous. Father got a book out of the library. Your letters mentioned girls now and then, but there were so many omissions."

"The women are as virtuous as you are, Alice."

She flushed and looked insulted.

"I hope I am!" she said hotly.

"I know you are, and that is why I used you as an example."

"And you didn't . . . ?"

"Didn't what?"

"Oh, you know. Get mixed up?"

"Nothing that happened could be called getting mixed up."

"You didn't have a native wife?"

"I married no one."

"Were you decent, John?"

If I interpreted her word my own way I could truthfully say that I was; but if I interpreted it her way, I would lie if I did not answer "no." Thinking of what Nattana and I had been to each other, I felt blood rush to my face.

"I did nothing I am ashamed of, Alice."

Her eyes met mine with hostility and daring.

"Did you do anything *we* would be ashamed of?"

The choice was between a lie, being misunderstood, and a long explanation that would not convince except momentarily. The rock of the family's morality was a barrier between us impossible to reduce.

"If you would be ashamed of anything I did, Alice, knowing all the facts, I would realize that the difference between us could never be bridged."

"You haven't answered my question," she said stoutly.

"I am not going to, any further than that. You ought to be satisfied that I am not ashamed."

"Well, I am not satisfied. You aren't the only judge."

"Nor are you. Each person must decide for him or herself."

"It would be a fine world if that were true!" she blazed.

"Alice," I said, "I want to make Hytha Nattana a present of a sewing machine. Will you help me to buy it?"

It was not in her nature to allow me to change the subject so abruptly.

"I don't like your attitude," she said. "It is so—darned superior. I see that you don't want to be frank. . . ."

"If frankness consists in saying I did something shameful I won't lie and say it."

"Shameful according to you!"

"I know no standard except one within myself for telling what is shameful."

"John!"

"The opinion of others is only a guide that sometimes is a false one, Alice."

"There are certain things that are always so!"

"Morality, Alice?"

"Of course! There are some things decent people don't do."

"I have done nothing decent people don't do!"

She looked at me consideringly.

"Why did you hint that you had?"

It was obvious that she was seeking a way to end the conversation with an appearance of understanding.

"I never intended to convey that idea, Alice."

She looked down, her large hat covering her face.

"Well . . ." she said. "I suppose it is all right." She looked up suddenly. "May I tell Mother?"

"Of course, Alice."

She sighed.

"You say this Miss Hytha is a friend?"

"Only a friend, Alice."

"Was that all she ever was?"

"Yes, Alice." This American lie was an Islandian truth.

"And there was no other woman?"

"None whom I knew so well as her."

"You want to give her a sewing machine?"

Our conversation flowed into smoother waters. Alice was a great help, giving herself wholly to the task of finding a suitable machine. We made a purchase and had it sent to the house to be on hand while I translated the directions into Islandian. In the succeeding days Alice typewrote these with practical suggestions of her own. A needlewoman herself she was able to put herself in the position of another one who had never used a sewing machine. She became interested in Nattana and in the latter's work and way of life, and I told her all about it. Thus, by carefully avoiding the obstacle of dogmatic morality, Alice learned sympathetically something about Islandia.

She was so sweet in her eager, intelligent helpfulness and also so pale and physically so weak swathed in her voluminous clothes that my heart was warm with grateful affection and pity. Toward the end of my stay at Medford I told her about Ek, Atta, and Ettera, and the life which the last-named had chosen to lead with her brothers.

"I would like to take you to Islandia," I said, "and set up a household like that. It would be good for you."

"In what way?"

"It would be so much more healthy, with much more 'outdoors,' more exercise, and fewer clothes."

"Fewer clothes? I have quite few enough."

"Your dresses would reach only just below your knees. You would go barelegged in warm weather—"

"I couldn't!"

"You would, because everyone else did. You would not wear such high heels nor such pinched-in shoes. You would walk more freely and get less tired."

She looked at me narrowly.

"Are you thinking of going back?"

"I am just supposing, Alice."

"You think I would like Islandia?"

"You ought to!"

"What would I do? Housework?"

"Some—no more than you do here."

"What else?"

"Whatever else you wanted."

"But I am useful here. I think we are doing a real service to the poor."

"You wouldn't have that, but—"

"What could I do that was useful?"

"Help build up our household. . . ."

"Make you comfortable, you mean? Would that be my life work?"

"I might marry. . . ."

"Then I would work for you and your wife? Is that what you plan for me?"

"You might marry."

"Oh no!" She shuddered, and then eyed me, saying:

"Would I find a man whom I could possibly get along with?"

"They are fine men."

"It doesn't sound attractive, John—a life spent working for someone else with no chance to be really useful or of service in the world!"

"You would be healthy and happy."

"I doubt it."

"I would like to have you with me."

She laughed.

"No thank you, John!"

"I might persuade you if I told you more."

"You couldn't! You couldn't! You have told me enough. I have my work cut out for me here. I like it. I—"

She paused sharply and made a forlorn nervous gesture with her hands.

"Of course, everyone wants something else," she continued. "I have wished—oh, never mind! I have given up expecting. But it sometimes seems—"

She stopped again.

"You are only twenty-seven, Alice."

"Only twenty-seven! and not attractive."

"You are attractive, Alice."

"It is a pity only my brother thinks so! But I really prefer it, and I have useful work to do, and I love it. And it isn't just 'building up a household'—it is helping the poor and teaching them how to live."

"You could weave as Hytha Nattana does or be an artist in Islandia."

"I would be either selfish or a drudge. I've got work, and I've got Mother and Father. You are a nice brother, but when you get down to work you will see."

The day came when I was to go to Uncle Joseph, and enough had been said to assure me that I was going to be allowed to labor in his office again. I had a farewell conversation with Father and Mother.

"I am so glad now," she said, "so glad my boy is going to work at last in the fine spirit you have shown, and so glad my boy did nothing we would be ashamed of in that country . . . Alice told me. I worried—I am so glad you are out of it at last!"

It seemed that so long as my morals were what she approved of and so long as I had work to do, nothing else mattered, such as happiness, contentment, or a feeling of integration with my surroundings; or perhaps in her opinion the world in which we lived was so well planned that these feelings would inevitably accrue to the man who worked hard and was moral. Time would show whether she were right or not. There was no appeal in the forms of immorality that America offered and I was going to work hard. She was a good mother, for provided she was sure that in these two respects her sons and daughter followed the right path she was unexacting.

On arrival in New York by the Fall River boat—taken to avoid the noise of trains—I telephoned to Uncle Joseph. He was very busy, his secretary said, but would see me at lunch. To kill time I went to the Metropolitan Museum to look at pictures, which were not a part of my life in Islandia, and I saw them with new eyes. Many, of a storytelling sort that I had once liked, seemed now to be of a past most arid and dead, like the decorations in my room; but others were eternal and moved me deeply. Yet what was most striking about all the pictures was their finish, their elaborateness, their sophistication. They made the carvings that I had seen upon and in Islandian houses crude and childish. Then a strange thing happened. I sat down and felt queer, and the pictures seemed indicative of a cerebration so intense and overbalanced that it was reflected back in the canvases themselves. My head hurt with it. Many of these artists had gone too far in their concentration upon their art. The fresh air of normal living was not in their painting. I went out into Central Park.

I met Uncle Joseph at his lunching club downtown. We were formal and a little distant. He asked about the Mora Treaty and why it had failed and again I told him all that I knew. In return I inquired what attitude was taken in the United States, and he replied that there were too many large fish in the sea at present for American businessmen to bother over their exclusion from one small fishing ground. . . .

"Unless," he added drily, "others are allowed to fish there, in which case we want our share. But a good deal of money was spent and it is going to be got back in some way. Islandia will have to open up sooner or later."

The raid at the Vaba Pass and the tension in the relationship with Germany were news to him, and he confessed that he had not been following Islandian affairs lately.

"Islandia is off the map for the present," he said. "All the same your knowledge of the language and of influential people there may come in handy. What you learned may be worth something some day though it is not much use now."

There were pauses in the conversation. Several times he inquired what my plans were and I said I did not know. We whipped a dead horse into a canter a good many times not only at lunch but in his office afterwards. He wanted me to ask for a job with him, but he had invited me to come and see him, here I was, and it was for him to make the move.

Finally I said that I was taking up too much of his time, that it was very nice to have seen him again, but that I ought to go.

"There is a place for you here, John," he answered almost painfully, "that is, if you want it. It is not much of a place now, but you may be able to make something of it."

"I can begin today, Uncle Joseph."

Arrangements were quickly made.

That evening I dined with him. His granddaughter, my first cousin once removed, was the only other guest. Uncle Joseph had two children—one a successful lawyer and married, the other a daughter, wife of a banker. His wife was dead many years and he seemed rather lonely, his gratitude to Myra Jephson for coming to dine with him too great—she should have regarded herself as the debtor; but she did not and left early for the theater. Instead I was the grateful one, for he obviously had it in mind to put me in the way of meeting young people through her.

Now that I was in his employment, our conversation was more intimate and personal. All the old animosities that had been forgotten reappeared in my memory but were quite dead. I liked him, was appreciative of his kindness in giving me a job after failing as consul, and felt stirrings of loyalty and eagerness to do my best.

We talked of the business and of the opportunity it presented. He had put me in a position to rise if I had any ability. I thanked him with warm feelings.

"I hope it will be a permanent thing," he said, and I remembered the invitation in my trunk. Was I deceiving him if I did not mention it?

"Take me on trial," I answered, "and let me take you on trial also, in case there is something else I want more to do."

"Of course," he said a little stiffly, "you must make your place with us and you must be satisfied."

There was a period of mutual hesitation and then he said he was going to be frank.

"Tell me all you think, Uncle Joseph."

"I don't know what is in your mind," he said, "but it looks to me as though you had a grand loafing time there in Islandia. You certainly did not make all you could out of your job as consul. I don't mind telling you now that I pulled wires for your appointment. You had a chance and you did not make much of it. You knew the language and you were friend of the most important family there though on the wrong side. I am not saying you could have done anything, not as things have turned out, but I looked for a sign that you would try to swing these people the right way. There was none."

"They were too good friends."

"That was your chance."

"One does not try to swing friends."

"You do in politics, and this was politics, not a social gathering."

"We talked," I said. "We talked as friends talk, stating our points of view, even arguing, but with no definite purpose of one converting the other. And I don't think I could have influenced them."

"You admit you did not try. That was a mistake."

"I tried in one way. I got up the Exhibition Ship."

"Was it your idea?"

"Mine and a man named Jennings."

Uncle Joseph smiled.

"He has been around looking for work—a seedy fellow. He said at first the idea was his, but when various firms got after him for the money they spent he said it was yours." But having spoken, he seemed annoyed. "Your idea was costly to a good many of my friends. They don't like to see money thrown away. They get after me, saying, 'Joe, where's that thousand that nephew of yours made me spend?'"

"Where is Jennings now?"

"He has gone West somewhere."

"You say he looked seedy?"

"Drank too much . . . It was a good idea, if it worked, but it didn't. That was all right, however; I don't complain of the Exhibition Ship nor of your failure to talk things up to a lot of hard and fast conservatives, but you did not help out your own countrymen. That is the main thing."

"There are two sides to that, Uncle Joseph."

"I know. They wanted you to do things you thought improper, but when you can't do a thing for an influential man, or think you can't, you ought to do something else for him that you can do. You had a fine chance to make an impression on some fairly important men, John. But you were too busy doing something else, God knows what . . . And why didn't you come home when you were through? You were through last June. It was time you quit. I know all that was happening. I saw you weren't the man for the job. When they got after you in the State Department I did not lift a finger to save you. You were wasting your time and getting nowhere. I wrote you to come home! And what were you doing besides?—Writing articles for the newspapers!"

It would have been interesting to know if Uncle Joseph had done more than fail to lift a finger.

"Why should I come home?" I asked.

"It strikes me that is obvious," he said with finality.

Next morning, February 5th, 1909, at 8:30 a.m. I walked into Uncle Joseph Lang's familiar offices as though I belonged there and went to the allotted desk on which was nothing but blotter, ink, pens, and two empty wire baskets. Within a few minutes a young woman brought me a letter and a file of correspondence. She remarked that I could dictate to her whenever I wanted to and retired. I read, and forgotten knowledge of the way things were done came back. Work had begun.

The day wore slowly through, long but absorbing, and at the end I had learned a good deal, remembered more from experiences during past employment, become familiar with the terms of a number of transactions, and had the satisfaction of a few small things definitely done. My position with Uncle Joseph had no title, no specialized set of duties were prescribed, and I did what was handed to me. I was not exactly a clerk or secretary, but felt as I had not felt before that I was the nephew of the boss on trial.

In the dark, with thousands of others, many of whom were younger than I with assured positions and much farther along the road to success, I went home to a boardinghouse and a room no larger than that at the Fains', but with a great deal more in it in the way of rugs, pictures, curtains, bedspreads, bric-a-brac, and all the rest needed to make it homelike and complete. Later I dined at a common table with strange people, whose welcome was to ignore me and to talk about house news and people unknown to me, but who at length hinted discreet questions in order to learn who and what I was, and after that conversed freely.

The office was a more interesting and pleasant place to be than the boardinghouse, but the latter had the advantage of cheapness. In the hours spent there I had tangible satisfaction in the thought that I was spending less than my income and earnings—but with no definite thought of what I was saving for.

On my first Sunday in New York I dined with my cousin, Uncle Joseph's daughter, Agnes Jephson, a woman of forty-five, her banker husband, their son, and another couple. Myra was week-ending somewhere. They were cordial. The meal was a good one.

"You have been away for a long time, haven't you?" said Agnes. "And now you are back."

It was quite true. Being back was the significant thing.

Attempting to do my share in conversation I told about Islandia, the only topic in my experience novel to these people, but it was soon apparent that their interest was fleeting and polite. To them, and to others whom I met, the mention of Islandia caused reactions as uniform and as inevitable as the antics of a jumping jack when the string is pulled. Islandia meant to them this and no more: an agricultural nation, remotely situated but lacking the interest and color of China and Japan once similarly closed, a country with its back perversely turned on progress, which would someday of course "open up" and become semicivilized; and it was a wonder that it had held out so long! When I tried to explain some of the Islandian theories of life (but at a loss to express them), if my hearers understood me, they found these theories quaint and that was the end of them. The Jephsons, like the people at the boardinghouse, were interested in the life going on around them, knowing no other; and I soon learned that the returned traveler, unless invited formally to lecture, had best remain quiet in a social gathering until he becomes sufficiently familiar with the local life to talk about that, though often this local life seems to him very dull!

In the particular local life around me as to its nonbusiness aspects I played as yet no part, nor through these cousins and my other cousins, Uncle Joseph's lawyer son and his family, was I likely to find a role. We were like two pieces of paper on which mucilage has been spread. We put ourselves carefully together with good will, but the mucilage had dried and we did not cohere.

They made some tentative suggestions as to future dates and suggested that I come to their houses often, though of course, they said, they were often out. I answered that I would do so; and the two pieces of paper fluttered apart with no regrets and quick forgetfulness.

At the office, however, I soon began to feel near a significant activity and then that I was a real part of it. The variety and cosmopolitanism of international commerce was fascinating even for one who spent most of his time in a small room viewing it all through papers. Often, however, there were contacts with men from different parts of the world, who did not talk business only. The life I lived was so absorbing that it had the quality of dazed sleep, and Islandia was reduced to a picture, bright and vivid, but seen at a distance. Boardinghouse meals and evenings were endurable with so absorbing a tomorrow to come. There was no need for anything more.

There was Gladys Hunter upon whom I ought to call. Her last letter written in October before she knew of my decision to return was only a brief note, timed to catch a steamer and sent so as not to break a correspondence, stating that she was busy and that she would answer my last letter by the next boat. This answer had not reached me. The last word I had had from her was this note, the last to her from me was mailed in November, three months before; but up to then our letter writing was uninterrupted. We wrote each other a little less often than monthly and I had a packet of some twenty letters, written from New York and various places in Europe, thick not because she wrote much but because she wrote a large hand. She always carefully thanked me for my letters as though I had done her a favor, always commented upon what I had written her, saying that it must have been fun or very interesting, and often matched an experience of mine with some similar one or some reading of her own. Sometimes she gave me American or European news not likely to be found in the newspapers, sometimes asked questions about Islandia, was brief about her own doings, said nothing as to her thoughts, and only once became at all personal, writing: "I am becoming very selfish because you write me such fine letters and I feel so honored. I can't come up to them but I do hope you won't stop!!!!" All I knew about her was how she looked in November, 1906, more than two years before when she was seventeen, that she had "come out" a year ago and had been in Europe, that she was nearly twenty now, and that her letters had been simple, restrained, intelligent, and charming.

Nevertheless I shrank from going to see her, perhaps dreading to exchange the Gladys who wrote letters for an unknown woman who might have a changed appearance, or else—and more probably —a little ashamed to face her. If the packet of her letters was thick, that of mine was thicker still and my handwriting was small. I had written her pages and pages of description, not a usual thing for a man of twenty-six or -seven to do to a schoolgirl whom he scarcely knew and who was not yet out; and in retrospect much of what I had said seemed sophomoric and excessive.

These things delayed my call until the middle of the month, but on a Sunday afternoon I went to an apartment house which had been the Hunters' last address. The janitor told me that Mrs. Hunter had died two months before and that Miss Hunter had immediately left.

He would not give me her address because to do so was contrary to rules, but a letter sent to the apartment would be forwarded. It was a sharp disappointment not to find her. That night I wrote her a letter of sympathy and said that I hoped she was within reach and that I could call upon her soon.

On Wednesday upon returning to the boardinghouse I found on the hall table a letter in her handwriting, which had changed from that in which she first wrote me and though just as large was more formed. She thanked me for my note and said that she had been in New York since the first of January, and that she was usually at home in the evening and would be glad to see me again. The address was within walking distance of my own.

Next evening I went there through slushy streets and found another boardinghouse not so attractive as that in which I lived and in which I thought I economized. There was an unpleasant smell of food in the dingy parlor which was a public meeting room in spite of pictures and bric-a-brac intended to make it look private and homelike. There I waited.

A tall young woman, as tall as I, strode into the room and came straight to me, and greeted me with a square look in the eyes, and the clasp of a long, slim hand.

"Hello, Gladys!"

"Hello, John!"

It was like calling a stranger by her first name, but there was pleasure in hearing this stranger's even, well-bred voice call me by mine. She was not the seventeen-year-old whom I had left nor she whom I had pictured when I wrote. She seemed older than twenty, more mature than she ought to look, with shadows under her fine clear eyes. She had certainly grown, but was too old and too dignified to be told as much. . . .

We were seated and she was asking me questions about myself, showing in them a flattering memory of things said in my last letters. She was at ease with me, taking charge of the conversation, while I searched to find the Gladys I knew. I interrupted her.

"What are you doing, Gladys?"

She crossed her legs nervously. Her forgotten, long-limbed, graceful awkwardness was suddenly remembered again. I pressed my advantage and took charge of the conversation. She told me briefly of her mother's death. She was studying commercial art at present.

789

She was going to have to work for a living. Her mother had been living upon capital. It was something of a shock. She had wanted to be a real artist but doubted her talent . . . Though brief, she was frank. Though she spoke lightly I knew that there was worry underneath.

Silent because thinking of this I gave her the lead again. Our conversation was an eager battle in which each sought to bring the other up to date, but did not object to paying the penalty of defeat by telling of him or herself.

Three boarders passed the open door and one by one they paused, looked in, and hurried on.

Gladys smiled and the smile became a laugh, complete, without shyness, full of humor. It was new, for there had been no wit in her letters, yet the phrase "I do hope you won't stop!!!!" with the four exclamation points had probably been written with just such a hearty smile. I looked at her and realized that the young woman before me had written me twenty letters with the same long white hands that I saw in her lap, and that her tired but amused, clear, brown eyes had read all the words my heated flying pen had written.

"I don't have many callers," she said, long dimples in her cheeks, "and the other boarders are curious. I'll tell them you are a distinguished diplomat. . . ."

"Who was asked to resign."

"You wrote me. You didn't seem sorry. So I didn't sympathize."

"There was no need."

"I am glad . . . I liked your letters."

"I liked yours."

"Mine? I wanted to write you better ones, but I couldn't. I didn't know how. I quite despaired at first. Our correspondence might so easily have died, but when I found that you were pleased with my efforts I had to go on."

"Didn't you want to?"

"Of course! For selfish reasons, but it didn't seem fair to make you go on when I gave so much less than I got."

"How funny that is! I felt all the time that I was in debt to you."

"Well, you weren't!" she said, and added, "You ought to write a book about Islandia. I have read quite a lot about that country." Her cheeks flushed a little. "You got me interested. There is no recent book that is any good."

"I can't write a book. I can't even explain Islandia. I lack proper words."

"I think you could. Your letters show it."

"My letters were full of ravings."

"Yes, they were, but there are lots of good things. I read one to Mother once, one I specially liked. She laughed and said, 'Your young man is rather flowery, isn't he, Gladys?'—I was so hot I could hardly speak to her."

Suddenly her face was concerned as though she feared she had gone too far. I laughed, for she was right. She looked relieved, saying:

"You know you said yourself in one letter, 'This sounds too extreme, but I'll let it go.'—I liked that. In letters it is all right . . . Do write a book!"

I had quite forgotten that I had ever split her into two Gladyses. At some time in the course of our conversation the two had flowed into one single continuous woman, who had grown up and had within herself all the qualities of both. When I went home that evening we had a "date" for the theater next week and we were going to talk about Islandia.

After I had been a month in his office and a pay check was due, Uncle Joseph of whom I had seen little asked me to lunch again. He told me that I was doing well, to which I answered that I found the work most interesting. He inquired as to my life outside business hours. When it appeared that his son and daughter had invited me to dine with them once and had done no more, he was annoyed.

"Those young people make me tired," he said. "When I am there and Agnes is called on the telephone and asked to dinner or the theater, if she has a previous engagement with some prominent person she will say, 'I am sorry but I can't; we are dining with the Morgans that evening'; but if her engagement is with people like you or me she will say, 'Oh, I wish I could. I would like to so much, but I am dining out that evening and I'm afraid I can't break it.' But she will break her engagement if the right people ask her. Joe is as bad." Uncle Joseph pondered a moment. "But I will see to it that you meet some of the right people yet," he continued. "You are young. I don't go out myself as I did. I am too busy and haven't the strength any longer. I have got to save myself for the office. But I'll do something for you."

He did not approve of my living in a boardinghouse.

"You have a position to uphold," he said, "and if it is a question of money. . . ."

I was afraid he would raise my salary without reason and tie me to him too tightly.

"Not that!" I said quickly, "but I want to save money. I am perfectly comfortable."

"Why do you want to save money?" It was a hard question to answer, but he spared me from doing so by asking, "Not thinking of getting married, are you?"

"Not at all, Uncle Joseph."

"You don't make enough yet to marry on. Wait a while. Be sure of your woman . . . Seeing any?"

I hesitated and then mentioned Gladys whom I had called on once, taken to the theater once, and with whom I was going to walk on Sunday morning. He asked who she was, and when he learned her circumstances, he said:

"That is a dangerous type. Watch out, John. Wait till you meet some of the girls I'll scare up for you. A right marriage will do you a lot of good."

"In what way, Uncle Joseph?"

"Every way!" he said sharply, and I knew that what he was thinking of was what is called "a good match," and I suspected that if I made one of which he approved he would help me on the money side.

Joseph Lang and Company among their various activities acted as agents for certain inland manufacturers in connection with their sales in foreign markets. There came to my hands a file of correspondence that showed the following situation: A buyer in France had sent to us an offer to buy the product of one of these manufacturers at a price somewhat above that at which they were then selling it. Our clerk in charge had promptly cabled back accepting the offer. The French buyer answered that one of his own clerks had made a wrong calculation and asked to be relieved. The order was for delivery some time hence and the manufacturers had in no way yet changed their position in reliance upon the miscalculated price.

It seemed to me quite clear that the Frenchman ought to be relieved and our relations with the manufacturer were such that the decision rested with us. I almost sent a letter to the buyer that the order was canceled, but at the last minute decided to consult Uncle Joseph. I showed him my letter, ready to go.

"What's this?" he said sharply. "He is liable, isn't he?"

"I think so—"

"Have you consulted Tuck?" Tuck was our attorney.

"No," I said. "The question of liability seemed unimportant."

"Why?"

"They made a mistake on the other side. Our principal isn't harmed in any way."

"We lose a commission."

"Does that matter, Uncle Joseph?"

"You wouldn't be here if it didn't! Are you afraid that Frenchman won't deal with us any more? Don't worry about that. We have an exclusive agency and he needs that product. He will come back again."

"I wasn't thinking of that either."

"What were you thinking of?"

"It seems unfair."

"It is a question of law. Ask Tuck. If they are legally liable, make them fulfill the order or pay for getting out. Don't be soft, John. We have been caught that way ourselves and we have had to pay. Don't let those Frenchmen put one over on you."

I consulted Tuck who advised us that the mistake of the French clerk was not such as to relieve the French buyer of his obligation to fulfill his order.

Here was the situation as it looked to me: The manufacturers and ourselves were making money that they and we never expected to receive in the normal course of things; the Frenchman was losing a sum of money which except for the mistake of a clerk he never would have had to pay; but there was an institution called the law which in the present instance prescribed this result . . . I wondered why . . . If Uncle Joseph had handed one of his friends to whom he owed ten dollars a twenty-dollar bill by mistake, he would despise that man if he did not rectify the overpayment, and the man himself would be scrupulous in doing so. Very likely the law would make him do it. Where was the difference? Of what importance was the fact that the Frenchman would not cease to deal with us if held to this bargain? Either I, or Uncle Joseph, or the law, or the situation that compelled the existence of such a law, was wrong.

I wrote the Frenchman as I was told to do, and felt sick in doing so, sick because I had to concern myself with such a problem of right and wrong, all the more because I was not at all sure that my own impulsive solution was not of a sort disintegrating to the intricate structure of business and commerce. Employed as I was I could not be individualistic and settle matters as accorded best with my own nature. Nor could I understand the solution that was prescribed.

This was but one problem among many. I wanted someone to discuss it with and thought of my own brother Philip and Dorn. From either of them I would get an opinion or a point of view freshening to my own.

Freshness and clarity were what I needed and they were hard to find in the life I led. At present there was nothing to do but go on to the next thing—and I went on.

Hard work made the days slip by and it was as absorbing as ever. Because I was absorbed all day with something interesting to do and with plenty of vitality to do it with I felt quite happy. The Frenchman episode was a setback, but there was too much on my mind to think of it long.

Then one day I was tired. Out of my window was nothing to see in the late dusk but the walls of buildings a dark gray-blue; a thin vertical strip of sky of the same color and a little lighter in tone; and, dotted upon the walls, squares of yellow light. From below rose the roar of traffic and of voices. I was tired, not as I had been tired in Islandia with a heavy contented longing for sleep; I was devitalized but wide awake with a brain overactive. I felt the stirrings of strong impulses, but my body was an inert thing and needed the stimulus of a drink or of something to quicken in it a vitality equal to that in my head. I wanted something to pull me together again and to make me even and whole, brain and body functioning as one.

I saw a stenographer putting on her coat in the frame of a yellow' window across the court on which mine opened. She looked attractive at a distance and the idea of her was alluring. I wanted a woman. The excitement and immense physical effort of possessing her would give me a semblance of unity, make me forget, ease the strain.. I wanted no gentleness with her, no love—hungry merely for the flesh of her. . . At the same time the idea of the aftermath of letting go in such a way was detestable. . . How easy to call this repulsion an instinctive morality! How easy to regard the act that I wanted as in itself wrong! Consciousness of a degradation as of sin seemed an inevitable part of the split that fatigue had caused. . . Would Dorn understand it? I would like to tell him about it—"See what this sort of thing does to a man!"

I knew, however, what others would say: they would prescribe another split in my functioning and tell me that I needed more exercise. It was laughable! Having autointoxicated my brain with a fatigue due to a sort of work of which it was heresy to disapprove, a man was advised to exercise his body and to fatigue it equally, jaded though it already was by the demands made upon it by his head. The root of the evil was the life itself, and at this root no one thought to strike. In the deceitful clairvoyance of weariness and tired nerves the whole theory seemed to me as futile and childish as that which in the Middle Ages prescribed a loathsome thing, such as the corpse of a rat cut open, as cure for the sores of a loathsome disease, the bubonic plague.

A few days later I went with Gladys to the theater again. She had not taken much pains with her appearance and had a slightly untidy, everyday aspect; but she was too naturally neat and fine looking, if not pretty, to be anything but a pleasing companion.

"Do you ever get tired out?" I said.

"I get awfully tired.—Do I look it?"

"No," I answered promptly, but it was a lie.

"Well, you look tired, John. You aren't so brown and healthy-looking as you were when I first saw you. You work too hard."

There was a kindly concern in her eyes.

"You also work too hard, Gladys."

"I know it, but what else can I do?"

"Gladys," I said, after wondering about all this, "I don't think we work too hard. Did it ever occur to you that the trouble is not the long hours but the nature of the work, because of the complexity of the life we are confronted with all day long, suggesting continuously a feeling of chaos?"

"I am too tired to work that out," she said, "but this is restful."

Either she referred to the fact that we were two congenial friends together or to the play which had a social problem for its theme with an apt solution, simplified and condensed for us by its author.

Spring came, not as a gradual change in the revolving year of which the senses are aware day by day, but as a sudden visitor to the city, like some distinguished man, whose presence was unexpectedly noticed.

"By the way, it is Spring now, I suppose!"

Spring meant little more than changing from a heavy to a light overcoat in air that was warmer but stronger with city smells, of vegetables, wet asphalt, roasting coffee, gasoline. In vistas of sky seen down street canyons, spring was sometimes apparent where white clouds showed against darker ones and both were edged upon a fresh blue, and there were pleasant showers.

April—and the sewing machine must have reached my friend Nattana, who would write me a letter of thanks from the Lower Farm where she probably now was, all difficulties with her father settled. . . Perhaps Dorna's baby was already born. It would be good to know that she was well.

For some reason I was glad to think that in Islandia it was not spring but fall.

Uncle Joseph had been true to his word. Invitations of one sort and another began to come. My cousins rediscovered me again. Evenings were filled. But people were already going away, saying that they hoped to see more of me in the fall. Their good will was great but I felt Uncle Joseph's influence behind it. I was accepted as his nephew, but as a young man, as myself, there was something that barred me from them. It seemed at times as though I had only a foreigner's imperfect knowledge of and interest in the things that interested them. As a businessman, however, I was more at home. It was my life.

May came, and during a walk one Sunday morning Gladys unexpectedly said that she was leaving New York in a few days not to return until fall, if ever. Her course in commercial art was ending and she had cousins in Vermont with whom she could live cheaply. She had talked about her work as I about mine, but nothing real had ever been said as to what she felt about it or where she thought it was leading her. Her mask dropped in spite of herself and the revelation hurt her. She strode along in her full skirt that seemed so needless a handicap, her face to the front but with her lip quivering like a child's. She was only twenty.

I walked with her, torn two ways, willing to listen, eager to help, but afraid to intrude. The personal that exacted nothing seemed best.

"I am sorry you are going," I said, "and I hope you come back. You have been someone to whom I could talk about things that have meant much to me. You have been a charming, dear friend. It has been good from the beginning, hasn't it, Gladys?"

"Of course!" she said briefly.

"You haven't had so much on your mind to talk about or you haven't wanted to. But I would like to be used in the way I have used you."

I felt her eyes upon me.

"Friends don't use each other enough," I said. "They are too afraid. Of course, it is good just to know you have a friend who stands by. I am all of that. I am also a pair of ears and I certainly like you."

"I like you," she said.

"I have some intelligence too," I added. "Crossing two intelligences even though one is ordinary often breeds good results."

"It is nothing much," she said with a little laugh, and then her voice changed. "Only—I'm no good. I don't know where my work is leading me. . . I haven't wanted to bore you with it of course—but I am not clever, and you have to be clever and facile to succeed in what I am doing. Others at the school have places and work for this summer, but I haven't. I haven't even any ideas any longer. And that isn't all! I know I ought to stick to it, and not be discouraged and give it up yet, but I am tempted to throw the whole thing over—bang! . . . I have so admired you. You haven't said so exactly, but you have told me enough for me to know that you don't wholly approve of what you are doing, but you go right on all the same. I wish I could do that; but I don't want what I'm doing and I never did. It was at best a *pis aller,* and now I think it is a blind *allée,* too!" She laughed with a catch in her voice at her own joke.

"What are you going to do this summer?" I said.

"I am going to do the other thing!" she answered hotly, "and spend money. I ought to be tramping the streets of New York getting some job near to the kind of work I've set out to do, or else learning stenography or something. Instead I am going to try to paint land-scapes in the hope I'll sell them, knowing I won't, and knowing I'm doing wrong all the time!"

"Gladys," I asked, "how much money have you?"

"I have—or rather I had—five thousand dollars, and I ought to spend only the income. I am doing as Mother did, using up the capital. Father did not leave her as much as she expected and though she economized a little she was used to living a certain way and kept on. She was spoiled and now I'm spoiled."

"Have you no relatives, Gladys?"

"None I care to sponge on for long. I have got to learn to support myself and I don't seem to be able to find a way, and meanwhile—"

She stopped abruptly.

"Your money gives you time to find it," I said.

"It is going fast."

She had shown an uncertainty and indecision which were the opposite of what I had thought characteristic. What was to be done for her if she had these qualities and were, as she said, without talent? Her life had been sheltered and she was "spoiled," that is, too much a lady. I felt a sudden impotence and remembered how easily and naturally others, Dorn and the Fains, had helped me. My trouble was not like hers, but had I been as poor as she was they would no less have taken me in. I paid them nothing, merely worked as I saw fit. In Islandia a case like Gladys's would not arise, but if it did what would happen? Gladys would find a place with friends, I was sure.

I spoke my thoughts, absorbed by the picture I was seeing: a farm, commodious, ample, not merely the single crowded house of a relative on whom one did not care to sponge too long; Gladys with a cottage like that of Nettera, or with a room of her own like mine at the Fains', doing some work for her hosts, as I had done, but also free to paint or to carve. I thought of the Lay River Farm. . . .

"I wish I had a place of my own where I could keep you," I said, "but I haven't such a place—not yet, though I'm thinking of one. But anyway at present I have money, more than I need. Let me be your good friend; you are so alone! Let me give you what you need, as a gift. There are ways in which you could repay me, of course. . . ."

"I haven't come to that yet."

Her voice was changed, hard, frozen, childish. . . I wondered what I had done, and suddenly the blood rushed from my heart. I saw over the treetops the tall buildings that hem in Central Park and knew where I was.

"Don't misunderstand me, Gladys," I said.

We walked on in silence.

"You have spoiled something that was very nice," she answered.

Before me was the tedious path of explanation and I shrank from embarking upon it.

"This country is a bad place," I said.

"I don't want to listen to you. I know it is, but that doesn't mean that I. . . ."

"You must listen to me. I don't want to lose your friendship."

"You have."

"It will be you who spoil something good."

"Can you blame me?"

"No, but I shall blame you if you don't listen."

"There's nothing to say."

"Yes, there is—"

"Nothing! I've met it before, at the school, but from you! I never thought. . . ."

She was walking faster and faster.

"Gladys, listen to me!"

"No, Mr. Lang."

"You are needlessly humiliating me."

"You have humiliated me."

"Not you! Where I have been, women's bodies aren't bought with money and I had no thought of buying yours."

"Oh!" she cried furiously, as though I had insulted her again.

"I was thinking of an experience of my own."

"Don't talk to me! I am going home."

I walked abreast of her and she was silent. Her steps were leading us toward an entrance to the park and if she once were upon a bus or trolley car, I felt that my chance would be gone.

"The Fains," I said, "took me in. You knew that, but I never told you that I was utterly miserable. They had a place where there was room for me. They were friends. I paid them nothing. I worked for them, naturally, but not during all my time and they did not ask it of me."

"You are not a girl!"

"I was not thinking of you as a girl but as my friend Gladys. I was thinking of myself in Islandia and of you there, too, and then of some way to do in this country what any friend would do for you there. The nearest equivalent to a place was money."

"Did you mean it as a loan?"

"No, as a gift, as a real gift, just as the Fains' hospitality was to me."

"You spoke about repayment."

"So that you need not worry over a sense of obligation."

"Oh!" she cried, pressing her hands to her face. "How can I know that seeing it did not work with me you aren't trying to make it seem something else?"

"You will have to have faith in me."

"How can I? You had been all right so far, but Mother told me never to trust men. She said they would be perfect for a long time and then when they got you at a disadvantage they would do some horrid thing!"

"Gladys, if I want anything of you I will say it so clearly that you won't have any doubt at all what it is. Will you listen to me? Have enough faith for that!"

Her pace slackened. She was willing to listen, she said. A park bench was the best place. I told her about my love for and loss of Dorna and all about the visit to the Fains'. With this background of reality I tried to make real to her what I had felt when I spoke, and it became necessary to tell her that Islandia was still very much in my mind because it was in my power to return there.

Instead of going home to our separate boardinghouses we dined together at a restaurant, and there the explanation continued, and became more than that. I wanted the country to live in her eyes. There must be no doubt in her mind at all. In the end she said:

"Forgive me, but you understand, don't you?"

"Of course, and forgive me for giving you a shock."

"It was a shock," she answered. "I couldn't believe in my heart that you meant it that way, but I knew no other way to act."

She promised with a smile not to tell anyone that she knew about Dorna and about the invitation I had received.

I took her to her door.

"If this were Islandia," she said, "and if I were very hard up,

I might accept your hospitality, but in this country it is better not. But anyway that problem is a long way off yet."

She left me cheerful, smiling, and I felt exhausted but serene.

The pace accelerated at the office but with it my ability to keep up. On looking back I had a feeling of achievement and saw many tasks finished satisfactorily. Every morning one wire basket was full and the other empty. My ambition was to leave in the evening with the first empty and the second full, and to have as many files of correspondence and contracts pass from the cabinets containing pending matters to those containing "dead" or "closed" ones.

The transactions for which these papers stood were sometimes unreal, but they became more and more living as time went on and Uncle Joseph and the older men took me more into their confidence. I had not been found wanting this time at any rate and I saw ahead of me financial competence and more. The family were delighted. Mother wrote that she was very glad that I had found myself at last. I was pleased also and thought of moving out of the boardinghouse and of having a small flat of my own—next fall perhaps—and of buying an automobile. Summer was not far and already I had a number of invitations for week ends and for my as yet indefinite vacation. Clothes in greater variety would add to my appearance and to the interest of life. There were other things that caught my eye, a liqueur set, a silver cigar box. I thought of going in for sport, of taking up golf or tennis, and of riding in the park. The John Lang of February, March, and April had been almost a recluse, with few invitations and but one girl to see and her not often; the John Lang of May and June had promptings to blossom into a promising young businessman about town.

Life took on a brighter color. With realization of greater means there was an expansion in desires. Alluring avenues opened. As yet I merely looked at them. A week passed in which I forgot all about the invitation to Islandia still in the bottom of my trunk. Remembering it I reaffirmed my decision, but now it was not to remain in America for a year but rather not to decide to remain until a year was over.

33

The United States: Summer

IN THE FULL WIRE BASKET of matters calling for attention was a letter from Islandia addressed in Dorn's handwriting. I had written him once, after coming to New York, and this was the first word from his country since I had left it six months before.

I put the letter aside to be read when the day's work was over, not because I was busy, but because it was threatening to present moods. Until night came that letter reproached me from an inside pocket for not being read at once; my best and dearest friend had written it; and it made my return to the boardinghouse hurried and impatient as though I expected to find there a message from someone I loved. But I waited until after dinner when I was alone in my room with no interruptions.

The square, odd-shaped envelope, the stiff hard paper, the black ink, and the firm bold handwriting that always looked as though Dorn restrained his vigor to penmanship with an effort, set vibrating the strings of elusive memories. There was a sensation as of closed doors about to open.

I had forgotten that it took force to tear Islandian paper.

The envelope enclosed another one as well as Dorn's letter, which was dated April 10th and had caught the mid-April steamer. On the second of that month Dorna's child had been born, a boy. Her labor had been difficult but not dangerous, and she and the boy were both well and strong on the eighth when he had last heard from the Frays. Nekka would give birth to his own child in September, and she was in the best of health.

He spoke of all whom I knew and cared for most, the Fains, Lord Dorn, the Stellins, and others, adding that he enclosed a letter from Nattana who did not know how to address me and who he was sure would speak for herself and the Hyths. He then reported upon the condition of the three Dorn farms briefly but fully as though I were one who had a right to know. Fak he was using himself and taking good care of. The political situation was favorable. There had been no attempt to reopen any questions settled by the repudiation of the Mora Treaty, and tension had greatly eased over the Vaba Pass raid. The German government had been informed by the British government that aggressive steps against Islandia would be looked upon unfavorably. A joint commission was investigating the matter still.

Then Dorn wrote:

> I think often of you. I know that you can live a good life in your own country and also a good life here. The question you must decide is which is the better one. I am afraid that merely because you find that the American life can be good you will choose it. A choice between two good things is the hardest choice there is. For myself I want you here and so do many others. The Mountain Farm or the Lay River Farm both wait for you. I forgot to tell you that the autumn coloring at the latter place is wonderfully beautiful and I know what this means to a New Englander. Something good is gone from my life with you not here.
>
> DORN

The fabric of contentment that I had built up was shaken. I hungered for the flavor of Islandia. . . But Dorn himself had warned me not to let love for an American woman play too great a part in my decision; neither must affection for him.

There was Nattana's unopened letter, which I did not want to read. In my emotions but not in my reason I resented her writing to me, yet knew that having received the sewing machine, write me she must whether she wanted to or not. For her sake I disliked resenting her letter. But something new had crept into my feeling about her—a sense of regret and of shame. I might dislike Alice's feeling toward such affairs as mine with Nattana, but to do so was very like adopting an attitude of which I equally disapproved, though what that attitude was I did not really know. There had been in the air and all around me, washing over me, waters of sex, a little tainted, known before I had gone to Islandia as consul and found again when I returned; waters from many sources some clean and some unclean, manifested in stories of employers and gay young stenographers, of rich men and actresses, and of commercial travelers and women on trains; manifested in masculine boasting and glorification of a man's supposedly irresistible desires; manifested in man's condonation, like the traditions of an exclusive club, of things women disapproved of because women being women disapproved; manifested also in women's outcry against a double standard, of their own invention, which they declared men imposed upon them; manifested in preachings of purity and chastity and against temptations of the flesh; manifested in many other ways, sprung from pride, vanity, animality, idealism, organization, and altogether confusing, conflicting, overemphasized, and troubling to anyone who wished to think clearly and simply. I was American and the thought of my relation with Nattana made me uncomfortable now. I picked up her letter and realized that I was also proud of myself because holding in my hands the letter of a woman I had possessed, even I—and at the same time I disliked having both these feelings and felt a distressed ache in my head.

At last I read her letter with a sort of lust:

Lang, my friend:

The machine for sewing stitches in cloth arrived and surprised me as nothing has in years. It was such an interesting idea of Lang's to make a surprise of it. I am very grateful for the trouble Lang took—and to think that it required a special vote of the council. I am also glad to have the machine as Lang will see.

It was brought to the Lower Farm, where I now am, in the strangest-looking box with American words on the outside which Father explained. He was as interested as I was. We opened it together and were slow to touch it lest we do something wrong and break it. We found the directions and read them together several evenings before we did anything. The pictures helped. Then at last we took out the machine very carefully and set it up reading the directions as we went along. Then we looked at it a long time. It is the oddest thing, unlike anything else I have ever seen. The first way we worked it was to wind thread on a "bobbin" from one of the spools that came with it. I worked the things called treadles with my own feet. Then we got it all ready and I took some cloth. It was late by this time. My heart was beating. I did what the directions said and there were stitches on the cloth more even than I could make them. It was a very exciting moment for Hyth and Hytha Nattana.

I think it will be useful. There are a number of problems to be worked out, one of which is of the proper thread. But already I have used it for sewing that does not have to be carefully done and it certainly saves time. This is of great importance to me now for I have all the work I want to do and am very happy in consequence. I have new ideas for blending colors and am at work on a dress (two shades of green) to wear at the Council Meeting in June.

Lang will be glad to know that Father and I settled everything to his and my complete satisfaction. There was no misunderstanding though we differed. He said there was a rule; I that there was only a custom. He said that he had made a rule for his children, his house; I answered that he could do so, but that the rule he had made was an unusual one. He declared that nevertheless it was the rule, and being a rule not a custom something must be done other than the punishment which nature inflicted on those who lived wrongly. I asked what good that would do; he replied that rules gained strength by being enforced. I told him that he was making a god of the rule like a foreigner and was sacrificing me to that god, and that my opinions and ideas would in no way be changed. "Even so," he said, "you will never forget the rule." I replied that the rule was the last thing to remember in connection with what I had done but rather the effect on myself and others, which was good rather than bad. He asked if I thought punishment was good. I said no. "Punishment for breach of the rule is one of the effects," he answered. I said, "Father, you are arguing round in a circle." He denied it. I saw that it was hopeless. The rule truly was his god and existed for itself and ruled him. He punished me by locking the door to my loom for a month. I rode horseback and helped with the cattle and got healthy and brown, and thought up new

designs. Since then he and I have been the best of friends and
I have promised to live his way while at home.

At the Upper Farm the new wing is finished. All Ek's
cattle will winter there for the first time. I have not been there
since a few days after Lang left when I also left. Ek, Atta,
and Ettera at last see a clear road before them. Work has lessened.

Nettera has begun playing again, and Bain is kind and
understanding. It is hard for him to live with a woman for
whom he has *ania,* to know that he is nothing but a friend to
her, and to find her uninterested in his household. He tries
to love her music and she tries to give him what he wants but
of course cannot. She is not to be pitied for she can always
absorb herself in her music, but I am sorry for him. He is
paying dearly for his mistake in marrying her. He should have
been satisfied with what he had, but it was true though blind
ania for him.

If there is more Lang wishes to know about the machine
or about anything else in Islandia within my power to tell him
let him write to his now and hereafter friend

NATTANA

The letter rebuked my resentment. Nattana made no claim upon
me. She alone of those I knew well had never expressed any wish
for my return. I felt her strength. She had enriched me. To feel regret
and shame was to feel falsely.

That night I dreamed an inconclusive, confused dream. Instead
of being here I was there and instead of the question of leaving the
United States was that of leaving Islandia. I had a farm which was
neither that of the Lay River nor of the Hail River Pass nor of any
other single place but was beautiful beyond words. I had a wife
who was Dorna, Nattana, and Gladys—now one, now another, now
none of them. I had a child, a boy. Upon me was a heavy obligation
to make a decision, and though I never made it and could not, endlessly reasoning in futile dream fashion, all the while I knew that
I was going to leave and be a cruel deserter for the sake of something that was fiery and sweet that was Dorna, Nattana, Gladys . . .
a child . . . a child who looked like me but was dark, who was
his mother, who was me, and who was unbearably dear.

Next day at the office again, full of "do it now" determination with reference to the contents of the full basket, I found that the usually firm structure of concentration and business thoughts was like a house among the foundations of which a dark undermining flood washes. Islandia was in my senses—I saw, smelled, and tasted it. It was in my blood as love is in the blood, welling up continually, insisting upon itself and its existence, whatever one thinks, whatever one's occupation. But in the practical world of a downtown office the emotions caused by two letters—one merely a recital of news and a word of friendship, the other a girl's naïve account of a new sewing machine, an experience with her father, and meditations upon her sister's marriage—and by an intangible dream were not such as any sensible man allows to affect him. As the day advanced the foundations became firmer and the flood was but a murmur.

The prosperity of Lang and Company was founded upon a great many small and moderate transactions methodically, carefully, and quickly performed. We were agents and forwarders for manufacturers and merchandisers, we also carried a few lines of our own, and we often bought and sold for ourselves. Similarly though to a less extent we were importers. The business was old, going back to my grandfather, but Uncle Joseph had made it what it now was. Lang and Company, however, was not all of Uncle Joseph, who was a larger figure than his firm. It was his bedrock, his steppingstone, his specialty, but he was interested in many other enterprises. His opinion was valued, he was often consulted, and he had many friends. Venturers in business liked to have him with them. Most of his money came from these outside investments, but for Lang and Company he had a deep affection and an undeviating interest. He was no absentee owner and made it a matter of his personal concern when anything happened likely to affect the reputation of the firm.

He evoked loyalty and affection from us, his employees. We also felt loyal to those for whom we acted or those with whom we dealt—that is, with the right ones, whom Uncle Joseph determined. Those who had been with him long knew which firms were the favored ones and which were to be dealt with at arm's length. From them the rest of us picked up the proper tone to adopt. The distinctions that were made at first seemed to me haphazard, and based on nothing tangible that I could understand. The Frenchman whose clerk made a mistake is a case in point. The determining factor was not wholly the profitableness of the relationship to us, but depended on other things. Nor was it the duration of the relationship, though that also seemed to be important. Gradually I came to see that there were right people in this business world just as there were in the social world, and that the two worlds, at least as far as I saw them, either overlapped or were the same.

The Frenchman needed a product for which we had an exclusive agency. Why did we press him to the limit and not a friend of Uncle Joseph's who made as bad a mistake? In both cases we were mere agents and the greater part of the profit went not to us but to our principals; but in the one case Uncle Joseph insisted that the profit be taken, and in the other let it go although it was not wholly his. I suggested that from the principal's point of view the two cases were the same, and Uncle Joseph declared that he did not care to act for anyone who did not grant him the right to use his judgment in such matters, and that his principals knew it! He had no doubts in his own mind how to act. I did not have his certainty. There was nothing in me that made the distinctions he made. He was admired for his business acumen. Sometimes it seemed merely an instinct, like a knack at playing a particular game, that informed Uncle Joseph who were of the business four hundred and who were not.

There were the same jealousies, toadyings, and heartaches among the favored and the not favored as existed in the social life with which I was becoming more familiar. The lines drawn were fluid and any man who by good fortune had certain qualities could with capital or with perseverance or with luck find his way into the favored classes, business and social. Uncle Joseph thoroughly believed that business was democratic and social life not, but it began to seem that both were the same, and that the democracy was greater in social life, at least with persons assured of their positions. For them it was easy; they could make no mistakes. What were the qualities necessary for admission to the inside of business? I tried to formulate them in my own mind and found myself faced with a hopeless puzzle, the more confusing the more I thought about it.

Associating with Uncle Joseph, however, gave me for myself more and more an "inside" feeling, and the attitude of others increased it. When I mentioned to a clerk in the office with whom I sometimes lunched that I had spent the week end with the Jephsons, he became almost at once less frank and more deferential. Before that we had been easy acquaintances; now there was stress in our relationship as though some force were making us unequal. Thereafter I found myself tempted to do what Uncle Joseph had accused his daughter, Agnes, my cousin, of doing.

Uncle Joseph was partly responsible for this uncomfortable pride falsifying to contacts with others. He urged me to go about and to see more people, telling me all about those I met and keeping himself informed as to what I did. Social activities increased and bred others, and he took me out of New York to his own summer house on Long Island near Huntington, an old comfortable place, neatly kept. I bought an automobile and no longer spent many evenings or any week ends by myself.

It was a hot summer evening in the middle of the week. Uncle Joseph and I were sitting on a wide porch that looked off over a wide lawn to a dense bank of trees that cut off the road. It was growing dark and the high street lamps were already lighted, but I had so placed my chair that the trees almost hid them. On the table between us were whiskies and sodas, more the latter and ice than the former. Upstairs was a large high-ceilinged room with a wide comfortable bed, a place usually cool before morning.

Uncle Joseph's cigar glowed.

"Mind my asking a question?" he said. This was unusual.

"Of course not, Uncle Joseph."

"There was a girl you were seeing in the winter, a Miss Hunter. Do you know about her father? I happened to hear."

"Very little."

"He was an upstate man, Syracuse, I think. He had a good business there. His wife came from Ohio or Indiana. She was not satisfied with Syracuse, so they came to New York and he started in business here. Roger Pendleton remembers him, a fine-looking man, but pressed for money a good deal of the time. He got along pretty well at first, but his wife was a spender, though an attractive woman then. Things did not go well. He overworked himself and died. He ought to have stayed in Syracuse. . . I thought you might care to know who the Hunters were if she hasn't told you."

What struck me first was the fact that Uncle Joseph had taken the trouble to find out, and next that he thought these things significant. He could not have said more plainly that the husband was a failure, the wife a spender, both outsiders, and the daughter therefore undesirable.

"Miss Hunter hasn't told me much about her parents," I said.

"Still seeing her?"

"No. She left New York in May. She has gone to cousins in
Vermont, but," I added, sorry to have to tell him, "she may return
in the fall, in which case I shall see her again. While I was in Islandia
I wrote her every month or so and she wrote me. I have sent her two
letters since and have had an answer."

"It is not serious, is it?"

For a moment I did not understand.

"I have never thought of asking her to marry me."

"I hope you don't think of it."

"I don't—but I like her."

"That is all right, I suppose. Don't like too many women. Reserve your likes for men."

"Why, Uncle Joseph?"

"Soft!" he said in the darkness. "There are two uses for women—
one is as wives. For that, if you pick the right one, they are the greatest gift God has given us."

"What is the other use, Uncle Joseph?"

"To make a fool of yourself with! But there is nothing better
for a man than a good wife. There was your aunt. . . ."

He was silent. *Ania* and *apia,* I thought, but *ania* sentimentalized
and *apia* degraded.

"I never met Aunt Betsy," I said gently.

"Too good for me."

He spoke with so much dramatic feeling that for a moment I
believed he was joking, but evidently he was not, for after a pause
he continued earnestly:

"You really ought to marry, John, and not wait too long either.
You are thirty now. I know that marriage is a costly matter these
days. Very likely you are thinking that you can't afford it. But if
the question comes up and the girl wants assurances, as any sensible
girl does, you talk to me first and I'll see what I can do." He paused
suddenly. "I hope there is no impediment," he said.

"What sort of impediment, Uncle Joseph?"

"I meant that I hope you didn't marry some native wife out there
who will turn up here and blackmail you."

"I married no one. I'm quite single."

"I am not sentimental," he said, "but I don't expect a man to marry a woman he can't care for, however good a match she may be. I have seen men try it and the marriage go on the rocks. But I do say this: a man is much better off married than not, particularly a young man, provided he finds the right woman and shows as much intelligence and common sense in choosing her as he shows in other matters. I would like to see you married and I would like to see you do as well in your marriage as you have done in other ways since you came back from Islandia. And if ever you have such a girl in mind and there comes up the question of money, you can count on me to back you, and I am going to give you a substantial raise in salary anyway. My own children have disappointed me in one way or another. You are my nephew. Your father can't do much for you, but I can!"

"Thank you, Uncle Joseph!" I cried, moved by the strong feeling with which he spoke, moved also by the sense of power which he gave me. . . Yet I hesitated also, and to make up for such lack of gratitude and for what I must answer, I rose and grasped his hand. "But don't think of raising my salary yet, not unless you are perfectly sure that the value of what I give to the firm is worth the increase. I don't need money now, and I don't really want it."

"That sounds well," he said, drawing his hand away, "but don't be a fool. If I want to treat you as a son, don't talk that way to me."

His last words were a shock, but I worked out what prompted him to speak as he had. If what I said were sincere, he was offended at the repudiation of his bounty; if a pose, as I think he thought it, he quite naturally felt contempt for me; but I could not explain to him that I meant what I said without doing to him what seemed to me the greater unkindness; his contempt meant nothing but I did not want him hurt. . . So I thought, and became suspicious of myself, for what he offered to give me became more attractive the more I thought of it. To accept his offers to the full was, however, another matter and not until the year of indecision between the United States and Islandia was over and I was released, would I let myself become his debtor.

Time passed quickly as it does when one is busy and also waiting for something to happen. Days at the office were shortened but were just as full, and hours not at the office were active ones. August came suddenly and I found that my vacation of two weeks, which had to be taken, was at hand. Plans had already been made between the writing of business letters, and I departed impatiently to enjoy my leisure.

Philip had timed his vacation to coincide with mine and we met in Boston to go down to his cottage on Cape Cod, where I was to spend a week at least and to be with the family. He was seven years older than I, shorter, slighter, with skin that lay close upon the bones of his face, with delicate features, wide, clear, light-blue eyes, and a look of purity and goodness. As a young man he wanted to be a minister, had he had the proper beliefs, but not having them decided to be a lawyer and went through the Law School with purpose and determination. Now he was successful in a conservative Bostonian way, but not wealthy as Uncle Joseph and his friends were.

Now we sat side by side upon the green plush seat of an American railway car, alone together for the first time since I had gone to Islandia. His face had its familiar look of thoughtful and refined eagerness, and of trustworthiness.

It was a hot Saturday afternoon and many other hard-working husbands and fathers like Philip were going to wives and children at their summer places. Some of these men hailed him by his first name with friendliness and respect and he responded with his bright clear smile.

He talked of the family. The car was crowded and smelled of people and of acrid coal smoke. We passed through Dorchester, the Quincys, the Braintrees, Brockton, and Middleborough, and I had a sharp memory of how I had felt as a boy and younger man making this journey on vacation visits to the Cape: a purgatory of dingy and insipid towns had to be passed through before one reached the greater spaciousness of an outdoor region with sandhills, pine woods, marshes, summer cottages, and sea. These thoughts, however, I did not bother to point out to Philip; he would perceive exactly what I meant but would feel it necessary to say a good word for the towns. While he talked I waited 'for purgatory to end, but for some reason the spaciousness that I expected was less, and all seemed the same.

He told me that Mother and Father were stopping at a simple hotel a few miles from his cottage so as to be near him and Mary and to be near their grandchildren and to be near me during my visit. Alice was coming later and then the whole family would be together. Mary was planning some picnics. Philip Junior was learning to sail and having heard that his Uncle John knew about boats looked forward to having me sail with him. He was thirteen now and Faith was ten. She had no friends of her own age and was something of a problem. He and Mary were trying new methods.

It was wonderful to have me visit them at last, he cried. To think that I had been at home six months and that he and I had had no real talks! They had heard nothing as to my experiences in Islandia which must have been most interesting. There were things he wanted to know, and Mary also looked forward to asking me questions.

There were a number of nice people near their place, among them Professor Bedloe, of the English Department at Harvard, and his wife, and Robert Howard, a doctor interested in sociology, and his wife. I would enjoy meeting them and talking to them.

"But," said Philip, "tell me about yourself, John." His eyes were clear, simple, and affectionate, with eagerness behind them. "How is Uncle Joseph? Have you seen anything of the Jephsons?"

In answer to these and other questions I told him all that I thought would interest him relating to these people, knowing that he would pass it on to Mother. Family feeling or rather feeling of family was strong in her and Philip. They were always eager for news of cousins and relatives whom they never saw and never wrote to. To them relatives were differentiated from the rest of mankind.

When all family information that either of us knew was exchanged, he asked how I liked being a New York businessman, and I was puzzled how to answer.

"The work," I said, "is too mental."

Philip laughed.

"Are you already pining for the simple life?"

"No," I answered, "I am not pining for anything."

"In our family," he said, "there are two strains, the intellectual and the nonintellectual. Grandfather and Uncle Joseph and Agnes are nonintellectuals. I don't mean they aren't just as intelligent as we are. Alice is, I think, one of them also. Father and you, as I always thought, and I are intellectuals. Father had an equal chance with Uncle Joseph to go into grandfather's business, but instead he went to college and that got him started on the other path. Uncle Joseph thinks Father is a failure and Father thinks that Uncle Joseph has turned from the best things of life, but also envies him. . . We all want you to be a success in business, but I have often wondered how you liked it; and when you say the work is too mental—well, I think you still are one of us, John!"

"I don't know which I am," I said, "if I am one or the other. The work requires all the intelligence I have."

"It isn't a question of intelligence but of what you are interested in most, intellectual things, thoughts, ideas, knowledge, or in non-intellectual things, material things."

"I don't know, Philip."

The conversation continued, and it sometimes seemed that Philip wanted me to differentiate between identities.

The day was hot, the journey long, and it was a great relief to leave the train. Twilight had begun, and by contrast to the close air of the car that of the station platform was fresh and invigorating. The departure of the noisy engine and long row of boxes on wheels brought a sudden deep quiet.

Mary came running up with Philip Junior and Faith. She was dressed in a plain cotton dress and her face and hands were brown. She was Philip's age, spare like him, young in all her movements, not exactly faded but a little dried, with eyes that had come to resemble his.

She was very glad to see me, she said—it was perfectly fine! She kissed me, but before I returned it, she was reprimanding Faith for tugging at her arm. She beamed in Philip's eyes, said that "Father and Mother"—meaning ours not hers—were coming over after supper, that she had two chickens to get for Sunday dinner in the village and must not forget they were coming over to dinner, it being John's first day—she was so glad to see me!—and hoped I would not mind simplicity after New York, that I looked so nice, that we ought to be starting, that I looked well, that she hoped Philip had not forgotten to go to Pierce's, and that she wanted so much to hear all about Islandia!

It was her energy that arranged us in a hired automobile and moved us away into the country quiet of a long sandy road among the pines with a moist evening smell of resin and of the sea.

The cottage was new, standing on a bluff above a sheltered bay, with pines behind it. To the north and to the south upon the scalloped shore were other bluffs and other cottages. Philip had bought ten acres. Beside the house itself was a stable for a driving horse and a wire-wheeled buggy, and bathhouses on the beach of fine yellow sand below the bluffs.

The cottage was unplastered, with a large room just inside the door, living room, playroom, library, music room all in one, everything except kitchen and dining room. Upstairs were bedrooms and a bathroom with modern plumbing. The bedrooms were large and therefore few.

"You can have the spare room till Alice comes," said Mary, "and then we will put you in with little Phil. You see it is very simple. We try to be simple in summer. We both felt that plaster spoiled the simplicity."

"It is no simpler than I was used to in Islandia."

"You must tell me about it. Don't bother to change. Come right down."

I heard her talking to Philip in the next room, her children walking downstairs, a rattle of plates from the kitchen. An electric light burned above the bureau. The arrangements for cleanliness were complete. But I wanted privacy, not to have to hear, not to be heard. The house was like a cage. Islandian houses had thick walls. Except at times of communal enterprise, as at the Upper Farm, one roomed alone. The simplicity of furnishings was here as great and more convenient if no more comfortable, but the simplicity thus achieved was thrown away by the lack of privacy. Too many sounds of other lives came to one's ears. . . .

That evening Father and Mother came in a carriage from their hotel. They and their two sons, Philip and I, and the wife of one of them, sat on the porch. Upstairs their grandchildren were asleep. We had met without many words but with a warm deep affection that was tangible and real like a thing in the air. Islandia had not altered so strong a thing. What was new to this gathering and therefore the subject of our talk at first was the experience of one of us, myself, in New York. It was incumbent upon me to make a report, and I was anxious that it should satisfy them. An important part was Uncle Joseph's attitude, including his promises for the future. These matters were, of course, confidential but those present were entitled to know them.

I knew as a son that the two questions which Father and Mother would most wish answered were these: was my future secure financially? was I contented with what I was doing? As to the first it was easy to reassure them; as to the second the best I could do was to describe the work I did and to say that it was absorbing. Whether or not I was contented now and would be in future was not a question that I yet asked myself. In order to complete the report which I had begun I described various incidents of my work and it took on color to me as I spoke. They listened so quietly that I stopped.

"It is odd to think of you as a businessman," Mother said.

"I would like to stay and hear more," said Mary, "but you won't have any breakfast tomorrow if I do."

Father asked Philip about a book, and went indoors to look at it.

"John," said my brother, "you are going to be able to answer questions I have wondered about. You are the first New York businessman I have had at my mercy. I want your candid opinion as to whether or not you think that a great deal of the abuse of big business nowadays isn't wholly unwarranted."

I answered him as best I could, knowing so little.

After Mother and Father had gone, Mary came out on the porch again and sat down.

"Now," she said with "at last!" in the tone of her voice, "now I can talk to you."

"Isn't it rather late?" Philip suggested.

"I am not sleepy and I don't think John is," she said almost as though pleading.

"I want to talk with you, Mary. I am wide awake."

"Tomorrow," she said, "will be hectic. The cook is in a terrible mood complaining of the extra work though she knew before she came.—Forgive me, John, but you are family and it doesn't make any difference so far as you are concerned.—I have got to help her and go for the ice cream. And Father and Mother are coming to dinner, and in the afternoon I have got to drive over to the club about the entertainment next week. And we are all going to the Bedloes' to supper, and I have the laundry to make out and deliver."

"All the more reason—" he began.

"My dear," she said, "this has been a hectic day, too, and the most restful thing possible is talking about something entirely different."

"You are hopeless," he answered.

"I don't want to be, Philip!—and I will be if I don't get outside myself sometime."

"I think you ought to go to bed, and have a good sleep."

"Damn bed! Tell me about Islandia, John! Is it any easier for women?"

I told her that the problem of the cook would not exist nor would there be any club to drive to, nor food to be fetched from a distance. She listened and brought each thing I said within the scope of her own experiences. It made the conversation more real but also prolonged it.

Philip was restive.

"You can't talk so many details tonight!" he said.

"I can't see it unless I know the details," she answered.

"You won't see it as a whole, Mary."

"If John stays long enough I will," she said, and asked how they handled the laundry. I replied that they all wore fewer and less fussy clothes and did not iron. That washing was otherwise much as here. . . .

"Mary," said Philip, "it is after twelve!"

"Well," she remarked, "my lord and master calls me and I must go. It seems to me that in Islandia the women probably work just as hard but that there is less wear and tear."

"Philip," I said, "Mary does see it as a whole."

As she rose he put his arm around her.

"Tell me more differences tomorrow," she said, and she went away with him, putting out the lights on the way.

There were other differences that struck me with a twist in my heart. There a father and mother, the sons and the wife of one, would have a common enterprise and the same *alia*. My own father would not be irked by and hostile to what I was doing, my own mother would understand it, and we would all talk happily together, interested in the same way in the same thing, and our differences would not create gulfs between us. There my wife's work would not be so sharply divided from mine. Nattana drove a wagon to the quarry as naturally as a man would have done. Her brothers helped Ettera in the kitchen.

Philip and Mary had worked out their own division of labor. She administered Sunday which was an all-day task, while he took charge of the children whom she had had with her all the week. But

817

Sunday was an exceptional day. During most of the week his work was at one place and hers at another.

For five minutes during swimming before dinner we discussed this problem. She had joined us on the run, as it were. He had said he wanted her to come. One of her tasks which she did not slight was being his wife.

She said that she thought it would be awfully nice if a husband and a wife could do more things together, but her ideas were indefinite. She was making such an arrangement real in her mind and until it was real she would not generalize.

"On the whole," said Philip, "I think the present arrangement is best. I am an expert at one thing, making money, and Mary at another."

"I have so many things to do that I am not an expert at any one of them," she said.

"You are an expert in doing the many things, Mary. Life is so complicated that one has to be an expert. If Mary and I each spent half our time at the other's job, neither job would be done anywhere near so well as it now is."

"I am not an expert at anything!" she cried. "I wish I were. I've got a mind."

"You are an expert, Mary—an expert wife."

"I can only make a halfway job of that, my dear."

"If life were simpler," I suggested, but Philip interrupted.

"That is a fallacy," he said. "Man's greatest happiness lies in being an expert, a specialist, and in doing one thing supremely well. The simple life gives him no chance to develop himself fully. He is too busy with diverse things."

"We try hard to be simple but it doesn't seem possible," said Mary. "Do you really like being nothing but a lawyer, Philip? There are lots of other things you want to be and do."

The cook appeared on the bank and called:

"Mrs. Lang!"

"I've got to go," said Mary. "So long as you are happy I'm satisfied."

She left us and climbed the slope in her bathing suit, moving swiftly.

"She really is an expert," he said, looking after her. "It takes an expert to keep so many different things in order. Her trouble is just what she said: she has a mind. Running the house and bringing up the children does not contain her or satisfy her. She is constantly trying to find some outside occupation which will, and she does not have the time. You have got her interested in Islandia, but it seems to me the last place for Mary. What possible outside occupation would she find there to take her mind off the household and the children?"

I told him about Ettera working shoulder to shoulder with her brothers, in all their councils, as much concerned and as significant a factor as they in the single enterprise of the Upper Farm.

"To those three it is your law work and her household work all one thing."

"We have outgrown anything so primitive," he said.

"Is that growth intentional?" I asked.

"It is evolution."

"Not in Islandia."

He laughed.

"Don't get too much attracted by theories as to the simple life, John. It is a frequent vice among intellectual men. You probably had a very good time there just as anyone does on a farm when it is a change and he does not have to be the farmer."

"You call it a vice," I said. "Maybe it is his natural reaction against something that his instinct tells him is excessive and abnormal."

"Try farming for a while. You will soon find out that it is not the highest life."

"Is business? Is law?"

"Whatever gives man the fullest scope to use his powers is the highest life. Of course, I can imagine a man contented with a farm conducted in a modern way on scientific principles."

"The Islandians don't call their principles scientific, but that is only a word. They have carried the art of farming and of living on a farm very far."

"Didn't you find them narrow, limited, lacking in interests?"

"I didn't."

"You may not be intellectual after all."

"I hope I don't fall into either one or the other of your two classes, Philip."

"You can't help yourself."

"Why can't you be both and not too much either one?"

"Life isn't made that way. There is a need for lawyers, scientists, thinkers, and a need for workers, businessmen. Our civilization is a result of just that differentiation among men."

"How do you know that a haphazard growth hasn't forced the differentiation upon us?"

"Because I believe in progress, John."

His eyes shone with a bright clear fire almost angry. There was no more to be said. My own head felt brittle; such a path of thought as we had been following filled me with a confused sense of unreality.

But such wrangles could not be avoided with Philip. The evening at the Bedloes' was all one long wrangle. Besides our host and his wife and Dr. Howard and his, there was a Miss Hyde to even the numbers of men and women. Conversation at first was slow, and then Philip with a light in his eyes stated again the division of men into two classes. For a few moments those present amused themselves by wondering to which group they belonged. Philip frankly announced that he was of the intellectual type.

"I know I am," said Miss Hyde.

"I'm not but I want to be," said Mary.

"I suppose I am," said Bedloe.

"Of course you are," said his wife, "very much one."

"What are you?" he asked her.

"I am too!" she replied as though resenting it. "We all are." She looked at me with a question.

Philip spoke for me.

"John is, but thinks he isn't. He is a businessman. What are you, Doctor Howard?"

"I am a scientist compelled to work for his living."

"Scientists are the highest type of intellectuals," said Philip.

"Where do artists come in?" asked Mrs. Howard.

"They are the lowest type," answered Bedloe, and everyone laughed.

Having thus started a topic of conversation Philip posed the question whether civilization was the result of the differentiation or *vice versa*. Everyone talked. After a while he brought in Islandia and called upon me to say what I thought. Instead I began to describe what I had seen. There were questions, frequent interruptions. Clever things were said. . . Adroitly in the end Philip, a lawyer, summarized it all with broad generalizations: man of course was progressing, going somewhere; everyone contributed his little push to the movement; men in the more highly civilized centers were developing many new skills, techniques, and ways of thought, each of which contributed some special direction to the direction of this great progress; a test for distinguishing between the civilized and the noncivilized was to be found in the variety or lack of variety in the lives of men. It was wonderful to be alive today!

Mary, Philip, and I walked home upon a path that rose and fell along the edges of the bluffs and through the sand of short beaches. A quarter moon danced among the pines and bushes inland.

In answer to her question I said that I had enjoyed myself, without waiting to consider whether this was true or not.

"Well, I did!" cried Philip, "even though I did most of the talking."

"You kept things going nicely," she said in her pleasant, comfortable, young voice. "But I don't know that we got anywhere exactly."

"I think we did. I have tested out my idea. Of course, it is a generalization and there are exceptions, but on the whole, broadly speaking, it is true. And it gives a reason for the way civilization is going—opportunities greater and greater for different kinds of men. What do you think, John?"

"I have been where the classification does not hold good and where civilization doesn't force differentiation and specialization."

"But as to a developed civilization, not one still primitive?"

"John hates to be too much one thing or the other," said Mary. "I'll speak for him because poor John doesn't think the way you do."

"How does he think, Mary?"

"He likes facts and I think he is interested in feelings."

"John," said Philip with a laugh, "Mary is as much as saying you are a nonintellectual."

"Are you, Mary?" I asked.

"Me? What?" Her mind had wandered and her head was turned toward the pale slaty blue of the bay. "I'm not classifying anybody. It is too lovely a night. I had an awfully good time, and it was a change, but now I'm tired. Why are you always classifying and theorizing, Philip?"

He was silent for some moments. Her words had a sharp edge that hurt him, I knew.

"Did I go too far, Mary?" he asked.

"Oh, no, Philip dear!"

"It is only an attempt to find order in things," he said gently. "I can't help it. I think and think all the time—"

"We all do, Philip," she interrupted. "I understand. We are all puzzled, and you don't lie down under it like most people and just accept and complain. . . I'm sorry I seemed to criticize."

"You didn't, Mary! But I do have to work things out. Life forces it on me. What do you think, John?"

"Your developed civilization has many unexplained and conflicting forces and rules," I said. "Anyone who really looks at it as you do, and is intelligent as you are, naturally wonders, and wondering thinks; and tries to arrange things in a pattern."

"That is just it!" said Philip. "And having found the pattern you have found the truth."

"Yes, if you *find* a pattern! But tonight you did not find one—you made one yourself. You fitted together generalizations not necessarily true."

"Perhaps," said Mary quickly, "you find out about your generalizations by seeing how well they fit. Philip said he was only testing his idea."

"I wish," I continued, a heating excitement in my brain, "that one did not always have this impulse to arrange things in patterns. I wish we were free of the wondering and could—oh, feel more!"

"You are Epicurean," said Philip, "and you are headed right straight for hedonism! Why do you want to feel more, and go backward?"

"Because we have had to think so much to get along—and it gets worse as civilization develops—that our knowledge of our feelings and our feelings themselves have had no chance to keep pace with our brains and to develop as our brains have. We are all so uneven!"

"No!" cried Philip. "What seems to you—because you are (excuse me, John) a materialist, a hedonist—to be an unevenness in man is only a higher evenness, a development, a change for the better."

"Philip!" I began, but he interrupted.

"I am not interested in having feelings. I want to think clearly above all things."

"Well," said Mary, whom we had forgotten, her voice coming cool and sweet in the moonlight, "I am terribly interested in Philip's feeling for me and in mine for him,—and at this moment also in the feelings you two have for each other."

It was an interruption that we both resented, a distraction.

"I am interested in what I feel about you, of course," said Philip, "but the point I was trying to make was this—"

"That John feels too strongly, and I think you do too," she said, "and all about nothing at all but mere ideas. Don't spoil an awfully happy evening."

We let her silence us, but I am sure that he as well as I continued his side of the argument in his brain, for, I thought, not only did one's capacity to feel not keep pace with one's head but the over-development of head falsified feelings or thwarted and atrophied them. . . My own feelings tonight were an example—and feelings thus falsified made my head ache. And Mary, whose head remained cool because she did not let argument heat her, felt truly and made peace. I wanted to tell her so, to tell her that she was Islandian, but it would only inflame Philip.

A week went by. There were many books in their house and much talk of them. Philip and Mary were readers, though how she became so familiar with what was within the covers I do not know, for much of her time was spent in putting away and arranging books like blocks. Philip was constantly handing me this or that work saying that I ought to read it, but the texts went arid as I read them. There were too many ideas half followed, too much dealing with inferences and generalizations. He told me that Islandia and going into business had spoiled my literary digestion. What did I want— fiction? I answered that Islandia had made me want things at first hand.

We sailed, we swam, talked, and wrangled. He made me contentious with a susceptibility to bad temper over what Mary called "mere ideas"; but as a result I thought deeply and often of the significance of Islandia, and what I had experienced there became more real than it had been since coming home.

But vacation was an irksome thing. I wanted something stronger than pleasant physical exercise and talk that was in the end confusing and unsettling. The solid things were the affections that he, Mary, the children, and Mother and Father and Alice roused, but they could have no adequate expression. The beauty of pine woods and water had its place and was good, but with Philip near it was too much analyzed. When a reason and excuse for going appeared unexpectedly I seized it.

34

Nantucket

THERE CAME a letter from Gladys hastily written but rather long, as though she had suddenly had a wish for the relief of talking to someone and had thought of me.

Her cousins, she said, had begun to keep at her and it had got on her nerves. For a while one could stand one's painting being regarded as a mild but foolish self-indulgence, and one was not much affected; but after a time and when one was always being asked seriously where it led to and seriously what one was going to do, one simply could not stand it! One couldn't paint, couldn't do anything. But, she wrote, her cousins were awfully nice to her and had invited her to live with them. They even took the trouble to find out if there wasn't a place for her in a local bank! But she simply had to get away whatever the cost. She was going to Nantucket for two weeks. She had friends there. She named the hotel where she was to stay and gave the dates of her arrival and of her leaving. She acknowledged my last letter and commented on the fact that I would have my vacation at the same time. She would look north over Nantucket Sound and she would think: there is John not so very far away. Maybe if he sails over to Nantucket he will come and see me.

The letter, however, had been addressed to the boardinghouse, and thence forwarded to Uncle Joseph's country place, and from there to Philip's. Only a few days more of Gladys's vacation remained. In five minutes a decision was made; she had given me invitation enough. I wrote at once to her hotel, telling her that I wanted to see her and would arrive one day and leave the day after the next, but that sailing to Nantucket was impossible for the waters on which I now was did not open on the Sound. For reply she sent a telegram stating what trains and boat I could catch, all worked out.

From the deck of the steamer bound to Nantucket the waves below seemed to crawl in irregular lines hastening onward together, with racing whitecaps on their lifted crests. The wrinkled water was a smoky blue under a fresh southwest wind.

As we drew near the dock I searched for her among the groups waiting to meet those arriving, and she was there, standing quietly, tall and young. I waved my hat. She saw me, nodded and lifted her hand, and remained where she was, not calling greetings and running along as others were doing.

Ashore at last I came up the gangway and found her, a little behind the rest. She seemed taller, dressed in a long white linen suit and a light-tan straw hat, with a white ribbon and a soft brim turned up at one edge and framing her face. Beneath the hat her hair was a dark wing. She looked fresh and well, not pale, tired, and harassed as she had been in New York. She was like a flower, last seen and known as a bud, and now startling and lovely in the fullness of its bloom; and I could think of nothing to say except to thank her for her telegram.

"With that large bag of yours," she said practically, "we had better take a hack."

The vehicle was old with rusty seats and she in her spotless freshness was out of place in it.

I asked her where I could lodge. She had arranged for a room for me in the "annex." It was the last one, for the hotel was crowded.

She was a little constrained and shy, not yet having really smiled, but it did not matter. Ahead of us was one whole day with a night before and a night afterwards and no worry over departures to lessen its hours. But I remembered her friends and asked about them, fearing they would rob the day of completeness. She answered that they had already gone.

"Then you are here alone, Gladys?"

"Yes," she said, "but it is all right. I look older than I am. People think I am twenty-five."

The drive was not long. We reached the hotel, a large, plain, white, wooden box pierced with windows and surrounded by a wide veranda.

While I was paying the hackman she slipped away saying that she would wait for me. Then, having registered and having been led across the street to the annex—a cottage usually tenanted by hotel employees

—and shown my room, a small one under the roof, I returned to the hotel to find her. Upon the veranda were many people sitting and rocking in the green porch chairs, and looking at the street. Their eyes followed me as I hunted for Gladys. Around the corner was a glimpse of the blue waters of the harbor and of a sandy shore beyond, pale as though seen through thin smoke. Fewer guests were here. I saw her suddenly, without her hat, her face bent a little forward and in profile. Her browned nape and her slender shoulders were almost childish, but her fine forehead and poised round head were dignified and noble. She was seated talking with a sunburned man of about twenty-three, who rose as I approached and soon left us.

Past the straight gray shingled wall of an old wharf on one side, a sailboat, minute in the distance, reefed, leaning to the wind, had come in sight. All that I saw was suddenly so brightly beautiful that it hurt.

Time lay before us, long full hours. I was happy and at peace. . . But she had moved restively. I turned to her and saw her face, puzzled, with her eyes upon me and wide open. "I wondered if you were ever going to say anything," she said. "You were silent so long."

"Ought I to have spoken?"

"Well! People usually do, don't they? I wasn't going to say anything until you did."

"You are right, Gladys," I answered, "but there was nothing in my mind that should be said. I was thinking how good this was. . . You wrote me that your cousins had been on your nerves. My brother has been on mine more and more these last ten days. It was a relief to get away from him, though I like him very much. We wrangled all the time."

She leaned towards me, her long hands clasped on the flat green arm of the porch chair. They were browned by the sun but her skin was fine in texture, and her tapering fingers were interwoven.

For a moment I forgot what I had been saying.

"You will tell me all about your cousins, won't you?" I said. "We will talk about many things."

"All right!"

She smiled her complete abandoned smile that lighted and covered her whole face and put long dimples in her cheeks.

"My brother Philip and I disagreed about the simple life," I began. "Philip thinks I idealize the simple life because I have been in Islandia, but it is only the social structure that is simple there. He is so inconsistent! As soon as I reached his house he and Mary his wife began telling me how simply they lived in summer—whereas she at any rate has a most complicated time. His idea of simplicity means chopping wood now and then, wearing different clothes, having no plaster on the walls, and things like that, all as a change from the way that he ordinarily lives."

"Is there any such thing as a simple life?" she asked.

"No; but there are different ways of living in each of which different things are complicated. There is no simple life unless you are a lizard—"

" 'The Perfect Life,' " she said with a smile.

"Have you read Stanning's *Fables?*—Can you read Islandian, Gladys?"

"A little. I have puzzled out some of Bodwin. He refers to Stanning's 'The Perfect Life.' "

"What do you think of Bodwin?" I asked her in Islandian. She looked at me with a thoughtful light in her eyes, and understood. It was like finding an unexpected and beautiful room in a house all of which I thought I knew.

"I read at first merely for the stories he told, not knowing anything else was there, but something else lay underneath. I wondered what it was and wished I were not so badly educated. I know nothing about philosophy, but there is a philosophy there, I am sure."

"I have never worked it out either. When I try to tell Philip what Islandians think, he says they are hedonists, and I answer that, if so, they are kind-hearted ones. He says that is absurd. So it goes, between him and me."

"What is a hedonist?" she asked. "I have never been to college."

"I looked the word up in the dictionary. Philip always has one near him. It comes from a Greek word ἡδονή meaning pleasure. The idea seems to be that happiness or pleasure is the greatest good, and that a hedonist arranges his life accordingly. But I never could get anything out of philosophical definitions. They are like bags open at both ends. So long as you don't touch them their contents remain inside, but when you lift the bags the contents run out."

"I wish I had been to college."

"You will get in time all you would have got there."

"Why do you say that?"

"You are quick to understand and you want to learn. You aren't prejudiced."

"I am full of prejudices."

"Would you die for any of them?"

"No—not for a prejudice."

"Then they won't stand in your way."

"I always feel at a loss with a person who has been to college."

"There is the fable about the two horses, Gladys. One started first and the other thought himself hopelessly outreached. The first waited a little, and when they were together they were perfect play-fellows, one no faster nor quicker than the other."

There was a look in her eyes that contradicted her humbleness.

"What else have you read in Islandian?" I asked.

"Oh, your *History of the United States*."

"You did read it! You wrote that you couldn't."

"When Mother was so ill, I took up Islandian. I needed some-thing utterly different from nursing."

So we talked until suppertime, when a great bell jangled.

She was in haste to enter the dining room, long and low with long tables. The china, the napery, the walls, the ceiling, and the uniforms of the waitresses were each a tone of white. Every place at every table was set exactly like every other one, and one felt like a trespasser in breaking such monotonous and perfect symmetry.

We were at a table holding ten persons. I was given a seat at the end as though for some reason I ought not to sit next to Gladys. We were the first to come.

"I am glad to be here ahead of the others. People stare so," she said.

"You are tall and lovely and fine-looking," I answered.

She looked at me in surprise.

"You must not flatter me," she said, and her voice was a little regretful but with sharpness, as though I had said something im-proper and wrong.

Others came to the table and she named me to the nearer ones in a shy hasty way.

The food was served in heavy white plates with many little dishes clustered around them like bumboats about a vessel in port. There was clatter and chatter. Looking for some vivid thing in the blank uniformity of tables and diners and other faces I found it in Gladys who was warmly colorful to my eyes.

She was right. Many persons stared, not so much at her, as at us, in a way neither hostile nor friendly but curiously, acquisitively, with eyes that would cling for a few moments like a fly with sticky feet. A woman of perhaps fifty, who seemed friendly and who called Gladys by her first name, and flattered her in subtle ways, began asking me questions about myself. It occurred to me suddenly that all these people were wondering what I was to Gladys, and it was as though unwelcome alien fingers were feeling us.

When supper was over I suggested a walk, and after a moment of hesitation she ran off to fetch a wrap, for the air was cool and damp and the wind still blowing. We walked through quiet streets of old houses—she, in a dark long cape, was the guide.

"Gladys, what shall we do tomorrow?"

"What would you like?"

"Let's go to a beach for the day."

She was silent.

"I am sorry," she said. "I am going sailing in the morning."

It was my turn to say nothing.

"I am sorry," she repeated.

"It is quite all right, but I did want the whole day."

"Do I know you well enough?"

"Isn't it rather a question of wanting to be with me or not?"

"I would have liked it," she said.

"What do you fear?—Me?"

"Not you."

"Other people, Gladys? Have they troubled you and talked about you?"

"I am alone here and have to be more careful."

"Do you care what any of these people think or say?"

"It is not that exactly . . . Of course I don't care! I shall probably never see any of them again, anyway. But Mother used to say that people expected the worst of you when you were alone, particularly if you were a lady. She said it was envy. She told me that the world was always on the watch, and that one could not be too careful."

"Have I exposed you to the eyes of this world by coming to see you here?"

"Haven't you?" she asked.

"Only to the eyes of persons whose opinion you don't care about. Their eyes are the only ones."

"It doesn't seem quite that," she said. "In New York one is lost in the crowd, but here . . . Isn't it rather doing as the Romans do?"

"That is safer," I answered, "and the Romans sometimes have ways of making you uncomfortable, but aren't you letting an unreal thing influence you?"

"I don't want to do anything outré," she said. "It is bad for a person. That is another thing Mother said."

"Would it be outré to spend a day with me? How would it be bad for you if you wanted it and had no fear of me, the only danger being that some persons whose opinion meant nothing would talk about you?"

"Perhaps I am foolish, but it seemed that if I were seen with someone else part of the day people would not think—"

"You said you did not care what they thought."

She pondered.

"Anyway," she continued, "I have promised to go sailing."

"Keep your promise, but give me the afternoon."

"Of course."

"And evening, too."

"I will."

We walked along together without speaking, and I fretted, for this conversation was like a fog sprung up between us.

"Gladys," I said, "why would it have made a difference if you had known me better?"

"Then I could have said you were an old friend of the family's, that I had known you from childhood—things like that."

"Why not say so anyway?"

"I have to tell the truth," she answered in a voice a little high.

"Do you have to tell the truth to people whose opinion means nothing and who have no right to any opinion, even when it loses you something you wished?"

"I really am sorry."

"Are you sure you have no fear of me?"

"None whatsoever," she said instantly.

"You have faith in me, a man you know, and you fear an abstraction, the eyes of the world!"

"You think I have been foolish?"

"It is worse than that. No, you are wise! But it is cruel that you have to have such a wisdom."

"We are taking it very seriously," she said.

"Yes, we are. Not the fact that we lose a whole day in exchange for the better part of one, but the reasons why we lose it."

"Do they seem to you all wrong?"

"Yes, they do . . . I had a day with Dorna of whom I told you. In fact it was two days. We set out in a boat and slept aboard, because of lack of wind. I knew her then less well than I know you. There was no world with watching eyes to be considered. There was no fixed idea as to the propriety or impropriety of what we did. They have a belief, however, that a young man and woman who do not plan to go on together should not be alone too long, because they know that sooner or later the horse of friendship ceases to carry them and they become attracted in a normal animal way."

"How long is too long?" she asked.

"It depends on the persons. A single day is not too long."

"I have never spent a whole day alone with any man. I've wanted to before. Mother did not approve."

"Did you—in yourself?"

"Of course I did. I thought her foolish and too little trusting in me. She said I did not know enough. Nevertheless," she continued, "the world is very real to me. Perhaps I'm not innocent enough."

"If you aren't, it is because the world has made you so. I can understand how it comes about. Suppose you and I had been away for two days as Dorna and I were—"

"Was that the sail from Doring Town to Dorn Island not long after you had been in Islandia?"

"Yes, it was."

"You wrote me about it, but did not say whom you were with."

"You were American. I was afraid of a wrong opinion."

"Of yourself?" she asked.

"Of Dorna."

"I would have been surprised, I suppose."

"Are you surprised now? Have you a lower opinion of Dorna and me?"

"Not of you, of course. I know nothing about her except from you. She seems to have been very lovely."

"She is, Gladys."

"You told me about her," she said gently, "and it was awfully kind of you . . . How I did misunderstand you!"

"The world standardized your ideas."

"Perhaps Islandia made yours a little impractical . . . But why are you willing to tell me you were with Dorna now, when you were not willing then?"

I had to think for a moment.

"Because it never occurred to me now that you really would have a wrong opinion."

"Well, I haven't!" she said firmly.

"Suppose you and I were away for two days in a boat, these people at the hotel would probably have a wrong opinion. And I will tell you why. They would not be thinking what sort of man and woman you and I are in ourselves. They would see that something has happened that 'isn't done.' They would be shocked because a conventional rule had been broken. If asked to justify the rule they would generalize about temptations, still not taking into account the personal you and me. Working backwards they would assume an evil because a rule had been broken. How would they know that we had temptations? How would they know that what we felt weren't the normal emotions of a good love? And what concern is it of theirs anyway? Yet they make it their concern because a rule was broken, not because of what we had done or not done—whether that was good or not in itself . . . It is the rigidity of the rule that makes trouble. Without it, men are at once free to think of the effect on others of what they do or don't do!"

"I don't know how I would get along without conventions," she said lightly. "I wouldn't know what to do."

"They are all right as suggestions for conduct," I answered, "but not as rules."

"I don't believe in them just because they exist. Mother used to say she despised them."

"Did she observe them?"

"Oh, yes. She said one had to."

Her mother was dead. Gladys loved her, but I thought of Mrs. Hunter and her teachings with distaste.

"She was not always consistent," Gladys continued, "and sometimes she told fibs."

"Yet you wouldn't say I was an old friend of your family's."

"She taught me not to lie, and I have never learned how to do it—I mean, to lie easily."

"What did you think of her fibs?"

"That she was wiser than I—and that I wasn't wise enough to know when to lie."

"Oh, the faith of a child!"

"I wasn't perfect," said Gladys. "You have been objecting to rules. Don't you think there ought to be a rule against lying?"

"No," I said. "You should tell the truth to those who have a right to know it, that is if it affects what they will do. But you have no duty to tell the truth to those who intermeddle."

"I don't agree to that at all!"

"And you must not condemn a person for lying unless you know they are lying."

"I don't. Weren't you taught not to lie?"

"Yes. To my father and mother a lie was so terrible a thing that though they were very gentle in other ways, if I lied I was whipped. The result was that for a long time I always associated lying with a stinging sensation on a certain part of me. That is all wrong!" Then I told about the occasion when Alice took upon herself the blame of something I had done to save me the loss of an excursion. "We both told untruths," I said, "but the feeling strongest in us was of union, of gratitude, of kindness, which wholly obscured any consciousness of guilt. That was childish reasoning, of course."

"What should your parents have done?" she asked.

"They should have found out our feelings and pointed out the consequences of carrying them too far and of reasoning as we did. Punishment was futile."

"How about Islandia?"

"There is very little occasion for it," I said. "Rules breed punishment." Then I told the story of Nattana's home-coming to the Lower Farm as described in her letter, but impersonally, adding, "All that the rule and the punishment it called for accomplished was to handicap this Islandian girl in doing a good work."

"She is not like everyone," said Gladys.

"Then she should not have been treated like an ordinary person. The rule should be fitted to her, not she to it."

"How can one tell if a person is ordinary or not? Rules must be made for the ordinary ones. There are more of them."

"In Islandia the social system is so much simpler that there is less need of rules for ordinary people. Judgments can be made to fit the individual. All is more flexible."

"I think, all the same," said Gladys, "that that Islandian girl was rather horrid to her father. She should have tried harder to think as he thought."

"But each understood the other's point of view."

"That is not enough. Why wouldn't she sacrifice her own opinion?"

"Isn't it better to be honest?"

"Not always—not in that way, I mean. I know that Mother was often unreasonable and inconsistent and unjust, but what did it matter if I could make her happy? Even if she did punish me, what difference did that make? I tried to be what she wanted me to be."

"You loved her," I said. "Did it make you happy to be what she wished?"

"It certainly did."

"You are quite Islandian, Gladys. I have been generalizing about rules and you have been thinking of the feelings of an actual person."

But I did not add that Gladys was inconsistent. For if she had really thought as her mother did, she would not have called her unreasonable and unjust.

We had come to an old windmill standing darkly upon a knoll. The moon, red, large, and round, was just rising. We turned and faced it. The wind, still blowing, tossed the folds of the cape she wore against my arm.

We went on along a dirt road. There were few houses and the land was flat and low, and as the moon rose the light became more white and the shadows sharper.

She walked well in spite of her long dress and I pictured her in the freedom of Islandian clothes. How lovely she would be, supple, unhampered!

The country I had left lay under everything else, like the mood left by a dream. She was not alien to it in any way. . . .

Sometimes she moved with her head bent and shadowed, then lifted it, and the moonlight touched her features. The sweet, strong reality of her being lay within the enclosure of all my perceptions, held there in suspense.

"You must not misunderstand about Mother," she said suddenly, and the current of her thoughts was clear: she feared that I would think unjustly of one she loved.

"I don't misunderstand," I answered.

"Mother had a hard time," Gladys continued. "She had been spoiled as a girl, and our money was going, going, all the time, and she did not know what would become of us."

"Had she no work she could do?"

"She told me once that there was nothing she was suited for . . . Whenever I find myself wishing that things had been different I remember how hard her life was. She was not brought up with the idea that she would ever have to work. My grandfather was quite well off for a while. She traveled and had luxuries . . . After she married Father she found life in Syracuse very narrow. Mother was cosmopolitan. Then Father did not succeed in New York . . . I don't remember him well. Mother used to say that he was a successful small-town man, and that he ought never to have left Syracuse . . . Of course, all the time Mother and I were together I didn't know that the money was going. She seemed to have enough for us both, and I thought that if she ever died I would—oh, be secure. She brought me up with the expectation of marriage as my fate. I never worried about anything but how to be a daughter that she would like . . . She did love me, John, I know she did. I was all she had."

"You loved her," I said.

"Of course." She walked with bent head, seeming to flow along the road. "You do understand her, don't you?"

"Yes," I said.

"Life was so hard for her."

"She had no *alia* to cling to," I said.

"What do you mean?"

"Aren't you tired with Islandia?"

"No, I'm not. Tell me."

"There, in Islandia, no girl as a child is given a taste of a more glamorous and exciting life than the one she may be called upon to lead. She knows that if she marries, what she will have will be similar to what she had. She will choose a man for himself, not for what he can give her. Nor after their marriage will she feel any inducement to change his life to another one. She will have a life that is permanent and secure, with great possibilities within itself to make it rich and good. *Alia* means one's love for one's home place and family as a going thing . . . Love of parents for children, of children for parents, and of relatives for each other, is not all of it but is the greater part. It makes the family tie strong and natural. All have a common object. Take my own case." And I told of meditations upon my own parents' love for me and of mine for them, and of Mother's and Philip's interest in relatives, saying: "These are all examples of a love that is partly thwarted, Gladys, and that would have a finer opportunity to bear fruit if there were true *alia* possible."

"Poor Mother," she said gently. "I wonder if she would have liked it there."

"Would you?"

"I?" She pondered . . . "I don't think I would be suited to Islandia."

"Why not?"

"I am too much puzzled about things. That Islandian girl you told about knew her own mind. I never would, in the same way."

"Do they seem so definite-minded?"

"Aren't they?"

"They are very ready with ideas about human relations. Their education is different, with less emphasis on facts and more as to the realities of human emotions and behaviors. Their education gives them great understanding."

Gladys was thoughtful.

"It is hard to know what to do," she said, and her words, suggesting an actual experience, roused curiosity. "Do they understand very well?" she asked.

"When a man has loved one of them and cannot have her," I said, "they believe in telling him all the reasons and in being perfectly clear to him."

"Did Dorna do that?" she asked shyly.

"Yes," I answered, "and knowing how dearly women guard the secrecy of their insecure decisions, I think she did a wonderful, kind thing."

"Isn't it kinder not to tell a man too directly? Won't it hurt him less if he learns gradually?"

"No, it won't!"

"Sometimes the girl isn't any too sure herself and can't be clear."

"She can tell him so."

"She may not want to—she may be afraid."

"An Islandian education would make it easier for her . . . Are you thinking of something definite, Gladys?"

"Yes, I am," she answered. "A man wanted to marry me. I was eighteen, but Mother approved. I didn't know what I felt. It seemed that I ought to marry. It would have settled certain problems . . . Then I found I couldn't! But I didn't tell him the reasons. It would have been impossible!"

"If you knew the reasons why couldn't you tell them?"

"Oh!" she cried, "how can a woman tell a man that she can't bear him except as a friend?"

"Why is it so hard? It is true, and there is nothing so final."

"Mother kept saying that I would get over what I felt. And she had left me so in the dark . . . How could I sit down with him and explain it all?"

"Yes," I said, "how could you, with no clear knowledge of the forces working in you? You should have been taught about them so that you knew them well and could speak of them. It would have saved you both much unhappiness, I am sure."

"One learns—"

"In such a long, painful way."

"I don't believe I know yet . . . Is one ever sure?"

"Those who are free of pressure can be sure."

We were coming to the hotel through a narrow street of old trees and of ancient handsome houses standing with quiet solid dignity in the moonlight and suggesting a gracious life as a rest from the hard life upon the sea, the salt of which was in the air.

She was thoughtful . . . and I wanted her to know certain things.

"I loved Dorna," I said, "and I was sure, very sure. Then I lost her . . . That was hard. But there is something in Islandia that gives you strength. And then she granted me this Reckoning in which we each became perfectly clear to the other. And now she is a memory of beauty, and I am quite free."

"And knowing her hasn't spoiled you for—Americans?"

"Oh, no, indeed!"

At my side she was wordless—a warm, lovely, moving darkness. . . .

We reached the hotel steps.

"Won't you come in?" she asked with hesitation.

"I had better not."

"Well, then—shall we say good night here?"

She stood a little above me, and I wanted her to remain.

"Tomorrow, Gladys. . . ."

"Shall we breakfast about eight?"

"Till then! And you will go sailing?"

"I promised. I'm sorry now. I see that I need not have done so."

"Don't worry over that."

"I'll be back at twelve and we can swim. Shall we say good night? I have had a happy evening," she said.

"Not too much talk?"

"A good many ideas to think about."

"Tomorrow we won't live so much in our brains."

She considered . . . lingered. . . .

"Good night!" she said suddenly.

Her long cool hand resting in mine made me tremble.

"Good night, Gladys."

She ran up the steps and vanished within. . . .

Crossing the street to the annex I climbed to my room, with its patch of ceiling and long slope of roof covered with slanted wallpaper, under which lay a cot bed. A washstand, bureau, and single chair in hard yellow pine were all its furniture. In the single, low, open window the curtain fluttered and the air was damp.

When the hard electric light was out, the moon, riding high, made a white barred patch on the floor. . . .

There had been too much thinking all these last days, not the good first-hand thinking of actual things, but thoughts removed from reality by various stages of generalization and theorizing. The life lived with intellectual people stimulated but one side of man's nature. And all this feverish mental activity had been turned loose on Gladys and was a poor way in which to treat her. . . .

Her brown long hands teased my senses. I desired her hands and all the length of her. There had been a pause, months of a natural restraint, and now the dam was broken.

The way in which I wanted her was not good. There was too much blood in my brain and I was split in two. Too much of the sort of thinking which the present way of life made inevitable resulted in a man's dividing himself into two beings instead of one—into the spiritual and the physical man. I wanted some good work in sun and air. I wanted to be whole again and not to feel the damnation of a desire that did not seem worthy even of the name *apia* . . . And were I not split I would not thus analyze and criticize myself.

We met formally at breakfast and played a game for the benefit of Mrs. Peters and others. She casually let drop the fact that she was going sailing, and I that I had some business matters to attend to and thought I would look over Nantucket.

She wore a shorter skirt of white piqué with full pleats making slim her black stockinged ankles. On her feet were low white shoes and above she wore a plain, rather thin waist that made the curving of her arms and her body seem almost too soft. It was a costume like that of hundreds of others, and her appearance so dressed with her hair done low, with a black ribbon, turned to mere pretense her assertion of being mistaken for twenty-five. She looked her age, which was twenty, and no more, but the clarity and strength of her face and eyes gave her a dignity and a protection greater than that which would have come from being five years older. Her social fears seemed laughable when one looked at her, but when one realized the teachings and perhaps experiences upon which they were based they were pitiful.

We let them rule us all morning, but when dinner was over and we had gone upon the veranda to decide what to do with the afternoon which they allowed us, they seemed destructive to what was natural.

"Let us go somewhere," I said, "and let's go soon. We will take supper with us and come back by moonlight. There will be a time of dark before it rises but that won't be long."

She hesitated, her eyes grave, and considering. Then they shone with a sudden brightness.

"All right! Where shall we go?"

I went to hire a buggy and she to arrange about the supper.

We met again and drove off in our vehicle, one high wheel grinding. Our vague destination was a beach and the sea. Everything was good, the smell of the horse, the feel of the smooth leather reins, the robe once green, now rusty, enfolding her knees and mine, the road moving or sliding beneath us, the town diminishing behind us, the rolling scrubby wastes around us and overhead blue sky with thin veils of cloud.

We told how we felt about natural things that we saw, discovering the happiest coincidences of observation—how stones in the road seemed to each of us to walk toward a carriage or a horse until close, suddenly to run in a single line, and after passing behind to walk away again. We talked about what conveyances we had traveled in and their differences; about horses and then about Fak often mentioned in my letters.

"He is still mine," I said. "Dorn uses him at his farm."

"I think I would know him if I saw him," she answered. "You described him so vividly."

We discussed the mare which was drawing us, a hack from a livery stable, spare, but not unwilling. Gladys told of the ancient horse at her cousins', and then of them.

"They are typical outspoken New Englanders," she said. "They believe that the more a thing hurts the person to whom they tell it the more honest it is."

I laughed and told her I liked her epigram. She looked at me in wonder.

We came to a fishing village of small frame houses, white or gray, perched upon a sandy cliff or crouched on the shore below. There we stabled our horse and with our lunch basket went on and down to the level of the sea.

Walking along the beach we watched great green waves roll in, rise, curl over, grow smooth on their concave side with a white flash, fall, break, and rush up the beach in foaming tongues. The seethe and trampling roar of the surf was in our ears, the sun hot overhead.

When the village had grown small, we sat down in the dry sand . . . There were a few words. Time passed. . . .

"It makes me sleepy," said Gladys.

"Why don't you sleep?" I asked, but she shook her head and sat erect running her brown hands into the sand.

I lay at length, one forearm supporting me.

She looked down at her hands, and all at once lay as I was lying. After a moment she put her head on her arm, attended to her dress over her knees, and sighed.

"Go to sleep," I said.

"You don't mind?"

At last, almost reluctantly, she relaxed and lay loosely, her feet drawn up a little way. Her eyelashes were black against her cheeks, which were smooth, softly flushed, and faintly freckled. Her lips were slightly parted and her blouse moved in the regular rhythm of sleep.

She was desirable. I wanted to lie down close to her, my face toward hers, and gently to slip my hand under her brown one that lay dropped upon the sand with curled fingers.

Watching her unguarded lips and hands and loosened knees— two rounded points through the pleating of her skirt—I remembered the hint she had given of offers made to her at the school where she studied, and also the man whom her mother had wished her to marry. How much had men had of her? I resented all who had ever touched her, and was jealous of the thought of Gladys quickening to any other man.

She was desirable, all of her; she would have denied it, yet it was a most precious possession and she had armor and weapons to protect it so that it would attain its proper destiny. She was one to rouse a strong desire. Would she be able to save herself from the pitfalls of *apia* in this confusing, blurred country, she whose dark nature was desirous as well as desirable? Would she see as clearly as Nattana had done if her heart once were stirred?

Her sleep, so natural and so flattering, must not be troubled. It was in itself surrender whispering of another greater one. She was alone and gallant, childish but strong. Her weapons and her armor were as important to me as to her. I wanted her to have a good love, for she was an *ania* woman. . . .

The sun declined and became misty, and the wind brought a damp chilliness. I laid her wrap over her as lightly as I could, but it waked her, and she sat up like one frightened, her opening eyes startled, and one cheek more flushed than the other.

"Have I been asleep?" she said.

"Yes, Gladys, but not very long."

"Oh, I am sorry! What have you been doing?"

"Lying here."

She looked at the cape which lay upon her knees.

"Did you cover me?"

"Yes, but it waked you."

"I was tired. There was this morning and swimming, and then last night I slept hardly at all—I don't know why."

Nor did I ask her . . .

She was cold and we went to the edge of the sea and walked along the beach. We watched the great rollers break, and ran down as near to them as we could come and raced back again to escape the rushes of sandy water and seething foam that pursued us in broad loops.

Her hair blew in damp wisps upon her bright cheeks. She stopped and looked at her feet and at the sea.

"I wish I could wade," she said.

"Why don't you?"

She shook her head.

I longed for the salty wetness and the drag of water about my body, and the rush of sand under my feet.

"I wish we could strip and go in all over," I said.

She looked at me a moment.

"I would love it," she answered, and she ran away over a glistening surface just left bare by a receding wave, which reflected the whiteness of her dress for a few seconds before it dried to moist brown sand.

The wind lessened and the sun was bright again.

We returned to the lunch basket and our cloaks, but on the way she was careless and a wave filled her shoes. We gathered a pile of driftwood and made a bonfire.

Her white shoes were gray with wet and covered with sand, her black stockings salty. It grew darker and we ate our supper. She put on her cape and was warm, she said, all but her feet.

"Why don't you dry your shoes and stockings, Gladys?"

She would not.

We waited for the moon. At last it rose from the dark sea, withered upon its upper edge. It was the signal and we climbed the sand-dune cliff and harnessed our horse in the shadowy stable smelling of hay.

As we drove back over the empty inner country, the grinding wheel sang us a tune.

We said many little things and no great ones, but each knew that the other was so happy as to be weary and drunk with it, ready for the night and long quiet rest.

Next morning she came to the steamer to see me off. There was a pressure of things to say but none was quite right.

"I have been perfectly happy," I said, and I took her long hand. She looked me in the eyes and her hand was given and all mine.

"I have not been so happy for years," she answered. "You spoil me."

"How have I spoiled you? You have been the kind one."

"Oh—for ordinary living. Perhaps it is Islandia."

She smiled but her eyes lingered a moment. . . .

From the deck of the steamer I watched her upon the receding wharf. She remained after most of the others had gone and became a vivid dot against the dark gray wall of the warehouse on the wharf— a dot, and then a pin point within which the promise of happiness was enclosed.

35

Finding Values

UNCLE JOSEPH hoped that I had had a good vacation and was ready
for business again. Things were not standing still, he said, and this
I took as a hint, and said that I was in good condition for work.

"Where have you been?" he asked, and I told him. He inquired
about the family and I reported.

"See that girl of yours?" he demanded suddenly.

"I spent a day with her at Nantucket."

"That's all," he said, but he called me back. "Take your time,
John. You have only just come home to the country where the finest
women are. Don't be caught by the first pretty face. Have a good time,
of course, but don't be in a hurry—Need any money?"

"No thank you," I answered.

"We have a talk coming."

It was September, and some of its glory of gold and red, blue
skies, and clear air was to be felt in New York City. On the Island
Farm in the Doring Marshes Dorn's child would be born this season,
early in the spring.

Six months in Uncle Joseph's office had brought a technical facility that made work easier and the reality behind details more clear.
It was pleasant being efficient in the service of and making money for
Lang and Company; therefore I postponed thinking about the decision I must make before the year was out. Uncle Joseph was entitled
to a trial without thoughts of something else. The daydreams consciously indulged were those of a successful New York businessman:
a great deal of work downtown but not under the compulsion of
coming and leaving at fixed hours; a house or apartment in the city;
a club there, though what for I did not know; theaters, dinners,
bridge with friends for city pleasure; a house in the country; a coun-

try club; golf; horses, perhaps, and a yacht; a wife; children no doubt; friends like myself; and some reading when I had time. I saw the picture and placed myself, John Lang, within the frame and moved myself about. There was a certain style to the whole. In time I would have a sensation of being someone and superior to something; later still I might find it natural. There was an elusive pleasure in the progress of success. Once the taste of it was really in my mouth I would know whether I wanted it or not. To bring it there I worked hard using all my intelligence and will, intent on pleasing Uncle Joseph.

Just when invitations were beginning, in mid-October, a note came from Gladys at her boardinghouse. She had promised to write me when and if she returned to New York, but had let nearly two weeks pass, saying that she had been very busy. When I called upon her she looked older and more slender than I remembered. There was much to talk about but also a disheartening feeling of distance, as though we both had subtly changed and were not quite fitted to each other in the city. Her eyes, however, were bright when she talked of the school where she studied.

"This summer," she said, "has made a different person of me. I am going to work hard to catch up. I cared too much before what happened to me. Now—nothing matters."

We made an engagement for an evening a week hence and said good night formally.

Was she the woman who said that I spoiled her for ordinary living? Was I the man who saw the promise of happiness enclosed within her person? Perhaps as a businessman I was no longer Islandian to Gladys, and therefore different. Perhaps the lovely afternoon and evening were the cause of our—what? Sentimentality? *Apia?*

She had lost a little of her flavor, and I was sorry, for it made living rather flat.

I wanted a thrill. Where would I find it? I was not the only man who after a hard day's work in an office wished either rest and relaxation or a thrill. There were thrills of various kinds that could be bought, such as certain plays, certain musical comedies among the more innocent ones. But the thrill I really wanted was one a woman could give, not merely by being looked at or heard sing in roles composed for her by another . . . Uncle Joseph understood this feeling. There was a suggestion behind some of his offers of money.

Like Mephistopheles when Faust, feeling a similar need, invoked him, Jennings dropped in to call, seedy no longer, on a business visit from Chicago.

He wanted the news, guessed he was settling down, and asked how that Godforsaken dump, Islandia, was.

"Hell of a place," he said. He was prosperous, well-groomed, with the same cherubic face as before, but his eyes were older with little rings beneath them.

"How's Mannera?" he asked.

"She went home, I think."

"Great girl, but she and that damn' country you liked so much got my goat. I went to the dogs as you may have heard. Johnny, you nearly ruined me with your Exhibition Ship!—But I am all right now."

He told me of his position and of the money he was making. After a while, however, his mind went back to Mannera.

"When she wouldn't come away with me—thank God!—I sort of left her to you."

"How did you?"

"I gave her a letter to give to you in case she needed a kindly hand."

"She never gave it."

"I thought she and you, who got along so well with those hide-in-the-woods people, might have something in common. You were so damn' good, though not half so bad that way as Harry Downs . . . I like my own kind," he said. "They are all hellcats, but you know their game."

"You have a low opinion of women, haven't you?"

"I have not. I know a nice girl when I see one."

We went on a spree of a mild sort. He talked of Islandia all the time and always with contempt.

"It did get your goat," I said, "and it has it still."

"The hell you say, you old devil!"

"Mannera was something to you that no other woman ever had been."

"Don't be so damn' wise, Johnny."

"If I ever go back will you come with me?"

"Do you suppose I want to see her old? Not I!"

"What made you like her? Give me a straight answer."

"She was kind of—oh, kind of simple. I don't know."

"Have you found a nice girl here?"

"Have I?" He was suddenly mysterious. "She's a fine girl and keeps me straight."

The idea of having a thrill was distasteful. But would it be so the next time it came? Then someday someone might tell me that a nice girl steadies a man. I would be degraded indeed if I took any woman for that purpose.

Uncle Joseph did not summon me for the "talk" which had been promised in the summer and again early in the fall. I worried, wondering where I had fallen short and if after two months I were already going stale.

Philip, coming to New York on business, dined with me, and I took him into my confidence as inevitably I must.

I told him of the Vaba Pass, of my good fortune in escaping, of the resulting invitation, and of Dorn's offer to me of one of two farms.

"And I may go," I said. "I shall decide before the first of the year finally and definitely. It is not a decision to delay. It must be one life or the other with no afterthoughts. They are very different."

"Why didn't you tell us?"

"Because I wanted to give your way of life a fair trial as other men live it, without arguments."

" 'Your' way!" he exclaimed. "My way isn't Uncle Joseph's way. There isn't any single way here. And you still are one of us, you know. Why don't you say 'our' way, or ways?"

"They differ among themselves but are all one contrasted to the Islandian way. . . ."

"That is just the beauty of our ways: they do differ so. But you have certainly given us news that will upset us." He studied me. "I wondered what had changed you so. You seem much more nervous and high-strung."

"Blame it on the fact that I have a decision to make. But I don't feel nervous or high-strung. An Islandian told me that I was a quivering jelly when I came there, but no one said so when I left."

"Maybe—you were always very sensitive—but at least you quivered in a way we all understood . . . That there can be a choice is hard for an intelligent person *to* understand. Haven't you lost by being less sensitive?"

"I believe I am more sensitive to real things."

"Do you credit Islandia?"

"Islandia and friends there."

"You would have had them here. Are they better?"

"My best friends now are there."

"Why don't you try making friends here?"

"I have."

"You are rather snobbish."

"Oh, Philip! Must I be so loyal to this place that my best friends must be countrymen?"

"Of course not, but you have picked up prejudices, shibboleths. Of course, prejudices are all right as a rule of thumb way of deciding the simpler questions of life, but when it comes to important matters they should be subject to change without notice."

"My trouble is not having them. Islandia has given me a temperament too fluid and too undogmatic to have prejudices enough to get along smoothly in this community, which is so complicated that we are always having to decide important as well as unimportant matters by rule of thumb."

"There you go, contradicting yourself. You have a prejudice in favor of the simple life—the Brook Farm, the Charles Wagner, the Rousseau fallacies!"

"Philip, don't accuse me of mixing up those theorists with Islandian reality. It is not simple there. I have been in several tangles and I know. Socially it is simple. Human relations are simplified also in consequence. But emotionally it is not so at all!"

"Islandia is an emotional Utopia evidently! That is pure hedonism."

"The emotions, the feelings, all that makes a man conscious of his existence, have freedom in Islandia, Philip!"

"Hedonism! But there is a higher thing."

"What?"

"The pure spirit of thought!"

"Abstract thinking is not so much stimulated, I'll admit—"

"What a loss, John!"

"What good do you get out of it but the pleasure of a mathematician?"

"The ordering of life in the best way extends from the spirit of pure thought downward."

"If you believe that, Philip, you are a lost soul. But we are not advancing. Let me tell you a few things which I don't like here."

"That doesn't make them wrong . . ." he said. "You are a sort of pragmatic individualist."

"You have called me all sorts of names. Be concrete, Philip. Tell me what you think is wrong with Islandia!"

"All right," he said, "I'll open . . . I have gathered from what you have said that the country is largely agricultural, that each farm is largely self-subsisting, and that except for marriages a man if born there dies there. That means a man's way of life is determined for him in advance. Therefore there is no scope for ambition. In consequence man becomes devitalized. There is no spur of change and opportunity. It is a fine place for a plodder and a security lover, but for a man with . . ." He paused for a word.

" 'A restless man,' " I suggested.

"No, 'a man with ambition.' If you go there it is a confession of weakness, John."

"Ambition," I said, "is a quality approved of because it often makes for the best life under conditions like those here; but it is not good in itself . . . Is it my turn?"

"Go ahead."

"As I see it, men are born with an impulse to be active and to do various specific things. In Islandia that impulse or vitality has outlets which are natural to man, taking into account the fact that he is a muscular, two-legged animal as well as a creature with a highly developed brain. The life here makes such demands that men to exist are compelled to expend their vitality in unnatural ways. As a result in Islandia men are more even, all-round beings who feel and enjoy things with a greater keenness—"

"Hedonist!" he cried.

"All right, Philip, I will accept your term of abuse and confute you with it.—Pleasure is the greatest good! But pleasure means one thing to an Islandian and another to you. Pleasure means to you pleasure of the senses either directly or vicariously through emotions in the mind. And here everyone has such a devil of a time surviving, and so many unpleasant things to do in order to live and survive, that they exalt the unpleasant things and decry the pleasant ones. Pleasure means to you something sinful, wrong, self-indulgent. If so, of course pleasure isn't the greatest good. But Islandia isn't for everyone. There are some who have so perverted themselves that the unpleasant things are pleasure to them—the reformers, those who wish to organize others' lives. But the perfectly normal man with normal desires, a mind, and muscular strength, is not so perverted. All I say is that the Islandian way gives him a better chance to have what he wants than this country."

"Islandia then is the hedonist's paradise!—What you call a perversion is not a perversion here!"

"Perhaps not, if surviving is the main thing with conditions what they are; but suppose men from the beginning had had as their chief interest the slow creation and preservation of conditions that made a kindhearted hedonism the better way in order to live and survive, wouldn't you say an alterer, a reformer, was perverse and out of tune?"

Philip shook his head.

"Men would be prevented from fulfilling their ambitions," he said. "There is no opportunity for the individual who differs from his fellow man."

"He is usually someone who has been or is in physical or mental distress, or an idler whose energy is not sufficiently exhausted."

"How can you say so! The reformers include the noblest of men!"

"That is equally true, and it is tragic that conditions make them so."

"John, you are so smug, so self-satisfied with Islandia—so selfish!"

"Me or they, Philip?—They aren't selfish. Their hedonism is kindhearted, yours is not. Man finds pleasure in kindheartedness. It is natural there. It springs from his gregariousness and the fact that his offspring aren't born in full possession of their powers like reptiles or insects from an egg."

"You mean they have some family feeling."

"Very much."

"You won't persuade me it is any better than ours."

Thereupon I told him what I had told Gladys about Islandian *alia,* and how it gave scope to "family feeling," and continuing I explained how *alia* and *ania* were interlocking emotions.

"That is very pretty," he said, "but you can't convince me that your Islandians are always perfectly satisfied with life with the same wife at home."

"They have no word for 'wife,' " I interjected, "except one which literally means: *alia*-sharing lover . . . But you are right. There is another conception: *apia*, desire for a woman or man not as an *alia* sharer.''

"I knew it! They aren't perfect."

"They recognize that Nature in her usual prodigal way has over-endowed men and women with attractiveness and susceptibility to each other."

"Well, what do they think of immoral relationships?"

"They have no word for 'immoral.' As to non-*alia*-sharing relationships, you must remember that the interlocking strength of *alia* and *ania* makes for a social institution that emphasizes the unfruitfulness of *apia* relationships to an extent unfamiliar to us here. We think of 'love' as the tie that binds. A man or a woman is much less likely to break up his or her home either for the sake of or because of *apia* or even a thwarted *ania* for someone else, because his wife and he share in a common *alia*."

"Nevertheless, you grant they are immoral."

"To them the term 'immoral' has no meaning. They have no standardized moral rules. They don't need them!"

"There you are wrong!" he cried triumphantly. "Morality is a normal human impulse, an instinct. All immoral people are abnormal."

"*Ania* is a normal human impulse, but not morality."

"But they are immoral, aren't they?"

"If you mean that men and women have sexual relations with persons other than *alia* sharers you are right."

"I don't mean that at all. I mean such relations with other than husband or wife."

"There is a difference," I said. "The first woman who agrees to share your *alia* with you is technically your wife, but if she deserts it, and another one takes up the sharing, the latter has first claim. They would favor such relations with her."

"That is immoral," said Philip.

"Yes, it is, but what difference does it make?"

"John, they have corrupted you! They have made morality unreal to you."

"I hope so—that is, if I live there."

"I can only say I hope you don't go to the dogs."

"Is taking a woman not your *alia* sharer, or your wife, going to the dogs?"

"Of course it is!"

"Then I've been there," I said in sudden rage, having no shame over my relationship with Nattana; but instantly I was sorry. He looked at me in surprise yet with a light in his eyes.

"That explains everything!" he cried. "But why did you lie to Alice about it? We all thought you had led a decent life."

"I lied as to the fact and told the truth as to the decency. Rules of morality, standardization of conduct, make lying reasonable and necessary!"

"You had a mistress, John?"

"Yes."

"I don't call that decent."

"Why?"

"Did you love her?" he demanded.

"We found out that it was not *ania.*"

"Then there is no excuse for you."

"Excuse! Excuse from what?"

There was a brighter glow in his eyes.

"If you want to know what I think," he cried, "I call any such relation with a woman beastly unless there is love to redeem it!"

"If my clean body and a woman's clean body come together, Philip, there is nothing beastly in it in the sense you use that word. It is good, I tell you! But we aren't so far apart, you and I. For a man's relationship to her may falsify him and her for later *anias.*"

"Suppose you are already married?"

"It may falsify an existing one."

"It is nice of you to grant that, John!"

"I don't grant it," I said, "I know it. It predisposes you to the less profitable, less fruitful, less satisfying things."

"There is hope for you! You do have it on your conscience."

"My—my what?"

"Conscience, John!"

"I don't know what you mean," I cried, clutching my head.

"Yes, you do."

"I am conscious of what I have done," I said. "I know what some of the effects are."

"You are sorry! You know you are!"

"I am not sorry!"

He paused.

"You had better go back there if you think like that!"

"Very likely I shall," I said, "if I am exposed to this sort of thing during the rest of my life here. I don't mean you personally, but the ideas you stand for."

He turned a little white.

"You have said a harsh thing, John."

"I am sorry. We are out of tune with each other."

"I hope you find tuneful persons there."

"Philip," I said, "Islandia has made discussions like this unbearable. I don't mind being called immoral but I do mind what you feel toward me when you call me so. I object even more to the sort of talk we had before we began to be personal. Once it was pleasant mental exercise. Now it is too real. I hate this life because of the confusion of it!"

"Thinking and talking about it is the only way to make it clear!"

"Thinking too much about it makes it even more confusing and sterile. I am only happy here when I am relieved of thoughts about it."

"Happiness is not the highest thing."

"How horrible to have to admit it!"

"No!" he cried, his eyes shining, "how glorious!"

"There is a gallant glory about you, Philip!"

"John," he cried, "you ought to find the right woman and marry her! You need a wife!"

"I want no woman to steady me morally. Nor do I want any woman as a way to escape unhappiness. It demands too much of her."

"You and she would find your greatest happiness in giving each other a helping hand."

"You and Mary!" I said.

He nodded, and I made no answer, for I was thinking that I wanted neither to help nor be helped, but rather to build.

Then having talked ourselves in and out of a condition of nervous anger, we were silent, felt brotherly again, and parted good friends.

October became November, and as previously I indulged daydreams of myself as a successful businessman, now I indulged those of myself as an ordinary Islandian but not with a whole heart. In spite of what I had declared to Philip my decision had not yet ripened . . .

In Islandia there would be work, not too much, most of it outdoors, work prescribed by weather and seasons; my house would be upon the land where I labored; The City would be rarely visited, but Dorn Island where I had *tanrydoon* would be my second home . . . For pleasure at my house there would be my own 'day' and the 'days' of others, music such as Nettera made, the look of what was mine, and the happiness of work there . . . There would be no other house that was mine and no club, but there would be horses and my boat; there would be friends, none quite like myself, but all persons of strong individuality—Dorn, Stellina, and new ones . . . There would be the smell of burning leaves in autumn, rain that meant more than the need of overshoes and an umbrella, sun enjoyed not merely because it brightened the world and made me warm, wind and clouds watched with daily interest, and the earth that was more than the foundation for my house and the place where my feet rested . . . There would be no theaters, no opera, no illustrated magazines, no developed sophisticated art, none of the highly flavored pleasures of the Western world; there would be heavy silences and few unnatural sounds; but there would be peace and a sense of dreaming, and I would be always learning new ways to labor and making new discoveries in growth of plant and animal . . . I would be sunburned and a little coarsened, with tongue far less glib than that which argued with Philip; my desires would be simpler, stronger, less nervous; and I would often be utterly alone. . . .

Once the loneliness of Islandia had been sinister and terrifying, but now I did not dread it. I feared something else, but what? Was it dying there away from persons who were my own kin and kind? Would any Islandian woman who became my wife, or *alia*-sharing lover, take their place? I might be wifeless all my days, finding no one, and yet, though a stranger, I had half won Dorna and wholly won Nattana halfway. There were lovely women who tempted courtship, but I remembered Stellina's words and her advice to marry my own kind. An Islandian woman would be a little too much mother and teacher. Whom could I persuade to go there with me?

These thoughts brought before me a picture of the farmer who deliberately sets out for town to find him a wife. A gentleman or a lady sees crassness in such a mission and believes that the union resulting cannot be the finest. The nobler people wait for love to happen like a miracle. But the farmer has three solid purposes—to find a bedmate who will share and satisfy his desires, to obtain offspring to work on his farm, and to procure a pair of arms suited to certain necessary labor. These purposes are discreditable only because love is left out and only if he desires offspring to work for nothing in place of hired men. Those who build their lives with no such clear purpose expecting, when the miracle of love happens, in some way to fit the woman into their scheme err in another direction. The ideal lies between the two: the love for a woman and a purpose in life coexisting, love *ania,* the purpose *alia.* Were I thoroughly Islandian, the miracle of love would naturally happen, the woman would be of my own kind, and the *alia* would stand waiting. But I was not thoroughly Islandian. John Lang going to settle there was exceptional. Since only an American woman would suit me, since married life there was the better one, there was some excuse for me to search for a wife.

But whom?

I knew many girls and had seen more, charming, desirable, givers of pleasure actual or potential. Among them was Gladys—but I liked her too much to play the role of the farmer to her. Unless I loved her wholly and completely I would not ask her to share an Islandian life.

I had seen her twice since her return to New York and after the talk with Philip early in November I went to call upon her at her boardinghouse.

The only place where she could receive me was the dingy parlor, but she, though pale again, was a clean bright jewel among shabby common stones. Her hair, which she did not wear in pompadour like most women, was brushed back in two shining wings, black in the thin yellow electric light from overhead. She wore a long dark red dress, like a loose glove, but not too loose anywhere. It hinted of, without revealing, her figure, but did not overload it. Nothing of her appeared except her head above a high collar and her hands out of long wristbands. The only close-fitting things were her stockings, and of them only the arch of her insteps and her ankles when she crossed her legs were to be seen.

If I were truly the farmer looking for a wife I would describe what I had to offer and ask her if she could cook and liked hard work, having no question as to her other qualifications. Though I was not yet the farmer I wanted to tell her about Islandia. Therefore, after showing a polite interest in what she had been doing, I led the conversation in that direction, saying that the time for a decision was drawing near.

She watched me with her intelligent eyes, the brown irises of which were crisply clear against the white.

"Help me to decide, Gladys."

"How can I help you?"

"By listening."

"I would love to."

She smiled, lifting her round firm chin, her eyes flashed darkly, and she assumed a listening position. I thereupon told her of the two contrasting daydreams, one as successful businessman, the other as ordinary Islandian but leaving out the wife in both for the present.

"One is a certainty, the other is not," she said. "How do you know you will be a successful businessman?"

"I don't, but I am not going to choose Islandia because I may be a failure here."

"That is sporting," she said, "but I wish the comparison was not between being a businessman here and an Islandian, but between something else and an Islandian."

"What else?"

"I don't think our best men are businessmen."

"But the men most thoroughly at home in life here, the men who live most naturally under present conditions, are businessmen. The rest are their parasites or critics."

"That is a very materialistic view."

"Which would you choose, Gladys?"

"If I were you or if I were I?"

"If you were John Lang."

She looked down and put her hands on her uppermost crossed knee, sighed, looked at me for a quick glance, smiled, and said a little grudgingly:

"Islandia sounds very tempting."

"Suppose you were yourself," I asked, "which would you choose?"

"What would I be there?"

"Somebody's wife, perhaps, or sister."

"As a sister—where would painting come in?"

"I wrote you about Catlina and her sculpture," I said. "You would be freer, because there are less sophisticated standards to live up to. Your art would be more lonely and less stimulated by competition

with others. But Islandian art is so little specialized that it is delightful and comprehensible in spite of its childishness, and the artists
seem quite happy."

"But I could paint?"

"Of course!"

"I am not much good at cooking and hard work."

"Do you dislike it, Gladys?"

"I have never liked what little I have done—but I might, John.
I am fairly strong."

"Suppose you weren't a sister but a wife?"

"If I loved the man, I would be happy anywhere. Islandia or elsewhere would not be the question."

"But suppose you could choose?"

Her eyes were dark and thoughtful. She shook her head.

"It isn't any of it very real," she said.

"I shall make it more real, Gladys. An American woman considers these things: first, does she want to live with and be the wife
of a certain man? second, if she becomes his wife will her life with
him be a livable one? If the first is very strong the second is less important."

She smiled mysteriously, but I continued:

"If the second is very strong it influences her also and quite rightly
so. If the first predominates and the second is ignored, the life is impossible, and we say she has thrown herself away for love; if the
second predominates she is a materialist or mistaken. But these are
the only two considerations here . . . There, however, there is a
third consideration. The Islandian woman—it is true of a man, also,
of course—sees herself as a builder of an *alia,* sharing his with the
man she loves. This is different from the second consideration, which
is more concerned with comfort, position, opportunity for work and
the like. Nor is it the same as the wish to have children. It is that and
more: to have them and to have them go on in a good life which
she and her husband have helped to build for them . . . The rudi-
ments of *alia* are to be found in our life here, but there it is a developed conscious emotion. To marry ideally in Islandia a woman considers three things: first, does she want to live with and lie with a
certain man? second, will her life with him be livable? third, is the
alia he offers her a good one : . ? It is true that usually the most he
can offer is a life as a farmer's wife, but I have written you all about

that life. You must have some idea what it is like. It is a good life, Gladys, for one who is strong and healthy . . . And it does make you healthy. It isn't like New York."

I paused, not remembering where the conversation had started. She was very still, her eyes veiled, and then she looked at me with gentleness.

"I couldn't think of all those things," she said. "The first one is the only one that would matter."

"Nevertheless, I know you would be happier if you had a good *alia.*"

"I would be happy anyway."

"There is another thing, Gladys. It is not just love—it is *ania*. To me it is perfectly beautiful. You look at a woman and you don't merely think, 'I want to have her and lie with her.' You think, 'O, this is the right one. This is my dear. She seems like me, my own, and yet is richly different. I want something of me and her to go on. I can't bear to have what I feel for her die . . . What would our child be like? She gives me such beauty that it must go on in our child . . .' You desire her, of course, Gladys, but there is no fever in it, no wish to possess and have done. Your desire is peaceful and deep . . . And if you have a good *alia* to offer her—"

"I know what you mean," she said.

We were both utterly silent.

She sat without moving. My blood rushed to my head. There was Uncle Joseph and the way of the businessman, and Gladys herself in her long dress with her slender white artistic hands, not robust like Dorna and Nattana—more like Stellina—very much an American. What would Islandia do to her?

"I haven't made up my mind whether to go or stay," I said.

Her eyelashes lifted quickly as though throwing off a burden.

"I hope you find *ania*," she answered. "I do, John, with all my heart."

"And I hope you also find it, Gladys . . . I did not find it with Dorna. I was—too immature, I think now. There was another woman. I wanted to marry her. We were friends and then we attracted each other. She and I were lovers for a while. We found that it was not *ania* and separated."

She bent her head.

"I have no secrets," I said. "If I go back there, she will not cross my path in that way again . . . I have lost something by that experience, but I have gained more."

"What did you gain?" she asked in a low voice.

"Beauty," I answered, "and knowledge which I an American had to learn and could not accept naturally—that love and desire are not the same things as *ania.*"

"What did you lose?"

"One rather likes to think that one has spent all of one's self upon one's best."

"I know," she said . . . "I like the idea of *ania,*" she added, after a moment. "It must make them a good people."

"Oh Gladys!" I cried. "You see! You see!"

She looked at me—her eyes narrowed as though I had hurt her.

December came and Uncle Joseph sent word that he wished to talk to me. From his office window was a glimpse between high walls of a slaty-blue wintry sea crossed by car floats, tugs, and ferries. He called to his secretary that he did not want to be disturbed and offered me a chair. He sat down at his desk and lighted a cigar, his face brooding, more lined than I had remembered it, old, but not unhappy.

"I am going to tell you something about this business," he began after a thoughtful silence, and he described it at length with a considered prophecy as to its future. The income which he derived from it was larger than I supposed.

"My father—your own grandfather, John—founded Lang and Company," he said. "It has made me, though I do not now depend upon it. I have enough to live on and to leave to Agnes and to my son without it. Nor are they interested in it. They have gone their own ways, which aren't mine. I don't want Lang and Company to die when I do. You may think that sentimental—very likely it is. I also want to see my brother's son have the chance I had—which his father passed by. I am going to take you into partnership beginning January first, and I am going to leave you my share in the business. I want you to keep it going as long as it makes you a good living. I can't ask more."

He raised his hand as I was about to speak.

"This is no new idea of mine. I have had it ever since my son decided to be a lawyer. I never mentioned it before because I wanted you to prove yourself first. Well, John, you have done so this last year. I had almost lost hope for a time, but now nothing would make me happier than to leave Lang and Company in your hands. You have found yourself."

With sudden clarity I saw all. Uncle Joseph, controlling my destiny, had by chance given me Islandia. The consulship was to him a test, in which I had failed, but he had given me another opportunity. In failing him I had found that which I wanted more than anything he could give me . . . Lang and Company was his *alia,* which he wished to perpetuate. His son had turned from it. The nephew must carry it on.

"Well, John?" he said, emotion in his voice. . . .

If I had known his intention when I went to Islandia I would have been another man. I would have stood as firmly as young Islandians stood. I would have spoken very differently to Dorna . . . Oh, bitter!

"Uncle Joseph!"

He had given me Islandia. Did I not owe it to him to make his *alia* mine? Islandia would never die in me.

"I may have been a little hard," he said, "in keeping you in the dark so long—"

"No!" I answered, "you were quite wise."

"That's how I looked at it," he said, relief in his voice. "I am glad you take it that way."

He must be spared one regret at least.

"It was better for me not to know, Uncle Joseph."

"And now, John, shall we settle it? I have the partnership articles in my desk. I will give you a third interest in the firm."

His generosity amazed me. My income would be multiplied six times. On January first I would already be a successful businessman —at thirty!

"I am sorry, Uncle Joseph, but I am going back to Islandia to live the rest of my life."

"Don't!" he said after a long dazed silence. "Don't ruin yourself! Don't be a fool!"

"It is the life I wish."

"What will you do there?"

"I shall take what money I have and buy a farm."

"You are no farmer."

"I know it, but I can learn."

"You will make a botch of it."

"Oh, no! I shall have good instruction and advice. The farm I shall buy is already a going thing."

"It is suicide, John! What of your family?"

"Father and Mother?"

"No—your children."

"It will be a good life for them—and they will be good Islandian farmers."

"Have you got a wife out there? Is that the trouble?"

"No, Uncle Joseph. There is no woman there to whom I am tied."

"Is it—a girl here, who doesn't want to marry a businessman?"

"No. I have no girl here who has made up my mind for me."

"John, listen to me! This is the most important decision in your life—important to me, too. I've set my heart on taking you into the firm. But it is your good I'm thinking of now. If you go you write finis on yourself. There is no future for you there, nothing . . . Why do you want to go?"

"Because for me it is a fuller, happier life, Uncle Joseph."

"And you can say that to me now!"

He shook his head.

We talked for a long time, but nothing that either of us said met the other's argument. The life that he wanted me to lead was his repeated. He had as much faith and contentment in his *alia* as any Islandian.

In a tangled rope the removal of one kink often makes the whole coil run freely. The hold that business had upon me suddenly ceased. There was nothing that I wanted in the life I had been leading, nothing I would regret. Instead there was the happy impatient longing of the lover for the mistress who does not deny him. No one of my kin really opposed my going though all pleaded with me to remain. My separation from them was a farewell and tore at my heart.

As to Gladys I had also made my decision, avoiding her lest the sight of her disturb it and put kinks in the rope again. Passage to Southampton was already taken for January 5th, 1910. I visited the family from Christmas over New Year's day and was in New York again on the third. On that day I called upon her.

We met in the same dingy parlor and she wore the same red dress that swathed her body and made her hard to see.

"I have wondered what had become of you," she said easily. "I suppose you have been very busy."

She smiled and the movement of her red lips, and the cling and lift of the upper one from the lower, sharpened the desire that I had been resisting.

"I have been busy getting ready to go to Islandia," I answered.

Her face became white and blood left the lips which I wanted to know with my own. Her chin quivered and one hand went to her breast but dropped again. Her eyes, however, conquered and remained steady. I looked at them as though not noticing the rest.

She smiled.

"I hope you will be happy," she said. The look upon her face, more significant than anything I had hoped for, filled me with a happiness that shook my resolution.

"Gladys . . ." I began.

She was staring at her hands in her lap and did not seem to hear her name spoken.

"I would like to know why you are going back," she said.

My answer had been already prepared. I wanted my reasons to be clear to her.

"Because the Islandian way is a better one," I answered. "There a man is not split so that body and mind fall apart, the one going too far from earth, the other sinking too low in it. Here the labor which is regarded as the highest knows the realities on which men live only at second hand. We think too much about thoughts and not enough about feelings and things. Men specialize and deal with fragments and not with wholes. We live in confusion. And our overintense brain life either desiccates the pure animal soul in man or makes an unmanlike beast of it. I know, Gladys! Desire becomes impure, perverse, a thing to be hidden and not to be faced . . . I love you and I don't trust my love. I have been here too long, and do not know my own mind!"

She looked at me, flame in her cheeks, with unflinching eyes.

"I want you, Gladys, but at present I am split and I must find myself . . . The best life for a man and a woman is a life with an *alia* which they share, united by *ania*. I have thought of asking you to come with me, but I am not going to. There is no one but you now in my life, but Islandia is a hard place and a lonely one for an American. There is no Islandian woman to claim me or to call to me. I would fear marriage with any one of them. They are wise and strong in ways strange to me. It is you or no one, Gladys. To live with a woman and to have children by her, working together on the same thing, specialists in a common enterprise and not in diverse ones, is the best life, my dear. I am not going to ask you to come with me merely because I know that it is better to have a wife there. I am afraid of such a choice. You are worth a better offer than that. Gladys, I can't know my own mind here. I am still too dazed by visions of the paths I might have followed. But after I have been there for a few months I shall know whether what I feel for you is *ania* or not, and I shall write to you."

All the while she listened without a word, smiling a little, her eyes watching me with a wisdom better than my own, and her cheeks were hot with a flush that fired my blood.

"You will write me anyway, won't you?" she said.

"Why, yes, Gladys."

Her blush deepened.

"I don't mean a' correspondence. Please not that again! I mean: you will write me even if you find out that it is not *ania*."

"Of course I shall."

"When do you think you will know?"

"In two months or three."

"That means I shall hear from you in May or June?"

"It is very long, isn't it?"

She smiled a little and looked down.

"If I were to remain here," I said, "I would know that I loved you enough to ask you to marry me."

"I don't want you to stay here!" she said quickly . . . "I don't know what I think or what I shall think . . . It is a long time, John."

Her eyes lifted with a look of warning. But I could not take back what I had said.

"When are you going?" she asked. I told her of my plans without eagerness and that I should not reach Dorn Island until February 23rd.

"There I shall see Dorn," I said. "He has given me the choice between two farms. One is unique. It is a ranch where horses are raised, a flat shelf high above a deep narrow valley surrounded by mountains. It is a romantic, wild, hard, beautiful place. The other is like a hundred other farms, in gently rolling country, on a stream that is not navigable, with mountains not very near; but there is a spot from which the sea can be reached only eight miles away . . . I don't know which to choose."

"Which would the Dorns wish to keep?"

"I don't know."

"Perhaps it isn't a good plan for a stranger in a country to be too unique," she said, "but I don't see how I can help you to decide."

"Which would you like the best, Gladys?"

"You mustn't let that influence you. And I should not know."

"May I tell you more about them?"

"If you wish to."

Thereupon I described the two farms in detail and she listened with attention but without a word, her smile wise, her eyes bright, her cheeks warm, becoming as I spoke more and more desirable and desired.

Abruptly I concluded, for if I stayed longer I would seize her hands and undo all I had said.

"I am going, Gladys."

She rose also, a look of surprise on her face. I took her hand and it was smooth fire against my own.

"I will see you again before I go," I said.

"No, please!" she answered. "Go and don't bother about me again until you get there, or even then if you don't want to. But write me one letter."

Her hand was firm and strong, and I felt her being behind it, supple, unsurrendered, desirable to all my senses.

"I will surely write you," I said.

"Good-bye, John."

"Good-bye, Gladys."

The air quivered a moment with other words almost said.

The night was cold and gusty with no sky overhead, only blackness into which vanished the perpendicular walls of buildings set at right angles to the hard flat street. I walked as though pursued. Islandia was an impossible dream, my decision unreal, America and

865

New York too strong in my blood and in my nature to break. I wanted Gladys and I would not see her again for seven or eight months, if then. I desired her. I wanted to strip off the wrappings of her red dress and find her within . . . I had not tried the door. I felt, but did not know, that it would have swung open. This was my opportunity and I had probably lost it, striving to attain a perfection which America knew not, too high above its entangling confusion . . . I was a fool to think of *ania* here. I should have seized my moment and bound her fast. My decision was a brain-made thing contrary to my heart and my blood, disconnected from my desire and made in fear of it. I talked about being split and I was split myself. My words were brassy, but her restraint rang like a clear silver bell. . . .

PA**VI**RT

36

The Decision

AT LAST I was at sea. I sat in a corner of the lounge with a novel and did not watch New York fade out in murk and smoke. The horizon lay ahead and would slowly encircle the ship, finally closing complete and whole. I was tired. There had been innumerable things to do, under pressure. Transforming all the property I owned into a draft upon the British Bank at St. Anthony which would give me gold was a complicated matter—disheartening because it seemed unfair to use money inherited from Lang and Company through my grandfather for the purchase of a farm in Islandia. I was untrue to the *alia* that America had given me; Islandian enough to regret a change . . . But that *alia* had played me false when I most needed it. The whip of necessity was required. Doubting horses must be spurred to go on. . . .

The lounge was a quiet place for there were few passengers. Seeing me weary Alice, who had come down to the boat to say goodbye, had told me that the sea voyage would be a fine rest . . . But what a life where one became so jaded that the night's sleep was not enough—where one must make a complete change! Over the horizon men and women sprinted and fell exhausted, rose and sprinted again. An even pace was impossible.

I had begged Alice to come with me—or at least to follow—but she had refused, saying that I mustn't think that because she was often discouraged and ill she was not satisfied with the life she led. I had told Mother that I had a home for her, but her answer was that it was too complete a change at her age—and there were her grandchildren, and Father, and Philip, and Alice. Father said that he could not imagine a life more barren. They all professed to be satisfied, but what held them to America were rather palliations than fulfillments. I told them that my house was theirs. . . .

I looked ahead to Islandia. I saw the austere beauty of loveless nature, hard work and sleep, friendship, and peace, but I had left behind what set life on fire.

The vessel throbbed. A door intermittently rattled. It was as it had been a year ago on the voyage to America. The clothes that Nattana had made for me were in my single trunk. I had few belongings . . . I closed my eyes and slept. . . .

Waking, I went on deck. The wind was sharp and full of winter ice. In Islandia it would be Sorn or summer. . . .

I went to the stern and looked back. It was dark, but the horizon was visible, unbroken.

America had vanished.

Returning to the lounge I found it deserted. The ship seemed empty.

Islandia-bound, I knew my own mind. The doubts that had clouded the clear fire of my senses and had confused my thoughts were suddenly gone, left behind in the overbuilt, too complex stress and turmoil of New York. America's revenge was to make a fool of me at the one time in my life when clear knowledge of myself was most needed. Considerations of little value had blocked the road of my progress. I wanted no one aspect of Gladys's being, but all. My mind ceased to take trial votes upon her various qualifications and desirabilities. I was split no longer. Become a whole I wanted the whole of her—as she was, perfect to me . . . She and I, whole and complete, rich and fruitful. . . .

This, I thought, is *ania*. It was simple when I found it . . . Very calm and happy I made plans to repair the errors of hesitation.

The steamer was carrying me eastward, widening at every moment the space between us, but there was no going back in person, nor was there any means of conveying a message through the air. I must wait. From Southampton on arrival I would send her a cablegram and a letter. Her response to the former would determine whether or not I returned to America, remained in England, or went on to Islandia.

That same night I began my messages, wishing that I had a better way to tell her these things. . . .

Cold green waves patterned with foam and bearing snowy crests against gray clouds lifted their moving hills as high as the decks. In the warm lounge or smoking room or in my stateroom I worked upon a letter to Gladys, striving to make it a perfect thing, writing slowly with long pauses of contemplation of her and of dreaming upon the life we would lead. Nor were they hopeless dreams as with Dorna, but dreams that could be realized. I saw the Lay River Farm —best for us because not "too unique"—and Gladys against its backgrounds of flaming autumn. It would be "Leaves" or fall when we came there. I saw her short-skirted and free in wind and rain; and my desire would be calm as a deep river and as strong.

On January 13th the letter was mailed. It was not long and it told her why I had come to know what I wanted sooner than promised, what she might expect life in Islandia to be, and how much I loved her. Only in one respect did I not give all to love: I made her no offer of any life but an Islandian one. In America I would begin to doubt again, not happiness, but the future. Our life must be founded upon a basis in which I believed. At the same time I sent her a cablegram:

DOUBTS HAVE CEASED WILL YOU MARRY ME CABLE ANSWER HERE IF YES WILL REMAIN OR RETURN TO NYORK OTHERWISE LEAVE FOR ISLANDIA EIGHTEENTH LETTER FOLLOWS

Every day I went to the office of the cable company, sure some reply would have arrived. None came. I explained her silence in many ways: she was dead; the message had not been delivered; she could not make up her mind and was waiting for my letter; she had answered to the wrong address . . . At my request the company sent inquiries and reported that my message had been delivered. Since no answer of "yes" had come to me, I concluded that Gladys wished me to leave for Islandia—that her reply was "no," which, she, ignorant of my cruel suspense, preferred to send in a letter.

Up to the last moment I hoped, and then lost hope and set sail on the *Greyton* for St. Anthony. Islandia was my solace as it had been when I lost Dorna, but hope had not died . . . There were too many straws at which to catch, yet none supported me. And robbing me even of these, such as they were, was the sharp fear that I had thrown

871

away my chance to win her by not returning. This was my punishment for not knowing my own mind in New York.

For six days we sailed south out of winter into subtropical seas and on the twenty-fourth came to the island port of call. It was possible but not likely that a message waited me here. I inquired, dreading a disappointment that would be no less great because certain.

A green envelope was handed to me by the purser in his office. Days believed real became a nightmare from which I had unexpectedly awaked. Through the open door to the deck was a glimpse of blue sea and dark-green hills dotted with white houses never seen before, existing in a new and changed world, but dim and remote in the faintness of my relief.

Her message read:

CABLE RECEIVED NINETEENTH HAVE LETTER YES ARRIVE
THE CITY APRIL FIFTEENTH   GLADYS

She also had become unreal, but now she lived again vivid in my heart and mind and to my eyes. Her answer was dated four days before. Whatever the reason for the delay in her receipt of my cablegram, her thought was clear: seeing that she could not catch me at Southampton she believed it best that I continue my voyage and she would follow. Nor was there any other reasonable course open to me, long as the journey would be for her alone. The steamer that would arrive on April 15th at The City came from the west coast and the German colonies, not from St. Anthony. It could only be caught by taking a German boat from Bremen or Cherbourg, which did not touch at this island port of call . . . Nor were there any certain connections by which I could return to Europe to intercept her.

Again I was punished for my doubts. Gladys must make her voyage to Islandia alone. All I could do was to tell her my happiness and ask her if she wished me to cable funds, directing her to answer me at St. Anthony.

A few hours later I was steaming south again, but now Gladys was mine, and the longing for her, heretofore held in restraint by doubt as to whether or not she would have me, increased in intensity, in impatience, and in happiness. A woman willing to give is doubly dear. . . .

Once more I knew the heat and calm of Caldo Bay and saw the dun cliffs of St. Anthony in the pale haze. There I had her answer:

HAPPY ALSO FUNDS SUFFICIENT   GLADYS

All I could do was to cable her again knowing that once I left St. Anthony it was the last message from me that she would receive and that the most I could hope for was a letter from her in March and already written. I told her that I would meet her at Biacra, M'laba, or M'paba if it could be arranged, otherwise at The City. No answer had come to this when on February 13th I went aboard the *Sulliaba* bound for Islandia. Nor was there any reason why she should answer. In two weeks or so she would herself be embarking for Europe on her way to me.

We left at noon of February 13th. In addition to the invitation to reside I had a certificate of physical fitness from the Islandian doctor who had succeeded Mannar. His language had sounded in my ears and my tongue had spoken it, bringing a change of mood as though a different-colored light had been thrown upon the world. The City was only five days away and soon this would be the language of all my speaking and of my verbal thoughts. English for some time, perhaps always, would remain the principal medium of communication with Gladys. Inevitably Islandian words would find a place in our conversation giving us greater clarity of expression in many things. English was stout, expressive, musical, subtle, and blurred. I loved it. We would keep it. We would never be wholly Islandian, for the English language and what it stood for was too strong in us.

Late in the long hot afternoon we passed Coäpa, and next morning I dressed in Islandian clothes, perhaps never to wear those of Europe and America again except to show them off to the curious— or to our children.

Late on the night of the sixteenth I woke and went to the porthole. The air was cool with a light wind blowing. Under a moon at the first quarter a headland lay slumbering in a pale, hazy glare. We had left the subtropics of the Southern Hemisphere. These were the Sosal Islands, part of the Province of Carran, and the most eastern and southern extremity of Islandia. I had come home but to a home in the making and not to one long known—dear as Gladys was, new and an adventure . . . I wished that I had known my *alia* from

873

birth, but it was not un-Islandian to acquire a new one as a woman does.

All day we skirted a visible coast, at first white mountains low above a dark horizon, later wooded headlands and little islands, with glimpses of farms. Miltain, Deen, and Hern—I saw a little of all three, and late in the afternoon the red cliffs of Storn.

Night came with a strong wind and a rough sea and then sleep with consciousness of something very dear approaching, so good, so natural, that I felt no need to wake and ask my brain what it was.

The City with its stone buildings of differing pale tints lay under the high sun of a late summer morning. It lay upon its three hills, familiar, various, lovely, and quiet. There was no other place like it, and for the sake of my *alia*-sharing lover I was glad of it and of all Islandia to which she was coming.

Once more the road! I traveled upon a hired horse and alone. All was green and warm and heavy with summer. In season it was like the latter part of August in the United States. In the air was the smell of cut hay. Every tree was in mature leaf, the beeches at the Bodwins' towering, massive. Only in the marshes of the Some River which I crossed at noon the second day was there any sign of the impending fall. There the grass was turning red and yellow. I rode on through Loria Town and in late afternoon came to the house of Lord Some. The day's journey was an easy one but I was tired, soft from the life which I had been leading.

Lord Dorn had been absent from The City, the Periers were French, the Bodwins I knew but slightly; here, however, were those who were not only Islandian but contemporaries and friends. With them came the sense of naturalness and of home so deep that consciousness of contrast and strangeness vanished. We spoke of the farm which I was to take and I told them of my wife who was to come. They in turn gave me news of friends, of Cadred and Soma now come home, of those at the farm in Loria Wood, of Dorn and Nekka and their child, a son, born in September, of young Stellin to whom Tora was now married, of Dorna who was in the East, and of the Fains.

After sleep I woke refreshed and at ease, and the road through dry Inerria was my own, leading me to lands that were mine. In the orchards the red apples were already ripening and the Islandian maize with its flaming crimson tassels stood high. The red and green in the fields, the yellow soil of sandy loam, the bright air under a hot sun, and in the distance the snow fields of Doan and Winderclorns pale and distinct but without bases against a hazy sky. . . .

Next day, the fourth on the road, already more firm and more thin, I rode in the morning up the valley of the Cannan River to the Inn at the Doan Pass, thinking often of Dorna, a lovely memory, with curiosity but no pain. Pain born of frustration keeps desire alight, but she and I, meeting at the end and parting as friends, gave each other what cured pain. She would not trouble Gladys's path.

After a night at the Inn I rode down into the West and saw again the plains of Lower Doring and the Marsh, like a dark motionless sea. From Earne I went by the ferries to Dorn Island and arrived in midafternoon at the Fisherman's Harbor.

The southwest wind was blowing fresh, bending the trees all one way with huddled leaves, and floating upon its vigor were soft pink clouds. I smelled salt air again and saw the pallid glare of clamshell roads.

Riding through the cattlefields I came to the house by its eastern side, past the school of Dorna the elder, and beneath the window of my own room, to the pepperbox tower, which seemed to have grown smaller. There in a sunny lee out of the wind, and close to the walls, a rug was spread, and the first Dorn I beheld was Dorn's baby lying on his back, his bent legs up, compact, pink, half-naked.

Nekka sitting against the wall at a little distance saw me and rose suddenly. She called my name. I dismounted and went to her. Handshaking was not the custom, but I took her hand and kissed her given cheek.

She stood for the Dorns, for their Island, for so much that was fruitful and dear. Her question and my answer went unuttered. She picked up her baby and we set out to find Dorn himself, who was cutting grain.

We came to the edge of a field where several men were swinging scythes, their arms brown and their shirts white amid the yellow falling stalks. He was there. Nekka with the baby held high on her breast called to him. He turned his head, stared a moment, and then came quickly over the stubble. We moved to meet him. His pace quickened to a run.

We caught each other's arms.

"At last!" he cried. "You did come back!"

"Yes . . . Islandia is too strong."

His face was dark with sunburn. His legs and arms, massive but fine, were like mahogany. He was magnificent and his white teeth, his white shirt, and the whites of his dark eyes were dazzling.

"For good?" he asked.

"For good."

He paused.

"The farms are still vacant."

"The Lay River Farm," I answered.

"You are one of us, now," he said.

My room, familiar, unchanged, was quiet. Drafts of salt air, subduing, restful, murmured and sang around the firm stone corners of the house. This was my home, my center, complete—and incomplete, for without Gladys my side was always empty. I was single, too much one. I wanted her to share with me this home-coming. There were fifty-three long days to wait.

That evening at supper when all were gathered—Lord Dorn, Faina, Dorna the elder, Marta, Dorn grandson now ten, my own friend, and Nekka—I told them of Gladys and how it was that I came alone. While telling of these things she became more bright and more necessary and I knew that the days before her coming would be a race against unbearable impatience. Yet all my hope rested upon sixteen cabled words. . . .

Nekka suggested that it was fortunate for me that cables existed somewhere else in the world.

"Perhaps," said Lord Dorn, "if they did not she would now be with John."

An important matter was soon settled. All members of the Dorn family except Dorna were present and also the Lord of the Province of Lower Doring in which the Lay River Farm was situated. Save for a few details the transfer of that place from Dorn grandnephew with assent of his kin to Lang was effected on the evening of my arrival; and I was a *tana*, or proprietor, of an Islandian farm with *tánrydoon* at Dorn Island. Henceforth I could go to the meetings of proprietors at Doring Town and vote when the Provincial Assembly met. The letter of invitation was my patent of naturalization. No one required me to abjure my allegiance to the sovereignty of the United States nor swear it to another nation.

The opportunity had come to discover if the emotion of *alia,* about which I had said so much in the turmoil of argument during the year just over, would be real in me and real in Gladys, both Americans and not brought up to it. At present, at any rate, the Lay River Farm seemed little more than the place to lay their heads which every house-hunting couple sooner or later finds. Love was the tie that bound us. So long as we were together it did not matter where.

When would we be together?

In order to meet Gladys at Biacra I must depart in a week, in which case there would be no opportunity to prepare the Lay River Farm for her and me. On the other hand we would be together at the French port for two of the three weeks which I must spend there. Which was the more important? M. Perier had cousins in Biacra to whom he would write and they would meet and safeguard Gladys; and Dorn suggested that I intercept her at M'paba, which could be reached by sailboat from the Island in three or four days at this season when the prevailing wind would blow from aft or abeam. In this case it would not be necessary to leave until April 7th, allowing me six weeks in which to make ready the farm. Gladys's early days in Islandia might prove difficult ones and if the house to which she came were smoothly running she would be much happier . . . Not without misgivings and also hurt myself at the postponement of our meeting I decided to accept Dorn's plan and to go to the farm within a few days, when he could come with me, in the meantime helping him with his harvesting. And there was still another reason. Nearly all the money I had, brought in gold from St. Anthony, had gone to pay for our house and land. Gladys and I were poor. Of all this I wrote her in a letter which she would find waiting at Biacra. . . .

For nearly a week I labored for Dorn four or five hours a day, learning as well as becoming fit. The Lay River Farm also had its grain fields. And every day we swam or rode or sailed and had long talks.

When the grain was cut we set out for my farm and spent two days upon the journey.

The air was hazy, the sun warm, but under its heat was a faint trace of coolness and of change. Fall was in the air like a thought of light before the flush of sunrise. We had come by way of Doring

Town and Tory and had branched from the National Highway ten miles·west from the latter place. The farm was approached by country roads through fertile country. We skirted the edge of low, forested hills—Doring Forest, covering nearly thirty square miles, only ten miles from home—and traveling northwest came at last to the Lay River. The unfenced stone bridge by which we crossed was at the boundary line of the Dartons' land and mine. They were my neighbors on the east. South across the river were the Adners, through whose farm we had come, to the west the Napings, and to the north beyond the pine-crested ridge the Rannals. In the midst of these dropped Lang, an American, and later would come his *alia*-sharing lover.

We rode up to the house on the knoll. Dorn offered to fetch someone from the two households of dependents, the Ansels and Stanes. Letting Fak wander I remained.

The long side, the front, faced southeast and along its whole length of perhaps sixty feet was a veranda or terrace paved with worn flagstones. At its outer corners and along its outer edge were five round columns, monoliths of a weathered gray-blue stone. These supported a heavily timbered roof that was also part of the floor of the second story of the house, which therefore was wider than the lower one.

Seated next to a column I waited for Dorn, looking down the sloping grass to the river a hundred yards away, its dark water flecked with sunlight. The willows in heavy leaf but just beginning to be sere occasionally heaved their masses of foliage in a light wind as though some creature were struggling underneath. Behind me was our house where we were to live all the rest of our days. . . .

Dorn came with most of the members of the two households, and I met them all again, this time as owner of the farm. In charge in the absence of the Dorns was old Ansel, a slender, weather-beaten, but wiry man of seventy, with a white beard and remote blue eyes. He was a widower and father of Ansel, a man of forty-five and like his father. With them of the Ansel family were Laya, Ansel's wife of about his age, and an unmarried son and daughter, of twenty-three and twenty-two. The only missing persons were old Ansel's brother, a bachelor who had gone fishing up the Lay River, and a boy of sixteen and girl of fourteen who were at school at the Rannals'. There also came Stane, a man of sixty, dark and heavy, and his sister Stanea, who was a little older and unmarried, Stane's three sons, men in the late twenties and early thirties, and Raina, wife of the eldest. Absent from this family were Edona, Stane's wife, and his two grandchildren, girl and boy, ten and eight, also at school.

As Dorn had told me there was no lack of able-bodied men on the Lay River Farm. My labor was not indispensable in order to make a living for Gladys and me and them. Indeed the farm was a going thing, necessary to all these persons who had known it for years and had carried it on. I was a stranger who must prove his right to live there. The knowledge that as proprietor I had certain rights and duties would mean little until actual experience made them real. I said to those who had assembled that I had come there to live, learn, and work, and that there would be more learning at first than useful work. We talked for a little while and then all went away, except old Ansel and Stanea, their heads together. Change of ownership in Islandia was rare and though they knew it as not unlikely to happen, they must have found it a shock and upsetting because the new *tana* was so ignorant.

Stanea remained because she was best suited for position of house dependent, that is, the person whose principal duty was housework. She was not needed at the home of her brother, and in the past when the Dorns came to the farm she had done this sort of work. Dependents, or *denerir,* were for a certain portion of their time nominally subject to orders from the proprietor. Actually what they should do was more a matter of mutual arrangement, the final responsibility for the farm as a whole resting on the proprietor, who was not an owner in the full sense of ownership in America. Households varied in what arrangements were made. It depended upon what was most useful to the farm as a whole. At the Hyths' Upper Farm there was no house dependent, for the labor of those who might have filled that position was put to better advantage elsewhere; Ettera did the work which Stanea would do for Gladys and me.

She was glad to come, realizing our greenness, pleased also to have the main house permanently occupied. She and old Ansel's brother had been its caretakers for many years. He would still help her.

With her and Dorn and old Ansel, I went over the house. There were many signs, not of decay, but of disuse. The somewhat meager furniture had stood for a long time in one spot. The air was a little musty and dead. Hangings were creased through being long in boxes. The linen was yellow from lack of sun. There were no pictures on the walls and the carvings were simple and few. It was an old plain house but still solid, with four large rooms below and six small ones above, more than Gladys and I needed.

Dorn stayed with me for a few days and then departed. We were to meet again on April 5th at Doring Town from which place I was to sail to meet Gladys at M'paba. And I was alone for a month at my own farm.

By day I worked or made visits or else explored the land that was mine. At any task to be done I lent a hand outdoors and in. I swung a scythe and tossed hay with the three young Stanes; gathered apples with the young Ansels and helped their mother, Laya, make cider and wine; fished with Ansel "brother" and cut wood with Stane; threshed grain and drove it to the mill to be ground; milked cows and curried horses—did many things, none well, and learned a little about all. Old Ansel came to me for decisions. I asked what he thought best and we agreed on that. There was no need of me; my place I must make, and in the meantime I would become familiar with all things and persons upon my domain and they with me, so that when I returned with Gladys I could truly bring her home.

I went to see my neighbors and attended their "days." From several miles around they came to see me, and I knew their faces, their names, and where they lived. I walked over the farm from end to end, crossways and back, following fences, about which I knew a little, and plunging into woods and thickets to find what was there, if it were only bright fall flowers and weeds under dark shadows. I traced the half mile of brook from the spring in which it began to its end in the Lay River. I found a deep pool and bathed there before supper.

There was less to be done for the house and little with which to do it. For Gladys I chose a room in the northeast corner where there was sun nearly all day long. It would also be mine if we were to live so closely—with five other rooms on the same floor. Until this was decided I would sleep in the room adjoining and there placed my things. A third with a south window I set aside for her studio and manufactured an easel to indicate its character, for there was nothing else. A fourth I dedicated to Dorn, to be his as my room at the Island was mine.

At night after supper, when Stanea had gone home, I wandered all over the house with a lanterned candle. On the lower story the floors were of stone. More rugs were needed, more hangings to make warm the coldness of the walls. The rooms looked empty by candle-light, the few pieces of furniture isolated. Would she care . . ? In the kitchen and pantries there was not much crockery or cutlery, and few cooking utensils, very little food laid by, but Stanea was quietly increasing the supply. We would not starve. We would not be cold and we would have shelter . . . There would come dark winter nights with gusty winds. Would she be lonely? What would she do with so few books and in a strange language? Would I be enough?

Upstairs the floors were of oak, rugs not so necessary. I moved hangings and furniture about so that Gladys's room at least would seem to her furnished. I spent a long time making it ready and Stanea kept it clean and bright. There was a bed, wide enough for two, its soft blankets in a chest at the head; a wardrobe empty of everything yawning for her clothes; rugs on the floor so laid that she could go anywhere without leaving them; hangings ready to be put up on the white stone walls when the weather was really cold; a bureau with empty drawers; a mirror which I knew she would find too small; a sofa with rugs, brought from another room for her to rest upon; a washstand with copper bowls and basin; a table where she could write letters; and an open fireplace, with fire ready laid, tongs and poker in place, and wood in the woodbox. On the table I placed all the books I had, and ordered more, thinking again of winter nights.

About March 20th, old Ansel returning from Thane which was our "town," brought back a heavy parcel and a letter from Gladys.

In an empty house before an open fire I read it.

New York, January 24, 1910

Dear John,

I must write you tonight in haste or not at all for otherwise this letter won't reach you any sooner than I do. I want you to know why I did not cable you at Southampton for you must have wondered and worried. On January 7th I went to my cousins for ten days without leaving any address at the board-inghouse and so did not get your cablegram until I got back on the eighteenth when it was too late to let you know my answer. I waited for your letter for two bad days not knowing what to do, so wanting to say yes to you somehow. By the time it came I had got my wits back and cabled to you my an-swer which you got. I am awfully sorry but Mrs. Gillingham (her landlady) *ought never to have receipted for your first cablegram when I was not there.* I am sorry when I think what you must have felt with me all the time so sure!

John, I do understand the doubts you had when you were in New York. It is an awful place! Tonight it is raining like mad. It is noisy and dirty and confusing and impossible to be yourself. You won't mind my saying that you did not seem to be your usual self the last few times I saw you. But your letter convinces me that you really love and want me. Even without it I would have come on the strength of your cablegram. And I would have accepted you when you came to call the last time, for I do love you. All I am sorry for now is that we have lost three months of each other, for I think your doubts were perfectly natural and I know what doubts are. Now I am very, very happy and I am already horribly busy getting ready to leave here and join you. I have things to sell and give away, good-byes to say, letters to write, things to get, etc., etc.

I shan't bring many clothes because I know Islandian clothes are different and suppose I must dress as they do. I shan't have any trousseau. I am also studying Islandian and since I have a month and can never go to an art school again I am taking intensive lessons. I am so happy that I find it hard to concentrate and be practical; nevertheless it is all the great-est fun I have ever had.

I am leaving here February 22nd on the *Groenland*. I have haunted steamer offices these last days. I take the *Kap Ostend* of the H.A.S.S. from Cherbourg for Biacra. I am going to change there to the *St. Anthony* rather than at M'laba because of the examination I have to take and because I shall be more at home in a French-speaking place. Two weeks are a long time to be there but it can't be helped. Do write me there if you can. I leave on April 8th and reach The City on the fifteenth as I cabled you.

I have quite enough money for the journey if you are worried about that, but afterwards I shall be penniless—almost literally. But I am not a bit afraid. This isn't the time for me to be cautious and saving. I am, however, bringing a large supply of paints, canvas, etc. You won't mind my keeping that up I know. You said I could paint in Islandia. Otherwise I shall come to you empty-handed, and you will have to get along with me and some paints and nothing else. I think from your letter that you will. You seem to want me. It makes me very happy. I did not know you loved me so much. Your letter has changed everything for me. The world is a different place. As for me if you want to know, I began to love you last winter. All *my* doubts vanished at Nantucket, but I had no idea you cared for me then. I saw that you did care that last day here, and all evening I wanted to tell you I loved you; but I thought you would rather have me be silent, for if I said anything it might have forced your hand in a way you would regret, or else you would have had to take it into account in making your own decision and I wanted you to be quite free. I don't know whether I did right or wrong. It was hard then but now I can speak.

I am so happy I can hardly write this, only weep with happiness. I do love you. I love you with all my heart and soul. There is not a bit of me left out. I hope so much that I shall be what you want, as your wife, or *alia*-sharing lover. Only in this do I have doubts, not for myself but for you. I know I shall be contented and happy as you will want me to be, leading the sort of life we shall lead at the Lay River Farm, but I doubt my ability to be what I want to be to you.

I think it best that I be honest with you as you were with me. Several men have kissed me. I did not really love them but I liked their kisses at the time. To one I thought I wanted to give more but I did not. I haven't a mild nature, John. I am sorry now about these things but I feel quite sure that they will not really spoil me for you. What I felt for them was

883

quite different. Only you have made me know what love is.

Thank you for making so clear what our life will be like. I see how different it will be, but even so I would have come anywhere if you wanted me, even if the life weren't so healthy and lovely and serene as ours is going to be. I am so happy, John. I shan't mind being among strangers for I shall have you who are my dearest. You say your friends will like me. I hope they do. I want to meet Dorn very much. I should love to visit the Fains. John, to think I shall really see the places you wrote about and with you and share them with you because you want me.

I love you, John. You say your love for me is *ania*. Mine is all there is and possibly can be, so I suppose it is *ania,* too, but I am a little afraid of strange words. I can only say—I love you.

I expect you will meet me at The City. For that day I live. You are my whole happiness and life now. I have no fears.

I must stop. I could go on and on but I am not saying much. I want this letter to reach you by one of the March boats.

I love you and I am coming. You love me and want me. I know you do. I am quite dazed. I long for you.

GLADYS

Outside the night was still, the moon four days from the full. I went down to the river. The water murmured softly. It seemed that I could not live or breathe until Gladys came. Nature all around me was like a motionless creature with open eyes, watching me, deep and incomprehensible. Here in Islandia one gazed into those eyes longer than one dared at home—found the unknown, was not afraid, and let it be unexplained. She loved me and I her. What would we find? Our minds would meet and our lips and hands. Our bodies would unite and separate stunned with what we felt. But there was another meeting, deeper than any of these, which they merely shadowed. Each to the other was an open door.

Later, at the house, I found the parcel, containing a flat plaque of stone carved with small figures. I recognized myself and Don prone on the ground. Over the fireplace, it could be let into the wall.

Whether heroic or not, my one significant deed would be memorialized in my own house for the line of Lang to see hereafter, with smiles, wonderings, and a feeling as of something mythical. "That is father . . . grandfather . . . great-grandfather . . . that happened five hundred years ago," they would say.

37

Gladysa

THE SEVEN DAYS from April 7th to April 13th were the most worrying I ever spent. In a boat of the intermediate type, owned by the
Dorns and carrying wares from The City consigned to Sevin in
Vantry, I set sail from Doring Town. The master of the vessel had
agreed to extend his voyage to M'paba. While it was a little late in
the season for the southwest winds to blow with the unfailing regularity of earlier months, no one thought that we would take more
than four days to reach M'paba, two hundred and forty miles away.
We had two days' margin, and a forty-mile average on a high seas
voyage was a snail's pace. Dorn, who saw us off, voiced what seemed
a needless caution.

"I will write to Perier to meet the *St. Anthony,* in case you are
becalmed and don't make M'paba, and he will bring her to the
Island."

It took us two days to reach the mouth of the Doring River and
a third to gain Grase Bay, in all not eighty miles. The fourth day,
April 10th, opened with a light breeze that fell flat within an hour.
At night we were in Fannar Bay ten miles south. I was rowed ashore.
It was impossible to reach The City by the fifteenth when Gladys
would arrive and impossible to tell her where I was. On the eleventh
the long-delayed wind blew fresh but it was too late to return to the
boat. She had gone. A farmer lent me a horse and at dawn I set out
for Dorn Island whither M. Perier would bring Gladys, and I
ground my teeth as I rode. At noon of the twelfth I arrived to find
that Dorn had a new plan. On that same morning he had sailed with
a picked-up crew in another one of their boats, hoping to intercept
the *St. Anthony* at sea. They had forty miles to go in forty-eight hours
against a strong head wind, and would lie hove-to under Hess Island

off the coast of Winder, close to which the steamer usually passed in the morning. If the plan succeeded I would see Gladys on the fourteenth or fifteenth. . . .

There was nothing I could do. My friends were on foot to catch my bride and bring her to me. The man to whom she had come half-way around the world failed to be at the places where she hoped to find him. I feared that she would imagine me dead or changed, and knowing herself penniless would suffer too much for any future peace of mind . . . And yet her coming so far was proof of her strength.

Upon Dorn I relied. He saw a solution and if he could find the *St. Anthony* and prevail upon her master to stop and transship Gladys, our meeting would come about in a way that would efface all our present troubles.

Nekka was another friend and also a nuisance. She wished to help us in every way possible; but she was Islandian, and not aware of the traditions and behaviors of Americans. To her Gladys and I were already married. She asked if there were any changes which I wished to have made in my room. I explained that at least in Gladys's eyes we were not married. Her brows wrinkled in her quizzical puzzled smile. I said that we were Americans and that to us marriage required a ceremony as well as an understanding.

"Haven't you said all that is necessary?" she asked.

"All that is necessary to marry at some future time, but not to be married now."

"You mean she may not want to lie with you at once?" she said.

"Yes," I answered, "not until we have formally had a ceremony."

"I can understand her wanting to recover herself after so long a voyage, and I will prepare a separate room for her . . . Still . . . I should think she would want to be with you as soon as she could, for it is going to be strange to her here . . . And I don't see what you can do for a ceremony."

"She will want one, I think. It will give us an opportunity solemnly to say what we feel."

"Lord Dorn can give solemnity to occasions," she suggested, "but he is away."

"It won't do any harm to be married American fashion, and Gladys will want it. I shall speak to him."

"Of course," said Nekka, "Dorn may come back without her. What will you do then?"

"What do you think the chances are?" I asked with a spasm of worry pinching my heart.

She went to the window. The southwest wind was pouring over the marsh with limitless power, and the sun winked out and in from behind the scudding clouds that rode upon the wind.

Nekka shrugged.

"I am an inland woman," she said, "and not 'one of them.' It seems to be blowing. I don't envy Gladysa out on the sea . . . But I shall be happy to do all I can for her when she comes—if she does. Is she a good sailor like those who live here?"

"I don't know. . . ."

Nekka's eyebrows lifted.

"And it is perfectly natural that I should not know about an American woman a great many things that I would know about an Islandian woman if she and I lived here all our lives!"

"One can know too much," said Nekka cynically.

The wind blew so strongly on the twelfth and thirteenth that there could be no doubt of Dorn's arrival at the place where he hoped to meet the *St. Anthony,* but the sea might be so heavy that transshipment of Gladys was impossible. In the Tower room I studied a map of the Winder Islands. There were places, close to which the steamer might pass where the force of the sea would be broken. But she might not go there . . . Her master might be unwilling to stop even so . . . Every possible cause of failure at one time or another crossed my mind.

On the night of the thirteenth the wind lessened and new possibilities had to be considered. As I lay in bed I thought of Gladys on the *St. Anthony* in her cabin expecting to see me on the next day but one, full of doubts and wonderings as I was, and of Dorn lying hove-to or anchored in his boat the *Maso,* under the high rocky shores of Hess Island. . . .

The next morning I went to the harbor with fishing rod and line against the chance of an early return of the *Maso.* The wind coming off the shore wrinkled the blue water in dark flying catspaws. Outside in the channel were rushing whitecaps. The pines of Ronan's Island were sharp with no atmosphere between me and them. It was a wild windy day, as clear as crystal, fall in the air; but the sun was bright and it was warm in the lee of the warehouses, where I cast over my line.

By this time the question of Gladys's arrival on the *Maso* was probably settled. She was either headed toward me or was going on to The City where I would not be.

The morning slowly moved. Fish were not likely to bite, but it was better to fish than to do nothing.

At noon a boat appeared in the channel, but not the *Maso*. She was too small and she came from the east. As she entered the harbor, however, and rounded to alongside the quay wall, I watched the figure of Lord Dorn and wondered why he had returned to the Island from Doring Town. The reason, which he gave when he landed, was Gladys and me. Before going to the house he sat down on the wall and took the fishing rod to try his luck. He had heard of all our complications in a letter from his great-nephew. He wished to be present at the Island when she arrived.

"She has been alone a long time," he said.

He believed that the *St. Anthony* would stop for the *Maso* and that the transfer would not be very difficult . . . I told him that Gladys would probably expect a ceremony of marriage and he understood as Nekka had not, and offered to do what I proposed.

"At any time," he said, "today or tomorrow, or later at The City, for I cannot stay here long."

He remained for several minutes but caught nothing.

Waiting was less tedious.

Nekka came with her baby and a rug and a basket, charming and graceful thus burdened.

"I thought that you might prefer not to go back to the house," she said, "and that you would not mind if we came and lunched with you."

She suckled her child, sitting quietly against the wall of the warehouse, white in the sun's glare. She left him asleep wrapped in the rug, and we ate the food she had brought and drank wine, cold to the lips but warm and smooth in the throat. Later, when the baby waked, she tried her hand at fishing while I held him, heavy, soft, lovable, with a body that moved with its own life.

We had little to talk about, but her presence was welcome.

"Gladysa has come a long way," Nekka said. "She must be very

sure of herself and of you . . . I can only imagine what it would be
like to go so far to a man. I wonder if I could . . ." She smiled and
was thoughtful. "I have been thinking about her all the time. I wish
I knew what her needs were. She may have none . . . there is you,
of course—but I would like to help her."

"You can help her as to clothes," I said.

"Oh, clothes! I will, of course, if she wants me, but. . . ."

She was silent for some time, and then reached her arms out for
her baby. I handed him to her carefully, his legs kicking. She held
him close, watching.

"Giving herself to a man makes a woman a different creature,"
Nekka said slowly. "She knows in advance that this will happen and
dreads it. That is why we are sometimes so hard to understand. I
think she is very brave. . . ."

She frowned as though this were not what she had meant to say.

"Still—it is best and we know it!" she continued more firmly,
"but. . . ."

Again she ceased speaking. She rose.

"I am going back to the house," she said. "I do hope the *Maso*
comes soon, for your sake and hers. I know you are going to be
happy, but waiting is hard . . . Everyone's problems are their own.
But you have something we don't have."

"What is it, Nekka?"

She smiled vaguely.

"You have come to each other from so far."

The afternoon began. I was alone again, making calculations as
to the speed at which the *Maso* would make the return journey.
Then I caught a fish, flat like a flounder. . . .

It was strange, almost like disloyalty, that in this place, which
was so much Dorna's, where I had felt so much and suffered so much
because of her, I waited for another woman, eager, untroubled by
any thwarted desire, longing only for this other one. I wished all
loves to be permanent—but why?

My shadow fell upon the water and grew long. It was late afternoon. I had almost ceased to worry and to wonder. . . .

Above the western end of Ronan's Island had suddenly come
the high peaks of two sails, tinted pink in the low sunlight. They

might be those of a vessel bound ahead to the town of Earne, but one sail swung over, and the two together moved sideways, and I knew it was the *Maso*. I ran to the end of the wall that enclosed the harbor, whence I could look down the channel between the two islands. The sails seemed to move over the tops of the pine trees like a great bird flying. Then the hull came in sight with a line of foam from her bow, and my blood was drawn to my heart.

The hull swung and pointed toward me, heeling a little, the great sails convexed to one side, hiding those on board. The *Maso* grew larger like a bird swooping down. The wind freshened. I saw a man on the upper rail, not Dorn, but one of the crew. The *Maso* came nearer, and another figure appeared, slender, dark, with a white floating scarf about her head, sharp against the sky.

I waved and shouted, though she could not hear. The man turned to her and pointed. She leaned to him, watching, and suddenly lifted her hand. . . .

She had come, she had come to Islandia! She was real, no longer a dream and a hope.

She stood clinging to a stay, and her face was a white dot watching. She was graceful, living, Gladys herself and no one else, the one laughing perfection, a release into happiness.

As the *Maso* bore down the channel with foaming bows and came abreast of my station, she turned as I turned, and I saw her features and her black hair under the scarf.

Dorn was standing at the tiller ready to sway upon it. The crew were at the ropes. Gladys faced about and hastened aft out of the way, awkward now, and I ran back to the quay lest she come there before me.

Along the road in the distance others were approaching—Lord Dorn, Nekka, Dorna the elder, Marta and her boy, and a man pushing a two-wheeled cart.

The *Maso* was heading into the harbor, her bow toward me, the stern hidden. Her great foresail dropped in billows of canvas that thundered for a few moments. She turned a little and I saw Gladys again, sitting on the rail near to Dorn. She waved to me and spoke to him, as though happy, excited, but self-possessed.

Instead of anchoring and warping in, the *Maso* charged on; her mainsail dropped, and she swung parallel to the dock wall, her speed decreasing, bringing Gladys toward me, a narrowing space of water between.

We watched each other, and I was near enough to see her smile. She wore a long, close-fitting, blue serge suit, coat and skirt. She suddenly was a stranger, one I feared but one I loved, as though I must win her again.

She stood by the rail, borne nearer and nearer, ten feet away, five, so close that I saw her eyelashes. I dared, and made a leap, half fell on the deck, and she and I were face to face.

She was smiling, but her eyes were pinched and in their corners was a wet gleam.

"Hello," she said.

I kissed her; she gave me her cheek.

The *Maso* was now alongside the quay and the crew were making her fast. Dorn was busy with the mainsheet.

I took Gladys's hand. I had her at last but did not seem to know her. Her coming was not an end but a beginning. And she was white, and dark under her eyes.

"Let's go ashore," I said.

"My trunks and my hat. . . ."

"They will bring them. Are you well, Gladys—all right?"

"Oh, I am well. And you, John?"

"I am myself again. The house at the Lay River Farm is all ready."

She uttered a sound like a moan, but her hand squeezed mine.

"Shall we go ashore?" I repeated.

She looked at the rail, two feet above the deck and the stone edge of the quay, higher yet.

"How can I get up there in this tight skirt?" she asked.

"I'll help you," I answered, and mounting on the rail offered her my hand. She hesitated and her face sharpened. Then she raised her skirt, took my hand, and came up to me. I saw her leg in a long black silk stocking with a seam down the back, and winced because she was troubled and because these things embarrassed her.

Lord Dorn and the others were now on the wall a few feet above us.

"I am Dorn," he said in English and he gave her his hand. The troubled look left her face, she smiled up at him, and made the long step gallantly.

They gathered around her, naming themselves and smiling, conscious of the barrier of language. She faced them, straight, slender, in her clothes which were so different from theirs.

She was American and I introduced her to them.

"Lord Dorn," I said, "and Hytha Nekka, the wife of Dorn who met you, and Dorna the elder, and Marta, and the youngest Dorn of all."

To each she gave her hand and none of them hesitated to take it. She smiled and seemed at ease, and I was proud of her but baffled by a passionate wish to smooth her path.

Nekka came near and looked in her eyes.

"We have a room for you. Our house is yours," she said in Islandian.

Gladys considered her words.

"Thank you, Hytha," she answered. "I understand what you mean. You are very kind."

We walked toward the house, Nekka on one side and I on the other, and Gladys's two trunks, her suitcase, her roll of umbrellas and rugs, her long overcoat, and a large soft-brimmed beaver felt hat followed on the two-wheeled pushcart.

She and Nekka talked together with slow, careful articulation. She said that the *St. Anthony* had been delayed for several hours by the heavy seas and that she had been sick but had recovered on the *Maso.*

Suddenly she gave me her hand and I took it, lacing my fingers among hers.

"Everything is going up and down," she said to me in English, "but I am all right now. Don't worry."

Her eyes were never still, her lips unsteady. I held her hand with gentle firmness, hoping she would find me real.

We came to the alley of beech trees. The wind rushed in the branches overhead and at the end of their long gothic arch the façade of the house glowed in the amber evening sunlight, the ancient stones and the vines sharply detailed.

"The Marsh is like nothing I have ever seen," she said, "but this could be at home."

We entered the house. Nekka and she went ahead to her room while the rest of us followed with all her baggage, Marta bringing her hat and the youngest Dorn carrying the rugs and umbrellas. The *deneri* of the pushcart and I carried one heavy trunk and Dorn the other. We set down her belongings in her room. The boy demanded what an umbrella was for, and with a smile she opened one and showed him. She thanked the various carriers and they retired, each with a word of welcome, until only Nekka and I were left.

She unwound her scarf and I saw her round fine head again, her disordered hair flattened upon it.

"It is very comfortable here and you are all very kind," she said to Nekka in Islandian.

Her voice trembled; she was white with fatigue, half sitting on the footboard of the bed.

"If there is anything I can do or anything you need . . ." Nekka was saying. Gladys's eyes wandered to me. She smiled a quick forced smile and looked down . . . Nekka slipped out of the door, closing it.

I took the limp weight of Gladys's hands and lifted them and my senses became aware of her living desirableness and value.

Her eyes rose to mine.

"Well—I am here," she said softly.

I led her to a bench and we sat down together.

"With everything I own," she added, nodding to her belongings.

"Including your paints?" I asked.

She indicated the heavy trunk.

"My paints and my most precious books."

I held her hands tightly.

"I am glad you are here at last!" I said, and I moved to kiss her, giving her time to avoid it if she wished, but though her eyes debated for a moment she gave me her lips squarely. . . .

She leaned her head back.

"Yet we hardly know each other," she said.

"I have wanted you and you me."

"Have I! Three months, John!"

"And now you are here, and I love you."

"I love you, but I can't believe in you . . . Everything is going like this," she said, and she drew her hand away and waved it.

I raised her to her feet and led her to the bed, her eyes never leaving my face.

"You must lie down and I will get you some *sarka*. It is like a sweet brandy."

When I returned she was lying on the bed with a rug over her feet. She sat up like a child taking medicine, her dark eyes puzzled and deep, and she sipped the hot smooth liquor, watching me over the edge of the glass. I took it from her and she lay back again.

"I love you. I have thought of nothing but life with you since I left New York," I said.

"And I do love you," she answered as though apologizing.

Leaning over her I looked upon her face, learning it. Her eyes were unflinching. Thoughts, worries, everything was washed away as by a rushing stream and nothing solid remained but the miracle of her face, unfamiliar, unknown, but real, and then more real, and yet more real again. I embraced her and kissed her lips many times, telling her that I loved her, and she was like a victim of my longings . . . But then, with a sigh, she lifted her arm and held me as I held her. She kissed me. The barriers that had separated us were broken. We had found each other.

Released, I was aware of the future again.

"When will you marry me, Gladys?"

"Whenever you say."

"Then it will be tonight."

She stared with questioning wonder, and then smiled a faint smile as though a little afraid, a little amazed. She nodded her head. . . .

Her voice spoke suddenly.

"I am so glad," she cried, "so glad to be here! I have been alone so long. You can't know—you can't ever know!"

I held her hands again.

"But it was fun," she continued, "it has all been fun—and funny too, lots of it! And everything really went very well, but there were such unexpected things. I was at Biacra for two weeks waiting for the steamer, and I found myself in society, playing tennis, going to parties. Madame Constant Perier was very nice to me. I stayed with them and they did lots for me . . . A man tried to persuade me not to go to Islandia. He was quite serious . . . Oh my John, as though I ever would stop on the way to you! And another man on the *Kap Ostend* asked me to marry him."

"You are mine," I said.

"I know it, but I did want you there to tell me so. You seemed so remote sometimes. I read your letter over and over. It has been here all the time." She touched her breasts. "It was only paper, but so dear . . . I did hope to find you at M'paba—but it is all right. It got worse the nearer I came. The first mate, however, explained that there had been an unusual calm so that if you were sailing to M'paba you might be held up somewhere—worse off than I was . . . He was awfully nice to me. I agreed to write him after I met you. Do you mind?"

"No," I said, but I kissed her . . .

"He said I might meet you at sea . . . I was quite prepared not to find you at The City . . . Then this morning! It was horribly rough last night and the *St. Anthony* is so small. I was miserable and decided not to get up, praying I would save some of my looks, determined not to make them worse by weeping. Then about noon I noticed that we weren't tossing so much and that the engines had stopped, but I was too sick to be really curious. Then the little cockney steward said someone wanted to see me. I had a moment of hope . . . Then a huge man filled the door of my cabin. It was like a dream . . . He said, 'I am Dorn, John's friend.' Shivers went up my spine. I asked where you were, and he explained how you had gone to meet me, and that as he knew you would not reach M'paba he had sailed out to intercept me. He said you were probably back at his house. He told me that I would have to hurry because the *St. Anthony* would wait only fifteen minutes. He offered to help me. I asked if he could pack my trunk and he began at once . . . I was so weak. I dressed with him right there. Once I would never have thought that possible, and he told me about you and did not look at me. He has such a nice voice. He meant you to me. He made you real. He was a friend all of a sudden. I'm crazy about him . . .

"Before I knew where I was I found myself on deck in the glare with an island nearby, an Islandian island! I don't know how I got down the ladder, I was pretty faint. He helped me. Everyone was laughing and cheering. I was just about a pin point, alive and wild with excitement. I felt I was being kidnaped by pirates. We rowed to the *Maso* in a little boat. The *St. Anthony* blew a salute!

"Dorn lifted me on board. They made a sort of couch for me in the open air on deck, and wrapped me up and gave me something to drink. I found sailing on the *Maso* much easier than the rolling and pitching of the steamer. I felt better at once. Dorn came and sat with me now and then. I called him just 'Dorn.' That was right, wasn't it?—When we reached smooth water, I sat up and ate something. The Marsh was just as you described it—all the little settlements so far apart. They told me when we came near the Island, and I got up . . . It was a wild adventure from the time I left New York—just as wild and improbable as could be."

"Does it seem so still?" I asked.

"No," she said. "I am at home at last." We embraced again.

The time sense, which life in Islandia had perforce developed, declared that it was not long before supper. We separated to change our clothes. When ready I returned to her room as agreed. Only shadows under her eyes showed the excitement, strain, and illness she had undergone. Her eyes themselves were brilliant, her color bright, her hair rich and dark.

"Will I look absurd?" she asked.

She wore a close-fitting dress of dark-blue and red chiffon, a tea gown, with silver beads on the bodice—fashionable, strange, and graceful. There was nothing like it in Islandia, and it became her.

"You are lovely," I said. "It is all right," and I held her and told her I loved her.

"What shall I do about clothes?" she demanded. "I can't go about in what I have."

"Nekka will help you."

"Did I make myself understood?—I have been reading and studying ever since I got your cablegram."

I linked my arm in hers and we went down to supper. In the anteroom where the Dorns gathered the blazing firelight gleamed ruddily upon the silver beads and the blue and red of her dress. She was startling and exotic in color, and prettier than I had remembered her with her young head held high. She made the Islandians seem plain and her face was as proud and as well-bred as theirs. They watched her, for she must have seemed strange to them, with her high-heeled silver satin slippers and her soft dress. They knew only wool and linen. She was also new to me, for I had known her as a child, a girl on vacation and at work, not as a young woman with other people.

We went to supper and she was quite at ease, talking Islandian courageously, sometimes looking to Dorn or me for a word but able to express herself in all simple things. I was proud of her for her ability and grateful for her effort to learn to speak Islandian before her arrival instead of later. She was the center of interest, and Isla Dorn, Dorn, Parnal, a young man stopping for the night, Faina, Dorna the elder, Marta, and Nekka were continually turning and speaking to her. I loved to watch her listening, intelligent eyes as she considered the unfamiliar foreign words, and her lips framing answers that were to the point. My thoughts flowed away to the Lay River Farm where I was eager to take her and to have her in the country upon land which was ours. Isla Dorn, as though aware of my wishes, told of "Lang's Farm," of its history, of its inhabitants, and of his gladness that we were to live there. He described my *tanrydoon* at Dorn Island (about which I had written her), and explained that she shared it with me. It also gave us, he said, a place to stop at The City or Doring Town. He spoke of us as though already married and her eyes became intent and bright. No one could have made her welcome more tactfully and graciously.

The meal ended and we returned to the anteroom, all except Lord Dorn. Gladys sat on the plain wooden bench next to Faina. Her knees were crossed and the upper leg hung straight down over the lower one, both hidden in the soft folds of her dress, so that only her pretty ankles were revealed. Her feet were proud and arched in the satin slippers. Behind her were bare stone walls. At her other side was Dorna the elder, with eyes that studied her covertly, dressed in a brown jacket, tan shirt, and short skirt that covered her knees. Her legs in brown woolen stockings were sturdy and muscular, and on her feet were sandals. Yet plainly as she was dressed, she was harmonious in every detail of costume and person.

With a chill of doubt I wondered whether Islandia would prove to be what Gladys wished. There was a look of romance in her thoughtful brown eyes. Until recently she had lived a life of many pleasures and excitements, of travel, theaters, and an interesting if shifting society. Her dress was not that of a woman who preferred plain things. It was costly, stylish, striking . . . What would she do with only plain colors? Would the artist in her rise to them as it did in so many Islandian women . . . ? And except for visits to her cousins she knew little of the country where all her life would be led. Would its silence be as oppressive to her as it had been at first to me?

Would she find durable satisfactions in a life of much physical work and exercise, much solitude, and long simple days . . . ?

What had I done in bringing her so far . . . ? She was here, she had miraculously come—a New Yorker, an American, with a gallant faith and an intelligent courage. She had come to me; and who was I to give her what she wanted? If I were her all she would find me insufficient. She must have something for herself, which I at most could show her . . . She was pitiful, for she had nowhere else to go, no one but plain John Lang, intent upon being Islandian.

Yet she truly needed me for what I was; and seeing her with Faina, Dorn, Nekka, and the others, dear but strange, I needed her as I had never needed anything—her of my own race and kind, to whom I could come close as I never could with them . . . The wisdom of Stellina had suddenly a startling significance. She had understood my needs. The barriers between me and Islandians were double, those of my civilization and those due to their long training in a different way of life. The first I had partly crossed with several of them but the second never could be bridged. With Gladys the only barriers were those of our civilization. The Islandian way of life furnished a means to break them down. Then truly she and I could understand each other and be *alia*-sharing lovers all our days; but there was a long way to go, for we were strangers and we were romantic, brought up to believe in impossible unities and perfections. The singing beauty of senses vibrating in unison must not blind us to the nature of the roads we must follow, alone but parallel, our oneness in our fruits but not in ourselves.

She looked across to me sitting upon the other bench and smiled shyly but intimately. Then her eyelids covered her eyes and she turned her face to the fire, and I remembered that she and I were yet to be married and that the time was set for this evening. What she was thinking was impossible to know.

I watched her for a little while and desire quickened and was strong and peaceful because she was in every way, in every part and as a whole, what I wanted—so perfect, so dear, so promising, that the happiness in my senses and my longing were equal. Yet she had only just arrived, she had been ill and under a strain; and all was new and strange to her including myself. She might be wishing to give herself and to have me; she might not; or she might know no more than that she was willing to do whatever I wanted, preferring herself to be led . . . This evening we would have the ceremony of marriage, for to that she had agreed. Afterwards I would ask her to lie with me. She could say "no" if she wished. Thus it must always be.

With quickening heart I crossed to where she was sitting and found a place between her and Dorna the elder, but because everyone looked up at my movement and watched us I delayed speaking. Then Dorn asked Parnal a question that drew the attention of his cousin and of the others, and Gladys and I had a moment of privacy. Her nearness like strong wine was breath-taking, her desirableness definite. I turned to her and found her dark eyes waiting, deep, gentle.

"Let us go to Lord Dorn," I said in English, "and he will marry us."

Her face became grave. She looked at her hands.

"I have a white dress I'd like to wear," she said, and suddenly I remembered. . . .

"Gladys, I have no ring. I never thought of it! They aren't worn here, but if you want one you must have it."

"I do," she answered slowly.

"Shall we wait till I can provide for a ring?"

She lifted her head and studied my face.

"You don't want to wait, do you?"

My impulse was to try to discover her wishes and to defer to them, but she had asked for my own.

"No," I answered.

"Then I don't want to wait either, but I should like a ring sometime."

"You shall have one."

"May I change to my white dress?"

"Oh yes!" I said. "And wouldn't you like to have Nekka come with you and help you dress?"

She looked at Nekka and at Dorn and then her eyes came back to me.

"I think so," she said.

"Now, Gladys?"

"Yes, John."

Her eyes met mine and we rose together. She went to Nekka and spoke to her. I followed them into the hall.

"Come to the Tower room when you are ready," I said. They departed, and I returned for Dorn. We went out of the room and to his great-uncle. The rest did not know what was happening.

None of the traditional things necessary to a wedding in the United States was to be had. I feared that she would miss them, blamed myself for my failure to provide for them. Not only was there no ring but there was no wedding cake, nothing. Dorn would be my best man, Hytha Nekka her maid of honor.

We placed logs on the central hearth so that the fire would be blazing brightly when she came. The bark flamed and crackled. Dark smoke went up the hoodlike chimney in wreaths and coils. Ruddy light leaped on the circular walls, toward which the corner pillars cast four radiating shadows.

"Dorn," I said, "I ought to give Gladys a ring. I did not think of it until a moment ago. And I have no flowers."

"She shall have flowers," he answered.

"They must be white ones."

"There are asters in the garden. But as to a ring—"

"A ring?" asked Lord Dorn, who had come to us.

"A ring, a finger band," Dorn said. "You have seen them on the hands of foreigners. They reveal the fact that a woman is married. John thinks that Gladys wants a ring, and he forgot."

"The only rings we have that would fit a finger are those on the armor of Dorn XVII."

Him I remembered as the admiral who defied the foreign Portuguese on Doring Quay and did not quail before firearms which he had neither seen nor heard of before.

"They are of iron," he added.

"She wants a ring now," I said.

With a lantern Dorn went out into the night to gather white asters and his great-uncle entered the armory where weapons and coats of mail of his ancestors were still kept, while I waited in the Tower room lest Gladys find no one there.

They returned before she came. The asters, like single chrysanthemums, were white, with a red flush at the base of the petals, moist leaves, and the clean aromatic odor of wild flowers; the ring, taken from the armor by breaking those linked with it, was grooved with wear in three places. Lord Dorn brought a rough cloth and gave both to me. I began to polish the ring, seated with Dorn before the fire.

Gladys entered, followed by Nekka, and her coming was sudden light and freshness in the room. Her eyes were serious and wondering. Her dress, of white silk, was simple and graceful.

We rose and I went to her with the flowers. She smiled with a quick grateful look in her eyes, but her lips trembled.

"I have a ring," I said, showing it to her. "It is of iron but from the coat of mail of Dorn XVII."

"The one who drove out the Portuguese?"

"Yes, and the one who was afraid of nothing."

"I shall love my ring," she said.

Lord Dorn was standing by the hearth. We went to him and stopped before him. Dorn and Nekka were a little behind us.

"Lang," he said in Islandian, "have you *ania* for Gladys?"

"Yes."

"Gladys, have you *ania* for Johnlang?"

Her eyes were fixed upon his face lest she fail to understand.

"Yes," she answered in a clear voice, adding in English, "I love him."

She turned her head, her eyes bright.

"Will you live with me at the Lay River Farm, Gladys?" I asked.

"Yes!" she cried.

I took her hand and slipped the ring on her finger.

"We are married," I said.

Her face was radiant with a light that dazed me. I kissed her, and her lips, soft under mine, responded eagerly.

"Is that all there is?" she asked wonderingly.

"What more can there be?"

She looked at Lord Dorn who smiled. Dorn came up to her, and held out his hand which she took.

"It is all according to our customs," he said. "You and John are married as we marry."

Her eyes thanked him with a flash of reassurance which we had not given her.

"We are glad that you two are to live together upon a farm which once was ours," said Lord Dorn. "We know that you will carry it on."

"I know nothing of farming," she answered, and she looked from him to me as though ashamed.

"There is no need," he said, and I held her arm.

"We will drink the health of you and John," Dorn said suddenly, and he went to a cabinet against the wall. I led Gladys to a bench facing the fire. She sat down, clutching her flowers, and I took my place at her side.

Lord Dorn watched us, his face troubled, seeking the proper word.

Dorn brought the ruddy liquor and filled four glasses, which he offered to us.

"The health of Gladys and John," he said. "May they be very happy." He repeated the same words in Islandian with a glance at his great-uncle, and raised his glass.

"Gladys," said the latter, doing as Dorn had done, "you will be happy here. We are glad that you have come among us. We love you already and we are your friends as well as John's. Many will love you."

She made a little bow and lifted her glass.

"You are all very kind," she answered in Islandian. "I don't know why I am . . ." but she could not think of the word for "crying." With a gesture she sipped from her glass, her hand shaking.

"We will leave you," said Lord Dorn.

"Good night to you both," Dorn added.

When they had gone from the room I took the glass from her and embraced her.

"Gladys, we love each other. We are going to be happy. I know we will be happy."

"It is not that. It is you."

She wept like a child and I held her against me, kissing her wet cheek.

"What of me?" I asked. "Have no fears for me."

"I keep thinking you need someone very different from me."

"I need only you. It is what you are that I love. We will go to the farm soon. You will find peace there, your own place."

"Whenever you say."

"You haven't seen it. You will like it."

"I want to see it. I want to go."

"We will ride. You have riding clothes, haven't you?"

"Oh yes."

"We could start tomorrow noon and spend the night at Doring Town, your trunks and things coming by boat. You will be happy there. We are in the same position, you and I. The place runs itself. What we can do we must find for ourselves together . . . And there is a room which can be your studio. . . ."

"I shall be happy," she said.

"And so will I. We are together now. That is enough."

She was quieter. Silence fell upon us. We watched the leaping flames, our hands fast together.

"This is a strange, fascinating room," she said at last.

"It is the heart of that Islandia which seeks to remain whole and unchanged."

"I am glad to have been married here . . . and I do like my Dorn ring."

She looked at the iron band upon her finger, and I at her, living, desirable.

"Will you come with me?" I said. "Will you sleep with me tonight?"

"If you want me?"

"I want you. Today has not been too hard?"

"No," she said with a little shake of her head.

"Will you come to my room?"

"If you wish."

"There is an open fire there. And it is always mine and now ours in this house."

We went through the chilly empty corridors of stone to her room. There we gathered what she needed and brought it to mine.

I lit the fire on the hearth and we sat down on the rug before it. Behind us the room was dark except where the firelight touched bright things, the copper pitcher in which she had placed her asters, the dark polished woodwork of the wardrobe. She gazed at the flames which brightened her face and made ruddy the white of her dress.

"Are there open fires at our farm?" she asked.

"They are the only way of heating the house," I said.

"Will it be cold?"

"Cold and still and clear, but without much snow."

"You said I should have a studio?" ·

"Yes, with a south window which is like a north window in the United States."

"There will be time to paint?"

"All you wish."

"Tell me about the farm," she said, holding out her hand. I de-

scribed the land, the house, the room I had prepared for her, seeing
it all as I spoke. . . .

"Kiss me," she said, and she held up her lips. "We will be happy
there."

The gently burning fire hissed and purred softly and busily. The
odor of burning bark mingled with that of the asters, moist and aromatic. I kissed her and looked upon her face and kissed her again.

"I need you," she said, "and you must take care of me. I once felt
quite self-sufficient, but I used it all up coming here. That is why I
wept this evening."

"I need you too," I answered, "and you and I will make a good
life for ourselves."

"You are always looking ahead, John. I see it in your eyes. I am
content with now."

"I want all my happiness with you at once. I see it as a whole."

"*Ania* and *alia*," she said softly. "I have been thinking about those
things."

The room became darker. Her face was so wonderful, her lips so
sweet, that I did not want to leave her for even a moment.

"Are you glad it is I?" she asked.

"There is no one else."

"Not Dorna? Not that other girl?"

"No," I answered. "You are my natural one."

"We both are Americans still. You don't seem so Islandian after
all. Yet I understand Dorn—or perhaps he understands me. I'm glad
he is our friend. Are there others as nice?"

"Many," I said, "and among them are women whom you will
like."

"I like Nekka already. She will be a friend . . . And she has
promised to help me about my clothes . . . But if we go to the farm
tomorrow, will there be time?"

"We don't have to go tomorrow."

"But you want to!"

"We will decide then."

"If you want to go we will. Clothes can wait."

I looked down into her tired, excited eyes. The fire was low, the
air growing cold.

"Let's go to bed," I said.

She drew slow deep breaths and tried to speak. I guessed her

905

thoughts which were my own. Strangers in this land we needed a time of adjustment and settlement. We would not have a child at once . . . Nekka had spoken to her.

Though we were shy with our eyes, nothing was strange to us. We prepared for bed as though we had known each other for a long time.

We lay in the dark, close together. Then for a moment her body was like that of another woman, the memory of whom was confused with the present. I held her and kissed her, wishing to be aware only of her.

Night deepened. A breath of cool air through the open window brought the smell of the sea and of salt hay. The Marsh was around us, eastward lay the plains of Lower Doring, and beyond them rose the high mountains, which she had not seen. To the north was our farm, clear to my eyes in all its details. The room where we lay was hers and mine for generations to come.

I held her closely, my hands around her and upon her, and knew the reality of her, the shape of her, her sweet odor, all that was Gladys. The house of the Dorns, the room, the bed, we two embraced, swam in the darkness. We were alone and there was nothing else in the world. We had wakened from the bad dream of anxious waiting— wakened in darkness to the perfection of each other.

Happiness pierced our hearts; we could not speak.

We desired, and came together. It was an incident and the whole of love. We gave ourselves, each to the other. We suffered complete change, touching the depths, knew exquisite pain, perfect release. We were equals and lovers. . . .

She lay very still, her weeping, her trembling over. Her arms that had clung tightly relaxed and became heavy. She quivered and slept. My being was like a dark river flowing on in the night. Images of the Lay River Farm flickered in the darkness, bright and promising. I held her lightly lest I wake her . . . There was tomorrow, the questions of her clothes, of moving her belongings, of horses to carry us—problems that did not matter. I was sinking down, conscious still of her inert warm nearness, loving her . . . Then sleep became profound and time passed.

The room was full of clean fresh air, a low sun rising in the east. We woke at the same time, not surprised for long to find ourselves together, but new each to the other. Still half-asleep we turned and embraced. . . .

I rose to make up the fire, for the room was cold. Gladys put on her red slippers and red and blue dressing gown and went to the window, her braided hair loose about her head and upon her back.

"I see mountains!" she cried. "John, it is a wonderful day!"

When the flames had begun to spread along the logs I went to her and put my arm around her. She leaned back against me. Desire, satisfied, made no demands but treasured her, giver of strength and peacefulness, curer of discords in body and spirit. All was right, and satisfaction was as tangible and real as pleasure itself.

The clear air brought the mountains near. They were a dark-blue rampart with gleams of rose-white on their irregular broken summits. The marsh and the plain were continuous, from the meadows at our feet, past the willows, to the far foothills, a sea of green and blue and hazy lavender. . . .

She turned and kissed me.

"I shall love it!" she cried . . . Then she frowned and took my face between her hands. "If only I can make you happy!"

"Be just what you are," I said. "Happiness will follow."

"Oh, I want to be better, to be more!"

"Don't try to be anything different."

Her eyes studied mine for a few moments.

"What are you thinking?" she asked.

"I was getting ready to think about today, but was in no hurry."

"You mean whether we go to the farm today or not?"

"Yes," I said, "but your hands are cold. Go back to bed until the room is warm."

She obeyed.

"What time is it?" she asked. "I forgot to wind my watch."

"I don't know."

"Where is your watch so I can set mine?"

"At the farm. I never use it."

"How do you know when to do things?"

"I guess . . . I know that we have plenty of time to dress before breakfast."

"When is breakfast?"

"I don't know what you would call the hour."

She shook her head.

907

"I have lots to learn, my Islandian! Oh, John, I do love you . . ."
I went to her and kissed her. After a little while thoughts quickened
in her eyes again.

"What shall I wear?" she asked. "I dread getting dressed. My
clothes are so different from anyone else's. What will people think
of me on the way to the farm?"

"No one will stare at you or bother you. I found that out when I
went about in European clothes."

She pondered.

"Could I get Islandian clothes at the farm? I can sew a little and
make my own, but I should need help."

"We can ask Nekka's advice."

"You want to go today, don't you?"

I thought before replying, for she had asked this question several
times and might be hoping for a negative answer. Yet I knew that if
I asked what she preferred, she would toss the ball of decision back
to me.

"Yes," I said, and I slid my arm beneath her, kissed her, and
looked into her eyes. "I want to go to our farm today. I want to be
with you on the place that is ours, I want you to see it, and I want to
possess you there, and our life together to begin."

Her eyelids dropped.

"We will go," she answered. "My clothes don't matter . . .
Don't you feel that our life together has begun?"

"Not wholly."

"I do. I am wholly yours, though. . . ."

She was silent.

"Though what, Gladys?" I prompted.

"I wonder if I am really married. You said we were. Lord Dorn
did not."

"Did something seem left out?"

"A little, but Dorn said it was according to the custom here."

"It is. All that is needed is for two people to announce their love
for each other and their intention to live together. We did that."

"Yes," she said. "Anyway I don't care. I am happy. I have
you . . . But the farm seems to be part of it in your mind."

Her eyes looked up into mine.

"The farm for you and me. You come first," I answered.

"I think I understand," she said.

"Never feel that you are secondary," I cried, "but to me it is all one thing."

"Don't be too Islandian," she pleaded gently, "or I won't know where I am. I love you. I've come to you, and I have given all of myself." She put her arms around my neck and trembled, but before I could speak her voice went on, "We will go to the farm today."

"It is yours as much as mine when you come to share it with me," I said. "I love you, Gladys—so much that I want the perfect thing, a place for us as well as you."

"It is all right," she whispered, "quite all right, John."

"And you are not too tired to ride?"

"Oh no. I slept well." She laughed lightly. "I feel up to anything."

"And this matter of clothes?"

"I don't care."

"We will ask Nekka's advice."

"All right. I want to do what you want."

I studied her face, wondering whether or not she were making too great a sacrifice.

"For the present," I said, "let us make decisions this way: I will propose what we shall do. You will know that whatever I propose can be changed. When what I propose is not what you want, you will say so. Promise me that."

In turn she watched my face, and after a while she nodded her head.

"That suits me . . . Mother said marriage was one long series of mutual concessions and adjustments. This is adjustment number one."

"We love each other," I said, "and therefore each wants to defer to the other. We must avoid the impasse of Unmeeting Wishes, which can be as bad as disagreeing." And this I explained as it had been explained to me.

"My first lesson in being Islandian!" she said at the end. "But I do love to do what you want."

"And I love to have you."

"I'll develop wants of my own—no fear! But for the present—"

"For the present you are mine."

She kissed me.

38

Home-Coming

GLADYS WORE the fourth dress in which she had appeared—a walking costume of brown tweed with shirtwaist and coat. Except for the length of the skirt and the snug fit of the coat at the waist it was not dissimilar to one type of Islandian costume. Having breakfasted, being late and therefore alone, we found Nekka with her baby on the rug in the sun on the east side of the house. With her we discussed the question of clothes and her advice was to spend a day or two in Doring Town and to obtain them there. We therefore decided to leave the Island at noon.

Leaving the two women together talking over details in the slow but apparently understanding manner in which they conversed, I went to make arrangements for our departure and for sending Gladys's belongings to the farm by water. The day was clear and warm with a light wind, more north than west, and I was impatient to be on the way to our own place.

Noon came. Gladys had spent the morning with Nekka, and came down from her room in a fifth costume. Except that she was vivid and lovely, she looked like a picture of "correct riding costume for ladies" come alive. She wore whipcord riding breeches, high cylindrical leather boots, a long brown coat with flaring skirts, a white shirtwaist with high piqué stock, and a brown felt hat. She was stylish and dashing, and everyone looked at her twice.

She was to ride a horse of the same breed as Fak and I the one lent me by the farmer at Fannar Bay. The clothes she needed for the journey were packed in a saddlebag and the rest of her belongings were leaving by boat as soon as the wind rose.

All of the household gathered at the door to say good-bye to us. There was a time of waiting until the lunch we were to take was brought. She was talking to Dorn, looking down and then up into his eyes, her cheeks bright with the long dimples of her smile, absorbed, happy-seeming, eager. I was glad of the liking that seemed to exist between them.

Nekka's eyes were upon Gladys's dress. I went to her to thank her for what she had done. Her face was a little troubled.

"I think Gladysa dreads going to the Lay River Farm," she finally said. "We had a long talk this morning."

"What does she fear?" I asked with a chill of dismay.

"She is hard for me to understand, but of course I know well the kind of life you will lead; and even though I have had moments of rebellion, it is a natural life for me; but she has been accustomed to ways of living that are apparently very different."

"I know it," I said.

"I don't want to worry you," continued Nekka earnestly, "but she is used to having a great many things happen every day. On a farm there can be as much, but one has to seek for it . . . Her mind jumps from thing to thing . . . I am thinking of you and of her too. I am afraid she will find it hard to quiet down to the life she will lead . . . She has traveled so much, and like all you foreigners she has been exposed to many shifting and changing interests every day."

"Perhaps her mind jumps because all is new to her. Remember she has had much to think about lately and is tired . . . Have you any suggestions, Nekka?"

"I would make life gay and various for her."

"Thank you," I said.

"It is a question of adapting oneself. *You* have learned . . . She will, I am sure. You both will be happy, I know."

She smiled but her face was not so confident as her words.

Dorn was helping Gladys to mount. I climbed upon my own horse and told her that I was ready. Good-byes were called. I rode on and she followed.

Looking back, I saw her with body half turned toward the diminishing group on the steps of the house, graceful and apparently at ease in the saddle.

Drawing my horse to the side of the road I waited until she was abreast of me. She came on, smiling.

"We are on the way at last," she said.

"I am glad of that!"

"So am I! They are nice, and I would have liked to be with them longer and to know them better, but I want more to be alone with you . . . Oh, John!"

She made a gesture of despair over the inadequacy of words.

The horses were fresh and restive. We let them run. She rode far better than I did when I came to Islandia. Nekka's words lost significance.

We came to Fisherman's Harbor and to the ferry just beyond. The boat was on our side of the creek and we went on board. She remained in the saddle. I tied her horse and mine and heaved on the rope with a strong pull to start us.

She began to laugh.

"I have never seen you do anything violent before! This is fun!"

I wondered if I should always refrain from violence toward her. . . .

The boat moved quietly over the water toward the landing on the opposite shore, the sheaves whirling and tossing water as the wet rope passed through them. On her horse, leaning forward to quiet him, she looked here, there, over the flat plain of marsh to the little cluster of the town of Earne, back at the Island, now and again at me, swaying on the rope. She was having many new thoughts and impressions which I wished to know and share, but I feared too close an interest in what she was feeling. I would take the journey as a matter of course, ready to talk if she wished but not explaining anything she could see for herself. What we experienced together was better talked about afterwards, not at the time.

The boat jarred against the landing and stopped. I made the knot that held the boat firmly but could be pulled out by a tug on the rope on the shore we had left.

I looked up at Gladys outlined against the blue vault of the sky, watching me with a smile of amusement which became gentle and friendly, when she met my eyes.

We rode on to the next ferry only a few hundred yards away and then out upon a wide table of marshland, where the sky overhead was a vast blue dome and objects on the horizon low and little. And I let Gladys see with her own eyes my happiness in being with her and in perceiving with senses quickened by her presence with the certain future before us full of richness.

We reached the last ferry across to the town of Earne, and signaled to the ferryman. Tying the horses we sat down on the dock to wait his coming, a gentle wind rippling the water, the sun warm on our backs.

She looked across at the town with its harbor and masts of ships, its walls and clustered roofs of houses.

"That is Earne, isn't it?" she asked.

"Yes, Gladys."

"I have studied maps. Doring is over there?" She waved her hand to the north.

"We can see it," I said pointing.

She came close and looked along my arm, and I pointed out to her the town, which was like a low couchant creature in the far distance with miles of flat dark-green plain between.

The ferry boat with vigorous rhythmic oars was coming over the water bringing others who were journeying into the Marsh as we were leaving it. One of these came up to us and named himself.

"Mart!" he said.

"Lang!" I answered, and turned to Gladys adding in English, "Say your name to him." She hesitated, but as he faced her she came out with it bravely:

"Gladysa."

"We heard that you were coming to Lang," he said pleasantly. "Marta at Dorn Island is my cousin. We are glad that you are here, Gladysa."

The curiosity in his eyes as to her costume was the merest flicker, no more than was the due of any woman who was lovely and well-dressed.

"I came yesterday," she said. "I know Marta . . . Now we are on our way to our farm."

"You will have fewer troubles there than in the Marsh," he answered. "There is more rain for one thing, fewer gales for another . . . We hope to see you sometime. Our house was his and now yours too."

"I'd love to come," she answered and glanced at me.

"Our house on the Lay River is yours," I said.

The ferryman was ready for us, and saying good-bye to Mart we led the horses on board, and having tied them went into the bow.

"Mart was nice," she said. "Are they all like that?"

"All are as polite."

"Did I behave properly?"

"Perfectly!"

"I did not know what name to give. I am not Miss Hunter. He would not understand 'Mrs. Lang.' And you said 'Gladys' sounded strange to them."

"They will think of you as Gladysa."

"Why shouldn't that be my Islandian name?"

"Do you like it?"

"I never liked my name, but it will do."

"You could be Huntera."

"I prefer to be Gladysa . . . It was odd to be called by your first name by a stranger . . . Why aren't you 'John'?"

"I became Lang at the beginning. It is already an Islandian name."

"Did you notice that he did not stare at my clothes?"

"Yes, but why should he?"

"But they are so different!"

"He takes you as you are. They are your affair to him."

"He seemed a gentleman."

"As to your clothes," I began, "perhaps you don't quite understand these people. Your dresses are becoming to you and fine in themselves. You have too good taste to wear anything wrong. Everyone sees that at once. Fashions don't matter."

"Still, when I see how free Nekka is in her clothes and her short skirts, I want dresses like hers. I have a little money left."

"And I have credit still with our agent at Thane and will have more when we have finished the harvest . . . We can afford new clothes for you."

"We will go shopping tomorrow! It will be fun!"

After landing at the quay we rode through the town and left it for the country with a suddenness characteristic of Islandia.

The horses, free of restraint, broke into a canter and we let them run as long as they wished. Mine outdistanced hers and when he was tired I drew him to a walk. She came up smiling and flushed.

"I felt quite alone for a while," she said.

"Our horses aren't matched."

"Dorn warned me . . . This one is mine. He gave it to me. He said it was a wedding present, that it would go well with your horse, Fak . . . May I keep it?"

"Why, of course!"

"I didn't know and was a little troubled. I ought to have told you before, but—"

"Does it make you uncomfortable to accept his gift?"

"Yes, if you have the slightest feeling—"

"Feeling of what—that he has some claim on you?"

"Of course he has none!"

"I know that in the European and American world it is unconventional for a man to make an expensive present to a girl. She feels placed under an awkward obligation. Perhaps there are relics of those feelings in you and me. Dorn may know of them as a fact, but they are not real to him . . . I know what he was thinking—that you and I would want to travel and ride together, and that there was no horse equal to Fak on the Lay River Farm. It may have been a sudden thought and impulse . . . Keep the horse, Gladys."

She turned to me bright eyes.

"Can I keep him? I want to."

"Yes," I answered, and said no more; but sometime I would try to persuade her that she was not so far under my domination as to make either my consent necessary or a request for it a courtesy.

"We shall be much better mounted," I continued. "We will make trips together."

"I hoped we could."

"Dorn thought of that."

"He is a darling! He gave me advice which he meant to be helpful . . . I have talked to him more than I have to you. I wish now I had not said quite so much. . . ."

"What did he advise?"

She looked at me with doubt, as though wondering whether she would not betray a confidence, and I did not ask her again.

To the left was the infinite flatness of the Marsh, to the right, the plain covered with trees and fields and pastures. Ducks and geese were gathering in the creeks ready to fly north. Sometimes a wedge of them cut through the sky. At intervals, as the road turned away from the groves and farm hedges and lay upon meadows or upon the marsh itself, the rampart of the mountains was visible to the east and ahead lay Doring Town slowly enlarging.

Many of my later Islandian journeys had been made alone. Now I had a companion. Conversation linked our minds and in the close contact that resulted there was something that became confusing and feverish after a time. Nekka had said her mind jumped from thing to thing. Was I finding Gladys to be what Islandians had found me, one who quivered with shifting feelings too active in the mind? What I wished now was silence in her company and to feel the flow of loveliness in water, land, and sky which her presence so greatly brightened. I wanted to be quiet with her beauty. I feared that if I looked her way she would wish to talk again, but equally I did not want her to feel that I was remote.

After a little while, therefore, when we came to a fresh water stream from the mountains, I suggested that we stop. We rode the horses into the stream and let them drink, then dismounted, tied them, and went ourselves to the westward edge of the road and sat down under low willows on their fallen yellow leaves.

She took off her hat. Her forehead was moist, her hair matted. She was solid, graceful, a little tired. Looking in her face, I saw it anew, not pretty at that moment but peaceful with some unknown and absorbing thought.

"Is all well with you?" I asked.

"Oh yes!" she answered without hesitation.

"No dreads, no worries?"

"Not a single one!"

"I love you, Gladys."

I laid my hand on hers and she smiled. The back of her hand was smooth and warm. Sitting motionless at rest, contentment quieting her face, she was desirable. I wanted her suddenly . . . and knew that there would come many moments like this when the natural thing was to love her and possess her, and yet time and place made it impossible. I remembered the fable of "The Perfect Life."

"I want you," I said.

She caught her breath with instant response, stirred, and her eyelids covered her eyes.

"It can't be here," I said.

She shook her head and looked at me with wide eyes.

We lunched and then I lay back, my arms behind my head, and looked up into the sparse yellow leaves of the willow against the sky.

"Let's both rest," I said, remembering the beach at Nantucket where she had at last relaxed and slept. Would she do so now . . . ? But she sat erect in her rather stiff costume, her starched stock snug around the soft pillar of her neck, her shoulders a little rounded, her eyes downcast.

"You make Islandia ten times more beautiful," I said. "Your presence is like a polish that puts a shine on everything."

She looked at me with a quick smile and then down again.

"I think you do love me," she said.

"I love you."

She shook her head in doubt.

"If only I can make you happy!"

"If only you will be happy yourself, Gladys. Worry about that, not about me."

"It is what Dorn said. His advice seemed to me a plea to be selfish."

"Tell me," I said. "We will talk about these things and learn together."

"Sometimes it seems so simple, but at others . . . I thought a great deal on the way here and was amazed at my presumption in coming to you! I told Dorn about my feelings. I had to talk to someone. I told him I was afraid I could not make you happy, that this was my one fear and doubt, the one thing I cared for. I said that I realized that you already had a life with which you were contented and which engrossed you, but one about which I knew nothing and feared I could not fit. He said that I must not worry about making you happy, but must first of all consider myself and take care of my own growth. He told me how I could be happy on our farm. He said I must not be afraid of silence or of solitude, that I must learn to let thinking drop and learn to live in what I was seeing, hearing, and feeling, for long periods of time. He told me to beware of trying to solve my problems solely by thinking! He said you were not a 'molding man' and that he was sure you were aware that I was only twenty and would change and grow and that you loved me as a growing creature. He said I was the goose that laid the golden eggs of happiness for you, and that if I wanted to be a good layer I must think first of my health and of myself and keep my peace of mind. He warned me not to think about laying eggs all the time or else I would worry myself into barrenness . . . He teased me, of course . . . I kept asking myself if he were really thinking of your happiness, as I was, or of mine. He was thinking of mine, I am sure."

"He was thinking of us both."

"He said you were also my goose . . . and we got into an argument as to whether male geese laid eggs. He said they did, and that the concern of both of us was to be productive healthy geese, in which case happiness would take care of itself!"

"Doesn't it seem good advice?" I asked.

"I don't know. If I followed it . . . I would feel I was robbed of something."

"Of what, Gladys?"

"I want to be everything to you," she cried passionately. "You see I love you so much!"

I was deeply moved and at the same time felt a sense of strain. . . .

"We will work together on the farm," I said. "We will find a way to use the force of love that is in us."

"But I don't know anything about farming!"

"That is a very small part of it—and neither do I!"

I sat up and took her hand which lay limp in her lap and which was warm from the riding glove in which it had been. The touch of her flesh changed the color of all things as when a dark cloud moves off the sun and floods the world with subduing light and heat . . .

"This is the moment for us to be lovers," I said. Her eyes looked into mine with surrender and alarm . . . "But we can't . . . We had better continue our journey."

We rode on, and the sun leaned over the Marsh converting its levels into a golden, hazy plain. After an hour we came to dark quiet woods. I did not tell her what lay beyond them, and when we emerged upon the river bank, Doring Town, standing above the blue water in the long shadows of late afternoon, with its many tinted houses and roofs, its gardens, walls and trees, and rocky shores, struck suddenly upon her unexpecting eyes. While we waited for the ferry I had my pleasure in seeing her face, glowing in the flood of low sunlight, startled and happy, all the lovelier and dearer because of lines of fatigue under her clear eyes.

She came to me, removed her gauntlet, and took my hand.

"It is just as you described it in your letters," she said. "I have in my mind pictures of all the places you mentioned."

She looked in my eyes.

"You ought to write, John," she continued. "You can. Your talent is too good to lose."

But the thought of writing was an arid and withering one at that moment.

"You ought to paint," I answered.

"I am going to try, my dear!"

"We both may need something of that sort," I said with a sense of foreboding that seemed causeless.

"Why 'need'?" she asked. "Because we aren't really farmers? I have wondered about you as a farmer."

"We aren't going home to be farmers," I answered.

"But it is a farm, isn't it?"

"Not wholly."

"What is it then?"

"It is my *alia*, Gladys, and it will be yours also."

"I wish there were a good dictionary of Islandian words in English!" she exclaimed.

"One has to evolve one's own definitions of things—when definitions are needed." Her hand was in mine. I wanted to squeeze her fingers till they hurt her.

"Someone is coming," she said in a quick voice, withdrawing her hand. . . . "I came to Islandia expecting to be a farmer's wife. Don't worry about that."

"You have come to live with me," I answered, "rather than to be anything."

"If we don't like it, we can try something else. We don't have to remain farmers."

My forehead was chilly with a sense of strain.

Other riders were gathering on the stone quay. After those from the town had landed we all went on board. Gladys stood close to me near the heads of our two horses.

"You are right," she said. "People don't stare at me. But did you notice that woman when she got off her horse? Her dress went above her knees!"

"Women here don't mind having their knees seen."

"They seem to like it!"

"They don't think about it one way or the other, any more than American women do about their hands."

"Knees aren't hands!"

Again came the sense of strain.

"You will become accustomed to knees," I said.

"I? I was not thinking of that."

"If you were thinking of the men here, they find no more impropriety in knees than in hands."

"I wonder if I ever can—"

"You let me see your knees."

"But I am yours now," she said gently, and I could argue no longer.

"They are good knees, narrow and in proportion," I said.

"Doesn't it make a woman more valuable to know that—her knees are yours only?"

"What she is and what she feels make her value."

"And you would not mind?"

"Gladys, I would not mind anything that was natural to you, even though it were the showing of all of yourself."

"Do you really mean that?"

"I do," I said, "if the feeling behind what you did was a true Gladys-feeling."

She uttered an ambiguous sigh of disagreement and surprise.

"I feel that I am yours," she said, "but sometimes you seem to push me away."

"No—I want you to come to me of yourself."

"I suppose that is Islandian!"

My mind wandered. We were approaching Doring Town.

"Over there is the Doring Palace where we are to stay," I said. She turned from watching me and uttered an exclamation at the high square building above its terraced gardens and rocky, quay-lined harbor, its upper parts in sunlight, the lower shadowed.

"John! It is so beautiful here!" she cried. "It is like nothing I have ever seen!"

Gently I took her arm and at the contact she stirred with a movement of acceptance and yielding.

The high arching bridge above the channel that led to Doring Quay was like Venice, she said. I pointed out the spot where Dorn XVII had confronted the Portuguese, wearing perhaps the very coat of mail from which her ring was taken. We mounted our horses and rode by winding narrow streets to the palace, sometimes ascending flights of low steps; and it reminded her of Clovelly, of Quebec.

The *deneri* in charge of the palace showed us to the room, which I had occupied many times, with a view northeast over the prowlike end of the Island and up the Doring River, the flat, fertile, tree-lined banks of which narrowed in the distance.

Gladys sank into a chair and said with surprise, as though just aware of it, that she was very tired.

"It is all so new and queer," she said, "and I have only been here twenty-four hours!"

There were still two hours or more before supper, which was to be late because Isla Dorn was expected to arrive by boat.

"Aren't you tired too?" she asked. I did not know how to answer, for physically I felt no fatigue but in my head was that sensation of tension which I had known in America.

"No," I answered. "But how tired are you? Is it too much for me to love you?"

"Never," she answered.

So I went to her and she yielded to my arms. I looked long in her eyes and saw weariness in them, worry, and doubts of herself, and fear as of something she could not understand, but also love and wonder. I seemed to see also the confused whirl of her thoughts, and I knew that what she needed was peace and that my happiest task was to give it to her. And yet at the same time, as though there were two I's, I wanted to forget her needs, to handle and kiss her with violence, to possess her angrily.

Split, I was forced to make a choice and chose what seemed best for her. I held her quietly, kissed her not too much, and strove to make my love a restful thing, and little by little the strain passed from her face. It relaxed and was lovely and still. . . . The peace I gave her flowed back to me, as though when her being was calm my desire was calm also. . . .

The room grew darker, but her eyes, looking up into mine, still gleamed. We said little, and that, our love. There were clasped hands, her weight against my arm, kisses now and then—and time moved smoothly like a deep river. . . .

It must end. I lit the fire and at her request all the candles. She wanted a bright light, she said, but gave no reason, and also asked me not to watch her dressing. I sat facing the fire, hearing behind me her footfalls and the sounds of brushing and the rustle of clothes, and wondering why I might not see.

"John," she said. "How am I?"

On her feet were her own low brown shoes, but she wore tan stockings turned over below the knee, a short skirt of darker brown, a long jacket of the same material, a shirt of green linen with wide lapels and green cuffs turned back from her wrists.

"You are an Islandian," I said, and she seemed more natural, more graceful, and better proportioned with her legs revealed.

"The dress and waist are Nekka's. She lent them to me and wanted to give them. The shoes and stockings are mine."

She held back the skirt to see her feet, and then her eyes looked up.

"How do you like me?"

"It becomes you," I said, but I was afraid lest I seem to condemn the clothes of her own selection which she had herself brought. "All the dresses in which I have seen you are becoming and charming."

This was not what she wanted and her eyes questioned.

"Nekka said the color was wrong. She seemed surprised that I was willing to take the dress and waist. . . . Do you think it wrong?"

The cinnamon brown of the jacket and the pale green of the skirt made her hair almost black and her skin very white. Perhaps this was what Nekka meant. . . . But the simplification and naturalness of her figure outweighed these defects.

"I thought you would like to see me as an Islandian," she said, disappointment in her voice. I had waited too long to answer her question. "But of course if it doesn't go—"

"It makes your figure lovely."

"My figure?"

"Yes."

Her cheeks had flushed.

"The color is becoming too," I said, seizing the moment when this was truthful.

"Nekka said the color of the dress I wore this morning was very good. She suggested that I shorten the skirt and wear with it a dark-green waist."

"Don't change the clothes you brought!"

"Do you really like them?"

"Oh, Gladys, I love them and you in them."

"That is a comfort. . . . Would you like me to wear this to supper?"

"Yes, I would."

"Are you perfectly sure? If I look all right to you nothing else matters."

"I am quite sure."

"In spite of my bare knees?"

"Yes, Gladys."

"I want to please you."

"You are lovely in yourself. . . . You do!"

She uttered a faint sigh. Something she wanted had not been said.

So natural was she to Lord Dorn and to the two other men present, his aides or secretaries, that they apparently did not notice her costume, and she seemed to forget her knees also, though once or twice her hand went to the edge of her skirt.

Next morning gray clouds covered the sky with flurries of rain. Doring Town was no longer the sunny Venice of summer, but bleak and windswept. Gladys was unprepared for such weather and borrowed my cloak and hood when we set out for the house of the weaver of whom Nekka had spoken. It was on Becney, and we went by a roundabout way stopping to look at vistas of channels or river, boats, quays, and carven façades, all new and strange to her.

At the weaver's we spent two happy and expensive hours, ordering a hooded cloak, several dresses of wool and linen, and then undergarments. He showed us fabrics that he had on hand, and discovering that Gladys was foreign and not very sure of her "colors," he ventured to advise her and promised to dye new fabrics that would become her.

"I will take into account that you will be darker," he said.

When we started back she asked why he had made that remark.

"Because he thinks that you will live more out of doors."

"I see," she said slowly. "Farmer's wife!"

"Lang's *alia*-sharing lover," I answered in Islandian.

I led her home through Fish Town, its wharves crowded with boats, and by way of the sea wall along which I had towed the *Marsh Duck*, and thence by Stone Island and the bridge under which we had passed the day before.

She seemed happy, holding my arm, eager to see all these things.

"This is really our honeymoon, isn't it?" she said. "And I shall like my new clothes—but things aren't cheap, are they?"

The next day was the one for which I waited and because it would be a long one on the road I suggested a quiet afternoon and early bedgoing. I wished her to be as fresh and unfatigued as possible when we came to the farm. I longed for it as a beginning but dreaded it as a test. If happiness eluded her there I did not know what I should do. Her remark, that if we did not like the farm we need not remain, was ominous in my ears. I saw myself hopelessly drifting without it, of little use to myself and to her, my life too dependent upon what she, a woman, could give me, too little my own to master and make grow.

The quiet privacy of an open fire in our room and rainy weather outdoors satisfied her. She was tired, content to rest upon the bed and to read the books I brought her from the library, wishing me to be near, and now and then to explain an Islandian word. She was ignorant of what I was feeling and seemed to be at peace. I envied her placidity, loved her from a distance, waited upon her with pleasure; but I did not want to be her lover until we were upon our own ground, for no peace would be in it, our minds too far apart. Yet as before her serenity increased my own. The quiet afternoon of reading and desultory talking was a happy one, and just before supper we had a brisk walk in wind and rain.

It was still dark next morning when I woke and knew by the feeling in the air that dawn was near. I rose and lit a candle. She lay inert, still sleeping, folded, rounded, relaxed, her hair scattered over her head so that she seemed faceless. I did not want to waken her from the quiet depths into which her dear and restless spirit had gone. I knew that I loved her, and whether Islandian or not I preferred my love for her to my *alia*; but at the same time I resolved to anchor her firmly to that *alia* and never to abandon it without certainty of defeat.

Leaning over her I touched her shoulder gently and spoke her name in a low voice lest she come back to consciousness through startled dreams. It was some time before her head turned. Through meshes of hair I saw her soft loosened lips, unset by any thoughts. I kissed her, and her arms closed round my neck. She was warm and sweet.

"What time is it?" she said.

"Nearly dawn and time to go."

Her arms did not loosen. I felt myself sinking and let myself go.

We were each other's, nothing else existed, each equally loving, giving, and taking, and our pleasure was pure without thought.

She moved about the room, dressing and packing, dazed and subdued, for she was discovering in herself what she had only surmised was there.

"I did not know I loved you so much," she said, "and I am so happy that we are going to the farm today."

Rain spattered out of the dark into our faces as we led the horses down the slippery steps and inclines to Doring Quay, the wet pavements of which glimmered in the light of scattered street lamps. The early ferry was ready to leave. We went on board, tied the horses, and found shelter in the well at the stern with several other huddled figures. Fearing for me who had no cloak she wrapped mine which she wore as far around both of us as it would go, and we sat close together.

The boat moved away from the wall. A man next to me whose face I could not see said:

"Garton of Vantry, near Sevin."

"Lang," I answered, "the Lay River."

From my other side came her voice naming herself.

"Gladysa."

I squeezed her hand.

"Lang of the Vaba Pass?" he asked.

"I was one of Don's men."

"We envy you and are grateful," he said. "And you are not an Islandian?"

"Now I am. I have my farm from the Dorns."

"You live there?"

"Yes," I answered. "But Gladysa has been in the country not quite three days, and has not seen it yet."

"We welcome you," he said, leaning forward toward her. "The Lay River Farm is fertile and beautiful."

"Thank you," she answered with a little hesitation. "I look forward to seeing our farm."

We had reached the river where the wind was blowing from the northwest. There was a perceptible sea and we heard the uneasy movement of the horses' feet, and I went to look to ours, leaving Gladys in the shelter, and remained at their heads until the waves quieted again. By this time a pale light from the east had spread over the water, and when I returned the shelter was no longer a dark pit. Five persons were there, separate figures, no longer merely darker shadows, but with faces that were still indistinct.

Garton was telling Gladys about Vantry.

When we came to the north bank of the river a subdued daylight had begun. There was no sunrise. The clouds in the east were too dense; yet they were not formless and full of rain but corrugated and hard.

We landed and I paid the ferryman from my dwindling supply of ready money. The completion of the harvest at the farm and the transportation to Thane of roughly one-fifth of it to meet taxes and to establish a credit with the agent there was much more than the gesture of a gentleman-farmer. Unlike most Islandians, Gladys and I had no surplus money stowed away against emergencies. Even though we would neither starve nor be cold without a cent to our names, we would be handicapped in many ways, our travel circumscribed, our clothes ragged and few, no new books to be bought, no replacements or improvements upon the farm.

We mounted our horses, Garton, who was alone, riding with us. Gladys saw for the first time a portion of the National Highway, but she said it looked just like an ordinary country road.

"Nine hundred years old!" I declared.

"The Roman roads in Europe are older," she answered. "This looks quite new and fresh and like home."

"It is home."

"It is going to be. It can't be home until I have seen where I am to live."

The sense of impatience mixed with dread returned a little, but our earlier unison still dwelt within me; a physical reality distilling peace.

We stopped at the Inn at Tory for a second breakfast. The rain had ceased and the wind had changed to the south, breaking up the clouds and uncovering growing patches of blue. Garton, a dark, good-looking man of thirty-five or forty, was still our companion and seemed to have been attracted by Gladys, riding at her side much of the time and telling her many things, some of which I did not hear. I was sure that she did not always understand him, but not sure that he was aware, so well did she uphold her end of the conversation. To see an Islandian taken by her and to see her ability to interest him promised well for her future pleasure, and I gave her every opportunity I could to discover her power by assisting her with a word when she needed it and by being not too much present in their conversation and not too obviously absent.

Ten miles beyond Tory our ways parted, for we left the highway and he continued on. He urged us to come to Vantry and to stop at his father's house. His eyes lingered upon Gladys and then he rode away. We turned into the road that eventually led to the farm by way of Doring Forest.

"Well!" she exclaimed. "What do you think of that?" Amusement, satisfaction, and a little doubt were upon her face. "He really seemed to like to talk to me. Was it because I am so different?"

"Islandians will like you."

"Why do you think so?"

"Your looks—"

"Oh no!"

"Your looks, your sincerity, your intelligence, your directness, and the novelty you are to them."

"The last is the only reason."

"Know yourself, Gladys, and you won't be so modest. You are attractive—"

"I'm not!"

"I am not the only one who has proved it."

"Who else?"

"The man who wanted to marry you several years ago, the man on the steamer, the man who wanted you to remain in Biacra, Dorn, Garton—"

"Not Dorn! He thought of me only as belonging to you."

"Are you sure? I am not. He would not think of you as anyone's."

"I don't agree, and the others—they meant nothing."

"You know you are attractive, Gladys. You know you are valuable and a strong lover."

"Do you want me to be conceited?"

"I want you to know and value your charm, your loveliness, yourself."

"Well, if it pleases you . . ." she sighed.

"Oh," I said, "be pleased with it yourself, my dear."

"You don't want me to be modest about myself?"

"I don't want you to decry yourself."

"I don't! Are you complimenting me elaborately or are you criticizing me?"

"I am trying to set you free."

"Don't I seem free?"

"Not wholly."

"I don't want to be free! I love you. I want to be yours."

"I love you to say that, when it means that you are glad to give yourself to me . . . but you aren't mine nor am I yours."

"I am yours," she said, her voice a little hurt, "or otherwise I would not be here. Isn't being yours properly Islandian?"

"A woman is a man's only so far as she is willing that he should lead her. But otherwise she is her own, very much her own."

"I feel that I am yours. Don't tell me I am not."

"I won't!" I said. "You are mine. I shall lead you and you must obey."

"I did not swear to obey," she answered with a laugh. . . . Her mind went back to Garton, and she told me what he had said to her, which was about himself, the Garton farm, the beauties of his province, and the white wonder of Mount Omoa at the head of the valley. His characterization of himself as "Garton-second-son" amused her, but he had also roused in her a wish to see Vantry and the mountains and valleys of the three northwestern provinces. Then as though making a confession she added that he had said that he was not married.

"One of two brothers often does not marry," I said. She asked me why, and I explained that it was due to an instinct or belief hostile to overcrowding a farm. This seemed to her unfair to those who could not marry.

"They are partly compensated by a greater interest in their nephews and nieces, who are more like their own children than nephews and nieces in the United States."

"That is not all of marriage," she said.

"Such men sometimes have lovers."

She was grave and then looked at me suddenly, a flush on her cheeks. She was thinking of Garton.

"Do you blame them?" I asked.

"Oh no," she said quickly.

I wondered what vague speculations were passing through her mind, warm enough to make her blush.

The road wound in and out around fields, groves and pastures, accommodating itself to the outlines of farms rather than determining them. Having traveled this way but once before, I had to give all my attention, and Gladys realizing the danger of being lost was content to ride behind in silence, her own eyes alert.

It was still morning and we were already halfway to the farm. The broken canopy of clouds had been driven far enough east to reveal the sun. The air was clear and fresh. We would arrive in fine weather resembling that of bright fall days in the United States. Her first impression would be of the farm at its loveliest—late afternoon with trees flaming. I rejoiced, wishing we were there, longing for its beauty and steadying peaceful work—for my own sake and for hers —dreading also lest she be disappointed.

At present she was happy and very pretty, riding now in broken shade, now in sun, smiling whenever her eyes met mine. The road was often like a lane and the horses' feet shuffled through fallen leaves; stone walls or hedges were close with glimpses of fields, stubble lands, and woods.

"It looks like home—or England," she called to me. "John, I am going to love it."

Happiness quickened in my heart.

Doring Forest was full of enchantment, the woods on fire. There we stopped to rest and water the horses and to eat the lunch brought from the palace.

Gladys folded her hands behind her head and lay back upon the cloak, looking up into the tops of the half-bare trees. This was as it should be; time was not pressing.

"I am not really tired," she said.

"The farm is not more than ten miles away, less than two hours."

"So near?" she answered vaguely.

"Sleep," I said. She shook her head from side to side, looking up at me.

"I can't—not here."

"You slept on the beach at Nantucket."

She smiled elusively.

"I was ashamed—but I don't believe I had slept all night. . . . When I saw you I knew I loved you. It was so sudden, so true, so wonderful. I did not want to sleep that night."

Her eyelids fluttered and hid her eyes.

Lying down at her side and taking her hand I felt the sustaining earth, than which one can go no lower and which therefore seems the foundation.

"Did you sleep?"

"Maybe," she answered, following a middle course between consistency and truthfulness. She rose a little stiffly and wearily but with willingness and we mounted the horses and rode on.

The road, not difficult to follow through the edges of the forest, descended into the intricacies of farmlands again. I rode ahead trying to recapture visual memories of turnings and to reconcile what I saw with what I thought ought to be. Whenever I looked back she was following, and there was happiness in riding on, in finding the way, and when turning to see her always there. . . . Where else could she go? Yet her will led her and she smiled when she saw my face.

The air was windless, the sky blue, shadows were lengthening, and the atmosphere was assuming a brilliance through which the grass in the fields green with recent rain, the trunks of trees, twigs against the sky, burning red and yellow leaves quivered with their color intensified. Gladys always following was herself as bright, moving with stillness against these glowing backgrounds.

We were already among farms like our own, gently rolling with no harsh slopes and no wide views, but with constant variety of beauty and richness. It was almost more than my heart could bear.

"Are we near?" she called, her voice tired but cheerful.

"Only a few miles," I answered, but I was not going to tell her until we were there. She must see the farm before she knew it was hers, waking up from her fatigue to know herself at home.

When, however, we had come upon familiar roads I drew up my horse so that we might ride abreast.

"Are you sure of the way now?" she asked.

"Yes, from now on."

"Then we must be really near."

"Not far. . . ."

"John!" she cried. "You are so white! What is the matter?"

"It is only a mile or so."

Her eyes watched me but I could not face them.

"You care a great deal, don't you?" she said in a voice of wondering discovery.

"For you most," I answered.

"My dear," she said, "my doubts don't mean anything."

We were riding along the edge of the Adners' farm, the road little more than a grassy lane between stone walls, gradually descending to the meadows of the hay. I saw with a throb in my heart like sickness the willows more yellow and with fewer leaves than when I had left them, the gray-stemmed, wine color of the beeches, and the roof and upper story of our own house. But her eyes were upon me, and she did not notice these things.

We reached the bridge and the water lay cool in the shadows. I drew in on the rein and let her go ahead. The feet of her horse beat upon the earth of our farm. The whole length of the house was in sight, a little above us, standing alone, the stone columns half in bright sun, and half in dark shadow. The light upon it was golden and still.

The road led on to the stables and barns. I rode my horse upon the grass, she followed, and we came to the front of the house and I stopped.

"Is this . . . ?" she said. I could not speak. Our eyes met, and she smiled a shy smile.

"It is!" she said, "and I shall love it." But she did not look about her. I dropped from my horse, tied him, and went to hers, and held him while she dismounted heavily. She was tired. Her eyes came instantly to me. Tying her horse also, I took her hand.

"Either you care terribly," she said, "or you are worrying about me. Don't do that, John."

Her voice ceased. I put my arm about her and turned her around. She leaned against me without a movement. It was utterly quiet, no other house in sight, nothing but autumn trees, blue sky, grass, the gleam of the river.

For me there was a sudden feeling of peace and eternity.

"I shall love it," she said. "I love you."

"I love you most," I answered and it hurt to say it. Then I took her hand and led her to the door, simple, massive, of oak without paneling, and half sunlit.

She drew a sharp breath and laughed.

"My own house!" she said. "I never had one!"

The hall with its sparse furniture was empty and simple, but the stone floor and stone staircase without a railing were swept clean. We entered the living room on the left with low deep windows on three sides, more furniture, and a few rugs. Over the fireplace the bas-relief of Don's death and my escape had been built into the wall. I led her towards it. . . .

"It looks like you!" she cried in a high voice.

"It is I."

"And that is—Don."

She turned towards me, her eyes wet.

"I don't know why it moves me so. . . . I had forgotten. You told me about it. I didn't expect to see it here. It is good. Awfully simple. . . ."

"I want you to see your room," I said, and I took her hand firmly.

"My room?" she asked, "not ours?"

"Ours if you wish."

"Then it is ours. I want to see it!"

I led her to the stairs and up, the yielded resistance of her hand tightening my fingers and then my heart.

"My trunks have come!" she cried. There they were amidst the simple, dark, Islandian furniture with their many-colored labels of hotels and steamship companies.

She moved about the room observing all that was there.

"Oh John, I have always wanted a simple room . . . and that lovely copper pitcher . . . it looks like a nice bed . . . and the fire irons hand-wrought . . . and plenty of room for my clothes. . . . The mirror!" she laughed. "It is rather small. I don't care."

She looked at her reflection.

"I'm a sight!" she said, and she turned to me. "You look just as tired as I."

"We can rest from now on."

She swung away.

"I wish I were prettier."

"Oh, Gladys!"

Prettiness was irrelevant. She was herself, and her I desired.

"Let me show you the studio—with nothing in it but an easel and a few chairs."

We passed through the door between the two rooms.

"There is more than that!" she cried.

Somewhere Ansel or Stanea had found a rug and a bench. There was a table, new-made, and the fire was ready to be lit.

"A south light," I said.

She sat down on the stool before the easel, and looked with absorbed eyes at the place where a canvas would be.

"Your paints are all here," I suggested.

"I know it. I was thinking of that. I shall paint." Her voice was full of purpose. "That bas-relief was so simply done. It is crude, yet awfully good. It looks like the work of an amateur just as everything of mine does. . . . I am wondering . . ." She looked quickly at me, her face eager and thoughtful.

"Here there aren't the same standards of professional perfection to discourage the amateur," I said, and I thought of the Metropolitan Museum of Art and its evidences of overintense cerebral art.

"What a relief!"

"You can do just what you please for yourself and for friends whose judgments have also not been professionalized."

She brightened with pleasure and amusement. Her face, lovely and young in outline as she looked up at me, with lips soft and red, and with her eyes clear and crisp in color and alive with intelligence, quickened my desire.

"There is another thing to think about," I said. "Painting in oils is unknown in Islandia. You can develop an art and manner of your own. You have all the time you want. You can give the Islandians something valuable which they lack."

Her eyes became fixed and her lips parted a little.

"John, do you think . . . really . . ."

"It is worth considering."

"And you!" she cried. "You have something in you. You can write. Don't be just a farmer."

"I hope not!"

Forces stirred in both of us, separate but shared.

"You make me crazy to begin!" she cried.

She rose and went toward the room which was to be ours, as though to carry out what she had just said. I followed her, and found her standing before the unlit fire.

"I know I shall be happy," she said thoughtfully. "But isn't it quiet?"

My thoughts knew that she was tired and that I was tired also, but beneath them another voice spoke more true than they. This was the time more surely than any other.

"I love you," I said, "and I want you."

She did not move. I watched her unchanged profile and she seemed unknown. The wish became stronger and more right, rising like a tide, bringing a sense of dreaming.

"No one will come?" she asked coolly.

"No one knows that we have come home."

"Could we have a fire? I am a little chilly."

I took the flint and steel from the mantel and kneeled before the hearth.

"I love you to ask me that way. . . . I'll undress," she said.

I had brought up the saddlebags, ridden the horses to the stable, and told Stanea of our arrival. Gladys had dressed again in a costume I had not yet seen, an afternoon frock of dark blue with red and yellow embroidery in wool. We had had a welcome supper of steak, salad, bread, apples, and red wine.

We went to the living room and I lit the fire there, but the room seemed rather bleak. We sat on a bench before the flames and made ourselves comfortable.

The evening wore on. We had little to say, for the spell was still upon us of a meeting in which nothing of either of us remained outside, each giving all and taking all, with pleasure that was laughing happiness in the care of our hearts, and contentment as deep as perfect sleep. . . .

"Tomorrow," she said after a long time, "I must—"

"Let's think of tomorrow tomorrow."

"Kiss me then."

I kissed her and we went to bed and slept peacefully in the stillness of our own house.

39

The Lay River Farm

THE MORNING SUN of a clear day filled the room with fresh white light. I looked at Gladys who did not know that I was also awake. She was lying on her back and her black lashes were lifted from her eyes. She was gazing at the dark rafters of the ceiling, and her face had the rapt look of a child happy in daydreams.

Cool air came through the open window. The world and the house were soundless. Stanea might have come already, but even so we could not hear her through the thick walls and floors.

Seeing me awake Gladys moved into my embrace. She was very happy, she said, speaking as though to reassure me.

"I have been thinking of all the things I can do, John. I suppose you will be going off to work quite early on most mornings."

"The only thing I have in mind now is the delivery of the equivalent in value of one fifth of what we have grown to the agent of Thane," I answered. "Of this, one half or one third will go to pay taxes and the remainder will be sold and yield us cash for what we have to buy. In a few days we shall drive to town with grain, perishable vegetables, apples, cider, and wine."

"Can I go with you?"

"When I say 'we' I include you. I hope you will want to come."

"I shall."

"By that time I shall have Fak again, and you can ride Gran"— the horse Dorn had given her—"and we will lead the one I borrowed. As soon as our goods are delivered we will ride on to Fannar Bay and return him."

"It will be fun. What are you going to do today?"

"Show you the farm and introduce the Ansels and Stanes to you."

A look of diffidence came upon her face.

"What shall I wear?"

"Your brown walking dress or the one Nekka lent you."

"I'll be Islandian," she said.

After breakfast we set out, following the road that led through the little valley where the dependents lived. There we stopped for a short time. We went on up a gentle ascent beyond their houses to a low saddle between the pine-crested ridge and a hill with beeches and oaks on its summit like a pompadour, all the rest being open fields. The road continued to the north and then east again to the Lay River which our lands touched at two places, for the river turned a right angle to the east of us. We reached the northern end of the farm a full mile from the house. Beyond us were the lands of the Rannals, steeper than our own.

We stopped on the bridge.

"The farm is larger than I thought," she said.

"A mile long by nearly half a mile wide. I have not half explored it yet. . . . We will go all over it and really know it, won't we, Gladys? and learn the wild places as well as the cultivated ones."

"I am going to enjoy being out of doors so much. New York. . . ."

We looked at each other and laughed.

"New York!" she cried, "noise, theaters, dirt, crowds, the elevated . . . ! Was I ever really there? I am not the same person at all! You married the New York one; are you going to like the one into which Islandia changes me?"

"You won't change."

"Won't I, dear! I'm changed already."

"Perhaps you are finding yourself."

"I wish I were sure what I was finding. I only know . . ." She paused and had to be urged to continue, "I only know that love is much more of a change than I thought it was going to be."

"For the better?"

"Yes, for me. I'm happy. . . . But how about you? What does it mean to you, John, to have me always with you, to be able—oh my dear—to love me and take me, to know I belong to you?"

Trying to find words for my feelings, I could think only of these: "Peace and power."

"What a funny thing to say!"

"Beauty also," I said.

"You love me, don't you?"

"I love you," I answered, yet the phrase added nothing to my meaning.

"That is all that matters to me."

We retraced our steps, climbing Pine Ridge, from which she saw, more real than it could be explained, the topography of our farm and those adjacent. The Goda Hills looked nearer than they were, and sixty miles away across the whole width of Doring Valley were white snow mountains, low but distinct.

Within a quarter of a mile and upon our own domain was a yellow grain field where Ansel and others were at work. We returned that way through a dense growth of pines. There Gladys met those who were absent when we called at their houses: old Ansel himself, Ansel "brother," Ansel, and young Ansel of twenty-three. The grandfather, son, and grandson were all of the same type, slender but strong, with a fine reserve and distinction in their faces. The two older of the three young Stane brothers were heavier and more commonplace in figure and face. She met them with a smile, steady eyes, and her wellbred directness.

They went back to work all except old Ansel, who spoke of delays and one thing and another, the effect of which was a plea to me to lend assistance in cutting and threshing their last field of late grain. Gladys had wandered a little distance away as though our talk of farm affairs were confidential, excluding her. I wished that she had remained to be a party to my assent to Ansel's request; but she had not and I gave it without her.

I went to tell her what I had done. She was watching a line of scythemen advancing into the soft uncut grain, leaving behind them the fallen stalks in flowing patterns.

"I wish I could do it!" she cried.

"You mean swing a scythe?"

"Oh no! Paint a thing like that, the yellow grain, their blue shirts and motion forward!"

"You can try."

She laughed in a tone that told me I did not realize the utter impossibility.

"Try it simplified," I said, "and not in a finished manner."

"I can't draw."

Further argument was useless. . . . I informed her of Ansel's request and my answer.

"Oh, of course!" she said. "Shall I go to the house?"

"Laya and Laina are going to bring lunch to us soon. Afterwards they and the children when they have come home from school will remain as gleaners. You could join them in that if you wished."

"I have unpacking to do."

"As you please. Stanea will be ready to get lunch for you if you go home."

"What would you like me to do?"

"What you most wish, but it is pleasant working in this way."

She looked uncertain, and to help her to decide I said:

"Stay and lunch with us anyway."

"All right. What shall I do until then?"

"You could go and help Laya and Laina."

"Will they want me?"

"They will be glad of your company."

She hesitated and then went in the direction of the houses, and became a diminishing figure moving slowly along the edge of the field.

I took a rake and proceeded after the advancing men. Their scythes had cut such even swaths and the fallen stalks lay in such regular arrangements that the motions of my rake were simplified. My labor soon fell into a swinging rhythm, physical movements repeating themselves. It was easier so and pleasanter, and I began to sing to myself any sounds that came into my head, not tunes that I knew. . . .

It did not seem long until Laya, Laina, and Gladys appeared through the gate at the far end of the field, little vivid moving figures. Their coming was the signal for us all to gather under an oak tree. Out of the wind the sun overcame the coolness of midfall weather.

We were ten in number and of all ages and Gladys was and looked the youngest. She and the other women had each brought a basket of meat rolls, fresh lettuce, nut bread, apples, and large flasks of diluted wine. We sat or lay on the ground beneath the oak tree, the grainfield before us yellow in the sun. I had worked long enough at different times to find such a meeting as this too natural to be analyzed, but her presence provoked again thoughts upon social relationships. I wondered whether she would think of these people as an Englishman thinks of his laborers and tenants—as inferiors entitled to exactly as much respect as they merited; or as some other races think of theirs—as equals in an inferior position which must be insisted upon or democratically ignored; and I watched for signs in her manner that would indicate her attitude. There was nothing to mar her usual friendly sincerity, nothing but a little stiffness that might be due to the strain upon her attention in understanding what they said.

Young Ansel had found a place near to her and was reclining on his elbow. I overheard a little of their conversation. He was telling her that everyone on the farm was glad to have the main house permanently occupied instead of being, as it had been, a dark and vacant place. It would be a pleasure to see lights in the house, to go there and find Lang and Gladysa at home. Life would be easier and more natural for everyone, the Ansels and the Stanes better friends. . . . Saying this he tossed a twig at the back of young Stane who looked around with a smile of recognition and good humor. . . . He was glad, too, he said, to have someone of his own age on the farm besides his sister. . . . It was odd, of course, to think that of the one hundred and fifty thousand farms in Islandia theirs should be one of the two or three whose *tanar* came from a foreign place; but Lang certainly was not and Gladysa did not seem to be unlike other people.

He looked up in her eyes as he said this as though hoping for some word or glance of reassurance, and of more perhaps. . . .

This was not the way that one who felt himself either an inferior or an equal in an inferior position would speak to his mistress. I saw Gladys studying him, but her friendly though noncommittal answers showed no indication that she thought him in any way forward. . . . Indeed, I heard her telling him her age and trying to work out her birthday in the Islandian calendar.

The looks he gave her were those of a young man attracted by a woman. I remembered Garton and even Dorn. Gladys had qualities that appealed to Islandian men. She was pretty, or rather handsome with brilliant eyes and a vivid face, and she was of a type less common there than in the United States. She was straightforward, gave herself wholeheartedly to a conversation, yet was also elusive because of her different ways of thinking. Young Ansel was handsome, attractive. I realized with a faint pang that he had seven years advantage of me in age, and that he had made this apparent; and I wondered as to the firmness of her love, founded now apparently upon nothing but the physical and mental Lang. Islandian men were often very attractive in both respects.

The lunch hour ended. The men rose and went to work. I turned to Gladys, who seemed doubtful what to do, and suggested that she take a rake and work for a while with Laya and Laina.

"Do you really need me here?" she asked.

"No, you aren't needed, but your work will help. It is a pleasant thing to do, also."

"If I am not needed . . . Another time . . . I think I'll go to the house and unpack. . . . But, John, if you want me to stay . . ."

"Do whatever you wish to do."

"Then I'll go." She moved away but came back.

"When will you come to the house?" she asked.

"At dark."

"Will that be suppertime?"

"An hour or so before."

"Would you like . . . Of course there is no tea."

"Ask Stanea to have some chocolate ready."

"All right. Well . . . au revoir." There was a trace of disappointment in her voice.

At dusk I walked home, pleasantly tired, peacefully eager for Gladys, her loveliness, her companionship. In the kitchen Stanea gave me chocolate to drink, and I was sorry that Gladys had not arranged to have it with me.

Upstairs in our room she was sitting before the burning fire doing nothing. She had changed to a dark-green silk dress that made her slender and American again. She was doing nothing, but both trunks and her bag were open and the room was in disorder, part of their contents scattered about. I dropped down beside her but hesitated to touch her, for I had been a laborer and was unwashed.

"I am glad you have come back," she said. "It seemed awfully long. . . . I thought of coming to meet you."

"Why didn't you?"

She did not answer. She had smiled at seeing me, but now her face was turned to the fire, and I saw the flames gleam in tears upon her eyelashes.

"What's the matter?" I cried, and I took her limp hand.

"I don't know. . . . It is so frightfully still. Everyone moves like a ghost."

"Have you been lonely?"

"Oh no . . . I am foolish. . . . In this house I feel like a cat in a new place. I don't know where I belong."

"We will make you a hearth and center of your own."

"That is the reason why I lit a fire."

"We will make a center for you in the studio. That will be your place."

"This seems more my place than any other."

"Don't you want one all your own? This room is ours now."

She shook her head. Her hand tightened. She turned to me a stricken face.

"Gladys, I have been working all afternoon. I've been hot and earthy. You are so fresh and clean."

"Do you think I care?"

I drew her over between my knees and held her tightly.

"I am very happy," she said against my shoulder with the quiver of gentle but hot tears. "John, everything is so unreal, even you—everything but your arms around me."

I made my clasp steady and firm, and kissed the smooth surface of her neck, which my lips could reach without disturbing her. . . .

After a while she sat erect again, kissed me, and went for her handkerchief.

"You are a comfort," she said. "Mother always declared that while some women could cry prettily it made me hideous . . . How does one get hot water in Islandia?"

"There are pitchers ready in the kitchen, I am sure. I'll get them."

"I shall learn in time. I washed in cold water and only want to bathe my eyes. I don't often cry, John."

With enough for us both in two large copper ewers, I returned. She was arranging the things she had taken from her trunk, but as soon as she had bathed her face, she sat down before the fire again, taking a book which she did not read.

Having laid out clean clothes I brought the copper tub from under the wardrobe, filled it with hot water, and stripped. . . .

I heard her voice.

"May I watch you?" she asked.

"Of course—always."

"I didn't know."

After a moment I glanced at her. Her eyes came to mine with a look captured but amused. Her cheeks were pink.

"You are rather nice," she said, turning away . . . "Oh, I wish—"

"What do you wish, Gladys?"

"It is all too perfect, too dear!" She leaned over, taking her face in her hands. "Now I am wishing I could draw figures and not make them look like grotesques! If you look in the studio . . . I meant to hide it but I won't."

As soon as I was dressed I went into the studio. She had dragged there the trunk containing her painting materials, and its contents were stacked on the floor and piled on the table. Sketches in oils had been set up on the bench and along the lower edge of the walls for want of hooks to hang them on. By candlelight I could only see their dim colors. On the easel was a canvas stretched on a frame. Upon this had been drawn in charcoal the outlines of the view from the window. There was no color except a single brush-stroke of white. But across the whole were the violent black marks which a child makes crossing out in a rage what it has drawn. There was a pleasant smell of oils and of turpentine, and on the floor a palette with worms of color squeezed upon it.

I returned to the bedroom, where she was still sitting before the fire. She did not move. Sitting down by her, I put my arms around her. She did not resist but gave nothing.

"When I first came here," I said, "I thought sometimes that I would die because of the silence and a loneliness that is in the very air itself."

She quivered. . . . Her hand reached mine.

"I suppose it is just a nervous reaction after doing so much for so long and never really by myself. . . . I am sorry," she said.

"I am the one to be sorry because you suffer."

"I'm not unhappy. I couldn't be, with you."

"For me," I continued, "that loneliness proved to be an anteroom to a more vivid reality than I had ever known before. One has to be lonely first."

"But I haven't been here a week yet. . . . I tried to paint. I couldn't. . . . You saw, didn't you?"

"Yes, but—"

"What do you think of me?"

"Think of you? I love you!—I want to hurry you through the anteroom. You must do things, Gladys."

"Do you think I am a fool?"

"No! No!"

"I do—I have so much."

"You have come halfway round the world, been married, settled in a strange house, started a new way of living, all in five days. You cannot accept such changes all at once. You are not yet wholly here."

"Don't!" she whispered as though frightened. . . . "You tell me to do things. What can I do?"

"We will go downstairs," I said, "and after supper we will finish unpacking."

She drew away as though startled, her eyes hostile. Was the taking of her things from her trunks and placing them in the chests and drawers of this house a surrender that she did not wish to make? I looked long in her face, for it seemed that she was slipping from me. . . . But she said:

"All right, John. I will do what you wish."

I banked the logs and extinguished all the candles but one. By its single flame we went through the dark, chilly, empty rooms to the stone staircase and down to the dining room, where there was light and food and wine.

Stanea coming through the door was ordinary, familiar, and yet strange, but soon Gladys was cheerfully talking with her. Others on the farm would not guess that she was moving in a dream.

What can one say to a dreamer that will not deepen the dream? If the farm were part of her nightmare I could not mention its activities; nor could I speak of the world to which she wished to wake but could not. There was the food on the table and her actual hunger, and there was our love for which I had no words. Longing to talk to her and make her laugh I could think of nothing to say, too much wondering whether her depression were due to fatigue and curable by time and rest or to unfulfilled expectation in her love.

I spoke of books, hoping that she would tell me of those she had brought. I found myself talking like a lecturer upon Islandian literature. She did her best to uphold the conversation, but dodged, telling me what books she had loved enough to bring with her.

As soon as the meal was over, she said:

"Shall we go and put the room upstairs in order?"

Once there I made the fire blaze up again, but as to the unpacking itself there was little I could do. I was like a taskmaster who sits idle while his servant works because forced to do so. Yet her manners were perfect, her smile ready, and I knew that she was trying her best. We, or rather she, did the task thoroughly and carefully, putting her things away as though to remain.

At last the room was in perfect order and her trunk and suitcase were empty, everything in place, but she had not softened and agony, like despair, gnawed in my heart.

There was but one way to win her back. I went to her and took her in my arms. She yielded passively. I kissed her to make her live and be quickened. She feared that her silk dress would be rumpled, and I took it off. Her quietness spurred me on, yet she was not unwilling, not indifferent, merely but half with me. I undressed her and with lips and eyes and hands adored her face and her body. Loving her this way, burning with a desire that I did not wish to satisfy too soon, I thought less of her and her needs and more of myself and mine. In the eyes of my mind the farm, my farm, lay vivid yet subdued, rich in the power to give me beauty and work I loved; and she, Gladys, was mine also, my woman, who gave my senses pleasure and my body comfort.

"Is this real?" I asked.

"Oh, yes," she answered. She trembled and clung to me. "I love you. I love this. . . ."

Her passion equaled mine but when I had possessed her she lay like one slain, only her dark eyes alive, deep and wondering.

I looked at her and I wished to weep. She was a child and in her nakedness simple and beautiful. I saw her slim shoulders, her breasts that were not large, her flat stomach, the dark hair, her graceful hips, her long thighs, her narrow knees, her slender feet. Trying to give her reality I had endangered my own. She was like a stranger unexpectedly come. Her eyes watched me as though she did not know me. Unreality had returned.

In the morning, however, she woke laughing, put her arms around me, told me that she was sorry that she had been so blue and that it was only a mood, and whispered that she loved me and that after what we had done she could not help being happy. Nor would she accept my suggestion that we spend the day together. I was needed in the grainfield. She felt like sketching and wanted to do the house from the bridge, but would probably join us during the morning and anyway at lunchtime.

Reassured I departed, with her kiss on my lips and her smile in my heart. Labor in the field lessened a nervous tension that remained from the night. The tasks we had to do upon the farm in order to move our fifth of the harvest were well in hand and the wagons would surely leave for Thane on May 1st, eleven days hence.

Late in the morning Gladys came. Everyone on the farm, except Stanea and the children at school, was in the field in order to complete the cutting of the grain that day.

She approached me with a manner at once shy and nonchalant, but did not appear to see me until she was quite close. Then she smiled and casually said hello.

"Hello," I answered, "I am glad to see you. I hoped you would come."

"I have been down at the bridge."

"Did you make a sketch?"

"Yes, and then I went to the house and did nothing much and thought I would come and glean with the others. What must I do?"

I took her to Ansela who was only two years older. The two young women smiled at each other and I left them to return to my job of raking the cut swaths into windrows. . . .

A little later, looking to where Gladys was working, I felt again the pang of the cruel taskmaster. The Islandian women, old and young, leaned over from the hips to gather up the scattered ears and put them in their skirts, held like a bag; but Gladys, apparently unwilling thus to show her figure, stooped like a person about to kneel, down and then up again, graceful yet awkward, half unwilling but obedient—and the ears she gathered she held in her hand like a bunch of flowers.

Edona called us from the oak tree. From different parts of the field all came towards her, and Gladys, whose face was smileless, had thrust ears of grain in her hair, their heads pointed together over her forehead, so that she was crowned like Demeter.

Young Ansel, who was watching for her, spoke to her, his eyes upon her head. During lunch old Ansel talked with me about arrangements for moving our crops, but I overheard at intervals Gladys's quiet voice telling the rapt young man the story of Persephone and of her mother's search.

The harvesting of the grain in this field was so far advanced that it was unnecessary for me to remain in the afternoon. I walked back to the house with Gladys, the yellow ears still crossed in her lustrous dark-brown hair.

I asked her if she wished to ride, saying that Gran and my borrowed horse needed exercise.

Rather curtly she replied:

"All right, John, we will take them out."

When we reached the house I found myself at a loose end. There were many things to be done, but I was giving the afternoon to Gladys and the ride was set for an hour or two later. Vaguely I thought of making love to her. . . . And she, I knew, was at a loose end also.

We drifted into the living room rather as though I had come to call upon her formally and neither knew how to entertain the other. She stood in profile by the fireplace as though warming herself at imaginary flames.

"How did sketching go?" I asked.

"It didn't go."

"I am sorry."

"Nor did I try to make it go," she said turning further away. . . . In the grainfield she had told a needless lie and my heart was cold with surprise.

"Didn't you feel that you could, Gladys?"

"I knew that I could not."

"What was the reason, do you think?"

"The reason . . . ? I told you yesterday."

"Was everything too unreal?"

"Yes—and not interesting. Too bleak."

"The wish and power to paint will come back."

"I don't know. . . . John, I am a failure."

"Gladys, you are not! I deny it."

"Nor am I of any use to you. . . . This morning I felt all right, quite happy. I went down to the river with high hopes. The young Ansel boy and his pretty sister and the two little Stane girls stopped to talk on their way to school. They were friendly and nice, but when they had gone there was nobody, nothing—just silence and water splashing. Oh! . . . I came back to the house, and wept for a while, and tried to write a letter to my cousins, and then I thought I would do what you had asked me to do. So I came to the grainfield in time to do some work. You saw me doing it. It was not much use. . . . That was my morning."

"Was it all dead and barren?"

"Of course not! I am quite all right."

"Gladys, if you are still blue, tell me."

"No, my dear, it does neither of us any good."

"Don't pretend to be happy if you are not. Instead, tell me. There may be ways I can help."

She looked at me gravely and took my coat in her hands.

"You are all I have," she said. "You are everything in the world to me. I am happy! But I don't want to spoil your happiness . . ." Her lips trembled. "I have come to you and given everything. I am yours. It ought to make me happy . . . I don't know what the matter is."

"Gladys, Gladys!" I cried, holding her hands. "Don't try so hard to be mine. Think of yourself."

She freed her hands and stepped back.

"If I am not yours," she said, "what am I? What have I got? You push me away."

Turning from me, she walked toward the door.

"You are my own darling Gladys, my *alia*-sharing lover!"

"Oh, John!"

She did not stop.

After moments of deadness I followed where I had heard her footsteps going. I found her lying on the bed with dry open eyes that did not look my way when I entered.

"You are no less my darling," I said, "when you try to find your own happiness."

She did not make any sign of hearing.

I looked at her, wondering how I could make her happy when she based her happiness upon being mine and was miserable notwithstanding—whether she were mine for my sake or her own . . . I thought of various things I might do for her, but she stirred beneath my gaze as though resenting it.

"Shall we ride?" I asked.

"Of course. I'll be ready," she answered.

I waited a moment and then returned to the grainfield.

Along the Lay River were grass-grown roads and lanes, with hedges and stone walls on one side or both, sometimes overarched with trees, sometimes skirting green open meadows. The river, now placid, now moving with a gentle murmur over rocks and shingle, was always near. By the lands of the Dartons, the Rannals, and the Sevins we rode through sun and the crisscross shadows of half-bare trees, with dry fallen leaves underfoot in heaps and hollows.

At the edge of an orchard of the Sevins' windfallen late apples lay in the road, and dismounting I hunted for a sound one among the leaves and brought it to Gladys.

I saw her even, strong, white teeth, the profile of her red, parted lips. The bite was a large one, and the apple, still a little green and cold, brought tears to her eyes. . . .

I laid my hand on her thigh and felt its soft supple muscles under the whipcord. She became very still, the apple upheld.

Desire came like a breath of flame and I knew that she shared it.

I pressed my face against her thigh and she placed her hand gently upon my head. Our accord was limited and I felt the knife of misery turn; but it was she who needed comforting not I.

"Forgive me for the way I behaved to you," she said. "I love you, John. I am really very happy."

"There is nothing to forgive. And if you cannot be happy here, we can leave the farm," I answered, and it was like dying for her.

"No! No!" she interrupted. "We will stay here. I have you, my dear, my dear John, and that is enough."

At that moment her horse becoming restive edged away. There was more to be said, but it seemed not worth the saying. We had made peace.

Turning our horses we rode home with growing impatience to be alone, to be lovers.

Ten days passed. Each was a little shorter and colder than the last and the nights had a breath of winter with the harvest moon waxing and waning, but the weather was still too lovely for peace when I was indoors. Fak had come back from his futile trip to The City, sent there to meet the steamer and for Gladys to ride home. We rode him and

Gran daily, and she seemed happy learning the roads and ways in the neighborhood of the farm.

These rides were not long, for I was very busy, but when I explained that the amount of work to be done was unusual, necessitated by the impending trip to Thane, she laughed and said it would always be so. Often I was gone from her for all the day except the time spent upon these rides together. She did not wish it otherwise, she said, and I believed her, waiting for greater leisure to come. Nor did she take part with me in the work upon the farm, although there were many things she could have done; but if they did not interest her there was no reason why she should do them. Instead, and in spite of the fine weather, she spent much time about the house, trying to impress upon its ancient and unyielding shell a little of her own personality—like a bird who finding a nest ready-made nevertheless rearranges it. Having formally asked my consent she hung upon the walls of the studio, living room, and dining room all of her sketches, selected, she said, out of "hundreds of failures" and putting them up not because they were good but because the house lacked color; and perhaps for the further unuttered reason that glimpses of Brittany and England, of Nantucket and Vermont, made this new and unreal Islandia in which she found herself seem still to be within the world. I did not scorn them as paintings as she did; there was no critic in me like that in herself to call them amateurish and commonplace. Their color was warm and bright on stone walls often cold and gray, and they were continuously welcome and pleasing in themselves, not merely because they revealed what visions her eyes had seen.

Though she had declared that the bedroom seemed more her place than any other, she proceeded to make the studio her own. There she brought her books from the table where she had at first left them with mine. She decorated the room with sprays of autumn leaves and over the bench before the fire she draped bright-colored shawls which she had brought. On the new table she laid a scarf and placed a tea set of old thin china, of the Thousand Sages pattern, which had been her grandmother's. She took from the kitchen a few copper vessels which Stanea did not use and set them up over the fireplace, and again asking my consent collected pieces of furniture and rugs that she particularly liked from unused rooms.

When not busy in this way she was writing here long letters to relatives and friends, so absorbed that I knew she was recapturing while thus engaged the flavor and color of the country that she still called home. In this room she also read her own books, only rarely browsing in the Islandian ones of mine, always scrupulous to ask first if she might borrow them.

About her books and her reading she did not speak and seemed uneasy if I showed interest in them, saying that she had chosen them in a hurry and mainly for sentimental reasons. They were not many; some were much worn. They included the poems of Tennyson, Keats, Kipling, de Musset, and Dante in Italian, *The Golden Treasury, The Oxford Book of English Verse,* and a collection of Scottish Ballads; a Bible, an Episcopal Prayer Book, and a small dictionary; Bulfinch's *Age of Fable* and Ruskin's *Stones of Venice* and *Seven Lamps;* Daudet's *Jack,* Hardy's *Tess* and *Return of the Native,* Thackeray's *Esmond* and *Vanity Fair,* Dickens's *David Copperfield,* Scott's *Quentin Durward,* Miss Austen's *Sense and Sensibility,* Miss Alcott's *Little Women;* three old school books; brochures with half-tone illustrations of Titian, Michelangelo, Giotto, Ghirlandaio, Rembrandt, and Botticelli; a portfolio of photographs of paintings mostly of the Renaissance; M. Perier's *History of Islandia,* Carstairs' *Travels* and *Against the Demiji;* and my *History of the United States* in Islandian, with my newspaper articles carefully pasted therein.

Often on coming home I found her curled up before the fire, one of these books in her hand, her eyes remote; and it was some time before her smile lost its vagueness and she was wholly aware of Islandia and me.

In the studio, where she was usually to be found, I felt like a guest and it seemed that she unconsciously treated me as one. Our common ground of conversation while there was the books we would import sometime soon and the mechanics of painting in oils. She had discovered gaps in her equipment. Some of these could be filled on the farm, but others required importations which we might not be able to make. We therefore planned to write at once for treatises on pigments and surfaces, in the hope that we could eventually learn and make good these lacks ourselves. Thus we talked much about painting, but during this period she did not touch brush or paints again.

Overcoming a shy reluctance rather than an actual unwillingness I persuaded her to attend three of the "days" of our neighbors. On a cold windy night with a full moon we walked to the Adners'. There

she met some of the Dartons, Rannals, Napings, and their dependents. My assurance that they would like her was confirmed and from
her manner she seemed to like them. Shyness apparently passed from
her as soon as she had entered the door. Her Islandian lost a little
of its fluency but she made up for it by her graciousness and her
smile. She seemed a little dazed and was flushed and very lovely, the
object of much attention and great friendliness. We did not stay
long, walking home under a high white moon that silvered the sleeping world as with hoarfrost. She held my arm tightly and asked many
questions in an effort to straighten in her mind the many persons she
had met. She declared that she had had a good time and the flush on
her cheek remained a long time, warm to my lips as I kissed her.

We also went to the houses of the Dartons and the Stanes. Young
Ansel, her contemporary, was present at all three places. There was
also a young Rannal of twenty-two, a young Sevin a little older, and
others. These men hung about her and with them her shyness seemed
less, her Islandian though fuller of mistakes more expressive. At the
Dartons' there was square dancing as at the Hyths' when I first went
there. Young people danced in the barn to the music of strings and
in the dim light of lanterned candles. The older men, the *tanar* of
which I was one, had the moving of their crops to Thane to discuss,
for it was custom that a group of neighbors lent each other their
wagons, a matter requiring some arranging which old Ansel had
shirked. Therefore I had to talk business, but I looked in upon the
dance and saw Gladys, prettier than I had ever seen her, going
through the figures with aptitude and grace, only occasionally forgetting. Whenever this happened there were many to set her right,
and her smile of apology was charming to see.

On the way home I told her that she was a belle.

"It almost seems so, doesn't it?" she answered, and for her to
admit as much was proof that the fact had been made very apparent
to her.

"They treat me as though I weren't married at all," she declared.
"I don't quite like it. I don't know yet how far they will go . . . Of
course it may be only politeness to a stranger."

She thrust her arm through mine and walked close to me.

"If you mind anything, John, say so. I am yours."

"Did you have a good time, Gladys?"

"Oh, yes. I loved it. It was fun. I haven't danced for years. But I wished you and I could do the boston together. I didn't quite like . . ." She stopped short, but I made her continue. "I did not like being apparently younger than you."

So we talked and she went to bed with the bright-eyed, absent-minded, sleepy contentment of one who is young and has been very happy at a party.

But Gladys was homesick and this was merely an interlude. I knew it by the way she clung to me at night, as though on the edge of desperation. Sometimes it seemed that only in close physical contact did she find the touch of reality. In no other way could I give it to her.

On the last day of April, in season the same as the last of October at home, our neighbors arrived in the morning with their wagons. These they left, departing with their horses, to return early on the morrow. We had done or would do the same thing for them. The day was spent in loading the wagons, six in all, two of ours and four of theirs. Of this labor old Ansel was in charge and I worked with the others under his direction. No ride with Gladys had been planned, and she had been quiet in the house these last few days, finishing her letters. In the late afternoon, when the stars were beginning to brighten in a sky made blue by our yellow lanterns, she suddenly appeared among us, wearing the cloak made for her at Doring Town. I saw her face in the gleam of a moving light, watching with interest the dark figures on the wagons and in and out of the barn.

We finished our tasks soon afterwards, and with it the most serious part of our labor for the year. The drive to Thane was in the nature of a holiday, and several of the *denerir* were starting off on travel and visits next day.

Laya and Edona together brought out to us pitchers of the hot and somewhat bitter Islandian chocolate so welcome after work when the air was cold. All the nineteen inhabitants of the farm were present, from old Ansel, who was seventy, to little Stanea, who was eight. I was glad that among these was the one who was my dearest, come of her own free will and seemingly happy.

Then instead of separating we remained in the barn. Old Ansel, pleased with the work at last accomplished, asked us all to sup at his house, but we were too many. Edona, Laya, and Stanea formed themselves into a committee which assumed the task of preparing a common meal. Gladys of her own accord offered her services. They departed with volunteers, and we who had worked hard during the day made ourselves comfortable here and there in the barn, talking in a reminiscent spirit of what had been done and of this year's harvest in comparison to others. I, a newcomer, listened and learned and enriched my knowledge of the farm.

The women returned laden and declared their intention of waiting upon us. We gathered on benches and on the floor. It was now quite dark outside and crisply cold, but in the barn there was warmth and the smell of cattle and of hay. Some sat in shadow and some in the rather dim light of the lanterns, which accentuated the character and beauty of their faces. Edona, Laya, Stanea, and Gladys moved about, now in dark, now in light, tending us well, our servants with gracious good humor, honoring us.

Ansel "brother," the musician of the farm, brought a wind instrument similar to that upon which Nettera had played for dancing. His music, however, was more like that of Ansel, whom I had heard with the Periers three years before, than like hers. Indeed, he was a remote relative. He played with increasing feeling melodies known to his hearers, sometimes not unfamiliar to me, full of allusions to something half-remembered. It was emotional music and I saw Gladys sitting rapt, her chin on her palm, her dark bright eyes intent upon him.

Young Ansel asked him to play for a dance. Then the young man proceeded to arrange the sets and came to Gladys. She looked at him with cool friendliness, shook her head, and then as though to apologize smiled the smile that a woman gives a man whom she knows admires her and whose admiration she wishes to keep though she has repulsed him.

If she did not want to dance she had some other wish, and I went to her to discover it.

"Let's walk," she said. So we said our thanks and good-byes and went out into the cold clear darkness, leaving behind us the dim yellow square of the barn door through which came the beat of the dance music, the sound of feet and of laughter.

She said nothing but linked her arm through mine assertively. We walked towards the pine-crested ridge. The night was without a moon but the stars were very bright.

She whispered that she loved me and that the music had stirred her—that she did not want to go in yet.

953

"I am happy," she added, "really I am! I like the way that we all of us met so informally and had supper together. I loved Ansel "brother's" playing—but dance music and dancing with young Ansel and the Stanes would have spoiled it."

I pressed her arm with mine and her fingers answered.

"You are much more silent here than in New York and Nantucket," she said, "but I think you understand what I am feeling even better."

"For some reason I seem to have lost the power of explanation."

"I am learning to know that . . . and I am losing it too. But I never thought that I should be more of a talker than you . . . It doesn't matter if you don't mind."

"I like all the ways in which you manifest yourself."

Her laugh was half a sigh.

"Tomorrow is going to be fun," she said.

"In a month or so we will make some visits—and travel. And people will come to us."

We were following the farm road toward the saddle between the two hills. Looking back we could see the light in the barn sinking lower than ourselves, becoming a small faint spot of yellow in the darkness. Reaching the spot where the road dipped down again into the blackness of trees, we stopped.

"Listen!" she said. We could feel the coldness of the falling dew. The sound of the music unheard was a memory in the brain that made absolute the actual silence.

She turned to me quickly and I held her, a dark figure of many soft woolen folds, enclosing within them a body, slender and supple, straining against mine. Her cheeks were cold, but her lips, crisp and soft, soon became warm against my kisses.

As though they were a wine too strong for her to drink, she gently but firmly freed herself. I heard her say in a low voice:

"What am I going to do? What am I going to do?"

I drew her arm through mine and led her home.

The grass in the fields was white with frost next morning, but the sun rose bright and when we gathered for the ride to Thane the ground was wet where the light fell, though hard and frozen still in the shadows.

The wagons were to be driven by Old Ansel as leader, Stane,

Young Ansel, Ansela his pretty sister, Stane Etteri or Three, and me at the end of the train. Ansel and Laya, Young Stane, Laina his wife, and his brother were departing on visits at the same time that we did. The three younger children of the farm were coming with us for the ride, and it had been planned that Ansel Etteri who was sixteen was to ride the horse of Fannar Bay and to lead Fak, burdened only with Gladys's and my saddlebags. But I overheard a remark of the boy's as he said good-bye to his father, and following it up learned that he was sacrificing a camping trip with companions in the Goda Hills to accompany us. I tried to find some way by which we could release him. The difficulty was that the Fannar Bay horse had to be ridden, and could not be led.

Then Gladys who was standing by volunteered.

"Let me ride him and lead Gran," she said. "Ansela Nekka"—who was fourteen—"could ride Fak."

"It is not easy to lead a horse of a different breed," I said, remembering other experiences.

"Ansela Nekka will help me." She looked at the girl who smiled an instant assent. "If it does not work I can drive the wagon and you can ride him."

Her eyes were eager for the adventure.

"All right. Go ahead! And you will do us all a favor."

"Am I not one of the 'us'?" she asked lightly.

"Very much one!" I answered.

The boy was a changed being and thanked her warmly, offering to see her fairly started after the wagon train was well out of the way lest the unridden horse bolt after it.

The six wagons started, leaving her behind with the girl and the three horses. Looking back, last in the procession, just before we reached a turn in the road I saw the little cavalcade about to start. Gladys, already on the restless Fannar Bay horse, was calling something to the girl who was riding Fak. She had taken charge of the expedition. I remembered the understanding looks which she and the boy and his sister had exchanged . . . wondered if sixteen and fourteen were not closer to twenty than my own age of nearly thirty . . . wondered if I had not brought her too far and subjected her to the strain of marriage too young. I worried about her—loved her —and, looking forward again, and braking the heavy wagon as we descended to the bridge, saw the broad back of Stane Etteri and beyond him the slender one of Ansela Attana. The fifth of the harvest was moving. Financial stringency was all but over. Winter work would not be unremitting . . . I would leave Gladys to her adventure. She would be happy succeeding in it alone.

Several times on the fourteen-mile ride to Thane I saw her behind me, holding in the Fannar Bay horse, followed by Gran and Fak with his young rider. Once she was near enough to wave her hand. She was mistress of her cavalcade. Again as we came near to Thane and emerged upon the marshes northeast of the town I saw her far behind me, but with her cavalcade still orderly and compact, coming along at a trot. I slowed up my span of horses so that she would not lose her way in the town, and we arrived at the agent's warehouses almost together. Young Ansel, who had come before me, was waiting to catch the bridle of her horse and help her down. I wished that opportunity had fallen to me, but Ordly, the agent, was coming up to talk business. Old Ansel, Stane, and I remained with him for some time. The others, Young Ansel, the two Anselas, Stane Etteri, his nephew and niece, and Gladys went off to the Inn for lunch, all younger than we, and she very pretty.

When I joined them, my business transacted, her triumph was an old story to her, and I feared that my praise and thanks fell flat. But I was free now and she was mine now for three days of travel before we reached home again.

There was a pleasant sense of leisure at the Inn, greater for us than for the others. As soon as the wagons were unloaded they must drive them back to the farm, but we had nothing to do but seek the house of Dorn IV, Commodore, in the Thane Marsh. They left before we did and it was like the breaking up of a happy party of congenial friends. At last I had Gladys alone and I told her again how well I thought she had done.

"If you are pleased that is all I ask," she said, "and I believe you are. I saw it in your eyes. I enjoyed it too . . ." And she described with humor and a little pride her trials on the road. She had met her difficulties with resourceful intelligence and I told her so.

She laughed as though she read me well and was amused. "You like me to be Islandian, don't you?" she said.

"Yes," I answered, "because it is what you naturally are."

"Oh, no, John dear, you don't know half the un-Islandian feelings I have."

"Tell me some of them."

"No," she said, shaking her head. "I am not going to let them bother you."

"They won't."

"They do!"

40

Alia

THE RIDE into the Marsh was a cold one, and the marsh itself bleak. There was a quickening thrill in the smell of the sea and marshlands and in seeing water that was salt; but Gladys, warm with her exertions and the fire at the Inn and tired also, suffered from the shrill, strong, west wind, particularly on the ferry.

"I like our farm better than any place I have seen yet," she said, but when we arrived she declared that she was frozen.

Dorn IV was away as usual, but Monroa and his sister Dorna, the widow of Granery, received us. They had heard of Gladysa—as was the case with nearly everyone who had formerly known me. Besides these, Granery's half-brother and his mother Luka; Monro, Monroa's brother but much older; and Resler, a captain of one of the Dorn boats, and Daila his wife, were guests at the house. Nevertheless there was a room for us, though a small one.

While we prepared for dinner Gladys said that she wished we had stayed at the Inn. I was a little uncomfortable against my first instinct, becoming infected by her doubts as to the naturalness of our dropping upon this household uninvited. But I argued that it was the thing to do in Islandia, that our hostesses would be surprised if they knew we had not come for lack of an invitation, and that the whole social scheme was based on such visits as this. She conceded that we seemed welcome, but contended that it was only their good manners; how could they want two simple country people like us when they had five other guests, all of whom were related to them by blood, marriage, or business? We were only so much extra trouble, comparative strangers, and she wished we had not come. It had been so cold, too. . . .

She was tired, reacting from her triumph, socially ill at ease, and therefore combative; at the same time, sitting half-dressed before the fire for its warmth, brushing her loosened hair, her cheeks wind-burned, her eyes bright, hostile, and elusive, she was so charming and desirable that I wanted to make love to her. The desire persisted but our difference of opinion rose and re-arose to thwart it.

She was still untouched when we went down to dinner.

"We have dropped into a house party, John," she whispered on the stairs. "Let's never do anything like this again. . . ."

Soon, however, I forgot all about this aspect of our visit, too happy in talking upon subjects other than farming with men and women whose chief interests were either professional or related to the sea, for Monro was a lawyer and Granery in the navy. Later, realizing that I was enjoying myself, I looked to see how she was faring. She was next to Resler. That sunburned man, with the authoritative eyes of the master of vessels, was listening with interest to what young Gladys was saying. Later Monro on the other side gave her the same attention. However shy she was before meeting strangers, once she was face to face with them, nothing betrayed that she had been or was ill at ease, and furthermore she knew how to hold them, men perhaps more than women.

She seemed specially lovely—but she often surprised me in this way as though she had within herself an inexhaustible spring of attractiveness—and I was impatient for the evening to end and to have her to myself. But when at last we were in our little room, the fire lighted again, she was bright-eyed with thoughts which she was eager to utter, and I delayed stopping them with kisses.

She had enjoyed talking with Resler, Monro, and Granery, she said. They were different from persons whom she had previously met in Islandia. She had told the sea captain of her journey and he had asked questions about the vessels she had traveled on and seen. Of course, he knew all about boats and she knew nothing, but she had seen types of boats that he had not. It had been fun describing them. And Granery was like other navy people that she had met, and Monro like other lawyers. It was fun meeting people who weren't farmers.

While she talked she slowly undressed, removing now a shoe, now a stocking, now the becoming frock of brown and red made by the weaver at Doring Town. I loved her very much, restrained myself, and listened to her.

"The neighbors and the people at the Lay River Farm are plain country people," she said. "I don't see much difference between *tanar* like the Dartons and *denerir* like the Ansels. I thought they would be like gentry and peasants in Europe, but the Dartons aren't any more gentlemen than the Ansels. Young Ansel is like a college man who hasn't happened to go to college."

"I understand what you mean."

"I like them all, John. I really do. I can become quite fond of some of them. But there is another class in Islandia. I discovered this at Dorn Island. Lord Dorn, Dorn, and Faina are aristocrats. I don't think Marta is one; she is more like the Dartons. I suppose the Dorna whom you liked so much was an aristocrat too. That may be one reason why she attracted you."

Gladys paused and looked at me as though for an answer.

"She has the qualities of one with a great tradition," I said. "And many Islandians have some of the qualities that we associate with aristocracy; but aristocrats as a class develop various traits aimed to preserve their exclusiveness and to accentuate their differences from others. The Islandians—"

"They are true aristocrats!" she declared. "I know what you mean. The Dorna who lives here is another one. So is Monroa. They have been awfully sweet to me . . . It does seem that you have friends among the best people."

"You will meet others quite as attractive," I said.

"Though I suppose," she continued, following her own thoughts, "that we are plain people ourselves, like the neighbors at the farm and the Ansels and Stanes. Mother always warned me not to think of myself as anything else, though she also said that we had something better than most so-called aristocrats and that any American who really cared could be as real an aristocrat as any of them . . . I never quite liked to think of myself as a plain person—but I suppose we are."

"I never thought whether we are or not. Of course outwardly our way of life is like that of many others—but that is also true of the Dorns." She was silently pondering these matters, and I went on: "We will take a trip soon and you will meet the people whom I like best. I want you to make good friends. You haven't any at all yet."

"No," she said slowly. "Nekka came nearest. We talked quite

frankly . . . But so far I like the men better. I seem to have less to say to the women."

"Wouldn't you like to have some woman for a close friend?"

"Yes, I suppose so, though I haven't yet seen anyone. I have wanted someone to talk to who isn't you."

"We will make visits."

"I should love it!" she answered, and laughed. "I know you think you have caught me . . . Well, you have. I did say that we should never again drop down on anyone uninvited, but it does seem to be all right."

"They will drop down on us; and if we did not do as they do we would cut down our contacts with other people too much."

"I am learning."

Wearing but a single garment she dropped upon the rug before the fire, and sat with her arms folded around her bare lifted knees, her hair loose over her shoulders, her long body folded and lovely.

"I am thinking of the future a little," she said thoughtfully.

"Travel and visits and friendships—"

"I know," she interrupted. "They make farm life more endurable."

"Gladys, have you found it unendurable?" I asked, lead in my heart.

"No, of course not! You know that. I am happy here. But as to friends and things away from the farm, I am thinking of you too. I don't exactly see you as a laborer all your days. That sort of life dulls a person."

"Has it dulled me, do you think?"

"A little. You don't express yourself as you used to."

"Don't we understand each other as well, Gladys?"

"Do we . . ? I wonder."

"We have not been very long together."

"I know it. All the times we have been together if added would be less than a month! There are—there were, I mean—other men whom I saw a great deal of, when Mother and I traveled. Some traveled with us, and there were at least two whom I knew better than I know you—and understood better, too."

She was so loose-limbed that she rested her chin on her knee.

"Did they seem to understand you better than I?" I asked softly.

"I think so."

"Are you sure you are not mistaking similarity of ideas for under-standing, Gladys?"

She was silent for some moments.

"Perhaps," she said, as though grudgingly.

"I love all the new things I learn about you."

"Oh, no—not all, my dear! I wish you did . . . But John, I am ambitious for you."

"What do you want me to be?"

"We have talked about your writing—but I wonder if you ever will . . . Seeing all these people tonight, I have been wondering . . . Couldn't you go into politics or something?"

"There are enough persons who have made a tradition and pro-fession of public service for generations to fill all positions."

"You mean that there is no opening?"

"That, and more. Their interest and ability has freed the rest of us."

"But there must be something, even here, that needs improving and reforming?"

"Nothing which others with greater training and knowledge cannot do better."

"I see that you aren't ambitious. Perhaps it is your nature and one reason you are here. And of course I realize that you are a new-comer with much to learn." Her voice rose suddenly. "But are you going to let your children be farmers all their lives? How about them and their future?"

Her words drew me to my feet. As I looked down upon her seated on the floor she seemed in her incomprehension like an enemy.

"Why do you speak of them as though they would be my chil-dren only?" I demanded. "They will be yours also, not mine, but ours, our children, with something of both of us in them. They will carry on both of us—our line in our place."

She sat unmoving.

She was, through me, the potential bearer of children who would inhabit the Lay River Farm, but within her dear round head, only the top of which I saw, with its loosened, floating, lustrous dark hair, were obstinate ideas, hopes, and wishes brought from another civili-zation, honestly hers but not mine.

Her slim arms, her knees, her thighs were bare; she was desir-able, unprotected, a field ready for sowing. When I spoke, had I told her the truth, or did I not think of her as a field and no more—her head and its ideas a thing apart and irrelevant—wherein I would sow my seed and raise what crop I wished . . ? But not yet would I take back what I had said.

I dropped to the floor at her side, but did not touch her.

"I care about our children more than you know," I said, "and about their future as well."

She turned her head so that I still saw only the top of it with the line of the parting of her hair.

"What do you yourself want our children to be, Gladys?" I asked. "Have you a clear picture of them in the future?"

The head was shaken, and after a moment she said:

"Have you?"

"Yes. They will succeed us at the farm. They will know it better than we ever can, and it will therefore be for them a larger and richer world in itself. It will give them shelter, food, and it will be their greatest pleasure. It will lie back of all their dreams. They will love it . . . They will have ambitions enough—don't fear!—but not ambitions of power over others, rather hopes and desires relating to creation, beauty, love, and work. The farm will lie beneath these hopes and wishes of theirs, a reality they know. Their ambitions will be just as broad and deep and all-absorbing as ambitions can be in the United States, but because of the farm they will be solid and such as can be realized. They won't have fretting ambitions as the result of discontent and a wish to escape confusion. And what we must be careful to do is not to infect them with the restlessness that is our heritage and which we have brought from our former homes."

"What do you mean?" she asked. "Do I seem restless?"

"Yes, you do, as I have been—and still am."

"No, not you. I am sorry if I seem discontented."

"Not that! But you have a belief in ambitions, Gladys, as something good in themselves. It is natural that you should. Our parents and teachers and friends were continually telling us all the things we must be. Think of them all! We must be a gentleman or a lady, a patriot, a success, a good citizen, unselfish, moral, a good 'mixer,' a leader. We were confronted by many objectives which it was our duty to attain and no one was definite, varying from person to person, and some were inconsistent with others. It was so confusing, though we did not know it then, that a large part of our thoughts were con-

cerned with reconciling indefinite ideas. No wonder that we are restless! No wonder our habits of thought make us unperceptive of the
real things!"

"Aren't we going to teach our children to be any of those things?"

"We must break them to the world they are to live in as puppies
are housebroken, but it is a simpler house with fewer rules requiring
less arbitrary training than the complicated world we have known.
We must also offer them all the opportunities we can—"

"For what?" she asked, and her shoulder jerked with a hopeless
shrug.

"To know beauty, to work, to live healthily, to find friends."

She sighed.

"I don't see it very clearly," she said. "But I have been thinking
about their friends and social connections."

A hot wave went over me—of tenderness, desire, and loving
pity—loosening the cold knots of thought and theory in my brain:
she had been thinking of our children! I waited for her thoughts.
And as though she guessed my mood she gave me her face at last.

"That is what I meant," she said, "when I told you I was thinking
of the future. I want them to have friends who aren't just Ansels,
Stanes, Dartons, but friends more like the Dorns."

"And I told you that we would meet other people, and their
children will be our children's friends."

"And I said I was glad."

I took her hand, held it, and was set on fire by it.

"There is another thing, Gladys. You have seen the marshes only
for a glimpse and our farming country which is unexciting. There
are other, different, lovely places—"

"I have also seen mountains—"

"At a distance! There is Storn, my dear, which is like Devon but
wilder and more spacious, and Winder, which I have not visited,
like Norway—"

"And Vantry! Don't forget Garton's invitation."

"There is The City like no other in the world."

"Your home once! I want to see it. We will go!"

I played with her hand and kissed it.

"John," she said, "I take back what I said about farm life making
you dull, and about not understanding. And I didn't know that you
felt as you do about our children."

I drew her nearer, but she resisted.

"But there will be a great deal of me in our children as well as you," she said.

"It is what I want. Aren't you glad also?"

"Oh! Of course! But how can you be glad?"

Her resistance ceased. I held her against me, thinking: why not have a child now? But she had been in Islandia less than a month. . . .

Two happy days followed. We visited the shipyard and docks, rode to Thane and picked up the Fannar Bay horse and returned him to his owner with a gift of a sack of apples and twelve bottles of wine. Declining an invitation to spend the night we rode to the house of Dorn III, the Judge. He was at home, and he and Gladys liked each other. Next day we returned by a new route, avoiding Thane, crossing the Lister River, and riding over the hills that separated it from the Lay. Thus we reached our farm through the lands of the Sevins and Rannals.

We left the horses, Fak and Gran, at the stable and walked to the house. It was late twilight, overcast, chilly, quiet.

She had been full of fun and gladness.

"Well," she said, "we have come home to the farm!" In her voice was a trace of sarcasm and hostility.

May—November in the United States—was a long month. The absences of the *denerir* increased the daily work to be done. I was happy and absorbed in the occupations of the farm, but it was unfair to Gladys to give them all the time I wished. There were many in which she could have joined either with me or near me; but she never came unless asked on each occasion, constrained by a shyness which I found hard to understand, but accepted, hoping that time would cure it. When asked she did what was requested of her obediently, cheerfully, willingly, but with so little heart in her work that I felt like a taskmaster and became shy in making suggestions. Yet several times when the work took us afield together away from the others she came with what seemed gladness. Thus we spent two happy half days upon the fences of the pastures. More often, however, when I worked she was in the house. Once or twice, however, she made sketches which she kept in her paintbox and showed me with so much hesitation that I did not really see them, unwilling to force her to betray them. Sometimes when I came home she told me

of walks she had taken, usually along the river lanes. Sometimes also
she rode Gran by herself. Every other day or so we went together on
foot or on horseback, but these expeditions were not easy to arrange.
Whenever I asked her to come with me she cross-examined me as to
whether I did not want to do something else more. The fact of the
invitation was not enough for her, and because of the ordeal to which
I was put with each one I dreaded making them. Yet on several days
of rain squalls and light flurries of snow we had a happy time in the
workshop making frames and stretchers for her pictures.

In the evenings we were together, nearly always at our own house.
We attended the "days" of three or four of our neighbors and had
the first one of our own with music by Ansel "brother," and dancing.
She was a charming hostess, at ease with the old, as young as and one
of the youngest. She seemed to enjoy it, but afterwards said that she
was thankful that it was over for another month.

She read a great deal and reading consumed her time but made
her restless afterwards, her mind active, and full of comparisons between Islandia and the United States, which we discussed at length
sometimes disagreeing, several times with heat. Yet she was fair and
read Islandian books as well as her own in English; the *Life of Alwina, Letters from the Moors,* fables, and verse. She had many
criticisms to make and often ended one of our arguments by crying
out that she wished she had some new exciting novel, and that she
missed newspapers and magazines.

Away from her I had many long and somber thoughts upon her
maladjustment to the life that I had given her. Remembering that it
had been several months before I had accepted Islandia I hoped she
would follow the same path and come to love the country and its
manner of living, its beauty, and its peacefulness as I had. There
was often, however, a sense of darkness—darkness by day when I
was away at work and when we talked or argued in the evening; and
it would have been a sad hard thing to endure had we not continued
to desire each other so much. In our passion there was always a flame
that we could light. When we were lovers or spoke of love there was
no disaccord; yet sometimes it seemed that we forced this light too
much, seeking the pleasures of our senses when not truly wanting
each other, because in them only had we a light in common. There
would follow a feeling of having abused her loveliness and of having
clouded my own fire, and the darkness would be deep and full of

ominous shadows like a coming storm. At work next day, however, I would find freshness again and with it hope.

June came and it was winter, the days short and often overcast, the air bitter, the ground hard. Gladys found the house cold in spite of roaring open fires, but she would not wear the warm garments of Islandian women. She wanted a steam-heated house and the freedom and lightness of thin underwear, and on harsh days hugged the hearth.

Early in the month there came a lovely day and when I returned from hard labor cutting wood, I found her wind-burned and tired. She had been for quite a long walk, she said. She was silent at supper, and I ascribed it to fatigue. Afterwards we went up to the studio where I made the fire blaze, turned the bench to face it so that there would be no drafts, covered it with rugs and cushions to make it soft, and there I laid her down. Her eyes lingered on mine, a question in them.

"You are very sweet to me," she said, as though it were something to which she was not entitled and which I was unduly kind to give. I sat on the floor by the bench. We seemed far apart, very much isolated. A strong wind had come up and it was growing colder.

I took her hand, but pressing her thumb against the side of mine she firmly released it.

"I wish the windows wouldn't rattle!" she cried.

"I'll tighten the fastenings," I answered, rising.

"Oh, don't!" she cried. "Stay where you are, please. Don't bother! It doesn't matter!"

I sat down again, looking into the fire, wondering whether I had done what she really wanted, obeying her instead of fixing the windows. She lay on the bench behind me and I could feel her eyes on the back of my head . . . Why had she taken her hand away? I could not blame her for not wishing to have it held. Perhaps something was wrong and in her time she intended to have it out with me. I waited, humiliated a little by the unexplained withdrawal, apprehensive of fruitless argument; and at the same time happy to be near her, physically content and peaceful though tired, and with a desire that also waited—not insistent but sweet and promising—which I felt sure that she would later reciprocate in spite of her quick refusal of her hand.

She broke the silence.

"You haven't asked about my walk," she said.

"Where did you go, Gladys?"

"We went along the river as far as the Sevins' and then back to the Upper Bridge, and I came to the house over the hill."

"We"! Who went with her? Did she wish me to ask?

"That is all of five miles," I said.

"It is a lovely walk. We saw a little gray wolf. It was the first I had ever seen . . . Young Sevin said they were harmless and came down from the hills in winter, but the little gray blur moving like a flash through the trees startled me."

Young Sevin had walked with her. Was it a chance meeting or arranged . . ? I waited.

"I have only seen them once or twice," I said at last. "They are more like foxes than real wolves . . . I'll speak of it to Ansel, for they go after poultry."

She made no answer for a long time. . . .

"John, what am I going to do?" Her voice was shaking. I turned to her, and her eyes met mine, steady but as though reproachful.

"What is the matter, Gladys?" I reached for her hand and then thought better of it.

At my gesture and question she uttered a sigh, turned her head away, and put her hands out of reach.

"Tell me what the trouble is," I said softly.

"What do you think?"

"I don't know, Gladys."

"Did you know young Sevin had come to see me—oh, five or six times?"

"No. I met him once when I was coming home from the barns . . ." My heart became heavy and beat.

"Well, he has—I have been to walk with him several times."

"Have you, Gladys?"

"I said so . . . Yes!"

What should I say—or think?

"I don't see why you shouldn't, Gladys."

"Is it Islandian of me?"

"Oh, Gladys! It isn't Islandian to be secret with me about it."

She uttered a little moan and I looked away.

"I haven't meant to be secret," she said.

"But you found it hard to mention naturally? Was that it?"

"Yes, I suppose so. You were so interested in other things when you came home. You often seemed so far off. And all the conventions here are so different."

"Don't worry, Gladys."

"I do worry—about lots of things. I can't help wondering . . . I know for example that Ansel 'brother' and Stanea used to be lovers and now are like an old married couple or special friends. She told me quite frankly. Did you know?"

"I thought it not unlikely, but I didn't bother one way or the other."

"Then there is you yourself—"

"I, Gladys?" I cried.

"Yes, John, you! Your attitude about that girl of whom you told me in New York. I have been wondering . . . You spoke about it as a natural thing—said you had gained . . . I have never asked you before."

She stopped abruptly.

"She lives nearly a hundred and fifty miles from here," I said, "and I have not seen her nor written her nor heard from her since I have been here, nor thought about her often. I have too much else. I have wondered several times what to do if her path crosses yours and mine. Sooner or later we are likely to meet—"

"You need not bother! I won't know."

"Would you like to know?"

"I don't think so . . . Perhaps, if you saw anything of her."

"If *we* saw anything of her."

"I don't care."

"If you do care, say so! She has no shame of me nor I of her. She would not mind my telling."

"That's just it! You have no shame. No one has, here! That is what upsets me so. I should think you would be ashamed . . . I would be."

"I am not so sure, if you really had deeply cared and found it natural. Your bringing up might tell you that you ought to be ashamed and you might think you were, but in your heart it would not be true."

"I ought to be!"

"Oh, no—not ashamed."

"Aren't you sorry?"

"I regret a little that it did not turn out to be my best. I told you in New York what I felt . . . Are you sorry?"

"I wish that it had not been—that you came to me as I came to you. But I have loved you. I still do, no one but you. I don't mind the fact so much as your—your not caring, being so satisfied about everything . . . What will happen to morals if people feel like that? Are there any morals here?"

"The rules of morality are negative ones, imposing prohibitions. Here the existing loves are so strong and so natural that they rule, and prohibitions aren't necessary."

"Oh, my dear—that is not true, people being what they are!"

"It is more true than in Europe and the United States."

"Well—I am an American still, I am afraid." There was shame and pain in her voice, and my heart throbbed and was like lead again.

"Have you something to tell me, Gladys?"

"What does it matter, if there are no moral rules?"

"Your own peace of mind."

"How about yours?"

"Yes, mine. Gladys, what is it?"

She was silent for a moment, and I held my breath.

"Young Sevin wanted to kiss me," she said.

"Did he kiss you?"

"Oh—once. He took me by surprise."

"When, Gladys?"

"This afternoon."

I took her hand and squeezed it till her knuckles cracked, pity and jealousy equally strong. I hurt her but she made no sound.

"I had to speak Islandian. I didn't know what to say," she cried in a hurried broken voice. "He had been all right. Oh, we had before that talked about personal things, I suppose. I had been a flirt, I guess—but not a bad one, John . . . You don't know what I have been through here! But today he wanted to take my hand and wanted to kiss me. Poor Sevin! It seemed to come so suddenly. Everything was all right, and then he began begging me. He said I was so lovely he couldn't stand it . . . And I tried to talk to him. My Islandian went all to pieces. I said he was forgetting that I belonged to you and that I was yours . . . He did not seem to understand . . . I told him we must not do these things or where would we stop . . .

Nothing seemed to make any difference to him. He kept trying to get my hand, and I was trying not to let him have it. He said I was the loveliest thing he had ever seen . . . Oh, John! I couldn't think of any words. I was terribly frightened. Then I suddenly said, 'I have *ania* for John, only for John.' He asked, 'Who is John?' I said, 'Lang! It is only Lang I have *ania* for. I have nothing for you—nothing, nothing!' I could not say the other word to him. He became very quiet then. He said he thought he had better not walk home with me. I said that I thought so too, and that he must not come to see me any more. He agreed to that, but said he wanted to explain himself.

"We stood on the Upper Bridge some time and I let him talk. He asked why I had not told him I had *ania* for you in the first place, that he did not understand me at all, that I was very hard to understand for he never could tell what I was feeling, that just as I seemed about to say something I didn't say it. How was he to know? he asked. I hadn't shown him a single sign to indicate that you and I were '*alia*-sharing lovers.' Of course he knew we lived together and thought we might be. He reminded me that he had asked me if I were happy in my *ania* and *alia,* and I had said no, but that I was trying to be. I did not think he meant by that question to ask if I loved you. I thought he meant, was I contented with my life . . . I tried to explain myself. Finally he went away, saying that he understood me now and would bother me no longer with his *apia*—he said that word . . ! He went away. I was so ashamed I wanted to die. I stayed on the bridge a long time, trembling."

I held her hand firmly. I laid my cheek upon it. I kissed it, so utterly limp that I could not be sure she knew that I held it.

"It is all right," I said. "It is quite all right, Gladys . . . I am sorry, very sorry you had this happen. Don't worry."

"It is not all right!" she cried.

"You said the right things . . . You love me."

"I know that I did at last, but—that is not all . . . Oh, John, my dear, I do love you. I knew it this afternoon, but I thought that when I married you I would never again have any of the feelings about other men that I used to have. I have been good and decent and all that, but I am susceptible, I suppose. I thought I never would be to anyone else but you. And I am. I was to him . . . until I saw what might happen and then—I was just sick with horror. I do love you! What is wrong with me? You will hate me, I am afraid."

"Never!"

"You have a right to hate me."

"No, only to be sorry because you suffer."

"Don't you care because I felt about him as I did?"

"What did you want of him?"

"To be kissed."

"What stopped you?"

"I belonged to you."

"Was that all?"

"What more could there be, John?"

"You do stir in me something that is like a blind wicked anger," I said.

"Do I, John? I am sorry."

"No," I answered. "You are glad! and I am glad too."

Our eyes met, and I rose and sat by her on the bench and looked in her face.

"Let's have this out," I said. "Do you feel like a sinner?"

She raised her chin and trembled.

"I do," she answered. "I do . . . Why don't you do something to me?"

"Do you know what I think?"

"What are you thinking?"

"You have great vitality. The life you are leading does not put it all to a good use."

Her eyes became still and her body was suddenly quiet.

"You mean I am lazy?"

"You aren't doing anything real, except being mine. That has proved not to be enough."

She turned her head away.

"What a thing to say!" she said.

"What are you thinking?" I asked. "We are going to have this out."

"You are right in a way: I am not being of any use to anyone, you least of all. But how can I be, if being all yours is not enough to you?"

"Gladys, doesn't the farm seem to be your place?"

"No. It is all yours, not mine at all. And I am all yours too. Everything is yours! I am throttled because you don't like me to be all yours. You are strong, serene, impersonal, and cocksure! Every day I am more dependent, more yours . . . You push me off. You are so cold."

"Not cold," I said. "Am I cold when I love you?"

"No . . . You seem to like my body. But that is not enough! I have given everything I am. I need you to lean on. You don't like me to be all yours . . . Oh, John, John, I am so afraid! It has been so beautiful, so perfect, so dear. I have been so happy! I am afraid I shall spoil it all!"

"You can spoil it," I said.

"Why do you let me spoil it?"

"Why do you let yourself spoil it?"

"Is it all my fault? If you think so why don't you make me do the right things? I am yours in spite of what you say."

"How can I make you?"

"Don't you see that I am just loafing and brooding—that I am homesick? Don't you understand my—flirting with young Sevin? I need to be made to do things. But you let me alone. You are so cold and impersonal about it all, when I need—"

"What do you need?"

"I need a strong hand. You are too nice to me. I am yours. I need to be told—oh, to work, to paint, to do things. I'll kick, of course, but if I do kick and refuse to obey you ought to make me—punish me, whip me, or something. I can't do it all myself."

"Shall I make rules and if you break them whip you like a child?"

"Our happiness is at stake. Don't you see I can't help myself? Nothing is the matter with you. You are perfect and dear. Only you don't. . . ."

She paused.

"Don't what?"

"I'll say what you don't like."

"Say it!"

"You don't do or say the right things to me. You merely love me and let me alone. You don't make me do what you want. Can't you see? I am yours. I want to be what you want. I don't know how by myself."

I took her hands and squeezed them enough to hurt her a little.

"I could do it," I said. "I could make you do what I wanted. I could whip you. I would rather like to whip you, Gladys . . . But, oh, the poison it would all be to both of us! Everything you did would

973

be done of my will and not of yours. You would obey, and inwardly reserve your freedom. You would hold fast to the right to criticize and rebel. All the burden and blame of what we did you would escape and shift to me. My poison would come from treating you whom I love—as mine. You aren't mine. I don't want you to be mine. There is nothing you have to do . . . Oh, Gladys, if you love me, give! Don't make me draw it from you, under the pretense that you are mine."

"Let me go," she said. I rose, and without looking at me, she swung herself from the bench and ran to the door of the bedroom. There she turned.

"It will be your own fault!" she cried, and fled through the door.

I settled the logs on the fire, lest they roll out upon the hearth. The bedroom was barred to me now; it would be a strange thing to go to her and sleep at her side after such a repudiation. Nor upon the bench where she had lain, warm with her body, her weight still imprinted on the cushions, would I lie.

She must not kill my happiness.

I went downstairs, but there was no place there where I cared to be. Outside the wind was blowing, full of that chilly dampness that foretells snow. It was very dark, and I waited on the porch until my eyes could see a little better. I walked down to the river feeling the road with my feet. Coming to the bridge I stopped, held by my own land, not wishing to leave it.

She should not kill my happiness, nor by her strong will to be mine force me to share her discontent and rob me of the power to give to her from my heart. She could leave me if she wished and I would aid her in every way, but if she remained with me she must share my *alia* and not escape the burden of it by centering her life upon me. There were more fruitful outlets for her vitality than by a struggle for the impossible, by the vain attempt to submerge her wishes and her will in mine. I loved her for her strength of purpose; she was pitiful; her strength craved an outlet and she saw nothing real but her love for me.

She was unfed. Love and desire were not enough. She was puzzled. She did not understand that because she was hungry, without an *alia* of her own, she had quickened to the passion of young Sevin in the midst of my own. She suffered . . . I loved her for the abundance of her strength. She was no weakling. I loved her and tears of love and adoration ran down my cheeks.

She should not kill my happiness; nor should her discontent, lessening what we shared, convert my *ania* into *apia*. We must not live alone upon desire and love, if love and desire were to remain fresh and refreshing. She and I must live outside our love as well as within it.

But neither must I shirk my task and find my happiness alone. She was not yet won and I must win her. I must take account of her thoughts, her attitudes, if I were ever to lead her to mine, but I must resist the temptation to accept them, to believe with her, to follow her lead.

After a long time peace came back to me, and I returned to the house. Feeling my way up the stairs and through the cold quiet rooms I came to the one that was ours. Here only was there life. Coming to the bed in the darkness I put out my hand and found her there.

"Gladys?"

"Yes, John?" Her voice was a whisper.

"Did I waken you?"

"No. I haven't been asleep. Where have you been?"

"For a walk—to the bridge."

"You have been gone a long time. Are you all right?"

"Yes, Gladys. Are you?"

"I am all right, John."

After several moments, I said:

"I am going to make you do something."

"What?" she asked in a low whisper as though afraid.

"Tomorrow morning we will rise early, pack our saddlebags, mount our horses, and go and see Islandia. Will you come?"

She made no answer. I laid my hand upon her.

"You are coming," I said.

"Yes, I'll come," she answered. "I shall love it."

"And now," I said, "I am going to sleep with you and to love you."

She uttered a low sigh and stirred.

"I feel . . ." she whispered, but I did not heed.

When I was lying by her I drew her reluctant body into my embrace, and she seemed after our quarrel unfamiliar, a stranger.

She began to weep.

"I am sorry," she said. "I feel unworthy. I feel that I ought to be—"

"Hush," I answered, kissing her mouth so that she could speak no more. And after a while I possessed her as though she were a creature with no wishes and no pleasure of her own. She seemed content to have it so, but my heart wept.

She became quietly happy and asked where I was going to take her in Islandia. I replied that all plans were vague and that all I had decided was to start tomorrow.

"It will be the greatest fun in the world," she said.

We drifted into sleep not knowing when it was.

41

A Bodwin Fable

NEXT MORNING we each packed two changes of costume in saddle-bags and added a few other articles of use and for pleasure; I went to fetch the horses and to tell Ansel that we were going; Gladys and Stanea prepared a lunch; and then we set out, thus casually and simply, for a week or a month. Low gray clouds were in the sky, the air was brisk and not too cold, and we rode down to the bridge in a flurry of large, soft, snow crystals that soon dotted with white her brown hood and cloak. Her face, looking out from its nunlike shelter —the only part of her visible, the rest wrapped and altered in outline—was red-lipped and red-cheeked in the sharp wind, wet from melting snow on cheeks and eyelashes, and happy as a child's.

We rode to Doring Town, lunching in a quiet place in Doring Wood while falling snow seethed on dead leaves, struggling against wind and weather that were rather a boisterous friend than a hostile enemy. She said that though her mother used to declare that the one truly satisfactory feature in modern times was the elimination of weather from daily life, she had always loved storms, and was glad to meet one really for the first time; but she was tired when we reached the palace and went to bed early.

Next day it was overcast but clearing and somewhat colder. Our destination was the Inn at the Doan Pass, a thoroughfare which to me was interesting and beautiful but no longer unusual or fearful. She, however, was doing something she had never done before: riding through a high pass in winter. The snow was deep in the higher places, and the road was reduced to a narrow, beaten trail. She was very much alive, excited, even a little fearful, responding keenly to the situation with all the sensations of dangerous but happy adventuring.

Charmed by her gallant companionship I was conscious of her feelings, experiencing what she was experiencing, and hoping that my old and painful memories would be covered over. The Doan Pass had been a place of suffering, and in my heart it had become a shrine dedicated to Dorna. Now I resisted the temptation to be once more her devotee. I tried to accept the significance of natural things and my present life with Gladys in their purity, uncolored by particular associations of the past. Any impulse to dwell upon what was not with me in reality cut me off from the beauty that was mine. But I was not yet Islandian enough to accept the Doan Pass for what it was. Voices called me to the shrine. I sought to set up another one and to worship there. I made passionate love to Gladys, and thus, having become a devotee, my other goddess exacted her due . . . I was not simple enough . . . My dear companion, who knew nothing of these conflicts, was delighted and a little overwhelmed to be loved so much; and next day when we rode down through the pines, the branches of which sagged under the weight of snow, while my heart bled for Dorna, she was saying that she had a Christmas feeling as though something wonderful were going to happen.

When, however, the roar of the Cannan River no longer sounded in my ears and we had ridden into autumn weather again upon the plains of Inerria, green with recent rain, I was all hers again. She was very happy, so young that her growing fatigue did not lessen it. After a night at the Inn of Inerria Town we rode on to the Somes', and there I decided to give her a day of idleness and rest. Like a child who once started does not want to stop she objected, but as soon as she was overruled she relaxed and took full advantage of her day of inactivity. She had brought with her Carstairs' *Travels* for reading, a sketchbook, and a diary begun when she left New York, continued until her arrival in Islandia, but a blank ever since. She now wrote of her present journey with a flying pen.

She was pleased with and was the pleasure of her hosts, Some XII, Broma, and Danninga, his mother. Upon the second and last evening of our visit, the clan of Somes gathered to meet her, word having been sent to those who dwelt in Loria Wood. This courtesy of theirs made us all stronger friends. She met Some I, the retired General, Marrinera, his wife, and the young Some with whom I had dug a trench and found the *darso* bulb. He liked her and was friendly and yet light-handed. That night when we were going to bed she said he made her less afraid of Islandian young men. The hurt of Sevin's behavior and her own response still rankled, yet she was loyal. Though Some seemed a finer, more trustworthy sort, nevertheless, she said, she could not help feeling that Sevin was a gentleman.

"I am to blame, John," she declared. "I should have made things clear at the start. He did not understand. You have been very nice about it . . . but I am glad we came away, though it really wasn't necessary. I love you! I love you! I love you!"

And she came to me and proved it.

Next day, June 9th, we rode to the Bodwins' accompanied by Some XII and Broma who were on their way to The City and the Council Meeting on the eleventh. We were all about the same age except for Gladys and she was old enough. Broma who had lately weaned her child was light-hearted with freedom and irresponsibility, singing as she rode, teasing us about our slower horses. Some, though Lord of a Province, was high-spirited also, infected by her and by Gladys who was happy with two new and jolly friends. We were bound for the house of Bodwin, Lord of Bostia, whose wife was Some's second cousin, instead of that of Bodwin the Marshal where I had heretofore stayed. Our destination was the dwelling of Bodwin the Younger, but no one thought to tell Gladys that she was doing the Islandian equivalent of visiting Shakespeare's house as the guest of his descendants. Not sure that she knew he was a Shakespeare I let her find out for herself.

At supper when the fact was revealed by our host in the course of casual conversation I watched to see how she would take it. Her eyes became fixed for a moment and afterwards I saw her looking about with new interest, taking note of walls and furniture. In the evening Bodwin, the brother of the Marshal, and Cania, his young and silent wife, came to see us. Gladys, an American woman, was a little of a curiosity to most Islandians and perhaps especially so to these people, for the brother of the Lord of Camia had also married a foreign woman, the only native Islandian who to my knowledge had done so. This woman, called Marya (without stress on the y) was Mary Alice Miller-Stuart, the daughter of Sir Colin, builder of Suburra, and dwelt with her husband near the Tanar River, about twenty miles away. She and her sister, Mrs. Gilmour, her brother's wife, an Englishwoman, and Gladys were the only foreign women permanently resident in Islandia, and of these Mrs. Miller-Stuart was hardly to be counted for she with her husband, Sir Colin's son, was as often in England. Gladys's realization of the fact that she was the only foreign woman, neither English nor of the Miller-Stuart clan permanently in Islandia, living an Islandian life, appealed to her imagination and made her eyes bright.

When we went up to bed she wanted to talk over these matters.

"I should like to meet Mrs. Bodwin—I mean Marya," she said, "and the Miller-Stuarts and Gilmours also. Am I likely to do so?"

"We will go and see them."

"Can we? Do you know them well enough?"

"Oh, yes. Instead of going on to The City why don't we ride to the Tanar River Bodwins' tomorrow and to the Gilmours' next day?"

"I should love to. I should like to see how the women get along, particularly Marya. I need friends."

"She is more than twice your age."

"I'd like an older woman—of my own kind—for a friend." Her eyes became thoughtful. "You see, Mother . . ." But she did not finish.

"We will go tomorrow."

"That would be fine—if you would. But it is for you to say. If you want to visit The City—"

"There is time enough—"

"All our lives," she said with a sigh. "Yet I can't help feeling that Islandia is only a temporary visit—that we are sightseers, as Mother and I were in Europe. I'm sorry if that hurts you." She put out her hand.

"It doesn't hurt me," I answered. "What you feel, you feel. But I also want you to adopt Islandia."

She listened with downcast eyes as though to a lecture. When I had finished she looked up with a quick smile.

"I am trying," she said.

"You are a darling, Gladys."

She shook her head.

"Oh no, I wish I were."

"According to what I feel you are a darling—"

"That doesn't make me one. I have failed you several times."

"You have been yourself and yourself is what I love. You are changing and growing. Accept all that comes naturally, and you will feel at home here in time."

"Haven't I tried?"

"Yes, but you have theories that stand in the way. You measure and compare rather than feel and learn."

She turned her face away.

"You look as though I were scolding you," I said, and I kissed her smooth warm cheek. She smiled but her eyes were grave.

"I am learning," she said. "Wait, John dear. And let me rebel, won't you please? Let me tell all my troubles to you!"

"Always!"

"They grow much less when I do. I need you—more than you know. I love you and need you, and you love me and don't need me, and that makes me hate Islandia at times."

"When we are equal we shall both be the happiest givers. One who is too much in need is handicapped as a giver."

"You odd man!" she said, and then as though it were hopeless she changed the subject. "Why didn't you tell me that this was where the great Bodwin lived?"

"Do you think him great?"

"You haven't answered my question!"

"I did not tell you because I was not sure what it would mean to you. This is just a house where people live after all."

"Were you afraid I would act like a tourist here?"

"Oh, no! But if Bodwin is not a great man to you I would rather have the place speak for itself."

"Do you think his works great?"

"I do, the more I know them. He voices Islandia better than anyone else."

"His fables provoke me," she said. "I feel as though he were talking to me in words of one syllable because that is all I am capable of understanding, but that at the same time he is expressing hidden meanings with a smile over my head to other people who are more knowing than I!"

"I have felt that way. . . ."

"All Islandia is like that sometimes, you included!"

"How about the young men you have talked to?"

"That is unkind!"

"Do they talk over your head with a smile?"

"Of course they don't!"

"Maybe it is only Bodwin and I?"

She fixed me with her eyes and looked at me a long time as though she did not know me, and were wondering what I was. Her eyes dropped finally and she shuddered a little.

"I love you anyway," she said gravely, as though it were a fact which she found true in spite of herself and with surprise . . . "And I'll try to like Bodwin . . . I have liked him very much. That is honest, John!" She rose. "I am going to bed," she said.

While she undressed, I took from my saddlebag a volume of the *Fables* to look for evidences of this quality that she found objectionable. While I was reading she came and looked over my shoulder, brushing her hair. Her nearness, her faint warm odor, was distracting. I put my arm around her, but read on. The hissing of the brush on her hair ceased, and I felt her cheek on mine.

I held the book for her to see, and thus with her eyes on the same page we read together but not aloud this fable:

"In that part of Bostia Province which is drained by the Tanar River the soil is black, and the farmers' greatest difficulty is luxuriance and rapidity of growth both of weeds and of what is sown. They are good friends and many of them come to Bostia Town to pay their taxes and to buy what they do not produce."

Her cheek moved.

"Like us going to Thane," she said.

We read on.

"A certain man from this district was said by his neighbors to be the surest and most helpful critic in all matters relating to the beauty of farm landscape and of carving in stone. His ability was all the more strange, they declared, because he himself had been unable to beautify his own farm and his efforts to carve in stone were failures; but they said, he is a true artist. I did not ask why, although I wondered what they meant.

"When I was adding a new wing to my house and was planting new trees and shrubs this man very kindly came to advise me. His name was Noral. He had no suggestions to offer but tested all of mine with a balanced judgment and a sure imagination. Without his advice my house and the trees around it would not have been the lovely thing they now are. Whence came this ability to help me from one who could himself create nothing?

"Later I visited Noral. He was an artist, not in trees and fields and buildings, not in stone nor in paint, but in his relations with the woman who shared his *alia*—an artist in *ania*. She grew as a flower grows, and his concern was not to train her like a vine nor to prune her like a fruit tree nor to graft alien branches upon the trunk of her being, though she loved him as some women do and would have permitted all these things had he wished them. He, however, enriched the soil about her and freed it of weeds and was careful that no blight descended upon her. She grew in her own natural form and produced her own flowers and fruits. Exacting nothing he was given much. He gave greatly and always from his heart. His hands were delicate upon her life but he loved her strongly. He had no wish to change her nor she him.

"While I lay at their house I heard their laughter together as untroubled as the song of birds."

Finishing before she did, I waited. . . .

"He was sweet," she said. "He is like you."

I drew her around beside me. Her dressing gown fell open and I held her to me and kissed her a little below her breasts, and my kiss, near the middle of her, was intended for all of Gladys, not merely for her body, but for her mind, her theories, and her rebellions also. She pressed her soft warm flesh against my lips.

"That kiss isn't only for me," she said above me.

"What else is it for?"

"You kissed your *alia* too, my dear John. I know you did."

"No, only you."

"Only me and your *alia!*" She laughed and freed herself.

Next day, June 10th, Bodwin and Danninga, Some and Broma, rode southeast along the National Highway toward The City while Gladys and I on Gran and Fak went northeast towards the Tanar River district by narrow country roads. The sky was overcast and the ground white with a light fall of snow. It was a day of black and white and gray, somber and a little dispiriting, but we were happy. The thread of Bodwin ran through our thoughts. Along this road Noral and Bodwin had very likely traveled. She hoped that there were still Norals in the region to which we were going. We talked about Bodwin and she marveled at the fact that the Islandia of his

day was so like that of ours, whereas Chaucer's and even Shakespeare's England were very different from the present one.

We lost our way once or twice but it did not matter. There was
chilly mist in the dark afternoon. The plowed lands of the Tanar
River farms, with snow between the furrows, showed how truly
black was the soil. We reached our hosts just in time not to be
benighted.

Mary Alice Miller-Stuart was so English that it was difficult to
call her Marya and not Mrs. Bodwin. She wore a wedding ring, but
so did Gladys. She was about forty-three, rather weather-beaten, with
bright color in her somewhat veined cheeks, a thin handsome face
more masculine than feminine, the blue eyes of one a little spoiled
in childhood, and a spare body of quick movements. Though born
in Islandia she had been educated in England, and by choice spoke
English to us. I had not met her before but knew her as the author
of a book on Islandian art.

She made us welcome in an overcrowded room filled with paintings, drawings, and bas-reliefs, European and Islandian, and some
English furniture, gave us tea, and deplored the fact that we had
come at this season and could not see her garden. She was glad we
had come to see her, and hoped she would see something of us, was
sorry Gladys lived so far away from herself, the Gilmours and her
brother and sister-in-law (who were in England now), and hoped
Gladys was not lonely. The foreign colony was small, she said, but
still they were all good friends. They made a point of Christmas, she
said, and all met at her brother's place in Camia, and she hoped we
would feel at liberty to come—and would we like to see some of the
specimens of Islandian art that she had collected . . . ?

That night Gladys and I did not have our usual talk summarizing
and commenting upon the day's experiences. She was too tired. She
had had a long talk with Marya, whom she was determined to call
Mrs. Bodwin, while I sat with Bodwin himself in his rather bare office
or study, sipping *sarka*.

Next morning it was still gray and gloomy and, once more upon
the road, we both were rather silent. She had not outslept her fatigue.
I wondered a little what she and Marya had talked about so long.
When we were a few miles from the house upon a muddy road of
dark earth she brought Gran up to Fak and looked me in the eyes.

"Well," she said, " 'Mrs. Bodwin' was very nice to us, wasn't she? But isn't she English!"

"She seemed so to me."

"Why does she stay here?"

"She married an Islandian."

"I suppose that is the reason . . . She gave me some advice."

"What did she tell you?"

Gladys questioned with her eyes.

"You seem so Islandian I hesitate to tell you. She kept thinking you were one and speaking as though you were, and then remembering you weren't and saying no doubt it would therefore be easier for me . . . She was very frank! The funny thing was . . ." She paused and laughed to herself. "It is a joke on me. The effect on me was that I didn't mind what you were, the more Islandian the better."

"What did she say?" I repeated.

"Many things. She said there were good doctors and that I needn't worry about having children, and that I seemed very young indeed—a mere girl, she said. She saw I wore a ring and said that Islandian marriage seemed so little like marriage that she had insisted on being married at the nearest Anglican church which was at St. Anthony. 'Bodwin was rather a dear about it,' she said, 'but Islandia is a man's place rather than a woman's.' Though Islandian men were gentlemen and faithful and well-bred and did not interfere with one, still they held themselves rather aloof. One had to learn to live very much upon one's own resources . . . Then she remembered and said, 'But you haven't married an Islandian, have you? And Americans are said to make very devoted husbands.' She asked me what I did and I told her about my paints. She was very discouraging. She said the Islandians had done charming things in the sort of pastels and colored chalks they used, and in black and white, but that there were no serious artists or art, and that for one to go on alone in oils was rather hopeless. She knew from experience. Still, she wished me well and advised me to go on with it while I could, and not to let it slip for I could not get it back again, and that I would be expected to nurse my own child and that to paint and nurse a child was not easy. She has had two . . . She talked and talked. I can't tell you half of what she said."

"Is she the older woman friend you want?" I asked.

Gladys shook her head.

"She made me awfully tired," she answered, "or maybe it was riding for so many days. And she was rather upsetting. She set my back up for some reason. She meant awfully well, I know, but I didn't like the way she talked about her husband, not directly of course, but as one of a class. I liked Bodwin—but I like all the men here. The more she talked the more I liked them. I kept thinking of you and how nice you are, as nice—oh nicer!—than anyone else I have met, and I thought about that fable we read night before last . . . Perhaps I am more adaptable. She was thirty-two when she married . . . I hope Mrs. Gilmour is different."

"She is, but she married an Englishman."

"I don't think the trouble is marrying an Islandian but remaining stuck in what you were before you married him. That has been one of my troubles."

"You are all right, Gladys!" I said. "Don't worry about your troubles."

"Rebellions aren't over yet!"

It was a hard day, the air penetratingly chilly and full of mists that shut us within a narrow world of muddy roads, and dark fences and hedges, all distance veiled. We crossed the Tamplin River near where the Tanar joins it, and struck north for the Tamplin-Reeves road, thereby lengthening the journey but lessening the chance of being lost. Gladys was tired indeed when we reached the dark walls of the University, but she was plucky and she quickened at seeing the dark arcades and cloisters, the bulk of old buildings, and the mysterious doors lighted by lanterned candles; and the Gilmours were sympathetic hosts.

They were alone, having sent their children to England to school. To me their house, wholly English, was a restless place with many odds and ends to attract the attention. In the United States the eye and the mind learn to eliminate when there is more than can be conveniently seen, but in Islandia one lost that self-protective ability.

But they had a piano, and after dinner Gladys, somewhat revived by the easy kindliness of our hosts, asked if she might try it. She sat a long time at the keys before venturing to begin. She did a few scales and chords and played charmingly Schumann's "Warum?" Then she at once took refuge in a deep chair and would not go back.

It was not until we had been alone together for some time that she said what was on her mind. She wanted a piano, but supposed it was impossible to get one even if we could afford it. . . .

"If painting fails me I must have something outside myself," she said as we lay together in the darkness. I told her that I would do what I could, and promptly she argued against even thinking of a piano. "I won't let the painting fail me. When I go back to the farm I shall take it up again in earnest. I am perfectly rotten at it but I am going to do portraits. I shall begin on Ansel 'Brother,' who is a character."

We remained at the Gilmours' the next day, most of which she spent in their library surrounded by books which she looked at rather than read.

"Isn't there anything modern in Islandia?" she asked, and I promised to investigate when we reached The City.

We discussed where we would go next, and as soon as I mentioned the fact that the Fains' was but a day's ride, she was eager to go there, even though the day would be a long one and Lord Fain away. The weather had become fine and her fatigue seemed gone. She said that though the University was fascinating, the Gilmours' was stuffy and she did not want to be in a city yet.

Therefore, early next morning, we were on the road again. More than once during the day I regretted the attempt. We did not reach Tindal until dark, and once more I went on foot up the endless defile of the Frays River. There was a moon nearing the first quarter, but the road often passed through pools of utter blackness. For a little while Gladys walked with me, the horses behind us, but mounted again with relief.

I remembered this same journey with Nattana and her two brothers, but there was no moon then, and all was very different.

Gladys was frank about her fatigue, saying that she had never been so tired in her life, but it did not affect her mood. She retained her happiness and thereby upheld mine. When we had passed through the familiar gates and pine wood and reached the house that I knew so well, she could hardly stand, but laughed at her plight.

Mara alone was at home. Lord Fain and his brother had both gone to The City. Gladys was too tired for a formal supper. Warmed milk was all she wanted, and a chance to lie down. She stretched out on the bed and said that she was too weary to undress and ached in every limb.

"I am all right, John. Don't worry about me. In time Islandia will make me tough. This is only temporary, my dear."

Her face was a little pinched, older, and stronger. I watched her, wondering what I could do for her. The thought of her suffering wrenched my heart, not so much now but in future. If I lost her I would want to die.

"Don't look so scared," she said. "Really I am all right! I'll be myself tomorrow."

"It is not that I am afraid, but that I love you. What can I do?"

"You can undress me."

I was her nurse, but felt myself her lover also, as I took off all her clothes, disturbing her as little as possible. She was as limp but as awkward as a large doll. Then covering her over and making up the fire I went to Mara, who gave me some oil of the sugar gum, which is mollifying and aromatic. Returning I set it before the fire to heat.

She was drowsing.

"What are you going to do?" she asked. I told her and she stretched luxuriously.

"I can't believe that I am really at the Fains'," she said sleepily. "I can hardly wait for morning to see it. It is like a dream. Islandia is a dream. . . One has a feeling one ought to be awake and that it is wrong to dream. That is one reason—my conscience."

"What do you think you ought to be doing?"

"Good to others, I suppose. I never did much. Mother and I sewed a little for charity. But I was always going to do more and at home there were things that could be done. But here there aren't any. One can't help being selfish. There is no escape from it, as there was at home."

"Aren't you glad there is no poverty?"

"It is bad for my conscience. . . I thought I might be the lady bountiful of the manor as women are in England and take a turkey in a basket to my grateful tenants. But they are as well off as I am. I have got to have something to do. I shall find it too."

"Painting, playing—things will occur to you."

"Not those, perhaps. Something I find by myself. I am not yours."

This was teasing, but I would not be teased.

"You are your own," I said.

"I shall be very independent."

"You are. Coming to me has not made you less so."

"I may do what you don't like."

"Be true to what you value, not independent for its own sake."

"To be true to what I value would make me wholly yours, and you don't want it."

I could think of no answer to this sort of statement except a straight denial. Instead I uncovered her and rubbed her muscles with the heated oil. With a new motive for what I did, caring for her body which I had enjoyed, yet seeing her naked and close, all the simple dear details that were Gladys, I felt her value in a new way, a value so great, so beautiful, so precious that my heart broke with love and I saw her blurred and glowing through tears. I adored her. She was my friend and perfect companion, my pleasure, and the certain path of my fulfillment. The word "love," the word *ania*—neither was enough. My touch was half a caress and I lingered over what I was doing, and she gave herself like a quiet lover, with closed eyes, relaxed and sleepy. . . .

I thought she slept and covered her again, and myself went to bed, but as soon as I lay by her side she came drowsily into my arms.

"If I am not yours, there is something special that is ours," she whispered.

There were many friends upon the Fain and Catlin farms, and next morning they began coming to see us, all urging us to stay long and to stop at their houses, but we had made up our minds to remain only a day. Gladys in spite of her fatigue was restless. She wanted to see The City and to meet other friends there.

Our visitors treated me with the ease and knowledge of past events characteristic of those with whom one had lived. Anor came, known to Gladys through my letters, with his son and daughter, and five of the Bodins; Bard and Anora, his wife, looking pretty and mysterious; Tolly, my friend, but not Tollia who was having school; four of the Keepings; Larnel and Larnella, the former stronger and older; and then Catlin and his daughters. The last two stayed for lunch.

It had been an invasion and Gladys was fatigued by it, becoming grave and silent. Nevertheless when Catlina Attana, the sculptress who had carved the bas-relief over our mantel at the Lay River Farm, invited her to see her studio, she went. The two young women were of the same age and I did not accompany them, thinking that perhaps Gladys might more easily find the friend she needed.

She did not return until late in the afternoon. Her eyes were a little inturned but bright. She was tired and glad to lie down. I expected her to speak of her visit, but instead she looked at me curiously and doubtfully.

"Is she here?" she asked.

"She? Who?"

"You know—that girl whose lover you were?"

"No—she is not here. This is more than one hundred and fifty miles from the farm."

"Is it true that she isn't here?"

"It is quite true, and I shall tell you who she is and end these doubts of yours—"

"No, please! I don't doubt you."

"I had better tell you."

"No! No! I won't listen. But these people seemed to know you so well. And the way one or two of them looked at you. Never mind, John. Only—there is no one here but you, and people are so strange, and I have no one but you."

"Did you like Catlina Attana?"

"Oh yes, but I was suspicious of her. That bas-relief she did of you, and sketches—and on the way back we stopped at an old mill and there is a portrait of you there. Evidently she has thought about you a great deal."

"I am only a subject, interesting because foreign."

"Perhaps that is all it is. . . ."

"Did you like her work?"

"Oh yes! I was much interested. It is all childish in a way, but intelligent and charming sometimes. It encouraged me. She is my age, she works alone, and she is doing something real. I told her about all my ambitions, and she was very helpful . . . If it had not been for what I was thinking—but that was like a dark cloud."

"You couldn't take her just as she was and for what you had to give each other?"

"No—I'm not Islandian. You are mine, you know."

"If you are not mine—you said you weren't, you know—am I yours, Gladys?"

"Yes, you are!"

"I love you and you only, and I am faithful."

"It is the same thing!"

"If it is the same thing," I said. "Then I am yours and you are mine."

"It is all I mean when I say you are mine and that I am yours. Haven't you understood that?" she said.

"I thought you meant something more."

She shook her head but a little doubtfully; and I knew that she either had changed without knowing it or did not speak the truth.

"Would you like to have Attana visit us sometime?"

"Well," she answered, "maybe we can ask her later."

The friend was not yet found.

We had a quiet supper, but other guests came in the evening, among them Tolly, who was a friend. He was a reader and I led him to talk with Gladys of Islandian literature in the hope that he would quicken her interest and tell her of something modern. I devoted myself to Larnel who had also come again. He confided to me that in the spring he had gone to the Hyths' and had asked Nattana to marry him. She was kind to him, he said, but refused to marry him, refused him everything, even friendship. "She is hard and cold," he added. I was secretly glad and yet until recently I would not have been such a dog in the manger. It was not because the Fains' farm was full of memories of Nattana. The whole affair with her had, in perspective, become a unified thing like a picture. It was full of beauty, bringing that ache in the heart which all beautiful things cause, but it was a picture merely, stirring no desire. Lately, however, like a wound which is thought healed but is not, the affair had become sore again because Gladys seemed to think that it necessarily must be a living, dangerous thing. I did not blame her for her fearfulness, but it threatened to create confusion, and difficulty where none need exist. It would mean nothing to her to be told that *apias* die, for she did not distinguish between *apia* and *ania;* nor that a woman's doubts are full of suggestion to a man, disposing him to new, or to the renewal of old, *apias*. She wanted new proofs constantly fresh. I wondered if I ever could give them. . . .

I watched her talking to Tolly in her friendly way wherein a man had the whole of her smiling interest and intelligence. It was not merely manner. She truly gave herself, and I knew suddenly what had quickened young Ansel and young Sevin and made men like her so much. It was giving, unconscious but complete so far as it went. While it lasted I had none of her. . . . I faced the fact and accepted it. It was hopeless to expect all, and stultifying to her if I made her give it. . . . Why could she not treat my affair with Nattana in the same way? She would have her answer: I had possessed Nattana. There was a difference, but was it a difference in kind and not merely of degree? She herself had been kissed within six weeks of her marriage to me. Was that a difference in kind or of degree?

How futile jealous wonderings were! She gave to me greatly. Why strive to attain an impossible, destructive whole? Yet she wanted it of me, I knew. She wanted all other affairs effaced. Because she wanted it I was put under compulsion and the freedom of my giving lessened. . . . Yet she tried hard not to exact too much.

As I watched her I felt a sudden shock of fear. The flush in her cheeks was almost hectic, her eyes too brilliant. She was too tired to go on traveling.

Later, when we were alone, she admitted that she was tired but declared that she was not *too* tired. She did not want to stay any longer at the Fains'. She would remain as long as I liked at The City and do nothing! Tolly (who was very nice) had given her a list of new Islandian books which could be got only at The City. She would read and rest all day long once we were there. . . . There was nothing the matter with her at all, except, if I must know, the coming of an event that happened to all women.

She had her way and we left early next morning riding to Reeves in one day, but stopping at the Provincial Palace instead of at the Gilmours', and to The City the next. The ride thrilled her and I was happy in her interest and excitement in what she saw and flattered by her memories of my letters. The City was exactly what she expected it to be, only much more beautiful, clean, and bright under a clear winter sun. Lord Dorn came to see her for a few moments, having no time for a longer visit. She gave him her hand and said with an unrepentant smile that she was sorry to use his house as a place of rest but felt that he would not mind. Did he? He laughed and shook his head. They said little more. They understood each other in a way that excluded and yet amused and pleased me.

She needed little care and frankly said that for the present she wanted to be let alone and to be by herself. I brought her an armful of the books upon Tolly's list, fables, poetry, and essays, all written within the last twenty-five years; and she read by the hour, very lovely with bright color in her cheeks, bent head, and absorbed eyes. I also hunted for a piano and by great good fortune heard of one that had belonged to S. Poloni, former Italian consul. As soon as I was sure I could buy it I told Gladys of my search.

"We can't afford it," she said.

I produced a piece of paper and showed her my figures.

"We can afford it," I answered, "if we live at home simply and forego luxuries and make only one more trip like this before the next harvest."

She watched me with her bright dark eyes trying to read my wishes and govern her own accordingly.

"What do you want? I am no musician. You won't hear much that is good."

"There is another thing to be thought of. You will have to tune it yourself."

Her face lighted.

"I think Ansel 'brother' and I could do that."

"All right. We will get it."

"No, John. There are surely things you want more."

"There is not one!" I lied, for I wanted a boat in which I could sail through the marshes.

She waited some time.

"I would like a piano," she said shyly. "And as to the simple life I'm content with that. There are no luxuries I want, and I think one trip like this will be enough for this year. . . Could I try the piano?"

"Of course! Any time."

"I think I'll get up," she said. "Could we go now?"

She enjoyed the walk along the quays, past the Western docks, and the Agency and Navy Buildings and the hotel, and across the Islandia River by the Botian Bridge, and thence north among the warehouses of the Alban docks to that of The City, where the piano was stored. It was a small grand, in good condition, but somewhat out of tune. She tried it and was satisfied, and felt so well that she was anxious to call upon the Periers who lived near, and who had come to see her. I was glad because in Marie or Jeanne she might find the needed friend. But it was M. Perier who attracted her and his daughters went almost unnoticed.

We returned at dusk over City Hill, arm in arm. Never before had it seemed so beautiful, so dear, so mine, with holiday in the air. I knew it now as most Islandians knew it, the place of government, meetings of friends, and trade, belonging to and serving all the countrymen.

The meetings of friends, however, were not occurring because Gladys, still resting, was seeing no one there. It was already June 19th and next day the council adjourned. She seemed so indifferent that I did not stress the matter to her, but I had a feeling of opportunity lost. I had learned that Stellina and both Moranas were in The City, as well as Stellin and Tora, Lord Mora, young Earne, and others. Dorna, however, was at the Frays again and for the same reason as before. Lord Hyth had come unaccompanied. I was content to have it so, and told Gladys that neither Dorna nor "that girl" were present.

Lord Dorn, however, took matters in his own hands and prevented our visit from being barren of meetings. On the night of the twentieth he assembled Tora, Stellina, both Moranas, Lord Mora, Lord Fain, and young Stellin to meet Gladys and me. Several postponed their departure in order to be present. Conversation was general with such distinguished men present. There was no opportunity for Gladys to make a friend, but at least she could say that she had seen these people, and they also had seen her. She was never lovelier in my eyes than now with a soft glow in her animated brilliance. She was at ease, aware that all these people were more or less significant friends of "her Lang." She was charming, and I was proud, congratulating myself for fine discrimination upon what I had really taken as a matter of course—the essential similarity of Gladys to these people making her at home with them and them with her.

The seating was cleverly arranged. Lord Dorn had Gladys on his right and Tora on his left. Royalty in Islandia did not exact the seat of honor. But beyond Gladys to counterbalance his age, Lord Dorn had placed Stellin. Opposite to her was Lord Mora. Morana, my princess, upheld the other end of the table with me on her right and Stellina beyond me next to Lord Mora. Opposite me was Lord Fain with Morana Nekka between him and Stellin. Gladys could not have been better placed, nor could I. The only fault was that she and

Stellina were far removed from each other, for my secret hope always was that Stellina would be the friend. I was very happy to meet these persons again and to have Gladys among them. Dorna and Nattana were out of my ken and except for Dorn these had done most to make Islandia beautiful. At my two sides were the loveliest of all my friends. I could say little to either of them except those simple facts that between friends are significant without amplification—facts as to life in the United States, my decision, the Lay River Farm.

At the other end, with Lord Dorn the host, Gladys need only exchange smiles. Lord Mora, across the table, courted her a little and spoiled her, watching her, careful not to make her self-conscious. I overheard him now and then and saw her talking and laughing, flattered but a little on the defensive. . . I hoped her evening was a success, that she was happy. I wondered, thinking of the Lay River Farm, dark, wintry, lonely. Would not this beauty and glamour but increase a contrast, accentuate what to her was its gloom. . . ? She was so pretty, so young, so dear that I wanted her days to be full of color. While her mother lived she had met many people of different sorts. I had condemned her to a life of closer but fewer meetings. . . Would she realize that occasions like this happened at only two seasons in the year and that all others lived as we did most of the time?

As though aware of my thoughts Stellina asked:

"Can I help you in any way to make Gladysa happy here?"

"Do you remember what you said the last time I saw you?" I answered, quickened by her understanding and by a sense of being supported.

"Yes, I remember. I offered to come and see you soon if you brought an American wife."

"You see I have. Will you come?"

"Of course, if you are sure." She paused.

"What do you think, Stellina?"

"I think she has in herself all she needs."

"She says she wants a friend."

"Am I the one?"

"You are the one whom I would like her to have."

"It will be her friend not yours," she said.

"Won't you come? I have thought about it a great deal. Are you willing to come on the chance that you are the one?"

"Yes, I am. But I think I shall bring someone else with me, perhaps two others. Can you house three of us—you and Gladysa?"

"We have room enough and our *denirir* are plenty."

"Would she be overwhelmed?"

"I don't think so."

"Can you ask her?"

I hesitated. I wanted Stellina to arrive as Islandians did, unannounced, expected in general but not in particular, lest Gladys worry over her personality in advance and misconceive it.

"I'll come," said Stellina. "You need not explain. If we are too much for Gladysa I shall know it and leave."

"I hope that doesn't happen."

"If she needs a friend it is worth trying. I shan't mind."

"I should be sorry."

"So should I."

She looked at me with her clear eyes, and what I thought of saying—that I hoped she and I would remain friends in any case—I left unsaid; for I knew that our relationship was such that I could lose her friendship because Gladys took it or because Gladys denied her, and yet still have what was most valuable of Stellina.

Later I was glad I had not said it; it would have colored our intrigue with a false light. As we left it I was free to be secret with Gladys.

The party had freshened rather than tired her. In our room she took my hands and said that she had had a wonderful evening, that they were as nice people as she had ever met, that she had never before seen such pretty girls as Tora especially, and Morana, and Stellina, that Lord Mora was all I ever said he was in my letters, that Lord Fain was a dear, and that the only trouble was that she wanted to know them all better.

"We could go on endless visits, couldn't we?" she cried. "Well, we will some day."

I told her how lovely she looked, and her eyes met mine knowingly, but she did not deny it as usual.

"Did I make any breaks?"

"Of course not!"

She laughed and kissed me.

"I liked your looks as well as anybody's," she said. She sat on my knee. "I love you," she cried. "You don't know how much—and in your way, too, as well as in mine."

"How is my way different?" I asked.

"It is Islandian. It makes me swim for myself and give you what I can. But my way is to think of myself as part of you—and part of me is now, at this very minute, part of you!"

She began to tremble.

"I want two things," she said, "and one is to be taken home soon."

At last she had spoken naturally of the Lay River Farm as home. My voice shook.

"Shall we go tomorrow?"

"Yes, please!"

"We will go tomorrow early."

"Thank you for that—for everything, dear John!"

"What is the other thing you want?" I asked, suddenly remembering that there were two wishes.

"I want you to love me and love me and love me," she said. I held her close and kissed her till she was breathless. It was not enough. . . .

42

Ania

WE WENT HOME by the shortest way, along the shores of Islandia Bay through Botian to the Inn at Some; then to Inerria on the second day; and the Doan Pass on the third. She surprised me by her strength, but she was rather quiet much of the time and at night wanted my arms. On the fourth day we rode down to Doring Town, and on the last took the familiar route by Tory and Doring Forest toward the farm.

It was late dusk when we passed through the Adners' lane, the snow on the ground a white glimmer. Ice tinkled under the bridge. We had been gone three weeks, and the farm had an air of change and as of time passed; but I suddenly found it again as after a night of sleep and forgetting one wakes to the knowledge of love. Because every day I woke thus with the thought of Gladys, I wanted her to share in this happiness, which was one with that which she gave me. On her horse, silent for a long time, she was indistinguishable, darkness that moved. . . I knew no way to tell her.

We rode to the house, which showed no lights. It was too cold to leave the horses standing. She would not remain alone. We laid our saddlebags on the veranda and went on to the stable. It also was vacant and dark, but warm with the heat of the other horses. The flint and lantern were in their accustomed places. The light showed her face, pale with eyes dark and large. She stood quiet while I cared for Gran and Fak, their hard journey over. When all was finished I went toward her, and then with no thought at all held her to me with all my strength.

"Can you understand," I said, "that I love you and because I love you I love home, and love for home makes me love you more? You won't mind my loving two things that really are one?"

"Don't, don't explain!" she cried. "I know, I know. And I haven't been kind always. It is home to me too. It has suddenly seemed like me."

We went to the house telling no one of our arrival. We wished no one to share it with us.

Thinking lately in the terms of the Islandian calendar, tired and preoccupied by our journey, we had forgotten that it was June 25th, my birthday. She remembered as we lay together.

"And I haven't given you anything!" she said.

"It doesn't matter."

"It does matter! I wanted to give you a present."

"I have all I want."

"Are you sure, quite sure?"

"I am perfectly happy."

"I may give you a present all the same."

"Don't bother," I said.

"I can't help bothering."

I kissed her. She was laughing.

It was the solstice and winter had begun, the season of Windorn. The farm like the sun stood still. There was no pressing work except the care of animals, but there were many small tasks and I gave half my day to them, working in a leisurely fashion, and gave the rest of the time to Gladys.

She was tired for a few days and then bloomed like a flower out of season. She never looked lovelier and she lighted the shadowy house on dark days. She was serene and seemed happy, interested in the books that we already had and had brought from The City, and in painting in her studio. Absorbed, she was a new person. Her face became grave, and if her lips smiled her eyes were absent. She seemed at times aloof, but I was careful not to break in on these moods. They changed, for she wanted me, wanted to be loved. Giving her to herself I had no less of her. And every day we walked or rode for a little while, and she was a lover of changing weather and a dear companion.

Two weeks passed quickly, and life seemed good, if a little idle, a little fallow. . . .

It happened that late one afternoon, when we had returned from a walk, I found a message that Ansel wished to see me and I went to his house. When later I came out of the warmth and light into the crisp cold night, the snow seeming blue, I saw a black shadow waiting.

"John," she said, and her voice was troubled.

"Has anything happened?" I took her arm but she was a little stiff.

"We have visitors. I took them to the stable. They are there now seeing to their horses."

My steps quickened but she drew back.

"Who are they?" I asked.

"Stellina whom I met at Lord Dorn's is one of them."

My heart grew warm but Gladys was troubled.

"Who are the others?"

"There is only one other. Her name is Hytha."

"Hytha!" I was suddenly a little sick and my voice was strange. It was not like Nattana to come and yet . . . Islandians had ideas of their own.

"Has she another name?"

"Yes, Stellina called her Nettera."

"She is not the one, Gladys. But I am going to tell who the one is—"

"No, you mustn't. You mustn't! You don't understand. I did not mind her coming if she were the one. I don't care so much as I did. Don't tell me, please. I don't want to know."

"But—" I began.

"I know I seem disturbed, but not really! Don't tell me. I don't care who your Islandian lover was. I understand so much better."

"Can you believe it is all over?"

"Oh yes! There are things you get over. Tell me it was that sort of thing, and I will never bother you again with my curiosity—or jealousy. I know, I know you love me and this place and what we mean to you."

"It is all over," I said. "It was *apia* but a beautiful one."

"That is all I need to know. And I don't mind its having been beautiful to you."

"I have beauty now."

"Don't compare us. We are different. I know we are."

"That is true. . . But the way I said Hytha, Gladys—"

"Don't tell me. I know all I need."

She ran away toward the stable and I followed her, and caught her at the door.

"I won't tell you," I said. "I promise."

The light from the lantern fell upon her face and she was laughing as I was.

Within we found Stellina and Nettera. The latter stood idle leaning against a post watching, but the former, in a way both dainty and efficient, was turning over straw to make a bedding for the horses. She wore a long cape of the flushed gray color that became her so well. It swayed and clung to her with her movements. The hood was turned back from her small pretty head, and she was as graceful as a Tanagra dancer, but more slender, more simple.

Gladys and I came forward, laughter still in our eyes perhaps, and our two guests smiled at us as we exchanged welcomes and greetings; and I knew without its being said that we were all glad of each other, both hosts and guests.

We walked to the house in couples, Gladys and Stellina ahead, while Nettera waited for me to extinguish the lantern and close the stable.

Our guests were cousins and when together a resemblance appeared. Both were slender, fragile seeming, delicately made; the faces of both had an inner serenity that they had won for themselves; both had the clearest of starry eyes, but Nettera's were haunted by dreams.

It was always a surprise to find her in the world and talking naturally of ordinary things.

She was glad to come and see us, she said, but never would have thought of it if Stellina had not written to her. She had not been away from the Bains', except to go home now and then—by which she meant the Lower Farm of the Hyths—since she went there to live. Stellina had asked Nettera to come with her to see Lang and Gladysa. They had met at Tory yesterday. Bain would not let her make the trip alone!

She spoke with a trace of annoyance.

"Why didn't you bring him here? I would have been glad to welcome him."

"Oh, there's the baby!"

"How is she?"

"She is well—like Bain. I have to think to realize that she is mine."

"And your music, Nettera?"

She did not answer for some time.

"I said I would play for you and I will."

"I want to hear you again, and so will Gladysa."

"Stellina said she was going to have a foreign musical instrument, a 'pianoforte.'" She pronounced the word with care and amazement, but her voice was eager. "Has it come?"

"Not yet."

"May I visit you again when it does?"

"Our house is yours, Nettera. . . . But why not stay till it does come?"

"When will that be?"

"It is coming by boat to Thane. It may be here in fifteen or twenty days."

She was silent again.

"No," she said. "If I stay away too long, I'll never go back. I want too much to wander over the country playing at people's houses, or playing by myself, and finding other musicians. But I have a baby and there is a man who wants me so much I can't hurt him."

"You will come again?"

"I'd like to hear the 'pianoforte.'"

Thus we left it.

"How is your sister Nattana?" I asked.

"Oh, she!" said Nettera, whose thoughts were elsewhere. "She works, she works, she works. There is a line in her forehead between her eyes. She flies out of the house and mounts her horse and rides. She comes to see me and takes me outdoors and we walk. Then after a while she isn't thinking of anything we are seeing or doing, but of weaving, weaving. 'Good-bye' she says, and back she goes."

"Is she happy?" I asked.

"She doesn't miss you," answered Nettera, "but . . ."

I waited for the rest but it did not come.

Our guests slipped into our lives most easily. Gladys ceased to worry over their entertainment and comfort. They were as little trouble as any two persons well could be, contented with everything, demanding nothing. There was no need for us to discuss what we should do. Seeing Stellina daily in my own house I discovered her anew. She became as familiar and as natural as a sister. In her presence all tension between persons ceased, and happy things came about of themselves. She had a quiet vitality that freshened the life of everyone about her. She went sketching with Gladys, she walked with her or with me or alone, she rode our horses, she read, she helped Stanea and visited the Stanes and the Ansels, and she said nothing that I can remember. She was perfectly one of us and there was never a moment when her rareness and charm left her.

Nettera was more like one on holiday, happy in her freedom and lack of obligation. Her child, her husband, her life at the Bains' she never once mentioned. Painting did not interest her but she was amused to pose for her portrait. Stellina on the other hand made attempts in oils. She and Gladys were much together, Nettera a little out of it, but Nettera enjoyed being alone. Once or twice she asked if she could come with me when I worked. She played whenever the spirit moved her, which was often. We learned not to ask her, though she always complied, for it was better when she came of herself, or suddenly burst into music at unexpected moments. Sometimes when I came home Stellina and Gladys would be in the studio, the latter attempting the former's portrait, Stellina idle or reading, and I would find Nettera by the rippling brilliant sound of her wood wind, either in the living room or kitchen, in her room or even ours, playing with eyes half-closed, flushed face, and her lips in the odd curve they took —playing with all her soul.

After they had been with us for ten days Bain appeared. He stayed with us a day. Nettera's clarinet was silent. He took her away with him; but she was coming again, she said, when the piano arrived.

Then Dorn came and spent two days with us and carried off Stellina to visit him and Nekka at the Island.

Our house was suddenly very quiet.

"It has been lots of fun and I have been awfully happy," Gladys said, "but rather strenuous and I haven't seen much of you."

She took my hand and we walked all through the house. No one else was there except Stanea in the kitchen.

"Don't go and work," she said. "Stay with me."

I remained and we went up to her studio. It was full of sketches half-done; two hopeless daubs of Stellina's, landscapes by Gladys that for me had the spirit of the farm, and the portraits that seemed crude on first glance but flashed the reality of Stellina and Nettera.

She looked about her, still holding my hand, and laughed.

"Your friend Stellina got me started, anyway," she said. "I think I shall go on now. She didn't lecture me either. . . She is a queer person. She is stimulating."

"Do you like her?"

"I love her. Who could help it? Everyone must."

There was a "but" in her voice.

"She is nice," continued Gladys. "I shall always be glad to see her. She puts me on my mettle. . . I needed that too. . . Did you know it? Did you arrange for her to come?"

"We talked it over, but I had nothing definite in mind."

"Did she?"

"She is too simple for that, Gladys."

"I am not so sure. She is clever."

"Is it cleverness? Isn't it rather sincerity?"

"She is beyond me, but I shall always love her and value her as a friend. . . And one can be sincere and clever too."

"She did not come here hoping to do something definite for you."

"No, not that."

"It is her heart that is clever."

"Too clever, too impersonal," said Gladys vaguely. . . "I am glad to know her though," she added. "I liked Nettera, too, though I don't feel I know her so well. But I am going to know her better when my piano comes. She has a wonderful ear. . . We are going to have a good time together. She is going to help me tune it. She says she thinks she understands our scale. I am going to play all the things I can. We will write for music soon, won't we, John? I'll try to teach her to read our music. I told her about Bach and Beethoven and Schumann. . . But she is another queer girl. She is so frank! She would tell you anything."

Gladys looked at me quickly and squeezed my hand, and I wondered if through Nettera Gladys had learned that Nattana was my lover. . . But that matter was settled.

"They are upsetting!" Gladys continued. "They are so much themselves. They are so nice! But I got talking to Stellina about morals and she doesn't seem to have any at all. It is all a question of whether she wants to give herself or not. She never has, she said, and probably never will. It all seems to be to them a mere matter of taste. . . She did say she wanted to be sure of *ania*. . . But perhaps that is the same thing in Islandia as being moral. . . And then Nettera! She has no morals at all! I naturally asked her about her husband and baby, and she said that it came in such an odd way it did not seem her baby at all!—John, I don't see how a woman can feel that way! And she said perfectly frankly that she had no *ania* for Bain and never had had."

"That is the reason, perhaps," I suggested.

"Of course it is!"

She released my hand and went to the bench and turned toward the fire.

"It is a funny world," she said. "You don't know what I feel. Here are you and I, and our love and our home seem absolutely solid. But what makes it so? It is the way we feel, I suppose. But is that all there is? Yet here that seems to be everything. It has a queer effect on me, John. I can't let things go. I can't take them for granted. I am not yours just because I married you and you mine just because you married me. I have got to take care of my feelings and of how I treat you and you of yours. That is all that will keep things from being loose. . . Take what happened with Sevin: I relied on the fact that I was married, not on what I felt. I was bored. . . Of course I didn't do anything except not prevent him from kissing me. Then I felt repentant because I had been untrue to our marriage. That was the main thing, not my feeling for you. I felt like a naughty girl. I wanted you to whip me. I really did. I thought if you got angry and let yourself go and beat me a little, the account would be balanced. But that wasn't your way. You were right, of course. I hated you for a while for being right."

"That is all over," I said.

"Oh yes, it is over. Your way made what we have more valuable but more fragile also. . . And take the case of Nettera! I ought to be shocked. I ought to feel she isn't the sort of person I could have for a friend or trust with you. That is what I would feel if I had married at home—I mean in the United States. When I seemed surprised because she didn't feel that her baby was her own, she said that she never wanted to marry Bain nor intended to marry him. She said he had wanted her so much and suffered so about it that it had seemed she ought to give him what he wanted. She did, and suddenly she found herself with the baby and married. Everyone seemed to expect her to marry him. She didn't realize till later that she did not have to do so. There were other men to whom she would much more like to give herself. But that would hurt Bain, and it didn't matter very much anyway; yet if it did really make a difference to her and to her music—John, I ought to have been shocked, but I wasn't. I wasn't even sorry for her, marrying the wrong man, because she didn't seem sorry for herself. But I thanked heaven for what you and I have!"

I sat down on the bench and we unconsciously fitted ourselves together in an embrace. The light of busy thoughts was still flickering in her eyes. I kissed her and watched the light change. . . .

"This is an odd way to spend a morning," she said. "We ought to be doing something useful."

"Shall we go somewhere and work?"

"No!"

"I am glad they are gone," she said.

"But you liked them?"

"Oh, yes. And I shall want to see them again."

"Have you found the friend you need?"

"They aren't what I thought I wanted. I don't need more friends than I have—or any closer ones."

"Who are your best friends here?"

"Lord Dorn is one. I told him I wanted someone I could think of as a father or an uncle, and he answered that if I really insisted he would try to be both, but wouldn't we be happier as friends? I said that I thought that too much to ask, because nieces and children were wished on you, but friends you made yourself. He told me that was the reason why he wanted to be my friend. I kissed him and he kissed me very nicely."

"Is Dorn a friend?"

"He may be someday. He is your friend now. He thinks of us as amusing children. . . But you are my best friend. You won't let me belong to you, and so I have to think of you as a friend."

"Do you want to be mine?"

"Always! And I always shall, but it isn't a good plan in Islandia. It makes me too different from other women."

The wood of the crimson birch burns with a hot flame and an odor pungent and spicy like incense. I noticed that when Gladys placed logs on the open fires she searched for those from this tree. Because our supply would not last through the winter I determined to increase it; but not wishing to change too much the appearance of things on a place where others had lived so long I first consulted old Ansel. We went to the northern part of the farm where a hilly pasture was bordered along its upper part by crimson birches. He told me that in the last fifty years they had encroached upon the cleared land and suggested that I cut these trees back to the original line.

"Leave a good-looking edge," he said. "We have always enjoyed the view from the road up the pasture to the white tree trunks and green leaves and red stems against the sky."

Here, for work in the open air, nothing else requiring to be done, I went for a few hours morning or afternoon as the spirit moved me. Here I was alone except once when Nettera came to visit me, playing her wood wind as my ax rang on the trunks of trees that had not the softening sap of spring.

Several days after Stellina had gone I came here in the afternoon. The sky overhead was clear, but all around the horizon was that winter murkiness into which the sun would later sink as a red ball. Eastward was the depression of the Lay River, southward and westward the rest of the farm lay hidden on the other side of the birch wood, and northward were higher hills. No habitations were in sight except the chimneys and roofs of the Rannals' half a mile northeast and a house a long distance from me beyond the Lay.

Cutting down trees was a small part of my labors; more time was spent in trimming the cut trunks, in piling them so that they would season, and in making heaps of brushwood to be burned. And I gave much thought to the appearance of the trees left standing and to the composition of the edge between grove and pasture as seen from below. The birch wood was a lovely thing and had an unprotected beauty of its own which I safeguarded. So dense was the thicket of crimson twigs above the white stems with their etchings of brown and white that it seemed like a red mist in the air. Though the sunlight sifted through, beneath the trees were dark hollows with blue shadows on their white-floored stillness. Here I did not enter, loving the purity of the drifted snow. In one place, however, were footprints, but they did not spoil it. Nettera had entered the wood and hidden herself. There she had played like a bird become humanly passionate. Her footprints remained, and in the silence of later days they whispered in my ears echoes of her haunting, elusive music.

Alive to the beauty of the birches and caring for that as well as interested in obtaining firewood, I was absorbed. Labor was dream-like, and meditations upon affairs beyond the pasture were incon-secutive, flickering pictures rather than thoughts. They centered upon Gladys and returned to her as to a problem. She seemed to me like one who had fought a battle, won a victory, and gained strength, but who remained idle afterwards. She had her painting, books to read, occasional visitors and "days," her own and others, and she had me. And I meant to her walks, rides, talks about books and painting—and a lover. We were happy but we drifted. In our common life we found in our senses the vividest reality. The rest was sometimes shadowy.

To me, whenever I let slip the chance to have what her lips and hands and body caused me to feel, it was like a precious opportunity lost forever. My desire for her was under a goad, and my wish for her had the recurrent quality of hunger for food. I felt vaguely the indignity of a slave. When I went away from her to work there was peace. Then as time advanced little by little images of Gladys entered upon and heated my thoughts.

So it was this afternoon.

The air was very still. I wondered whether or not to touch fire to a pile of brush. The sun was on the edge of the murk becoming red, and shadows were lengthening on the flushed snow. I would love to see the flames brighten as dusk increased, but the large pile would take a long time to consume and would delay my return to Gladys's lips and arms. . . .

She was moving along the road at the foot of the pasture. My heart was wrenched with loving pity through which desire went like a flame. She was little, a dark figure, the only living thing in the midst of quiet miles of snowy fields and groves of bare trees. Her presence here was unusual and foretold trouble, whether she were walking alone or were coming to me.

She turned at the gate to the pasture and advanced up the slope in the different way that she always had when she sought me elsewhere than in the house, not looking at me, leisurely in her pace, as though not wishing to admit that it was I whom she was seeking.

"Hello," she said as she came near. Her manner was casual but she was a little breathless. She stopped at some distance from me and seated herself upon the pile of birch trunks, and became round-shouldered like one tired. "Don't mind me. Go on working!" she added.

"I am glad to see you. I am glad you have come."

"Oh, I got bored at the house."

I went toward her.

"I was thinking and thinking about you," I said.

"Were you?" Her voice was indifferent but gentle. "What were you thinking?"

It was hard to make precise in words vague thoughts that were rather desires.

I sat down by her.

"You needn't stop working for me," she said.

In her relaxed position her back made a long simple curve. Her knees were side by side and her short skirt just covered them. The pillar of her neck was young and her cheeks were smooth to her long black eyelashes. Her lips were parted. She was desirable and my senses quickened, but because the unknown mood that brought her might be at odds with love, she was half a stranger. Yet because she was not wholly mine I longed to have her the more, was eager for the half-violation.

"It is lovely here, isn't it?" she said. "But I didn't mean to stop what you were doing. I'll be quite contented sitting here, watching you work. . . ."

"I love you, Gladys."

"Do you? Is that what you were thinking?" she asked more softly.

"It is part only."

"What else were you thinking? Tell me." Her voice was sweet if remote. She turned her face to me, and her voice and her eyes melted my resistance suddenly.

"I love you. I have been wanting you." I laid my hand on her knee.

"Well, here I am."

"You didn't come for that—"

"No, but does it matter?"

She did not deny whatever her mood might be. She was mine to lead where I wished and to have. But a rule denied me, that we were not yet to have children.

She seemed unconcerned; desire was strong and a temptation. I could not trust myself to embrace her as I wished, for violence was within—but neither could I let her go. Sinking on the ground at her feet I put my arms around her knees.

"I want you too much," I said, "too much and too often. There is no end to it."

"Why not do as you wish?" she answered, and was my kind foe on the side of temptation. Her head was against the sky, but I saw the dark gleam of her eyes.

"No," I said, "not now. We are not to have children yet."

Her knees quivered.

"Do you want a child?"

My heart beat and my arms tightened. The beauty of Gladys was like a breath of wind that stripped from desire the garments of temptation. What was wrong because of a rule suddenly became right.

"Yes," I said. "I love you and I want a child by you that is mine; but you, Gladys, there is you—"

"Don't bother about that if you want me."

"And you—you are willing?"

"I am willing."

I rose and took her hands.

"Will you come?" I said.

We went into the hollows among the birches. The snow was soft beneath us, and the twigs and branches were a mist of red over our heads. Her eyes never left mine. She was my victim, quiet and kind. All my heart and will went toward her. Pleasure was as right as sleep, and complete like death.

It was darker and colder. I kindled a blaze but the pile of brush was slow to catch fire. When I turned to her she was seated on the birch trunks, her arms upon her knees, her face hidden.

I went to her and knelt by her.

"What is it? What is the trouble? Are you sorry?"

Her head shook. I pleaded with her to tell me, felt for her hand and found it trembling.

"It is the one thing I wanted," I said.

"You are sure?" she whispered, "because if you are not . . ." She could not speak.

"All is perfect," I said. "You are beautiful. All needs are satisfied. We have each other. Enjoyment isn't enough, and the only way is to make something that is ours and goes on. . . ."

"I came to tell you," she said as though not hearing. "I could not keep it back any longer. Then when I was here I couldn't say it, because you thought I was being true to what we agreed. But I haven't been true to that. I haven't done anything to prevent having a child since you and I almost quarreled in May before we went on our journey. You told me I wasn't yours and that you would not rule me. You made me think of myself not of you. And that is what I have done. It was not revenge either, not to get back at you. It was just being myself, what I wanted for my own sake—not to bother . . . not to please you. Oh yes, it was also to please you, to give you something you wanted for your farm, your *alia*. . . ."

I found her cheek with mine.

"I don't know whom it was to please," she said. "I am all mixed up . . . But I am going to have a child. There's no doubt any longer. And you will have to forgive me."

"It will be all the sooner," I said, and I could think of nothing else except to hold her and kiss her and tell her that I loved her and was glad. And after a while as though becoming aware at last, she relaxed, and I drew her into my arms.

The pile of brushwood was a sheet of flame. Heat and bright light were upon us and the darkness, come nearer, was an invisible wall. I tried to convince her of what was perfectly clear to me, so happy at fresh realization every few moments of what she, whom I held, held within her, mine and hers, that my words seemed futile.

"It gives us power," I said. "It justifies us. We are here now. Islandia isn't a dream any longer. It seemed so until now to me—"

"To me, too."

"And it makes you mine and me yours. It unites us. We have everything now. Something more than our feeling for each other makes our love solid. Don't you see that, Gladys?"

"Yes, that is what I thought. But I ought to have told you before."

"It makes no difference. It has postponed my happiness for a month or so, but that doesn't matter now. Not telling me was your only rebellion. Doing as you pleased was right. It was—"

"I know what you are going to say: that it was my way of showing *ania.*"

"I was going to say: 'love.' "

"It is the same thing. Our love is."

Much later under a moon nearly full we went homeward.

There Stanea handed me a letter brought that afternoon. It was from Dorna. Gladys moved away up the stairs.

The letter read:

John:

I have known for a long time of John's marriage and recently, through my great-uncle, of the great loveliness and fineness of Gladysa. I wish him and her perfect happiness. And I am happy too to think of him settled in Islandia with one worthy of him. I would have come to greet him and Gladysa but for reasons he perhaps can guess. My second child, a son, was born seven days ago. I am well and so is he. I have two boys now.

Sometimes I think this: that what John and I can never have, and wish for no longer together, may yet be accomplished in another way. For he may have a child which will meet one of mine, a boy and a girl. And if he wishes it he and I might bring them together when they are ripe for *ania.* Let us think of this at least.

DORNA

I took the letter, which concerned our child, to Gladys to read. She was changing her dress and my heart stopped at the sight of her. She was the one who had been courageous—and by herself. She was only a child, but such an intelligent, such an interesting, dear, and strong one!

She read the letter and seemed unconcerned, and gave it back to me, with a little that smile which one woman has for the wiles of another.

"Isn't it rather early to think of matchmaking?" she said. "And do people make matches here?"

"Not as in Europe and the United States. Nearly everyone is eligible."

"Do you want what she wants?"

"Her blood is good blood, but I don't like his."

"Ours is plain American," she said.

"We are Islandians, Gladys."

"I know what you mean."

Afterword

Islandia was first published in April, 1942, eleven years after my father's death. France was occupied, Singapore and Java lost, Australia threatened. "Abroad," an out-of-date word, had become "overseas." Many people unable to travel obeyed the publishers' suggestion that they spend their vacations in Islandia.

The country of Islandia forms the southern and temperate portion of the Karain subcontinent, which lies in the Southern Hemisphere. It is inhabited by a white race, ancient in history, agricultural in civilization. To this country in 1908 the young American, John Lang, goes as the first American consul, to discover a world that is alien yet compelling, traditional yet free, strange yet totally plausible—so much so that, when reading his adventures, one soon finds it impossible to accept the fact that Islandia never existed—except in my father's imagination.

So real has Islandia seemed to many readers that they cannot let it go; they are compelled to write a sequel, or some other commentary. The late Elmer Davis, both enthralled and irritated by a civilized country which supplied him with neither coffee nor tobacco, wrote a (privately circulated) entry for the *Britannica Year Book* of 1943, in which Islandia was opened up to foreign trade; coffee drinking was spread through the influence of a small Dutch colony; and finally, "after a heroic but brief resistance," Islandia was incorporated in the Greater East Asia Co-Prosperity Sphere.

This novel represents only a part of the total Islandia papers. The original novel, containing close to six hundred thousand words, was so vast as to be virtually unpublishable, particularly during a wartime paper shortage. It was in this form, however, a manuscript contained in seven thick spring binders, too heavy for me to carry by myself, that it was accepted by the publishers. Aside from its own attraction, the book owes this acceptance to two people, my mother and Leonard Bacon. In a demanding routine, which included four children and a job, my mother learned to type and transcribed the twenty-three hundred pages from my father's longhand. After her death, Leonard Bacon made himself a salesman for the book with a characteristic energy and devotion which had, like him, a quality of seeming larger than life. It would be hard to imagine a more perfect friend for an author, or for a book which survived him.

With the intelligent and sensitive help of Mark Saxton, then an editor of Farrar & Rinehart, I cut the original novel by about a third. This is its form today. As I indicated in a note in the original edition, my father knew the exact lineaments of every scene John Lang saw, down to its geological causes, and enjoyed describing such things. Much of the cutting was of this sort of leisurely observation. Also, as Mr. Basil Davenport pointed out in his essay on the Islandia papers, published as a companion volume to the novel, my father's writing became more succinctly his own as he went on. The bulk of the cutting, therefore, was in the early part of the book.

My father knew the country so well because he had considered it and traveled around it in many guises. In one, he constructed its history, a scholarly work entitled *Islandia: History and Description,* by M. Jean Perier, whom readers of the novel will recognize as the first French consul to Islandia.

This document, of about 135,000 words, is the major part of the remainder of the unpublished Islandia papers. In addition, there are a large volume of appendices to the history, including a glossary of the Islandian language; a bibliography; several tables of population; a gazetteer of the provinces with a history of each; tables of viceroys, judges, premiers, etc.; a complete historical peerage; notes on the calendar and climate; and a few specimens of Islandian literature. There are also nineteen maps, one geological. To use Leonard Bacon's phrase from the introduction he wrote to the first publication, here one discovers "the very Devonian outcrop of Never Never Country."

The writing of these documents; the drawing of maps; the plotting of typically Islandian devices such as the sailboat, the ski, the saddlebag; were fitted into a life otherwise not out of the ordinary.

Austin Tappan Wright was born in 1883, in Hanover, New Hampshire. His father, John Henry Wright, was a professor of Greek and Latin, and later became Dean of the Harvard Graduate School. His mother, Mary Tappan Wright, was the author of several novels, which took place in a college town of her own concocting called Great Dulwich.

My father grew up chiefly in Cambridge, and was, like Lang, a member of the class of 1905 at Harvard. After graduation, he entered the Harvard Law School, where, in his final year, he was on the *Law Review*. During a break in his law-school career, he studied at Oxford and traveled in Europe. After graduating from the law school, he practiced law for some years with the firm of Brandeis, Dunbar, and Nutter of Boston. In 1916, he decided that he preferred the career of teaching, and became a professor of law at the University of California in Berkeley and, later, at the University of Pennsylvania in Philadelphia. According to a memorial paper by Professor Lloyd of the University of Pennsylvania Law School, his most important work was in the field of corporation law, although the course which gave him the greatest personal pleasure was admiralty. He was killed in an automobile accident in Las Vegas, New Mexico, in 1931.

The makers of Utopias, the inhabiters of imaginary countries are often assumed to be, and sometimes are, unhappy in, or split from, the real world. "Utopias," said *The New Republic*'s reviewer in 1942, ". . . grow out of wants, frustrations and dissatisfactions, and the grown man who resides in one has been beaten down by experience and/or environment."

I can give no impressions of my father from an adult's point of view. Children accept the personalities who are already there, particularly when these personalities know what things should be treated seriously. When I decided to swim the English Channel, my father was agreeable, but said I must go into training. For part of a summer, we swam up and down the coast of East Chop in Martha's Vineyard, going one dock farther every day. When you asked questions, he gave straight answers. I wanted to know why he was a Democrat, and he said, "Because of the Hawley-Smoot tariff."

We did not go to church, which disturbed some friends and relations. Accused of neglecting this part of our education, my father instituted a summer school for my brother and me, the two oldest.

We read H. G. Wells's *Outline of History,* and were so delighted with the beginnings of the world, dinosaurs and Pithecanthropus Erectus, that we invented our own prehistoric animals. Mine—I have never before written down its name—was the Menyeloothic me-goofey. At another time, the summer course included ancient history, which Papa felt our schools neglected, and navigation, in which we had a formal examination in the dining room, part of which consisted of tying several knots in a given time limit. Then we were each separately taken on what was grandly referred to as a cruise in my father's eighteen-foot knockabout, spending the night on board, and loaded down, according to my mother, with enough food for a week. I remember that on my cruise I formally plotted our course, using the tide table, even though our objective was a buoy I could see quite clearly across the water in the distance.

From our sailing experiences evolved the Plup family. My younger brother continually demanded, "Lemme pull up the centerboard," and became Lummy Plup. From this, for reasons I cannot possibly fathom, we three others became Bozo, Goozoo (me), and Fabian (my sister) Plup. Discovering the Plups, my father joined them. He was, he said, Old Epaminondas Plup. My mother, of course, was Angelina.

My father's sayings stick in my mind. One, which I did not quite understand at the time, was "This is synthetic gin, which makes for ginthetic sin." (Like Sir Thomas More, he was fond of puns.) Another I often think of when trying to get a taxi at five o'clock on a rainy afternoon—roughly the original circumstances—"Every apple has a worm in it."

He refused to let us sit down while going up mountains, because he did not believe in the "rush-very-fast-and-sit-down-and-pant" school of climbing. If tired, you went more slowly and had a piece of Sportsman's Chocolate. Walking in the city, he swung a cane, which we noted as a mild oddity, along with his habit of taking his hat off while talking from a telephone booth to our mother.

We took for granted his capacity to draw what we demanded. I felt both annoyed and indulgent when, at my request that he do me "a galley with oars," he drew a ship's kitchen complete with steaming pots on the stove, and two oars over the doorway. Eventually he drew a splendid galley; in color, with me, wind blown, in the stern. He also constructed things—a gorgeous cardboard ferryboat for my younger brother, which came apart in the middle and became a tug and barge, But most of all I believe that we admired his ability, as a sign of disgust, to turn his lower lip inside out, something which none of the rest of us, except my sister, can do.

When he reported that he had fallen in love with Marlene Dietrich in *Morocco,* and that the finish of the picture had reduced him to tears, we insisted on going to see it. Sitting in an avid row, we were spellbound with pleasure when Marlene followed Gary Cooper into the desert, discarding her high-heeled shoes, and Papa, on cue, pulled out a large handkerchief and burst into heart-rending sobs.

He enjoyed music, but felt he had a poor ear—music was my mother's department. However, he liked to sing, somewhat off key, "Fair Harvard," in which he became silent on the high notes, indicating them by a gesture; "Jubilo"; and a song I have never heard elsewhere, which began, "What's the use of all these cunning little babies growing up to ugly men?"

My mother's birthday was our most elaborate celebration. Every year, we performed a sort of spoken cantata with the same refrain, said in unison. Besides, each of us had a solo, written in verse by my father, commenting on the present. Throughout their marriage, he wrote her little poems.

He was controlled; only once do I remember provoking him to violence. The situation could be summed up in, "You will sit there until you eat your prunes," and we did. Finally my father's patience snapped. He forced me to eat a token prune. Afterwards I told him this was unfair—I could have sat there as long as he. He thought this over and apologized.

He understood the explosive and tentative loves of children. On an impulse I presented him with my precious possession, a red plaster rabbit. He did not urge me to take it back. Later on, in the course of the evening at the theater, I fell in love with an actor, who was a friend of the family, and cried all night because I had not managed to tell him that he was good in the play. Next day my father, without comment, planned a walk, in the course of which we called on the actor. I was given, as, grown up, one seldom is, another chance. (The actor said he had been better on Friday.)

We always knew about Islandia, although apparently my father did not talk very much about it outside the family. We had ideas of what it looked like, from comments like, "This view looks like Islandia." Our boat was called *Aspara,* the Islandian word for seagull.

My father originated Islandia as "my island," when he was a child. This is why the name is the only exception to the rule that there are no silent letters in the Islandian language. Occasionally he shut my uncle, who was younger, out of Islandia, and my uncle created his own world, Cravay. After my grandfather's death, they discovered that he, too, had mapped an imaginary world.

Thus Islandia began to take shape in the Mauve Decade, the era which Thomas Beer says started when "They laid Jesse James in his grave and Dante Gabriel Rossetti died immediately." The country began to be documented and its history written around 1908, a time when what John Lang calls "the new Western civilization" was full of confidence. The novel was probably begun at about the same time and later put aside, to be taken up again sometime in the twenties. It was finished within a year or so of my father's death. Most of the writing of the novel, therefore, was in the decade of Stopes (Marie) and Scopes (trial), of synthetic gin and various sorts of what was still considered sin, the period of the early novels of Huxley and those of Lawrence, both writers also aware of the split human being.

Now *Islandia,* first published in wartime, is reissued in what passes for peacetime, as we begin to make passes at the immemorial moon. Where are the Islandians in this?

My instinct would be that at present Islandia is very much the same as it was in 1910, when the novel ends. Probably the Hundred Law, limiting the number of foreigners in the country at any one time to a hundred, is still in effect. Here, there are people who remember the *Maine,* and the *Arizona,* and the end of battleships. There are ladies, now not very old, who in girlhood were told that they must never lie down on a beach. As Lord Dora points out, with us, the son and father are of different civilizations and are strangers to each other. But in Islandia it seems impossible that life could have become what he calls "too swift to be real." Judging from Islandia's trenchant past, the country could not have changed without ceasing to exist—something which is, of course, impossible for an imaginary country to do.

★　★　★

For those who would like to know a little more about the background of Islandia, a very brief account of M. Perier's history follows. Unfortunately, since it is particularly addressed to foreigners, this book has not yet been published outside of Islandia. In addition to a historical account, M. Perier describes flora, fauna, social institutions, etc. The book is supported by a bibliography of foreign works, of which the author lists sixty. It contains titles like the following:

> Busted, Henderson R.: *Exclusion of American Ships from Islandia.* Baltimore, 1861.
> Reprinting various reports, letters, and other material relating to the controversies over the whalers, to the Spigott mission, etc., and advocating another attempt to collect indemnity.

> MacPherson, Rev. James: *Spreading the Gospel in Heathen Islandia.* Edinburgh, 1828
> An account of the author's work near Mitain during his first three years in Islandia.

> Schwink-Schwanstein, Gottlieb Schwerin: *Islandia, and the World's Supply of Coal, Iron and Precious Metals.* Berlin, 1905.
> Arguing that the world will soon require that Islandia's mineral resources be fully developed, and working out a method how under German Management they may be fairly distributed.

"Historic fact is indistinguishable from legend until the year 800 A.D.," M. Perier begins. This is the date of the Descent from the Frays ("ledges"). Before that time, the Islandian nation, of thirty-three families, was penned up on the southern slopes of the mountain range. "The rest of the world," according to the Chronicle of Clisson, was inhabited by Bants, "black of face. . . clad in skins, dwelling in forests, and murdering the sons of Om wherever they were found." In the Descent, the Islandians were led by Alwin (literally "swim-river," *vide* Matwin—"broad river"), who gave his name to the first dynasty of Islandian kings.

During the next four hundred and fifty years, the Islandians cleared the country of Bants and established their own state. Throughout subsequent history, however, there are many wars against the Bants and other races who established themselves in the continent—the Karain, a mixed race of Bant and Saracen blood, and the nomad Arab Demiji of the Col Plateau. In recent times, European colonists, seeking trade relations with Islandia, have complicated the picture.

Against the background of recurring Karain wars, M. Perier shows us Islandia developing her characteristic institutions. Unlike Europe, Islandia never passed through a feudal period, partly because traditionally farms have been small, each one providing enough to support only two or three families. There was, however, a struggle for power, between nobles influenced by Christian missionaries and the king. In an exciting series of intrigues, the power of the hereditary nobles was finally and permanently broken in 1200. Since that time all nobles have been elected by the people of their provinces as provincial lords, although there is a tendency to continue electing members of certain families, who are trained to govern.

Islandia's constitutional monarchy, on the other hand, was established as the result of a fortuitous accident, the disappearance of Alwin XVII. While attacking the Demiji near Mobono, Alwin was cut off from his armies and vanished into the ranks of the enemy. His death never having been established, he is still king of Islandia. Five years after his disappearance, the National Assembly, a congregation of the whole people and an ancient institution dating from the time of the Descent, was called together and voted that Alwin's son should become the acting king, to hold office only so long as he was chosen to that position by the Assembly. All kings since formally refer to themselves as "By courtesy, king of Islandia."

Characteristic of Islandian history has been the presence of strong exclusionist sentiment. Christian missionaries came early to the country and established themselves. Because they allied themselves with the nobles in the struggle for power, they were expelled in 1200. During this expulsion, Bishop Anthony met the death for which he was later canonized as St. Anthony of Miltain, although, according to M. Perier, Islandian records show that the Bishop died of dysentery as a result of "eating green oranges, of which fruit he was passionately fond." Missionaries and other European settlers have been permitted to settle and have been expelled at various times since, most notable after the crisis of 1841, when the English,

French and American governments, supported by the expansion party of Lord Mora, attempted to force foreign trade and exchange of diplomatic representatives on Islandia. As a result of this crisis, the Hundred Law was passed.

Yet Islandia has taken certain things from the outside, particularly the European, world. The Islandian alphabet we formulated by Christian travelers to the court of Alwin XI although Islandian is not a European language and its origins remain obscure. The printing press, the compass and the secret of glass were brought back from England by a young Mora who visited there in 1600. After the crisis of 1841, Islandia decided to introduce a degree of industrialization, and an English engineer designed for the Islandians a separate industrial town near The City, to which he gave the Latin name of Suburra. Here farm implements are made and, although little information is given out about it, the navy is built and equipped. Since 1472, when the offshore volcanic islands of Carnia, Kernia and Ferrin were discovered, Islandia has been assured of large supplies of copper, iron and other minerals.

Islandians have tended to associate Christian missionaries and would-be settlers with fears about venereal disease and demands on Islandia's resources. Very few Islandians have ever become converts (the Islandian word for convert means "tight thinker"), and foreign commentators have wondered whether this was due to the fears of the existence of a developed Islandian religion. Much has been written on the subject, and conclusions vary. Professor Zinckhauser of Columbia states that since all races so far have had some religion, the Islandians must also have theirs, and since they are primitive, this religion is a combination of polytheism and superstition. Professor Borden disagrees, remarking that "The Islandian, not being material minded, needs not the counterirritant of religion." M. Perier (who never gives opinions of his own) notes the existence of Islandian temples, called "Houses of Quiet," some of which, like the Romanesque cathederal in Miltain, were formerly Christian churches. No services take place, but Islandians visit them, either to sit silent in the spacious interiors or, in bays set apart, to make some sort of statement, "a sermon, a parable, a confession usually to a small audience, sometimes to empty walls."

The ancient hymn to Om, who may or may not be the Islandian god, has been remarked on by all the scholars, though their comments on it do not solve the problem. I quote a few lines:

Om
Cannot be seen with eyes,
Nor heard with ears,
Nor felt with the hand.
Om is great because Om
Is what man cannot understand. . . .

Does Om bid you do evil?
Does Om bid you do good?
Evil and good are alike to Om.
Go not to Om for guidance in petty matters,
But it is well for men to sit in the Halls of Om
And, so sitting, to be lost in his darkness,
And, so sitting, to be dazzled by his brightness,
And to know that Om is. . . . .

I am in the field before the rain.
I am seeking my horses in the hills. . . . .
Am I not pleasing to Om,
I, Man, walker on the ground,
Son of Om?

Elmer Davis, and other writers, decided that Islandia is in the South Pacific. Both Lang and Perier assume that everyone knows where the country is, so neither mentions latitude and longitude. M. Perier does say, however, that the Karain subcontinent is not on the Spanish side of the Pope's line, which I have been told by so eminent an authority as Dr. John K. Wright, former head of the American Geographical Society, means that Islandia cannot be in the Pacific proper. Dr. Wright has studied the situation. He also feels that the Atlantic is too crowded.

Since everything else is so carefully documented, and since this is the only reference I have found to what might be called outer geography, I feel the matter cannot be definitely settled. At the moment when M. Perier mentioned the Pope's line, I believe he had slipped out from under my father's watchful eye. Everyone may speculate, but under the ciucumstances I feel it would be more polite not to.

Sylvia Wright